Lawrence Sanders

Three
Complete
Novels

The
McNally Novels

Also by
Lawrence Sanders

Lawrence Sanders

THE TOMORROW FILE

Three

THE TANGENT OBJECTIVE

Complete

THE TANGENT FACTOR

Novels

G. P. PUTNAM'S SONS   New York

G. P. Putnam's Sons
Publishers Since 1838
a member of
Penguin Putnam Inc.
375 Hudson Street
New York, NY 10014

The Tomorrow File © 1975 by Lawrence Sanders
The Tangent Objective © 1976 by Lawrence Sanders
The Tangent Factor © 1978 by Lawrence Sanders

Library of Congress Cataloging-in-Publication Data

Sanders, Lawrence.
    [Novels. Selections]
    Three complete novels / Lawrence Sanders.
        p.   cm.
    Contents: The tomorrow file—The tangent objective—The
tangent factor.
    ISBN 0-399-14661-X
    1. Detective and mystery stories, American.   I. Title.

PS3569.A5125 T53   2000   00-039016
813'.54—dc21

Printed in the United States of America

10 9 8 7 6 5 4 3 2 1

This book is printed on acid-free paper. ∞

Book design by Patrice Sheridan

Contents

Lawrence Sanders

Three
Complete
Novels

The Tomorrow File

"We can no longer afford an obsolete society of obsolete people."

—President Harold K. Morse

Second Inaugural Address

January 20, 1988

Organization of the Department of Bliss (1988)

Department of Bliss (DOB)
Director (DIROB)
Headquarters Staff

Prosperity Section (PROSEC)
Deputy Director (DEPDIRPRO)

Wisdom Section (WISSEC)
Deputy Director (DEPDIRWIS)

Vigor Section (VIGSEC)
Deputy Director (DEPDIRVIG)

Culture Section (CULSEC)
Deputy Director (DEPDIRCUL)

Satisfaction Section (SATSEC)
Deputy Director (DEPDIRSAT)

Organization of Satisfaction Section, DOB

Satisfaction Section (SATSEC)
Deputy Director (DEPDIRSAT)
Headquarters Staff

Division of Research & Development (DIVRAD)
Assistant Deputy Director (AssDepDirRad)

Division of Security & Intelligence (DIVSEC)
Assistant Deputy Director (AssDepDirSec)

Division of Data & Statistics (DIVDAT)
Assistant Deputy Director (AssDepDirDat)

Division of Law & Enforcement (DIVLAW)
Assistant Deputy Director (AssDepDirLaw)

Book X

X-1

She was naked, riding without saddle. In the cold moonlight her green hair was black, her slender corpus as pliant as a rod of white plastisteel.

The thunder of hooves on hard-packed sand faded. I looked about slowly. The great earthquake of 1979 had taken up this section of coast south of San Francisco and shuffled it like a pack of stone cards. Much had been destroyed, many had perished. But the quake had created new cliffs and coves, sand beaches and clever openings through which the sea came murmuring.

Her house was above, built on stone. I sat in a kind of beach gazebo, infrared heated, and waited patiently.

I heard the sound of hooves again, thundering, thundering. . . . She reined up, the sea behind her, and slid smoothly from the stallion's back.

She held up an arm. The em in an earth-colored zipsuit, standing behind my sling, left the gazebo and went down to her. He took the reins and led the whuffing horse away. I watched them go. That horse was partly my triumph.

In 1985, an extremely virulent form of multivectoral equine encephalitis had swept the globe. Almost 60 percent of the world's horses had stopped. The East claimed the outbreak had started in a Maryland laboratory operated by the US Army's Research & Engineering Section. They were working on mutant viruses. I knew that to be operative. The East said the outbreak of encephalitis was deliberately planned. I think that was inoperative.

Fifty years previously, breeders would have despaired of replacing this epizootic loss of horse flesh in anything less than a hundred years. We did it in five. We used artificial insemination, artificial enovulation, genetic manipulation, and a new category of hormonal and enzymatic growth drugs that reduced the natural equine gestation period to three months. The program was a dramatic success.

But that wasn't the entire reason I admired the stallion as it was led away. Because, as I saw from the first day I was assigned to the Planning Section of the SOH (Save Our Horses) Project, the same techniques we employed—

a crash program to restore a grievously endangered species—could be used for the human race in the event of nukewar.

My paper outlining such a program caused considerable comment, much of it favorable. It certainly led to my present service. My name was Nicholas Bennington Flair. I was an NM (Natural Male). My official title was Ass-DepDirRad. That is, Assistant Deputy Director of the Division of Research & Development, of SATSEC, the Satisfaction Section, of DOB, the Department of Bliss, formerly the Department of Public Happiness, formerly the Department of Health, Education and Welfare.

The ef waving her white arm at me from the beach was Angela Teresa Berri. She was DEPDIRSAT, Deputy Director of the Satisfaction Section of the Department of Bliss. She ruled me. I took up a magenta alumisilk cloak and went down to her.

When I proferred the cloak, she thrust it away with a short, angry gesture. We paced slowly down the deserted beach. Her corpus was not trembling in the chill sea wind. I guessed she had taken a mild Calorific tablet to raise her body temperature.

"Nick," she said. Abrupt, almost rude. "Do you remember that night in Hilo, two years ago, the last night of the International Genetic Control Association meeting?"

I turned my head to look at her in astonishment. Remember? It was a silly question, and she was not a silly ef. Of course I remembered. Not because it had been a particularly memorable evening, but because it was practically impossible for me to forget anything.

Fortunate in having a superior natural memory to begin with, I also took monthly injections of Supermem, a restricted drug administered to everyone in my Division, and annually I underwent surgery for hormonal irrigation of my hippocampus and electronic stimulation of my amygdala. In addition to all this, I was an honor graduate of the GAB, the US Government's Academy of Biofeedback, where I had majored in theta.

We strolled along the beach, her long, thin fingers on my arm. Her nipples were painted black, a tooty fashion I found profitless.

"What did we do after we left the meeting in Hilo?" she asked. Demanded.

"We stopped at the Hi-Profit Bar for a vodka-and-Smack."

"And then?"

"We went down to the beach, took off our plastisandals, and waded in the wet sand back to our hotel."

"And then?"

I couldn't understand the reason for this examination. She was on Supermem too; she remembered that evening as well as I.

"And then?" she insisted.

"We went up to our suite. We used each other. We both took a Somnorific and I left in the morning to fly back to the mainland."

She smiled briefly, tightly, and turned me around. We went back to the gazebo. She put on her cloak then. We climbed to the house, passing a lower level of Thermaglas. Inside I saw a young em bending intently over a work-bench, doing something with a portable Instaweld tank.

"Beautiful home," I said. Our silence was beginning to disturb me as much as her questioning.

"It's not mine," she said. Too fast. "It belongs to a friend Who's away. I borrowed it for my threeday. Nick, thank you for coming. You were right on time."

We turned to smile at each other. Because, of course, I had arrived before she summoned me.

X-2

I had been in bed with Paul Thomas Bumford, my Executive Assistant. He was an AINM-A, an artificially inseminated male with a Grade A genetic rating. We had been users for five years, almost from the day he joined my Division.

Paul was shortish, fair, plump, roseate. He wore heavy makeup. All ems used makeup, of course, but he favored cerise eyeshadow. Megatooty, for my taste.

Strangers might think him a microweight, effete, interested only in the next televised execution. In fact, he was one of the Section's most creative neurobiologists. I was lucky to have him in DIVRAD.

It had been a dyssynaptic evening. It started with a long, angry meeting with my Chimerism Team. I had ordered them to produce a fifteen-minute cassette film on our progress to date. I had approved the preliminary script. It ended with a two-minute closeup sequence of a cloned grizzly bear cub (*Ursus horribilis*) that had been fitted with human hands (to provide the ap-posable thumb) easily performing a variety of simple mechanical tasks: picking up small screws, handling a sheet of paper, turning a valve, etc.

But the rough-cut of the film we viewed was all wrong. It was too cute. The bear cub in the experiment was a natural-born comedian. It didn't help when the voice-over narrator kept referring to him as "Charlie." It was an amusing film. But the intent was not to amuse. Far from it.

When the lights came on, Horvath, the team leader, an NF, and her film producer looked at me expectantly. I stared at them in silence. Paul Bumford said nothing, made no movement. He knew my moods.

Then I made the following points:

1. The experimental animal was to be referred to only by its breeding code: UH-4832-A6.
2. All shots of the bear cub cavorting were to be cut.

3. More footage would be devoted to the actual transplant, and more voice-over to the use of immunosuppressive and learning drugs developed by DIVRAD.

Then the arguments began. I let them shout. I would have my way, but they wouldn't understand why I was so intransigent. They had no need to know. Finally, grumbling, they took their foolish film back to their lab.

"What was that all about?" Paul asked, when we were on our way to *La Bonne Vie*, one of the less execrable restaurants within the government compound.

"Obsolete history," I said. "You weren't in Public Service during the Presidency of Morse. He was our first scientist-President, the first Chief Executive to understand the consequences of the Biological Revolution. He had a doctorate in microbiology, you know."

"From where?" Paul asked sharply.

"London. At the time, they were doing some marvelous things over there. Now they're just coasting. No love. If you want input on the quality of Morse's mind, scan a paper he delivered on July 16, 1978, at a meeting of the American Chemical Society. We have a spindle in the film library. He completely demolished the icebox theory."

"Now you've lost me completely," Paul said. "What was the icebox theory?"

"In the 1970's, neuroscientists were becoming increasingly concerned about the political, social, ethical, and economic consequences of their service, as well they should have been. The icebox theory was suggested. Biological research wouldn't be halted or curtailed, but discoveries would be stored away, put on ice, until the public had a chance to debate fully their possible consequences."

"The public!" Paul burst out laughing. "What the hell do they know about it?"

"Precisely. That's what Morse said. He also pointed out that by putting biological discoveries in an icebox, we were condemning a lot of objects, particularly children, to pain, subnorm lives, or early stopping. But most important, he said that by keeping research completely free and unfettered, we were increasing the possibility that means might be discovered—chemical or electronic—to increase learning to the point where we *could* understand all the potential problems of the Biological Revolution and cope with them."

"Beautiful logic."

"Yes. And had luck. A week after his address, von Helmstadt in South Africa published his definitive study on the results of oxygenation of the fetus. Those kids could learn at an astonishing rate. It proved exactly what Morse had said. A remarkable em."

"You met him a few times, didn't you?"

"Once. I met him once."

It had been an early spring. We strolled along slowly. The compound was a bleak place at night—and not much more inviting during the day. The wide cement walks had been intersected with squares of green plastigrass. There were a few plastirub trees, some bearing wax fruit. The floodlights went on automatically at dusk, freezing everything in a white glare. And the fence, of course: chainlink with triple strands of barbed wire at top. A total of six double gates, with guardhouses.

"How did Morse stop?" Paul asked. "Assassinated?"

"Never been definitely determined," I lied. "A lot of rumors. Anyway, on the day he took office, Morse started working on the Fertility Control Act. We *had* to have it. First of all, it insured zero population growth by federal licensing of procreation. But in addition to Z-Pop, it gave us the beginnings of genetic control by law. Morse finally got the FCA passed a few months before he stopped in 1990. And ever since, obsos have tried to chip away at it. The latest is an amendment that would allow unlicensed breeding between natural ems and natural efs."

"You're against it?"

"I'm against anything that weakens the FCA. So is DEPDIRSAT. So is DIROB. But this time the obsos have some clout. It comes from two directions: the Department of Peace and the Department of Creative Services. The generals want more bodies because it increases their options in the event of a popwar. The labor pols want it because they're getting a lot of kaka from union leaders whose objects are steadily dwindling as consumption declines under Z-Pop."

A two-em security patrol passed us, sauntering slowly. They had flechette guns slung over their shoulders. Each had an attack beast on a chain leash. The beasts were a new mutant our San Diego Field Office had developed: DNA from hyena, jackal, and wolf. Prototypes had no tails, but more recent models were bred for tails, to improve their balance when attacking.

"So that's why the film is being made?" Paul asked. "To defend the FCA?"

"Right. It's intended for Public Service distribution only, with a restricted PS-3 rating. You won't even be able to view it, legally. But it's political clout. It holds out hope to the generals that the possibility of sending chimeras into battle isn't as remote as they may have thought. And it scares the Department of Creative Services, because if we can put animals to work on assembly lines, what's going to happen to their precious unions?"

"I'm computing," Paul said. "A promise and a threat, all in one."

"Correct," I said. "Maybe now we'll get an answer to the great CR debate. In Conditioned Response, which has the higher efficiency—the promise of reward or the threat of punishment? How do you opt?"

"Threat of punishment," he said. Promptly.

"I'm not so sure. And there's another factor involved that makes me want to defeat that amendment to the FCA. If natural ems and natural efs are permitted to breed without licensing, it's only a matter of time—little time—before naturals will consider themselves as elite. Then our society will become structured strictly by genetic classes."

"Now you're talking like an obso. There's elitism right now. The scientific elite. And it exists because we *are* elite."

"*That's* a lot of kaka."

We turned into the restaurant. We had to wait almost ten minutes, but finally got a table in the Executive Dining Room. We didn't need menus. Few in the restaurant did. Most of the customers were from my Division, all on Supermem.

If I was asked to name the greatest technological discovery of the past fifty years, I would have to say it was the synthesizing of protein from petroleum, first in the lab and then in a commercially viable process. If I was asked to name the most disastrous technological discovery, it would be that same development.

When my square of prosteak, rare, was put before me, surrounded by propots and probeans, I knew I was in for a mild attack of RSC. Sighing, I fumbled in the side pocket of my bronze-colored zipsuit for my pill dispenser.

About a year previously I had become aware of a curious and bothersome mental irregularity. It first occurred after my annual hippocampus and amygdala treatment. In effect, my memory, triggered by a sight, sound, smell, or almost any other input, ran wild. I could not control a flood of associative memories that engulfed my brain and temporarily extirpated my ability to respond normally to subsequent stimuli, or to learn, deduce, or fantasize.

After the second attack, I went to my Memory Team leader, a molecular neurologist, and described the symptoms. He was not at all surprised. I was suffering from RSC, Random Synaptic Control. It was fairly common in both ems and efs who had been memory-conditioned in the 1975–1985 period. It was due to an inaccurate stereochemical configuration of the hormone administered. Therapy was by ingestion of a corrective hormone isomer.

If Proust could write a novel of that length inspired by a piece of madeleine soaked in tea, you can appreciate why a plate of food derived from petrochemicals and artificial flavorings might drive my synapses out of control. The memories came flooding in. . . .

. . . my father's shrewdness. He was a successful toy manufacturer with a BS in chemistry. When the production of protein from petroleum was announced as commercially feasible, he had immediately put a lot of love into companies producing spices, flavorings, and seasonings. He made a bundle, and then, as he followed the chemical journals carefully and noted the inevitability of synthetic salt, pepper, thyme, tarragon, garlic, curry, mustard, dill, etc., he withdrew with a tremendous orgasm that made him a decamillionaire in new dollars.

. . . my mother's adamant refusal to consume *any* synthetic food or drink, and especially artificially flavored whiskies made from petrochemicals. She existed in an alcoholic stupor maintained with a rare Eastern vodka produced from natural potatoes.

. . . Millie's service. The young ef was a CF-E, an embryo-cloned female with a Grade E genetic rating. She was a packer in the Qik-Freez Hot-Qizine factory in Detroit. It was possible she had packaged the prosteak I was about to eat. Millie and I were users.

...almost atavistic memories of the taste of farm-fresh eggs, vine-ripened melons, cucumbers, fresh beef, gravel-scratching chickens, wine made from grapes....

I popped my RSC pill. Paul watched me sympathetically.

"Bad?"

"Not too," I said. "There are some memories I can do without."

"Tememblo?"

"Too gross," I said. "It erases everything."

Tememblo (Temporary Memory Block) was a restricted drug we had developed. Given by injection, it produced complete forgetfulness, either immediately before or after the events, for periods of one to forty-eight hours, depending on its strength. But the duration of the effect was limited.

Paul was instantly alert and interested.

"You're suggesting a specialized memory inhibitor?" he said. "To block, say, a color memory without inhibiting a scent memory?"

"Something like that." I nodded. "But we can't take it on now. Better put it in the Tomorrow File."

We no longer smiled at that, though it had started as a joke.

Soon after Paul Bumford joined DIVRAD, he sent me a memo tape suggesting that every individual in the US have his BIN (Birth Identification Number) tattooed on his forearm. The idea was preposterous, but I admired the organization of his argument.

I called him in and explained why his suggestion was impractical for social and political reasons.

"If it's the cosmetic effect of the tattooing that might offend," he offered, "we could use a skin dye visible only under ultraviolet light."

"Paul, you're not computing. We still have some objects in this country who have harsh memories of Germany's Third Reich, the concentration camps, the arm tattoos. If I suggested such a program, all hell would break loose."

"Obsoletes," he said. "They can be manipulated."

"Obsos," I agreed. "And they probably could be manipulated if I felt the project was important enough. But I don't. Do you know how long it took us to get the National Data Bank accepted? Five years! By a massive-all-media effort to convince objects it was not a computer but just a highly sophisticated filing system. *Files*, not dossiers. And it was only after the Fertility Control Act was passed that we were able to assign Birth Identification Numbers. You must learn that what is practical and useful scientifically is not necessarily practical and useful socially, ethically, or economically. And especially politically."

"I still think it's a good idea," he said stubbornly.

"As a means of personal identification? Well . . . maybe. About as good, and bad, as fingerprints, I'd guess. But we're working on something much better.

He came alive. "Genetic codes?"

"No good. Not in the case of identical twins or clone groups. Ever hear of forensic microbiology?"

"No."

"Suggested about 1970. But nobody did anything about it at the time because most of the biomedical research then was therapy-oriented. But this could be big. Right now I have only one object serving on it. Mary Bergstrom, a neurophysiologist. She's good, but she needs help on the microbiology. I want you to serve with her."

"Will she rule me?"

"No. You'll be equals, reporting only to me. I'm very interested in this. I'll code you and Mary the IMP Team, for Individual Microbiological Profile."

He reached for his memo tape.

"Then I guess I can erase this."

"Don't do that." I smiled, putting my hand on his. "Have it transcribed and filmed. "It's not a *bad* idea. But for the future. Put it in the Tomorrow File."

"The Tomorrow File?" He liked that. He smiled.

We became users that night.

Since then, whenever we—together or separately—came up with an idea that could not be developed because of the current social, economic, or political climate, we put it in the Tomorrow File. Paul kept the film spindles in his office safe.

We finished our dinner.

"How do you feel?" Paul asked. "The spansule work?"

"Fine," I said. "So far. Knock on wood." I rapped the table top.

"That's plastic," Paul said.

"Old habits stop hard," I said.

"Yes." He nodded. "That's the problem."

We went back to my apartment. Paul wanted to watch the AGC Network—Avant-Garde Cable. They were presenting Walter Bronkowsky on the Leopold Synthesizer, playing his own symphony, *Variations on the Rock of Ages Mambo*. We watched and listened to about five minutes of Bronkowsky twiddling his dials and flipping his switches. Then Paul and I exchanged grimaces. He tried other channels.

It was a new laser-holograph three-dimensional set, with a one-meter box. But all we could get were sit-coms, talk shows, and the tenth rerun of *Deep Throat*. So we went to bed.

Paul's mucus membranes were gainfully tender. Our investment had endured long enough for each to be attuned to the physical and mental rhythms of the other. We were, for instance, able to go into alpha together.

Recently, almost as a hobby, Paul had been researching ESP. He had evolved a theory that during sexual arousal, as during moments of other emotional stress—fear, anger, etc.—the ESP faculty was intensified.

We had been conducting a series of experiments to test this out. Before sexual relations, Paul or I would write a single word or simple phrase on a piece of paper, keeping it hidden from the other. During using, the sender attempted to transmit mentally the word or phrase he had written, and the other to receive mentally the identical word or phrase.

Results had been inconclusive but encouraging enough to continue. That night Paul was sending.

After we summited, and our respiration and cardiac rates had returned to normal, Paul asked, "What was it?"

I hesitated a moment, then said, "Ultimate pleasure."

Paul switched on the lamp, reached to the bedside table. He picked up his note and unfolded it so I could read what he had written: "Ultimate pleasure."

I shook my head. "Not conclusive. Too subjective. It may have been an emotional or purely physical reaction on my part."

"Not so," Paul said. "You've never used that phrase before. And besides, it *is* objective. It's a subject I've been thinking about a long time. I put a memo on it in the Tomorrow File. It proposes the development of an Ultimate Pleasure compound. In pill form. Cheap. Addictive. No toxic effects. No serious side effects. Working directly on the hypothalamus or affecting the norepinephrine-mediated tracts."

"That's interesting," I said.

I turned off the bedlamp and we went to sleep.

I was in the middle of an REM dream when I was awakened by the chiming of the bedroom flasher extension.

"Flasher" was not the correct name for this device, of course. Technically, it was a Video Phone. Why flasher? Because the new devices had spawned a new breed of obscene phone callers. The conventional table or desk set consisted of a 3 dm viewing screen with a 5 cm camera lens mounted above and centered between the video and sound control dials and the push-button station selector.

The obscene caller, ef or em, stood before the flasher so the face could not be viewed by the camera lens, and exhibited naked genitalia after calling a selected or random number. Such callers, and there were many, were termed "flashers." The device took its popular name from them.

I pulled on a patterned plastilin robe and sat before the flasher on my bedroom desk. Paul climbed out of bed and stood behind the set where he could not be photographed. I flicked the On switch. The color image bloomed blurry and shaky, then steadied and focused. It was a pleasant-faced black ef, wearing the blue zipsuit of a PS-7. We stared at each other.

"Mr. Nicholas Bennington Flair?"

"Speaking."

"Mr. Flair, are you AssDepDirRad?"

"I am."

"Would you insert your BIN card, please."

I motioned to Paul. He rushed to get my card from my discarded bronze zipsuit.

Meanwhile the ef was looking at my image and then down at her desk, obviously comparing my features to a photo. Paul handed me the BIN card over the set. I inserted it in a slot under the screen. The ef read her output, sent by the magnetic-inked numbers on my card. She seemed satisfied.

"Mr. Flair, this is DIVDAT in San Francisco. We have a message to you from Angela Teresa Berri, DEPDIRSAT. May I show it?"

"Go ahead."

The printed message came on.

It was a memo, dated that day.

FROM: DEPDIRSAT.
TO: AssDepDirRad.
SUBJECT: IMP progress report.
          You personally rush urgent latest. Emergency. /s/ Berri.

The operator came on again.

"Did you get that, sir?"

"I did," I told her. "No reply, and thank you."

The screen went dead, a little white moon fading, fading. . . . I flicked the Off switch. Paul and I looked at each other.

"She's on a threeday," he said finally. "Someplace south of San Francisco."

"I know."

"That report she wants—I wrote it. Strictly NSP—No Significant Progress."

"I know."

"Listen," he said, "are you sure that was from her?"

"I'm sure."

"You are?" He looked at me narrowly. "Oh-ho! Section code. I get it. 'Rush urgent latest. Emergency.' R-U-L-E. Verification code—right?"

No idiot he.

"Right." I nodded.

I looked at the bedside digital clock.

"If we hurry I can make the 2330 courier flight from Ellis. Let me shower, shave, and dress. First, you lay on a cart and copter, and book me on the flight. Then put on some clothes and get me an Instox copy of that report from your office. Meet me outside in twenty minutes."

He nodded and we started rushing.

Twenty minutes later he handed over the sealed report and drove the electric cart to the copter pad at the other end of the compound.

"Nick," he said. "Be careful."

"Careful?"

"Something's up. If she really needed that report, which I doubt, it could have been scanned to her. But she started with 'You—You personally....' "

"That's right."

"What is it?"

"I have no idea."

"You have no idea—or I have no need to know?"

"I have no idea."

"Will you flash me after you see her?"

"No. If possible I'll take the return flight. I'll be back before dawn."

"Nick, I grabbed a couple of things in my office—amitriptyline and the new iproniazid. Want one?"

"I'd like the fast upper but I'm not going to take it. I better play this straight."

He parked in the shadow of the hangar, cast by the floodlights on the pad. The copter was waiting there, rotor slowly turning. Paul and I kissed.

"Take care," he said lightly.

I made the 2330 hypersonic from the airfield that had formerly been Ellis Island. We landed in San Francisco two hours later, and most of the time was spent circling over the Atlantic and Pacific Oceans, going and coming through the sonic wall.

Arrival was approximately 0130, New York time. I was coptered and then driven to Angela Berri's seaside home in less than 30 minutes. According to my digiwatch, I walked down to the beach just before 0200, New York time. But just before 2300, local time.

Ergo, I had arrived before I had been summoned. Amusing.

X-3

We came up from the beach into the main house. Angela Berri led the way into a living room-office-den, then closed and locked the door behind me. She motioned me to a white plasticade armchair, then switched on a cassette of a gamelan quartet. I remembered she fancied Eastern music. She turned up the volume of her hemispherical sound system. Too loud. The windows fluttered. She went to a small office refrigerator and, without asking my preference, poured us each a glass of chilled Smack.

She sat down behind the red plastisteel desk.

"You brought the report I wanted, Nick?"

"Yes. Here."

I leaned forward to scale the sealed envelope onto the desktop. She tore it open, scanned the report swiftly, tossed it aside.

"What is the status now?"

Curious. She received weekly progress reports, and I knew she listened to them. She had a double doctorate—in molecular biology and biochemical genetics. She would understand exactly what we were doing on the Individual Microbiology Profile Project.

But dutifully I replied, "Everyone in the Department of Bliss has been tested and coded."

"New employees?" she asked sharply.

"Not those coming aboard in the last six weeks. But we have everyone else. The computer has been programmed. We're tuning up now. We should be able to start blind tests in a day or two."

She nodded. "I'm beginning to work on my budget recommendations," she said tonelessly. "I must adjust the allocation for IMP."

Curiouser. She knew as well as I that no specific allocation had ever been made for the IMP Project. The new dollars came from my discretionary fund, as did the love for all pure research projects. Congress and the public were interested only in hardware. We hid the rest.

She came over to me and stood directly behind my chair.

"I'm glad you could bring the new report personally, Nick."

But it was not a new report. She had scanned it two weeks ago. What was—

Then, standing behind me, she began lightly stroking my temples, jawline, beneath the chin, with her fingertips. My initial reaction was ego-oriented. I knew she took profit from me, and thought she might want to use me. But then, as those cool fingers continued to search the outlines of my face, I knew what was happening.

That interrogation on the beach had been to assure her that I was who I claimed to be, Nicholas Bennington Flair. That I remembered events that only she and I had shared. But it was inconclusive. An object's memories could be drained, to be learned by another object. I had helped develop the drugs to do it.

This probing of my face with her fingertips was to confirm that I was the em I appeared to be, Nick Flair, and not the product of clever surgeons using the new Juskin. It was a synthetic product, bonded to natural skin by a technique not unlike welding. It left no scars or seams, but it did leave an invisible welt at the line of juncture that could be felt.

She feared me an impostor—a not unreasonable fear. Two months previously the Statistics Projection Chief of the Department of Agribusiness, formerly the Department of Agriculture, had proved to be an impostor, in the employ of a cartel of grain dealers. The original Chief had been assassinated.

She went back behind the red desk and sat there, staring at me. We both sipped our plastiglasses of Smack while she tried to make up her mind. I thought idly that the reason for her senseless questions about the IMP Project had been inspired by her suspicion that this room was being shared. That was also the reason for the high volume of the gamelan tape. The sound was sufficient to set up random vibrations of walls and windows, in case anyone was sharing with a long-distance laser beam.

I turned the glass of Smack in my palms. The Jellicubes of "ice" didn't melt. Unfortunately. They looked like little blocks of squid.

Smack was interesting. It was the best-selling soft drink in the world, by far. It had a sweetish citric flavor. Other soft drinks tasted better, but Smack had an advantage they didn't have: it was addictive.

The original formula was a serendipitous discovery. In 1978, Pace Pharmaceuticals, in St. Louis, was doing research on a drug that might be effective against the so-called "fatty liver" caused by alcohol addiction. Eventually, they found themselves working on the physiological effects of alcohol, caffeine, and nicotine.

Two years later, Pace had produced a powder that was, in solution, admittedly physically addictive. But it did not require increased dosage to provide mild euphoria over a long period of time. More important, Pace claimed, it produced absolutely no harmful physical or psychological effects.

It was a nice legal point. Pace decided to meet the issue head-on. They fought it through the courts for seven years. By the time the Supreme Court decided, in 1987, that addictive substances were not, per se, illegal, providing they had no toxic effects, Pace was ready with "Smack! The Flavor You Can't Forget!" It was widely rumored that two Associate Justices and five law clerks became millionaires overnight by prior knowledge of the decision and purchase of Pace stock. This may or may not be operative.

What was operative was that Pace's addictive formula was now licensed for chewing gum, toothpaste, ice cream, mouthwash, and candy bars. As the obsos were fond of saying, "Better living through chemistry."

So there I was, sipping my Smack like millions of others throughout the world, and watching Angela Berri struggle to make up her mind. It really didn't take her long. She rose, pulled heavy drapes across all the Thermapanes. She returned to her swivel chair, unlocked a desk drawer, drew out a tape cassette, placed it squarely in the middle of the desk blotter. She stared at it. I stared at it. Then she raised her eyes to give me that hard, tight half-smile of hers. I looked at her, computing.

When, at the age of twelve, I announced to my father that I had been accepted at the government's new National Science Academy, under the Accelerated Conditioning Program, and that I intended to make a career of Public Service, he gave me a sardonic look and said merely, "Save yourself."

It was five years before I understood what he had meant. As I moved up in PS, I became increasingly aware of the plots of Byzantine complexity and Oriental ferocity that swirled through government, and especially Public Service. Unless you were utterly devoid of ambition, it was impossible to remain aloof. You had to ally yourself with the strong, shun the weak. More important, you had to join the winners, reject the losers. It called for inching along a political tightrope. You hoped that you would master the skill before falling.

Now Angela Berri was presenting me with what I guessed to be essentially a political choice. I hesitated only a moment. In politics, as in war, it is better to make a bad decision than no decision at all.

Without speaking, I raised my eyebrows and jerked my head upward to point my chin at the tape cassette.

Without speaking, she motioned me over to stand next to her.

Without speaking, I picked up the cassette and examined it. It appeared to be a standard commercial cartridge, providing about thirty minutes of tape on each side. The clear plastic container was unlabeled.

Without speaking, she took a pad of scratch paper and a gold liquid graphite pencil from a side drawer. I watched her movements carefully.

She tore the top sheet of paper from the pad and placed it off the blotter, on the bare plastisteel desktop. She didn't want to risk the second sheet of the pad or the desk blotter picking up even a faint imprint of what she would write. She scribbled a few words, then looked up at me. I bent over her. I smelled a pleasing scent of her sweat, the stallion's, and the exciting estrogen-based perfume she was wearing.

I read what she had written: "For you only." I pondered a few seconds, then took the gold pencil from her fingers. Directly beneath her note, I jotted, "Paul Bumford?" She read it, raised her eyes to stare at me a moment, then nodded. Yes.

She took a ceramic crucible from a side drawer, crumpled our shared note, dropped it in the crucible. From another drawer she took a small bottle of a commercial solvent, Deztroyzit. The cap was actually a dropper with a bulb of plastirub. She dripped two drops onto the crumpled note. It dissolved. We watched the white smoke curl up. Acrid odor. In a few seconds the paper was gone. Not even ashes left.

I slipped the tape cassette into the side pocket of my zipsuit. We walked to the door without speaking.

In the hallway, the young em was just coming up from the lower level workshop. He was carrying a beautifully crafted model of an antique rocket. I think it was a Saturn.

"Nick," she said, "this is Bruce. Bruce, meet my friend, Nick."

We smiled at each other and stroked palms. I judged him to be about twelve. No more than fourteen. Handsome. Big.

"Bruce's clone group is being conditioned for Project Jupiter," she said proudly.

"Lucky Bruce." I sighed. "I wish I was going."

But of course I was much too old. I was twenty-eight.

Bruce, not having spoken, left us and carried his rocket to an upstairs room.

At the outside door she put those long, slender fingers on my arm.

"Nick, thank you again for bringing me that IMP report."

"Sure."

"Perhaps when I get back we can use each other again."

"A profit!" I said. I meant it. She was an efficient user.

"For me, too," she said.

I made the return flight with minutes to spare. There were fewer than twenty passengers scattered around the cabin of the 102-seat hypersonic. It was a waste of the taxpayers' love. But if you worried about wasting taxpayers' love, you shouldn't be in Public Service in the first place.

Takeoff was right on the decisecond. After we were airborne, the Security Officer came down the aisle returning our BIN cards, surrendered for identification check at the boarding gate. As we circled out over the Pacific, I stared at my card. I had, as required by law, provided a new color Instaroid photo the previous year. But I felt many years older than that long-faced, rather saturnine em who stared back at me.

The BIN card noted I was 182 cm tall and weighed 77 kg. (The US had completed switchover to the Metric System in 1985.) Hair: black. Eyes: Blue. Race was not noted since by assimilation (especially interbreeding), classification by race, color, or ethnical stock was no longer meaningful (or even possible). Creed was not noted since religious persuasion was of no consequence.

My BIN was NM-A-31570-GPA-1-K14324. That is, I was a Natural Male with a Grade A genetic rating, born March 15, 1970, who lived in Geo-Political Area 1, and whose birth registration number was K14324. The invisible magnetic coding made it almost impossible to forge a BIN card. Almost, but not quite.

I put it away when the stewardess came down the aisle, pushing her cart of nicotine, caffeine, alcohol, Smack, Somnorifics, tranquilizers, decongestants, antidepressants, antibiotics, diuretics, steroid hormones, and nonnarcotic sedatives. In her white zipsuit and white cap, she looked exactly like a pharmaceutical nurse making the rounds in a terminal ward.

I asked for a two-hour Somnorific, but all she had was one-hour or three. I took the one. I settled back in my seat, the alumistretch strap holding me securely, and turned the inhaler over in my fingers before removing the seal.

About five years previously, the Space Exploration Section (formerly NASA, now a division of the Department of the Air Force) had let a contract to Walker & Clarke Chemicals to develop a controlled hypnotic. SES had found that on extended flights and tours of duty in the space laboratories, the crews frequently suffered from boredom and/or insomnia. SES wanted a precisely timed sleeping pill, inhalant, or injection with no side or toxic effects.

After some clever molecular manipulation of glutethimide, a nonbarbiturate hypnotic, Walker & Clarke came up with a powder that oxidized when exposed to air, releasing a gas that had the required somniferous effect when inhaled. After tests, the Space Exploration Section accepted the new product and felt it safe enough to license for unrestricted use. They claimed it was nonaddictive.

"It is nonaddictive," Paul Bumford agreed, "unless you want to sleep."

Anyway, Walker & Clarke, after a massive preproduction advertising campaign ("Don't wait for sleep; make it come to you!") brought out Somnorific—plastic inhalers of precisely controlled strengths, from one to twenty-four hours. You peeled off the foil seal, waited about ten seconds for oxidation to take place, plugged the Somnorific into each nostril for a deep inhalation, and away you went.

Initially, Somnorific was a colossal failure. Customer complaints mounted, unopened cartons were returned to jobbers by drugstores, to wholesalers by jobbers, and to Walker & Clarke by wholesalers.

Investigation soon proved where the problem lay: customers were simply not waiting the required ten-second oxidation period despite clearly printed instructions for use. They were yanking off the foil seal, plugging the bullet-shaped containers up their noses, and taking deep breaths. Nothing.

I knew all this because Tom Sanchez, Director of Research at Walker & Clarke, had brought his troubles to me. We sometimes did favors for lovers in the drug cartels. They, in turn, helped us on sweetheart legislation. In this case, I assigned the problem to my Human Engineering Team.

They came up with the solution in one day. It was a classic. They recommended that the foil seal on each Somnorific inhaler be attached with a more tenacious adhesive. It was now difficult to pick off with your fingernails. When you finally got the damn thing off, it stuck to your fingertips and you had to ball it up between thumb and forefinger before you could flick it away. By that time, oxidation was completed and the Somnorific ready for use. We were all manipulated, in small matters and large.

I finally flicked the foil seal off my fingers, took two inhalations of my one-hour Somnorific, and was gone: black, deep, dreamless.

I must have drifted into natural sleep after the hypnotic wore off because we were letting down when I awoke. The hypersonic had no windows or ports. But there was a cabin telescreen, and I saw we were over New York harbor, coming into Ellis. I could see the Statue of Liberty. For safety, they had outlined it in red neon tubing when the airfield went operational. It didn't spoil the lady's appearance as much as you might expect.

A SATSEC copter was waiting for me. That was Paul's doing, and I appreciated it. A few minutes later we landed on the pad in the compound. Paul was seated in an electric cart near the hangar. He leaned out to wave to me. I walked toward him, brushing the side pocket of my zipsuit with the back of my hand to make certain I still had DEPDIRSAT's tape cassette.

Paul waited until I climbed onto the plastivas seat next to him.

"What was it?" he asked eagerly.

I fished out the cassette and showed it to him.

"What's on it?"

"I don't know. For our ears only. We better go to your lab."

He nodded and started the cart with a jerk. He was a miserable driver.

Geo-Political Area 1 was a megapolis that ran along the Eastern Seaboard from Boston on the north to Washington, D.C., on the south. During the decentralization of government offices during the Presidency of Harold Morse, the DOB had assigned SATSEC to a complex of office and residential buildings on the lower tip of Manhattan Island.

The development had originally been called Manhattan Landing. It was excellent for our purposes, including offices, apartments, shops, restaurants, and small parks. The three level underground area had been converted to laboratories and computer banks at a cost of 200 million new dollars. Like all government compounds, ours was surrounded by a high chainlink fence, with constant security patrols, closed-circuit TV, infrared, ultrasonic, and radar monitors.

My apartment was on the penultimate floor of the highest residential building, since I was a Division Leader, PS-3, the third highest rank in Public Service. Paul Bumford, a PS-4, lived one floor below me. Angela Berri, a PS-2, had the penthouse. DIROB, the Director of the Department of Bliss, a PS-1, had his home and office in Washington, D.C.

Paul and I drove directly to A Lab, fed our BIN cards into the Auto-Ident, and took the executive elevator down, down, down. Another Auto-Ident check to get into the general lab area. To enter Paul's personal lab, he had to speak his name into a live microphone. It automatically checked his voiceprint with the one on file in the Security Computer. Then the door could be opened with his magnetic key. It was all a game. Everyone knew the whole system could be fiddled, but we all followed regulations.

Over in a corner of the lab, the fluorescents were on high intensity. Mary Margaret Bergstrom, an AENOF-B (an artificially enovulated female with a Grade B genetic rating), was serving with a polarizing microscope. She looked up in surprise when we entered. Paul waved to her. She nodded briefly and went back to the scope.

"What's she doing here at this hour?" I asked. It was not yet dawn.

"She serves all hours." Paul shrugged. "She's got no social life, no hobbies, no bad habits."

"Unless you call playing a flute naked in front of a mirror a bad habit."

Paul laughed. "Oh, you heard that story, too."

We went into his private office. He turned on the lights, locked the door behind us, pulled the plastopaque shade down over the glass window that looked out into the general lab area.

I checked the Sharegard monitor on the wall. It was supposed to register the presence of any unauthorized electronic sharing devices. Sometimes it worked. At the moment it showed a normal reading.

"When did you have your last sweep?" I asked.

"About a week ago. We were clean then. They found an unauthorized transistor radio over in B Lab. Some clone had been listening to the dog race results."

"Beautiful. Let's get on with it."

Paul took out a portable cassette deck. The cracked plastic case was held together with plastitape.

"Earphones," I ordered.

I used an earplug set. Paul did, too, but in addition he clamped on a theta helmet: small steel plates, held about three inches from his temples. They sent a weak electric current, about 7 cps, through his hippocampus. Paul was studying biofeedback but had not yet mastered the skill of going into theta at will.

He inserted Angela Berri's tape cartridge and pushed the On button. He looked at me. I nodded. He pushed Start.

"This morning, at approximately 1045 EST, the corpus of an em was discovered lying in a bed in an apartment on West Seventy-fourth Street in Manhattan. The em was identified as Frederick Halber. That's H-a-l-b-e-r. The corpus was discovered by the guardian of the building in company with a uniformed officer of the New York Peace Department. The guardian had been alerted by flasher from Halber's employer. Halber had failed to show up for service that morning and wasn't answering his flasher. The employer is Pub-Op, Inc. You know that outfit, Nick.

"The New York Medical Examiner made a preliminary diagnosis of coronary thrombosis. The corpus was taken to the New York City Resting Home. His 'next of kin' listed in Halber's service file at Pub-Op, Inc. was a cover name for his control. That was how I was notified.

"The real name of the stopped em was Frank Lawson Harris. He was in PS, on my Section's Headquarters Staff, assigned to undercover service, reporting only to me, through his control. The Director of Bliss and the Assistant Deputy Director of the Security Division are not aware of this activity. They are not, repeat, *not* to be informed.

"Nick, I want you to find out what you can about how Harris stopped. I do not believe it was a coronary thrombosis. I believe he was assassinated. Claim the corpus from the NYC Resting Home and perform a complete autopsy, including tissue and organ analysis. Preferably, do it personally. If not, concoct a believable cover story for whoever does it. Lieutenant Oliver of the New York Peace Department will cooperate on releasing the corpus and allowing you access to Harris' apartment.

"I will be back tomorrow. I hope you will have answers by then. I know I can rely on your loyalty and discretion. Destroy this."

The voice stopped. Paul turned off the machine. We removed our earphones. We looked at each other.

"What do you make of that?" I asked finally.

He ticked points off on his fingertips:

"One: Angela Berri is involved in a covert and possibly illegal activity of X kind for Y reasons.

"Two: Her immediate ruler, DIROB, is unaware of this activity, as is the

Department's Security Chief. Why? Either her activity *is* illegal or *they* are personally involved in an illegal activity which she has uncovered or suspects.

"Three: Her covert activity is organized and of some duration, since she has a system of controls for her agents and has enlisted the assistance of at least one officer of the New York Peace Department. And since she suspects Harris was assassinated, her activity is serious and not just ordinary politicking.

"Four: Halber's—or rather, Harris' employment at Pub-Op, Inc., is probably of some significance since we depend on them a great deal in our estimation of the Satisfaction Rate.

"Five: If Harris was in service with the Department of Bliss, his file is available to us, and we have an IMP on him."

He paused a moment, then: "How was that, Nick?"

I held up a finger. "Six: You and I are now involved, whether we like it or not."

"We can refuse to do anything."

"And risk Angela's vengeance? I know the ef. Good-bye careers."

"What do you suggest, Nick?"

"Do what she orders," I decided. "I interpret this tape as an order from our ruler, not a request. And you so interpret it. Agree?"

"Agree."

"Do not destroy the tape. It is our only hope in case this whole thing blows up. I'll keep a file on all this in my apartment safe. When you're finished with the tape, return it to me. From then on, we'll discuss this only in the open or in a closed area where the possibility of sharing is minimal."

"Understood."

"Tomorrow morning, or rather this morning, I'll get Lieutenant Oliver on the flasher and make arrangements to get into Harris' apartment. We'll take IMP samples. And I'll claim the corpus. Can you do the PM?"

His face went suddenly white. "I can, but don't ask me, Nick. Please don't ask me!"

I was shocked by his vehemence.

"All right," I said gently. "You don't have to. But I haven't done an autopsy in more than ten years. I'm not up."

"Mary!" he burst out. "Mary Bergstrom can do it! She does them all the time. She *likes* to do them."

"What will you tell her?"

He thought a moment.

"That the New York Peace Department requested our cooperation because the case demands a transmission electron microscope, an energy-dispersion analyzer, and a lot of other hardware they don't have."

"You lie very well." I nodded approvingly. He grinned. "Will she ask questions?"

"Not Mary. She'll do what I tell her."

"Fine. Tell her to get everything on color tape. She'll have the corpus later today. I'm going to sleep. You keep the cassette until you run the voiceprint. I'll call you after I've spoken to Lieutenant Oliver in the morning."

He locked the tape cartridge in his office safe. Then he opened the door. I put a hand on his arm.

"Paul, that beachhouse of Angela's out on the coast. . . ."

"Yes?"

"She told me she doesn't own it, that she borrowed it from a friend. But she moved around in it like she's lived there all her life."

"Oh?"

"There's a glassed-in gazebo down on the sand. And a small stable. I saw a stallion and at least one em server. The whole thing has got to cost at least a hundred thousand new dollars, plus upkeep. On Angela's rank-rate?" I pondered a moment. "Paul, does the Section have a contact in that area who could make quiet inquiries and find out who actually owns the house?"

"Sure," he said promptly. "I know just the em. An attorney in Oakland. DIVLAW let one of his clients plead *nolo contendere* in a case of mislabeling chlordiazepoxide. It might have been an honest packaging error, but I doubt it. Anyway, they ran a good recall, and no one got hurt. But if we had fought it, the client could have drawn a five-year reconditioning sentence instead of a ten-thousand-dollar fine. That lawyer will do anything we ask."

"Take care of it. 'I know I can rely on your loyalty and discretion,' " I quoted solemnly. He laughed.

Paul went over to talk to Mary Bergstrom. I went back to my apartment, to sleep. I didn't need a Somnorific. I had an REM dream of an ef galloping a black stallion. She had a death's-head.

X-4

I awoke irritably at 0700 when my radio alarm clicked on to the strains of "Esperanti Street Songs." We were enduring one of the periodic Esperanto revivals, although linguists had proved—to my satisfaction at least—that the world had more to lose from a universal language than from a profusion of national tongues. The only valid universal languages were music, scientific symbology, and gold.

I did twenty minutes of slow hatha asanas, followed by twenty minutes of meditation. I showered, shaved, used my ultrasonic tooth strigil. I applied light pancake makeup, a rosy shade; my skin was rather sallow. Just a touch of lip rouge. An eyebrow darkener. My hair was still black, but my eyebrows were beginning to go gray. Probably an enzyme deficiency. I dressed while drinking the day's first glass of chilled Smack, laced with a packet of high-potency vitamin concentrate. I also ate two probisks. They tasted as you might expect: anise-flavored sawdust.

As usual, I arrived at my office before any of my three secretaries. Each was assigned one of the three general areas into which I had divided my responsibilities: (1). Day-to-day activities of DIVRAD; (2). Relations with Satisfaction Section and the other three divisions it ruled; (3). Relations with food and drug manufacturers, makers of prosthetic devices and organs, commercial laboratories, biomedical academies, neuroscientific associations, etc.

I found three neat stacks on my desk awaiting me, each left by one of my secretaries. All included memos, letters, and papers to be scanned; tapes to hear; films to see.

I glanced first at two bright-red teletyped messages. One was the weekly Satrat (Satisfaction Rating) Report from DIVDAT (Division of Data & Statistics). It showed the national Satrat was up .4 percent. That was encouraging.

The second red teletype was less encouraging. It was a medical report from SATSEC's Rehabilitation & Reconditioning Hospice No. 4, near Alexandria, Virginia. It stated that Hyman R. Lewisohn, the government's foremost theorist, showed no improvement under continued treatment. Lewisohn was suffering from leukemia. We had been trying a new manipulated form of methotrexate, with apparently no improvement. We might have to add vincristine and cytosine arabinoside. I jotted a note on the teletype to flash the Chief Resident at R&R No. 4 and discus it. Lewisohn's survival was the responsibility of my Division. I did not take the duty lightly.

I then went through everything else rapidly, making three new stacks of my own: (1). Requiring immediate attention; (2). Leave till tomorrow or for a week at most; (3). When I had time. Or never.

I was still at this organizing procedure when Ellen Dawes, one of my secretaries, came in. She was an AINF-B, a female bred by artificial insemination. I had long ago decided that the Examiner who had assigned her a Grade B rating had been more impressed by her personality than her genetic code. I didn't blame him a bit.

At the moment, as she stood in the doorway and held a plastic cup out to me, her eyes were as wide as those of an addict preparing a fix.

Without speaking, I went to my office safe, inserted my magnetic key, swung open the heavy door. I withdrew the five-pound can that had cost me fifty new dollars on the black market. She watched me measure out five tablespoons into her plastic cup. She licked her lips. Her eyes were still glistening.

"Thank you, Dr. Flair."

"Thank *you*, Ellen."

We both laughed. She left with the precious grind. I put the can back in the safe and locked the door. Fifteen minutes later Ellen was back with a steaming mug, put it carefully on my desk on a little plastimat. I didn't touch it until she had left to enjoy hers with the other two secretaries, both ems.

Then I sat back in my swivel chair, took a sip, closed my eyes. It was so hot it burned my lips. But I didn't care. It was the genuine thing. The last can I had bought, from an unfamiliar pusher, had turned out to be mostly chicory, oregano, and ground-up peanut shells. But this was real coffee. Possibly from Columbia State.

It was 0942 before I could get through to Lieutenant Oliver of the New York Peace Department. My office digiclock showed 1020 before I had things organized. Then we left the compound.

Paul and I led in an internal-combustion-engined sedan. I drove; Paul never could learn how to shift gears. His IMP equipment was in the back seat. Behind us came a fuel-cell-powered ambulance driven by Mary Bergstrom. With her were two laboratory attendants. They were both young gene-variant ems, bred by electrical parthenogenesis before we had satisfactorily solved the problems of chromosomal injection of the egg. Their appearance was normal, but both suffered from Parkinsonism. It was controlled with an improved form of L-dopa.

We stopped at the New York City Resting Home, after driving around the block three times before we found a parking space. I went inside with Mary Bergstrom.

There was no problem; Lieutenant Oliver had already alerted them. I signed the release form. Before Mary and the attendants took the cadaver away on a wheeled stretcher, I zipped the body bag down far enough to take a look.

Face contorted in agony. Bulging eyes. Rictus. Deep lateral scratches across the thoracic area. It was difficult to imagine, but he might have been handsome. I wondered if he and Angela had been users.

The guardian let us into the apartment. I locked the door; we looked around. All the furniture, the rugs, the prints on the walls, the linens, the plates and cutlery, even the clothing in the dressers and closets appeared to be leased. That was not unusual. Few people owned more than trinkets and minor personal effects. Styles and fashions changed rapidly; you could trade in all your belongings annually and lease new, tooty "possessions."

Paul began unpacking his equipment. I wandered about. The guardian and the officers who had removed the corpus had already polluted the air, the rugs, possibly the furniture. It was not an ideal situation for gathering IMP samples.

I went into the nest. Neat and clean. A row of six-hour Somnorifics in the medicine cabinet, along with the usual array of unrestricted drugs. Nothing unexpected. Paul started taking adhesive patches from the sink. I went into the living room. Cold, cold. . . . Who had lived there? No one had lived there. A ghost maybe. It was empty of human track. The bedroom wasn't much better. But the bed was rumpled, the thermal blanket thrown back, the plastisheet still showing an indentation where Frank Lawson Harris had rushed to an excruciating stop.

Near one leg of the bed a glint caught my eye. I bent over to stare at it. It appeared to be the foil seal of a Somnorific inhaler, balled up and flicked away. I went to Paul's case for a little self-closing plastic envelope. I slid the balled-up Somnorific seal into the bag and pressed the lips tightly together. I slipped the envelope into the pocket of my zipsuit. I went back into the nest. Paul was on his knees, sleeves rolled up, probing down into the toilet drain with a long, flexible instrument we called an "eel." It had a rounded, adhesive knob on the end.

"I'm going now," I said to Paul.

"Right."

"There are Somnorifics in the medicine cabinet. Bring them along."

He didn't answer. He was intent on what he was doing. He could probe a toilet drain, but he wouldn't do a postmortem or even look at a stopped em.

I went back to the compound. I had a lot of service to get through, heavy because in two days I was due for a threeday and wanted to train to Detroit, GPA-3, to visit my parents. And Millie.

First I took the little plastic envelope from my pocket and sent it down to A Lab for analysis of the Somnorific seal. Then I went back to scanning the daily team reports. My Division was organized into teams: Nutrition Team, Transplant Team, Genetic Team, Biochemistry Team, etc. We did a tremendous amount of original biomedical research. In addition, we performed the functions of what was formerly the Food and Drug Administration. We tested all commercial drugs and foods for purity. Well ... maybe not for purity, but for nontoxicity. And our field forces inspected production facilities regularly.

I was proud of the fact that DIVRAD was self-supporting. That is, we developed new foods, drugs, artificial and cloned organs, new laboratory equipment and techniques, etc. These, when not restricted, were licensed for commercial production. The fees received more than paid for the expenses of DIVRAD.

Only two other governmental departments were self-supporting. One was the Atomic Energy Commission of the Department of National Resources (formerly the Department of the Interior). The other, of course, was the National Contribution Commission (formerly the Internal Revenue Service), a division of the Department of Profitability (formerly the Department of the Treasury).

(Incidentally, all these name changes of government departments were not made by whim. They were decreed by the Office of Linguistic Truth, OLT, formerly the Office of Governmental Euphemisms, OGE.)

The following morning, Angela Teresa Berri returned from her threeday in California. I met her by chance in the corridor outside her office. We chatted casually, all-colored zipsuits moving by us on both sides.

Finally, the corridor reasonably clear, she murmured, "Anything?"

"No," I whispered in return. "Not yet. It's very complex. I'll contact you when I have something. Or nothing."

"Who else knows?"

"Paul Bumford."

She looked at me steadily. Greenish, flecked eyes.

"You trust him, Nick?"

"Of course."

She nodded, and was gone.

Late that afternoon, A Lab returned my little plastic envelope with their report. They had identified the inclosed object as a standard Somnorific seal. Hardly earth-shaking news. But on the underside of the seal they had discovered minute quantities of a substance they "believed to be" (typical scientific hedging, there) 5-HT.

Now, 5-HT—5-Hydroxytryptamine—is known to biochemists as serotonin. Nanogram amounts of platelet-bound iso-serotonin were found. And platelets are particles suspended in human blood, formed by bone marrow, and necessary in the clotting of blood and the sealing of injured blood vessels.

It was interesting.

The following morning, at 1030, Paul Bumford, Mary Bergstrom, and I were in my apartment, seated in plastivas slings drawn up around my new 3-D TV set (leased). The shades were down, the door locked, the flasher disconnected. The set was switched to Tape.

I leaned forward so I could see her, past Paul.

"Mary, what lens did you use?"

"Infinite focus," she said in that cold, toneless voice of hers. "Wide angle. Electronic zoom by voice-actuated switch. But no sound. There was no need for sound."

"Of course not," I said. I leaned back, pressed the Start button of my control unit.

The guard glass flickered. Wild images. Then, as the lasers took hold, the holograph image steadied in the box. We were looking at the pain-racked features of the stopped Frank Lawson Harris. Focus was sharp, colors were lifelike—or rather, unlifelike.

The naked corpus was stretched out on a stainless steel table, slightly tilted, with a run-off channel at the bottom. Mary stood behind the table, masked, gowned, gloved, scalpel in hand.

She gave us a running commentary, in person, her voice flat, without inflection.

"Closeup of features. Contorted. Agonized. Notice lips drawn back from teeth. Rictus. Long view of total anatomy. Limbs twisted. More than normal rigor. Notice hands half-clenched. Now this—close-up of lateral scratches in thoracic area. Analysis of tissue under object's fingernails proved scratches self-inflicted. Clawed at chest. Long shot again. Here—close-up of genitalia. Penis and testicles flaccid. Now . . . autopsy begins. I'm going in. Butterfly incision. Firm skin. Good muscle tone."

I was fascinated. I was aware that Paul Bumford was not watching.

"Everything normal," Mary continued tonelessly. The camera zoomed in to show her knife at work. "Now I'm going into the chest cavity. Heart normal but aorta unusually small to the touch. My first clue. Liver somewhat fatty but not pathologic. Here's a close-up. Healthy."

I watched the tape hum along. I admired her technique. She was sure, deft, unhurried. She removed the organs swiftly, put them gently aside.

"Now I'm into the stomach cavity. Normal. Except for that abdominal aorta. Unusually tortuous. You'll see a close-up in a second. There it is. Rigid, nodular. Now I'm at the pancreas. Everything out. Everything normal. Intestinal tract normal. Within four hours prior to stopping object had consumed proveal, propep, natural starch—possibly spaghetti—red petrowine, and a few other things. I have it all on my taped report. Now I'm in the lower abdominal area. This took more time than is shown, of course. I cut and spliced the Instaroid tape so you wouldn't get bored. Genitalia normal. There they are. Testicles large but soft. I'm going into them now. Ejaculation two hours before stopping. Penis small. Here, close-up, discoloration on glans. Analysis showed it to be Amour Now, a popular brand of lip rouge. Color: Passion Flower."

A sound came out of Paul Bumford next to me. Whether it was a groan, a sigh, or a giggle, I could not tell.

"Into the legs now," Mary Bergstrom continued, staring intently at the TV screen. "Nothing unusual. Good musculature. Strong. Good skin tone. But here again, close-up, tortuous and sclerotic femoral arteries. That completes the tape of the PM. Now we go to the tissue slides."

Paul straightened in the sling, took his hand from his eyes, looked at the TV glass.

"Cross sections," Mary narrated. "Gross slices, gold-palladium coated. For the SEM. Arterial. One: Internal carotid. Two: External carotid. Three: Thoracic aorta. Four: Abdominal. Five: Common iliac. Six: Femoral. Now we go to venous. One: Jugular. Two: Iliac. Three: Subclavian. Four: Vena cava. Finally, sections of those 'healthy' organs. One: Heart. Two: Liver. Three: Kidney. That's it."

The tape wound to whiteness. I pushed the Off button. We sat there in semidarkness, in silence. I couldn't believe what I had seen.

Paul Bumford spoke first.

"J-J-Jesus Christ!" he burst out. "Are those cross sections for real?"

"I have the shavings," Mary Margaret Bergstrom intoned. "I have the slides. It's all in my report."

After my initial shock, I began to realize what had happened to Frank Lawson Harris. Those arteries and veins looked like obso iron pipes, the inside surfaces so encrusted with rust that flow was slowed and finally choked completely. It would take years, maybe a century, for iron pipes to become that obstructed. I suspected the stopped em's circulatory system had been plugged in minutes, and the intensive venous involvement suggested a nonphysiologic process.

I stood and raised the shades. We blinked in the strong south light.

"Anyone want anything?" I asked.

"Something stronger than Smack," Paul said. His voice was shaky.

I had been saving a bottle of natural apple brandy for a special occasion. This seemed like a "special occasion." I poured three small glasses—real glass—and served their drinks, then brought mine. I stood before them, leaning on the TV set.

"Paul?" I said. "you all right?"

"Fine," he said defiantly. "I'm fine."

"You saw the tissue slides. Diagnosis?"

"Extensive, widespread infractions involving multiple organ systems."

"Mary?"

"I concur."

"Any idea what caused it, Paul?" I asked.

"Ingestion. Injection."

"Not ingestion." Mary Bergstrom shook her head. "I'd have found traces in the stomach lining or intestinal tract. Not injection. I went over the object carefully with a high-powered magnifier prior to PM. He was clean."

"Inhalant?" I suggested.

They looked at me.

"Possible," Paul said.

"Probable," Mary said.

"All right." I nodded. "Now what did he inhale?"

"Something," Paul said. "Something that caused wild, uncontrolled platelet agglutination and limpid deposition."

"Serotonin," Mary said. I looked at her, surprised and pleased. She had learned a lot, outside her discipline. "It's got to be the serotonin. Probably a manipulated form of 5-HT. The East uses it as an interrogative technique. By injection. Very painful. Very. But this must have been by inhalation. Stopping him almost instantaneously."

"I concur." I nodded. "The military played with it in the obso days of hypothesized chemwar. But they rejected it. Too lethal."

"Too lethal?" Paul cried. "For a nerve gas?"

"Use your brain. It killed instantly. So we wipe out all of France. Seventy-five million humans stopped, plus all other warm-blooded animals, including those marvelous geese with their synthetic-hormone-injected livers. What do we do for foie gras then? Seriously, what would the military do? All those corpora to flame. Vegetation gone too, if we wanted. What's the point? War is geography. That's why the military put lethal gas in the icebox and switched to temporary incapacitators. Knock 'em out, walk in wearing masks, take away their weapons, wait for them to wake up. Then they go back to work, the horses pull, the dogs bark, the birds sing, and those geese feel their livers expand. Beautiful. Simple and humane. But at onetime, back in the 1970's and '80's, a 5-HT gas existed. Probably still does. In a deep cave somewhere in Colorado."

I paused.

"The New York Peace Department will be very interested in this," I continued smoothly. "Mary, you did a fine service."

If I had told her she was gorgeous, she couldn't have blushed a deeper hue.

"Thank you," she said faintly.

"Run a lung slice to confirm. I think you'll find it. Then put the object back together again. Paul will give you the final disposition."

She nodded to us and was gone.

"A very bright ef," I said, after the door closed behind her.

"Sometimes she scares me," Paul said gloomily.

"Pure intelligence is always scary. You've never met Lewisohn, have you? There's a creative intellect that's terrifying."

" 'Final disposition'?" he said. "You told Mary I'd give her orders for the final disposition of the object. What?"

"That's Angela's problem. I'm going on a threeday in exactly"—I looked at my digiwatch—"three hours and fourteen minutes. Angela knows you're in on this. Catch her alone and ask her what to do with it. She'll probably want it flamed."

"Probably."

"All right. Now let's get to you, what you found. Did you bring back those Somnorifics in the medicine cabinet?"

"You told me to."

"What were they?"

"Analyzed? Six-hour Somnorifics."

"Uh-huh. What else?"

He finally shook off his depression, came alive, started talking rapidly.

"Habitual and recent presence in the apartment of an ef, approximately twenty years old, one sixty-five centimeters. Long, blond hair, trimmed recently. She uses Quik-Eeze Creme Shampoo. She wears tooty shoes. Spike heels. One pair is oxblood red. No Reason perfume, a complete synthetic. Amour Now lip rouge. Color: Passion Flower."

"Ah-ha," I said.

"Let's see . . . what else? Slight nasal drip. Low-grade bronchial infection. Fuchsia eye shadow. Ugh! Oh: here's an oddity; I don't think she's on the pill or any other fertility control. Blood type is O-Rh negative. That's not Harris'. She was recently on a threeday or vacation in a hot, southern climate." He paused. "Want to know how I know all this?"

I looked at him.

"I know exactly how you know all that. You used chromatography, electrophoresis, spectrophotometry, polarizing microscopes, X-ray refraction, the scanning electron microscope, and our very best energy-dispersion analyzer. All this high-priced equipment on hairs you found on the backs of chairs and the sofa. Ditto on stains from hair shampoo. Position of stains gave you height. Then we have rug indentations for the spike heels and rug stains for shoe color. Pillowcase stains and scents for lip rouge and perfume. You might have used the Olfactory Analysis Indicator there. Eye shadow from pillowcase or bathroom towel, which would also give you perspiration specimen, which would give you a partial immunoglobulin profile. Nasal drip and bronchial infection from discarded tissues in the bathroom wastebasket."

"And the vacation in a hot, southern climate?"

"Skin flakes all over the place."

"Gee, boss, you're real smart."

"That's why I'm an Assistant Deputy Director, and you're my Executive Assistant."

It was a mistake. I knew it the moment I said it.

"All right, all right," I said hurriedly. "Did you find an exhausted Somnorific inhaler? Near the bed? Anywhere in the bedroom? In the apartment?"

"No. No sign."

"I checked with Lieutenant Oliver. His ems didn't find it either. They took Instaroids of the scene in the bedroom. No empty Somnorific inhaler."

"Is it important?"

"Yes. But let's get on with it. I've got to catch a train. What about the IMP samples?"

Now, I shall be as brief as possible. Microbiologists interested in pursuing the subject further are advised that more than a hundred references exist on film spindles. The journals of the American Society of Microbiology might be a good place to start.

As I had told Paul Bumford, the idea of microbiological identification of the individual began as a forensic concept, the purpose being to establish the presence of a suspect at the scene of a crime. I felt this was of peripheral importance. Microbiology, I was convinced, could be used as exact means of personal identification of the general populace, far superior to appearance, physical measurements, fingerprints, voiceprints, hair, teeth, blood type, etc.

All humans are hosts to an incredible number and variety of microorganisms. Some exist within the skin, some without. Some are pathogenic. Most, fortunately, are inert or beneficial. Indeed without the "good" protozoa, bacteria, fungi, and viruses, we simply could not exist.

IMP, Individual Microbiological Profile, was a project concerned only with the external microbial populations that humans support on skin, eyes, nasal passages, genitalia, throat, anus, mouth—whatever organs of the body are exposed to the atmosphere.

After two years of research, the IMP Project (a temporary horizontal organization drawing specialists from all my teams) selected the fifty most common permanent and semi-permanent microorganisms to be found on the human body. Each was given a quantitative rating of 1 to 10, depending on the profusion in which it was found on a particular object's surfaces.

We then took IMP samples from every member of the Department of Bliss—quite an undertaking when you consider there were more than half a million in DOB service. And "taking an IMP sample" involved analysis of saliva, sputum, perspiration, semen, vaginal scrapings, skin scrapings, nasal and throat discharges, urine, and feces. Fortunately, most of these analyses were automated.

Having coded IMP's for the 500,000-plus DOB personnel, we fed the information to our largest DIVRAD computer and asked for duplicates. There were none. That was encouraging, but hardly surprising.

We were about to start testing computer retrieval of IMP information. If the blind tests were successful, I intended to suggest a campaign, low-key at first, to make microbiological analysis obligatory nationwide. We would then include every American's IMP in his file in the NDB (National Data Bank).

"I was able to get a good IMP of Harris from his apartment," Paul Bumford said. "His dirty laundry, sink, bed, atmosphere, rugs, toilet seat, and so forth. What I couldn't get, Mary furnished from the corpus. But we already have Harris' IMP on file. I presume you want a blind identification test. Right?"

"Right."

"But why an IMP on anyone else I could find?"

I didn't answer his question. "Did you get an IMP on the unknown blond ef?"

"A partial. Fairly accurate, I would say. Thirty-two definite factors out of the fifty. Nine possibles. That leaves nine unknowns. And where does that leave us? Nick, do you think the blond ef is in service in DOB? Is her IMP on file?"

"Could be. Harris was in DOB. It's possible his user was, too."

"Possible, but chancy. There's something else on your mind. I can tell."

I paced around, looking down at the floor, hands jammed into my zipsuit pockets.

"A crazy idea," I muttered. "You'll laugh at me."

"I've never laughed at one of your ideas in my life and never shall," he vowed.

"I thank you," I said. Everything was all right between us again. "The crazy idea is this: Of those fifty microorganisms included in the IMP, I think about half could be inherited."

He sucked in his breath. "My God," he said, "you are incredible."

"If I'm right," I went on, "if twenty-five or thirty factors out of the fifty— particularly those in the respiratory tract—are inherited, then maybe if that mysterious blond ef who sucked Harris' cock the night he was stopped isn't actually in service in DOB, with an IMP on file, then maybe she's related to someone who is. What do you think?"

He looked at me, shaking his head.

"Mary scares me, and you scare me," he said. "What do I think? Definitely possible."

"Yes. Now here's what I want you to do while I'm gone. Take your construction of Harris' IMP to the Computer Team. Tell them you're running a preliminary blind test and see if they validate it. Then try input of the unknown blonde's IMP. I know it's incomplete, but *try* it. If the computer comes up with zilch, ask Jim Phelps if he can reprogram to give you a list of DOB people with identical quanta on the IMP factors you *do* have on the blonde. Follow?"

"Of course. I'll have it all for you when you return. You better get moving. Say hello to your parents for me."

"Thank you, I will. I'll be back in time for the Section meeting on Thursday. Meanwhile, keep the mill grinding."

"Bastard!" He laughed. He took Mary Bergstrom's cassette from my TV set and started out. The tape cartridge reminded me of something.

"Paul."

He turned back.

"This is for the Tomorrow File."

He brightened. The TF was his baby.

"I know you weren't watching the PM. That's all right. But you heard Mary's narration. Did you hear her say that the stomach was normal, the heart was normal, the pancreas was normal? And that the liver was slightly fatty but not pathologic?"

"So?"

"Paul, those organs were grossly normal. Microscopically, of course, they were totally infarcted. But if they *had* been totally normal, they would still be shoved back into the object and flamed. The waste! You know the figures on donated organs, in spite of that last telethon. And production of artificial and cloned organs just isn't enough. We don't have the love we need to increase production. Patients are waiting, hopefully. And we're going to flame a healthy heart, liver, pancreas, stomach. And every time anyone stops naturally and is flamed, we lose retinas, kidneys, hands, arms, legs, gonads, and ovaries we can use, that we need."

"Nick," he said soberly, "you were the one who taught me the difference between what we *should* do and what we *can* do."

"I know, I know," I said impatiently. "That's why this is for the Tomorrow File. The first sanitation laws this country passed, more than two hundred years ago, established the government's interest in and concern for public health. Then laws, laws, and more laws. Sanitation, hygiene, drinking water, sewer systems, inspection of meat plants, then Medicare, then hospitalization insurance, government payment for kidney dialysis, genetic counseling, then national health insurance, then the Fertility Control Act, the licensing of procreation. It's all been gradually, gradually evolving, coming to a time when we must realize the citizen's corpus is the government's responsibility."

"And property?" Paul said.

"Well . . . its concern, certainly. We should not flame healthy organs; that's all I know. They're too valuable. They could be used for research, transplant, or frozen for the nukewar bank. They're a national resource and should not be wasted."

Paul computed a moment.

"It would mean a federal license for stopping," he said. "Government inheritability of the corpus."

"I know." I nodded. "That's what troubles me."

He looked at me steadily.

"The future belongs to the untroubled," he said.

X-5

They had restored direct New York-Detroit train service in 1983. It was the southern route, via Philadelphia, Canton, and Toledo, Ohio. I took the Bullet Train. It was gas-turbine-powered, with a linear motor. We moved at 480 kph, riding on a cushion of air about 1.5 cm above the track. Beautifully smooth, quiet, comfortable. The service in the dining car was excellent, the food detestable. But no one complained. They had no basis for comparison.

I had taken a compartment. This was a threeday, but I had brought along a case of papers, film spindles, tapes. Fortunately, I didn't need to carry clothing or toilet accessories. I kept a civilian wardrobe and complete kit in my suite in my parents' home.

The morning I returned to GPA-1, three days hence, I would be expected to attend the monthly executive conference of Satisfaction Section. This was, of course, ruled by Angela Berri, DEPDIRSAT. Present would be the Assistant Deputy Directors of her four divisions. The five of us (DIVLEG had two Assistant Deputy Directors) would sit facing Angela across the white plastiglass table in the conference room. Behind each of us would be seated our Executive Assistant. In my case, that would be Paul Bumford.

Angela Teresa Berri was a rigorously efficient manager. Each Division was allowed ten minutes, no more, no less, to present and discuss a single topic.

The topic I had selected for discussion in this particular meeting was Project Supersense.

Almost fifty years ago, neurosurgeons believed they had isolated "pleasure centers" in the human brain that could be excited by implanted electrodes. It became obvious, years later, that the term "pleasure center" was something of a misnomer; there was no single center of pleasure in human brains, or even in a single brain. Pleasure was generated in a series of "islands of concentration" in the pathway leading from the forepart of the hypothalamus to the cortex. Tickle one, and the object was no longer thirsty. Excite another, and hunger was satisfied. Titillate a third, electrically or chemically, and sexual pleasure was produced.

After lengthy experimentation on animals, a technique was evolved by which needle-thin electrodes could be implanted in the human brain. Energizing the titanium-alloy electrodes with a mild electric current gave the object a feeling of well-being. One neuroscientist termed it "reward" rather than "pleasure." Exact placement of the electrodes was crucial, but not as difficult as you might expect. During neurosurgery, the object might be administered an anesthetic sufficient only to allow cutting through the scalp and drilling a hole in the skull.

Once the surgeon was through the meninges, the patient could be conscious and responsive during surgery. Fortunately, the stuff of the brain itself cannot register pain. So a surgeon implanting electrodes could probe and test, probe and test, asking the wide-eyed object, "There? There? What do you feel? What's happening? Are you happy?"

Originally, after correct emplacement, these electrodes were fixed with glue to the object's skull, with a bit protruding beyond the scalp. Wires were attached to carry the required electric current. Later, using hardware developed in the space program, a microminiaturized radio receiver, battery-powered, was taped to the object's skull. Upon receipt of a radio signal, it stimulated the object's "pleasure centers." Thus he was ambulatory, free from entangling wires.

Still later, a microminiaturized radio transmitter, battery-powered, was attached to his belt. The receiver was implanted beneath his scalp for cosmetic reasons. An object could now stimulate his own brain, giving himself a jolt of pleasure, or reward, by pressing a button on his belt kit.

The purpose of all this research and development was therapeutic, to relieve the symptoms of epilepsy, depression, schizophrenia, etc.

But as frequently happens, what began as a biomedical blessing became a medical craze. It was estimated that more than two million Americans had had electrodes implanted in their brains for the sole purpose of self-stimulation. The operation was not inexpensive, and even with the development of plastitanium, the presence of electrodes (or any foreign matter) in the brain presented certain risks, especially during violent acceleration or deceleration of the object. In a car crash, for instance. But the risks did not lessen the human hunger for new pleasures. They never do.

Now enters Project Supersense. It was my idea. I realized that the brains of these two million electrode-implanted Americans were being stimulated by a radio signal, self-produced. I saw no reason, considering the state of our technology, why a film—either in a movie theatre or on a TV set at home—could not be coded along its edge, just as sound is synchronized to the visual image, to send a signal to all receivers under the scalps or within the skulls of the "Mind-Jerkers," as the people who had opted for the electrode implant operation were popularly called.

Then these two million, watching a film on any subject, would be automatically stimulated to pleasure, thirst, pain, hunger, or eventually any other appetite or emotion, if neurobiological research continued at its present rate. Their titillations would be synchronized with the scene being shown on the film. Mind-Jerkers would feel greatly increased sexual arousal during a love scene, increased pain during a torture scene, increased fear during a horror scene, increased glee during a comedy scene.

I discussed this concept with Paul Bumford. He enthusiastically concurred that it was feasible. It was assigned to my Psychobiology Team. After investigation and research, they reported the plan practical, valuable, and eagerly awaited a go signal to develop the necessary hardware and film synchronization techniques in conjunction with the Electronics Team.

It was the file on Project Supersense that I was reviewing and attempting to evaluate on my train trip to Detroit. I was trying to decide whether to recommend going ahead with it or stopping it.

The railroad station in Detroit occupied a concourse on the two lowest floors of a new high-rise crematorium. Carrying my case, I took the express elevator to the copter pad on the roof. My father's copter was waiting. In his inimitable style, the four-seater was painted a startling Chinese red. On the cabin, in block lettering of vibrating purple, it read: FLAIR TOYS: THE TOYS WITH A FLAIR! Subtle.

The pilot was a young ef with flaming blue hair. She wore a Chinese-red zipsuit. Across one breast the expected legend was embroidered in that jarring purple. But she was so pneumatic it read: "flAIRToys." She told me she would drop me at the house, have something to eat, then go out to the airport to pick up my father, who was coming in on a commercial flight from Denver. He had a factory out there.

We tilted out over the Detroit River and almost immediately began our descent over Belle Isle to Grosse Pointe. She hovered a moment over my father's beautifully tended estate, then let down on the front lawn. My mother wasn't too far away, near the water. She was seated in a garden chair of white-painted iron. She was wearing one of her gowns of flowing silk, all pleats and ruffles. Her thin arm poked out, resting on the table alongside. Her fleshless fingers grasped the glass.

I looked around for Mrs. McPherson. She was nearby, a wooden statue with folded arms, standing under a small copse of young elms. She never let my mother out of her sight. Never.

I walked slowly down to the garden chair.

"Mother," I said softly.

"Who?" she said vaguely. She looked up at me, dazed and faraway.

"Nick."

"Who?"

"Nicholas, your loving and devoted son."

Her face cracked into a million pleased wrinkles.

"Nicholas, my loving and devoted son," she repeated, reaching out her arms. "Come kiss me, chappie."

And so I did.

"How are you, Mother?"

"'I never saw a purple cow,'" she said.

"What?"

"'I never saw a purple cow, I never hope to see one; But I can tell you, anyhow, I'd rather see than be one.'"

"What on earth is *that?*"

"Long before your time."

"Mother, it's nonsense."

"Isn't it?" she said delightedly. "Isn't it just! You're so handsome."

"Mother's beauty, father's brains."

"You're lucky," she said, and we let it go at that.

"This world . . ." she said.

"Yes, yes," I said. "Let's go up to the house. It's getting chill, and we have so much to talk about."

I got her onto her feet and gave her my arm. We walked slowly, slowly up the slope.

"Nicholas, my loving and devoted son," she mused.

"I am that."

Behind us, trailing but catching up, Mrs. McPherson trundled along, somber in the dusk.

"Are you in love, chappie?" She used the word in the obso sense.

"Not at the moment, Mother."

She laughed again. She had been a great beauty. But she had resigned from the world; she no longer belonged.

When I got mother inside, Mrs. McPherson took over and helped her upstairs to her bedroom. Charles smiled a welcome and took my case. I didn't know what Charles was. Obviously an obso em, he had to be an NM—but I knew nothing about his genesis. I suspected he might be from GPA-2, from the Tidewater section of what was formerly Virginia.

I went into the library. I mixed a vodka-and-Smack, mostly vodka. Coming home always did that to me. I could analyze my reactions, but it didn't help. I wandered about the library. Almost two thousand books my father had never read.

I was finishing my second drink when I heard the copter overhead. I went outside and stood on the floodlighted porch. I admired the youthful way he leaped from the copter and came bounding across the lawn toward me.

"Nick-ol'-as!" he shouted as he came. "Nick-ol'-as!"

It was his joke. He never tired of it.

He caught me up in a great bear hug. What a ruffian he was! He pulled me close. He smelled of a lot of things: petroscot, a testosterone-based cologne, a scent of something softer—probably from a quick embrace with that blue-haired ef copter pilot.

In the library, under overhead light, his face, beneath his makeup, seemed old and tired. But his manner hadn't changed: loud voice; jaunty walk; hard, decisive gestures; barked laugh; the need for physical contact—fingers on arm, arm around shoulders, shoves, pats, strokes, thumps. It was his way.

He poured us drinks, a petroscot for himself, one of my mother's potato vodkas for me. We hoisted glasses to each other and sipped.

"You seem perky," I said. "Who's the new tootie?"

He barked his laugh.

"You wouldn't believe."

"I'd believe."

"Ever catch *Circus au Natural?* It's on Thursday nights at 2300."

"The contortionist?" I said.

"You bastard!" He barked again. "You know everything. Hungry?"

"Starved."

We went into the cavernous dining room. We sat next to each other at an oak table large enough to seat twenty. It was genuine oak, all right. When they destroyed an obso building and found reusable oak planks they fashioned them into tables for the wealthy. But first they dipped the planks in caustic, beat them with chains, drilled in fake wormholes, and then used a stencil to make false rings where wet glasses might have rested. *Then* they coated the whole thing with Plastiseal.

My father didn't give a damn about food. Put anything in front of him—he'd eat it. But he had a special fondness for new foods, synthetics, laboratory spices, and refinery flavorings.

After dinner, dominated by his long, loud discourse on the success of his new sex dolls, we moved back to the library for a natural brandy. He continued his monologue there.

The sex dolls were not obscene. They were the result of a government contract he had won to produce small Juskin dolls, efs and ems, to teach sex education to four-year-olds. The dolls were naked and complete with genitalia. They had proved so popular that my father had started commercial production. They were now available in three sizes: 28, 60, and 90 cm tall. Many adults bought them.

Chester K. Flair had long experience in the industry. Originally, he had been employed as a research chemist by a toy and doll manufacturer. He came up with a suggestion for a doll that vomited when you bent it forward sharply. The vomit was a viscous compound containing bits of sharp plastic. You fed it into the doll through a stoppered opening at the nape of its neck. Refills of vomit were to be available in half-liter bottles.

Also, my father cleverly suggested adding a stain to the fake vomit so that after regurgitation, the doll's dress was stained ineradicably. The doll's owner (her parents, actually) would then be forced to purchase a new costume. This doll, my father was convinced, would be an immediate commercial success. He called it Whoopsy-Daisy.

His employer rejected the idea. My father then married the woman who became my mother. Her name was Beatrice Susan Bennington. With her money—she had an inheritance of 50,000 old dollars—my father resigned his service, formed his own company and, with additional financing, started production of Whoopsy-Daisy. His confidence was vindicated. It was an almost instant success. He expanded his corporation to include the production of conventional toys, dolls, and novelties. He was a very knowledgeable and shrewd businessman.

When I was nine years old, one of my father's designers came up with the extraordinary idea of a baby doll that defecated. The "feces" were plastic turds, fed into an opening in the doll above the coccyx.

The production of the Poo-Poo Doll, as it was called, meant an enormous investment in new dies, formulae, patents, machinery, etc. I remember an incident that occurred during this period. I was then ten years old, and my father still had fantasies of my "following in his footsteps" and becoming a doll manufacturer and director of his enterprises after he retired. He insisted I accompany him to a bank meeting for the purpose of securing a large loan to finance tooling-up for production of the Poo-Poo Doll.

I listened to my father make his presentation to a tableful of hard-faced bankers. He demonstrated a handmade prototype. He explained, with charts, color slides, and samples, that he was basing his estimate of potential income not only on the initial retail purchase price of Poo-Poo but on continued consumption of packages of fresh plastic turds and miniature paper diapers.

They listened to his sales pitch expressionlessly. When he finished, they turned to look at each other. He was asking for a great deal of love. Finally, one banker with a skin of parchment made a tent of his hands, stared thoughtfully at the ceiling, and said, "I know we have dolls that piss. But dolls that shit? Isn't that in rather poor taste?"

I rarely forget anything. But *that* I particularly remember.

My father got his loan. The Poo-Poo Doll proved to be the sensation of the industry. It made millions of new dollars.

My father ended his Panegyric to Sex Dolls abruptly. He poured us each another brandy, then flopped onto the leather couch facing me. "So what's new?" he asked.

I recognized that apparently casual "What's new?" My father was fearful of aging, especially of the loss of physical strength that aging imposes, particularly of the diminution of his sexual vigor. I knew he would never lose the hunger. His terror was of being deprived of the ability to satisfy it.

"Nothing much," I said. "We're fooling around with several things at the moment: a manipulated form of vitamin E that's had some interesting results on rats; a new steroid we're constructing; and the pituitary transplant program is continuing. I really think we'll find the answer there, in the anterior lobe."

"How about injection of testosterone? I think that's the most obvious answer. After all, I have a BS in chemistry."

I refrained from sighing. This was the Bachelor of Science who had flashed me from Hong Kong to ask if there was really any aphrodisiacal benefit in swallowing a ground-up tiger's tooth, as he had been assured by a Chinese apothecary.

"Androgen would be the most obvious answer," I agreed. "If it worked. It's been tried for years, for a half a century, and it doesn't. But there are so many psychological factors involved, it's difficult to make an objective evaluation of the results. We can clone ovaries easily, but we're having trouble with testes. So that leaves direct transplant. Would you like to leave your nuts to science?"

"Fat chance," he scoffed. "When they flame me, my nuts are going to be where they've always been—between my legs. Who knows, I may go to heaven and need them."

"Fat chance," I repeated, and he laughed.

We sat a few moments in silence, staring into the cold fireplace.

"Something bothering you?" he said finally.

"Not bothering me, exactly, but perplexing me."

"What is it?"

"I have a Section conference when I get back. I have to make a recommendation to go ahead on a project or to stop it."

"What is it?"

Ordinarily, I don't like to discuss DIVRAD's business with outsiders. The indepsec stuff I never do, of course. But it suddenly occurred to me that I might benefit from his practical judgment and shrewdness. I briefly explained Project Supersense to him, how film scenes could be synchronized to give Mind-Jerkers increased stimulation. He listened closely, fascinated. He was always fascinated by anything that affected sexual pleasure, however indirectly.

"What do you think?" I asked him when I had finished.

"How many Mind-Jerkers are there in the country?"

"About two million. Maybe seventy-five percent adults."

"How would they pay for this?"

"I don't know. We'd license the process, I imagine. The people who make TV tape cassettes might be interested."

"I doubt it. Two million isn't much of a potential market these days. Is there any other way of producing the same results? Say by a pill?"

"Not at the moment there isn't."

I didn't tell him about Paul Bumford's memo in the Tomorrow File on the UP—the Ultimate Pleasure pill.

"Then forget about Project Supersense. Stop it." He rose and began to pace about the library. "Try for a pill that increases pleasure. Why a pill? The two big C's of modern merchandising: Convenience and Consumption. You've got to have a product that's convenient to use, and that is consumed by use, and has to be repurchased periodically. The safety razor was the greatest product ever invented. The makers could give it away, because then you had to buy their blades. That's where the love was. Ditto the camera. What goddamn good is it without film? No, forget about Project Supersense. Strictly a one-time sale. Put your people to work on a pleasure pill."

"It's not as simple as you think," I objected. "First of all, what *is* pleasure? No one can define it. Too subjective. To an obso ef suffering from arthritis, pleasure might simply be absence of pain. To a young em, pleasure might be parachuting from one hundred fifty meters. To me, pleasure is this glass of natural brandy. To you—well, I know what pleasure is to you."

"Don't say it!" He barked his loud laugh.

"What I'm getting at is that there are no objective criteria. How can we possibly start synthesizing a pill? We don't even know what we're looking for."

I finished my brandy and stood up. I pleaded tiredness and work to do. He didn't object. He had work to do, too.

The copter was still on the front lawn, and I supposed the ef pilot was in the guesthouse, waiting.

My parents' home had been built in 1904 by a wealthy Detroit brewer. I was born a little after midnight in my mother's bedroom on the second floor.

The house was a charming horror, a dizziness of gables, turrets, minarets. My father had compounded the insanity by adding a glass-enclosed terrace, a futuristic plastisteel guesthouse, and a boathouse on the river done in Tudor style with beams brought from England. There was an antique coat of arms over the doorway with the motto: *Aut Vincere Aut Mori*. I told my father it meant "I shall conquer death," and no one ever enlightened him. He was pleased with it, and had *Aut Vincere Aut Mori* engraved on his personal stationery.

My suite was on the third floor. A huge bedroom had a four-poster bed, two enormous armoires that held most of my civilian clothing, chests of drawers, an ornate, gilt-edged pier glass, a few faded prints of sailing ships on the walls. An open doorway (no door) led to a modernized nest. Then there was a small study that was all business: desk, swivel chair, film spindle racks, reading machine, a tape recorder that took cassettes, cartridges, and open-end reels, a TV set, a small refrigerator, and file cabinets.

The final room was my "secret place." It was always kept locked. I had, as far as I knew, the only key. Each time I left to go back to GPA-1, I glued a fine thread from jamb to door, about 20 cm above the floor. The thread had never been disturbed.

Two walls of this hideaway were the lower slopes of the mansard roof, interrupted by two gabled windows facing south and east. The inside walls and ceiling were plaster, painted white a long time ago. Now they were almost ocher. There was a frazzled rag rug on the planked floor, a sprung Morris chair with the leather seat and back cushion dried and cracking. There was a metal smoking stand, a bottle of my father's natural brandy and a single glass, a small bookshelf that held four books.

That's all there was. Nothing very significant. Except for the four books.

In 1998, most "books" were published on film spindles, designed for lap and desk reading machines. The few actual books printed were paperbound. To buy a hardcover book, you had to patronize a rare book store, an antique shop, or a merchant who sold secondhand junk. Practically everything ever published had been reproduced on microfilm. It took up so much less space, people simply sold or gave away their actual books, or threw them out. As my father would say, the film spindles were convenient.

In 1992, to escape a sudden and unexpected summer shower, I had ducked into a tiny decrepit antique bookstore on Morse Avenue (formerly Second Avenue in Manhattan). I had passed it a few times previously, and was vaguely aware it specialized in obso art books. How it survived I do not know, since you could buy film spindles of most of the world's great art, and the color reproduction in a viewing machine was incomparably more vivid than on a printed page.

Waiting for the summer squall to pass, I idly picked up and leafed through a heavily illustrated catalogue of an art exhibit that had been held in New York in 1968. The artist was an em I had never heard of. His name was Egon Schiele.

It would be melodramatic to declare that coming upon that old art exhibition catalogue by accident on a rainy summer afternoon changed my life. It did not change my life, of course. I continued my service in DOB as before (I was then Executive Assistant to AssDepDirRad). I visited my parents, ate, slept, used around; nothing in my life changed.

But something in me was altered. I knew it now. How I was altered by seeing the work of Egon Schiele, in what manner and to what extent, I did not compute then and did not now.

Egon Schiele was an Austrian painter, born in 1890, stopped in 1918. He was twenty-eight. He was the son of a railroad server. He lived in poverty most of his life. He was imprisoned, briefly, for "immorality," for having shown some of his drawings to curious children. He died of influenza, on the day of his wife's funeral. She also died of influenza.

Those were the bare bones of the em's life. They tell you little, and what they do tell is without significance. The meaning lies in the man's work.

If you stared for hours, as I had, at the self-portraits, you would see the depth of demonic possession in that face, and you would be disturbed, as I was disturbed. Did I like the work of Egon Schiele? I did not. But it obsessed me. There had not been a single day since 1992 when, at some time, awake or asleep, I had not suddenly remembered one of his drawings or paintings. With pain, and the sense of loss.

I had purchased the exhibition catalogue, and the obso shopkeeper promised to try to find more of Schiele's work. About a month later he mailed me a note—handwritten!—saying he had located another catalogue of a different Schiele exhibition. I bought that one, too. During the following years I was able to buy another book, in poor condition, of sketches Schiele had made while in prison.

Then one day the owner of the shop where I had purchased the catalogue flashed me, in great excitement. He had heard of an obso ef, a widow, a recluse, who owned a biography of Schiele. It was, reportedly, in mint condition, an enormous volume of 687 pages with 228 full-page reproductions (84 in color), plus 612 text illustrations. She would accept no less than 1,000 new dollars for this prize. I bought it immediately, sight unseen. It was a prize.

Those were the four books in my secret place: the life and work of Egon Schiele. I had never seen any of his originals (most were in museums in Pan-Europe). I had never been able to locate prints or large reproductions. Schiele's name was not included on the list of artists whose work was available on film spindles.

On the cover flap of the largest book, an unknown editor had written: "The anguish of the lonely, the . . . despair of the suffering, the desolation of the desperate, are the moods Schiele expressed. . . . The themes are genesis and decay, longing and lust, ecstasy and despair, suffering and sorrow. . . ." This was all true, but it was not the entire truth.

I sat in my creaking chair, alone in the world, turning pages to feed on those wonders. Yes, there was gloom there, pain and desperation. But I was once again shocked by the colors, the forms, the beauty he had seen and I had not. There was something indomitable there, something triumphant.

It was after midnight before I closed the book, switched off the light, locked the door, went into my bedroom. Even in bed, my lids resolutely shut, I saw an explosion of color, pinwheels, great rockets and fireworks, all created by that long-stopped em whose eyes stared at me so intently from the self-portraits.

I awoke at 0900 to the roar of the copter ascending: Chester K. Flair commuting to his office and factory near Mt. Clemens. The copter thrummed away, the noise faded. Then I heard gasping caws of delight: water birds over Lake St. Clair. I went to the south window but could not see them in the fog. But I heard their cries.

The break in my daily routine was welcome. I pulled on old slacks, a heavy turtleneck sweater, worn moccasins. In the kitchen, with Miss Catherine bustling about, trying to force a "good, hot, solid breakfast" on me, I had only a glass of orange concentrate in cold Smack and a cup of something called coftea. It tasted like neither. To please Miss Catherine, I ate one slice of toast. Most of it anyway. Every year our bread became fouler and more nutritious.

Then I wandered out onto the grounds. The fog was lifting from the lake. I could still hear the birds. I went down to the shore. I found a flat stone and tried to skip it over the surface of the water, but it sank instantly. I picked up another stone, almost perfectly round. I bounced it on my palm. How could a stone seem so alive?

I strolled about, no plan or destination in mind, just meandering. I passed the garage, the boathouse, the guesthouse, the empty stable. Once we had a horse, a gentle mare named Eve, with a back as broad as a desk, so fat you couldn't possibly fall off. Eve had died during the equine encephalitis epizootic in 1985. My mother had wept.

I sat on the cold, wet grass under an oak tree. I rubbed my cheek against the rough bark. I chewed a blade of grass, bitter and pulpy, and spit it out. I poked a finger down into the moist soil.

My mother came down for lunch, sweeping into the glass-inclosed terrace like an obso queen.

"Good morning, chappie! It's going to be a beautiful day. I just feel it!"

She held up her face to be kissed, then insisted I sit next to her at the table. It was glass-topped, on an ornate wrought-iron base. It was set with linen placemats, Georgian silver, a crystal vase of mums. Everything had been leased. The mums were plastic.

The lunch was delightful, except for the food. My mother was in a manic mood, laughing, shrieking, clutching my arm, telling me outrageous stories of the two young ems who had purchased the estate next to ours. Apparently, both wore false eyelashes, and one had a small gold ring suspended from his nasal septum. Mother was delighted with them; they had brought her natural crocuses they had found on their grounds, in early spring.

"What are their names?" I asked.

"Who, Nick?"

We went on to something else. She was like that now, and deteriorating. Her attention span grew shorter and shorter each time I came home. She would not seek help, and my father would not force her. Nor would I.

Later we strolled about the grounds, trailed by Mrs. McPherson.

The afternoon passed. It was a glory, the air washed, earth scented. We went back to the terrace, and Charles threw open all the windows. Another glass and pitcher were put on a small table next to the soft chair where mother lolled. I lay on the couch. Once we sang a song together, a children's song I hadn't heard in years: "If you needed a man to encourage the van...."

Then, the pitcher almost empty, she fell silent. Her eyes became dazed: that faraway look I had noticed on greeting her the previous day. I looked around for Mrs. McPherson. She came out of the house and led my mother away.

I went upstairs to bathe, shave, clean my teeth with an old-fashioned brush, and apply makeup. I dressed in a manner I thought would please Millie: a collarless jacket of purple velvet with a lavender shirt and mauve jabot. My knickers were fastened below the knee with gold buckles. My hose were black lace. My shoes were shiny plastisat, with heels higher than I was accustomed to. But I wouldn't be doing much walking.

A few years previously my father had a brief enthusiasm for antique and classic cars. He had purchased twelve before his interest waned. He sold them all off (by then he was collecting Japanese armor), and I bought one of them, a 1974 Ford Capri. I kept it in our Grosse Pointe garage. It would have been useless in GPA-1.

I drove the Ford into Detroit, the gift I had brought for Millie on the seat beside me. It was a combination powder and music box, made of plastic, with a tiny ef and em on top who held each other and twirled in time to the music. It was dreadful. Millie would think it a profit.

I had arranged to meet her at a restaurant-cabaret in a crumbling section of the city, down near the river. I had no fear of appearing there in the costume I was wearing. Most of the young factory ems who frequented the place would be dressed in similar fashion, many more elaborately. Last year it had been plastipat tights and Wellington boots.

I had met Millie Jean Grunwald at a basement cockfight. We had both bet a winner, and stood next to each other in the collect line. I won much more than she, and invited her and her girlfriend to join me at the bar for a drink. They accepted happily. I ordered a magnum of "champagne." They adored it, so I said nothing, but drank as little as I could. I thought it might contain methanol.

They went off to the ef nest together. When they returned, the girlfriend departed suddenly, giggling. I suspected they had flipped a coin for me. Whether Millie had won or lost, I did not know.

She had a large one-room apartment over a porn shop. It was almost a loft, reasonably clean, decently enough furnished with leased possessions that were obviously in their third or fourth setting. But there were a few personal touches: a calendar showing a young ef hugging a kitten, a plastic imitation of an old-fashioned round-faced clock, a crimson sofa pillow stamped "Use Me."

She answered all my questions readily and with great good humor. She was fourteen then, a CF-E, and she served as a packer at the Qik-Freez Hot-Qizine factory. She traveled to and from work in an electric bus. She was paid 125 new dollars for a four-day week (twenty-two were take-home pay), plus two two-week vacations every year, plus free lunches every working day of the factory's products which, she assured me, were the best foods ever, sold in all the tootiest restaurants in the world.

She was jolly, companionable, undemanding. I could relax with her. When she came in from the nest (it was outside in the hallway), I stood up as she entered. She blushed, smiled shyly, and murmured, "Thank you." When she asked if I would like to use her, I said it would be a profit.

Afterwards, I offered her ten new dollars "to buy a gift." She would not take it. I urged her then to accept a plastigold brooch I had on, the kind of cheap trinket I wore on my excursions into the "lower depths." She was delighted with it.

That had been two years ago. I saw her every time I came to Detroit to visit my parents. I brought her presents and took her wherever she wanted to go. I think she liked me. But it was hard to tell; she liked *everything*.

Apparently something had gone wrong in the chromosomal manipulation of the embryo from which her group had been cloned. She was not quite a variant, but her Grade E genetic rating was warranted. Once I saw her trying to shove a grossly oversized plastic stopper into the narrow neck of a bottle. Her brow was furrowed, her eyes puzzled. Her spatial cognizance was especially deficient, her vocabulary limited, her speech rapid to the point of spluttering. But she was a sweet ef, not incapable of treachery but unaware of it. I liked her. I may have felt a sense of responsibility.

She was standing outside the restaurant-cabaret when I arrived, although I had told her many times to wait inside if I was delayed. Her face lighted up when she saw me. She came running to throw her arms about my neck, and smeared my lip rouge.

The restaurant was crowded, noisy, and smelled of phenol. Too many small tables had been jammed in under a low ceiling; the atmosphere was milky with smoke. But Millie loved it, waving to acquaintances as we threaded our way to our table.

We had an enjoyable dinner: wretched food, but served with great verve by a flatfooted obso waiter who obviously recognized a good thing when he saw one. He would get his pat.

Millie chattered unceasingly, sometimes with a mouthful of food. She told me about her mean supervisor at the factory, about her girlfriend Sarah who had consumed a liter of petrorye "straight off" on a dare, and had to be taken to a hospital to have her stomach vacuumed, about a kitten she had found abandoned, named Nick, for me, who had stayed two days and then departed for parts unknown.

I listened to all this, smiling and nodding. DIVRAD was far away. I ate my prochick, drank my petrowine, and asked myself no questions.

Millie was wearing a tooty transparent blouse. Her breasts had been painted in red circles, like archery targets. There was what appeared to be a wide aluminum "gut-clutcher" about her waist, fastened in front with a brass tongue, shackle, and iron padlock. The key hung from a wire loop about her neck. She wore a minikilt, her legs bare from calf to buttock. Her boots were synthetic fur. From the zipper tabs hung the "flying penis" ornament that was the current rage, advertised on TV with a remarkable animated film and the endlessly repeated demand: "How tooty can you get? How tooty can you get? How tooty can you get?"

After dinner I asked our solicitous waiter if any natural brandy was available. Regrettably no. But he promised something just as good. It turned out to be a fruit liqueur. I think it was natural. Much too sweet for my taste, but Millie loved it.

The lights dimmed, a siren sounded, the diners screeched in anticipation, and a Master of Ceremonies darted through the curtain onto the minuscule stage. He was wearing an enormous codpiece, the batting popping out through a rip. The audience roared with laughter. He told several jokes ("I'm in mourning tonight. I lost my wife. But she found her way back home").

Then the nude chorus line came kicking on. One had a scar from a recent Caesarian section clearly visible. Another one astounded me; I thought I might have discovered the first case of steatopygia in the Detroit area.

After the dance routine, the next act was introduced by a professional type as being a "serious sex lecture." It was two marionettes, nude ef and em, cleverly manipulated, demonstrating various copulative positions. Father would have loved it.

This was followed by an em transvestite who sang a song about his continual "hard luck," with the rhyming lines you might expect.

Then came two nude ef acrobatic dancers who were quite good.

The chorus line came on again for a tired number in which they wore animal masks. The ef with the *gluteus* that was the most *maximus* I had ever seen was the gorilla.

The final act, the "star attraction," lasted less than five seconds. The room was darkened completely. A single blue spotlight centered on the stage. The curtains parted briefly. There stood a naked em, obviously a genetic variant, with a circumcised *membrum virilis* at least 60 cm long. The audience gasped. The curtains closed. The house lights came on. There was a great snapping of fingers.

"Shall we go?" I asked Millie.

She profited from driving at high speed. I enjoyed it, too, though I rarely had the opportunity. We drove out to an automobile testing track we had discovered in the River Rouge area. For a ten new-dollar pat, the bearded obso night watchman would unlock the gate and allow us onto the track. It was oval-shaped, the end curves so steeply banked that it was impossible to climb them until I had the car up to top speed.

Around and around we went, Millie screaming with delight as we moved higher and higher, lying on our side as we neared the tops of the almost vertical end curves. It was a cloudy, moonless night. Only the fan of white from the headlights, rushing ahead of us, showed me the edge I was shaving.

On the final go-round, I switched off the lights. Then just the faint light from the sky provided dim illumination. Wind-howl, engine roar, and the pleased whimpering of Millie next to me. . . . I plunged through the darkness.

"Y'gonna stop yesself one of these nights," the bearded watchman said when we left.

"That's right," I said.

He shook his head. "This world. . . ."

I remembered my mother had spoken the same words in the same tone. "This world. . . ."

Back in Millie's apartment, I handed over her gift. She tore off the wrappings as a child might, almost frantically, ripping. She was delighted with the musical powder box and set the miniature couple to dancing, around and around, watching them with a pleased smile, head cocked.

Her body was young, young, the skin nylon, the flesh natural rubber. There was a patch of golden lanugo over the lumbar vertebrae. Her painted breasts stared at me like shocked eyes. I rolled atop her and penetrated. Her lips drew back in a lupine grin.

She had told me, "I like using the most," and that was operative. But she had a habit that amused me at first, then distracted me, then angered me, but that I eventually conditioned myself to ignore. During using she would continue her conversation, telling me of a prank they had played at the factory (they had put the supervisor's purse on the assembly line, and it had emerged at the other end wrapped tightly in plastic and frozen as hard as a plastibrick). Or of a tooty pair of black plastisilk panties she had seen, imprinted with crimson mouths. Or of her desire to learn to drive, to drive endlessly, at high speed, anywhere.

While she recounted these things, during using, her cardiac rate increased, her breathing became shallow and rapid, her eyes glittered, a sweat covered her plump thighs. She continued chattering, linking her heels behind my knees, grasping my buttocks to pull me deeper, talking, talking, until she summited, interrupting her recital for a small shriek, then gabbling again while her body continued to pump in diminishing rhythm and her fingers probed gently into my rectum.

I arrived back at my parents' home in Grosse Pointe about 0400 the following morning. I went immediately to bed and slept until almost 1300. Without a Somnorific.

X-6

The return to GPA-1, thirty-six hours later, was a series of small accidents that almost added up to disaster.

1. The Bullet Train left the Detroit terminal right on schedule. It moved about ten meters and ground to a halt. A small em had tumbled off the platform, onto the tracks, and broken his right tibia. It was almost an hour before he was attended to and taken away.
2. East of Canton, Ohio, streaking for Pittsburgh, we hit the last section

of four-unit articulated truck-train, driverless, on the new AUS-1 automated highway. No one was injured or stopped, but it took almost three hours to clear away the wreckage and the hundreds of plastilap bags of probeans scattered all over the right-of-way.

3. In New York, getting close to conference time, it took me twenty minutes to get an electric cab. At Fourteenth Street we ran into a traffic jam and sat without moving for another twenty minutes. I was beginning to sweat under my zipsuit.

I signed in at the compound with ten minutes to spare. I swung aboard one of the open-sided, slow-moving cart trains that made continual circuits of the compound, driverless, following a wire laid under the pavement. I was in my office in five minutes. Paul Bumford was waiting with his big green accordion file.

"You like to live dangerously, don't you?" he said.

"Thank God for accidents," I said, "or we'd start thinking we can predict *everything*. What's hot?"

"Lewisohn's condition has stabilized. Everything else can wait."

"Good. I have the Supersense file. Let's go."

We waited for the executive elevator to take us up to the conference room.

"Were you faithful?" he whispered.

I looked about casually. No one in sight. I patted his cheek softly.

"Not to worry," I said.

We were the last division heads to arrive, but it was another minute before Angela Teresa Berri made her entrance. We all stood up.

The Satisfaction Section of the Department of Bliss was rigidly organized into four divisions:

- Division of Research & Development (DIVRAD). I was Assistant Deputy Director in charge (AssDepDirRad).
- Division of Security & Intelligence (DIVSEC). Burton P. Klein was AssDepDirSec.
- Division of Data & Statistics (DIVDAT). The AssDepDirDat was Phoebe Huntzinger.
- Division of Law & Enforcement (DIVLAW). The two Assistant Deputy Directors were identical (and, according to rumor, incestuous) twins, Frank and Frances von Liszt. Both, naturally, were called "Franz," to their delight.

In addition, Angela Berri, Deputy Director of Satisfaction (DEPDIRSAT) had her own headquarters staff. She ran a tight ship, especially on matters that affected policy rather than mere planning and operations.

"Nick, you lead off," she commanded.

"Project Supersense," I said, glanced at the digiclock on the wall, and began. . . .

Without consulting my notes, I delivered a concise recitation of the history
and current status of the project, costs to date, estimated costs to completion,
estimated potential income. I ended in a little more than five minutes by
stating, "I recommend Project Supersense be stopped."

"Comments?" Angela asked, looking at the others.

Burton Klein was the first to respond. He felt Project Supersense should
be continued. I knew he would; he had plastitanium electrodes implanted in
his brain. He was a Mind-Jerker. He said he did not feel a potential market
of two million was negligible. It could be exploited for a lot of love.

I replied with a condensed form of my father's lecture on Convenience and
Consumption, pointing out that if synchronized movie films were made available, nothing would be consumed; it would be a one-time sale.

"Not necessarily," he said. He claimed that Mind-Jerkers would purchase
large libraries of the high-stimulant movie films. And, he pointed out, the
same technique could also be used on film reels of books for reading machines.
"Even on tapes of music," he added.

It was an idea that hadn't occurred to me, and I was silent.

"Anyone else?" Angela Berri inquired.

Brother and sister Liszt passed. Phoebe Huntzinger agreed with Klein.

Angela asked me if we had anything in present status that could be leased.

"No," I said, "nothing patentable. At this stage, it's just a concept."

She nodded. "Stop it," she said crisply. "Too limited. Phoebe, you're next."

One of the responsibilities of Data & Statistics that we were all interested
in, that the entire government was interested in, was the Satisfaction Rate
(Satrat). Data was gathered daily; Satrat Reports were issued weekly.

Briefly, the Satrat measured the quality of life in America, what percentage
of Americans were satisfied with their lives and the way things were going
and, conversely, what percentage were dissatisfied.

The testing was done by a dozen commercial and academic organizations,
under government contract, that specialized in public opinion polling. One of
the companies was Pub-Op, Inc., in which Frank Harris Lawson was serving
when he was stopped.

The polling involved in calculating the Satrat included everything from
yes-no questions to essay-type questionnaires seeking in-depth reactions,
emotions, hates, fears, prejudices, etc. The technique had evolved from social attitude and motivational testing of the late 1970's when it was recognized that the public's well-being could no longer be judged solely by
economic indicators: income, growth of the Gross National Product, employment, etc.

The Satrat was extremely important to policymakers, from the President
and Chief Director to Congress and the courts. By closely monitoring the

public's social attitudes, laws could be passed or repealed, funds spent in one direction rather than in another, potential dissension smothered before it escalated into an intractable crisis, etc.

Phoebe Huntzinger, with her army of demographers, multivariant analysts, and linear regression statisticians, was the ef who provided the precise weekly social barometer, with the aid of an extremely sophisticated computer, of course. Her ten-minute contribution to our monthly conferences was invariably not a problem seeking a solution but merely a review of where the Satrat had been, where it was now, and her predictions of where it would be in a week, a month, a year, five years from now.

She was a black ef with a Grade A genetic rating that was fully deserved. She spoke languidly, almost lazily, but question any of her conclusions and you'd find yourself sinking slowly in a quagmire of sine waves, hyperbolic functions, and angular velocities that would do you in. Right now, her report was optimistic: The Satrat was up and rising. The near future looked fair, the far future glorious.

No questions were asked.

The third offering was from the von Liszts, heads of the Division of Law & Enforcement. Usually their monthly reports involved their continual struggles with lawyers and the courts. The main problem was inheritance. The development and increasing use of artificial insemination, artificial enovulation, parthenogenesis, self-fertilization, cloning, etc., had created a legal jungle through which lawyers and judges moved cautiously, no paths (precedents) to guide them.

As one eminent jurist remarked. "The Biological Revolution has raised law into the realms of poetry."

But on this day, the von Liszts' report did not concern inheritance; it dealt with a proposed legal change in the IC (Informed Consent) Statement.

By law, we were forbidden to experiment on human objects without first obtaining their signed IC Statement. Prior to signing, we had to explain to them, whenever possible, the potential results of their cooperation. That "whenever possible" was our legal out, of course. When testing a new drug on a human object, for instance, who could possibly predict the potential results, even after lengthy testing on animals?

Most of our testing on human objects was done on prisoners in federal penitentiaries. The IC Statements were easy to obtain. The prisoner was paid one new dollar a day for submitting to the test, or he hoped his cooperation would be a factor when his parole or reduced sentence was up for consideration, or he feared refusal to sign an IC Statement might count against him in such a legal proceeding.

Patients in government hospitals represented a different problem. If they were obviously incompetent to scan and/or understand what they were signing, the IC Statement had to be signed by next of kin. It was invariably signed, relatives fearing that not signing might jeopardize the patient's treatment in the hospital, and hoping too, of course, that the proposed experimentation might result in a cure.

The third class of human objects of experimentation were formerly in government service but were now confined to Rehabilitation & Reconditioning Hospices "for psychiatric observation for reasons of public security." A little trick we had picked up from the Russians.

The "psychiatric observation" part was valid enough. If their acts had been antisocial, it was *prima facie* evidence of a disturbed mind. The second part, "for reasons of public security," was validated by the first; obviously, a disturbed mind represented a potential threat to public security.

A lot of kaka had recently been published in facsimile newspapers and publicized on TV news programs that when these patients signed Informed Consent Statements, it was under physical torture or threat of torture. This, I could testify, was absolutely inoperative. No patient in a government R&R Hospice signed an IC Statement under duress.

It was true, of course, that those patients were frequently under hypnosis, under the influence of drugs or electric and electronic behavior conditioning. But that was part of their therapy. The fact that they signed IC Statements while undergoing treatment in no way nullified the validity of those statements.

That was our policy.

The increasingly vociferous objections to that policy came mostly from the Society of Obsoletes (SOO), a loosely organized association of obsos (generally people born prior to 1970) whose activities were usually laughable, concerning such things as antivivisection campaigns, letters to newspapers denouncing televised bullfights and executions, parades to protest the federal licensing of prostitutes, meetings to object to the legality of Smack and other addictive drinks and foods, and similarly hopeless causes. Most of these were simply a nuisance.

But their current program against the existing Informed Consent Statement was a little more serious. It appeared to be well organized, cogently reasoned, and presented to the public with thoughtful moderation.

To counter the efforts of SOO, Frances and Frank von Liszt suggested the IC Statement be reworded to include phrases stating that the undersigned fully understood the significance of what he was signing, that he had been offered no reward—financial or otherwise—for signing, nor was he signing under any physical, mental, or psychic duress.

Having concluded their presentation, the von Liszts were silent. Angela Berri asked for comments. Burton P. Klein and Phoebe Huntzinger gave approval to the revised form. I had no objection. I asked if making even this minor affirmative response to the Society of Obsos' desires might not encourage them to increase their demands.

"Once we give in," I pointed out, "they'll up the ante. Then where do we end? Sooner or later we'll have to answer them with a loud firm 'No!' It might be better to fight them on this. We could easily win with a well-planned media campaign stressing the anticipated therapeutic benefits to be derived from human experimentation. If we surrender on this small issue, they undoubtedly will be inspired to escalate their demands."

"What do you think of that, Burton?" Angela asked Klein directly.

She surprised me. After the way he had savaged my report on Project Supersense, she seemed to be deliberately pitting the two of us, for what reason I could not fathom.

"Mountains out of molehills," Klein growled. He was an enormous NM; heavy through the shoulders and torso, with ridiculously spindly legs. His face was all eyebrows. He had a Grade B genetic rating, but I suspected most of his talents were in his muscles. Of course, in his service that was of some importance.

"Look," he went on, "it's just the wording of the IC Statement we're concerned with here. It won't restrict us at all. Give those old idiots what they want and shut them up. They're no threat. No one takes them seriously."

There was silence for a moment. We all looked at Angela. She looked at Burton Klein.

"I'll think about it," she said finally. "I may discuss it with DIROB."

That seemed to satisfy Klein. He smiled. He thought he had won.

"All right, Burton," Angela continued. "Let's hear from you now and wind this thing up."

The report of AssDepDirSec was a compendium of statistics and percentages. It concerned the numbers, categories, and frequencies of acts of assassination, kidnapping, sabotage, terrorism, and threats against PS, academic, and commercial research laboratories. Klein rattled off the figures so rapidly that he was finished in three minutes flat. I don't think the others had caught the significance of what he had said. I was conscious of Paul Bumford shifting his position and moving uneasily behind me. I knew *he* had, and was trying to alert me.

"Wait a minute," I said, even before Angela had asked for comments. "Burton, if I understand you correctly, acts of assassination, sabotage, and terrorism against scientific research facilities are up almost five percent from last month and more than fifty percent from what they were a year ago?"

"That's right," he said stolidly.

"Well, you seem very calm about it. Aren't you concerned?"

"Sure, I'm concerned. I'm taking steps. I've organized a working committee of government, commercial, and academic security directors. We're exchanging intelligence. We're beefing-up security precautions. And we're working closely with the BPS on this."

The BPS, Bureau of Public Security (formerly the Federal Bureau of Investigation), maintained the data bank on domestic criminals and dissidents.

"Well, what's the pattern?" I demanded.

"Pattern?"

"Yes. What *kind* of installations are being bombed and burned and sabotaged?"

"All kinds. There's no pattern. Listen, I realize this is serious, but our violence rate isn't so bad when you compare it to the big picture."

"The big picture? What big picture?"

"The national incidence of violence, against banks, corporation offices, universities, insurance companies, government compounds, railroads, oil fields, laser-fusion power stations, airlines, and so forth. In some categories—bombings, for instance—our growth rate is actually *lower* than the national average."

I stared around the room. I don't think any of them caught it.

"It doesn't compute," I said. "Burton tells us the incidence of terrorist attacks against research facilities is fifty percent larger than it was last year and growing at a rate of five percent a month. He adds that the growth rate of national terrorist activity is even higher. But Phoebe tells us the Satisfaction Rate has never been higher and is rising every month. Just what the hell is going on?"

Angela stared at me a moment. No expression.

"Yes, yes," she said quietly, "it's something to think about. Well . . . I believe we've accomplished a great deal. Good meeting. I thank you all. Adjourned. Nick, could I see you for a moment?"

There was a gabble of relieved voices, pushing back of chairs, gathering of papers and files. The room emptied. Paul waited for me near the door, I went up to Angela.

"Yes?"

"I want to see you and Paul tonight. Come up to my place. At 2100."

"Fine. We'll be there."

She nodded and was gone. I sank down into her chair, began rubbing my chin. Paul came over to stand close to me. I looked up at him.

"What Klein said about using the Project Supersense synchronization technique on filmed book reels and sound tracks—we should have thought of that."

"I know." He nodded miserably. "I'm sorry."

"Not your fault. Mine. Put it in the Tomorrow File."

"Too late," he said. "I'll explain to you later tonight."

"We've got to see Angela at 2100. At her place."

"I'll be back by then."

"Back?"

"I have to leave the compound tonight."

I nodded.

"Aren't you curious as to where I'm going?"

"Should I be?"

"I may have a user on the outside."

"So?"

"Couldn't you be just a wee bit jealous?"

"All right, Paul." I sighed. "Where are you going?"

"Tell you when I get back."

Sometimes he acted like a flirtatious ef. I let it pass.

"What's gotten into Klein?" I asked. "He seemed out for my balls."

"I noticed that. I was hoping you'd pick up on his report. I should have known you would. An Instox copy was circulated yesterday. I scanned it and got curious. I borrowed their rough data. They wouldn't let me take it out of their office, but I scanned it. There is a pattern to the terrorist attacks against scientific facilities."

"Had to be," I nodded. "What is it?"

"About seventy percent are against laboratories doing procreation and genetic research."

"That's interesting," I said.

The problem with the four-day week, for executives, was that we were compelled to serve twice as hard during the first six hours we returned from a threeday.

I went down to my office from the SATSEC conference and dug into the three stacks of documents on my desk. As usual, I organized my own three stacks: Immediate, Soon, Later. Included in the Immediate pile were the daily progress reports from team leaders that had accumulated during my absence. Most were routine; I scribbled my initials to indicate they had been scanned. They would then be microfilmed and filed. But one report was of particular interest to me.

It was from my Gerontology Team. With some diffidence, the leader was bucking along a suggestion made by one of his young servers—a bright ef. I scanned her name again to make certain I'd remember it.

She had run a computerized actuarial study of what it cost the government to maintain an indigent and nonproductive obso until the object stopped. She had included costs of food, clothing, shelter, and medical care. The dollar total was shocking. And when I saw the grand total for all such objects, I was astonished. What I could do for the young, vigorous, and productive with all that love!

The bright ef on the Gerontology Team had suggested an unusual approach to the problem. It was called GAS (Government-Assisted Suicide) and proposed the government offer 500 new dollars to any indigent and nonproductive obso who signed up. Stopping would be painless, by ingestion of pills provided free of charge by the government. The benefit would be awarded thirty days prior to stopping, to be used for any purpose the object desired, or it could be bequeathed.

Assuming a minimum of 10 percent voluntary acceptance of GAS, it was estimated that, even after payment of the benefits, the savings to the government would be almost two *billion* new dollars annually. I could scarcely believe it. But the report stated: "Computer printout available if desired."

I made two Instox copies on my office machine. The original report, initialed, would be microfilmed and filed. On one copy I wrote "Original thinking. F&F," initialed it, and marked it for return to the Gerontology Team leader. The "F&F" was Division shorthand for "File and Forget."

The second Instox copy I put in my pocket, then drew it out to red-pencil every reference to "Government-Assisted Suicide." I was writing in "Government-Assisted Peace" when Paul Bumford came in. The other offices were dark; everyone else had left.

"You've got to eat," he said.

"I suppose so," I said. I rubbed my eyes. "What time is it?"

"After 1900."

"I've got to come back. Pick me up here and we'll go to Angela's together. Will that give you enough time?"

"Plenty."

"Here's something for the Tomorrow File."

I handed him the corrected report on Government-Assisted Peace. He scanned it rapidly.

"Nick, it's good."

"I know."

"Not for action now?"

"No way. Talk to that ef who worked it up. Creative thinking there. She could be your second secretary."

He grinned. "For that I'll buy you dinner. *La Bonne Vie?*"

"I suppose so."

"You eat and I'll talk. I've got a lot to tell you."

He ate, too, of course, but he did have a lot to tell me. We sat at a corner table, Paul spoke in a low voice, his lips close to my ear.

He finished his recital.

"You don't seem very surprised," he said, disappointed.

"I'm not. Angela's original tape was the input. She said not to inform DIROB."

"Oh. I had forgotten that."

"I hadn't."

"Do you trust her?"

"Yes, I trust her. In this."

"She's *such* a bitch."

"I know. But I think she's onto something here. It could benefit us. Let me do the talking tonight. Pick up your cues from me."

"Nick, I always do."

"Play it very tight. Don't volunteer *anything*."

"Where thou goeth, there goeth I," he said.

We left and separated. He headed for the gate. I went back to my office. I had completed the Immediate stack. Logically, I should have started on the Soon. But there was a file in Later I wanted to scan.

When a server in PS was sent to a Rehabilitation & Reconditioning Hospice "for psychiatric observation for reasons of public security," and had signed an Informed Consent Statement, the first task given him was to write a report or dictate a tape detailing his activities during the past year, two years, five— for as long a time as his interrogators believed would be of value.

In this account, the object sometimes revealed names, places, dates that were frequently useful to AssDepDirSec, or BPS or UIA, in uncovering others who harbored antisocial tendencies. The object was usually assisted with memory-intensifying drugs, hypnosis, electric stimulation of the hippocampus, etc. The journal the object produced invariably made fascinating scanning.

It was particularly fascinating in this case, since the object had been a genetic biologist attached to the Denver Field Office of my Division. He and his wife had been principals in a criminal trial that had created headlines in the nation's facsimile newspapers and was the subject of endless TV gabble shows. It was popularly known as "The Horse Triangle Murder Case."

The couple wanted to breed, desperately. Since both were Naturals, with good genetic ratings (hers was an A; his a B), they had no trouble obtaining a license. But the em's sperm proved sterile. No amount of hormonal or enzymatic therapy was successful. It may have been a genetic variance. In any event, the ef opted for artificial insemination, wanting to experience—according to the subsequent testimony of her friends—the "glory of birth," whatever that may be. The em opted for artificial enovulation, but his wife refused to carry another woman's fertilized egg.

Their arguments on this decision became rancorous. Neighbors testified that on at least two occasions peace officers had to be called to calm the squabbling couple. Finally, apparently, the husband surrendered and agreed to artificial insemination. Since he ruled the local sperm bank, and was entitled to the discount allowed all government servers, he provided the sperm injection, and even immunosuppressive drugs which, he assured his wife, "were necessary to prevent rejection of the sperm." Ridiculous. In any event, the ef became pregnant.

In the fifth month of pregnancy, it became obvious to the ef's obstetrician that he was not dealing with a normal fetus. X-ray and internal telescopic TV examination proved the ef had been impregnated with equine sperm. The immunosuppressive drugs had served well, as they usually do. The wife underwent surgery for removal of the equine fetus, but suffered a massive hemorrhage on the operating table. She stopped. The husband was charged with premeditated murder, but local authorities surrendered him to us. Not without a lot of arm-twisting.

The journal of the object dictated in the R&R Hospice had no political significance. It implicated no one else. It was merely the confession of an em, of good intelligence, who wanted to breed but was unable. In simple language, the object recounted his emotions, his motives, what compelled him to do what he had done. The object was obviously jerked, but his account had a curious human logic all its own. It was almost convincing.

I was sitting there, still staring at the file, though I had long since finished scanning it, when Paul Bumford returned.

"You said you had some new iproniazid in your office?" I said.

"When did I say that?"

"The night I flew out to the West Coast."

"My God, Nick, don't you ever forget *anything*?"

"I wish I could."

We stopped at his office, and I popped two, dry. Then we walked over to the apartment complex. I asked Paul for the computer printout and he handed it over. A short list. Twenty-nine names with their service title and BIN's. All members of the Department of Bliss. I folded the printout and slid it into the inside breast pocket of my zipsuit.

"I just flashed the Section's contact in Oakland," Paul said. "That's what I've been doing. It was my third call. I thought it best to flash from outside the compound, from a commercial pay station."

"That's wise."

"Angela's beachhouse south of San Francisco is owned by the Samatin Foundation. It's a small outfit. About ten million new dollars' endowment."

"What do they do?"

"Give grants for the study of exotic disorders—frambesia, beri-beri, tsutsugamushi fever, icthyosis. Things of that sort."

"Where does their love come from?"

"I thought you'd never ask. Mostly from Walker & Clarke Chemicals and from Pace Pharmaceuticals and from Twenty-first Century Electronics."

"Oh-ho," I said.

"Oh-ho, indeed." He nodded. "Dear Angela is on the suck. That's why she gave you that quick stop on Project Supersense at the conference. She's going to peddle the concept."

"She wouldn't dare."

"Want to bet?"

"No." I looked at him curiously. "You're enjoying this, aren't you?"

"A profit." He laughed. "I think I have a talent for it. Devious motives, complex plotting, smart guesses, and shrewd digging. When you get to be DEPDIRSAT, I want to be your AssDepDirSec."

"You have it," I said, the iproniazid beginning to serve. "Let's go get it started."

Angela met us at the door and led us into the huge living room. She offered a box of cigarettes. Bold, a good brand of *Cannabis indica* with crimson filters. They were legal. I declined, but she and Paul Bumford lighted up.

"Well, Nick?" she said. The cigarette bobbed. "What have you got?"

I narrated our retrieval of the corpus, the autopsy, and what was revealed by the tissue slides. I described the apartment. Frank Lawson Harris had probably been stopped, I told her, by inhaling a platelet-associated 5-HT nerve gas contained in a six-hour Somnorific. She was a molecular biologist; I didn't have to spell it out for her.

"There were other Somnorifics in the medicine cabinet?" she asked.

"Yes. All six-hour. All checked out normal."

"How did the assassin get him to take the one that stopped him?"

"Offered it to him in person, pretending it came from the medicine cabinet. Or, if the killer wasn't there, by simple manipulation. Five Somnorifics in the medicine cabinet. Four of them against the back, neatly lined up. The fifth one, the lethal one, out in front, at the edge of the shelf, by itself. If you wanted to sleep, which one would you take? But I think the killer was there and handed the fiddled Somnorific to Harris personally."

"Why do you think that?"

"Otherwise the killer would have had to return to the apartment to retrieve the used inhaler. We didn't find it. Neither did the Peace Department. But the killer forgot the crumpled seal."

"All right. Go on."

I described Paul's efforts in gathering IMP samples at the murder scene. The stopped em's sample had been coded and run through the computer in a blind test. It checked out: it was the IMP of HARRIS, Frank Lawson, PS-5, Hdqtrs Stf SECSAT, AINM-B-70973-GPA-1-M76774.

I then explained our inferential postulation of a blond ef at the scene, how her IMP sample was completed as far as possible and compared with the computerized records to determine duplication of inheritable IMP factors.

"Clever," Angela said. "Whose idea was that?"

"Mine," I said. "Paul did the workup. We've bred a list of twenty-nine possibles."

"Let me see," she said, holding out her hand.

"No," I said.

She looked at me a moment, then leaned forward to stub out her cigarette slowly.

"No?" Angela Berri repeated, looking at me suddenly.

"Not until you tell us what this is all about. Paul and I are risking R&R on this. We need to know more."

She leaned back on the sofa, turned slightly sideways, slumped. Her long green hair fell across her face.

"Oh, Nick," she said. "Don't you trust me?"

I turned to Paul Bumford.

"Are you catching this?" I asked him. "Great performance. A lesser talent would have pulled the zipper lower and wiped away an imaginary tear."

Paul grinned. Angela straightened up on the sofa, took a sip of wine, lighted another Bold.

"How many doctorates do you have now, Nick?" she asked casually.

"What difference does it make? It's like collecting medals. The best soldiers have none."

"What if I tell you nothing?" she said.

"We'll have to take what we have to DIROB and hope for the best. We have evidence that we acted under orders."

"Nick, you must learn not to give people ultimatums."

"I never do. I'm not giving you an ultimatum; I'm giving you a choice."

"A fine distinction."

"A distinction nevertheless. Well?"

"Come out on the terrace. It's not too chilly. Bring the wine."

I heard a small sound from Paul, an exhaled sigh. We followed her out onto the wide terrace. It extended around three sides of the penthouse and overlooked the brightly lit compound. But the terrace was not lighted. We sat on pillowed garden furniture in a dark corner.

"You heard the reports of Phoebe Huntzinger and Burton Klein at the conference today," she started. "Nick, you said it doesn't compute. It doesn't. I became aware of the conflict about six months ago. Phoebe's computer said the Satrat was going up, slowly but steadily. Klein reported increased terrorism against scientific installations. Actually, the national terrorism rate is much worse than he stated this afternoon. I see departmental reports; you don't because you have no need to know."

She didn't either, but I made no comment.

"So either Huntzinger or Klein was giving me inoperative input," Angela went on. "I knew it wasn't Klein because of those departmental reports on assassinations, bombings, sabotage, and so forth. Most of it is pillowed; the public isn't even aware of it. But it *does* exist, and it is serious. That left the Satrat."

"Phoebe Huntzinger?" Paul burst out, disbelieving.

Angela shook her head.

"Not Phoebe. I'll swear she's clean. It's her computer. It's being fiddled. And very cleverly. Not electronically."

"GIGO," I said. "Garbage in, garbage out."

"Exactly." Angela nodded. "All the Satrat input comes from about a dozen public polling organizations, commercial and academic. They've been infiltrated. The tapes they supply to Phoebe's computer are inoperative."

We were silent. I pondered the enormity of what was being done, if Angela was correct. The Satisfaction Rate was the temperature, pulse, cardiac rate, and EEG of the nation, all the life signs computerized into one important index. We were in trouble—if Angela was correct.

"How did you decide Phoebe's computer was being fiddled?" I asked her. I knew, but wanted to lead into another question.

"If Phoebe's Division was clean, and I was certain it was, there was no other possibility."

"All right. Assuming it was exterior sabotage, why didn't you call in Burton Klein and dump the problem in his lap? He's Security Chief."

"He had his hands full with the bombings. And I had to consider the possibility that, somehow, he was involved."

She spoke a little more rapidly when she was lying. Many people do, thinking fluency proves probity.

"Besides," she went on, "I had no evidence. Just suspicions. So I handled it myself. I placed undercover agents in four of the public opinion testing organizations we have under contract. Each agent reported to a control I trusted who reported only to me. Results were nil until about three weeks ago. Then Harris, assigned to Pub-Op, told his control that he was onto something. Someone, rather. An ef who lived in GPA-1 and worked at Pub-Op as an analyst of essay-type questionnaires. But she had access to the coding and taping room, and had a Master's in computer technology. She had the capability to fiddle their Satrat tapes."

"What's her name?" I asked.

Angela took a deep breath.

"That's why I've been playing this cloak-and-dagger game. Her name is Lydia Ann Ferguson. She's the daughter of Franklin L. Ferguson, Director of the Department of Bliss. Is his name on your list of possibles?"

"Yes," I said. "Have you ever met her?"

"About a year ago, at a party in DIROB's home in Washington. She's blond, about the age and height you mentioned."

"Were she and Harris users?"

"Yes, for the past three weeks."

"It can't be only her."

"Of course not. This is nationwide. Well organized. Dedicated people, very intelligent, very dangerous."

"What do they want?"

"I have no idea. At the moment, apparently, all they want is to destabilize the country."

"Maybe," I said. "What were your plans?"

"For Harris? I was hoping he'd get some hard evidence on Lydia Ann Ferguson. Then I'd have her committed and decant her. Her father would raise hell, but he couldn't stop me."

"He'd have to resign," Paul put in.

"Would he?" Angela asked, as if the idea had only at that moment occurred to her. This ef was toxic. "I suppose he would. Well, I was certain that under interrogation Lydia Ann would implicate others and tell us what is going on. But Harris was stopped. I suppose she did it."

"I suppose so," I said.

We were all silent then, running through the permutations and combinations. Finally Paul spoke: "Nick, are we in?"

"Yes."

"Then you could do it."

"Take Harris' place? No way. They know me at Pub-Op."

"Not take his place, but do his service. With Lydia Ann Ferguson."

"Yes," Angela Berri said. "Yes. You could do it, Nick. With your body and that smile, what ef could resist you?"

"Thanks a lot," I said. "But no, thanks."

"My annual Section Party is scheduled a little more than two weeks from now," she went on, ignoring my protest. "Ferguson will fly up for it, I know. I condition two clone efs for him every year. He wouldn't miss it for the world. I'll ask him to invite his daughter. She's in the city; it's logical. You'll meet her then, at a party of a hundred people."

"Is she profitable?" Paul asked.

"Yes. Very."

Paul was silent.

"Well, Nick?" Angela said.

"I'll meet her," I said, deciding suddenly. "I guarantee nothing."

"Don't be so modest," Angela said. "I *know*."

We moved back inside. The three of us stood there awkwardly, not speaking.

"Paul," Angela said finally, "I wonder if you'd mind leaving us? I have some things to discuss with Nick. Not concerning this matter. Section activities."

"Of course," Paul said genially. I knew he was furious.

Later, we lay naked in her bed, resting.

"Nick," she said, "do you trust Paul Bumford?"

"That's the second time you've asked me that. The answer is still the same: Yes."

"He's *such* a bitch. . . ."

X-7

One of my duties as Assistant Deputy Director of Research & Development was to conduct distinguished visitors on tours of the Division's facilities. The sight-seeing groups were generally of two types: politicians and scientists.

On the morning of Angela Berri's annual party, at which I was to meet Lydia Ann Ferguson, my first scheduled service was to conduct a group of visiting Japanese pols on my portion of a Section tour.

The tour progressed as expected—and ended as expected: They asked to see our most famous project—Fred. Or rather, Fred III, since Fred I had stopped after forty-eight hours, and Fred II after seven months. Fred III was the severed head of a Labrador retriever we had succeeded in keeping alive for more than three years.

As they clustered about the oversized, sterile bell jar in which Fred existed, I explained the project briefly in their language. A liquid nutrient was constantly circulated through Fred's natural blood vessels. A computer and automatic pump controlled temperature and pressure. A continual EEG signal registered on a cathode ray oscilloscope, and all other life signs, including hormonal and enzymatic levels, were monitored.

The Japanese watched, fascinated, while I shined a bright light in Fred's eyes. The pupils contracted. I spoke his name softly into a microphone: "Fred!" He heard it from the little speaker inside the bell jar and his muzzle lifted. I pumped in a synthetic odor akin to fresh beef. His mouth opened and he began to salivate.

I finally drew the visitors away from the bell jar and accompanied them down an underground corridor to the computer room where Phoebe Huntzinger would take over. I found myself walking alongside an em I recognized as a prince of the Imperial Household.

"Tell me, please," he said in a low voice, "what do you hope to learn from this experiment?"

"We have already learned a great deal, Excellency. The construction of the equipment necessary, the formulation of the liquid nutrient, the nature of consciousness the rate of brain cell stoppage, and so forth."

He finally asked the question invariably asked by visitors. "Is it possible that such a technique could be applied to humans?"

"It is possible." I nodded. "Anything is possible. There is no problem that cannot be solved."

We bowed to each other when we separated. I went back to A Lab, to Paul Bumford's office. He was inside, but the door was locked. He was intently scanning a long roll of computer printout. It had folded up around him, in a loose pile almost as high as the desk. He looked up, rose to unlock the door. He locked it again behind me.

"Well?" I asked.

I had persuaded Angela to requisition the raw data of the previous week from the public opinion polling organizations that provided input for the computation of Satrat. Then, without Phoebe Huntzinger's knowledge, Paul had run a comparison of the raw data with the tapes supplied Phoebe.

"Angela's right." He sighed. He sounded almost disappointed. "Nine of the twelve tapes are inoperative."

"Strange," I said.

"What's strange?"

"Angela said she began to suspect the Satrat was being fiddled six months ago. The logical thing for her to have done then would be to run the kind of test you just did. That would have confirmed her suspicions and she could have stopped the faking. But instead she let it continue while she set up her little spy network."

"I suppose she thought it was more important to discover who was doing it."

I nodded and stood up, knee-deep in computer paper.

"Make a tight roll of this," I told Paul. "I'll add it to the file in my safe. I have to go to the bank. I need some love. Then I'll be in my office until 1700. Stop by the apartment about 1900. We'll go up to Angela's together."

"What are you going to say to Lydia Ferguson when you meet her?"

" 'Happy to meet you, Lydia.' "

"Be serious. I mean after, when you talk to her. Are you going to ask if you can see her home?"

"First I'm going to ask if she likes Italian food."

"Italian food? What's that got to do with anything?"

"You've forgotten. Mary's autopsy report. Harris had consumed proveal, propep, spaghetti, and red petrowine four hours before he was stopped."

I went over to the branch of the American National Bank located within the compound. The ANB was one of Lewisohn's ideas. It had been sold to the Congress as a "standard by which civilian banking could be judged." A lot of kaka, of course. Lewisohn realized that, with more than five million adult servers, the government was missing a good bet in not establishing a bank to cater to their financial needs. The ANB offered a full range of services. How would you like to be a banker with five million depositors?

I handed over my BIN and told the server how much love I wanted. Checks were obsolete, it was paperless banking. A computer checked my account, okayed the transaction, made the debit, and I was handed my 200 new dollars. Fast and painless. I didn't like to think of what would happen if the people fiddling the Satrat computer decided to fiddle bank computers. Instant chaos.

I walked back to my office slowly, wondering if there was any possible way to obtain a printout of Angela Berri's bank account. I was still pondering her use of a beachhouse owned by a foundation financed by corporations to whom we sold licenses and, on occasion, gave invaluable free assistance. It might be interesting to compare the dates of her deposits, for instance, with the dates of contract grants to Walker & Clarke Chemicals.

But even if I could obtain her bank record, I couldn't believe that intelligent, ambitious ef would be stupid enough to deposit any more than a reasonable percentage of her rank-rate in the American National Bank. If she was on the suck, she was hiding the love somewhere else. There were many ways to do it. I could compute a few original methods myself.

I omitted lunch and devoted the afternoon to catching up on my "correspondence." It went swiftly, since practically all communication was done by minicassettes. The dictation machine could make an original tape and up to five copies simultaneously, in case of multiple mailings. I usually made only an original and one copy for filing.

I rejected, as politely as possible, practically all the invitations I received to address conventions of professional associations, contribute to scientific journals, take part in symposia, engage in televised debates, etc. I accepted a few speaking engagements, offered by prestigious commercial and academic groups. Not solely for the personal prestige but because of the esteem my Division enjoyed. It was important, politically, to hyperactivate our image.

I got back to my apartment about 1730, stripped down, went into the kitchen, and mixed a tall vodka-and-Smack. It was petrovod—but with Smack you couldn't taste the difference.

Of course, the day wasn't over yet.

I took a bath. Something I rarely do, preferring to shower. But as a PS-3, I rated a tub. It seemed silly not to take advantage of it occasionally.

I dressed with more care than usual. A two-piece suit of the light blue metallic (the jacket collarless), and a turtleneck sweater of white plastisilk, woven with black bugle beads. I wore formal hoshoes of black nylon and black plastikid. My makeup, as usual, was minimal. I did wear a silver brooch studded with lapis lazuli. It had been given to me by Mother. She said it had belonged to *her* mother. It was pleasantly obso.

I was on my second vodka-and-Smack when Paul arrived.

Unfortunately, he was not very prepossessing, physically, but he did very well with what he had. I noticed first the sequined eyeshadow and lip rouge, and a small, star-shaped beauty mark at one side of his chin. He was wearing a plum-colored velvet suit with a ruffled blouse of puce lace.

"What would you like?" I asked.

"You," he said.

"To drink."

"Vodka, please. By itself. Chilled."

We slumped at opposite ends of the couch, sipping our drinks.

"I have something good for the Tomorrow File," I said lazily, "but I don't want to discuss it now. Let's just relax."

"Nervous?" he said.

I laughed. "You're hyper."

"It is important."

"I suppose so. Have you ever met DIROB?"

"No. Never."

"Meet him tonight. Introduce yourself. You've got to start meeting the movers and shakers."

"What's he like?"

"Pleasant enough. Dry palm-stroke. He smiles too much. And a gloss to him. Like all upper-rank pols. Hair, suit, eyes, skin—he *shines*. Not science-conditioned. He came up through social engineering. But don't take him lightly. He's survived. He smells the wind."

Paul nodded. "I'll be ever so worshipful. By the way, Mary Bergstrom hit the national lottery for a thousand."

"Good for Mary," I said. "Finished? Let's go."

Last year her apartment had been transformed into a *fin de siècle* Parisian bordello, all red velvet, black lace, and frolicking plaster cupids. This year her decorator had opted for a jungle village, with natural plants in tubs.

Angela Teresa Berri moved through the undergrowth smiling, white teeth gleaming against a skin dyed a tawny brown. She wore a sleeveless gown that appeared to be aluminum foil with a bonded surface of stretch plastic. It came high on her thorax, cleaved to her body, ended in a hemline of points halfway down her hard thighs.

If anyone doubted she wore nothing beneath, it was only necessary to view her from the back. She was almost completely exposed, low enough to display the Y-division of her buttocks. She wore no shoes, but leather thongs ringed her toes and wound tightly to her knees. She had a golden serpent thrice encircling her left bicep. The snake's eyes were rubies.

Only she could have worn such a costume and made it believable. She was more than an ef, more than human. She was a primitive power. A force. It radiated from her. It went beyond sexuality.

Everyone in the Section with a rank of PS-4 and higher had been invited and was there. In addition, three other Deputy Directors were present, and a party of five had flown up from Washington, D.C.: DIROB Ferguson and his staff. All five were ems; none was accompanied by his wife. The Chief Director, it was rumored, had been invited but had sent his regrets. Something about another famine in Bangladesh.

No attempt was made at formal introductions. I slipped sideways through the crowd, carrying my sweetish petrorum punch in a plastic coconut shell, greeting familiar friends and acquaintances, sliding palms with two of Ferguson's assistants I had not met before. Both had the gloss I had mentioned to Paul: the polish that increases in brilliance as you move up in Public Service, like a waxed surface drying to a hard shine.

Finally I came face to face with the Great Man himself, Franklin L. Ferguson, Director of Bliss.

"Good evening, sir," I said. "Nice to see you again."

We stroked palms automatically while his glazed eyes sought to focus.

"Flair!" he finally burst out, with a politician's memory for names. "Nicholas Flair!"

"Right, sir."

He smiled proudly. "Never forget a name. Let's see—you're a scientist, huh?"

"Yes, sir."

"I met Einstein once. When I was a youngster."

"Did you, sir?"

"Sure did. As nice a guy as you'd want to meet."

We went through this routine every time we met. It no longer annoyed me.

"See m'daughter?" he said.

"No, sir."

"Around here somewhere," he said vaguely.

A chubby ef from the Division of Law & Enforcement was thrust tightly up against him by the press of the throng. She giggled.

"Well there!" he said, and slid an arm about her waist. I left them to their rapture.

It was better out on the terrace. Too chilly for most of the guests. The air quality for the day had been deemed "Unsatisfactory" but at least it smelled all right. You could see stars. In an hour, if I waited, I'd see Skylab No. 14 flash high overhead, southwest to northeast. There were efs and ems up there, serving, snoring in a Somnorific sleep, or watching *Circus au Natural* on TV. I wondered how my father's contortionist was doing.

I was staring down in the brightly lit compound, watching a two-em security patrol saunter along the chainlink fence, flechette guns slung over their shoulders, when I became aware of someone standing at my side. Blond ef. Approximately twenty. About 165 cm. I supposed the object was Lydia Ann Ferguson, and Angela had suggested she slip out onto the terrace. "Say hello to that very handsome em over there by himself."

She, too, was staring down at the chainlink barrier around the compound.

"Outside, the animals," she said.

I turned to her. "What an odd thing to say."

"The fence is to keep the animals out, isn't it?"

"No. I serve here. The fence is to keep the animals in."

She laughed at that.

"Nicholas Bennington Flair," I said.

"Lydia Ann Ferguson," she said.

We stroked palms.

"Your father is Director of Bliss, isn't he?"

"Yes," she said. "He is."

"He rules me," I said. "If you get a chance to talk to him—a deep, close, personal daughter-to-father communication—would you mind mentioning that the new PS-3 zipsuit doesn't have any inside breast pocket, and I, for one, object?"

She laughed again. She laughed very easily.

My first response was negative. I was not usually attracted to very feminine efs with a soft serenity and an air of self-assurance. I could not endure sympathy and suffocating charm. I always thought they must smell of lavender and suffer from primary dyspareunia.

"Hungry?" I asked. "I can get a big dish of food and bring it out here. Save you from fighting the animals."

"I'd like that."

"I think it's pseudo-native slop," I said. "Shredded coconut, rice balls, papaya, poi, roast pork, raw fish—things like that."

"Sounds good."

"It does? What kind of food do you really like?"

"I like all kinds. I enjoy eating."

Good-bye, Sherlock Holmes.

"Grab a table for us," I said. "I'll be right back."

I was returning through the mob with a heaped platter, moving cautiously to avoid sliding a chunk of pickled octopus down an ef's bodice, when Angela Berri caught my eye. She raised her brows in question. I nodded.

Lydia and I chatted casually while we sampled Angela's "native delicacies." Some had a surprisingly pungent flavor, to epithelial end organs atrophied by a constant diet of petroleum-based synthetics. The raw fish was especially good.

I asked Lydia where she served. She said she analyzed and coded essay-type questionnaires for Pub-Op, Inc. She asked me what my duties were. I was as brief as possible.

"Sounds fascinating," she said.

"Not really. Just routine. Most of the Division's responsibilities concern testing and approving or rejecting new commercial products: drugs, prosthetic devices, foods, toys, paints—things of that sort."

"But don't you do original research and development?"

"Oh, yes. A limited amount."

"You have Fred, don't you?"

"Yes, we have Fred."

"What are you interested in mostly, Nick? I mean you, personally?"

"Me? Oh . . . I don't know. I guess my main interest is in procreation research and genetic engineering."

She nodded, without speaking, and we resumed our nibbling. We talked of several inconsequential things, a pleasant enough conversation but hardly significant. She was patting her lips with a plastinap when, quite unexpectedly, she asked; "How is Hyman Lewisohn?"

Lewisohn's illness was not a secret. It had been announced on all the TV news programs and published in facsimile newspapers. Anyone who viewed or scanned knew he was suffering from leukemia and was under treatment at a government hospital. What *was* unusual was that she should ask me about his condition, as if my responsibility was common knowledge. It was not. Perhaps Daddy had been talking too much.

"His condition has stabilized," I said.

She said she thought she'd thank Angela and leave; she wanted to get home early. I told her that her chances of getting a cab after midnight were minimal and, if she'd allow me, I'd call the motor pool and see if I could requisition a car. If I could, I'd be happy to drive her. She hesitated a moment.

"All right," she said finally. "Thank you."

I went inside and made the call on the compound intercom in Angela's bedroom. I noted with some amusement that all her closets and dresser drawers were fitted with locks. A secret ef. I finally got through to the schedule server. He promised me a sedan in half an hour.

I went back into the noisy living room. I found Lydia Ann Ferguson standing just inside the terrace door, looking with some distaste at the clamorous bacchanal swirling about her. I told her it would be a thirty-minute wait. It obviously distressed her.

"We could wait in my place," I offered. "I live one floor down. It's quiet there."

She had no fear. Daddy's rank would protect her.

"Oh, yes," she said. "Thank you. Let's go."

In my apartment, she wandered about examining my library of TV cassettes. I handed her a drink and we sat at opposite ends of the couch, exactly where Paul and I had sat a few hours previously.

"Ballet and Greta Garbo." She smiled. "You're quite a contradiction."

"I am? I don't understand."

"I thought all that interested you was science."

"No. Other things interest me. Occasionally."

"You're a Renaissance man," she said.

"Now you're jerking me." I smiled.

"No, really. I know your reputation."

I could have made a smart answer to that, but let it pass.

After a moment she said, "Angela Berri is a beautiful ef. Don't you think so?"

"Oh, yes. Very beautiful. She rules me, you know."

"I wish you wouldn't say that."

"Would it be better if I said she was my boss? The Office of Linguistic Truth tells us that words like boss, work, job, and labor have a pejorative meaning."

"Like 'love'?"

"Oh, that's not pejorative. Just meaningless in the obso sense. 'Profit' is much better."

"And 'use'?"

"That's economical," I said solemnly. "Instead of a four-letter word, we now have a three-letter word."

She didn't change expression. I had the feeling I was being given a test and wondered if I was passing or failing.

She looked at her digiwatch.

"Another fifteen minutes," I said. "Then we'll leave." I'd be as relieved as she. I wasn't enjoying this.

"That's a profitable brooch you're wearing."

"Thank you." I unpinned it and handed it to her. "Hammered silver and lapis lazuli. It belonged—"

"Damn!" she said.

"What's wrong?"

"Stuck myself on the pin." She sucked her thumb.

"Here," I said, rising, "let me take a look."

Good-bye, Sherlock Holmes. Hello, Lady Luck.

I squeezed her thumb. A small drop of dark red blood rose to the surface. I dabbed it away with my handkerchief.

"I'm a medical doctor, among other things," I said. "Shall I treat you?"

She looked at me, puzzled.

I kissed the ball of her thumb.

"All better?" I asked.

She laughed. "You're a very good doctor. Profitable bedside manner. I'll recommend you to all my friends."

"Thank you. I need the practice."

It went over her head.

"Are you really a medical doctor?" she asked.

"Of sorts. I am many things, of sorts."

She smiled mechanically.

"Let me get a fresh handkerchief," I said. "Then we'll leave."

In my bedroom, I folded the soiled handkerchief carefully and placed it in the top dresser drawer. Paul Bumford had analyzed perspiration on a towel in Frank Lawson Harris' nest and found the type of IgA associated with blood type O-Rh negative. Not Harris' type. We'd see, we'd see. . . .

She lived up on West End Avenue, near Ninetieth Street. It took us almost a half-hour to drive, and I don't believe we exchanged a dozen words. I was certain I had failed.

We pulled up before an obso town house that must have been a hundred years old, converted into apartments. It had remarkable carved stone trim in a classical Greek pattern. I got out of the car and went around to her side. We stood a moment on the sidewalk. I looked up at the building. It needed cleaning, badly, but the lines and proportions were there.

"It was designed by Stanford White," she said. "Do you know who he was?"

"Yes. American architect. Stopped by Harry K. Thaw at the original Madison Square Garden in 1906."

She shook her head. "Do you know *everything*?"

"Everything." I nodded. Something flickered across her face so quickly I couldn't catch it.

We walked up the stone steps together. I waited while she found her key and unlocked the door. She stood a brief moment, her back to me, then turned suddenly.

"Come in," she said.

It was as fast and unexpected as that.

X-8

Angela Berri, Paul Bumford, and I began meeting one or two times a week in my apartment, at about 1730. Angela welcomed this arrangement; she had an almost paranoiac fear that her apartment was being shared.

The first few meetings were devoted to planning and operations. We all contributed opinions and recommendations. Angela listened intently to Paul and me, but the final decision was hers. There was never any doubt about that.

The most immediate problem, we all agreed, was the rigged Satisfaction Rate.

In any bureaucracy, one soon learns that an error is *never* admitted. It is corrected, as discreetly as possible. Only when it is of enormous magnitude, impossible to gloss over without a conspiracy of impracticable size, is one's superior advised. The ruler, then, being ultimately responsible, may be capable of arranging the gloss.

So our initial discussion was of ways and means to accuratize the Satrat, make it absolutely operative. Paul's analysis of the fiddled tapes had shown it was presently too high by at least 10 percentile points, perhaps as much as 15. Suddenly to reduce the Satrat by that amount in one week would be disastrous. There would be an incredulous outcry, perhaps a formal investigation. Down go we all.

After a lengthy discussion of our options, we decided on this plan: Angela would send a routine memo to Phoebe Huntzinger, suggesting that, in the interest of accuracy, it would be wise of Phoebe to work from the polling organization's raw data, rather than from the coded computer tapes they supplied. The first organization selected for the new system would be one of the three whose tapes, Paul's analysis had determined, were *not* fiddled. The second and third companies asked to supply raw data would also be, apparently, uncompromised organizations. The purpose of this was to avoid alerting those who were fiddling the inoperative tapes to the fact that their activities were suspect.

It was decided that the restoration of the Satrat's accuracy should take place over a period of six months. The loss of 10 to 15 percentile points in such a period would alarm government rulers certainly, but not, we hoped, to such an extent as to cause them to question the Satrat's exactitude.

I go into such detail in this matter to illustrate the complexity of our discussions and the depth of our concern.

The Satrat was Angela Berri's responsibility. Paul Bumford's assignment was to analyze in much greater detail the incidence, types, and locations of terrorist activities against government, commercial, and academic scientific research facilities. Angela said it would be no problem for her to requisition the raw data from Burton Klein's Division of Security & Intelligence. But it was an enormous service Paul would have to provide, in addition to his regular duties. He asked if he might enlist the aid of Mary Bergstrom, without telling Mary the reason for their activity.

"What is your reaction to the Bergstrom ef, Nick?" Angela asked.

"She has a Grade B genetic rating, but I suspect the Examiner had a subjective reaction. She is very closed-off. I can't get a control on her. I have no doubts at all about her intelligence. Grade A plus, I'd judge. Paul tells me she is discreet, and he can control her. Her service on Harris' autopsy was profitable."

"I vouch for her," Paul said. "Absolutely."

Angela thought a moment.

"All right," she said finally. "But tell her as little as possible."

At the fourth meeting we discussed my service. I had already informed them that Lydia Ann Ferguson and I had become users.

"Her blood type checked out," I said. "Two nights ago I learned she is not on the pill or any other fertility control. I believe that verifies her presence in Harris' apartment beyond a reasonable doubt."

"And she stopped him," Angela said.

"Probably." I nodded. "We know she had the capability and opportunity of fiddling the Pub-Op tapes. Harris' reports to his control show that he knew it, too. Then he blew his cover, by accident or deliberately. Perhaps she meant more to him than just a user, and he told her who he was and tried to get her out, tried to convince her to tell who her rulers were and save herself. So she stopped him. Either on her own or on orders."

"It computes." Paul nodded.

"Yes. Now there are three possible roles I can play to uncover her degree of involvement in this intrigue, plot, conspiracy—whatever you want to call it. And to identify who is ruling her. One: I can play the clown, a microweight snagged on alcohol, cannabis, sex, anything. She or her rulers might find me useful. Two: I can pretend a heavy profit. For her. Beneath that pleasant, charming self-assured manner is a strong ego drive, an operative passion. I told you what a furious, violent user she is. She might respond to a similarly undisciplined passion in me. Third: I can act the Public Service malcontent, dissatisfied with the orders he is given, disgusted with official government policy. Reactions?"

I had expected Angela to opt for the third possibility. She approved of the second. But the real surprise was Paul. I had expected him to select the first role. He argued for the third, vehemently. My own choice was the third. After almost an hour of sometimes rancorous debate, we convinced Angela; she agreed I was to play the rebel looking for a cause.

"Good," I said. "I'll go ahead with it. There is something else. Lydia's apartment should be shared. Angela, I know you don't want to bring Klein in on this—at this point in time—but is there anyone else in DIVSEC you can trust?"

"No," she said decisively. "I don't want them alerted. But I know an em who can handle it. A private investigator. He's served me before."

I looked at her with wonder, trying to guess how many strings dangled from those long cool fingers, how many marionettes jerked when she gestured.

"Leon Mansfield," she said, looking directly at me. "Peace of Mind, Incorporated. At 983 West Forty-second Street. Got that?"

"Yes."

"Don't flash him, go see him. Mention my name, but tell him nothing except that you want Lydia's apartment shared. He'll ask no questions. Just reward him."

"How much?"

"Start with a hundred. Cover it in petty love."

I nodded. We separated then. I think we all had the sense of events set in motion, a quickening tempo.

Late that night, wearing a robe, I lay on the couch to watch a televised debate that involved one of Hyman R. Lewisohn's innovative ideas. He was much on my mind. After stabilizing, his blast count had fallen dramatically. We went to a manipulated methotrexate. His survival was important, of course. Even more important was that therapy did not cloud the functioning of that marvelously clear, seminal brain.

Late in 1982, Lewisohn had proposed the United States of America open its federation of sovereign states to other nations. Upon application and approval, countries beyond our mainland, beyond the seas—just as Alaska and Hawaii—would be accepted for statehood with all the rights and privileges inherent thereto.

A foreign nation becoming one of our states could retain its native language, if it wished, but English would also be taught in the schools. Each nation joining, like a mainland state, would be entitled to two Senators, and Representatives commensurate with its population. The United States of America would become simply the United States. The abbreviation would be changed from U.S. to US, for semantic reasons.

The suggestion for a worldwide US was proposed in a special message delivered to the Congress on January 15, 1983, by the then President, Irving Kupferman. Enabling legislation was passed by Congress on October 21, 1983 (by a 2-vote margin in the Senate, incidentally).

The Dominican Republic was the first nation to make application, and won immediate approval. At once, teams of social engineers swarmed in. Enormous amounts of love were spent. It was vital that the first foreign state should become a showcase of the Lewisohn Plan. So it did. The birthrate dropped, public health improved, average annual income rose, and roads, factories, new towns, and an American life-style appeared almost overnight.

Realizing what was happening, Puerto Rico applied almost immediately for statehood. They were soon followed by Mali, Chad, Ecuador, Taiwan, Colombia, Upper Volta, and others. In 1998, the United States, US, consisted of ninety-seven states and was growing at an average rate of three new states per year.

The most recent development was a tentative inquiry from Great Britain. There was a great deal of domestic British opposition, of course. Crowds gathered before Buckingham Palace and sang an obso song, "Rule Britannia!" But the great majority of Britons, and their rulers, were weary of their endless economic crises. Pan-Europe (formerly the European Economic Community) had been referred to by President Kupferman as "ten Switzerlands," and he was right. The main problem was whether Great Britain should be admitted as one state, which we preferred, or as three states—England, Scotland, Wales—as they preferred. That was the subject of the TV debate I was viewing.

My doorbell rang. Paul's distinctive ring: three shorts, one long. He wasn't aware he was ringing Beethoven, and I never told him. I switched off the TV and went to the door.

"Interrupting you?" he said.

"No, no. Come in. Drink?"

"No, thanks. Mind if I have a Bold?"

"Of course not. May I have one?"

"I thought you were off."

"One won't hurt me."

I had sworn off cannabis cigarettes almost a year ago. After we lighted up, and I took the first deep draught, I wondered why.

"What were you doing, Nick? When I knocked?"

"Watching a debate on TV. Should Great Britain come in as one state or three?"

"Which do you prefer?"

"I couldn't care less—as long as we get them."

"Why so important?"

"Seventy million underconsumers there. Through necessity, not choice. But I want them for different reasons. England has some of the most originative neurobiologists in the world. Scotland's surgeons and biomedical doctors are the best."

"And Wales?" Paul asked.

"Well . . . we could use some good poets, too."

He laughed.

"Nick, can we talk business for a minute?"

"Sure. As long as you like."

"Remember the night of Angela's party? You and I had a drink down her before we went up, and you said you had something for the Tomorrow File. What was it?"

I looked at him. "Paul, your memory is improving."

He blushed with delight.

"You really think so?"

"No doubt about it. How's the theta coming?"

"Progressing."

He was beginning to imitate my speech patterns. Short phrases. Laconic. I was amused—and touched.

"Stick with it," I advised him. "Big advantage. Yes, I have something for the Tomorrow File. Inspired by a letter I received that afternoon from an obso. An old, old obso. He was a Nobel Prize winner a long time ago. An environmentalist. It had been a good brain then. Senile now. Atheromata, I suppose. We've made some great advances there, but too late to help him."

"You're suggesting a new antiatherosclerosis drug?"

"No. A drug to *reverse* the effects of atheromata, to flush out those clogged arteries, particularly in the brain."

"Brain cells can't regenerate."

"Thank you, doctor," I said with heavy sarcasm. "God damn it, Paul, don't lecture *me* on physiology. It seems to me that in a case like this—an old, old obso with what was originally a fine brain—a drug that could reverse atherosclerosis would be invaluable."

"You mean, keep objects alive for one hundred twenty-five, one hundred fifty, or two hundred years?"

"Well . . . if that was necessary. But not for everyone, of course. Can you imagine the social and economic chaos that would result if we shoved the average lifespan up by fifty years? No, it would only be for selected individuals. Or perhaps just their brains."

"What's the point?" he asked. "Why not a *new* brain?"

"We could start with an infant's brain," I acknowledged. "One with a Grade A genetic rating potentiality. But even that would not guarantee its creativity. A brain that over a period of years had demonstrated inventive genius—like that old obso's brain I mentioned—that would be best. But in addition to regenerating it in a biomedical sense, we would also have to erase its memory, totally. Get rid of old habits, conditioning, prejudices, conceived opinions, and so forth."

"Didn't you suggest that for the Tomorrow File once before?"

"No, I suggested a selective memory block, less gross than Tememblo. What I am now suggesting is *total* memory erasure. Perhaps a manipulated isomer of eight-azoguanine might do it. Something like that. Well . . . it's for the future. Add it to the File."

Paul nodded. "Now I've got one. Remember that ef on the Gerontology Team? The one who suggested a program of Government-Assisted Suicide?"

"Of course I remember. Maya Leighton. Only I changed her suggestion to Government-Assisted Peace. I told you she might be your second secretary. Did you speak to her?"

"Yes. We've had two lunches."

"And?"

"Tall. Imposing. Wide shoulders and hips. Narrow waist. Red-haired. Wears her zipper down. A good brain, Nick. Really good."

"Rating?"

"Well . . . Grade B, but some very original thinking. She's been working on another idea. She's running a computer study on what it costs the government to maintain nonproductive objects of any age who have a Grade F-Minus genetic rating."

Genetic ratings were assigned by a government GE (Genetic Examiner) to every infant at the age of two, and updated every five years after that. The Grade F-Minus was assigned to all those in the retarded, feebleminded, moronic, imbecilic, and idiotic classifications, the single rating used for all of them since differentiating criteria did not exist.

"She says her preliminary findings indicate a program of euthanasia," Paul said.

"And what did you say?"

"I told her that ideas and programs that were logically and scientifically sound were not necessarily politically, socially, or economically feasible."

I laughed. "You're learning. She seems to be terminally oriented, if her first two suggestions are any indication of the way she thinks."

"Not necessarily," Paul said. "You marked the memo about her first idea as 'Original thinking. I believe that inspired her to try something along similar lines. Besides, is her suggestion any more impractical than the required abortion of embryos with untreatable genetic defects?"

"You may be right. Well, if you want her for a second secretary, go ahead. Angela won't object after all we've been doing for her."

He stared at me a moment.

"What's bothering you, Nick?" he asked.

"Remember your telling me Angela's beachhouse was owned by the Samatin Foundation, and the corporations that financed it?"

"Of course I remember. We decided she's on the suck."

"Yes. Well, we suspected it. That's what's been bothering me. This afternoon I went over to Data & Statistics and asked to scan the films on sales of licenses to Walker & Clarke Chemicals, Pace Pharmaceuticals, and Twenty-first Century Electronics. You know the mechanics of a license sale?"

"A product or process we developed is put up for license and advertised. Sealed bids are submitted."

"Right. To Angela. At the cutoff time and date, the bids are opened. High bidder wins exclusive license. During the past four or five years, those three companies have been winning their licenses with late bids, some of them submitted just hours before closing. And they've been winning with bids just a few hundred thousand and, in some cases, just a few thousand new dollars higher than the second-highest bid."

He looked at me, his eyes growing larger as he realized the significance of what I was telling him.

"Nick," he said, not believing, "has she been scanning previously submitted bids and tipping them off?"

"Something like that. I don't know her technique. Perhaps it's as primitive as steaming open the envelopes and resealing them. Maybe it's a fluoroscopic or ultrasonic scanning process. However she's doing it, I'm convinced it's being done."

"But I thought all the big drug companies work together?"

"They do—on cutting up world markets for aspirin, birth-control pills, tranquilizers, antibiotics, sulfas, steroids, and things like that. But on new, untried products and processes, it's every em for himself."

"Then Angela *is* on the suck?"

"I think so."

"But *why*?"

"A very ambitious ef. With expensive tastes. And the talent for applying a knee to a groin that politics demands. Plus a complete lack of conscience. There may be psychopathology there."

"My God."

"That's not all. Now compute this: When I returned the filmed record to the file clerk at Data & Statistics she remarked—quite casually—that those were certainly popular records, that Security Chief Burton Klein had been in just a week ago scanning the same films."

Paul's eyes grew even wider. "Nick," he said, "what the *hell* is going on?"

"Let's go to bed," I said.

I sat up, my back against the headboard, and let him do what profited him most.

Then we snuggled down beneath the thermasheet and held each other. He was soft and warm, his pheromones sweetish.

"Pleasure?" he said.

"Oh, yes! And for you?"

"Pleasure."

"The last time I was home, my father talked about a pill that would give pleasure. I didn't tell him about your suggestion in the Tomorrow File for the Ultimate Pleasure pill."

"The UP pill."

"Right. But I explained to him how difficult it would be to synthesize, since pleasure is so subjective. What does pleasure mean to you?"

"Physical orgasm, for starters."

"And?"

"I'm not sure, Nick. A kind of surrender?"

I propped myself on one elbow and looked down at him.

"Surrender? That's interesting."

"Is it?"

"Yes. I think the first problem is to differentiate between pleasure and happiness. How about this: Pleasure is momentary; happiness, or content, is lasting. Well . . . at least longer than pleasure. Agree?"

"Agree."

"Then, for you, the orgasm is momentary pleasure, but the surrender is happiness?"

He was silent.

"Surrender implies mastery," I said. "Therefore you find happiness in submitting?"

Still he was silent.

"Surrender, or submission, means the recognition of a power greater than your own. Since I am obviously not coercing you by physical force or threat, you submit voluntarily, to obtain happiness. That's why you accept me as your master."

"Oh?" Paul said. "Is that what you think?"

I spent a few hours the next morning scanning and initialing monthly reports from Field Offices of the Division of Research & Development. These FO's, now scattered all over the country and soon to be established beyond the mainland US, had their origins as the National Institutes of Health which, as recently as 1980, were centered in Bethesda, Maryland. At one time, the eleven Institutes, plus several other divisions and units, constituted the world's finest biomedical research organization. They had perished.

They had simply been phased out of existence, budgets strangulated, because of their directors' intransigence in dealing with Washington. The scientists refused to face political realities.

Their epitaph was delivered in 1979 during a Senate committee hearing on a proposed NIH budget. The committee listened to the stubborn demands of the scientists. Then Senator R. Vachel Krumbaugh (R-Oklahoma) gave his reaction to the press.

"A bunch of goddamn Joan of Arcs," he snorted. "We can't burn 'em, but we can sure as hell fire 'em."

Sometimes idealism can be a terminal virtue.

At 1030 I left the office, left the compound, and rode up to Forty-second Street on the Seventh Avenue IRT. I hadn't been in the subway for years. The air-conditioned cars were on rubber-tired wheels; the ride was quiet, fast, endurable. But the graffiti hadn't improved.

It wasn't difficult to find 983 West Forty-second Street; it would have been difficult to miss it. The six-story obso studio building stood alone on one side of a block-square area that had been leveled, then excavated for the foundation of an enormous office-apartment-theater complex. Why 983 still stood, I did not know; perhaps the owner was holding out for more love, or fighting eminent domain through the courts.

In any event, the exterior sidewalls of 983 were ancient brick, showing scars and ruptures where supporting buildings had been ripped away. In front, some of the wide windows had been covered with tin. The stone stoop was littered with garbage, I looked up at what had once been a graceful façade, curlicued and embellished with carvings. On the third floor, on a dusty glass window, was painted a gigantic gilt eye and the legend: LEON MANSFIELD— PEACE OF MIND.

I picked my way up the steps, into the dark interior. It smelled of urine, boiled cabbage, damp wood. The office directory, hanging crazily from a single nail, showed a violin repair shop; a wedding photographer; a wigmaker; an association to liberate Latvia; a personality development school; a union of kosher butchers; and Leon Mansfield, Peace of Mind, Inc. I climbed the creaking stairs and followed a scuttling cockroach to Mansfield's door.

I listened a moment, my ear close to the wood. I heard feet shuffling rapidly, harsh breathing, a muffled cry. I knocked firmly.

The man who flung open the door had eyes the color and consistency of phlegm, and a nose that went on and on. He held a rusty fencing mask under one arm; a bent foil dangled from his fingers. The cuffs of his soiled trousers were snugged with bicycle clips. He stared at me.

"Mr. Mansfield?"

"Yes."

"My name is Nicholas Flair."

"Yes?"

"I'd like to speak to you."

"On a professional matter?"

I nodded.

"Come in, come in."

He closed and locked the door behind me. He came close to me. I amy hypersensitive to personal odors. His was musty. It wasn't the building; it was him.

"Nicholas," he said. "From the Greek. Meaning 'victorious army.'"

I must have shown my surprise.

"Names are a hobby with me," he explained. "My own name, for instance. Leon means lion. I'm like a lion. Know what a good name for a Chinese gangster would be? Tony Kimona. Sit down."

He removed two wooden dumbbells from a cracked leather chair, dusted the seat with a blood-stained handkerchief. I sat down and looked around.

A fencing foil fixed to the wall, pointing out into the room. A kitchenette in a small alcove with a sinkful of dishes rimmed with the golden halos of synthetic egg mix. A chess game laid out on a table. Obso books and magazines and newspapers everywhere. A brittle theatrical poster for a performance of *Ah, Wilderness!* tacked to the wall. A clipped ad from a defunct magazine pinned to the lampshade: a plump beauty pouting a crimson sheath, her eyes dark with unrequited love. Beneath, the legend: "My constipation worries are over."

And dust clinging to everything like a wet sheet.

He dropped his fencing mask and foil onto the floor, removed the bicycle clips from his ankles. He folded into a swivel chair behind the desk, began biting furiously at the hard skin around his thumbnail. His eyes never left mine. I guessed him to be forty to forty-five, in that range.

"Doesn't look much like a detective's office, does it?" he said, speaking rapidly, spitting out bits of skin.

"I've never been in a detective's office before," I said. "I can't judge."

"I'm not a detective," he said, almost angrily. "I'm a social investigator."

I was almost ready to rise and walk out.

"Who sent you to me?" he demanded.

"Angela Berri," I said.

I was staring into his eyes. When I spoke Angela's name, the pupils of his eyes contracted. I was certain he had done it consciously. Whether he was a student of biofeedback or whether it was a natural gift, I did not know. But it changed his appearance. Before, his face had been thin, bony, hard: whacked from a block of walnut by a hasty sculptor. But in those slanted planes, deep and stubbled hollows, crisscrossed ridges and lines, had been a kind of obso charm. Then his pupils contracted, and the stricken face became. . . .

"Angela Berri," he said in a toneless voice.

He unfolded abruptly, strode over to the chessboard, moved a pawn.

"You play chess?" he asked, studying the board. "I have a theory about it. Sex is sublimation for chess. Everyone wants to be a great chess player, but most lack the ability, the drive, the passion. So they substitute for it by using. Defend, attack, checkmate. Sex imitates chess."

"You're joking?" I asked.

"Joking?" he cried. "Mr. Nicholas Flair, I never joke. Life is a tragic thing. Know what a good name for an English farmer would be? Lester Square. What did Angela Berri tell you about me?"

"Nothing. Only that you might be able to help me."

"What's your problem."

"My user."

"Ef or em?"

"Ef."

"Cheating?"

"I think so."

"Evidence?"

"You mean like letters?" I asked him. "Or suspicious behavior? No, nothing like that. Just a feeling I have."

"A feeling." He nodded. "And you want me to find out if this feeling is right or wrong?"

"Yes," I said. "I want to know the truth."

"Oh-ho," he said. "The truth. Oh-ho. Believe me, Mr. Nicholas Flair, you wouldn't like it—the truth. But find out about your user I can. You want her followed?"

"No." I said. "I want her apartment shared."

He went back behind the desk again, sat down heavily in the wooden swivel chair.

"Would you wish for a drink?" he asked formally. "I have something special."

"All right. Thank you."

He took two mismatched empty petrojelly jars from a desk drawer, blew into them. Something flew out. Then he removed a bottle from a bottom drawer, placed it gently on the desk. I leaned forward to examine the faded label. Slivovitz. Obviously quite old. He poured us each a small drink, recorked the bottle carefully. We raised glasses to each other, then sipped. He looked at me.

"Well!" he said.

"I must tell you, Mr. Mansfield, it tastes exactly like petronac."

A small sound came out of him. It may have been a laugh.

"Well . . . it *is* petronac." He sighed. "But the *bottle*—that's something special. No?"

I nodded and finished my drink.

"Angela Berri" he said dreamily. "How is the dear lady?"

"Fine."

"This ef of yours—you want her apartment shared?"

"Yes."

"She live alone?"

"Yes."

"What kind of a building?"

"Old townhouse on West End Avenue, near Ninetieth Street. Nine other apartments. I think all or most of the tenants serve during the day."

"And this user of yours—she serves during the day?"

"Yes, from 0900 to 1500."

"You have keys?"

"No."

He shook his head. "Doesn't matter. When do you want me to start?"

"As soon as possible."

"Give me the address, name, and apartment number. I'll go up today. How will I contact you?"

"I'll flash you."

"No, no," he said quickly. "I have no flasher. I'll call you from outside, from a phone, not a flasher."

I thought a moment. I wasn't pleased with the idea.

"I'll give you my apartment number," I said finally. "Call me there if you have to. Identify yourself as 'Chess Player.' Just tell me where I can meet you. Don't say anything more. Don't repeat anything. I have a good memory."

He nodded, as if such clandestine arrangements were the most natural thing in the world. As perhaps they were.

I opened my purse. I gave him the slip of paper I had prepared with Lydia Ann Ferguson's name, address, and apartment number. I added my flasher number. I was still holding my wallet. I looked at him, about to speak....

"Angela Berri told you a hundred new dollars?" he said.

"Yes."

He nodded. "The dear lady. All right—a hundred. To start."

I handed over the love, stood up, started for the door.

"Mr. Nicholas Flair," he said, voice dead.

I turned. He was staring at me.

"I don't carry a gun," he said. "Never touch them."

I looked at him in astonishment.

"Why should I be interested in that?"

"Just thought you should know."

I was halfway out the door when he stopped me again.

"Know what a good name for a brawny Scotsman would be?" he said. "Jock Strap."

I went back to my office and popped an Elavil. I don't know why that meeting with Leon Mansfield had depressed me so much. The physical surroundings, of course: decay, destruction, must. But also the em himself, with his quick alterations of antic wit and ...

I called the commissary for a bottle of Smack and a package of probisks. That would hold me until my dinner with Lydia Ann Ferguson. I went back to scanning the monthly Field Office reports.

I had some excellent objects serving me. Young, talented, innovative. I was proud of them and, as far as possible, kept my hands off and let them run. Many of them could have made much more love on the outside. But they wouldn't have the freedom. What corporation, for instance, would finance a team of ten genetic biologists to investigate color blindness? Everyone knew it was caused by a defective gene in the X chromosome. Where was the love in that?

But the corporations would be intensely interested if they knew the results of that team's work: Manipulation of the defective gene that could quite possibly lead to manipulation of a similarly defective gene that caused baldness. Genetic engineering sometimes led to chemotherapy for symptoms of the genetic variance. "Bald? Take Shaggy!" We could license *that* drug for zillions.

I went back to my apartment and took a one-hour Somnorific. I arose at 1830, showered, dressed carefully. I decided to wear a new wig I had purchased recently, a "King Arthur," down to my shoulders, silver-blond. As I tootied up, I rehearsed how best to play my role as a Public Servant malcontent, looking for a cause to which I might totally dedicate my energy, talent, and sacred honor.

I had my hand on the doorknob when the flasher chimed. I went over and flicked the switch, but no image came on. Flashers could receive voice calls from conventional phones.

"Hello?" I said.

"Hello?" a voice said. "Who's this?"

"Whom are you calling?"

"This is Chess Player."

"Oh. This is Nicholas Flair."

"There's a Mess Hall on Seventh Avenue between Eighteenth and Nineteenth. In half an hour."

He clicked off. I looked at my digiwatch. If the meeting didn't take too long, I could still be on time. And even if I was a few minutes late. . . . Lydia was a patient, sweet-tempered ef.

The chain of popular Mess Hall restaurants had been started in 1989 as one answer to the rising prices of restaurant meals. An ingenious entrepreneur—an ex-nightclub publicist—had bought up a supply of Army surplus compartmented steel trays. They were the key to the low-cost fast-service Mess Hall operation. Meals were served cafeteria style, only one selection a day; no menu, no substitutions, no seconds. The day's choice was posted in the window: Monday, beef stew; Tuesday, hamburger; Wednesday, fried chicken; and so forth. If you didn't like the main course offered that day, you didn't eat there; nothing else was available.

I saw Leon Mansfield from the sidewalk. He was seated at a table near the plate glass window. His steel tray was empty. He had pushed it away and was playing a chess game on a small pocket set. I went inside. I took the chair opposite him. He didn't look up.

"Nice perfume," he said.

"Thank you. Please make this fast."

"I put in two," he said. "One in the flasher in her living room, one behind the dresser in her bedroom. Transceivers. I'll pick up in a white van marked 'Kleen-Eeez Laundry.' Sound-activated recorders, so I don't have to be there."

"You have any problems?"

He finally raised his eyes from the chessboard and looked at me.

"Problems? No, I have no problems. But you—you got a problem."

"Oh? What is that?"

"Her place was already shared when I got in."

I thought about that for a moment.

"How many?" I asked.

"One. Under the slipcover on the side of the armchair in the living room. Butcher's work. A straight mike. The wire goes down through the floor."

"Into the apartment below?"

"It goes through the floor. That's as far as I could trace it. I left it there."

"Thank you," I said.

"Give my best to Angela Berri," he said. "The dear lady."

I met Lydia, on time, at an eastside Italian restaurant. The place was half-empty. With the love they charged, that was understandable. But they knew me. I *think* the wine they served was made from grapes.

"You must be very wealthy." Lydia smiled, studying the menu.

"Not on my rank-rate," I said. "But occasionally I have to get out and unwind."

"Let off pressure?"

"Exactly. How about the veal? *And* peppers. *And* spaghetti. *And* a bottle of red wine."

Frank Lawson Harris' last meal. Her expression didn't change.

"Sounds marvelous," she said.

She looked quite profitable. Not tooty—but then she didn't have the body for it. Wide shoulders, heavy bosom, thick hips. She was smart enough to wear a loose, flowing shift. It tightened across her nipples, then draped straight to her knees. Seductive without being obvious.

Her face was broad, too. High, clear brow. Wide cheekbones. Rather Slavic. Her neck was soft, almost puffy. Her eyes were large, slightly protuberant. I wondered if she might not be suffering from occult hyperthyroidism. Probably not. Her mind was certainly not dulled, and I could detect no signs of irritability. She seemed as serene and self-possessed as ever. A very pleasant ef.

I asked her questions about her service as we dined. She was quite open about it. She was currently analyzing and coding essay answers to the question: "Do you approve of, disapprove of, or have no opinion on televised transvestite beauty pageants?"

"Did objects know what a transvestite is?" I asked.

"Interviewers were instructed to explain only when asked. Most of them knew. Even children. Some of the replies we received were hilarious."

She quoted some of the essays. I didn't think they were particularly hilarious. But I smiled or laughed each time she paused expectantly in her recital.

"What do *you* think about them?" she asked suddenly. "And televised bullfights and executions?"

I shrugged.

"Why does the government allow it?" she demanded.

For the first time I caught a glimpse of an anger behind her placidity. In bed she was a wanton. Now I saw a hint of an emotional (if not intellectual) passion that might equal the physical.

"The government allow it?" I laughed. "Lydia, you *are* naïve. The government *encourages* it!"

"But *why*?"

"For very practical reasons. Psychological studies have proved that violence and sex on TV act as a catharsis, a visual safety valve for hostility and aggression."

"I don't believe that," she said sharply.

"In any event, it's not the main reason why—"

I was silent then while the waitress removed our emptied dinner plates. She brought us a pot of espresso (mostly chicory) and, proudly, fresh apples (two). They were huge, bright, red. And mealy and tasteless. But Lydia appeared to be delighted with hers. I watched her large, strong teeth chonk into the fruit. When she swallowed, her entire soft throat convulsed. It was oddly exciting to watch.

"What is the main reason that the government encourages permissiveness on TV?" she asked finally.

"Well, in the media industry there are two main cartels: print media and electronic media. They claim to be complementary. In a few significant ways they are. But actually they are quite competitive, especially in obtaining advertising revenues. Now the government cannot license print media. The last time they tried it, in 1990, the result was catastrophic.

"But the government does have some ways of manipulating the electronic media. This they can do legally since all radio and television stations must be licensed by a government agency. It's easier to influence an industry whose very existence depends on official grant. And for that reason, it's vital to the government that the electronic media grow while the print media decrease in importance. So the government encourages permissiveness on TV. People who once could only scan sex scenes in books and magazines, can now view it—in three dimensions and color. Thus the electronic media attract larger audiences. Thus their advertising revenue increases. Thus they grow stronger, make more love, and the need for TV station owners to retain their licenses becomes even more imperative. Thus stronger government control of their editorial policies. That's why you see fornication and bullfights and executions on your home set. Do you follow all that?"

She seemed shocked. I thought what I had explained was obvious to everyone.

"I can't believe it," she said.

"Believe it. It's operative."

"But don't you—you personally—object to government control of media? Any media, in any form?"

"I'm just an em following orders," I said. "What can I do?"

We finished our coffee in silence. She opened her purse, then paused to look at me.

"Do you mind if I touch up my makeup?" she asked innocently. "I know I shouldn't do it at the table."

In some ways she was delightful. Almost as ingenuous as Millie.

"Please do." I laughed. "I might even touch up mine."

"You don't wear much."

"No, not much. A friend of mine has been after me to use eye shadow."

"Oh, no," she said quickly. "Please don't do that."

I watched her apply lip rouge.

"Beautiful color," I said. "What is it?"

"The color is called Passion Flower. Does that jerk you? The lip rouge is Amour Now."

"*That* jerks me," I said. "Amour now or later?"

She tried to smile mysteriously, but she was too open and honest to bring it off. We both laughed and left the restaurant hand in hand. It had been a profitable dinner.

We went to a nude performance of *Swan Lake* at Lincoln Center. The audience seemed to enjoy it—oohing and ahing whenever the em star performed a *grand jeté*—but I found the whole thing absurd. I think Lydia did, too. At least, she made no objection when we left before it ended. We stopped at a federal grogshop where I bought a lovable bottle of cherry liqueur which the manager assured me was made from real cherries. I also bought Lydia a national lottery ticket. She laughed happily.

"If I win I'll give you half," she vowed.

"Good. An ef in my Division won a thousand a few weeks ago."

"I want to win a million."

"I hope you do. What will you do with it—after you give me my half?"

"I'll buy a farm," she said dreamily. "Somewhere far off. Lonely and deserted. I'll buy animals—dogs and horses and cows and chickens and cats. And I'll raise my own food. I'll have a little lake, and I'll swim every morning. I'll listen to the wind and watch the stars."

I think she was serious. But of course there were no places like that anymore.

We went back to her home by taxi. The cabs had changed; they were electric now. The drivers hadn't changed; still choleric and unpleasant as ever. We also had to endure a Cab-Alert installation that flashed color slides at ten-second intervals and, by recorded messages, advised us what to do about wet armpits, bowel irregularity, and a breath that wilted flowers.

Lydia had an apartment that reflected her personality: unassertive, pleasing, calm. I had to keep reminding myself this was the ef who provided Harris with a going-away present: the fiddled Somnorific.

"Sit over there," she said casually, motioning toward the slip-covered armchair in the living room. "It's the most comfortable chair I have. Would you like this cherry stuff in Smack or on ice—or how?"

"Just straight," I said. "And just a small glass. It's sure to be sweet."

Obediently, I sat down in the armchair. She was right—it was comfortable. While she was in the kitchen, I ran my fingertips lightly over the slipcover on both sides. Leon Mansfield had been right, too; it was amateurish; I felt the bump of the mike. When she came in from the kitchen, I was leaning back, relaxed, my mouth close to the concealed bug.

"Cheers," I said, lifting the plasticup she handed me.

She pulled a hassock across the floor and sat at a lower level, near my knees.

"But you don't seem so cheerful tonight," she said. "Depressed?"

"A little."

"Your service?"

"I guess so. It's been bothering me for some time now. Recently it's become worse."

"Want to talk about it?"

"Want to, but can't."

"Security classification?"

"Yes."

"I won't repeat it."

That was a giggle. She wouldn't have to.

"Oh, Lydia, it's not that I don't trust you. I know you wouldn't do or say anything to endanger me. Or your father."

That startled her, but she recovered quickly.

"I can't believe you and Daddy would do anything wrong," she said.

"Depends on your definition of wrong, doesn't it? Tell me this: Is it wrong to refuse to obey the legal order of your ruler when you feel, in your heart of hearts, that the order you are given is immoral?"

She was silent, staring at me.

"Nick, I can't make a decision like that for you."

"I know you can't. I'm not asking you to. It's all mine."

"But maybe it would help if you talked it out."

I shrugged.

"I doubt it, Lydia. I've been over and over it, again and again. I've considered every possible argument, for and against. And I just don't know what to do."

"Nick, for God's sake, what *is* it?"

I sighed. "Well...I might as well tell you. But don't—please, please, don't—breathe a word of this to anyone. It involves behavior control. Or, as it was once euphemistically called, 'behavior modification.' But I'm talking about behavior control by chemical means, not by psychological conditioning."

"You mean by giving an object a pill or injection?"

"I wish it was that simple. But it's not a single object I'm talking about; it's an entire population. Look, the principle is an obso one. More than seventy years ago we started putting traces of iodine in table salt. It practically eliminated goiter in this country."

I paused to see if she reacted. If she, as I suspected, might be a victim of hypothyroidism. But she showed nothing but fascinated interest.

"Then we put chlorine in our water to make it potable," I continued. "Then fluoride—all chemicals."

"But they're like—like medicine!"

"Right. No one but the ignorant could possibly object. But we established the principle of involuntary ingestion of chemicals by government decree. All right, now take this situation: We have a prison riot. The warden and several guards have been seized as hostages; the prisoners threaten to kill them. They're destroying the prison. We can go in with armored tanks and flechette guns. Sure, a lot of objects will be stopped, but the riot will be over. Now every prison in the country is supplied water from a central source, pipe or tank. Wouldn't it make more sense to put tranquilizers or hypnotics in the drinking water to subdue the entire prison population without loss of life? Wouldn't you opt for that?"

"Yesss," she said. "I guess I would."

"What about Harlem, or Watts, or any other ghetto being torn apart by a race riot? Rather than an armed confrontation, wouldn't you prefer that the riots be calmed by adding say, a soporific, to their water supply? Only for as long as it took to end the riot? Then the authorities could discuss the issues involved with objects not inflamed by blood lust or an uncontrollable urge to burn, baby, burn. Wouldn't you opt for the drug?"

"I don't know," she said slowly. "Now it's getting complicated. I might approve if it meant saving lives."

"It would," I assured her. "But it's become more difficult than you imagine. Because now we have a whole arsenal of drugs that affect behavior. We can make an object as fierce as a tiger or as mild as a kitten. And not only a single object, mind you, but by adding the chemical to food or the water supply, we can manipulate populations—in prisons, schools, towns, cities, nations, the world."

"You're talking about chemical warfare."

"Not necessarily. I'm talking about behavior control—although I admit the fine line between that and chemwar gets finer each day."

"But you said you had a particular problem?"

"I do. About a year ago—well . . . a little less than that—an African nation was admitted to statehood in the US. We can do a lot for them—socially, economically, medically, culturally. But they have one tribe, about ten thousand objects, who are national fanatics and oppose US statehood. These objects are primitives—unbelievably cruel, without conscience, burning and looting and stopping. They can cause absolute chaos in a young state trying to pull itself up from the mud of ignorance and poverty. The other objects in the state number about four million. They want nothing but a peaceful existence, a chance to improve their standard of living and educate their children. Should the ten thousand rebels be allowed to thwart that desire? Most of the dissidents live in one very restricted area. Most of them draw their drinking water from one lake. We could calm them all tomorrow by sending planes over the lake to drop a few centiliters of a clear liquid. That would be a temporary solution. We could make it a permanent solution simply by substituting a different chemical. You understand?"

"Oh, yes. Oh, yes. I understand."

"But if we poisoned the lot, the international outcry would be—well, just something we don't want. So a decision has been made at the highest possible levels of our government. It will be a two-part program. First, the rebels' water supply will be treated with tranquilizers and antiaggression drugs. That will take care of the immediate problem. The long-range cure—if you can call it that—is to stop the tribe. Our prosterility drugs are not as dependable as they might be, so it was decided to take advantage of a genetic deficiency from which the rebels already suffer naturally."

"Which is?"

"Sickle-cell anemia. We've practically wiped it out in this country. Genetic manipulation led to an oral drug. In developing the inhibitor, we also learned how to synthesize a stimulator. We can stop the entire rebel tribe in one generation. Long enough to forestall any international accusation of genocide, and short enough not to endanger the social and economic development of the state. I have been ordered to work up the technology: drugs required, amounts, preferred methods of delivery, and so forth. And that, Miss Ferguson, is my problem. Now give me advice."

She sat there, hunched over on the hassock, chin cupped in palms.

"You're not going to do it, are you?" she asked quietly.

"I don't *want* to do it!" I cried. "If I don't, my career is over. But that's the least of my worries. There's always the R&R Hospice 'for psychiatric observation for reasons of public security.' They'll never let me walk away from this. Not knowing what I know."

She nodded, reached forward, took my hands in hers.

"We'll work it out," she whispered. "Somehow."

"Don't talk to your father, for God's sake," I said roughly. "That's the last thing in the world I need—the Director of Bliss learning I had mentioned this to anyone."

"No," she said. "No, I won't talk to my father."

She rose and smiled down at me. A sad, understanding, sympathetic smile. The last smile Harris had seen before he began clawing at his chest?

"Another drink?" she asked.

"No, thanks. I'm all knotted up. It won't help."

She nodded, took my empty glass, went into the kitchen, then into the bedroom. I waited, wondering what she was doing. Then she came to the bedroom door and stood there for a moment, erect, arms down at her sides, palms turned forward. She was naked. She looked like an anatomy chart. I rose, turned off the lamp, moved to her.

Whatever control she possessed, and she had displayed a great deal, fell away from her in bed. The pleasant self-assurance disappeared, and something raw took its place. If she was not a practised user, she was an ardent student. I could understand Harris' infatuation. There was nothing she would not do.

The body was overwhelming, slightly tumescent, a fever to her flesh. She had an almost demoniacal strength, thrashing, bucking, flailing. And uttering animal cries. Her odor was dark, fern-rot and bog. I know it may scan ridiculous, but I was never certain she was conscious of my presence. Surrendered to a paroxysm of sensuality, she was simply lost and gone, rutting her last minute on earth and howling with delight.

Long afterward, her great breasts puddled out, nipples bleary, soft thighs spread, she looked at me with dazed eyes, coming back slowly from wherever she had been. I may have hated her then.

Smelling of her, I showered quickly and dressed. I bent over the bed to kiss her goodnight. A strong arm curled around my neck, pulled me close.

"Yes," she whispered.

In the lobby, I looked at the mailbox of 2-B, the apartment directly below hers. Dr. and Mrs. Henry L. Hammond. I knew him—or knew of him.

I circled the block slowly. Finally, on Ninetieth Street between West End Avenue and the river, I found the Kleen-Eeez Laundry van. It appeared deserted. I rapped on the side. A small circular flap, concealed in the lettering, slid aside. An eye stared at me. The flap closed. A moment later the van's rear door was opened. Leon Mansfield motioned to me.

I climbed in and closed the door behind me. The interior was dimly lighted with a low-wattage red bulb. It was fitted out with electronic equipment: tape recorders, shortwave radio transmitters and receivers, locator, tape splicer, etc. There was a canvas cot with a filthy blanket. Mansfield was seated at a make-shift desk, earphones clamped to his elongated skull. He turned one of the earphones around and waved me close.

I moved next to him, breathing through my mouth. I had had enough of other objects' odors for one day. I pressed my ear to the turned pad.

Man's voice: "We'll discuss it tomorrow."

Lydia: "Yes, Henry. As long as you got it all."

Henry: "We did indeed. Perfectly."

Lydia: "He's very troubled."

Henry: "We'll discuss it tomorrow. Get a good night's sleep."

Lydia: "Give my best to Alice. Good night."

Henry: "Good night."

Click. The tape stopped.

Leon Mansfield removed his earphones. He rewound the tape, stopped the machine, removed the reel. He fitted a fresh reel on the spindle, threaded it through. He handed me the reel he had removed and two more.

"This is what I have so far," he said tonelessly.

I was waiting to hear him comment about those bedroom sounds he had picked up, but he said nothing. I climbed out of the back door of the van, carrying the reels.

"Thank you," I said.

"A pleasure," he said.

X-9

On the morning following my dinner with Lydia Ann Ferguson, I flashed DIV-SEC (Division of Security & Intelligence) and requested a complete profile on Dr. Henry L. Hammond from the National Data Bank. I was certain I'd hear from Assistant Deputy Director Burton P. Klein within the hour, demanding to know the reason for my request. I underestimated the em. He came storming into my office thirty minutes later, banging the door behind him.

"Come on in, Burton," I said genially.

My irony was wasted.

"What the hell is this about Dr. Hammond?" he shouted.

I looked at him critically.

"Calm, Burton, calm," I said. "You want me to quote correlative statistics on hypertension and mortality? Now sit down and relax. I don't like that high color in your face."

It worked. He threw himself into the plastivas sling at my deskside, breathing heavily, glaring at me, but gradually quieting.

He was a bear of an em, carrying an overweight torso on slender legs. He was ugly. Ungraceful. His voice was too loud, his manner boisterous, his personal habits disgusting. (He picked his nose, rolled the detached matter between thumb and forefinger, flicked it away.)

But he could no more dissimulate than he could play a toccata on a harpsichord. I took no profit from him, but I admired his openness. He was what he was: take it or leave it.

"Dr. Henry L. Hammond," I said. "Yes, I requested a profile. I'm thinking of asking him to serve on a consultant basis."

"What the hell for?"

"Burton, it's just routine," I said softly. "Hyman Lewisohn has leukemia. You know that. Lewisohn's survival is my concern. He's not responding to drugs. So I've drawn up a contingency plan if his condition continues to deteriorate. One step in that plan is parabiosis. Hammond is an expert in parabiosis. That's all there is to it."

"What's parabiosis?" he demanded.

At least he made no attempt to disguise his ignorance.

"Parabiosis is a surgical process by which two objects of the same species are linked physiologically. Hopefully for a short time. One object is healthy, one diseased. By linking their blood vessels, the healthy one takes over, or assists, the life processes of the diseased object. It has worked many times in renal failure. That pertains to kidney malfunctions. And it has worked, experimentally, with leukemic patients. That's why I want Dr. Hammond. If parabiosis becomes necessary in Lewisohn's case."

In his blunt manner, he went directly to the essence of the problem.

"Where do you get the healthy object to connect him to?" he asked.

"Volunteers." I shrugged. "Prisoners condemned to capital punishment. Others. We can work it out."

"Do you know what you're doing?" he asked finally.

I was startled. I thought at first he was questioning my professional competence. Then I saw, from his bemused manner, that it had been a rhetorical question. What the hell, he wanted to know, was going on?

I had seen that same manner in, and heard the same question from many other objects, some much more intelligent than Burton Klein. It sprang from an inability to accept change. It was a psychological condition quite similar to shock. Things were moving so fast, society evolving so rapidly, some objects simply could not cope. Mutation followed mutation so swiftly that after a while catalepsy was the only means of survival.

"Burton," I said gently, "you've been serving too hard."

"Yes, I have," he agreed. He scrubbed his face with his palms. "Things have been piling up. These terrorist attacks. I don't know where to start. And—"

"And?" I prompted when he paused.

"And other things," he muttered. "I don't know whom to trust anymore."

"Sleeping well?" I asked him.

"Somnorifics."

"How often?"

"Every night."

"That's not so good. Want to check in? Here or at a Hospice? We'll give you a workup."

"No," he said decisively. "Not now. My annual comes up in September. I can wait till then."

He got up heavily, started for the door. Then he turned.

"Listen," he said. "You talk to Angela Berri more than I do."

It wasn't a question. I didn't answer.

"You should know—"

But then he stopped, turned around again, and marched out, leaving my door open. I stared after him.

We met in my apartment about 1800. Angela Berri told us the program to accuratize the Satrat was proceeding on schedule. No problems. She and I looked to Paul Bumford.

Paul had been serving long hours; it showed. His weight was down. His naturally fair skin had an unhealthy pallor. There were dark rings under his eyes. With his vanity, I knew that must gall him. He had applied pancake makeup, but the shadows were still discernible.

"Mary Bergstrom and I have been using the King Mk. IV computer in A Lab," he reported. "I thought it best not to take the chance of alerting Phoebe Huntzinger to what we were doing."

"Good," Angela said.

"But the King is limited," Paul went on. "Especially in storage. Anyway, we broke down and coded the raw data on terrorist attacks. Nationwide. Only on the mainland. Incidents in outlying states are normal. We programmed for dates and times, types of attack, number of objects believed involved, types of installations hit, results, duration of attacks, methods of approach and escape, types of sabotage, and so forth."

"And?" Angela demanded.

"These are preliminary printouts," Paul said. "But I think they'll hold up. It may be a nationwide conspiracy, directed from a central command. I can't say definitely. I'd guess yes. Operations appear to be organized by Geo-Political Areas. Each GPA exhibits distinct characteristics. In GPA-6, for instance, bombings predominate. In GPA-3, it's kidnappings. Times of attack and numbers of objects involved convince me the whole is organized, structurally, along GPA lines."

"Any uniformities?" I asked.

"Mostly procreation and genetic research facilities, in all GPA's. Most significant: Attacks on procreation and genetic research facilities are 82.3 percent sabotage. That indicates interior collusion. Turning a thermostat down a few degrees. Enough to destroy a culture. Poisoning rats' meal. To stop a cancer-sensitive strain it's taken thirty years to breed. In our Denver Field Office labs, a hundred aborted fetuses were uncovered over a weekend."

"Jesus," Angela breathed.

I tried to control my anger. What in God's name did they think they were doing?

"Those are my gross conclusions to date," Paul finished. "It's big. It's serious. No hint of who may be behind it. No suggestion of foreign influence. Obviously a great number of objects, including SATSEC personnel, are participating. Questions?"

"Any captures?" I asked. "Defectors? Informers?"

"None."

"Any love stolen?" Angela asked.

"Now that's interesting," Paul said. "The answer is yes. Terrorism against banks was in the usual pattern. Large sums were taken. But I think the bank hits were a diversion."

"Nice diversion," I said. "Dual purpose. Muddy the waters and finance the whole operation. Good brain there."

"Paul, you've done excellent service," Angela said.

He straightened and brightened.

"Another two days," he said. "Then we'll be finished. What's next?"

"Me," I said. "I'm next. These are the tapes supplied by Leon Mansfield. Recorded yesterday. He told me Lydia Ferguson's apartment was already being shared before he got in. The bug leads to the apartment below hers. Occupied by Dr. and Mrs. Henry L. Hammond."

Angela Berri showed no reaction when I spoke the name. I was watching for it.

"So what you hear," I went on, "has already been shared by her rulers. I knew it when I spoke. Here we go. . . ."

I started the machine. Angela and Paul leaned forward, hands clasped, heads down. During Lydia's animal cries in the bedroom, I watched them closely. Neither reacted. They listened intently, right up to Henry's last line. I switched off the machine.

Then Paul raised his head, looked at me admiringly.

"How did you ever think of that African idea?" he asked. "Using an anemic stimulator on a rebel tribe?"

"It just occurred to me. I thought it was exactly the type of activity a dissident group would be looking for. Something to discredit the US in the United Nations."

"Genius," Paul enthused. "Genius!"

Angela Berri was silent.

"Who is Dr. Henry L. Hammond?" Paul asked.

"I know him. I never met him personally, but I heard him address a meeting of the American Association for the Advancement of Science in 1993. On symbiosis. A brilliant paper. Then he disappeared, for years. This afternoon I ran a DIVSEC profile on him."

Then Angela came alive.

"DIVSEC?" she said sharply. "Did Klein question it?"

"Of course." I nodded. "But I soothed him. I told him I wanted Hammond as a consultant because I was considering symbiosis for the treatment of Lewisohn. Which I am."

She started to speak, then thought better of it.

"Hammond's profile was interesting," I went on. "He headed a team at CIT that did the research on symbiosis. More failures than successes on human objects, but definite progress. Six months after he delivered the paper at the Triple-A S, he resigned, went to Japan, and served in a Zen Buddhist monastery for two years. How does that jerk you? Then he returned, married his former secretary, and took service at CCNY teaching a very primary course in something called Human Dynamics. As far as I can discover, it's a lot of kaka. Hammond and his wife live in the apartment directly below Lydia Ferguson's. Alice Hammond rules a government daycare center on Broadway and Seventy-third Street. She's a PS-7. About six months ago they applied for and were granted a procreation license. Ef. Their political involvement, to date, has been minimal. Both are registered Independents. She belongs only to several scientific societies."

"Obsos?" Paul asked.

"No. He is twenty-seven, she is twenty-four. Both, for some unknown reason, underwent primal scream therapy about two years ago. He should have known better. Anyway, there you have Dr. and Mrs. Henry L. Hammond who, possibly, are now listening to tapes similar to those you just heard."

They both straightened up, leaned back on the couch.

"Well . . ." Paul said finally. "Where do we go from here?"

"I know where *I* go," I announced. "This afternoon Lydia called. She just had a wonderful idea. The people downstairs, the Hammonds, have had her for dinner twice. So she feels she owes them an invitation. Will I come for dinner on Thursday to meet them?"

"Watch yourself," Angela said.

Late that night—not too late, about 2330—I was seated naked on the edge of my bed. I should have swung my legs under the thermasheet and tried to sleep. But something was puzzling me.

Paul Bumford, the last time we had been under that same sheet—not the *same* one, but an identical one—had said his happiness derived from surrender. To me, I presumed. Or at least to physical mastery. And last night I had proof of Lydia's happiness in surrendering to—well, to something. The mastery of her own flesh perhaps. There was a link there, between the two, but I couldn't analyze it.

My flasher chimed. I went over to the bedroom extension, sat down, flicked it on. The image was Angela Berri.

"Nick," she said, "why did you have to use the African idea?"

"Angela," I said, "what difference does it make?"

"What if they ask for documentation?"

"I'll tell them the truth: all oral orders, no documentation exists. It doesn't, does it?"

"Not to my knowledge," she said.

"Good. Besides, that was three years ago. It's operative, isn't it?"

Then she looked at me, eye to eye, on the screen.

"Perfectly," she said. "One of the most lovable ideas you've ever had."

"Thank you, teacher," I said.

She smiled and switched off.

I was the last to arrive at Lydia's apartment. But she wasn't upset. Just happy, apparently, to see me. I kissed her cheek, left her to serve in the kitchen, went into the living room to introduce myself.

Dr. Henry L. Hammond had changed little, physically, since I had seen him at the AAAS meeting five years ago. He was a big em, stalwart, with a natural Valkyrie hair style and a full, blondish beard. His lips were an intense cherry-red, but I did not believe it was makeup. His palm stroke was dry and hearty.

His wife, Alice, obviously pregnant, was small, mousy, and seemed composed mostly of grays: gray hair, a grayish tinge to her skin, a gray silk dress, gray plastipat shoes, a necklace and bracelet of slate chips set in pewter. She was quiet, contained, watchful. The more dangerous of the two, I judged.

Hammond and I chatted briskly. Inconsequential topics: the high cost of food, the difficulty of getting cabs when it rained, the dearth of decent housing in New York. Finally, his wife spoke.

"Where do you serve, Dr. Flair?" she asked.

I told her. She nodded, with a half-smile. Then she rose awkwardly and went into the kitchen, presumably to help Lydia with the dinner.

"Pardon me, Dr. Hammond," I said. "My memory may be playing tricks, but didn't you serve on parabiosis?"

"Oh, yes," he said casually. "But that was a long time ago."

"You're no longer in the field?"

"Oh my, no. I took a two-year sabbatical to visit the Orient. When I returned, I discovered I was simply out of it. Things had moved along so rapidly in my absence that it would have taken me years to catch up."

"I know exactly what you mean." I laughed. "Sometimes I'm afraid to take a threeday. The world progresses while I'm away."

"Progresses?" he said. "Well, it certainly changes."

"And what are you doing now?"

"Conditioning. At CCNY. Basic stuff on human motivations. But I find it very satisfying. Teaching the young, I mean."

Then we were called to dinner. We sat at a round plastisteel table in a small alcove. The table was lighted with electric candles, the little bulbs shaped like flames, with flickering filaments.

Lydia had prepared a casserole in her microwave oven: prorice and proshrimp—shaped and tinted like the real thing. It also contained slices of green propep, bits of natural ham, and natural onion. It was edible.

We went through the confusion of passing plates about, spooning out the main dish, dividing a prolet salad that could have used more synthetic herbs and spices. Then, all served, we settled down to consumption.

Dr. Hammond was wearing obso clothes: flannel slacks and a rough tweed jacket. He withdrew a pair of yellowed ivory chopsticks from his inside breast pocket. He manipulated them with great dexterity, demonstrating how it was possible to pick up a single grain of rice. His wife gave me the impression of having witnessed this trick previously, too many times.

"Mrs. Hammond," I said. "I haven't—"

"Alice," she interrupted gravely.

"Alice." I smiled. "A first-name basis is profitable. Call me Nick. I haven't yet congratulated you and your husband. When is the child due?"

"The last week in August."

"Congratulations! Ef or em?"

"Ef," she said.

"Wonderful."

"We wanted an em," she said.

Lydia and Hammond were silent, bending over their plates.

"I'm sure you'll be delighted with a little ef," I said. "You'll see."

"Dr. Flair, do you—"

"Nick."

"Nick, do you approve of the government licensing pregnancies and dictating the sex of the child?"

"Approve of it?" I said cautiously. "Perhaps not approve. But I accept it. I recognize the necessity."

"What is the necessity?"

"Why . . . it's the Fertility Control Act."

"I know. But what is the necessity for *that*?"

"Well . . . it's very important, socially and economically. When sex predetermination drugs were developed, a few years before the FCA was passed, it was discovered that half a million ems more than the norm were being bred annually. Parents opted for them. Lewisohn was the first to point out the dangers of that. At the time, more than fifteen years ago, they were very real dangers: increased male homosexuality due to a gross surplus of ems, psychological deprivation of efs when they were old enough to realize they were not first choice, a decline of culture consumers since efs predominate in this market, and so forth. All the FCA does is decree the most favorable social and economic ratio. Computerized estimates are made annually of how many babies are to be bred. The government still authorizes more ems than efs, I assure you. But you probably know the statistics of ef and em longevity rates. Even today, widows over sixty-five far outnumber widowers of the same age. But we're slowly bringing the numbers into balance. And, most important of course, the FCA has achieved Zero Population growth. Now, as longevity increases, we're considering going to Minus-Z Pop. To ensure every living object adequate breathing room and a decent environment."

"You make it sound so logical," she said.

"It *is* logical."

"But isn't the FCA a restraint of individual freedom?"

"No doubt about it," I said promptly. "Like traffic laws and required radiation inoculation of children. For the common good."

"All I know," she said, "is that we wanted an em baby and are not allowed to have one."

"It's a weakness I have," I acknowledged sadly, "to speak in statistics and percentages and ratios and Z-Pop growth. But these things are part of my service. I tend to treat objects as numbers. I forget the personal traumata that may be involved in obeying a very logical and practical government decree."

"You see the forest but not the trees," Henry Hammond said.

"Right," I agreed. "But you must realize I've been conditioned to do exactly that."

"Well," he said, "at least you recognize it as conditioning."

"Yes," I said. "I do."

"Nick," Lydia said suddenly, "can a hypnotized object be made to do something against his will? Something he knows is morally wrong?"

I looked at her in surprise.

"Of course," I said. "If the hypnotist is clever enough."

"You mentioned conditioning," Alice said. "Can a conditioned object be made to do something against his will? Something he knows is morally wrong?"

It was a beautiful orchestrated performance. I wondered if they had rehearsed it.

I knew the operative answer to Alice Hammond's question, but it didn't fit my role.

"You've opened a different can of worms," I said. I tried to appear disquieted. "There's been a great deal of research on the subject, but no definitive answer. As yet."

"How do you feel about it?" Henry Hammond asked. "What's your personal opinion?"

I paused a long moment, staring down at my empty plate.

"I'd say no," I said finally, in a low voice. "I believe, regardless of the length or intensity of conditioning, an object's operative nature will eventually surface."

They said nothing. Their expressions didn't alter. But I felt I had scored points. It was all a lot of kaka, of course. They were talking about psychological behavior modification. If I wished, I could describe to them the effects of an existent drug that simply demolished all their airy-fairy theories. They were such innocents, playing a game the rules of which had changed while they were picking up a single grain of rice with obso chopsticks.

I insisted on helping Lydia clear the table and sterilize the dishes. The Hammonds went into the living room. I couldn't overhear their conversation. It wasn't important; I'd be hearing soon enough on Mansfield's tapes what they had discussed.

I learned sooner than that. After our chores, Lydia and I joined them in the living room. Talk was desultory. Nothing significant. Until....

"By the way, Nick," Dr. Henry Hammond said, "Alice and I have a summer place, up near Cornwall. Know where it is?"

"On the river, isn't it? South of Newburgh?"

"Glorious view," Alice said.

"Built on the ruins of an Indian trading post," Henry said.

"Almost a hectare of land."

"Clean air," Alice said.

How could I resist?

"Alice and I are going up on Friday morning to open the place for the season," Henry went on. He paused to light an enormous oompaul pipe, puffing mightily, blowing out great clouds of blue smoke. He was really a ridiculous em. "We were wondering if Lydia and you would care to come up for Saturday? We're having a few interesting people in."

I had been planning to start a threeday on Friday morning, but I didn't hesitate.

"A profit," I said. "Lydia?"

"Oh, yes." She nodded. "Sounds like fun."

"Can you get a car?" Henry asked. "You could train to Newburgh, and we could pick you up there. But a car would be easier. It's a profitable drive."

"No problem," I said. "I'll requisition one from the motor pool. One of the advantages of serving our beneficial government."

We all laughed. I was in.

I returned to the compound shortly after midnight. Paul must have tipped the gate guard to flash him when I signed in; he was waiting outside my apartment door.

"I was worried. The whole thing worries me. Is it going to be all right, Nick?"

" 'The future belongs to the untroubled,' " I quoted him.

He had the grace to blush.

I let us in, locked the door behind us.

"What happened?" he asked.

"Wait a minute. Let's get Angela in on this. I'll tell you both at the same time."

"You can't. She flew down to Washington this evening. The Deputy Directors are meeting with DIROB tomorrow. Cabinet meeting on Thursday."

"Shit." I thought a moment. "She usually stays at the PS hostel, doesn't she?"

"Well, she checks in there. God knows where she sleeps." I grinned at him.

"Try to get her, will you? I'll pour us a petrovod. I need it."

Paul was still on the flasher when I returned to the living room He finally got through to the Public Service hostel in Arlington. Yes, Angela Berri was registered there. No, she was not in her room. Yes, she had left a number where she could be reached. Paul repeated it, then switched off.

"That's DIROB's private number," I said. "He must be having a buffet dinner for his Deputy Directors and headquarters staff before the meeting. He usually does."

"*Before* the meeting? Why not after?"

"Who knows? Maybe they've all lost their appetites by then. Try her there."

I stood behind Paul, playing with his ear while he punched out DIROB's number. He got the image of an em server in an earth-colored zipsuit. There was a lot of noise, people moving in the background. Finally Angela came on.

"Yes, Paul?" she said crisply. "Where are you?"

"Nick's apartment."

"Can it wait?"

He looked up at me. I shook my head.

"No," he told Angela.

"Call you back in five minutes," she said, and switched off. Paul arose, and I took the chair in front of the flasher. Angela was back on in about three minutes. This time she was seated at a desk in what appeared to be a study or library.

"You look lovely," I told her.

She smiled. "Thanks. Is that what you called to tell me?"

I laughed.

"There's more. They want me to meet people. This Saturday. At a place near Cornwall. That's up the Hudson. Just south of Newburgh."

She thought a moment.

"Yes," she said finally.

"I've already agreed," I said. "But the place should be shared. Or at least scouted. And fast."

She nodded.

"Send Mansfield. Give him three hundred. You have it?"

"I can get it."

"Good."

"I don't know the exact address."

"Just give Leon the name. Let him take it from there. Tell him to call you when it's set."

"Right. Enjoying yourself?"

She made an O of her mouth, extended her tongue, wiggled the tip lasciviously.

"Wicked ef," I said.

She switched off.

"You heard all that?" I asked Paul.

"Yes. Bitch! Who's the meeting with?"

"Very vague. 'A few interesting people.' You'll hear the tapes."

"Are you in, Nick?"

"Almost certain. I played it very cozy tonight, but they think they have me in a bag. That African business I invented to tell Lydia. They've got it on tape."

"Oh-ho," he said. "Blackmail."

"Well . . . just call it pressure."

I had no way of contacting Leon Mansfield, other than making that annoying trip up to West Forty-second Street. He had given me no number to flash; he wasn't listed in the directory. I decided to wait till noon, hoping he'd call by then.

I spent the morning doing a workup on my Division's budget for the coming year. It was axiomatic in Public Service that you inflated your proposed budget by approximately 20 percent, knowing it would be cut by approximately 10-15 percent. Fiscal game-playing.

Ordinarily, I would have stuffed all the raw data into a computer, pressed the button, and let it chug out the estimate in minutes. I would still do that, eventually. But there was a factor involved that few other government budget-makers had to wrestle with.

A great number of projects my Division was serving on were classified. Some were unknown to the Chairmen of the ruling Congressional committees. A few were even unknown to Angela Berri and DIROB. I had to conceal funds for these projects by diluting them to several other known and approved programs. And, of course, I could make no records of this double-entry bookkeeping. Budget-making was not particularly difficult, but it was time-consuming.

I was still hacking away at it, about 1115, when Leon Mansfield flashed me from a public booth. This time he was on camera. He looked weary.

"Same place as last time," he said. "Half an hour."

He switched off. I cursed the em. But I had no choice. I drew a propane-powered sedan from the motor pool and drove up to the Mess Hall on Seventh Avenue. I had the 300 new dollars in my purse. Parking, as usual, was a nightmare. Finally I pulled into a restricted zone. I stuck a card, "Psychoanalyst on Call," on the windshield. Someone in my Division had them printed up as a joke. Incredibly, they sometimes worked.

Leon Mansfield was at the same table near the plate glass window. He looked seedier than ever. He had a package with him. I slid into the chair next to him.

"Couldn't we have met at your office?" I asked.

"No. I don't have an office. They tore the building down yesterday."

"I suppose you've been moving," I said.

He shrugged. "I left everything there. Nothing I wanted."

I had a sudden, sharp attack of Random Synaptic Control. Images flickered by. . . .

. . . the wreckers' ball flinging high against a blue sky.

. . . tons of steel crunching into stone carvings on which an Italian immigrant had served slowly and lovingly 100 years ago.

. . . great clouds of acrid dust, jagged holes in the walls, crumbling brick, wooden staircases knocked flat, a gigantic gilt eye staring up from the rubble.

. . . and all the odd detritus of Mansfield's office obscenely exposed, opened to the wind. Blowing away: posters, books, magazines, photos, pictures—all blown and scattered.

I took a spansule from my side pocket and popped it dry. Mansfield watched me with interest.

"On something?" he asked.

"Increases my sex drive," I said. He lost interest.

"Got some tapes for you," he said listlessly. "Slow job."

"It's quickening," I said. "Dr. Henry L. Hammond. He's on the tapes. The apartment below Ferguson's."

"The em who's sharing?"

"Yes. He owns a summer place. Near Cornwall. That's—"

"I know where it is."

"He and his wife are going up Friday morning. I want you to get there first. Share it, if you can. If not, just scout. Take some Instaroids. I'll need to know by tomorrow. Can you handle it?"

"Sure. How much did she tell you to give me?"

I took the love out of my purse, passed it to him under the table. He riffled the bills with a grubby thumb.

"Three hundred," he said. "The dear lady. Never too little. Never enough."

"I thought it was generous," I said.

"Hmm?" He looked up at me, through me. "Generous? Oh. You misunderstood me, Mr. Nicholas Flair. Yes, it's generous for the service."

"Then what did you mean by 'Never enough'? Never enough for what?"

He shrugged and tried a ghastly smile.

"Dreams," he said.

His personal problems had a very low priority rating on my Anxiety List. I started to leave, then sat down again.

"Just out of curiosity," I said, "when did you stop believing my story about a cheating ef user?"

He looked at me in astonishment.

"Stop believing? I never started. You said Angela Berri sent you."

I took the package of tape reels and left. Out on the sidewalk, I glanced back. He had taken out his pocket chess set and was continuing the game that seemed never to end.

On the following afternoon I met him again at the Mess Hall. He told me what he had done at the Hammonds' summer place and handed over another envelope.

"How can I get in touch with you?" I asked. "Do you have a new office or an apartment?"

"No. I'm living in the Kleen-Eeez van."

"Living in it?" I said. "Where do you wash up?"

"Subway toilets," he said.

Great conspiracies. Nationwide plots. Vital plans astir. Important state secrets endangered. And one of the principal actors living in a laundry van and using subway toilets. It called for a 100-year Somnorific.

That evening we gathered in my apartment, standing at my white plastisteel service table, the overhead fluorescents pulled low.

"Here are the Instaroids that Mansfield took," I said, passing them around. "This is a rough map he drew of the site. The house is just south of Cornwall on Hudson, before you get to the state park. The dirt access road leads off Route 218, crosses abandoned railroad tracks here, curves toward the river. The house is on a bluff overlooking the river."

"Nice-looking place," Paul remarked.

"Hammond told me it was built on the ruins of an Indian trading post, and it looks it. The foundation is natural fieldstones set in mortar. The rest is all wood. Hand-hewn beams. The originals. Very obso. Some of the knee braces and rafters are modern. Glass windows with plastisteel storm shutters. Poor security, Mansfield reports. He got in with no trouble. That em is a whiz on locks. Downstairs: one large living-dining room, kitchen, small pantry, toilet. Upstairs: one bedroom, a study-library, a nest. Lots of obso furniture."

"Inside walls?" Angela asked.

"Painted plaster. The walls are unusually thick. But emplacing cameras would be a structural service. We don't have time."

"So?" she asked.

"Paul, let me have those shots for a minute. Here, Angela. And here. Two obso phones. One in the downstairs living room, one in the upstairs study."

"Did Mansfield share them?"

"No. He was concerned about an electronic sweep."

"Smart," Paul said.

"Oh, yes. He guesses something of what's happening. So he put a tap on the line. It's an overhead wire, on poles, coming down the access road form the highway. He says it's a direct wiretap, the best he could do in a short time. The transmitter is concealed under a plastic insulator close to one of the poles. Mansfield claims it's invisible from the ground. He'll receive in his van, parked off the highway, about a kilometer away, hidden in the trees. All right so far? Angela?"

"If they sweep the house electronically—and I think they will; I think Mansfield is right—can they detect the phone line sharing?"

"I don't know. Paul?"

"Doubtful," he said. "Unless they measure power loss. That could only be done through the phone company."

"All right," I said. "We'll go with the phone line tap. We'll get all incoming and outgoing calls. But that may be nil. We need interior conversations. Question: Should I be wired? Personally?"

"How?" Paul asked. "Something taped to your ribs? Too dangerous, in case of a search. Dental implant? Rectal implant? Ingested transmitter? All detectable."

"Aren't we crediting them with more talent than they probably possess?" Angela said.

"No," I said. "Paul's right. And it's my cock. I say no."

That ended wiring me for hi-fidelity broadcasting.

"There are other solutions," I said, "but they all require time to set up. We could use a laser to pick up window vibrations. Or an ultrasensitive telescopic mike. But all that involves heavy equipment, difficult to conceal. I don't see us getting any physical evidence. We'll have to go with my memory. I'll take a Supermem intravenous and try to stay in theta as much as I can."

"My God," Paul said, "with several people gabbling around you? Practically impossible."

"I'll try," I said. "We have no choice. Angela, another problem."

"What?"

"Look at this map. Cars coming off the highway turn onto the dirt access road and head down toward the river. Those abandoned railroad tracks are set in an obso wood crossing. But—here, scan this Instaroid—the planking has shrunk and been worn away. If you were driving, you'd naturally slow down before bumping over the tracks. Foliage on both sides. If Mansfield could conceal remote-controlled cameras, we could get photos of the visitors."

"Marvelous," Angela said.

"Great," Paul said.

"Here's the problem," I said. "I have no way of reaching Mansfield to tell him to emplace the cameras tonight. And the Hammonds are going up to-morrow morning."

"No problem," Angela said. "I'll get in touch with him tonight. As soon as I leave here. I'll tell him what we need. He'll have the cameras in before the Hammonds get there tomorrow morning."

"You have a number for Mansfield?" I asked.

"I can contact him," she said.

I didn't pursue it.

"All right," I went on. "then we're set on the sharing for Saturday. Now sit down and listen to the tapes."

We moved to the living room and sat in a row on the couch. We listened to the dinner party at Lydia's. None of us spoke until the machine clicked off.

"Very good, Nick." Angela nodded approvingly. "You manipulated them beautifully."

"I liked your answer to the question on conditioning," Paul said. "Fancy footwork."

I rose, went over to the machine, changed reels.

"Just a little more," I said. "The Hammonds were obviously in no hurry to leave, so finally I left. This is the conversation after I departed."

I started the tape.

Lydia: "He's nice, isn't he?"

Alice: "You like him, Lydia?"

Lydia: "Yes. Very much."

Alice: "Be careful. You know what happened last time."

Lydia: "This is different."

Henry: "Well, in any event, I think he'll do. Clever. Creative mind there.

But not deep, of course. I'll wager he's never answered a koan or known satori."

Alice: "Yes, dear. I think he's going to be very valuable to us. Lydia, you've done a fine service."

Lydia (faintly): "Thank you."

Lapse of eleven seconds.

Lydia: "I do like him, you know. I wouldn't want anything to happen to him."

Henry: "We all know the risks involved. He'll know them, too. Before he volunteers."

Alice: "I think we should go now, dear."

There were the usual thank-yous and goodnights. Then the sound of a door closing. I switched off the machine.

"That's all," I said.

"You're definitely in," Paul said. "No doubt about it."

Angela looked at me. Curious expression.

"The ef profits from you," she said. "Mightily."

"That needn't concern us," I said. "What stresses me is that on all the tapes we've heard, hours of them, there's been no mention of the stopping of Harris."

"My God, you're right," Paul said.

"I was hoping for a confession," I said. "Or at least an obvious reference."

"Oh, but there was," Angela said quickly. "On that last tape, Lydia said she liked you. Alice said, 'Be careful. You know what happened the last time.' Then, at the end, Lydia repeated that she liked you and hoped nothing would happen to you. She was making a reference to what happened to Harris."

"Possibly," I acknowledged. "It's one interpretation. Another could be entirely innocent. Alice merely referring to an unhappy affair that Lydia had in the past. Then Lydia, at the end, expressing a normal anxiety that something might happen to me if I join in on the bombings. It's just not definite. We haven't tied them to Harris' stopping with any physical evidence. Well . . . no use worrying it. Perhaps I'll get what we need this weekend. Let's hope so."

After they left, I sat in my suspended plastifoam sling and went into my own blend of alpha and self-hypnosis. I came out of it twenty minutes later, calm and relaxed. As far as I was concerned, it was as good as Hammond's satori.

I had brought home a single file to scan. It was an abstruse report from my Genetics Team. It concerned a process known as "auto-adultery," which one of our laboratory wits had dubbed "masturbation carried to its logical conclusion." Briefly, it was a technique of taking the DNA from the egg of one human ef and using it to inject another egg from the same object and fertilize it. The child bred would be, genetically, entirely the ef's, with no em sperm involved. In the process we were developing, entry into the "mother" egg was made by laser surgery.

The technique was still experimental, of course, but the concept had been proved feasible. There was no reason why it could not be made generally available. I hesitated to imagine the social, political, and economic consequences. Even more important, I had doubts of its genetic value.

Even assuming a Grade A genetic rating of the efs selected for such procreation, wouldn't there be a deterioration of the gene pool, simply by the loss of variety supplied by the em sperm? In other words, would we be risking a kind of inbreeding, a never-ending reproduction of identical efs? (An ef's cell contains no Y chromosome.) Perhaps it was em chauvinism that conditioned me, but I felt the dangers were real.

What it all came down to, I computed, was—what kind of a society did we want? Ten years from now? Fifty? A hundred? We had not yet decided that.

It was best, I thought, to cultivate pragmatism, trying to cope with each change as it developed. The science of futurism had its limits, doomed to failure by the invention, discovery, development of mutations impossible to foresee.

One thing I was certain of: There was no way, *no* way to halt change. Or even to postpone it. Declare a moratorium on all scientific research, destroy all laboratory equipment, dismantle all the paraphernalia of science, and still you would have someone, somewhere, ef or em, pacing in a drafty attic perhaps, scrawling symbols on a blackboard, erasing, scribbling more.

We could not stop the future. We could only hope it didn't stop us.

We arrived at the dirt access road a little before 1145 Saturday morning.

"There it is," Lydia said.

She nodded toward a marker at the roadside: a large pseudo-folkart cutout of a human hand, one finger pointing toward the river. The knuckles had HAMMONDS' POINT painted across them in flaky red paint.

"Cutesy," I said.

I turned slowly onto the dirt road, slowed even more as we bumped over the rusted railroad tracks. I looked about casually. If Mansfield had installed the cameras, he had performed a good service; I didn't spot them.

I had expected the "interesting people" to be there before us, waiting. But only a single car was parked outside the house. I guessed it to be about a 1980 model. Hammond had a yen for the obso.

He came out the front door, waving, as we pulled up. He was wearing a brown corduroy suit, suede bush boots, a checked flannel shirt. He was smoking his silly pipe. The country squire.

We had brought them a two-kilo package of probisks, the round container a reasonably accurate plastic imitation of an old English biscuit tin. Of course, it was labeled "Olde English Tea Biscuits." Hammond was delighted.

We went into the kitchen where Alice was preparing food. She kissed

Lydia's cheek, smiled at me. Even in a cheerfully patterned "rustic" dress, she was a gray ef. Lydia stayed with her while Hammond took me on a tour of the grounds. We went first to the edge of the cliff overlooking the river. The view was magnificent. He swept his arm around in a fustian gesture.

"Imagine all this as it was originally," he commanded me. "Virgin forest as far as the eye could see. Untouched. Unspoiled by the hand of white men. And then, coming up the river in their birchbark canoes, a band of red Mohawks, with the pelts of mink and otter and beaver to trade."

I was tempted to ask, "Do you really think the Mohawks traded this far East? And did they really have mink pelts?" But I wouldn't interrupt his glorious oratory for the world.

It continued as we wandered about the house. He pointed out the thick stone walls of the foundation.

"Actually a fort," he revealed. "Not all the Indians who arrived came to trade."

Politely, I admired everything. In truth, it was a pleasant place on this mild spring afternoon. I heard birdcalls. As promised, the air was clear. The sky was cloudless azure.

"And now," he said, "the *pièce de résistance*. Follow me. . . ."

Pièce de résistance, I mused. That must be Mohawk for "unwilling squaw."

We went back into the kitchen. The efs looked up from their service.

"I want to show Nick the tunnel," he said, excited as a boy.

"Henry, you'll muck up everything," Alice snapped at him.

"Just take a minute."

With his heel, he pulled a rag rug aside. It had concealed a trapdoor with an iron ring set into a recess so the floor was perfectly flat. He looked for my expression of surprise. I obliged.

"Y'see," he explained, "in case of Indian attack, they held them off as long as possible from behind the stone walls. But if push came to shove, they nipped down through here. Now follow me. Watch your head, Nick."

He bent and, with some effort, raised the trap.

"Original hinges," he said proudly. "Hammered iron."

He took a cadmium-celled lantern from a kitchen shelf and led the way down a narrow wooden staircase. I followed cautiously. At the bottom, we stood on a packed earthen floor. He moved the light about. It was a small chamber, not too deep; we had to stoop. The walls appeared to be marl. It was cooler and damper than the upstairs rooms.

"Probably used for a fruit cellar," he said. "To store apples and such during the winter."

"And firewater," I said maliciously.

"What? Oh, yes. That, too. Now follow me closely, Nick, and watch your head."

He led the way into the small opening of a tunnel cut through the clayey earth.

The walk, or creep, took only a few minutes. We came up against a barred iron gate, fastened on the inside with an obso chain and padlock. We looked out onto the surface of the river, a few meters below us.

"Escape?" I said.

"Right!" he said triumphantly. "Out through this gate and you practically step onto the beach."

"You think they kept a boat moored?" I asked.

"Shouldn't wonder," he said portentously.

He looked at me expectantly.

"Amazing," I breathed.

He seemed satisfied.

We retraced our steps. When we came to the wooden stairway leading up to the kitchen, he paused and played his torch behind the steps. He found a small box, held it out to me. He beamed the light to illuminate the contents. I peered in.

"Arrowheads," he whispered. "Three. Genuine. Indian. Arrowheads. I found them in the dirt floor of the tunnel."

"Amazing," I repeated.

He nodded solemnly in agreement. Dolt.

We had a reasonably profitable lunch. We filled our plates from the pot of stew simmering on the obso electric range and brought them to the dining table in the big room. There was also a large bowl of greens.

"All from plants in the woods," Hammond bragged. "All natural. You've never tasted anything like this before."

That was not reassuring. During our tour I had identified at least three toxic species, including a particularly noxious toadstool. But I said nothing. Nor did I make any reference to the missing "interesting people" I had been invited to meet.

We all served in the cleanup after dinner. Then we sat in chintz-covered chairs in the living room while Hammond lectured on Oriental philology. His accent was atrocious. Finally, recalling his duties as host, he brought out a small bottle of something. He and I took drinks; the efs declined—thus proving their superior intelligence. Lydia was making a valiant effort to stay awake. Alice knitted placidly, pushing back and forth in an obso wooden rocker.

It was close to 1630 when we heard the sound of approaching cars. Hammond stopped his monologue immediately, rose, looked out the window.

"Here they are," he announced. I thought his manner suddenly tense, but perhaps not.

The four objects who came through the door, ef and three ems, had arrived in two cars. I could not see the license plates, but perhaps Mansfield's cameras had caught them.

The newcomers were dressed casually. The taffy-haired ef was wearing a jolly plaid zipsuit with an overjacket of plastifur. Two of the ems had black turtleneck sweaters. They looked like brothers. One carried a small cassette machine. I knew what *that* was. Those three were young. The other was an obso, perhaps forty. He was a short, barrel-shaped em, chunky through the shoulders. He had a great, black walrus mustache. Dyed, I suspected.

I recognized him immediately. Dr. Thomas J. Wiley. He was a genetic biologist who had won several prizes for his services on shortening normal gestation periods by enzymatic manipulation. I had studied with him at Harvard. But that had been almost ten years ago; I doubted if he'd remember me. He did.

"Nicholas Flair!" he said, coming toward me with outspread arms. "After all these years! How nice to see you again."

He gripped me in a surprisingly strong embrace, then withdrew to slap my arms while he examined me critically.

"Yes, yes." He nodded. "A few more lines. What, no fountain of youth from that respected Division of yours?"

"Not yet, sir," I said. "We're serving on it."

He nodded again, suddenly sober.

There was a flurry of introductions. The tall, willowy ef was Martha Wiley, the doctor's daughter. She was also serving in her father's specialty. The two ems were, as I had guessed, brothers: Tod and Vernon DeTilly. Tod was a nuclear physicist, Vernon a neuropharmacologist. It was Tod who circled me casually, glancing occasionally at an instrument on his wrist. I was happy I had not swallowed a transmitter.

Chairs were brought from the kitchen. We settled in a rough oval, only Dr. Wiley standing. He was evidently the leader.

"Well," he said genially, "here we all are. Dr. Flair, we know you for a very brilliant, very talented young man. You see? I do not say 'em.' Man. We would not waste your time. Also, we have a long drive to make, another visit, so I will speak bluntly and to the point."

I looked at him in puzzlement, then looked around at the others. They were all staring at me.

"You see, Dr. Flair," he continued, "all of us in this room are members of a secret organization that—"

I rose hastily to my feet, held up a hand.

"Please, Dr. Wiley," I said. "I think perhaps I better leave."

"No," he said. "I think perhaps you better stay."

"If it's anything that might compromise my official—"

Now he held up his hand.

"We do not have the time," he said. "Vernon, play the tape."

Obediently, the DeTilly em pressed the Start button of the cassette machine held in his lap. I heard my own voice. . . .

"About a year ago—well . . . a little less than that—an African nation was admitted to statehood in the US. We can do a lot for them—socially, economically, medically, culturally. But they have one tribe, about ten thousand objects, who are national fanatics and oppose statehood. These objects are primitives. . . ."

Dr. Wiley made a gesture. DeTilly stopped the tape. I turned slowly to look at Lydia. Her face was flushed but her chin was up; she returned my stare without flinching.

"Lydia!" I said with shocked disbelief.

"Following orders." Wiley shrugged. "Playing an important role."

"Oh, yes," I said bitterly. "I presume this secret organization of yours has high ideals?"

"The highest," he said.

"But you are quite willing to use despicable means to achieve your ends—is that it?"

"Any means!" he said in a passionate voice. "Any means, including violence, murder, terror, blackmail, that will bring this obscene government of yours to its senses."

How I wished I had *that* speech on tape. We'd have popped the lot of them into R&R and drained them.

"I don't wish to debate the morality of what you're doing."

"No," he agreed unexpectedly. "The time for debate has passed. Now is the time for action."

I was waiting for him to say, "Those that are not for us are against us." But his daughter said it.

"Dr. Flair," she said solemnly, "those that are not for us are against us."

I looked around the oval of staring faces.

"Time, Dr. Flair," Wiley warned.

"I don't understand," I said. "What do you want?"

"We want you to serve with us to the limit, and beyond, of your energy, talent, and devotion to the cause."

In how many forgotten revolts and revolutions had those ringing words been spoken?

"You're asking me to risk my career to—"

"No," he interrupted. "We're asking you to risk your life. Well?"

"You can't expect me to decide now, this minute?"

"Can and do. Well?"

I collapsed back into my chair, sat a minute with lowered head, hand covering my eyes. What melodrama! Finally I straightened up, raised my head, looked at Dr. Wiley.

"At least tell me what you want me to do. So I can make an informed judgment."

"Informed judgment?" he repeated. He smiled suddenly, full lips pulling back from big white false teeth. "Yes, I remember Nicholas Bennington Flair and his informed judgments. Your fellow students called you 'The Thinking Machine.' Did you know that?"

"I heard."

He slapped his palms together briskly. "All right. So you can arrive at an informed judgment—we want, primo, all documentation of that little African assignment mentioned on the tape."

"Impossible," I said. "No documentation exists. All oral orders."

"I told you," Tod DeTilly said.

"A disappointment." Wiley shrugged. "But not fatal. Secondo, that famous severed head in your lab. Fred."

"What about him?"

"A photo or film of that head has never been released to the media. Correct?"

"Yes, that's correct. Why needlessly antagonize antivivisectionists and dog lovers?"

"Exactly. But I am certain such photos and films do exist. We want them, or copies of them."

I sat back, crossed my knees, put back my head, stared at the ceiling, apparently deep in thought.

"Dr. Wiley," I said flatly, "what proof do I have—or *any* evidence, for that matter—that you are what you claim to be, members of a secret organization?"

"I assure you we are. Nationwide, and growing daily."

"So you say. But how do I know it's not just the seven of you present in this room? Just seven hotheads. You want me to risk my life for you seven?"

They looked at each other, back and forth. Finally, Alice Hammond spoke:

"Tell him, Tom," she said flatly. "If he decides not to come in. . . ." She shrugged.

I knew what that shrug meant. The sweet ef. . . .

"You've heard of the Society of Obsoletes?" Wiley asked me.

"Those lunatics?" I cried. "Surely you don't—"

"Wait, wait—" He stopped me. "What you see in the Society of Obsos are eccentrics: antivivisectionists, ecology freaks, health food fanatics, occult religionists. That is exactly what we want you to see. That is the public image of the Society: a conglomerate of harmless loons writing letters to the media, marching in silly parades, making ineffectual demonstrations. But the Society is actually a two-tier organization. The second layer, the basic one, hidden, secret, is composed of professionals like ourselves. Scientists, mostly, but also teachers, businessmen, union leaders, journalists, academicians, politicians— all bound together in one determination: to stop the US Government from pursuing the course it is on, and to steer our society's destiny in a different direction.

"What direction?" I demanded.

"If my phrases sound obso to you, forgive me. But there are no new words or better words available. A society of personal liberty, freedom, justice, equality. A diversified society of individual choice, not decree by the Public Service. Does that satisfy you?"

"Dr. Wiley," I said earnestly. "I believe you are sincere. And the other objects in this room are sincere. But sincerity isn't enough. Can you give me evidence—any evidence at all—that what you've told me is operative?"

Again they looked at one another, heads swiveling.

"We've gone this far. . . ." Martha Wiley said.

"Dr. Flair," Tod DeTilly said, "you know about the recent wave of bombings, assassinations, kidnappings, and sabotage against scientific research facilities?"

"I've heard of them," I said cautiously.

"I'll bet you have." He laughed. "Not all of them were made public. Correct?"

"Yes."

"I will name a few that were *not* made public," he said. "The only way we could know about them is by having planned them and carried them out. Will that convince you?"

"Yes."

"In your Denver Field office, a hundred aborted fetuses destroyed. A cancer-sensitive strain of rats poisoned in Dallas. A cyclotron sabotaged in Illinois. A neurosurgeon assassinated at Berkeley. Is that sufficient—or do you want more?"

"That's sufficient," I said. "I'm convinced."

"Well then," Dr. Wiley said genially, "now that we have delivered our secrets to you, let's return to the secrets we want you to deliver. I have already mentioned the photographs or films of Fred. In addition, we have prepared a little list. Martha?"

She took a paper from her purse, unfolded it, rose to hand it to me. I scanned it swiftly. I was genuinely shocked, and let it show. I looked up at Wiley, feeling a sour smile stretch my face.

"It appears you have infiltrated my Division," I said . . .

"Oh, yes." He nodded. "We have objects everywhere."

Again I scanned the list. All the material they wanted—letters, reports, statistical studies, tapes, films—all concerned classified projects. Some had a higher priority than others, but none were known to outsiders—supposedly.

"Very technical material," I commented. "Quite specialized."

"I believe we will be able to compute it, Dr. Flair."

"I'm sure you will," I acknowledged. "But if this is the sort of thing you're looking for, why on earth do you want a photo of Fred? What possible good will that do you?"

"Surely you're not as obtuse as that, Dr. Flair?" he said. "Media exploitation."

"Oh-ho," I said. "You've decided to go public?"

He laughed.

"A nice way of putting it," he said. "Yes, our national leadership has decided the time is ripe to bring our activities to the attention of the public. To publish our aims. To make an appeal for public support. The reproduction of Fred's photograph and films in facsimile newspapers and on TV will show even the most indifferent citizen exactly what the government is doing, and show it in shockingly dramatic fashion. The secret material we are asking you to furnish will provide added ammunition. It will be a two-part program of public enlightenment and education: What we are against and what we are for."

I scanned again the list I held in my hand.

"I can't simply walk out of the compound carrying all this," I said. "If you have members inside, you must be aware of our security precautions."

"Oh, sure," Vernon DeTilly said, grinning cheerfully. "Your problem is getting the material out of the files—right?"

"That's not the big problem," I said. "I could manage that—at great risk. But how do I get it out of the gate? Every package is opened and searched. I am required to open my purse and empty my pockets every time I pass through, no matter how many times a day. X-rays. Metal detectors. Ultrasonic detectors. Odor analysis. The instrumentation is extremely effective."

"Microfilms?" Tod DeTilly suggested. "Or microdots?"

"In what kind of carrier?" I asked. "And by what means—swallowing? No, thanks. Not this mass of material."

"Broadcast?" Vernon DeTilly said. "To a mobile receiver parked outside the fence?"

"Impossible. We are constantly monitored electronically. They'd be on me in seconds."

"Mail?" Henry Hammond asked.

"Packages fluoroscoped," I said. "Letters opened on a random basis."

"Isn't restricted material *ever* taken out of the compound?" Lydia Ferguson asked faintly, then blushed at having ventured to speak in this august assemblage.

"Of course." I nodded. "But then you need a pass signed by your ruler. In my case, that would be Angela Berri, DEPDIRSAT. In addition, the gate guard is required to flash the ruler signing the pass to verify its authenticity."

"A problem," Dr. Wiley agreed. "It will be difficult, I know. But we have great faith in your intelligence, creativity, and talent at synthesizing an informed judgment."

"What you're saying," I told him, "is that I have no choice."

"That is correct, Nick," he said gently. "You have no choice."

"How do I contact you?"

Wiley looked at Hammond.

"I'll be in the city next week," Hammond said to me. "Alice is staying out here, but you can flash me at our apartment."

"By Monday," Dr. Thomas J. Wiley said.

"Monday?" I was incredulous. "You're only giving me two days to come up with a viable plan?"

"I told you," he said. "We have great faith in your talent."

I drove Lydia Ferguson back to New York through the gathering twilight. It was a trip made in morose silence.

"I'm sorry, Nick," she said once.

I didn't answer.

"I suppose you hate me," she said sometime later.

I didn't answer.

But then, the lights of Manhattan glowing across the river, I thawed.

"No," I told her, "I don't hate you. I know you did it from a deep belief."

"Oh, yes." She sighed. "A deep, *deep* belief."

She put her head on my shoulder, hugged my arm. We drove up to her door that way.

She asked me to come up. If I hesitated, it was because I feared she might want me to listen to all her rationalizations of her deep, deep belief. I had had enough histrionics for one day. But her motives were simpler.

"Please?" she said, touching me.

When we were naked in her bed, she teased my body with hot fingers.

"You're so profitable, Nick," she murmured. "You've used a lot of efs, haven't you?"

"No," I said, "you're the first. You routed my maidenhead."

She laughed.

"And ems?" she asked.

"Of course."

"I've never tried it," she said.

"With ems?"

"Don't be silly." she giggled. "You know what I mean."

"I'm bisexual," I admitted. "By intellectual choice and physical predilection. I think most objects are, admittedly or not. The sexual preferences of obsos were conditioned by biological necessity and hence by society. Neither prevail today. Efs can procreate without sperm. The preservation of the species is no more vital than its limitations. Now we can indulge our operative natures, which are androgynous."

"What does all that mean?" she asked.

"That I like to use both efs and ems."

"Oh, yes," she breathed. "Use me."

Perhaps her betrayal of me, via the tape on the African incident, excited her, empowered her. She was aggressive, bold, a leader now, not a follower. Even while taking profit from her strong attack, I puzzled her motives—and mine. Once again it came back to mastery and surrender, but on a primitive level.

Even with my ears pressed flat between her sweated thighs, I pondered if what we felt was not operative on a social and political, perhaps even a philosophical level. It would not be the first time that physical spurs had a counterpart in moral and mental passions. Indeed, some obso thinkers believed it all one: a finite quantity of "life force," dammed in the gonads, sure to break out in the cortex. It was interesting.

I resolved to move Paul Bumford's suggestion of an Ultimate Pleasure pill, the UP, from the Tomorrow File to an active project. It would require an immense amount of service: analysis by neurophysiologists of the physical nature of the orgasm, analysis by neuropsychologists of the emotive factors involved, and finally synthesis by specialists who, to my knowledge, did not yet exist: neurometaphysicians. It might be necessary to condition an entirely new breed of scientific investigators before the problem of the UP could be solved. Difficult. Arduous. But I hardly dared envision the reward. Simply the world and all.

X-10

Later—for months—I was to wonder to what extent the events of the following week were due to planning or due to chance. But that kind of deliberation is fruitless, of course. You become immobilized in a thicket of determination, free will, and accident. A lot of kaka. Every object must make a choice between speculation and action. I had opted for action. I was willing to endure the consequences of that choice.

One curious consequence—I confess frankly—was a haunting suspicion that the satisfaction I felt in Lydia's bed that Saturday night sprang from a subconscious realization that I was using a doomed ef. But I didn't wish to compute that thought further.

Sunday:

In the morning I picked up a packet of Instaroids from Leon Mansfield at the Seventh Avenue Mess Hall. They were good, clear photos of the four visitors and the license plates of their cars. I delivered the packet to Angela Berri. By evening, she had obtained the home addresses of the four. I believe she served through Lieutenant Oliver of the New York Peace Department. It wasn't important; we never employed the input.

At our evening conference, I addressed Angela and Paul for almost an hour, describing the Saturday meeting at Hammonds' Point. I used the actual words of the participants as much as possible.

"So," I concluded, "that is what happened. We have no physical evidence of their complicity. I have the list they gave me—the restricted material they want. But the list itself proves nothing. Common bond paper. Smudged fingerprints. A dicto-typeprinter we might identify, if we ever find the machine. They are intelligent, wary objects."

"Is Dr. Wiley the leader?" Angela asked.

"Of them? Yes. But I think his authority is limited. He spoke of 'our national leadership' in a tone that leads me to suspect he is not a member. If Paul's analysis is operative, if their activities are organized on a Geo-Political Area structure, then I'd guess Wiley is director of GPA-1. But he may be only their recruiting chief."

"Suggestions?" Paul said.

"When I saw that escape tunnel leading to the river bank, I thought it would be simple and obvious. Mansfield could plant incriminating material in there, from the river exit. I'd arrange a meeting with all of them. We'd alert Burton Klein and his bully boys and take the lot. We'd have them cold. But then Henry Hammond said his wife would be out there all week. We can't have Mansfield prowling around. Too much risk. We can forget the tunnel."

"I agree." Angela nodded.

"I need a solution by tomorrow," I said. "The deadline. Here's a scenario—a little complex, but I think it will serve. I call Hammond tomorrow. I will obtain the material requested and deliver on X day at Y hour. His question: How will you get it through the gate? My answer: I will bribe the gate guard. That simple. I have fiddled the whole security setup by bribing the key object. His question: How much? My answer: Fifty thousand new dollars. Hammond will then say he has to check with his rulers—that probably means Wiley—and flash me back. All right so far?"

"With me," Angela nodded.

"Me, too," Paul said.

"All right," I went on. "Hammond flashes me back. Now it begins to get cute. His rulers are interested. But can I trust the guard? Meaning, can they trust me? They suspect I may want the love for myself. Or perhaps that fifty thousand will be for the guard, but it will just be the down payment on a blackmail plan that will go on and on. Hammond is a loon. I can manipulate him, implant the possibility of blackmail in our first conversation. I agree that the guard may prove to be too greedy. So I suggest that when I deliver the material, I bring the guard with me. They take still photos or tape of the guard receiving the payoff. Then they've got him hooked. He can't blackmail; he's implicated. They're home free—they think."

"Who plays the guard?" Angela asked.

"I will," Paul said.

"No good." I shook my head. "They're inside, in my Division. They might have a file on you. It's got to be an object they know nothing about. A low-rank object. Angela, you've got to draw an em from Burton Klein."

"No," she said definitely. "Not yet. He'll have to be called in eventually, when we take them, but not yet."

She rose and paced about my apartment, hugging her elbows. What an ef! Tight and tough as a tungsten coil. A brain that, by nature or conditioning, targeted instinctively. And the power she exuded! Not because of her rank. Put her on a factory assembly line and it would still be there. I wanted very much to be using her at that moment.

"Leon Mansfield," she said decisively. "He'll do. We'll dress him up in a gate guard's zipsuit. What the hell is it? Brown? Tan? Nick, will Mansfield do?"

"No," I said. "He's got to be in Public Service. That's the whole point of having them photograph the payoff. Evidence of attempted bribery of a Public Service employee to obtain restricted documents."

"We can sign Mansfield on as a temporary consultant," she said.

"It might serve." I nodded. "I think so. Obviously, they won't have a line on him. They won't be able to check out his Public Service record. If the meet is soon enough, it will go. Yes, I think we can fiddle it. All right. I set up the meet. I bring the evidence. Mansfield plays the gate guard. They take photos of him accepting the love, photos we'll use later to prove bribery. Then Klein moves in. Timing. It's all timing."

"Yes—timing," Angela agreed. "But we can structure all that. Paul?"

"Nothing wrong I can compute," he said slowly. "Nick, do they carry weapons?"

"They didn't on Saturday," I said. "I'm sure of that. Wiley said they had a trip to make, another visit. They wouldn't risk a random stop-and-search on the road. These objects are not simpletons."

"All right," Angela said. "Let's go ahead with it."

"After I have it set up," I said. "I'll brief Mansfield. Then I'll brief Burton Klein."

"But at the very last minute," Angela warned. "His Division may be infiltrated, too."

She thought of everything.

Monday:

0945. I flashed Dr. Henry Hammond from a station outside the compound. I told him I thought I could diddle a gate guard. But the object had a Grade D genetic rating, and I wasn't sure I could trust him. If the guard cooperated, it would be from cupidity, not from a desire to overthrow the US Government. Hammond said he would have to "consult my rulers." I gave him my apartment code.

1745. Hammond flashed me back. He said his rulers approved of the plan, "in principle," but needed to know the gate guard's name and how much love he wanted. I told him the guard was Leon Mansfield, and he'd probably want 50,000 new dollars.

2330. Hammond flashed me again and said his rulers instructed me to offer Mansfield 25,000 new dollars.

Tuesday:

0930. I flashed Hammond and said the guard would take 35,000, but no less. He said he'd relay the message.

1840. Hammond flashed me at my apartment and said the 35,000 was acceptable. But could I compute any way to ensure the future silence of Mansfield other than stopping him, since his rulers avoided personal violence whenever possible. A giggle, that. I answered by saying that the most obvious solution would be to make the payoff before witnesses, in an isolated place where the transaction could be photographed. Like Hammonds' Point. He said he'd get back to me.

Wednesday:

0830. A call from Hammond to my apartment. He was off camera. He said his rulers approved of the plan. I was to bring the material requested to his summer place on Saturday, at 2030 precisely. I was to be accompanied by the bribed guard, Leon Mansfield. No one else. At that time, 35,000 new dollars would be turned over to Mansfield and the deal would be filmed. I said that was just dandy. I was almost certain they meant to stop Mansfield and reclaim their funds.

I was about to leave for my office, thinking of how to brief AssDepDirSec Burton Klein on what would be expected of him, when my flasher chimed again. My father came on screen. He didn't look well.

"Nick," he said, "Mother's ill." His voice was unsteady.

"Bad?"

"Yes. I think so. She's in bed. I don't know. Bradford is here. He says she's just going. She won't eat."

"Can he get some fluid into her?"

"He says it'll have to be under sedation."

"She wants to die."

"Nick, make her live."

"How? We can strap her into machines. Shove tubes into her veins. Keep her heart pumping. Is that what you want?"

"No," he said. "You?"

"No," I said. "Let her go with will."

"I remember how it was at first," he said. "When we—"

He stopped suddenly. The brute wept. I waited patiently.

"Ahh," he said, "memory is a curse."

"Is it?" I said. "Put Bradford on."

"I can't," he said. "He's upstairs with her. He said about two weeks. Maybe more. Nick, I've got to go."

"Go?"

"Our plant in Connecticut. There's been a tragedy. We've lost a whole run of Poo-Poo Dolls. They're falling apart on the shelves. Something went wrong."

"Yes," I said.

"I stand to lose half a million."

"Yes," I said. "When do you want me?"

"As soon as possible."

I couldn't get a government hypersonic to Detroit. The regular flight had been suspended since six months previously, when a courier plane letting down over Lake Erie had swamped a pleasure boat with the sonic boom. Six objects had drowned. "The investigation is continuing. . . ."

"I'll get a commercial flight from Kennedy," I told my father's flickering image. "I'll be there at 1223."

"I'll hold my jet until you come in," he said. "I'll have the copter there to take you to Grosse Pointe."

We switched off. I moved precisely. I flashed my own office. One of my secretaries was in. I told him to book me on commercial Flight 128 to Detroit, leaving at 1058. I told him to requisition a Section copter to get me to Kennedy. I flashed Paul Bumford's office. He wasn't in yet. I left a message: I was leaving on a threeday; he was to call Angela Berri for details. I flashed Angela's apartment. Her serving ef came on. She said her ruler was showering. I told her to get Angela to the flasher. Angela came on, wet, hair dripping, a big pink plastowel wrapped around her.

"What, Nick?"

"My mother is ill. I've got to take my threeday now."

"Take as long as you need."

"Can't. The meet is on for this Saturday."

"It's set?" she asked, coming alive.

"Definitely. Less than an hour ago Hammond flashed me. It's Saturday night at 2030. I'm to be at Hammonds' Point with Mansfield and the things they want. Paul will contact you. Have him pack the classified material in a bag, a box, a carton—anything. A transmitter at the bottom. Are you tracking?"

"Yes."

"Burton Klein will receive. The code is—listen carefully—the code is, 'That's everything you wanted.' Repeat."

"That's everything you wanted."

"Correct. Then Klein moves in—fast. I'll be back by noon on Saturday. I'll pick up the carton and Mansfield and drive up to Hammonds' Point. Any problems so far?"

"Nooo," she said slowly.

"Angela, you'll have to brief Klein and Mansfield. Will you do that?"

"Of course," she said briskly.

"The important point is the timing. Klein will have to be in position before

'I get there. Show him the Instaroids and map of the site. And Mansfield will have to be rehearsed on his role."

"I compute," she said. "Not to worry. Everything will be set by the time you get back. Nick, I'm sorry about your mother."

I was about to switch off when suddenly she held up her palm.

"Nick," she said, "will Lydia Ferguson be there? On Saturday?"

"I don't know," I said. "Is it important?"

"Yes," she said. "We want to take as many of them as possible. Especially Lydia. To tie them in with stopping Harris."

That made sense to me. I looked at my digiwatch.

"I'll flash Hammond," I said. "I'll arrange it."

"Good service, Nick," she said.

I took another few minutes to call Hammond. I explained I had to go out of town on personal affairs, but I would return in plenty of time for the Saturday meeting. I asked him if he'd drive Lydia Ferguson up to Hammonds' Point. I'd meet her there and drive her back to the city Saturday night.

"Of course, Nick m'boy," he said genially. "Of course."

X-11

I had time to scan two files on the flight to Detroit. The first originated in the Culture Section of the Department of Bliss. It dealt with the problem of televised executions. Ratings were down. Although not stated in the memo, it was in the state's interest—as I previously explained—to keep TV viewing audiences at optimum levels.

Capital punishment had been legislated in 1979, but only for federal crimes. Originally, these included treason, espionage, military desertion, kidnappings in which the victim was stopped, bombings or hi-jackings of interstate carriers, and assassination of government servers.

Over the years, the list of capital crimes had been enlarged to include all kidnappings, all homicides, threats and acts of terrorism against the state, use of and trafficking in restricted drugs, forgery of federal specie (including BIN cards), acts of public terrorism, defiling the US flag, willful political dissent with the intent of overthrowing the government, and "slanderous and/or libelous actions taken against public servers."

The guilty were executed by electric chair. Not only was it a popular TV special, but it was believed that TV exposure of capital punishment had a socially beneficial effect on those contemplating similar crimes.

In any event, ratings were off. The CULSEC memo asked for suggestions for more "visually stimulating" methods of execution that might regain the lost audience. The answers seemed obvious to me. Hanging, garroting, or even the revival of the guillotine would certainly prove more visually stimulating. And when these methods palled, as I supposed they eventually would, there was always drawing and quartering.

I scrawled quick notes on the border of the memo. One of my secretaries would transcribe them into acceptable officialese.

The second file, a thick one, was labeled "Hyman R. Lewisohn." It concerned the health of the em who, more than any other object, was the source of innovative ideas for the social, political, and economic progress of the US.

Lewisohn's genius had come to the attention of the government in a curious manner. Early in 1973, at a diplomatic reception in Teheran, an aide of the economic counselor to the US Embassy had been chatting with the Shah.

"That was quite an article by your Professor Lewisohn," the Shah mentioned.

"Ah yes, Excellency," the aide said, as smoothly as he could. "Remarkable." The Shah looked at him closely, then smiled.

"Yes," he said. "Quite remarkable!"

An hour later a coded cablegram went to Washington: RUSH URGENT RECENT ARTICLE PROFESSOR LEWISOHN.

The article and the author were finally tracked down. Hyman R. Lewisohn was an obscure professor of economics at an obscure Midwestern liberal arts college. His article had been contributed ($25 honorarium) to an obscure monthly trade journal of the petroleum industry.

Working with only a primitive desktop computer, Lewisohn had proved, quite simply, that petroleum was too valuable to be burned as fuel. His theory was based on estimates of the finite quantity of petroleum in the world. He then computed the future cash value of heating oils, kerosene, gasoline, lubricants, naphtha, and similar products versus the future cash value of plastics, chemicals, drugs, dyes, fertilizers, and—a pure conception at the time—synthetic protein.

Lewisohn was offered a US Government post. He refused. The rank-rate was doubled. Again he refused. An Undersecretary of State was sent out to talk to him. It must have been a bewildering interview for the public server.

Hyman R. Lewisohn was the orphan of immigrant German Jews. He was a victim of achondroplasia, with the enormous bulging forehead common in such cases. In addition, he had a crop of coarse red hair, paid absolutely no attention to his grooming or even to his personal cleanliness, and deliberately discouraged personal relationships by a rude and offensive manner. This included expectorating on the floor, loudly deriding the opinions of others, lewd gestures, and so forth. But he had one thing going for him: He was a genius.

Eventually, he stated his terms for public service. He was to be paid 100,000 new dollars annually. Living and working quarters were to be provided, with a relatively small, compact, versatile computer. His expenses for periodicals were to be paid, including the obso romantic novels to which he was addicted.

The government agreed immediately, making the most lovable bargain since the purchase of Alaska. We had bought the power of Lewisohn's creativity.

And now that power was stopping. The file I scanned contained the most recent contingency plan from the Chief Resident at Rehabilitation & Reconditioning Hospice No. 4, near Alexandria, Virginia. It was not encouraging. The obso em was not responding to treatment. Bone marrow transplant was recommended. I realized I had to go down there myself and scan him. His continued existence was—well, essential. That was all I could say.

When I came down the ramp at the Detroit airport, I was met by the blue-haired copter pilot. She was wearing her Chinese red zipsuit with the embroidered "flAIRToys" across one breast. The other disembarking ems looked at her voraciously.

"I'm supposed to guide you," she said archly.

"Oh? Where?"

"To the private plane area. Your father's over there, waiting at his jet. And the copter's parked there."

My father was standing at the cabin door of the sleek twin-jet. There were three objects with him. One em was Ben Baker, his production manager, carrying a plastic box. The other two were assistants, one ef, one em. Introductions were made. We all stroked palms.

"Thanks, Nick," my father said. "I knew I could depend on you."

"How's Mother?"

"No change. Ben, show him."

Baker took the lid off the box he was carrying, held it out to me. I bent over to look. The stench drove me back.

"Jesus Christ!" I cried. "What *is* it?"

"What is it?" my father repeated bitterly. "When it left our Connecticut factory five weeks ago it was a perfect Poo-Poo Doll. Something happened."

"Something sure as hell did," I agreed.

The mess in the box was putrescent. It stank. The plastic body of the doll had deteriorated, decayed almost to the point of liquidity. The rot had discolored the dress, stained the hair, even corrupted the little plastiglass eyes. It was a small corpus. Fetid.

"Ben," I said, "what caused it?"

"I wish I knew," he said miserably. "That's the most automated toy production line in the world. Computerized quality control. Bells go off if anything isn't just perfect. Automatic temperature and fluidity controls. Foolproof. Fail-safe. But we lost a whole run."

The ef assistant spoke up.

"Everything since that run has been perfect," she said. "We've done heavy analysis. They look fine."

"How long did the bad run last?" I asked.

"A week," Ben Baker said. "Actually a little less than six days. Before, the dolls were fine. After, the dolls were fine. But during? Murder!"

"We can't let it happen again," my father said furiously. "Never!"

On that happy note we separated. I watched my father's jet take off. Then I took the copter to Grosse Pointe. The ef pilot didn't stop chirping.

"What's your name?" I interrupted once.

"Beryl," she said. And started up again.

We landed on the front lawn. I handed my case over to a sad-faced Charles and went immediately to my mother's bedroom on the second floor. Shades and drapes were drawn. But enough late afternoon light came through to pearl the room. Mrs. McPherson was seated woodenly at my mother's bedside. I went over to the bed, picked up the feather hand, tried to find a pulse.

Head turned. Eyes opened slowly. Widened in consciousness. Then recognition.

Weakly: "Hullo, chappie."

"What's this?" I said sternly. "What's this?"

"Terminal nostalgia," she said.

I caught my breath.

"Don't fake me, chappie," she said.

"Have I ever?"

"No," she murmured. "No, no, no." In diminishing volume until I couldn't hear. "No, no, nooo. . . ."

I went over to one of the windows. I think I leaned my head against the frame. I was alert, aware of my own symptoms. Mental dislocation. Lightheadedness. Something new: Physical vertigo. Weakness in the knees. A tilt. I thought I might fall. . . .

. . . annual visits to the cemetery at Mt. Clemens when I was a child. The grave of an older sister who had stopped at the age of three months from a respiratory infection. "Susan Bennington Flair, May 3, 1967—August 14, 1967." A smirking granite cherub.

. . . natural bacon frying for breakfast. A treat on Sunday morning. The kitchen filled with the scent. Dividing up the thick Sunday newspaper, a section to each. Gobbling bacon, shouting news items to each other. Rollicking.

. . . my parents dressed to go out. Mother in a strapless black velvet gown. Her bare flesh glowing. *Glowing!* Excitement and electricity. Her naked body moving inside the gown, bursting to spring free. A choker of small diamonds, no brighter than her sparkle. Goodnight, Nick! Goodnight! Goodnight!

. . . a midnight storm when the thunder. . . .

I flipped a spansule into the air, caught it in my mouth. A salted peanut. I swallowed it down. In a few moments the trembling ceased; memories faded.

I went back to my mother's bedside. I saw the dark green jar on the bedside table, picked it up, spilled a few of the pills into my palm. I recognized them.

"Did Dr. Bradford tell you about these?" I asked Mrs. McPherson.

She nodded.

"Please don't leave them at the bedside." I moved the jar across the room, to a dresser top.

I ate alone in the gloomy dining room. I sat at one end of the long oak table, surrounded by lost whispers and forgotten laughs. I had a slice of pro-ham, a cold salad made of propots, two slices of natural tomato—ruby red and mealy. I did what I could with it all, forking it down, staring at the walls, listening to echoes.

Then, in the library, I poured a large natural brandy. I took it up to Mother's bedroom.

"I'll stay awhile," I told Mrs. McPherson.

She nodded and left. I sat in a cane-backed armchair, sipping my drink, watching the bed. Occasionally my mother stirred, moved uneasily, groaned or muttered. It was not natural sleep. That dark green jar contained a potent barbiturate.

I went over to the bed, put my hand lightly on her hot forehead. She relaxed, calmed; the moans ceased. I was standing there, feeling the paper-thin skin beneath my fingers, when Mrs. McPherson returned. She was carry-ing a tray of dishes, covered with a large plastinap. She hadn't been gone more than fifteen minutes. She wasn't giving an inch. Mother was *hers*. I left the two of them. Together.

It was a black night, mild and moonless. A tug hooted somewhere. A jetliner droned over. Then the silence crept back. I walked slowly down to-ward the water, peering about for the garden table and chairs. I found them, finally. I sat there in the dark, sipping my brandy slowly, almost tonguing it.

I stirred, eventually, when bright lights flashed on in the guesthouse. I heard loud music. New jazz. It was probably Beryl, dancing about in her red zipsuit or inspecting her bare breasts critically before a mirror, peering at them through a cloud of cannabis smoke. I went back to the house and called Millie. No answer.

I poured another brandy, took it up to my suite. I showered, dressed in tooty civilian clothes, called Millie again. No answer. I finished the brandy in two gulps. There was an effect now, a welcome lack of caution, irresponsibility triumphant. I drove into Detroit, singing.

Millie wasn't at her apartment. I started a crawl of taverns we had visited together. I drank a petronac, petrovod, petroleum—whatever I saw first; it made no difference. I didn't find Millie. By midnight I was moving sideways through a blurred world, slipping by everyone, giggling.

I found her finally. I was in a tumultuous place, somewhere, raised my head from my drink, looked in the mirror. A stranger there. And over his shoulder, across the room, there was Millie, sitting with another ef and two tooty ems. I swung around on the barstool, so quickly that I spun off, stag-gering.

"Hey," I yelled. "Hey, Millie!"

I went banging toward them, knocking into tables, chairs, shoving objects out of the way. A burly em suddenly stood before me.

"Be good or be gone," he said pleasantly.

I got a knee into his groin and he went down, mouth open. Grinning, I clawed my way toward Millie.

"Hey, Millie!" I called joyously.

Then I was in an alley. I was on the bricks, slime under my cheek. I doubled over, drew up my knees, covered my face with my hands.

They took me with their boots. Not speaking. Just breathing hard. It hurt. How it hurt.

Just before I went out, I heard an ef screaming, "Stoppit! Stoppit! Stoppit!"

I came up slowly. Through a bloody haze I was staring at a plaster ceiling, paint chips peeling away. My chest was cold and wet.

I looked down. Millie was rubbing a plastinap of Jellicubes along my ribs. I looked around. Her apartment. And two uniformed bobs from the Detroit Peace Department, watching. One held my BIN card, one my purse.

"Oh, Nick," Millie said anxiously. "Are you tip-top?"

Beautiful question.

"Tip-top," I nodded. "What time is it?"

"Almost 0200. How do you feel?"

"I told you. Tip-top. Would you make me some coffee?"

She scurried off. I slowly swung my legs over the edge of the bed. Cautiously, I sat upright. Something was wrong on my left side. I probed gently.

"Broken?" one of the bobs asked.

I took a deep breath. No sudden, sharp anguish. Just dull pain.

"I don't think so. Contused perhaps."

"You want to press charges?" he asked.

"That wouldn't be wise," I said. "Would it?"

"No," he said. "It wouldn't."

"Did I cause any damage?" I asked.

"You kicked an em in the balls," the other bob said. "The manager."

"Can I have my purse?"

I took out my wallet, riffled the bills. I thought some love was missing. But I had spent a lot.

"You think fifty will make him feel better?" I asked.

"Fifty will cure him," one of them said.

I handed over the fifty, then added twenty more.

"Sorry for the trouble," I said.

"It happens." One of the bobs shrugged. "But an em like you—in a place like that. You want to watch it."

They both nodded virtuously. I was given back my BIN card. They departed. I was getting out of my clothes when Millie returned, bringing a plasticup of something black and steaming.

"Oh, Nick," she said sorrowfully, looking at me.

"I vomited?"

"Yes, you did."

"Not in here?" I asked, horrified.

"No. In the alley. When they were picking you up."

I took a sip of coffee. If it had any flavor, I couldn't taste it. It wasn't important. It was hot and wet. I took slow sips as I continued undressing.

"I'll wipe off your clothes," Millie said. "With a damp rag."

"Thank you." I smiled. "Later. Is my face all right?"

"Your right ear is a little scratched. From the bricks. But you can hardly notice."

I examined myself. Red blotches on shoulders, arms, ribs, hips, thighs, calves. I knew what color they'd be tomorrow, and the next day, and the next. And I could feel the pain starting in my back and buttocks. A complete service.

"Do you have any tape, Millie?"

"Tape?"

"Any kind. Mending tape? Electrician's tape?"

"Nooo, I don't think so. Nick, should I go out and get some?"

"At 0200? Thanks, dear, but no. Do you have an old thermasheet I can rip up? I'll send you a new one."

"Don't say that. You don't have to give me anything."

I tore long strips. I held one end in place, then slowly revolved. Millie wound me like a mummy. I kept telling her to keep it tight. Finally my thorax was wrapped, armpits to waist. It still hurt. But it would hold. I tucked in the loose end.

"I'm sorry, Millie," I said. "Please excuse me. I know I ruined your evening."

"Oh, Nick . . . I was so happy to see you again. Why didn't you call?"

"I tried."

It seemed a ridiculously formal conversation. A naked em, chest mummified, standing before a fully dressed ef.

"Another coffee?" she asked.

"No," I said. "Two liters of cold water."

"Do you think—" she asked tentatively.

"Let's try," I said. "But you must be very gentle."

"Ever so gentle," she cried happily. "I'll do *everything*!"

But I didn't let her. For some reason I couldn't compute, it was important to me that I give her profit. I never penetrated her child's body that night, not once, but I employed lips, tongue, fingers, eyelashes, toes, until she was screaming with delight, and I had to hush her, fearing the neighbors would call the bobs again.

It went on and on. She seemed insatiable, but I would not end until she signaled me. Finally, she pushed me away and lay back exhausted, rosy and sweated.

"Who is Lydia?" she gasped.

"Lydia?" I said. "I don't know any Lydia."

"In the alley. Just before you passed out. You said, 'Lydia.'"

"Did I?" I said. "That's interesting."

Late the next morning I watched while Dr. Bradford examined my mother. She was awake, babbling nonsense.

"Yes, yes," Bradford kept saying. "Yes, yes."

I followed him out into the hallway. He was a short, thick, comose man. About my age. Competent.

"Well, doctor?" I asked him.

"Well, doctor?" he said ironically. "You want her force-fed?"

"No. You want off the case?"

He thought seriously about that.

"I should," he acknowledged.

"Strap her in—"

"Oh, don't give me all that kaka," he exploded angrily. "I've heard it all before. I simply have to do nothing—right? As if sins of omission are less tainted than sins of commission."

"You want off," I said stonily, "you're off. It won't change things."

"Goddamned son of a bitching bastard!" he cried furiously. He actually stamped his foot.

"My sentiments exactly, doctor," I said.

"Ahh," he said. "The dear lady."

This quote from Leon Mansfield startled me.

"Would you come up to my rooms, please?" I asked him. "A professional consultation. I have some natural brandy."

"Only sensible thing I've heard today," he grumbled, and followed me up the stairs.

I poured us each a glass. Then I stripped down. He took a look at the colors.

"Pretty," he said. "Hit by a truck?"

"Two of them," I said. "Check the ribs, please."

He helped me unwrap the stripping of torn sheet. He probed me gently.

"Breathe deeply," he commanded. "Again. Again. Pain?"

"No punctures," I said. "No fractures. I think."

"Confusions," he said. "Here and here. Drive back with me. We'll take some plates."

"No," I said. "It's not that important. I'll have it done when I get back to New York. I have wide tape here. Just strap me up."

"Idiot," he growled.

"Exactly," I agreed.

He taped me up. We finished our brandies. He wanted to give me a meperidine. I insisted on a codeine. It took me another brandy to get it. By the time he departed, he was feeling no pain. And neither was I.

I wandered about the grounds. A gray, overcast day. I was gray and overcast. Codeine plus hangover. But I was computing in a dazed kind of way, jumping circuits.

I think I ate something. I know I visited my mother again. We held hands and chatted away like magpies. Mrs. McPherson didn't seem shocked, but I know Mother and I were trading absurdities. It pleased Mother. I think. It certainly pleased me.

Afterward, the pain coming on again, my whole body aching, I debated: Another codeine? No, I decided. Because the anxieties were worse than the pain. So I popped a new manipulated amitriptyline I just happened to have in my case. It worked on me like a hypnotic. Get rid of the anxieties and then you can sleep.

I slept until noon. I took a sponge bath and shaved carefully. I was tracking. A little deliberate, a little dulled, but functioning. My bruises hurt like hell. I accepted the pain gladly. I had been lucky and I knew it.

I spent most of the day with Mother. She had been off barbiturates for almost twelve hours; I thought it safe enough to allow her the natural vodka she craved. I cut it with water, but she didn't notice. Her color improved, her spirits perked, she laughed.

The copter had taken off for the airport at 1700, to pick up my father. At 1730, I took a bottle of natural brandy and glasses out to the lawn table. I waited for him there, not drinking. It was almost 1840 before I heard the copter throb. Beryl came slipping in neatly, hovered, set down gently. A skillful ef.

Ben Baker got out first, then turned to assist Father. He climbed out wearily, clumsily. Sad to view. They ducked low as the main rotor revved, then slowed to a stop. I stood, called out. They saw me and came over. Both were obviously fatigued, depressed.

"Nick," my father said.

Ben Baker nodded briefly. I gestured toward the brandy.

"Medicine," I said. "Doctor's orders."

They accepted gratefully. Father downed his in one gulp, shuddered, drew a long breath, then held out his glass for a refill. We all sat down at the metal table.

"How is she?" my father asked.

"Better," I said. "A little. I got some fluid into her."

"Eat?"

"No. You have any luck?"

Baker shook his head gloomily.

"Can't find it, Nick," he said. "Checked out everything. It couldn't have happened, but it did."

"And might happen again," Father said. "Goddamn it to hell!"

"Faulty input?" I suggested.

Baker shook his head. "No way. We're still using plastic from the same shipment. It's up to specifications."

"Maybe heavy analysis of the spoiled doll will tell the story," I said. "Wait for that."

Neither seemed cheered by the possibility.

"Ben," I said, "give me a rough idea of how the doll is made. The process. Just the highlights."

"We get the plastic in pellets," he said. "Mix for flesh color desired. We market the Poo-Poo worldwide. White, pink, tan, yellow, red, brown, black. The plastic is melted down, poured hot into alloy molds. Front molds and back molds. The Poo-Poo tubing and devices are laid in the back mold. The front is pressed on and heat-welded. Excess is sheared. The complete body is dunked for cooling and washing. Then it goes for eye insertion, facial stenciling, wig-gluing, dressing. These are semihand operations. Then inspection and packing. Shipping. That's it."

"But the plastic is controlled?"

"Absolutely. Fluidity and temperature. Automatic."

"What about the molds?"

"Steam-scalded after every impression. Practically sterile."

I computed the problem a few moments. We all watched the night creep in, darkness flowing around us, coming from the lake like fog.

"Ben," I said, "where does the factory get its water?"

"What water?"

"When you wash the hot doll bodies to cool them and rinse off scrap."

"In a tank," he said. "Constantly running, constantly flushed."

"Where from?"

"The Connecticut River. We pump in one end and have a gravity flow out the other."

"Is the intake filtered?"

"What are you getting at, Nick?" my father demanded.

"Ben, is the water intake filtered?"

"A gross filter. Just to take the crap out. Nick, we don't *drink* the stuff."

"What's upstream from you?"

"Nick, I'm not following."

"What is this?" my father asked again. Bewildered.

"What kind of factories are upstream from you?"

"Oh—let's see.... A foundry. Alloys. A bauxite refinery. Some small tobacco-processors. A rayon manufacturer. A few others. I don't know them all."

"Do they exhaust into the river?"

"Not if they want to stay out of jail. You know the law."

"But an accident? Or maybe a quick dump at night, hoping no one could trace it? Like that rayon factory, pouring carbon disulphide into the—"

"Jesus Christ!" he shouted.

He stood suddenly, spilling his brandy all over the table. He began running awkwardly toward the house, elbows flopping out at his sides.

"What?" my father cried in alarm. "Where is he running? What's happening?"

"Calm down." I soothed him. "He's going to flash your Connecticut factory to order objects to check on accidental or deliberate spills in the river from upstream plants. The ruined run of dolls was probably rinsed in polluted water. Maybe carbon disulphide sludge from the rayon factory. Why didn't you dunk the hot doll bodies in sulphuric acid and be done with it?"

"Oh, God." He groaned.

"You've got to monitor the water intake," I told him. "Constant analysis. It can be done automatically."

"Nick-ol'-as!" he shouted, leaned over, pounded my back. My bruises. I tried not to wince.

"You've got to come into the business," he said. "*Got* to!"

"Let's not go into that again."

"Nick, I'm getting old," he said piteously. "I need help."

He watched Beryl finish strapping down the copter. She glanced toward us, then waggled off toward the guesthouse.

"You need help?" I said scoffingly.

"Not with that." He giggled.

He dragged me up to the house for dinner, hugging my arm, laughing like a maniac.

"I feel twenty years younger," he declared. "I want to buy you something. Anything. What would you like?"

"Nothing," I told him. "You know I've got everything."

It was almost 2200 before I could get away from them. I pleaded a heavy schedule on the following day. I left them in the library, glassy-eyed and belching, trading coarse and not very funny jokes. I felt sorry for Beryl. Briefly.

I looked in at my mother on the way upstairs. She appeared to be sleeping. Mrs. McPherson was sitting there, ramrod straight in her chair. But her eyes were closed. They opened when I put a wool blanket softly across her.

"Thank you, son," she whispered.

At the top, in my suite, I checked the glued thread from the jamb to the door of my secret place. It had not been disturbed. I switched on the light, locked the door behind me. I stacked the four books alongside the sprung Morris chair, poured a brandy, settled down. . . .

Egon Schiele had done many nudes, em and ef. The thighs were deliberately spread, genitalia represented in almost finicky detail. I found these portraits so harrowing, I could not view them without dread. The artist had gone beyond sexuality. I sensed something of death in beauty, beauty in death.

At this point in time, I wanted only to look into the eyes of the self-portraits. There was a demented possession there. But perhaps I considered it "demented" simply because it was foreign to me, not part of my conditioning.

When you cannot comprehend what is being said, if an object seems to be wildly pleading in a language utterly unknown to you, then your instinctive reaction might well be fear. Terror. That was close to what I felt, staring into the burning eyes of Egon Schiele. I strove to compute. There was something for me there. I wanted to learn what those eyes knew.

X-12

I called Ellen Dawes from the Detroit airport, told her what flight I was taking, asked her to have a Section copter meet me at Kennedy. She must have alerted Paul Bumford; he was waiting at the compound pad when we let down.

"Nick," he said, "what happened to your ears?"

"Stumbled and scraped it on a brick wall. Nothing serious."

"How's your mother?"

"All right, thank you. Are we set?"

"Everything ready. We've got—"

"Wait a minute. Let's go over it with Angela."

"Can't. She's gone down to Washington."

I thought a moment, then nodded.

"That's Angela," I said. "So she can be the first to tell DIROB his daughter was arrested for homicide and crimes against the state."

"More likely tell the Chief Director," Paul said. "Anyway, she's made arrangements for an open line to DIVSEC from 1990 on."

I glanced at my digiwatch.

"We've got time. Come up to my place. I need a fresh zipsuit. You can fill me in there."

In my apartment, Paul followed me into the nest. When I stripped down, he saw the taping and bruises. His eyes widened.

"My God!" he breathed. "Nick, what the hell happened?"

"Nothing happened. A disagreement."

"Are you all right?"

"Of course. Minor aches and pains, that's all."

"What's under the tape?"

"Jesus Christ, Paul," I shouted. "Don't stress me. Possibly a crack or two. I'll have a plate taken tomorrow. I'm functioning. I'm perfectly capable of winding up this whole thing. Now . . . what have you got?"

He pouted.

"All right." I sighed. I patted his cheek. "I'm sorry I yelled at you."

He brightened.

"I don't mind, Nick. Really I don't. I know you've been pressurized."

"Just tell me what's happening."

"Burton Klein has been briefed. He and a squad of twenty objects left here at midnight. They're in position now, reporting every ten minutes to DIVSEC. So far everything is quiet, no unusual activity."

"Good."

"Before we left, Klein picked out a car for you, a white sedan. There's a beeper under the hood. Klein will track you in."

"That was smart."

"The car is in the motor pool now, under guard. The carton of material is in the trunk. I assembled it. Everything on the list."

"Transmitter?"

"At the bottom. We've got omnidirectional mikes: they'll pick up everything. The Electronics Team rigged it. We checked it out here, but Klein will stop you on the road up there for a final check."

"Were you there when Angela briefed Klein?"

"No, she briefed us separately. But I talked to Klein later. He's a pig, Nick, but he knows what he's doing."

"As long as he knows the code."

"He does. He said to ask you if you wanted a gun. You can draw one from DIVSEC if you want it."

"A gun? What for? These objects aren't thugs."

"I told that to Klein. He said maybe you should carry one—just in case."

"No, thanks. I don't anticipate any violence. If Klein knows his service, no one will be injured."

I came into the living room, zipping up my fresh uniform.

"Now what about Mansfield?" I asked.

"Angela said she briefed him and furnished a gate guard's zipsuit. She said to pick him up at 1700 at 'the usual place.' That's all she'd tell me. She said you'd know where it is. Do you know, Nick?"

"Yes."

"No one tells me anything," he grumbled. "Anyway, are the times right?"

"Barring accidents. If I'm to pick up Mansfield at 1700, I better leave here in about"—I glanced at my digiwatch—"in about forty minutes."

"Can I come with you, Nick?"

I smiled at him.

"No way. But thank you, Paul."

"You will be careful?"

"Of course. Anything else?"

"No, I . . . Oh, yes, another thing: Angela has already given orders for their interrogation. After Klein takes them, they're to be separated and sent to Hospices 2, 4, and 7. She said we'd get better results if we kept them apart."

I shook my head admiringly.

"She thinks of everything," I said.

"She surely does," he said. "Bitch!"

We ran through the whole thing once more to make certain the timing and communications were as foolproof as possible. Paul said he'd wait at DIVSEC headquarters for news of how the raid went. That reminded me of something else.

"Did Angela arrange for an Uncle Sam?" I asked.

The law allowed the security section of any government department to make arrests for crimes against the state, providing the arresting officers were under the command of a server of the Bureau of Public Security (formerly the FBI) of the Department of Rewards. (The DOR had originally been called the Department of Justice, then the Department of Merit, then the Department of Virtue, and now the Department of Rewards. Everyone agreed the title was not quite right yet. The Office of Linguistic Truth was working on it.)

In any event, the law requiring a BPS server to be in command when arrests were made by security officers of other government departments was easily circumvented. A token BPS officer was requisitioned, but in nominal command, and the necessary documents executed. The borrowed BPS object, who was rarely present at the time and place of the arrests, was known in Public Service circles as an Uncle Sam.

Paul assured me Angela Berri had remembered to requisition an Uncle Sam. The required papers had been filed in Washington. Everything was legal.

I picked up Leon Mansfield at the Mess Hall on Seventh Avenue at 1700, after driving the white sedan around the block twice, despairing of finding a parking space, and finally double-parking in front of the restaurant. I could see him inside, playing his chess game. I honked the horn twice. He looked up, saw me, folded his little chessboard, put it in his pocket, and came out to me.

He was wearing a soiled raincoat, but took it off before he got in the car. His tan zipsuit, a gate guard's uniform, fitted reasonably well.

"Who's winning?" I asked him.

"What? Oh, you mean the chess game. Well, when you play yourself, you win and you lose. Am I right, Mr. Nicholas Flair?"

"Right." I nodded and swung into traffic.

He didn't say a word while I maneuvered over to the West Side Freeway.

"Did Angela Berri give you your orders?" I asked, as we headed north.

"I have my orders. The dear lady."

After that, there was no more talk. He seemed unusually reticent. I was just as happy; his cryptic comments, always hinting at something beyond the obvious, were wearisome.

When we were about thirty meters from the access road to Hammonds' Point, I slowed down, trying to spot the sign. An object came out onto the highway, signaled us to a halt with a swinging lantern. There was a red filter over the lens.

He was wearing a white plastisteel helmet with transparent faceguard. His body was bulky in nylon-alloy armor: cuirass, cuisses, greave. He looked like an obso baseball catcher, before soccer became the Great American Game. He came around to the driver's side.

"Dr. Flair?" he said.

He turned the torch on my face, briefly.

"Yes," he said. "I've seen you around. I'm Art Roach, X-0 of DIVSEC. Flair is here."

I looked around, thinking he was speaking to someone else. But then I saw his throat mike. The miniaturized transceiver would be in his helmet.

"Where's Klein?" I asked.

"Roger," he said. "Pull off to the side a moment. Please."

His voice was cold, cold. I pulled onto the verge, cut the motor. The silence out there had a ring to it.

Roach came back to my side.

"Yes, sir," he said. "Will do. Where is the package, Dr. Flair?"

"In the trunk."

"Can we run a communication check? Please."

Obediently, I got out of the car. I unlocked the trunk. Roach backed off a few paces and motioned me to him.

"Say something," he said. "Please."

" 'I never saw a purple cow,' " I recited. " 'I never hope to see one. . . .' "

"How was the voice level?" Roach asked. "Very good. Yes, sir. I'll tell him. Dr. Flair, Klein wants you to wait here a moment. He's coming up from the communications van. No smoking. Please."

In a few moments Klein appeared, coming out of the brush. I would have recognized that big, square torso and spindly legs anywhere, even brutalized with helmet, faceguard, armor. He was carrying a flechette gun slung over one shoulder.

"Burton," I said, gesturing toward his armament, "is all this necessary?"

"Regulations," he said. "You're transmitting loud and clear. You can go ahead."

"Are they here?"

"Yes. About an hour ago."

"All of them?"

"Martha Wiley is missing. You want to wait for her?"

I thought a moment.

"No," I said, "do you?"

"No," he said. "Let's take what we've got. Listen. . . ."

"Yes?"

"What's Mansfield doing in this? He's not PS."

"Just bait," I said. "We needed someone they couldn't check."

"I don't like it. Something smells."

"Burton."—I sighed—"we had to set up a bribery trap."

"I should have been handling this. How can a bribery charge stand if he's not a PS?"

"Angela said she'd sign him on as a temporary consultant."

"I don't like it," he repeated. "She says my Division is infiltrated. That's a lot of kaka. I trust every one of my ems."

"Burton, will you calm down? Everything is set; let's get it over with. You know the code?"

" 'That's everything you wanted.' "

"Right. Then you move in. Come in fast, Burton."

"I know my service."

"And take plenty of photos, still and tape. All the objects, the love, the restricted the material—everything."

"I know my service," he repeated stubbornly.

I started back to the car, but he put a hand on my arm. I turned. He switched off his throat mike.

"Flair—"

"Yes?"

"How are you going back? After it's over?"

"I'll drive back," I said, puzzled. "With Mansfield."

"Let me come with you. Mansfield can go with my ems."

"Well . . . sure."

"Will you wait for me? It may take some time before we get them searched and on their way."

"What's this all about?"

"I just want to talk to you. Alone."

"All right, Burton. I'll wait."

"Thanks. I've got to tell someone. I don't know how to handle it. Go ahead now."

I got back in the car and started up. We bumped slowly over the railroad tracks, pulled up at the side of the house. The porch light went on. Henry Hammond came out, peered down at us. I got out of the car, lifted my hand to him.

"You're late," he said. And went back inside.

Leon Mansfield got out of the car, carrying his soiled raincoat draped over his arm. I went around to the rear trunk, opened it again, unleashed the carton. I left the trunk lid open. Mansfield followed me up the steps, into the house. Hammond switched off the porch light, closed and locked the door behind us. I looked around. Lydia Ferguson. Alice Hammond. Dr. Thomas J. Wiley. Tod and Vernon DeTilly. Henry Hammond.

I caught their excitement immediately. Eager eyes on the carton of goodies I was carrying. I moved toward the wooden dining table. Lydia cleared it hastily of a bowl of wax fruit and two pewter candlestick holders. I smiled at her, set the box carefully in the middle of the table. I jerked a thumb over my shoulder.

"Leon Mansfield," I said.

They started how-are-yous and nice-to-meet-yous, but Mansfield interrupted roughly.

"Where's my love?" he demanded.

Wiley pointed at a black plastic case on one of the chairs. It looked like an obso doctor's bag.

"Right there," he said, smiling. "But Mr. Mansfield, surely you don't expect us to hand it over until we have examined what we are buying?"

"Nothing to do with me," Mansfield said harshly. "I don't know what it is and I don't want to know. I done my job. I want my love."

"Of course, of course," Wiley said smoothly. "But just in case you may, some day, decide you want more than agreed upon, surely you'll have no objection if we photograph your receiving the love?"

Mansfield looked slowly about the circle of faces. Pupils contracted in his phlegmy eyes. That thin, pointed face became cruel. I fancied even the tip of the long, prehensile nose quivered. He convinced *me*.

"Cute," he said harshly. "Goddamned cute."

Vernon DeTilly moved slowly around until he stood between Mansfield and the door. He put his back against the door, folded his arms.

"Well, Mr. Mansfield?" Dr. Wiley asked genially. "What is it to be?"

Mansfield hesitated, apparently pondering. Tod DeTilly helped make up his mind. He went over to the black plastic case, unlatched it, upended it over the couch. The contents spilled out. Packets and packets of new bills in the brilliantly hued abstract designs adopted in 1989.

Mansfield stared at the spilled love. He actually licked his lips. The em was a natural thespian.

"Take your lousy pictures," he said hoarsely.

They had a camera prepared, threaded with a reel of color. Instaroid. They turned the lamps toward Mansfield, switched on the overhead light so he was brightly illuminated. Tod DeTilly photographed him taking a bundle from the hand of Dr. Wiley, counting a sheaf, stacking the packets of bills.

"Fine, fine." Wiley chuckled. "That should do nicely, Tod. Now just one more thing: Let's take a look at the presents Dr. Flair has brought us."

We clustered around the table. The carton was unstrapped. I removed the lid, began taking out documents, tapes, reels of film, a box of slides, specimen jars, etc. As I emptied the box, I cautiously probed beneath. But the Electronics Team had done good service; the transmitter was below a false bottom. I tilted the carton to show Wiley it was empty.

But he and the others were too busy to pay attention. They were eagerly, almost frantically shuffling through the mass of material. Each item bore a red label, RESTRICTED, and below, in small type, a warning that unauthorized viewing or disclosure was a capital offense.

"Excellent," Dr. Wiley crowed. "Excellent!"

"That's everything you wanted," I said in a loud voice.

Burton Klein was right: He knew his service.

It seemed to me I had no sooner spoken than the room, the house, the entire world was bathed in a brilliant, white, almost phosphorescent light.

"You are surrounded," a thunderous voice boomed out. "You cannot escape. This is Division of Security, Department of Bliss.

Open the door. Come out one at a time. Hands on top of your head. You are surrounded. You cannot escape. This is Division of Security, Department of Bliss. If you come out now, one at a time, hands on top of your head, you will. . . ."

The deep, resonant voice thundered on and on, never ending. That tremendous noise and the blinding light had the effect intended: We stood shocked. Trembling. Small, helpless animals shriveled by fear.

Dr. Thomas J. Wiley recovered first. He realized at once what had happened.

"*You*, Dr. Flair?" he shouted. "Your informed judgment?"

I didn't answer.

He turned to the others, tried to smile, didn't quite make it.

"All of you," he yelled, to make himself heard above the thundering voice from outside. "Do as they say. Do not resist. There is no hope. God help us all."

He went to the front door, unlocked it, swung it open. Then he put his hands atop his head and stepped through. Almost immediately the thundering voice ceased, cut off in mid-sentence. The glaring floodlights dimmed.

I looked at Lydia Ferguson. Her head was bowed. She was blushing and would not glance at me.

The behavior of the others was predictable: Alice Hammond, proud, feeling her gravid abdomen. The DeTilley brothers, furious and frustrated, about to follow Wiley out the door. Henry Hammond utterly destroyed, riven by terror.

I looked through the open door. There was a circle of armored ems. Their pipe-barreled flechette guns were pointed at the house. I saw the burly figure of Burton Klein coming toward the steps. He pushed up his faceguard.

"Move out," he shouted. "Make it—"

Then everything came apart.

Klein had one foot on the lowest step.

I heard three sharp cracks from inside the house. Next to me. Three rapid shots.

Klein's heavy face disintegrated into red pulp.

He went down.

The surrounding ems opened fire. Boom of flechette guns. Whiz of steel darts.

Dr. Wiley was safe. Tod DeTilley was safe. Both stood, guarded, beyond the firing line.

Vernon DeTilly was on the porch, hands on top of his head. The fusillade caught him, tore him apart.

Then I was on the floor, head turned sideways. I could see Lydia Ferguson. She was on the floor, eyes closed.

Alice Hammond was down too. Spouting blood from a hundred punctures. A sieve. Henry Hammond was behind the couch. I could not see Mansfield.

I heard a high, cracked voice: "Stop firing! Stop firing! Stop firing!"

Was that me?

Silence.

I raised my head slowly. An armored monster stood braced in the doorway. A black pipe pointed at me.

"Flair," I cried. "I'm Flair!"

"Who fired?" Art Roach demanded.

"I don't know. I didn't see."

"Where's Mansfield?"

"I don't—"

But then we heard the boom of a fletchette gun, muted. From down near the river. X-0 Roach turned and ran. I climbed shakily to my feet. Armored ems came crowding through the door.

It took almost two hours to get it sorted out.

Burton Klein was stopped. So was Vernon DeTilly. Alice Hammond was going. She aborted: a stopped ef fetus. But we had Wiley, Tod DeTilly, Lydia Ferguson, Henry Hammond.

We photographed everything: the living prisoners, the corpora, the scattered love, the restricted material on the table. Roach confiscated the bag of bills. I made him sign a receipt. I repacked the DIVRAD carton, locked it in the trunk of my white sedan.

Then I went to the river, sliding and slipping down the bank, grabbing at trees to keep from falling. An armored em was guarding the corpus of Leon Mansfield. He had been sliced in two. Literally. At short range, a flechette gun will do that.

"He came through that tunnel," the em said excitedly, pointing to the opening a few feet above us. "I waited for him to unlock the gate. He dropped to the beach. I told him to freeze, but he raised a pistol. So I blew him away."

"What kind of pistol?"

"Rocket. Every slug carries its own power."

"I know."

"Good penetration at short range," he said professorially. "Inaccurate at long. I guess he stopped Klein."

"I guess so." I nodded. "You were stationed here? By this tunnel exit?"

"Sure."

"Who ordered you?"

"Klein did. He said there was an underground tunnel, and they might try to escape. I figured he was right because when he placed me here, we found a boat. Tied up right over there."

"A boat?" I said. "Birchbark canoe?"

"What?" he said. "No, it was a little plastic runabout with an electric kicker. We took it away last night."

I turned to go back.

"Hey, Dr. Flair," he whispered.

I stopped. He looked about furtively.

"See what I found in the pocket of his raincoat," he said.

He showed me. Three. Genuine. Indian. Arrowheads.

"You think I should turn them in?" he asked.

"No, keep them," I said. "They're not important."

So I drove back to New York alone. No Leon Mansfield. No Burton Klein. I tried to think of nothing. I tried alpha. I tried self-hypnosis. Failure. So I gave myself over to it. Remembering. Computing. I did not, honestly, believe I could have foreseen from the input.

Paul Bumford was waiting for me when I drove through the gates of the compound. I didn't get out of the car. He came over to my window and bent down. His face was ashen.

"Burton Klein was stopped?" he said.

"Yes. And Leon Mansfield. And Alice Hammond. And Vernon DeTilly."

"My God," he breathed. "Nick, what happened?"

I tried to keep my voice as normal as I could.

"Listen carefully, Paul," I said. "I want you to go to the pad, requisition a copter, and go over to Ellis. There I want you to check passenger registers for the twenty-four hours preceding and following the stopping of Frank Lawson Harris. Only the hypersonic flights to and from San Francisco."

"Nick," he said, "what am I looking for?"

"Goddamn you!" I screamed at him. "Can't you follow orders? Get moving!"

He stumbled away, shocked, glancing back nervously over his shoulder.

I tracked precisely then. I returned the sedan to the motor pool. I got a receipt for it. I returned the restricted material to the NDO's (Night Duty Officers) of my Genetics, Chimerism, and Neurosurgery Teams. I got receipts. I returned the empty carton and concealed transmitter to the NDO of the Electronics Team. I got a receipt. I was functioning.

Then I went back to my apartment. I took a hot shower, taped ribs and all, and pulled on a plastisilk robe. Butterflies in flight on a dark-green background. I mixed a large vodka-and-Smack. I turned out all the lights, settled down in the darkness.

I was on my third drink, almost dozing, when the doorbell chimed. I rose, switched on lights. I opened the door.

Paul stood there, trembling. I pulled him inside, locked the door behind him, handed him my drink. He drained it, just swallowed it down as fast as he could, then looked about wildly, gasping.

"N-n-n," he stammered.

I got him over to the couch and seated. He bent far over, head down between his knees. That was encouraging; he was beginning to function. I went into the nest to get two phenothiazines from my cabinet. He popped the slugs dry without asking what they were.

We sat quietly for a while.

"When did you compute it?" he asked finally.

"On the trip back."

"Do you want to know what I found? Or *do* you know?"

"I can guess. I may not have the times exactly right. Angela flew to San Francisco the day before Harris was stopped. On the night he inhaled the fiddled Somnorific, she flew back. She was in New York for two or three hours. Maybe four. Then she turned around and went right back to California."

"Close enough." He groaned. "Nick, what are we going to *do*?"

"Do? We're not going to do anything."

"You mean she's going to get away with it?"

"Yes," I said. "She is."

"But her name is on the passenger register!"

"So? She came back because she forgot something. Or she had an important meeting with a pol or a supplier that night. Do you really want me to take those passenger lists to the Chief Director and claim they are proof that Angela Teresa Berri committed homicide?"

"Then she did it?"

"Of course."

"Herself?"

"Had to be. Harris would let her into his apartment. Gladly. He was on her Headquarters Staff. She had probably used him before. So she used him again—and left a present. The fiddled Somnorific."

"Then she went back for the container?"

"Oh, no. She was in California by then. Mansfield picked it up. He could get by any lock. He had a talent for it."

"But why would he do it?"

"For love. He had dreams."

"What about tonight? How did she fiddle that?"

"Double, triple, quadruple-cross. At least. She promises Mansfield a lot of love to assassinate Klein. She tells him there's an escape tunnel Klein doesn't know about. Then, in her briefing of Klein, she tells him there's an escape tunnel to the river, and he better guard it. Pretty?"

"But you were scheduled to brief Klein and Mansfield. Until your mother got worse, and you went on a threeday. What if you had been here to brief them, and told them both about the tunnel, and warned Mansfield it would be guarded?"

I shrugged.

"She would have thought of some other way to stop them."

"I can understand her stopping Mansfield. After all, he knew she had stopped Harris. But why Klein?"

"That's sad." I took a deep breath. "He wanted to drive back with me. Said, quote, 'I've got to tell someone. I don't know how to handle it.' Unquote. He probably had evidence that Angela is on the suck."

Suddenly, unexpectedly, Paul laughed. It might have been the phenothiazine.

"But why us?" he asked finally. "Why did she bring us into this whole thing?"

"Paul"—I sighed—"you still don't compute this ef. She doesn't think the way we do. We see problems. She sees opportunities. That's very *political* thinking. We must learn to think that way."

"Nick, I'm not tracking."

"Let's imagine we're Angela," I said. "Here is her input of, say, a few months ago. One: She's on the suck and learns that Burton Klein suspects it. Two: She realizes the Satrat is being fiddled. That's serious; it's her responsibility. Three—very essential this: She has a hyperactive desire for power. Political power. Up the PS ladder. Become Director of Bliss. Sooo.... She assigns Frank Harris to Pub-Op, Inc., to help uncover the Satrat rigging. He comes up with the name of Lydia Ferguson. Beautiful. To you and me—a problem. To Angela—an opportunity. But Harris isn't moving fast enough. Maybe he has an operative reaction to the ef. It's possible. I know. And Klein is getting closer. Now Angela has to consider a time factor. How much time has she got before Klein blows the whistle? Or someone in Washington starts wondering why the Satrat is so high while the terrorism rate is increasing?"

"My God," Paul breathed. "I'd have cracked."

"Would you?" I said. "Not our Angela. She breathes better when the oxygen is thin. She computes carefully. Probably all of three minutes. I'm not joking. She's not a thinker; she's a feeler. Primeval. She stops Harris. She brings us in to make certain she can pin a homicide conviction on Lydia Ferguson via the Individual Microbiological Profile she knows we've been working on. If Lydia is taken for homicide and crimes against the state, her father, DIROB, has to resign. *Has* to. At least. If he can avoid arrest himself on suspected complicity. It all computes for Angela. A dream. Klein is stopped. Mansfield is stopped. And along the way, Frank Harris, Alice Hammond, and Vernon DeTilly are all stopped. Angela couldn't care less."

He shook his head in wonderment.

"Nick, she scares me."

"Does she? She is of our species. She belches, farts, pisses, defecates, bleeds, stops—even as you and I."

"What do you suppose she's doing now?"

"Now? This minute? Probably gulping the Chief Director."

"Nick!"

"I mean it. Within a week she'll be DIROB."

"And you?"

"I'll be Deputy Director of the Satisfaction Section."

"You'll take it?"

"Of course."

"Payoff?"

"Well . . . really a token of her regard. Angela doesn't have to do it. She knows that. I couldn't prove a bit of what I've just told you. But she'll toss me a bone to keep me happy. That's the way she functions."

"What about me, Nick? Can I be your Assistant Deputy Director of Security and Intelligence?"

I looked at him pityingly.

"Paul, you still haven't computed how this ef's brain works. It's my guess she'll move up to DIROB. Her first official act will be to transfer Security and Intelligence to Washington, as part of her Headquarters Staff. She doesn't want another Burton Klein situation."

He nodded despondently.

"But if I get DEPDIRSAT, you can have Research and Development. With Mary Bergstrom as your Executive Assistant. And three secretaries. Corner office. Does that please you?"

"Sure, Nick."

I looked at him sympathetically.

"It's difficult to acknowledge you've been played for a fool, isn't it?"

"Yes," he agreed. "Very difficult."

"It is for me, too. Let's go to bed."

"Oh, yes!" he cried.

I punished him until we were both panting with pleasure. Finally I pushed him away. We lay gasping.

"ESP?" I asked.

He nodded.

I turned onto my side, scrawled one word on a pad on the bedside table. Then we set to again, flopping like spawning salmon.

Later, not having disengaged or even moved, I said drowsily, "What is it?"

"One word, or more?" he asked.

"One."

"Revenge!" he said.

I showed him my scribbled note: "Patience."

"Oh, God." He groaned. "How could we have been so far apart?"

"Not really," I said.

Book Y

Y-1

So it came to pass in the Department of Bliss. . . .

Angela Teresa Berri became DIROB. I, Nicholas Bennington Flair, became DEPDIRSAT. Paul Thomas Bumford became AssDepDirRad, with Mary Margaret Bergstrom his Executive Assistant.

Angela Berri's first official edict as Director of Bliss, as I had predicted, transferred the personnel, duties, and responsibilities of the Division of Security & Intelligence to her headquarters staff in Washington, D.C. It reduced my Section to three Divisions, but I was not disappointed.

I told Paul: "At least it proves I'm beginning to compute the way she does."

"It also means a lot of problems for us," Paul grumbled. "Now we are required to go to her for a security check on anyone. And as for investigating her, forget it."

"You're too easily discouraged," I said. "What any brain can do, a better brain can undo. Remember, as DEPDIRSAT I now award contracts to independent servers and suppliers of my Section."

My complacency was stopped almost immediately.

Angela Berri's second edict came in the form of a printed notice, return receipt requested. To all ranks, PS-3 and higher. . . . Henceforth, all bids involving contracts in excess of 50,000 new dollars would be processed by DIROB's headquarters staff.

"Well?" Paul said.

"Pretty," I acknowledged. "She's still one step ahead of me—and anyone else in the Department computing heavy larceny. Notice the cutoff limit—fifty thousand new dollars. That's the way this ef operates: Scatter crumbs to the peasants so they won't become too jealous of cake on the lord's plate."

"What are you going to do about it?" Paul asked.

"At the moment? Learn my new service."

That is what I did. I believe Paul Bumford served just as diligently learning the duties of his new rank. I assisted him when I could, but it wasn't often. He came up to my penthouse apartment a few times, usually to ask questions about those privy matters he had not been aware of: the restricted projects I had initiated.

In turn, I received little assistance from Angela Berri in mastering my new service. I could appreciate that; she had her own new service to rule, more intricate than mine. I saw her at monthly DOB meetings in Washington, but most of our contacts during the early summer of 1998 were on the flasher, brief and businesslike. We were both learning to swim in new waters.

After one of those DOB staff meetings, at a reception at her luxurious apartment in the Watergate Complex, she called me into the study. Art Roach was present, standing by the door while Angela and I talked. Roach was now Chief, Security & Intelligence, for the entire Department of Bliss.

My initial impression of the em had been correct; he *was* cold. A tall, rawboned figure. Close-cropped hair, so blond it was almost white; pink scalp showed through. Large, protuberant ears. Bloodless lips. Eyes as colorless as water.

He listened, blinking slowly, as Angela told me that Lydia Ann Ferguson, Dr. Thomas J. Wiley, Tod DeTilly, and Dr. Henry L. Hammond had been drained.

"Could I scan their journals?" I asked. "Or hear the tapes?"

"You have no need to know," Angela said.

I computed the reason for that: Lydia Ferguson hadn't confessed to stopping Frank Harris.

"I hope you destroyed the organization," I said.

"Not completely," Angela said. She was toying with a letter opener on her desk. A miniature Turkish scimitar. "Art and I felt it would be unwise to stop the entire apparatus. Others might start a similar association under another name. By leaving a skeleton of the Society of Obsos intact, we can infiltrate it. Keep an eye on their activities. Learn the identities of new recruits. Clamp down any time we want to. Nick, we've got to get the terrorism level down and the Satrat up."

"I hope, at least, you've cleaned out my Section," I said blandly.

"Of course," Angela said blandly. "Almost a hundred objects."

"That's fine," I said blandly.

I repeated this conversation to Paul Bumford the following day.

"Do you think what she said was operative?" he asked.

"Operative to the point where I asked about SATSEC. After that, a lot of kaka. I'm certain we still have members of the Society of Obsoletes in the Section. But in addition, we now have Art Roach's doubles. Save yourself, Paul."

He nodded grimly.

Y-2

It wasn't until after the July Fourth threeday that I felt I had mastered the routine of DEPDIRSAT. I could begin to act on what I had been computing since Angela Berri made a fool of me. At that point in time, my plan was vague. My only input was the ef herself: shrewd, ambitious, greedy. The shrewdness I could not condition. The ambition I was powerless to control. I could manipulate the greed.

It began innocently enough. Everything I did had to appear innocent. I asked Phoebe Huntzinger to have dinner with me at *La Bonne Vie*. It couldn't have been more public.

The Assistant Deputy Director of the Division of Data & Statistics was an uncommonly attractive ef. Not yellow, not tan, not café au lait. Not bronze, nor dark. She was *black*, with a purplish undertone to the epidermis.

She must have carried Benin genes; the characteristics were unmistakable: aquiline nose with splayed nostrils; almond-shaped eyes, large and slanted; wide, sculpted lips curved as artfully as a bow. It was not difficult to imagine that more than a century ago she might have been a favorite of the Oba's court in southern Nigeria. Now she ruled one of the largest computer installations in the US. Not too surprising. The Bini were famous for their prowess with numbers.

We ordered. I lighted her cannabis cigarette.

"How's the new service, Nick?"

Her voice was deep, throaty, without being thick. Good resonance.

"Getting settled in. I think I'll find it profitable."

"Good. Anything I can do to help. . . ."

"Thanks, Phoebe. I may take you up on that. I see the Satrat's down again."

"I know." She sighed. "It irritates me. The raw data we're processing now from the polling contractors is uniformly lower than their tapes of just a few months ago."

"Don't worry about it," I soothed her. "It will stabilize soon."

She raised those huge, lustrous eyes to stare at me. Her expression didn't change.

"Fiddling?" she said.

I nodded.

"It's been stopped," I said. "Just keep using the raw data."

"I knew it had to be that. Nick, it's going to make my long-range predictions inoperative for awhile."

"I know."

"It would help if I knew the time period when the fiddled tapes were supplied. Then I could excise that and reconstruct my projective curves."

"I can't tell you that, Phoebe, I honestly can't. I just don't know. Do the best you can with what you have."

We had a profitable dinner. I kept her talking about her service. She was voluble about the regenerative potentialities of computers: devices capable of breeding. I found it interesting.

"Phoebe," I said finally, "I want you to take a trip."

"A trip? Where to, Nick?"

"The Denver Field Office. You know they're doing most of our cyborg research. I see their reports, and they've been stalled fro months now. They're working with soft laser beams, precisely aimed, to pick up electrical activity from the central nervous system, much in the manner of an EEG. Then the signals are amplified and analyzed by computer with a typewriter printout."

"What hardware are they using?"

"A Golem Mk. III."

"Very good. What's the problem?"

"They've been able to pick up sensations from the objects' brains and iden-tify them: colors, scents, sounds, and so forth."

She was interested now, leaning forward across the table.

"Shape identification?" she asked.

"Yes, on a primitive level. The object is shown a circle, square, star, cross, and the computer spells it out: circle, square, star, cross. Good results. But they're stuck there. They can't pick up conceptions."

"The problem may be in the equipment or in the technique. The laser beam may not be sensitive enough. It may be poorly aimed. Their signal booster may not be strong enough. The Golem may be poorly programmed."

"That's why I'd like you to go out there, Phoebe. Check into every phase of their technology. See if you can suggest improvements. All right?"

"Of course, Nick. I could use a change of scene. But why the sudden interest in cyborgs?"

"Lewisohn's condition. He shows no improvement. I'm trying to foresee every eventuality."

The next day, about 1400, I flashed the copter pad. I asked if Phoebe Huntzinger was there, They told me she had taken off for Kennedy about an hour previously. I thanked them and switched off.

I went over to her office. Her Executive Assistant was a sluggish em with the unlikely name of Pomfret Wingate. Known as Pommy. He was the or-ganizer and director of the Section's little-theater group. They called them-selves the Masque & Mirth Society. Atrocious players.

I chatted with Pommy a few minutes. Or rather, I listened to Pommy chat, describing the Society's coming season that would include a nude performance of *King Lear*.

Finally I mentioned casually that I was serving on the budget and wanted to scan a list of contractors and suppliers the Section had dealt with for the past five years.

"Surely, Mr. Flair," he said. "But it won't include anything over fifty thousand new dollars. Those reels were sent to Washington. DIROB's orders."

"I know," I said. "I just want to scan the small fry so I can make an informed estimate of expenses for the coming year. Could you get that for me?"

"Surely, Mr. Flair," he said.

I sat at Phoebe Huntzinger's cleared desk, running reels through her viewing machine. I made heavy notes in case anyone looked in and wondered what I was doing.

I was looking for a regular supplier who specialized in one particular product, who was not located on the East Coast, and who operated with a limited physical plant and few servers. I found three possibles.

I finished in an hour, returned the reels to Pommy, thanked him profusely.

"Surely, Mr. Flair," he said. "Don't forget the nude *King Lear* on October tenth."

"Who's playing Lear?" I asked.

"I am." He giggled. "Nothing but a beard!"

"Wouldn't miss it for the world," I said.

I took the list back to my office and sat computing the three candidates. I looked them up in a thick *Directory of Contractors and Suppliers*, as an indepsec publication of the Department of Bliss. One of the three was eliminated immediately. It was too large; it was publicly owned. A second I set aside because of its sole product: electronic prosthetic devices for the armless and legless. I couldn't see any logical justification for a sudden increase in its sales.

The third supplier listed was small, located in San Diego, California. It specialized in hallucinogenic drugs: mescaline, cannabis, bufotenin, lysergic acid diethylamide, etc. Its sales to SATSEC had averaged about 30,000 new dollars annually over the past five years. The directory stated it was a privately owned corporation, employed twenty-four servers, had a good credit rating, owned a somewhat obso physical plant valued at approximately 200,000 new dollars. There was no record of any government prosecution or even investigation of illegal trafficking, mislabeling, or unexplained loss of inventory. Unusual for a company producing hallucinogens.

The name was Scilla Pharmaceuticals, Inc. I wasn't sure I could afford it, assuming they were open to a tender. I spent the evening computing my personal finances.

Over the years, my mother and father had each given me 50,000 new dollars, the legal gift limit. It was tax-exempt and would reduce taxes on their estates when they stopped. And although I had never lived frugally, I had managed to save a small proportion of my rank-rate, lecture fees, love from writing assignments, etc.

I kept my cash balance in the American National Bank to a necessary minimum. Most of my assets were in common stocks of publicly held corporations. About 50 percent was invested in Flair Toys, my father's company.

I trusted his acumen. The other half was almost all in drug manufacturers. I usually knew, weeks or months in advance, when a pharmaceutical company was close to the solution of a difficult research problem, and might announce a new commercial product shortly.

In 1979, all stock exchanges in the US had been merged into one, the Consolidated Stock Exchange, CSE. For a monthly leasing fee, they provided an electronic push-button device, slightly smaller than a shoebox, that tied in with your flasher line. Simply by punching out the symbol of your stock, the current price was shown on a small screen.

That evening I ran my list of love affairs through the stock scanner (popularly known as the "suicide machine"). The total came to a little more than 150,000 new dollars. A few miscellaneous investments in insurance policies, government, and municipal bonds, etc., plus my ANB balance, brought my total to almost 200,000 new dollars. It would, I judged, be sufficient, either converted into cash or as collateral for a loan.

I flashed Paul Bumford. He came on screen in a dressing gown, holding an official record I recognized as a directory of DIVRAD objects serving in Field Offices. He was still learning.

"Paul," I said, "you've been serving too hard. Come on up for a few minutes."

"Nick, I really better—"

"It's a lovely night," I said. "But wear a sweater or jacket. We'll sit out on the terrace and have a drink."

He stared at me a moment. Then he computed.

"Ten minutes," he said.

"Fine," I said lightly. "See you then."

The last few months had mutated him. He was no longer pudgy. The girlish flush was gone from his skin. The face was thinner, harder. His whole bearing was more confident. He carried himself with an almost authoritative arrogance. Serving as administrator of so many objects had done that.

We took our vodka-and-Smacks out onto the terrace. It was a gorgeously mild night, but at that height the wind had an edge. We sat in the shadowed corner where, not too long ago, we had plotted with Angela Berri. My penthouse was swept electronically once a week. But that meant nothing. The sweeper might be reporting directly to Angela Berri. Or to Art Roach.

I went through it as briefly as I could. It wasn't even a plan. It was a plan for a plan. I blocked it out for him, suggesting what might be done, alternative approaches, what we might hope from luck and chance. I finished.

"Well?" I asked.

"Complex," he said.

"Richly complex," I agreed. "But only in the details. The overall design is elegant. Almost pretty. I gather you're not interested."

He leaned forward, hands clenched between his knees. He almost hissed. I was startled by the venom in his face.

"You think I haven't been computing this?" he demanded. Voice low and intense. "Every minute. Waking and sleeping. Ways. Means. Methods. Plots, Plans. Including inviting her out to lunch, saying, 'Oh, Angela, look at that woman in the funny hat,' and then slipping a bomb in her drink."

"I know," I said sympathetically. "But that's stupidity."

"I *know* it is," he said passionately. "I knew it when I thought it. But I thought it, Nick, I actually *thought* it. Your way is best."

"You're sure?"

"I can't better it. Dangerous. For both of us. But the possibility of success is there. Jesus, Nick, you've got to be so *careful*."

"Not only me," I said. "You, too. Then you're in?"

"Whatever you ask," he said.

I leaned forward. He leaned forward. We kissed. Then we leaned back. Both of us took a deep breath. Knowing we had crossed a line.

"What's first?" he asked.

"That lawyer in Oakland—the one who discovered who owns Angela's beachhouse. What's his name?"

"Sam Gershorn."

"Flash him tomorrow. From outside the compound. Tell him you have an obso friend who's retiring and thinking about the San Diego area. Ask Gershorn if he can recommend an attorney in the San Diego area who handles investments, especially industrial properties and real estate."

"I'll do it tomorrow."

We started to rise from our chairs, then Bumford settled back. He touched his lips with two pressed forefingers.

"What input do you have on Art Roach?" he asked.

"Not much. Subjective reactions. Not a profitable em. Potentially violent."

"Yes. I've been making a few cautious inquiries. Here and there. He used around the Section a lot. All efs. A stallion. And not nice. Rough."

"Psychopathic?"

"Probably. Sado. He put one ef into a hospice. About a year ago."

"I didn't hear anything about that."

"Angela glossed it."

"She did?" I pondered that tidbit. "Yes, that makes sense. That's how she knew Burton Klein was investigating her. Roach was her em inside DIVSEC. She bought him by covering up his assault. I told you: She doesn't see problems, she sees opportunities."

"He's a danger, Nick. As much as she is."

"I know."

"We should get a control on him."

Paul was right. I computed the problem, then forced myself to compute the opportunity. It would be difficult, with Art Roach stationed in Washington. But it could be fiddled.

"You're not going to like it, Paul," I said.

"I told you, whatever you ask."

"Your new secretary. Maya Leighton."

"What about·her?"

"Bisexual?"

"Possibly. I think so. Why?"

"Is she using Mary Bergstrom?"

"I doubt it. Maybe. I don't know. Is it important?"

"Very. We can't afford to alienate Mary. Can you find out if they're users?"

"I'll try."

"Paul, *do* it. Casually, humorously, if you can. If not, a direct question."

"All right. Then?"

"I've got to use Maya."

"Nick!"

"Got to."

"I don't follow."

"To set up Art Roach."

"Ahh."

"You don't profit from the idea of my using Maya?"

"No."

"Paul, it's necessary."

"I know, I know. How will you get her together with Roach?"

"No idea. Yet. I'm just winging it. But the first step is determining if she's right for the service. What do you think? Is she ambitious?"

"Very."

"Sexually curious?"

"Yes."

"On anything? Smoking? Drinking? Popping?"

"On *everything*. But she functions. And very well."

"So?"

"Yes. You may be right, Nick. You always are. I'll set it up."

"No, *I'll* set it up. Friday night. You and Mary Bergstrom and Maya Leighton come up about 2100. We'll have a few drinks, smoke a little hemp, talk a little business. Nothing about *this*. Understand?"

"Of course."

"During the evening, I'll get Maya aside and suggest she leave with you and Mary, and then come back up here about a half-hour later. You know nothing about it."

"I compute, Nick."

"She may return or she may not. If she doesn't, we'll have to find another ef. If she does, I'll take it from there. Paul, are you certain you control Mary Bergstrom?"

"Certain."

"Are you users?"

"No."

"Then how do you control her?"

"Well. . . . Well, we talk. I listen to her. I even listen to her play the flute. She doesn't have any friends. So I—"

"Paul? What is it? Do you have an investment in this ef?"

"Nick, I sweat to you, I don't know. I don't really know. That's operative. I do know she'll do whatever I say."

"That's good enough for me. Let's get moving on this."

"Thank God! At last!"

After he left I had another drink. I paced the floor. I knew what was bothering me. *I* should have thought of the idea of getting a hook into Art Roach. Paul Bumford was not only becoming more confident, he was creating fresh and operative ideas. I wasn't certain that development was lovable.

I took an eight-hour Somnorific.

Y-3

On Friday morning, I sat down to a breakfast of dissolved orange-flavored concentrate (500 mg of ascorbic acid per teaspoonful), probisks, and a hot cup of coftea. As I munched and sipped, I scanned the front page of my facsimile *Times*.

The lead story, under a three-column head on the *left*-hand side (human behavior analysts had finally realized that most non-Judaic objects scanned from left to right) carried a Washington, D.C., dateline. It concerned a speech delivered by Angela Berri, Director of Bliss, to the national convention of the Actuarial Guild of America. Angela stated at the outset that the ideas she would express were based on the concepts of Hyman R. Lewisohn.

A radical revision of the Social Security laws was proposed. An object who had contributed to the SS fund all his serving life, and to which his employers had contributed, would have an equity in that fund. It would not end when he stopped. It could be bequeathed. It would be part of his estate.

Such a law, if enacted, would mean a revolutionary adjustment of Social Security deduction rates. An upward adjustment, of course. It would also mean the US Government was getting into the life insurance business. I could well believe the New York *Times* report that Angela's proposal had been greeted by the assembled actuaries with "incredulous murmurs."

That was of no importance to me. What I found of interest was Lewisohn's basic conception. For some time, I had suspected that all the ideas from his prodigious brain were not simply fragmentary answers to fragmentary problems. I imagined that extraordinary em had conceived a Plan, and every suggestion he made was part of a visualized design.

That filthy, cantankerous dwarf was putting together a new world, *his* world. I could not perceive its delineation. But I knew, *knew*, there was a grand Lewisohn Plan. He was creating a mosaic, a piece here, a piece there, chuckling obscenely. I found it a stress to manipulate SATSEC. He read his obso novels, vilified his doctors and nurses, scorned the rot of his corpus, and jauntily encompassed us all.

The moment I arrived at my office I flashed the Chief Resident at Rehabilitation & Reconditioning Hospice No. 4. He came on screen almost immediately, with his habitual manner of expecting every call to presage disaster. Dr. Luke Warren was a perennially worried little em. His field was biomedicine, and he was good. Not just competent, but *good*.

"Luke," I said, "how are you?"

He told me—at length. I had heard the story before: Hyman R. Lewisohn was destroying his sanity.

"Insulting, is he?" I asked. Knowing the answer.

"Insulting? Nick, *that* I could take. But he's obscene. Yesterday he threw a full bedpan at the morning nurse. His language and habits are filthy. The only way I can get anyone to attend him is to bribe them with extra threedays. We had to put him in restraint to clean him up, and then he complained to the Chief Director who ordered me never to do that again. He pulls out his tubes, spits out his pills, urinates on the floor. Nick, he's a beast."

"I know, I know," I said. "Luke, you've got a megaproblem; no doubt about it. How is he responding to treatment?"

"Not good. Want to go to marrow transplant?"

"No. Not yet. It'll incapacitate him for too long. Have you ever used the BCG vaccine with irradiated tumor cells?"

"A few times. Nick, it just postpones the inevitable. I think we'd do better to go to the marrow now."

"Tell you what. Suppose I come down next week and we'll talk about it. Maybe I can persuade him to stop acting like a depraved child."

"Oh, God, would you do that? It would be a big help."

"I'll flash you on Monday and we'll set a time. Don't tell him I'm coming. But alert your team; I'll want a colloquy."

I switched off and looked at my next week's schedule. That would be an all-day consultation. Lewisohn was suffering from acute myelogenous leukemia. There were several methods of treatment; if one didn't serve, you tried another. You hoped the patient would hang on until you found something effective.

Ellen Dawes came in for the morning ration of real coffee. She was her usual smiling, pleasant, unflappable self; a good way to start a hectic day.

When Angela Berri had moved to Washington, she had taken two of her four secretaries with her. That left me two short. I brought Ellen with me. Now I was one down. Paul Bumford, with the addition of Maya Leighton, had his appropriate three. But of course, I had wall-to-wall plasticarp while his, in my former office, ended twelve inches from the baseboard. Also, I had a private nest, a small kitchen, and windows on three sides.

I had an 0930 meeting scheduled with Frances and Frank von Liszte the twin Assistant Deputy Directors of the Division of Law & Enforcement. I went over to their conference room, at their request, since they wanted to make a presentation that involved big charts, graphs, visual aids, etc. Also, they wanted the top objects of their staff to be present. As I had expected, the meeting dealt with the legal problems of inheritance generated by the Biological Revolution.

At that point in time, we had developed fourteen methods of mammalian reproduction, seven of which had been used successfully on human objects:

1. Artificial insemination
2. Artificial enovulation
3. Parthenogenesis
4. Fertilization *in vitro*, the fetus brought to "birth" in an artificial placenta
5. Auto-adultery (resulting only in ef offspring)
6. Embryonic cloning
7. Sexual intercourse

This list, of course, did not include embryonic or gonadal transplants, which posed similar legal problems.

In artificial insemination, did the child inherit from the mother's husband or from her donor? Could the husband sue for divorce on the grounds of adultery—even if he had agreed to the impregnation but changed his mind later?

In artificial enovulation, did the child inherit from the ef who bore it, from the ef who donated the fertilized egg, from the em who provided the sperm, or from the husband of the ef who bore the child?

In cloning, where as many as twenty identical offspring had been produced from a single embryo, did all progeny inherit equally?

I had heard all these problems discussed before, endlessly. But in that morning's conference, new input was added. The von Liszts, after a great deal of research, had come up with reasonably firm statistics on the number of objects in the US bred by methods other than using. They also displayed charts showing computerized projective curves on the number of such objects to be expected in five, ten, twenty-five, and fifty years. It was brain-boggling.

"Well," I sighed, after the presentation, "what solution do you suggest—or was this just a preview of my future migraine?"

I derived a lot of profit from Frances and Frank von Liszt. They were attractive twins with their infantile complexions, flaxen hair, light blue eyes, young profiles. I could believe the rumor that they used each other. Why not?

Now, speaking alternately, they explained what they proposed. They were getting nowhere with bar associations. The debates on recommended legislation were futile. What the von Liszts suggested was an official government "position paper" that would at least give a basis for logical and informed discussion by interested jurists.

I questioned them and their staff closely. Did a child born of electrical parthenogenesis have *any* legal father other than a dry cell? If clones were brought to "birth" at different times, either in an artificial placenta or by implant, would the one born first be the senior, inheriting from the natural father?

It was a lively discussion. I enjoyed it. I had no law degree, but I knew molecular genetics better than they. I finally approved of their plan to draw up a preliminary government position paper. I also suggested they give some thought to a discussion with academics of the government's Science Academy with a view to creating a new field of Biological Jurisprudence: objects conditioned in genetics *and* law.

I went back to my office, not optimistic that their proposed position paper would ever be allowed distribution to the civilian bar associations for which it was intended. Too controversial. And if it was distributed, would it help clarify the issues? The kaka would continue, perhaps even intensified.

Paul Bumford was waiting for me. I took him into my inner office and closed the door.

"All set for tonight?" I asked.

"Yes. We'll be up about 2100."

"No fancy dress. Just an informal get-together."

I was speaking to the suspected sharer as much as to him. He computed.

"Another thing, Paul," I said. "Please get out a Telex to all the Hospices asking how many parabiosis volunteers each can furnish for a leukemic victim. Don't mention Lewisohn by name. The less publicity on this the better."

"You're going to parabiosis?"

"Not immediately. Just preparing. Anything else?"

"No, that's all. Walk me to the elevator?"

"Sure."

In the crowded corridor, a zipsuited throng was noisily waiting for high-speed elevators to take them down to the building cafeteria.

"San Diego," Paul murmured. "Hawkley, Goldfarb and Bensen. Got that?"

"Yes."

"Hawkley is the only senior partner still alive. Sam Gershorn says he's one year younger than God. But he has some smart junior partners."

"Good. Can you come up early tonight? Just you. About 2030. The efs at 2100."

"Uh-huh. Important?"

"No. Just talk. For the Tomorrow File."

"Fine. I'll fix it. See you at 2030."

As DEPDIRSAT, I carried weight at the motor pool. I had first choice of the Section limousine, a huge, black, diesel-powered Mercedes-Benz. Reserved for my exclusive use was an electronically powered two-door Chevrolet. I took the small sedan and drove up to Canal Street, to one of the public flasher stations scattered around the city. I wore a light raincoat over my zipsuit.

I sat in a small booth and after about five minutes of spelling the names for Information operators, I finally got through to Hawkley, Goldfarb & Bensen in San Diego. I made certain my raincoat was zipped up to the neck; my uniform wasn't visible.

A plumpish, matronly secretary came on.

"Hawkley, Goldfarb and Bensen," she said, in a surprisingly deep, emish voice. "May I serve you?"

"Could I speak to Mr. Hawkley, please? My name is Nicholas Flair. I'm calling from New York."

"I'm sorry, sir. Mr. Hawkley isn't in today. Could you speak to someone else?"

"To Mr. Hawkley's secretary, please. I'd like to make an appointment to meet with Mr. Hawkley."

"Just a moment, please, Mr. Flair. I'll see if she's in."

She went off-screen. A full-color reproduction of one of Van Gogh's self-portraits unexpectedly took her place. And I was treated to a symphonic rendition of Bach's *Jesu, Joy of Man's Desiring*. It was a new device introduced about a year previously. When a commercial operator had to hold a call, she switched on a gadget that simultaneously showed an "ageless painting" and played "immortal music." So the caller wouldn't get bored waiting. I wondered how long it would be before there were similar gadgets showing illustrations from the Kama Sutra and playing "Gimme Head Blues."

When Van Gogh disappeared, and Bach was cut off in midstrain, the ef who appeared was very young, very blond, very—

"Yes, Mr. Flair?" She dimpled. "I am Mr. Hawkley's private secretary. May I serve you?"

"I'm calling from New York," I repeated. "I'm coming out to San Diego next week and would like to make an appointment to meet with Mr. Hawkley to discuss possible investments in real estate and industrial properties in the San Diego area."

"And may I ask who referred you to us, Mr. Flair?"

"You may ask, but I won't answer. It's not important."

She didn't seem shocked, or even surprised by my answer. She was making no notes. I suspected our conversation was being taped.

"Would Tuesday afternoon at 1500 be satisfactory, Mr. Flair?"

"Fine. I'll be there."

"In case Mr. Hawkley is unable to keep the appointment, how may I get in touch with you, sir?"

"Unfortunately, I'll be out of town and unavailable," I said. "But I'll check with you Tuesday morning to confirm the appointment."

I stopped at a government grogshop in the neighborhood and picked up four bottles of Bordeaux. The clerk swore—"On my mother's grave"—the wine had been made from real grapes. I didn't believe him for a minute. In the early 1980's the multinational cartels had started buying up French vineyards. The prices of natural wines and brandies went so high that the only things left for most objects to drink came out of oil wells.

In my office, I had Ellen Dawes get through to Phoebe Huntzinger at our Denver Field Office. It took almost fifteen minutes to locate Phoebe in Denver's Computer Room. When she came on screen, she was wearing white paper coveralls. She looked her usual cool, imperturbable self.

"Nick," she said. "How are you? Checking up on me?"

"Of course," I said. "I thought you might have taken off for Rio. How are you, Phoebe? Any luck?"

"A little. We've tuned the laser and boosted the amplification. The signal is stronger now, sharper, but preliminary tests still don't show much more than they did before."

"Still no conceptions?"

"No. Just sensations and inconclusive tests on simple words like 'Go.' 'Come.' 'Walk.' 'Run.' Things like that. Then we tried emotive words: 'Cry.' 'Shout.' 'Frown.' 'Scream.' 'Smile.' And so forth. A little progress there."

"Fine. I think you're on the right track. Who's the Team Leader?"

"An em named Stanley. That's his last name. Peter Stanley. Know him?"

"No. Good?"

"Well. . . . He's enthusiastic'."

"That helps. Is he around now?"

"Just went out for coffee, Nick. Anything I can do?"

"Phoebe, the problem there may not be the technology. It may be in the experimental objects. When Stanley gets back, suggest he try hallucinogens on the objects prior to test. Especially lysergic acid diethylamide. If it intensifies sensation the way the freaks claim, it may get a conception through to the computer."

"Wild idea," she said.

"Worth trying. Probably nothing, but you never can tell. If he's short on hallucinogenic drugs, tell him to requisition more. I'll approve."

"I'll tell him, Nick. It's nice out here. I profit from it."

"Don't stay too long. You might not come back."

I was assigned a private serving em from the Maintenance Department to keep my penthouse in order. He was ordered to serve six hours a day, four days a week. I suspected he served about ten hours a week and watched TV the remainder of the time. It was cushy duty. Knowing the customs of the lower Public Service ranks, I supposed he had paid his ruler something for the assignment. In any event, my apartment was kept reasonably clean. I could detect no pilferage or search of my personal effects, so I was satisfied.

The em, a bearded obso, was just going off duty when I arrived home. I gave him one of the bottles of wine I had purchased and told him not to come in on Saturday until after 1200. He asked no questions; the wine was answer enough.

I undressed, slid into bed, napped until 1900. Then I rose, showered, pulled on a fresh summer-weight zipsuit. I wore no underwear. I switched on a music cassette—Vivaldi's *Four Seasons*—opened one of the bottles of Bordeaux, and sampled it. It might not have been produced from grapes, but a clever chemist had compounded it; it was light, dry, with good body and bouquet. Only the acrid aftertaste betrayed its test-tube origins. I tried a drop or two on a plastowel. The stain washed out immediately. That was encouraging. I once performed a similar test with a "genuine grape Burgundy." Not only was the stain indelible, but two hours later there was a hole in the towel.

The air conditioning had been turned on full all day; the apartment was almost painfully cold. I stepped out onto the terrace, sliding the thermopane door closed behind me. I wandered around to the west side. The setting sun looked like a human ovum.

It was a hot July evening, the atmosphere supersaturated, the air smelling distinctly of sulphur. There had been an inversion layer over much of GPA-1 for the past two days; objects doing outdoor service wore masks over nose and mouth, glared at the murky sky with red-rimmed eyes. I went back into the chilled interior thankfully. It might smell of Freon, but it was better than breathing smoke, ash, soot, hydrogen chloride, carbon monoxide, sulphur dioxide, and air that had been filtered through too many lungs before it was my turn.

Paul Bumford arrived promptly at 2030. I poured him a glass of wine. I noted he was wearing a minimum of makeup.

"Let's go out on the terrace for a moment," I said. "I hate to do this to you; it's brutal out there. But I want you to see the sunset. The one advantage of air pollution; magnificent sunrises and sunsets."

We stood at the rail, watching the sun slowly stop. I talked rapidly in a low voice. I recounted my San Diego conversation and the call to Phoebe Huntzinger.

"That Denver project is one possibility for increased use of hallucinogens," I explained. "Tonight, when the efs are here, I'm going to bring up the subject of the Ultimate Pleasure pill. We'll discuss methods of development. Follow my lead. Volunteer nothing. Let one of them suggest a hallucinogenic approach. Compute?"

"Yes. But aren't we going at this ass-backward? We don't have the factory yet."

"We will," I said. "Scilla or some other. While we're serving on the factory, we've got to plan increased need for LSD, mescaline, and all the rest. Check your files of ongoing projects, and see what you can do. On Tuesday, you'll have to go to San Diego with me. A perfect cover: I'm taking you out to meet the Field Office objects and familiarize you with their service. All right?"

"Fine."

"I'll make the arrangements. We'll take the courier flight out Tuesday morning. I'll come back Wednesday morning. You stay on a day or two, serving with the FO. I'll see Hawkley on Tuesday afternoon. I'm taking civilian clothes, but all you'll need are zipsuits."

"Going to use your real name, Nick?"

"Have to. Sooner or later I'll have to identify myself and sign papers. We can't afford the dangers of a fiddled BIN card. Besides, the Field Office is in San Diego, and my father has a factory out there. There must be a hundred objects in that city who know me by sight. Too risky to forge a new identity. I'll chance it."

"How will Hawkley contact you?"

"On Monday I'll go uptown and lease a mailing address, or desk space— whatever it takes. If I have to show my BIN card, I will. But if I pay in advance, I doubt if they'll want identification. See any flaws?"

He pondered a moment.

"What if Hawkley doesn't go for it?"

"Then I'll stay on another day, or until I find a sharp attorney who can handle it all and keep me hidden."

"Nick, you're taking all the risk. I'm not doing anything."

"Oh, but you will," I assured him. "You will, indeed. If the deal goes through, you may have to pay a visit to Scilla. You'll have good cover: You're checking the facilities of your suppliers. And while you were visiting the DIVRAD Field Office, you thought you'd stop by and say hello, and so forth, and so forth. But all that's futuristic. Right now, the important thing is to get control of that factory and build up its sales. Let's go back in; I'm beginning to sweat."

"You said you had something for the Tomorrow File. Can you talk about it inside?"

"Good point. No, I'll give it to you now. This morning I had a long meet with DIVLAW. They want to draw up an official position paper on how inheritance should be handled in all methods of reproduction. You're familiar with the problems?"

"Yes."

"Incredibly complex. No precedents in litigation. DIVLAW's solution is fragmentary, a hodgepodge. No solution at all. How's this for the Tomorrow File: All created objects, *all* objects, regardless of reproductive technology, become wards of the state. No orphans. No bastards. No daughters. No sons. All objects created have legal equality. The government acts *in loco parentis*. And inherits all. Well?"

"Nick? Are you serious? *No* inheritance? *No* family at all? It would take a century of conditioning."

"It could be done in less," I said. "The difficulty isn't liquidation of the family as a social unit. That's been going on for generations. The sticking point is individual motivation. If an object was prevented by law from bequeathing love to heirs, would the object lose desire to amass it?"

"You mean, how would government inheritability affect the profit motive?"

"Well . . . call it the acquisition drive. A desire to succeed in a capitalistic society. That's the problem."

"Nick, answer me one thing?"

"What's that?"

"Do you have a plan?"

"A plan?"

"A design. A coherent view of the future. The suggestions you've made recently for the Tomorrow File seem to fit a pattern. I can't visualize it. But I sense something there."

I was startled. Exactly what I had thought about Lewisohn's ideas that morning. Paul was no fool. This needed thought, review of my own suggestions, long and careful computation to determine if synthesis was possible. And if it was, would my plan and Lewisohn's be complementary or antithetical? It was interesting.

"I have no plan," I said shortly. "Let's go inside and cool off."

Mary Margaret Bergstrom was a husky ef, solid as a stump, and as shapely. Her face reflected nothing of her intelligence. Features heavy and coarse. Complexion sallow. I looked in vain for animation. The eyes were, if anything, wary. She seemed to have suffered, in the past, some awful hurt, and was determined not to risk pain again. But perhaps I was romanticizing. It was quite possible she was simply overconditioned. It was happening frequently with younger scientists: pure objectivity and complete incapacity to make value judgments.

I courted her while Paul and Maya Leighton inspected my cassette library. I lighted Mary's cannabis cigarette, kept her wine glass filled, strove desperately to find a subject, other than our service, that might rouse her. I found it by accident when I congratulated her on hitting the national lottery for one thousand new dollars.

Within minutes we were having a lively discussion on gambling—odds, horse vs. dog racing, soccer vs. jai alai, roulette vs. chemin de fer, poker vs. gin rummy, and the mathematical possibilities of winning at the daily numbers drawing. Maya and Paul joined us; talked quickened, gestures became more vigorous. I opened the second bottle of wine.

At this point in time, the US Government, in addition to sole ownership of the nation's grogshops, also sponsored lotteries and operated a nationwide chain of betting parlors. All gambling was legalized in 1983, and prostitution a year later. Casinos and bordellos were now as much a part of government activities as day-care centers and veterans' hospitals. The income from bets on sporting events alone was sufficient to reduce the personal contribution rate (formerly the income tax rate) by 5 percent.

I discovered that Mary Bergstrom was an addicted gambler. I wondered if Paul had been aware of it. If so, why hadn't he told me? Mary's knowledge of odds, spreads, points, combinations, and all the other details of wagering was encyclopedic. We listened, fascinated, while she described a system of winning at roulette she was devising with the help of a King Mk. IV computer. We resolved to make a visit, *en masse*, to the Central Park Casino as soon as Mary's system was perfected.

Then our conversation became more general. I drew them into a gossipy discussion of personalities in SATSEC, who was using whom, what marriages were planned, divorces scheduled. My news that Pomfret Wingate was to play the lead in a nude performance of *King Lear* sent the efs into almost hysterical laughter.

"Well"—Paul shrugged—"if it gives him pleasure, why deny him?"

"And speaking of pleasure," I said, rising to turn off the cassette player, "here's a puzzle for you all. What is the greatest pleasure, the ultimate pleasure, a human object can know? Paul?"

"Physical orgasm," he said promptly.

"Mary?"

"Gambling," she said. "And music."

"Maya?"

She was a queenly ef, almost as tall as I. Soon after entering my apartment, she had taken clips from her coiled red hair and let it tumble down her back, to her waist. Her official zipsuit had obviously been altered to display her body to advantage: wide shoulders and hips, narrow waist, long legs.

She had enormous hazel eyes, generous mouth, impudent smile. Her eye shadow was mauve, the false lashes extraordinarily thick. Her ears bore huge clamp rings, not on the lobes but on the pinna. A tooty fashion. Her zipper was pulled low enough to exhibit cleavage. She wore a black velvet mouche, star-shaped, on the upper, shiny bulge of the right breast.

When I spoke her name, asking her the ultimate pleasure a human object could know, she raised her leonine head slowly in a cloud of cannabis smoke and looked at me mockingly.

"The greatest pleasure?" she said. "Almost any pleasure if you surrender to it completely."

"Now that is interesting," I said, "because—"

"Wait a minute, Nick," she said. I think she was smiling. "We've answered. Now it's your turn. What do you think is the ultimate pleasure?"

"That's easy," I said. "Danger."

"Physical danger?" Mary asked.

"Possibly. Perhaps a better word would be peril."

I believe I lied successfully.

Then we were all talking at once. We smoked up a storm, finished the wine, started on petrovod and petronac. The conversation bubbled, ebbed, exploded anew: sex, cannabis, alcohol, drugs, art, music, gambling, danger, dancing, crime—which might be the most pleasurable?

"All in all," I said finally, "you pays your love and you takes your choice. Too bad we can't come up with something to intensify the pleasure of the means we select."

"Drugs can do that," Mary said. "Or so it's said. I've never tried them."

"Drugs?"

"Hallucinogens," Maya said.

"That's an idea I hadn't thought of," I said slowly. "Paul, we might consider that."

"What's this all about?" Mary Bergstrom asked.

"Paul and I were discussing the possibility of developing a pleasure pill, the Ultimate Pleasure pill, the UP. Then we realized we couldn't start until we knew what we were looking for. What *is* the Ultimate Pleasure? There are four of us here. We have at least four different answers."

The efs were interested now, leaning forward intently.

"I still think it could be done," I said. "Hallucinogens would certainly be one line of approach. Paul, this is DIVRAD's service. Why don't you and Mary and Maya try to come up with a plan, a system of attack. What are the immediate goals? Intermediate? Final? How many servers will we need? What specialties? How large a budget? Should we try it here or farm it out to a Field Office? Or is it so big and complex that we need several teams working on it in several places? Could you do that?"

"Of course," Paul said. "The first target, obviously, is a basic conception of what we're looking for. Mary?"

"It could be physiological," she said slowly. "Or emotional. Or mental."

"Or something even deeper," Maya said.

"Deeper?" I said. "Instinctive."

"Perhaps," she said. "Something like that."

Paul and Mary started discussing how they might begin to outline a plan of attack on the problem.

"Maya," I said, "come on into the kitchen and help me make some coffee."

"Real coffee?" she asked.

"Close enough," I said. "After another petronac and another Bold, you won't know the difference."

She laughed and followed me into the kitchen. I asked her to leave with the others and then return a half-hour later.

"All righty," she said blithely.

It didn't seem to make any difference to her.

After they all left I switched the air conditioners to exhaust and got rid of the cannabis smoke. I cleaned up the living room, stacking plastiglasses and ashtrays in the sink. I washed my face with cold water. Gradually the buzzing in my brain dulled to a pleasant drone. I stood erect, closed my eyes, lifted my arms sideways and attempted to touch forefingers over my head. I didn't miss by much.

I might have been reasonably sober, but Maya Leighton was still flying when she came back. She strode in, kicked off her sandals in the living room, and was in the darkened bedroom before I got the front door locked. I left one lamp on, then followed her into the bedroom. Her zipsuit lay in a crumpled heap near the bed. I picked it up, shook it out, draped it over a chairback.

"Sleepy?" I asked.

"Far from it."

Her voice was full, musical, but not as confident as she intended. A slight tremor there. I looked at her, the bed dimly visible in nightlight from the undraped windows. She stared back at me, eyes enormous and black. Glistening. The huge earrings lay on the bedside table.

"What is that on your left thigh?" I asked.

"A tattoo," she said.

"A tattoo of what?"

"A scarab," she said.

"Scarab? That's a dung beetle."

"Yes. A dung beetle. Bite it."

I bit it.

She was lying on her right leg, hip, shoulder. Head pillowed. Hair flung. A lush Circe. Her body was more than baroque. There was extravagant opulence. It came perilously close to being a caricature of an ef's body.

There was a bursting heat in her. Almost feverish. Eyes half-closed, glimmering. Mouth half-open in a pant. But she was conscious and aware. She did not surrender, as Lydia Ferguson had, to her own sensuality. But to my demands. A fine point, but significant.

I used her. Or did she use me? I knew my motive. It was, I thought, more devious than hers. But still. . . .

She seemed hypersensitive. I suspected drugs, but could taste nothing on her lips or tongue but sweet saliva.

I used her painfully, but I could not daunt her. I had to know, you see. I left bruises and the marks of teeth on that tumescent flesh. She did not object or cry out. But opened herself to me, urging on the night.

Y-4

The hypersonic wheeled out over the Atlantic, accelerating, gaining altitude so rapidly that G-force pressed us back against the semireclining seats. I viewed the telescreen as the coastline fell away. We circled again, then passed through the sonic wall with a barely perceptible shudder. The plane straightened, headed west for San Diego at a gentler climb. We pulled up our seatbacks. The white-clad stewardess began pushing her cart down the aisle. Paul Bumford returned to his facsimile *Times*.

"Nick," he said, "look at this."

I glanced down, then settled back, closed my eyes.

"I scanned it," I said. "At breakfast."

It was a short item. Only a few lines. . . .

The corpus of a young ef had been washed ashore near Falmouth, Massachusetts. It had been identified as Martha Wiley, daughter of Dr. Thomas J. Wiley, noted genetic biologist, who had been taken two months previously, charged with subversion and crimes against the state.

"Probably suicide," Paul said.

"Probably," I agreed, my eyes still closed.

Then the stewardess paused at our seats. We each took a plasticup of coftea. Paul also took a package of probisks. He dunked them in the hot brown liquid.

"You're losing a secretary," I told him. "I'm taking Maya Leighton onto my staff."

"All right. She'll work out then? With Art Roach?"

"I think so."

"How will you bring them together?"

"I'll find a way."

"How much will you tell her, Nick?"

"As little as possible. I don't think she'll pry too much. As you said—a good brain."

"I've been thinking about it," he said. "Suicide, I mean. For the Tomorrow File. Making suicide illegal."

"I agree the numbers are horrendous," I said. "Especially among the young. But what do you propose—making suicide a capital crime?"

"I know that's senseless, Nick. But what if the law decreed capital punishment for the suicide's immediate family? Wouldn't that be a deterrent?"

"No," I said. "Suicides are usually in a hyperemotional state. Or extremely neurotic or psychotic. Don't expect them to compute rationally the consequences of their act."

"Did you like her, Nick?"

"Maya? Very much. A puzzle."

"How so?"

"Total surrender. But I can't compute the reason."

"She recognizes it. She suggested it when you asked her to name the ultimate pleasure. So it must be deliberate choice."

"That's what she said. But she may be rationalizing a weakness. We all do it. You are cowardly; I am cautious. You are miserly; I am prudent. You are a spendthrift; I am generous. We all conceal—no, not conceal, but prettify our weaknesses."

"What is your weakness, Nick?"

I laughed.

"My fatal flaw? I want life to have charm."

I closed my eyes again, leaned back, relaxed. I could feel a gentle forward tilt. We had already started letting down for the Pacific.

"I still think suicide belongs in the Tomorrow File," Paul said stubbornly. "A law making it illegal. With penalties stiff enough to make would-be suicides think twice."

I opened my eyes to stare at him.

"Why do you feel so strongly about it, Paul?"

"Because it fits right in with what you've suggested—about the government inheriting healthy organs from stopped objects. And all new objects becoming wards of the state, no matter how they were bred. If those suggestions are valid, then suicide becomes a crime against the state. If you stop yourself, you're destroying government property."

"That's interesting," I said.

We came in low over Point Loma. The cabin telescreen showed a fine view of the harbor: pleasure boats, tuna fleet, Coast Guard cutters. After the jammed frenzy of the N.Y.-D.C. axis, the Southern California scene was open, yawning, whitewashed in the summer sun.

Paul and I splurged, taking one of the new steam-powered cabs to the Strake Hotel in Chula Vista. It was Paul's first trip to San Diego. I pointed out the DIVRAD Field Office as we drove by. He was impressed by the heroic bronze statue of Linus Pauling in front of the main building.

"But it's a small installation, isn't it, Nick?"

"Larger than you think. The labs are underground."

We claimed our hotel suite. I flashed Hawkley's office and confirmed my appointment at 1500. Then we cabbed back to the FO, arriving a little before 1000. They had been alerted to our coming; we were taken directly to Lab 1 where the Chief was waiting for us.

The San Diego Field Office specialized in molecular and biochemical genetics. Their list of accomplishments was impressive.

The servers were remarkably young, eager, innovative. They spawned a thousand new ideas annually. Most proved loveless, but it didn't seem to discourage them. I had noted that about DIVRAD servers: The farther they were removed from the political pressures of New York and Washington, the more freewheeling and creative they became.

The Chief of the FO was one of my favorites, Nancy Ching, a jolly yellow ef as cute and plump as an Oriental doll. On my last trip to San Diego, Nancy and I had become demented on plum wine and amphetamine, and had used each other with much giggling delight.

She greeted me with a hot, smeary kiss, grabbed our arms, and dragged us on a whirlwind tour of her labs, chattering incessantly. She spoke a rapid patois of technical jargon and tooty slang. I caught about half of it; Paul seemed to have no trouble at all. In a few moments he was talking in similar fashion. Two of a kind.

Suddenly Nancy stopped, tugged me around to face her.

"Oh, Nick," she said, "DIROB flashed you just before you arrived. You're supposed to flash back at once."

"Why on earth didn't you tell me that before?"

"Because I wanted you to myself. Let her wait—the bitch!"

I glanced at Paul. He was looking at her admiringly. I knew she had made a friend for life.

"You can flash from my office on the second floor," Nancy said. "I'll give Paul the fast, thirty-cent tour, and then we'll join you up there. I've laid on a gorgeous lunch for you in the conference room."

I sat at Nancy's desk while the FO operator put me through to Washington. Angela Berri came on screen.

"Nick," she said, "what the hell are you doing out there?"

"Good morning, Angela," I said.

"Good morning, Nick," she said. "What the hell are you doing out there?"

"Showing Paul the scenery."

"When are you coming back?" she demanded.

"I'll probably return tomorrow morning. Paul will stay on a day or so to learn what's going on."

"I want you in Washington on Friday night. A dinner with the Chief Director and his wife. At their home. It's important."

"It's awkward," I said.

"Why?"

"I have an appointment in Alexandria on Friday. To examine Lewisohn."

"Fine. Come over to my place in the evening."

"Angela, I'll have my new secretary with me."

"What for?"

"To take notes."

"Nick, when did you ever need notes?"

"Since I got a new secretary."

That thawed her. After she stopped laughing, she said, "Bring her along. We'll find something for her to do."

"Maybe Art Roach can entertain her for the evening," I said casually.

"Why not?" she said.

"Who'll be there? At the dinner?"

"Just you, me, the Chief Director and his wife. I've got something to discuss with him."

"While I keep the wife busy?"

"Of course. Wear your uniform and decorations."

"Where do we stay? At the Alexandria Hospice?"

She thought a moment.

"No," she said. "Come to my apartment. I can put you up overnight. Separate bedrooms, I presume?"

"For whom?" I asked.

She smiled and switched off.

I finally found Nancy and Paul in another corridor. They were standing before a closed door, staring through a small square of transparent glass. On the inside, I knew, it would be a mirror.

". . . third month," Nancy was saying as I came up to them. "All vital functions normal. A strong, healthy ef. We decided on a rhesus monkey."

"Compatible DNA," Paul said.

"You plenty damn smart for a white em," Nancy said perkily. "Get your call through, Nick?"

"Sure," I said. "Nothing important. What have we here?"

"Take a look. Fertilization, *in vivo*, with rhesus sperm. And a new interspecific drug we've been working on. Normal gestation period. The object is coming along nicely."

I stooped a little to peer through the glass. Lydia Ann Ferguson was sitting on the edge of the bed. Hands folded in her lap. She was staring out through the window, beyond the white bars, at the endless blue sky.

It came on fast. . . .

. . . dissecting a frog when I was seven years old. Taking out the heart and putting it carefully aside. Watching gravely while it continued to pump, for minutes in diminishing rhythm.

. . . the look of surprised hurt on a child's face in Central Park. The string of his helium-filled balloon had slipped from his fingers. The blue balloon floated slowly upward. Then, caught by the wind, it whirled away.

. . . George Bernard Shaw: "Liberty means responsibility. That is why most men dread it."

. . . in a darkened car. A street on upper Manhattan. A warm hand touching me. "Please?" she had asked. "Please?"

I fumbled in my pocket, found the dispenser, popped a spansule.

"Nick?" Paul said anxiously. "You all right?"

"Yes," I said. I jerked a thumb toward the glass. "Very impressive, Nancy. Now what do we have to do to get something to eat around here?"

"Right now," she said. "I warn you, Nick—all my Team Leaders will be there. We're ganging up to you."

"Don't tell me," I said. "Let me guess. You want more love?"

"How on earth did you know?" She giggled.

It was a delightfully noisy, confused lunch. Almost everything served had been grown in the Field Office's hydroponic beds. The few protein substitutes were made from soy rather than petroleum. I hadn't had such a flavorful feast in months.

As we gobbled, we squabbled. The usual kaka: pure versus applied science;

the impossibility of an absolute value judgment; action versus speculation; the influence of technology on the future of science; and so forth, and so forth. I had heard it all before. I let Paul attempt to answer their questions and respond to their complaints. It was time he learned to handle, to control, to manipulate these free and sometimes abrasive debates. I thought he did rather well.

Finally, I glanced at my digiwatch. Almost 1330. I pushed back from the table and stood up. The room quieted. Everyone looked to me.

"Lousy food," I said. "About what I'd expect in a dump like this."

They laughed delightedly. Strange. The young prefer insults. How old must one be to learn to accept gratitude gracefully?

"And now," I continued, "I expect to be presented with the bill. Let me guess. . . . You are against further love being spent on chimerism by transplant. You are in favor of enormous sums of love being spent on chimerism by genetic tinkering. Well, this is my decision. . . ."

They were silent, staring at me expectantly, wide-eyed. . . .

"My decision," I said, "is that Paul Bumford, your new ruler, will make the decision. Good-bye, all. Stay happy."

I marched out, to a chorus of groans, boos, laughter, catcalls. Paul came running after me into the corridor.

"Nick!" he gasped. "You're not serious?"

"I'm serious." I nodded. "It's your decision. Make it."

I changed into civilian clothes at the hotel. I took a cab to Hawkley's office, in a new skyscraper overlooking Balboa Park. The building was as cold and sterile as an operating theater. The offices of Hawkley, Goldfarb & Bensen weren't much better. They occupied the entire thirty-fourth floor, and appeared to be carved from a single block of white plastisteel. If a robot had taken my hat I wouldn't have been a bit surprised. It was not encouraging.

I gave my name to the matronly receptionist. She murmured into an intercom. I stood waiting. In a few moments a knobless panel opened in the wall; the young, blond private secretary came out to collect me.

"Mr. Flair?"

"Yes."

"Follow me, please."

"To the ends of the earth."

I had hoped for a dimple. But there was no reaction. I followed her haunches down a long, apparently endless corridor. On both sides of that nightmare alley doors led away to—to what? Offices? Closets? Cells?

There was no human sound. A slight hum of machinery. Or perhaps I was humming to myself. We went through a door to another, much shorter corridor. At the end, a door. What a door!

It was oaken, the wood looking as though it had been excavated from primeval ooze and laid out on desert sand to dry and bleach. The outside hinges were unpainted iron, fancifully wrought, fastened to the wood with clumpy studs. There was no hint of plastiseal, no sign of any futuristic fakery.

"I'll buy the door," I told the blond ef.

"He'd never sell it," she said.

She bounced her knuckles off the wood. Like rapping the Great Pyramid of Cheops. Then she swung the door outward. It moved with nary a squeak.

"Mr. Nicholas Flair," she announced.

I stepped inside, past her. She disappeared. I heard that massive door thud shut behind me.

If there had been a single feature of that remarkable room unconvincing or not essential, I would have thought it more stage set than office. But I did not see anything leased, and there was nothing I did not want to own.

It was obso, of course: pine paneling; curtained windows; maroon velvet drapes; a mahogany desk; shelves of leather-bound law books, glassed in. And brass lighting fixtures with green shades, buff ceiling, watercolors of ancient sailing ships, a table of carved walnut, a liquor cabinet made from a campaign chest: inset hardware and brass corners. Over all, a musty, antique odor; paste wax and oil, old wood and polished metal.

The obso em sitting motionless behind the enormous desk belonged there: fly frozen in amber. He appeared to be ninety, at least. He was not bald, but white hair had thinned to a halo. Keratoses of scalp, temples, backs of hands lying palms down on the black desk blotter.

Clear, almost colorless eyes. Penetrating stare. A hooked beak, fleshless. Lips that had faded into the surrounding skin. A haze of eyebrows and lashes. The corpus thin to the point of emaciation.

The voice was shockingly deep, strong, resonant. I had expected a frail whisper.

"Forgive me for not rising," he said. He moved a finger toward a thick cane hooked over a corner of the desk. "I move as little as possible."

"That's quite all right, sir," I said.

He did not, I noted, ask me to be seated.

"Sir. . . ." I said. And paused.

He gave me no encouragement. He was stone. Posture, manner unyielding. I knew at once it had been a mistake. Not fatal—but still a waste.

"I am interested in making an investment in the San Diego area," I said rapidly. Determined to speak my piece and leave with as much dignity as I could salvage.

"Investment?"

"Yes, sir. Preferably in real estate or industrial properties."

"You have something specific in mind?"

"Scilla Pharmaceuticals. They are—"

"I know them," he said shortly. "No, I'm afraid I can't help you."

That was clear enough. I turned, took two steps, had my hand on the huge brass doorknob when he spoke my name for the first time.

"Mr. Flair," he trumpeted. "Dr. Nicholas Flair. Deputy Director of something called the Satisfaction Section. Of something called the Department of Bliss. Of something called the Government of the United States of America."

I took my hand off the knob, turned back.

"That is correct," I said.

"The name Flair is not unknown in this city," he said coldly. "I like to know who is coming across the country to see me. It wasn't difficult to find out."

"I didn't think it would be," I said. "I admire your thoroughness—if that's what you want from me."

"It isn't," he said. "I couldn't care less what you think of me."

"Then our business is at an end, sir," I said.

Again I turned to go. Again his voice stopped me.

"Your father is wealthy," he said. "Has a good reputation. You seem to be in no need. You hold a responsible government job."

"So?" I said.

"Just to satisfy an old man's curiosity," he said. Eyes squinting. "Why should a young man in your position want to invest in a drug manufacturer that sells to the government you work for? Shoddy, Mr. Flair. I don't like shoddy."

I looked at him. It was obvious what he thought.

"My motive is not what you suspect," I told him.

"Oh? Then what is your motive?"

I should have walked out then, of course. But I wanted to make a chip, at least, in that icy superiority.

"My motive, sir?" I said. "Revenge."

If he had been given adrenalin IV, the result could not have been more astonishing. The sunken cheeks flushed. The cold eyes took on a sparkle. He pushed himself upright in his straight-backed chair.

"Revenge?" he said. "Revenge?"

I stared at him, astounded by the sudden change in his appearance. He had, literally, come alive. He raised a steady hand, pointed across the room at the polished liquor cabinet.

"On the lower shelf, young man," he said. "The squarish decanter and two balloons, please."

I hesitated a moment. Then I did as he asked. I brought the bottle and brandy snifters back to his desk. He waved me to a leather armchair. Then he unstoppered the decanter, poured the two glasses one-third full, pushed one of them toward me. His movements were slow but not tremulous. We lifted, nodded, sipped.

I almost gagged. It was liquid fire. He smiled happily. I thought it was a smile; there was a crinkling.

"Burgundian," he said. "From the grape dregs. An acquired taste. Like revenge. Tell me what you think I should know."

I kept it brief. I did not mention Angela Berri by name. I said only that my target was an object in a high government position who was on the suck. I outlined my plan. He listened intently, not interrupting. But his eyes never left mine.

I finished. I waited for his reaction.

"An outlandish scheme," he said finally. "Farfetched."

"Yes, sir," I agreed. "It's a great advantage. The object couldn't possibly conceive of anyone going to all that trouble."

"And expense," he said shrewdly. "It's going to take a lot of money."

"A lot of love," I said mischievously.

"Money," he repeated stubbornly.

I laughed. "Money it is," I said. "How much?"

"How could I possibly know at this time? A lot. You want complete ownership? Or will a partnership suffice?"

"Ownership, if possible. Or any arrangement that will give me access to the offices. The chief executive must be ruled by me."

"I see." He pondered a moment. "Of course, you want your name kept out?"

"Of course. I thought you might be able to set up a dummy corporation, or some kind of a holding—"

"Don't tell me my business," he said crossly. "There are many new discoveries and products of which I am not aware, I'm sure. But now you're talking about something as old as Cain and Abel. We used to call it a 'fuzz job.' "

"I don't believe I've ever heard the expression."

"To fuzz the ownership of a particular property. Hide it behind layers of owners of record. Lots of papers. That's the secret: lots and lots of legal documents. The true ownership can always be traced, of course. But only after a great deal of time and effort. By then, we will have accomplished our purpose."

"*Our* purpose?" I repeated. "You're willing to take this on?"

"Oh yes," he said. "It's human. Very human indeed. It almost convinces me that there's hope for you yet."

"Hope for *me*?"

"For you, your generation, your world. That it's not all urine specimens and computer printouts. There's some blood left."

I smiled politely and lifted my glass.

"To blood," I said.

We made what arrangements we could: his payment, maximum love to be expended, transfer of funds, communication. He suggested the code. Thirty years previously he had written a thin book: *Early Monasteries of Southern California*. It had been privately published. He still had a dozen volumes left, and gave me one. If he sent me a letter of numbers, including 19–3–14, it would mean the fourteenth word of the third paragraph on page 19. Simple and unbreakable. Providing, of course, the key wasn't known to the interceptor.

I leaned across the desk to shake his frail hand just before I departed. I knew a palm stroke would offend him.

"Mr. Hawkley," I said. "A pleasure."

"Yes, young man." He nodded. "It will be a pleasure. You must tell me all about it. When it's over."

"When it's over," I agreed. "Meanwhile, sir, our Gerontology Team has come up with—"

"No pills, no pills," he said sharply. Then, to soften his refusal, he patted the brandy decanter gently. "This is my medicine."

I left him then. No fear of failure. With my ideas and energy and his experience. . . . But the euphoria may have been due to the marc. Put *that* in a pill and my fortune was made!

Y-5

At that point in time, according to regulations, I should have turned over to Paul Bumford complete rule of the Division of Research & Development. I did not do so for the following reasons:

1. Paul, although able and talented, was inexperienced in the administration of many objects, despite his previous service as my Executive Assistant.
2. There were a number of ongoing projects in DIVRAD which I had originated or to which I contributed. I could not withdraw my personal service suddenly without loss of creative momentum.
3. The transfer of the Division of Security & Intelligence to Angela Berri's headquarters had left me with only three divisions. Two of these—Law & Enforcement and Data & Statistics—practically ran themselves; they required a minimum of administrative supervision. Hence, I could devote more time to DIVRAD.

If my future actions were questioned, if I was called to account by a Board of Inquiry, those were the three explanations I would have given for my conduct—and all were operative.

But the real reason I could not—had no desire to—relinquish the rule of the Division of Research & Development was considerably more complex.

The popular belief was that laws (policies) of the US Government were made by the Legislative branch and administered by the Executive. It was cynically believed that the Public Service (formerly Civil Service) was a necessary boondoggle of bookkeepers, accountants, statisticians, computerniks, clerks, etc.—mindless and servile paper-shufflers interested only in obtaining the highest possible rank-rate for the least possible effort.

A dangerous assumption.

Actually, it was quite possible for a bureaucrat to make policy. In fact, it was frequently a required part of his service. Congress might legislate the broad outlines of policy. But inevitably, it was a lot of kaka until bureaucrats translated law into action. How they translated it was, in effect, how US society functioned and evolved.

I had, long ago, realized that the Division of Research & Development, of the Satisfaction Section, of the Department of Bliss, wielded political clout far beyond its size and status on the government's Table of Organization. No object, ever, surrenders power voluntarily. I was not about to yield the enormous power of DIVRAD to Paul Bumford, or to anyone else.

The governing factors were these:

1. The Executive, Legislative, and Judicial branches of the US Government did not yet fully appreciate the significance and consequences of the Biological Revolution and the increasing contribution of all scientific disciplines to the political world and the manner in which life would be lived. The general public was almost totally unaware of what lay ahead—not in 100, 50, or 20 years, but tomorrow.
2. After the death of President Harold K. Morse, there was no one object in the higher echelons of government who, by conditioning or inclination, was capable of recognizing what was happening. A few Congressmen had degrees in science. Most were woefully ignorant. Even the staffs of Congressional committees whose service was to oversee DIVRAD's budget and operations did not have the necessary expertise.

Power abhors a vacuum. I rushed in. I cannot list here, for want of space, the areas in which I—*I*, personally—could make national policy through DIVRAD. And not policy of little importance, but policy that would affect the society we lived in, and society for generations to come. A single example will suffice. . . .

Annually, an item of X-million new dollars for "gerontology research" was included in DIVRAD's requested budget. Congressmen and staffs of the ruling committees assumed the love was for investigation and cure of biomedical disorders of the aged. During my tenure at DIVRAD, the requested sum was never reduced. Never. It would have been politically inexpedient. The rapidly growing number of obsos were voters. And increasingly vocal in their demands.

So, annually, I was granted X-million new dollars for gerontology research, with no restrictions as to how the sum was to be spent.

The legislators had no more knowledge of gerontology than they had of molecular genetics.

I had several options, including:

1. Prolong life itself. That is, attempt to extend the physical life span to, say, 100 or 125 years, by heavy research into the mechanism of stopping. But that might leave us with an enormous population of senile, dribbling oldsters, to be supported by the taxes of younger generations. The care of obsos was already an onerous economic burden. How long before euthanasia of all those over Y years of age was legislated?

2. Improve the middle life. That is, devote those X-million new dollars to research in arteriosclerosis, arthritis, senility, and other deteriorative disorders, to ensure a relatively healthy old age without appreciably increasing the longevity rates. But to what purpose? The obsos would still be retired nonproducers and nonconsumers.

3. Extend immaturity. Spend those gerontology research funds to prolong youth, keeping the young young for a longer period, so that one-half of an object's life might be spent in conditioning, the second half in producing, and all of it in consuming.

These were but three of the options I faced in determining how gerontology research love was to be spent. I have simplified my choices, of course. There was an almost infinite number of additional factors to be considered.

For instance, the human species is by nature conservative. That is, objects resent and are fearful of change, despite the fact that change is the only constant of biological and political history. This abhorrence of change becomes stronger as objects grow older. Obsos cannot cope with change. It bewilders them. So even naturally intelligent and well-conditioned oldsters frequently waste their energy providing obsolete answers to obsolete questions, like bad chess players. Did we really want a society of doddering conservatives?

I go into such detail to illustrate my thesis that bureaucrats *can* make vital policy. And, more than any other department of Public Service, DIVRAD made policy that affected the life and future of every object in the US and, eventually, every object on earth.

That was why I was unwilling to relinquish this awesome power. Sometimes it is necessary to cultivate madness.

My activities during the several days following my visit to San Diego provide a more precise conception of my responsibilities and the decisions I was called upon to make.

Leo Bernstein ruled the miniteam conducting research on the severed head of Fred III. At the age of eighteen, Leo was, in my opinion, one of the top three biochemists in the world. Certainly the fattest. When he was thirteen, Leo had published a brilliant theoretical paper on the virus causing plantar warts. It had led to chemotherapy for rodent ulcers of the face and scalp, and suggested an entirely new approach to the treatment of all epidermal carcinomas.

Leo's only defect was that he knew exactly how good he was.

He waddled into my office, tossed a computer printout onto my desk, lowered himself sideways onto a chair, and with much grunting effort hoisted his bulging thighs over one of the arms.

"Make yourself at home, Leo," I said.

He couldn't be bothered with irony, small talk, or common courtesy.

"Take a look," he commanded. He gestured toward the printout. "We checked the numbers three times. It's operative."

I scanned the printout. It was stupefying. I had been away from the lab too long. Things were moving too fast.

"Where the hell's the bottom line?" I said.

"On the bottom. What's the matter, teacher?" he jeered. "Can't keep up?"

I forgave talent anything, including distended egos. I scanned the printout again. Again. Finally I computed the meaning.

It was exciting, but I wouldn't let him see my pleasure. In brief, what Leo's team had done was to stabilize the deterioration rate of Fred's brain. They hadn't yet halted the natural stopping of brain cells and loss of electrical power. But they had firmed the *rate* of decline. A small step, but an important one.

"Not bad," I acknowledged. "But a breakthrough it ain't."

"Don't jerk me." Leo grinned. "It's great and you know it."

"What are you using?"

"You'll never guess."

"That's why I'm asking."

"Ergotamine."

My astonishment drew a burst of laughter from him. But he didn't know the cause of my reaction. Ergotamine is an alkaloid of ergot, with a chemical structure similar to that of lysergic acid, a hallucinogen. Marvelous. Everything was going my way.

"Excellent," I said. "Nervy thinking. Stick with it."

"Of course," he said. "Increasing the dosage. I'll have Fred's deterioration ended in a month."

"Leo," I said, "if you're ever going wrong, may I be the first to know?"

He laughed again, made a rude gesture, grabbed up his computer printout, waddled out of the office. He was an obese young em. But no fat around his brain.

Maya Leighton came into my apartment wearing a floor-length plastilap cloak in kelly green and an enormous tooty nosering of braided elephant hair. As usual, there was about her an aura of febrile expectancy. From my conditioning at the Science Academy I suddenly remembered an obso medical term: thyrotoxicosis. But perhaps I was playing doctor.

I took the cloak from her shoulders. She was wearing an em's shirt, the tails rolled up and knotted beneath her gourdish breasts. There was a wide span of naked torso. Smooth, tanned. A large umbilicus with a protruding yolk stalk, a little tongue. Beneath were rough pants, belted low on the pelvis. Wisps of pubic hair sprouted like sprigs of parsley. Between heavy bosom and wide hips, that incredibly slender waist.

"We're going to Alexandria on Friday," I said. "You and I. To the Hospice. I want to take a look at Lewisohn."

"All right," she said equably. "That will be nice. Can we drive?"

"Good idea. We'll start early. Take our time. Do you drive?"

"Oh, yes! May I? Part of the way, at least?"

"Of course. We'll stop for lunch along the way."

"A picnic lunch."

"Or at some amusing roadside restaurant."

"Maybe near a lake or river."

"We'll eat outside. With wine."

"We'll throw crusts to the swans."

We both laughed. I leaned to tongue her breasts.

As usual, Maya was eagerly complaisant, almost perversely so. Mastery excited me. I felt no sadistic tendencies, but still. . . .

We showered together, tissues raw and swollen. I mentioned, as casually as I could, that after the Alexandria visit, we would go into Washington where I had a dinner engagement.

"But you won't be left alone," I told her. "We'll stay at DIROB's apartment."

"All right."

"Her Chief of Security will take care of you," I said. "His name is Art Roach."

"All right."

"He has a bad reputation."

"Bad?"

"He's a rough em. You understand?"

"Yes."

"Will you be careful?"

She laughed and presented her great soaped ass to me.

I had a two-hour conference with Frank and Frances von Liszt and their top attorneys of the Division of Law & Enforcement. It was a relaxed, unstructured meeting. I had convened it to discuss progress in an ongoing project to write an addendum to the Fertility Control Act. When completed, the proposed law would be submitted to Congress for debate and, I hoped, legislation.

The new law would require compulsory sterilization of habitual criminals, the feebleminded, insane, drug addicts, chronic alcoholics, and those suffering from incurable genetic disorders and/or abnormal sexuality.

I felt very strongly on the need for such a law. You must realize that the service of DIVRAD fell into two time-frames. We were seeking to prevent mental retardation and physical disorders by genetic engineering; i.e., we were trying to improve the quality of the gene pool of the future.

Simultaneously, we were seeking to cure living victims of those same disorders, and thus improve the quality of life in the present. Sometimes, happily, a discovery in one time frame also proved efficacious in the other. More frequently, our successes in genetic engineering far surpassed our victories in the treatment of existing victims. Hence the need for compulsory sterilization.

I wanted to present a proposed law as logical and complete as possible. As usual when dealing with subjects as sensitive as this—a law that limited personal liberty for the public good—the main difficulty was precise definition of terms. What was insanity? Feeblemindedness? Abnormal sexuality?

Source material covered the long conference table. With as many opinions as sources. No consensus. I could see the von Liszts and their staff were bewildered and disheartened by this mass of conflicting views.

"Look," I told them. "You're getting bogged down in a quicksand. Don't consult any more authorities. Don't scan any more learned papers or listen to distinguished scientists and scholars. You have quite enough here to assimilate."

"But it's so contradictory," Frances burst out. "Nick, we just can't reconcile all these viewpoints."

"Impossible." Her brother nodded. "And not only disagreement on definitions of the physical and mental disorders warranting sterilization, but also a zillion objections to such a program on religious, ethical, and political grounds."

"Now you're getting into value judgments," I warned him. "In an area where there are no universal values. We cannot let ourselves become involved in a moral debate. It would go on forever, never be settled, and nothing would be accomplished. Somehow we have to create a situation in which we are above such a debate—or beyond it. A situation in which opposition is, if not hopeless, at least ineffectual."

"And how do we do that?" one of the attorneys demanded. "You're asking for guaranteed success."

"No," I said. "Just better odds than we have now. All right—give me a minute and then I'll throw you some raw meat."

They quieted, lighted up their Bolds, whispered softly to each other. I sat where I was, at the head of the table, looking with some distaste at the mounds of research. A lot of thoughts there. Ideas. Theories. Kaka. If I let it, science would be pushed back to the four elements, demonology, dowsing, and belief in the soul.

"All right," I said loudly. "Here's what we do."

Heads snapped up. They looked at me expectantly.

"For some time I haven't been satisfied with the Genetic Rating program. It was originally established under the Fertility Control Act to be exactly what its title indicates: classification of objects by genetic quality. The big error was to as-sign to human examiners the authority to determine Genetic Ratings. There are good GE's and there are bad ones. But all suffer from one defect: They are hu-man. It was inevitable that subjective judgments would be made. The entire Ge-netic Rating program should have been computerized from the start.

"That will be our first step. The switch to computerization can be made by administrative decree without enabling legislation. I anticipate very little opposition. As a matter of fact, I think the move will draw general approval. You've all heard the stories of bribery of GE's, and other rumors as to how they are influenced by personal and political considerations. The main oppo-sition will come from the GE's themselves when they learn they're being replaced by a King Mk. V. But there aren't enough GE's to cause a major flap, and they'll be assured of transfer to other services with a rank-rate equal to or more than their present love.

"Now I want you to work very closely with Data and Statistics in planning the programming for determining Genetic Ratings. Make certain that minus-ratings of sufficient weight are given for precisely those disorders for which we will eventually require sterilization."

A gasp ran around the room. They turned to look at one another. They understood now what I was planning.

"Once computerized Genetic Ratings are operational—we should be able to do it in a year, at most—the Sterilization Addendum will then be submitted to Congress. We'll have to give it an attractive title—like the Gene Pool Improvement Act, or something like that. It will be based solely on Genetic Ratings. The opposition will then find no human objects to debate. You can't argue with mechanical thinking. Having already accepted computerized Ge-netic Ratings, they'll find it difficult to object to the use of those ratings to improve the quality of life today and the quality of the gene pool tomorrow. I don't say they'll be completely silenced. Of course, they won't be. But we'll have broken their teeth. I think we can win this one, and the plan I have outlined is exactly how we'll do it. Any questions?"

There were no questions.

Phoebe Huntzinger returned from the Denver Field Office. She marched into my office. Her usual placidity was not evident. She was disturbed and trying to control it.

"Phoebe," I said, "how was the trip?"

"The trip? Fine. I like it out there. Would you believe they still have snow up in the mountains?"

"I believe. You like the objects?"

"At the FO? Some good brains there, Nick."

"I know. So what's the problem?"

She tried to laugh. "It shows?"

"It shows. A crisis at Denver?"

"Not so much a crisis as just plain, everyday, run-of-the-mill stupidity."

"Can it be glossed?"

"What? Oh, sure, Nick. It can be handled."

"All right. Then there's no crisis. Now what is it?"

"Do you know how they're running this game?"

"On this particular project? Roughly. Nine laser beams pick up the CNS electrical activity. They scan in overlapping disks, like radar beams. Right so far?"

"Right."

"Electric synapses show on screen and at the same time the bedside computer determines location, duration, and strength of the cerebral signal. That information is amplified and fed into the master computer for translation into printout. From a trigger in the brain, we get an actual word in type. Correct?"

"Correct. Pretty good for an old em like you. Is there *anything* going on in this Section you don't know?"

"Cut the kaka. What's the problem?"

"You're hoping for a conception from the experimental object. A complete declarative sentence. Nick?"

"Yes."

"Impossible."

"Why impossible?"

"What do you think is the vocabulary of the master computer? How many signals is it programmed to accept and translate into words?"

"Oh . . . I don't know. Three thousand? Five thousand?"

"Two hundred."

"You're joking?"

"I'm not. That computer can never give you a conception, Nick. It only knows two hundred words, and almost all of them are adjectives and adverbs. Few verbs. No pronouns. It's great for picking up sensations and emotions. Hot. Pink. Green. Soft. Blue. Happy. Red. But a complete conception? Forget it. Unless your idea of a declarative sentence is: 'Sad red warm hurt cold loud.'"

I got up, moved to the window, stared out into murky sky. I tried to control my anger. I knew there were two factors that negated the best efforts of the best futurists: human genius and human stupidity. You could construct the greatest mathematical model in the world, but all your agonized planning could be brought to dust by a leukemic dwarf creating a new idea in a hospice bed or by a stupid scientist who neglected an experimental element so basic that no one thought to question it.

I turned to face Phoebe Huntzinger. I tried to smile. She tried. We both failed.

"Not fatal," I said. "Peter Stanley?"

"The Team Leader? Yes, Nick. That's his name."

"I'll take care of him. Phoebe, does this project interest you?"

"Yes. Very much. Let me serve on it, Nick. The things I do around here are routine. My Division runs itself. You know that."

"All right. That master computer in Denver—a Golem?"

"Mk. III."

"What's the storage potential?"

"Vocabulary? Maybe ten thousand words tops, on the basis of input from the bedside computer."

"Flash WISSEC. They've got basic vocabulary lists from five words to fifty thousand. Ask for copies of one, three, five, and ten thousand words. Program Golem to its limit. Got that?"

"Sure."

"What about the in-brain technology? Any chance of a foulup there?"

"I don't know, Nick. It's not my field."

I nodded. "I'll take care of it. As soon as you get your word lists, get back to Denver and start the reprogramming. Thanks, Phoebe."

She smiled warmly at me.

"Nick, if I wasn't married, I'd suggest you and I use each other. One night at least."

"Why not?" I said. "Your wife won't mind. By the way, Phoebe, that Denver project never has been named. I've been carrying it on the budget under Gerontology Research. I think we'll bring it out of the closet now and give it a name. Make the servers feel they're on something important. We'll call it Project Phoenix."

"Whatever you, say, Nick."

Paul Bumford returned from the San Diego Field Office on Thursday morning. He flashed my office to report in. On screen, he appeared thin, hard, drawn.

"Tired?" I asked him.

"Busted my ass," he said. But he was not grumbling. If anything, he seemed proud of his labors, confident of his mastery of his new power.

"How did you resolve the chimerism debate?" I asked him.

"I told them I would phase out the transplant program and provide more love for genetic manipulation. Nick?"

"Excellent. Good judgment."

"I passed the test? Thanks, teacher."

"Paul, break the news gently to the Chimerism Team here. Better yet, just don't mention it. Reduce their love gradually over a period of a year. Eventually, they'll get the message."

"That's what I planned to do," he said crossly. "How about a serveout and swim later today?"

"Fine. At the DIVSEC gym. Meet you about 1700."

At 1630, I left my office and walked over to the small gym and swimming pool on the compound grounds. It was not the large communal gym-pool, available to servers of all ranks, but was located in what had formerly been the headquarters building of the Division of Security & Intelligence.

When Angela moved DIVSEC to Washington, leaving behind only a guard company for compound security, their offices were assigned to objects from other divisions who required more room for their service. The small gym and swimming pool that had formerly been reserved for the exclusive use of DIV-SEC had now, by my decree, become a private facility for the use of PS-4 rank and higher.

Paul was serving out in the gym when I arrived. He was using the horizontal wallbars. Arms stretched over his head, he had suspended his body a few inches above the floor. With his back pressed against the bars, he was slowly raising and lowering his legs from the hips.

I had changed to plastilast briefs in the locker room. Paul was wearing a plastilast clout. His body had always been androgynous. But now he had lost weight; he had a waist; I could see his rib cage. He was no longer pudgy. I fancied even his skin tone had changed. It was no longer blushed. And it was taut. Plump curves had disappeared. Muscles were discernible.

"You're looking good," I said.

I jumped up to grab a bar alongside him. I began to replicate his exercise, lifting my legs from the hips, slowly, then slowly lowering them.

"Nancy Ching?" I said. "What's your input?"

"Superior," he gasped. "Elegant brain. Good ruler. Her servers follow."

"Use her?" I asked. "After I left?"

"Yes," he said. "At her cottage, north of La Jolla Bay." I felt something.

"Fine." I exhaled. "She's profitable."

"Election," he said, trying to breathe deeply as he exercised. "Off-year election out there. Local Congressmen."

I turned my head to look at him. His lovely body was sheened.

"Don't tell me Nancy is involved? She'll stop her career."

"No, no. She just mentioned this obso in office will probably be returned. She said he's a clunk."

"So?"

"His support is mostly from obsos. This is for the Tomorrow File. My idea. Nick, why should obsos have the vote? No one under sixteen has it. Why objects over, say, fifty or sixty? It's not right. They don't produce, and their consumption rate is nil."

"Disenfranchise the obsos? Good. Solve the political problem of their conservatism. Excellent thinking, Paul. Add it to the File. Let's go to the bikes."

They were bicyclelike mechanical contrivances bolted to the floor. You could adjust the tension on the pedals. An odometer showed meters and kilometers. Paul and I mounted onto the saddles.

"Set it at five," I told him. "One new dollar on a kilometer."

"You're on," he said.

We began to pedal madly.

"That thing in Denver," I said. "Printout from brain signals."

"Yes."

"I coded it Project Phoenix."

"Oh?"

"The computerization was mucked."

I told him what Phoebe Huntzinger had told me, how the computer vocabulary had been shorted.

"Oh, God," he groaned.

"Get rid of Peter Stanley. He's the Team Leader."

He turned his head sideways to glance at me.

"Terminate him with prejudice?" he said slowly.

"Not permanently, you idiot. Transfer him. A tsetse fly station in darkest Africa—something like that. Just get rid of him."

"All right, Nick."

"I want you to go to Denver and check out the in-brain technology. There may be a balls-up there, too."

"Nick, for God's sake, I've got a full plate."

"Then send Mary Bergstrom. She can compute what's going on."

He was silent. We were both pedaling our stationary bicycles as hard as we could. Gripping handlebars with sweaty hands. Knees plunging up and down. Leaning forward. Gasping. Striving.

"What's stressing you?" I panted.

"You," he said. "What you're doing. Goddamn it, Nick, it's *my* Division. I rule it. I'm AssDepDirRad. Can't you let me make the decisions?"

"You object to my decisions?"

"No, but let *me* make them. Your decisions are operative, but I want to make them first. You've been acting like a—like a—" He paused in fury and frustration. "Like a mogul!" he burst out, pedaling crazily.

"Mogul?" I shouted. "I haven't heard that word in years!"

"Well, that's what you are—a mogul."

We pedaled away furiously, glancing occasionally at each other's odometer. We were about equal. I strained to draw ahead.

"Power," I gasped. "I recognize the symptoms."

"Because you suffer from it yourself."

"Right! You don't seek it out. It seeks you. It's a passion, a virus. It's incurable."

"You've got it and I've got it."

"Yes. Can't we serve together?"

"Sure," he said.

"One kilometer," I said, peering at my odometer. I stopped pedaling, swung off the saddle. I stood trembling, knees water, heart thudding. Paul stopped pumping, swung slowly from his machine.

"You win," he said. "Owe you a dollar."

He walked away. Steadily. Not looking back. I glanced at his odometer. It showed slightly over one kilometer.

I took one hand off the wheel and placed it delicately on her hard, tanned thigh. She was wearing a miniskirt. Fresh zipsuits and makeup were in a small overnight case on the back seat.

"Look what I have," she said.

She unzipped her purse. I took my eyes off the road a moment to glance down. A red dildo.

"Got a jerk for Indians?" I asked her.

She laughed.

"I like the color: Come-Along Red. Nice?"

"Oh, yes," I said. "Electric?"

"Ultrasonic."

"Turn your bones to water," I warned her.

"I don't care."

"Shock therapy?"

"Well . . . it just feels good."

"The endless problem of therapeutics," I said. "Risk versus benefit."

She laughed again and hiked her little skirt higher.

"You're cute," she said.

I had been certain the day would prove a disaster. It began in rain, what Hibernians call a "soft day." Gray, wet, endless. Not gusty or sweeping; nothing as dramatic as that. Just a slow, unreeling curtain of drifting water. Polluted enough to stain cloth.

I requisitioned a hydrogen-powered sedan from the motor pool. Speed and acceleration were not the best, but it could churn out 100 kph without faltering. Just what we needed for the run south.

Except that every driver in New York was going to Alexandria, Virginia, that Friday morning. Or so it seemed. It took us an hour to get through the new Morse Tunnel to Jersey City. The freeway south was clogged, an infarcted artery: stop start, start stop.

Then suddenly, almost instantaneously, it ran free. I moved the hand accelerator switch. At the same time the curtain of rain lifted. Someone rolled it up. Just like that. The sun was there in a clearing sky. Blue. Maya Leighton sighed and pushed out her long legs. And I put my hand lightly on her bare, cool thigh. It might, I thought, it just might serve.

"Maya, where are you from?"

"GPA-5."

I guessed Iowa.

"What made you pick geriatrics?"

"I want to live forever."

She switched off the air conditioning and lowered the window on her side. I lowered mine. The fresh air seemed washed. Sunwarmed. She took off her jacket, unbuttoned her blouse to the waist, put her hand inside. She began to hum. Not a tune, a song. Just a hum, a not unpleasant drone. Her eyes were closed.

"Maya, what do you want?"

"Excitement," she said drowsily.

"I can give you that. Pain, too."

"That's excitement," she said faintly.

I thought she might be napping. She was a lazy animal. She required long hours of sleep.

I drove steadily, letting the astronauts zoom by. The wide road lulled. Suddenly, without willing it, I was at peace. We—she, I, the car—were floating and stationary. The new world revolved beneath our wheels.

I made the long curve onto the new elevated freeway that had been completed north to Mt. Holly. Eventually it would link with the Morse Tunnel to Manhattan. At that point in time, it was completed from Mt. Holly south to Washington, D.C. Once on it, you were captive. You could turn off for Philadelphia, Wilmington, or Baltimore. Otherwise, you had no place to go until you saw the Capitol.

"Good-bye, swans," I said.

"Good-bye, roadside paradise," she said sleepily.

"We'll pull off," I promised her. "They don't let you starve. Exactly. Do you prefer a fake English tavern or a fake German biergarten?"

"You decide," she murmured. "You say."

Her hand flopped limply sideways. Into my lap. Her fingers tightened gently. She began to play.

"Keep that up," I warned her, "and the result will pop my zipper and poke up through the steering wheel. Then some idiot will cut in front. I'll make a hard turn, and fracture my engorged penis. You, naturally, will then provide medical attention. And I will go to my very important dinner engagement this evening with my *Laternenpfahl* in splints. Is that what you want?"

"You're mad," she giggled.

"I suspect so," I sighed.

She turned sideways on the passenger seat, lying with her head in my lap, her hips turned. I took my right hand off the wheel and slid it into her unbuttoned shirt. I pinched a nipple as hard as I could between my knuckles.

"Yes," she breathed.

We stopped for lunch at one of the approved turnoff "Rest-Ur-Haunts." This one was a fake Italian ristorante. We dined under an outside arbor, enclosed by washable plastic lattice. Overhead were clumps of purple plastirub grapes and green leaves. On the tables were imitation empty Chianti bottles, fitted with plastiwax candles and flame-shaped bulbs with flickering filaments. Battery-powered. The false bottles even had browned, peeling labels. It was swell.

We returned to the car trading small belches from the proveal, propep, natural spaghetti, red wine. Frank Lawson Harris, where are you now?

She surprised me: an uncommonly skilled driver. She was relaxed, almost negligent. Hands lightly on the wheel in the approved 10–2 position. Fast, but not careless. Skirt pulled up to her pudendum. Eyes on the road. Elbow on the window rest. Sensitive touch. But excited.

"Can I go faster?" she said.

"Sure."

We went faster. I responded to that, remembering Millie and me whirling around that darkened track in Detroit.

"Whee!" she said.

As usual, speed took me out. I could forget my mad Potemkin's Village scheme to hang Angela Berri by her soft heels, forget the groans of today and the moans of tomorrow. The whispers of yesterday.

"Are you wearing anything?" I asked her.

"Beneath? No."

"Will it bother you?"

"Yes," she said. "It will bother me. *Do it*."

I twisted my body sideways. She spread her legs eagerly. I buried my face. She tasted of . . .

"Petronac-flavored," she said. "A new douche."

And so we sped into the Nation's Capital.

I took the wheel then. It cost almost two hours to get through Washington traffic, across the Potomac, down into Alexandria. But I welcomed our slow progress. It gave me time to compute the ef at my side.

There were contradictions. I knew—and Paul Bumford concurred—that she had a sharp, alert brain. But I found her, physically, a yawning animal, almost indolent, willing server to sensuality.

Her scientific discipline was geriatrics; all her conditioning had been directed toward alleviating the ills of the aged and the extension of life. Yet she had come to our attention by her suggestions for two euthanasic programs.

She had told me glibly, "I want to live forever." But my original take on her had been correct: She *was* terminally oriented.

There had been a brief moment in my life when I had believed there was still hope for the human species if there remained but one unpredictable object. But that was youthful romanticism. After I squirmed into the snakepit of national politics, I realized that a ruler must equate the unpredictable with the unreliable. The future was too important to leave to whim.

We were rolling through the lovely Virginia countryside when I decided there was less to her than met the eye. She would not be a problem.

Hospice No. 4 offered a pleasant prospect: several hectares of plastiturf surrounding small plots of natural meadowland, trees, a well-groomed orchard. The buildings were three levels high, constructed of antiqued plastibrick with plastirub ivy attached to the south walls. A curved driveway of Glasphalt led to the portico of the Headquarters Ward. A small spur of this driveway turned off to the receiving and emergency building, marked with a large sign: WELCOME WARD.

The various buildings were in a loose cluster. They were, I knew, connected by underground passageways. Utilities, power sources, computers, and classified labs were also underground. It was a design that was, with minor modifications, standard for government hospices all over the US.

Also standard was a single building that stood apart, unconnected to the others by above- or below-ground passages. It looked exactly like the other wards. The only difference was the plastisteel wire netting over the windows. The netting was molded white. You could hardly see it in the late-afternoon sunshine.

This was the Public Security Ward. It was in this building that objects guilty of politically unacceptable behavior were rehabilitated and reconditioned. It was also where government servers guilty of activities inimical to the public interest were drained. It was also where most of our scientific research on human objects was conducted. Generally, this was limited to the testing of new pharmaceuticals. More esoteric research was the province of my Field Offices.

I do not wish to imply—that is not my thrust at all—that this building was a prison ward of dark dungeons, beatings, torture, starvation, or any other kind of repression whatsoever. Quite the contrary. It was a reasonably clean, cheerful, bright, efficiently operated facility. It was open at all times to duly authorized inspectional or investigative bodies of the US Congress, and was so inspected and investigated frequently. We had nothing to hide. Everything was legal.

It must not be inferred that at this point in time the US was what the Society of Obsoletes termed a "police state." The communications media were still privately owned and allowed to express their views freely, even if those views were critical of government policy, as they sometimes were. Private property rights were still cherished and protected by law. And the public could still vote, choosing between the two political parties. In fact, during the Presidential election of 1996, 16 percent of the qualified electorate had cast ballots. So the US could hardly be called a police state. Far from it.

We were no sooner parked, getting out of the car, when a group of white-clad figures debouched through the main door of the Headquarters Ward. They awaited us on the porch. I recognized Dr. Luke Warren.

"Welcoming committee?" Maya Leighton asked.

"Yes," I said. I was about to warn her not to speak unless spoken to, to follow my lead in all things—but then I thought better of it. Let her behave as she wished. It would give me additional input on her potential.

We went up to the porch. Introductions and palm stroking began. I gathered fresh evidence of a new social habit I had first noted a few months previously.

The palm stroke had generally replaced the handshake by the mid-1980's. Human behavior analysts believed its origin was the palm slap of black "studs" and "cats," widely used in the 1960's. The violence of that gesture was modified in the palm stroke that had become an almost universal token of friendly greeting. Originally the palm was offered with the hand held vertically, thumb and fingers closed. Palms were pressed as much as stroked.

I had noticed a new modification that signaled status. The server, or inferior, was, more and more, offering his hand in a semihorizontal or sometimes flat position, palm upward. Almost in supplication. The ruler, or superior—by rank, wealth, age, or fame—would then stroke the proferred palm with his own hand turned downward. Almost a benediction.

So we went through the ceremony. All palms were turned up to me. All palms were turned down to my secretary. I was amused, and took care not to show it.

Besides Dr. Luke Warren, the Chief Resident, the only other object of significance to this account was Dr. Seth Lucas, introduced as the junior resident who had day-to-day responsibility for Hyman Lewisohn's condition. It was the first time I had met Lucas, although I had scanned his file before approving his assignment to the case.

He was a tall, thin (almost scrawny) black with the somewhat glassy stare of a contact lens wearer. His features were quite ordinary. He was nineteen years old and was an honor graduate of the Science Academy's Accelerated Learning Course. He had majored in biochemistry and specialized in psychopharmacology. His record in Public Service had been excellent, but not brilliant. A tiny red tab in his PP (Psychological Profile) called attention to "potential racism against blacks."

Dr. Luke Warren bustled about, gnawing crazily at his upper lip, blinking like mad, continually running both hands over his bald pate, as if to press water from his nonexistent hair. He wanted to shepherd us into the colloquy immediately. It was all set up. It was all planned.

I told him that was impossible. I wished to make a personal examination of our famous patient first. Face fell, shoulders slumped. I had dealt his always frail confidence another stout kick. Too bad. In certain objects, one cultivates apprehension. They perform best when fearful or even desperate.

So, with Dr. Seth Lucas showing us the way, Maya and I went to see Lewisohn.

"Seth," I remarked to the black doctor. "Seth. The evil brother of Osiris."

We were walking down a wide, polished corridor, stepping aside occasionally to avoid bustling nurses, pushed beds, wheeled equipment.

"That's right," he said, not smiling. "Seth, the evil brother of Osiris. That's me. Except my brother's name is Sam. Sir."

I looked at him curiously, remembering suddenly.

"Didn't you publish recently?" I asked him.

Then he came alive. Smiling. He looked even younger when he smiled. Little boy playing doctor. White paper gown. Electronic stethoscope hung around his neck.

"Yes, I published," he said. "About six months ago. In the *Psychopharmacology Bulletin*. You scan it?"

"Sure," I said. " 'The Influence of Cocaine on Catecholamines in the Treatment of Schizophrenia.' Right?"

He laughed with delight.

"Right! What did you think?"

"Elegant organization," I said. "But you're full of kaka."

He bridled.

"How so?"

"The results of that experiment of yours can't be replicated. We tried. I think your problem may have been contaminated coke. What's your clearance?"

"Red-3," he said.

"I'll get it raised to Red-2," I promised him. "Then I'll send you some restricted stuff they're doing in the Spokane Field Office. I think you'll be interested."

"Thank you," he said gratefully. "I'd like that."

We stopped outside Lewisohn's suite. I stepped into a nest across the hall to scrub my hands with germicide and dry them over the hot air outlet and ultraviolet beam. As habitual and meaningless as a devout religionist crossing himself as his bus speeds past a church.

I went back to the door of the suite where Maya and Lucas were waiting.

"How's he doing?" I asked him.

"No better, no worse. An hour ago the count was—"

"All right"—I interrupted him—"I'll get all the gruesome details at the colloquy. What's his mood?"

"Today, not so bad. It scares me."

"Scares you? Why?"

"I'd rather have him ranting and raving."

"I compute." I nodded. "Well . . . we'll see. Maya, when we go in, stand away from the bed where he can see you. If I look at you, clear my throat and raise my chin a little, you go over to the window and look out. Have your back turned to him and bend to look out. Bend far over. Got that?"

"Of course."

"When you turn back into the room, have the top button or the top two buttons of your blouse open. Then come over to stand close to the bed. Understand?"

"Yes."

Dr. Seth Lucas had been looking back and forth from Maya to me during this exchange. But he said nothing. He didn't grin.

"Let's go," I said.

It was a conventional VIP hospital suite. The electrically operated bed dominated. Emergency equipment was hidden behind a screen. A private nest with tub and shower. A parked electric wheelchair. A separate sitting room with sofa and two armchairs of orange plastifoam. A 3-D laser TV set. There were books, papers, tape rolls, and film reels everywhere. A viewing machine. A facsimile newspaper machine. Two flashers and three phones, one in red fitted with a scrambler. A small, desktop computer. Rolls of computer printout.

When we entered, Lewisohn was in bed. The top third raised. He was scanning a thick manuscript through spectacles that looked like the bottoms of obso bottles.

He didn't look up until Dr. Lucas closed the door behind us. Then Lewisohn pushed his glasses down on his mottled nose and stared at us over the rims.

"Dr. Nicholas Bennington Flair," Lewisohn said in his harsh, grating voice. "Born too late. Should have been a Borgia. One of the bad ones. A poisoned dirk at your belt, a poisoned ring on your finger. Wooing a lady with a love song on a lute. Kissing her just before you murder her so you might rule a duchy inherited by her weak brother to whom you have been supplying young boys and drugs from the East."

I looked at him, trying not to show my shock. It had been almost six months since I had last seen him. The deterioration was evident. He was stopping.

"Still reading those crappy novels of yours?" I said disgustedly. "No wonder we can't get any service out of you."

Observers usually thought our insults, our obvious hostility masked a hidden and deep affection. I wasn't so sure.

His eyes slid away from me and locked on Maya Leighton. He continued to speak to me while he stared at her.

"Think you're going to prod me with those filthy fingers of.yours?" he demanded. "Be gone. I don't need you. I don't need anyone."

I glanced at Maya, cleared my throat, raised my chin a little. She moved casually to the window. Lewisohn's eyes followed her. She bent far over to peer out. Her legs were slightly spread. The miniskirt hiked up farther on her long, tanned legs.

"Who's she?" Lewisohn shouted furiously. "What's she doing here?"

"Maya Leighton. She's a doctor, too."

"Doctors!" he shouted. "I'm surrounded by doctors. I'm up to my asshole in doctors. All of you get the hell out of here."

But his voice lacked his usual ferocity. He continued to stare at Maya's bare legs. I moved closer to the bed. I looked down at him.

It is extremely difficult to generalize about the symptoms of leukemia. In many cases there are only minimal signs of physical deterioration; the gradual stopping may be concealed by rosy cheeks, a sweet breath, grossly normal vital functions. But the rot is there: milky blood, tumerous bone marrow, a serious lowering of the defense mechanism against infection.

In Lewisohn's case, however, degeneration of the corpus was plain. Tissue had shrunk. That dwarfed body seemed even smaller, more distorted. The coarse red hair had thinned to a fuzz. Features had condensed so that the protruding forehead was obscenely bulging. Pale lips. Sluggish eyes. Pinched nostrils in a thick nose. I bent over him.

"Get the fuck away," he said. "Don't touch me, you Italianate bastard."

All diagnosticians have their individual bags of tricks. In this case, diagnosis of the disease wasn't necessary; I knew what was stopping him. But I wanted to know more about his condition. I leaned far over to sniff his breath. Foul. Sour predominating. His skin also had a stale scent. I inspected his fingernails. Milk-tinged with bluish half-moons. I pinched the skin on the back of one hand. The ridge slowly, slowly flattened out. But not entirely.

He let me tinker with him because Maya had turned from the window and come back to the bedside. She had unfastened the top two buttons of her blouse. The shining cleavage between her heavy breasts was clearly visible. Lewisohn had pushed his glasses back into place. He was still staring at her. She regarded him gravely.

"Hello, Maya," the old man said in a low voice.

"Hello, Mr. Lewisohn," she said in a soft, tremulous voice. "I can't tell you what an honor it is to meet you. I'll never forget this moment."

She sounded as if she meant it. Perhaps she did.

"Pull up a chair," he said to her.

I went back to the door where Dr. Lucas had been standing silently, arms folded. I motioned him outside. We closed the door, leaving Maya inside with Lewisohn.

"Not good, is it," Lucas said.

"Are you usually given to understatement?" I asked with more sharpness than I intended.

"Dr. Flair," he started, "I've been—"

"How do you get along with him?" I interrupted.

"As well as anyone. My father was a son of a bitch to live with. I'm used to it. We jive one another."

"Jive? I haven't heard that word in years. Who runs the tests? Who takes the blood?"

"I do."

"What do you want?"

He was startled.

"What?"

"What do you want, Seth?" I repeated patiently. "From your career. From life. Want to serve in a hospice?"

"Jesus, *no*! I'm just putting in my time."

"Well then?"

"Research," he said promptly. "I profit from that."

I nodded. What I was computing might work out.

"I can do that for you," I said. "What will you do for me?"

He looked at me shrewdly. If he had agreed immediately, I would have canceled him on the spot. But he was trying hard to be prudent. Still, I caught his excitement.

"What do you want me to do?" he asked cautiously.

"Not much at the moment. I want you to talk to Maya Leighton, as much as you can. Observe her. Get some input. Then I'm going to flash you tomorrow and ask if you believe you can serve with her. You'll rule."

"Sure," he said. "I'll do that."

"Fine. Where's the colloquy?"

"Conference Room B. Downstairs."

"I'll find it. You wait for Maya. The two of you come down together."

I opened Lewisohn's door. Maya was sitting at his bedside, holding his lumpy hand. Leaning forward. Loose blouse gaping. Her legs were crossed. Cool, tanned thigh. The other calf bulging sweetly.

"Get the fuck out of here!" Lewisohn roared.

"Up yours," I snarled at him. "Serve a little and earn your keep, you monster. Maya, five minutes."

She nodded. I closed the door.

"Give them five minutes," I said to Lucas. "Then knock at the door. Maya will come out."

I went down to the colloquy, synthesizing. I needed a friendly base in the Washington-Alexandria area. Hadn't someone said war is geography?

Conference Room B was crowded when I entered. A chair had been reserved for me, front row center, next to Dr. Luke Warren. I took my place. Lights dimmed.

The colloquy had been beautifully organized. Warren was on top of his service, though no one would ever convince him of that. It began with a fifteen-minute presentation. He had put the entire thing on tape.

We had the whole story in color: tissue slides, magnified computer print-outs, filmed microanalysis, blowups of those deranged leukocytes dancing about madly, color comparisons of serum, charts, percentages, projective curves. I was vaguely aware of the door of the conference room opening and Maya and Seth Lucas entering. But I was concentrating on the screen. It was not encouraging.

Then the tape ran blank, lights came on, we all blinked. Warren turned to me and gestured toward the stage. A podium had been set up there, to one side. I rose, moved up the two steps, turned to search those young faces. Young! There was even a group of five thirteen-year-olds assigned to the Hospice by the Science Academy for practical training as part of their conditioning. That had been my idea and I was proud of it.

"First of all," I started, "before we get into a screaming match—"

There was a titter of laughter.

"—I'd like to congratulate Dr. Luke Warren and his associates for one of the finest scientific presentations I've ever seen. Luke—well done!"

There was an enthusiastic snapping of fingers. Warren ducked his bald head, blinked ferociously, gnawed his upper lip, blushed happily. First the kick, then the pat. That was how this object had to be manipulated.

I went on. "Now then, I have just examined the patient. I hadn't seen him for six months. His physical deterioration is obvious and ominous. Question: Is that deterioration due to the disease itself or to the irradiation treatment? Oh—before anyone eagerly volunteers—let me say that I will listen to anything you have to offer. I welcome your opinions. But the final decision must be mine." I paused. "After all, it's my ass that's in the sling."

That won them and loosened them. They roared with sympathetic laughter. The give-and-take became fast. Sometimes angry and heated. Consensus: Physical deterioration was basically due to the nature of this disorder in this particular victim. Similar deterioration, though rare, was not unheard of. But it had been compounded by the radiation treatments, which should cease immediately.

"I concur." I nodded. "We're getting nowhere. Even worse, neither is the patient."

Again, laughter. I knew, of course, that Warren had planned this colloquy to condition his young staff as well as to inform me. He had been exactly right to do so.

"Second question," I said. "What do we do now? With the understanding that it is not sufficient to keep this object's vital functions animate. I hope you all recognize that his service as this country's most creative theorist is necessary—no, it's *essential* to the future of our society. He must not only be kept alive, he must be kept capable of serving. And if that isn't enough, we must also consider the personality and character of the em himself. I am sure you are all aware of what a quiet, gentle, cooperative, profitable object he is."

Loud groans and laughter. They knew him.

"So that's our input. One: Keep him alive. Two: Keep his brain functioning. Three: Tailor our treatment so it will not adversely affect his willingness to contribute his very unique service—I mean this very seriously—to the planning of our future world. Dr. Warren, is this symposium being taped?"

"Why, yes," he answered nervously. "I thought—"

"Excellent," I said. "I'm glad it is. All right—let's have suggestions on where we go from here."

It was a wild-and-woolly session and I profited from every minute of it. I think what gave me most pleasure was that I could keep up with them. I had fears, occasionally, that my increasing service in social and political fields might leave me lost in the disciplines from which all my power stemmed—scientific expertise. Things were moving so rapidly, on so many thrusts, that to fall behind was to perish.

The first suggestion offered, predictably, was for bone marrow transplant. I explained, for the umpteenth time, that this difficult, painful treatment would incapacitate Lewisohn for long periods of time. During which his service would be lost to the US. The Chief Director would never approve.

Second suggestion: Connect him to a strainer. This was our name for a machine that operated in a fashion not unlike kidney dialysis. Briefly, the strainer sieved useless, immature leukocytes from the bloodstream. It required a three-hour connection every twenty-four hours. I knew Lewisohn well enough to know he would never allow it. He didn't want to live *that* much to endure the strainer for the remainder of his days.

Several additional suggestions offered by the young Oncology Team at Rehabilitation & Reconditioning Hospice No. 4 were brilliant, none the less brilliant for the fact that I had already thought of them and included them in my contingency plan. One was the injection of laboratory-grown antibodies. We had recently made great advances in breeding specific antibodies *in vitro*. Some had proved efficacious in the treatment of multiple myeloma.

Another suggestion came from a bioimmunologist. She suggested treatment with tuberculosis vaccine and dead cells from stopped leukemic victims. Excellent.

I was wondering if anyone might suggest parabiosis. Dr. Seth Lucas did. The treatment was relatively brief, he argued. Lewisohn would have to be connected to his partner about an hour a day.

"And how do you suggest we persuade him to do that?" I asked. "To have his veins and arteries tied to a stranger at his side, for whatever period of time? You can't sedate him every day. He'll compute what's going on and fight it. One call to the Chief Director, and that's it."

"Easy," Lucas said. "We build a special suite. Partitioned. Tubes lead from Lewisohn through a blank plastiwood wall. He'll never see his partner. We tell him we're monitoring his blood. I think we can get him to lie still for that. He's fascinated by machines. We'll tell him it's an automatic blood an-alyzer, a computer. He'll go for it. We should have no trouble getting objects to connect him to. And it's better than a strainer; there's a possibility of a cure."

I was profited. I had selected the correct object for the scheme I had in mind.

"Not bad," I acknowledged. "We could even make up an inoperative com-puter printout to show him. Thank you, Dr. Lucas. And thank all of you. Dr. Warren, if you will be kind enough to furnish me the original tape of this conference, it will be of great help to me in making an informed judg-ment."

I paused. Then, slowly, I descended the two steps of the stage to stand on the floor of the conference room. On their level.

"A final note," I said. "A personal note. A sermon, if you will. My text is cancer, and the long, arduous search to find a cure. Many of you are aware, I am sure, that in obso days it was believed this disorder was a single disease for which a single cure might be found. It was only with the passage of years, and much service, that science became aware of the complexity of the problem. Cancer, as we now know, is many diseases with many causes, many symptoms, and demands many cures. Today we take most of those cures for granted. I ask you to remember the time required to produce them, and the services of thousands of objects, singly and in teams, that contributed to those cures. But I don't wish to rehash medical history. I only want to point out that the conquest of cancer, to date, is the most frighteningly complex task science has ever undertaken. Even today, when computers relieve us of much of the analysis and synthesis, we still don't know all the answers. This colloquy today is evidence of that! My thrust is this: On a personal level, I ask you not to be disheartened by complexity. On the contrary, I urge you to accept complexity. In fact, to seek it. You are individually capable of computing far more than you are now called upon to do. Life is no longer simple—if it ever was. Science is no longer simple. And certainly our society and the world are no longer simple. They are organs of incredible complexity. And to understand them, to manage them, we must, each of us, become infinitely complex ourselves, capable of assimilating, computing, and acting on millions of bits: facts, ob-servations, emotions, instincts, experience, and so forth. Do not fear complex-ity. Do not be dismayed if human values and aims prove to be just as complex as the conquest of cancer. Open your mind to the complex. Train your mind to encompass more, more, more. Then the future will truly belong to us. Thank you."

They all stood to snap their fingers frantically. I was not certain they com-puted what I meant. But I did.

. . .

Following the Watergate scandals of the 1970's, heavy structural changes had been made in the US Government. In 1979, a weak—and frequently witless—President had signed an Executive Reorganization Bill. In the words of a political commentator of the time, "Today, with one stroke of his pen, the President reduced the White House to the size of a privy."

Briefly, the ERB legislated the removal of all departments and agencies from control of the Chief Executive. What had been the Cabinet became independent Public Service Departments, ruled by PS directors. All departmental directors were ruled by a Chief Director who was appointed by the President with the advice and consent of the Congress. The Chief Director could be, but need not be, a PS server. He had tenure to the age of fifty-five unless removed from office upon conviction of wrongful acts, carefully spelled out in the enabling legislation.

In effect, the Chief Director became the manager of the US, ruling through the Public Service. The intent was for the PS merely to administer laws passed by the Legislative Branch.

In the almost twenty years the Executive Reorganization Bill had been law, two results had become increasingly apparent:

1. The President's role was reduced to that of a titular "head of state." He visited abroad and received foreign dignitaries. He awarded honors and presided over national ceremonies. He addressed the citizenry on the need for morality, law, order, patriotism, and the prompt payment of voluntary contributions (taxes). He kicked out the first ball on the opening of the soccer season. He met with delegations of Indians, Boy Scientists, and crabby veterans of World War II. He launched atomic-powered dirigibles and chatted, via TV, with our colonists on the moon. He barbecued proribs on the White House lawn and spent at least two days in each nation that elected to become a new state in the US. But his administrative powers were nonexistent. The Chief Director ran the government.

2. The purpose of the ERB had been to curtail the swollen power of the Executive Branch. That it did. But it also created a fourth branch of government, the Public Service bureaucracy. By 1998, it ruled 89 percent of *all* government servers (96 percent, including the military), and had amassed more political power than the other three branches combined. As pointed out previously, we not only administered the laws of the US, but in the manner of bureaucrats everywhere, in all times, we *created* policy.

Our present Chief Director, Michael Wingate, had held office for seven years. His particular interests were economics and foreign policy. He was said to be science-oriented, and I believed that to be operative. Although I had never met him personally, I had received a cordial handwritten note from him thanking me for my assistance on "our recent project." He was referring to my suggestion for the use of a sickle-cell anemia stimulator on the recalcitrant African tribe.

The Chief Director and his fourth wife lived in a pleasant, unpretentious home (surrounded by a guarded, barbed wire fence) in the Georgetown area. I drove Angela Berri from her Watergate apartment in her smart, steam-powered sedan. We were both wearing zipsuits with decorations. Angela was carrying a thin, shiny briefcase linted to her wrist with a silver-alloy handcuff and chain. She didn't tell me what the case contained and I didn't ask.

The security precautions at the gate were as stringent as those at the compound in GPA-1. We were not allowed entrance until our BIN cards and voiceprints were electronically scanned, approved, and recorded. Then came visual identification by closed-circuit TV to the house. Then the gate was opened. The surrounding lawn was brilliantly illuminated by floodlights.

A serving em in a black zipsuit opened the steel-backed front door. But before he could close it, the Chief Director came rapidly toward us, smiling, hands outstretched. My initial reaction was to the em's warm charm. Then I was surprised by his shortness. In his TV and film appearances, he had seemed much taller. But that could have been manipulated, of course.

I knew something of his background. It was interesting. He was forty-two, a Natural Male, and married only Natural Females. His father had been a successful inventor, mostly of gadgets and small electric and electronic devices. But one invention, a machine for "aging" whiskies and wines almost instantaneously, had proved enormously lovable. It exposed alcoholic beverages to actinic light. It could not produce a twenty-five-year-old cognac in seconds, but it could take the raw edge off petroleum-based alcoholic drinks and make them potable. It was used in almost every distillery in the world.

Michael Wingate inherited his father's wealth at the age of twenty. He could have spent his life in indolence. But he earned a doctorate in social engineering and came to the attention of the government with his PhD thesis on the practicality of direct TV broadcasts to foreign countries via satellite. His ideas had been adopted, but objections in the United Nations became so heated that the US was forced to sign a covenant that restricted all international satellite radio and TV broadcasting to UN control.

(As I dictated the previous paragraph, I became suddenly aware that Michael Wingate's background was not too unlike my own. This was an insight that had not occurred to me before. Perhaps it explains why I was prepared to take profit from the em even before meeting him.)

Wingate joined Public Service, rose rapidly in rank, and was appointed Chief Director in 1991. His brilliance was almost universally recognized and his wit admired.

"Angela!" He smiled. She bent slightly to take his kiss on her cheek.

He turned to me and beamed.

"Dr. Flair!" he said. "This *is* a pleasure. I've been waiting a long time for this meeting."

That solved a question that had been puzzling me: Why had Angela called me to Washington? She was too crafty to initiate contacts between her servers and rulers. Now it was obvious: *He* had commanded my presence.

His palm stroke was slow, firm, dry. He looked like a beardless Santa Claus: white hair, rubicund complexion, pug nose, blue eyes twinkling merrily. An appearance, I knew, that served him well in the political jungle. His brain was quick, dark, devious. He preferred the plot to the plan.

"Grace will be down in a moment," he said. He chuckled suddenly, for no reason I could tell. "Let me show you about. Then we'll have a drink in the library before dinner."

He bounced ahead of us, full of energy and delight. Throwing doors wide, pointing out antiques: rugs, paintings, sculpture, porcelain—all on loan from the National Gallery. This home and all its furnishings were owned by the US and provided as the "Georgetown White House" for the use of the Chief Director.

It was larger than the exterior had indicated. Three early Federal houses had been combined, walls removed or archways and doors inserted. Rooms ran into rooms. Ceilings soared. Quaint cubbyholes abounded. Colors were light; fresh flowers were everywhere. It was all bright, cheerful, comfortable and pleasant.

But still. . . . In almost every room black zipsuits moved casually, shadows, ems and efs. None of them obviously armed. One em, in a red zipsuit, an officer, stood aside to let us pass, grave and reserved. Servants all. But members of the Chief's personal guard. Formerly the Secret Service. Now officially called the Household Staff. They were everywhere. Michael Wingate ignored them.

Finally, he led us into the library. He had, I noted, a need to touch. His hands were on my arm, shoulder, back. He stroked Angela's hair, clasped her waist, held her hand briefly. When he poured an already mixed beverage from a plastic decanter bedded in a bucket of Jellicubes, he handed us each our plastiglass, then curled our fingers about it with both hands. An interesting tic.

"Well," he said happily, holding up his glass. "Happiness and long life to all."

We smiled politely. I looked about. Like my father's library in Grosse Pointe. With one vital exception: These books had been read. I could tell: uneven rows, stained bindings, bookmarks poking up, a few lying on open shelves, bindings down, spread wide.

"Dr. Flair," the Chief Director said. He paused. "Nick? All right?"

"Of course, Chief."

"Nick, how is Lewisohn?"

I gave him a brief, concise report. The em's deterioration. The best we could hope for. The worse we might expect. What I proposed to do next. He listened intently, head cocked to one side. The bright smile on the lips, but not in the eyes.

"Nick," he said. "I'm sure you understand the importance of this em's survival?"

"Yes, sir. In a functioning condition."

"Precisely," he said. "Functioning. We need that."

"Chief," Angela said, "from what Nick says, it may require a heavy outlay. The use of—uh—volunteers. A new staff. And perhaps—"

"Anything." He waved away all the details. "Don't even pause to question it. Whatever you need. My responsibility. You have full authority. Is that clear, Nick?"

On that last question, the velvet glove split and I saw the iron fist: blue eyes deepening, lips pulled tight, the whole face suddenly harder, austere. This em would not suffer failure lightly.

"I compute,"I nodded. "You have my—"

But then the library door opened suddenly. The Chief's wife stood framed. Angela and I rose to our feet. Wingate, the happy bunny once again, bounded over to take her hand and lead her into the room.

"Ah. . . ." he said. "Oh. . . ." he said. "Grace, you look lovely. Just lovely."

So she did. My first reaction, purely visceral: I must use this ef.

She was a head taller than he and, I judged, half his age.

Bare feet, spatulate, with big-toe rings set with clusters of red stones. Garnets?

Loose-flowing gown in a flowered pattern. Natural silk perhaps. Sleeves to her wrists. Draped to her ankles. High on her neck.

Long hands. Smooth, tapered fingers. Tanned. A tiny gold chain for a wedding band.

Dark eyes. Violet? Brown? Heavy brows. Curved brows swooping down on veined temples.

Wide mouth. Full lips. Slightly parted. Glistening. Upper teeth somewhat protuberant. Long canines.

Sharp nose. V-chin. Sinuous neck.

What little I could see of her flesh—ankles, feet, wrists, hands, neck, head—was complete, an almost discernible line about her. She was within. Contained.

Hair the color of fresh ashes. As fine and fragile.

Sculpted ears.

I would lick those first.

"Please forgive me," she said, smiling at Angela. Giving me a flick. "I tried three sets of earrings, then gave up."

Thick voice. Almost syrupy.

We all—even Angela—waited on her. Her presence demanded it. Though her manner was never less, nor more, than quiet, attentive, sympathetic, un-

derstanding. But she seemed so *sure*. A teacher. Even her laughter was detached.

It was an unmemorable dinner—surrogate food—served efficiently but
with no panache by black zipsuits. A natural Israeli white wine was palatable;
a red petrowine, actinized, was not. One amusing detail: Angela Berri ate her
entire dinner with her right hand, the briefcase still shackled her left wrist.
No one commented. I wondered, idly, if the Chief Director might have the
only key. If so, he made no effort to relieve her discomfort.

He dominated the conversation during a gelatinous pâté, cold potato soup,
an entree of chilled canned salmon (molded inexpertly into the shape of a
fish), a salad of prolet. This synthetic lettuce was produced in endless sheets,
the rollers stamping the veins and crinkles of the natural leaf. Then the sheets
were cut into small squares and merchandised in plastic bags. It might well
be used to stuff mattresses.

Chief Wingate, in a droll, eye-rolling manner, recounted his tribulations in
dealing with a small, emerging nation of the Far East. Its representative in
Washington had expressed interest in joining the US. Diplomatic tactics in
this case demanded gifts, bribes, long letters swearing undying fealty to the
current monarch, and, finally, supplying the Ambassador with the corpus of
a popular TV star, a comedienne who weighed about 100 kilos.

"And how did you get her to cooperate, dear?" Grace Wingate asked.
Dutiful wife, feeding her husband lines. "Bribery?"

"Oh, no." He chuckled. "She agreed voluntarily. Didn't even have to appeal
to her patriotism. She said no one had asked her for years and years!"

Laughter fluttered around the table. Artificial lettuce.

"Is it worth the trouble, Chief?" Angela asked.

"I think so." He nodded. Serious now. "Not from any great contribution
they can make, but simply from their numbers. Almost four million. Their
resources aren't all that exciting, although there may be oil off the coast. But
we must constantly keep in mind our need to increase our consumer pool.
Nick, what do you think?"

His sudden, direct question startled me. I had a distinct impression I was
being interviewed.

"A Zoo Nation," I said.

"Zoo Nation?" He looked at me quizzically. "I've never heard the term
before. Yours?"

"I believe so. Yes, sir."

"How do you define a Zoo Nation?"

"An undeveloped—or underdeveloped—political entity that has nothing to
offer but its history, hunger, culture, and poverty. Limited natural resources.
And most of those can now be synthesized. Or adequate substitutes produced.
No science and no technology."

"Surely they could be developed as a viable nation," Grace Wingate said
sharply.

I turned to look at her.

"To what purpose?" I asked. "Assuming it could be done. I'm not certain it could be. Science and technology progress at a geometric rate. Attempt to raise a Zoo Nation to our status—or Russia's, or China's—and by the time that was accomplished we'd be so far ahead they could never catch up. Never. But I think they could achieve a reasonable level of prosperity as a Zoo Nation, a well-ordered Zoo Nation. Income from tourism and handicrafts. Assistance with their sanitation and public health. Perhaps some light cottage-industry. A limited amount of education. Bring the first-rate brains to the mainland for advanced conditioning. But don't expect to make a Japan from a Chad. Develop it deliberately as a Zoo Nation, Encourage its native culture. Make it a kind of human game park, protected, allowed to grow. Within limits."

"Limits?" Wingate said. "Z-Pop?"

"Or Minus-Z. Depending on arable land, rainfall, birthrate, disease, and so forth. A computer study would give you the optimum population. The vital factors are not to expect too much from or promise too much to a Zoo Nation. There is quality in nations, just as there is in objects."

"Mmm," the Chief Director said. He stared at me. Pausing as the servers removed our dinner plates and brought dessert. Thick slices of the new strain of seedless watermelon. They had removed the flavor with the seeds. But the coffee was genuine. With an oily film from poorly washed cups.

"Interesting," he continued. He slipped a saccharine pill into his coffee. "You judge national quality by the degree of scientific and technological development?"

"Of course." I smiled. "My conditioning."

"And how would you rank the US?" he asked. "Compared to, say, Russia, Pan-Europe, China?"

"Forget Pan-Europe," I said. "They have the brains but not the love. As for Russia and China, I can give you only an uninformed judgment. I am not cleared for restricted research in the physical sciences."

"What is your 'uninformed judgment'?"

"In the biomedical disciplines? Compared with Russia and China? Grossly equal. We're ahead in molecular biology. Russia is ahead in bioimmunization. China is ahead in psychopharmacology. But still, as I said, grossly equal."

"But you feel we're not doing enough?"

"Not nearly enough."

He threw back his head and laughed.

"I get that thrust from all sides," he said finally. Spluttering. Wiping wet eyes with his plastinap. "But rarely as openly or as honestly. What do you suggest we do?" Then, ironically: "I'm sure you have many ideas on the subject, Nick."

I caught an angry glance from Angela Berri. But I ignored her wrath and his irony. I didn't care. It was an opportunity. I would have been a fool to avoid it.

"Yes." I nodded. "I have many ideas on the subject. The Science Academy and the National Science Advisory Board were steps in the right direction. But not enough. There must be clear communication between the scientific community and government. A continuing dialogue. And in a participating, not merely an advisory capacity."

"I thought most scientists were deliberately—even enthusiastically—non-political," Chief Wingate said mildly. "If not antipolitical."

"Obso scientists were," I acknowledged. "And are. Many younger scientists are activists. They—we—recognize that science has always been political. That is, it is based on the values of the society in which it exists. The same holds true for art, of course. And economics. No human activity exists in a vacuum. All are influenced by and, in turn, influenced the social medium. Today, science is the megafactor of tomorrow. We ignore it at our peril."

"You feel very deeply about this," Grace Wingate said softly.

"Yes, I do. And it's operative. Remember, we are the first species that can control its own evolution. Compute *that* and its consequences."

"And what do you suggest?" the Chief asked. Somber now. "For today? Where do we start?"

"A separate department under your rule, sir. The Department of Creative Science. Bring together all the government's scientific activities in one efficient and effective political body. Right now, the government's scientific activities are scattered all over the place: atomic energy and solar research in the Department of Natural Resources; weaponry and chemwar research in the Department of Peace; plant biology research in the Department of Agribusiness. Et cetera. The most important, the most promising projects in basic research are restricted. So the overlapping and duplication of effort are disgraceful. I realize that sometimes this state of affairs is desirable: planned disorganization with several teams working on identical projects unknown to each other. But in this case, the disorganization is unplanned. There is no centralization, no firm management. Science demands control, political control, for optimum value to the state. Conditioned political scientists are the answer. If a purely objective scientist, working alone in his lab, was to come up with a guarantee of physical immortality, a public announcement of such a development would simply wreck our economy and our society. We make a thousand discoveries a year, none as world-shaking as that, but the consequences of every scientific advance should be evaluated economically and politically before it's made available. A Department of Creative Science could do that. Am I making sense?"

"A great deal of sense." Chief Wingate nodded. "A great deal indeed. I agree with your thrust. And I thank you for expressing your views so lucidly."

He glanced at the digiclock on the wall, then looked to his wife. A signal apparently passed between them, although I did not catch it. Grace Wingate rose to her feet. We all followed.

"Nick," the Chief Director said, "I'd like a favor from you."

"Of course, sir."

"Angela and I have things to discuss. My wife has a meeting to attend. May I prevail upon you to accompany her and see her safely home?"

Mrs. Wingate smiled faintly.

"My profit," I said.

We separated. The Chief led Angela into the library, his arm linked in hers. She still carried that thin briefcase. Grace Wingate asked me to wait a few moments while she changed.

When she came bouncing down the stairs, I was startled by her costume. She had suddenly lost five years. At least! Long ash hair flamed down her back. A middy was closed with a loosely knotted light blue scarf. A white pleated skirt stopped just above her bare knees. She wore white plastivas sneakers. If she had tried to sell me Girl Scout cookies, I wouldn't have been a bit surprised.

She smiled at my reaction to her appearance.

"Well!" I said. "Are we going to a marshmallow roast?"

Then she laughed, took my arm, led me to the door. We waited silently while the heavy bolts were drawn, the door swung open. Two outside guards accompanied us to a waiting diesel-powered Mercedes limousine. Chauffeur and guard in the front seat, closed off from us by a shield of bulletproof glass. The windows also had the green-tinted nylon layer. As we rolled through the opened gate, a sedan with four black zipsuited occupants followed us closely to Wisconsin Avenue, M Street, and onto Pennsylvania Avenue.

"We're visiting the President," I guessed.

She laughed again. A throaty, gurgling laugh. She seemed freer, relaxed, glad to be out from behind that barred door.

"I'm going to church," she said. Hint of mischief in her voice. "I'm a religionist. Did you know that?"

"No, Mrs. Wingate, I didn't. Which religion?"

"Beist."

"Deist?"

"Beist. I'm sure you've never heard of it. It's very new."

"How many members?" I asked her.

"Oh . . . perhaps a hundred."

"That's not a religion," I said. "It's a cult."

"Beist," she repeated. "We have a small chapter here, and in New York, and in San Francisco. But we make no effort to recruit. If objects hear about us and want to attend meetings, they are welcome. We ask nothing from them. We own no property. Meetings are held in members' homes or, as tonight, in offices or stores. It's all very informal. Unstructured. We hope to keep it that way."

"And what does a Beist believe?"

"A force. A Life Force. We prefer not to define it. We accept the mystery. We welcome the mystery. We say the individual is not immortal, but the human species is. We say all life is growth, with purpose. To merge finally, and become one with that Life Force."

"Vaguely mystic," I murmured.

"Is it? Perhaps. You said tonight at dinner that we are the first species capable of directing and controlling our own evolution. We accept that. We say the human species, now, today, is the highest form of life but will direct its evolution, over thousands and thousands of years, to a higher form, something finer, that will eventually become one with the divine essence of the universe, the Life Force."

She stopped suddenly, turned sideways from the waist, stared at me.

"Well?" she demanded. "What do you think?"

"You want me to be honest?"

"Of course. You must always be honest."

This last was uttered in such a sweetly innocent tone that I could not scoff.

"Mrs. Wingate," I said, "I can't—"

"You may call me Grace," she said.

"Thank you. Grace, I'm glad your new faith encompasses manipulated evolution. But when you speak of a Life Force, a divine essence, you lose me. Consider my conditioning. All scientists—well, certainly most—equate the individual corpus with a clock. Nothing divine about a clock. Dial, hands, wheels, pivots, gears, springs: a mechanical device. Reproduce it exactly—so many teeth in the gears, ratios just so—put tension on the spring or provide some other power source, and away it goes. Tick-tick-tick. Nothing mysterious there. Similarly with the human corpus. But infinitely more complex. Not only mechanical, but electrical and chemical. Still, the corpus is *stuff*, no matter how complex. Bone, blood, tissue, cells, enzymes, hormones, glands, organs, skin, muscle. All *stuff*. And the time will come when we can produce it all, assemble it correctly, and then away it will go, the heart beating steadily— ca-thump, ca-thump, ca-thump. But no finger of God will poke down through the clouds and touch it. No divine essence will be injected. No Life Force will be needed. It will be purely a laboratory product, a reasonable facsimile of the real thing. We're closer to that synthesis than you might think. Where does that leave Beism?"

"But don't you see?" she said excitedly. "We accept all that. It's all part of the purpose. To evolve into something finer and better. When you can create a living human in the laboratory, won't you try to improve on it?"

"Probably. In fact, undoubtedly."

"Well, there you are!" she said triumphantly. "You're part of it, part of the Life Force, whether you recognize it or not. And—Oh, we're here. Nick, would you like to attend? You don't have to, of course. But you're welcome, if you'd like to come in."

"I'd like to very much."

This particular meeting of the Beists was held in the back of a commercial laundry on Sixteenth Street, behind the White House. There were, perhaps, thirty objects present. There was one ef in the uniform of a naval commander, and I recognized the junior Senator from South Dakota. The others were a diverse lot. Most, apparently, middle class, but with a sprinkling of artisans, zipsuits from several Public Service ranks, a few adolescents, a few obsos, a tall, dignified em in Arabic robes.

The congregation stood against the walls, or sat on a miscellany of folding chairs, or perched on cold pressing tables and laundry machinery. The mood seemed light, carefree, informal, lively. There appeared to be no ceremony or ritual. Grace Wingate left me a moment to whisper to a plump young ef with stringy hair and a complexion disfigured by a bad case of *acne vulgaris*.

Grace rejoined me. I had "reserved" a seat for her alongside me on a long metal sorting table. If we had leaned back incautiously, we'd have fallen into empty wire bins labeled Shirts, Skirts, Sheets, Towels, Drawers, etc. Just the place to seek the divine essence.

The dumpy young ef stood up before the gathering. Gradually, the congregation quieted. The ef introduced herself as Joanne Wilensky. She welcomed newcomers. She regretted there was no literature on the Beist movement to distribute, but suggested those interested might question any members present after the formal meeting was concluded.

"We can't answer all your questions," she said. A smile that made her almost pretty. "Because we don't know all the answers. Beism is as much a seeking as a knowing. Perhaps you can help us. We hope you can. Does the secretary have anything to report?"

The junior Senator from South Dakota rose and read two short letters from the Beist chapters in New York and San Francisco. Both reported increased attendance at their most recent weekly meetings and growing membership. The secretary announced with some pride that he now estimated the total number of Beists in the US at almost 200. Fingers were snapped.

Joanne Wilensky then asked if anyone else cared to speak. An em in a bronze-colored zipsuit rose and stated he was about to be transferred to Yuma, Arizona. He requested permission to start a Beist group there. The congregation voted approval enthusiastically. The wave of the future.

The Wilensky ef paused a moment, surveying the group slowly. She was a dowdy figure, shapeless, in a wrinkled plasticot dress.

"Is she the minister, or priestess, or guru?" I whispered to Grace Wingate.

"Sort of. It all started with her. But we take turns leading the meetings. She doesn't get paid or anything. She's a presser in this laundry."

"Scientists believe—" Joanne Wilensky began in a hesitant, stammering voice—and then she proceeded to tell us what scientists believed, repeating almost word for word the comparison of a clock to a human corpus. I had made to Grace Wingate in the car. I had seen Grace speak to her, but I was startled at how accurately the Beist leader was repeating my thesis.

"But the life of the clock comes from a coiled spring," she stated. "Or from an electric outlet. Or from a battery. Where does the life of a human come from? Not from on high, the scientists say. Not from the finger of God poking down through a cloud. Then from where? Why should this combination of blood, tissue, cells, and organs result in animate life? Because, say the scientists, it is the nature of the materials used, being so constituted that in proper combination life begins. That is no answer at all. *Why* should the constitution of the materials be of such a nature? *Why* should the proper combination of those materials result in a beating heart? It is the *why* we seek. It may or may not be the touch of a Divine Creator. It may or may not be the blind functioning of chance. God or accident: Is there any difference? But we believe there is a reason, a purpose. We know not what. But we ask the scientists this question: Why do they exist? Or we? Or stones, stars, fish, and the universe? Why a something and not a nothing? Nullity, complete nonexistence, would prove nonpurpose. Existence presupposes purpose."

And so forth, and so forth. A stew of not especially new ideas. She made the mistake so many religionists make of trying to justify their faith by reason. Then they're in my court, and I can slaughter them. If I started a new religion, I would have but one law, one justification: Believe. Faith confounds reason.

I said much the same thing to Grace Wingate on the ride back to the Georgetown White House.

"Don't you believe in anything?" she asked me.

"Of course. In the immortality of the human species and the ability of science to ensure that immortality."

"But to what purpose?"

"My Personality Profile says that I am goal-oriented. That is true, but in the short run. I am essentially pragmatic. I am not concerned with teleology. A lot of kaka. A waste of time. There's too much to be done today. For tomorrow."

Suddenly, unexpectedly, she put a hand on mine. She leaned toward me.

"Will you be my friend, Nick?" she asked. A whisper.

"Of course." I smiled. "Do you have to ask?"

"Do you know what was in Angela's briefcase?"

"No. I obviously have no need to know."

She sat back, huddled into the corner of the wide seat. She stared at me thoughtfully a long moment. In the gloom she seemed suddenly older, despite the girlish middy, the ashen hair misting about her shoulders. I was conscious of the bare legs, the curve of her upper arms.

"I want to tell you," she said.

"I don't think you should," I said.

"I *want* to."

"Please don't. It's wrong for you to talk about restricted material, and dangerous for me to listen."

"Then I'll tell my husband you tried to worm it out of me, that you tried and tried to get me to reveal what's going on, but I refused to tell you."

I looked at her in astonishment. Shocked by her resoluteness.

"Why would you want to do that to me?" I asked her. "I have done you no harm."

Then she was weeping. Hand over her eyes. Shoulders hunched, shaking. Hair a scrim about her face. Little sounds came out of her. My hand crept sideways, found her free hand. She gripped my fingers with surprising force.

"All right, Grace," I said gently. "What's this all about?"

"Angela," she said. "And Mike. What she's doing. With Mike. To Mike."

Mike? Chief Director Michael Wingate, manager of the US. It sounded odd. Did President Harold K. Morse's wife call him Harry? Probably. And here was Grace Wingate worrying about Mike. Knowing Angela, I thought she probably had cause for worry.

"Grace." I said her name softly. I gripped her hand tightly. "I want to be your friend. Tell me what is in Angela's briefcase."

We were on M Street, approaching Georgetown, and she spoke rapidly in her deep, throaty voice. What she told me seemed anticlimactic. But I did not at that point in time fully compute the Washington world. I was not conditioned to assigning operative political values. It was my first experience as a major mover and shaker. Later, when I learned the techniques of power politics, I realized the importance of what Grace Wingate told me that night.

This had been the sequence of events:

1. Hyman R. Lewisohn had run a definitive computer study of the US Government's assets in real property. The inventory included public lands, military bases and hardware, natural resources (estimated), power generating facilities, and such real estate as shipyards, factories, homes, universities, hotels, motels, schools, zoos, wholesale and retail businesses, etc. Most of the last-mentioned had reverted to US ownership upon the default of government loans or for nonpayment of voluntary contributions.

2. The total proved simply astonishing. The US was by far the largest landholder, the largest shipbuilder, the largest *everything* in the world. This enormous capital had been amassed not deliberately but by a slow process of accretion, almost by accident. The US Government now owned and operated, either directly or through license, hamburger stands and swimming pools, parks and playgrounds, macaroni factories and airlines, golf courses and bordellos, bridges and distilleries, shipping lines and private mints, an orchard in Florida, and a trout stream in Oregon. Even whole towns that had grown up about military bases.

3. It was determined that all these enterprises were under the direction of or operated by several Public Service departments. Natural Resources handled public lands and parks. Commerce handled hotels, motels, factories, stores. Bliss handled nursing homes, hospitals, recreation facilities. Agribusiness handled farms, food processing plants, supermarkets. And so forth.

4. Lewisohn's plan was to maximize income by bringing all US Government profit-making properties under the management of a new Public Service department, the Department of National Assets. He argued that by centralized control, modern management techniques, stricter accounting procedures—by operating US-owned business as an efficient conglomerate might—income from government property could be increased by 38.6416 percent and result, if desired, in a 4.2674 percent tax reduction.

5. Chief Director Wingate, his staff and directors were enthusiastic about Lewisohn's proposal. But the creation of a new Public Service department would necessitate enabling legislation from Congress. Wingate wasn't so enthusiastic about stirring up the Whigs (formerly the Republican Party). And they would certainly be stirred up by the revelation of the incredible total of real property held by the US Government that would have to be made in any Congressional hearing on a bill to create the proposed department.

6. Angela Berri had suggested a way out of the difficulty. Instead of a new department, a new section in the Department of Bliss, which she ruled, would be established. New sections were purely an administrative matter and required no Congressional approval. The new section would perform all the functions of the new department proposed by Lewisohn. It was a detailed prospectus for this new section that Angela was carrying in her chained briefcase to discuss with the Chief Director.

Dear Angela! For an ef on the suck, I could understand how tempting the new section must seem. All that love rolling in from government properties all over the world. If she skimmed only one-tenth of one percent, she'd be the wealthiest ef in the world within five years. Temerity! Greed!

"I'm not sure I can do anything about this," I said slowly to Grace Wingate. "If your husband wants to avoid a Congressional confrontation, I can't see any choice but to opt for Angela's plan."

She turned away from me, staring out the window.

"She owns you, too, I suppose," she said dully. "You've probably used each other."

"Yes, we've used each other," I said. "No, she doesn't own me. Give me a little time. Maybe I can compute something. If you want me to be your friend, if you want me to help you, you must trust me. Can you do that?"

She turned to look at me. Despair in those dark eyes.

"I have no choice." she said. "Do I? I have nowhere else to—I can't let her—They—she and Mike—Nick, I want to keep my husband! But she—and she thinks I—you don't *know* what she—"

"I know, Grace," I murmured. "Believe me, I know. I'll do everything I can. I'm on your side."

She leaned forward, kissed my cheek swiftly, pulled away. We stopped before the barred gate. Guards came over to inspect us.

We found Angela Berri and Chief Wingate seated casually in a parlor-type room in the front of the house. It was furnished with three TV sets, a game table, a cellarette on wheels, and slightly worn chintz-covered armchairs and sofas. Angela no longer had her briefcase. There was nothing in the manner or appearance of either of them to indicate how their discussion had gone. Perhaps I imagined they were seated an unusual distance apart.

Wingate rose to greet us.

"Good meeting?" he asked his wife.

"Oh, yes."

"Let's have a nightcap," he said.

He glanced at me, made an almost imperceptible motion of his head. Obediently, I followed him over to the cellarette. He busied himself with the bottle of apricot-flavored petroqueur and four small, stemmed glasses.

"Did you attend?" he asked in a low voice.

"Yes, sir. I did."

"Reactions?"

"Certainly not apocalyptists. Quite the contrary. I think they're harmless."

"They are," he said. "At this point in time."

"Not politically oriented," I observed. "Unless what I saw was a front."

"No, it's operative," he said. "I had them profiled. Nick, that suggestion of yours for a new Department of Science...."

"Department of Creative Science, sir."

"Yes. Spell it out in a personal letter to me. Purpose, organization, staff, estimated budget, and so forth."

"Be happy to, sir."

He handed me two filled glasses, looked swiftly at the chatting efs, turned back to stare into my eyes.

"No need to go through channels," he said quietly. "Bring the prospectus directly to me. Don't mail it. No endorsement copies. You compute?"

"Yes, sir."

We each carried two glasses back to the efs. Wingate handed one of his to Grace; I gave mine to Angela. We sat in a rough square, efs at the ends of a sofa, ems in distant armchairs. Each in a corner.

"Nick," the Chief said, rather languidly, "that suggestion of yours for a new Department of Science.... I wonder if you appreciate the political problems involved in getting a new Public Service department approved by Congress? The opposition would be heavy: the small but loud group that is against any extension of PS hegemony, obsos, the antiscience faction, antiabortionists, most religionists, rulers of existing government research sections in other departments, and industrial lobbyists with sweetheart contracts with those sections. A can of worms. It wouldn't be easy to get the enabling legislation passed."

"I'm sure it wouldn't, sir."

"But suppose we decided to make a fight for a new department," he said casually. "Any suggestions on tactics?"

I caught a warning glance from Angela. Wingate was, I knew, drawing me out on the possibility of creating Lewisohn's new Department of National Assets. He had no way of knowing I recognized his stalking-horse. Nor did Angela. She was concerned only that I might say something to endanger her plan. But I could safely ignore her warning; I could always plead ignorance and innocence.

"I don't believe the establishment of a new department would present insuperable difficulties, sir," I said pompously. Ingenuous I. "It seems to me one way to approach the problem would be to introduce—at the same time you introduce the new department bill—another bill so controversial, so certain to arouse strong passions and angry dispute, that with all the howling going on—media debates, demonstrations, strikes, boycotts, and so forth—why, you might stand a much better chance of slipping by your new department bill with a minimum of opposition."

He stared at me a moment. Expressionless. I risked a quick glance at Angela. If looks could stop, I would have been cremated in my armchair.

"A throwaway bill," Wingate mused. "Something we know will be defeated. But we put up a valiant fight. It takes off the heat. In other words, a decoy bill. I do believe you have a talent for politics. What you suggest—"

At that precise instant. Explosion. Loud. Heavy thump. Ground tremble. Inside me. Tinkle of broken glass. Softer thump. Wisconsin Avenue or all around? Shake and flutter. Looks. Frozen. Cuaght. Shatter of automatic rifle fire. Boom of flechette guns.

Wingate: "Down on the floor! All of you!"

Angela a cat. Up. Two quick steps. Soft, gymnastic roll onto one shoulder. Then. Under a table. Hands and knees. Spine arched. Head up. Lips drawn back. Snarling.

Door burst. Black zipsuits.

Ems kneeling. Glass breaking. Another thump. Mirror shattered. Myself moving in a dream. Stop-action. Down on one knee. A razor stripe across the back of my left hand. Shallow slice. Dark blood welling. No pain.

Wingate at the window.

"Goddamn it, get down! Sir!"

A red zipsuit inside. Door slammed and bolted.

"Down! Down! Down!"

Grace Wingate gliding to her husband. Grasping his shoulders. Turning him. Interposing her body between him and the jagged windows. Hugging him close. Looking into his eyes. Angela spitting. Furious. The efs magnificent.

A chatter of gunfire from black zipsuits at the windows. Smoke. Smell.

Sharp crack. Whine of steel splinters. Portrait of John Quincy Adams with three eyes. Final burst. A human wail. High-pitched scream.

Silence. We wait. Trembling. Black zipsuits reload. With shaking hands. I look down. A few drops of urine. Nothing shows. But I know. Wingate goes to the cellarette. Begins to fill glasses. Steady hands.

"Oh," he breathes. "Ah," he breathes. "The worst this year."

He turns. Sees my blood, starts toward me. I wave him away, knot a handkerchief, pull it tight with my teeth. Angela crawls out. Straightens up. White.

"Stay here," Wingate says. Rushes out.

The black zipsuits are still at the windows. Not moving. I take them brandies. They drink. Not taking their eyes away from the night.

Wingate comes back with a kit. My wound is ridiculous. A slice across the knuckles. Already clotting. I dab it, tape it. The bandage stains slowly. Then stabilizes. Angela grips my arm, her grin a forgiveness. Grace Wingate kisses my cheek. Again. Soft, yielding lips. Syrupy as her voice. Her body would come apart in my hands. Just disintegrate. No. Unfold. And reveal mysteries.

"We lost an em on the gate," Wingate reported. "Three injured. They lost four stopped. Two injured. All of them. We think."

"Who?" I asked.

He shrugged.

"Oh . . . who knows. Animals."

The Chief ordered an escort to see us back to the Watergate Complex. A gray sedan preceded us. Driver and three armed guards. A gray sedan followed us. Driver and three armed guards. The red zipsuited officer in command was an ef. She insisted on ushering us safely inside the door of Angela's apartment. When the door was closed, locked, bolted, chained, I glanced through the peephole. A black zipsuit stood outside.

"Welcome to Washington," Angela said. "District of Columbia."

"But the love isn't bad," I said, and we both laughed.

When Maya Leighton and I had arrived late that afternoon, I had been impressed by the apartment. Now, after an evening in the Wingates' pleasant, comfortable, lived-in, slightly shabby home, these rooms seemed stagy. Everything glistened or glowed. Ashtrays were not only empty but polished. Artificial elegance.

When we had arrived, Angela had not yet returned from her office. A serving ef in an earth-colored zipsuit let us in, showed us the two double bedrooms, nests. We bathed separately, changed into our uniforms, waited with a drink for Angela's return.

She rushed in, stroked palms, gave Maya a sharp, searching look, then disappeared to dress for dinner with the Chief Director. While she was absent, and Maya and I sat in silence, sipping vodka-and-Smack, Art Roach rang the chime. He was wearing his red zipsuit.

What a chilly, bloodless em he was. He inspected Maya Leighton drowsily, blinking. I recognized the look. There are certain surgeons who enjoy cutting. The two departed, for an evening of fun and frivolity. I had already warned Maya. I could, I told myself, do no more.

Now. Angela and I safe inside the guarded door. We were sunk in uncomfortably soft armchairs. Enveloped. Drowning. She stared at me.

"You're a fool, Nick," she said. Finally.

"A fool? How so?"

"When the Chief asked you how he might pass a bill for a new department."

"So? I answered him as honestly as I could. Would you have me stutter, 'I don't know,' or 'I have no idea.' Then *he* would have thought me a fool. And *you* a fool for giving me my rank. Is that what you wanted?"

"Oh . . . no." She sighed. "I suppose you're right. You just didn't know."

"Know what?"

"Nothing. You have no need to know. I wonder if your secretary is home?"

I waved toward the door of the second bedroom.

"Take a look," I told her.

She rose, kicked off her shoes, padded to the bedroom door. She opened it, peered in cautiously, closed the door.

"She's here. Sleeping naked."

"Any obvious cuts, bruises, contusions, welts, or scratches?"

She looked at me curiously.

"Ah," she said, "I see you know Art Roach. No, she looks rosy and whole."

We looked at each other and laughed. We were both very vulgar objects.

"Speaking of wounds," she said. "How's yours?"

"I'll survive," I said. "How often does that happen?"

"Assault on the Chief? Third time this year. It's always pillowed. The neighbors are all in PS. No one talks."

"He was good. So was his wife. Lovely ef."

"Yes."

She looked toward the bedroom door. Seeing, I knew, the naked Maya sprawled sleeping.

"I'm charged," she said.

"That's understandable." I nodded. "Violence. Danger. Adrenalin."

"Don't you feel it?"

"Of course. Flip a coin?"

"Don't be silly. Is she het or bi?"

"Bi. I think. Don't really know, ma'am."

"Would you mind if I tried?"

"Not at all. But Roach probably just used her."

"So?" she said. "That just makes the cheese more binding."

"You're a dreadful ef." I laughed.

"I know." She smiled coldly. "Dreadful. An object inspiring dread. And don't you ever forget it, Nick."

She went into Maya's bedroom. Closed the door behind her. In a moment I heard a burst of laughter. Then murmurings. Then silence.

I stood up, stretched, looked around. I poured myself a petronac at her futuristic bar, then slumped down again in that womb-chair. I sipped the brandy and, for a moment, plotted her destruction.

I couldn't compute it through. Too many variables. I thought of Grace Wingate. What she . . . What I . . . I couldn't compute it through. Insufficient input.

I came around to Lewisohn's suggestion for a new Department of National Assets. His Grand Plan was becoming increasingly evident. I should have seen it before. Opening the United States to foreign nations. A national bank. Converting Social Security to conventional insurance. And now centralizing the management of the nation's real property. The leukemic dwarf was creating a corporate state. Eventually, a corporate world. It was that simple and elegant.

I could live with it, I decided. I moved to the other bedroom. Undressed slowly. I could live with it. Every successful corporation, conglomerate, multinational company depended on research and development for growth. Enter Nicholas Bennington Flair. Machiavelli in a silver zipsuit.

I inhaled an eight-hour Somnorific and plunged out.

Y-6

In the forty-eight hours following my return to GPA-1 from Washington, I made a number of administrative decisions that were to have far-reaching effects important in this account.

I constituted a "Group Lewisohn" that would be responsible for the continued creative functioning of our famous patient. The Group would be headquartered at Rehabilitation & Reconditioning Hospice No. 4 at Alexandria, Virginia, and would be under the nominal rule of Dr. Seth Lucas. Second in command would be Maya Leighton. I transferred her to GPA-2 and briefed her on what I expected from her. In the treatment of Lewisohn . . . and in the treatment of Art Roach.

I informed Angela Berri of the creation of Group Lewisohn (later, Maya Leighton was to refer to it, in my presence only, as "Group Lewisohn") via a conventional, low-priority mailed memo.

I flashed Seth Lucas, told him his new assignment, and instructed him to proceed with the construction of a suite designed for the parabiotic treatment of Hyman R. Lewisohn as he, Lucas, had described it during the colloquy at Hospice No. 4.

I also remembered to have his security clearance raised to Red-2.

I had a heavy four-hour meet with Paul Bumford. We dealt with a plan for drawing and storing an Individual Microbiological Profile for every object in the US, as a means of positive and precise identification. Then our discussion turned to our project for developing UP, the Ultimate Pleasure pill. We agreed basic research fell into three gross areas: physiological, psychological, mental. Overlapping, of course. There was a fourth, worrisome research area: metaphysical in nature. But we could not define it and postponed action until more input was available.

We decided to organize three miniteams in our field offices: physiological in Houston, psychological in Spokane, mental in Honolulu. None would be aware of the final goal of their service. Simply that we wanted to determine the origins of pleasure.

Paul had an additional matter to discuss. In the most recent bulletin of the Bureau of Public Security on current crime statistics, he had noted that the arrest rate for use, sale, or possession of restricted drugs was up 0.4 percent.

"It's statistically insignificant," he admitted. "But I think it's large enough to justify action. In fact, action might be a plus if someone in Congress or the media picks up on it."

"So?" I asked him. "What do you suggest?"

"A study of possible chromosomal damage due to habitual use of hallucinogens. Having Nancy Ching set up a team out in San Diego.

With increased need for hallucinogens for research. From Scilla Pharmaceuticals, of course."

"Paul," I said, "I'm proud of you. And when you send out your directives on the UP Project, be certain to mention the use of hallucinogens as one possible approach."

On the evening of the second day I picked up a long coded message from Simon Hawkley at my mail drop. I spent most of the night decoding it with the aid of his book on the early monasteries of California. I completed the service about 0430, and fell into bed. Exhausted.

I was awakened at 0740 by a flash from my father in Grosse Pointe. My mother had stopped in her sleep the previous night.

I gave the orders I had to give. I didn't anticipate being absent more than three days.

"Can I come with you?" Paul Bumford asked.

He had met my parents. Once. My mother had liked him. My father had not.

"All right," I said. "Thank you. I may stay on a day or two, but you come back right after the funeral. Let's take the Bullet Train. A few more hours will make no difference. We'll try for a compartment. I have a lot to tell you. In camera."

I had time to make some purchases in the enormous compound PX before we left. I wondered if Lewisohn had included the worldwide PX chain in his list of the US Government's real property. Probably. At eight-six new dollars for a middy blouse, it had to be a lovable enterprise.

Aboard the Bullet Train to Detroit, we sprawled comfortably, uniforms unzipped, shoes kicked off. We pulled the shades; the landscape en route was not inspiring. I told Paul first about my establishing Group Lewisohn in Alexandria.

"Advance toward the guns," he remarked.

"Exactly," I said approvingly. "Paul, you're becoming very perceptive. Washington is where the action is, and we need a base there. Maya's proximity to Art Roach can do us no harm. She's been instructed to supply me with a profile on him. Everything: personal habits, sexual kinks, daily routine, prejudices, speech patterns. And so forth."

"What do you hope to learn?"

"Anything. Maybe after he uses, he talks. Some ems do. Is he left-handed? What pills does he pop? Does he use a lighter or matches? I want to know everything about him. Now take a look at this . . ."

I took a paper from my briefcase and handed it across to him. It was my decoding of Simon Hawkley's long message.

Yes, Scilla Pharmaceuticals in San Diego would probably be amenable to a takeover, if the love was right. The current owner, Anthony Scilla, was fifty-two and had recently suffered two mild strokes. His family was urging his retirement. The company had strong union contracts with two years to run. Scilla himself had even stronger loyalties to his executive staff. Terms of sale would probably include rank security for top management.

Paul Bumford scanned this financial kaka quickly. But when he came to the bottom line, he slowed. Lips pursed. He emitted a low, hissing whistle. Then he looked up at me. I was suddenly aware he had stopped using eyeshadow. His makeup was much more subtle than it had been.

"Nick," he said, "I was going to offer to help out. To throw my little pittance into the pot if it would help buy Scilla. But my contribution would be pissing in the sea. You can't manage this, can you?"

"I couldn't last night," I admitted. "After I decoded, I was ready to reject the whole thing and try to concoct a new plan. That was last night. Then this morning I woke up, my mother has stopped, and I'm her sole heir. That's what I mean by chance and luck. Who could have computed . . ."

"A sweet ef," he said in a low voice. "I took profit from her. Very much."

"Yes," I said. "And she profited from you. "Terminal nostalgia,' she said. She knew. It's true. Nostalgia is desperation. When you can't cope. It'll probably take a year for probate. Mother had the faith of a French peasant or Chinese shopkeeper: Paper is no good, put everything in gold or diamonds. So it will take time to realize. But I know my father will lend against it."

"A sweet ef," he repeated faintly.

"Yes, yes," I said impatiently. A little angry, perhaps, that his grief should seem greater than mine. "But I now have the funds. Zero in on that. Let's futurize . . . Assuming Angela takes the bait, and assuming we're able to obtain hard evidence that she's on the suck, where do we go from there?"

"Go?" Paul said. "Why, we take her."

"Take her? How? Go to Art Roach, the ruler of Security and Intelligence, and demand her arrest? No way. He's her creature. He'd have us both in a Cooperation Room so fast we wouldn't know what happened until we were given the Informed Consent Statement to sign."

"Then, if we have the evidence, don't go down. To Roach. Go up. To the Chief Director."

"Yes." I nodded. "That's logical. But life isn't logical. Politics isn't logical. No, strike that. Politics is logical. But a different kind of logic. No value judgment implied, but *different*. Not the linear logic of science. Infinitely more complex. More input. More variables. Angela and the Chief Director are users."

"Oh, Jesus." He groaned.

I told him about the dinner with the Wingates at the Georgetown White House. He interrupted once.

"Nick," he said, "I've been meaning to tell you. Wingate. Chief Director Michael Wingate. Phoebe Huntzinger's Executive Assistant is Pomfret Wingate, the em who's going to play *King Lear* in the nude. I thought he might be related to the Chief Director. Remember Franklin Ferguson and Lydia Ann? But there's nothing to it. They're not related. Chief Wingate is an NM, and Pommy is an AINM."

"Good," I said. "Glad you thought to check."

But I was disturbed. The possibility should have occurred to *me*.

I continued describing the dinner with the Wingates. Paul listened intently, bent forward, head lowered. I related everything except the final armed attack against the Chief Director. Paul had no need to know.

"What's your reaction?" I asked when I finished.

"Involved," he said. "But more plus than minus, I think. We should be able to manipulate Grace Wingate. She asked for help. She might provide more to us than we can offer her."

"Well . . . equal, certainly. One hand washes the other. But I agree with you that she's an important factor. Or will be when we go to the Chief Director with evidence of Angela's snookering."

"Beism, you said?"

"Yes, Beism. Not Deism."

"Sounds wild. And with a New York chapter?"

"That's what she said."

"Nick, suppose I look them up and join the group. Wouldn't that help?"

I didn't like it. I didn't know why at that point in time, but I instinctively rejected the idea.

"I could do that, Paul."

"No, no," he said earnestly. "Too obvious. You told her your objections to Beism. You came on strong for science. She wouldn't accept a sudden conversion. Nor would her husband. It would look exactly like what it was: opportunism. But I could do it."

"To what purpose?"

He grinned at me.

"If you want a precise scenario, I can't supply one. But it might help. Nick, I want to help."

He half-rose to his feet, leaned across to me, kissed my lips. The caress surprised, pleased me.

"Long time since we've done that," I breathed. "Too long."

"Yes," he said. "All right then if I become a Beist?"

His reasoning was valid. But still . . .

"All right," I said reluctantly. "But keep it pillowed."

"Sure. Now, Nick, about this Department of Creative Science—where did *that* come from? It's not in the Tomorrow File."

"I know it isn't. But the Chief Director asked me for ideas on how to bring scientists into government. I winged it."

"And brilliantly," he said. "Have you prepared the prospectus yet?"

"No. Who's had time?"

"Can I provide some input? Wild ideas? Include them or not, as you like."

"Of course. All contributions gratefully accepted."

I think we both dozed. When finally, slowing for the Detroit terminal, I opened my eyes, Paul Bumford was awake and staring at me.

Later, when I was to recall the events of those two days, scenes and images were remembered in short takes. Out of sequence. A badly spliced film. I thought at first it was an extended attack of Random Synaptic Control. Then I realized that, because of emotional strain, the alcohol I drank, the pills I popped, those two days were recollected as a discontinuous series of incidents. In my memory a time frame did not exist.

Paul and I were elevated to the roof of the high-rise crematorium surmounting the Detroit terminal. My father's helicopter was awaiting us. A new ef pilot: dark, thin, Petulant mouth.

Paul glanced at plane and pilot. Then looked sideways at me, raised his eyebrows.

"My father's toy," I said.

I had resolved to take no drugs before her funeral. It was to be a kind of penance. The only penance I was capable of. I was not capable of it.

After the burial of the urn, after my weeping father, weeping Mrs. McPherson, weeping Miss Catherine, and weeping Charles had stumbled back to the house, Paul and I stood staring at the freshly turned earth.

Through the trees, drifting, came the two young ems, neighbors who had

so amused my mother. Wispy creatures from the adjoining estate. Both barefoot, wearing identical plasticot caftans decorated in an overall pattern of
atomic explosions.

They were carrying armloads of natural flowers: something long-stemmed
and purple. They asked if they might leave them on my mother's grave. I
nodded. They put them down gently.

"She was a beautiful human being," one of them said. The one with a ring
in his nose.

"Yes," I said. "Thank you."

"Who were *they*?" Paul breathed when they ran away. Startled fauns.

"Friends and neighbors," I said.

"The kind of ems who give homosexuals a bad name," Paul said. "Flits."

"You've changed," I told him. "You wouldn't have said that a year ago. In
that tone."

" 'When I was a child,' " he quoted, " 'I spake as a child. When I became
a man, I put away childish things.' "

"Now I'll give you one," I said. " 'Upon what meat doth this our Caesar
feed, that he is grown so great?' "

Paul wrote:
    In your prospectus to the Chief Director re the establishment of a De-
partment of Creative Science, I presume you will include an introduction
explicating the relationship between science and politics. Do not neglect
to point out that the development of birth control pills and their wide
acceptance affected the Women's Liberation movement of the 1960–1970's:
a classic example of how science and technology influence sociological
change.

"What data banks does your company buy from?" I asked my father.
He looked at me curiously.

"Consolidated or Federated," he said. "Occasionally some of the smaller
ones. Why?"

The government's National Data Bank was the largest, of course. It maintained a complete computerized file on every object in the US. It issued BIN
cards, recorded genetic history, military service, political activity, criminal accusations and convictions, credit rating, income taxes, marital status, awards
and honors. Everything. By law, information stored in the NDB could not be
revealed to anyone outside the government, or inside for that matter, who
could not prove a need to know.

But private data banks had proliferated. Several attempts had been made
to curb their activities by licensing, as Sweden had. But in 1998, there was
little regulation of their operations. Most of the commercial data banks were
specialized, dealing with such things as credit rating or personal interests or
purchasing habits, etc. If you wanted a list of all seventy-year-old obsos in the

US with an annual income of 10,000 new dollars and an active interest in shuffleboard, there was a data bank to provide names and addresses. Or if you wanted information on a specific object, for whatever reason, enough love paid to enough data banks would buy a profile almost as complete as if you had free access to the National Data Bank.

Sometimes I wondered how long it would be before the definition of "privacy" in your dictionary began "Obsol." And how long before it began "Obs."

"I want a profile on Angela Teresa Berri," I told my father.

"Ah," he said. "DIROB. She rules you, doesn't she?"

"Yes," I said. "And I also want a profile on Art Roach. He's ruler of Security and Intelligence of the Department of Bliss. That's why I don't want you connected with it in any way. Can you scam it?"

He didn't ask why I wanted the information. My father wasn't afraid of me, but I thought possibly he was in awe of me.

"I think I can do it." He nodded. "I'll place the orders through a supplier who owes me. What do you want?"

"Everything," I said. "Down to the moles on her ass."

"She has them?" he asked.

"She has them," I said.

He laughed.

"All right," he said. "But it'll take time."

"I have patience," I told him.

My mother's corpus was cremated, according to law. By custom, flaming took place following the funeral ceremony, lay or religionist. Then the plastilead urn containing the ashes of the stopped would be placed in a deposit box in a high-rise crematorium. A simple marker attached to the door. The long corridors of deposit boxes were decorated with frequently changed bouquets of plastirub flowers.

But in this case, my mother's corpus had been flamed soon after stopping. The urn had been delivered to a local church for the service. My father intended to bury her ashes on the grounds of our Grosse Pointe estate. It was illegal, but he had bribed local authorities. I approved of his arrangements.

The service was held in an Omni-Faith church, across Mack Avenue from Sunningdale Park. It was an A-frame structure of white plastisteel panels inset with long, narrow windows of colored plastiglass in abstract patterns. Rosy light fell on the altar where the gray urn had been placed. The church was crowded. I was surprised by the number of objects. I had expected her obso friends. But there were so many young objects present. Adolescents. What their relationship to my mother had been, I did not know. But they may have been strangers, their attendance due to simple curiosity in a church service.

It was a short ceremony. The pastor said she was not gone. Though she was stopped, he said, the memory of her kindness, beauty, and good humor would endure. We would recall her many charitable deeds, he said. We would speak her name, and tell children of her. So she would remain alive. A small choir sang a rock lament.

Millie Jean Grunwald was delighted with my gifts. Gifts for her. Gifts for me.

"Oh," she kept saying. "Oh, oh, oh."

The gifts were a middy loosely tied with a light blue scarf. A white skirt that ended above her bare knees. Plastivas sneakers. And a long wig of ashen hair (nylet) that flamed about her shoulders.

How artful. Carrying her tenderly to the bed. Ministering. She a surrender, wavering. Slowly the scarf, the middy, the skirt. I held my breath. It was sacred. I guided her fingers. She opened the mystery to me.

We were so slow. Just drifting. I wasn't sure when sperm spurted. If it did. It made no difference in my dream.

"You're going to be rich," my father told me. "Not rich rich, but rich. Everything she had is yours."

"How much?" I asked.

"Oh . . . maybe half a million new dollars."

New dollars. Interesting. They were always "new." In 1979, Lewisohn had persuaded the US Government to go to an Index System. The original idea was Brazilian. Lewisohn improved on it. Everything in the US economy—prices, wages, interest rates—was linked to the Cost of Living Index. As the index rose, as it did, inexorably, so rose every other economic factor in an intricate relationship.

The setting up of this system had required ten years of intensive computerized service, calculating the monetary, financial, and economic equations. The terms of all outstanding contracts—mortgages, bonds, stocks, insurance policies, etc.—had to be renegotiated. It was a horrendously complex task.

Yet, when completed, the Index System served reasonably well. It demanded, of course, that the US dollar be devalued, or you'd need a wheelbarrow of dollars to purchase a loaf of bread. "Revaluation" was the term used, rather than "devaluation," for semantic reasons. After each revaluation, old bills were declared obsolete and without value. New dollars, in new designs, were put into circulation.

The Index System proved to have one unexpected benefit: It halted hoarding completely, either by misers or by objects seeking to hide illegal cash from the government. No longer could the criminal conglomerates store bills in safe deposit boxes. After each revaluation, old dollars could be exchanged for the new currency at government banks. Questions were asked.

"Half a million new dollars," I repeated to my father. "I imagine probate and sale of the gold and other assets will take at least a year."

"Probably." He nodded.

"Will you lend against it?" I asked him. "I may need large sums for a short time."

"Of course," he said. "As much as you want."

"I insist on paying interest," I said.

He was offended.

Paul wrote:

In the prospectus for the Department of Creative Science, it will be necessary to make certain projections, describing the role of science and technology in the world of tomorrow. Just as inevitably, objections will be made that our vision of the future is "inhuman." It is important that we stonewall this attack. One approach: Point out the subjective nature of the term "inhuman world." What is human? What is inhuman? Cro-Magnon man might very well have found Renaissance Italy inhuman. Queen Victoria, I am certain, would have thought amniocentesis inhuman. Yet today it is accepted casually as a proved and useful diagnostic technique. I am convinced the technology we suggest today will similarly be accepted casually tomorrow.

We were in the library. Drinking brandy. Paul, my father, Ben Baker, my father's production manager, me. After a while we could talk.

"Hey, Nick," Baker said. "Look at this."

He brought a box from a corner, lifted the lid under my nose. The putrescent corpus of a Poo-Poo Doll. The same stink.

"Not again?" I said. "Another bad run?"

"What are you looking at?" Paul said.

The production manager shoved it at him.

"My God!" Paul cried. "What *is* it?"

I told him about the Connecticut River spill, the polluted rinse water in my father's factory, the ruined dolls.

"But this one is deliberate," my father said. "We got those doll bodies so they decay within predictable time limits. And that's not all we've got. It's going to be big, Nick."

I looked at him. Not certain.

"What's going to be big?"

"I'll tell you," he said. "A couple of weeks after we solved—after *you* solved the problem of the spoiled run—I went over to Ben's place for an outdoor barbecue. Ben's youngest daughter—What is she, Ben? Five? Six?"

"Penny is five," Ben Baker said. "Smart as a whip."

"Right," my father said. "Well, when I got there, Penny and some of her friends were having a funeral for her pet turtle which had just died. They were burying him in a cigar box. Regular funeral: ceremony, procession, a grave, a piece of cardboard for a marker. The kids were crying. It was the real thing."

"Did exactly the same thing when our canary died." Baker nodded.

"Right," my father said. "Well, Ben and I got to brainstorming a doll that stops. Get it? The Die-Dee Doll. After the kid buys it, it begins to decay. I mean the body of the doll and the face just fall apart. The eyes sink. The hair falls out. I knew it could be done. After all, I have a BS in chemistry."

"And I suggested a death rattle," Ben said. "We could do it with a fused Japanese battery and noisemaker. The kid hears the death rattle, at any hour of the day or night—we can't program it *that* accurately—and knows her doll is dead. It's all falling apart by then."

"Right," my father said. "Then the little ef has the funeral. Now get this, Nick—this is where the love comes in. The basic Die-Dee kit is just the doll itself: young, pretty, blue eyes, blond wig. Other colors for other ethnic markets, of course. But the accessories! First of all, a model doctor's kit: toy stethoscope, plastic scalpel, bandages—the works. Then, when the doll rattles and stops, a plastic snap-together coffin. Get it now? And a little shovel and a plastic marker for the grave. A blank marker, shaped like an obso tombstone, so the kid can write on it the doll's name and age and whatever else. Well? Nick? What do you think? About the Die-Dee Doll?"

I stood up slowly and poured brandy in all the glasses.

"Well," I said. "That's quite a conception. Unusual. You'll get a lot of flak on it, of course."

"We're prepared for it," Ben Baker said.

"Right," my father said. "We've already got the go-ahead from our house child psychologist. Excellent emotional catharsis, he says. Teaches the child to feel. Second of all, we've paid out some good love for a motivational research survey. Kids between the ages of four and ten, both efs and ems, are fascinated by stopping, Nick. Third of all, we went to an independent psychological testing lab. That cost ten thousand new dollars, Nick. We got some big names in child psychology. Really big. You'd be surprised. They substantiated our in-house em. The Die-Dee Doll is recommended for emotional catharsis. Aids normal adjustment to stopping."

"Well, Nick?" my father asked.

"I think you've got a winner," I said.

Paul Bumford caught my warning glance and kept his mouth shut.

"I told you!" my father said. He leaned forward to slap Ben Baker on the knee. "I told you Nick would go for it!"

"When do you go into production?" I asked.

"As soon as we can get approval," my father said. "The sooner the better."

He and Baker began to exchange their coarse jokes. I signaled to Paul and we withdrew. Paul was sleeping in a second-floor guest-room. I stopped in with him for a nightcap and a Bold.

"Nick," he said, as soon as the door was closed, "that idea—that Die-Dee Doll—" He choked on the name. "—That will have to come to my Division for approval."

"Of course," I said mildly. "Why do you think my father and Baker were giving us that sales pitch?"

"Well, I'm not going to approve it."

"Oh? Mind telling me why?"

"Two reasons I can think of offhand. One, the projected sale of a toy doctor's kit along with a doll inexorably fated to stop. So the young ef, or em, is conditioned to the inefficiency of medicine and science."

"A possible result," I admitted. "If the child makes the connection, comes to that conclusion."

"Has to!" he said hotly. "Secondly, the child is conditioned to an image of stopping as putrescence, ugliness, and stench. Even the word 'die' is used. That goes against our national psychological thrust that has taken generations to reinforce. We don't want a society of objects pondering on stopping. Before you know it, they'll all be sitting around naked, cross-legged, contemplating their navels. Do we want a world of mystics or a world of producers and consumers? I'm going to reject the Die-Dee Doll, Nick."

"I can overrule your rejection, you know," I said.

"Are you going to?"

"We'll talk about it when the time comes," I said.

Paul wrote:

I would not favor a conventional bureaucratic hierarchy for the proposed Department of Creative Science. Rather than a Director served by deputy directors and assistant deputy directors who are specialists in one scientific or technological discipline, I recommend the Director rule a board of "Omnists" that would constitute his second line of command. These "omnists" I see as objects conditioned in several scientific and/or technological disciplines and who can appreciate the interrelationship of those disciplines. "Renaissance man" was the term used for both objects of wide interest and expertise in several arts. I suggest the term "omnist" to describe a Renaissance object of science.

I was preparing for my visit to Millie Jean Grunwald. Paul Bumford knocked on the door of my suite. When I answered, he handed over a sealed manila envelope.

"My notes on the prospectus for the Department of Creative Science," he told me.

I weighed the envelope in my hand.

"You've been serving," I said.

"Yes. I wanted to finish them here. I'm taking a late flight back tonight."

"The copter will take you to the airport." I said.

"Yes," he said. "Your father arranged it."

"Well. . . ." Strained silence. "Have a good flight. I appreciate your coming."

He nodded.

"I'll see you back in GPA-1," I said.

He looked me up and down. My tooty costume.

"Going somewhere?" he asked.

"Yes. Into Detroit."

"Ef or em?"

"Ef," I said.

"Nice?"

"*My* toy," I said.

I sat in my "secret place," staring at the paintings of Egon Schiele. Searching for answers. As always, I was dazzled by those explosions of color, the raw sensuality, the brooding despair, the probing so deep it seemed to me a scalpel rather than a paintbrush had exposed the live nerve and set it tingling.

And, as always, the answers eluded me. I was convinced they were there, but I could not decode them. Suddenly I had an infamous thought: I wanted Egon Schiele alive. Then I could take him, send him to an R&R, into a Cooperation Room where, after he had signed an Informed Consent Statement, I could drain him and learn what I sought. But the em was stopped. And I could not read the testament of his art.

Paul wrote:

Re planning for the DCS, the problem of projection is always the same: What kind of a world do we want in 20, 50, or 100 years? Agreement will be difficult, if not impossible, but planning *must* be started unless we are to leave the future to chance and accident. Our Tomorrow File is certainly a good beginning.

Nick, I know the quality of your mind, and I wish you would give some thought to the eventual establishment of social classes based on procreative techniques. From highest to lowest: Natural, Artificial Insemination, Artificial Enovulation, Placenta Machine, Embryonic Cloning, Parthenogenesis, etc. Within each class, of course, status would be determined by genetic quality.

I wasn't enthusiastic about this suggestion. My first impulse was to reject it. But I could not reject it totally. As Paul requested, I computed it.

The heavy conflict, to any object of reason, is between the tomorrow you desire and the tomorrow you expect.

Y-7

By the mid-1980's, the US Postal Service had reached such a nadir of inefficiency that in desperation Congress had amended existing law to allow the establishment of commercial postal services. Although their rates were higher, they did provide some degree of privacy and some assurance that a letter mailed from Point A to Point B would not end up in a dusty pigeonhole at Point K. Gradually, the US Post Office was reduced to the handling of parcels and a service called Instamail by which open letters were electronically scanned at Point A, broadcast to Point B, reproduced in facsimile on a standard form and, one hoped, delivered to the addressee. No privacy, of course, but useful for form letters and nonconfidential correspondence.

I had instructed Maya Leighton to send me reports on Art Roach via commercial mail, addressed to my rented box number in the Times Square section of Manhattan. On August 14, I left the compound in uniform and drove uptown. I flashed Simon Hawkley's office in San Diego and told his secretary I would be out there the following Tuesday and would contact Mr. Hawkley upon arrival.

I then stopped at my mail drop and picked up the first report from Maya. As I was coming out of the building, an obso em, handsome, well dressed, looked scornfully at my silver zipsuit and said clearly, "Jinky shit."

I think everyone in Public Service had experienced this kind of personal hassle. One reason why the wearing of official uniforms outside government compounds had been made voluntary rather than mandatory.

A few hours later, in my office, I scanned Maya Leighton's report, laughed aloud, tossed it across my desk to Paul Bumford.

Subject from GA-8. Georgia, I think. Cracker. No wonder he's so silent. Every time he opens his mouth he betrays his conditioning. Or lack of it. Brains in his penis. He's very brainy. Heavy signet ring middle finger left hand. Loose kidneys. But frequently constipated. Doctors himself. *Everything!* But mostly laxatives and nasal sprays. Pimples drive him wild. Very clean personally. Rushes to the nest after using. Can't pass a mirror without glancing at his image. With approval. Nick, a beautiful, *beautiful* ass! You wouldn't believe! A muffin! Loves steam rooms, saunas, massage. Exercises strenuously every day. But hooked on the saunas. A kind of ceremony? Not intelligent—but shrewd? Hoo-boy! Nick, I was amused at first. Now he's beginning to wear. Such a child. When he starts calling me "Mommy" I resign. He has absolutely *no* pubic hair at all. Well, of course, he has. But it is so blond, so fine, you must get up very, very close to see it. Miss me, you fork-tongued bastard?

Paul scanned the letter swiftly. Then he laughed, too.

"Sardonic ef," he said. "What do you want done with this?"

"Dictate it onto a belt," I said. "Leave out all personal references to me. Then send it down to your Neuropsychiatry Team and order them to start building a Psychological Profile."

"It would be a lot easier if we could get into the Personnel Files and scan his original PP."

"It would," I agreed, "but we can't. He rules those files. What do you want me to do—flash him and say, 'Oh Art, by the way, could you send me a copy of your PP? I want to know what makes you jerk.' No, this is the only way to do it. I don't need it on Angela because I compute that ef. And we'll be getting background and financial input on both of them from my father's private data banks. Just tell the Neuropsychiatry Team the subject is an object applying for sensitive service and we need a preliminary profile. No problem."

"Nooo," he said slowly. "No problem."

I stared at him.

"What's *your* problem?" I asked. "Something inoperative here?"

"No, no," he said hastily. "I was just computing. For the Tomorrow File."

"Oh? What?"

"These Psychological Profiles—they're part of the Personnel File of everyone in Public Service. Right?"

"And the military. And universities. And academies. And every decent-size company, corporation, foundation, and conglomerate in the US."

"In other words, they're valuable?"

"Valuable? Invaluable! They cull out the nuts. And objects too ambitious or too creative for a particular service. What are you getting at?"

"Everyone should have a Psychological Profile. Every citizen of the US. To be included in the National Data Bank."

I shook my head.

"Illegal," I said. "A PP requires a value judgment. By law, the NDB can only be a repository for raw data."

"So change the law." He shrugged.

"For what purpose? What benefit?"

"Nick, you know what's been happening to the Satrat."

"Yes. It's soft."

"Soft? It's limp! And terrorism is increasing."

"How do you know that?"

"I hear things, Nick. Just as you do. Bombings, kidnapping, assassinations. All over the place. Well, if we had a Psychological Profile in the National Data Bank on everyone, computerized, maybe we could weed out the violence-prone, the crime-prone, the nonproducers and the underconsumers. A PP updated every five years, or two years, or annually, would certainly flash warning signs. It could cut down on terrorism, reduce crime, give us a clearer picture of the number and identity of enemies of the state."

"Yes," I said promptly. "I think you've got something there. It's interesting. Add it to the Tomorrow File. And while you're at it, send me a tape of the entire file. I want to include some of our items in the prospectus for the Department of Creative Science. There's a meeting of DOB early next month. While I'm in Washington, I'll deliver the prospectus to the Chief Director."

"Nick," he said, not looking at me, "are you going to mention me? You know, as source of some of the ideas?"

"Not to worry," I said. "I'll spell your name right."

He grinned at me then. I could remember when it was a little boy's grin.

I took a commercial jet to San Diego. It stopped at St. Louis, Tulsa, Phoenix. But I didn't regret the time lost. I used it to dictate notes into my Pockacorder, organizing ideas on the prospectus for the Department of Creative Science. I knew I not only had to convince the Chief Director of its value, but I had to provide—in a brief document—sufficient ammunition to make it politically viable. I had to manipulate his mind from concept to reality.

I decided, in the introduction, to move swiftly from the specific to the general.

"As recently as two hundred years ago, ours was an agrarian society. An em might spend his lifetime in the same log cabin, chinked with mud, in which he had been born. He woke to a cock's crow, washed in well or stream water, donned garments woven and sewn by his wife, ate a breakfast of foods raised on his own land, turned his fields with a wooden plow pulled by a horse, sold what extra produce he could for needles and glass, read his Bible by candlelight, fell exhausted onto a rope bed covered with a straw tick. Ignorance, poverty, near-starvation, and hard, grinding, endless labor. Muscle labor.

"Today, two centuries later, the average em wakes on a plastifoam mattress when his radio alarm clicks on. He adjusts the temperature of his shower by regulating taps through which flows water brought from hundreds of miles away. He cleans his teeth with an ultrasonic strigil. He dons garments knitted of fibers made from petroleum. He drives an electric-powered vehicle. He serves in aseptic, air-conditioned surroundings. He rules machines that provide brute labor. He eats foods, nutritional foods, vitamin-enriched, of an astounding variety. He is able to learn from or be entertained by an amazing array of sight, sound, and scent appliances. He lives longer and he lives better.

"Science and technology have effected this change from the society of two hundred years ago. Revolution is a mild word for it. But since science advances exponentially, the next two hundred years will be, not revolution, but change so fundamental that those living today have less possibility of visualizing it fully than the em of 1800 conceiving today's world.

"With these advances in medicine, comfort, personal fulfillment, and increased opportunities for all objects, have come new problems: the possibility of nukewar, uncontrolled population growth, despoilment of the environment, a shortage of energy, etc., etc. It could be said that science and technology have created these problems.

"If this is operative, then science and technology can solve these problems. When the need becomes imperative, the human brain will find a solution. Otherwise, we would be apes, would we not?"

I played the tape back and listened intently. It would need greasing, but the gist was there. It was at once a challenge and a promise. It was almost a crusade. I felt it would impress Chief Director Michael Wingate because he would recognize the political potential. No one is against tomorrow.

I called Hawkley, Goldfarb & Bensen from the jetport and was told Simon Hawkley would see me at 1400. I purchased a map of San Diego at the newsstand. I sat down on a plastic bench, put my attaché case flat on my lap, spread out the map. I found the approximate location of Scilla Pharmaceuticals. I refolded the map—not on the original creases, naturally—left the terminal and rented a diesel-powered two-door Ford sedan, one of the new Shark models. The attendant gave me directions on how to get to the La Mesa area, to Alvarado Road.

I am conscious of having dictated the preceding paragraph in simple, declarative sentences. It is indicative of my actions at that point in time. After reflection and planning comes the go or no-go decision. This is the stage, I believe, at which most objects falter. Anyone can reflect. Anyone can plan. The crunch comes with the move from thought to action, a giant step that requires energy, resolve, and a willingness to accept change.

In any event, I became aware that once the go/no-go decision was taken and I had opted for action, a linear logic all its own took over. A led to B which led to C, etc., almost with no volition on my part. Pilots speak of "the point of no return," the exact second when their diminishing fuel leaves no alternative but to continue the flight, they hope to their destination. I believe I reached my point of no return on that hot afternoon of August 20, 1998, in San Diego, California.

Did I believe in omens? Yes, I believed in omens, and Scilla Pharmaceuticals was a pleasant surprise. The main building was small, two stories high, built of cinder blocks painted a celery green. The architecture was inoffensive. There was a loading platform, several smaller outbuildings, a circular drive of white gravel. The landscaping was attractive: trees, bushes, shrubs, lawn— all obviously well tenued, neat, clean. There was a chain fence around the area, a smartly uniformed guard at the gate.

I drove past slowly, staring, made a U-turn and drove past again. I was briefly tempted to stop, go inside on some pretext or other, and take a look at the interior. But I decided against it. I was satisfied with my first impression: a small, clean, moderately prosperous drug factory. It seemed to fit my needs exactly.

A few hundred yards past the gate the road was bordered by trees for a short distance. The shoulders of the road were wide; a driver could safely pull off onto the verge. Traffic, at that time of day, seemed minimal. At night, I guessed, it would be practically nonexistent. We could park in the shadow of the trees with our receivers and recorders.

I drove slowly back toward the business section, computing possibilities and variables. The difficulties were numerous, but not unconquerable. Mostly physical problems: equipment, timing, tactics. I might even bring it off by myself, but it would be awkward. I needed assistance. Which brought me back to something, or someone rather who had been troubling me. Paul Bumford.

He was, of course, my co-conspirator. Having divulged so much to him, having made him privy to my motives and plans, I should not at that point in time have even questioned his further involvement. He was already in. I could not deny it. But still. . . .

A year previously there would have been no problem. He was then my creature. But the events of the past six months—the smashing of the Society of Obsoletes' conspiracy and Paul's elevation to AssDepDirRad—had given him power. That was, as I had told him, a virus. He was as much a victim as I. But I knew it for what it was. And could, I thought, cope, recognizing the responsibilities and dangers of power. But did Paul?

I drove directly to the offices of Hawkley, Goldfarb & Bensen, and spent almost fifteen minutes searching for a parking space. Finally I did what I should have done in the first place: I parked directly in front of the building in a No Parking zone. A uniformed doorman seemed to pop up out of the Glasphalt sidewalk, but I had a five-dollar bill folded, ready to slip into his palm.

"I'll only be a few minutes," I said.

He glanced at the bill.

"Take your time," he said.

Up to the thirty-fourth floor in a high-speed elevator that smelled of an estrogen-based perfume. Then down those chilled, empty corridors. The massive plank door swung shut behind me. Thudding. I was not conscious of having stepped into the past. I had stepped into an executive's office on the star Arcturus. It was all foreign to me, including the unwrapped mummy propped behind the mahogany desk. Those exhausted eyes stared thoughtfully at me. Again, the scrawny neck stretched from a starched white collar, a shiny alpaca jacket.

"Sir," I said, "I trust I find you in good health?"

He demanded language like that.

He waved me to a chair. He already had the decanter and two balloons ready. He poured me a half-glass with a slow, steady hand.

"I live, young man," Simon Hawkley said.

We plunged right in. He had a sheaf of papers ready and flipped them over steadily, explaining what he proposed. My initial investment would be in a new corporation formed for the purpose of establishing a franchised chain of porn shops. Quite legal. The porn shops would then purchase controlling interest in a new company formed for the purpose of establishing a drive-in three-dimensional laser movie theater. Which in turn would invest its assets in a new factory to produce redi-mixed frozen salads with forty-eight different artificial seasonings. Which would. . . . A classic "fuzz job."

"To accomplish all this," Simon Hawkley said at one point, "I will need a power of attorney from you, young man. This is where a certain degree of trust on your part is essential."

"A degree of trust, sir?" I said. "I always thought of trust as complete and absolute, or nonexistent. You have my trust, Mr. Hawkley."

He liked that. The silver lips compressed in what I hoped was a smile.

I signed all the documents he shoved toward me. I wrote out a check for an enormous sum drawn on a Detroit bank where my father's loan against my inheritance had been deposited in my name. Hawkley immediately called in the bountifully hindquartered secretary. She took my check and BIN card and departed to open my account.

We raised glasses, sipped, looked at each other. Quite solemn.

"Now then—" I began.

"Now then," he rumbled in that surprisingly deep, resonant voice of his. "Now then, you will need a personal representative at Scilla. Under the terms of sale, the executive staff stays on. You are allowed to bring in a chief executive. I have a man for you. I vouch for him completely. Agreed?"

"Agreed."

"He is on our payroll, so your expense will be minimal. He is young, intelligent, sharp. Versed in business law. He will spend a minimum of two or three hours a day at Scilla, familiarizing himself with the operation. Auditors will go in every month. You will not be—uh—I believe 'scammed' is the new word, Mr. Flair."

"That is the word." I nodded. "But it never occurred to me that I would be scammed, sir. But there is—"

"Our man," he rumbled on, "whom you will meet shortly, will occupy the private office of the former owner, Anthony Scilla. Now, you will want the office shared. I recommend Chauncey Higgles, a British organization of excellent reputation. They have a branch office in this city, on Market Street. We use them frequently. Dependable. Discreet. The salesperson you want to deal with is Mrs. Agatha Whiggam. I have alerted her to your interest. She tells me that Higgles has in their files complete floor plans of Scilla, as they do of almost every other building, office, store, and factory in the city. I suggest you follow her instructions."

I looked at him with admiration.

"Mr. Hawkley," I said, raising my glass to him, "we're two of a kind."

"Umm," he said.

He swung slowly back and forth in his high-backed leather swivel chair. He gazed at me dreamily from those faded eyes.

"Mr. Flair," he said, "you are an adventurer."

"Yes, sir," I said. "I expect so."

"Perhaps a buccaneer?"

"Perhaps," I agreed.

Again the stretched smile. I think he saw himself in me. I know I saw myself in him. Strangely enough, I had never felt that sense of identity with any object except Angela Teresa Berri. And here we were, plotting her destruction. If the three of us ever got together, we could rule the world and all its suburbs.

The blond secretary returned with bank forms, a receipt, a book of checks, my BIN card. I signed where I had to sign, including a dozen blank checks. I kept only my BIN card; he retained the other documents.

"We'll wait for your Detroit check to clear," he said. "But unless you hear from me differently, you may proceed with your plans in two weeks."

He was speaking to me, but his eyes were following the haunches of the young ef as she marched out of the office. The massive door boomed shut behind her.

"Art is long, and time is fleeting," Simon Hawkley said.

"Yes, sir," I said. I wasn't certain what he meant. If anything.

He sighed, looked down at his liver-spotted hands.

"The man you are about to meet is Seymour Dove," he said. "He is neither a clerk nor a junior partner. But he occupies a very special position in this office. Originally, he trained for the stage. He is very handsome and has great presence. He also had enough intelligence to realize the theater—stage, movies, TV—did not offer the rewards he desired. So, at a relatively late age— his middle-twenties—he took a law degree and minored in business administration. But his previous stage experience has proved valuable, as I have reason to know. Also, he is a happy man. That helps."

"Yes, sir," I agreed. "It surely does."

He slowly slipped an obso hunter from an inside pocket, flicked it open, glanced at the face, clicked it shut, slid it back into the hidden pocket.

"Mr. Dove will be with us in two minutes."

If only I could manipulate SATSEC as efficiently.

Initially, Seymour Dove overwhelmed me. Dismayed me. I saw a big, beefy em, handsome and brutish, clad in harsh, bright California colors. A horseblanket-plaid jacket, fire-engine-red slacks, a lace shirt unbuttoned to his navel, capped teeth, bronzed skin, red hair so perfectly teased it had to be a wig, makeup artfully applied, plastigold sandals on bare feet, enormous sunglasses that not only blanked his eyes but covered half his face. A sight.

"Hi, dads," he said.

I turned to look at Simon Hawkley in astonishment, Was this—But he was silent, regarding me gravely. I turned back to Seymour Dove. He was pulling up a chair, unasked, beginning to speak rapidly in a flat, hard voice, totally unlike his flutey "Hi, dads."

"Here's what you want," he started. . . .

Then, as he spoke, I caught on. He wasn't wearing clothes; he was wearing a costume. He was auditioning for a role. He would wear those garments as chief executive officer of Scilla Pharmaceuticals and earn a reputation as a microweight, a playboy. But he'd watch the books. He'd report to Simon Hawkley the moment he got a nibble from Washington. He'd keep his private office sacrosanct and oversee the sharing installation.

"Is that about it, dads?" he asked, switching back to his stage voice.

I stood up, leaned across the desk to shake Hawkley's paper hand. Then I stroked palms with the seated Seymour Dove.

"My worries are over," I said.

The California whites gleamed at me.

"Depend on it," he said.

Y-8

On September 10, Paul Bumford came to my office to discuss matters of mutual interest. He had been serving tough; his thinned-down physique and almost gaunt features showed it. But he was cool, precise, informed. If he had problems—and I knew he had—he showed no signs of being unable to handle them.

Finally, after we had concluded the agenda agreed upon, he returned to me an Instox copy of the DCS prospectus I had submitted to him for comment.

"Well?" I asked.

He grinned. "Nick, it's magnificent."

"Really?"

"Really. If he rejects it, he's a fool. But he won't reject it."

"How do you know?"

"I just feel it."

I laughed. "Well . . . I trust your instincts."

"Do you? Nick, don't change a word of it. It's great. And thanks for the plug. More good news . . . Mary Bergstrom and Phoebe Huntzinger are back from the Denver FO. Everything on Project Phoenix is go. Mary made some suggestions on the scanning areas of the lasers. Phoebe says the computer is as ready as it'll ever be. Tests started yesterday."

"Fine," I said. "That's fine."

I consulted some notes on my desk pad. I was conscious of him staring at me. I looked up. Our eyes locked.

"So much going on," I said, "I thought it best to make notes."

"Of course." He nodded.

"Now then," I went on, "the DOB (we pronounced it Dob) is meeting on Tuesday of next week. Do you have time to go down to Washington with me?"

"I'll find time."

"Good. And I want Mary Bergstrom to come along. We'll drive down on Monday, directly to the Alexandria Hospice. They'll put us up for the night. I want you and Mary to meet Group Lewisohn."

"Why?"

"Oh . . . just to familiarize yourselves with their operation," I said vaguely.

"In other words, I have no need to know?"

"At the moment, no," I agreed. "But you might."

"Oh? Your contingency list for Lewisohn?"

"That's right."

"The trouble with contingency plans," he said, "is that they all have a built-in defect. The objects who devise them can't resist trying them out to see if they'll succeed."

I thought it time to show my teeth.

"Are you objecting to my efforts to keep Hyman R. Lewisohn alive?" I asked coldly.

"No, no!" he backed off hastily. "My God, Nick, you're touchy lately."

"I admit it." I sighed. Having made my point. "The moment we get the Scilla business concluded, I'll be my usual sweet self again."

"Scilla," he said. "Ah-ha! I've been saving the best news for last."

"What about Scilla?" I asked sharply.

"I've gotten the need for hallucinogens to over a hundred thousand new dollars during the next fiscal year. Projected."

I smiled. "Paul, that's great. Just great!"

"Yes." He nodded. "I won't be modest. It's great."

"All right, now here's what you do: Send me a Request for Suspension of Bidding form. State that you'll need the hallucinogens in the amounts detailed for the purposes noted. State that Scilla has been our supplier in the past and you recommend them on the basis of tested purity of product, responsibility for delivery, and so forth. And the amount involved, in your opinion, is not sufficient to advertise competitive bidding among the drug cartels. Then I'll put my endorsement on it, forward it to Data and Statistics, and they'll send it on to—"

"Got it right here," he said.

He picked the document from his case, glanced at it briefly, placed it on my desk with a flourish.

I laughed. "Paul, you're way ahead of me."

"That's right," he said.

We estimated it would take about a week for the request to clear Data & Statistics in GPA-1, and another two weeks to be processed by Angela's Purchasing Department in Washington. If she was going to take the bait, it couldn't be before late September, perhaps early October.

I was content to wait. I would be patient. Sometimes anticipation is more satisfying than realization.

I wasn't so patient with the preliminary reports Paul was receiving from his Neuropsychiatry Team: the psychological profile of Art Roach. Of all scientific jargons, sociological gobbledygook was the worst. Closely followed by psychiatric guck. I wanted objective judgments. I received such kaka as "anal positive . . . cyclothymic personality . . . severe status orientation . . . probable overcompensating inferior . . . possible paranoiac schizophrenia, etc., etc."

In my disciplines, a gene is a gene, a cell is a cell, a virus is a virus, and a brain is never a mind. I wanted their language to be as exact.

Finally, in desperation, I posed a series of questions, through Paul. The answers that came back substantiated my splanchnic opinion of the em.

Art Roach was shrewd without being intelligent. He was deeply conscious of the circumstances of his birth—he was a bastard—and his lack of conditioning. To reinforce his self-esteem, he pampered his corpus—mirrors, massages, saunas, laxatives, and nasal sprays. He was motivated by status almost totally. His sadistic sexual behavior served to obliterate his essential belief in his own unworthiness. He was a slave striving to be a master.

To my question, "If status is threatened, is this object capable of violence?" the answer was unequivocal and mercifully short: "Yes."

The private data bank reports on Angela Berri, sent by commercial mail to my father and forwarded by commercial mail to my letter drop, were less revealing. I scanned the background material swiftly: "NF . . . born in Chicago . . . father a bartender . . . etc., etc." It wasn't important. No one had roots anymore. History was inoperative.

The quality of her brain had been, apparently, recognized at an early age. She received advanced conditioning, then was accepted by the Science Academy at the age of thirteen. I was already aware of her doctorates and of her career after she entered Public Service.

Something I hadn't known: She had been married at the age of eighteen to an em named John Findlay. He had suicided three weeks after their marriage. No details provided. None were necessary. I could guess.

I spent more time scanning reports of her personal finances and credit rating. At first glance, they revealed nothing. Her total wealth was substantial, but nothing that could not be accounted for by her annual rank-rate. She neither deposited nor withdrew sizable sums at regular intervals. Her expenditures seemed to be what might be expected of an ef with her income. The totality did not form a mathematical model of the greedy object I knew her to be. Until . . .

I was scanning an Instox copy of her household insurance policy. I zipped the fine print. It seemed normal. I went back for a slower scanning. Ah! She was paying insurance premiums on more than 100,000 new dollars' worth of personal jewelry and furs. This in an age when some of the wealthiest efs leased their jewelry and furs. The policy had a footnote to this assessment: "See Appraisal Affidavit No. 6-49-34G-2-B."

I searched for this document, but it was missing from the file. No matter. She could not resist adorning her corpus—with gems and costly furs that were hers alone.

So I believed the insurance policy, without yet knowing how she had managed to cover the purchases of 100,000 new dollars' worth of jewelry and furs. I was saddened, because greed seemed to me so drab. There are more admirable vices.

I decided to take the limousine to Washington, D.C. These trappings of official majesty counted for something in the Nation's Capital. In Manhattan, the new breed of pimps selected the identical vehicles: big, black, sedate, silent, powerful. Tooty cars to drop off street whores along Park Avenue.

Our chauffeur was a perky, red-wigged ef with the face of a choirboy and a corpus to match. I wondered how much love she had paid the ruler of the motor pool for this cushy assignment. Whatever, she seemed to be happy; her humming never ceased. Finally, Paul leaned forward and pressed the button that raised the bulletproof, soundproof plastiglass partition between driver and passengers. Then he settled back. Mary Bergstrom was seated solidly between us, knees together. So we drove south. Stiff. Rarely speaking. A grim trip.

At Rehabilitation & Reconditioning Hospice No. 4, we went immediately into colloquy with Group Lewisohn. In addition to Dr. Seth Lucas and Maya Leighton, the Group now included a hematologist, a neuropsychologist, two oncologists, an interne, three nurses, a dietitian. We went over the most recent scannings quickly. There had been little change, physically, since my last visit. No grave deterioration, but no improvement either.

"It's not the scannings that bother me so much," Lucas said nervously. "But I think there's been a loss. The object refuses to let us test motor ability. So the loss may be psychological. But I'm convinced there's a growing lassitude there. Maya?"

"I concur," she said promptly. "He doesn't grab my tits anymore. Physical? Psychological? I can't say. Both, probably. But there's a definite slowing down. One symptom is a lengthening of verbal response. Nick, we're with him every day, so we can't determine its significance. You haven't seen him for weeks; you'll be able to compute it easier than we can."

"All right." I sighed. "I'll take a look. Is he serving at anything?"

"At something." The psychologist nodded. "Lots of books, computer printouts, confidential reports. He hasn't volunteered any information and, of course, we haven't asked. But his morale is degenerating. No doubt about it. It may be due to his current service or it may be physiological in origin."

"Thank you, doctor," I said. I meant it ironically, but he missed it.

"You're welcome," he said.

"Is it depression?" I asked him.

"Close to it."

"Is he eating?" I asked the dietitian.

"Poorly. We're giving supplements by injection. When we can. He's a difficult patient."

"The understatement of the year." I looked at the blood em. "Doctor?"

"Nothing's serving," he said gloomily. "A very stubborn case."

Then we all sat in silence a few moments. I was thinking—and I presumed the others were computing along similar lines—how important the survival of this disgusting, magnificent object was to my own career. His life had become my life. I would not let him go without a struggle.

"The parabiosis suite?" I asked Lucas.

"Almost finished. Want to take a look?"

"Yes. Paul, you and Mary and Maya come along. Then we'll beard the ogre in his den. I thank all of you."

The new suite designed for the parabiotic treatment of Hyman Lewisohn had a fatal flaw. I pointed it out as calmly as I could. The purpose of the massive and lovable alteration of three hospice rooms was to shield him from the fact that his veins and arteries had been snugged with the veins and arteries of a healthy "donor" or "volunteer" or "partner" whose natural immunity might help rid Lewisohn's circulatory system of the proliferation of immature white cells.

Lewisohn, I knew—we all knew—would not willingly endure this vital linkage. He scorned personal relationships, intimate relationships. They sickened him. He gloried in his independence, in his uniqueness. To such an extent that he rejected every opportunity for friendship. I do not wish to dwell too long on the neuropsychiatric motivation of this em's behavior, except to point out that his physical ugliness, his achondroplasia, was undoubtedly the gross motivating factor. But unfortunate as that might have been, it may also have been the stimulus of his creative energy. Such things happen.

In any event, I had no wish to "cure" this psychic twitch. In fact, it was to my interest that he continue to function as before. My only concern was his continued existence and ability to serve. Nothing more.

So I pointed out to Dr. Seth Lucas that the dividing wall erected between Lewisohn's new suite and the room in which the donor would reside was much too thin. Sounds would carry. Lewisohn would become aware of some object existing on the other side of that partition through which ran the tubes and wires necessary for the exchange.

We spent almost an hour planning how the dividing wall might be improved: widening, the addition of insulation, the use of ultrasonic baffles, the placement of Lewisohn's three TV monitors to mask sounds from the donor's chamber, etc. Maya Leighton proposed that visitors' chairs and Lewisohn's computer be placed on the side of his bed away from the wall, manipulating his attention in that direction. An excellent suggestion.

Then we all trooped down one floor to examine the patient in his present quarters.

I saw at once what Maya Leighton and Seth Lucas had meant by the object's lassitude. His obscene insults were as vituperative as usual. But they came fitfully, in bursts, almost as a duty to maintain his reputation. Or his ego image. But between outbursts were periods of a condition distressingly akin to catatonia: head turned aside, eyes unfocused, jaw hanging slackly. That enormous skull seemed more distorted than ever; the corpus had shrunk. Skin on neck and shoulders hung loosely, without tone. Spittle gathered in the corners of his mouth. Maya wiped it gently away. He looked up at her dully. She took his hand. I watched. His fingers did not curl about hers.

I remember thinking, bitterly: The bastard is going.

I introduced Mary Bergstrom and Paul Bumford. He did not acknowledge their presence. Finally, he gathered enough energy to demand of me when he'd be out of this "dungheap."

"Soon," I promised him. "We're moving you to a new suite. Upstairs. More room. More privacy. You'll like it there."

He cursed me mechanically, then lost interest, looked about vaguely. Seth Lucas fussed at him, watching the electronic monitors. The little white spheres bounced across the black screens or traced graceful curves. Thankfully, there were only minor aberrations. *Ping-ping-ping. Ka-voom, ka-voom, ka-voom. Ahh-waa, ahh-waa, ahh-waa.* Soft sounds of existence.

I noted Paul surreptitiously examining a pile of books stacked at the bedside. There was the usual disorder of computer printouts, folders, manuscripts, envelopes with the red tags of restricted material. But I could not believe the em was capable of serving productively in his present state.

Outside, we held an impromptu, low-voiced colloquy in the corridor.

"Paul?" I asked.

"Going."

"Mary?"

"I concur."

"Yes." I agreed. "Seth"—I turned to him—"you have that list of potential donors from FO's and hospices. Start bringing them in for serological work-ups. Begin with twenty. We'll make our initial choices from them."

"Right."

"Get a crew on that wall immediately. Prepare to start parabiosis next Wednesday. I'll come down with a surgical staff from GPA-1 to help you with the hookup. Now . . . where can we get a vodka-and-Smack in this necropolis?"

They all laughed. Dutifully.

On our way to the Executive Lounge, I drew Paul Bumford aside for a moment.

"What were the books, Paul? Alongside Lewisohn's bed?"

"I only saw three of them: *The Methodology of Modern Revolution. A Psychohistory of Terrorism.* And *The Roots of Social Discontent.*"

"Oh?" I said. "That's interesting."

Beds had been reserved for us in Transients Quarters. I could forgo the honor; let Paul Bumford and Mary Bergstrom endure those hard cots. I knew Maya Leighton had leased a small apartment in Hamlet West. I pleaded my need in doleful tones. She had a dinner engagement that evening with Art Roach. I told her what to do: Flash him and cancel it, claiming a sudden medical emergency.

"And so it is," I assured her.

"So it is," she agreed. "It'll be wonderful losing him for a night. How much longer do I have to jerk him, Nick?"

"Three months max," I told her. "But probably only a month. Maybe a little more. Can you endure?"

"If you say so."

"Maya, your reports have been a big help."

"But he's such a yawn, Nick, *such* a yawn. There's nothing *to* him. After the novelty has worn off."

I insisted on cooking dinner for us. It took an hour's touring of local markets to find a natural steak, four small, sad natural potatoes, a natural Spanish onion. We settled for green probeans, a plastipak of synthetic scallion greens, a half-kilo of prorooms—"Taste-engineered to please the most discriminating palate." And a liter of actinized brandy.

It turned out to be an unstructured, improvised, and rather splendid evening. At least, I enjoyed it, and I tried to please Maya. Her profit, being part of mine, *most* of mine, was important to me. Also, at that point in time, I was in need of mindless bliss. She was always in need of mindless bliss. This is merely an observation, not a value judgment.

I baked the minuscule potatoes in Maya's microwave oven, chilled them swiftly in the quik-freez section of her refrigerator, then sliced them and fried them with chopped onions and scallion greens. The steak was microwaved, the probeans and prorooms cooked together, then turned into the frying pan at the last moment for a coating of oil and seasoning. The whole thing was palatable, eminently palatable.

Perhaps our enjoyment was whetted by the brandy. We attained a level of beaming inebriation and held it for hours, not becoming maudlin, slovenly, physically uncoordinated. But relaxed in an almost floppy state, grinning continually, occasionally teasing, playing like puppies. I could not recall ever feeling such a sense of physical belonging with another object.

Late in the evening, she leaped from my lap—we had been munching each other—hauled me to my feet, tugged me toward her bedroom.

"I have something to show you," she said.

"You've had toothbud transplants on the labia majora?"

"How did you guess?" she giggled.

What she had to show me was a shelved cupboard filled with all the paraphernalia of a sophisticated sexualist.

"Why, Maya," I murmured, "I didn't know you cared."

"I joined the Thrill of the Month Club about three years ago," she said. "But I've only been collecting seriously in the last year. I have some rare items here."

"Rare, indeed," I agreed.

Dildos: wood, rubber, plastic, steel; capable of being filled with hot water, metal bearings, mercury; or vibrated electrically or ultrasonically. Japanese Ben-Wa balls; German breast oscillators; French ticklers; US artificial vaginas; British Electro-Cops; inflatable sex dolls, ef and em, life-size, fitted with wigs and costumes, with heat elements and vibrators; coitus splints; molded tongues covered with nodules; clitoral stimulators; penile extensors; desensitizing cremes, lotions, and sprays to delay orgasm; vibrating fingers; dildo harnesses; vibraginas; penis rings; studded penis sleeves; open-mouthed rubber masks; double-vibrators for vagina and anus; purse-sized vibrators; erotic statuary; a "gun" with a penis barrel that "ejaculated" when the trigger was pulled; false breasts; condoms and vibrator sleeves of every conceivable abrasive design; jellies, oils, sprays. And much, much more.

"I don't know how they can sell that stuff," she said. Vestigial morality there. "Isn't there a law against it, Nick?"

Her naïveté amused me. Yes, there was "a law against it." Several. But it was deliberate government policy not to enforce those laws. The reason given for the government's inaction was the doubtful constitutionality of those laws and the subsequent difficulties in obtaining convictions.

The operative reason why the government allowed—allowed? Encouraged!—the increasing technologizing of sex was the continuing need to achieve and maintain Zero Population Growth. Anything that contributed to Z-Pop was in the public interest. Hence this proliferation of false penises and artificial vaginas (the expensive models trimmed with mink). Similarly, the federal government had quietly passed the word to state and local law enforcement agencies to overlook laws still on the books making homosexuality and lesbianism criminal offenses. Z-Pop was more important.

"Now then," I said, rubbing my hands before this cornucopia of mechanical delights, "what shall we start with?"

Maya had a pharmacopoeia in her nest. I made full use of it the following morning. After a liter of cold water, a vitamin injection, an energizing inhalant, and two methylphenidate spansules, I began to believe my original diagnosis of ambulatory quietus had been exaggerated.

The brandy bottle was quite empty, but I found a new half-liter of petrorum in the cupboard under the milk. I mixed a large rum-and-Smack and sipped it while showering and using Maya's dipilatory face creme. I called for a cab. While waiting, I examined my features in the bedroom mirror. Except for a small bite mark low on my neck, there were no obvious signs of the previous night's debauch. And certainly no psychic scars.

Maya was still sleeping. That great, lush corpus sprawled across the rumpled sheet. Tangled hair. Slack flesh. Bruised breasts. Smeared makeup. I heard the doorbell chime—the taxi driver—and bent swiftly for a final lick.

"Who?" she said drowsily.

I laughed, and left.

We took the limo into Washington, Mary Bergstrom sitting between Paul and me, as before. During the trip I questioned both on Group Lewisohn personnel and operations. Generally, their reactions were favorable, though both felt Dr. Seth Lucas, while talented, was too young and inexperienced for the responsibility he held. I agreed, which was one reason I ruled his decisions so closely. Also, of course, if Lewisohn survived, I wanted no doubt as to whom the credit belonged. If that seems egocentric, allow me to point out that I was also quite willing to accept the consequences of failure.

We pulled up before the old HEW Building on Independence Avenue, now headquarters of the Department of Bliss. Three limousines were parked in line before us. Two were identical to our own hearselike vehicle. The third was a white Rolls-Royce.

"That belongs to DEPDIRCUL," I told Paul. "He thinks it enhances his image."

Paul snorted.

He and I got out of the car, carrying our attaché cases. I leaned down to speak to Mary.

"Sight-seeing?" I asked her.

"I'd like to," she said faintly. "This is my first visit to Washington."

"Take the car," I told her. I glanced at Paul. "Suppose we all meet right here at 1600 this afternoon for the trip back?"

"Thank you," Mary said. "I'll be here."

Paul nodded. We stood there a moment, watching the limousine pull away.

"That was kind of you," Paul said. "Lending Mary the car."

"I'm a kind em," I said. "Some kind. Paul, after the conference I want you to move around. Talk to objects you know on Headquarters Staff. Not Security and Intelligence, but others. Talk to reporters. Then go up to the Hill. Check in with the staff members. If you bump into a familiar Congressman, stroke palms and tell him what a splendid service he's doing. But the staff members are more important. Buy lunch or drinks."

"What do you want?"

"Anything on terrorism rates. Current social discontent. We know the Satrat is soft, but I don't think it's giving us an operative scan. The demographics may be off."

"You're thinking about Lewisohn's books?"

"Yes. I believe he's serving on possible solutions. And if the Chief Director assigned it, the situation must be getting near flash point."

"Nick, we better move faster on the UP pill."

It took a lurch of my brain to realize he was already computing the social, economic, and political consequences of a drug that provided Ultimate Pleasure. Particularly if the manufacture and distribution of that drug were controlled by the government.

"Right," I said. "We'll review progress on the trip back. Now let's walk into the cage."

We marched up to that ugly heap. There were a few reporters lounging about, a few photographers. No TV coverage.

"Get them, Larry," a voice shouted. A photographer stepped in front of us, aimed his camera, clicked the shutter.

The shouter, a reporter named Herb Bailey, on the Washington Bureau of a news syndicate, came strolling forward to stroke our palms.

"Nick," he said. "Paul. You two look full of piss and vinegar."

"At the moment," I said, "Paul's full of vinegar, and I'm full of piss. Got to get inside, Herb."

"Sure," he said. "But just for the record, Deputy Director, do you anticipate any earth-shaking decisions resulting from this meeting of the Department of Bliss?"

"Just for the record," I said. "No comment."

He shook his head dolefully. "The Dragon Lady runs a tight ship. What about off the record?"

"Herb"—I sighed—"this is a routine monthly meeting of DOB. We have nothing heavy pending on the Hill. Zilch. Now let me ask you a question: Why the photographer catching Paul and me? We're not news."

"You will be if you get blown up inside." He grinned. I glanced toward Paul.

"Happy Herby," I said. "The public servants' best friend."

"Herb," Paul said, "are you sticking around until the meeting ends?"

"I suppose I'll have to," the reporter said disgustedly. "Just to get the canned handout."

"Buy you a drink?" Paul asked.

"That's the best bribe I've had this week."

The Department of Bliss, at that point in time, was organized into five gross divisions:

1. Prosperity Section (PROSEC), ruled by a Deputy Director (DEPDIR-PRO), was responsible for all welfare, poverty, and antihunger operations, plus what was formerly Social Security, now called Personal Happiness.
2. Wisdom Section (WISSEC), ruled by DEPDIRWIS, controlled all fed-

erally financed conditioning programs, from nursery schools to universities, including the Science Academy.

3. Vigor Section (VIGSEC), ruled by DEPDIRVIG, administered public health laws, including HAP (Health Assurance Plan) that had replaced Medicare, Medicaid, etc.

4. Culture Section (CULSEC), ruled by DEPDIRCUL, was in charge of all government programs in communicative and performing arts, including what had formerly been the Federal Communications Commission, Commission of Fine Arts, American Battle Monuments Commission, Architect of the Capitol, National Foundation on the Arts and the Humanities, etc., etc.

5. Satisfaction Section. My section, SATSEC, of which I was DEPDIRSAT.

Angela Teresa Berri, DIROB, also had a constantly expanding Headquarters Staff. Its two main groups were: (1) Security & Intelligence, ruled by Art Roach, which in addition to the duties indicated by its title, also controlled all personnel files of the Department of Bliss; (2) PUBREL, the public relations and publicity group for the entire Department.

And, of course, Angela now had a small army of Administrative Assistants, assistant AA's, legal counsels, specialists, secretaries, clerks, and Congressional liaison representatives who did the Department's lobbying on the Hill.

The monthly meeting of DOB was held in a cavernous conference hall which Angela Berri, thankfully, had had redecorated. Each Deputy Director was supplied with a comfortable swiveled armchair upholstered in real white leather. On the glass before him, exactly positioned, was a carafe of ice water, a plastiglass, two sharpened pencils, a pad of legal-size yellow paper. Behind each DEPDIR sat his Administrative Assistant, in a straight-back, upholstered chair. All proceedings were taped.

In addition to the tape engineer, Angela was served by her chief legal counsel, her AA, her executive secretary, the chief of PUBREL, and Art Roach. They like everyone else in the room, wore the zipsuits of their rank.

The structure of these meetings was quite unlike the conferences of SATSEC Angela had ruled in GPA-1. According to Public Service regulations, all departmental conferences began with the reading of what was properly called the "Menace," a statement rattled off by DIROB's Administrative Assistant:

"Accordingtoregulationfortysixdashbeesubsectiononethreedashkayoftheinter nalsecurityprovisionsofthePublicServicecodeasamendedbysubsectiononeohtwod ashgeeadoptedsixMarchnineteeneightynineallpresentareherebyinformedthese proceedingsarerestrictedandanythingsaidheardscannedorobservedwithinthecon finesandlimitsofthismeetingaredeemedofaconfidentialnatureandnothingshall bedivulgeddisclosedproclaimedrevealedormadeknowntoanyobjectgroupor . . . etc.,etc."

Penalties were not specified. They didn't have to be.

After this cheery introduction, Angela would speak, usually briefly, bringing us up to date on the progress of legislation affecting DOB. She would then relate any additional information of governmental plans and activities she thought might be of value or interest to her Deputy Directors. At this particular meeting, after running quickly through an especially dull recital of Congressional action, or inaction, Angela concluded by saying:

"You may be interested to learn that the Chief Director has decided to ask for enabling legislation establishing a new department of Public Service, to be called the Department of National Assets. The DNA will rule the management and income of all real property of the US. Any questions?"

She looked directly at me. With hostility. What an ef! I knew she blamed me—partly, at least—for her loss in this particular political cockfight. I did admire her then: the tailored gold zipsuit, pointy breasts, whippy corpus bathed in the soft beam of a spot directed onto her chair. A wig of parsley curls. Her witch's face perfectly symmetrical, almost frightening in its lack of blemish. So composed. So *sure*. Exuding power as naturally as sweat. I could look at those green-painted lips and marvel where they once had been. On me.

"Nick," she said tonelessly, "you seem amused."

"Only because of the name of the new department," I said smoothly. "Department of National Assets. DNA. That's my Section's abbreviation for the molecular basis of heredity. Deoxyribonucleic acid. The double helix. Why we are what we are. It seems an apt title for a department dealing with national assets."

There were a few smiles, a relaxation. I think the others were vaguely conscious that an unpleasant confrontation had been avoided.

"Very good, Nick," she said. "Well, let's get started. Anyone?"

Problems presented and discussed during that particular meeting—with one exception—were of monumental inconsequence. My own report, though deviously contrived, could have had little significance to the others present. I said that my Division of Research & Development had noted an increasing arrest rate for drug abuse, and we had started a research program to determine possible chromosomal damage from habitual use of hallucinogens. They all looked at me blankly.

The reports of the other Deputy Directors were equally as enervating.

DEPDIRCUL read a long, numbing research study on the feasibility of including commercials in the US Government's satellite broadcasts to every nation wealthy enough to own TV receivers. The conclusion was that commercials of products distributed internationally would provide a dollar revenue approximating 83.4 percent of the total cost of providing the world with free US films, US cartoons, US news programs, artfully interspersed with short features on happy US servers on the assembly line, tuna fishing off California, the splendid array of electric bidets available to US citizens, and the white-washing of Mt. Rushmore.

Heavy interest in buying commercial time on US satellite TV broadcasts had already been expressed by Kodak cameras, Ford cars, IBM typewriters, Pepsi-Cola, and Jiffi condoms ("I'll be with you in a Jiffi!").

It was decided to recommend to the Chief Director that such commercial time be sold.

DEPDIRWIS, a tall, gaunt ef with a reported predilection for young, plump boys, complained of the scruff she was receiving on the government-sponsored program to provide methylphenidate tablets for hyperactive children in elementary schools. It was the same drug I had popped a few hours previously to overcome hangover depression. With the children, of course, the reaction was exactly the opposite: It sedated them.

It was agreed a new public conditioning program would be necessary to convince unreasonably anxious parents of the benefits of the drug to their children. It was so ordered.

I came alive only during the presentation by DEPDIRPRO. This fussy little em, a prototype bookkeeper, droned through a list of depressing numbers that revealed how much love the US Government was expending on indigent, nonproductive, and underconsuming obsos. Including costs of food, clothing, shelter, medical care, etc.

I was alerted because it had been Maya Leighton's memo on exactly the same subject, when she had been a member of my Gerontology Team, that had first brought her to our attention. I remembered her suggestion, now in our Tomorrow File. I was conscious of Paul Bumford shifting position behind me, and knew he remembered it, too.

DEPDIRPRO begged for possible solutions to his dilemma, saying:

"The annual drain on the US Treasury is rapidly approaching the point where it will no longer be financially tolerable. To say nothing of the essential unfairness to young, productive, consuming, taxpaying objects of our population."

"At the moment," Angela Berri said immediately and crisply, "the possibility of euthanasia is not politically expedient, and I want no discussion of the subject. But I will welcome any other suggested solutions for this serious problem."

There was almost a minute of silence. Then I raised my hand, tentatively. "Nick?"

I told them SATSEC had been aware of this problem for some time, that it was difficult and vexing, that we had expended a great number of object-hours brainstorming the situation. And we had evolved what might be, at least, a partial solution.

I then, briefly, explained the program of Government-Assisted Peace: X dollars paid to each indigent obso who signed a life-release statement, that sum to be spent or bequeathed before painless suicide, the means of which would be provided by the government at no extra cost to the object.

I pointed out that details would have to be refined: the amount of the grant, the wording of the voluntary release statement, the time allowed between signing and stopping, and so forth. But SATSEC estimated, I lied casually, that a minimum of ten million new dollars annually, and probably more, could be saved by the plan. *Not* euthanasia, I emphasized. Purely voluntary.

Again there was silence while they all stared at the water carafes on the table, at the walls, the ceiling, anywhere but at each other. Finally Angela turned to her Public Relations chief.

"Will it play in Peoria, Sam?" she asked.

He hunched forward in his chair, a benign, rubicund em with flashing rings on three fingers.

"If you want my tip-of-the-tongue reaction," he said, "I would say yes. We got a motivation study here, of course, and we got some in-depth emotional analyses. But like I said, my instinctual gut feeling is go."

"Vic?" Angela turned to her legal counsel.

"In my opinion—" he began.

"Yes or no, Vic," she said sharply.

"I think we can manage it."

"Very well, Sam." Angela nodded at the PUBREL chief. "Move on it, Good computing, Nick. Anything else? Anyone?"

"Strange," Paul Bumford said as we moved out of DOB headquarters into that bright afternoon sunlight.

"What's strange?" I asked.

"That PROSEC business and Government-Assisted Peace. I had no idea that items in our Tomorrow File might be implemented so soon."

"That's what we're creating it for, isn't it? It's not just a Christmas list. It's a plan, a practical program that may not be feasible today but that we expect to be tomorrow."

"You're right, of course." Paul nodded. "But tomorrow has become today so quickly. It's just the speed that surprises me. Well . . . there's Herb Bailey waiting for his drink. I better start my rounds. Where are you off to?"

"Chief Director," I said shortly. "To deliver the prospectus for the Department of Creative Science."

"He's out of the country," Paul said. "Left yesterday for talks with the British on their joining the US."

"I know," I said. "I'll leave it with his wife."

"Oh-ho," Paul said.

I stared at him.

"We agreed she may prove lovable to us."

"No argument, Nick," he said hastily. "I may soon be meeting the ef myself."

"Oh?"

"I joined the New York chapter of the Beists. A national convention is planned for next month. Here, in Washington."

"Where are they going to hold it—in a phone booth?"

As anticipated, I had trouble at the gate. They took an electronic scan of my BIN card, ran a voiceprint check through their central computer, made me walk through a metal and explosives detector.

(Since 1981, by UN agreement, all explosives legally manufactured any-where in the world contained a radioactive signature.)

After all this, I was told the Chief Director was out of the country. I expressed chagrin at my ignorance, then asked to see Mrs. Wingate. Reluc-tantly, they flashed the main house and I showed my phiz on screen. Grace Wingate vouched for me, I was allowed entrance, escorted to the bolted steel door by an armed guard.

She waved aside the zipsuited butler and held her hands out to me.

"Sorry about the fuss, Nick," she said. Somewhat breathlessly. "How *are* you?"

"Well, thank you. And you?"

"In shamefully good health, doctor. Hungry? A drink?"

"A drink would be nice. I just stopped by to drop off a report the Chief Director wanted delivered personally. It's restricted."

"I'll make certain he gets it personally," she assured me. "Let's go in here. . . ."

She led the way into that same slightly shabby, chintzy parlor-type room where we had all been seated when the bombs boomed and flechettes sang during my previous visit. The portrait of John Quincy Adams still had a third eye.

She looked about vaguely.

"Oh dear. No ice."

She pressed a concealed button. A black zipsuit materialized instantly from somewhere.

"Modom?"

"Some Jellicubes, please, John."

"Immediately, modom."

She waved me to the lumpy couch. She seated herself gracefully and looked at me with sympathetic interest.

"Have you been busy, Nick?" she asked.

I had the oddest impression of a little girl stumbling about in her mother's high heels, pearls down to her knees, wearing a crazy chiffon gown and oversized garden hat. With makeup awkwardly painted on in patches.

But Grace Wingate was wearing tawny pants so tight they could have been sprayed on. A knitted tank top of some sheeny material, cut wide at neck and arms. Ashen hair flung loose. Spatulate feet bare. About her neck, partially covering the cleavage between her tanned breasts, was a silvery, oversized reproduction of a snowflake, hung from a leather thong.

"Your necklace," I said. "Beautiful."

She grinned with delight, forgetting I had not answered her question.

"I do thank you. It's a new alloy of silver, palladium, and platinum. It was given to me by the manufacturer. But of course we're not allowed to accept gifts. So Mike paid for it. The wholesale price. That's all right, don't you think, Nick?"

I laughed. "Yes, I think that's all right. Perfectly legal. It's lovely."

"Well, they're all over now, but this is the first striking of the design."

She looked down at the gleaming snowflake, stroking it. Her long fingers were close to the soft bulge of her breasts. Fingernails touched her sinuous neck.

I could not fathom her. She seemed an odd combination of the fey and the profound I could not analyze. That line that enclosed her sculpted corpus appeared to complete her. But I had the sense of a force bursting to spring free. I just did not know. She was unique in my experience.

The black zipsuit returned with a tub of Jellicubes, then disappeared. I mixed vodka-and-Smacks for both of us. We hoisted plastiglasses to each other, smiled, sipped delicately. Then we sat in silence. I wanted her to make the approach. Finally. . . .

"You said. . . ." she murmured faintly. Then stopped.

"Yes, Mrs. Wingate?"

"I asked you to call me Grace. Will you not?"

"I want to," I said. Still smiling. "But it's difficult. Your husband is very important."

"I know. Oh, God, do I know. Nick, what have you—"

I pursed my lips and pressed them with a forefinger. So dramatic! A Restoration comedy. She rose and moved toward French windows. I joined her there. We looked over a rather scrubby garden. A kneeling em, head shielded with a white riot helmet, was loosening dry soil about azalea bushes.

"You must be patient," I urged her. "I promised to help, and I shall. Grace, tell me—are you certain? Of your husband and Angela Berri?"

"Oh, yes."

I had to force her, not only for my own need to know, but to make her face it and say it.

"Are they users?" I asked.

She tried to speak but couldn't. Finally she nodded dumbly. I wanted to tongue that vulval ear revealed as her fine hair swung aside.

"Do you have any letters, documents, tapes—any physical evidence?"

She looked at me scornfully.

"*Physical* evidence? I have all the *physical* evidence I need. Nick, a wife *knows*!"

"Yes, yes," I said quickly. Convinced.

She put a hand on my arm.

"Nick," she said, "you're my only hope."

In retrospect I can be objective. But at that particular moment in time, I was so overwhelmed by her proximity, her presence—scent, the matte of her skin, dark eyes, syrupy voice—that I would have said anything, done anything to prolong the interview.

"I asked you to have patience," I repeated. "A month, two months, possibly three. No longer."

"Then you'll—you'll—" She couldn't finish.

"Yes," I told her. "Then I'll stop Angela Berri, or myself be stopped. Is that guarantee enough?"

We stood motionless, not speaking. Did her look turn to sympathy? To pity? To acquiescence? To complaisance? I simply did not know. A pulse fluttered low on her neck. I wanted to swoop and kiss it still. Strange that even then—so early—I was aware of what was happening.

There was a sharp rap at the parlor door. The moment shattered. We turned back into the room. A black zipsuit announced scheduled visitors. I made a polite farewell, leaving my prospectus to her.

At the doorway, smiling her good-bye, one hand rose almost languidly and touched the back of my head, my neck.

"Thank you, Nick," she said.

I was lost, I thought suddenly. For some reason I did not wish to compute, the thought pleased me.

It took almost two hours, in a cab, and visits to five jewelry shops before I was able to locate and purchase an exact replica of Grace Wingate's necklace—a silvery snowflake swinging from a leather thong.

But I was only ten minutes late for my meeting with Paul Bumford and Mary Bergstrom in front of DOB headquarters. I climbed into the back of the limousine, and we started off for New York immediately.

"Well?" I asked Paul.

"Worse than we supposed," he reported. "Very heavy social unrest. They're pillowing most of it—but who knows for how long? Bombings, assassinations, arson, kidnappings. A complete mosaic."

"Who?" I asked.

He shook his head. "That's what's so weird. Everyone agrees it's not organized. Just a kind of general discontent."

"But *why?*" I said loudly. Angrily. "They never had it so good."

"The pee-pul." Paul shrugged. "Who knows?"

"Show them," Mary Bergstrom muttered sullenly.

We both, Paul and I, looked at her in astonishment. But she volunteered nothing more, and we went on as if she had never spoken.

The remainder of the trip was spent reviewing input from the Field Offices at Houston, Spokane, and Honolulu, dealing with the physiological, psychological, and mental sources of pleasure. Even these preliminary reports generated grave questions. We drove through gathering darkness, debating the nature of happiness.

Y-9

I visited my Times Square mail drop every day. Nothing from Simon Hawkley. Anxiety growing. My position was perilous. I was owner of a factory selling drugs to my own department of government. I knew what the results of discovery would be.

Finally, on September 20, rainy, windswept, I found a short, coded message from Hawkley. Just three series of numbers. Decoded: FISH BITING. CALL.

I called San Diego from a corner booth. We kept our conversation as brief and cryptic as possible. A letter had arrived at Scilla Pharmaceuticals from Headquarters, Department of Bliss. It was signed by an Edward T. Collins. His title was Commercial Coordinator, Security & Intelligence. It stated that since Scilla was engaged in the production and sale to the US Government of restricted drugs, according to Public Law, Section DOB-46-H3, subsection 2X-31G, the premises, the production methods, and the distribution procedures of Scilla were required to be examined and approved periodically. At 1500, on September 29, Mr. Art Roach, Chief, Security & Intelligence, would arrive at Scilla to make such an inspection.

I told Simon Hawkley I would get back to him with instructions for Seymour Dove well before Roach's arrival.

I discussed it with Paul Bumford that night.

"You really think they're taking the bait?" he asked.

"Definitely," I told him. "Those *in situ* inspections are customarily made by a road crew, PS-4's, conditioned for that service. I never heard of an S-and-I chief inspecting a factory personally."

"You don't seem too happy," he said.

"I'm happy enough. I suppose, subconsciously, I was hoping Angela would make the approach personally. But I should have known better. I should have known she'd use Roach as a bagman, keep a level between her and the overt act. Then, if push came to shove, she could terminate him with prejudice. Well, we'll have to manipulate roach and compromise her through him. Let's get started on the scenario. The first consideration is the time frame. . . ."

There was never any doubt that Paul and I would have to be in San Diego when the trap was sprung. In fact, we'd have to be there a day or two earlier to help install and test the sharing equipment in Seymour Dove's office at Scilla, and to instruct and rehearse him in his role.

"Getting out there with a legitimate cover should be no problem," I said. "I have a backlog of threedays. You can go out to inspect Nancy Ching's operations in the FO. The problem is—where do we stay? The letter Scilla received states that Roach will arrive at 1500 on September twenty-ninth. But what if he takes a threeday and gets there on the twenty-seventh, or maybe just a day earlier to scout the ground? His profile says he is shrewd, clever, suspicious. We're so close now, Paul, we can't take the chance of getting out there early and discover we've checked into the hotel where he's staying. Am I being paranoid?"

"My God, no!" Paul said. "We can't leave anything to chance. It's risky enough as it is. How about Nancy Ching's place on the beach?"

"Think she'd let us have it?"

"Of course."

"Yesss," I said slowly. Computing. "I think that would serve. We'll stay out there as much as possible, going into the city only when it's absolutely necessary. That should reduce a chance meeting with Roach to the ult min. Now let's talk about what equipment we'll need. Chauncey Higgles, Limited, will supply the heavy stuff. But we'll need cameras, film, maybe some personal devices. Just in case."

We served long hours for three evenings. We went over the Personality Profile of Art Roach, trying to determine how he might react in certain situations. We pored over the Federal Criminal Code to determine what kind of evidence we'd need to stop Art Roach and Angela Berri.

Finally, the scenario was in a form where anything added or subtracted would just be tinkering. We agreed to go ahead with what we had. I sent a letter to Simon Hawkley the following morning by commercial mail. Merely: "Arriving Sept. 27. Adventurer."

After our planning was completed, in the few days prior to September 27, I served hard, clearing my desk for the threeday I announced I was taking. I doubted any emergency would arise. But if it did, I told Ellen Dawes she could contact me through my father in Grosse Pointe, Michigan. I sent my father a letter instructing him to forward any messages for me to the San Diego Field Office.

We arrived in San Diego, on a commercial flight, a little before 1100, Pacific time, on the morning of September 27. We rented a black, two-door Dodge sedan, a Piranha, with a high-performance eight-cylinder internal combustion engine. Nancy Ching had closed her beachhouse for the season, but had readily agreed to lend it to Paul. She had promised to leave the keys in the sand under the first step of the porch.

We drove directly there, stopping just once to pick up vodka, Smack, some sandwich groceries. It took us about an hour to get the place aired out, to unpack, and settle in. Then I called Simon Hawkley to announce our arrival. I told him from then on, I would deal directly with Seymour Dove at Scilla and keep my contacts with him, Hawkley, to a minimum. He approved of my caution. I thought he might wish me good luck, but he didn't. Perhaps he didn't think I'd need it.

I then called Seymour Dove at Scilla, told him where we were, asked when he could join us. He said two hours. I told him we'd be waiting. And so we did. Wait. We spent the time discussing unexplored approaches in the development of the UP pill. I know I felt no nervousness about our current activity. If Paul felt any, at this late stage, he hid it very well.

I had alerted Paul, but still he was startled when Seymour Dove sauntered in. A vision in peacock blue, including blue sunglasses, blue sandals, blue bone earrings, blue eye shadow, and a blue, feathered hat left over from the road company of *The Three Musketeers*. He grinned at us, whites flashing against that incredibly tanned skin. Then he twirled slowly for our inspection, arms akimbo.

"Jerk you?" he said.

Paul laughed, and we all stroked palms. We made vodka-and-Smacks and prowurst sandwiches. Then we started on the details of the scenario.

We all agreed that the sharing operation should be kept as simple as possible. Seymour Dove pointed out that with the number of servers at Scilla, assigned to all levels of the main building, including the basement, it would be practically impossible to place clandestine wiring and power sources without being observed. We would have to opt for self-powered devices. The critical danger was that such devices could usually be detected by a portable meter, or even a wrist monitor. Art Roach might well be carrying or wearing either.

I believed I had the answer to this problem. In scanning the Chauncey Higgles, Ltd., catalogue, provided by Mrs. Agatha Whiggam, I had noted a new (1997) device which seemed almost to have been designed with our mission in mind.

It was a conventional, one-meter TV receiver, a console model available in three furniture styles: Contemporary, Traditional, and Mediterranean. It was not one of the new 3-D, laser-holograph sets, but still utilized a cathode tube. However, installed within the tube, photographing through the plastiglas faceplate, was a miniaturized TV camera, picking up both sight and sound. It was powered by the electric current supplying the television set.

Its greatest advantage was that the set was always "hot." That is, diminished power was constantly fed to the picture tube so that, when the viewer clicked the On button, it was not necessary to wait ten seconds for the set to warm up; the image appeared on screen almost instantaneously. Thus, if the set was checked with a meter, of course it would show a power flow, for a very innocent reason.

We agreed that such a set, designed for home or office, would be entirely appropriate in the executive suite of Scilla Pharmaceuticals. The monitor was small, compact, and would easily fit into the back seat of our rented Dodge sedan. The monitor consisted of a loudspeaker, a 20 cm viewing screen, and a TV tape attachment by which voice and visual communication could be recorded. We, in turn, in the car, could talk to Seymour Dove via his TV set.

So it was decided that Paul and I, with the monitor, would park in the copse of trees bordering the road that ran in front of the Scilla plant. The trees, fortunately, were in the opposite direction from that Roach would probably take in arriving at the factory by taxi or rented car. The chances of his spotting and recognizing us were minimal. And our parking area was well within the claimed range of the TV camera transmitter.

Then we went over Seymour Dove's role. Several times. I gave him a page of dialogue we had prepared: questions to ask Art Roach, the answers to which, we hoped, would implicate Angela Berri. Dove was a quick study. He scanned the page swiftly, nodded, handed it back.

"All right," Paul said. "Let's try it. Pretend I'm Art Roach."

They went into the suggested dialogue:

Paul: "So you see, Mr. Dove, if you want that contract, it'll cost you."

Dove: "How much?"

Paul: "Ten percent."

Dove: "Ten? My God, there goes my profit."

Paul: "Not at all. If the contract figures out to a hundred thousand, bid a hundred and ten. You'll get it. No loss to you. You get the hundred. We get the ten. Up front."

Dove: "Up front? Jesus! How do I know I can trust you. No offense to you, but I've never seen you before. I've never even *heard* of you. You're in Security and Intelligence. All my dealings up to now have been with Satisfaction Section."

Paul: "Who did you deal with in SATSEC?"

Dove: "The last purchase order was signed by Nicholas Flair. But before that, it was Angela Berri."

Paul: "That's who you're dealing with now."

Dove: "Berri? But she's Director of Bliss."

Paul: "That's right."

Dove: "You mean she's in on this?"

Paul: "She's in all right. She's your guarantee."

Then Seymour Dove looked at me, troubled.

"Something wrong?" I asked him.

"I don't know," he said hesitantly. "Look, I don't want to damper this thing. I'll serve on it. You ems know what you're doing. You know the objects concerned. But . . ."

"But what?" Paul asked.

"I've been involved in deals like this before," Dove said, shaking his head. "Believe me, it's never that easy."

"Well," I said, "you know what we want. If Roach doesn't follow the scenario, you'll have to play it by ear."

"That I can do." He nodded.

I admired the em. He appeared to welcome the challenge. A new role at the San Fernando Playhouse. He was the star and would get great reviews. He had the unreasoning confidence of all actors.

We spent the following morning and early afternoon installing and testing the equipment. Paul and I picked up the monitor at the Chauncey Higgles, Ltd., warehouse on Sampson Street. Then we drove to our stakeout under the trees. Higgles delivered the fiddled television set to Scilla Pharmaceuticals in a van chastely marked "New World TV Service & Repair." Seymour Dove had it positioned at one end of his long office, against the wall. The hidden camera covered practically the entire room. The image we received on the small monitor screen was remarkably detailed. Not as bright as I would have liked, but adequate. Sound reception was excellent.

Paul drove me back to the beachhouse, then left to put in an appearance at the Field Office and take Nancy Ching to dinner. I went for a swim, then walked down the road to a seafood restaurant and gnawed futilely at a rubberized abalone steak afloat in an oleaginous sauce. Finally I gave up, returned to the cottage, made two more prowurst sandwiches. I washed them down with vodka-and-Smacks, while watching a televised execution. A rapist-murderer was being hanged. It was messy. But I imagined the ratings would be lovable.

We were in position by 1430 the next day. Well off the road. Practically against the tree trunks. We had brought sandwiches and cans of Smack. Not so much to assuage hunger, but as an excuse for parking in case a highway patrol car stopped to look us over.

Paul sat in the back seat, tending the monitor. I sat up front, behind the wheel. I held the mike, on a short cord. We both watched the screen. Dove's office was empty.

At 1440 an ef secretary came in and placed a folder on Seymour Dove's desk. She scratched her ass before departing. I don't believe either Paul or I smiled.

Dove entered the office about 1450. He came over to stand directly in front of the television set.

"Receiving?" he asked softly.

"Fine," I said. Just as softly. "Picture and sound good."

He stood motionless a moment.

"Would you like to see my impersonation of President Hilton?" He grinned.

"No," I said. It was the first time he had evidenced nervousness.

He went back behind his desk, sat down, began to scan papers in the folder the secretary had left.

1455.

1500.

1505.

Dove glanced once toward the TV set, seemed about to speak, then thought better of it.

At 1525, Dove's desk flasher chimed. He switched it on. We could see no image on the flasher screen. It was obviously a phone call.

"Seymour Dove," he said. His voice was steady and loud.

We couldn't hear the reply.

"Yes," Dove said. "How are you, Mr. Roach? . . . Yes, sir, we're all set and waiting for you . . . I see . . . But what about the inspection? . . . I see . . . Well, yes, of course . . . When? . . . Yes, I can make it by then . . . of course . . . The Strake? Yes, I know where it is . . . Shall I ring your room? . . . Fine. See you then."

He switched off the flasher. Sat a moment in silence. Rose heavily and came over to the TV set. He looked directly at the screen.

"It's no-go," he said. "He's not coming out to inspect. He wants me to meet him at 1700 at the Strake Hotel."

Paul and I stared at his miniature image on the TV monitor. Then we looked at each other. I wondered if my face was as pinched and drained as his.

I spoke into the mike: "We'll drive down to the plant. Can you meet us just outside the gate? Across the road."

"Sure," he said. "Will do. Sorry, Nick."

We moved down the road, pulled off into the shoulder opposite the Scilla gate. In a few moments Seymour Dove came out into the main building, walked down the graveled driveway.

"Sorry, Nick," he repeated.

"Not your fault," I said shortly. "I should have trusted your instinct. It was too easy."

"Where are you meeting him?" Paul asked. "His hotel room?"

"In the lobby," Dove said. "At 1700. I suppose we'll go someplace from there. Some safe place. His room, a restaurant, maybe just a ride. In *his* car. He's cute."

We were all silent. Trying to compute a way.

"Look," Seymour Dove said finally, "you told me you brought a body-pack and some other trinkets from New York. Want to wire me and hope for the best?"

"Negative," I said. "If he's this cautious, he's sure to be carrying or wearing a monitor. If he discovers you're powered . . . well, just forget it. No, I think all you can do now is meet with him and see how much you can salvage from the scenario."

"I'm willing to testify if you want him on extortion or bribery conspiracy."

"Forget it," I told him wearily. "Just your word against his. All it would accomplish would be to start them checking into the ownership of Scilla. That I can do without. How did he sound?"

"Roach? Sharp, hard, no hesitation. He's done this before."

"Shouldn't wonder." I sighed. "All right, meet him. Can you come out to the beachhouse later and fill us in?"

"Sure, Nick. Shouldn't take more than an hour or so after 1700. Unless he chisels a free dinner. I'll get to you as soon as I leave him."

Paul and I returned the TV monitor to the Higgles warehouse. Then we drove back to La Jolla Bay in silence. The beachhouse seemed airless and deserted. The sun was beginning a long, slow slide into the sea. From the porch we could see a few naked swimmers, a picnicking family group, a couple of nude efs suntanning on plastilume sheets. There were no birds.

I had bought a liter of lovable natural brandy. We were going to drink it to celebrate our triumph. We drank it to numb our defeat. The bottle was almost half-empty when Seymour Dove stalked in. He slammed the door behind him. He went directly to the brandy bottle, poured a glassful, drank it off the way I'd drink a glass of Smack. Then he looked at us.

"That em," he said, "is one cold monkey."

We said nothing. He took off his jacket, kicked off his sandals, slumped into a plastivas sling.

"You'll never guess where he took me," he said.

"Wait, wait," I said hurriedly. "Don't tell us. Let me compute this. I'll tell you where you went."

Suddenly it was important to me that I got this correct, that I could reason where a man like Art Roach would take a prospective victim to dictate terms. I reviewed everything I knew about Roach. Input, storage, retrieval.

"I'll tell you," I said. "He took you to a steam room or sauna."

"My God," Dove said. "You're exactly right. A sauna. How did you know?"

"I know Roach," I said. Feeling better. "He dotes on saunas and steam rooms. And where can you be certain the man you're cutting isn't wired? In a sauna or steam room, of course. Where you're both bareass naked."

"Well," Dove said, "I'm glad you turned me down on the body-pack. I don't know what he would have done if he had spotted it while we were undressing. And he was wearing a wrist monitor. I haven't met many objects who scare me, but that em is one of them. Be careful of him, gentlemen. He bites."

"How much did he want?" Paul asked.

"A modest five percent. I followed your scenario. He did, too—up to a point. I said five percent would kill my profit. He said to add it on the top. But he wanted the five percent up front. I asked what guarantee I had that if I paid the love, I'd get the contract. That's when he departed from the script. He said the only way I could prove his sincerity—that's the word he used: 'sincerity'—was *not* to pay the love. Then I wouldn't get the contract, and I'd know positively he hadn't been scamming me. Beautiful?"

"He never mentioned Angela Berri?" I asked.

"Never. Not once. He implied he had complete rule of contract awards. He was the only object I had to deal with. No one else."

"How does he want the payoff?" Paul asked.

"If I agree to his terms, I go to Washington on October 20 and check into any hotel. I call him at the hotel where he lives—the Winslow on N Street. I act like an old friend unexpectedly in town, looking him up. He'll give me instructions on delivery then."

"Uh-huh." Paul nodded. "At a place of his choosing. And you're to bring the love in cash. Small, untreated bills. Nothing larger than a twenty. In nonconsecutive serial numbers."

"However did you guess?" Dove said.

We all laughed. I don't know why, but suddenly we all had the idea we were still alive.

"Well?" Dove asked. "Should I plan to be in Washington on October 20?"

"Sure," I said. "With the love. I'll be in touch with you or Simon Hawkley before that."

We sat a few minutes after he left. I think what most pleased both of us, although we didn't mention it, was that our basic premise had proved out: Roach *was* on the suck. And by reasonable inference, so was Angela Berri.

"Paul," I said suddenly, "let's get out of here. Let's go back. Right now."

"Nick, we've got reservations on a morning flight."

"So? Change them. Get on the flasher. See if there's a flight tonight we can make. I've got to get moving. Even if it's only from Point B to Point C."

We made it, with minutes to spare. The jet was only one-quarter filled. In fact, there was only one other passenger in the first-class cabin. He had his left leg encased in a heavy cast. It stuck out into the aisle. We stepped over it carefully on the way to our seats.

"Sorry," he said cheerfully. "Skiing. I zigged when I should have zagged."

We smiled sympathetically.

After takeoff, we each took our three free drinks: vodka-and-Smacks. They lasted to Phoenix. There we started on what remained of the natural brandy, which we had thoughtfully brought along. We nursed it to Tulsa. Pleading dehydration, we got two more drinks from the stewardess and sipped those to St. Louis.

Meanwhile, we had been brainstorming the logistics of the payoff: Seymour Dove to Art Roach, Washington, D.C., October 20, 1998. We came up with many ingenious scenarios. A lot of kaka. The only possible solution was to have Seymour Dove swallow an internal mike and transmitter. Or implant a set in a molar or the rectum or in the external auditory meatus. But if Art Roach wore a wrist monitor, he could detect any of those. Checkmate.

At St. Louis, our crippled fellow passenger debarked, slowly and painfully, leaning on crutches. We watched him move himself up the aisle to the open door, assisted by the stewardess.

"My God," Paul said, "he must be dragging twenty pounds of plaster in that cast."

"Probably plastiment," I said. "Half the weight, one-third more strength."

"Why not an inflatable splint? One-hundredth the weight."

"Can't use an inflatable splint," I said. "Not on a load-bearing break."

We took off from the new St. Louis jetport, heading for GPA-1. The fenced compound. Home. I closed my eyes.

"You want to sleep?" Paul asked.

"No. Go up to the galley. See if you can wheedle some more booze."

He came back in a moment, giggling.

"Well?" I said.

"Look," he said.

I opened my eyes. He had four miniatures of vodka. He handed me two.

"Stole them," he said.

"Good em," I said. "Fine service."

I twisted off the little plastic cap. Drained half in one swallow. Closed my eyes again.

"Paul," I said dreamily.

"What?"

"Ever see an inflatable splint?"

"Of course I've seen an inflatable splint. Are you drunk?"

"Just enough. A double sleeve of opaque heavy-gauge plastic. Compressed air forced between the sleeves. After inflation, it's hard as a rock. Keeps the fracture rigid. Right?"

"Nick, for God's sake, what's all this about inflatable splints?"

I opened my eyes.

"Very scientific. Very objective. Given: Two objects. Problem: To share their conversation. Known factor: One object cannot be equipped for sharing. Ergo: Equip the other."

"I know, I know," Paul said. Impatient now. "But *how?*"

I told him.

"Nick. . . ." he said. Almost choking. "You're either mad or a genius."

"Can't I be both?" I asked.

Y-10

I had decided to grow a beard and mustache. No reason that I could analyze. Just whim. I wanted something vaguely Vandyke, but perhaps a bit more squarish.

I had showered and was standing naked in front of the nest mirror. I was inspecting five days' growth of beard, debating whether it was long enough to trim, when my doorbell chimed. I padded out.

"Yes?"

"Nick, it's me. Paul."

I let him in, relocked the door. He followed me back to the nest. He sat on the toilet seat lid, watched me fuss at the new growth with a little pair of fingernail scissors.

"Itch?" he asked.

"It did the first few days. What's on your mind?"

"You don't really want to know, do you? Not everything!" I sighed, put down the scissors, pulled on a robe.

"All right, let's have a nightcap. Just one. Then you can tell me."

He followed me into the living room, sat on the sofa. On the edge. I knew his moods. He was winding himself up to something. I brought us each a petrorye on Jellicubes, and sat down opposite him.

"All right, Paul," I said, "let's have it."

"Your father's application for permission to manufacture, distribute, and sell the Die-Dee Doll came across my desk today."

"And?"

"I'm going to reject it. As being 'Inimical to the public interest.' "

"Yes. You told me you would."

"Nick, I'd like a chance to explain the reasons for rejection to your father."

"You know I'll probably overrule you on the doll?"

"Yes, I know that."

"But you still want to explain your position to my father?"

"Yes. It may sound silly to you, but I keep thinking I can get him to withdraw it."

"No way," I said. "He smells love. But you rate a try. Paul, we've both been serving hard. Suppose we take a threeday together to Michigan?"

"Sounds good," he said. Brightening. "Let's do it."

"Fine." I rubbed the new hair on my chin. "Maybe by the time I get back objects will stop asking if I forgot to shave."

He tried to smile. That night he looked—somehow sad. He had the look of an em who had come to some momentous decision he meant to carry out, though it would bring him no profit.

I came close to bringing out the bottle of petrorye and asking him to stay the night. I believed then, and I believe now, that he would have accepted gladly. I also believe that it would not have altered what happened.

We took the Bullet Train to Detroit, treating ourselves to a compartment. With two bottles of natural wine to lubricate the trip. It was October 8. There was a threat of winter in the air: wind with a bite, smell of snow, a lowering sky. The feel of things coming to an end.

This time the copter pilot was an em—was my father changing his religion?—but wearing the usual Chinese red zipsuit with the usual logo embroidered across the chest. On the short flight to Grosse Pointe, he told us Father was out of town but was expected back the following day.

Miss Catherine had prepared a cold supper for us, served by Mrs. McPherson in the echoing dining room. Both Paul and I were ravenous, and ate hugely. The meat dish was some kind of processed pork substitute, a cold, lardlike loaf. Side dishes came from a nearby food factory where fruits and vegetables were grown in enormous plastic greenhouses. Humidity, temperature, artificial sunlight, carbon dioxide, soil nutrients, and water were rigidly controlled. The resulting produce was enormous in size but, though unquestionably natural, was something less than tasty. They were "working on the problem." I suspected it was the soil used: reprocessed and dried sludge from Detroit sewers.

We dawdled over ersatz coffee and my father's decanter of natural plum brandy. Our conversation was meandering and rather bawdy. Mainly, it concerned the government's puzzlement over what to do about an international airline that had recently started "The Sultan's Flight," US to Europe. The ticket cost included, according to the advertisement, "a single act of normal coitus" with one of the young hostesses aboard. Consummated in small, curtained cubicles called "Harem Huts." It all seemed to be legal.

Finally, before midnight, we straggled upstairs.

We wasted the following day—a delightful experience. Somehow it made us superior to time, to spend it in such a profligate manner. We wandered about the grounds, had a lazy lunch on the terrace, skipped stones over the water (Paul was quite good), and chased a squirrel through the woods.

When my father arrived, late in the afternoon, we were waiting for him on the porch. He came bounding up the steps, grabbed me in the usual bear hug, shouted "Nick-ol'-as!" several times, stroked palms with Paul, bundled us into the library, shouted for a tub of Jellicubes, vodka, Smack. When Mrs. McPherson brought the tray, I noticed my father was using up what remained of my mother's natural potato vodka. I couldn't expect him to pour it down the sink. I don't know why I felt a pang.

He immediately began a loud and enthusiastic account of what he had been doing: rushing from Connecticut to Indiana to North Carolina, setting up production facilities for the Die-Dee Doll. Paul's lips compressed, his face congealed, he set his drink slowly and carefully on the floor alongside his chair.

"Mr. Flair—" he started. Voice cold and steady.

"—an entirely new concept," Father burbled on. "A system of snap-together assembly that should—"

"Mr. Flair," Paul repeated. Louder now. He stood up.

"—in terms of—" my father said. And paused. Suddenly.

"I'm going to reject your application to produce the Die-Dee Doll," Paul said. Again loudly. Distinctly. "As a matter of fact, I already have. As being inimical to the public interest."

"What?" Chester K. Flair said shakily. "What are you talking about?"

"Yes, sir. The Die-Dee Doll. I've rejected your application to produce."

"Jesus Christ," my father breathed.

He sat down heavily, took a long pull of his drink, looked at us, back and forth, with hurt, bewildered eyes.

A marvelous act. Paul would never know. But I saw at once that my father had already considered the possibility of rejection and computed how to handle it.

" 'Inimical to the public interest'?" he said. Incredulously. "How can you *say* that?"

Paul repeated, in greater detail, the reasons he had already stated to me. I thought they were valid arguments. Finally—this was a new one—the concept of burial in the ground in a plastic coffin conditioned disobedience to the federal law requiring cremation.

My father listened closely, and gave every evidence of growing perplexity.

"Paul," he said, "it's just a toy. Nothing more. I'm not out to condition or recondition the kids. I must tell you—and I swear it—I really don't compute what you mean. How could a toy do what you say it does? Listen, I've got the signed statements of some of the best child psychologists in the country. Really big names. They all say the same thing: The Die-Dee Doll will do no harm. In fact, it will do good. *Good*, Paul. 'Emotional catharsis.' 'Normal adjustments to stopping.' 'Relieves irrational childish fears.' I've got the papers to *prove* it, Paul. All right, if you insist on the last part, about the burial, I'll change it. Instead of a coffin, we'll supply a little cremation oven. How about *that*, Paul? The kid can burn up the stopped Die-Dee Doll, oven and all. Will that do it?"

Paul looked at me with a kind of wonderment, shaking his head.

"I'm sorry, Mr. Flair," he said. "My rejection stands."

He turned, marched from the room, closed the door softly behind him. My father watched him leave, then stared at me.

"What's *with* that little butterfly?" he demanded. "He eats my food, drinks my booze, sleeps in my house—and then he pulls this kaka?"

"He's doing what he thinks is right," I said mildly.

My father grunted. He mixed us fresh drinks. He took his to a club chair opposite mine, slumped into it, regarded me gravely over his raised plastiglas.

"You can overrule him, can't you, Nick?" he asked quietly.

I nodded.

"You going to?"

"I haven't made up my mind yet."

"Well...." He sighed. "Do what you think is best. Don't let our father-son relationship affect your service. Just judge me like any other applicant."

"I will," I said solemnly. He was hilarious.

"Now let's talk about other things," he said. "You been getting those private data bank reports on Angela Berri and Art Roach?"

"Yes," I said. "Thank you. They've been very helpful."

"Good," he said. "I had a lot of trouble setting that up. But as long as the reports are getting to you and helping you, that's all I care about. And the love? Have any trouble with the transfer from the Detroit banks?"

"None whatsoever," I said. "The love was there when I needed it."

"Glad to hear it," he said. "Anything I can do for my boy really makes me happy. Well, Nick, let me know what you decide on the Die-Dee Doll."

"Of course," I said. "As soon as possible."

Suddenly he was looming over me, grinning down at me, his great paw crushing my shoulder.

"Thanks, *son*," he said. "Now I think I'll take a little stroll and relax."

"Who is she?" I asked.

"Who?" he asked innocently. "Oh." He laughed. "Oh ... in the guesthouse. Well ... she's a musician."

I held up a hand, palm out.

"Please," I said. "Don't tell me what she plays."

He was still laughing when he went out the library doorway, banging the frame on both sides with his wide shoulders as he went through.

I finished my drink. Then, from the library phone, I called Millie Jean Grunwald. Thankfully, she was at home. Better than that, she was entertaining a girlfriend. They were watching a Spanish bullfight on the telly, via satellite, and eating sandwiches of prorye spread with premixed peanut butter and grape petrojelly.

"Yum-yum," Millie said.

I asked how she and her girlfriend would enjoy the company of two young, horny ems.

"Yum-yum," Millie said.

I went up to Paul's room, walked in without knocking. He was standing at a window, staring out into the darkness. Hands thrust into his pockets.

"Come on," I said. "We're going into Detroit."

"What for?" Dulled.

"Life."

"No. You go ahead without me, Nick."

"Don't you want to meet my girlfriend?"

He turned then to look at me. I knew; he *was* curious.

"Three's a crowd," he said cautiously.

"Four, in this case. She's got a girlfriend visiting. Don't know who. I probably never met her."

"Well..." He hesitated. "Listen, Nick, what did your father say after I left?"

I told him exactly what my father had said. He was aghast.

"My God," he said. "Between father and son? That kind of interaction?"

I shrugged. "That's the way we are. That's the way we all are."

"I'm glad I never knew who my father was."

"It can be an advantage," I admitted. "At times."

"Then you're going to overrule my rejection? Approve the Die-Dee Doll?"

"Do I have any choice?"

"Nooo," he said slowly. "I guess not."

I thought it time to bring him up to speed.

"Before you hate him, or me, too much, Paul, remember that what he did for me also benefited you. Enough of this kaka. Let's get tracking."

On the ride into Detroit, we stopped for a two-liter jug of red petrowine. I think we were both in the mood for something harsh and primitive.

Paul was shocked, perhaps a bit frightened by the dark, bricked street down near the river. The suppurative smell of things. Echoing footfalls. Feeble pools of light from obso streetlamps. The apartment over the porn shop. A display of dusty phalli.

"Nick," he said. Looking up at the cracked windows. "Do you come here often?"

"Every time I'm in Detroit."

"And you've never had your throat slit?"

"Every time I'm in Detroit."

He laughed. "Now I understand your bruised ribs. You were lucky."

We rang, were admitted, climbed the creaking stairway. The efs awaited us at the top of the stairs, arms about each other's waist. Millie, with all her bountiful blessings, looked like the mother. The girlfriend's name was Sophie. No last name volunteered or requested.

During the late 1980's and early 1990's, for almost a decade, a series of great droughts and famines had bloomed like a firestorm across Southeast Asia, India, Africa, South America. It was said that 500,000,000 objects stopped. That may have been operative. No one would know. The "developed nations" (what does that mean?) did what they could with token shipments of proteins, fats, vitamins, etc. It was all useless. The world listened to the chuckles of Malthus.

The famines were, at first, given heavy media coverage. Until it became a bore. We stared at staggering animals, stopping objects, cracked earth, withered foliage. Heard the cries of the victims, animals and objects. So similar.

What impressed me most was the expression on the faces of the very young. Outrage.

Sophie had much that same look. And curiously, she had the physical appearance of a famine victim: joints poking out against parchment skin, thinness to the point of emaciation, faintness of speech, eyes abnormally large. I guessed that, like Millie, she was one of a flawed clone group. Paul didn't flinch.

We drank quite a lot of the red petrowine. We danced. I recall that at one point, Paul and I engaged in a kind of adagio routine with Sophie, throwing her back and forth between us. She was a loose rack of bones. She adored the rough play, urging us on with piggish squeals. Millie couldn't stop laughing.

What else? Paul crawled across the floor on hands and knees, Sophie perched on his back. Her sleazy shift was pulled up to her waist. The naked pelvis was a shadowed hollow. Bones jutted whitely. Wiry hair bristled. Millie and I applauded this performance wildly. We were then sitting up in bed. About Millie's neck, suspended from a leather thong, the silvery snowflake hung between sweated breasts. My gift to her.

Then we four were naked. A tangle on the crumpled sheet. Paul and I drank wine from them. This amused us all. But the alcohol stung when they took us into full mouths. We bit their flesh. To screams. The taste of the two efs was quite different: Millie soft, sweet, pulpy; Sophie tart, hard, astringent. Paul and I knocked foreheads as our tongues met in some viscous trap. We discovered Millie was able to suck her own nipples. Sophie locked her heels behind her head and pouted that bearded mouth to all. We knew the world would end the next instant.

During that fevered night I lurched out into the hallway, found the nest. And there was Paul, standing on the closed toilet, his head and shoulders out the opened window. He appeared to be inspecting the rear wall of the adjoining buildings.

"Paul, what are you doing?"

He came inside slowly, climbed down.

"I had to get some air," he said. "I thought I was going to faint."

"Sorry," I said.

"About what?"

"Sophie."

He stared at me.

"Nick," he said, "believe this. It's operative. The best orgasm I've ever had in my life."

"Oh?" I said. "Why?"

"Why? Why? I'm not sure."

"Try."

"Complete mastery. I owned her."

"That's interesting," I said.

Physical pleasure demands deliberation. Passion is for beasts. The second half of that *Walpurgisnacht* was cool, muted, considered. Occasionally painful. We all moved slowly in a grunted dream. Some things we could not do. But tried.

By dawn we were emptied. I slept on the floor. When I awoke aching, I found the other three on the bed, spoon-fashion, hands grasping swollen flesh in sleep.

I moved them about. Slowly, gently. They did not awake, but muttered, groaned. It was more pained stupor than sleep. I arranged the efs on their backs, knees raised and spread. Paul turned, twisted, his flaccid genitals plastered to his thigh.

It was Egon Schiele, of course. I had recognized it the moment I saw their rawness. Now, exposed, I dimly glimpsed a truth and began to understand. It went beyond sexuality. To a primitive something. A dark mystery I could not deny. It drew me, this wonder long sought. It was almost a revelation.

Paul and I got home safely. I bathed and went to bed. I presumed he did the same. I know I didn't see him until late that afternoon. I was forcing myself to eat some food, on the terrace, and trying to stop a bursting thirst with a tall vodka-and-Smack. Paul took his place opposite me, nodding. He was quite pale. I suppose I was, too.

Later, carrying a second vodka-and-Smack, we wandered out onto the grounds. We wore flannel bags, heavy sweaters. There was, thankfully, a nip in the wind. It dried sweat, brought a welcome chill. I did not mention the previous night. Nor did Paul. I think we were both too awed by what we had done.

"About the UP pill," I said. "Are you up to speed?"

"Yes."

"Reactions?"

"On the physical factor, I can see a reasonable hope. Houston says it will definitely be addictive, psychologically if not physiologically. I see it as a combined narcotic and euphoric. I think the chemistry can be solved."

"I concur. But you don't sound too enthusiastic."

"I'm not. Nick, if all we want is the world's greatest physical jerk, we might as well go to an opium-based derivative, or an amphetamine, and have everyone in the country on the nod or grinning their way through life in a semipermanent state of goofiness. That's not what we want, is it?"

"You know better than that."

"Honolulu was equivocal. They didn't say yes, and they didn't say no. Except for Ruben's report."

"Oh-ho. You caught that. Know the em?"

"Never heard of him before."

"I served with him on a memory project. Very quiet. Shy. A chess genius. With a fantastic ability to go straight to the jugular of a problem. You notice that while everyone else in Honolulu was trying to analyze the mental factor in happiness, only Ruben realized it may consist of no mentality at all. What was it he said? 'The total absence of conscious ratiocination may prove to be the dominant mental factor in states of euphoria.' That's pure Ruben. It's even the way he talks."

"He also said, in his report, 'Mental happiness may result from complete absence of responsibility.' Interesting."

"Yes. Well, Spokane was unequivocal. They said flat-out that, psychologically, happiness is such a subjective state that there is no common denominator. Do you believe that?"

"I don't want to, Nick. If it's true, we can forget about the UP pill."

"Well, I don't believe it. Paul, we'll never get a pill with one hundred percent effectiveness. What pill has? Even aspirin is ineffective on some subjects. If we can jerk even seventy-five percent, I'll be satisfied."

"You have a very low satiety level."

I laughed. We continued our stroll. Wandering through the trees. Crunching dried leaves underfoot. I began to believe I might live.

"What is Lewisohn up to?" Paul asked abruptly.

"I was wondering when you'd get curious. As nearly as I can tell, his plan is mainly economic. I don't believe he's done any computing on the social organization it will demand. He probably assumes social form will follow economic function."

"What's the economic plan?"

"A corporate state," I said. "That's as close as I can come. Evolving into a corporate world. All means of production owned by the government. Planning takes over the role of the marketplace."

"The individual buys stocks or bonds in the government?"

"Possibly. Perhaps the total of voluntary contributions determines an object's share. I don't believe Lewisohn has yet considered the problems, the social problems."

"It would have to be authoritarian. The government."

"Of course. But no more than, say, General Motors or IBM. A benevolent despotism. Written into law. You better make notes on this in the Tomorrow File."

"Yes. I will. It implies a class society, doesn't it?"

"If Lewisohn has computed it at all, he probably envisions economic classes: rulers, managers, servers. Not too different from what we have now."

"With free vertical movement between classes?"

"I would imagine so. Paul, why are you so interested in Lewisohn's plan?"

"Because right now he's serving on social unrest. But I see nothing in his proposed world, as you describe it, that would eliminate the unrest."

"The UP pill might."

"Perhaps. But we agreed we don't want something to keep servers perpetually dopey. They've got to produce. How about the UP pill as a reward?"

"For producing? Now you're just substituting a drug for love. That solves nothing."

"Yes. Yes, Nick, you're right. Let me compute this a little more."

On the following day, in our compartment aboard the Bullet Train to GPA-1, Paul returned to the subject.

"If the purpose of the UP pill is to curb social unrest," he said, "then it cannot be considered by itself, a new drug, *in vacuo*. It must be developed in the context of the social situation."

"In other words, you're saying we should work backward from the purpose? Determining the social goal, then developing the UP pill that achieves it?"

"In a way. Nick, we've got to create a *political* drug."

"A political drug," I murmured.

"Exactly. The UP pill must be effective, physiologically. But it cannot succeed as we want it to unless it is encapsulated in a social organization that reinforces it. One has no greater value than the other. But both sustain each other, mutually dependent."

"Are you saying then that purely *physical* joy—Ultimate Pleasure, if you will—is sufficient if the social organization is so computed as to provide the mental and psychological factors of operative happiness?"

"Yesss," Paul said slowly. "That's about it."

"Yes," I said. "I think so, too. Let's serve along those lines."

We came out into the low ceilings and rancid, littered corridors of the Pennsylvania Station in New York. At one point in time a huge railroad depot had stood here. Modeled after the Baths of Caracalla. With enormous, delicate, soaring spaces that dwarfed objects and at the same time, strangely, enobled them. But that cathedral was before my time. I never knew it.

Y-11

On October 15, I was to take the 1300 air shuttle to Washington, D.C. But I had several official duties to get through that morning. Paul Bumford accompanied me on my rounds. Whenever we had the chance, whenever we were alone, we went over once again the details of the scenario for the next five days.

Our first visit was to C Lab where Paul's Memory Team leader was staging a demonstration for us. They had been serving on the physical transfer of memory from one object to another of the same species. They had developed a derivative of purified RNA, from the donor object, hyped with a chlorinated uracil. Since, at that point in time, we had an evidentiary indication that memory was both a chemical and an electrical process, the Memory Team was experimenting with a very low-frequency current, in the range of human theta waves, to boost the effect of the injected chemicals.

In this case, the donor was a young em chimpanzee. He had been trained to pull a lever that released a food pellet. Positive behavioral conditioning. He was then sacrificed. Lovely word. RNA was extracted from his brain, purified by a newly developed cryogenic process, and combined with the uracil compound.

This mixture was then injected into the internal carotid of an untrained em chimp of the same breeding group—a "brother" of the donor. At the same time the untrained chimp was fitted with a metal helmet, self-powered, that generated the theta waves.

We all crowded around the one-way glass window looking into the chimp's room. In a moment, a lab server carried him in. The chimp's arms were clamped about the ef's neck. She gently disengaged him, set him in the middle of the floor, left the room. The chimp stared about curiously. He looked like a little, hairy astronaut.

"Haven't been starving him, have you, Ed?" I asked the Team Leader.

"Sure," he said cheerfully. "We need all the help we can get."

"As long as you haven't trained him," Paul said.

"I swear," the Team Leader murmured.

We watched the chimp in silence. He rose to all fours, put his head back, yawned. He scratched his ass. Exactly like the Scilla secretary Paul and I had watched on the TV monitor in San Diego.

Then the chimp looked around, bounced up and down once or twice as if to loosen his muscles. He ambled over to the food dispensing panel.

"He's going for it," someone breathed.

Almost without pausing, the animal reached up, yanked the lever, released it, lifted the metal cover of the chute, removed the food pellet, popped it into his mouth and began to chew, grimacing.

"Son of a bitch," someone said. Wonderingly.

Strangely, there was no elation. I think we just looked at each other, stunned. I know I was trying to compute the significance of what I had just seen. What it meant. What it could lead to. Physical transfer of memory. The power!

"Congratulations, Ed," I said finally. Shaking his hand. "Try it again. And again. And again. Publish nothing. It looks good."

He took me aside for a moment.

"How's the RSC, Nick?" he asked.

"Fine," I lied. "No problems."

"Good. When are you due for a hippocampal irrigation?"

"February."

"See me before then. We've been serving on something new."

"Will do. Congratulations again, Ed. Very impressive."

If we had one triumph that morning, we also had one disappointment. We stopped by Phoebe Huntzinger's office in the computer complex. I knew she had been monitoring Project Phoenix in Denver. She had come to feel it was her baby. Baby wasn't growing.

"Nothing," Phoebe growled. The moment we walked in. "Nothing plus nothing gives you nothing."

Her heavy brogues were propped up on a desk littered with books, pamphlets, journals, papers. Paul and I pulled up chairs facing her.

"Mary Bergstrom checked out the brain technology," Paul said. Defensively. "She says it's operative."

Phoebe nodded glumly. She was fretted by this problem.

"Nick," she said slowly, "if it was a nice day out, and I passed you in the hall or outside, what would you say to me?"

I looked at her.

"All right, I'll play your game," I said finally. "I'd probably say, 'Hello, Phoebe. Nice day.' "

"Precisely," she said. Bringing her feet down from the desk, hitching her chair toward us. "You'd say, 'Nice day.' But you'd say it like, 'Niceday.' In effect, you wouldn't use two words, an adjective and a noun. You'd use one word, 'Niceday,' as a kind of label for the kind of day it was. Compute? You'd not only say, 'Niceday,' but you'd think, 'Niceday.' A combination of two words, a union that describes verbally *and in your mind* the kind of day it is. You don't think 'nice' and then think 'day' and then put the two together. You get input from the sky, the sun, the air, and then your brain leaps immediately to the label, 'Niceday.' "

"So?" Paul said. He was interested now. Leaning forward to stare at her.

"See this kaka?" she said. She pushed at the stacks of books on her desk. "Linguistics. How we are conditioned to think in words. But more than one object suggests we don't think in words at all. Not individual words. A lot of our thinking is in phrases, even sentences, that constitute labels. Niceday, howareyou, hardrain, hotsun, cutekid. Compute? Nick, send me out to Denver. I want to reprogram that damned Golem to pick up a couple of thousand basic, primitive verbal labels in the English language. I can make up my own list from all this—" Again she shoved at the research on her desk. "And it may help us pick up coherent thoughts. It certainly can't do any harm. All we've done so far is print out a few individual words."

"Phoebe," I said, "sounds to me like you'll be making Golem sensitive to clichés."

"All right, all right," she said. "Clichés. Call them that if you want to. That's what ninety percent of human speech consists of, isn't it?"

"Cynic," I said. "Well, you may be right. Clichés may be the basis of rational speech. We've got to start somewhere. Paul? Reactions?"

"Phoebe," he said, "how will the computer print it out? In a series of words without space breaks?"

"No, no," she said. "It's a simple circuitry trick. The thought will be picked up by the input bank as connected phrases or sentences. The printout from retrieval will be properly spaced and punctuated."

Paul looked at me.

"Nick, let's try it," he said. "Nothing to lose."

"Right," I said. "Phoebe, have a good time in Denver. Orrather, have a goodtime."

October 15, 1998.

1630: I arrived at Rehabilitation & Reconditioning Hospice No. 4, Alexandria, Virginia, via taxi from the airport. I immediately sought out Chief Resident Luke Warren and informed him I would be his guest for the next five days. During which I intended to monitor the reactions of Hyman R. Lewisohn to the new parabiotic treatment. Lewisohn had already been connected to the first "volunteer," a young em from Texas. He was a former border guard of the Immigration Service who had been found guilty of actions detrimental to the public interest in that he accepted bribes to allow unlawful immigration across the border. From the US into Mexico.

I also told Dr. Warren I would need accommodations in Transient Quarters and the use of a radiotelephone-equipped car during my stay. He made the arrangements immediately, apologizing for the only radiophone car available, a diesel-powered, four-wheel-drive Rover.

1645: I called Paul Bumford in New York, reported my arrival, gave him the number of the mobile phone in the car assigned to me. I then called Angela Berri's office at DOB Headquarters to report my whereabouts. I had intended to speak only to an assistant or secretary, but Angela herself came on the flasher screen.

"What's up, Nick?" she asked.

"I am," I said.

She tried to smile. It wasn't only my feeble joke; she seemed worn, features honed down to tight skin on sharp bones. I thought her manner subdued, if not depressed. Her service as DIROB could account for that; I had learned that routine administration can be more wearying than the most demanding creative assignment.

I told her I'd be in Alexandria for the next five days, personally ministering to Lewisohn. She accepted the news casually.

"How about dinner or a drink?" she asked. "Whenever you get a chance."

"A profit," I said. "May I flash you at any hour of the day or night?"

Then she became the "old" Angela, did something with her mouth and tongue, and switched off, smiling wickedly.

1710: I drove to the first public phone booth I could find and called Seymour Dove in San Diego. I gave him two phone numbers: the R&R Hospice and my radiophone-equipped Rover. He told me he expected to check into the Morse Hotel in Washington, D.C., by noon on October 20. With the 5,000 new dollars, as demanded by Art Roach.

1730: I returned to the Hospice. Dr. Seth Lucas was off-duty, but Maya Leighton was there. In her private office. Feet up on her desk. Tanned legs spread. Leaning far back in a tilted chair. No panties. The tattooed scarab showed. She was leafing through a unisex fashion magazine (*TOOTY: For Those Who Dare!*). She saw me at the door. Her chair slammed down. She came out of it as if propelled.

"Look at the beaver!" she marveled. Stroking my face with both palms. "Look at the dickety twitcher! A devil! Nick, now you look exactly like the Devil!"

She groped my testicles and pursed for a kiss.

1750: I looked in on Lewisohn, leaving Maya to prepare for her evening with Art Roach. She said he always left before midnight, to drive back to his hotel suite in Washington. I told her I'd call to make certain the coast was clear before I came over.

Lewisohn was sleeping, and so was his donor. I checked the instrumentation, then went back to the Group Lewisohn office to scan the most recent reports. Lewisohn's blood count had stabilized and was holding. The donor's leukocyte count was up. That was to be expected.

Reading the record of this radical treatment, I wished, briefly, that Dr. Henry L. Hammond was alive and available for consultation. But after his arrest in the fiascoed Society of Obsoletes' plot, he had been drained and his corpus assigned to the National Survival Bank. That facility ruled the storage tunnels in the Tetons where the US Government kept its hoard of frozen sperm, fertilized and unfertilized eggs, blood, organs, and complete corpora. In case of a nukewar. They were continually in need of fresh deposits.

2030: I stopped time at a porn movie. Single ems were encouraged to hire young, lubricious efs ("hostesses") for companionship in small, foul-smelling balcony cubicles (one lumpy sofa), or simply to sit alongside during the performance and supplement the action on the screen with whispered promises or threats, whichever you preferred.

2315: I parked down the block from Maya's apartment, concealed in shadow. The street was as I remembered it. Her apartment was on the ground floor of a two-story town house. It had both a front and a rear entrance. Important to our plan.

2350: The windows of her apartment suddenly blazed with light. I scrunched down further in the seat of my Rover.

0020: Art Roach strode quickly from her front door. Turned to wave. He got into his four-door, black Buick, an official "command car," and drove off. Still I waited.

0100: I found a phone booth, called Maya. She said that as far as she could determine, he had forgotten nothing. If he followed his usual pattern, he wouldn't return that night.

"Hurry," she said.

0125: She was in a surly mood. She admitted it.

"It's that pile of kaka who just walked out of here," she said wrathfully. "He thinks he owns me. Nick, for God's sake, how much longer?"

"Five days," I said.

She came alive. Rushing at me, flinging herself atop me. She was wearing only an em's undershirt, something thin and clinging, with shoulder straps and deeply cut armholes. One breast plunged out.

"But you have to do a favor for me," I said. "One final favor. Then we're home free."

"Anything," she murmured. She was rubbing her cheek against my new beard. "I'll do anything."

I explained slowly what would be required of her. She listened intently. Her questions were to the point: "But what if he—" "But what if we—" I had the answers ready. I gave her the fail-safe alternatives to all his possible reactions to the scenario.

She agreed immediately. But I don't believe her motives were those I anticipated. There was her dislike of Roach, of course. But something more. I sensed it. A tasting of power. A feeling of mastery. It was something new for her. She found it sweet.

We went over the script, in detail, two more times. She provided additional valuable input: Roach was right-handed; he smoked continually, at least two and sometimes three packs a day; he wouldn't touch cannabis; he didn't use a lighter; he was continually running out of paper matches. When he lighted a cigarette, he cupped both hands around the match and cigarette, like a sailor in a gale. Excellent.

I told her that her role would begin on the evening of October 18. She would invite Art Roach to a dinner in her apartment. A dinner she would prepare for him.

"Anything unusual in that?" I asked. "Anything to make him suspicious?"

"Of course not. We've had dinner here a dozen times. He likes to eat with his shoes off."

I took a white envelope from my inside pocket and handed it to her. It contained 500 new dollars. Various denominations. She opened it. Thumb riffled the bills. Widening eyes turned up to me.

"It's not for this Roach thing," I said hurriedly. "It's from me to you. For putting up with my nonsense. I didn't have time to get you a gift. Buy yourself a pretty."

She was one of those objects sexually excited by the sight of love. I could tell. She felt the bills. Flipped through the stack again and again. Did everything but smell it. Excitement growing. The power of love.

October 16.

1040: I called Paul again at GPA-1 and asked him to call me from an outside phone. When he returned my call, I told him what additional equipment we'd need. He said there would be no problems; his Electronics Team carried most of the devices in stock and could easily assemble what they didn't have. The Neuropharmacology Team could provide the remainder. Paul had merely to tell the team leaders their cooperation was needed on an urgent classified project. They would ask no questions.

1110: I spent almost two hours with Group Lewisohn, giving the patient a workup. I could only bully, but Maya Leighton could wheedle. Between us, we got what we wanted. All gross indicators were encouraging. Even his color and skin tone had improved as his rejuvenated blood was returned to him through plastirub tubing.

His disposition, of course, was as repellent as ever. Only Maya's pattings and strokings allowed us to complete our tests. We were filing out when he suddenly shouted, "You bastard!"

Naturally, we all turned around, startled. His ugly mouth stretched in what I assumed to be a grin.

"You all know what you are, don't you?" He chuckled. "Flair is the particular bastard I want at the moment. The rest of you get the fuck gone."

The door closed behind them. I came back to his bedside.

"I should let you stop," I told him. "You're more trouble than you're worth."

He could accept that kind of language. It confirmed his misanthropy. It comforted him.

"Look at the beard," he said. "The lean and hungry look. Ah there, Cassius. Or Iago." He stared at me. "No," he said. "A cut-rate Machiavelli." The idea seemed to amuse him. Then:

"Where do those tubes go?" he demanded.

They led from his arm through the thick, soundproof wall separating him from the former Texas border guard.

"Continuous blood analysis," I said glibly. "Constant monitoring on a linked computer. We put it behind a wall so the noise wouldn't disturb you. Want to see the latest printout? It looks good."

"Fuck you," he grumbled. "No, I don't want to see the latest printout. You'd fake it, you monster."

He was right. I would.

"Now what the hell is this?" he shouted.

He took a manuscript from a stack alongside his bed and threw it at me. I caught it in midair. Glanced at it. An Instox copy of my prospectus for a new Department of Creative Science.

"Oh?" I said. "The Chief Director sent you a copy?"

"Oh?" he said. Burlesquing my innocent tone. "The Chief Director sent you a copy? Just what are you plotting, you devious whoreson?"

"Plotting?" I said. Righteous indignation. "I'm not plotting anything. I suggested the idea to the Chief. He was interested and wanted to see it expanded. That's all there is to it."

He stared at me.

"It's all a mouse in a cage to you, isn't it?" he said finally.

"Now look," I said. Anger in my voice. Feigned? I don't know. "If you're going to give me the canned lecture on science versus humanism, forget it. I've heard it from better brains than yours. I've heard it in a hundred lecture halls, conditioning sessions, symposia, and colloquies. You know what it all adds up to? Kaka. Rich, refined, intellectual kaka. Let other objects debate, endlessly, morality and value judgments. I won't spend a microsecond wringing my hands and pleading, 'What does it all mean?' To act is all. I'm just not teleologically oriented. I'm only interested in the tomorrow I can compute and plan. The future that can be manipulated."

"You think scientists can do a better job than politicians?"

"We couldn't do worse, could we?"

"Yes," he said.

Which, from him, was almost praise.

"Who's this Paul Bumford you mentioned?" he said.

"You met him. A small, slight em. He was with me the last time I was here."

"Oh. That one. The one memorizing the titles of the books I was reading." That shook me.

"He's got some fresh ideas," he went on. "And you're giving him credit."

"Of course," I said. "They were his ideas."

Again I saw that caricature of a cynical grin. Lips drawn back, yellowed teeth showing it in an ugly rictus.

"Round and round it goes," he said. "And where it stops, nobody knows."

"I don't know what the hell you're mumbling about," I told him, "and I don't think you do either."

He turned his face to the wall through which his blood was disappearing, to reappear young, cleansed, whole. I took his silence for dismissal and left. The old fart had bounced me.

1400: We took Maya's tooty little sports car. We spent all afternoon finding the right location. It had to be on a secondary road between her apartment and a tavern, an all-night drive-in movie, a cabaret, a grogshop—something like that. The road, preferably, would be bordered with trees. The spot selected should be within quick walking distance of a public phone. In a booth, store, gas station—anyplace. Any phone available around midnight.

We didn't find the perfect spot, of course. But the one we selected would serve. Light traffic in the afternoon, probably less at night. Direct route from Maya's apartment to a roadhouse called the King's Pawn. Maya said she and Art Roach had been there before. They served food and featured a transvestite pianist after 2100. There was a roadside phone booth a five-minute walk from the place we selected. Most of the road ran through a wood.

2200: I drove my Rover back to the selected location to inspect it at the anticipated time of action. It looked better. It was quite dark. Traffic was minimal. Trees menaced on both sides. The road itself was a paved two-laner. The shoulders on both sides sloped down steeply. Nice.

October 17.

1020: It is hardly an original observation: The basic motivation of all living things is self-interest. This is, to be sure, a generalization. As operative and inoperative as all generalizations. But still, the hard rock of self is there. In *Homo sapiens*, it may be—usually is—slicked over with various camouflage: patriotism, mercy, devotion, sacrifice, altruism, duty, and so forth. Sometimes you can hardly see the rock.

In manipulating Dr. Seth Lucas, my only problem was in determining where the young black's self-interest lay. As expected, it proved to be a melange.

"Seth," I started, "I haven't had a chance before this to tell you what a fine service you've been pulling with Group Lewisohn."

I believe positive behavioral conditioning is more useful than negative.

"Thank you, Dr. Flair," he said. Straightening. Consciously mature. "It's been great experience for me. I've learned a lot."

"Nick," I said. "Any problems?"

"Nothing I haven't been able to handle. Nick. Lewisohn himself is my heaviest migraine. But I knew that before you organized Group Lewisohn."

"All the indicators show go," I said. "We'll just have to wait and see. Meanwhile, Seth, I have a heavy migraine myself. I'm hoping you can help me."

"Of course," he said. "Anything I can do, Nick."

We were in his tiny office, seated at his desk. We were both sipping a plasticup of brown liquid the Hospice cafeteria called coffee. I rose from my chair, walked lightly to the corridor door. I yanked it open suddenly, peered out cautiously. I locked it shut from the inside.

"What the hell?" the kid said. "Nick?"

"Seth," I said, "I'm going to ask you to do something for me. I know the request will sound strange to you. All I ask is for you to hear me out. I'll explain what will be required of you. Then you can say go or no-go. The decision is entirely yours. Whichever way you decide, it shouldn't have any effect on your rule of Group Lewisohn. Will you listen?"

"Well . . . sure. Nick."

Speaking slowly, earnestly, I explained to him that a certain object (unnamed), a server of DOB, had been accused of activities dangerous to public security. I had been ordered to cooperate in proving or disproving those accusations. I would need his, Dr. Seth Lucas', professional assistance.

"This object," I said, "this em, will be brought into the Welcome Ward at approximately 2400 tomorrow night. You will be informed of the exact time of his arrival. Then you will send for me. I will be sleeping in Transient

Quarters. This object has a security clearance equal to mine, higher than yours. Are you aware that such an object can only be treated by a medical doctor or psychiatrist with an equal or higher clearance? It's regulations."

"Oh sure," he said hastily. "Nick."

I doubted he had ever heard of that regulation. But it was operative.

"So I must be in attendance before this object is treated in the Welcome Ward," I said solemnly. "From that moment on, he will be my responsibility."

"Will he be injured?"

"Not at that point in time. But he will be unconscious."

I then explained what would be required of him. His features grew increasingly bleak as I related details. He was spooked. It was understandable. Nothing in his conditioning had prepared him for activities of this nature.

"Of course," I said offhandedly, "if you would feel safer if you had a direct order, signed by me, to account for your actions, I'll be happy to oblige."

"No no no," he said hurriedly. "That won't be necessary. I just don't see—"

I leaned forward, grasped his arm, lowered my voice.

"Seth," I whispered, "I'd like to tell you more. I really would. But there are certain things you have no need to know. And believe me, it's better that way. Just let me make one thing perfectly clear: If you do this, you'll be performing a valuable service for the Department of Bliss. And for your country. I can't make you any promises, but I'm sure you'll find, a few weeks from now, that your Department and your country are not unappreciative."

I thought then I had touched all bases. And so I had. He was bewildered, shaken, frightened. But he was in.

1640: Paul Bumford and Mary Bergstrom arrived. They had come down from the GPA-1 compound in my limousine. No chauffeur; Mary did the driving. The heavy equipment was locked in the trunk. Paul was carrying the drugs and small devices in a plastic shopping bag advertising "Maxine's Smoked Salmon and Imported Delicacies." I remembered Leon Mansfield sleeping in a laundry van and using subway toilets. It's the bizarreness of existence that continually bemuses me.

They settled in at Transient Quarters and made their presence known around the Hospice. Paul seemed charged, brittle, almost fatalistic. He didn't smile or laugh very often. But recently he had become increasingly serious. If not solemn.

Mary Bergstrom I never could compute. I had no input on *her* self-interest. Paul said he controlled her, and had proved it. But to me, she was essentially an unknown quantity. I thought her cold, introverted, frustrated. Unattractive and rather dull. None of this, of course, affected her usefulness.

1900: I treated us all—Maya, Mary, Paul, myself—to dinner at a restaurant recommended by Dr. Luke Warren.

It was a crowded room; we didn't discuss business. But afterward, we drove to the scene of the crime. We parked; Paul, Maya, and I got out and took a look. We couldn't see any difficulties. Paul approved. We were there almost five minutes, and not a single car passed on the road.

We drove back to the Hospice. Maya transferred to her sports car. We followed her back to her apartment. She pulled into the driveway that curved around to the back entrance. We parked right behind her. Paul and I got out and joined her. He handed over the drugs. They were in three small plastic containers, Color-coded caps: red, white, and blue. Red held the anaphrodisiac, white the instant narcotic, blue the thirty-minute narcotic.

Then I showed her the matches. Apparently an ordinary packet of paper matches. An ad on the cover for an IUD with the legend: "Close cover before striking."

"The moment he lights up," I told Maya, "turn your head away. Have your window down. Get your head outside and breathe fresh air deeply. Got that?"

"Sure," she said. "How long does it take?"

I looked at Paul.

"Probably within thirty seconds," he said. "A minute at the most. Make certain he doesn't fall forward and hit his head on the dash. We don't want him to injure himself."

He meant it seriously. Maya and I laughed.

I tore two matches from the folder. Holding them at arm's length, I struck them. They flared. I turned my head away. They both burned halfway down, then went out when the saturation was consumed. I dropped them onto the gravel driveway.

Then I placed the match folder on the shelf over the dash.

"You'll drive?" I asked Maya.

She nodded.

I positioned the matches directly in front of the passenger's seat. I bent the cover open.

"Don't use them by mistake," I cautioned her. "We want you wide awake."

We went back to the Transient Quarters barracks. I thought sleep would come easily; I had done everything that could be done. But at 0200 I shoved a six-hour Somnorific up my nose.

October 18.

1000: Dr. Seth Lucas reserved two rooms in the Welcome Ward, as I had instructed. Into one, he moved a portable laserscope and the other equipment we'd need. He locked the door. I had told him if he got any flak, refer it to me.

Sure enough, Dr. Luke Warren found me in the offices of Group Lewisohn. He asked why it was necessary to reserve two of his precious rooms. He was unexpectedly determined. I think he was astonished by his own temerity.

"Departmental business," I told him. It had worked once; I tried it again: "If you want a signed order, I'll give you one."

"Butbutbut...." he stammered.

"You have no need to know," I said coldly.

1930: I phoned Maya Leighton's apartment from the Hospice. She answered : "Hello?"

"Is Jack there?" I asked.

"Sorry," she said, "you've got the wrong number." And hung up.

Signal. Our pigeon was in the coop.

Paul and I departed in my Rover. Mary Bergstrom took the plastic shopping bag up to the locked room.

2030: We were parked down the block from Maya's apartment. All our lights were out. I had a feeling of inexorableness and could wait patiently. Paul was in a voluble mood. He may have popped an energizer. I let him talk.

2140: The lights behind the shades of Maya Leighton's apartment went out. Paul and I straightened in our seats, peering.

"She got him," I said softly. "Clever ef."

2145: Maya's tooty little sports car backed swiftly out of the driveway, swung around in the street, paused, headed off. We followed, well back. Paul had the infrared binoculars out, pressed to his eyes.

2150: "Normal," he reported. "She's driving. Normal. Normal."

"All *right*, Paul," I said. "Just tell me if anything happens."

2205: "There!" Paul cried. "Flare of match on his side. He's lighting up! He's using the matches! He's using the matches!"

"We'll soon know," I said.

2210: The red sports car slowed appreciably. We pulled up until we were trailing by twenty meters. A bare arm came out of the driver's window. A hand flapped at us languidly.

"Marvelous, marvelous ef!" I laughed. "He's out."

"Oh, yes!" Paul giggled. Almost hysterically. "Oh, yes! Oh, yes!"

2235: She pulled off the deserted road, into the shadow. Her car was tilted downward, hanging up on the steep shoulder. We parked right behind her. Paul and I got out, hurried up to her car. I was on the driver's side.

"Go?" I asked her.

She was lighting a cigarette. With her own lighter.

"Cake," she said. "You manipulated him beautifully. Clunked almost instantly. Dropped cigarettes and matches in his lap. I've got them. He started to fall forward, but I pulled him back."

Paul had the door open on the passenger's side. Feeling for a pulse in Roach's neck. Lifting his eyelids.

"Pulse slow," he reported in a low voice. "He's under deep."

I went around and helped haul Art Roach from the car. We finally got him unfolded, lying on the shoulder of the road.

Maya Leighton got out and joined us. She left the driver's door open. She took a final puff of her cannabis, dropped it to the ground, rubbed it to shreds under her foot. She looked at her car.

"Good-bye, sweetie," she said.

"I'll pay all expenses," I assured her. "It'll be as good as new."

The three of us got behind the car and pushed it over the shoulder of the road. It crunched down into the trees. The right front fender crumpled. The car tilted crazily.

We hauled Art Roach down there, dragging him on pavement, gravel, short scrub. To mess him up. We arranged him artistically. On his back, arms flung wide, one ankle hooked over the sill on the passenger's side. The door had sprung and he had been thrown out of the car. What else?

We climbed back onto the shoulder of the road.

"Let's have the drugs, Maya," Paul said. He was tracking now.

She gave him the fiddled matches. Roach's cigarettes were tossed down atop his corpus. Paul inspected the three plastic containers before he slipped them into his purse. There was one anaphrodisiac capsule missing. Maya had slipped that into Roach's' first drink. To cool his ardency. Make him more willing to leave the apartment. If he had refused to leave, the instant narcotic would have smashed him in the apartment. Then Paul and I would have wrestled him out of there into Maya's car, and the plan would have proceeded on schedule. If he had agreed to visit the King's Pawn, but hadn't used the narcotized matches en route, Maya still had the thirty-minute narcotic pills to fiddle his last drink at the roadhouse. He'd have clunked on the trip back. Fail-safe.

Maya Leighton looked at me, squared her shoulders, lifted her chin.

"All right, Nick," she said crisply. "Let's have it."

Without pausing to reflect, not wanting to reflect, I slammed her in the jaw with the heel of my hand. She went flying back down into the gully, one hand out to break her fall.

She sat up on the ground, shaking her head groggily. She looked at her palm. It was scraped raw, beginning to ooze blood. She wiped it on her blouse. Ripped two buttons open. Took clips from her hair, let it fall free. She climbed to her feet. Came up the bank to us. Rubbed a bloodied palm across her face.

"You'll pay for all this, you bastard." She grinned at me.

"Any time," I told her. "A profit."

I made certain she had small coins in her purse. Then she started walking down the road to the public phone. Paul and I got into the Rover, drove back to the Hospice, undressed, slid into our cots in Transient Quarters. I may have been whistling.

2350: A nurse came down between the two rows of cots. She was carrying a flashlight. A puddle of white light jerked along at her feet. I closed my eyes.

She leaned over me, shook my shoulder.

"Dr. Flair," she whispered. "Dr. Flair, wake up."

"Wha'? What? I sat up suddenly. "What is it?"

"Dr. Lucas asks you to come to Emergency. At once, doctor."

"What's wrong? Is it Lewisohn?"

"No, not Lewisohn. The ambulance just brought in two accident cases. Maya Leighton and an em. Dr. Lucas says it's urgent, doctor."

I began to dress. I waited until she had left the barracks. Then I tapped Paul and Mary Bergstrom. Their cots were side by side.

"They're here," I said. "Let's go."

The interne ruling Emergency was completely confused. The night dispatcher had sent an ambulance in answer to Maya's phone call. By the time it returned with Maya, bruised but conscious, and Art Roach, unconscious, Dr. Seth Lucas was on the scene. After Maya had identified Roach as Chief of Security & Intelligence, DOB, Lucas had refused to touch the case and warned the befuddled interne not to interfere. At that moment he sent for me.

"You did exactly right, doctor," I told him. In a loud voice. Everyone listening. "This em can only be treated by me. Regulations. Let's get them upstairs. Paul, you and Mary assist. Dr. Lucas, please give us a hand. We'll take them on the wheeled stretchers."

"I can walk," Maya protested.

"Just lie still," I told her sternly. "You may have internal injuries."

We wheeled the two stretchers rapidly into the elevator. On the second floor, we paused in the corridor outside one of the reserved rooms. The unlocked room.

"Mary, Seth," I said, "you two take Maya in, get her cleaned up. A big bandage around that hand. Hospital gown."

"No way," Maya said. Climbing off her stretcher. "I'm mobile. And I'm not going to miss the fun."

It didn't seem the right moment to assert my authority over her. If I had any.

"All right," I said. "Let's get on with Roach."

The five of us got in each other's way getting him off the stretcher onto the hospital bed. Finally, I made the two efs and Paul stand clear. Seth Lucas and I stripped Roach down. Maya's first report had been accurate: The em was blessed.

"It looks like a baby's arm with an apple in its fist," I said. The standard encomium. "Paul, let's have the syringe first."

He took his plastic shopping bag from the closet, extracted a hypogun. There was a sealed vial in the case. Actually a cartridge to fit the gun.

"I'll do it," Paul said.

If he wanted to demonstrate his complicity, fine.

"In the neck," I told him.

He loaded the gun expertly, cocked it by pulling back the spring-operated plunger. He placed the muzzle on the side of Roach's neck, pulled the trigger.

There was an audible "Pflug!" sound. The indicator on the gun showed empty. Paul replaced it in the shopping bag.

We had decided on a purazine compound in a liquid that could be sub-cutaneously injected. We administered two cc's. It would produce a temporary memory block for approximately eight hours prior to the time of injection. The memory erasure with this particular compound was not permanent. Within a week or two, Roach would remember everything. By then, we hoped, it would make no difference.

He was lying naked, supine on the hospital bed. I pulled him across to the left side. I straightened his left arm. Now everyone was serving. Roach's dig-iwatch was removed from his left wrist, placed on the bedside table.

"The signet ring?" Mary asked.

"No, no," I said hurriedly. "Leave it on. Identification that it's really his arm. He'll recognize it."

The portable laserscope was brought close. The bed had to be raised electrically so that Roach's arm could be slipped easily into the image tunnel. Then the laserscope was moved to one side. Dr. Seth Lucas wheeled over a sturdy stainless steel table covered with a towel on a square of plastirub padding. On the table were two natural-rubber blocks and a surgical mallet.

Roach's forearm was laid across the rubber supports. Just below his elbow and just above his wrist. The arm was supported about five cm above the table surface.

"Seth," I said casually, "give it a whack."

I had intended to break Art Roach's arm myself. But after Paul had proved his loyalty by administering the memory inhibitor, I computed it might be wise if Dr. Seth Lucas also performed an overt act.

Lucas picked up the surgical mallet. Suddenly his face was glistening with sweat. He looked at me. Appealing.

"Try for the radius," I said. "A simple break. Not a compound fracture."

Almost blindly, he hit Roach's arm. Too close to the wrist, and such a light tap I doubted if it would bruise the skin.

"Give me that," Mary Bergstrom growled. She grabbed the mallet roughly from Seth's nerveless hand.

We moved in closer. Mary pursed her lips, studying the white, almost hairless arm. She pulped the flesh feeling for the bone position and thickness. Then, with a look of utter concentration, she raised the mallet and smacked it down.

We all heard it. I was convinced Roach's arm had been shattered into a million pieces. But no, it appeared whole. No jagged splinters of bone protruded.

"Laserscope," I ordered.

Paul and Lucas (breathing heavily) held Roach's arm immobile while the table was rolled away and the laserscope moved close. The arm was slid into the tunnel, the set switched on. We crowded around the viewing screen. There it was: a definite hairline break in the radius, midway between elbow and wrist.

"Beautiful, Mary," I said. "Just what we wanted."

"Thank you," she murmured. "Another tap? A light one, just to enlarge it?"

"No, no," I said hastily. "This will do fine. Paul, take the plates, from various angles. Make certain the signet ring shows."

We took a holder of 3-D holographic laserpix. Dr. Seth Lucas departed with the film to have it processed by the night crew in the lab. We wheeled the tables out of the way. Paul and I moved Roach back into the center of his bed while Mary pressed the two sections of his cracked arm tightly together.

Paul took the inflatable arm splint out of his bag of tricks and handed it to me. I slid my hand inside, felt about cautiously.

"The Electronics Team did a good service," Paul said.

He was right. The self-powered transmitter was no larger than a postage stamp, and almost as flat. What bulk it had came from the plastifoam padding in which it was encased. So it wouldn't press into the arm and impede circulation.

We gently pulled the limp plastic sleeve over Roach's cracked arm. It reached from just below his elbow to the limits of the metacarpals, the large knuckles. His fingers, and that signet ring, hung free.

We attached the bottle of compressed air provided by Dr. Seth Lucas. We began to inflate the splint. Slowly. Smoothing out the wrinkles. Pulling it taut. I kept an eye on the splint valve. When the dial showed the recommended pressure for the splint, I gave it an additional two psi, cut it off, detached dial, tube, valve nipple. The splint was rigid, hard as plaster.

"Let's check it out," I said. "Paul, you go. We'll keep talking."

I gave him the key to my Rover. We had put the receiver on the back seat, covered with the topcoat I had brought down from GPA-1.

Paul left. Maya Leighton said, faintly, "I think I better sit down."

Mary and I whirled to look at her. She was suddenly quite pale, forehead moist. Mary got to her first, helped her into a chair, felt for her pulse. I rummaged through Paul's shopping bag, found the half-liter of natural brandy I had asked him to provide. I poured a double dollop into a Hospice plastiglass, held it to Maya's lips.

"A little at a time," I told her. "Gently, gently. You deserve it all. You were magnificent."

"I was, wasn't I?" She smiled wanly. "Did you have to break his arm?"

"Yes." I nodded seriously. "We did. We could have put the splint on a whole arm and told him it was broken. But what if he insisted on proof? Show him someone else's plates? What if he wanted to see it himself on the laserscope, or asked for another doctor, another set of plates? Or went to another Hospice? Also, we couldn't put a bugged splint on Seymour Dove's arm. Roach is very cautious, very careful. He'd have been immediately wary of taking a bribe from an em with his arm in a splint. Roach would have suspected an implanted bug. But it won't occur to him that *he* might be shared. This way, he won't take the other em to a sauna or steam room. And because the splint covers his left wrist, where he usually wears his digiwatch, he'll have to wear the watch on his right wrist. That reduces the possibility of his wearing a wrist monitor and discovering he's a walking broadcasting station."

"You thought of everything," Maya marveled. Sipping her brandy.

"We tried to anticipate every eventuality." I nodded. "But tonight was just preparation. We're not home free. Now we—"

The door was unlocked. Paul strode in. Grinning from ear to ear.

"Clear as a bell," he laughed, "We're home free."

"Mary," I said, "will you take care of Maya? Get her cleaned up, into a hospital gown. Bandage that hand. Maybe a romantic head bandage, a turban, would be nice."

Maya looked at me.

"What I've got aching you can't bandage," she said.

That brandy had served quickly.

October 19.

1010: I was in the offices of Group Lewisohn. Had been since 0800. A Hospice nurse was sitting with Art Roach. Her orders were to call me the moment he showed signs of regaining consciousness. When the call came, I grabbed up the file of laserpix and went directly to his room. He was sitting up in bed, looking as ridiculous, helpless, and furious as any object wearing a short paper gown slit up the back. He gawked when I came in.

"What are *you* doing here?" he demanded. Instantly suspicious.

"Nurse," I said quietly, "would you leave the room, please."

After the door closed behind her, I went up to his bedside. I lifted his right wrist. Pressed the inner surface professionally. Not bothering to count.

"How are you feeling?" I asked sympathetically.

"Lousy," he said. He repeated: "What are *you* doing here?"

"I've been here for five days. Treating Hyman Lewisohn. Angela knows where I am. When you were brought in, they called me. Because of your security clearance." I added virtuously: "Regulations."

"I know the regulations," he said angrily.

Suddenly he realized what I had said.

"Brought in?" he said. "Brought in from where? When?"

"Don't you remember?"

He groaned, rubbed his free hand across his forehead.

"I don't remember a damned thing since—since—what day is this?"

"October 19."

"Then it was yesterday. The eighteenth. I was sitting in my office at Headquarters. About 1600. I was signing requisitions. That's the last thing I remember."

"Oh-oh," I said. "That doesn't sound so good. Let me take a look."

Fear came into his eyes. We had been counting on his hypochondria.

"What is it?" he gasped. "What's happened to me?"

I didn't answer. I pressed him back onto the pillow. I shoved up his eyelids, beamed a pencilite into his pupils. Then I felt his skull, fingertips probing through his fine, brush-cut hair.

"Hurt here?" I asked. "Here? Here? Here?"

"No. No. NO! Goddamn it, doc, what's wrong?"

I don't like to be called doc.

"Loss of memory might indicate possible concussion," I said coldly. "But I see no gross indicators. Eyes clear. No cranial contusions. But that amnesia bothers me. Maybe we should take some tests."

"What kind of tests?" he cried desperately.

"Very simple," I said cruelly. "We go into the brain with a needle—local anesthetic; you won't feel a thing—and draw off some fluid for analysis."

"My brain feels fine," he said. Shaken. "Just fine."

"Sure it does," I said softly. "The brain has no capacity to feel pain inflicted on itself. You think everything's normal, and then—" I snapped my fingers.

"My God," he breathed.

"Well," I said briskly, "we'll discuss that later. Now ... how's the arm?"

"This?" he said. He raised the inflated splint in front of him and looked at it with wonderment. "What the hell *is* it?"

I shook my head. Discouraged.

"You really don't remember, do you? You broke your arm. We put it in an inflatable splint. Want to see the plates?"

I held the laserpix to the light. I pointed out the hairline fracture. He saw his own signet ring.

"Will it heal okay?" he asked anxiously.

"It should," I said. Doctorial hedging. "You'll have to carry it in a sling for about two weeks. I don't anticipate any complications. Any other aches or pains?"

"My neck," he groaned. Rubbing it. "Here, on this side. It hurts."

Where Paul had shot him with the hypogun. I inspected it carefully.

"Just a minor bruise," I told him. "If that's all you've got, you're lucky. After that accident."

"Accident?" he cried. Horrified. "What accident?"

"Oh, that's right. Amnesia. Well, do you remember having a date with Maya Leighton?"

"Yes. Yes, I remember that. I was supposed to go to her place for dinner last night."

"Very good," I nodded approvingly. "Now do you remember being there?"

"No. I don't remember that at all."

"Oh. Too bad. Well according to Maya, you arrived on time, had dinner, and then, about 2140, you both decided to go out. Some cabaret or tavern. The King's Pawn, I think it was. Does that ring any bells?"

"I don't remember going there last night. But I know the place. We've been there before."

"Well, you and Maya were on your way there. Maya was driving. It's a two-lane road. A semitrailer was coming in the opposite direction. Some nut swung out to pass just as the truck went past you. Maya swerved to avoid a head-on. Her car went off the road, down into a gully, banged into the trees. Thankfully, she wasn't driving too fast. The doors were sprung, you were both thrown out. No one stopped to assist. Maya came to, and, when she couldn't bring you around, staggered down the road to call for help."

I could almost hear his synapses clicking.

"Who did she call?" he asked.

"The Hospice. Here. She knows the regulations. She wouldn't call the local cops. So they sent out an ambulance from the Welcome Ward to bring you and Maya in."

"What happened to the car?"

"Maya's sports car? Banged up considerably. Ruined the front fender. Probably need new doors. It's in a garage over in Hamlet West."

"How's Maya?"

Sweet em. I thought he'd never ask.

"Maya's doing fine. She's got a bad hand and scalp lacerations, but we can't find anything worse."

"Listen, doc, can you gloss this? I mean, I don't want to get Maya in any trouble."

It was his own muffin ass that was troubling him.

"Well...." I considered thoughtfully. Frowning. Chewing my lips. "I can probably gloss it at this end. Lose the file, and so forth. As a personal favor to you...."

"Oh sure, doc. I'd really appreciate it."

"Look," I said. "Suppose we do this. Suppose you stay here until noon tomorrow. You'll be able to gloss that at your office, won't you?"

"Well ... maybe," he said doubtfully.

"I'll take another look at you tomorrow morning. If everything shows go, you can check out. By noon. October twentieth. Then you can consult the Medical Section at Headquarters if you need further treatment. How does that sound?"

"Sounds fine," he said. Almost laughing. "Sounds real good."

Why shouldn't it? He could make the meet with Seymour Dove.

"There's your digiwatch," I told him. "Your zipsuit, underwear, shoes, and so forth are in that closet. I have your identification, BIN card, wallet, and keys in a downstairs safe."

"Keys?" he said. "Was I driving?"

"You drove over from Washington. Your car is parked in front of Maya's apartment. I'll have it brought over here. Anything else?"

"Can I visit Maya?"

"You better stay flat on your back as much as possible if you want to get out of here tomorrow. But I'll send her in for a short visit. She's just next door."

"Good, good," he gurgled. "Maybe she can fill me in on what happened."

And maybe the anaphrodisiac was wearing off.

1845: Paul had connected two tape decks to the receiver in the back of the Rover. One was temporarily switched off, the other was operative and voice-actuated. We ran through the tape that evening.

Most of it was kaka: Roach snarling at nurses, Roach trying to lure Maya Leighton into his hospital bed for a session of rub-the-bacon. "No way," Maya said firmly. Apparently pointing to her turban bandage. "Can't you see I've got a headache?"

Roach made two phone calls. We couldn't share the entire conversations, of course—just his part. One call apparently went to his office. He explained he was personally investigating a "serious security problem" at R&R Hospice No. 4, and expected to return to Headquarters the following day.

The second call apparently went to his residence hotel. He told them he would be absent for a day, but was expecting an important phone call from a Mr. Seymour Dove. He gave the hotel his phone number at the Hospice and instructed them to tell Mr. Dove to contact him there.

I immediately called the Morse Hotel and left a message for Mr. Seymour Dove. He was to call *me* as soon as he registered.

And so the checkers went flying about the board.

October 20.

1135: I was in the Group Lewisohn offices. Paul was monitoring Roach's gimpy arm in the Rover, moved to a deserted end of the Hospice parking area.

Seymour Dove called me from the Morse. I explained the situation, told him to call Roach's hotel and then call Roach at the Hospice as he would be instructed. I asked him to give me ten minutes before making the call to Roach.

1150: I was out in the Rover with Paul when we heard Roach's phone ring. His conversation went like this:

"Harya. . . . Yeah. . . . What hotel? . . . Real good. You got it? . . . Fine. . . . No problem. . . . Be in the lobby at, oh, say 1400. I'll meet you there. . . . Yeah, 1400. . . . Right. . . . See you then."

After he hung up, I called Dove's hotel room on the Rover radiophone. I told him to meet Roach at 1400, play the role he was expected to play, and try to follow the original San Diego script as closely as he could.

"We'll be shared?" he asked.

"Yes," I said. But I didn't tell him how.

1210: I went up to Roach's room. He was alrea[dy] [strapping his] digiwatch onto his right wrist.

"Harya, doc," he said genially.

He had the splinted arm in a sling, a wide strap [around his] right shoulder.

"How does the arm feel?"

"Real good," he said. Rapping the splint with his [knuckles.] all."

I went through the stethoscope charade. Lifted his lids to peer into his eyes. Took his pulse.

"Well . . . all right," I said doubtfully. "But check with your Medical Section as soon as you get back."

"Oh, sure. Where's my bumf?"

"Right here." I handed him all his identification. He began stuffing it into his pockets. "Your car's out in front," I told him. "Take care of yourself."

He was still checking to make certain no one had raped his wallet when I walked out. I went directly to the Rover. Paul had all the equipment ready. We were away and heading toward Washington before Roach came out of the Welcome Ward.

1410: We were parked across from the Morse Hotel. We saw Art Roach come down the street, striding purposefully. Actually, we heard him before we saw him. His arm was picking up street noise: honk of horns, screech of brakes, a siren, bits of passers-by conversation. Paul got his Instaroid movie camera fixed and focused before Roach turned in to the hotel.

We picked up a lot of lobby gabble. Interference from somewhere. Then, suddenly, voices clear enough to understand. Both tape decks were running now:

Roach: "Car accident. A kid ran out and I had to go off the road to avoid hitting him."

Dove: "My God!"

Roach: "Nothing serious. Come on outside."

In a moment, they came through the powered revolving door, Roach first. Seymour Dove was carrying an attaché case. Paul got busy with his camera, adjusting the telephoto lens. They crossed the street to the park, looking both ways.

"Good shot," Paul murmured. "Got them together."

He continued to photograph the two men. They walked through the park slowly. No conversation. Roach looked about, spotted an empty bench that apparently appealed to him. He led Dove over to it. Seymour set the attaché case down between his feet.

"Very good," I said approvingly. "Can't share a random park bench, can you, Art?"

the Rover away from the curb, circled until I found a parking
across the park, almost facing them. Paul got film on the two of them,
talking together. Then switched off the camera.

Roach: "—out in time. But it worked out real good. Mind opening your
coat?"

Dove: "My coat? What for?"

Roach: "Just standard operating procedure."

We saw Seymour Dove unbutton his violet velvet topcoat. We saw Roach
pat all the pockets, feel the seams.

Roach: "Now your jacket."

Dove: "What is this?"

Roach: "Just take a second. The jacket. . . ."

We saw him give Dove a quick frisk, patting pockets, waistline, trouser
legs. He even bent over to feel Dove's moccasins.

Dove: "I'm not shared, if that's what you're afraid of."

Roach: "Afraid? Not me. But if you're bugged, *you* better be afraid. Did
you bring it?"

Dove: "Yes. Five thousand unmarked new dollars."

Roach: "Small bills? Unmarked? Out of sequence?"

Dove: "Just the way you told me. It's in twenties."

Roach: "In the case?"

Dove: "Yes. Want to take a look?"

Roach: "Why not? Is it locked?"

Dove: "Yes."

Roach: "Just bend over casually and unlock it. Then hand it to me. Slowly."

"Get this," I said to Paul hurriedly. "It's the actual payoff."

Paul switched on the camera again. I watched Dove lift the attaché case.
Roach took it from him, placed it on his lap. He opened the lid halfway,
peering inside. He inserted his right hand, began pawing.

Dove: "It's all there. Five thousand new dollars."

Roach: "I know you wouldn't scam me. I'm just making sure there's nothing else in here."

Dove: "A bug? Would I do that? Listen, I'm taking an awful chance by
doing this."

Roach: "What do you think *I'm* taking?"

Dove: "But how do I know I'm not throwing it away? If you don't come
through, Scilla Pharmaceuticals is stopped. We've made heavy investments in
raw materials and new machinery. We need that contract."

Roach: "Don't worry. You'll get your contract."

Dove: "I wish I had a guarantee."

Roach: "This five thousand is your guarantee."

"What a good little boy he is," I whispered to Paul. "This time he's following the scenario."

Roach: "Can I have the case?"

Dove: "Sure. Take it. Here's the key."

Roach: "I'll return it to you."

Dove: "No need. It's yours."

Roach: "Thank you very much. Real good doing business with you." We watched the two ems stand, stroke palms. They separated, Roach carrying the case in his free hand. He walked across the park, angling away from us. Dove headed back to his hotel. We watched Roach.

"He won't go to Headquarters." Paul frowned.

"Doubt it," I agreed. "Not with the loot. He wouldn't go directly to Angela's apartment at the Watergate, would he?"

"I don't know," Paul said. Worrying it. "I don't think so. She wouldn't allow it."

"No. She wouldn't. Maybe he'll go directly to a bank, put it in a safe deposit box. But I don't think so. He'll want to count it. Examine it. That means his place. The Winslow on N Street. We'll lose him in this traffic if we try to follow. Want to take a gamble?"

"Sure. The Winslow it is."

We left the park, headed for N Street.

"We've got him, haven't we, Nick?" Paul said happily.

"Screwed, blewed, and tattooed," I agreed. "He's down the pipe. One down, one to go."

We were parked across the street, near the corner, when Roach drove up to the Winslow Hotel in his official black Buick. He got out, carrying the attaché case. We heard him say, "Be down in twenty minutes, Al," to the doorman. Then he went inside.

"Now what?" Paul said.

Suddenly, at his question, I felt a curious lassitude. Having come so far, I wanted to rest. Hadn't I done enough? Hadn't enough been accomplished? I had to flog my resolve, telling myself it would all be wasted if I didn't finish. But I was weary.

"Got any uppers?" I asked Paul. "Amphetamine? Anything?"

"The Pharm Team gave me a new methylphenidate. Experimental. No results yet. Want to chance it?"

"Sure," I said. "I have nothing to lose but my balls."

He fished around in his shopping bag. He came up with a plastic container of spansules as big as suppositories.

"For whales," I said. "Where's the size for humans?"

"This is them." Paul laughed.

I sighed. "Give me one. Maybe there's a water fountain in the lobby."

We had a big, horsey briefcase among our gear. We packed it with everything I thought I'd need.

"Are you still getting him?" I asked.

Paul moved his head closer to the receiver speaker. He turned up the volume, cautiously moved the tuning knob. What we heard could have been

Roach moving around in his hotel room. It could have been anything. Then we heard a toilet flush.

"That's him," I said. "On my way. Get it all. If you hear anything bad, or if I don't come out within an hour, take the other tape to the Chief Director."

I started to duck out of the car. Paul pulled me back, kissed me on the lips. I was surprised. And pleased.

"Take care, Nick," he whispered.

He had said the same thing to me on the helipad of the compound when I was starting off to meet Angela Berri in her California beachhouse. Was that aeons ago? Or yesterday?

There was no water fountain in the hotel lobby. But there was a unisex nest in the cocktail lounge. I went in there, used a cupped palmful of water to bolt down the giant energizing spansule. I could almost feel it thud into my stomach.

Do something, I urged it.

I was turning to leave when an ef came out of one of the toilet booths, adjusting her skirt. She looked at me.

"I suck cocks," she said.

"Who doesn't?" I said.

It was a stuffy obso hotel, with a color photograph of the Washington Monument over the registration desk. Not the kind of place that encourages wandering about the corridors. I called Roach on the single house phone. It rang seven times before he answered.

"Yes?"

"Art Roach?"

"Yes. Who is this?"

"Flair. Dr. Nicholas Bennington Flair. I'm downstairs. I've got to see you."

"What the hell for?"

"About your condition. The results of the tests we took. It's very important that I see you at once."

He panicked. "Oh, my God! What is it, doc?"

"I must see you immediately. What room?"

He was standing outside his door. He practically pulled me inside.

"What is it, doc?" he demanded. "What about the tests? What's wrong with me?"

I sat down near a glass cocktail table. I set the briefcase at my feet, opened it, took out the threaded tape deck. He watched me. First in astonishment. Then warily. His attaché case was not in sight.

"Nothing wrong with you," I said. "Cracked arm. That's all. But you're strong as a horse. And not much smarter. Sit down. Something I want you to hear."

I stared at him. Slowly, almost tentatively, he slid into a chair at a diagonal to mine. Not across the table. Clear of the table.

I switched it on. We listened to his entire conversation with Seymour Dove. When it came to an end, I switched off the tape.

"There's another tape," I told him hastily. "Exactly like this one. Elsewhere. And films of the entire meet."

"And I suppose the bills are marked?" he said bitterly.

"What else?" I shrugged.

That was inoperative, but he couldn't be sure.

We sat in silence for at least a minute. Then he stood. I stood.

"Motherfucker!" he shouted.

It was more an expletive than an accusation.

Then he came at me. Good arm reaching for me.

I was not unmuscular, and I had a kind of desperate courage. Not quite hysterical. But even in that state it would never occur to me to strike an opponent with my fist if a more effective weapon was at hand.

I bent to slip his lunge, picked up a heavy plastilead ashtray with rounded edges. As he was starting his turn, I clipped him just to the left and low on the occipital area.

He went down, going "Houff!" Then he was still.

I replaced the undamaged ashtray on the table. I bent over him, felt for pulse and respiration, peeled back his eyelids. He was already blinking, snorting, curling up into the fetal position. I patted him over and found a weapon, a short-barreled rocket pistol.

Then I went back to my chair, sat down, lighted a Bold. My hands were trembling slightly. I abhor violence. I sat silently, staring at him.

"I'm all right, Paul," I said loudly. "Everything's fine."

After a while, Art Roach roused. He looked at me from the floor.

"You're fast," he said admiringly.

"Thank you," I said.

He glanced at his pistol on the table in front of me. No way. He climbed to his feet, staggered over to his armchair, sat down heavily. He lowered his head between his knees.

"Dumb-ass," he said dully. "I'm a dumb-ass."

I didn't say anything.

"You come here with enough to take me," he said in a grumbling voice. Shaking his head. "But you don't just take me, like you could. So you want to talk deal. Right?"

"Right," I said.

"Stupe," he said mournfully. "I've been a stupe all my life. What do you want?"

"Her," I said.

"Oh, Jesus." He groaned. "Do I gotta?"

"Yes," I said. "You gotta."

I didn't have to spell out for him what would happen if he didn't "gotta."

He knew. But he was a pro and wanted to know how it had been fiddled. I told him: the phony accident, the memory block, the broken arm, the shared splint. It had been *his* arm, but he wasn't angry.

"That was *beautiful*," he breathed.

"Yes," I said. "Now let's get to it. I know she's on the suck. Where does she hide the love?"

It was an interesting story. He had been shrewd enough to keep records, figuring they'd be a bargaining factor if Angela ever decided his activities were contrary to the public interest. From that, I guessed he had his own private little scams going which she tolerated as long as he didn't become too greedy.

I had thought her method of concealing her booty would be original and complex. It proved depressingly simple. There was, it seemed, a well-organized band of thieves serving at the National Data Bank. They were all assigned to the Stopped Section where, according to law, the BIN cards of all stopped objects were returned, flamed, and their names and registration numbers erased from the master computer tape.

BINS of stopped objects flowed into the NDB at a rate of approximately 10,000 per serving day. It was not difficult for the crooks to extract from this flow certain BIN cards expressly ordered by a growing list of customers. The going price had risen to 1,500 new dollars per card.

Angela Berri had a standing order for cards of stopped efs whose age and physical description approximated hers. The stopped efs were victims of accidents, disease, murder, suicide, etc. When Angela purchased such a card—the unlawful possession of which, incidentally, made her liable for execution, under certain circumstances—she merely attached her own photo, sent Roach to a large city to open a bank account under the stopped ef's name and number.

Once a year, under her orders, he closed out each account and moved it to another bank, under new identification. This was to thwart annoying investigation by the Voluntary Contribution Commission of the Department of Profitability. They hadn't even come close to her.

Roach had a complete record of her current deposits, which he handed over to me. I also received a lengthy list of government contracts on which she had received kickbacks. And a neatly written journal of her other peculations: unlicensed dealing in grains and other foodstuffs; part ownership of a small refinery producing methanol ostensibly for sale as a solvent, though a goodly percentage of the output was diverted to a distiller producing champage; and—Angela! Shame!—ownership of a very posh, very secret Washington, D.C., bordello called, by its habitués, "The Sexual Congress." This last was, of course, completely illicit, since the US Government had a monopoly on bagnios.

That would seem to be enough, I told Art Roach, packing up my goodies. I would do everything I could to pillow his involvement in these disgraceful shenanigans. He might be called on to testify, but I doubted if that would be necessary. He might even be able to retain his rank-rate and continue to serve as Chief, Security & Intelligence, DOB.

He brightened at that.

"You'll be taking over her spot I suppose," he said. "Real good."

I looked at him in amazement.

"Whatever gave you that idea?" I said.

"Why else would you be doing this?" he asked.

I could have explained to him that Angela Teresa Berri had grievously wounded my amour proper, and in that area I was as sensitive as a Sicilian. But he would not have understood. Besides, there might be something operative to what he suggested. Not a vulgar ambition to have the title Director of Bliss. But an almost unconscious thrust for power.

I didn't answer him, but turned to go. He spoke before I reached the door.

"I told her to watch out for you," he said.

"Oh?" I said. "Why?"

"Listen," he said, "it takes one to know one."

I wasn't certain I knew what he meant by that, and didn't want to know. I took the elevator down, my spirits rising as the cage descended.

I could move mountains. Do anything. I told myself it was me, *my* talent, *my* will. But way down deep in that prune I called my heart, I knew it was partly, mostly, that experimental energizer. That wonderful whale-sized spansule. I was on air. Not walking on air. Just on air. Floating.

I leaned down to talk to Paul through the opened car window.

"That new methylphenidate . . ." I said.

"Yes?" Paul said.

"Make notes. Too euphoric. Loss of visual perception. Slight mental displacement. Some verbal slurring. No obvious impairment of muscular coordination. Improved audition. Ego inflation. Got that?"

"Yes," Paul said. "I'll remember. Want to stretch out on the back seat awhile, Nick?"

"No," I said, "I do not want to stretch out on the back seat. Did you get all the Roach stuff?"

"I did," Paul said happily. "A complete tape. That's it, isn't it, Nick?"

"That's it," I said. Climbing into the car. "That, indeed, is it."

I picked up the mobile phone, punched the numbers of the Chief Director's residence.

"Who you calling?" Paul asked.

"Grace Wingate."

"What the hell for?"

"Wheels within wheels," I said mysteriously. I tried to wink. Both eyes closed at the same time.

Mrs. Wingate wasn't at home. They refused to tell me where I might reach her.

"That reporter," I said to Paul. "Herb Bailey. What outfit does he work for?"

"Federal Syndicate."

"Right," I said. "Make another note on the new energizer. Negative memory effect."

I finally got through to Herb Bailey and asked him if he could discover the whereabouts of the Chief Director's wife.

"I probably could," he said. "Why should I?"

"Because I will then give you the scoop of a lifetime, Scoop," I said.

"Are you drunk?" he demanded.

"Of course I'm not drunk. Do me a favor, Herb. And I have got something for you."

"Fat chance," he grumbled. But he left the line open, was gone a few minutes, finally returned. "The Society Desk says she's scheduled to visit a school for retarded clones this afternoon. It's in Chevy Chase. The New Hope School."

"Thanks, Herb," I said. "I appreciate it."

"What's the something you've got for me? You running away with the Chief Director's wife? She's a prime cut."

"No," I said shortly. Displeased. "It's something else. If I give it to you, can I join the Anonymous Sources club?"

"Sure."

"Keep an eye on the Department of Bliss for the next few days," I told him. "Big shakeup due."

"No kidding?" he said. Interested now. "How big?"

"Enormous," I said, and hung up.

"Was that wise?" Paul asked.

"The Washington game." I shrugged. "Besides, I'm tired of being wise. I think I'll be foolish awhile. You better drive. In my manic mood, I'll be worse than you. I want to go to the New Hope School for Retarded Clones in Chevy Chase."

"She's there?"

"Yes. Visiting. Not enrolled."

"Should I wait for you?"

"No. You go back to the Hospice. Make a copy of that film in case of accidental erasure. And better make Instox copies of the records Roach gave me. In the briefcase. You never can tell...."

"Now you're tracking," Paul said. "Where are you going after you see Grace Wingate?"

"Things to do," I said. "Worlds to conquer. I may not be back to the Hospice until tomorrow."

"When are you going to see the Chief Director?"

"Also tomorrow," I said. "It's all in the Tomorrow File."

As we drove off we heard, via Roach's broken arm, a toilet flush.

By the time Paul had located and delivered me to the New Hope School for Retarded Clones, in Chevy Chase, the giddy effects of the methylphenidate had evaporated, leaving dregs of vague anxieties and dim terrors. A year was ending. A century would soon end. I shivered inside my silverized zipsuit. I should have worn my topcoat; the wind was a knife.

There were three limousines parked at the curb. Black zipsuits stood near the cars. They inspected me coldly. Apparently I didn't look like a potential assassin; they allowed me to walk up the brick path and enter the school. The exterior was white enameled tiles. It looked like a subway station turned inside out.

I asked for the Chief Director's wife. I was told she was completing her tour and would be out soon. I waited patiently, staring at children's crayon drawings taped to the walls, wondering how old the "children" were.

She came out eventually, surrounded by a retinue of Administrative Assistants, social secretaries, guards, a few reporters, photographers.

I stood, took a step forward. She prepared to exit, glanced up. Startled. Then the fading smile grew again. She came over to me, hand outstretched. We stroked palms. I had the impression of rigidity beneath cool softness.

"Nick!" she said. With pleasure. I thought. "What are *you* doing here?"

"I must speak to you a few minutes," I murmured. "Alone. Before you get in your car. It's important. Anywhere we can go?"

Lips tightened, paled. She was wearing a smooth helmet of white felt. It covered her ears. Her hair was tucked up, out of sight. The wide-collared natural wool coat, simple as a smock, left the long stem of her neck exposed.

"There's an outdoor playground," she said. Tentatively. "Around to the side. I think it's empty now. All the—ah, children are inside. We could go there. But only for a few minutes. We have another stop to make. At an orphanage. They're expecting us."

"The playground sounds fine," I said. "It won't take long."

She went back to speak to her assistants. They looked at me doubtfully. But eventually they all filed out ahead of us. Then she led the way around a curved walk to a small, fenced playground.

We sat apart on a slatted bench. I glanced about. Already there was a black zipsuit at each of the playground's three gates. They were all regarding us gravely. For the first time I realized the full import, and danger, of what I was doing: a public tête-à tête with the wife of the most powerful man in the US Government.

"Have things changed between you and your husband?"

"No," she said shortly. "If anything, they're worse. We had an argument last night. Screaming. I cried. I'm so ashamed. And ashamed of bothering you with my problems."

She tried to smile.

"It's still . . . *her*?"

"Yes. Nick, I don't know what she's done to him. He can't break loose. I think he wants to. Really. But she seems to have him under some kind of—of a spell. I know how foolish that must sound."

"No, no. Not foolish at all."

I spoke mechanically. I was computing. I had assumed Chief Director Michael Wingate was merely a victim of Angela's sexual expertise. But her ownership of an illicit bordello opened another can of worms. It would not be difficult for Angela to share the private rooms of the Sexual Congress. What a leverage that evidence might give her! Over the Chief Director, Congressmen, journalists, lobbyists, Public Service executives, judges—the whole political bestiary of Washington, D.C. She had murdered; blackmail was within her ken.

"How did it end?" I asked. "The argument?"

"It didn't end. It will go on and on. Until our marriage ends. I know."

"No," I said positively. "That's not going to happen. Take a gamble?"

Lids raised. Dark, somber eyes stared into mine.

"A gamble?" she said. Smiled suddenly. "What odds?"

"Long," I admitted. "But it's my gamble as well as yours. I'm taking it."

She stared at me a long moment. Once again her features ran that curious gamut of emotions; perplexity to sympathy to pity to . . . what?

"All right," she said. Stiffening her back. "What is it?"

"Here is what you must do . . ." I started. Coaching her. Nicholas Bennington Stanislavski Flair.

She must go to her husband that very evening. She must present him with an ultimatum. No, not an ultimatum exactly, but a declaration of her intent. Either he would agree never to see Angela Berri again, or she, Grace Wingate, would simply leave him. Pack up and walk out. I told her exactly how to conduct herself during the meeting: state her resolve, make no threats about adverse public relations, speak quietly in a firm, dignified tone, wear something sexy. But subtle. Keep the interview as short as possible. Speak her piece, tell him the decision was his to make, she loved him and wanted to continue as his wife. And he must decide within twenty-four hours. That was most important. Within twenty-four hours.

"Can you do all that?" I asked her.

"Yes," she said.

Two hours later I was seated in the cocktail lounge of the Morse Hotel. I had asked for Seymour Dove at the desk. But he had already checked out, was on his way back to San Diego. So I was drinking a vodka-and-Smack by myself. My first opportunity to spend leisure alone for many, many months. I was enjoying it.

I dined somewhere. A crowded, horrendously expensive French restaurant. It required ten new dollars slipped to the maître d' to bypass the crowd waiting to claim their reservations. The food was undeniably natural—but what was the use? The best chefs in the world couldn't compensate for its lack of flavor. Within a generation or two, the sense of taste would be as debased as the sense of smell was at that point in time. Sighing, I dug into my "baked potato." What they had done, of course, was to salvage a blackened shell, discarded by a previous diner, fill it with cheaper mashed potatoes, and shove it under a microwave broiler for a minute to give it a realistic crust.

I had two natural brandies at the restaurant bar on my way out. A black ef, wearing an obso nun's robe, scuttled through the door and succeeded in handing out small pieces of paper to several bar patrons before the maître d' and two waiters hustled her out of there. My paper read: REPANT FOR THE TIME IS AT HAND. Even the holy couldn't spell. I strolled out in an expansive mood. This was my world. Let others waste their days weeping.

I spent hours walking Washington that night. From Lafayette Park to the White House. Down Pennsylvania Avenue to the Capitol. Around to the Library of Congress. Back to the National Gallery of Art. All the way down the Mall to the Lincoln Memorial.

It was easy to feel indulgent about Washington, D.C. Despite the presence of foreign embassies, of couriers arriving and speeding off to every corner of the earth, despite its architecture—some of it incredibly gross, some incredibly elegant—Washington remained insular. A marbleized village. A company town. Its one product was government; its one raw material was power. Departments and offices and agencies and facilities had been distributed all over the US. But no one doubted where the thrones were.

Eventually, I went to a phone booth. I called Angela Berri. It was almost a reflex, an automatic response, an emotional knee-jerk. My soul had received a light tap below the patella.

Her greeting sounded fretful, weary. But after some idle chitchat, she seemed to thaw; her voice warmed.

I suggested an immediate picnic on the White House lawn.

She suggested a naked *pas de deux* on the Capitol steps.

It went on like that for a while, each suggestion topping the last in outrageous public lewdness. Finally I asked her to join me somewhere for a drink. She said she was too exhausted to consider stirring from her apartment. But she wanted very much to see me. I was to come to her Watergate apartment at once.

Which was what it was all about in the first place.

Exhausted, she may have been. Without makeup or uniform. But I saw no diminution of her unique primitive force. If anything, her languor only heightened, by contrast, the flash deep in her eyes, the electricity of her sudden gestures. She was wearing a black silk robe. Carelessly. A plain robe. It gaped at neckline and thigh. A full sleeve fell back to reveal a bare arm. That pampered body was cut into white sections. An effect at once abstract and stirring.

She gave me a straight petrovod on Jellicubes. She was not drinking, but she was smoking—something. I could not identify the odor. Not cannabis. She saw me sniffing.

"Perfumed hash." She smiled. "What to try?"

"No," I said. "Thanks."

She smoked slowly. A small, jeweled pipe. I sipped my drink slowly. She crossed her knees. The robe fell back. One bare foot bobbed.

"I'm weary, Nick," she said suddenly. "I've begun to flip in and out. Occasionally. Is that bad?"

"Anxieties?" I asked.

"No. Not really. Nothing I can't handle. Just a—it's difficult to describe."

"Flipping in and out?" I asked.

"Reality," she said. "You play a role long enough, hard enough and the role takes over. You're all role."

"Disorientation," I said. "Want something for it?"

"Yes," she said. Rising. Holding out her hand. "I want something for it. Come along."

None of Maya's hardware for her. Not that night. Just her depilated body and a curious need for tenderness. For warm affection. For close, protective snuggling. The ruler ruled. The master mastered.

The problem was. . . . The problem was. . . . Well, the problem was this: Was her mood operative or plotted? Was her soft languor real or structured? Was her surrender valid or scenarioed? I didn't know. For certain. And not knowing, I would have been a fool to assume anything but falsity.

That's the way we were. That's the way we all were.

No sexual sophistication that night. No tricks, gimmicks, gigs. Just a slow, lazy petting to arousal. At one point we lay slightly apart, not touching. I could not compute the rapture.

I would have preferred her to ravage me. Absolution? That lacking, I could only serve her. I was a knight, and gathered her close. A young body came bonelessly into my arms.

Usually we laughed with delight. That night we were silent. Obediently she lay upon her back, spread silken thighs. Curled snake arms about my neck. Linked snake legs about my back. But silently, in a shy, docile manner. I penetrated her as gently as I could, as deeply. It was her mood.

There was some illumination from the nest light. I arched my back to see her face. Eyes closed. Lips slightly parted. Gleam of wet teeth.

"Don't go away from me," she murmured.

I bent to scrape my new mustache and beard across her breasts. She responded to that; I could feel her return. From wherever she had been. She had no right to try to escape. We are all here. Fingernails rived my shoulders. Legs tightened.

She was velvet on steel: the languor suffused with steamed blood she could not deny. But no further murmurings, whispers, cries, moans. In silence, deliberately, we used each other, sensing when our rhythm was one.

I don't know how long we lasted. A lifetime, I suppose. Eventually, of course, we could no longer control our deliberation. Our rhythm controlled us; conscious will eroded. My fingers slid to join my penis. I had one wild, frightening impulse to tear her apart. But that was gone almost as quickly as I recognized it.

Our summit was calm, satisfying. Certainly for me. And, I believed, for her. We flowed together in a kind of dance. Her extended arms and legs now feebly stroking the air. My pelvis squirming in rut. Open mouths were slicked together; tongues beat a slow tattoo. Good-bye. Good-bye.

Y-12

Early the next morning I took a cab back to the Hospice in Alexandria. I found Paul, Mary, Maya, and Seth Lucas having breakfast together in the cafeteria. I drew a plasticup of black coffee and joined them, pulling up a chair.

"How's Lewisohn, Seth?" I asked.

"Well . . . all right."

"What does that mean—'Well . . . all right?' "

"Count's up. Just a bit. Not appreciably. Not significantly."

"How often do you take it?"

"Every eight hours."

"Take it every four. Keep me informed. Mary and Paul and I will be leaving this morning."

"Everything all right, Nick?" Paul asked.

"Everything's fine," I assured him. And then. "Coming up roses. Load the limousine. We'll be starting back this afternoon."

I showered, shaved, trimmed beard and moustache, donned a fresh zipsuit. With decorations. I waited until Dr. Seth Warren was about to start his rounds, then requested the use of his office. I told him I would soon be gone. He happily granted my request. I knew I made him nervous. But then life made him nervous.

I had decided to start with Chief Director Michael Wingate's Administrative Assistant, a capable ef named Penelope Mapes. The headquarters of the Chief Director were located in the obso Executive Office Building. Since the Presidency had been reduced to what was essentially a ceremonial role, the White House was completely adequate for the Chief Executive's activities.

I sat behind Dr. Warren's cluttered desk and flashed the Executive Office Building. When an operator came on screen, I identified myself and asked to speak to Administrative Assistant Mapes.

"Just a moment, please, sir," the operator said.

I saw her punch buttons furiously. But Penelope Mapes didn't come on screen. Instead, I got an em I recognized, although I had never met him

personally. His name was Theodore Seidensticker III. His title—unlikely anywhere except in Washington, D.C.—was Executive Assistant in Charge of
Administration to the Administrative Assistant.

I identified myself as he inspected my silver zipsuit and decorations. I asked
to speak to Penelope Mapes.

"Sorry, Dr. Flair," he said stiffly. "The Administrative Assistant is not
available."

"Not available." That meant she was in conference, in the nest, ill, nursing
a hangover, stopped, or under the desk of Theodore Seidensticker III enjoying
a little *fellatio alla veneziana*. That last remark suggests my mood of the moment.

I then asked to speak directly to Chief Director Michael Wingate. Seidensticker looked at me pityingly. He said that was quite impossible. The Chief
Director was in conference and had a full calendar for the remainder of the
day. Checkmate. We sat and stared at each other.

The Executive Assistant in Charge of Administration to the Administrative
Assistant was a tall, bony, sniffy character with a cold, Brahminical look. Even
his posture was designed to demonstrate his uprightness. He was reputed to
be the Lord High Executioner of Wingate's court. I decided, that moment,
he was just the em for me.

I explained, as briefly as I could, that I had a matter of the greatest urgency
to lay before the Chief Director. A matter of the greatest sensitivity. Allega-
tions had been brought to my attention indicating conduct inimical to the
public interest by an object high—very high—in the Chief Director's administration.

He didn't consider, hesitate a moment, or ask any questions. It was evidently a situation with which he was not unfamiliar.

"I will see you at 1200 precisely, Dr. Flair," he said tonelessly. "Please bring
whatever documentation you have in your possession."

We left the Hospice amidst fond farewells. I stroked the palms of Warren
and Lucas. I kissed Maya's cheek. I promised to return as soon as possible. A
prospect that sent Warren into a paroxysm of blinking, pate-stroking, lip-
gnawing.

Mary parked the limousine at the curb outside the Executive Office Building. I told Paul I expected to be an hour, no longer. He agreed to wait right
there, in case I was finished earlier. I marched into the building, carrying my
loaded briefcase. Ted the Stick was faithful to his word; he saw me at precisely
1200. *Precisely*.

I had prepared my story. I told him that a month previously I had been
visited by the chief executive of Scilla Pharmaceuticals of San Diego. A drug
manufacturer with whom SATSEC had had lovable dealings in the past. He
had claimed he was the victim of extortion by Art Roach, Chief, Security &
Intelligence, Department of Bliss. If he paid off Roach, he was guaranteed a

government contract. I had advised Scilla to play along. A meeting was arranged, the Scilla president was shared, and this was the result.

I then played the Art Roach-Seymour Dove tape for Theodore Seidensticker III. Watching his face as we listened. No change of expression on those horsey features.

I had then, I went on, confronted Art Roach with the evidence of his criminal behavior. He had been immediately contrite, even tearful, but claimed he had attempted the shakedown under direct orders of Angela Teresa Berri, Director of Bliss. Since she ruled him, he followed her orders, knowing what he was doing was contrary to the public interest, but fearing to disobey her. His career was at stake. To prove his horror and disgust of her illicit activities, he had compiled a record of her infamy. This he had delivered to me voluntarily, trusting in the mercy of those who would judge his own participation in her nefarious schemes.

I then placed the remaining evidence before Seidensticker: the list of fiddled contracts, grain deals, the methanol refinery ripoff, ownership of the Sexual Congress. He donned steel-rimmed spectacles to scan the documents slowly and carefully. Perhaps I imagined it, but I thought his thin lips pressed thinner still when he learned of Angela's proprietorship of the bordello. Could Ted the Stick be a regular customer? (Every Thursday evening. 1800 to 1900. Precisely.)

Finally he pushed the material away with the tips of bloodless fingers. Ugh. Dirty stuff. He took off his glasses, massaged the bony bridge of his nose.

"If possible, sir," I said, "I would like to ask for compassion for Art Roach. He is not an intelligent em. I believe his story, that he acted as he did under orders."

I owed Roach nothing. But he had certain specialized talents that might be of use to me in the future. It was worth one tentative effort to save him.

"Roach isn't important," Seidensticker said. Voice of doom. "Angela Berri is."

"Can it be glossed, sir?" I asked anxiously. "Allow her to resign for reasons of personal health?"

He pursed those knife lips, considered the matter gravely. A gourmet inspecting a menu.

"It might be possible to gloss," he acknowledged, "if it was not for that distressing business involving the National Data Bank. That gang must be cleaned out, and all their customers taken. With so many objects involved, it will be almost impossible to put a pillow on the affair. No, I'm afraid Angela Berri must pay the penalty prescribed by law."

He didn't smack his lips. Exactly.

He leaned toward the flasher, punched a number. Three digits. I couldn't see the screen from where I was seated, but it was obvious to whom he was speaking.

"Sorry to interrupt the Chief Director, sir," he said in a lackey's voice. "But something of the utmost urgency has come up. I have Dr. Nicholas Flair with me, and—"

"Who?"

"Flair. Dr. Nicholas Flair. Deputy Director of Satisfaction Section, Department of Bliss. He has brought a matter to my attention that I believe demands the Chief Director's immediate decision, sir."

Michael Wingate's office was impressive. And quite unlike his home. It occupied half of the top floor of the EOB. Cold, futuristic decor and furnishings. It was divided roughly into thirds. A serving area: plastisteel desk, swivel chairs, maps and charts on the walls, flashers, phones, Telex printers, etc. A sitting area with a chromium cocktail table, inflated chairs and sofa, radio and television sets. A dining area: a glass table large enough to seat eight, pantry, a well-equipped bar, a stereo set with a screen for film cassettes.

Seidensticker knocked on the outer door and waited for the "Come in!" before he entered. I followed a few paces back. The Chief Director was in the "parlor" area, seated on the inflated couch alongside a short, plump, obso hausfrau. I recognized her at once from newsphotos and TV appearances: Sady Nagle, Deputy Chief Director for Domestic Affairs. (When her appointment was up for confirmation, a Congressional critic grumbled, "My God, she's so ugly she couldn't have had a domestic affair in her whole life.")

The Chief Director rose to greet us. He nodded at Ted the Stick, then turned to me with a strained smile. The pleasant, twinkling Santa Claus was gone. He seemed to me an em under considerable strain. I could guess the reason for his tension. The twenty-four hours his wife had given him were ticking away.

"Nick," he said. "Good to see you again."

"My profit, sir," I said.

He introduced me to Sady Nagle. She was across the room. I bowed in her direction. She smiled sweetly, bobbed a great mass of iron-gray hair. She was so ugly she was charming.

"Nick, entertain Sady for a few minutes, will you? Mix a drink if you like or ring for the steward."

He and Seidensticker went back to the office area. The Chief Director sat down heavily behind his desk. The Executive Assistant was carrying my briefcase. He stood at Wingate's elbow and began to lay out the evidence: tapes, film, lists, journals, notebooks. He leaned far over Wingate, whispering, whispering. . . .

"May I get you a drink, Miss Nagle?" I asked.

"Sady," she said. In an unexpectedly hoarse, emish voice. "Tea would be nice. For that you push the little button over there by the pantry door. Then

Tommy comes in. He knows how I like my tea. In a real glass. And whatever you want."

I did as she instructed. I pressed the little button, a red steward appeared immediately, listened to my request, nodded, disappeared.

"Come sit here," Sady Nagle called to me. Patting the couch beside her. "You're really a doctor?"

"Really."

"So tell me, Nick . . ." she went on. "I can call you Nick?"

"Of course."

"Tell me, Nick, what kind of a doctor are you? Head? Foot? Stomach? Heart? A professor maybe?"

"All kinds," I told her.

"Good." She smiled approvingly. "So tell me, doctor, what do you recommend for an endless headache?"

"Two aspirins every four hours," I said. "Endlessly."

She laughed until her face was pink.

Her tea was brought, and my iced Smack. We had a most enjoyable conversation. I had never met an object who could *listen* as well as she. She asked personal questions about my birthplace, my parents, why I wasn't married. But never did I feel she was prying; I felt she *cared*.

She was said to be a political genius, the one object in the US perfectly attuned to the wants, needs, ambitions, and dreams of the political hierarchy and the public. And to their sins and weaknesses. I could believe it. It seemed difficult to withhold a confidence from her, and impossible to deceive her. I think her gift, in addition to that ugly, grandmotherly appearance, was that she could never represent a threat. She was sympathetic, disarming, and so worldly-wise and understanding that if I had suddenly blurted out, "Sady, I have just betrayed an ef I admire," she might pat my arm and say, "You shouldn't have done that, sonny." And I would then be less horrified by my deed than by the realization that I had diminished her good opinion of me.

"Nickola," she whispered. Leaning close. "What you and the Stick brought up . . . it's serious?"

I nodded.

"I knew," she said sadly. "I could tell. The poor boy is so upset today. His stomach? I asked him. But he said no, it's not his stomach. Not his feet. It's his wife, no?"

"Partly," I said. I could keep nothing from her.

"That poor girl," she said sorrowfully. "So lovely. I tell you, Nickola, what we women have to put up with you wouldn't believe."

I was rescued by the Chief Director. In a cracked, almost angry voice, he called, "Nick, would you come over here a moment, please."

When I got to the desk, he was standing at a window, staring out.

"Does Angela know anything of this?" Wingate asked. Tonelessly. "Is she aware that *you* know?"

"No, sir," I said. "Not to my knowledge."

We stood there silently another minute. At least. Then the Chief Director turned to us slowly. I hoped I might never again see an object's face so tortured. He was a stranger, twisted out of shape. Blank eyes looked at me without seeing. Then slid over to his hatchet.

"Take her," he said harshly.

An hour later I was curled up on the back seat of my limousine. The radio was on, turned low. The current jerk-and-jag star, Jock Rot, was singing, "If you don't like my artichoke, please don't shake my bush." I went to sleep to that.

I slept all the way to Manhattan Landing. It was a good sleep, deep and dreamless. At the guardhouse of the compound I picked up an urgent message from Ellen Dawes, asking I flash her the moment I returned.

We left Mary to return the equipment to the night duty officers and the limousine to the motor pool. Paul and I went up to my office.

Paul kicked off his shoes, sprawled wearily on my couch. I stood behind my desk, flipping quickly through the red messages.

"Satisfaction Rate is down point five," I said.

Paul groaned.

I tossed the messages aside. Sat down in my swivel chair, put my feet up on the desk. Paul and I drank in silence. I don't know why we didn't feel more elation. We had done what we set out to do.

"Will you get DIROB?" Paul asked. Languidly.

"No," I said. "I don't think so. Directorships are in the political realm. I don't have enough clout."

"Surely you'll get *something* out of it?"

"I got what I wanted," I said. "Didn't you?"

He didn't answer.

I finally called Ellen Dawes. She said Phoebe Huntzinger had been trying to contact me all day. Phoebe had said it was very, very important, and I was to flash her at any hour of the day or night, whenever I returned.

"Thanks, Ellen," I said. "I'll flash her right now. Sorry to bother you."

I switched off long enough to break the connection, then switched on again and punched the number of the Denver Field Office.

"What is it?" Paul asked.

"Phoebe Huntzinger in Denver," I said. "Probably about Project Phoenix. Says it's important."

Paul got up, came around to stand behind me, watching the flasher screen. The Denver Field Office operator came on. I asked for Phoebe Huntzinger.

"Yes, *sir*, Dr. Flair!" She grinned. "At once, Dr. Flair, sir!"

"Now what the hell?" I muttered.

The flasher flicked to a scene of bedlam. A mob in the background. Shouts, calls, laughter, screams. Total confusion. A naked ef dancing about.

"Jesus Christ!" Paul said. "Have they gone mad?"

Then Phoebe was on screen. Grinning and more than slightly drunk. Holding a plastiglass of something.

"Nick!" she screamed. "Nick, you old fart!"

She was bumped, shoved. Objects kept poking their heads over her shoulders to get on camera.

"Phoebe," I yelled, "what the hell is this? What's happening?"

Someone shoved a piece of computer printout at her. She held it close to the flasher camera eye. Our screen filled with print. Paul and I leaned forward to see.

XXXXXX I XXXXXX

XXXX I FEEL XXXXX

XXX I FEEL GOD XXX

XXXXXXXXXXXXXXXX

We scanned it. Looked at each other. Realization growing.

"Phoebe!" I screamed. "Phoebe!"

The printout was jerked away. She was grinning at me again.

"We did it, daddy!" she yelled. "We really did! The first declarative sentence! A conception! Brain to computer printout! Untouched by human hands!"

" 'I feel god'?" I repeated. "What is—"

"No, no!" she screamed. "It's a little booboo in the circuitry. 'God' wasn't fed into the memory bank. It should be 'good.' 'I feel good.' We can correct it. No problem. A little slippage. 'I feel good.' We did it, Nick!"

"Put it up there again," I yelled at her.

She held up the computer printout.

XXX I FEEL GOD XXX

Paul was laughing now. I was too. Everything we had bottled up for days, weeks, months came bubbling out. All our disappointments, fears, tensions, anxieties, terrors. All released. We hugged each other, roaring, screaming, tossing papers into the air, dancing wildly, stamping our feet.

XXX I FEEL GOD XXX

We had done it. Done it! Picked up an object's thought and printed it. Negated will. Tapped the brain. We were all one now. All one!

XXX I FEEL GOD XXX

Book Z

Z-1

Chief Director Michael Wingate sent me an Instox copy of Angela Teresa Berri's voluntary statement. It was delivered by courier and stamped "FYEO-S&D" on every page. For Your Eyes Only—Scan and Destroy.

Clipped to the sheaf of manuscript was a small, handwritten note: "Thanx. M. W." So apparently he was appreciative of my service.

I saved the mss. for late-night scanning, in the privacy of my apartment. I had succeeded in purchasing a case of natural beer, allegedly of Dutch origin, from a black-market pusher. The entire case was chilling on the bottom shelf of my fridge. Scanning Angela's *mea culpa* seemed as good an occasion as any to sample my treasure.

The medical report attached to Angela's statement described an ef of basically good health, in a somewhat debilitated state. At some point in the past, she had been hysterectomized and had undergone plastic surgery for the implantation of polyurethane sacs of silicone gel to increase the rotundity of her buttocks. I had not been aware of either operation.

The psychological diagnosis listed strong competitive drive, oral orientation, possible narcissism, positive self-esteem, and other labels of a similarly general nature. The final notation—"severe depressive anxiety"—was, I would say, normal under the conditions in which she had found herself following her arrest. But the citation of severe depressive anxiety served another purpose. As I well knew. It justified treatment by cocaine or some other alkaloid to relieve the symptoms. The report ended as I knew it would: "Subject signed Informed Consent Statement voluntarily." Of course.

In 1998, the judicial system of the US operated approximately as it had for 200 years. An object charged with a serious criminal offense was tried by a jury of his peers in a public court. However, in 1991, the Public Security Control Act created an additional court within the federal judiciary. It was designed to deal solely with crimes against public security or prejudicial to the public interest. Trials under the PSCA were held *in camera*. Rather than a jury, the verdict was decided by a board of appointed judges whose security clearance was sufficiently high to enable them to hear and consider evidence of a sensitive nature. Appeal could be made through higher channels in a manner similar to that specified in the Code of Military Justice. But in the great majority of public security cases, especially those involving objects in

Public Service, full confessions with a signed and witnessed Informed Consent Statement reduced most trials to an automatic plea of guilty before a single judge.

That was what happened to Angela Teresa Berri. Her sentence, as prescribed by law: "To be determined in such a manner as to maximize the convicted object's future usefulness and benefit to the State." The trial judge, after accepting and recording the guilty plea, invariably released the corpus of the convicted object to the US Government's Chief Prosecutor. That officer, in turn, usually transferred the corpus to the Public Service Department in which the object had been a member. The convicted object was then assigned to "service of the greatest public benefaction."

I opened another bottle of that delightfully biting beer and began scanning Angela's statement. It had been transcribed from dictated tapes. There was a great deal in it that was discontinuous, some that was irrational, and some merely gibberish. Considering the conditions under which the statement had been given, that was understandable.

I turned first to that portion of Angela's confession dealing with the conspiracy of the Society of Obsoletes, previously described in this record. I was concerned as to Angela's account of my activities and involvement in that affair. But nothing she said implied any serious improprieties on my part. In fact, she gave me generous credit in helping thwart the plot of Dr. Thomas J. Wiley, *et al.*

I then started at the beginning and scanned straight through. Finishing the manuscript and my fourth bottle of beer just before 0200. It was interesting. Not only had she murdered Frank Lawson Harris, but she had manipulated the suicide of her husband when she was eighteen.

Her ownership of the Washington, D.C., bordello, the Sexual Congress, was a fairly recent business venture. It had not been used for overt blackmail attempts, although she was aware of the membership. She had a few other minor scams going of which Art Roach was unaware.

There was no mention of her relationship with Chief Director Michael Wingate. But of course I might have been supplied an edited copy of her statement.

The final page of the manuscript was a copy of a document assigning the corpus of Angela Teresa Berri to Hospice No. 17 for "service of the greatest public benefaction." This Hospice was a small facility, near Little Rock, Arkansas, that was, and had been for many years, engaged in a single project: the chemical synthesis of human blood. I scanned their reports regularly. The most recent had announced the survival of a human subject for twenty-two hours following complete transfusion of a newly formularized fluid.

Incidentally, the assignment to Hospice No.17 was signed by the new Director of the Department of Bliss. He was Chapman, the fussy little bookkeeper type who had formerly been DEPDIRPRO. I told Paul I was not disappointed. But I may have been.

. . .

Four days after the Congressional elections, Paul and I received invitations to a dinner party to be held at the Chief Director's residence in Georgetown, to honor B. Anthony Chapman, the new Director of the Department of Bliss. Such an invitation was a polite command. In the lower left-hand corner of the card was printed "Decorations, *s'il vous plaît.*" From which I inferred this was to be a gathering of official guests only: all Public Service. If civilians had been invited, the instruction on expected dress would have included "Red tie, *s'il vous plaît.*"

Paul and I discussed our travel arrangements. We agreed that guests would probably include the Chief Director's personal staff, directors of all Public Service departments, section deputy directors of Bliss, and some division assistant deputy directors. We would be fools to arrive at this august assemblage in a battered, dusty cab after having taken the air shuttle to Washington. We opted for a drive down in my limousine. Chauffeured, of course.

En route, we reviewed our options on the Ultimate Pleasure pill. We agreed it was no longer a go/no-go decision; the problem now was how to formulate the directive to the Houston Field Office, what parameters to set for the new drug they were to develop.

"By its very nature it would have to be addictive," I pointed out. "In any social context. To be of any value. Psychologically addictive, if not physiologically."

"Physiologically addictive," Paul said definitely. "*Must* be. You know the numbers on cannabis, amphetamines, barbiturates. We're looking for a universal drug. That demands physiological addiction."

"Well . . ." I said slowly. "I suppose you're right. Psychological addiction is too chancy. But we want a formula with a constant effect. Something that doesn't produce tolerance. Easily self-administered. That means ingestion or inhalation."

"You're ruling out the needle?"

"Aren't *you?*" I said. Surprised.

"No. Nick, I think you're missing an important factor here: administration of the UP as ritual or ceremony. Popping a pill or sniffing an inhaler can't do it. But the needle can. Penetrating the corpus. A sacred rite. It needn't be intravenous; a subcutaneous injection would serve as well. Better. But there should be a period of preparation required, sanctified or holy equipment, a *process* of administering the drug as involved and satisfying as taking communion. Nick, we've got to PR this thing. Part of the jerk must come from the act itself."

"Any suggestions?"

"Yes," he said determinedly. "I ultimize the UP as something like those disposable one-shot morphine Syrettes they put in first-aid kits. Needle attached. Sterile. No danger of serum hepatitis. The UP shot attractively packaged, difficult to unwrap. This must take time. The used container must be turned in before a new one is awarded. To help prevent OD's."

"Awarded?" I picked up on that. "Is that how you see it, Paul? As an award?"

"Has to be," he said firmly. "For any service that benefits the state. To mildify terrorism. To reward increased production or consumption. To ensure military discipline. Whatever might be in the public interest. Production and distribution rigidly controlled. Public execution for illegal manufacture, sale or possession. It might even be used as a reward for limiting procreation. Another factor in the Z-Pop campaign."

I looked at him with something like wonder.

"You've really been computing this," I said.

"Yes." He nodded. "I have. I see it as cocaine-based. If we can't get Bolivia or Peru into the US, we can cultivate the shrub in factory-farms. In addition to the coke, we'll want an addictive factor. That's where it gets dicey. Almost any addictive factor will add a tolerance problem. But I think we can strike a risk-benefit balance. And an aphrodisiac. Perhaps an orgasmic trigger. It's going to be one hell of a cocktail. Can I get Houston moving on a crash basis?"

"Crash away," I said. "Top priority, top security. Weekly reports. Send me an Instox of your directive."

"Will do," he said happily. "Now we're moving. Nick, I—"

He stopped suddenly. I turned to stare at him.

"Well?" I asked.

"It's something for the Tomorrow File."

"Oh? What is it?"

"I don't think you're going to like it."

"Come on, Paul, don't play cozy with me."

"Well, it's not actually my idea. It's Mary Bergstrom's idea. With an assist from Maya Leighton."

"Mary? Maya? What the hell *is* it?"

"Well, when we were all down in Alexandria, the night you disappeared after you braced Art Roach, I took the two efs and Seth Lucas out to dinner. Talk got around to Z-Pop. I explained how difficult it was to achieve when longevity rates were increasing every year."

"Paul, I hope this doesn't concern euthanasia for obsoletes. You know it's politically inexpedient."

"No, no. Not euthanasia. I explained the arithmetic of population growth to them, how a reduced fertility rate is nullified if life span continues to increase. So then we started talking about longevity. Mary said longevity was primarily characterological. Inherited trait. Then Maya said, if it was genetic in origin, why couldn't it be engineered? Nick, we all started talking at once. Maya said, to her knowledge, no one has ever done any heavy research on the chromosome pairs that carry the long-life genes. Mary said she saw no reason why they couldn't be identified and manipulated. She futurized a predetermined life span. Adjustable to the needs of society. Nick? Reactions?"

"Yesss," I said slowly. "For the Tomorrow File."

"And it's definitely *not* euthanasia," Paul said triumphantly.

There were as many black zipsuits as guests milling about the barred gate to the Georgetown White House. There was no relaxation of security precautions. Invited guests and wives, husbands, children, relations, users, friends— all, one by one, filed through the metal detector, showed BIN cards and invitations, were identified by voiceprint or vouched for on closed-circuit TV.

Then up the driveway to the steel-paneled door. Inching along the reception line. Chief Director Michael Wingate. Grace Wingate, Director of Bliss B. Anthony Chapman. Mrs. Chapman. A fluttery ef with the face of a parrot. Rapid palm strokes. Smiles. Move along. Murmured phrases.

Then into the gathering crush. All doors thrown wide. Black zipsuits bearing trays. Paul shoved his way through; I followed in his wake. Pausing to stroke palms. Smile.

"Paul, I need a drink."

"Here. In here."

He elbowed. Pushing. He would have his way. He drew me to a bar. His eyes were shining. There he was. Being entertained in the home of the Chief Director of the US Government. Mama would have been so *proud*. I looked at him closely. Who *was* he?

"Nick, what's wrong?"

"Nothing's wrong."

"You look so strange."

"My genial, party look."

"There's Sady Nagle! There. Over there."

"Would you like to meet her?"

"Of course. They say . . ."

Noise increased. In volume and intensity. And heat. The crush. I lost Paul. I found myself with an empty glass. Edging back toward a bar. Then I was dancing with Theodore Seidensticker III, sliding in the opposite direction. We did a mad tango, revolving to get around each other.

"Ah there," he said. He did something with his face. I think he intended it to be a friendly smile. It frightened me.

"What happened to Roach?" I asked him.

"Who? Oh. Very cooperative. Demoted. Fined."

"Thank you," I said piously.

We scraped past. I had a terrible urge to goose him. I envisioned him suddenly plunging forward. Outraged and shaken. The full glasses he was carrying splashing on an ef wearing a tooty evening gown with portholes through which bare breasts bulged strabismically.

The doors of the dining room were thrown wide. The buffet awaited. Disposable food. Come and get it!

Objects were so deliberately casual. What a jerk! The slow saunter. Not really caring. Hunger was vulgar. Then the nonchalant inspection. Then the heaped plate. Where *was* she? I searched the crowd.

"Are you Nick Flair?"

"I am. Penelope Mapes?"

"Yes. The Chief Director's AA. I've been wanting to meet you."

A short, plump ef, downy as a bird. Enormously efficient at her service. It was said. But at this moment flushed, breathless. Her palm stuck.

"He speaks so highly of you."

"He's very kind."

She pushed or was pushed tightly against me. I thought her pneumatic. If her pudendum was depressed, her buttocks would expand. Compress her bicep, and the fingers would swell. Penetrate her with a respectful rod and, hissing faintly, the corpus would deflate in your arms. An empty envelope of skin smelling faintly of lavender.

I didn't like this party. Where *was* she?

"He speaks so highly of you," Penelope Mapes repeated throatily. Eyes glazed. Staring at my beard.

"Would you like a ringlet?" I asked. "To tuck beneath your pillow?"

"Oh, *you!*" she said.

Paul rescued me by squeezing nearby. I reached out, dragged him close, pushed the two together, introduced. Paul was delighted. The Chief Director's Administrative Assistant!

"Oh, *you!*" she was saying as I slid away.

The thought of heaping a plastiplate with that gelatinous food was more than I could endure. I had another vodka-and-Smack.

I stroked many palms. Supinely with departmental directors. Vertically with deputy directors. Pronely with assistant deputy directors. Joe Wellington, the Chief Director's PR Chief, insisted on shaking hands. As his left hand gripped my right arm just above the elbow. Numbing.

"Nick baby!" he said.

"Joe baby!" I said.

A billow of cannabis smoke parted and there she was. Centered in a semicircle. More a golden chemise than a sheath. Quite short. Bare arms. Bare legs. Golden sandals. Ashen hair bound up in a high swirl. The completed nakedness apparent. Lips parted. The teeth. Glistening. Head slightly lowered to listen to the em beside her.

She was wasting herself on him. On them. On everyone but me. Dark, somber eyes rose and caught my stare. Lips bowed in a quick smile. She looked slowly away. That brief lock of glances cut into. . . .

"Nick!" the Chief Director shouted. "So glad you could make it!"

He was Santa Claus again. Perhaps that had been Angela's fatal flaw. She had one role that devoured her. This em flipped a dozen masks off and on. Quik-change.

"Marvelous party, sir," I said.

"Is it?" he said. Chuckling. "Not when you're giving it! Got enough to eat and drink?"

"Plenty," I assured him.

"Good, good. Paul Bumford here?"

"Yes, sir."

"Find him, will you? Both of you upstairs in about fifteen minutes. Second door on your right."

"Yes, sir."

"Hello, hello, hello!" he caroled. Bouncing away. Stroking every palm in sight. Touching. Patting. Feeling. Pressing. Physical contacts for everyone. I turned to search for her, but the cannabis curtain was down.

"What's this about?" Paul asked.

"I have no idea," I said.

We trudged up the stairs. Second door on the right. A black zipsuit inspected us coldly.

"Do we knock?" I said. "Or walk right in?"

"Both," Paul said. He rapped sharply, paused a second, opened the door. We entered. I closed the door respectfully behind us.

It was, I supposed, an upstairs sitting room. Small. Cluttered with odds and ends of obso furniture. Many chairs. Many. Two couches. Stained prints on the walls.

Chief Director Michael Wingate. Deputy Chief Director for Domestic Affairs Sady Nagle. Administrative Assistant Penelope Mapes. Assistant to the Administrative Assistant in Charge of Administration Theodore Seidensticker III. Chief of Public Relations Joseph Wellington. All of them suddenly sober, suddenly solemn.

"Sit anywhere," Wingate commanded. Short, abrupt gesture. Santa Claus had departed. Genghis Khan had returned.

Paul and I listened in silence to what he had to say.

He told us the prospectus for the new Department of Creative Science—which he understood was the result of our joint efforts—had been distributed for comment. To certain selected objects in Public Service, Congress, the judiciary. Also, to objects in the highest echelons of academe, science and law, labor and industry, organized religion, and consumer/environmental Gruppen.

"Although I myself was high on the DCS—" Wingate said. Somewhat wryly. "—it was necessary to test the political viability of the product. Too many causes lost—even just causes—engender an impression of ineffectuality. Not only in others, but in oneself."

I began to appreciate this em's talents and experience.

He continued, looking mostly at me, but shifting his glance occasionally to Paul. His assistants sat mute, regarding us both without expression.

Wingate said initial reaction to the concept of a Department of Creative Science had been almost universally favorable. But the great majority of advocates—even those most enthusiastically supportive of the role of science and technology—were troubled and/or dismayed by what they considered to be our alarmist predictions of the future. What he wanted to learn, Wingate said, was had we included those predictions of extreme change in an effort to bolster our case? If we had, he felt we were guilty of oversell. Or did we sincerely believe tomorrow would produce the problems we had envisioned, necessitating the solutions we had suggested?

"Sir," I said, "new problems demand new answers."

"Sonny," Sady Nagle said. In the kindliest of tones. "Even if those terrible things you predict should happen—and I'm not saying you're all wrong; some of them I can see starting today—you suggest such radical solutions you scare us. Because what you suggest, sonny, is impossible. Just impossible."

"Why impossible?" Paul demanded.

"First of all, sonny," she said, turning to him, "some of your ideas are illegal. Just that—illegal. Other ideas, which may be legal, are a spit in the face of what remains in this little country of morality, religion, tradition, and social order."

"I don't think you understand," Paul said hotly. "I don't think any of you really understand. You just don't grasp what we're trying to tell you. And that is what President Morse said ten years ago: This society is obsolete. It's creaking along, parts falling off, levers jamming, fuses blowing, the whole outmoded mechanism coming to a shuddering halt."

It was too late to switch him off or try to mollify what he was saying. He was on his feet now. Pacing. His voice louder. They were all listening intently. Following him with their eyes as he strode about the room.

"Illegal?" he demanded. "Then change the laws. Tradition? As ephemeral as slavery and dueling. Morality? Someone said it's all a matter of time and geography. Religion? Valuable, but only as a function of the state. Social order? It is what the government says it is. Yes, the solutions we propose are radical. Or may appear radical. Because the problems are new. Have never been faced before. Zero population growth. Energy crunch. World-wide terrorism. Ecological decay. Genetic engineering. Nuclear blackmail. All relatively new problems. That not only demand new solutions, as Nick said, but demand a new way of computing. Of seeing the interdependence of all human activities. A lot of things that have been cherished for a long, long time will have to go. *Must* go! There are no absolutes. Free elections? Free speech? The Bill of Rights? Freedom of worship? Personal privacy? They've all been restricted during times of crisis. And they are all relatively young concepts. Some of them less than two hundred years old. They worked well for that timespan.

But we can no longer afford them. We must compute new concepts, a new Bill of Rights, to see us through the approaching crisis. And it is coming. As certainly as I know the reality of our presence here, in this room, I know it is coming. And the only way to even begin to cope is to put away the slogans of yesterday, the shibboleths of today's political system and social organization. I put it to you this way: Is there one of you who would not voluntarily relinquish your individual freedom if, by relinquishing that freedom, you helped guarantee the survival of the human species? That is not just a 'what if' question. It is an exact statement of the choice we may some day soon be facing. Yes, Nick and I suggested a radical program. Because only strange new ideas can ensure the survival of our society. Of our species. That is what we're really talking about—survival. The Department of Creative Science will be the first step toward bringing science and technology into a policymaking role in the US Government. Reject it, and you reject the future."

He ended suddenly. I could hear the sounds of the party downstairs: laughter, cries, music, the stomp of dancers. But in that frowsy room, silence banged off the walls. No one moved.

Finally, Chief Director Michael Wingate drew a great breath. He looked about slowly. Not seeking reactions, but reassuring himself as to place and time. Then his eyes came to Paul and stayed there.

"What I shall say," he stated in a low, firm voice, "does not imply concurrence with everything Paul said. Nor should my total agreement with his views be inferred. However, I have decided to go ahead with exploring the most feasible scenario for establishing a new Department of Creative Science. I ask you all to submit your ideas to me as soon as possible. I thank you for your close attention. I suggest we now return to the party, singly or in twos. So as not to attract attention or comment. Thank you."

Paul and I were the last to leave. He was still shaking. I thought it best not to say anything at the moment. We rejoined the throng downstairs. We were separated.

I wandered through the thinning crowd. Objects were waving, calling, departing. I smiled my way into that chintzy sitting room. John Quincy Adams' third eye had been repaired.

Then fingers touched my wrist.

"Nick," Grace Wingate said. Somewhat breathlessly. "I haven't had a chance to thank you."

I looked down upon that soft hand laid upon my arm. She drew me gently into an alcove. We were both smiling determinedly: hostess and guest in a polite and inconsequential dialogue.

"I don't know how you did it," she said, "and I don't want to know. But she's gone, Nick. She's gone!"

I nodded.

"I don't know how I can ever repay you," she said.

"You look lovely, Grace," I told her.

Too ingenuous to accept praise casually. Her hand rose automatically to her gathered hair. Fingers poked at floating tendrils. I thought she flushed with pleasure, suddenly conscious of her body. She glanced down at the glittering overskin.

"Nick, is it—is it too—"

"No," I assured her gravely. "It isn't too."

If she was suddenly conscious of her body, I was suddenly conscious of my. . . .

"Do you ever walk out?" I asked. The fool's smile still pulling my face apart.

"Walk out?"

"Casually. Shopping. A museum. A matinee."

Then she understood.

"I don't," she said. "I can't," she said. "I won't," she said.

"Lovely party!" someone cried. Drifting past. Grace lifted a hand. Head turning. Tilted.

I couldn't breathe. That line of completion enclosed her like a sharp halo. She was an ancient child. As fresh and knowing. The open, tender parts of her, pristine, might exude a scent of new worlds. I had dangerous visions of mad profits. Reason fled.

"I couldn't," she murmured.

Blackmail was not beyond me. At that moment. Nothing was.

"After what I—" I said. And paused.

"The Beists," she said. Finally. "Paul is a member. Can you come to Washington? He can bring you. I'll be there. Nick?"

Suddenly we were up to our assholes in idiots. Chattering and laughing. All I could do was stretch my smile to pain and nod at her over the heads of surrounding guests. She had tossed me a crust. I would have taken a crumb. I watched the hostess move, laugh, throw back her glistering snake head. I entered into that vulval ear and rested.

Paul and I started back for GPA-1 at 0215. We traveled through the new day. Languid with exhaustion.

"Listen," Paul murmured, "do you think they took me seriously?"

"I don't know if they did," I said. "I did."

"Did I frighten them?"

"Probably."

"Good. But it served. Didn't it, Nick? We got what we wanted."

"Yes," I said.

Z-2

At that point in time, mid-November, it seemed to me the whirligig increased speed. I, who had opted for action, became aware of the lure of rapid movement for its own sake. Without reason or destination. I felt a curious unease. The world on a fulcrum. Teetering.

During that period I suffered a severe attack of Random Synaptic Control that lasted almost five minutes and left me riven.

Even more disquieting was Hyman R. Lewisohn's lack of affirmative response to parabiotic therapy. Unless his vital readouts showed a sudden and unexpected upcurve, my prognosis was negative. The physioanalytic computer concurred. I returned, once again, to my contingency plan.

We had exhausted conventional protocols long ago. Arabinosylcytosine. 6-Thioquanine. Daunorubicin. L-Asparaginase. Vincristine IV. Prednisone. 6-Mercaptopurine. Methotrexate. Cyclophosphamide. Ara-C. Hydroxyurea. We had tried them all in dozens of combinations and protocols suggested by the pharmacoanalytic computer.

In addition to therapy for the acute myelogenous leukemia, Lewisohn had been and was being treated for leukemic infiltration of the nervous system. This called for intrathecal (injection into the spinal fluid) of methotrexate and aminopterine, as well as oral pyrimethamine. We had ended radiation therapy.

We had shifted to more experimental compounds of limited value. With no better results. Although, for a brief period, the object responded to 1-2 chlorethyl-3, cyclohexyl-1-nitosourea.

We had tried unblocking antibodies with a compound based on the original Moloney regressor sera. We had then turned to immunization with tumor antigens, utilizing living tumor cells pretreated with Vibrio cholerae neuraminidase. Nothing served.

The penultimate therapy, in which we were then engaged, parabiosis, was an attempt to transfer immunity with lymphocytes from immunized donors. The donors had underachieved the norm. In fact, the second had unaccountably developed leukemic symptoms from Lewisohn's infected blood.

I have presented this brief precis of Lewisohn's therapy to justify what lay ahead for him: the final step in my contingency plan. I had become convinced it would prove absolutely necessary. There was no choice.

Shortly after the hookup with the third donor, I went down to Alexandria to scan the most recent computer printouts. I saw no indications of improvement; the em was going. All the staff of Group Lewisohn concurred. I took their signed statements to this effect.

I was sitting in Lewisohn's room, close to his bedside. A roll of printout on my lap. But I wasn't scanning it. I was staring at him, computing what had to be done. The place. The time. How many objects would be needed. The chances of success. It never occurred to me, of course, to tell him what I planned. I could imagine his reaction. The horror.

He was somnolent. Heavily drugged. He had not stirred when I entered the room. I sat patiently, wondering if Paul had been correct. He had said all contingency plans have a built-in defect: the author wants to ultimize them, to see if they'll serve. That dictum was just operative enough to disturb me.

Lewisohn's eyes opened. Finally. He was staring directly at me.

"Jack the Ripper," he rasped. He made a weak gesture. "Where do those tubes go? The ones to the wall?"

"I told you a dozen times. We're monitoring your blood. Instant analysis. It looks good."

"Thank you, Doctor Pangloss," he said wearily. And looked away.

I nodded toward the stack of books at his bedside.

"What are you serving on?" I asked him.

"Go to hell," he said. "Besides, it isn't important."

"What *is* important?"

"The weakness," he said. "I can't think. It's draining me. Give me a pill."

"What for?"

"I'm sick and tired of being sick and tired. One pill. An injection."

"No way," I said. "We're not through with you yet."

"What good am I to you? My brain is mush."

"It'll come back," I told him.

"When?"

"Soon. Soon."

"My brain is dying."

"No," I said. "The corpus. Not the brain."

He turned his head slowly. Looked at me. I feared I had said too much.

"You devious devil," he whispered. "What are you plotting?"

"I'm planning to make you well," I said. "To end your pain and your weakness. Is that so bad?"

He began to curse me then. Forgetting his suspicions. Which was what I wanted.

During November and early December, Paul Bumford and I spent an increasing number of hours in Washington, D.C.

Out of all the confused and contentious meetings and conferences and colloquies of those weeks, the scenario for the Department of Creative Science was slowly structured. We could not have come to the necessary compromises without the knowing counsel of Joseph Tyrone Wellington. Of all objects! The Chief Director's Public Relations Chief.

I had always thought the em a microweight. With his petrobon complexion. Wirewool muttonchops. "Nick baby!" A breath of cold cigars. Shallow, blue eyes. Lips remarkably rosy, brownrimmed. A smile on the face of the tiger.

But the Chief Director did not surround himself with fools. Soon after Wingate's go decision, Joe Wellington took me aside and cautioned me not to take public relations lightly. "The trick," he said, "is to cross-fertilize substance and image so the resultant hybrid has the strengths of both and the weaknesses of neither. Example: God as substance, Jesus Christ as image. Think of the crucifixion as a PR scenario, and you'll compute what I mean."

With his aid, the following proposals were drafted for the Chief Director's consideration:

1. I would remain as Deputy Director of Satisfaction Section, Department of Bliss. But I would be appointed to Director (Temp.), enabling me to wear a crimson tab on the right shoulder epaulette of my silver zipsuit. The purpose of this promotion was to signal Congress and the public the importance the Chief Director attached to proposed legislation establishing a Department of Creative Science.

    I would continue to reside in the compound at GPA-1, but make frequent trips to Washington, D.C.—two or three times a week—to rule the DCS operation there and to consult with the Chief Director and his staff. This arrangement would also ensure my continued rule of Project Phoenix, the Fred III research, the UP project, personal care of Lewisohn, and several other restricted projects.

2. Paul Bumford would be promoted to Deputy Director (Temp.), with the crimson tab on his bronze zipsuit. A small office would be established in the Capital, ruled by Paul, and he would take up permanent residence in Washington.

    Paul's main responsibility would be personal relations with Congress and members of committee staffs. Via Sady Nagle. My main responsibility would be public relations with rulers and organizations of all scientific disciplines. Joe Wellington would manipulate lecture tours, convention addresses, symposia, TV appearances, planted magazine articles, perhaps a ghost-written book, etc.

3. At the same time we pushed the concept of a Department of Creative Science, we would also urge the establishment of a Joint Committee on Creative Science by both houses of Congress. To oversee the budget, plans, and activities of the new Public Service department. Something for everyone.

The Chief Director approved of the main thrust of our program *in toto*, making only a few minor adjustments. For instance, we had suggested Paul's Washington office be established in the headquarters of the Department of Bliss. Wingate rejected this, pointing out that it would give the impression of

DCS being ruled by or an offshoot of DOB. He wanted DCS to parturiate as completely new and independent. He was right.

Paul's service as AssDepDirRad was taken over by Edward Nolan, formerly leader of the Memory Team. Mary Bergstrom was moved to Washington to serve as AA in the DCS office. Paul and I, jointly, leased a furnished home in the Chevy Chase section. The new Metro link extended out there. Since a Metro link was also operating to Alexandria, transportation to Hospice No. 4 would be simplified.

The house Paul and I shared in Chevy Chase was pleasantly decrepit. It was an obso structure, brick with wood trim, badly in need of pointing and painting. The furnishings seemed to have been accumulated rather than selected: they were of all periods, in various stages of disrepair. But the house was adequately heated, undeniably comfortable, and had more rooms than we would possibly need. Shortly after we took possession, Paul asked me if Mary Bergstrom could take over one of the bedroom-nest suites since she was not happy in the studio apartment she had found on Franklin Street. I saw no reason to object. Mary moved in.

We had a carefully programmed housewarming, of course. Catered. A pro forma invitation was sent to the Chief Director and Mrs. Wingate. They sent their regrets. A previous engagement. But everyone else we invited put in an appearance. Even the Chairman of the Senate Government Operations Committee and two influential members of the House Government Operations Committee.

More important, we had an excellent turnout of media reps, Congressional administrative assistants, and general counsels and staff members of both GO Committees. Their cooperation was essential if we were to win preliminary approval of the DCS and move enabling legislation onto the floors of both Houses for debate and vote.

Sady Nagle served as hostess, and Joe Wellington had brought over his entire staff to make certain things moved smoothly. It was a large, friendly, noisy party; we hadn't skimped on alcohol, cannabis, or food. Everyone recognized it as a lobbying ploy, but the AA's and committee staff members were flattered by the attention we paid them and the importance we obviously attached to their goodwill.

I limited my drinking and played the genial host strenuously. As did Paul Bumford. We had previously agreed I was to manipulate the media reps while Paul concentrated on the pols. The arrangement served well.

"Good party," Herb Bailey assured me. "As parties go in this town. At least the booze isn't watered."

"What do you think, Herb?" I asked him. "Have we got a chance?"

"Don't be so impatient," he told me. "You'll learn that there's time, and then there's Congressional time. No one's in a hurry in this town. Or they might get all the nation's business cleaned up in a month or two, and have to go back home to their constituents. Who the hell wants to do that? By the way, I never thanked you for the lead on the DOB shakeup. Thanks. Got anything else for me?"

"Yes," I said. Solemnly. "Something very big indeed."

"Oh? What is it?"

"I'll keep an eye on what you write about the DCS before I decide whether to give it to you."

"Jesus Christ," he said disgustedly. "You're learning fast."

"I learned that at my father's knee."

"Which reminds me," he said. "My little girl has been pushing me to buy her one of your father's new Die-Dee Dolls."

He didn't have to say more.

"Don't spend the love," I told him. "I'll have one sent out to you from the factory. You should get it in time for Christmas."

"Thanks, Nick," he said gratefully. "I appreciate that."

I knew he would. One of the Government Operations Committee Representatives left early for another party. He took Maya Leighton along with him. I knew *he'd* appreciate *that*. Politics is objects. But so, it may surprise you, is science. In many respects. Winning a research grant, manipulating the race to be "first," earning credit for a discovery, or scamming your team leader—all are not too unlike getting a piece of legislation through the US Congress. The stakes may be higher in Washington, that's all.

After the final guests straggled away, Sady Nagle and Joe Wellington joined Paul and me for a final coffee and postmortem. We agreed the housewarming had been a success. An effective kickoff for the DCS campaign.

"I wish the Chief Director had been here," Paul fretted. "It would have made it more important."

Nagle and Wellington laughed.

"Sonny," Sady said, "believe me, he's got more important things to worry about. He's given you a chance. What more do you want?"

"He's testing the water," Wellington explained. "If he sees the DCS is going, he'll link himself more closely. If it doesn't look good, he'll pull clear. He has his personal image to consider. You heard what he said: He can't afford too many failures."

"This isn't going to fail," Paul said coldly. "I guarantee that."

After Sady and Joe departed—kisses all around; Washington had adopted many of the conventions of show biz—Paul and I lingered over a bottle of natural brandy we had *not* served our guests.

"What's bothering you?" I asked him.

He looked at me thoughtfully.

"I must never forget how perceptive you are of my moods," he said.

"That's right, Paul," I said lazily. "You must never forget that. So what's bothering you?"

"Sady Nagle is an obso. You know that."

"And?"

"She's never had any memory conditioning."

"Paul, she's Deputy Chief Director for Domestic Affairs. The Chief's political expert. She's supposed to know more about what keeps the country ticking over than anyone else."

"You know how she keeps her records?"

"How?"

"On file cards. Would you believe it? A card for every Congressman, for every governor, for every magnamayor and minimayor in the country. One for every big pol and little pol. Superlawyers and superbankers. Judges and wardheelers. Business execs, labor barons, college presidents, and professors with clout. Prime TV and newspaper factors. In other words, the Establishment. Movers and shakers. She's got them all. Thousands and thousands of file cards. With name, address, phone number, date of birth, brief physical description, political affiliation, voting record, marital status, conditioning, personal likes and dislikes, if any. And so forth. Then she's got a cross-file on dates. She sends out birthday cards, anniversary cards, condolence cards. To the pols and to their parents, spouses, children, grandchildren. It's incredible!"

"Seems to serve." I shrugged. "She's on top of the political scene. The Chief Director depends on her."

"But that card file's so *obso*," Paul said angrily. "Nick, do you know how Judidat functions?"

"Judidat? Is that the legal outfit?"

"It's a legal service. Available to attorneys. At a lovable fee, of course. Suppose an object is indicted for homicide. Or any other crime. The defense attorney retains Judidat. They come into the community where the alleged crime was committed. They do a public opinion poll in depth. Heavy motivational analysis. Everything goes into a computer, and they get a complete personality profile of objects whose sympathy is with the accused. Say the PP show white, em, under thirty, limited conditioning, strong parental influence, conservative politics, deep religous leanings, undersexed, whatever. All right, now the defense attorney knows what to look for in the voir dire. He tries to get a jury as close as possible to the Judidat profile. Then, after the jury is selected, Judidat moves in closer to construct life histories and psychological profiles of the individual jurors. Into the computer again. Out comes an analysis that dictates the thrust of the defense attorney's arguments, what questions to ask, what areas to avoid, what triggers to pull. How, in fact, to manipulate the jury. Judidat's attainment rate runs around ninety-plus."

"Paul, what *is* this?"

He was smiling at me. A sly smile. Almost ferrety.

"Nick, I want to bring one of Phoebe Huntzinger's whiz kids down from GPA-1 to study Sady Nagle's silly file card operation. And then to design software to get the whole thing on tape. Set up a political Judidat process so we can run Congress through a computer and get the most effective arguments for the DCS, what areas to avoid, what triggers to pull. We'll start with

Congress, but eventually we'll include everyone in Sady's file. The entire Establishment! The whole power structure! Think what that could mean to us—and the Chief Director too, of course. Instant analysis of the viability of proposed legislation. Accurate percentile predictions of success. What buttons to push for maximum response."

"You think Sady will lend her file cards to your computernik?"

"No way. Not voluntarily. She sleeps on them. But you and I know there are ways. . . ."

"Forget it," I said loudly. "Too much risk. Alienate Sady and we're stopped. Just forget it. It's for the Tomorrow File."

"The Tomorrow File?" he said furiously. "This is for today. Right *now*. We can't wait. Nick, we can get the whole thing set up on a computer in GPA-1. Top security. Crash priority. We can have it serving in time to give us the answers on this DCS project."

"No." I shook my head. "Absolutely not. It would obsolete Sady Nagle completely and probably get Wingate questioning our motives and solutions again. We narcotized him the first time around. Something like this would revive all his suspicions. Put it in the Tomorrow File."

"For God's sake, Nick!" he shouted. "We've got to start moving the Tomorrow File to actuality. You said so yourself. You said it's not just a Christmas list; it's a plan of action!"

"But you're moving too fast. You'll clever us both right into Cooperation Rooms. Being drained. Forget it!"

He didn't accept it easily. An ugly pout twisted his mouth. He jumped to his feet. Slammed palms together. The sharp crack of something breaking irretrievably. Then he put his hands on his hips, stalked angrily about the room. He didn't look at me. Finally he stood with his back to me. I heard him take several deep breaths.

"All right," he said. Controlled voice. "All right. We'll do it your way. I'll put it in the Tomorrow File."

"Good. That's best, Paul. Really it is."

"Are you going to tell the Chief Director about the UP project?" he asked suddenly.

He caught me by surprise. I couldn't compute his sudden jink.

"Why . . . no. I hadn't planned to. We having nothing to show him, Paul. Not yet. It's just a concept."

"But it's a political drug."

"Sure, if it authenticates. But what's the point of telling him now?"

"Just a thought," he said casually. "I'm going to bed."

A week before Christmas, 1998, I drove down to Washington from GPA-1 in my official sedan. I was carrying gifts for Paul, Mary Bergstrom, Maya Leighton, and Seth Lucas. And a liter of natural bourbon for Joe Wellington, a jeweled owl's head brooch for Sady Nagle, a natural silk scarf for Penelope

Mapes. I also had a gift for Grace Wingate: giant hoop earrings of hammered silver. But still undecided if I might risk the giving.

I had not endured the aggravating traffic jams on the New York-Washington freeway merely to celebrate the birth of Christ in the Nation's Capital. A meeting of the D.C. Beists was scheduled for the evening of my arrival. Hopefully, it would provide an opportunity for my first meeting with Grace Wingate since the Chief Director's reception for DIROB.

Paul had transferred his membership from the New York chapter of the Beists to the Washington organization. He suggested, in view of our new ranks and close identification with the Department of Creative Science legislation, it might be discreet to wear civilian clothes to the meeting. I concurred. I slipped the tissue-wrapped silver earrings into the pocket of my tweed jacket and carried a vodka-and-Smack into Paul's bedroom while he finished dressing.

I sprawled on his chaise lounge and watched him fuss with butterfly bowties in front of a wardrobe mirror.

"Polka dot or paisley?" he asked.

"Paisley," I said. "More festive. Is this going to be a Christmas party?"

"Something like that," he said. "We're all supposed to bring something. I had a cake delivered. We have a place of our own now. Did I tell you that?"

"No. You didn't."

"Oh, yes. A meeting hall over a delicatessen. You can get heartburn on the elevator. With a uninest and a small room for administration. I'm secretary-treasurer."

"Congratulations."

"Thank you. More than two hundred members, and growing. I think I can make something of it."

"Why?"

"It's a giggle."

"Paul."

He turned to stare at me. How he had changed in the past few months! Now he looked like a young Napoleon: broad brow, brooding eyes, sweet lips, a darkling cast to his expression. Withal, a cold, firm resolve in those effeminate features.

"I know you think it a giggle," he said.

"But *you* don't?" I asked.

After our blast over computerizing Sady Nagle's card file, I thought our relationship had regained its former tenor: open, candid, easy.

"Oh, I suppose it's a laugh now," he said. "Like all religions. But I see something in it."

"And what is that?"

"Primus: Beism is not only *not* antiscience, but whatever codified beliefs it expresses advocate increased scientific research and social change. Secundus:

A new society might do worse than encourage a state religion. As a kind of emotional spine. A new patriotism."

"Oh-ho," I said. "Pope Paul."

"The first." He grinned.

The new Beist meeting hall was simply a large, square, dusty room with a stage at one end, elevated two steps above the floor. It was almost filled when we arrived. The number of Beists surprised me. I had a fleeting impression of having left pregnant rats in a cage and returning a few nights later to find the cage crowded and swarming.

Paul left me to claim one of the cane-backed chairs on the rostrum. Reserved for the governing board. The last time I had attended a Beist meeting, the movement seemed unstructured, with no desire for rulers. I wondered what role Paul had played in this nascent power pattern.

I glanced about casually. I could not see Grace Wingate.

The meeting was called to order with the banging of a gravel. We all found places on those hellishly uncomfortable chairs. Joanne Wilensky, as dreary and acned as before, welcomed members and newcomers. She called on a chapter officer to make a membership report.

This ef, wearing the zipsuit of a PS-3, read a short statement. There were now Beist chapters in fourteen towns and cities. Total national membership was estimated at close to three thousand. I was astounded. It seemed to me very rapid growth for such a rinkydink cult.

Then Secretary-Treasurer Paul Bumford was called on to make his report. It was a remarkable performance. Without notes, he delivered a concise, number-filled account of his office. He spoke for almost ten minutes. Without hesitation or stumble. His memory conditioning was obviously successful.

Even more surprising to me was what he said. The Washington, D.C., chapter of the Beists now had a bank balance exceeding ten thousand new dollars. Paul said that since the only existent office equipment was an obso typewriter (donated), he strongly urged that the sum of three thousand new dollars be approved for the purchase of a new electric typewriter, a mimeograph machine, stationery, and the requisite office supplies. His suggestion was put in the form of a motion and overwhelmingly adopted.

The evening's speaker was then introduced. He was Arthur Raddo. A young em with lank blond hair falling untidily over his forehead. Enormous eyes with a fervid stare. Flat lips he licked constantly. Wearing a wrinkled, soiled zipsuit of a PS-5. His physical appearance gave the impression of limp ineffectuality. But his voice was unexpectedly loud, passionate. Still, I was certain he was a frail.

He said that up to that point in time, the Beists had been content with rather vague canons and implied scripture. What was needed, Raddo proclaimed, was a start on structuring the Beists' beliefs, to put them into written form, in a sort of Bible to which all members might voluntarily submit and adhere.

In addition, he said, such written prescriptions would serve as a basis for proselyting. For the time had passed when Beism could be content with the casual addition of the bored and curious and lonely to its membership rolls. The time had come to move actively to build numbers, require discipline, exercise power.

If Beists were sincere about the evolution of the human species into a single superrace, he said, then they must devise a program to purify the blood. That was the phrase he used: "purify the blood." But he never defined it, and I could only assume he actually meant to improve the gene pool. Although he never concretized how this was to be done. "Purify the blood!" he kept shouting. "Purify the blood!"

"We cannot stand still and talk and hope," he concluded. "We must sacrifice ourselves if the future is truly to belong to us. To the single, divine human race."

There was a moment of silence. Then an enthusiastic snapping of fingers. In spite of his nuttiness (surely there was pathology there), it had been a well-organized speech. Point led to point. A was easy to accept. If you accepted A, you had to accept B. And, of course, B led to C. I could hardly believe this insipid object was capable of such artfulness.

The meeting was brought to a close by the Wilensky ef's announcement that a contributed "holiday feast" was available to all members and guests in the administration room. There was a swift surge of hungry Beists.

Paul chatted a moment with other officers on the platform, then came down. We moved toward each other.

"Well?" he said. Smiling. "What did you think?"

"About what?"

"The speaker, for starters."

"A wowser," I said. "Where does he serve?"

"I'm not certain. Bureau of Printing and Engraving, I think. He comes on a little heavy, I admit. But every religion has its fanatics."

"How long have you had a board of directors?" I asked curiously.

"Oh . . . a few months," Paul said vaguely. "The membership was getting too large. We needed some kind of formal structure. Environment determines social organization, you know. Then you get a positive feedback."

"What the hell are you talking about?" I demanded.

"Oh, look," he said. "There's Grace Wingate. She's waving at us."

So she was. I moved slowly through the throng. Never taking my eyes from her. She watched me approach. Smiling. Paul had disappeared. So had everyone. And everything. She was wearing a bottle-green silk sheath. A black suede coat about her shoulders. Sleeves hanging empty. Her hair was down. She was beautiful. I could not compute why.

"Nick!" she said. "Merry Christmas!"

"Merry Christmas to you. Are you as well as you look?"

"Better." She laughed. "You can drop my hand now." And laughed again. "What a rogue you are!" Determinedly light.

"Was," I said. "Have been. Not now."

The smile faded slowly.

"Would you like something?" I asked. "Food? I can get it."

"No, nothing, thank you. We were at an embassy party and were late getting away. So sorry we couldn't get to your housewarming but... you know."

In another moment we'd be agreeing what a severe winter it threatened to be and wasn't it a shame that the entire crew of Sealab 46 had been lost when the hull unaccountably cracked.

"I really must run," she said nervously.

"Can we sit a moment?" I asked.

"A moment," she said. Finally.

And all during this our eyes had not unclinched. Had not wavered. Somewhere around us was movement, laughter.

"I have a Christmas present for you," I said. Suddenly deciding. "Will you accept it?"

Appreciable hesitation. Then: "Yes," she said.

I handed over the tissue-wrapped package. Her eyes lowered as she unwrapped it softly, timorously, just far enough to see what it contained. "Ahhh," she breathed. Then looked up at me again.

"Beautiful. Nick, they're beautiful. I thank you."

"Yes," I said.

"But I have nothing for you."

I stopped myself. I could have told her.

"Grace, am I to see you only at Beist meetings? Must I join? Is there no other way?"

It troubled her. But I had to know. If she wanted it no-go, now was the time to signal me.

"I am never alone," she said. In such a low voice I could hardly hear.

"Never?"

"Not outside. But. . . ."

"But?"

She shook her head. Ashen hair flaming.

"This is very wrong," she said.

"Not wrong," I said. "Just difficult. Couldn't you come to New York? For shopping or the theater?"

"I could," she said. "But with a secretary. And guards. Always guards."

I was deliriously happy. Because, I thought, my only problem was logistics.

"Grace," I said, "come to New York. Plan a week or two in advance. Tell your husband. Tell him that at your reception I invited you for lunch the next time you were in New York, and you're going to take me up on it. Send me a note when you'll arrive. Does that sound all right to you?"

"Yes."

"Will you do it?"

"Yes. What about the secretary and guards?"

"I don't know. At the moment. I'll think of something."

I hoped my erection was not obvious. I wondered why our flat words seemed to me the most erotic conversation I had ever had. Our eyes locked again, promising. . . .

"Do you sleep naked?" I asked her.

She caught her breath. Went quite pale. Those somber eyes seemed to grow in size and intensity. Dark beacons. I thought her lips trembled. A knuckle went to her teeth.

"Nick," she said. "Please. Don't."

"Do you?" I persisted.

"Yes," she whispered. At last.

"Think of me?" I asked.

She nodded dumbly.

"Here we are," Paul Bumford caroled brightly. "Best cake in the house. If I have to say to myself."

He was balancing three plastiplates with slices of chocolate layer cake, three plastiforks. He sat down with us, and Grace Wingate remarked how lovely the lighted Christmas trees looked along the mall.

We had finished the cake, were standing, beginning our farewells when a black zipsuit came pushing through the crowd of Beists. They fell silent as he passed. Drawing back. Watching him. No expression.

"Ma'am," he said to Grace Wingate.

"What is it, Tim?"

"We just got a call on the car phone. Do you know if Director Nicholas Flair and Deputy Director Paul Bumford are here?"

"I'm Flair," I said. "This is Deputy Director Bumford. What is it?"

"Sir," he said, "the Chief Director would like both of you to join him at his Georgetown residence as soon as possible."

Paul and I glanced at each other.

"Mrs. Wingate," I said. Bowing slightly. "It's been a profitable evening. Merry Christmas and Happy New Year."

"Oh, yes," Paul said. "From me, too."

"Thank you both," she said. Wooden smile. "Perhaps I'll see you at home."

Penelope Mapes met us at the outside door. Led us through the hallway maze to the library.

"I called your place in Chevy Chase," she said. "Mary Bergstrom told me where you were. Are you both Beists?"

"Paul is," I said. "I'm just an innocent bystander."

The plump squab giggled dutifully.

"Penny, what's this all about?" Paul asked.

"Penny." That was interesting.

"I'll let the CD give you the gruesome details," she said. Knocked, and swung open the library door. Chief Director Michael Wingate rose from behind the desk.

"Nick!" he said. "Paul! So glad you could make it."

He introduced us to the other two ems in the room. But I knew one of them well. And recognized the other. We all stroked palms.

Dr. Winston Heath was Chief of the National Epidemiology Center in Frankfurt, Kentucky. I had known him for years: a cold, unemotional technician. Capable but limited. No imagination. He was the palest live object I had ever seen. Blanched.

The other em was R. Sam Bigelow, Chief, BPS—the Bureau of Public Security (formerly the Federal Bureau of Investigation). In all the photos of him that appeared in newspapers, magazines, books, and in his frequent TV interviews, he looked like a frog. In person, he looked like a frog. A suspicious frog. He glowered at Paul and me. Not looked, but glowered. I felt immediately guilty.

We found chairs. Penelope Mapes faded into the background. That ef had made effacement a fine art. I wondered if Chief Director Wingate demanded her presence for the same reason gynecologists insist their nurses be present during an internal: to forestall cries of rape.

"This conversation is restricted," the Chief Director mentioned casually. "I need not quote applicable law. I'm certain you're aware of the penalties. The situation is this:"

Then, speaking rapidly but distinctly, Wingate related the pertinent factors. Two weeks previously, there had been a heavy outbreak of botulism in GPA-11 (Idaho, Wyoming, Montana, and both Dakotas). Since then, slightly more than 1,200 cases had been reported. Of those afflicted, approximately three-fourths had stopped. During the same time period, seven botulism cases had been reported from East Coast areas, sixteen from the West Coast, and scattered cases elsewhere.

"Dr. Heath," the Chief Director said, "will you take it from here?"

"Average number of botulism cases annually per total population for the past ten years," Heath said in a dead, lecturer's voice, "is 2.17. For the entire US. Naturally, our first thought was massive food poisoning. A bad shipment of canned *something* into the stricken area. Although that would not account for the cases on the East and West Coasts and the few scattered all over the US. But we computed that it was possible that tourists, traveling through GPA-11, had taken some of the spoiled foodstuff home with them. We immediately sent an investigative team into GPA-11, of course. They found absolutely *no* evidence of food poisoning. In fact, victims came, for the most part, from families who consumed identical meals. But only one object of several was poisoned. It could not have been the water supply since, as you know, the *Clostridium botulinum* is anaerobic. And besides, the water supply was ruled out because only a relatively few of the total population were affected. Most botulism results from inefficient home-canning. No evidence of that. As you are probably aware, commercial canning processes have been so completely automated, with such a multiplicity of quality controls, that the risk factor in commercial food processing is practically nil. That's it. Any questions?"

"Stop rate, doctor?" I asked.

"It's 76.1967, doctor."

"Age of victims, doctor?" Paul asked.

"Between nine and eighty-three, doctor. Very few of the very young. At the age of fifteen, the curve begins to rise. Slowly. It accelerates at maturity. Reaches a peak at fifty-plus, then declines slowly. One odd incident: the stopping of a four-month-old ef from botulism. The single infant case recorded."

"Any common denominators, doctor?" I asked. "Industrial pollution? Occupation? Clothing? Sports? Drinks—soft or alcoholic? Any drug intake common to all?"

"Negative, negative, negative, doctor," Dr. Heath said bleakly. "We've checked it all out."

"You're certain it's botulism, doctor?" Paul asked.

R. Sam Bigelow looked at him coldly.

"We're certain," he said. "Heath told you what it is. We checked it out in the Bureau labs. That's what it is."

The Chief Director turned to me.

"It's not over, Nick," he said. "Case incidence is beginning to decline slowly, but projective curves show more than a thousand objects eventually stopped."

"What was the diagnosis of the local physicians, doctor?" I asked Heath. Worrying it.

"Botulism, doctor." He nodded. "Some of them recognized it immediately and were able to reverse it. Some missed it completely. It *is* rare these days, Nick; you know that."

"We've been able to pillow it," Chief Director Wingate said. "The media have been very cooperative. No one wants panic."

"You said victim age peaks at fifty, doctor," I said to Heath. "Do you see any significance in that? Lowered resistance?"

"Can't see it, doctor." He shook his head. "There were many juveniles. Afflicted objects over the age of eighteen constituted 71.83 of the total. It appears to be an adult disorder, but not exclusively so."

We were all silent then. Staring blankly at each other. I computed what I had heard. The detail that impressed me most was that Dr. Winston Heath, Chief of the National Epidemiology Center, still believed that *Clostridium botulinum* was anaerobic.

It was not his fault, of course. The doctrine of "need to know," applied to scientific research, is stupid—and frequently fatal. As witness that stop rate of 76.1967 percent.

I glanced at R. Sam Bigelow's toadish scowl, then addressed the Chief Director.

"Sir," I said, "are Paul and I to assume, by the presence of the Chief of the Bureau of Public Security in a colloquy involving a public health problem, that there is reason to believe the epidemic may be—"

"Now look here, you—" Bigelow growled at me. Frog eyes popping.

But Wingate waved him down.

"No, no," he said. "A very cogent question. Nick, about two years ago a black revolutionary group tried to contaminate Denver's water supply. Last year, a group called SON . . . Ever hear of them?"

"Yes, sir," I said. "Society of Nothing. Around San Francisco. Mostly senseless assassinations. They were in all the media."

"Right." He nodded. "We took them just before they were about to feed cyanide gas into the air conditioning system of a federal think-tank in Oakland. We have absolutely no evidence of any terrorist participation in this botulism outbreak. We have received no letters or threats. We've checked our undercover agents carefully. No hint of any activity. No one in the media has received letters or threats. It may be just a medical fluke. Something no one will ever be able to explain. But I've got to cover all bases before I bring the matter to the attention of the Joint Committee on Internal Peace. That's why Chief Bigelow is here. That's why you're here. I need all the help I can get. I keep thinking that if it happened once, in GPA-11, it can happen again. Anywhere. Surely you can understand my concern."

"Of course, sir."

"Any ideas?"

"None at the moment, sir. Paul?"

"None." He shook his head. "Can we have some time on this, sir?"

"Of course." Wingate tried to smile. "You two are the very lively brains pushing a Department of Creative Science. I'm hoping you—and science— can make a significant contribution toward solving this problem. You understand?"

We understood; the velvet glove was peeling off the iron fist.

Everyone rose; the meeting broke up. Penelope Mapes came out of the shadows to open the door for us. But before we disbanded, I had the opportunity to draw Dr. Winston Heath aside.

"Doctor," I said, "it's been a pleasure seeing you again. How is the family?"

"Fine, doctor," he said. Brightening as much as a skeleton with skin can brighten.

"And that boy of yours? Scheduled for the moon colony, wasn't he?"

"That memory of yours," he said. Shaking his head. "Yes, he's up there now. We get a teleletter every week. He wouldn't be anywhere else. Enjoying every minute."

"Paleogeology, isn't it?"

"Yes, that's his discipline."

"Fine. Fascinating stuff. Doctor, about this botulism business—I don't for a moment doubt your analysis, or the diagnoses of the attending physicians, or the backup opinion of the BPS labs, but tell me—was this done on the basis of the clinical picture?"

"Of course, doctor." He looked at me strangely.

"Of course, of course," I soothed him. "Entirely understandable. Do you think you could send me some bits and pieces at GPA-1? Maybe a little blood? Just to confirm your findings. Substantiate your judgment. You know the kind of hardware we have. Excellent stuff. Some experimental. It would help us. Give the labniks a problem—right? A challenge. Who knows?"

He was thoroughly confused. As I meant him to be. All he could assimilate was that supportive testimony on his analysis could do him and the National Epidemiology Center no harm.

"Of course, doctor," he said. "Happy to cooperate. Most of what we have is frozen. But we do have some pickled stomach, I believe, and a few other things. And some very interesting slides. I'll send you what I can."

"Fine, doctor," I said. Clapping him on the shoulder. "Just fine. All contributions gratefully accepted."

"We both laughed."

"Since the matter is of such high priority and top security," I said. Leaning closer. Lowering my voice. "—Perhaps you better send it by personal courier."

"Of course, of course."

"Doctor," I said heartily. Slapping his palm. "It's a pleasure serving with you on this."

He couldn't blush with happiness. But he became less pale.

"And, doctor," I murmured, "I'm looking forward to serving much closer with you in the future."

I may have winked. I meant, of course, that the National Epidemiology Center would become part of the Department of Creative Science, and I would be ruling him. But the whole bit was lost on him. A very dull em.

"My God," Paul said. "Wouldn't it be marvelous if we could compute this botulism thing? What a leg up for the DCS!"

"Yes," I said.

We were driving back to Chevy Chase from the Georgetown White House. Paul was in an ebullient mood.

"It would solidify us with the Chief Director," he said. Almost laughed. "He'd get behind us all the way."

"Yes," I said.

"How the hell are they getting botulism, Nick? Got any ideas?"

"Ideas?" I said. "Not a one."

"That question you asked the CD about Bigelow being there—you think it's a programmed operation? Terrorist?"

"Could be."

"But *how*?"

"Don't know, Paul."

"But the motive? No letters, no threats. Even if it was an outfit like the Society of Nothing, they'd make phone calls to the media, and so forth. You know how high the ego factor is with terrorists. Why would anyone do it without taking credit?"

"What?" I said. "Oh," I said. And grimaced. "I don't know, Paul. Maybe just to destabilize the government. As basic as that."

Paul was silent. I thought he was shaken. Then he made one of those increasingly frequent jinks that vaguely disturbed me.

"Nick, we need a security officer," he said.

"What?"

"At the DCS office. We're adding objects. Expanding. And dealing with a lot of classified bumf. We need a security officer. For starters. And eventually, a security staff."

"So? Get one."

"How about Art Roach?"

"*Roach?* Why him?"

"Nick, he's down to a black zipsuit. He'd be grateful for the chance. And we own him, Nick. I've still got his tape with Seymour Dove. He'll behave. And he knows his service. Doesn't the, Nick?"

"I suppose so. All right. Maybe we owe him something. Bring him over from DOB. Serve through Penelope Mapes; she'll arrange it."

"Right, Nick. Now we're beginning to move. Don't you feel that, Nick? That things are coming our way?"

"Yes," I said.

I took a hot shower. As hot as I could endure.

I slipped naked into bed. Knowing I would be long awake. I wanted to be.

When I had been shopping for a Christmas present for Grace Wingate, I had seen—in a unisex boutique in Manhattan's Olympic Tower—a tooty blouse of a gauzy, see-through fabric. Artfully imprinted on the front, in color, were female breasts. When the blouse was worn, you could not be certain what you saw was real. That was the jerk.

Lying immobile, awake in bed, my jerk was in not knowing if the ef was real, existed or created. My own illusion. *Why?* Her neck was too long. Chin too pointed. Nose too thin. That flame of ashen hair. Undoubtedly tinted. Undoubtedly. The voice too fruity. And was there not an absence of fine intelligence? She did pick up on things. But not immediately. Certainly not Angela Berri's sharp wit. And certainly not Millie Jean Grunwald's young, tender innocence. And certainly not Maya Leighton's skilled and enthusiastic sensuality. But still . . . Still. . . .

What? *What?* Why was I willing to risk all, everything, for a convoluted ear?

Z-3

I served tough on institutionalizing the speeches I was to deliver to establishment groups all over the mainland US. And, if time allowed, in overseas suburbs.

I was jotting additional notes in my office in the GPA-1 compound when Ellen Dawes buzzed to tell me a courier had arrived with a delivery for me. Personally signed receipt requested. It was a steel box from the National Epidemiology Center, sealed with metal straps and plastiwax marks.

I signed for it, shoved it under my desk. I flashed Bob Spivey, leader of the Neuropharmacology Team. This wasn't his discipline—it wasn't anyone's, actually; we had no special chem-an team—but Spivey ruled an em named Claude Burlinghouse. The Sherlock Holmes of chemical analysis.

When Spivey came on screen, I explained what I wanted.

"Extreme priority and security," I told him.

"You want Claude, I suppose?" he asked.

"Who else? Robert, this stuff is mucho toxic."

"The fishbowl?"

"I'd say so, yes. How soon?"

"What have you got?"

"Bits and pieces of a corpus long stopped. Botulism indicated."

"Oh-ho," he said.

"Yes," I said. "But not necessarily inert."

"Three days?" he asked.

"One," I said.

"Settle for two?" he asked.

Laughing, we agreed on two. He said he'd send a messenger to pick up the specimens.

Then fat Leo Bernstein banged my door open. Without knocking. As usual. I watched Leo lower his bulk slowly into a chair, drape his bulging thighs over one of the arms.

"How long since you've seen your piccolo?" I asked him. Cruelly. "Without a mirror?"

"Who wants to see my piccolo?" He shrugged. "Not me. Nick I'm out of a job."

I stared at him a long moment. I knew the brain that hummed away in that lardy carcass. But if he didn't chisel off some of the blubber, that brain would be smothered to a stop in another ten years. I didn't want that.

"What do you mean out of a job?" I asked him.

"Fred is stabilized. No weight loss. The EEG is firmed. That hound's brain is immortal. Until someone pulls the plug. Doesn't that make you feel glad all over?"

"Congratulations, Leo."

I knew how many long hours he had served on the project. There wasn't another biochemist in the US—in the world!—who could have done it. The fat slob was a genius.

"Want to see the bumf?" he asked.

"No. I'll take your word for it."

"So I'm out of a job."

"Don't say 'job,' " I told him. "Say 'service.' "

"Say shit!" he said. Disgustedly. "Anyway, I'm finished. Got nothing to do."

"Oh?" I said. "Well, there is. . . . No, forget it."

He looked up.

"What?"

"No, nothing. Sorry I mentioned it. Just forget it, Leo."

"Goddamn it, what *is* it?"

"Leo, I'll flat with you. It's a top priority service. Hot security. Right up your plump kazoo. But I don't think you're the em for it."

"Why the hell not?" he demanded angrily.

"Leo, I told you," I said patiently. "It's top priority. I need the answers yesterday. That means I need an object with energy. Active. Someone who can get around. Look at you; you're a blob. Too bad. You'd have gotten a lot of profit from it."

"Nick, what the hell *is* it?"

I shook my head.

"Can't tell you. Ult sec. You have no need to know. But you talk about the head of Fred III being immortal. The object who comes up with the answers to this tickler *will* be immortal. And no one will ever pull the plug on *that*."

He groaned. I had him then. And knew it.

"Look, Leo," I told him. "I'll put you on this if you'll do something for me."

"What?" he said. "Anything!" he said.

"Lose three pounds a week. Promise, and I'll assign you. Then I'll weigh you. Down in the gym. We'll check every week. The first week you lose less than three pounds, you're off the project. How about it?"

"Sure, sure," he said. "I'll drop three pounds a week, Really I will, Nick. Easy."

"At first," I said. "Not after a month or so. But you stick to the three-pounds-a-week loss until I get you deflated. I'll tell you when to stop. Agreed?"

"Agreed," he said. "Sure, agreed! What is it, Nick? What's the project?"

"Just what you've done on Fred III," I said. "But for a human object."

We stared at each other. But really only I was staring at him. His eyes were on me, but his stare was inward. He was immediately computing, calculating, analyzing, figuring, determining the parameters of the problem, how to define it, how to encompass it.

"I'll need more staff," he said.

"As many as you want."

"Big budget for Tinkertoys."

"You'll get all the equipment needed."

"I can go so far *in vitro*," he said. "But sooner or later I'll need human volunteers."

"You'll get them," I said. "And I get three pounds a week."

"Goyische Shylock," he said.

I gave Bob Spivey and his Neuropharmacology Team—particularly Claude Burlinghouse—the two days he had requested for heavy analysis of the specimens forwarded from the National Epidemiology Center. I was certain, almost, what they would finalize. But I needed confirmation.

The fishbowl was in K Lab. Similar installations were frequently shown on TV and movie screens. A sealed, glass-enclosed room. No one within. Objects stood outside, manipulating specimens with long, jointed, remote-controlled grabbers. Stuff was brought into the fishbowl via a sterile lock. Chemanalysis computers were inside. Readouts or printouts were outside.

It was a slow, careful process. Especially when dealing with toxic and/or radioactive matter. The human factor was still important. In the handling, choice of technology, selection of equipment, presentation of evidence. Experts ruled our world. And not only attorneys and CPA's.

Standing outside the fishbowl with Bob Spivey and others on his team—all of us in white paper gowns and caps, like so many eager butchers—I watched with fascination while Claude Burlinghouse manipulated his stainless steel arms, hands, and fingers inside the glass. With deliberate, beautiful delicacy, he slid a mounted, microshaved specimen into the slot of a chemanalysis computer. A steel hand reached up slowly. A shiny forefinger pushed a button.

Burlinghouse turned to us.

"That's it," he said. "The last. Lousy specimens."

It took less than a minute for the final analysis. It was but one of a dozen that had been completed during the previous two days. An ef operator, sitting at the console of the master pharmaceutical file computer, added the information to what she had already stored. She faced both a cathode readout screen and an electric printout typewriter. She could have her choice or could combine the two. For instance, if she punched the readout button and then typed on the input board: $CH_3COOC_6H_4COOH$, the screen would immediately read ASPIRIN. Impressed?

But of course the master file computer was capable of infinitely more complex tasks than that. In its memory bank it had stored more than a million recipes consisting of elements and compounds. Fed input by the physiocoanalytic and chemanalysis computers, it would ponder a millisecond or two, then tell you what the stuff was you had submitted. Or, if it was an original mixture, unstored, the computer would laconically remark, on screen or typed, UNKNOWN.

I knew what was coming—and it did. The operator pushed buttons, and almost immediately the screen showed: RESTRICTED416HBL-CW3.

Bob Spivey, Claude Burlinghouse, the others—all looked at me. Disappointed.

I stared at the screen. Then said, "Erase. Everything."

Horrified, she looked to Spivey for confirmation. He nodded. Obediently she pushed a button to wipe the screen. Then she got busy blanking the input from the satellite analytic computers.

"Thanks, Robert," I said to Spivey, Stroking his palm. "Flame the specimens. Thank you, Claude." Stroking his palm. "Just what I wanted. Good service."

I strode away. Leaving them all floating. But they had no need to know.

Next stop: the office of Ass DepDir Rad. Edward Nolan, the em who had taken over from Paul Bumford when Paul moved to Washington. Ed was absent on a threeday. But I got no hassle from his Executive Assistant: She readily allowed me access to his safe. The combination had not been changed since it had been my safe, or since it had been Paul's safe. So much for security. And the drug code book was still on the upper shelf, left-hand corner. I was certain I remembered, but I felt it wise to check. I flipped pages, scanned, and there it was: 416HBL-CW3. Just as I recalled it.

It had started almost fifty years previously with the US Army's Office of Research & Development, as it was then called. *Clostridium botulinum* was but one of hundreds of protozoa, fungi, and bacteria they tinkered with in developing positive approaches to chemwar: poisons, pollutants, nerve gases, incapacitators, hypnotics, etc. At that point in time, it was believed *C. botulinum* toxin was the most virulent. Since then, of course, improved products had been developed.

We now skip to 1988. Interest in *Clostrium botulinum* had waned. There were simpler and more efficient means available.

But in 1988, a US intelligence sleeper in the Soviet Union reported a laboratory in Vitebsk had suddenly organized a restricted research project on botulism. The report was confirmed by other sources, and the flap was on.

Several US scientific agencies were put on a crash basis to develop: (1) Botulism as a viable chemwar agent: and (2) A defense against botulism used as a viable chemwar agent. One of the agencies assigned to this service was the Division of Research & Development, SATSEC, DOB, Which was how I became intimately acquainted with *Clostridium botulinum*. I was eighteen at the time.

Approximately six months after the Phase II alert, it was learned that the

Vitebsk lab was doing exactly what had been reported: It was researching the causes and prevention of botulism. Because there had been an outbreak of food poisoning in the Pinsk area, caused by spoiled canned blintzes. The Vitebsk research led to improved commercial food processing in the Soviet Union.

But before our Phase II alert was rescinded, civilian scientists under contract to the US Army had succeeded in developing a fully aerobic strain of *Clostridium botulinum*, easily cultivated *in vitro*. Suspended in glycerol, it could be sprayed on standing crops or dumped into water supplies. Quite lethal. To my knowledge it was only used once, in a field test. An obscure Marxist revolutionary in Guatemala had been manipulated into accepting a good Havana cigar. The tip of the cigar had been painted with the new compound. He lighted up, puffed, rolled the cigar around his lips. "Too sweet," he remarked. His last words.

That was 416HBL-CW3—the aerobic strain of *Clostridium botulinum*. It was in the specimens forwarded from the National Epidemiology Center. It was what was stopping all those objects in GPA-11. I had no doubt that the epidemic was programmed. But how, and by whom, and for what reason, I hadn't the slightest idea.

I intended to fly to Washington the following day to bring my discovery to the attention of the Chief Director. But late that same afternoon I received a note, via commercial mail, from Grace Wingate. Pleasant but cool. She and her aide would be in New York the following day on a shopping trip. She was writing to take advantage of my kind invitation to lunch. If that was possible, I could make arrangements through her aide. Number given.

416HBL-CW3 could wait. There was no rush, since there was no antidote. I immediately flashed the social secretary. A very imposing dragoon of an ef came on screen.

"Louise Rawlins Tucker speaking," she said crisply. "Ah, may I be of service?"

"I identified myself."

"Ah yes, Dr. Flair," she said. Consulting a list on her desk.

"We have you down for luncheon tomorrow in New York. Will that be satisfactory?"

"Yes, of course," I said. "What time will—"

"Ah, we have you down for 1300," she said. "We prefer the Café Massenet, since the premises are familiar to our security staff. Ah, will that be convenient?"

"Yes. Very."

"Ah, splendid. The party will consist of Mrs. Wingate and myself. And security staff, of course. But they will not be dining with us. The headwaiter, Henri, will have a secluded table for us in your name."

"Thank you. And I—"

"Ah, please be prompt, Dr. Flair," she said. "We do have a very tight schedule. Looking forward to meeting you in person."

I was about to return the compliment, but she clicked off. Ah.

It didn't give me much time. But I had computed how Grace Wingate and I might be alone together. Briefly. And not in my apartment, a motel room, or a lavish suite in one of the *maisons d'assignation* that had become the Park Avenue equivalent of hot-pillow joints. It was too early in our relationship to plan such a maneuver. And with her aide and security guards in atten-dance. . . .

I flashed a rental agency that specialized in elegant antique and classic cars. I knew exactly the vehicle I wanted; my father had had one in his collection: a 1972 Jaguar XKE. The agency had two available, one black and one fire-engine-red. I chose the red. In January, 1999, it would be impossible to be inconspicuous in a car like that, regardless of the color. I slid my BIN card into the flasher slot. While they were verifying my credit rating, I made arrangements for the car to be delivered to the compound gate at 1200 the following day.

It was, I knew, not a car that accommodated more than two comfortably.

The next morning I flashed Ellen Dawes and told her I would not be in the office until late that afternoon. If any insuperable crisis arose, I could be contacted at the Café Massenet after 1300.

"Nothing less than the end of the world," I told her. "On second thought, not even for that."

"I understand," she laughed.

"And I left you the coffee ration in the top file drawer. Under C. For coffee."

She giggled delightedly.

I had decided on civilian clothes. A suit of Oxford gray flannel with a Norfolk jacket. Shirt of white natural linen with a Lord Byron collar. Plas-tisilk scarf of sky blue. Black plastipat moccasins with tooty tassels. I wore a plaid cloak thrown casually over my shoulders. I smelled of elegance.

When I checked out at the compound gate at 1210, there was a gang of security guards around my red Jaguar, admiring the lines and listening to the chauffeur's lecture on the car's performance potential.

"What a cock-bucket!" one of them marveled.

"You going cruising for cush, Dr. Flair?" one of them asked.

"No," I said, "I'm taking my dear old grandmother for a spin in the coun-try."

I don't think they believed me. I signed for the car, handed the chauffeur a pat, slid behind the wheel. If I smelled of elegance, the car smelled of love. Natural glove-leather upholstery; natural burled-walnut dash. If burial had been legal, I would have opted for that car as my casket.

I pulled up in front of the Café Massenet. Directly in front. I had an instantaneous audience: passersby pausing to goggle at the car's sensuous lines. When I alighted, carrying my plaid cloak, I attracted almost as much attention.

"Big porn star," someone said knowingly.

The doorman awaited me under the canopy. I had his pat ready.

"I'm Dr. Flair," I said. "With Mrs. Wingate's party."

"Of course, Dr. Flair."

"I'd like to leave the car right there."

He glanced down at the folded bill before slipping it inside his white glove. "Of *course*, Dr. Flair!"

"I'm Dr. Flair," I said to the headwaiter. "With Mrs. Wingate's party."

"But of course, Dr. Flair! An honor, doctor!"

He snapped his fingers. Someone took my coat.

"I am Henri," he murmured. "Allow me."

He removed a minuscule bit of lint from my shoulder.

"This way, if you please, doctor," he said. "Mrs. Wingate's special table."

Heads turned to watch our passage. The trappings of power. The only objects who scoff are the powerless.

It was unquestionably the best table in the room. Secluded, but with a fine view of everything. I was the first to arrive. As I had planned. I bent my knee. A chair was gently nudged under me. The pale pink napery was so stiff it was difficult to bend.

"While the doctor is waiting?" Henri suggested diffidently. "A something?"

"A something would be nice." I nodded. "Perhaps champagne as an aperitif?"

"Oh, excellent," he chortled. "May I suggest a '91 Piper? It was a very good year."

"The Piper will be fine," I said.

"And just in time!" he cried. "For here are the ladies!"

If my entrance had occasioned glances, theirs attracted stares. The preceding black zipsuit marched past me, hand in pocket, into the restaurant's kitchen. And stayed there. Presumably guarding a back entrance. A second sentinel, an ef, took up a position behind and to one side of our table. Impassive. The third remained near the entrance. I relished every minute of it. The panoply!

"Mrs. Wingate," I said. Having risen. "How nice to see you again. And you must be Louise Rawlins Tucker. A profit."

When we were all seated:

Grace: "Nick! Did you see that antique car parked out front? What a beauty! It's all red, and so lovely!"

I (negligently): "The Jaguar? Oh, yes. It's mine."

I knew, instinctively, that Louise Rawlins Tucker, personal aide and social secretary to the Chief Director's wife, would be important to our scenario. During lunch I paid court. Not neglecting Grace Wingate, but trying to make the duenna feel she was guest and partner more than server and chaperone.

It was not difficult. Though her physical appearance was offputting—she was more yeoman than dragoon—she had an easy manner and a pretty wit. More significantly, she had an obviously deep affection for her young charge. That made us co-conspirators, did it not?

The luncheon ritual went swimmingly. Louise was wearing a dove gray flannel suit, not too unlike my own in cut. That was good for a laugh. Grace was wearing—I could not have been conscious of it since I did not remember it.

Once, while I was speaking, she reached up, listening, looking into my eyes, and twirled a vagrant strand about her finger. Slowly twisting and stroking. Ems have gone to war for less.

About Louise Rawlins Tucker:

She was an obso, quite large, with enough lumps and blotches to remind me of leonine faces. But she was obviously not a victim of *Mycobacterium leprae*; simply an unfortunate, unprepossessing ef. With a wry, self-deprecating charm that included amusement at her own officiousness.

I wondered—part-wondered—if she sensed my interest in Grace Wingate and might not be a closet romantic. Because, under my gentle prying, she revealed that she had devoted most of her adult life to the care of her widowed father. A professor of Romantic Literature at Georgetown University.

"Isn't all literature romantic?" I asked.

"Ah," she said.

Then, upon her father's stopping, she had created a whole new life for herself.

"I don't know what I'd do without Louise," Grace Wingate said fondly. Putting her soft, tanned hand on the other ef's claw. "Just perish, I suppose."

"Ah, I'd do anything for you, angel," Louise Rawlins Tucker vowed. Fiercely. "*Anything*."

I had the oddest notion that she was speaking to me. A promise. And a warning.

When we went outside, preceded and followed by black zipsuits, there was an admiring audience circling the red Jaguar. The doorman looked on benignly.

"Nick," Grace Wingate said, "is it really yours?"

"For the day," I said. "A ride?"

"Oh! What a profit!"

She looked to Louise Rawlins Tucker.

"Grace, you can't," her aide said. "We're running so late."

"A half-hour," I pleaded. "Around town. Through Central Park. You and the guards can trail us."

"Louise?" Grace said. "Please? May I?"

"Ah," the yeoman said. Looking at me. "Well.... Twenty minutes. No more. We'll be right behind you."

So they were: two black limousines following my every turn. I didn't care. I was alone with Grace. I laughed. She laughed.

"You *are* a scamp!" she said. "Do you ever run out of ideas?"

"Never," I said. "But this is a one-shot. We can't do it again."

"No," she said. Regretfully. "I suppose not. Oh, Nick, it's *such* a car."

It was. It handled like a muscled ef. I turned smoothly into Central Park, heading north, making the grand circuit. Children were sledding. Booting a soccer ball through the snow. Chasing. There were dogs. Objects were sauntering. Couples. Users, I supposed.

"Grace," I said.

"What?" she said.

"Nothing," I said. "Just Grace."

She put her hand lightly on my arm. A few months previously she had told me of her love for her husband. How she would do anything to preserve her marriage. And now she was. . . . But I didn't think less of her for that. It made her infinitely more precious. Idealism was for scoundrels. I wasn't that. Quite. Nor was she.

"Grace," I said again.

"Yes?"

"What are you wearing?"

"Didn't you notice? Brute! I wore it just for you."

"All I could see was you."

She could not snuggle; the limousine was close behind. But her arm moved sideways. Hand probed. I moved up casually in my bucket seat so she could clasp my waist.

I took a deep breath.

"I love you," I said.

It didn't hurt.

"Yes," she said.

"Will you say it?" I asked her.

"No," she said. Quite low. "Not yet."

"But you shall?"

"I think so. Please, Nick. Time."

"Oh, yes." I nodded. "As much as you want. And then I shall have your ears."

"My ears?" She was astounded.

I told her how I worshiped her ears. She was amused. And touched. I thought.

"I'll cut them off and mail them to you," she said. "Dear, sweet Nick." She touched my beard. Quickly.

"What are we to do?" I asked.

She thought a long moment. But I knew she had already computed it.

"Do you like Louise?" she asked.

"Yes. Very much."

"She lives alone in this big house in Chevy Chase. Not too far from where you and Paul live. Since her father stopped, she has become very social. Her parties are famous. Very tooty. Mike is away a lot. Out of the mainland. It would be all right if I went to Louise's parties. Mike would approve."

"Would Louise? I mean, would she invite me?"

"Yes. If I asked."

"You trust her?"

"With my life."

"Exactly," I said. "It may come to that."

"I'm willing. Are you?"

"There's a sharp curve up ahead," I said. "To the left. I'm going to speed up suddenly. We'll be around the turn before the limousines catch up. They won't see us. I can bend to you. You can bend to me. Briefly."

"Yes," she said.

So we did. We kissed. Oh.

The next day I took the air shuttle to Washington. I had flashed ahead to set up a facial with the Chief Director. Penelope Mapes came on screen.

"I've got to see him," I said.

"No, Nick," she said. "He's got a full plate."

"It's about GPA-11," I said.

"Oh," she said. "Take a beat."

She went off screen. Then came on a moment later.

"Should Bigelow be there?" she asked.

"Yes."

"Take two beats," she said. And disappeared again. Finally she came back on.

"Got you in," she said. "At 2030 tonight. Here, at the EOB."

The shuttle got me to Washington an hour before my meet. I took the Metro to the Lafayette Square stop. I was carrying no luggage. I intended to stay overnight, but I had clothes and toilet gear in the Chevy Chase place. As I did in Grosse Pointe. It would, I thought, be nice, some day, to settle. Put down roots. Obso thinking. To settle was to stop.

I was still early for my meeting with the CD. I walked in, unannounced, to the office of the gestating Department of Creative Science. After all, it was *my* office. In the basement of the EOB. A suite of three rooms, in the disarray of enlargement. No one about. Machines shrouded. But in the inner office, Paul's sanctum, lights and the sound of voices. I pushed open the door. Paul, Mary, Maya Leighton, Seth Lucas, Art Roach.

"Ah-ha," I said. "Gotcha."

"Hey, Nick." Paul said. Genially. Uncoiling from his swivel chair behind the desk.

"Dr. Flair," Roach said. Solemnly. "I haven't had a chance to thank yawl for what you did."

"Sure," I said. "We stroke you, you stroke us. Keeping an eye on the stamps and petty cash around here?"

Then they were all silent. Suddenly.

"Art just took over," Paul said. "A few days ago. Doing good service. Some creative ideas. What gives, Nick?"

I thought the mass was stressed. But when you lived in a paranoiac world, you learned to breathe suspicion.

"Got a meet with the CD, Paul," I said. "Can you make it?"

"About the DCS?" he asked anxiously.

"No. Something else."

"Nick, I have a meeting of the Beists' finance committee."

"Go," I said. "By all means." I turned to Seth Lucas. "How's your patient, Seth?"

"Just stopped by to say hello," he said.

"Lewisohn did?"

"No, no," he said hurriedly. "No change in Lewisohn. Maya and I came over for a seminar."

"Oh?" I said. "What seminar?"

"Not a seminar," Paul said testily. "How many times do I have to tell you, Seth? It's not a seminar, it's a hearing. House Committee on Science and Astronautics, Nick. I wanted to condition Seth and Maya to the drill. They may be called upon to testify."

"They may indeed." I nodded.

"See you later, Nick?" Maya smiled at me. "After your meeting?"

It was pulling in all directions. Stretched and disturbing.

"I may be a while," I said.

"Seth is going back to the Hospice," she said. "I'm staying over with Mary out in Chevy Chase."

"Fine," I said. "Maybe I'll see you there. Paul, can I talk to you for a minute?"

It had been a curious exchange. No structure. I could not compute it. It was my fault, I supposed, for barging in suddenly.

Paul followed me out into the corridor.

"That business in GPA-11," I said. Low voice. "It's a manipulated strain of *Clostridium botulinum*. Aerobic."

He looked at me. Startled.

"My God," he breathed. "How did you get onto that?"

"Heavy analysis of specimens from the National Epidemiology Center. The strain was developed during chemwar research in 1988."

"Never heard of it."

"You wouldn't. Not the original research. Before your time. But it was listed in the restricted drug code book. I'd have thought you'd remember. Didn't you scan it when you were AssDepDirRad?"

"Well, sure," he said. "But Nick, there must be a hundred stews in that book."

A serpent began to stir.

"Close to it," I said.

"Well, there you are," he said. "How is it administered?"

"No idea," I said. "I'm telling Wingate right now. Then it's Bigelow's migraine."

"Oh? He'll be there?"

"Of course."

"Well, don't take any kaka from him, Nick. I happen to know his status is fragile."

"My son, the pol," I said.

Chief Director Michael Wingate and Chief of the Bureau of Public Security R. Sam Bigelow were seated in the dining area of the CD's office when Penelope Mapes ushered me in. The remains of a meal littered the table. Both ems appeared frayed.

"Well, Nick?" the Chief Director demanded. "What have you got for us?"

"Sir," I said, "I had heavy analysis done on specimens sent from the National Epidemiology Center. That outbreak in GPA-11 is caused by a manipulated strain of the botulism bacterium. It's aerobic. Meaning it can exist in the presence of oxygen."

"I don't believe it," R. Sam Bigelow said angrily. Frog face going in and out.

"It's not important what you believe," I said. I was, I admit, relieving my growing hostility on him. "It's operative."

"Now see here, you—" he began.

Wingate raised a hand. Bigelow's mouth snapped shut. The CD stared at him.

"Why didn't Heath know about this?" he said coldly. "More to the point, Sam, why didn't you know about it?"

"Listen, Chief," Bigelow said hotly, "you can't expect the Bureau's labs to know about every poison developed by the Department of Bliss."

"It wasn't developed by the Department of Bliss," I said. "This particular poison was developed by the Department of Peace. In a Phase II alert, ten years ago."

"Shit," Bigelow said disgustedly. "All right. Write it down. We'll check it out."

I looked around for something to write on. Penelope Mapes was at my elbow instantly with pencil and scratchpad. I jotted the name of the bacterium and the code number and slid it across the table to Bigelow.

"Any cure, Nick?" the Chief Director asked.

"An antidote? No, sir. Not to my knowledge. The alert was canceled before we went that far."

"Shit," Bigelow repeated. And glowered at me as if I had personally stopped every one of those victims in GPA-11.

"Then the outbreak is programmed," Wingate said. No idiot he.

"Yes, sir." I nodded. "No doubt about it."

"Any idea how they're doing it?" the Chief Director asked.

"No, sir. Not really. You might have the field investigator check out fiddled cigarettes and cigars. But it's a very long shot, considering the age-victim numbers. It's something else. Got to be."

"Don't worry, we'll find it," Bigelow grumbled.

"I'm sure you will," I said equably. The toadish em bored me. Suddenly the whole fracture bored me. Not half so significant as a soft kiss, in a closed car, on a swift turn, in Central Park.

"Grace told me you entertained her at lunch in New York. Michael Wingate said. Walking me to the door. "That was kind of you, Nick."

"My profit, sir."

"Yes. And thank you for your service on this business. We'll take it from here."

It was late, but I was able to draw wheels from the EOB motor pool. I drove to Chevy Chase slowly. Much had happened in the past hour that I wanted to compute. But all I could reckon was my own obsession.

I estimated her weight at about fifty kilos. All stuff. Wind it up and set it ticking. No different. It was operative that she was comely, but so were millions of other efs and ems. Why she? No great beauty. No great wit. She was simply who she was.

I drove in a glaze. What bemused me was my chilly somberness in computing all this. And my total disregard of the possible consequences. Dreaming of her, even doom seemed a profit.

Z-4

From an address to a cadre of fourteen-year-old neuro-physiologists under accelerated conditioning at Duke University, Durham, North Carolina, February fourth, 1999:

"There was a time when a conditioned obso, expert in his discipline, might spend a lifetime studying Sumerian script. I suggest to you that this was less discipline than self-indulgence! (Laughter)

"I will not insult your intelligence by calling you the 'wave of the future.' I will say only that today, and tomorrow, your brains are needed. There is vital service to be done, a world to remake, and it is to enlist your aid in remaking that world that I am here tonight.

"When you leave this hall, you will be given Instox copies of HR-316, a bill to establish a Department of Creative Science in the Public Service, as submitted by the Chief Director to the House of Representatives for debate and approval. We hope!

"I would like to call your attention to Division III, Section 8 of that bill. It deals with staff organization of the proposed Department. You will find frequent mention of the term 'omnists.' I would like to take a few moments, if I may, to analyze for you what our computing was on this subject, and why we created the term 'omnist' to describe the scientist of tomorrow."

From an address to the National Association of Drug Manufacturers at their convention in Miami, Florida, February fifth, 1999:

"All right, having now outlined the new bill, let me ask and answer the question: 'How will the Department of Creative Science affect your organization and the future of drug biz in the US and in the world?'

"Let me make one thing perfectly clear: We haven't yet moved the bill out of the House Committee considering it, and already, amongst those serving to do exactly that, aspirin consumption is up three hundred percent! (Laughter)

"Seriously, I believe the DCS will prove the greatest boon to the drug industry since the synthesizing of steroids. Not because there is any one division, section, paragraph, or even a single word in the bill that applies particularly to the drug structure. But because the fundamental belief of the new Department of Creative Science will be in the holistic nature of science. The goal of all science is the improvement of the species. It's as simple as that. And it is there, precisely, that you and your industry will be expected to play a crucial role.

"I suggest to you that the time has passed to consider drugs within a limited, therapeutic frame of reference. Up to this point in time, you have been engaged essentially in producing a negative pharmacology: antiheadache, antiarteriosclerosis, antipimple, antidepression, and so forth.

"We, who are devoting our energies, talents, and brains to the DCS, believe the time has now arrived to develop a positive pharmacology. We are irrevocably committed to serving closely with you in researching a whole new spectrum of physical strength and mental health stimulators, to enable the human race to cope with the future and to fulfill its potential as the most creative species the universe has ever seen." (Applause)

From extempore remarks to a symposium of hostile media students at the University of Missouri, February 8, 1999:

"What on earth makes you think you are the anointed? To sit in judgment on the actions of objects in high places? To scorn their talents, misrepresent their motives, ridicule their sacrifices?

"You are falling into exactly the same trap that demolished the reputation of professional economists in the 1970's. They saw their occupation as a discipline apart, existing in *vacuo*, with its own laws, precepts, equations, logic, and goals. Then they awoke one day to discover it was all mush. They had neglected to consider the political factor, the social element, and all their fine computing amounted to a heap of kaka because their imput was faulty.

"I suggest that you ponder that example. Do you really believe you can write your news stories, shoot your documentaries, film your interviews, compose your editorials, from some slightly yellowed and stained ivory tower where reality is not allowed to intrude? Such an attitude is worse than foolish; it is dangerous. You are of this world. Your service is of this world. You deny the future at your peril."

From final remarks to a meeting of graduate neurobiologists at the National Science Academy, February 11, 1999:

"The important thing is not to waste time searching for answers to questions for which there are no answers."

I delivered 12 speeches in eighteen days, and took part in 6 symposia, 8 colloquies, and submitted to 16 radio and television interviews. I visited nursery schools, academies, colleges, universities, laboratories, factories, power installations. I stroked innumerable palms, smiled until I feared my face would crack, and was photographed in close conversation with a former President. His breath was foul.

Joseph Tyrone Wellington provided a PR staff of four. An advance em moved one day ahead of us, confirming arrangements, making contacts, setting up local media. Traveling with me were: (1) A technical em who checked out public address systems, seating arrangements, local radio and TV coverage, etc.; (2) A security em in civilian clothes who was responsible for antiterrorist planning and travel arrangements; and (3) An extremely tall, attenuated ef named Samantha Slater. "Just for laughs," Joe Wellington had whispered. Winking.

In fact, Samantha was remarkably competent and held the entire safari together. She got us where we had to be on time, paid motel bills, carried an inexhaustible pharmacopoeia, and, from the first day, when we surrendered to the hysteria, she and I used each other with profit. Frequently. Everywhere. Once, standing up in a phone booth. Once, blue with cold, on a hotel terrace. Her corpus was incredible. Like using a worm.

We finally got to Detroit where I addressed a formal dinner meeting (red tie) of richnik industrialists. I told them that, if they didn't know it already, research and development were their only guarantee of continued growth.

And the proposed Department of Creative Science stood foursquare for research and development. Applause was generous.

So generous that I told them that as industrial managers, they must also learn that innovative ideas in political and social orbits could be just as lovable. This time the applause was polite.

We had structured a break upon reaching Detroit. The rest of the party went on to Buffalo where I would rejoin them in two days. I cabbed out to Grosse Pointe and fell into bed. Coming down slowly from my energizer high. I awoke fourteen hours later, wishing Samantha Slater was there. She could twist her . . .

My father was away for the day on a business trip. Mrs. McPherson, Miss Catherine, and Charles seemed delighted to have my company. The weather was miserable. Extraordinarily cold. So I stayed indoors all day and the four of us played cartel bridge, the new form of contract that had been devised in 1996. We had an occasional pitcher of hot flip.

"Another small glass, Mrs. McPherson?" I'd ask.

"Oh, sor!" she'd say. "Well . . . just to keep the freeze away."

Miss Catherine helped her to bed. Charles snoozed where he was, in a library chair. They were good obsos, all of them, and had absolutely no connection with what was to follow.

I called Millie Jean Grunwald early in the evening. She sounded happy to hear from me. But Millie was always happy. I made arrangements to pick her up at 2030. Despite the weather, Millie wanted to go. I was in a similar mood.

I drove slowly through a thick night. Wet snow. Wipers licking at the windshield. I thought again of Samantha's talents. Millie was waiting for me in the doorway of her building. The porn shop, at street level, was dark, empty.

After she bounced breathlessly into the car, kissing me, and her door was closed, I gestured toward the deserted store.

"What happened?" I asked. "Out of business?"

"Uh-huh." She nodded. Then giggled. "One day they were there, the next day they were all cleared out. Nick, you should see the roaches and mice that have been coming upstairs to me since the shop closed."

Millie had a sleazy plastivet cloak across her shoulders. She pulled it open proudly to display her tooty costume: a blouse of strips of fabric gathered at neck, wrists, and waist. But gaping to reveal her naked torso. Nipples nuzzled through. And purple tights imprinted with a great orchidaceous growth, sprouting from her crotch with stems, leaves, flowers down her legs and around her ass. Boots of silver plastikid.

"Loverly," I said. "Really, it is. But the snowflake around your neck. Too much, Millie."

"But you gave it to me, Nick."

"I know. But it detracts from the overall effect."

Obediently she took it off. I slid it into my purse.

"Much better," I assured her. "Millie, you're beautiful."

"Oh, yes," she sighed. Slumping contentedly. Head falling sideways onto my shoulder. "I feel beautiful when I'm all dressed up."

She knew exactly where she wanted to go: the Lords Sporting Club. I had never heard of the club, but guessed what it might be.

The Lords Sporting Club was set off Gratiot Avenue in a whitewashed, one-story, cinder-block building. I judged it had been a former garage or supermarket. A single dim neon sign said simply: LORDS. With a red outline of a fighting cock beneath.

Parking space was ample. But lovable. So was the admittance. Behind a dock, just inside the door, a large primate in a crimson mess jacket inspected us coldly.

"Member, are you?" he asked. His voice had the peculiar harsh raspiness I usually associated with laryngeal nodules.

"Unfortunately no," I said. "May I join?"

"Twenty for a card for one," he said. "Entitles you to bring a guest. Ten each for tonight's show."

I looked at Millie. Her eyes were shining.

"All right," I said. "Credit on my BIN?"

"Love," he said.

I counted out the forty. He held each bill under ultraviolet light before he accepted it. Then he took a blank membership card from a stack.

"Name?" he asked.

"Smith," I said. "James Smith."

He wrote it in swiftly. Shoved the card across to me.

"A lot of your relatives inside," he said. Not smiling.

"All named John?" I asked.

"How did you guess?" he said.

"Take care of that throat," I said.

The interior was one large room. A crowded bar at one end. A uninest at the other. The backless bleachers were ranked about a pit of hard-packed earth. A fence of chicken wire separated the pit from the downfront rows. The room was hot, fogged with cannabis smoke, raucous with the cries of vendors and markers. But it was not completely filled; we found aisle seats about halfway up to the ceiling. Stifling.

"Isn't this exciting?" Millie said delightedly.

It was a five-match exhibition. The first event, a cockfight, was just concluding when we took our seats. One of the birds was staggering, dusty, torn. The other stalked relentlessly. The outcome seemed obvious. I looked about.

A very tooty audience. I saw one em with a metallic codpiece, artfully jointed like the arm of a medieval suit of jousting armor. There were several efs bare to the waist. Poor Millie, with her gaping strips, seemed almost overdressed. One ef, an unzipped cape hanging from her shoulders, appeared to be wearing a skinsuit in a pattern copied after Mondrian. A second look revealed she was naked, the squares and lines painted on her flesh. The em across the aisle from me wore a giant gold-plated phallus on a chain about his neck. It would not have been remarkable except that it was decorated with a small, violet ribbon bow.

There was a sudden roar. I looked back to the pit. The victor had sunk a spike into the eye and brain of the vanquished. There was a rapid flurry of feathers, a spreading stain. Handlers came forward to remove their birds. Attendants sprinkled fresh earth and swept the pit clean.

There was a harsh crackling from the loudspeaker. Then a voice boomed clear: "Second event of the evening coming up. Champion My Own Ripper versus Champion Devil's Delight."

If you wish to name your dog Champion this or that, there is no law against it. The scurviest mongrel in Christendom might be called Champion La Belle Dame Sans Merci, and no one would sue. The two dogs led into the pit were "Champions" of that order. I thought there might be a few vagrant bull-terrier genes in both, but the rest was up for grabs. One was a dirty white, the other a dirty buff. But both showed encouraging ferocity. Straining against their choke leashes, snarling, yellowed teeth naked. Eyes wild. Slavering. Doping there.

"Eight for five on the white," a frantic voice screamed in my ear. "Three to two on the tan."

I turned my head.

"Ten on the white," I said.

"You've got it," he shouted. Marking it down.

More noise now. Almost every seat filled. Objects leaning forward. Tense.

"Gentlemen," the steward said solemnly. "Pit your dogs."

It was a good fight. Even before it started, Millie's fingers were clamped on my knees. Pressure increased as the bout progressed. I was scarcely conscious of it. Staring at the action in the pit. Trying to follow the whirl of straining bodies. Jaws snapping for the killing bite.

Both dogs were quickly blooded. White with his left hindquarters ripped. Buff with a shoulder matted with gore and pit dirt. A feral roar ripped the room. Atavistic. "Kill 'im, kill 'im, kill 'im!"

It ended suddenly. White finally found buff's throat. He would not let go despite buff's wild writhings and tumblings. Then the bite of throat ripped free. Buff stood a moment on quivering legs. The heart still pumped. Hot blood sprayed over the first few rows.

"Ahhhh," everyone breathed.

The marker paid me off without comment or expression.

The third event was ridiculous. Two efs, one white, one black, clad in tiny *cache-sexe* with aluminum cups over their breasts, belabored each other with padded gloves. The audience grew restive during this farce. Then I saw the reason for the chicken-wire fence about the pit. It wasn't to protect the customers from violence, but to protect the performers. All the missiles fell harmlessly into the first few rows. Occasioning a few private squabbles that were more enjoyable than the languid action in the pit.

But the fourth event restored the crowd's fever. Two bare-knuckled ems, wearing only aluminum cups over their genitals. Both were heavily muscled, not young, and both showed scarcely healed scars and purpled bruises from similar, fairly recent bouts.

"Twenty on baldy," I said to the marker.

"You've got it," he shouted. Marking it down.

The encounter was strangely stirring. I could observe it, analyze it, reject it. But I was moved, physically and emotionally, in a way I could not compute. Part of it, I told myself, was empathic: identification with the crowd's mood. And with Millie's. She was quaked. Her fingernails dug deeply into the side of my thigh.

The bout lasted for a single fifteen-minute round. There was one judge, but only to warn on fouls. Decision-making was vested in the audience. They made clear from the start that the shaggy-haired gladiator was their favorite. If the fight went the full fifteen minutes, and came to a roared vote, my "twenty on baldy" was down the pipe.

It went down sooner than that. Shaggy opened a barely healed cut over his opponent's right eye. Blood streaked baldy's face, mixed with dust from the pit floor to cast a clown's mask.

Baldy was willing, if inexpert. As long as he could, he kept thudding his huge fists into shaggy's torso. You could see the reddened marks on chest, ribs, solar plexus. And, when baldy saw a target, on back and kidneys. The only results were clearly audible *whumps*, but they slowed shaggy not a whit. Methodically, precisely, he cut baldy's face to ribbons. Completely closing one eye. Goring the other. Ripping the lips loose. Breaking teeth.

Baldy's torn left ear was hanging crazily. Both eyes were blinded. Forehead, cheeks, and chin looked like filleted beef. He swayed on his feet. Arms fell slowly to his sides. He slouched. Clotted eyes peering up at the noise booming down. His knees sagged.

Shaggy had no need for skill then. No fancy footwork or artful dodging. He stood planted, estimated the distance, drew back stone knuckles, crashed them into baldy's nose. Great gouts of blood spouted. The defeated em toppled face down as if someone had axed him.

They dragged him off, sprinkled fresh earth, swept the pit smooth.

"Enjoying it?" I asked Millie.

"Nick," she said. Holy tones. "It was the most marvelous thing I've ever seen. I came."

"Good on you," I said. "Let's have a drink before the next bout. I'm thirsty."

We had miniatures of vodka-and-Smack, warm, purchased from a vendor at horrendous cost. Then, since the final attraction seemed delayed, we each had two more.

I shall never know whether the last bout on the evening's card was genuine, fixed, or—as I suspected—a sophisticated theatrical turn in which the participants were not opponents, but partners in a choreographed athletic ballet.

They entered the pit naked. The raucous audience fell silent, since both were quite beautiful. Catcalls, at the moment, would have been infratooty.

The young ef, introduced as Janet, was tall, slender, with purplish hair down to her waist. Small breasts, but well formed. Elongated nipples, faint aureole. Pubic hair shaven. Protuberant *mons veneris*. Flat abdomen. Excellent musculature. A cold, composed face.

The young em, introduced as Eric; was about the ef's height. Almost as slender, with a well-defined rib cage. Enlarged gastrocnemii indicated a dancer or runner. He was circumcised. Length of the penis was not unusual, but the thickness was. Hirsute scrotum. Well-developed pectorals and deltoids. His blond hair would have reached his shoulders, but was pulled back and gathered with what appeared to be a pipe cleaner.

The only things worn, by both fighters, were brown natural-leather gloves. Skin-tight.

At the gong, they moved cautiously toward each other. Lightly. Delicately. Bodies were turned slightly sideways. Hands and arms were held extended, waist-high. I wondered if, instead of a boxing match, this was to be judo, jujitsu, karate, kung fu, or any of the other Oriental martial arts.

It apparently was to be a combination of all, for the first blow essayed was a lightning-fast kick Janet aimed at Eric's groin. His reactions were swift: He drew back just enough to slip the flashing heel, then chopped the edge of his right hand across Janet's breast. I could hear her hiss.

I could hear it because that vociferous mob was, unexpectedly, suddenly silent. Perhaps there was a susurration, a low moan, a whispered, "Ahhhh." But no shouts, cries, cheers, jeers. Even the vendors and markers were quiet.

If it was a choreographed dance, it was an uncommonly brutal one. She kicked continually, almost turning her back to him as her foot slashed sideways. Aimed always at his testicles. He depended mostly on his hands and elbows, going for her unprotected breasts. Striking with scraping blows, using the edge of his gloved hand.

I could hardly believe it had all been programmed. Both gladiators were shiny with sweat, welted from blows taken, quivering from blows launched and missed. Eric was bleeding from thigh rip. One of Janet's breasts was suddenly livid.

Then, after about five minutes of careful maneuverings, great leaps, rapid flurries, and just as artful withdrawals, they appeared to be carried away by the primitivity of their conflict. This, too, may have been programmed. But speed increased, movements became wilder. More and more frequently we heard the smack of tightly gloved fists on young flesh, crack of heel or edge of foot against bone and tendon. Gasps and sobs for breath. I fancied I could smell them. Their young sweat. Hot blood. Even their charged fury.

They couldn't have been pulling those punches and kicks; I swear they could not. Flesh became lumped and rare. Slick with blood, mottled with pit dust. And when the gong sounded, ending the bout, they refused to stop. But now they were grappling close, straining against each other. It appeared he was trying to throw her to a fall, one heel hooked behind her right knee, pinioning her wrists as she strove to smash a gloved fist into his gonads, and she was biting his ear while his head swung wildly, butting her, and their slippery loins were pressed, smacked, again and again, and then, finally, a great roar went up from the crowd and, in cadence, we all shouted, "Draw! Draw! Draw! Draw!" Like the caw of waterbirds over the lake, and it was all so stupid, and Millie was actually weeping, and I had an erection that would never end. Ever. And we, Millie and I, the crowd, stumbled slowly away, and I passed the primate in the crimson mess jacket, still behind his dock, and he stared at me bleakly and rasped, "Enjoy yourself? Mr. Smith?"

I ignored him and bought Millie a souvenir from a vendor. A small stuffed pit dog. Its coat dyed with realistic bloodstains.

I have said that passion dooms profitable using, and it does. Millie and I were tuned to a tight, tinny pitch, but nothing we did that night opened the gates we wanted thrown free. I know it was so with me; I believe it was so with her. If that last fight had been a designed ballet, then I blamed art. For always offering the receding carrot. Beauty. Mystery. Ecstasy. I wanted only the now. The flat and tasteless now.

I was worse than her; I could not stop talking that night. To her sprawled, unhearing, somnolent corpus. All my problems. All my troubles. Stress pouring from me in a hemorrhage. That sweated bed became a confessional, and I meandered on about *Clostridium botulinum* and Grace Wingate and what I planned to do to Hyman R. Lewisohn. She did not hear me. But even if she had, she would not have understood. She was a poor, retarded clone with punched breasts and punished thighs, and what could she compute of the Department of Creative Science?

At some point in time, during that verbal diarrhea, I came around to Egon Schiele, whose art, I then realized, I had been sedulously avoiding for so long. There was something there, I said aloud, something there, something in his paintings and drawings frighteningly akin to what I had just seen: Janet and Eric seeking to chop each other to deadening pain.

It was all beyond me. I glimpsed rather than saw. Until I grew weary with disemboweling myself to a gently snoring Millie. I switched off the lamp. Listened awhile to the soft scuttling of mice displaced from the vacated porn shop below. And, finally, fell asleep.

Then back to Grosse Pointe the following morning. Curiously refurbished from the previous night's folly. As if I had been flayed and then fitted with a smartly tailored suit of Juskin. Guaranteed blemish-free.

The house seemed crowded. My father had returned, bringing with him his production, marketing, and PR staffs. Ben Baker was the only object I knew. I was introduced to the others: names and faces of no significance to this account.

I sat in on the afternoon session, listening to the set speeches and the colloquy that followed. It soon became evident to me that the Die-Dee Doll was an intoxicating success. I learned that production shortfalls had limited love input during the Christmas selling season, but a new assembly plant had been brought onto line, and sales were overachieving in the postchris period.

"Ethnic markets are incredible," the sales chief enthused.

"Much better than projected. Take Africa. We're airlifting the DD-4, 5, and 6 models: light tan, dark brown, black. The DD-6 in tribal dress is moving exceptionally fast. We're getting reports from our field ems that in some places, back in the bush, natives are worshiping the dolls!"

I gathered that, all over the world, little efs, and some little ems, were anxiously watching their Die-Dee Dolls, waiting for the rattle that presaged the end. In Scotland, Die-Dee Dolls in kilt and plaid. In Hong-Kong, in miniature cheongsam. In Japan, in kimono and obi. In California, in bikini (topless). In Greenland, in plastifurs. And so forth. All over the globe the final rattles sounded on the wind, and children rushed to inter the remains.

Then the meet was over; guests began departing by car and by copter. Finally, my father and I, alone, moved into the library. Giving Mrs. McPherson and Charles a chance to clean up the littered dining room.

"Nick-ol'-as!" my father shouted. Clapping me on the shoulder. "Good to see you, boy. You look peakish. Serving hard?"

"Very hard." I nodded.

"Little medicine for the doctor," he chuckled. Pouring us snifters of brandy. "I'm hearing and scanning a lot about you these days."

I said nothing.

"How's it coming?" he asked. "This Department of Creative Science? Think you'll slip it by?"

"We're hoping."

"It sounds good to me," he said stoutly. "I've spoken to a few objects about it. Heavy objects. They're sympathetic. But they'd feel better if they knew who'll be Director. I tell them you. Right?"

"Probably."

"Counting on it?" he asked shrewdly.

"Sure. But no guarantee."

"I wish you were in Washington. That's where the action is."

"They've got me on the road, doing the PR. That's important, too."

"No doubt about it," he assured me. "Very important. But Washington. . . . Paul Bumford's handling things there?"

"Yes. He's running the temporary DCS office."

"Uh-huh. Well, you know the obso stories about the traveling salesmen?

How much cush they get away from home? But no one mentions how much the old lady gets at home, while hubby's away. You follow?"

"Oh, sure." I nodded. "I follow. But I trust Paul."

"Uh-huh. But D.C. does strange things to young fellers. It's like their first drunk. Their first lay. A taste of what it's all about. I've been computing. . . . Suppose this: Suppose, unofficially, I organize a committee. 'Businessmen for the DCS.' Something like that. Get some big names. Lean a little on the Washington crowd. Would that help?"

"One hell of a lot. Thank you, Father."

"And while we're leaning, we can pass a few nudges that our cooperation depends on your becoming Director. How does that jerk you?"

"I like it, I like it!" I said. As enthusiastically as I could. "I'd really appreciate that."

"Good as done," he said. Finishing his brandy in a gulp. "Well. . . . I've got a few little things to do."

I must have looked amused.

"I don't want to talk about this one, Nick," he said.

"All right."

"No jokes. Please."

"All right," I repeated patiently. "No jokes."

"This one may be serious," he said solemnly. "I'm really jerked."

"Glad to hear it."

"Would you be sore, Nick? If—"

"If you married again? Of course not. It's your life."

"Well, I haven't decided," he said. "If I do, you'll be the first to know."

"If you do," I said, "I think I better be the second to know."

"Nick-ol'-as!" he said fondly.

On to Buffalo. A speech there, and at Rochester. A private conversation with the Governor in Albany. A symposium at MIT and a colloquy at Harvard. Then back to Manhattan Landing while the others continued on to Washington.

"So nice." Samantha Slater smiled. Slowly stroking my palm. "I'm looking forward to our next tour."

"My pleasure," I said.

"Oh, no," she said. "Mine."

During the twenty-six days I had been absent, I had kept in contact with Ellen Dawes in GPA-1 and Paul Bumford in Washington, D.C., via a Portaphone, a portable radiotelephone in an attaché case. With a scrambler attachment. Paul had nothing urgent. The methodology of the programmed nutbreak of botulism in GPA-11 was still unsolved. HR-316 was coming up for amendment votes in the House Government Operations Committee. The

DCS office in EOB basement had been expanded. Art Roach had added two black zipsuits to his staff. And, oh, yes—there was a hand-addressed letter to me from Louise Rawlins Tucker. I asked Paul to open it and read it to me. Louise thanked me for the enjoyable lunch and invited me to a dinner party the second week in March, date and time to be confirmed later. I told Paul I'd take care of it when I returned.

"Louise Rawlins Tucker," he said. "She's Grace Wingate's AA, isn't she?"

"Social secretary," I said.

Ellen Dawes' news wasn't as welcome. Nothing catastrophic had occurred in my absence, but the Satisfaction Rate continued to decline, and Lewisohn's vital signals continued to deteriorate. And there was a courier-delivered letter from the Bureau of Public Security. It was marked "FIA"—For Immediate Action. That, in BPS nomenclature, was akin to California canners marking a jar "Gigantic olives."

"Hold it for me," I told Ellen. "If it was really hot, the courier would have waited for a reply. Miss me?"

"Oh, yes," she said. "We're running out of coffee."

Dear, sweet Ellen. I needed her, occasionally, to snub me back to operative values.

I was glad to get back to GPA-1. To shower with a large cake of perfumed soap. To mix a big vodka-and-Smack with a slice of natural lime from three I had found in Florida. Generally to unwind. I pulled on a tattered, soft-as-silk zipsuit and old moccasins. I riffled through the personal mail that had accumulated in my absence. Bills, mostly. Some invitations to speak, write, submit to interviews, attend symposia. One of the latter, on megapopulation, was to be held in Reykjavik. Seemed an odd place for it. Why not Calcutta?

Later in the evening, about 2130, I pulled on a hooded oilskin and dashed across the snowy compound to my office. My desk was piled high. I zipped through it swiftly.

Hospice No. 17 in Little Rock reported that a "volunteer," who had been given a total transfusion of newly formulated synthetic blood, had lasted eighty-six hours. Possibly Angela Teresa Berri. But eighty-six hours wasn't bad; they were getting there.

Phoebe Huntzinger had submitted a lengthy status update. Progress was continuing on Project Phoenix. Coherent conceptions were being drained from volunteers' brains with increasing frequency and heightened sensitivity. Her use of the word "drained" excited a realization of how valuable the new technique might prove in interrogative procedures.

Leo Bernstein's report consisted of three words: "No significant progress." But I knew Leo; nothing was significant to him except the solution. I was certain he was achieving.

I finally came to the For Immediate Action message from the Bureau of Public Security. It was obviously a form letter, composed and produced by computer, with the signature of R. Sam Bigelow printed in water-soluble ink that smudged if you rubbed it. The real thing.

The letter stated the BPS was conducting a "routine inventory" on samples of the restricted toxic substance 416HBL-CW3. In 1988, a number of samples of this substance had been delivered to various research facilities, one of which was the Department of Research & Development, SATSEC, DOB. Records indicate, shipment of and signed receipt for 5 cc of the aforementioned substance. I was to inform BPS if the 5 cc were still in possession of DivRad. If not, I was to explain when and for what purpose any or all of it had been used. Reply requested instanter.

The letter angered me. I was not angry with R. Sam Bigelow; he was just performing his service, trying to trace all known quantities of the aerobic *Clostridium botulinum* in glycerol. I was angry with myself. After the analysis in K Lab, when I had looked up 416HBL-CW3 in our restricted drug code book, I had scanned the large green star after the definition. But the proper synaptic closure had not been made. I had not interpreted that green star. It signified that a restricted drug so marked was in our pharmacology library.

Then I recalled my few moments of talk with Paul Bumford in the basement of the EOB, when I had told him that 416HBL-CW3 was the causative agent in the botulism outbreak in GPA-11. I remembered that brief conversation had disturbed me. Was it because that, subconsciously, my mental lapse was nagging? That I knew I had missed something, but could not dredge it to the surface? I had had to postpone my annual hippocampal irrigation. Perhaps that had been a mistake if my memory was beginning to stammer.

No matter. All I had to do now was to verify that existence of 5 cc of 416HBL-CW3 in our pharmacology library and so inform R. Sam Bigelow. I could not recall anyone in DivRad ever requesting and using any of the damned stuff. We had no need to paint cigars or spray our neighbors' tomatoes.

Once again, oilskin clad, I dashed across the compound. Because of the snow, the automatic car-trains were not running. I slotted my BIN card, was further identified by voiceprint check, and was allowed entrance into B Lab. Down in the third sublevel I followed a maze of underground tunnels to the drug storage area. The empty white corridors went on and on. When, good little mouse that I was, I arrived at my goal, I would receive a food pellet.

There was a night staff in the outer office of the pharmacology library: two objects playing three-dimensional chess, one kibitzing. They looked up when I came in and started to rise. I waved them down.

"I can find it," I said. "Go on with your game."

They settled back.

"Still snowing out, Director?" the kibitzer asked.

"Still." I nodded. "You may be here for days. Nothing to eat but aphrodisiacs."

They grinned at me and went back to their game. I went to the file computer, switched it on, punched the readout button, and typed 416HBL-CW3 on the keyboard. Almost immediately the screen showed: RESTRICTED SECTIONXXXROOM GXXXBIN 3XXXSTACK 4XXXPOSITION RXXX END IT.

I wiped the screen, turned off the machine, went through an inner door to the storage area. The restricted section was at the end of another long, deserted corridor. Shining plastiasb tiles underfoot, white walls and ceiling, fluorescent lighting. Subway to nowhere.

The glass doors to the restricted section were locked. As they should have been. I pushed the buzzer. Nothing happened. No one came. I knew what the problem was. Vinnie Altman, the obso night guard of the restricted drug library. And *his* problem was petroport. But he was inoffensive, serving out his final years to retirement. It was easy to overlook his mild alcoholism and taste in scanning matter.

I leaned on the buzzer again. Finally I saw him. Blinking, shambling toward the door. Carrying a magazine. He peered at me through the glass. Then his whiskey face creased deeper. He turned off the alarm, opened the two locks, slid the door aside.

"Hey there, doc," he said. "Long time no see."

I didn't mind when *he* called me doc. I stepped inside. He closed the door. The locks and alarm connected again automatically. I took the picture magazine from his hand. Danish porn for export. It was called *Gash*. So it was. All of it.

"All I can do is look," he said.

"Look but don't lick," I said. "The ink may give you a bellyache."

"That ain't where my ache is," he said. "Please sign the register, doc."

I signed the register, a big ledger, with date, time of entrance, name. While Vinnie Altman leaned over my shoulder. Watching. He exuded petroport fumes.

"I know what I'm looking for," I told him. "Go back to your education."

He shuffled over to a corner desk. The half-liter of petroport was probably in a drawer. He rationed himself. One half-liter per night. No more. Just enough to make him forget the long, empty corridors.

This area of the pharmacology library was larger than you might have expected. Mostly due to the shielding needed for the radioactive drugs. But those were in special vaults equipped with automatic dumbwaiters. The other brews, everything from cobra venom to a synthetic nicotine we had developed for treatment of vascular hemorrhage, were stored on open shelves.

It was easy to find Room G. I switched on the overhead light. I searched around and found Bin 3. In it, last on the right, was Stack 4. I ran my finger along the position labels: L, M, N, O, P, Q, and there was R. I raised my hand to lift it down. And stopped. It was a small glass flask. Airtight stopper. A line had been etched around the bottle. The marking 5 cc was clearly visible. But the level of the liquid in the flask was appreciably below the etched line.

I didn't touch the bottle. Just stood there with my hand outstretched. Evaporation was impossible. Not that quantity. What else? I could not believe there had been a research project using 416HBL-CW3 which I could not recall. But then I hadn't remembered that green star in the restricted drug code book.

I switched off the light. Closed the door softly. Walked slowly back to the outer office. Vinnie Altman was tilted back in his swivel chair. Feet up. *Gash* clasped on his lap. His head was back. Eyes closed. Mouth open. He was snoring.

"Going to check the withdrawal file," I said gently.

He didn't stir. I tiptoed quietly over to the metal cabinet.

Each restricted drug had a file card. It showed, on one side, the initial deposit stored, at what date, and any additions made, at what date. The other side showed withdrawals. An object withdrawing a restricted drug had to write date, quantity, signature.

I slid open the 400 drawer slowly, easily. I looked to Vinnie Altman. He hadn't moved. The buzz was constant. I flipped through the cards. I found 416HBL-CW3. I lifted it out carefully. By one corner: Holding the file open with my other hand. With the tips of my fingers.

The card showed an initial deposit of 5 cc of 416HBL-CW3 on November 3, 1988. There had been no additions since the original quantity was stored.

I turned the card over.

There had been one withdrawal.

On November 18, 1998.

Two cc.

I looked for the signature.

It was there.

Nicholas Bennington Flair.

In my own flamboyant scrawl.

Z-5

Two days later I was on my way to Denver. For a personal inspection of Project Phoenix. Lewisohn's condition was deteriorating so inexorably that I knew I had to expedite my scenario for his survival. While he still had sufficient strength to endure it.

Aboard the jet, sipping my fourth vodka-and-Smack of the day, puffing my third cannabis, I reviewed my actions in re the fiddled 416HBL-CW3 file card. I was satisfied that I had done all that a crafty object might do.

My first reaction, of course, upon viewing my own signature, had been akin to, say, witnessing an act of levitation. "I see it but I don't believe it." Then I thought possibly I *had* taken the *Clostridium botulinum* and had signed the file card under the influence of hypnosis. Either by a clever operator or by drug. In the precarious world of politics, at that point in time, you learned to breathe the volcano's fumes.

But the date, November 18, 1998, precluded the hypnosis theory. On that particular day, I had been in Washington, D.C., conferring with Joe Wellington. I was certain. Later, my memory was verified by a notation in my appointment schedule.

Then, still staring at the file card, still shaken, I had the wit to check the register. That big ledger in which every visitor to the restricted drug library had to note date, time of entrance and exit, signature. Sure enough, "Nicholas Bennington Flair" had entered the library at 2320 on November 18, 1998, and exited at 2345.

But I was gratified to see that the signature on the register was identical with the signature on the 416HBL-CW3 file card. I don't mean the two signatures were similar; they were *identical*. To every hook, dash, curlicue. Vinnie Altman still snoozing, still gently snoring, I brought the file card over to the ledger to compare the two.

No object ever duplicates a signature exactly. Ever. But, of course, those were not signatures. Closer examination proved that. The pressure of pen throughout had been uniform: no faintness or heaviness of line. Ergo: not writing at all, but printing or inscribing with a mechanical or automatic device. The methodology then became apparent.

Like most executives, my form letters were printed and signed by an office computer. When the quantity desired was limited, and mass distribution unnecessary, identical letters were Instox duplicated from a signed master. When many letters of varied subject matter but of routine nature were prepared, they would be typed from my dictated tapes by Ellen Dawes' assistants, scanned by her for accuracy, and "signed" with a small, portable imprinter. This was a mechanical device not unlike a postal cancellation meter. It contained an ink supply. A lever depressed a plastisteel cut that was an exact (photographic) reproduction of my signature. The cut was an em equivalent of an engraving. The "signature" looked authentic. But being mechanically reproduced, pressure was uniform throughout.

The problem of my "genuine" signature appearing on file card and ledger having been solved, to my satisfaction, I next turned to how it had been snookered. My signature meter was usually kept in my office safe. To be requested by Ellen Dawes when there were a number of letters to be "signed." Then returned to me. But not always. When I was absent from the office on those Washington trips, or the PR expedition, the meter was turned over to Ellen. She should have kept it locked up. Knowing her, I didn't suppose she did. But even locked in my safe it would not have been secure. What was?

Having relatively easy access to my signature meter, how would a terrorist group planning to steal a quantity of *Clostridium botulinum* have proceeded? Putting myself in their place, with their arcane but obviously powerful motivation, I plotted a possible scenario. During the twenty-four hours following my discovery of the missing 416HBL-CW3, I put the plan to a field test. With certain refinements.

My preparations may sound complex; they were actually not. I sent Ellen Dawes to the stationery stockroom for paper, envelopes, pads, pencils, rubber bands, paperclips, and a quantity of several forms. Including 100 blank restricted drug file cards. I only needed one. Which I filled out for 416HBL-CW3. I showed an authentic initial entry of 5 cc on November 3, 1988, and no additional deposits. The withdrawal side I left blank. I "aged" the card by scraping it several times across the surface of my office plasticarp. When I finished, it looked ten years old. Reasonably.

I then paid a casual visit to A Lab, wandered about until my presence was ignored, and filched a 5 cc flask of glycerol. I then left the compound, briefly, to purchase a half-liter bottle of petroport at a federal grogshop. I brought the bottle to the Pharmacology Team Lab and told them I needed it doped with an instant hypnotic and a memory eraser. A restricted project. No questions were asked. The seal was carefully lifted, screw top removed, contents contaminated, the bottle restored to its original appearance.

Then, just to prove to myself the fiddling could have been carried out by a single object, I donned a greatcoat over my zipsuit and filled the pockets with my signature meter, the newly prepared restricted drug file card, the small flask of glycerol, the half-liter of fixed petroport. No problem of storage.

"Vinnie," I said. After he had turned off the alarm, unlocked and opened the door. "This is just a social visit. Someone gave me this jug of happiness. Thought you might like it."

I handed over the dozied liquor.

"Why, doc," he said. Coming out of his fog for a moment. "Mighty nice of you. Have one with me?"

"You go ahead," I said. "A little too sweet for me."

We went back to his desk where a copy of another Danish magazine, *Clit*, was spread wide. As it should have been. I waited while Vinnie poured himself a plastiglass of my petroport.

"Over the hills and far away," he said. Raising the glass and draining half of it.

Thankfully, he was seated when it hit him. I took the glass from his hand before the remainder spilled. His head had fallen sideways. He was snoring busily.

I went back to Room G, Bin 3, Stack 4, Position R. My original idea had been to bring in an identical glass flask filled to the etched line with 5 cc of pure glycerol. But close investigation by the Bureau of Public Security would have revealed the substitution. Also, I would have had to remove the original flask, taking it with me in my pocket when I left. The notion of striding on icy pavements carrying a glass bottle of enough toxic bacteria to stop the entire population of the US was not an endearing prospect.

So I merely removed the stopper of the original bottle and poured in enough pure glycerol to bring the level up to the etched line. I did this as porcupines fornicate—very, very carefully. I doubted if even heavy analysis of the contents would reveal the dilution.

I replaced the original bottle in its original position. After wiping the glass free of prints. Turned off the lights. Returned to the outer office. Carrying the remainder of the pure glycerol. Vinnie Altman was still snoozing comfortably, the eraser busily at work in his brain destroying the memory of the previous hours.

I then removed the fiddled 416HBL-CW3 card from the file and substituted the new card I had prepared. It looked right at home. But before I did that, I satisfied myself that my signature meter could have been used to imprint my name on file card and register. It could have. Easily. But I didn't record a notice of my current visit, of course. No need.

I remembered to pour the dregs of Vinnie Altman's drink back into the bottle and then take with me the remainder of the contaminated petroport. I switched off the alarm, opened both locks, exited, slid the door softly shut behind me. Alarm and locks connected automatically. Beautiful. I had done what I could to pillow the attack upon me.

In the jet, beginning the descent to the Denver airport, I reflected again, briefly, on the problem of who had been responsible. For the programmed outbreak of botulism in GPA-11 and for the attempt to fix the blame on me. Some terrorist group, I supposed. Perhaps frantic leftovers from the Society of Obsoletes' conspiracy who had not yet been terminated. But it was fruitless to wonder.

It was much more profitable to fantasize on Louise Rawlins Tucker's dinner party to be held the following Sunday. I had confirmed date and time by flasher. She had said casually, open-eyed, "I think you'll know most of the objects, Nick. They're fun. Grace Wingate promised to come."

The Denver Field Office had been alerted to my arrival. There was an official limousine awaiting me at the gate. I did not find those trappings offensive. At the complex itself, Phoebe Huntzinger met me at the door. We went immediately to a colloquy with the new Project Phoenix Team Leader, a yellow em named Thomas Lee, and his young staff.

I listened for more than an hour. Their progress startled me. Although I should have been habituated to rapid research. As explicated in my prospectus to the Chief Director on the Department of Creative Science, I had stated that the accelerating rate of scientific discovery was mainly due to four factors:

1. The increasing use of computer technology, especially for automatic chemo-and physioanalysis.
2. The increasing early conditioning of the young. By oxygenation of the fetus and a hyperprotein diet for selected infants, the US was producing what a French astrophysicist had called (sorrowfully, I thought) a "generation of genii."

3. The easy availability of human objects for research. This element alone contributed immeasurably to public health and happiness.
4. The exponential factor involved: discoveries leading to discoveries, a geometric progression of scientific knowledge. Our conditioning techniques and development of brain-expanding and memory drugs were hard-pressed to embrace the complexity of today's science. It had become a race, as the obso writer H. G. Wells said, between education and catastrophe.

So I tried not to appear too startled by the progress of the Project Phoenix Team. I listened to their triumphs and their defeats. Nodded. Made a few pertinent suggestions. Then we adjourned to their operating theater to observe an object currently under usage. I did not inquire about the volunteer's antecedents. It would have been infratooty.

She was a young ef. About fourteen, judging from her pubescent breasts and scrabbly pubic hair. She was tightly strapped, naked, into a mechanism roughly resembling a barber's chair. Taped with electronic sensors; IV feeding that included a mild hallucinogen. Atop her head, descending to her eyebrows, was an enormous stainless steel helmet from which radiated the spokes of the soft laser transmitters and receivers, on swivel attachments.

The operating theater was a jumble of hardware. Many primary readout screens: one for each laser scan. Computers to monitor the object's vital signals. A transmitter to the Golem computer in a sublevel. Readout and printout machines for computer retrieval. And, touchingly, a pink bedpan.

We watched, quiet, while technicians made minute adjustments of the last rods.

"Sending," someone said. Watching an EEG transmitter screen.

Machines went into action. The sounds were a symphony. *Ka-tah, ka-tah, ka-tah. Chingchingchingching. Beep-o, beep-o, beep-o.* And underneath all, a deep, disturbing hum. We looked to the Golem computer readout screen.

XXXI WANT TO GET OUT OF HEREXXX

XXXMUST YOU DO THIS TO MEXXX

XXXPLEASE LET ME STOPXXX

I turned to the operator.

"Could I have a printout on that, please?"

"Yes, sir."

She pushed buttons. Held the screen image while the printer chattered briefly, 350 wpm. She tore off the screed, handed it to me. I scanned it, passed it to Phoebe Huntzinger.

Phoebe scanned it.

"What do you find significant in that?" I asked her.

She scanned it again.

"Nothing special, Nick."

"All one-syllable words," I said.

"Nick, I told you Golem is limited. We're using a ten-thousand word vocabulary storage, plus phrase linkups. We're pushing the limit now."

"Phoebe, I'm not blaming you," I said. Smiling. Touching her arm. "You've done wonders. Just gives me ideas, that's all. Thanks for the show. Let's eat."

But that brief demo at the Denver FO led to consequential imperatives. (Loverly words—no? Obsos would have said, "Far-reaching consequences." But language changes. As it should. Otherwise we would still be chanting, "Whan that Aprille with his shoures sote. . . .")

When I returned to GPA-1, I began to move objects about. I sent Leo Bernstein to Hospice No. 17 in Little Rock, Arkansas, for brief familiarization conditioning on their service on the formularization of synthetic blood. I pulled Seth Lucas out of Hospice No. 4, temporarily, and sent him to the Denver Field Office to serve with Tom Lee, the Team Leader on Project Phoenix. And I brought Phoebe Huntzinger back from Denver to Manhattan Landing.

"Big service," I told her. "Clear as much storage in your computers as you can. Program two-hundred-thousand word English vocabulary, plus a thousand-item vocabulary of foreign words and phrases. Particularly those applicable to economics and government. Got that?"

"Sure, boss. Going to tell me what this is all about?"

"No. Then after you have your pachinkos programmed, set up a direct wire link with Denver. For send and return. So we can scan the input down here and interpret."

"All *right*, Nick. You don't have to draw a diagram."

"This Tom Lee—what's your take?" I asked.

"A brain," she said. "He's eighteen. Makes you feel obso—right?"

"In this juvenocracy, everyone makes me feel obso. Get hopping, Phoebe."

I sent a restricted, detailed letter of instruction to the eighteen-year-old Team Leader Thomas Lee. I ordered him to prepare a contingency logistics plan to transfer Project Phoenix from the Denver FO to Hospice No. 4.

I sent a formal letter to R. Sam Bigelow at the Bureau of Public Security. I stated that in answer to his such-and-such, dated such-and-such, my personal visual inspection had confirmed that 5 cc of the substance 416HBL-CW3 was still in the possession of SAT-SEC, and records indicated no withdrawals for any purpose whatsoever.

Then I flashed Penelope Mapes, requesting an interview with the Chief Director. Times synchronized to my satisfaction. He would be leaving for a week's tour of exmainland States on a Saturday, just one day prior to Louise Rawlins Tucker's dinner party. Fine. Penelope Mapes promised me fifteen minutes with him on the afternoon of his departure. Megafine. I remembered the comment of a lab ef who had been involved in a successful research project.

"How you doing?" I asked her.

"Just great," she had said. "Everything's coming up penicillin."

I arrived in Washington on March 15. Many happy returns, Julius Caesar.

I stayed at the Chevy Chase place and spent two full days with Joe Wellington and staff, including Samantha Slater, planning the logistics of a PR excursion through the Midwest. Touting the glories of a Department of Creative Science to Establishment Gruppen. It was, I sometimes felt, a contentless ceremony. Except, of course, the ceremony itself was meaningful.

I also spent a full day at temporary headquarters of the DCS in the basement of the Executive Office Building. The babe was healthy and growing. An enlarged suite of six offices, still in the process of expansion. More noise, more objects, more franticness. There is nothing quite like political growth. It is at once fascinating, exciting, disturbing. Something like the proliferation of *Neisseria gonorrhoeae* on a petri dish.

Paul Bumford and I—Mary Bergstrom sitting nearby, a silent fury—went over the political scenario. The original bill, HR-316, submitted to the House of Representatives by a Congressman from Alabama (a "sweetheart" of the Chief Director) had, of course, been overcast. A process similar to artificially inflating a requested budget by 20 percent. Knowing you'll be cut back to your desired goal. In this case, proposed amendments in the House Government Operations Committee were nibbling away at the original bill. But nothing that hadn't been anticipated and programmed. To quell wild beasts, you toss them raw chuck. When they are surfeited, the broiled sirloin is slipped by. So it was. So it always has been.

"By the way," I said to Paul. "Something for the Tomorrow File. A federal TV cable system. The only channel. All sets licensed."

"Got it," he said. "Excellent. Especially for agitprop."

My meet with Chief Director Michael Wingate was scheduled for 1430. I was ushered into his crowded EOB office. I had an opportunity then to observe the manager of the US in action. Surrounded, crushed by advisers, aides, secretaries, guards, applicants, patrons and clients, servers and masters. Penelope Mapes was there, of course, and Theodore Seidensticker III, Joe Wellington, Sady Nagle, and a varied assortment of concerned objects from Senators to hypersonic pilots and navigators plotting the CD's flight to our overseas provinces.

Then Michael Wingate exhibited to me another side of his multifaceted character: the efficient executive. Cool under pressure. Welcoming stress. The em of almost instant decisions; a barely preceptible pause before the "Yes" or the "No." And withal, remarkably genial, pleasant. Brooking no serious opposition, you understand. Not even from Senators. But the negative always glossed by the physical gesture: palm stroke, pat, embrace, caress, playful punch. It was a marvelous performance. To watch.

"Nick!" he said. Genuine pleasure. "So glad to see you!"

I believed it. That was his gift. A charm so intense it conquered all.

"About GPA-11?" he asked.

"No, no."

"You've discovered how they're doing it?"

Then I divined part of his secret: He never listened—totally.

"No, Chief," I said. "I'm sorry to report I have not discovered how they're doing it."

"Bad business," he said sternly. Shaking his head. "Bad business."

In our following conversation, interrupted a dozen times, I finally was able to make clear to him why I had requested the audience. Hyman R. Lewisohn was stopping. Using conventional therapy, there was no hope for the em's survival. But I wanted to attempt radical surgery. I didn't explicate further. But before that eventuality, I wanted the Chief Director to convene an ad hoc committee of the nation's foremost civilian physicians, hematologists, oncologists, etc., to make an independent analysis of Lewisohn's present condition. And to make a prognosis. They would have open and complete access to my personal files and to the records of Group Lewisohn.

Chief Director Michael Wingate looked at me closely.

"Why do you want an outside opinion?" he asked.

"For my sake, sir," I said. No expression. "And for yours."

His glance sharpened. You could see the knife edge thinning. And glittering.

"All right," he said. "Yes," he said. "I'll order it immediately."

He motioned to an aide and began dictating a tape-recorded memo that would result in the convening of a committee of civilian scientists to investigate the present physical status of Hyman R. Lewisohn. And to prognosticate his fate. I tiptoed away while he was dictating. He waved to me as I departed. He was already surrounded by the mob. Seeking his favors. His most precious was, I hoped, waiting for me.

The home of Louise Rawlins Tucker was on Oxford Street, about two kilometers from the place Paul and I leased in Chevy Chase. The house was well-sited; it had a university air: obso red brick, aged ivy, extravagant grounds, an air of staid respectability. Its most salient feature, for my profit, was a walled garden. Now sere, with patches of blued snow still lurking in the shadows. Flagstoned walks. Bare trees and withered brush.

"I don't like evergreens," Louise Fawlins Tucker said firmly. "Ah, what is?"

There was a charming arbor. It would, I hoped, be painted in the spring. Before the wild grape sprouted. There were two semicircles of benches: wood-slatted seats about a shallow depression that might have been, once, a pond. Fish? Lilies? Anything.

The dinner party was for twelve. Precisely seven ems and five efs.

"Ah, it is best to have two wandering ems," Louise Rawlins Tucker said firmly.

I had sent, at great expense, natural gladiolus. Enough to fill several vases and metal pots throughout the downstairs area. The splotches of soft color enlivened the dim, somewhat depressing interior. Louise Rawlins Tucker inspected my gift with great favor and thanked me.

"Regardless of what objects hint," she said, firmly, "you can't be all bad."

"And what do objects hint?" I asked.

"Ah," she said.

We dined, a sedate but pleasant party, from a buffet of adequate but unimaginative dishes. The proshrimp were undercooked, the prolet salad distressingly flaccid. But there was an excellent bowl of natural pasta with a prosauce hyped with what I guessed to be prorooms and natural Italian garlic sausage. Quite good. I had a second helping.

"You'll get fat," Grace Wingate said to me.

"More of me for you," I murmured.

"Awful em," she whispered. But she smiled.

Other than that brief exchange, we had engaged in no other talk except polite greetings after her late arrival. She spoke to the others; I spoke to the others. Slowly, gradually, I found myself cast in the role of a "wandering em." I was content, trying to compute the status of the guests.

They all seemed to be acquainted which, naturally, made me feel the outsider. Although I met nothing but gracious thaw and smiling pleasantry. All obsos except for Grace and myself. Two of the ems and one of the efs were Georgetown professors. A Vermont Senator and his wrinkled daughter. An ef from the higher echelons of CULSEC, DOB. Another ef, crippled, a poet who, she told me, composed by a complex word-chess-move code. I couldn't compute it. She showed me a sample poem she just happened to have with her. I couldn't compute it.

But I should not carp; they were all profitable objects. Or at least inoffensive. In their tweeds and quilted skirts. Bangles and hunting stocks. Neuter objects. Precisely the background for Grace Wingate and me. For our scenario. Might as well suspect that assemblage of leprosy as of passion hidden in their midst.

The after-dinner drink, as you might have predicted, was medium-dry sherry. The glasses were elegant crystal, just large enough for an eye douche. I waited until Grace Wingate was temporarily alone. Then carried my miniature sherry over to her.

"Warm in here," I said. Brilliantly.

"Yes," she said. Distantly. "Isn't it."

"There's a garden," I said. "I peeped through the draperies. How does one get out there?"

"A side door from the kitchen," she said. Faintly. "A walk leads around."

"Five minutes?" I asked.

She nodded.

"Bring your cloak," I said. "It's cold."

Carrying that ridiculous sherry, I stalked determinedly through a back hall, past two serving objects in the kitchen. They didn't even look up when I unchained the side door and stepped out. I was wearing a winter-weight zipsuit. But still the cold shocked, tingled skin. I walked about, apparently inspecting withered shrubs and frozen lawn. Breathing deeply. Plumes of white. Then I sat cautiously on one of the scabbed benches under the bare arbor.

She was with me in a few minutes. Wearing a hooded cloak that framed her face. A cloud of russet wool, and those paled features. She sat alongside me. Billowing down onto the bench.

"Not for long," she said breathlessly.

"Long enough," I said.

I maneuvered between her and the house. Anyone watching—why would anyone do that? Want to do that?—would see only my back. Perhaps the top of her head.

I set the little sherry glass aside. I took her hands. She withdrew her arms into the loose sleeves of her cloak so that our clasped hands were enveloped.

"You're freezing," she said.

"No, no," I said. "Not now. First of all, I know you trust Louise. The others?"

"They couldn't care less," she said.

"Yes, I suppose so. Grace, I can cope with my own danger. But not yours. If there's any—"

"You think I care?" she asked scornfully.

I stared at her. It was an instant when, I thought then and I thought later, we came whole to each other. Why else should I suddenly be sickened by my life's turbidity? The time's? I wanted lightness, clarity, simplicity, elegance, airy laughter and spidery beauty. I wanted Grace.

"Your husband doesn't listen," I told her. "Not really."

Her eyes widened.

"How did you know? No, not really. He doesn't. Nick, I have so much to give."

I may have looked at her in amazement. I would have laughed at that dumb line from a lesser ef. But if absence makes the heart grow fonder, it also makes it more flatulent. I was prepared to believe her; she *did* have so much to give.

I took by trying to absorb her. Not only somber eyes, patrician nose, soft lips, glistening teeth, sharp chin, stalk neck, but *her*. We spoke in low voices, short sentences. Exploring. We were emotional archaeologists. Not digging with shovels. Crass that, and counterproductive. But with dentist's pick, jeweler's loupe, camel's-hair brush. Gently uncovering and examining. Learning each other. Sentences getting longer. Voices murmuring off into sighs. Warmed hands clasping tighter.

"I've wanted," she said, "all my life to become devoted. Completely. To someone. Or something. I love Michael. But he's not the all I wanted. I see that now. I thought Beism might offer what I need. I don't think so. I need a—a target. Nick, are you a target?"

"I think so."

"*My* target?"

"I want to be. But it's your determination to make, isn't it?"

"All mine?"

"Well ... no. But I must change my nature."

"That's a great deal to ask," she said gravely.

"Yes." Nodding. "But I want to. Grace, I really *want* to. That's something, isn't it?"

We both sighed. Happy with our anguish.

"What is it?" I asked her. Nicholas Bennington Socrates Flair.

"What is love?"

She shook her head.

"Devotion," she said. After a moment. "That's what it is for me. It may be something else to you. Pleasure. Duty. Whatever."

"Devotion?" I mused. "To what?"

"Oh," she said. Looking about. "To anyone. Or anything. Worthy."

"Am I worthy?" I asked her.

"I don't know. Yet."

"Are you worthy? Of my devotion?"

"Oh, God, yes," she said. "I *know*."

"We may die," I said. Using a word that was not officially approved.

"I don't care," she said. Looking again into my eyes. "Do you?"

Suddenly I didn't.

"No," I said. Gripping her sweated hands inside the covering cuffs. "It's meaning, isn't it?"

"Oh, yes," she breathed. "Oh, yes. Oh, yes. Meaning. That's what I want, Nick. Meaning."

"Love," I said.

"Love," she said.

We circled down from our panting high to discuss ways and means. The house of Louise Rawlins Tucker would be our "safe place." Grace assured me she could arrange for access during afternoons. Servers absent. So we plotted. With the sad acknowledgment of how small plans must bring grand ardors low.

I suppose, later, we stroked palms politely, and nodded on parting. Then we were inside, her cloak was over her arm. I saw the simple chemise of slithery silk. Imagined the living flesh glowing within. Humid scents and clever crannies. I hoped she dreamed the same of me. And thought she might.

About ten days later, I was in Bismarck, North Dakota, addressing the annual convention of the Association of US Historians. I was not about to tell historians that history was inoperative. That it no longer offered precedents. Some of my remarks:

"As historians, you must know that most civilizations have perished. Or are perishing. Birth, growth, stop. It is the fate of most objects and most societies. Some in a wink, some longer. Some by interior rot, some by external aggression.

"But, as you also must know, some political, religious, and social corpora have continued to exist. For aeons. Not in their original form, true. Not with their original structure, laws, directions, methods, goals. But by evolving. Adjusting to new input. It is the one lesson, the one great lesson, history can teach us. *Change.* Either change conquers us, or we embrace change, learn to profit from change.

"I am here tonight to discuss with you a change in the Public Service branch of the US Government, the proposed establishment of a Department of Creative Science. I want to suggest how I feel this new Department will change the history of the US and, eventually, change the history of the world. To help us all adjust to new input, and to help us all survive. Because that, essentially, is what we're talking about—survival."

And so forth. And so forth.

I was back in the motel. In my room. Lying naked in bed with Samantha Slater. Both of us breathing like long-distance runners. Having had our first offs. One of her amazingly long, slender, hairless legs was clamped between my thighs. Her flesh could have been squeezed from a tube. I hugged it. Just the one leg. It was enough.

My Portaphone attaché case buzzed.

"Kaka," I said.

I disentangled, got out of bed, stumbled over to the desk. The case continued buzzing while I fumbled about, pulling the curtains, turning on a lamp.

"You're all red," Samantha said.

"I wonder why?" I said. I got the case open, switched it on.

"Flair," I said.

"Nick? Paul here. Go to scrambler."

"Wait a minute," I pressed the button, turned the code indicator. "What is it, Paul?"

"Nick!" Excited. "I think I may know how they're doing it. I mean the botulism. In GPA-11."

"How?"

"Are you alone? Can we talk?"

"Reasonably."

"Look, tonight I was in the office. Helping to get out the mail. We've had a postal metering machine on order for weeks, but it hasn't come yet."

"So?"

"So we've been using stamps. Licking a stamp and putting it on every envelope. So a few days ago Senator Blamey went into Bethesda for a hernia operation. I guess you scanned it."

"No. I didn't. Paul, it's hardly an item that might excite my interest."

"Well, look," he said. Almost stuttering in his frenzy to get it out. "Blamey is important to us. He's Chairman of the Senate Government Operations Committee, you know. Well, I thought—"

"Paul, will you get to it?"

"Well, I thought it would be a nice gesture to send him a personal get-well-quick note. From all of us at DCS. You compute?"

"Yes, Paul," I said wearily. "I compute. So?"

"So I wrote out the letter, handwritten, and addressed an envelope. Mary Bergstrom folded the letter, put it in the envelope and sealed it. Then she licked a stamp and stuck it on the envelope."

"Paul, what is this?"

"That's when it hit me! Nick, don't you see? I haven't looked into it, but surely there's a possibility. What if the botulism guck is in the glue on the stamps? Wouldn't that account for the number of victims in GPA-11? The age range? The scattered outbreaks elsewhere? Tourists traveling through GPA-11 and buying stamps they used when they got back home? Nick, for God's sake, all the victims are getting the dose from licking US postage stamps!"

"Jesus Christ," I said.

"What do you think, Nick? Nick? Are you there, Nick?"

"I'm here," I said into the transmitter. "What about the infant who stopped? It wouldn't be mailing a letter."

"The four-month-old?" he said. Still speaking rapidly. Still stammering with excitement. "*One* infant, Nick. Well, what if the mother or father wrote a letter, sealed it in an envelope, then licked a poisoned stamp. And *then* picked up the kid and kissed it on the mouth! That's possible, isn't it?"

I was silent.

"What is it?" Samantha Slater asked lazily from the bed.

"Nick?" Paul said. "Are you still there, Nick?"

"I'm still here," I said crossly.

"Well . . . what do you think?"

"A possibility."

"What should I do, Nick? Wait till you come back?"

I computed a moment.

"No," I said. "Don't wait. If it's contaminated stamps, there's still a lot of them around. Get to the CD as soon as possible. Tell him what you suspect. Tell him to bring R. Sam Bigelow's bloodhounds in on it. They'll run a search and analysis. Confirm or reject. But do it immediately."

"Right," Paul said. "Understood. Thanks. Nick. I really think this is it."

"Could be," I said.

"I'm off," he said.

"Good on you," I said. But he had already disconnected.

"What was that all about?" Samantha Slater asked as I crawled slowly back into bed.

"About licking," I said.

"How nice," she said.

Z-6

Paul Bumford is an ultrabrain," Chief Director Michael Wingate said gravely.

"Yes, sir," I said.

"A very lovable em," he said.

I nodded. I was not, I admit, too delighted with these tributes.

"Paul suggested to me how it was being done," the CD went on.

"The poisoned stamps. Bigelow's crew went in and verified it. Fortunately, they were twenty-cent stamps, used mostly on postcards. If they had been the twenty-five cent denomination for first-class postage, we estimate the stop ratio would have had a ten-factor increase. We picked up the unsold stocks of contaminated stamps at the post offices and put out a general alert."

"Public?" I asked.

"Had to be," he said grimly. "No other way. But the flak didn't last long, and we were able to limit media coverage mostly to GPA-11. Nick, one of the many things this service has taught me is the public's short attention-span. Fifty years ago a botulism outbreak like this would have been an horrendous scandal. Screaming headlines for weeks. But the Great Stamp Recall lasted in the news for two, three days. Just another catastrophe. We've all learned to live with disaster. It's part of our environment. Drought, famine, crime, earthquake, terrorism, revolution, war, radioactive fallout. If you've seen one child burn to death on TV, you've seen them all. So what's new? Too much. Too many words. Too many images. The attention span shortens. It has to. We once thought alcoholism and drug addiction were psychic surrogates for suicide. Then we realized alcoholism and drug addiction are self-defense mechanisms: the object protecting itself from depression, psychosis, or worse. Right, doctor?"

"Right," I said.

"So our attention span shortens," he went on. Broodingly. "As it has to. Must. If we are to survive."

I had never heard him talk at such length. Or so intimately. He seemed to me weary. Physically weary. Kept pinching the bridge of his nose and squinching his eyes. Those jolly Santa Claus features were slack, gray with fatigue. But I would not presume to prescribe for him. I was not his personal physician. It had nothing to do with the fact that I hoped to guzzle his wife.

"The stamps, sir," I said to him gently.

"What? Oh, yes. The stamps. . . ." He came back from somewhere. "Well, it's been determined they were printed here in Washington. The glue on the back is purchased from a commercial supplier in fifty-gallon drums. It's trucked to Washington, held in storage until needed on the press. The operation is called 'gumming.' It's done after printing but before perforation. The adhesive could have been fiddled at any step along the way. Bigelow's objects have been placed in services where they can watch what's going on. And, of course, the warehouse and printing areas are being shared. I think it was a one-shot thing. Demented. I base that opinion on the absence of any obvious motive. No letters. No threats. No demands."

"I still feel it may have been an attempt to destabilize the government, sir. Or perhaps in the nature of a laboratory experiment. A trial run to test the technique."

"Maybe. Naturally we're doing everything we can to make certain it doesn't happen again."

We were seated in his top-floor EOB office. Just the two of us. It was night. The curtains blotted out the lights of Washington, the glare bathing the White House. The only illumination came from a chrome lamp on his cluttered desk. It made a round pool of light. But farther out, from the corners of the room, the darkness pressed in.

"Well . . ." he said. Pushing himself erect in his swivel chair.

"Anyway, Paul Bumford did a fine service. I'll keep an eye on that young em."

"Yes, sir."

"But all this is by the way. The reason I called you in tonight is the report on Lewisohn. From that committee of civilian doctors you asked me to convene. They're in remarkable agreement—for doctors. Prognosis negative. Just like that."

"What is their survival estimate, Chief?"

"Three to nine months. In that area."

"Any suggestions for treatment?"

"Nothing you didn't think of. They were very complimentary about the number and variety of protocols you have tried. Very ingenious, they said. Now then . . . You mentioned something about radical surgery as a last resort. What exactly is it?"

"Chief," I said cautiously, "just how important is Hyman R. Lewisohn? How far will you go to keep his brain functioning?"

He rose heavily from behind the desk. Stretched his arms wide, arched his back. I heard the snap of vertebrae. Then he shrugged his shoulders, rolling his head about on his neck. A tired, stiffened em, trying to loosen up. He began pacing back and forth across the office. I moved around so I could watch him. He went into the darkness, then came back into the pool of light. Darkness and light alternating. While he talked . . .

"Lewisohn," he said. "I'll tell you about Lewisohn. It's not enough to call him our best theorist. He's more than that. All his conceptions have a hard, pragmatic core. He's a genius without being a visionary. Let me give you a for instance. Years ago—it was during President Morse's second term—Lewisohn was asked to run a research project on the possibility of global war. You *ask* Lewisohn, you don't order him. Instead, Lewisohn turned in a monumental study of the history, causes, methods, and results of conflict between nations. The entire methodology of international competition. It's still a classified document—highest classification—but I can tell you it's remarkable. Lewisohn dealt with conventional warfare, nukewar, genwar, econwar, chemwar, popwar, and a dozen other possible collisions between governments. He then analyzed the resources of the US for each type of struggle. His conclusion, which has been the unofficial policy of the US ever since it was formulated, was that the security and prosperity of the US would best be served by agriwar. Agricultural warfare. An aggression in which food becomes the primary weapon. Lewisohn computed that a heavy increase in our total acreage under cultivation, plus crash programs to develop new cereal strains and new sources of protein, would provide the 'armory' we needed. You probably know the results of those classified research programs. Lewisohn argued that by becoming the world's larder, we would, in a sense, be providing ourselves with a certain measure of insurance against nuclear attack. What foreign government would want to risk contaminating our land with radioactive fallout and endangering our agricultural productivity? But Lewisohn pointed out that, because of the population explosion, the US would never be able to feed the entire world. Therefore he recommended a system he called 'political triage.' PT for short. Basically, PT is based on the realization that food was then in short supply and would be for the foreseeable future. Therefore food must be used strategically and tactically as an offensive weapon. Since we could not feed the entire world, we could best serve our own interests by our choice of who buys our wheat, who gets our corn, who is shipped enough soybeans and fertilizer to allow them to continue to exist as viable nations. And at what level of subsistence. Some nations inimical to us would have to go down the pipe. Others we could maintain at a starvation level, a malnutrition level, or, if we wished, a comfortable level approximating our own calorie-consumption rate. Hence the term 'political triage.' It was a breathtaking concept that Lewisohn devised. And, all in all, I would say it served us well since it was implemented. At least we've avoided nukewar. All due to Hyman R. Lewisohn. This government will go to any lengths, *any*, to keep his brain functioning. We need him. It's that simple. Does that answer your question?"

"Yes, sir."

"Now you answer mine. What is it you want to try on Lewisohn?"

I told him.

He heard me out. Still pacing into shadow, and into light. When I had finished, he came back behind his desk.

"What chance of success?" he asked. Harsh, cracked voice.

"I'd guess between thirty and fifty percent, sir," I told him.

He nodded, shoved back, continued to stare at me. Horror there?

"I suppose you want my authorization?"

"Yes, sir." I nodded. "I'll need it. In writing."

He made a sound. A grunt? Snort?

"All right," he said. "Go ahead. Supreme security."

I had asked Paul to wait for me in the DCS office. Then we'd drive out to Chevy Chase in one of the official cars that had been assigned to his department. Strange. How I thought of it as "his department." Well, he ruled the daily administration, so I supposed the preconception was normative. It was probably everyone's.

He and Mary Bergstrom were alone in the inner office. They looked up questioningly when I walked in.

"All set?" Paul asked. "We're hungry."

"In a minute," I said.

I sat down across the desk from him. I noticed he had extended his swivel chair to its full height and had equipped it with elevated casters. It put him at a higher level than the object sitting across the desk from him. I was amused. A typical gig of Potomocracy. He had learned fast.

"Got a Bold?" I asked him.

He slid a package across the desk.

"Hitting the cannabis hard lately, aren't you?" he asked.

"Am I?" I said. "I wasn't aware of it."

"How did the meeting go with the Chief?"

"Fine. It was about Lewisohn. We're going ahead."

"Going ahead? With what? The em is stopping."

There was no way I could keep it secret from him. I had no desire to. I needed a capable AA in the Washington area. He'd have to be told, and Mary Bergstrom, and all of Group Lewisohn.

"This is top security," I said. "You both know the regulations."

Then I outlined the scenario. About halfway through, Paul rose to his feet. He leaned across the desk to me. Knuckles down. I thought at first that, like the Chief Director, he was horrified by the plan.

Then I saw it enraged him. I ignored his fury.

"Group Lewisohn will serve as nucleus for staff," I went on.

"I'll rule all personnel. Phoebe Huntzinger will rule the computer setup in GPA-1. I'll bring Tom Lee and Project Phoenix down from Denver to Hospice No. 4. When they're positioned, we'll switch the direct-wire link. Alexandria to New York and return. We'll pick up a time lag there, but of no consequence. Leo Bernstein will also move his project to Hospice No. 4. I'll start recruiting the surgical team immediately. Paul, I want you and Mary to handle the logistics down here. Try to get the one with Operating Theater D. It's the largest building. We'll need living quarters and feeding facilities for the entire staff inside the building. And recreation—movies, TV, music, games, and so forth. Everyone will be locked up. No one in, no one out. Until it's done. You'll have to structure the security screen. Art Roach can tell you what you'll need in the way of personnel and equipment. But don't tell him what—"

"You idiot!" Paul screamed. Face livid. Entire corpus trembling with anger. "You microbrained idiot! Do you realize what you're doing?"

"I'm hoping to save Lewisohn," I said. As calmly as I could. "That's my prime responsibility."

"Save Lewisohn?" he shouted. "Kaka! Nothing can save that em. He's stopping! You understand? He's practically stopped now. Thirty percent, you said. That's chance of success. And for that you're endangering the whole Department of Creative Science?"

"It has nothing to do with DCS," I said.

"It has everything to do with DCS," Paul yelled. Slamming a palm on the desktop. "*Everything!* You don't know politics. You just don't know. You think when we fail on this stupid Lewisohn caper that Congress is going to be sympathetic to our plans? 'The operation was a success, but the patient stopped.' Oh, they'll profit from that! All the butchers out to gut our bill. You think you can keep Lewisohn's stopping a secret? In this town? No way! And you and I will take the blame. So why trust us with something as important as the DCS?"

"You're overreacting," I told him.

"I tell you, I *know*, You don't know, but I do. I deal with these objects everyday while you're running around the country having tea with professors. This town will forgive anything but failure. When Lewisohn stops, you and I stop with him, as far as our political careers go. And maybe the DCS stops too. Right in its tracks. But even if the bill is passed, with the sperm drained out of it, they won't touch you and me with plastirub gloves. The two bright young lads who stopped Lewisohn. What in God's name were you thinking of?"

"There's a chance the operation will succeed," I said.

"A chance!" he scoffed. Still trembling. Face twisted with his wrath and frustration. "Thirty percent. Some chance! Don't you think the whole DCS is chancy? I can tell you it goddamned well is. But if that gamble isn't enough, you've got to pile chance on chance, endangering something I've served on every minute for the past six months."

"*You've* served?" I shouted. Rising to my feet. Leaning across the desk so that our faces were inches apart. "*You've* served? And what have I been doing—fluffing my duff? Whose idea was it? Mine! Who wrote the prospectus? I did! Whose record and reputation convinced the Chief Director to go along with the DCS? Mine! All mine! You're just a server here, and don't you ever forget it. I've watched you swell and preen and gloat over the miracles you've accomplished. Kaka! Ripe, rich Kaka! You've got the brain of a server, the talents of a server, the ability of a server. That's all you are, that's all you'll ever be."

Then we were both screaming at once. Spraying spittle in each other's faces. I was vaguely conscious of Mary Bergstrom still sitting woodenly, expression stony. I knew where her sympathies lay. But I didn't care. I didn't need Paul *or* her. If necessary, I could do it all myself.

Finally I pounded a fist on the desk.

"All right!" I shouted. "All right! All right! Enough of this. Enough!"

We both quieted then. And drew back. Breathing hard. We were not physically violent types, either of us. But I could taste the bile in my mouth. Smell a sudden change in the odor of my own perspiration. I think possibly if the confrontation had continued for another few minutes, we'd have been at each other's throats.

"All right now," I said finally. Trying very hard to keep my voice steady. "I'll make it simple for you. I'm *ordering* you to assist on Operation Lewisohn. *Ordering*. Do you compute that? If you choose not to cooperate, please tell me now. I will then report your decision to the Chief Director. All clear?"

He turned his back to me. Stood facing the wall. Staring at a framed photograph of the Capitol. The silence went on and on. I lighted another cannabis with shaking hands. And waited.

Finally Paul turned to face me. Unexpectedly he was smiling. A tepid smile, but operative.

"Sure," he said genially. "I'll cooperate, Nick. We both will—won't we, Mary?"

I looked at her. She nodded. Without speaking.

"Good," I said. "I'll flash Luke Warren in the morning and tell him you'll be out there tomorrow and to give you everything you need. Get moving on this."

"Will do," he said lightly. "Should we go home now?"

"No. I think I'll take the shuttle back to New York. I want to get started on a personnel roster. You can drop me at the airport."

"Anything you say, Nick," Paul said. The smile warmer now. "You're the ruler."

About three hours later I was standing on the terrace of my GPA-1 penthouse. Staring down at the lighted, deserted compound. I had showered. Mixed a large vodka-and-Smack. Pulled on a robe. Unbelted. Before starting the preliminary Table of Organization for Operation Lewisohn, I had stepped outside. Just for a moment.

It was an unusually balmy night for early April. Sky clotted with thick clouds. Wind mild, with a hint of fairer days to come.

Spring is surely the saddest season. One thinks: "My God, *again?*"

I found I was not replaying the scene with Paul. Nor even computing the

Lewisohn scenario. I was dreaming only of Grace Wingate. Wishing she was standing, loosely robed, alongside me. Barefoot, as I was. We would stand in silence, for a while. Then we would ...

It had scarcely begun, and yet I knew the end. I think now the most precious passions have within them the seeds of stopping. Hope is, after all, an immature emotion. The astringency of end brings to even the sweetest affair a balance of flavor. Comfortable on the palate. So that one tastes with a sad, knowledgeable nod, and murmurs, "Good."

Poetry by Nicholas Bennington Herrick Flair: "Gather ye rosebuds while ye may; the thorns come soon enough."

As I began preliminary structuring of the Operation Lewisohn scenario, I saw the problem devolved into four elements: personnel, equipment, setting, timing. All these factors were crucial to the success of the experiment, but the selection of the most skillful servers available was, I felt, of prime cruciality. I would need:

1. Surgery team
2. Computer team
3. Project Phoenix team
4. Leo Bernstein's team

In addition to these four major groups (I made a note: "Gowns to be color-coded"), I would also require such supernumeraries as a Chief Nurse and assistants, Equipment Chief and assistants, a Chief Anesthesiologist and his associates, and a Production Team who would serve as medical stage directors, getting everyone in place on cue, timing the operation to the second, and coordinating the entrances and exits of the other players to avoid a mob scene in Operating Theater D. There was also, of course, Hyman R. Lewisohn himself.

Having determined the parameters of the personnel requirements, I began drawing up "optimum skill profiles" of the objects needed. These would go to Data & Statistics to be coded, then fed into our OA (Object Ability) computer. We would then, hopefully, get a selection of names of objects in Public Service who could perform the services required. I would make the final choices myself. It was, perhaps, regrettable that I was limited to Public Service by the "supreme security" nature of the assignment. There were many talented civilian scientists, some close friends, who from a vapid idealism had refused to sign the Oath of Allegiance. Thus limiting their careers. The US Government had the love.

All this took time. It was slightly more than a week before requisitions went out all over the world, calling in surgeons, anesthesiologists, medical equipment specialists, computerniks, and surgical managers with experience in directing long and complex operations. I estimated the entire Lewisohn scenario, from first knife slice to final hookup test, would take a minimum of fourteen hours.

Meanwhile, I had satisfied myself that Paul Bumford and Mary Bergstrom were serving as promised. An entire building at Hospice No. 4 was taken over for Operation Lewisohn. To the anguish of Dr. Luke Warren. A fence was constructed, a security screen implemented. Arriving staff members found themselves temporary prisoners within a restricted area. They slept in the "Lewisohn Building," ate there, found recreation there, and communicated with the outside world only through a censor control board.

I estimated later that the total cost of Operation Lewisohn ran well in excess of one million new dollars. The subject of this governmental largesse was continued on parabiotic therapy with a special IV diet designed to maximize his physical stamina, if only temporarily, to help him withstand the trauma of what awaited him. I avoided all personal contact with him during this period.

Neither Paul nor I allowed Operation Lewisohn to impede our efforts to move enabling legislation for the Department of Creative Science through the House of Representatives. Hearings before a subcommittee of the House Government Operations Committee were scheduled to begin during the third week in April. A favorable vote there would almost ensure passage by the full committee. HR-316 would then pass to the House Rules Committee for scheduling of floor debate.

There were many strings to pull, many egos to lave. At that point in time, our primary concern was the structuring of a roster of sympathetic witnesses to testify in favor of the bill at the hearings of the subcommittee of the House Government Operations Committee. We had carefully orchestrated a group of civilian scientists, academics, enema doctors, sociologists, hygienists, energeologists, science historians, gerontologists, and nuts-and-bolts businessmen. The last were enlisted with the assistance of my father's committee: Businessmen for the DCS. He had delivered.

Two days before the hearings were to commence, I went down to Washington. I stayed at the Chevy Chase place. I flashed Louise Rawlins Tucker, and told her my whereabouts and plans. She returned my call an hour later and said I'd be welcome to join her for lunch the following day. At her home. At 1300. Her manner was grave.

I walked from our Chevy Chase place. A solitary pedestrian on a gray, weepy day. A black raincoat buttoned over civilian clothes: Norfolk jacket, turtleneck sweater, flannel slacks. I tried to walk briskly, purposefully. A neighbor on an errand. Some neighbor. Some errand.

"Out for a stroll, Dr. Flair?"

"Oh, yes. On my way to seduce the Chief Director's wife, thank you."

If I had stopped to ponder the consequences. . . . But I did not stop to ponder. Could not. I think, perhaps for the first time in my life, I "was not in full possession of his faculties." Journalese for nuts. But that's not operative. Quite. I was aware of what I was doing but could not forbear. A unique experience for me. A not unpleasant one.

If Louise Rawlins Tucker or a server had answered my ring, I might have burst into tears. But neither did. After the third ring, the door opened. It was she. She! Grace Wingate let me in. Closed the door swiftly behind me. We smiled at each other. Shakily. I think we both said, "Well!" at the same time.

She busied herself taking my coat. Turning away to hang it in a hallway closet. She was wearing a strapped tanktop in pink. Shoulders and arms bare. Pinkish-purple slacks chained low on her hips. Sandals. My hammered silver earrings. When she came back to me, I touched them. We both laughed. Brief blast. Put arms about each other's waist, walked slowly back into the house. Then it was all right. Easy.

There were cucumber sandwiches, I think. And cocoa. It wasn't important. We sat apart and talked. Rapidly, frantically, breathlessly. There was so much to get through. So much to learn.

Her father had been in the Foreign Office. Retired now. That was how she had met Michael Wingate—at a Department of International Cooperation reception. Her mother collected cut glass in a hobnail design. Her one brother, older, married, two children, was with the Permanent Trade Mission in Peking. She had broken her leg at the age of thirteen. Skiing. Her tonsils were out. She was ashamed of her teeth, fearing they were too large, protuberant. She had studied dance. She adored broiled natural shrimp. Green and blue were her best colors, she thought. She worshiped my beard.

I did my best to reply in kind. Telling her about myself. Even imagining things to make myself more attractive in her eyes. To mogrify my image. A desperate stratagem, I admit. But you cannot love another unless you love yourself. She watched me steadily. Gaze never flickering. Finally, sandwiches merely nibbled, cocoa merely sipped, I moved over to sit alongside her on the couch.

We clasped hands and talked, talked. . . . Circling each other. Tentatively. Then spiraling closer. Each new revelation breeding another.

She told me her husband was a brilliant em, and kind, thoughtful. But he had a hundred guises, was all things to all objects. Withal, a secret em. Because there was a wall around the core of him. She could not penetrate to what he was, really, essentially. He wouldn't let her. And, above all, she wanted to be close to someone. So close that she could lose herself. Surrender.

I warned her. I said that my moral sense was atrophied. That I had used many objects, ef and em, for my own profit. That I connived without conscience. Betrayed. That I was ego-oriented and goal-directed. Sometimes without ruth. But for all that, I had not murdered. Personally. She might think that last merely a matter of degree. But degree was all—was it not? Absolutism was the mark of a crabbed and dingy brain. And although I had—

It was then she leaned forward and pressed soft, warm lips on mine. To silence me.

"I don't care," she whispered. "About all that. You can hurt me. Nick. If you want to."

I shook my head. "I don't want to hurt you. I want to know you."

We stared into each other's eyes. And learned more than all our words. Those dark, somber eyes. Widening to bring me in. I drifted hair back from her ears. She sat erect. Trembling slightly. I felt her ears with my fingers. Probing.

"That . . ."she said.

"Oh, yes," I said. "I know."

We felt each other. Still seated, we touched. Explored. Hair. Features. Neck and limbs. Torso. Our hands fluttering. Her bare shoulders. My arms. Her waist. My chest. Legs. Yes, and ankles. All. I caressed her toes, bared by her sandals.

During that almost somnambulistic ritual, we realized—I know I did; I think she did—that we would not use each other that day. The recognition lightened us, freed us.

She was, Grace Wingate was, to me, all sweetness and light. A large corpus but fragile, elegant. In texture and movement. Complete with the buoyancy of youth. And beyond sexuality, there was, in those somber eyes, dark glance, the unknowable that sucked me in, drew me in. I wanted to dive.

"I love you," I said.

"Why do you love me?"

I told her all. Corpus. Somber eyes. Soft lips. Vulval ears. Flame of ashen hair. Touch of her skin. The naked body moving within what she wore. Toes I longed to suck. The pouting navel I imagined. The ache to become one with her. Need to . . . what? Merge? Melt into each other. Penis and vagina welded. A two-backed beast. Ultimate linkage. Then, Siamese twins. Heart and all visceral organs joined. One beat. One throb. One thought.

It did excite her. The conception. A mirror of her secret hope. She began to say why she loved me. Just as graphic. Obscure eyes flaming now. As she came alive. Words she had thought but had never spoken. Stuttering from her moist tongue. Her fantasies and mine. Combined.

She told what she would do to me. For me. Bravely. In such tones that I had to know she was willing to transform dreams of reality.

That brief afternoon was as dear as a dream recalled. Later, I remembered, we sat in the walled garden. Our secret place. Both of us cloaked against a raw drizzle. Clasping hands. We the only source of heat and joy in the universe. Radiating. Then we did not speak; we could already be silent together. With profit.

It was strange that parting—as we had to, eventually. It was a small defeat. A small stop. We both had the sense that such a necessary, practical thing as parting, that afternoon, somehow reduced our passion. Stupid, I know. But there it was.

"We must make it up," she said gravely. "So strong together that parting can mean little. Nothing. No effect."

"Even better," I said. "To make us stronger. You compute? Strong enough to be apart and loving more."

"We'll age well." She laughed. Kissing my palm. Before I slipped out the door. "Like good wine."

"Or music," I said.

"Music." she nodded.

Back to this world. The hearings opened on HR-316, A Bill to Establish a Department of Creative Science within the Public Service of the US Government, and went exceeding well. Joe Wellington had arranged for complete media coverage. Including live TV broadcasts on the federal (formerly educational) network. The parade of favorable witnesses was impressive. Their credentials were undeniable, their statements (as instructed) were short and pithy.

Questioning by subcommittee members was brief and superficial. The Congressmen were not venal. (In this regard.) Simply uniformed. We were dealing here with scientific matters of great complexity. Even the subcommittee's staff, though they might be science-conditioned, could grasp only part of what we proposed. Let alone foresee the consequences. So that opening statements and questioning dealt mainly with such matters as medical research on geriatric disorders, new methods of utilizing solar energy, the efficacy of inoculation against venereal diseases, genetic manipulation to prevent crime, and so forth.

But all this was froth. No one questioned, thankfully, the philosophy of the bill. No one asked what influence the proposed Department might wield on the political and social infrastructures. No one wondered how the future might be tilted by giving to science and technology an authoritative, policy making role in the US Government. I believed that role would be benign. But no one asked.

I think, by the fourth day, we had all relaxed. Knowing it was going well. HR-316 was on its way to becoming the law of the land. Paul and I, having set new events in motion, turned back to pendulating projects.

"This UP thing," he said. "Houston has been expediting it. As per orders. They're up to Mk. 7. They claim results."

"Tested?"

"On prisoners. Three stoppages on Mk. 4. But that was traced to contaminated containers. They've got a prototype package for the new brew. Want to try?"

He knew my insistence on testing new drugs personally. Either by myself or members of my staff.

"The Mk. 7?" I said. "Sure. Fly in a sample. I'll try it at Chevy Chase

tomorrow night. Have Seth Lucas bring over a diagnostic kit. And tape recorders. I've always wanted to know the Ultimate Pleasure."

"It's got an orgasmic trigger," he said.

"Thanks for warning me," I said. "Tell everyone to stand back."

By 2100 the following evening, we were prepared. In my bedroom at the
Chevy Chase place. In attendance were Paul, Mary Bergstrom, Maya Leighton,
Dr. Seth Lucas. Three tape recorders and Lucas' diagnostic kit. This was a
small, portable juke, developed by DIVRAD's Electronic Team. Circuitry
based on space technology. Taped sensors provided input on pulse, respiration,
skin temperature, blood pressure, EEG, etc., all signaled on separate screens
and recorded on paper tape automatically. With time indications along the
edge.

I lay naked, the taped wires leading from my corpus to the gizmo. Lucas
fussed over that. Paul and Mary handled stopwatches and recorders. A fascinated Maya Leighton held a towel.

"Your Thrill of the Month," I told her.

"Better," she assured me.

Seth checked out his pinball.

"All circuits go," he reported.

"All right, Nick," Paul said. Nervously, I thought. "I'm going to hand you
the pack. The moment you take it, we start the clock. You scan the printed
directions, follow them, open the pack, self-administer."

"Yes, doctor," I said. "Let's have it."

He took the UP Mk. 7 from a brown paper bag. It was a clear plastic kit.
Very small. No larger than, perhaps, a plastisealed tube of glue or a dozen
nails.

"Give us verbal response as long as you can," Paul said. "Don't worry about
coherence. Just babble."

"Right," I said.

"This is exciting," Maya said.

Paul handed me the package.

"Start time," he said loudly. "Two one three eight point four six. *Now!*"

I scanned the instructions slowly: "This UP injection is the sole property
of the US Government. It has not been licensed for manufacture, distribution,
or sale by any other agency, business, group, or individual. Unauthorized
manufacture, distribution, and/or sale is in direct violation of Public Law
DIVRAD OL962341-B2, and subject to penalties inherent therein. To receive
an additional UP injection, this package and its contents (needle and emptied
tube) must be returned to your local distribution center."

"Simplify instructions," I said. "Means nothing to wetbrains." I continued
scanning:

"To use the UP injection, follow these steps carefully:

"One: Open plastic case by tearing slowly along perforated line A-B."

Obediently, I attempted to tear along the perforated line A-B. It didn't serve. I broke a fingernail.

"It doesn't tear," I said.

"Correct," Paul said. "It's not perforated. The dotted line is just printed on. The whole idea is to consume time and make the object frantic. Keep trying."

I finally ripped the cardboard backing off and got the clear plastic cover loose. Paul and Mary glanced at their stopwatches, made notes of my progress.

"Two: Unscrew plastic cap from needle of Syrette."

"We need another word," I said. "Objects won't know what 'Syrette' means. And the dammed top won't unscrew."

I finally pulled it off. There were no threads; it was merely pressure-applied.

"Another time-waster?" I asked Paul.

"Ritual," he said. "Go on."

"Three: Push exposed needle with a sharp, quick motion into any area of the corpus below the neck."

"No good," I said. "That might include anus, genitals, nipples, navel, et cetera. Instructions should be more explicit. Perhaps limiting target area to arms, legs, buttocks, and so forth. I'll take it in the thigh."

Their tape decks were recording my comments. Seth Lucas was watching his screens and dials. His tape, too, was running.

"Slightly heightened signals," he reported. "Nothing abnormal."

"Here we go," I said.

I jabbed the needle into my right thigh.

"Four: Squeeze from the bottom of the tube. Using thumb and forefinger of the right hand (if right-handed) or thumb and forefinger of the left hand (if left-handed), make certain the full and complete contents of the Syrette are emptied through the needle."

"Who wrote these instructions?" I asked. "Gertrude Stein?"

I compressed the tube as directed. From the bottom to the top. It was an opaque container; I didn't know if it was a clear liquid or a milky creme.

"Five: Withdraw needle from skin and put Syrette carefully aside. Remember, you cannot be awarded another UP injection unless you return the used and emptied syringe to your local distribution center."

I pulled the needle from my thigh. Rolled over carefully so as not to disturb my taped sensors, and placed the emptied Syrette carefully on the bedside table.

I had expected it to start with a gentle euphoria. Either a numbness or a tingling. But it was a jolt.

"A hit," I heard myself say. "It's got to beeee...."

"Pulse and respiration rising," I heard Seth Lucas report. "Skin temperature up. And he—"

That was the last I heard from anyone. Then I could hear only myself:

"Got to stretch it. That intro. Now. Sweat and vibrations. Memory going. Sphincter contracting. Auditory nil. Numbness beginning now. Fingers. Toes."

Then I could no longer hear myself.

There were the hackneyed hallucinogenic visual reactions moving swiftly through clouds that gradually brightened to swirls of color. Great blobs of brilliant hues everywhere. (No music; no sound at all.) Then the colors clearing, drawing back: the reverse of a drop of oil on water. Enormous well-being then. Peace, and a divine carelessness. Ultimate don't- give-a-damnness.

I see a chair. Or couch. The center of the image is clear. The edges are blurred, with striations of light. A vignette. An ef is seated. An obso ef, but not unhandsome. A heavy, scarred, and pitted face. Almost emish, but attractive. Strong. She is wearing an em's blue serving shirt. Not buttoned, but loosely tied about her heavy breasts. She is leaning back. Bare stomach and torso are soft. There are precisely three rolls of avoirdupois. I note them clearly. She is wearing faded denim shorts. Ragged. Torn off from pants. Belted with a brass buckle in a lion's-head design. Her knees are up, and spread. Bare feet on the edge of the chair. Or couch. The skimpy shorts are pulled tight across her pudendum. It is divided into two plump halves. Bulging.

I come into the picture. From the blurred edge. Coming into focus. We speak. But there is no sound. I touch her bare knee.

"You can do what you like," she says. "Hurt me if you want to."

"I don't want to hurt you," I say. "I want to know you."

I spread her knees wider, standing now between them. I scrape the insides of her naked thighs gently with my fingernails. She closes her eyes.

I kneel. I rub my mustache and beard along her legs. Then begin to kiss. Lick. I pause to look up. Her eyes are open. Somber.

"Untie your shirt," I tell her.

She obeys. Pulls the knotted shirttails free, opens them wide. Her skin is coarse, bruised. Her liberated breasts swell down. They are heavy eggplants. Purplish. Glossy. Aureoles are hardly distinguishable; nipples are retracted. I lean forward awkwardly. I blow gently on one nipple. It begins to grow. When it has extruded sufficiently, I touch it softly with my wet tongue. Her entire body leaps convulsively on the chair. Couch. I pulp the elongating nipple between my lips. The other begins to extrude. Her breasts harden. She slumps sideways. I ease her down. Put a pillow beneath her head. Her hair is quite long. Black without luster. Streaked with gray.

I take her hand, make her cup a breast. Then I kiss her lips. Lightly. Our tongues serving. As we flicker, I push her hand and breast upward. Pull her head forward, down. Her breast is full enough so that we can both kiss and suck. Simultaneously. Tongues circling the erectile nipple, meeting, circling. The taste is sharp, almost acrid.

Now her breasts are slick. Slipping from my grasp. I draw back from her.

Gesture toward her shorts. Then they are gone. The opened shirt gone from her shoulders. She is naked. I am still wearing my silver zipsuit. Red tab on right epaulette.

I begin. Moving her hands and fingers to show her how she must hold herself for me. Her knees are up. Then her feet. High in the sky. A cloud beneath her hips. Warm moisture collects on my mustache and beard. She adores the beard. Worships it. I nuzzle deeper, straining my tongue. She groans.

I slide her fingers lower. Demonstrate how I want her buttocks prized apart. My fingers are coated with petrogrease. I slide into the brown rosebud.

"Am I hurting you?" I asked anxiously.

"Deeper," she says.

My forefinger probes slyly. She begins a slow paroxysm. My other hand fumbles at her navel. Exploring slickly.

Her movements become stormy. Unruly. I manipulate her. First here. There. Together. It crescends. The bruises on her coarse flesh become livid. Bright violet and yellow splotches. Then, with a great pelvis heave, she summits. I hang on, continuing my service.

I turned my eyes upward to see her expression. I saw Paul Bumford. Leaning over me.

"Nick?" he said. Anxiously, I thought. "You all right?"

"Time?" I asked.

He glanced at his stopwatch.

"From the moment you took the package," he said, "about seventy-three minutes."

I looked about the room. Seth Lucas was checking the dials and long strip of paper tape. Mary Bergstrom was regarding me curiously. Maya Leighton was grinning, the clotted towel wadded up in her hands.

"Total time disorientation," I reported.

"Get this:" I said. "Euphoric physical weakness. Visual disacuity. Total auditory loss. From the looks of that towel Maya is playing with, I gather I summited. But no memory of it. No psychic guilt. No hangover. No regrets. Quite an experience. *Quite* an experience. How much time elapsed after I stopped talking?"

They all looked at me queerly.

"You never stopped talking," Paul said. "Not for a second."

I groaned. "You mean you've got it all on tape? Even the eggplants?"

"Even the eggplants," Maya giggled. "And the bruises."

"That was interesting," Paul said. "Nick, do you agree that—"

"Please." I held up a hand. "Let's have no cut-rate psychoanalysis of my personal hangups. We're just trying to evaluate a new drug. Do you think my verbal outpouring was a result of the UP?"

"Nooo," Paul said slowly. Judiciously. "That particular reaction hasn't been reported in any other test. I think it was just your conditioning. A desire to give us—if you'll excuse the expression—a blow-by-blow account. Let's go through some physical and mental coordination workups now. Seth, how does he look?"

"Parameters back to normal," Lucas reported. "Pulse, respiration, and skin temperature just slightly higher, but nothing significant."

"You summited, baby," Maya Leighton said decisively. Enviously? "You really ultimized."

A few hours later I was in my bedroom, robed, serving at my desk. Knock at the door; I called out, and Paul entered, carrying his vodka-and-Smack, and bringing me one.

"For this relief, much thanks," I said. "Hamlet." I took a big gulp. "I'm trying to rough a report on the UP while it's all fresh. You might send it on to Houston."

"Of course. Your posttests proved affirmative. Any late reactions?"

"Warm lassitude. Pleasant. Slight physical weakness. No mental or psychological effects I can detect. Paul, if possible I'd like them to work on that initial jolt. See if they can mildify it. A slower lead-in would be more effective. Another thing that disturbs me: Shouldn't I have been physically conscious of the orgasm?"

Paul computed a moment. Frowning.

"No," he said finally. "Not necessarily. The fantasized experience apparently was psychologically satisfying. To such an extent that you summited. While still under the UP, you felt no sense of loss, did you?"

"No."

"And when you came out of it, you felt satiety. Correct?"

"Correct."

"Then your objection now is based on your conditioning to conventional orgasm. Did the UP satisfy you?"

"Yes. Definitely, yes."

"Well, then it achieved the goal. In your case, apparently, the psychological, or psychic, ruled the physical. The effect of the UP won't be identical on all objects. Some will be aware of physical orgasm. To some objects it might be great art, music, poetry, cruelty, suffering—anything. It's formulated to be generic."

"Yes. Still, I'd hardly call an involuntary emission the Ultimate Pleasure."

"Not even in the context of your fantasy?"

"Well . . . that's a thought. It was quite a go. Strange."

"Nick, could I—no, no! Don't hold up your hand. I'm not going to analyze your dream. At least not try to individualize it. But to universalize. . . . The problem, we agreed, is not the UP injection itself, but the surrounding social and political environments."

"So?"

"Would it be reasonable to interpret your fantasy as one of submission? Total surrender?"

I computed a moment.

"I think it could be interpreted that way."

Paul nodded. Thoughtful.

"You haven't had a chance to scan the Houston interviews. But the same factors turns up in a surprising percentage of experimental object tapes."

"What factor?" I asked.

"The slave factor," he said. Looking at me steadily.

I blinked at him. I had an unpleasant feeling that he had gone beyond me. That he was off somewhere. In realms I could not appreciate.

"Let's get this straight," I said to him. "Are you suggesting the slave factor may be primary to Ultimate Pleasure?"

"Yes," Paul said. Definitely. "All indicators point that way."

"And?"

"If it proves out, it should give us a valid guide to the essential nature of the political society that might enforce and enhance that pleasure."

I stared at him a long moment. He *was* ahead of me. Computing in spheres that had never concerned me.

"You *have* made a giant step," I said.

"Yes." He nodded. "I have. Look, Nick," he said earnestly, "we agreed a political drug could only function with optimum effect in a society that complements it. Neither of us brainstormed the structure of that society. If, after additional testing, the slave factor in the UP proves to be valid, wouldn't you say it constitutes a steer to the nature of the society required?"

I shook my head.

"Maybe that UP injection does have residual and negative mental effects. Paul, there's something inoperative in your computing. It just doesn't scan. I don't know where you're off. I can't isolate it. I just feel you're wrong. In any event, assuming what you say *is* operative, what do you propose now?"

He hunched forward on his chair. Very serious. Very sincere.

"Nick," he said, "this Operation Lewisohn gives us a marvelous opportunity for a field test. About half the staff have already come aboard at Hospice No. 4. The remainder should be reporting in a week or so. What if I call in a miniteam of psychoneurologists from Houston as observers. We divide the staff of Operation Lewisohn into thirds. Mixed disciplines. One-third a control group. One-third on placebos. One-third on the UP. Placebos and UP injections awarded for good service and extended hours. And so forth. Let the psychoneurologists run a computer study. Analyzing hours served, efficiency, morale, physical condition, and so forth. When Operation Lewisohn is over— whether it succeeds or fails—we should have a concretized idea of the value of the UP in a realistic productive situation."

"Good idea," I said. "Let's do it."

A year ago, even six months ago, it would have been my idea.

I checked on the progress of Operation Lewisohn at Hospice No. 4, finalized plans with Joe Wellington for a PR gig through the Midwest, sent three dozen natural roses to Louise Rawlins Tucker, and then returned to GPA-1. There I spent a day serving with Phoebe Huntzinger and her computerniks. They were programming our largest hardware, a King Mk, V, with a 200,000-word English vocabulary, plus additional foreign words and phrases.

"More, Phoebe," I said.

"More?"

"Pick up a dictionary of profanity and obscenity. Add it to your storage. Shouldn't be more than a thousand bits."

"Profanity and obscenity," she repeated. "I wish I knew what this was all about."

"It's better you don't," I told her. "Rush your wire link with Denver. The moment it's through and tested, let me know."

"And then?"

"Then you pull it," I laughed. "And switch to Alexandria, Virginia. When I tell you."

"Whee!" she yelled. Tossing papers into the air. "Insanity incorporated."

It wasn't. Really. It was carefully structured. With a timetable and flow chart. I had called in a project systems em with top security, and he had served on the logistics. We had allowed wiggle room, but as of that date in late April, we were right on schedule. As to equipment and objects. We had prepared fall-back positions and fail-safe alternatives. I was satisfied we were contravening Murphy's Law.

The twenty-eighth of April. About 2315. I was in my apartment at Manhattan Landing. Packing to begin the Midwest PR tour in the morning. Computing how many Somnorifics I might need, when the flasher chimed. Paul came on. Visage grave and pulled.

"Paul?" I said. "What is it?"

"It's an open line," he said tensely. "I'll cheat on what I say. Keep your questions glossed. Got that?"

"Yes. What is it?"

"The business in GPA-11. The stamps. Sam's stakeout. Follow that?"

"Stakeout? In D.C.?" I asked.

"Yes. I got all this from Art Roach. He got it from pals in BPS. Not complete. Anyway, about an hour ago, another attempt."

"Ohhh," I breathed.

"Caught him. One em. Contaminating the adhesive. Follow?"

"Yes."

"Tried to put a tranquilizer dart into him. Sam's servers. But before it worked, he gulped. Suicided. Got that?"

"I think so. Instant?"

"No. But he's stopping. No way. You understand? A mouthful."

"That should do it," I said.

"You know him," Paul said.

"What?"

"Not know him. But saw him. I knew him. Met him. Talked to him. Raddo. Arthur Raddo. That pale, blond fanatic. At the Beist Christmas meeting."

"Oh-oh," I said. "The wowser."

"Yes. Served at Bureau of Printing and Engraving."

"Anyone else?"

"No word. As of now. Just him."

"Motive?"

"Not known. Sam is checking."

"I can imagine. No doubt?"

"None. He had a little bottle of the stuff. Five cc. It broke when he fell. A TDT had to move in."

I was silent.

"Nick, it's not good. The Beist connection."

"Maybe no connection at all."

"That's what I'm hoping. Or that the CD will pillow it. Because of you-know-who."

"Yes."

"I think he was just a loner."

"Hope you're right. But why?"

"No idea."

"Anything else?"

"No," he said.

"Thanks for flashing. Let me know what happens."

"Will do. Have a good trip."

"Thanks."

We switched off.

Arthur Raddo. The young em with lank blond hair falling untidily over his forehead. Enormous eyes with a fervid stare. Flat lips he licked constantly. Wearing a wrinkled, soiled zipsuit of a PS-5. His physical appearance gave the impression of limp ineffectuality. But his voice was unexpectedly loud, passionate. Still, I was certain he was a frail.

That was the em who had poisoned thousands of objects in GPA-11.

But that wasn't important. At the moment. What was crucial, to me, in Paul's staccato report, was the 5 cc flask Raddo had been carrying. The bottle that smashed when he suicided. That required calling in a Toxin Decontamination Team. A 5 cc flask of *Clostridium botulinum* in glycerol.

I immediately went into the same drill. Pulled on a raincoat. Slogged through a rainy night to B Lab. Down to the third sublevel. Into the pharmacology library. I went through a charade of looking up acetylsalicylic acid in the file computer. Because I remembered 416HBL-CW3 was stored in the restricted section in Room G, Bin 3, Stack 4, Position R.

I finally buzzed a dozing Vinnie Altman awake. He let me in and I signed the register while he breathed petroport fumes in my face. He wanted to talk. I didn't.

I went directly to the room, the bin, the stack, the position. Extracted tooth. A gap. The 5 cc flask was gone.

I stood there. Staring at the emptiness. Smelling the piercing, pinching odor of manipulation. I had been. That forgery. The 2 cc taken, the bottle left. What else would I do but replace the missing liquid? Remove the original file card. Sign a letter to R. Sam Bigelow stating that *my* visual inspection had verified the original deposit of 416HBL-CW3.

And when the BPS snoops, alerted by the smashed 5 cc flask in the hand of the stopping Arthur Raddo, decided to check personally on all amounts of *Clostridium botulinum* issued to research Gruppen in 1988, how would I explain its absence from my pharmacology library? And my official letter stating it was intact and untouched?

Strangely, my first reaction was admiration. I remembered what Art Roach had said after I had explained how we had broken his arm in order to share him.

"That was *beautiful*," he had breathed.

So was this. Beautiful.

Then I felt sick.

Z-7

From an address to an international convention of neurobiologists held in Chicago, Illinois, on May 3, 1999:

"There is no precedent in history for what is happening. Those who look to the Mechanical Revolution of the Nineteenth Century or the Technological Revolution of the Twentieth Century for aid in coping with our problems will look in vain.

"For the Biological Revolution of the Twenty-first Century is unique in human experience. It deals not with materials, equipment, and tools—not with *things*—but with objects, members of the species *Homo sapiens*. It is revealing to us not only how to change objects already in existence, but how to alter our own evolution. To change both for the better, I hasten to add, so we might more easily deal with and plan for the radically transformed society that tomorrow will inexorably bring.

"As neurobiologists, you know there is nothing absolute in human nature. Nothing that cannot be manipulated for the greater health of the individual and the greater good of society. What are these alterations in the corpus we must seek if we are to insure the physical and mental health of citizens of the Twenty-first Century? Suppose we start with the brain, and consider what neurobiological manipulations may be of benefit to the gene pool of the future. . . ."

And so forth. And so forth. Kaka.

Worst of all, I didn't even have the consoling presence of Samantha Slater's wormish corpus in my hotel room. At the last moment, Joe Wellington had revised the travel scenario.

"Sorry, Nick," he said, "but I need Samantha here in D.C.-ville. HR-316 is coming up for a vote next week; it's no time to scatter the troops."

It was downputting, but I couldn't stamp my foot and pout. After all, it *was* for the DCS. As I boarded the jet for Chicago, a slender em in a checkered cap bumped into me. As I entered the hotel lobby in Chicago, a plump em in a checkered cap jostled me.

A less mentally healthy object might have suffered an onslaught of paranoia. First Joe Wellington's squelch of my amour propre. Then what might have been a tail by a confederation of checkered-capped enemies. All this on top of the disappearance of the 5 cc flask from my pharmacology library.

That was no irrational suspicion. The bottle was gone, and I was responsible for it. I had glossed it as best I could by filling that accusing gap in Position R, Stack 4, Bin 3, Room G, with an identical 5 cc flask of pure glycerol. But it was literally a stopgap measure. Temporarily, until R. Sam Bigelow's noses came to check volume and analyze contents. Before that happened, I would be able to discover who was manipulating me, and for what purpose. I hoped.

After Chicago, the PR safari moved on to Minneapolis, Omaha, Denver. In the last city, I spent a day at the DIVRAD Field Office with Tom Lee, reviewing his logistic plan for moving Project Phoenix to Hospice No. 4 in Alexandria, Virginia. He had projected well. I made a few minor alterations—more to assert my authority than from any real need for change; a server's plans are *never* totally operative—and then gave him the go for the move.

On to Oklahoma City, New Orleans, Memphis. Speeches, colloquies, interviews, symposia. My only pleasure was in writing and mailing a letter, every day, to Louise Rawlins Tucker. Addressed to her. Intended for the eyes of Grace Wingate. I wrote, I suppose, many foolish things. But they gave me much joy. I had never before known the happiness of stripping oneself naked in words. Surprisingly therapeutic.

And eventually, back in Washington, D.C., May 26, 1999. On the day I returned, the subcommittee of the House Government Operations Committee passed HR-316 with but one dissenting vote. I was in time for a sedate orgy at the home of Penelope Mapes to celebrate our initial victory. I had hoped Chief Director Michael Wingate, and wife, might be present. They were not. But Louise Rawlins Tucker was.

"How is she?" I asked.

"She's lonely," she said.

"She got my letters?"

"Of course."

I looked at her with admiration. She was taking a dreadful chance. She turned back to me then. Smile fading. Eyes hardening. Not an ef I'd care to cross.

"I told you," she said. I could scarcely hear. "Hurt her, and I'll—"

"I know, I know," I said hurriedly. "I believe you. I have no wish to hurt her. I told you that. And I told her. If something goes wrong, the CD will save her. But you must save yourself."

"And you?"

"I'll worry about it when the time comes. If it does."

"It'll be too late then," she said. Suddenly, embarrassingly, her eyes filled with tears.

I stared at the dragoon of an ef. The big, blotchy face. Like seeing a rhino cry. I couldn't compute it.

"When may I see her?" I asked softly.

"Tomorrow. Noon. My home."

"I thank you," I said. And moved away.

I left the party while Paul and Mary Bergstrom were still there. Carefully computed. I went back to our Chevy Chase home. Directly to Paul's bedroom. His desk was unlocked. After five minutes search, I found the membership list of the Washington, D.C., chapter of the Beists. I was startled by their rapid growth: more than five thousand names. I scanned Arthur Raddo's address until I was certain I had it. A scurvy neighborhood on Sixth Street.

I located, with difficulty, two lovable liters of natural California pinot noir. I carried them both to the safe house. One for us; one to be left behind for that stern obso ef who was risking too much for our joy.

The door was opened to my third ring. For the briefest of microseconds I was panicked by the sight of a stranger. But no, it was Grace Wingate. Wearing the same middy, blue scarf, pleated skirt, white plastivas sneakers she had worm to the Beist meeting the first night we met. What had delayed recognition was a heavy wig of russet hair. Drawn back, braided into a single plait that hung down her back. Thick and long as an em's arm.

She laughed delightedly at my astonishment. Whirled to exhibit. The pigtail flung out and struck me lightly across the face. I caught it. Held it to my lips. Thick hair. Strong. Scented.

"What on earth?" I said.

"It's real human hair," she said eagerly. "Not synthetic. From France, I think. Or Bulgaria. Some place like that. Do you like it, Nick?"

I pulled that live hawser in, hand over hand, until her back was against me. Tightly. I moved the woven plait so that it curved over her shoulder, hung down her front. I reached around to clasp it there.

"Wanton!" I whispered in her ear.

She glanced back at me. Mischievous.

"Yes, I am," she said. "With you."

It was a creamy noon. Breeze hinting of summer heat. Altocumulus high in a pellucid sky. On such a day; why should I glance about casually at the windows of strangers, overlooking our garden, our secret place, and wonder where hypersensitive parabolic microphones might be emplaced?

We sat on a curving bench in the arbor. The poor, peeling lattice that seemed fated to know July as bare and forlorn as it had endured December. The entire garden had that feel: gentle decay and soft sadness. All colors muted. All scents fragile. Even a cricket's chirp faint and hesitant.

After some initial chatter, she seemed to sense my reverie, and was quiet. Then she leaned close, back half-turned so that I might caress her glossy plait.

"You do like," she murmured. "Nick? Don't you?"

"Oh, yes. Very much."

"More than my own hair?"

"Not more than," I said. "But as much as."

She giggled softly. "I can never catch you out."

"I've had a lot of experience," I said.

I left off stroking that rope of vibrant hair. How could hair, as nerveless as a fingernail, so pulse with life and seem responsive to a touch? I slid a hand beneath her loose middy. Up. Stroked, with timorous fingers, her naked back.

"Oh," she said.

I sat without moving. Regarding with wonder my wandering hand. It was not I, but my scampish fingers that searched, smoothed, probed. It was not I, I swear. That vagrant hand had its own mind, and would have its way. I felt it palm her cool, quivering flesh. Arch to scrape nails from arm to torso. Then, sneaky hand, it shifted furtively to circle her. Pull her closer. Until sly fingertips could touch her bare breasts. And stealthily search out a nipple soft and yielding as a bud. My wayward hand stopped there.

After a few minutes—my hand and I motionless—she turned to glance at me.

"Nick?" she said.

I was silent.

She moved away to face me. The lifeless hand fell limp from beneath her blouse.

"You look so strange," she said.

"Do I?" I said. "I feel strange. Something strange is happening to me."

I stood up. Shakily. Leaving my wine glass on the slatted bench. I wandered about that shoddy garden. Kicking gently at doomed plants. They would never make it. Never. I went back to sit beside her, take her two hands in mine.

"Do you believe I love you?" I said. "Love you more than any object or thing in this world? Do you believe that?"

"Yes," she said. Gravely. "I do believe that."

"You scanned my letters. You must know how I feel about you. The fantasies."

"They were beautiful," she said softly.

"I could only hint. Imply. I didn't want to compromise you, or Louise, by writing a complete scenario. You compute?"

"Oh, yes."

"It seemed to me that if we could use each other, I might very well stop with profit. I imagined how it could happen. Many times. In great detail. Scents. Tastes. The touch of you. A wildness."

"Don't you think I've thought the same? Many times? Mad dreams."

"I know, I know. And yet . . . and yet, a while ago, when I touched your sweet breast, I knew suddenly it would be a defeat. For me. For you. For our love."

"A defeat? Nick, I—I'm not sure I understand."

"You think I do?" I burst out. Almost angrily. "It doesn't scan. I know it doesn't. I know you bought that lovely wig for me. I was so excited when I felt it. And when I touched your body, I thought: It will be *now*. This afternoon. We will do it now. I can't tell you what that was. Rapture."

"And then?"

"A cold fist clamping around my heart. That using each other would defeat us. Our Love. What love. What is it, Grace? Tell me. Do you know? I love you more, now, at this moment, than ever before. But why should I feel this? That using will ruin us. What we are to each other."

"You feel it will—will *soil* us?"

"I don't know." I groaned. "I just don't know. I've used hundreds. Efs and ems. You know that. I told you that. I've done things you might think perverse. I never felt defiled. Or that I was corrupting my user. I never felt guilt. Never! But then—but then . . ."

"But then?" she prompted.

"But then I've never loved before. I thought it was an obso vulgarity. Now, loving, I think I want it to be new. All new. Oh, I must sound a choice idiot! I'm sorry, Grace. I wish I could analyze exactly what I felt and could explain it to you. All I know is that it's important to me. The most important thing in my life. Can you tell me? Please! Tell me what it is."

She put her arms about me. I put mine about her. Mouths close without kissing. The moment stretched without breaking.

If she had demanded we use each other immediately, I would have obeyed. And been potent, I knew. Exhibited my expertise, taken profit and given it. But I was right: It would have been a defeat. I think she sensed it, too. For we had never been closer than on that magic afternoon, in that secret garden. Realizing that everything that had gone before was preliminary. Now we were exploring a frightening realm. Where intimacy was so profound that it was mixed with fear of the unknown.

From that day on, my life became trichotomous. All the tangled skeins twisted into three strands. The strands braided into one rope. Like Grace's glossy plait. There were a few stray tendrils: the campaign for the Department of Creative Science, and so forth. But my main concerns devolved into: My relations with Grace Wingate and the shattering self-analysis that demanded; the rowen of the botulism outbreak in GPA-11 and the missing flask of 416HBL-CW3 from the GPA-1 pharmlab; and Operation Lewisohn, the most complex administrative project I had ever ruled. A hundred talented servers to be directed and managed in such a manner as to ensure that minimal 30 percent success possibility I had predicted to the CD.

When the entire staff had gathered in the Lewisohn Building in Hospice No. 4, I convened the first general assembly in Operating Theater D. Staff sat on the tiers of polished benches that rose high above the actual operating area. They were behind glass walls that were attached to the ceiling. I stood in the arena. Speaking to them via a PA system.

As per orders, they were all wearing the color-coded paper gowns and caps of their groups. Green for surgeons and anesthesiologists. Blue for Leo Bernstein and his servers. Brown for the Project Phoenix Team. Gray for Phoebe Huntzinger's computerniks. White for nurses. Red for the Production Team. Purple for Operation Directors. These colors had not been picked by whim; they had been selected with the aid of the psychoneurology miniteam from Houston. They had advised that red and purple represented high authority to most objects. A centuries-old conditioned reflex. The miniteam itself, present to administer Ultimate Pleasure injections and placebos to the Operation Lewisohn staff, and to analyze the results, wore zipsuits.

"Colleagues," I began, "I welcome you all, and thank you for being here. The fact that you had no choice in the matter doesn't change that sentiment one whit."

Their laughter came to me faintly from behind the glass walls.

"Before continuing my remarks," I went on, "I would like to introduce our Chief of Security, Art Roach, who has a few pertinent remarks of his own. Art . . ."

He was still wearing a black zipsuit, although we had already forwarded a recommendation for his promotion to red. When he took over the microphone, I was surprised to note that he was almost exactly my height and weight. I had always thought of him as a taller, heavier em. But that was before he became my server.

I had feared his necessary comments would be an embarrassing ramble in a fried-fritter accent. But again he surprised me. Pleasantly. His address was short and to the point. He reminded them all of the Oaths of Allegiance they had signed, and of the penalties resulting from betrayal of that Oath. Quoting copiously from official regulations, without notes, he told them that they were, in effect, to be held incommunicado for the duration of Operation Lewisohn. Communication with the outside world could be made, if absolutely necessary, only through a Censor Control Board. Every effort had been taken to make their off-hours as pleasant as possible. Any suggestions for additional recreation facilities would be welcome.

He did it all very well. Just a few "yawls." There was a polite snapping of fingers when he concluded. I took over the mike again.

"All right," I said. "Let's get to it—what you're doing here. Some of you brought from halfway around the world. At great government expense, incidentally. I want to start by talking about the brain. The human brain. . . .

"A piece of gray cheese. It's not so large. You can easily hold it in one hand. An elephant's brain weighs four times as much. But in proportion to corpus weight, it's smaller. Otherwise, elephants would be sitting where you're sitting now. (Laughter) But I don't wish to discuss the physical properties of the human brain. You know all that. You better know it, or we're doomed! I want to discuss with you today the human brain as a national asset. Or, if you will, a national resource.

"In the present state of the world today, I suggest to you now that a nation's essential strength is not in its minerals, its agriculture, its wealth, or its armaments. But in the quality of the brains of its citizens. Compute that a moment. A nation is no stronger than the brains of its citizens. And the ideas those brains create.

"In the US, we have learned, and are still learning, how to improve the quality and functioning of this essential natural resource. Isolation of the 'smart genes' and genetic manipulation. Megaprotein feeding of the mother. Oxygenation of the fetus. Scientific conditioning of the child. Positive drug therapy for memory. And so forth.

"But the growth of a nation's brain pool is not only a matter of genetics, diet, drugs, conditioning. Other factors are involved. In a sense, great brains breed great brains. History is replete with examples of times—relatively short periods—when 'schools' of great brains flourished in politics, art, literature, science, music, and so forth. There seems to be an interaction. Great brains inspire great brains. Or perhaps, more exactly, great ideas inspire great ideas. So there is an exponential factor serving here. A nation's brain pool improves at a geometric rate.

"Are you still with me? Or are you now saying to yourself, 'Enough of this historical and political kaka. What are we doing here?' Fair enough. What you are doing here is to preserve, for the US Government, the continued functioning of one of the greatest brains this nation, or any nation on earth, has ever possessed. This is what we're going to do. And this is how we're going to do it. . . ."

I had them then. As I continued speaking, they shifted forward in their seats. Fascinated. Leaning to me. These were very brainy objects themselves; it didn't take long for them to realize they were involved in a radical and risky scientific project. But a characteristic of the human brain I had not mentioned—the absolute need to solve a mystery, to conquer the unknown— had taken hold. At the end, I casually remarked that anyone who objected to the purpose of Operation Lewisohn would be excused, without prejudice. Not one object opted for out. I hadn't anticipated there would be.

Those early rehearsals were ridiculous. Pure chaos. Even such a simple process as washing-up and sterilization became incredibly complex when a total of almost 100 objects were involved. When the preliminaries were solved, and we moved to positions, cues; and timing on the actual operation—more confusion. Paul Bumford generated an excellent idea. He suggested we paint circles on the floor. Color-coded to match the gowns of the various teams. The circles showed clearly where members of each team were to stand. Numbers within the circles designated various individuals.

With such stratagems; we gradually began to execute a coherent scenario. Four hours each day were spent merely planning physical movements and walking through our paces. Remaining hours were spent in team lectures, colloquies, and symposia in which actual techniques were discussed, demonstrated, attempted. Like well-trained gunners, each object had to know (and be proficient at) not only his own service, but the service of every fellow team-member. In case of emergency.

It all began to coalesce. I was definite progress.

As ruler of Operation Lewisohn, I had, of course, the perquisite of free, unquestioned entrance to and egress from the Lewisohn Building at Hospice No. 4. But with the stress of early organization and the pressure of preliminary rehearsals, it was June 5, 1999, before I had an opportunity to slip away. To requisition a black sedan from the motor pool. Start out early in the evening to locate the residence of the late Arthur Raddo. My investigation had to begin somewhere.

As I had anticipated, Raddo's address on Sixth Street was in a neighborhood that had once, long ago, been fashionable. Even elegant. It had seeded. There was a government bordello or betting parlor on almost every corner. Between were licensed shops offering porn, Graeco-Roman massage, high colonics, sporting events, and a type of specialized entertainment called "Sadie Moscowitz." This was a vernacular corruption of sadomasochism. Much as, years previously, marijuana had been debased to "Mary Warner."

I parked outside the area, on a shadowed sidestreet, and walked slowly toward Raddo's address. I was wearing civilian clothes. It was still early in the evening; the streets were crowded. Tourists, mostly, I guessed. With a heavy representation of pimps, jostlers of all sexes (including children), steersmen for illegal bagnios, black-market pushers, illicit drug sellers, etc. All, victims and predators thronging quik-thaw petrofood stands, taverns, handjob joints, cabarets, grogshops. A strange, roiling neighborhood for the home of a devout Beist. But perhaps Arthur Raddo hadn't had the love to move elsewhere.

His building was slightly more presentable than the others. Slightly. An obso red-brick high-rise. Some of the windows on the lower floors were broken. Blocked with squares of cardboard or tin. The usual litter and graffiti. The unattended lobby smelled equally of urine and carbolic.

There was a "Raddo, A." listed on the lobby directory. Apartment 2-H. I opted for the dimly lighted staircase rather than chance an elevator. The outside door of 2-H had once been handsome wood. Now the jamb and area around the lock had been slashed and hacked. I heard voices from within: the never-ending litany of a broadcast. I pressed the bell. Not only was there no answer, but I didn't even hear the bell ring. I knocked sharply. Again. Again.

Finally: "Who is it?" a voice called out. An ef's voice. Surprisingly light and cheerful. Almost a carol.

"Mrs. Raddo?" I said loudly. Wondering: A mother? A widow?

"Yes?" the carol came again. "Who is it?"

"I'd like to talk to you about Arthur," I said. Lips close to the door.

There was a pause. Then the clicking of at least three locks and bolts. The sound of a heavy metal bar being withdrawn. Squeaking.

The door was opened to the length of a short, heavy chain. A bright blue eye peered at me.

"I'd like to talk to you about Arthur," I repeated. Hurriedly. "Just a moment. My name is Flair."

"I'm not supposed to talk to anyone about Arthur," the clear voice said. "They told me."

"I'm a reporter," I said. "I'm serving on a feature. A very sympathetic feature about Arthur. I need some information."

"Will it be on the TV?" she asked.

"Of course," I said. More confident now. "But I need to know what he was really like. The truth."

"The truth about Arthur?" she breathed.

"Yes," I said. "Exactly."

The door closed, the chain was slipped. Then the door was opened. She let me in.

"I'm Mrs. John Raddo," she chirped. "Arthur's mother."

An obso ef. About sixty to sixty-five, I judged. Blued-white hair teased into tight curls. A wig? Short, plump, almost merry in appearance.

She closed the door behind me, then served on the locks and bolts. I watched. Fascinated. Finally, the heavy steel bar in place, she tried the door. Beautiful. She led the way down a dim hallway to a semilighted room.

"You're interrupting my favorite program," she said. Not angrily. Archly. "You must promise not to speak until it's over."

"I promise," I said.

We took two sprung armchairs facing the TV set. She immediately picked up what appeared to be a square of knitted wool (A sweater back? The start of a scarf?) and began manipulating large bone-needles rapidly. The blue yarn flew from a bag on the floor. Even as I watched, entranced, her nimble fingers finished a row and started back.

"I just love it." She sighed. "It's a rerun, but just as good as the first time."

I looked then at the TV set. Surprisingly, it was the same model I owned: holographic laser, 3-D. Very lovable.

I recognized the program she was watching: *The Twenty-six Best Positions*. Original programs from October to March, reruns from April to September.

Permissiveness on television had come much later than in books, magazines, movies, and on the stage. TV executives had moved cautiously, carefully, following a scenario pioneered by book publishers. First, in the late 1970's, they presented self-help programs on achieving emotional maturity. Followed, in the early 1980's, by increasingly frank discussions of the importance of sexual fulfillment in a happy marriage. These were mostly talk shows: seminars and symposia of physicians, psychologists, sexologists, and so forth.

By the late 1980's and early 1990's, television was presenting shows that were totally sex-oriented. There was one network series, *Have No Fear*, that appeared in the 1991–1995 period, very high ratings, that effectively glossed anxieties objects might still have about the dangers of masturbation, fellatio, and the use of dildos and similar gadgets of technologized sex.

Public objection to these televised lectures on sexual techniques proved to be less than anticipated. For years, ice-brained conservatives had been fulminating against sex education in the schools. "A child should be taught about sex in the home." Television executives did exactly that. In the home, the living room, bedroom, den, patio, library, kitchen. And at your friendly neighborhood tavern.

The Twenty-six Best Positions was by far the most popular program. Rated in the top ten shows for the past three years. On primetime, in 3-D, and living color. With instant replay. The participating objects changed every year to provide variety.

I watched a close-up of a young blond ef licking the glans of a young blond em.

"Aren't they *cute?*" Mrs. Raddo chortled. Knitting busily. "*Videotape Magazine* says they want to get married, but the sponsor won't let them. Afraid it might hurt their ratings."

I waited patiently as the famed psychologist who hosted the program provided a running commentary for the action on the screen. Finally, the half-hour program ended with a trailer for the following week's hour-long special on anal intercourse.

Mrs. Raddo leaned forward to switch off the set.

"Thank you for waiting," she said. Sighing again. "I so enjoy the *Twenty-six*. Watch it every week. Wouldn't miss it. Not even the reruns. I've seen *Mutual Masturbation* four times. What did you say your name was?"

"Flair, Mrs. Raddo," I said. "I just have a few questions. First of all, I'd like to present my condolences."

"Condolences?" she said.

"On Arthur's stopping."

"Oh," she said. Then nodded. As sadly as that merry phiz could. "Arthur was a good boy."

"I'm sure he was," I said. "What I—"

"When will it be on?" she asked. "The TV show? About Arthur?"

"Probably next fall," I said.

"The new season." She nodded wisely. "Primetime?"

"I expect so."

"You'll want a tape interview with me, of course?"

"Of course," I said promptly. "That's why I'm here. Just for background to give the host some leads on questions to ask."

"Yes, yes." She nodded briskly. "That's how it's done. I know all about it. You'll make a tape, then edit it down for the timeslot."

"Exactly," I said.

She nodded again. Happily. Busy fingers twirling the long needles. The patch of knitted wool grew before my eyes. Longer and longer.

"Mrs. Raddo," I said, "did Arthur have any friends?"

"Of course he had friends," she said firmly. "Lots and lots of friends. Arthur was a very popular boy."

"Could you give me any of their names and addresses?" I asked. "We'd like to interview them, too."

"Oh, I never met them," she said gaily. Blue eyes twinkling. "Arthur never brought any of them here. 'Mother,' he used to say, 'this is *your* home.' "

"Well, he must have met them somewhere," I said. "Did he go to any special place you know of? A restaurant, perhaps? A tavern? A cabaret?"

"Oh, Arthur wouldn't go to any place like *that*," she said. Needles flashing. "Never drank. Never smoked. Never took drugs or any of the nasty things young people do these days. Arthur was a good boy."

"I'm sure he was," I said. Desperately. "But he must have gone out occasionally. Some place in the neighborhood?"

"Well . . ." she said. Needles suddenly still. Head cocked to one side. "Let me think . . . He did. Yes, he did go out. Something Greek. He would go to something Greek."

"A Greek restaurant?"

"Oh, no. I don't think so. More like a private club. Where he could meet his friends in a nice atmosphere."

"But with a Greek name?"

"Yes, I think so. He mentioned it once, and I asked him what it meant, and he said it was a Greek god."

"A Greek god? Bacchus? Zeus? Appollo? Poseidon? Adonis? Pluto?"

"Adonis," she said triumphantly. "Yes, that's it. Adonis."

"You're sure?"

"Oh my, yes. Adonis. I remember very well now. That was the private club Arthur went to. He met his friends there."

"Frequently? Once a week? Or twice? More?"

"Oh . . ."She considered. The needles twirling again. "I'd say at least once a week. I remember it now because he usually went when *The Twenty-six Best Positions* came on. Like tonight. 'Mother,' he'd say, it's *your* program.' "

"Thank you very much, Mrs. Raddo," I said. Rising. "You've been very helpful."

"And when will the crew be around?" she asked.

"The crew?"

"The camera crew to tape the interview with me."

"Soon, Mrs. Raddo. Quite soon. You'll be hearing from us."

"Isn't that nice!" she said happily.

I was halfway down that dim hallway when she called me back. Knitting needles and wool clutched on her lap.

"Yes, Mrs. Raddo?" I said.

"There was one friend," she said slowly. "I never met him, of course. Personally, I mean. But in the last few months he called Arthur several times and they spoke on the phone. I don't have a flasher. Though I'd dearly love one. But do you know how much—"

"Mrs. Raddo," I said, "did Arthur mention his name? His friend's name? While he was speaking to him on the phone?"

"Well, not his last name," she said. "I never heard Arthur mention his last name, and I never asked. But he did use his friend's first name."

"And what was that?" I said.

"Nick," she said.

I heard the rumble of muffled drums.

Z-8

During the month of June, rehearsals for Operation Lewisohn progressed, and increased in complexity. The subject was kept animate on parabiotic therapy and massive injections of steroidal stimulants. This protocol resulted, I knew, in a false set of vital signs. His color might be rosy, blood pressure stabilized, respiration normal. But he was, for the purposes of the US Government, a vegetable. Incapable of serving. A temporary condition. I hoped.

Our basic scenario underwent constant, almost daily revision. For instance, in the cold outline of the original script, the Surgery Team, having finished their task, would move out and Leo Bernstein's Team would move in. Impossible. We had to phase out the surgeons, one by one, as we phased in the hematologists. This called for neat cooperation, microsecond precision.

We were still spending four hours a day on walkthroughs and timing. The confusion had lessened; there was no more pushing, shoving, stumbling.

When the entire staff of Operation Lewisohn were not engaged in the endless drills or sleeping exhaustedly in the unisex barracks, they were practicing their disciplines. I was especially interested in and concerned with the activities of the Surgery Team. Assigned an operation that had never before been performed.

The ST was under the rule of Chief Surgeon Dr. George Berk. A tall, slender ex-soccer star from HMS. He ran a tight ship. When he said "Go," his servers went. When he said "No-go," they froze. He had the macho to enforce his edicts. I didn't like to recall how young he was. Made me realize I was one year away from being an obso. Even his mustache was more luxuriant than mine.

To assist Dr. Berk and his staff, I had purchased two beautifully designed and engineered humanoids from a medical equipment manufacturer in Dachau, West Germany. They were custom-made, patterned on Hyman R. Lewisohn's exact measurements (taken while he was heavily sedated). Even to the proportions of his ears and the length of his penis.

The dummies were covered with Grade D Juskin, which closely approximated Lewisohn's coarse epidermis. Within was a plastitubular circulatory system through which a bloodlike fluid was pumped by an atomic-powered "heart." The mannequin also "breathed": the chest rose and fell. When skin was cut, the humanoid "bled." Interior organs were of various plastics: solid, sponge, glass, rubber, etc. The models had been designed to cry out when "pain" was inflicted (a cut, punch, pressure) unless a specially formularized anesthetic was first administered. This was simply a gas that temporarily neutralized the "voice-making" machinery.

The mannequins were marvels of engineering. The two replicas of Hyman R. Lewisohn had cost the US Government 100,000 new dollars each. But parts not destroyed in surgical practice could be returned to the West German factory for credit against future purchases.

The manufactured Hyman R. Lewisohns proved of invaluable assistance to the Surgery Team. They were able to plan their own surgical schedule, estimate volume of blood loss, practice on an inanimate object that reacted much as would their eventual subject.

It was, I admit, an eerie experience when I first saw the two Lewisohn replicas. Lying naked, side by side, on a wide operating table in the Surgical Team lab. We had sent over photos, hair and nail clippings, under ultrasecret precautions, and the results were astounding. There was the dwarf corpus, bulging brow, thin fringe of reddish hair, brutal features, thick lips. Had the reproductions snarled obscenities at me, I wouldn't have been a bit surprised.

If the Lewisohn copies shook me, they shattered Maya Leighton. She was not horrified by them. "Fascinated" is the operative word.

Maya had been serving as my Executive Assistant during those early stages of Operation Lewisohn. Like Paul Bumford and Mary Bergstrom, her attitude had gradually changed from cold cooperation to hopeful enthusiasm. In Maya's case, the sight of those two "breathing" reproductions of Hyman R. Lewisohn ended whatever final doubts she might have in the value of the project.

"What is it?" I asked her. Wanting to know why the sight of those two mechanical objects had so affected her.

She shook her head. "Exciting," she said. Almost in awe. I still didn't know. Then.

The Surgical Team busied themselves with the mannequins. Meanwhile, Leo Bernstein's Team had been serving with live "volunteers." I had set an arbitrary limit of three stoppages. But after what he learned from the research project at Hospice No. 17 in Little Rock, Arkansas—the development of synthetic blood—Leo's practice on human subjects resulted in only one stoppage. And that, he suspected, was due to an allergic reaction. He stated confidently that he was ready to go. Knowing Leo, I believed that was operative.

So it all slowly came together. The equipment of Project Phoenix Denver was airlifted down, set up in Operating Theater D. The direct-wire link with Phoebe Huntzinger's huge computers in GPA-was established and tested. We ran endless game-plans, gradually pushing our own electronic equipment to the ult. Problems arose. Were solved. Defects were discovered. Replaced. Backup equipment was readied (standby generators, a secondary commercial wire link, ect.). The machines were taken as far as we could stress them. That left the objects. The pressures were enormous.

Perhaps Grace Wingate kept me rational. Or, at least, kept me from becoming monomaniac. I know I came from my clandestine meetings with her purged and refreshed. For instance. . . .

A soft, rainy afternoon in early June. Too wet for our secret garden. We stayed in Louise Rawlins Tucker's great empty house. Curled up in each other's arms on a sagging sofa. Watching the rain fall. Listening to the old house creak. I had brought her a set of antique Greek worry beads. Amber. Strung on a silken cord. We were handling the polished spheres between us. Fondling them. They were warmed by our touch.

She said—what did she say?—oh, yes, she said that our decision not to use each other would lead to a love that would be "new . . . all new." Then I laughed softly. I told her she was quoting me, my first speech on the subject, word for word. Then she reminded me that, a few moments previously, I had been speaking about devotion, and had quoted her, almost word for word. Then we both laughed. Hugging each other tighter.

Because you see, we were adapting to each other. More than that, assimilating each other. Words, emotions, thoughts, attitudes, philosophies. We really were becoming one.

Later, she said, "Nick, do you believe in telepathy?"

I had sudden, total recall of Paul and me. A long time ago. In bed together. Exchanging slips of paper. ESP. Had we communicated?

"Telepathy?" I said. "Ambivalent, I guess. Why do you ask?"

"A book I read," she said. "Years and years ago. I think it was in my mother's library. I remembered it last night. For some reason."

"A book?" I said. "What kind of a book?"

"A novel. An obso romantic novel. I must have been quite young when I read it. Twelve? Fourteen? Around then."

"It must have impressed you," I said. "What was it about?"

"I don't recall all the details, dear. But it was about an ef and an em in love. Deeply in love. One of them stops. I think it was her. It might have been him. It makes no difference. The partner who had stopped returned from beyond the grave. They used each other. The live one and the stopped one. The novel said that their love was so strong, so mighty, that it conquered stopping. Nick, do you believe that is possible?"

I looked at her. Conscious my face was twisting.

"You're crying," she said. In wonderment.

"No, no," I said. "Well. Perhaps. A little. I'd like to believe it, Grace. It's very moving."

"But do you believe it?"

"I don't know. Just don't know. Do you? Believe it?"

"Yes," she said firmly. "I believe it. And that is exactly what I shall do. Or, if you go first, what you must do. Promise, Nick?"

"I promise," I said. Did I groan? "And if we both stop? Together?"

"We'll find a way," she said confidently.

We stared at each other. So close our eyelashes were brushing. At that proximity, all focus is lost. Pupils become worlds. One falls, swimming. A sweet dizziness. It was, I thought, a kind of parabiosis. Two linked by a vital look. But a two-way flow. A merging.

The exhilaration! An ecstasy to so surrender. It was passing the point of no return, not caring. The freedom! Spirit ballooning. Everything "new . . . all new," and we might come home to a fresh world.

Any wonder that I left her, each time, "purged and refreshed"? Nothing significant but her. Our love. I cannot say why.

We left Louise's home separately, of course. I departed first. Rode the Metro link into Washington. I went directly to the Executive Office Building where I had a two-hour confabulation with Joe Wellington and his top staffers. Including the serpentine Samantha Slater.

Subject was my third and final PR gig that would take me through the Far West. Conventions, universities, think tanks, laboratories, computer installations, etc. We assumed HR-316 would be approved by the full House Government Operations Committee. The shove was to bring it to floor vote before the summer recess.

After the meeting, I walked slowly toward the Hill. Delaying my return to Hospice No. 4 as long as possible. The Mall was torn up, bordered with construction trailers and heavy equipment.

It was to be the Capital's celebration of the advent of the Twenty-first Century. A series of houses was being erected in a long line from the General Grant statue to the Washington Monument. They were intended to demonstrate the progress of American homes from 1700 to 2000. One home for every fifty years. Beginning with a log cabin and ending with a plastic modular structure. The theme: "You never lived so good!"

I was surprised by the rapid progress of construction. But most of the obso homes were authentic, borrowed from museums, historical societies, national monuments, etc. Disassembled, trucked to the Mall site, and put back together again. The 1850 home, an antebellum Mississippi slave shanty, was already complete. It stood in a small field of plastirub cotton plants. Looking unbearably forlorn. I watched activities on the Mall for almost an hour. Servers were fitting stained glass windows into the walls of the 1900 home: a Victorian bordello from Chicago.

Then I went back to Operation Lewisohn.

We had tried to anticipate every possible contingency. Including such dire emergencies as fire, explosion (terrorist bombing), power failure, and so forth. But, as frequently happens in planning of such complexity, we had overlooked an obvious and imperative need. It was Paul Bumford who brought the matter to the attention of the Executive Staff.

"Look," he said, "assuming the operation is a total success, a direct-wire link is established with the computer installation at GPA-1, the Project Phoenix scanners are serving perfectly, and Leo Bernstein is delivering everything he's promised. Then what?"

"What?" someone said.

"Then what?" Paul repeated. "We haven't planned a permanent installation," he explained patiently. "Where do we move Lewisohn? Where does he *live*? What measures should be taken for his privacy and protection?"

They all looked to me. Waiting. I admit it was my failure. I should have foreseen the problem and solved it. I computed then as rapidly as I could. But all the solutions I plotted had obvious drawbacks.

"I'd prefer he not be moved," I said slowly. "Too much risk. The ideal siting would be underground, but. . . ."

"Let's do this," Paul said briskly. "Leave him *in situ* at the conclusion of the operation. Theater D offers a lot of advantages. Plenty of walk-around space. Facilities for sterile observation. And so forth. After a reasonable survival period, we call in architects. There are several possibilities. The entire Operating Theater could gradually be lowered underground if the proper preparations were made."

"Cost a mint," someone said.

"Use the cost," Paul said. "Another possibility: Convert the entire Lewisohn

Building into a gigantic bunker. Reinforce the roof and walls. Put a bomb-proof shell over the entire building. Cost less than an underground installation, and probably just as effective."

"Good computing, Paul." I nodded. "Call in some high security architects and get cracking on plans."

I was not gruntled by his imaginative analysis and solution of the problem. I should have anticipated him.

The remainder of that day was spent observing the Surgical Team run a stopwatched rehearsal on one of the Hyman R. Lewisohn humanoids. Maya Leighton was with me.

They were coming up to performance level. As the mock operation progressed, the team built up to full strength. Then gradually decreased in number as, during the actual operation, they would be phased out by Leo Bernstein's Team of hematologists.

I watched two complete runthroughs. When they started the third, I decided I had seen enough. On the following day they would begin practicing actual surgical procedures, cutting into the first Hyman R. Lewisohn dummy. Still intact on the operating table. Chest rising and falling rhythmically. Shining glass eyes staring at the ceiling.

"I can't stand the thought of that cafeteria food tonight," I said to Maya Leighton. "Or the unisex barracks. Too much snoring. Too many groans."

"My place," she said promptly. "I've got two natural ham steaks in the freezer. And some other stuff. We'll pop it all into the microwave."

"Stay the night?" I said.

She looked at me. Surprised.

"Of course," she said. "You think I'm asking you just for my hams?"

Then we both collapsed. Almost hysterical laughter.

"Let's stop at a grogshop first," I said. "What would you like?" She told me.

"To drink," I said.

"Oh . . . anything," she said. "Have you ever tried avocado brandy?"

"I never have," I said grumpily, "and don't intend to. Let's go. Leave the transcribing of those tapes till tomorrow."

"Yes, ruler," she said.

"Oh-ho," I said. "It's going to be one of those nights, is it?"

"I hope so," she said.

Four, perhaps five hours later, we were in the bedroom of her apartment. Not completely rational. We had drunk things. Popped things. Inhaled things. Injected things.

Maya had purchased a curious garment for herself. It must have been quite lovable. Natural rubber in a grayish-beige shade. Almost flesh-colored. Almost. It was not unlike a skin diver's wet suit. But it had gloves, feet, a hood that covered her face and hair.

Her eyes glittered through two small holes. There was an elevated, ventilated V over her nose. Mouth completely covered. All of her pressed tightly in this elastic envelope. I had helped her pull it on. Even with the aid of zippers and a powdered interior it took almost thirty minutes for her to become enshrouded. The most harrowing feature of this monstrous garment was, I thought, the carmined lips painted across her rubbered mouth.

She lay on her back, quite still. Arms at her sides. Legs slightly spread. I watched her coated breasts rise and fall regularly. The heart pumped. Fluid coursed through her vascular system. Beneath the two skins.

To me, the sight of her was at once shocking and exciting. It recalled the paintings of Egon Schiele: sexuality and dread. I couldn't begin to compute it. Darkness so profound that . . . A primitivity there. Something so crude and elemental that it stirred a forgotten bog.

Those flickering eyes. Tight rubber convexing to nipples and belly, concaving to navel and vulva. The sticky sheen of the second skin. Artfully placed seams. I bent over to stare into the eyeholes. A peer into the past. Aeons ago. The ooze. She did not assist when I put my hands upon her. Nor did she resist.

I won't attempt to analyze the psychopathology of what we did. It is not one of my disciplines.

A few days after that (blank) night—I use (blank) here to indicate a deficiency in the English language. I want a word that means you'd like to forget it but you can't. "Haunting" is close, but not exact—I found a note in my Lewisohn Building office asking me to buzz Paul when I had some open time. I buzzed him.

"Paul? Nick. I'm open. What is it?"

"Nick, could you come down here? I have something to show you—some computer printouts. Too clumsy to lug up to your office."

So I went to his office. The computer printouts weren't all that extensive. But I went to his office. I mention this because. . . .

"You don't have to scan all this kaka," he said. "Just take a look at the bottom line."

It was a preliminary report, not authenticated, from the miniteam of Houston neuropsychologists who had been running the Ultimate Pleasure testing of the Operation Lewisohn staff. Preliminary it may have been, but the results were astonishing. On an arbitrary 1 to 10 scale, efficiency of the control group showed 6.9; of the placebo group 7.7; of the actual UP group 9.6.

"It's serving," Paul said. Trying hard to keep the enthusiasm out of his voice. Trying to be the cold clinician. "The UP group is definitely hooked. Their production norms are incredible. Performance excellent. And wait till you scan the personal interviews. They'll serve until they drop for another UP injection."

"What about the slave factor?" I said.

"Confirmed. It exists in 84.8 percentile points of the total UP group. According to computer analysis of fantasy factors."

"So?" I said. "What's your recommendation?"

"First of all, I want to finalize the study here. I don't anticipate ultimate numbers will vary significantly from what we already have. But Operation Lewisohn is a special case. I want a full-scale field test. Nick, do you think your father will cooperate? Let us run a project in his factories, on the assembly lines?"

I computed a moment. "I'm sure he will," I said. "Especially if it results in increased productivity."

Paul laughed. "That's what I figured. We'll pick three generally similar factories. Plants engaged only in assembly. One factory is the control; servers get nothing. Servers in the second plant get placebo injections. In the third they get the real thing. I assume your father keeps object-hour productions records?"

"Of course. Has to. For the unions."

"Right. Well, those will give us statistical norms. Then after, say, six months of the test, we should have a clear idea of the effect of the UP on industrial production."

"And then?" I asked.

He paused a moment. The pouts had disappeared. The softness, the boyish indecision. A ramrod now, but not strutting. He had stressed himself, and found he could hack it. From that came the self-esteem he had needed. He had been in my shadow, a coattailer. Now he was . . . what? I didn't know. I literally did not know. A stranger.

More, he was moving into areas I could not compute. I was older than he: a prime factor. But age alone could not account for our growing estrangement. There was a fundamental disparity. I felt it, and I trust my corpus. What he undoubtedly saw in me as a weakness, I saw in him as a lack. I tried (sometimes failing) not to begrudge his enormous talents. I think, in all honesty, I must admit this: At that point in time, he began to frighten me.

"And then?" I repeated. After he had been silent for almost a minute.

He took a deep breath.

"Well," he said, "it's obvious, isn't it? We must do some heavy brainstorming on the theoretical structure of a society that can maximize the value of the UP. After the gross outlines are postulated, we can get on with effectualizing it. Translating theory into practice. Just for starters, we should increase our research efforts in the area of biobehavioral controls. We've got to minimize the terrorism rate."

"Scratch that last for the moment," I said. "Let's discuss the nature of this society that will maximize the value of the UP. How do you see it?"

He looked at me. Then shrugged.

"It's apparent, isn't it?" he asked. "We agreed the UP would be a political drug. Serving at max efficiency in a society that complemented it. That, to me, can mean only a heavily structured authoritarian government. Designed to take full advantage of the UP's slave factor.

He was going too fast.

"You're projecting the government as master?" I asked him.

"Yes."

"And the citizen as slave?"

"Yes. All indicators point to that relationship as the foundation of Ultimate Pleasure. Nick, it scans. No responsibilities. No decisions to make. No fears of the unknown. A planned existence. Absolutely free."

"You're equating slavery for freedom?"

He computed a moment. Then nodded.

"You can put it that way. If it pleases you. Yes. As a matter of fact, it's operative. Conventional freedom, like morality, is a luxury. But the world cannot afford it. It's like economic competition. We both know how *uneconomic* that is. How unlovable. Today, and certainly tomorrow, only absolute authority can produce absolute freedom."

"Absolute authority?" I said. "You mean absolute tyranny?"

He seemed to be doing a great deal of shrugging.

"All right," Paul said. "Call it tyranny if you wish. Absolute tyranny produces absolute slavery which provides absolute freedom which produces absolute happiness. Does that startle you? It shouldn't. Your Ultimate Pleasure resulted from a sexual fantasy of complete submission."

"Granted," I said. "But I think you're making a fatal error. It's been nagging at me since we last discussed this. I think it's this: We agreed that the UP would be maximized in a society that complemented it. A society that offered a political atmosphere in which the UP could be utilized for the greatest good of the individual. But you're starting with a political drug of known effect and tailoring a society to fit the individual's needs."

"Why not?" Paul said. "Society exists to fulfill the individual's needs."

"Ah-ha," I said. "That's where you're off. Society exists to fulfill *society's* needs. Otherwise, rape would be legal and opium would be sold in slot machines. The desires of the individual are in constant conflict with the needs of society. That's what law is all about."

"You're saying society must always be in conflict with the needs of its citizens?"

"Not their needs, Paul, their *desires*. Their fantasies. Their brutal dreams. In the perfect world, there would be no conflict. But objects being what they are, society must guard the preservation of the species against individual aggression. Look. . . . Society sets certain standards of human behavior. In our codified laws. Simply to keep the jungle from creeping in. Society cannot be constituted to pander to the lowest levels of human behavior. It must set criteria of behavior—sometimes impossible criteria, I admit—to which objects can aspire."

"That's rank romanticism," Paul said.

"Is it?" I said. "Your projected society is better? A tyranny that exploits the grossest instincts of the species? I thought you were a Beist. Believing in the human species and its eventual evolution in something divine."

"I'm a Beist for reasons of temporary strategy," Paul said. "You know that. I'm no wowser. I told you the world of tomorrow has a better chance of success with an emotional and/or religious factor. Slogans. Ritual. Flags. Prayers. Songs. The whole PR schmeer. But there is nothing in my projection of an authoritarian political society that negates what the Beists stand for."

"I think we better discuss this again," I said. "After Operation Lewisohn is concluded. I think we have a lot to talk about."

"Yes," Paul said. Quirky smile. "I think we do."

On July 2, 1999, I set out again, in civilian clothes, to the neighborhood of the late Arthur Raddo. There was no Adonis Club, restaurant, or tavern listed in the D.C. directory. So, once again, I parked on a sidestreet and ambled onto the stage. Same scene. Same actors therein. I wondered if the curtain ever came down. Certainly the sets were never shifted, the cast never changed.

I listened patiently to all the jostlers who approached me. Drugs, natural foods, Sadie Moscowitz, ef prostitutes, ems, infants. Whatever my heart desired. I let them finish their pitch, then I made mine. Where was Adonis?

It didn't take long. Less than an hour. Then an obso transvestie supplied the input. Adonis was a private cellar club. Members only. I bought the address for ten new dollars.

There was nothing outside to mark it. No sign. No lights. I stumbled down a short flight of brick steps from the street. Kicked gently at a steel door. A small panel, eye-level, slid open. I could see nothing. Darkness inside.

"Yes?" a pleasant voice inquired.

"I'd like to come in," I said.

"Sorry, sir," the pleasant voice said. "This is a private club. Are you a member?"

"No," I said, "but I'd like to join."

"Sorry, sir," the pleasant voice said. "New members must be recommended by a present member. Are you a friend of a present member?"

"I'm a friend of Arthur Raddo," I said. "I *was* a friend of Arthur Raddo."

"Just a minute, please, sir," the pleasant voice said.

The panel slid shut. I waited outside that black steel door for not one, but several long minutes. I was about to kick again when the door swung open. Not wide. Just enough to let me slip through. Then it was cracked shut and bolted behind me.

Complete darkness. A soft hand on my elbow guided me. Across a plasticarp. I came up against a piece of plastisteel furniture. A desk. I fumbled, touching. A flashlight came on. Pointed down at an open ledger.

"Sign here, please, sir," the pleasant voice said. "Twenty new dollars. Cash. No BIN card. All drinks and food purchased in cash. You are allowed to bring a single guest each visit."

"You want my name?" I said foolishly.

"We want *a* name, sir."

I signed "Mickey Mouse." It didn't even raise a chuckle. A beautifully manicured hand came out of the darkness to take my love.

"This way, Mr. Mouse," the pleasant voice said.

The inner room, the cabaret, was not so Stygian. But dark enough. I could make out, dimly, a stage, tables, booths, a bar. I thought the objects in the room were both ems and efs. The costumes fooled me for a moment. All ems.

"Table or bar, sir?" the pleasant voice asked.

"Bar, please," a said.

I was gently guided. When I could touch the bar, a swiveling barstool, the warm hand left my arm. I didn't turn to inspect him. I couldn't have made him out. What illumination there was in the room came from the weak floods focused on the stage.

"Sir?" a pleasant voice said. In front of me. I peered.

"Dr. Bartender, I presume?" I said.

"Yes, sir."

"Natural brandy, please."

"Yes, sir. Water on the side?"

"Please."

The pupil is a remarkable organ. After ten minutes I could discern the small snifter of brandy before me on the bar. I could even see, dimly, the bartender who had served me. A luscious lad. There were a few other singles seated at the bar. But most of the members at tables or in booths were couples or parties of four. Very quiet. Very restrained. No raucousness. Possibly the most genteel frail joint I had ever visited.

The lights pointed at the stage went off. The room was in total darkness. Then the lights came on again. Bright. Blinding. A loudspeaker clicked on.

"Ladies and gentlemen, the management of *your* Adonis Club is proud to present, by popular demand a return engagement of that exciting star performer—*Tex!*"

Curtains parted. To the recorded strains of Brahms' "The Rose Breaks Into Bloom," a tall, muscular em clumped onto the minuscule stage. He was wearing the black leather costume of a motor-cyclist. Complete with tinted bubble helmet that concealed hair and features. The tight jacket, pants, heavy boots seemed to have a hundred zippers, a thousand metal studs. The zippers were languorously slid open, in approximate time to the music. As the audience sucked its breath. Nothing better being available at that point in time.

Brahms seemed to repeat three times. Eventually, the strip-biker was down to tight bikini panties and that opaque helmet. Striding the dusty stage on bare feet. The corpus was that of a weight lifter: enormously developed deltoids, biceps, quadriceps. Attractive Roman fold about the pelvis. As I should have anticipated, the buttocks were extraordinary. Peachy. When he finally removed the panties and stood naked (except for that concealing helmet), his family jewels proved to be rhinestones. No matter; the audience approved. There was a frantic snapping of fingers. He took six curtains calls. On the final call, he removed his helmet. That was a mistake.

I turned back to my empty brandy glass and signaled for a refill.

"Have one with me?" I asked the bartender.

"Sorry, sir," he said. "We're not allowed to drink with members of the club."

"Have one with me?" I repeated.

"Thank you, sir," he said.

He mixed something swiftly behind the bar. Raised the glass briefly to me, in thanks, drank, then lowered the glass out of sight. In that darkness, even I, closest to him, could hardly see what he was doing.

"Arthur Raddo," I said. "Did you know him?"

"Who?" he said.

I reached across the bar to clasp his hand. And transfer a ten.

"Arthur Raddo," I said. Wriggling my hand free. "Did you know him? Artie? Ever see him?"

"Artie," he said. "Wasn't that a shame?"

"Yes," I said. "A shame. A tragedy."

He liked the word.

"A tragedy," he repeated. "Yes, it was a tragedy."

"He came in here often?"

"Oh . . . not often. Once, twice a week. Like that."

"With anyone?"

"Not at the bar. He came to the bar by himself. Up to a few months ago."

"And then?"

"He came with a friend. They sat at a table. I wouldn't know about that."

I sighed. I was running out of tens. So I gave him two fives.

"Ask, will you?" I urged. "Any waiter who might have served him. Artie's friend's name, and what he looked like. The friend, I mean. What the friend looked like. Can you do that for me?"

"Well . . ." he said doubtfully. "I'll try."

"Do," I said.

"You're so sweet," he said.

I sipped my brandy while he was gone. Trying to make out my own features in the artificially antiqued mirror behind the bar. My face was wrinkled with wavering tendrils of gilt. Guilt? Who was I? I couldn't make me out.

"Yes," a voice said. And there he was again. Looming close to me out of the gloom. "Artie came in several times with a friend. Not *with* a friend. He met him here."

"Name?" I asked.

"Artie called him Nick."

"Uh-huh," I said. "Did you ask what he looked like? This friend of Artie's?"

"About your height," the bartender said. "About your weight and build. With hair about your shade."

"And with a mustache," I said. "And a Vandyke beard. Just like mine."

"Exactly," he said. "How did you know?"

"Thank you very much," I said.

"I adore you," he said.

I went reeling out of there. Remembering an experience I had at MIT when I was being conditioned on computer technology. There had been a power lapse—not a failure but a lapse—and the computer I was serving on had run wild. It had spewed out incredible nonsense until we brought it back to norm. While it was out of control, the readout screen had scanned: "Bicycle boys never into tile sky shall." That was precisely my mood at that point in time: "Bicycle boys never into tile sky shall."

But it was to be compounded. I departed that dungeon and wandered back to my car. Not computing at all. Not at all. Toward me, on the crowded sidewalk, came lurching a very tall em. Apparently drunk. Picking his nose thoughtfully.

And wearing a checkered cap.

Z-9

Opening remarks delivered at a conversazione of scientists of various disciplines, University of California at Berkeley, July 16, 1999.

"It can hardly come as a surprise to most of you here tonight that, for the past fifteen years, the foreign policy of the US Government has been based on our agricultural production. Particularly of cereal grains. This agriwar, in which admittedly we have used food as an aggressive weapon, has reduced the danger of nukewar to an irremin. For which I think we all, regardless of our political tilt, can be thankful.

"Wait—wait just a minute! I do not want this colloquy to degrade into a debate on morality. Since when has morality been a scientific discipline? I'll say only that, having spent most of my adult life in Public Service, I know it is a fatal error to confuse personal morality with political morality. The two, I assure you, have nothing in common.

"But the thesis I wish to propose to you tonight—and which I hope will be the subject of frank and lively discussion—is that the period in which the superiority of the US in agriwar was the base of our foreign policy and national security is drawing to a close. The production of protein from petroleum, the improved strains of natural grains, the development of protein from the improved strains of natural grains, the development of protein from plankton, the exciting discoveries in the area of weather control, the increasing use of soybeans in the production of synthetic foods, factory farms hydroponic gardens: all these, plus the worldwide gains in achieving Z-Pop, have reduced the importance of food as a weapon of foreign policy.

"What I suggest to you now is that it is time to consider a new basis for our national strength. The twenty-first will, in my opinion, be the Century of Sciwar. And unless we immediately establish the proposed Department of Creative Science, bringing scientists of all disciplines into policymaking roles in the US Government, we are doomed to become a second-rate power."

That was the last meeting of my final Public Relations tour on behalf of the DCS. I flew directly from San Francisco to Detroit on an official courier plane. Hypersonic operations had once again been approved for the Detroit area.

I was exhausted. Throat raspy. Unable to compute clearly all the problems that beset me. I suffered three attacks of RSC in California. Of increasing severity. During the last, I remembered a stuffed giraffe I had played with as an infant. I couldn't have been much more than one year old at the time. It was, by far, my most ancient memory. If I went back any farther, I'd recall swimming lazily in my mother's womb.

I arrived at our Grosse Pointe place in time to have lunch with my father. Just before he departed for a week's tour of his overseas factories.

"Nick-ol'-as!" he shouted. I submitted to the expected bear hug.

He brought me up to tick. The Die-Dee Doll was a tremendous success. Worldwide markets. Eighteen ethnic models. Forty-seven national costumes. Love pouring in. Demand increasing. The problem was production. Not in raw material shortfalls, but in assembly. And just when he was convinced the problem was insoluble, along comes that little butterfly Paul Bumford with a request that he cooperate in a field test of a new drug that might double his production norms.

"Nick, did you know about that?" my father demanded.

I told him yes, I knew all about that.

And did I think it would really serve? Would it raise his unit assembly rate?

"I think it will," I said.

"That's good enough for me," he burbled. "I'll flash Paul a go. That's one bright em. I misjudged him. I admit it. What is this stuff, Nick?"

"An injection," I said. "Self-administered."

"What does it do? Make 'em serve faster?"

"No," I said. "No recorded effect on muscular coordination, physical speed, or anything like that. It's a reward for increased production. That's all I can tell you."

"A reward?" he said. "Better than overtime love?"

"Much better," I assured him. "And much cheaper."

"That's for me." He laughed. "But we'll have to make it voluntary. You know that, don't you, Nick? The unions will insist on it."

"Of course."

"Paul knows it?"

"I'm sure he does. We'll get Informed Consent Statements from everyone injected."

"You think they'll go for it? The servers?"

"When the word gets around, they'll be lining up for shots."

"Wonderful!" he yelled.

"Yes," I said. "Wonderful."

I stood on the porch. Waving as my father's helicopter lifted off the front lawn. He hadn't married the musician. I didn't think he would. But his new black ef copter pilot seemed to be about two meters tall. With a corpus as pliant as whalebone. Green hair down to her arse. My father's vitality depressed me.

I slept ten hours. Breakfasted voraciously on orange petrojuice, proham, powdered eggs, propots, two slices of soybread, and three cups of coftea. I spent four hours playing cartel bridge with Mrs. McPherson, Miss Catherine, and Charles. Then went back to bed for another eight hours. I awoke convinced that I would find solutions for all my problems and never again see another checkered cap. I called Millie Jean Grunwald.

It was then almost 2400. I woke her up, I knew, but I had never known her to speak to me in anger, or even pique. She seemed delighted when she recognized my voice. I think she was. She told me to hurry; she had so much to tell me.

I hadn't brought her a gift. But I went up to what had been my mother's bedroom, and on the top shelf of a closet, wrapped in pink tissue paper, I found an obso French doll. One of those long-legged, long-armed, fancily dressed, floppy figures young efs once left sprawled on their counterpanes.

Into Detroit, in the antique Ford Capri. To Millie's darkened street. The deserted porn shop. But her lights were on. She awaited me.

As I had hoped, the French doll delighted her. Millie would never be allowed to breed, not with her genetic rating, and perhaps she knew it. Or sensed it. She adopted the doll as her very own immediately. Insisted on taking it into bed with us. Perched high on a pillow, its painted lips smiled down on our naked corpora. Eyes opened wide in enthralled astonishment.

Millie had gained at least ten kilos since I had seen her. Too much Qik-Freez Hot-Qizine at her factory's cafeteria. She had scarcely any waist left. The breasts were fuller, and buttocks, thighs, calves. Even upper arms and feet. I didn't care. All of her was soft. That young, globular ass was particularly comforting. Her flesh had a fresh, infant scent. She tasted of warm milk.

I had intended only to hold her. Listening to her long, involved accounts of what had happened to her supervisor's husband, how her girlfriend's boyfriend had betrayed her, and what a local florist had suggested to her (Millie): a free natural philodendron for a fast blowjob in the stockroom.

But there was so much of her. Her almost matronly breasts hardened under my negligent urging. Long nipples stared at me expectantly. Plump thighs parted. Knees raised and widened. The lower mouth yawned. In all conscience, could I reject her when she was already humid? And panting? And I was already humid? And panting?

I maneuvered her to hands and knees. Then pressed her head and shoulders gently downward. Until her face was turned sideways onto a pillow. Live hair flung out. Great hips and buttocks raised to me. Sleek and round. She reached up to pull the French doll down to her. Cuddled it. Kissed its pouting lips. Stroked its long, tight sausage curls. Crooned into its little ear.

She was conscious of me on a physical level. The slow writhing of her pelvis demonstrated that. But as her corpus quickened, den became lubricious, ass heatened and tautened in my grip, she never left off crooning to the doll. Whispering into its tiny ear as I, insensate, thrust. Both of us slaves. Both of us masters. I didn't know.

I do know that when I felt the onset of orgasm, could no longer restrain, I withdrew and directed jets of hot semen onto her soft buttocks and dimpled back. Watching the birdlime drip and run. Wondering why I was doing what I was doing to this child. And she smiled, smiled, nodded, nodded, and whispered secrets into the ear of my mother's doll.

Hours later—one or several; I wasn't aware—she shook me awake. Frantic. She had switched on the bedlamp.

"Nick," she said, "wake up. Please wake up, Nick."

"What is it?" I said.

"Listen," she said.

I listened. A squeaking. Clicking. Sudden scamper.

"Mice in the walls," I told her. "Coming up from the basement. Try to forget them. Go back to sleep."

"I saw one last week," she said. "It ran across the floor and went down a hole where the pipe is. There in the corner."

"A little one or a big one?" I asked.

"A big one, Nick. *Huge!*"

"How gig?"

She held her forefingers about 10 cm apart.

"A little one," I said. "*Mus*, not *Rattus*. They won't hurt you."

"They'll bite me."

"No, Millie. Not mice. They won't."

"They'll run over me and, you know, get between my legs. And bite."

I sighed.

"All right, Millie," I said. "I'll fix it so they can't get up here."

I got out of bed, naked, and went into her tiny kitchen. I found some rags under the rusted sink. Brought them back to the big room.

"I'll stuff them around the pipe," I told her. "Tomorrow you must buy some plastisteel wool, pull the rags out, and stuff the wool all around the pipe. They can't gnaw through that. Do you understand, dear?"

"Plastisteel wool," she repeated.

"Right. You stuff it around the pipe where I'm going to put the rags in for tonight."

"Around the pipe," she repeated.

"Right," I said. "Then complain to the super or the owner. Tell them to set traps or scatter poison. Tell them you'll complain to the Health Board."

"The Health Board," she repeated faintly.

I knew she'd never remember. But I'd do what I could. I got down on hands and knees, began to jam rags into a wide circular crack between a vertical steampipe and the old, wooden floor. There should have been a metal flange about the pipe; there was none.

I was stuffing the rags into the crevice when I glanced at the wooden baseboard. The pipe was in a corner; walls and baseboard came to a *V* behind the pipe. The baseboard had been nailed in place, then painted over. But two nailheads protruded. Not more than 1 cm each. I bent forward to examine them. I had seen similar electronic devices before: nailhead microphones. Topping spikes inserted in drilled holes in the wood.

I knelt there for several minutes. Staring at them. I remembered the night with Millie when I talked, talked, talked. About things she could have no interest in. About things I should not have talked about. To anyone with less than Red 2 security clearance. Poor Millie. She would never have *any* security clearance. Not even Red 10.

Millie's apartment had been shared. I had told her things she could not—no way!—comprehend. But Maya Leighton's apartment? Was that also shared? Had I told her things? Our last evening together, when she had worn that dreadful rubber suit, had I spoken of the botulism outbreak in GPA-11? That I might have told her didn't depress me half as much as the fact that I could not remember if I had told her or not. And the safe house? My secret garden with Grace Wingate? Was that also shared? Was *I* being shared with new drugs, new technologies I had not been told about because I had no need to know? I was not without fear. What object is?

I grasped one of the protruding nailheads tightly and began to move it back and forth. I loosened the attached spike in the drilled hole. Finally I was able to withdraw it. Slowly. Carefully. There was a wire soldered to the end. It led into the wall.

That suddenly vacated porn shop below began to make sense.

"Come back to bed, Nick," Millie called.

"In a minute, darling," I said. "Millie, is there a back entrance to this building? A back staircase?"

"Nooo," she said. Frowning. "Not exactly. There's a fire escape. It's all dirty."

"How do you get to that?"

"Out in the hall. That window right next to the door to the nest. You have to climb out the window to get onto the fire escape. But it's all dirty."

"Do you have a flashlight?" I asked her.

"Flashlight?" she said. Worried. Trying to understand, to remember.

"I'll look," I told her. "You go to sleep. I'll be back in a few minutes."

I pulled on zipsuit and socmocs. I went back into her kitchen. Finally, in the back of a drawer filled with a miscellany of cheap household gadgets, I found a small, square plastic lantern.

Out to the hallway, down to the window next to the nest door. I unlocked it, but couldn't raise it. It appeared to be painted shut. I leaned against the frame on all four sides. Then strained upward on the sash. The window didn't move. Back to Millie's kitchen, carving knife, back to window, point of knife inserted between sash and frame, run all the way around.

Finally, window open a few cm, I could get my fingertips into the crack and heave upward. Once the paint seal was broken, the window ran free. I got out onto the fire escape. Millie had been right; it was all dirty.

I rested a moment on the encrusted, slatted iron landing. But it was a warm, muggy night; I was never going to get any cooler. I stepped down cautiously onto the counterweighted stairway. As I proceeded, it swung slowly lower. Gripping the filthy handrail, I went down step by careful step. Finally the base touched the ground. I scampered down.

I was about to step off the fire escape ladder onto the paved rear courtyard when, suddenly, mercifully, it occurred to me that the moment I stepped off, the counterweighted section of ladder would rise again. I would be marooned in that fetid courtyard forever. Archaeologists would find my dried bones in a million years and contrive elegant theories to account for my presence there.

I looked about frantically. Still standing on the bottom step of that cantilevered staircase. No weight within easy reach. Nothing but a barred window. Bars on the outside. There was no alternative. Still standing on the swinging escape ladder, my weight keeping it down, I skinned out of my zipsuit. Twisted it into a tough rope. Tied arms about one of the window bars, legs about a vertical handrail support on the rusty ladder. Naked, except for socmocs, I stepped onto the paved courtyard. Still gripping the handrail of the counterweighted ladder. Relieved of my weight, the end began to rise. I let it swing up slowly. Then the knotted zipsuit snugged taut. The end of the ladder was only about a meter above the ground. I could pull it down easily.

Third problem: an unbarred but locked rear door to the deserted porn shop. But there were six small panes of glass. I broke the one nearest the lock with the heel of a socmoc. Reached in cautiously through shards still in the sash. Turned a swivel latch. The door opened creakingly. I was in.

Used the weak flashlight then. Down a musty corridor. Into what had apparently been the main salesroom. Shading the light carefully with my fingers so that it could not illuminate the dusty front window, possibly alert a prowling bobcar. I moved it about slowly. Slowly. Inspecting. Fascinated dread. I thought again of Maya Leighton lying motionless in her earth-colored rubber suit. Painted lips. Glittering eyes. And—and all. . . .

Detritus of a lost civilization. Broken phalli. Ripped vaginas. Melted dildos. Vibrators long stilled. Torn photos. Dried condoms. Cracked leather masks. Rotted artificial tongues. False breasts puddled. All the technologized sex run down and stopped.

A sexual necropolis. Dust everywhere. And mouse droppings.

Finally, in a small inner room—office? stockroom?—I found the wires leading down from Millie's apartment. The bare ends dangled over a wooden table relatively free of dust. The recorders had been placed there, of course. The operators had sat there, on that rickety three-legged stool. They had been emplaced for some time; the floor was littered with empty and stained plastic coftea containers, sandwich wrappings, dried bread crusts, fruit rinds, old newspapers. I shuffled through the last. They scanned a time period of almost five months. Long enough.

. I went back the way I had come. Closed the door. Locked it. Pulled the escape ladder down. Unknotted and retrieved my zipsuit. Mounted to Millie's floor. Climbed in through the window. Closed it and locked it. Took a tepid shower in Millie's nest, with a thin sliver of petrosoap that raised no lather at all. Dried on a ragged square of thin petrocot. Then went back to the big room. Switched off the bedlamp. Climbed into bed.

"Everything all right?" Millie asked sleepily.

I turned her gently onto her stomach. I squirmed down until my face was at her tail, burrowing. I parted, probed, then pressed her buttocks tight to my fevered face.

"Everything's fine," I said to her anus.

Millie had to serve the next day, and awoke early. I was vaguely aware of her moving about. Dressing slowly. Doing something in the kitchen. Talking nonsense to the French doll that she carried about with her for a while. Then propped carefully in the corner of the couch. I wanted, desperately, just another hour or two of sleep. But I awoke, wide, when I heard her unlock the door.

"Millie," I called.

She turned back.

"Nick," she said, "I'm sorry I woke you. Go back to sleep. Stay as long as you like. Just click the door when you leave."

I got out of bed. Padded across the room to her. Took her tightly into my arms.

"You are a dear, sweet ef," I told her. "And I don't know what I'd do without you."

She flushed with profit. Hugged me tightly.

"We *do* have fun, don't we?" she said.

"We do indeed," I agreed. "Remember me, Millie?"

"Remember you?" she said. Puzzled. "Of course I remember you. You're Nick."

"I mean tomorrow." I laughed. "Will you remember me tomorrow?"

I knew she wouldn't, but I kissed her on the lips and thanked her again. She was happy because I was happy.

"I'll remember you tomorrow," she assured me. "Tomorrow's Friday. Right?"

"Right," I said. And watched her go.

I did sleep another two hours and got back to Grosse Pointe before 1100. Mrs. McPherson told me Paul Bumford had flashed twice from Washington, D.C., and I was to contact him the moment I returned. I went into the library and used the flasher there. After two wrong numbers, I got through to Paul in the DCS office at the EOB. He came on screen.

"Nick," he said, "where have you been?"

"Sleeping," I said.

"Millie," he said. "Well, listen Nick, are we still set for July twenty-sixth? For Operation Lewisohn?"

"As far as I'm concerned. I'm leaving in a few hours. Be down there tonight."

"I had this idea...."

"So?" I asked. "What idea?"

"We should make an official record. On videotape. Can I effect a communications team? To get it all. For history. I'll borrow objects and equipment from Joe Wellington's PR staff."

I computed a moment.

"The basic idea is go," I told him, "but Joe is not to be involved. He has no need to know. Besides, this is a very specialized type of production. Contact Ed Nolan at GPA-1 and requisition the objects who photographed that intravaginal documentary. Remember it? With the microminiaturized IBM TV camera?"

"Of course I remember it. Fine. I'll get them down here instanter."

"No interference with performing objects. Maybe they can set up platforms out of the way. And some effective commentator. Ron Nexler. That's his name. He did the voice-over on the chimera short. Remember that?"

"Nick, will you stop saying, 'Remember that?' I don't forget; you know that."

"If you say so. Bring the objects and equipment in. We'll have them set up, then have more walkthroughs to make certain they won't interfere with the actual surgery."

"Got it. With Ron Nexler giving a running commentary?"

"Yes. He's scientifically conditioned. No brain, but very glib. He's just right for the service."

"I'll get on it. It should be solidified by the time you get back tonight. I thought you'd want a permanent record, Nick."

"Yes," I said. "I do. Thanks, Paul. By the way, my father is going to flash you a go signal on the UP field test."

"Great," he enthused. "I'll start putting it together. Everything's percolating. Right, Nick?"

"Right," I said.

There was time before my father's copter would pick me up for the trip to the airport. I went to my third-floor aerie. The glued thread, door to jamb, was undisturbed. I sat down with the works of Egon Schiele. I lighted a cannabis. Alone.

As I turned those familiar pages once again, staring at that strong, baleful sexuality, I slowly became aware that I was never going to solve the mystery of Egon Schiele. What was the meaning behind those stopped eyes? What significance in the helpless, tormented nudes? The dread in the sight of exposed, pitilessly detailed genitalia? I could penetrate so far, but no farther. Then my descent was blocked. I was left with a horrified fascination I could not analyze.

Curiously, my failure to comprehend the work of Egon Schiele did not depress me. In fact, it led me to a realization I found oddly comforting:

There are questions to which there are no answers. There are problems for which there are no solutions.

Six hours later I was in the Lewisohn Building, Hospice No. 4, Alexandria, Virginia. Operation Lewisohn was scheduled to start at 0800, July 26, 1999. The staff spent the remaining hours in rehearsals, practice, drills. The Operation Directors devoted their time to running game-plans through Phoebe Huntzinger's computers in GPA-1. Testing our scenario for possible flaws. We programmed for every possible combination of disasters: power failures, linkage breakdowns, sudden stopping of the subject, terrorist attack, and so forth.

Difficulties were encountered, and overcome. For instance, the computer warned of incapacitation of key personnel. So we established an intraproject medical group, to minister to disabled staff members. We took extraordinary precautions to guard against food poisoning on the evening of July 25. We had already structured a fail-safe Table of Organization: Each object was numbered in relation to the importance of the assigned task. Thus, if Chief Surgeon Dr. George Berk, Green One, was unable to perform, his place would be taken by Green Two. And so on; everyone moving up a rank. Standby objects were present to fill in the lowest echelons.

At midnight, July 25, all operating staff were ordered to use a six-hour Somnorific. At the same time, the Command Staff was administered low-power, time-controlled energizers. The final countdown began. The last checkout of equipment, power supply, electronic linkages, and so forth. Phoebe Huntzinger's computers were gradually brought on line. Operating Theater D illuminated. Emergency supplies opened. Instrument sterilizers wheeled into position. Laser scanners put on warm-up. Amplifiers tested. Readout screens and printout machines switched to On.

The results of these preparations were all reported on monitor screens to Command Central. Paul and I had agreed that I was to remain there, ruling the entire project, while he roamed the assembly rooms, corridors, labs, washup lavatories, operating area, and so forth. Reporting progress and stoppages directly to me, and only me, via a Portapager on an exclusive wavelength.

Next to me in Command Central, on my right, Maya Leighton sat at a wide desk. With Mary Bergstrom as backup. They each had a throat mike and a copy of the final schedule. We had positioned loudspeakers throughout the building.

I watched the enormous wall digiclock rotate the seconds. At 0729:45, I looked to Maya. She was watching me. I raised my hand. At 0729:59, I pointed a forefinger directly at her. She began to read quietly from the schedule. Her amplified voice boomed from the speakers:

"0730. Transportation Group to stations. Green Team and White Team to standby."

The objects assigned to the task of bringing Hyman R. Lewisohn into Operating Theater D moved to their designed positions: his hospital suite, hallway, elevator, etc. The Green Team (surgeons and anesthesiologists) and White Team (nurses and aides) moved to their assembly areas. I could watch these activities, and all the actions that would take place that day, on a bank of TV monitor screens.

These belonged to the Communications Team. The commentator, Ron Nexler, sat at a control board on my left. The videotape editor sat next to him, making a rough mix as the images came in. Neither em took his eyes from the monitor screens. As Operation Lewisohn got under way, I saw the mobile videotape camera operator, powerpack on his back, move from one area to another. Taping the preliminaries. He, in turn, was videotaped by the fixed cameras.

Ron Nexler spoke softly into a desk mike:

"Good morning, ladies and gentlemen. This is Ron Nexler speaking to you from the Lewisohn Building in Hospice No. 4, Alexandria, Virginia. In a very few moments we will witness an incredible surgical operation that has never been attempted before in the long history of the human race. This is a historic moment, an exciting moment, and we hope to show you every step in this astounding scientific achievement that may very well revolutionize the future of the world."

"0740. Green Team and White Team to washup. Transportation Group to alert. Countdown will begin by minutes from 0755 to 0759. By seconds during the final minute."

Quiet in Command Central. I watched the clock. Listened to Maya's voice, coming over the loudspeaker, and to Nexler's voice, being taped. Paul patted my shoulder, then left to begin his rounds. I scanned the monitor screens. Normal.

"0754. Coming up to mark. Transportation Group to final readiness. Green Team and White Team to alert. Countdown to start begins . . . *now!* 0755.

"0756.

"0757.

"0758.

"0759, and 60, 59, 58, 57, 56, 55, 54. . . ."

As the numbers dwindled, I could see objects all over the building glancing nervously at wall digiclocks and taking deep breaths.

". . . six, five, four, three, two, one. *Start!*"

"Ladies and gentlemen, this tremendously involved and complex surgical procedure has started. I will attempt to provide a minute-by-minute account of what is taking place. But please bear with me if the image you see does not correspond to my commentary. This is a solemn and extremely intricate project, and we in the communications field must, quite rightly, take second place to all the wonderful objects contributing their time and their talents to make this great endeavor a resounding success.

"Now you see the door of Hyman R. Lewisohn's hospital room being opened. The Transportation Group is moving in to begin their assignment. The subject has already been sedated sufficiently so he can be disconnected from all his tubes and needles. Nothing but an incoherent, muttered protest from him. Jake, could you move in closer and get that moan again, please? Now they've got him on a high, wheeled stretcher and have started him out of that room where he has spent so many lonely, pain-racked hours. Moving him toward the elevator bank. A door is being held open . . ."

"0803. Green Team and White Team to positions. Subject on the way to Operating Theater D."

"Now, folks, the endless drills and rehearsals are paying off. Notice there is no stumbling, no bumping, no confusion. Every object knows the task required and the exact physical position and movements assigned. All serving together like the selfless angels of mercy they are."

"0805. Green Team and White Team to alert. Blue Team to assembly."

"Ladies and gentlemen, what impresses me most at this crucial moment is the absolute silence of the servers as the subject is wheeled through the wide doors of Operating Theater D. Now you can see, through the magic of a portable videotape camera, the preliminaries as Lewisohn's corpus is transferred to the operating table and draped. Now the anesthesiologists begin their important service. Notice they glance occasionally to the vital signs monitors against the walls. But mostly they are listening, listening intently, to the beeps, thumps, and whistles of amplified aural signals. All these indicators are reproduced here in Command Central. I have just spoken to Dr. Nicholas Bennington Flair, the brilliant ruler of this incredible scientific project, and he informs me that Lewisohn's cardiac rate, although erratic, is presently within acceptable parameters, pulse is strong, and other vital signs are encouraging."

I saw, on a TV monitor, the Chief Anesthesiologist nod to the Chief Surgeon. Just after Maya Leighton announced: "0821. Blue Team to standby," the Chief Surgeon spoke briefly into his throat mike.

"I'm going in," he said.

"Ladies and gentlemen, the actual operation has begun."

I thought then, and I think now, it was the longest day of my life. It was not only the slight click of the wall digiclock as the minutes ticked over in Command Central. Nor Maya Leighton enunciating her orders precisely: "Blue Team to alert. Green Team begin withdrawal in precisely five minutes. Brown Team to standby." Nor Ron Nexler's never-ending, "Ladies and gentlemen, the next miracle you are about to see. . . ." And so forth.

It was the slow, deliberate pace of what we did that day that stretched minutes to hours. I knew it could not be hurried. Should not be. But I longed for it all to be over. Done with. Finished. Won or lost. One way or the other.

It did not go perfectly. What human plan does? But we were able to cope with emergencies, improvise when required, substitute, invent. Considering the radical nature of the operation, I cannot see how our basic scenario could have been improved.

The surgeons were finished by 1600. Meanwhile we had been phasing in Leo Bernstein's Blue Team. Who, in turn, were phased out as the Project Phoenix servers, Brown Team, wheeled up their equipment and began positioning the laser scanners.

As servers came off duty, I noted they did not disappear to the cafeteria or barracks. I knew they were as worn and weary as I. Yet, almost to an object, they went immediately to the observation benches behind the glass walls in Operating Theater D. Where they could witness the climax of the project. Hunched over. Leaning forward. Elbows on knees. Chins on fists. Staring. Staring.

I had left my swivel chair only twice that day. To go to the nest. But I was on post when the first faint signal was picked up from Lewisohn's brain by the Brown Team, at 2139 on the evening of July 26, 1999. About five minutes later, they detected a signal they felt was precise enough to amplify and attempt to translate in the GPA-1 computer vocabulary. The signal was transmitted over our direct-wire link. We waited. The printout machine chattered briefly: WHAT?

It wasn't much, I admit. But if Lewisohn's brain had stopped at that instant, I would still have deemed Operation Lewisohn a success. As the word spread of what we had done, I heard a great, muffled roar go up from everyone, everywhere, throughout the Lewisohn Building. Maya Leighton kissed me. Even Mary Bergstrom kissed me. There was a continual snapping of fingers, stroking of palms. Paul came rushing back to Command Central. I realized then his total commitment to, and belief in Operation Lewisohn. For behind came laughing servers with bottles of petropagne, natural brandy, petrovod, chilled Smack. Many nice liters of many nice things. A celebration Paul had provided. We celebrated.

Meanwhile, Brown Team were still fussing with their laser scanners. Making minute power adjustments in the amplifiers. By the time I got down to Operating Theater D, they were transmitting a stream of utile signals to GPA-1. Returns were mostly gibberish, but that was understandable; Lewisohn's brain hadn't yet been totally flushed of sedatives and anesthesia. Leo Bernstein was personally monitoring the blood serum pump and adjusting the data processing monitor that gave a continuous scan and printout of brain weight, electrical power output, oxygen level, and so forth.

The head of Hyman R. Lewisohn had been severed from his corpus. It had been placed beneath a giant bell jar. Five times the size of the glass dome enclosing the head of Fred III, the Labrador retriever. Lewisohn's head existed in a sterile environment. Laser rods, instruments, the loudspeaker wire, etc., all penetrated the protective covering, but were attached with contamination-proof seals.

The head had been cut off below the larynx, slightly beneath the voice box. But Lewisohn could not speak, since there were no lungs to provide airflow across the vocal cords. Hence the need for the scanning equipment of Project Phoenix. The head would be maintained in an animate status in a manner similar to that used to keep Fred III alive, with an oxygenated blood pump. Brain weight and electrical output were monitored constantly. Lewisohn could see, and he could hear. Hence the small loudspeaker inside his bell jar.

When I first approached Lewisohn's head, the eyes were closed. The skin tone appeared waxen to me. But Leo Bernstein didn't seem unduly concerned, so I refrained from questioning him. He and two members of his staff were still adjusting flow rates and formulae. The Project Phoenix servers were just as busy. Making microadjustments on the laser rods. Watching their screens to provide maximum overlap of the scanned areas. Tuning their amplifiers on phoned advice from Phoebe Huntzinger in New York. I spoke with her briefly.

"Congratulations, Nick," she said. "You did it."

"*We* did it," I said. "Thank you."

"It was your idea," she said. "What's next?"

"I'll think of something," I said. And we both laughed.

I watched Lewisohn's head. Keratotic scalp showing through the scraggly fringe of reddish hair. Distorted skull. Bulge of domed brow. Gross features magnified by his pallor. Rubbery lips, drooling slightly. Certainly not as attractive as Fred III.

Finally, the eyes opened. Slowly. Lids rose like a weighted curtain. I moved closer to the bell jar. Picked up the small hand mike. Waited.

Eyes appeared dulled. Lifeless. But even as I watched, I saw a definite improvement. Consciousness flowing in. Animation growing stronger.

"Folks," Ron Nexler's low voice said, "Hyman R. Lewisohn's head appears to be recovering from the shock of this historymaking operation. His eyes are opening wide, and, yes, they're turning now to inspect. . . ."

I turned sharply. Nexler was at my side. Staring with fascination at Lewisohn's head. But not too fascinated to remain silent; he was dictating into a portable tape deck. Over his shoulder, the mobile videotape camera operator was recording the awakening of Hyman R. Lewisohn. For history. For one insane instant I wanted to beat them both to stopping with their own equipment. But the fury passed. They were doing their service. As I was doing mine. I turned back to Lewisohn's head.

The eyes were fully open now. Sclerae and cornea clear. Brighter. Pupils slightly dilated. The eyeballs turned slowly in complete circuits. Left. Up. Right. Down. They made two complete inspections. Surveying the inside of the glass bell jar. Distorted images of all of us outside, peering in. I knew the brain must be computing. As I anticipated, the eyes turned downward once again. To inspect the base of the bell jar. No corpus. If Lewisohn had still possessed a heart, it might have stopped at that instant. Instead, the printout computer began to chatter softly. I stepped over to it, but scanned the readout screen rather than wait for the permanent record. The translated electrical signals were not in coherent form. Understandable.

WHAT? GLASS DOME. DREAM? ALIVE. MOVEMENT THERE. OBJECTS. WHAT'S HE DOING? ABOVE. ALL SIDES. BELOW? NOTHING. NOTHING? A BASE. RODS STICKING IN. WHAT? A LITTLE SQUARE BOX. WHERE? ALIVE. YES. PAIN? NO PAIN WHO? HOT! CHRIST, IT'S SO HOT!

"Leo!" I called.

But he had been scanning the printout as it flipped from the machine. He saw it almost as soon as I did. He jerked a downthumb at one of his servers.

"Take him off five degrees and hold," he ordered.

Temperature and humidity inside Lewisohn's home were adjusted gradually downward. The computers started clacking again with scarcely a pause. It is difficult, if not impossible, to stop thinking completely. Try it sometime. The closest you can come is to think. "I will not think."

Computer readout showed that Lewisohn still did not comprehend what had happened to him. I judged it time to tell him. Primus: I wanted to anger him, keep him "talking." I guessed increased brain activity at that point in time would help rid the neurons and supporting nutritive structures of the effects of preoperative drugs and anesthetics.

Secondus: There was much we had to learn of the functioning of a detached human brain, and we had to learn it fast. For instance, did the brain have to sleep, without the need to recover from physical exhaustion? The Fred III research project had indicated that sleep is as much a function of mental recovery as of physical. But in humans? We simply didn't know.

The microphone leading to the loudspeaker within Lewisohn's bell jar was small, hand-held, with a volume control calibrated from 1 to 5. I set it at 1, and moved close to the glass. Maneuvering cautiously to avoid disturbing the projecting laser rods.

"Lewisohn," I said. In a normal, conversational tone.

It had no effect on him. His eyes did not blink. I adjusted volume control to 2.

"Lewisohn," I said again.

Eye reaction this time. Flickering briefly in the direction of the loudspeaker within the bell jar. He probably heard it as a whisper. I moved the volume control up to 3.

"Lewisohn," I repeated.

He heard that all right. Rapid blinking. Eyes focused on loudspeaker. I moved my head as close to the glass as I could.

"Lewisohn," I said, "move your eyes slowly, slowly to your left. As far as you can without feeling pain. You should be able to make me out. This is Nicholas Bennington Flair. How do you feel, Lewisohn?"

Why didn't I stand directly in front of the bell jar where he could see me without turning his eyes? Because in front of the bell jar, as close as we could get it to minimize distortion, we had set up a small viewing screen. On which Lewisohn would be able to scan books, newspapers, reports, computer print-outs, etc.—all to be taped at his command. For his exclusive viewing.

"How do you feel, Lewisohn?" I repeated.

The computer printout began its soft chatter. I switched off my microphone. I looked about. Paul Bumford was standing nearby, talking with Tom Lee, Team Leader of Project Phoenix.

"Paul," I called.

He came over immediately. I drew him close. Spoke in a low voice.

"Paul, interrogation of Lewisohn will be difficult if the interrogator has to run back and forth from microphone to computer to scan Lewisohn's response. A longer cord on the mike is no answer. Then you wouldn't be able to monitor his facial reactions. Get on the flasher to Phoebe. Ask her how long it will take to program the entire stored vocabulary into vocal responses. It can be done; the hardware's available. Her computers will trigger spoken words on tape. The words should be recorded by some em with vocal qualities similar to Lewisohn's natural voice. There must be tapes of him speaking *somewhere* they can use as models."

"Right." Paul nodded. "I'll get on it at once."

"I don't want the Chief Director in here until he can actually have a 'con-versation' with Lewisohn's head. Talk to him and apparently hear Lewisohn 'talking' back. Much more impressive."

"I concur," Paul said. "Marvelous idea."

"Meanwhile, assign a server to tear off printout from the machine as it comes in and hustle it over to me. Two servers would be better."

I went back to the bell jar. To my original position. I switched on the microphone.

"Lewisohn," I said. "Here I am. Nicholas Bennington Flair. Can you see me?"

The computer chattered. In a few seconds a strip of printout was held up in front of me. I scanned it: I CAN SEE YOU. WHAT HAVE YOU DONE TO ME?

I took a deep breath. Then I told him. Exactly. Everything. I came down hard on how new and revolutionary it was. How he would have stopped without it. How civilian physicians had examined him and his medical history and had agreed that he was doomed. But now his brain was, as far as we knew, as close to being immortal as any animate thing could be. "Immortal." I thought that was the key word and kept hitting it. "You will be immortal." "Your brain will never stop." "The world's first immortal object." Etc., etc. I described the precautions that had been taken and would be taken to ensure his safety: A fail-safe power supply for the machines that kept his brain alive. Gradually improved blood supply as we learned more about his needs. More physical comfort inside his bell jar. A bombproof and sabotage-proof shelter. Whatever he wanted to scan. Even his dumb romantic novels. All converted to tape and projected on the viewing screen before his eyes. No more pain. Above all, no more pain. And he could continue to serve. To serve the US Government which, in gratitude, would keep his brain animate and active. Forever.

Even before I finished speaking, the return from the GPA-1 computer came in. Was torn off in a jagged strip, rushed over to me, held before my eyes.

I had expected a stream of invective. Obscenities. Endless, gabbled curses. Blasting me for what I had conceived and what I had done. I expected that condemnation, and I wanted it. It would be a signal of Lewisohn's "normality." But I also wanted the judgment for myself. For reasons I could not compute.

But it was a brief message: MAYA. I WANT MAYA. TO TALK TO. TO SEE. MAYA.

I looked at the torn scrap.

"What?" I said into the microphone.

The response came through.

MAYA, it scanned. I WANT TO SEE MAYA LEIGHTON: BRING HER CLOSE. I WANT TO SEE HER. TALK TO HER. OR I WON'T SERVE.

I stared at that pumpkin head. Glaring eyes. Outraged. Like the starving children of Pakistan.

"Yes," I said. "All right, Lewisohn. I'll get Maya for you."

Z-10

On August 4, 1999, I was in my penthouse apartment. At the compound, Manhattan Landing, GPA-1. Trying to serve my way through four weeks' accumulation of bills, bank statements, dividend checks, scientific journals, personal correspondence, kaka.

My flasher chimed at about 2130. It was Seymour Dove. Calling from San Diego.

"Seymour!" I said. Pleased. "Good to see you again. How have you been?"

He wasted no time on pleasantries. His face, on screen, was expressionless.

"Nick," he said, "do you remember the address of the beach-house where I met you?"

"Sure. It was—"

"Don't say it," he broke in quickly. "How many digits in the number?"

I instantly became as serious as he.

"Three digits," I said.

"Correct," he said. "Keep them in mind, then duplicate the three. Now you've got a six-digit number. Right?"

"Right," I said.

"Add this number to those six: five one two seven six three one. Got that?"

"Five one two seven six three one. Correct?"

"You have the sum of the first six digits plus the seven-digit number I gave you?"

"I have it," I told him.

"Can you call me at that number, in precisely one hour?" he asked. "Call, don't flash. It's important."

"Will do," I said. I started to say "Thank you," but he had already switched off.

Precisely an hour later I was calling him from a public phone booth outside the compound.

"Seymour," I said, "what's this all about?"

"First of all," he said, "Simon Hawkley stopped two nights ago. In his sleep. I sent you a letter, but you probably don't have it yet."

Silence.

"I'm sorry to hear that," I said. Finally. "A gentleman. I was hoping to see him again. And tell him . . . But things . . ."

"But that isn't why I called," Seymour Dove went on. "I still have a friend at Scilla—the secretary—and about an hour or so ago she told me a government nose has been around. Investigating the sale of Scilla. Who the present owners bought the property from and when."

"Uh-huh," I said. "Did she say what agency?"

"Bureau of Public Security."

"Uh-huh. One nose?"

"Yes. An em."

"He wasn't wearing a checkered cap by any chance, was he?"

"Wearing a checkered cap?"

"Yes. Did she mention it?"

"Wait a minute. I'll ask her. She's in the bedroom."

I waited patiently. Finally he came back on.

"No," he said. "She says he wasn't wearing any hat at all. Why did you—"

"Thanks very much, Seymour," I said. "I appreciate your calling. It was kind of you."

"You'll be all right, Nick?" he asked anxiously. "Even if they trace it?"

"No problem," I said. "Thanks again, Seymour. Sorry to hear about Hawkley. Did he leave anyone? Wife? Children?"

"No," he said. "He was alone."

I was about to say "Aren't we all?" but then realized how fatuous that was. So I merely said good-bye and broke the connection. I didn't think Dove was in any danger. He was a born survivor. Was I?

Investigation of the Scilla plot . . . That could prove fatal. If they traced ownership to me during a period when Scilla had been selling hallucinogens to my Section. How had the BPS been alerted to Scilla?

I had hypothecated a scenario to account for the missing 5 cc flask of 416HBL-CW3. For the fact that a known terrorist, Arthur Raddo, had a friend named "Nick" who looked like me. (Anyone could introduce himself to Raddo as "Nick," and anyone of my approximate height and weight, disguised with dark wig, mustache and Vandyke beard would resemble me in the dimness of the Adonis Club.) My hypothetical scenario even accounted for the sharing of Millie Jean Grunwald's apartment in Detroit.

Assume a terrorist group, perhaps survivors of the Society of Obsoletes' conspiracy, were authors of the plot against me. Perhaps in revenge for my role in the stopping of Hammond, Wiley, DeTilly, and the others. Assume such a dissident organization might very well have members in SATSEC. Living and serving in the GPA-1 compound. It would not be too difficult for a laboratory server to manipulate the theft of the *Clostridium botulinum*. And to forge my name on the withdrawal card.

The subsequent removal of the entire flask had been masterfully planned and executed. And timed. Since it occurred after I had answered R. Sam Bigelow's inquiry. Stating I had verified the existence of the bottle by personal inspection.

The motive for effectualizing the botulism outbreak in GPA-11 was more complex. Their prime desire, I assumed, was to implicate me in a horrendous crime. But I suspected there might have been other reasons: The whole operation could have been in the nature of a "laboratory experiment," an exercise in terrorism to hone planning techniques, and test the determination, skill, and loyalty of members.

It might also have been a deliberate attempt to destroy the Beist movement by incriminating one of its members. It was quite possible that the late Arthur Raddo was duped. A selected pigeon. Perhaps his control was an em he knew as "Nick." A bearded em he met only in the dimness of Adonis and from whom he took his orders and received the flask of 416HBL-CW3.

There were many unknowns, many possibilities. The terrorist organization scenario was not a neat, elegant solution. But I felt it explained most of the bizarre occurrences that had been bedeviling me. It might even account for the continued presence of those checkered-capped snoops, if the organization was large enough.

But now, after computing what Seymour Dove had told me, I realized a new factor had appeared in the equation: the interest of the Bureau of Public Security. Perhaps they had been alerted by their analysis of pure glycerol in the replaced 5 cc flask in my pharmlab. But I doubted that; I would have been informed of any BPS investigation in GPA-1. Or would I? Perhaps the BPS told my servers I had no need to know. Perhaps the discovery that the bottle supposed to contain 416HBL-CW3 now contained no *Clostridium botulinum* was enough to set R. Sam Bigelow's noses on my track. Hence the investigation of Scilla. Perhaps the ems in checkered caps were BPS snoops. It wouldn't be the first time they had used the technique of open and obvious surveillance to panic a suspect and start him running.

I debated if it might not be wise to go to R. Sam Bigelow, or even Chief Director Michael Wingate, and tell either, or both, that I was being manipulated. I decided it would not be wise. Because either, or both, might be doing the manipulating. Why would they desire my destruction? Because the CD had learned of my secret meetings with his wife. Possibly . . . Maybe . . . Perhaps . . .

I stayed in GPA-1 for almost a week. Serving on my official duties as DEPDIRSAT and cleaning up my personal obligations. It wasn't until late in the week that I realized I was settling my affairs. As an object might do contemplating a lengthy trip. Or . . .

When I left the compound, I flew to Washington, D.C., took the Metro to the Chevy Chase place, and left my luggage there. Showered, changed zipsuits, and went back to the Metro for the long ride to Alexandria. There I could requisition wheels from the Hospice No. 4 motor pool.

Construction had already started on converting the Lewisohn Building into an ultrasecure bombproof shelter. The heavy, windowless walls were up to the second floor. I had to show my BIN card and official ID three times, and be identified twice by voice-print check, before I was allowed into Operating Theater D. There was a ten-object staff in attendance, twenty-four hours a day. They had been ordered to stay out of Lewisohn's sight as much as possible.

Lewisohn's head, in its domed greenhouse, sat in lonely splendor in the middle of the softly lighted theater. As I approached, I saw he was scanning a computer printout projected on the small screen in front of his bell jar. I stood as close as I could and waited patiently until he noticed me.

"Nicholas Bennington Flair!" came booming through a loudspeaker atop the computer readout screen linked to GPA-1.

The voice startled me. I knew they had completed the taping of the computer vocabulary. But I had never heard the voice before. It was remarkably like Lewisohn's natural voice: harsh and yet precise, loud and angry, with an occasional phlegmy splutter.

I looked more closely at Lewisohn's head. He was still staring at the viewing screen. But his eyes were not moving; he was not scanning. I picked up the transmitting microphone.

"Yes," I said. "This is Flair."

"Satisfied?" the canned voice asked.

"Yes," I said, "I'm satisfied. The operation was a success, and the patient survived. And is serving, I see. Are you satisfied?"

Stupid question. He didn't answer. For which I was thankful.

"What are you serving on?" I asked him.

"You wouldn't understand," he thought.

"Try me," I said.

Then the lids slowly rose. Reptilian eyes focused, stared at me.

"You have no need to know," the mechanical voice crackled.

The words shivered me. It was a common enough phrase. Probably justified in this instance. But I had become abnormally sensitive to such slights. Did everyone know something I didn't know?

"Are you getting everything you want—uh—need—uh—ask for?" I said. Difficult, talking to a head.

"Yes."

"Does Maya visit you?"

"Yes."

"Every day?"

"Yes. I want to be alone with her. I want a screen around us. So those grinning apes can't watch."

"I'll arrange it."

There were many others questions I wanted to ask. Can a disembodied head still love? What form of political society did he envision for his corporate world? Did he believe, as Paul Bumford obviously did, that instinctive sexuality was an operative base on which to predicate the political nature of *Homo sapiens*? Had he done any computing of the existence of a primitive slave factor in the psychology of our species? And much, much more.

But the sight of Lewisohn's head did not encourage conversation. Particularly of an intimate nature.

"All right," I said. "I'll leave you now."

"I don't want to see you again," he thought. "Ever. If you continue to come here, I will stop serving. I will tell the Chief Director that."

"Very well," I said. Understanding. But saddened. "I won't come again. Good-bye, Lewisohn."

Then the obscenities started. Loud, rancid virulence, spewing from the loudspeaker. The serving staff looked up, startled. I turned away. Followed by that screamed filth. Created in his brain. Transformed into electrical signals. Scanned by laser. Amplified electronically. Transmitted to the GPA-1 computers. Translated, triggering taped vocal responses. Returned to Operating Theater D. Verbal excrement flung at my back as I walked out of there.

I plunged into the DCS campaign. Serving in Paul's office in the basement of the EOB. At that point in time, late August, 1999, our staff had incubated to more than fifty objects. Following what seemed to be an inexorable law of megagrowth in all bureaucratic agencies. Most of our servers were assigned to Congressional liaison, and it was to this area that Paul and I devoted most of our time.

The signal from the Chief Director, based on Sady Nagle's estimate, was that passage in the House was assured. We switched our push to the Senate. Profiting from experience, we concentrated on the staffs of individual Senators and of the subcommittee and full committee that would first consider the new Department.

Attempting to convince individual Senators was counterproductive. Difficult though it may be to believe, in August, 1999, only eighteen members of the entire US Congress had a scientific background. The great majority were lawyers, businessmen, ex-soccer stars, and former television performers. They simply did not have the conditioning to comprehend our proposals. Some staff members had, at least, a rudimentary understanding of our numbers, computer studies, plans, and projections. It was their utilization we sought.

As I endured an apparently endless succession of lunches, conferences, cocktail parties, private colloquies, and dinners, I realized the enormity of what President Harold K. Morse had accomplished. He had established an executive advisory board of scientists during his administration. He had enlarged the Science Academy and helped bring it to a level of conditioning efficiency surpassing West Point, Annapolis, the Air/Space Academy, and the Academy of International Cooperation. I became aware that our Department of Creative Science was merely one more step—but perhaps a quantum jump—Morse might have effectualized a decade earlier. If he had not stopped.

I spoke to Grace Wingate about this. Recalling my meeting with President Morse in 1990. Shortly before he suicided.

"I thought he was assassinated," she said.

"No," I said, "I don't think so. The only object who could possibly benefit from his assassination would have been his VP. And he didn't have the brain—or the ambition—to manipulate it."

"How did you meet Morse?"

"He called me in. I had published a very minor, almost poetic paper on the nature of genius."

"The nature of genius? Nick, isn't that outside your disciplines?"

"It is now. It wasn't then; I was young."

"What did you say about genius?"

"I took as my text: 'Full many a flower is born to blush unseen, / and waste its sweetness on the desert air.' Thomas Gray. Not so, I said. I argued that genius unknown is genius nonexistent. Like a tree falling unheard in an isolated forest. It produces no sound. No receiver. Genius, I said, must be appreciated to exist."

"Do you really believe that?"

"I was certain at the time I wrote it. I'm not so certain now. Anyway, that paper was how I came to meet President Morse. It was published in an obscure Southern Literary journal. But he scanned it. I believe he scanned *everything*. He called me to the White House, and I had a marvelous hour with him. What a brain!"

"What did he talk about?"

"Everything! He dazzled me. He seemed to know all I knew, and a lot more besides. A very inquiring brain. A curious brain. Always asking, always prying."

"About what?"

"Well, for instance, he recalled an obso gerontological theory: that every object, at birth, has a built-in clock. The clock is wound for a finite number of heartbeats, respirations, and so forth. When the clock runs down, the object stops. And nothing can be done to keep the clock ticking. That theory has been demolished now, but it was potent at the time. President Morse wondered, almost casually, if the same theory could be extended to human emotions. Suffering. Enthusiasm. Pain. Hope. And so forth. If we were born with a finite quantity of each. And when they were expended, they were gone. Depleted. Never to be renewed."

"Nick, he *did* suicide?"

"I have no doubt of it. Grace, I've never told anyone this—it's still ultrasecret—but after Morse stopped, I was assigned as a member of an ad hoc committee of physicians to investigate. Our report was unanimous. It's filed away somewhere. He had always been a light drinker, but we found operative evidence of heavy alcoholic intake followed by massive barbiturate ingestion. There was little doubt about it. It was deliberate. He suicided."

"But why?"

"You want my theory? That's all I can give you—a theory. His wife. A dreadful ef. But he needed her. I think—this is just my own hypothecation—I think that he finally used up all his need. It was depleted. And he found that, without it, he didn't want to live. No reason to live. Does that make sense?"

"Is your need for me depleted?"

I groaned and took her into my arms.

We were in our safe house, our secret garden. A late August day so fulsome it was almost blowsy.

"Nick, you seem . . ."

"Seem?"

"So—so reflective?"

"Do I? Talking of President Morse, I suppose. Remembering."

"You have such a marvelous memory."

"A curse. Sometimes."

"You mean it's nice to forget?"

"The brain's natural therapy. Only occasionally it doesn't serve. Things buried must be dredged to the surface. And faced. Examined."

"Nick, do you know everything?"

"Everything," I assured her solemnly.

We laughed. Hugged. Then I drew back, looked at her for the first time.

I had kissed, or touched, almost every part of her. Except for those hidden places I wanted to keep inviolate. Sacred. The smooth brow I could assimilate. And vulval ears. Pale flame of hair, soft lips, sharp nose, somber eyes, pointed chin. Her whippy corpus. So important. But not important. *Her*. The giving. Hers and mine.

Neither of us restrained, and we made mad vows of what we might cheerfully do at the other's bidding. Suffer. Suicide. It was a game. With the grave significance of all games. I needed her so much. And she needed me. I *knew*.

We sat together that afternoon until the sky deepened. Mostly in silence. Occasionally exchanging trivia.

"What's your favorite color?"

"Have you ever eaten natural rabbit?"

"Can you swim?"

"Do you like the scent of gardenia?"

"Do you ever pray?"

"Who was the first object you used?"

Still exploring. Still learning. Still going deeper. To profound places of such intimacy that, I think, we were both shocked. But could not end. Having come that far, we could not see a limit. We must go farther. Deeper yet. And so we did.

Strange, the way we disrated to obso speech:

"I love you. Do you love me?"

"I love you. Do you love me?"

"I love you."

And didn't think it strange.

Finally, inevitably, we had to separate. I gave her the gift I had brought. A tiny jeweled scarab. A dung beetle. With a little clamp clasp. It bewitched her. She pressed it to her lips.

"Can you wear it?" I asked. Anxiously.

"Always," she said. "Hidden."

We both laughed with joy.

And that's how we parted.

I stayed in Washington, D.C. for several days. A period preceding and following Service Day. I spent most of my time in the DCS office in the EOB, although I visited Hospice No. 4 several times prior to September 8. I made no effort to see Lewisohn's head, as I had promised him. But I monitored his progress via daily status reports from the medical staff assigned to him. And I viewed films that had been made of him, without his knowledge, by a microminia-turized camera concealed in the viewing screen in front of his bell jar.

On the evening of September 8, 1999, I returned late to the Chevy Chase place. Having spent the day in Alexandria completing my final report on Operation Lewisohn. Paul Bumford and Mary Bergstorm were home, watch-ing a live TV broadcast from the US Government's permanent moon colony. Potable water had recently been discovered, at a depth of approximately 10 kilometers.

I waved to them, went into the kitchen to mix a vodka-and-Smack. I took it up to my room. No plans except to relax. Perhaps scan some scientific journals that had accumulated. Listen to some music. I was in a cautiously euphoric mood. I had heard nothing more about the Scilla investigation. I had not seen another checkered cap. The Arthur Raddo business already seemed ancient history. It would, I told myself, all go away. Still, I thought it might be wise to find a new safe place to meet Grace Wingate. In affairs of this sort, as in crime and espionage, habitual patterns prove fatal.

Shortly before midnight, Paul knocked on my door. Carrying his own brandy and one for me.

"Busy?" he asked.

"Come on in," I said. "How are things on the moon?"

"Those lunatics." He laughed. "Because of the discovery of water, they're talking about an enormous increase in the size of our colony. Eventually ap-plying for admission into the US as a state."

"Oh?" I said. "That's interesting. And what have you been up to?"

He slouched into a club chair facing me. Put his brandy glass to his lips. Stared at me.

"Well?" I asked.

"On the Ultimate Pleasure project," he said. "I received a preliminary report today. From Ben Baker, your father's production manager. Only on the factory in which servers are getting the actual UP injection. For the past week, production was up 69.8 percent."

"Sounds good," I said.

"Good?" Paul said. "Incredible! When you consider that only 38.6 percent of the servers signed the Informed Consent Statement. But that 38.6 percent accounted for the total production surplus. Your father should be delighted."

"He will be," I said. "Nothing from the control or placebo factories?"

"Nothing yet. Should be in this week. Nick, have you given any more thought to what we discussed?"

"Brainstorming a society to maximize the UP?"

"Yes."

"I've computed it. Some. I still feel you're overvaluing the UP. It doesn't make sense to me to predicate a political infrastructure on sexuality."

"You think that's what I'm doing, Nick?" This with a tinselly smile.

"Aren't you?"

"Far from it. But even if what you allege is operative, moral philosophies have been based on sexuality; why not political philosophies?"

"I'm not tracking."

"Nick, I'm not overvaluing the UP. Per se. I'm utilizing its most salient characteristic: the slave factor. If preliminary numbers hold up, it's present in approximately 85 percent of all UP fantasies."

"And so?"

"I think the slave factor is more than a symptom of sexopathy. I believe there is also emotional surrender, political surrender. Even, in obso terminology, spiritual surrender. In other words, 85 percent of all objects obtain their Ultimate Pleasure from total devotion, or submission, to objects, ideas, or ideals outside themselves. It's this principle of abasement I want to utilize in predicating a new political structure for our society. It maximizes a very basic, very instinctive human drive the UP has uncovered."

"And what about the unaffected 15 percent?"

"Ah." He nodded wisely. "You *are* tracking. Nick, those 15 percent of objects impervious to the slave factor are the big, unanswered question. A lot of heavy research to be done there. I think the answers will be found by psychobiologists. Can I activate a team?"

His sudden question caught me off balance. He was going so fast, pushing so hard, that I was dazzled. I needed time to compute. I waffled. . . .

"What do you think such a project would find?" I said.

"You want me to guess? That's all I can do at this point in time—guess. Nick, I believe research psychobiologists will find a common denominator in those 15 percent of objects unaffected by the slave factor. In addition, I think they'll find a definite correlation with genetic rating. All, or most of those 15 percent, will be found in the top and top-plus GR's."

"And what will that mean?" I asked. Knowing his answer.

"Nick, don't you see? It demands a class society based on genetic ratings. The managers would be immune to the UP, but able to utilize it objectively for the good of society. Can I activate that research project?"

"No," I said. "I won't approve it. If I learn you've started it without my permission, I'll stop it and have you up on charges."

His face turned to stone.

"Why?" he said. Barely audible.

"Because you're starting with a preconception. Paul, you and I both know that any research project can prove anything you want it to prove. If strongly ruled. Contradata is simply disregarded. Even the structure of the project itself—organization, selection of personnel—weights the results. You already know what you want your project to find. If I let you go ahead, they'll find it. You know it and I know it."

"You mean I'd falsify results?" Squalid smile.

"Let's just say you'd misrepresent conclusions."

"So you don't trust me?"

"On this particular matter—no."

He stood up. Trying very hard to keep himself under control. But his voice, when he spoke, was pitched higher than normal. Not hysteria, but a furious anger that threatened to break into screams and shouts.

"Nick . . ." he said. Drew a deep breath. "I'm trying to trail-blaze, and you're stonewalling me. I've noticed, more and more, you've been influenced by obso moral considerations. You've been corrupted by humanism. It's decaying your judgment and perverting your decisions. You were the em who preached total objectivity. Presenting a façade of humanitarianism was to be part of the scenario. That was operative, and I believed it. I still believe it. But now you have defected. What is it, Nick? Don't you have the courage to follow your convictions to their logical ends? Well, I do. And I'm not alone; I can tell you that.

"Something you haven't realized. . . . All your brave words about the Tomorrow File not being a Christmas list, and how we had to effectualize it as soon as possible—a lot of kaka, Nick! That's exactly what it is for you: a Christmas list, a never-never inventory of brilliant ideas. Created so you can postpone actions you know are inevitable but don't have the courage or energy or desire to fructify.

"The Tomorrow File *is* tomorrow, Nick—and you know it! Right now we're on the edge, the verge, the fulcrum. The balance is shifting. The change will be enormous. Overwhelming! And the Tomorrow File is the scenario, the Department of Creative Science the organism. I thought we'd do it together. Everything we projected. But you've become an obso, Nick. In your computing. You're no longer able to keep up. You can't accept change. You've been passed. Events have gone beyond you. And ideas. You're no longer able to translate scientific principles into political doctrine. I don't know why; I don't know what's happened to you. I could guess, but I won't. All I know is that your retrogression is sad. Personally, to me, sad. But you can't stop us, Nick. That's not a threat; it's a resolution."

He marched out of there. I inhaled an eight-hour Somnorific and found darkness.

I came out of it about 0830 on the morning of September 9, 1999. I lay awhile in bed. Sheet pulled down to my waist. Hands behind my head. Staring at pale sunshine washed through the curtained windows. Was Grace Wingate lying alone as I was then? Perhaps I had been wrong. . . . We had been wrong. . . . I wasn't sure. . . .

Light knock on the door. Then it was opened immediately. Paul, carrying a tray. Orange petrojuice, toasted soybread, a pot of coftea, cups, saucers, cutlery, petrobutter, natural grape jelly, paper napkins.

"Peace offering." He smiled. Radiant smile.

"Greeks bearing gifts." I laughed. "Bring it over here."

He sat on the edge of my bed. We breakfasted there. Sharing the same knife, same tub of butter, same jelly.

"Listen, Nick," he said. "About last—"

"Don't talk with your mouth full."

He swallowed obediently.

"About last night," he said. "I'm sorry. But it's important to me."

"I compute," I said. "Paul, if we can't talk to each other as operatively as that, we've got nothing."

"Right," he said. "Well, I'll forget about that research project."

"No," I said, "don't forget about it. Paul, I'm not trying to demolish your theories. It's just your timing I object to. Let's get the Department of Creative Science finalized. Once that's in existence, the stratosphere's the limit. But at this point in time, we've got to walk tippytoe. Gloss all our activities on the UP. If it ever gets out, we're stopped. You compute that, don't you?"

"Oh sure, Nick."

"But that doesn't mean your ideas might not be operative. But for the future. Put it in the Tomorrow File."

"I already have." He grinned mischievously.

We both laughed. He took the tray from my bed, set it aside. Then he skinned out of his robe, slipped under the sheet. Close to me.

"What's this?" I said.

"One guess," he whispered.

"Wait," I said. "Wait just a minute."

I slid out of bed, got a liquid graphite pen and a pad of paper from my desk. Brought them back to the bed.

"ESP," I said. "Let's try it again. A two-word phrase."

"Right," he said.

We both scribbled. Then turned into each other's arms.

His corpus had become firmer. Harder. But still beneath that incredibly tender, limpid skin. Through which I could feel the rushing course of blood, heartpump, the rising heart of sexual excitement.

He put his soft lips to my nipples, loins, thighs. A sweet butcher. Carving me up. His breath was young. All of him scented. We traced each other. Flung the sheet aside. Rolling.

His eyes fluttered, closed. I eased him onto his back. Knees rose and parted. Conditioned reflex. The pleasure I felt was not heightened by penetrating an em. But heightened by guilt at surrendering to the demands of my own corpus. Brain denied. Animal all.

We fumbled some.

"Out of practice," I gasped.

He grunted.

But we finally linked, moaning. His hips pillowed. My back arched. Both of us in heat. Lightly sweated. We held back. As long as we could. Ultimizing the swoon.

We summited in a fury. Nails. Crying out. As elemental as a storm. Something despairing there. I pronged as deeply as I could. Wanting to split him. Rend. And he wanting to surrender. Rend. Sur*render*. From *renda*, to tear? Or from *rendre*, to give back, yield? What difference? Who was slave and who master? Both of us slick and coughing with our passion.

We pumped in deescalatory rhythm. Then rested until the slime dried and stuck us fast. Disengaged cautiously. Pulled away.

"Oh," Paul breathed. "Oh, how beautiful."

"Yes," I said.

We lay in silence for minutes. Both upon our backs. Staring at the brightening sunshine streaming through the window. Watching the mad motes dance.

"What did you write?" I asked him.

He showed me his paper: "Ultimate Pleasure."

I showed him mine: "Checkered cap."

He looked at me.

"Checkered cap?" he said. "Nick, what does *that* mean?"

"Just a thought, I said. "A vagrant notion."

"Well"—he sighed—"it didn't serve. We're far apart."

We lay in silence another five minutes. Resting. Sharing a single cannabis cigarette. Watching how the white smoke bloomed and billowed up into the strengthening sunlight. Finally:

"What are your plans for today?" he asked lazily.

"Back to GPA-1," I said. "But before I leave, I want to visit that Twenty-first Century exhibit at the Mall. After I see that, I thought I'd walk over to Union Station and take the Aeroglide home."

"Oh, yes," he said. "That's fun. It really does feel like you're riding on air."

"You've taken it?" I said, surprised. "When?"

"While you were on the PR tours," he said. "I had to go to New York, and the airports were socked in."

"Why did you have to go to the compound?"

"Talk to Phoebe Huntzinger," he said. "About the direct-wire link for Operation Lewisohn. And once to check out Leo Bernstein's scenario for moving his equipment down."

"Oh, yes," I said. "Of course. Sure."

"Well. . . ." He yawned. "I better get back to the political world. Have a good time at the Mall exhibition."

He got out of bed. Pulled on his robe and belted it. Smiling at me. A beautiful em! Then he leaned down. Kissed my lips. Patted my cheek with his fingertips.

"Take care," he said lightly.

I spent a slow morning showering, shaving, dressing, packing. It was almost noon when I took the Metro to the Mall. Carrying a thin attaché case of reports, papers, journals. Kaka to scan on the train trip north.

Finishing touches were being applied to the Twenty-first Century Celebration Festival along the Mall. Servers were testing the lighting of an enormous sign that would flash YOU NEVER LIVED SO GOOD! every three seconds until the turn of the century. Ropes were up, keeping out the general public until the following week. But that week was a preview for US Government servers; my BIN card and official ID got me past the guards with no trouble.

I started at the log cabin, circa 1700, from Plymouth, Massachusetts, and wandered slowly through American homes of 1750, 1800, 1850, 1900, 1950, up to the present. I had come prepared to scoff at this patent public relations stunt. But I found myself fascinated. Touched. Unaccountably troubled.

The obso homes had been built or assembled with careful attention to authentic detail. They might be placed in artificial settings of plastiturf and plastirub shrubs and trees. But the structures themselves were the originals or accurate reproductions. Using primary materials. The houses were complete to bed linens, pictures on the walls, tables set for a meal, rugs, bric-a-brac, etc. They were even "inhabited." By actors dressed in appropriate costumes. Silently moving through their obso roles: serving, dancing, gathering about an ancient harmonium to mouth the words of long-stopped songs.

What impressed me so? First, the *texture* of these obso homes. Rough-cut wood. Nubby plaster. Carving. Crude painting. Hooked rugs. Odd shapes. Rooms that were not boxes. I was made doubly aware of the charm of obso texture when I entered the "Home of the Present." All smooth, glossy, bland, perfect. Obso homes were palaces of error: ill-fitting beams, three steps up or down from room to room, a bow window where a flat square would have served as functionally well.

And the whimsy! All shapes of stained glass inserts. Enormous brass door-knockers. China bulldogs on the hearth. Dried flowers under bell jars. Framed tintypes on a mahogany piano. A cast-iron wood-burning stove as artfully decorated and embellished as an altar. The *humanness* of it all!

I came out of the Twenty-first Century Celebration Festival chastened by a vague feeling that I had been bred too late. I would have flourished in those obso days. Perhaps lecturing on anatomy at Johns Hopkins to an audience as bearded as I. Returning to a gaslit home of gleaming wood and glittering crystal. Logs snapping in the fireplace. Wife and children. No amusements but our own company. Conversation. Laughter. Singing.

So I exited the "Home of the Present," still thinking of the past. The way they lived. As I passed through the guarded gate, a tall, heavyset em stepped into my path. Our eyes locked. He nodded once, briefly, turned and walked quickly away. He was wearing a checkered cap.

I looked about. There were three black official sedans parked in file along Fourteenth Street, in front of me. Another on Washington Drive to my right. Another on Adams Drive, to my left. Black zipsuits standing outside each car. Watching me.

I walked slowly toward Fourteenth. A group of three, led by a short, chubby ef in a red zipsuit moved to intercept. I stopped. The officer came close. The three black zipsuits moved quietly around me.

"Dr. Nicholas Bennington Flair, sir?" she said.

"May I see your identification, please?" I said.

"Certainly, sir," she said.

She showed BIN card and official ID. A lieutenant of the Bureau of Public Security.

"Very well," I said. "I am Nicholas Bennington Flair."

I proffered my BIN card and ID. She scanned them quickly. Returned them to me.

"Thank you, sir," she said. "Dr. Flair, I have orders to take you."

Silence. We stared at each other.

"On whose authority?" I asked her.

"Warrant from the Chief Prosecutor, sir," she said.

"May I see it, please?"

"Of course, sir."

She pulled her zipsuit down far enough to extract a folded paper. A warrant for my taking. "On suspicion of activities contrary to public interest." Nothing unusual about it. But I scanned it slowly.

"Thank you, lieutenant," I said. Returning the warrant to her.

"I must now read you a statement of your rights, sir," she said.

"That won't be necessary," I said. "I know my rights."

"Please, sir," she said. "I'm required to recite it. I *must* recite it."

"Very well," I said. "Recite it."

She withdrew a crumpled card from her opened zipper and began scanning it aloud. I had the right to remain silent, I had the right to legal counsel of my choice. I could call at US Government expense. If I could not afford legal counsel, the US Government would provide such counsel without charge.

"Do you fully understand what I have told you, sir?" she inquired anxiously.

"I fully understand it," I assured her.

"Thank you, sir," she said gratefully. "Would you sign this release, please? It states only that I have explained your legal rights to you, and that you fully understand them."

She pulled a third paper from her bodice. A walking file cabinet. I scanned the release swiftly. She had a pen ready.

"What can I write on?" I said.

She turned her back to me and bent over slightly. On her broad, soft back, I scrawled my signature on the release. She returned all documents to her body and zipped up.

"Thank you, sir," she said.

"Thank *you*," I said. "Now what?"

"This way, please, sir."

They walked me to one of the black sedans. Before I got in, my attaché case was taken from me and I was patted down. Quickly. Expertly. Then I was seated in the rear between two black zipsuits. The lieutenant got in front, next to the driver.

It didn't take me long to realize where we were going. Across the Arlington Memorial Bridge. Past the A&N Country Club. Down into Alexandria.

"Hospice No. 4," I said aloud.

No one answered. No one spoke.

To the building set off by itself. The Public Security Ward. With white plastisteel mesh over the windows. Surrounded by plastiturf. They hustled me into the main entrance hall. Lined with stainless steel tiles. The room marked Admittance was divided by a wire grille. Several objects, ems and efs, in white hospital garb, were serving on the other side. They looked up when we entered. A small yellow em came over to the opening in the grille and stood behind a counter.

"Who made the take?" he asked.

"I did," the red zipsuited lieutenant said. "Object's name: Nicholas Bennington Flair." She slapped down the warrant. "On authority of the Chief Prosecutor."

The yellow em behind the grille turned to a data processing machine and began to type. Talking as he served.

"Flair, Nicholas Bennington. Warrant BPS-91641-99G. BIN card and ID, please."

I fished them out again, handed them over. He slid them into an electronic verifier, then typed out the numbers on his report.

"Personal property?" he asked.

One of the black zipsuits handed over my attaché case. It was unlocked. The yellow pawed through it swiftly.

"One attaché case of papers, reports, magazines. Empty your pockets, please."

I dumped everything onto the counter. He began to sort it.

"One ring of keys. One pigskin wallet containing forty-six dollars in bills, three credit cards, and assorted membership cards. One handkerchief, white. Thirty-eight cents in change. One digiwatch, silver finish, marked 'Loxa.' One black comb, pocket size. One container of white spansules. Correct?"

"Correct," I said.

"Dentures or prosthetic devices?" he asked.

"None," I said.

"Object is assigned number 4 dash 618 dash 99," he said.

"Sign the receipt, please," the ef lieutenant asked the yellow.

They exchanged and countersigned papers. She waited until he had typed up an inventory of my personal possessions in quadruplicate. I signed all copies. She signed all copies. He signed all copies.

The BPS servers waited patiently until two objects appeared in the corridor. Coming toward us, Heels clicking. Their images were distorted by the stainless steel walls and polished floor. Two big ems. White hospital garb.

"Right," the red zipsuit said. When they had taken their places on each side of me. "That does it."

"Thank you, lieutenant," I said.

"Thank *you*, sir," she said.

I was taken to a room in the back of the ward, on the ground floor. White desk, chair, metal detector, electronic monitors. The obso ef behind the desk, wearing a nurse's uniform, looked up when I entered with my guards.

"Flair," one of them said. "Nicholas Bennington: 4 dash 618 dash 99."

"Undress, please," she said to me. "Everything. Including shoes." I stripped naked. All my clothing was folded neatly, put into a white metal box labeled with my number. A receipt was typed out in quadruplicate. We all signed all copies.

I was given a cursory medical examination. Blood pressure, heart, temperature.

"Step through the frame, please," she said.

I stepped through. Nothing buzzed. She moved an electronic wand around my head, back, legs, arms. She looked into my ears with a lighted probe. Examined my armpits. Tapped my teeth lightly with a little hammer. Felt my scalp and beard, fingers prying under the hair.

"Bend over and spread your buttocks, please," she said

I did so. She explored my rectum with a rubbered finger.

"Shower," she said.

They took me through a clear glass door into an adjoining room. I stepped into a tiled shower stall. No projections inside. No curtain. One of the guards turned a knob. A hot germicidal spray.

"Scrub your hair," one of the guards shouted. "On your head, chest, armpits, nuts, and ass."

I did as directed.

The water was finally turned off. They motioned me out onto a plastirub mat before a panel of infrared lamps. By the time I was reasonably dry, beginning to sweat, they had ready a pair of paper slippers and a one-piece paper suit. Styled like a zipsuit but closed with strips of paper tape.

They took me out into the corridor again. I shuffled along, trying to keep the heelless slippers on my feet. Trying not to trip on the long cuffs of the paper suit. They stopped me before a bank of elevators.

One of them pressed a button and leaned forward to speak into a small microphone inset in the tile wall.

"Pearson and Fleming," he said loudly. "Coming up. We have one: 4 dash 618 dash 99."

Then both guards turned and stared at a small closed-circuit TV camera mounted near the ceiling.

A loudspeaker clicked on.

"You are cleared to Three. Room 317."

An elevator door opened. We stepped inside. Another TV camera. The door closed. We went up. Door opened. We stepped out to face a white-clad guard sitting in the corridor behind a desk surmounted by a battery of TV monitor screens.

"Pearson and Fleming," one of the guards reported: "4 dash 618 dash 99 to Room 317."

The seated guard looked at his teleprinter.

"All correct," he said.

We moved to the left until we came up to a gate of steel bars. And another TV camera. We stood there a moment. Then the barred door slid sideways. Into the wall. We walked down the corridor. I heard the gate thud shut behind us.

We walked to where another guard waited outside a closed door. He held a clamp pad of teletype duplicates.

"Four dash 618 dash 99," one of my guards told him.

The em outside the door looked at me.

"Name?" he said. "Last name first, followed by first and middle names."

"Flair, Nicholas Bennington," I said.

"All correct," he told my guards. Then made a small checkmark on his pad.

He withdrew a ring of magnetic keys from his pocket. He unlocked the door. Room 317. They all stood aside. I entered. The door was closed and locked behind me. It looked like painted wood, with a small panel of clear glass. But when they clanged it shut, I knew it was steel.

I took a few steps into the sunlit room and looked about.

"Good afternoon, Dr. Flair," a metallic voice said. "How are you feeling?"

Z-11

I wish to go on record as stating that during the approximately six weeks I spent in Room 317, Public Security Ward, Hospice No. 4, Alexandria, Virginia, I was not physically abused or maltreated. I was provided with a fresh paper suit and paper slippers every week. The food brought to my room was plentiful, though bland. For some bureaucratic reason, I was not allowed salt, pepper, or any other seasonings. Although I requested them.

My sleep was never deliberately disturbed, and I was furnished with most of the scanning material I asked for. I was not allowed newspapers, news magazines, radio, television, a watch or clock, or a calendar. Nor was I allowed Somnorifics or any other drugs. However, during the fourth week, I contracted a very mild viral infection, and the nurse who had conducted the initial examination arrived to administer an injection. She would not tell me what it was, but it served excellently; I recovered fully within three days.

That was the only medication I received during my stay. Of course, it was possible that my food was drugged. Or even the water flowing from the tap in the small nest attached to Room 317. But several times a week I conducted a self-examination. Taking my pulse and testing muscular and visual coordination. I never found even a hint of covert drug administration. It was operative that shortly before, during, and for a brief period following my interrogations in the Cooperation Room, pulse rate increased. But this was undoubtedly due to a stimulated adrenalin flow, and was to be expected under the circumstances.

I exercised, faithfully, in Room 317. An hour after awakening and an hour before sleep. I practiced Yoga, isometrics, and my own version of T'ai Chi Ch'uan. In place of Somnorifics, I used self-hypnosis, alpha, and transcendental meditation. I would say that, during the six weeks of my stay, my physical health was excellent.

The objects with whom I came in contact were remarkably few. The morning guard who brought me breakfast, took me to and from the first interrogative session of the day, and who brought me lunch, was a hulking but pleasant em who said his name was Horwitz. The afternoon guard who took me to and from the second interrogative session of the day, and brought my evening meal, was a squat, muscled ef who said her name was Kineally. I called her "Princess." She liked that.

And of course, I was on nodding acquaintance with several corridor guards, head guards who watched the TV monitors outside the elevator bank, and the gate guards. I never learned any of their names. Some were polite, some were not. But there was no physical brutality. Never. At least not to me. And none that I personally witnessed. On several nights I was awakened by screams coming from nearby rooms. But they may have been the results of nightmares. It was possible.

I masturbated twice a week, on Tuesday mornings and Friday nights. Usually I slept soundly and woke refreshed. The scanning material that was provided kept my brain active and inquiring. When I wanted surcease from purely cerebral computing, I imagined what the objects looked like who spoke to me. The two Voices.

Voice No. 1 spoke to me only in Room 317. The loudspeaker was concealed behind a ceiling air-conditioning vent. This Voice was concerned with my physical well-being and daily routine. Had I slept well? Did I require anything special in the way of relaxation? A paper chess set perhaps? Were my bowel movements regular? And so forth. I was able to respond to these questions merely by speaking into the air. A sensitive microphone, probably concealed in the same vent, picked up every tone, whisper, belch, fart. As far as I could determine, Voice No. 1 was on duty 24 hours a day.

I recall once, awakening at what I judged to be about 0300, I said, into the air, "Are you there?"

Voice No. 1 came back: "I am here."

It was the Voice of Room 317. I never heard it anywhere else. I had little doubt that Voice No. 1 had me under constant surveillance. Through mirrors inset into the walls of the bedroom and nest. Even my masturbation was shared, although Voice No. 1 never alluded to it. The two-way mirrors were the only decorations in the small area. The furnishings were one bed, one chair, one desk. The toilet in the nest was seatless. The sink had recessed fixtures. As did the shower stall. I was supplied liquid soap, in small amounts, in a plastic container. The single tumbler was soft plastic. Impossible to slit wrists or throat with that. Toilet paper was supplied to me each week in thin pads. Along with paper sheets, pillowcases, and a paper towel. I controlled the air conditioning and heating in the room via a thermostat, and the illumination via a rheostat. Although the overhead light could never be completely extinguished.

"You've got the VIP Suite," the Princess told me. "You should see some of the others."

"I can imagine," I said.

"No," she said. "You can't."

Voice No. 1 intrigued me. Androgynous. At times it was definitely emish: heavy throatiness and deep overtones. Other times it was efish, almost flutey. It could be both in the same sentence. Running back and forth, soprano to baritone. The effect was not displeasing, but I could not believe it was a natural voice. I computed it might be the voice of someone I knew, a voice I might identify, and so it was being electronically distorted.

During my second week in Room 317, I asked Voice No. 1, "Are you ef or em?"

The answer came back: "Yes." Followed by a brief laugh of such a variety of tones that I became absolutely convinced Voice No. 1 was being filtered and amplified. For what reason other than that stated above, I could not guess.

Voice No. 2, that of the Interrogator, was definitely an em's voice. I heard it only in the Cooperation Room. It was beautiful. Deep, resonant, with a booming, organlike quality. A diapason there. Never less than harmonious. With a unique, echoing quality. It was only later that I began to detect a fruity, actorish dissonance.

I was taken to the Cooperation Room twice a day. At times I computed as being approximately 1000 and 1400. During the first two weeks, sessions were quite brief. A half-hour or so, I reckoned. Later, I spent two full hours in the morning and two in the afternoon. This regimen was, obviously, structured.

One fact I have neglected to mention: I never saw any objects but the guards. Although I was certain the other rooms on the third floor were occupied. On my short trips down the corridor to the Cooperation Room, I heard sounds of movement behind locked doors. Once I heard singing. Once I heard an ef's voice reciting Shakespeare: "Tomorrow, and tomorrow, and tomorrow...." And frequently I smelled things in the corridor. Smells of objects. Sweat. Feces. Other things. So I knew I was not alone on the third floor, although it seemed so.

The Cooperation Room to which I was taken for my daily interrogations (seven days a week) was located in my wing of the Public Security Ward; it was not necessary to pass through any of the barred gates in the corridor to get there. It was a long, narrow room, soundproofed with white plastibest panels. There was a small mirrored panel set into each of the walls. For surveillance and filming, I presumed. The Interrogator's voice came from an overhead ventilation duct, as in Room 317, and I answered by speaking into the air. In a normal tone of voice.

During my interrogative sessions, the room contained only an enameled steel table, about card-table size, and a single plastilume chair. Both of these were immovable. Bolted to the floor. The chair so close to the table that I had to bend my knees and sidle into the seat. I noted several other ringbolts, steel loops, and small steel boxes set into the polished floor. Around the room, at baseboard level, were many electrical outlets and small connections that looked like electronic jacks. None of these were used during my sessions. Illumination came from rose-tinted fluorescent fixtures on the ceiling. Not an especially pleasant light, but not too annoying.

I had an impression that, for each session, the Cooperation Room had been hastily prepared for my interrogation shortly before my arrival. Frequently the floor showed damp patches: evidence of recent mopping or flushing. Once I noted a reddish-brown stain on the floor directly under my table, missed by the cleaning server. Invariably, when I entered the room, I smelled artificial pine. The air had obviously been sprayed heavily with a scented deodorant.

On our first exchange, I learned the Interrogator was humorless.

"For the record, doctor," Voice No. 2 boomed from the overhead loud-speaker, "please state your name, rank, and address."

"Name:" I said, "Flair, Nicholas Bennington. Rank: Director (Temporary) of the Satisfaction Section, Department of Bliss. Address: Room 317, Public Security Ward, Hospice No. 4, Alexandria, Virginia."

"No, no," he said. Somewhat testily. "I mean your permanent address. Where you lived before you were taken."

I spoke it into the air. I felt I had scored a point. He had said, "Your *permanent* address," hadn't he? That obviously meant my stay in the Public Security Ward would be of short duration. Confidence came flooding back. I relaxed.

I had already spent some time computing how best I might reply to pro-longed questioning. Reply operatively to everything that was a matter of rec-ord. Protect, insofar as possible, friends, associates, and assistants. Pillow when I was able to, or gloss. Where I was certain no evidence existed, then deny, deny, deny. Stonewall. But in such a manner that I could not later be accused of deliberate deception. "I don't remember," would serve. As would, "I don't recall," "I have no recollection of that," "I cannot state from personal expe-rience," and similar phrases.

But during the first two weeks of brief interrogative sessions, I had little need to waffle. Questioning was direct and straightforward. It was also shal-low, and seemed to be antilogical. For instance: "Are you acquainted with an ef, residing in Detroit, Michigan, named Millie Jean Grunwald?"

"Yes, I am," I said.

I naturally expected the next question, or questions, would explore the nature of my relationship with Millie. Instead, the next question was: "Did you know the late Simon Hawkley, an attorney of San Diego, California?"

And so it went. Short, blunt questions. Apparently designed only to put on record the fact of my acquaintance with or knowledge of a long list of objects.

Some of the names, admittedly, surprised me. Burton P. Klein. Alice Ham-mond. Leon Mansfield. Joanne Wilensky. Vernon DeTilly. I remembered them all. But was somewhat shaken that the Interrogator knew them.

I volunteered nothing. Absolutely nothing. But occasionally I tried to ex-plain my relationship to the named object. Invariably, the Interrogator would interrupt, and in his orotund voice, say, "Yes, yes, we'll get to that later."

It took us three days to serve our way through a long list of names that apparently included every object I had had contact with since January, 1998. Several names I did not recognize. The Interrogator made no effort to prod my memory. He merely accepted my negative answer and went on to another name. Were the strangers a control group, to test my veracity?

One question I found disquieting.

"Are you acquainted with Mrs. Grace Wingate, wife of the Chief Director?" the Interrogator asked.

"Yes," I said. "I am acquainted with Mrs. Wingate."

He went on to another name. Louise Rawlins Tucker.

Finally, having apparently exhausted the list of objects with whom I was known, or suspected, of having had contact with during the preceding eighteen months, the Interrogator started over again. This time he probed my relationship with the objects named. How we had met, how often we met, were we users; did we have any financial dealings, etc., etc. But again, he forbore from prying too deeply. Limiting his questions to surface relationships. It was at this point in time that Voice No. 2 took on a sonorous, almost a pompous quality. Like a prosecutor designing his inquiries as much to influence a jury as to elicit information from the defendant.

Each evening, back in Room 317, I computed the day's interrogation. I determined what I handled well, and what badly. I tried to hypothecate future areas of inquiry. Most of all, toward the end of those initial two weeks, I attempted to analyze the Interrogator's methodology. That he was following a heavily structured scenario, I had no doubt.

My first reaction to my taking had been, I suppose, like that of many objects in similar circumstances: It was all a horrible mistake. A file had been displaced, or a computer had been faultily programmed. An object could be executed on the testimony of one crossed circuit.

But those first two weeks of interrogation convinced me that it was, indeed, *I* who had been deliberately taken. On orders. I could not compute it. Less than a month previously I had received a letter from the Chief Director almost fulsome in its praise of my service on Operation Lewisohn. "One of the nation's finest young creative scientists." That is how Chief Director Michael Wingate referred to me in that letter. And now I was languishing in a Public Security Ward, charged with activities contrary to the public interest. It was incomputable.

Beginning with the third week of questioning, the Interrogator dropped his politesse. No more "Please" or "Would you. . . ." or "Doctor" or "If you please. . . ." Inquiries became shorter, more brusque. I thought the tempo of interrogation also quickened. I scarcely had time to complete my reply before the next question was hurtling down at me. This effect, too, I presumed, was programmed. But I had little time, or inclination, to analyze technique. I was too concerned with my own defense.

"You stated you know Millie Jean Grunwald."

"Yes, that's correct."

"How long have you known her?"

"Three—no, four years."

"How did you meet her?"

"At a cockfight."

"In Detroit?"

"Yes."

"Where was this cockfight held?"

"I don't recall the address. A basement club. Somewhere down near the river."

"You were introduced to Millie Jean Grunwald at this club?"

"No. I had won a bet, and asked her and her girlfriend to have a drink with me."

"What was the girlfriend's name?"

"I don't remember. If I ever heard it. Which I—"

"What are your relations with Millie Jean Grunwald?"

"We are friends."

"Friends? Flair, how many doctorates do you have?"

"Several."

"Millie Jean Grunwald is a retardate clone. You are aware of that?"

"Yes."

"But you are friends?"

"Yes."

"Do you use her?"

"We use each other."

"Frequently?"

"Whenever I'm in Detroit. Perhaps three or four times a year."

"Do you give her gifts?"

"Yes."

"Love?"

"No."

"Have you ever discussed restricted matters with her?"

"She wouldn't understand, I assure you."

"You haven't answered my question. Did you ever discuss restricted material with Millie Jean Grunwald?"

"I don't remember."

"You don't remember? Flair, you have made that claim several times. Yet you are reputed to have the best memory in the scientific community."

"I was forced to skip my hippocampal irrigation this year, and I'm overdue on theta brushup conditioning."

"I see."

"Interrogator, you have made *that* claim several times. 'I see.'"

"You object to it?"

"It reminds me of an object who says, 'Let me make one thing perfectly clear.' Then I know I'm to be the victim of obfuscation."

"I see."

As sessions lengthened, I endured similar bursts of short, blunt questions about almost every object on the Interrogator's list. I had no opportunity to extend or explain my answers. Attempted explications were cut short. Subjects were shifted with bewildering speed and increasing frequency. Several times I found myself still speaking of the last object when a new name had been introduced. The Interrogator then snapped a command to pay closer attention to his questions.

Some objects, being stopped, I made no effort to defend. Simon Hawkley was one. Angela Teresa Berri was another. No one could touch them now.

"You and Berri were users?"

"Yes."

"Frequently?"

"Several times."

"Her apartment, yours, or elsewhere?"

"Her apartment, mine, and elsewhere."

"You have stated that you suspected her of activities contrary to the public interest."

"That's correct."

"Why didn't you communicate your suspicions to her rulers?"

"To whom? I had no knowledge of how extensive her conspiracy might be. Perhaps her rulers were involved."

"Did you think the Chief Director might be involved in her peculations?"

"Of course not."

"Then why didn't you go to him?"

"I—well; it didn't occur to me. I didn't know him personally at that point in time."

"Our records indicate that Angela Teresa Berri introduced you to the Chief Director. Is that correct?"

"Yes."

"So she was still animate when you met him. Personally. Why didn't you tell him of your suspicions then?"

"Because they were only suspicions. I had no hard evidence."

"But you have stated that you knew she had assassinated Frank Lawson Harris and had manipulated the stopping of Burton P. Klein and others."

"That's correct. I *knew* it, but had no evidence to prove it."

"Now about the Scilla business in San Diego. . . ."

By the end of the fourth week, I was no longer amused by the Interrogator's increasingly bombastic voice and denunciatory tone. I was too concerned with avoiding contradictions in my testimony and attempting to convince the Interrogator that although some of my activities might have been technically illegal, my actions benefited the US Government: A conspiracy of terrorists had been exposed and a corrupt government official was stopped. I made no love from this.

"Not even from your final sale of Scilla?"

"A very minor amount, I assure you. Hardly a tenth of my income for the year. If making love was my motivation, I would have retained ownership."

"Perhaps you became frightened."

"That's absurd."

"Is it? Let's go back to the Society of Obsoletes' conspiracy.... How well did you know Dr. Thomas J. Wiley?"

"I told you, I studied with him for a brief period of time."

"Did you like him?"

"Yes."

"Admire his brain?"

"Well ... yes. Not his ideas, but his brain."

"What contact did you have with him between the time you studied with him and the time you met him at Dr. Henry Hammond's summer home?"

"No contact."

"None?"

"That's correct."

"We have in our possession a program of a symposium held at the University of Chicago on July 14 to 17, 1997. The guest list shows that both you and Dr. Thomas J. Wiley attended."

"That's possible. There were more than a hundred objects at that symposium. I didn't know he was there and didn't speak to him personally."

"Were you and the late Lydia Ann Ferguson users?"

"The *late* Lydia Ann Ferguson?"

"Yes. She's stopped. Were you users?"

"Yes."

"Frequently?"

"No. A few times."

"Did you admire her?"

"Yes."

"Her brain, no doubt?"

"No. She was a silly ef. But I admired her."

"Listen to this tape...."

Through the overhead loudspeaker came my own voice. Explaining to Lydia Ann Ferguson that I had been ordered to expedite a project that would cancel a dissident tribe of a friendly African nation. That tape should have been erased a long time ago. I tried not to reveal my shock.

"Is that your voice speaking, Flair?"

"Yes."

"The project you are discussing with an object unauthorized to receive such information was, actually, a project you conceived and finalized some time previously. Is that correct?"

"Yes."

"An ultrasecret project?"

"Top secret."

"Very well, top secret. Why did you reveal it to this unauthorized object at that point in time? She had no security clearance."

"In the first place, that conversation was couched in such general terms, she could not possibly make the connection with an actual project. In the second place—as I have stated several times before—my role was that of an undercover agent, with orders to infiltrate the conspiracy."

"Whose orders?"

"Those of Angela Teresa Berri."

"Berri is stopped."

"I know that. But you'll find in her confession a full explanation of the part I played. She praises what I did."

"We are aware of that. But nowhere in that confession does she state that she ordered you to disclose classified material to an unauthorized object."

"Ask Paul Bumford. He knew about it."

"We shall ask him. Now listen to this tape...."

Again it was my voice. This time explaining to Wiley, Hammond, the DeTilly brothers, et al., how I would manage to remove classified material from the compound at GPA-1.

I waited until the tape finished. Then exploded....

"I've told you and told you," I shouted angrily into the air. "I was serving as an undercover agent. It was the only way we could catch them in the act and provide enough evidence to convict.".

"In the Scilla matter, concerning the crimes of Angela Teresa Berri, you stated you did not take your suspicions to a higher authority because you didn't know how far her conspiracy extended."

"And because all I had were suspicions. No hard evidence."

"But that doesn't hold true for the Society of Obsoletes' conspiracy, does it? You had more than suspicions in that case. You had hard evidence. A group of terrorists had attempted to suborn you. You had their conversation on tape. With your direct testimony, that would have been sufficient to convict. So why didn't you take the whole matter to the Bureau of Public Security?"

"Angela Teresa Berri," I said. "I did it the way she ordered me to do it."

"Angela Teresa Berri is stopped," he said hollowly, "and cannot testify to that."

"I know," I groaned, "I know."

What irked me, continually, was that what I had done was not all that awful. Illegal yes, but not awful. It had been done, was being done, and would be done by hundreds—thousands of objects in academe, multinational corporations, governments, and so forth. It had been, was being, and would be pillowed or glossed. The world would not falter for it. Good frequently resulted. Why was I being singled out for persecution and punishment? Where was the protection of my rank?

And all those "activities contrary to the public interest" I was alleged to have committed—why, they were peccadilloes, chaff, compared to my activities beneficial to the public interest. Operation Lewisohn. The over and covert research projects I had conceived. The public health programs I had initiated. They could change the world! Lessen human pain. Reduce the anguish of future generations. Did my life's service count for nothing?

"Now about the Die-Dee Doll. . . ."

"What has that to do with me?"

"It is manufactured by your father?"

"That is correct."

"It is extremely lovable?"

"So I understand."

"Records indicate that the initial application for a license to manufacture, distribute, and sell the Die-Dee Doll was rejected by your Executive Assistant, Paul Bumford. Is that correct?"

"At that point in time, he wasn't my Executive Assistant. He was Ass-DepDirRad."

"But he rejected your father's application?"

"Yes."

"On what grounds?"

"The word 'Die' in the name. The inclusion of a coffin and tombstone in the doll kit. Other reasons."

"Legal reasons?"

"Yes."

"But you overruled Bumford's decision?"

"Yes."

"Why?"

"The Die-Dee Doll is a toy. A plaything. It isn't all that important."

"It isn't? At the time you overruled Bumford's decision to disapprove the Die-Dee Doll license, was this before or after your father loaned you the love to purchase Scilla Pharmaceuticals?"

"What?"

"Did your father loan you the love to purchase Scilla Pharmaceuticals before or after you had overruled Bumford's decision to deny him a license to market the Die-Dee Doll?"

"I don't remember."

The curious thing was that I *didn't* remember. I literally could not recall. It bothered me.

"Listen to this tape. . . ."

My voice again. Babbling to Millie Jean Grunwald. Spilling out my worries and misgivings about a number of classified projects. We had just seen Janet and Eric battle at the Lords Sporting Club. We had returned to Millie's apartment. Unsatisfactory sex. Then I had talked, talked, talked. To a sleeping Millie. And to the recording machine below in the deserted porn shop.

"Yes," I said dully. Although I had not been asked. "That's my voice."

"Why did you tell this unauthorized object of these matters?"

"Perhaps I was drugged."

"Drugged?"

"It's possible. At the Lords Sporting Club. In the drinks I bought. Interrogator, there are drugs to make an object speak, contrary to his will."

"Who would drug you?"

"I don't know. Someone," I said foolishly.

"How well did you know the late Arthur Raddo?"

"I've told you, I didn't know him at all. Never met him."

"But you were aware of his existence?"

"He gave a speech. At a Beist meeting I attended. I told you that, too."

"This was the Christmas, 1998, meeting of the Washington, D.C., chapter of the Beists?"

"Yes."

"Mrs. Grace Wingate was there?"

"Well. . . . Yes, I believe so. She came in later."

"Did you speak to her during the evening?"

"Yes."

"Alone?"

"Yes. No. I don't remember. I spoke to a number of objects that evening."

"But not to Arthur Raddo?"

"No. Definitely not."

"Raddo's mother, in a sworn statement, asserts he had several telephone calls from a friend he called 'Nick.' "

"So? A lot of ems are named Nick."

"Employees of the Adonis Club, in sworn statements, have testified that the late Arthur Raddo was frequently seen on the premises with an em he called 'Nick.' An em who answers your description."

"A clever manipulation," I said. "A control em in a terrorist organization is known to Raddo as 'Nick.' The control is approximately my height and weight. He is disguised in wig, false mustache and Vandyke beard. In the dimness of the Adonis Club, he could easily pass as me."

" 'In the dimness of the Adonis Club'?" he repeated. "How did you know the Adonis Club is dim? Have you been there?"

"Once."

"For what purpose?"

"After I heard that Raddo had suicided. While in possession of a bottle of—"

"Yes? A bottle of?"

"Nothing. It's not important."

"I think we will end this session at this point. We will resume at our afternoon session."

Back in Room 317. Voice No. 1 caroled, "Your fresh paper sheets will be up shortly."

"You go to hell," I screamed into the air.

"Dr. Flair!" Voice No. 1 said. Shocked.

"About the five cc flask found in the hand of the suicided Arthur Raddo," the Interrogator said that afternoon.

"Yes?" I said. "What about it?"

"You stated it was the reason you went to the Adonis Club."

"Well, goddamn it, it was!"

"Soothe yourself," Voice No. 2 said unctuously. "Soothe yourself. Take it easy. Take all the time you need. Just tell me exactly what happened."

It all came pouring out of me. Spluttered. It was a plot. A skillfully structured scenario. Of long duration. I had been manipulated. I told the Interrogator of finding the partially empty flask of *Clostridium botulinum*. My own name forged to the withdrawal card.

"Why didn't you go to the Bureau of Public Security immediately?"

"I thought I could discover the instigator. I didn't know how high the conspiracy extended."

Then, I said, when I heard of the 5 cc flask found with the suicided Arthur Raddo, I rechecked the GPA-1 pharmacology library. The entire bottle was missing. So I had replaced it. With a flask of pure glycerol. I needed time. Time to compute. Time to attempt to determine the connection between Arthur Raddo and the ongoing conspiracy to destroy me.

"So your letter to R. Sam Bigelow, stating you had verified the existence of the original deposit of 416HBL-CW3 by personal inspection—your own phrase: 'by personal inspection'—that statement was, in fact, false and misleading?"

"No, no," I protested. "Not at all. Not false and misleading. Simply inoperative."

"And you say you concealed this vital information from higher authority because of your desire to uncover the plot to destroy you?"

"Yes."

"And who did you imagine was the creator of this plot?"

"I hypothesize a terrorist organization. Perhaps the remnants of the Society of Obsoletes' conspiracy."

"That Society was canceled. All the members were taken."

"Not all of them," I said triumphantly. "Angela Berri allowed some of them to exist, to continue their activities. It's a common enough ploy. So she could keep them under surveillance. So they might lead her to other members, more important members, of whom she was not aware."

"A very ingenious explanation. Do you have any proof that this was, indeed, the intention of Angela Teresa Berri?"

"No proof, no. But it's obvious, isn't it? And they singled me out for revenge for the part I had played in erasing Wiley, Hammond, Lydia Ann Ferguson, and the others. It all synthesizes. It all computes."

Silence. I knew I wasn't convincing him. Worse, I wasn't convincing myself.

"Look, Interrogator," I said. As calmly as I could. "What possible reason could I have for becoming involved in the structuring of that botulism outbreak in GPA-11? Remember, I was the object who went to the Chief Director and the Bureau of Public Security Chief and told them about aerobic botulinum. Doesn't that prove I wasn't involved in it?"

"Not necessarily," he boomed.

"Well, what possible motive could I have for such illogical actions?"

"You have the reputation of being an ambitious em."

"So? A lot of objects are ambitious. It's characterological of intelligence."

"It wouldn't be the first time an ambitious object had artfully planned and executed a crime, using a cat's-paw as the actual perpetrator, and then assisted in the solution of that crime. To earn praise for his talent. To earn commendation from his rulers. Advancement in rank."

"That's nonsense!" I shouted.

During the final week of interrogation, I cannot say my mood was serene. I was deeply troubled; I cannot deny it. I knew quite well what was at stake. Me. But I did not panic, except for a few brief occasions when the Interrogator's engorged voice was not to be endured. I approached the interrogation sessions with trepidation. Not because of the questions I might be asked. But in anticipation of being subjected, once again, to those overcocked tones that flowed from the ceiling loudspeaker and seemed to fill the room.

What preserved my sanity, at that point in time, was my self-esteem. I do not know why a strong, healthy ego is generally held in such ill repute. In the circumstances in which I found myself, my vanity was my salvation.

I know many neuropsychiatrists believe that character is the psychosis we show to the world. And that the slyly contrived conception each of us has of himself is the psyche's defense mechanism against despair and madness. All this may be operative. But it is, I think, beside the point.

All I know is that I functioned in such a manner as not to degrade my vision of myself. I might tolerate the pity, or scorn, or loathing of others. I could never endure my own pity, scorn, loathing.

"And was it also part of this 'secret conspiracy' that you allegedly commanded your servers to inflict grievous bodily harm upon the corpus of a security officer of the US Government? To wit, deliberately break the arm of one Art Roach?"

"Are you humoring me, Interrogator?"

"Answer the question."

"As I've told you many times, the Art Roach scenario had nothing to do with the plot against me. Breaking his arm was the simplest way to procure evidence of the corrupt dealings of Angela Teresa Berri. It succeeded brilliantly. As soon as the evidence was obtained, I took it directly to Theodore Seidensticker III, of the Chief Director's staff."

"You told him about breaking Roach's arm?"

"I did not. He had no need to know."

"I see."

"Are you drugging me, Interrogator?"

"Drugging you? How would we drug you?"

"In my food. My tap water."

"Have you detected any drug?"

"No, but it may be something new. With no gross symptoms. A drug to make me talk."

"Surely you'd know about a drug like that, wouldn't you?"

"No," I said. "Not if I had no need to know."

I may have cackled then.

I think, in my continual computation of my dilemma, the factor I found most difficult to integrate into the overall equation was the role of Chief Director Michael Wingate. I could not believe he was unaware of my predicament. My absence would certainly have been noted by Paul Bumford and by other friends and associates. The CD could hardly be in ignorance of my whereabouts. A brief phone call or message could have freed me. "To be released for the benefit of the public." But the command never arrived. I could not account for it. Until the final interrogative session. . . .

We had been reviewing, once again, the actions I had taken to effectualize the purchase of Scilla Pharmaceuticals in San Diego. And the precise amount of love I received on the final sale, above and beyond the original purchase price and my expenses.

Then, at the end of the session, a totally new subject was introduced. I was immediately cautious.

"Did you ever meet the late President Harold K. Morse?"

"Yes."

"How many times?"

"On one occasion."

"And that was?"

"He called me to the White House for a short conversation after he had scanned a paper I had published."

"What was the subject of your published paper?"

"On the nature of genius."

"You never saw him again?"

"Not until he stopped."

"Ah, yes. You were, were you not, a member of a committee of physicians appointed to investigate the stopping of President Morse?"

"That is correct."

"And this committee, of which you were a member, then filed a report. Which was immediately classified top secret."

"Ultrasecret."

"Very well, ultrasecret. That document has never been declassified. It is still ultrasecret."

"So?"

"I will now ask you a question concerning that classified document. Consider carefully before answering. The question is this: Have you ever divulged the existence, contents, meaning, or conclusion of that document to any object unauthorized to receive such information?"

My reply was prompt.

"No," I said. "Never."

"This interrogation is now concluded," the Interrogator boomed. Fruity voice burbling. "Remove the object."

I waited until I was back in Room 317 before I let myself compute the significance of the final question I had been asked. I lay supine upon the paper sheet, hands behind my head. I stared upward at the ceiling vent.

"Did you have an interesting session, Dr. Flair?" Voice No. 1 asked softly.

"Yes, thank you. Very interesting. I think if you don't mind, I'll skip dinner tonight."

"Oh, I'm sorry, Dr. Flair, we can't do that. The food must be brought to your room. If you choose not to eat, that's your decision, of course. But we must make it available. Regulations, you know."

"All right. Bring it up."

"Thank you, Dr. Flair."

"Thank *you*."

The reason Chief Director Michael Wingate had not intervened in the proceedings against me now seemed evident: He was aware of my relations with his wife. The final question revealed that.

I had told only one object on earth of my service on the committee to investigate the stopping of President Harold K. Morse. That object was Grace Wingate. At our last meeting. If the Interrogator had brought up the subject, it could only mean that he had evidence of my imprudence.

The fact that he had saved the subject for the final question in the concluding interrogative session, and then had delved no deeper following my denial, convinced me that the question had been intended to serve as a signal. The Chief Director was notifying me that he was aware of my interactions with Grace, and he was abandoning me. Turning his back. Walking away. Leaving me to my destiny.

There was no other explanation for that brief question. "*I know*," the Chief Director had said, in effect, "and now you know that I know."

I experienced, I admit, an initial terror. But other objects had stopped, and so should I, and so shall you. I consoled myself with that, as best I might, and resolved to act in such a manner as not to tarnish my conception of who and what I was. If self-esteem had betrayed me into seeking revenge on Angela Berri, and led to my downfall, then self-esteem would, at least, enable me to stop with as much courage and dignity possible under the dismal circumstances.

My evening meal was brought and placed on the table.

"Proveal," the guard reported. "Propots and some kind of white slimy stuff for dessert. Looks good."

"Thank you, Princess," I said.

The steel door clanged shut behind her. I didn't even rise to inspect the plastic tray with its plastic plates of plastic food. I lay on my back, watching the light fade. The darkness move in. Then I computed a problem that had to be faced.

If the Chief Director knew of my love for his wife, knew I had told her of my service on the Morse Committee, then our meetings in the safe place, in our secret garden, had been shared. Or she had betrayed me. One or the other.

It was possible, of course, that she had been forced to speak. But I didn't think it likely that Michael Wingate would do that to his wife. No, she had either spoken voluntarily, or our love had been shared, recorded, made a matter of dossiers and investigative projects. Even in that empty, deserted garden, sharing would not have been especially difficult.

She would not betray me. Could not. I knew her too well to believe that. Still. . . . The worm gnawed.

I reviewed again those intimate conversations that had been such an awesome revelation. That had introduced me to the glory of opening myself, totally, to another object, and of entering into her. The two of us one as we explored an unknown world. It was an experience of which I had never known I was capable. Had never known existed. As if I might leap from a high place and discover I could fly. As breathless and shocking and deliriously pleasurable as that.

It was quite dark outside, the illumination in my room at its lowest setting, when I came to a conclusion that almost syncoped me with its simplicity. Its purity. Whether our meetings had been shared or Grace had betrayed me was actually of no consequence. Nothing that had been done—for whatever reason—could take from me the exaltation of our love. I did not regret it. That was the operative factor: I did not regret it.

I would never know if she had betrayed me. Never. Even if our love had lasted a millennium. If we had a hundred, a thousand, a million intimate meetings. Even if we had used each other. I would never have learned her sufficiently to know if she was or was not capable of treachery.

For she was, essentially, finally, unknowable. I recognized that now. Unknowable. She was, and I am, and you are.

What will we do when the mystery is gone?

A-1

The office of the Director of the Department of Creative Science was a long box of a room. Conference area at one end. Desk, chairs, communication equipment at the other. One of the two ems in the room, wearing the gold zipsuit of a PS-1, sat in a swivel chair behind the desk. The other em, red zipsuited, stood facing him.

On the wall, behind the Director's desk, a plastic overlay graph was framed and illuminated with its own little lamp. In grease pencil markings of three colors, it was clearly shown that the Satrat and production of the Ultimate Pleasure injection were ascending curves, following almost identical percentage increases. As these two lines rose, a contrary curve, descending, marked the plunging terrorism rate.

The Director switched a tape deck to Fast Rewind. The two ems waited patiently until the empty reel filled up and the machine clicked off. Then the Director removed the full reel and placed it carefully in a cardboard carton alongside his desk. The legend on the carton: "Good-Cheer Skinless & Boneless Portuguese Sardines." It contained a vast number of tape reels.

"That should do it," the Director said. "You're certain this is the original?"

"I'm certain," the officer said.

"No copy was made?"

"No copy," the officer said. "I know better than that."

"I hope you do," the Director laughed. "I'll prepare the transcription personally for the Chief Director. What about the Informed Consent Statement?"

"Signed, sealed, and delivered," the officer said. "Original to the Chief Prosecutor. Copies to BPS and to our files."

"Good. How did you get him to sign it? Drugs? Hypnosis? Shock therapy?"

"Yawl won't believe this," Art Roach said, "but we didn't have to use anything. He really did sign it voluntarily. He was happy to sign it."

"Oh?" Paul Bumford said. "That's interesting."

The Tangent Objective

1

Brindleys was a private club. Small enough so that one knew everyone. Large enough so that one didn't have to speak to them. So when Tangent saw Julien Ricard at the crowded bar, he found a place down at the other end and kept his eyes lowered.

It didn't work. He felt a heavy hand on his shoulder and looked up.

"Hullo, Ricard," he said, shrugging off the hand. "What're you up to?"

"This and that," the Frenchman said. He was a tall man. Not as tall as Tangent, but tall enough. On the right side of his face was a purple birthmark shaped like the boot of Italy. And there, on his neck, Sicily.

"How about a chop?" he asked. His voice was querulous, almost whining. He had the reputation of being a mean drunk.

"Can't," Tangent said shortly. "I'm waiting for Tony Malcolm."

Ricard didn't expect to be asked to join, and wasn't.

"Thick as thieves you two," he said nastily.

"Aren't we," Tangent said equably. "Here he is now. Tony! Over here . . ."

"Hullo, Peter. Ricard. I called for the corner table."

"Good. Let's grab it."

They walked away from the Frenchman. He looked after them, glowering.

"Bad-tempered scut," Tangent said.

"Isn't he," Malcolm agreed. "So you're off to visit your Zulus again? Good evening, Harold."

"Good evening, gentlemen," the old waiter said, pulling back their chairs. "The usual?"

"The usual," Tangent said. "And a rare steak for me. It'll be a while before I see a piece of beef I can trust."

They had a leisurely dinner. The dining room was crowded; there were others within hearing. So they traded small talk: the most recent London bombing, a movie star's suicide, the famine in Bangladesh. By the time they were on cheese and port, the room had emptied out; the tables next to theirs were vacant.

"Peter, you sounded excited," Malcolm said.

"Was," Tangent said. "Am. Tony, I need something."

"Ah?"

"You mentioned once you had a broker you used to buy stock on the New York exchange."

"That's right. On Lombard Street. Old, established firm."

"Can he cover for me? Buy in another name or something? Hide it somehow?"

"He does for me. No problems so far, knock on wood. Why? Onto something good?"

"Good? You wouldn't believe. Starrett Petroleum. I saw our top secret report on the Asante exploration today. We'll have oil coming out our ears. As an insider, I'll get my ass in a sling if I wheel and deal. Can your man get me five thousand shares and keep it under the table?"

"I don't see why not. Should I get in?"

"I'd advise it, Tony. One problem: our exploration lease expires in two months. That's why I'm going down there tomorrow, to renegotiate."

"Trouble?" Malcolm asked.

"In Africa? *Always* trouble. But I think I can swing it."

"They know about the oil?"

Tangent looked about casually. "No," he said. "We scammed their report. You won't have to tell Virginia about *that*, will you?"

"Not at the moment," Malcolm said.

"You bastard!" Tangent laughed. "Well, take care of my five thousand shares, will you?"

"Of course. Tomorrow. Now you do something for me."

"What?"

"Stop by and see my man in Mokodi. Bob Curtin."

"Dear old Bob," Tangent said. "Anything wrong? He been acting up?"

"That's just it," Malcolm said. "He hasn't been acting at all. He files once a week with Virginia. I get a copy, and believe me, Peter, it's nothing. His reports read like travel brochures. I can't believe Asante is that quiet."

"Believe me, Tony, it isn't."

"Maybe the sun's got to him."

"It wouldn't be the first time. But after that little deal he pulled in Germany, I'd have thought he'd be anxious to please."

"That's what I thought. Now I think maybe he left his nerve in that Berlin alley. Take a look at him for me, will you, Peter? I'd like to get your take."

"Sure. Want me to send a bullet?"

"No, no. When you return will be soon enough. No crisis. Curtin will probably ask you when I'm going to pull him out. Tell him he better change his luck."

Tangent laughed, and they debated awhile, lazy and uncaring, then decided on a cognac. The old waiters moved about slowly, setting up for the after-theater crowd. Brindleys allowed ladies in the dining room, but not in the bar or grill. And not, of course, in the small sleeping suites upstairs. Although there were stories . . .

"Tell me about Asante," Malcolm said.

"What do you want to know?"

"Everything. Well . . . about ten minutes of everything."

"Third-smallest country in Africa in land area," Tangent recited. "A population of about eight hundred thousand, although they've never taken a census. It's a thin, wedge-shaped silver of land between Ghana and Togo. Runs north-south. About thirty miles wide on the coast. On the west is Lake Volta. On the east is the Mono River. South is the Atlantic Ocean. At the northern tip, Asante, Ghana, Togo, and upper Volta all come together at a map position called Four Points. It's near the village of Dapango. But no one's ever surveyed or marked the national boundaries, so there's a lot of smuggling back and forth. The local politicos scream about it, but don't do much to stop it. Actually, it benefits everyone."

"My God, Peter, you're a walking atlas."

"Tony, it's my *business*. Let's see . . . Asante is now a monarchy. Used to be a French colony. Got its independence in fifty-eight. It's at a break in the West African rain forest. Like Togo and Dahomey. The savannas come down to the sea. There's a hilly area in the north with fine hardwoods, but generally Asante is agricultural. Cotton, wheat, coffee, yams, corn, citrus fruits, barely, cassava—stuff like that. They've got a brewery, two textile mills, a factory that makes African 'art' for export. It's all junk; you know that. There's also an asphalt plant."

"Minerals?"

"Phosphates, iron ore, one active gold mine. Every once in a while someone picks up a diamond."

"What about Mokodi?"

"Capital and largest city. It's on the coast, with a good harbor and port facilities. Offshore is the island of Zabar. It's connected with Mokodi by an old ferry that runs three times a day. We found the oil southwest of Zabar. It'll drive Shell over the edge. They spent millions off the Dahomey coast and have zilch to show for it."

"Mokodi endurable?"

"Very much so. Clean. Wide, tree-lined boulevards. The French know how to plan a city. Lots of public gardens and parks. The electric power works. The water's good. There's a serviceable telephone system."

"Radio or television?"

"One radio station. No television. One daily newspaper."

Tony Malcolm looked about benignly, a cherub in houndstooth. An unknowing member of Brindleys had once said of him: "There's less there than meets the eye." Those in the know who heard the comment had smiled secretly and kept their mouths shut.

"What's Asante's bottom line?" Malcolm asked.

"Need you ask? Hairy at the heels. Know any African country that isn't? Except possibly Nigeria and Zaire. France holds Asante's bonds and notes. Most of their funds come from tourism. The highest building is the Mokodi Hilton, on the beach west of the port area. That's where our offices are. Air-conditioned, thank God. Tony, it's not a *bad* country. The crime rate is very low. Get convicted of murder, and you get your head chopped off. Crooks work out their time in the phosphate mines. Owned by the king's brother-in-law. Naturally. The streets of Mokodi are swept every morning and hosed down every afternoon. There are nightclubs, theaters, restaurants, sidewalk cafés."

"Sounds like a tropical paradise," Malcolm said.

"That's Mokodi," Tangent said. "The only part of Asante that most tourists see. But in the small villages of the uplands and grasslands, kids paw through dungheaps looking for undigested nuts."

"Oh-ho," Malcolm said. "Like that, is it?"

"Like that," Tangent nodded. "King Prempeh the Fourth—calls himself the Avenging Leopard of Bosumtwi, for no apparent reason—is bleeding the country white, you should excuse the expression. Him and his relatives. They own everything."

"On the take?"

"Of course."

"Secret police?"

"What did you expect? Nasty thugs. The chief is called the 'Nutcracker.' Because when he—"

"Please." Malcolm held up a hand. "I can guess."

"The joke down there, when you hear of his latest depravity, is to say, 'That's what makes the Nutcracker sweet'."

"Very funny," Malcolm said. "Ha ha."

"Well, that's Asante. As African countries go, it's not as good as the best, not as bad as the worst. I like it."

"Oh? Why?"

"You'll have to go down there and see. It gets to you, Tony. Sooner or later."

"Well, it seems to have gotten to my man Curtin sooner. I've learned more about Asante from you in the last ten minutes than I have from Curtin in the last six months. You'll check him out, Peter?"

"Sure. And you'll take care of the stock buy?"

"A pleasure. When's your flight?"

"Noon."

2

They were in position before dawn. Their attack was from the east, so the rebels would be blinded by the rising sun. Captain Obiri Anokye commanded the frontal assault by a platoon of joyous Ewe-speaking troopers armed with MAS 49 rifles and glaives, short machete-swords issued to every Asanti soldier. Their orders were to shout, scream, fire blindly, and charge bravely.

The rebels would then abandon their encampment and stampede down the path to the shore of Lake Volta. There, along the trail and on the beach, Sgt. Sene Yeboa and his men would be waiting for them with automatic weapons.

It had all been worked out on maps and sketches with the aid of the beautifully crafted lead soldiers belonging to Alistair Greeley, chief teller of the Asante National Bank. Captain Anokye and Greeley had spent an evening bending eagerly over rough maps, moving the little soldiers about, soldiers in the brilliant dress uniforms of British dragoons and French cuirassiers. Sgt. Yeboa had been present and had looked on, bored. War was not his business. Battle was.

It was Captain Anokye who had suggested coming in from the east, with the new sun at the back of the attacking platoon.

"Very good, Captain," Greeley had nodded. "Very good indeed."

So it was. The Little Captain waited patiently until fire rose out of the earth. Then he led his men in a wild charge, shouting, screaming, plucking triggers. Rebels came popping from their lean-tos, squinted into the glare, then turned to flee down the trail to the lake. Only one unarmed rebel stood to face the attacking force. He folded his arms and regarded the onrushing soldiers with grave sadness. Captain Anokye shot him dead.

In a few moments they heard the chatter of automatic fire from the direction of the trail and lake beach. Captain Anokye ignored it; he knew Sgt. Yeboa's worth. He led his men in a quick search of the rebels' shelters. They found four women, three infants, a naked boy of nine, perhaps, or ten. Like the man who had been killed, the boy stood erect, folded his arms, regarded the soldiers gravely.

"You are a full man," the Captain assured him, in French. Then: "Do you speak Akan?" he asked, in that language.

The boy was silent, but his eyes flickered.

"Go alive," the captain said, in Akan. "Tell your leader, tell the Nyam, that I am Captain Obiri Anokye, and I would speak with him. I will meet him at such a place as he wishes. I will come alone, with no soldiers, no weapons. If he wishes to kill me, he may kill me. But first, I would speak with the Nyam. Tell him that."

Then Captain Anokye went down to the shore of Lake Volta. The only rebel still alive was Okomfo, the traitor who had informed, telling of the location of the encampment, the number of people, the weapons. He was grinning.

"Was it not as I spoke?" he asked, in Hausa.

"It was as you spoke," Captain Anokye agreed.

"I will be rewarded?" Okomfo asked.

"Surely," the Little Captain said.

Lt. Solomon was put in command, with orders to bury the dead rebels, then march the soldiers back to the Mokodi barracks. Captain Anokye returned to his Land Rover. He sat in the back, alongside the traitor Okomfo. Sgt. Yeboa drove, his favorite Uzi submachine gun on the floor at his feet. The two soldiers put on large, aviator-type sunglasses. The sky was flaming. There were no signs of rain. Of anything.

They bounced through grassland to Asante's single paved highway. Then Sgt. Yeboa turned north. It took a moment before Okomfo realized what was happening.

"We are not journeying to Mokodi?" he asked.

"No," Captain Anokye said. He drew his Walther P38 from a hip holster and gently placed the muzzle behind Okomfo's left ear. "We are not journeying to Mokodi. We are journeying to Shabala."

Okomfo groaned softly. "I have a good wife and two small ones," he said. "They shall live?"

"They shall live," the Captain promised. And Okomfo was comforted.

Shabala was not even a village. It was a crosstrail accumulation of flattened gasoline tin huts, several of them broken, leaning crazily. The rebels had raided this place a month ago. They had killed most of the men. They had taken what food there was: wheat, barely, okra, a few pumpkins, shea nut butter, some yams. And they had driven off three cows and two goats. Okomfo had been one of the raiders.

Captain Anokye delivered the traitor to the survivors of the Shabala massacre. He and Sgt. Yeboa, sunglassed, sat silently in the Land Rover and watched as the rebel was lifted off the ground and his hands and feet nailed to a billboard that advertised, in French, "Coca-Cola: The Pause That Refreshes." The men finished their job of crucifixion and stepped back. The women moved in. No one spoke.

Okomfo's singlet and trousers were cut away from him. He was wearing soiled underpants. These too were cut away. A hempen cord was knotted about his penis and testicles. At the end of the cord, between his spreadeagled legs, was attached a small reed basket. A stone was placed in the basket. Another would be added each day. Okomfo would be given water. Enough to keep him alive as his genitals stretched and stretched and stretched until the weight of the added stone burst penis and scrotum. Then the man might die.

"A good lesson for all traitors," Sgt. Yeboa said virtuously.

"Yes," Captain Anokye agreed. "Their traitors, our traitors. But there is another reason. The Nyam will hear of this death and understand. I, Captain Anokye, have given him Okomfo. Perhaps, in return, the Nyam will give something to me."

"Yes *sah!*" Sgt. Yeboa said, and both men smiled.

3

The Ruler of Asante, King Prempeh IV, lived in a palace that had originally been the quarters of the French governor. It was a handsome, flat-roofed, four-storied building of imported stone. It was air-conditioned, but King Prempeh, in one of his extravagances, had decreed that the old, four-bladed electric fans, suspended from the ceilings, be retained and kept operative. They sent currents of chilled air drifting through the palace rooms. The effect was not uncavelike.

On the morning that Captain Obiri Anokye was defeating the rebels at Lake Volta and witnessing the crucifixion of the traitor Okomfo, King Prempeh IV was in his audience chamber on the ground floor of the royal palace. The King was seated at the head of a five-meter-long conference table, crafted of a single slab of pinkish mahogany. Prempeh sat in a throne-like armchair, the largest chair in the room, reinforced with iron braces to support his enormous bulk.

The current jape making the rounds of Mokodi's outdoor cafés, discotheques, and waterfront bars was that the personal tailor of King Prempeh IV was a direct lineal descendant of Omar the Tent-Maker. It was true the King's court uniform would have provided enough white silk for the saparas of two ordinary men. Sagging the expanse of white across the King's bosom was a dazzling array of medals and orders, many from other African rulers, but most self-awarded.

At the moment, the King, who was fond of stroking his medals, was more fascinated by the gold Patek Philippe watch that encircled his right wrist. It was a gift brought from Geneva by Peter Tangent, who had had the foresight to order the watch attached to an expandable band twice the circumference of an ordinary band. It gripped the King's plump wrist comfortably, and he had been king enough to accept it.

Two hours previously, there had been others present. Along one side of the table, on the King's right, in precisely spaced chairs, were seated the Crown's closest advisers: Prime Minister Osei Ware; Commander of the Armed Forces General Opoku Tutu; Minister of Finance Willi Abraham; and the King's personal secretary Anatole Garde, a Frenchman.

Opposing them across the gleaming table were four executives of the Starrett Petroleum Corp., headquartered in Tulsa, Okla., and New York, N.Y. The oilmen were led by Peter A. Tangent, Chief of African Operations, who worked out of Starrett's London office. The others were J. Tom Petty, General Manager of Starrett's Asante explorations; his legal counsel, Mai Fante, an Asanti; and Dr. Hans Apter, a German petroleum geologist employed by Starrett under contract. Apter had been brought along to provide whatever technical information might be required regarding Starrett's explorations off the southwest coast of the Asante island of Zabar.

Since the King was a Muslim, as were his advisers (except Garde, a Christian), no alcoholic drinks were served. But there was a thermos of chilled orange juice before each man, a plastic cup, and a small bowl of salted groundnuts. No one drank or nibbled until the King drank or nibbled. Since he did not, they did not.

The discussion was conducted in French, with Mai Fante whispering a running translation into the ear of monolingual J. Tom Petty. The leadoff speaker, at the King's command, was Minister of Finance Willi Abraham. He was a small, fine-boned, gray-haired man wearing a dark business suit of European cut. He was a graduate of the Wharton School of Finance. His personality profile in Peter Tangent's private file included:

"Phenomenal memory . . . soft-spoken but hard bargainer . . . does what he can to counter King's profligacies . . . refused two bribe offers . . . will accept contributions to Asante's schools . . . oldest son killed in war for independence . . . likes fine bindings . . . chess . . . HWC." This last was Tangent's shorthand for Handle With Care.

Speaking slowly in a clear, dry voice, without notes, Abraham reviewed the history of the Asante-Starrett relationship. A lease for preliminary oil exploration, including underwater explosions, had been granted for a period of three years, at a fixed annual fee. That three-year period would expire in two months. At that time, Starrett had the option to withdraw completely from Asante waters or, if they desired to continue operations, to negotiate terms of a new lease.

On the basis of the most recent report submitted by Starrett, the Minister said, tapping a heavy binder of documents on the table before him, it appeared there definitely was oil beneath the sea off the southwest coast of the island of Zabar. What did Starrett now propose?

"With all due respect, Minister," Peter Tangent replied, "I submit your use of the word 'definitely' is not justified by our findings. In fact, it is a word rarely used in petroleum exploration anywhere, at any time. Our industry is, as you know, beset by thousands of unknowns and imponderable."

"On page eighty-two," Abraham said, "under the heading 'Summary,' it is stated that there is a good possibility of a large field, somewhat oval in shape, that might prove to be recoverable by conventional offshore drilling techniques."

"A 'possibility,' yes," Tangent said. "And 'might prove to be recoverable,' yes. But we are a long way, many, many months, from actually proving the oil is there. And we are years away from determining if it is recoverable in sufficient volume to justify the enormous outlay my people must make for development."

"What do you want, Tangent?" Prime Minister Osei Ware asked bluntly.

"We respectfully suggest, Prime Minister, that the original lease be extended for an additional two years at the same annual fee. It will give my people the opportunity—"

A short bark of laughter came from King Prempeh IV, and Tangent ceased speaking.

"Impossible," the King rumbled. "I am sure you are aware, my dear Peter, that you are not the only people interested in profiting from Asante's oil."

"Your Majesty," Tangent said, "with all due respect, it has not yet been proved beyond a reasonable doubt that oil actually exists beneath Asante waters. I would like, with Your Majesty's permission, to ask Dr. Hans Apter, our famous geologist, of world-wide renown, to describe exactly what we have and have not found."

"It's all in the report, isn't it?" General Tutu asked impatiently.

"It is, General," Tangent acknowledged. "But perhaps Dr. Apter could expand a bit and convey to you gentlemen the tentative nature of our findings. Your Majesty?"

"Oh, very well," the King said grumpily. "Keep it short. This isn't my only meeting this morning, you know."

Tangent nodded at Dr. Apter. Speaking a heavily accented French, the German scientist described the process of determining if fields of oil lay beneath the sea bottom. After five minutes of an extremely technical lecture that had General Opoku Tutu nodding sleepily in his chair, Peter Tangent interrupted . . .

"Yes, yes, Dr. Apter," he said. "Very interesting, and we all appreciate the information. But what these gentlemen wish to know, I'm sure, is whether an oil field exists in the Zabarian exploration area."

"I cannot say for a certainty," Dr. Apter said promptly. "No one can. Perhaps yes, perhaps no."

"So you can see," Tangent said earnestly, speaking to all the Asantis, "an extended period of exploration is certainly justified under the terms of the original lease."

"If you haven't definitely located oil in almost three years," Willi Abraham said, "why do you feel more time will enable you to make that determination?"

"What we propose," Tangent said, "is to bring over two offshore drilling rigs from the U.S.—at great expense to my people, of course—for drilling delineation wells. They should give us an answer to the question of whether there is or there is not petroleum in sufficient recoverable volume beneath your seas to justify further development."

"You want to start drilling?" the King said. "Under terms of the original lease? What kind of fools do you take us for?"

"No, no, Your Majesty," Tangent said hastily. "Not commercial drilling. Not at all. Test wells, that's all. Merely a logical extension of our exploration to date."

"Peter, Peter," the King said reprovingly. He waved a fat forefinger at Tangent. "The colonial days are over."

"I am well aware of that, Your Majesty. But what we propose is, I think a far cry—"

"You have told us what you propose," King Prempeh said. "Now I shall tell you what I propose. Willi?"

Peter Tangent attended to the Asante proposition without change of expression. But as he listened to Mai Fante's translation, J. Tom Petty's beef-and-bourbon complexion deepened; the big man rolled almost frantically in his chair. Tangent looked at him sternly. Petty gradually calmed under Fante's whispered entreaties.

What the Minister of Finance proposed was a two-year lease giving Asante seventy-five percent of all future profits derived from the sale of Zabarian oil. These terms would be subject to renegotiation at the end of the two-year period.

Tangent showed nothing of what he felt.

"I shall, of course, relay Your Majesty's suggestions to my people," he started.

"Not suggestions," Prempeh said. "Terms."

"Very well, Your Majesty. Terms. In all honesty, I must tell you they will find them unacceptable. Surely Your Majesty is aware that in many oil-producing nations of Africa and the Middle East, the customary division of profits is approximately fifty-fifty and, in several cases, sixty percent or more to the corporation or consortium providing the funds for exploration, drilling, the construction of pipelines, and so forth."

"And I am sure *you* are aware, Mr. Tangent," Willi Abraham said, "that in several oil-producing nations of Africa and the Middle East, *all* oil-production has been nationalized completely, and the sovereign state is the sole owner of resources beneath its territory and the only party to profit therefrom."

"True, Minister," Tangent acknowledged. "But those conditions only came about after many years of heavy investment by the oil companies and the development of productive and profitable wells over known oil reserves. Asante has yet to produce a single barrel of oil."

"And you think we won't?" the King demanded.

"I didn't say that, Your Majesty."

"Tell your people there are others who are interested, if they are not. Others from the East. Need I say more? You have heard our terms. Give us your answer as soon as possible. This audience is at an end. Peter, stay a moment. I wish to thank you personally for your gift."

The chamber emptied slowly, the others bowing themselves out backwards. Then the door closed. Prempeh motioned Tangent closer. The American moved around to take the chair on the King's right. He watched Asante's monarch hold his thick wrist aloft and turn his new watch this way and that, admiring the flashes of reflected light.

"Very handsome, Peter."

"Thank you, Your Majesty. May it bring a lifetime of health and happiness."

"Fourteen karat, I suppose," the King said casually.

"Twenty-four, Your Majesty," Tangent lied.

"Oh?" the King said. "Excellent. Peter, about this oil lease..."

"Yes, Your Majesty?"

"Your nation is so wealthy, and mine so poor."

"True, Your Majesty. But, of course, Starrett Petroleum is a very, very small part of the United States. I am sure Your Majesty has seen our most recent annual report. After-tax profits have declined alarmingly."

"Still... I have so many responsibilities, Peter. So many demands on my time and energies. And so my personal funds."

"I am sure you do, Your Majesty."

"You wouldn't believe how much I contribute to private charities. These are things never made public. I am not a mean man to boast. But I assure you the drain is enormous."

"I am certain it is. Is there any way my people may be of service to Your Majesty in this regard?"

"Peter, you know there is no disagreement between us. This matter can be settled between men of good faith."

"Of course, Your Majesty."

"Suppose, Peter, after a period of hard bargaining, I reduced my terms to fifty-five percent. For my Treasury. After expenses of production, distribution, and marketing have been deducted, of course. Do you think that would be evidence of my good faith?"

"It would, indeed, Your Majesty. But after such a noble concession, I would think it only proper for my people to make a concession on their part. Perhaps some means of assisting Your Majesty with the drain on his private funds."

"Oh? The idea hadn't occurred to me, Peter."

"I am certain it hadn't, Your Majesty. May I suggest to my people a fifty-five-percent share of all profits to the Asante Treasury, and an additional one percent to Your Majesty personally to insure continued support of those private charities Your Majesty mentioned?"

"Mmm... I think perhaps ten percent would enable me to do more for the poor of Asante."

"*Ten* percent, Your Majesty?"

"That is still only sixty-five, Peter. Ten less than my original terms."

"Quite so, Your Majesty. Of course. And the mechanics of delivering our aid to the private charities?"

"Oh, that can be worked out," the King said casually. He flapped one stuffed, beringed hand. "Surely you have business in Zurich?"

"Surely, Your Majesty."

"Well then . . ."

"I shall certainly present Your Majesty's generous offer to my people. I shall relay their answer before the expiration of the current lease. I hope a mutually beneficial arrangement can be quickly negotiated."

"Excellent, excellent," the King beamed. "I wish you success in all your endeavors. Will you be in Asante long?"

"Only another day or two, Your Majesty. Regrettably."

"It has been a pleasure to meet again with you," the King said. Then he switched to Akan. "Go in good health, and return in good health."

Tangent replied in the same language:

"May health, love, and wealth be yours; and time to enjoy them."

The King's secretary, Anatole Garde, was waiting outside the door to the audience chamber.

"All finished?" he asked.

"Completely," Tangent said.

Garde glanced about the corridor. Two members of the palace guard stood at parade rest at both sides of the chamber doorway. The guardsmen wore white spatter-dashes and carried Colt .45 automatic pistols in white leather holsters suspended from pipe clayed belts.

"You might stop by Minister Abraham's office," Garde murmured. "He wanted to speak with you."

"About what—do you know?"

"Not really. He said there was someone he wanted you to meet."

Tangent nodded, walked down the chilly hallway to the Finance Minister's suite. The receptionist was a young, perky Asanti woman, hair braided and corn-rowed, wearing a smart vermilion Apollo that came to her knees.

"Peter Tangent," he said. "The Minister—"

"Oh yes, Mr. Tangent," she said. Brilliant smile. She had spoken to him in English. But when she whispered softly into her intercom, it was in a language he did not understand. He thought it might be Twi.

"The Minister will be with you in a moment, sir," she smiled. "Would you care to sit down?"

"I'll stand, thank you," he said. "I've been sitting all morning. I need a stretch."

"Sir, you have a lot to stretch," she giggled.

He laughed, and nodded.

"Sir, I have been studying feet and inches in my English class," she said. "May I say that you are six feet tall and six inches tall?"

"*Very* good," he said admiringly. "Actually six-five."

"Is that tall for Americans, sir?"

"Yes, Quite tall."

"I want so much to visit America," she said. "I wish to visit Bahstan."

"Boston," he said.

"Are you certain, sir?" she said doubtfully. "My brother is studying to be a doctor there, and when he was back last year, he called it Bahstan."

He was saved from an explanation of American accents by the sudden entrance, from an inner office, of the Minister of Finance.

"Escort you to your car, Mr. Tangent?" he said, speaking French.

"An honor, sir."

"About that oil report . . ." the Minister said aloud. Then, as they came out into the corridor and he closed the door behind him, he said nothing more.

They exited the palace and walked slowly across the broad plaza that led to the Boulevard Voltaire.

"How much did he want?" Willi Abraham asked.

"Minister, I don't know what you're talking about."

"I'd guess ten percent," the Finance Minister said. "There's a man named Anokye."

"Who?" Tangent said. Bewildered. "What?"

"Obiri Anokye. He's an army captain. Look him up. You may be interested."

"Why should I be interested in an army captain, Minister?"

"A pleasure meeting you again, Mr. Tangent," Abraham smiled. "Captain Obiri Anokye."

He turned away and almost trotted back to the palace. Tangent watched him go, then began levering himself, joint by joint, into the Volkswagen he had rented. The other Starrett employees had arrived in the company's chauffeured white Mercedes-Benz limousine. J. Tom Petty had offered it to Tangent for his exclusive use during his stay, but Tangent thought it too conspicuous. Now he wondered if it was any more conspicuous than a red Volkswagen with the driver's head protruding through the opened sunroof.

4

That Nigger Sonofabitch!" Petty said furiously.

"Watch your language," Tangent said sharply. "You keep talking like that and Starrett will be out of Asante completely, and you'll be peddling enchiladas in El Paso. Is that what you want?"

"But seventy-five percent? Jesus H. Christ!"

"It's not your problem," Tangent said coldly.

Starrett Petroleum Corp. had leased the entire penthouse floor of the Mokodi Hilton and, at great expense, had converted it into offices, a conference room, a "hospitality suite," living quarters for J. Tom Petty and his assistants, and bedrooms and baths for transient VIPs. There was an added advantage: On the hotel roof, up an outside iron staircase, was a helipad. It could accommodate the Sikorsky S-62 that made frequent flights to the *Starrett Explorer*, the ship engaged in searching for oil off the coast of Zabar. The *Explorer* had a helipad on her afterdeck.

Tangent and Petty were seated in the manager's office, an attractive room decorated with African art. Not the dross sold to tourists or exported by the shipload, but good pieces—ancient and modern—of wood, bronze, fabric, fur, shell, copper. None of it could be taken from the country without a special export license, difficult to obtain. But there were other ways . . .

"Well, what are you going to do about it?" Petty demanded. "Seventy-five percent? They sure got civilized fast!"

Tangent was silent.

"And look at this piece of shit," Petty went on, lifting and letting fall on his desk a copy of the exploration report submitted to the Asantis. "It cost Tulsa a mint. I knew it wouldn't work. That field proves out bigger every day. There's an ocean of oil out there!"

Tangent glanced about the office.

"I hope you're clean," he said.

"What?" Petty said. "Oh . . . sure. The whole floor is checked twice a week. No bugs."

"Don't count on it," Tangent said. "And don't go running off at the mouth about an 'ocean of oil.' I've got a report to file. I'll need the code book."

Petty opened a small desk drawer safe, handed the little red book to Tangent.

"Pete, I'm going to grab a drink and a chicken sandwich. You hungry?"

"Not right now."

"Christ, no wonder you're so skinny. Need me for anything this afternoon? I want to go out to the ship."

"No, you go ahead. I have enough to keep me busy."

He waited until Petty departed, then took the manager's swivel chair behind the desk. In spite of the air-conditioning, the leather seat cushion was uncomfortably warm. From Petty's heavy buttocks. With a twist of distaste, Tangent rose immediately, lighted a Players, and strolled about the office. Giving the cushion a chance to cool.

He liked this room. He had selected many of the works of art himself. There was one small bronze statue Tangent particularly fancied. Dogon workmanship, he thought. A squatting male figure with enlarged erect penis. The statuette had a dark green patina, but the extended penis was bright. Every visitor stroked it, laughing. The workmanship had that sure, airy, amusing appeal that Tony Malcolm admired in African art. Tangent took the statue from its little teak base and slipped it into a manila envelope. Then he sat down on the cooled cushion to compose his report to the Tulsa office, with copies to London and New York.

He wrote it out in longhand (typewriter ribbons could be deciphered), keeping it as brief as possible. He detailed King Prempeh's final offer. He recommended that no decision be made at that time since almost two months remained of the initial lease period. He hinted that other options might be open to Starrett Petroleum, that he was exploring them and would report if they proved viable.

He then transposed his message into company code. He tore up and burned his original draft in the heavy marble ashtray on Petty's desk. He returned the code book to the desk safe and spun the dial. He rang for a secretary, an Asanti, and asked her to cable it immediately. Then he took the Dogon statuette in the manila envelope and headed for the elevators. He stopped suddenly, returned to the office area, knocked on Mai Fante's door and entered.

The Asanti attorney looked up from his littered desk, smiled, motioned to an armchair. Tangent slumped, hooking one knee over a chair arm. Fante sat back in his swivel chair, swinging gently back and forth.

"Quite a session, wasn't it?" he said. He spoke English.

"Beautiful," Tangent said. "Mai, I want to thank you for keeping Petty under control. The man is an animal. Out on the ship, an animal is exactly what we need. But not in a palace."

"My sentiments exactly," Fante laughed. "But...." He shrugged in the traditional Asanti gesture: shoulders heaved, hands raised with palms up, eyes rolled to the heavens. Almost Italianate. "What can you do?" it said. Or, "It is the will of the gods." Or, "The entire world is mad, and every wise man knows it."

"Obiri Anokye," Tangent said. "An army captain. Do you know him?"

"The Little Captain?" Mai Fante said, grinning. "Everyone in Asante knows of Captain Anokye."

"I don't," Tangent said. "Tell me about him."

"A small man," Fante said. "But with a large pride. He leads his men personally, always. In every action he is out in front. That is rare for an Asanti officer."

"For *any* officer," Tangent smiled. "Is he to be trusted?"

"I believe so, yes. His men love him. They will follow him anywhere. He has become a legend, almost. There is a song about him, sung in our cabarets."

"Oh? Do you know it?"

"Difficult to translate in rhyme. Something like this: 'When the bullets begin to fly/Who is sure to be passing by? The Little Captain. When the action is at the front/Who is first to bear the brunt? The Little Captain.' Then the chorus goes: 'Bibi, Bibi, the big Little Captain who is first in the people's hearts.' Something like that. I told you, it is difficult to translate."

"It's interesting," Tangent said. "What is his background?"

"Born in Zabar," Fante said. "A large family. He had to end his schooling to help out. So he joined the army as a private. But he has continued to study on his own. He speaks French, of course, and English very well. Some German and Italian. Several African languages. He likes history, biography, political science. He is what you would call a quick study."

"Oh?" Tangent said. "How do you know all this?"

A mask came down over Mai Fante's face. Tangent had seen it many times before: The African asked a question he does not wish to answer and yet does not wish to appear rude by not replying.

"I have loaned him several books," Mai Fante said finally. "On occasion."

Tangent switched away from Fante's personal relationship with Captain Obiri Anokye.

"Is the Little Captain a friend of Anatole Garde?" he asked.

"The King's secretary?" Fante said. Astonished. "Friends? Not to my knowledge."

"Any connection?"

"Nooo . . . Unless, of course, it might be the Golden Calf." Fante giggled to indicate what he was about to say was a joke, of no significance. "Garde is a regular customer, and it is said that Captain Anokye is fond of Yvonne Mayer, who manages the Golden Calf." The attorney added quickly, "But all that is just street gossip."

"And Minister of Finance Willi Abraham? Any friendship or connection with Captain Anokye?"

Again the mask descended.

"Not to my knowledge, Mr. Tangent."

"Thank you," the American said, rising. "You have been most helpful, and I appreciate it."

"Please forgive my poor service," the attorney said, in Akan.

Tangent replied in the same language: "The wise man is never too old to learn and is thankful."

He could not endure the thought of folding himself once again into that rented Volkswagen. So he took the first taxi in line outside the Mokodi Hilton. To his pleased surprise, it was a 1968 Chrysler, spacious, spotless inside and out. But around the passengers' compartment was displayed a selection of men's and women's leather sandals, tied to the upholstery, with pricetags giving the cost in West African francs, the CFA.

Since the cab was not equipped with a meter, Tangent thought it best to arrange terms before starting.

"The American Embassy, please," he said. "It is on the Boulevard Voltaire, one square north of the palace."

The driver turned to look at him. A face of a thousand wrinkles.

"But of course," the old man said. "I know it well. A splendid place. But a far journey."

"Surely not so far," Tangent protested.

"Far enough," the driver said. "But I shall drive you comfortably and in complete safety. What do you have—Dollars? Pounds? Francs? CFAs? Cigarettes?"

"I would prefer to pay in American dollars."

"A pleasure. A journey of such length will require ten American dollars. The dash is extra, of course."

"Surely the journey is not of such great length. It seems to me a payment of five dollars, including dash, would be generous."

"Oh, sir! Surely you make a joke? Five dollars including dash? Surely a joke! What would I tell my woman and little ones? So hungry!"

They warmed to their task. Other passengers entered cabs behind them, but no horns were honked. The game was going on everywhere.

"The smallest child needs medicine," the driver said. "A terrible pain. Here." He thumped his chest.

"I am not a wealthy man," Tangent whined. "I have arrived penniless in your beautiful country to seek my fortune."

They finally agreed on $6.50 for the fare, with the dash extra, to be determined by the comfort, convenience, and speed of the trip. They started out in high good spirits—and with a sudden jerk that almost snapped Tangent's neck.

"Such a beautiful day, one is thankful to be alive," the driver said happily.

"One is indeed," Tangent murmured, as they barely avoided a collision with a slow-moving bus crammed with Asantis, and more clinging to the running boards. At the United States Embassy, Tangent climbed out trembling. He was still carrying the manila envelope with the Dogon statuette. He paid the driver the $6.50 and added a dollar dash.

"May you be blessed," the driver said.

"And you," Tangent said. "For driving me with such bravery."

"A trifle," the driver said modestly. "Sandals?"

"Not today, thank you."

"My wife's cousin makes them," the driver said sorrowfully. "The workmanship is not exceptional."

The Marine guard at the Embassy gate was chatting up a bird and paid no attention as Tangent walked across the tiled courtyard and pushed open the massive bronze door. The receptionist, reading an overseas edition of *Time* at her desk, looked up as he entered.

"Back again, Mr. Tangent?"

"Back again," he said cheerfully.

"The Ambassador's not here, you know. He's up in Monrovia for some kind of conference."

"I know," Tangent said. "It's Bob Curtin I'd like to see—your cultured Cultural Attaché. Is he in?"

"Let me find out . . ."

She picked up her white phone, dialed a three-digit number, spoke softly.

"He's in," she told Tangent. "Go on up."

"Second door on the left?" he said.

"Right," she said.

"Second door on the right?" he asked.

"No, on the—" Then she realized he was teasing her. "Oh, *you*," she said.

"Give my best to Selma, Alabama," he smiled.

"How I wish I could," she said. "I tell you I can't *wait*."

Bob Curtin was standing outside his door. He looked thinner, drawn, and the hand he proffered was soft and without strength.

"Peter," he said. "Good to see you."

"Bob," Tangent said. "You're looking well."

"And you're a liar," Curtin said. He laughed suddenly, a harsh bark.

They sat at opposite ends of a leather couch. Tangent handed over the manila envelope.

"Can you get this in the pouch, for Tony Malcolm?"

"Sure. What is it?"

"Take a look."

Curtin withdrew the Dogon statuette.

"Nice," he said. "Tony will flip. When you get back, ask him when the hell he's going to get me out of here."

"He told me you'd ask that. He said to tell you maybe you better change your luck."

"Don't think I haven't tried," Curtin said bitterly. "What's Tony been up to?"

"This and that."

"Are they still talking about me?"

"No one's talking about you, Bob. It's all past history."

"Not for me it isn't. I'm still stuck down here. Peter, it could have happened to anyone."

"Of course."

"I didn't panic, I swear I didn't. I really thought he was going for his gun. You know me, Peter; you know I'm not a trigger-happy kid. I've been in the business a long time. But I had to protect myself. I'd do exactly the same thing if it happened today."

"It was just bad luck, Bob. Everyone knows that."

"If he had just said something before he reached for his ID. I honestly believed he was going for a shoulder holster. It was his own fault."

"Look, Bob, be reasonable. The West Germans were very sore, and they had every right to be. One of their best men. So Virginia took care of his family and tucked you out of sight for a while. Memories are short; you know that. You'll be back in London one of these days. You haven't been put out to pasture."

"And you're full of shit," Curtin said morosely. "If I had any guts I'd resign, but what the hell would I do—write a book about Virginia?"

"I wouldn't advise it."

"I don't know—everyone seems to be doing it these days. Peter, I honestly thought the guy was going for his gun. That alley was dark, and he had been—"

"Bob, for God's sake stop brooding about it. It happened, and it's over. Finished and done with."

"Not for me it isn't."

"Tell me what you know about Captain Obiri Anokye."

Curtin looked up suddenly and stopped biting nervously at the hard skin around his thumbnail.

"What do you want to know about him for?" he asked "He's just another army captain, with more balls than most."

"Is that how you see him?"

"Sure. What else? Do you know something I don't know?"

"I never heard his name until today."

"Where did you hear it—at the palace? When you were getting that reaming on the oil lease?"

"Oh, you heard about that," Tangent said.

"Peter, this is Asante. *Everyone* heard about it. Who mentioned Anokye's name?"

"Willi Abraham."

"That's odd. I don't know of any connection between Abraham and the Little Captain."

"There is none—if you can believe my local attorney."

"But you don't?"

"I just don't know. Is this Anokye politically involved?"

"Not to my knowledge. All he's interested in is military stuff. He's a steady customer at USIA. The *New York Times* every day. And they got him a lot of U.S. Army and Marine Corps field manuals he requested. Nothing classified."

"What kind of manuals?"

"Tactics for small infantry units, ambushes, street fighting, house-to-house fighting—stuff like that."

"Bob, have you filed anything on Anokye with Virginia?"

"Of course not. Peter, he's just a lousy army captain. They'd think I was really around the bend."

Tangent said nothing. Curtin blinked rapidly several times, bit angrily at the skin of his thumbnail.

"You think I *should* file on him?" he asked.

"Wouldn't do any harm," Tangent said. "Cover yourself."

"I guess you're right," Curtin sighed. "Even if nothing comes of it. Shows I'm on the ball—right?"

"Right," Tangent nodded. "You ever meet this Anokye?"

"No, I never have. But I heard him speak at a rally of war veterans. A real rabble-rouser. He had them screaming and crying and jumping all over the place."

"Oh? What did he speak about?"

"The usual crap—Asante for the Asantis. The glorious future that lies ahead. With liberty and justice for all. But he made it sound fresh and new. They ate it up. I think if he had said, 'Let's take the palace,' they'd have been right behind him."

"Better put that in your report to Virginia."

"I will. I'll get it off tonight. I guess I should have done it before. This sun down here is scrambling my brains."

"And you'll get that dingus off to Tony Malcolm?"

"Sure. In tonight's pouch."

"Thanks, Bob."

Tangent rose to leave.

"Sam Leiberman still in the country?" he asked casually.

"As far as I know," Curtin said. "Where's he going to go? If he goes back to Kenya or the Congo, they'll cut his nuts off."

"Can he get into Togo?"

"I don't see why not. What's your interest in Leiberman?"

"I've got a delivery to make in Lomé."

"If it pays enough, Sam will make a delivery in Cairo. He lives over Les Trois Chats down in the dock area."

"Thanks again, Bob. I'll find him."

"Tell Tony I'm doing a helluva job down here."

"I'll tell him. See you around."

5

The Asante Royal Air Force consisted of two old Broussards and a twin-engined Piper Aztec. The Royal Navy included four motor launches, mounting search-lights and machine guns, assigned to antismuggling operations, and a smart corvette, *La Liberté*. This craft was a gift from the French government when Asante achieved independence in 1958. It was reserved for the King's exclusive use—for holiday cruises along the coast, close to shore; for ceremonial receptions for foreign dignitaries; and, it was whispered, for certain dockside revelries when King Prempeh and his ministers tired of their wives and orange juice.

The Asante Royal Army was somewhat more impressive. It consisted of two infantry brigades, the 3rd and 4th, with several smaller shared support units of light artillery, tanks, engineers, etc. The two brigades alternated in their occupancy of the Mokodi barracks. While one was stationed in the capital, the other was in the field, on maneuvers, and manning garrisons in smaller Asante towns and villages.

All the armed forces were under the command of General Opoku Tutu. Third Brigade was commanded by Colonel Ramon de Blanca, a cousin of the King, and 4th Brigade was commanded by Colonel Onya Nketia, the King's youngest son. But Colonel Nketia, only 25, spent most of the year in France, allegedly improving his military expertise. Mostly on the Place Pigalle, if foreign tabloids (not allowed in Asante) were to be believed.

In his absence, 4th Brigade was commanded by Major Etienne Corbeil, an ancient leftover from the French administration. He had stayed on to help organize and train the new Asante army. Now, arthritic and somewhat senile, he rarely moved from headquarters and left the training and day-to-day administration of 4th Brigade to Captain Obiri Anokye.

Following the action at Lake Volta and the business at Shabala, Captain Anokye and Sgt. Yeboa returned to the Mokodi barracks. The day was spent supervising close-order drill, calisthenics, lecturing on small-unit tactics, inspections, weapons instruction, map reading, a film on personal hygiene and, at 1900 hours, a Brigade review and trooping of the colors. The Asante national flag was alternating vertical stripes of red, white, and blue, superimposed with a large green star that bore in its center a fulgent sun. Brigade and company flags were somewhat more subdued.

Following the evening review, one-third of 4th Brigade remained on duty while two-thirds were allowed liberty, as was the nightly custom. Since most of the soldiers lived in Mokodi, or had girlfriends there, they went to their homes for their evening meal, taking their rifles and glaives with them. This custom resulted in a great saving of rations. Also, it was felt, the presence of armed, uniformed men on the streets of Mokodi was a deterrent to crime and civil insurrection.

Captain Anokye presided over the officers' table in the general mess hall. Officers ate the same food as enlisted men. That night it was an excellent, highly flavored shrimp and chicken stew, with eggplant chunks and tomatoes included. Side dished were rice and fufu—yam dumplings. Dessert was fresh pineapple.

As was his custom, the Little Captain read a book while eating. It was propped up on a specially designed stand of twisted copper wire his father had made for him. Oblivious to the chatter and laughter of his lieutenants, Captain Anokye spooned in his stew and read with great interest of the exploits of General Thomas Jackson during the American Civil War. Jackson's deployment of small but highly mobile forces against a numerically superior enemy was impressive. He seemed to depend on speed, Anokye noted, and the ability to feint, turn, strike, withdraw, strike again miles away. The loyalty of his men made it all possible, of course. Not so much their loyalty to the Confederacy, but loyalty to Jackson himself. He didn't command; he led.

Anokye finished his meal before anyone else, snapped his book shut, motioned to his lieutenants to remain seated, and strode away. He was still wearing his dusty sweat-streaked field uniform: tan, camouflaged denim dungarees, canvas gaiters, leather boots, web belt, holster and pistol. His limp-brimmed forage cap was tucked under his belt.

He went to his office and spent two hours catching up on paperwork: Brigade accounts, records of courts-martial, inventories of weapons and supplies, muster rolls, etc. He stacked all the completed documents in his Out basket, for delivery to Major Etienne Corbeil. It was doubtful if the old man had the ability or desire to read the reports before scrawling his spidery initials of approval.

Then Anokye wrote out a terse account of the morning's action: personnel involved, huts destroyed, rebels killed. He singled out Sgt. Yeboa for a sentence of praise, and noted that the reconditioned MAS 49s had performed well. But he reiterated his frequent suggestion that his men be equipped with a modern weapon, preferably an automatic carbine or assault rifle. He favored the Kalashnikov AK-47, but did not mention it in his report lest it might be thought he had been bribed by the Russians.

Paperwork completed, he closed up shop, turned off the lights, and walked rapidly to the compound gate, returning the faced-palm salutes of passing soldiers. He could have taken his Land Rover, but he didn't intend to return until dawn, and didn't wish to park a Royal Army vehicle outside the Golden Calf.

He walked on the dirt sidewalk of the Boulevard Voltaire. Farther downtown, of course, sidewalks were paved. But here they were packed dirt. After a while he paused to unlace his boots and remove them along with his wool socks. He stuffed socks into boots, tied laces together, and hung the boots about his neck. He strode along in his bare feet, grinning with pleasure at the feel of the good Asante earth beneath his toes.

A glorious night. A sky that went on forever, a million stars, a quarter moon as sharp as a glaive. Anokye was not a religious man. Technically, he was a Christian; his family were members of the small Mokodi Baptist community. But on such a night it was natural for a man's spirits to quest. Perhaps the old beliefs were best: the Onyame (from whom the Nyam had taken his name), the okra, the sunsum, the ntoro. Many, many beliefs and many, many gods. This night had room for all of them: Africa's and those of every nation on earth. It was all one.

He walked steadily for almost an hour before turning off on the wandering street that led, eventually, to the home of Professor Jean-Louis Duclos. He paused in a shadowed place to pull on socks and lace up his boots. Jean would not object to bare feet, but his woman, an Asanti, Mboa, whom Jean-Louis called Maria, would be offended by a barefooted Asanti officer entering her home.

Duclos was a Martinicain. He had journeyed to Paris to complete his education at the Sorbonne, hoping to become a professor of history and political science. But in Paris, Duclos had discovered he was a Negro—and what that meant in France, Europe, the world. Unwilling to return to Martinique, he had brought his university degree to Asante where he obtained employment as a teacher of history at the Mokodi lycée. It was not the life he had dreamed.

He was drinking raw Algerian wine when Captain Anokye arrived, and had the exaggeratedly slow, precise movements of a man who has drunk too much and thinks to conceal his condition from observers. He was a handsome man, a light fawn, with straight hair, blue eyes. His study was lined with books, old and new. Over the door lintel was an angry red blotch where a bottle of wine had been shattered.

His woman, Mboa, or Maria, was small, blue-black, quiet and dignified. Her hair was corn-rowed, and she wore an ankle-length lappa in a tie-dye design of light browns. She spoke a mellifluous Akan and was inquiring, politely, of Obiri's health, that of his parents, his family, etc., when Jean-Louis interrupted angrily.

"Speak French," he shouted, in that language.

"French, French, *French*! I've told you a thousand times."

Maria glanced timidly at him, then looked away hurriedly. She moved with a sinuous grace, bringing Captain Anokye a clean glass, pouring wine from a carafe, adjusting pillows on the low couch, opening the shutters wider to let in the cool night air.

"For the love of God, stop fussing," Jean cried.

"Haven't you anything better to do?"

Anokye, familiar with such scenes, made no comment and kept his features impassive. It was their hell.

"Stupid nigger," Duclos muttered, after Maria had left the room. "She remembers nothing."

Anokye took a small sip of the warm wine. He would have preferred a beer, but if he asked for it, and Duclos had none, the Martinicain's pride would be wounded and he would scream at Maria for not keeping a "decent house." So the Little Captain sipped his warm wine and told Duclos of the morning's action.

Jean-Louis listened intently. He said nothing of the slain rebels. His interest was solely in the possibility of a meeting with the Nyam.

"Is it necessary?" he asked.

"I believe it would be wise," Anokye nodded. "He is not totally without teeth. His men follow him bravely. Why should I wish to kill Asantis, my brothers? We all desire a free Asante. I will speak to him of this."

"Tell him that Africa's war is not one of class," Duclos said excitedly, "but one of race. Tell him that colonialism is not dead, but still exists in the white bankers who own our bonds, the white publishers who tell us what we may read, the white merchants who own our stores, the white profiteers who sell us guns and cars and beer and shoddy cloth." Duclos' voice became louder; he rose and began to pace about the room. "Tell him that Marxism is an invention of the white devils, a European religion that has nothing to do with African wants and needs and beliefs. The Nyam must be made to understand that the struggle is against *white* exploitation. That our black rulers are running dogs of the white imperialists. Look at this nation! This poor, impoverished nation! The King amasses a fortune in white European banks while his sons and daughters and cousins buy their whiteness in France with Asante taxes. Tell the Nyam there can be no freedom for us, no liberty, no happiness, until all white power is destroyed in this country, and eventually in all of Africa, cut out like a malignant cancer. Only then can we build a black Asante and a black Africa, true to our color, our history, our traditions, our gods. Will you tell the Nyam all this?"

"No," Captain Anokye said.

There was a brief moment of silence. The professor looked at him in astonishment.

"No?" he repeated. "But—but I thought you believed these things. As I do."

"What you believe and what I believe are not important at this time. Words are not important. Actions are. If I was to tell the Nyam he must totally reject his Marxist beliefs, then *he* would reject *me*. I must persuade him to be pragmatic. Let him continue to read his thick books of Marxist philosophy and his thin pamphlets of dialectic and revolutionary tactics. It is not important. What is important is that now, *today*, he and I must join forces to destroy the monarchy and save our people from starvation. When the King is gone, and the palace is ours, then we may debate the nature of Asante's future. But now, *today*, that is not our problem. Our problem is to seize power. As soon as possible. And it will come sooner if we join forces and plan together. If I was to speak to his as you propose I would be as great an enemy in his eyes as the King. Jean, do you understand? We need help from whatever quarter we can get it."

"I see, I see!" Duclos said. Almost shouting. "Expediency. Yes! Very good! Then, when the palace is ours, we shall rid our society of the white leeches and create a truly black Asante. Very wise, Bibi; very wise indeed. May I tell the others of this strategy?"

"If you wish," Captain Anokye said gravely.

"I will compose a letter," Duclos said. Filled with enthusiasm. "A magnificent letter to all the others. Explaining exactly what you have told me. The time for action has arrived! How does that sound? The time for action has arrived!"

The Little Captain nodded. Professor Duclos rushed to his desk, pulled paper and pen forward, began to write frantically. Anokye watched him a moment, then went quietly into the kitchen. Mboa was sitting on a reed stool, knees spread wide. She was peeling a small eggplant. He stood before her, and she looked up. Timorous smile.

"For stew?" he asked, in Akan.

She nodded.

"Do you grind the seeds?" he asked her.

"Of course," she said. Laughter in her voice. "Always."

He put a hand lightly on her bare shoulder. His hand was almost as black as her matte skin.

"You love him," he said. More statement than question.

She looked down at the work in her lap, but her hands were still.

"He loves you," he said in a low voice. "But he cannot say it. To you or to himself. Does he beat you?"

"Sometimes," she said. "But not hard. Do you speak the truth? Does he love me?"

"Would he beat you if he did not? He is beating himself, his love for you."

"Yes," she said wonderingly. "That is true. Obiri, will he marry me?"

"That I cannot say. Yes, if he is to survive. But I cannot say."

He bent swiftly to put his cheek against hers. Then he departed.

6

Peter A. Tangent had visited 39 of Africa's 61 nations and knew well the myth of "this divine little native restaurant where prices are so *cheap!*" Claptrap. The best food was in Africa's big cities, because the best produce was sold there, for higher prices, and the best African chefs emigrated there, for higher wages. The price of an excellent dinner in Casablanca, Abidjan, Cape Town or Kinshasa was comparable to what Tangent was accustomed to pay in New York, London, Paris, or Rome. There was one difference in Africa: The service was better. It was cheerful.

His favorite restaurant in Mokodi was the Zabarian, specializing in seafood. It was close to the waterfront, within walking distance of the Mokodi Hilton. It was a modest building of whitewashed stucco with a red-tiled roof. The main dining room was air-conditioned. It was said that Felah, the Asanti bartender, was capable of mixing any drink a customer might name. Tangent had tested his expertise on a Pink Lady and a Bees' Knees, and hadn't stumped him.

But that night, Tangent was content with a Beefeaters martini, up, served in a frosted glass with a tiny prawn immersed, instead of the conventional olive, lemon peel, or onion. The American didn't object to the taste, but thought the little shrimp looked exactly like a miniature fetus floating in amniotic fluid. Not an appetizing fantasy.

He had called for a reservation and asked to be seated outside, on the open terrace. From his table, he could see the flickering torches of fishing boats and, beyond, the dim lights of the island of Zabar. Asante was on approximately the same latitude as Venezuela, and at that time of year, on the coast, the temperature rarely went above 85°F during the day, falling to 75°F at night. The rainy season would bring mugginess, but now the air was warm, clear, scented. Tangent wore a lettuce-green voile shirt, Countess Mara tie in navy blue, a suit of raw, cream-colored silk. He was comfortable.

After two martinis, he dined on an appetizer of crayfish lumps in a hot sauce, a broiled local fish similar in flavor to Florida's pompano, and a mixture of tiny eggplant chunks fried with groundnuts. There was a flinty '69 Muscadet and, later, coffee laced with a local brandy that was chocolate-flavored. He had, Tangent acknowledged, come a long way from Crawfordsville, Indiana.

He signed the bill and left a generous dash, in CFAs, for the waiter. He knew that in Asante the dash was customarily given before the meal was served. It was not a custom Tangent approved of or followed. He slipped an additional American fiver to the maître d', then stopped at the bar for a final Remy Martin.

"Felah," he asked the bartender, "do you know of a place called Les Trois Chats?"

The black did an exaggerated burlesque, rolling his eyes skyward until only the whites showed.

"Oh, Mr. Tangent, sir, please don't ask me," he begged. "I would not want it on my soul that I had directed you *there!*"

"That good?" Tangent asked.

"That *bad!*" Felah said. "All kinds of nasty-nice things there. Ask for Sweetpea."

"No, no," Tangent said. "You've got me wrong. I'm going to meet a man."

"Of course you are, Mr. Tangent," Felah said solemnly. "You are surely going to Les Trois Chats to meet a man. To be sure, Mr. Tangent, sir."

They both laughed.

"I'll summon you a taxi," Felah said. "A driver you can trust."

"Your cousin?" Tangent asked.

"How did you know?" Felah said. All mock innocence. "Anyway, he'll get you home safe. What's left of you."

"Another problem," Tangent said. "I need a bottle. Say, Johnnie Walker Red. You think your cousin might be able to help me out?"

"That cousin of mine," Felah nodded, "he's *helpful.*"

"Tell me, Felah—is there anything in this world money can't buy?"

"There is indeed, Mr. Tangent," Felah said. "The love of a good woman. But don't tell Sweetpea *that!*"

Twenty minutes later Tangent was seated in the taxi of Felah's cousin, drawn up outside a dockside bar. There was a neon sign, almost completely dark, and on the clapboard wall an enormous primitive painting of three cats fighting. Get that to a Madison Avenue gallery, Tangent thought, and your fortune would be made.

"This is it?" he asked the driver.

"Kootchie-koo," the drive said.

Tangent gave him 50 French francs.

"Please wait for me," he said.

"Kootchie-koo," the driver said.

"I won't be long," Tangent said.

The driver was still grinning when Tangent pushed through the wooden doors. Half-doors really. Swinging wooden shutters. The Last Chance Saloon. He entered into bedlam. Noise. Dust. Music. Laughter. Shouts. A fight. But there were fascinated tourists in conducted tours. It might all very well be a put-on. "Harry, I got to tell you I was in this fantastic place in Mokodi, and you wouldn't *believe* . . ." It was possible.

He gave the fat bartender an English pound. His wallet was a file drawer of currencies.

The bartender was white. If washed. His hand devoured the bill.

"Sweetpea is busy," he said. "Sit down, relax, take off your shoes. She'll be—"

"Sam Leiberman," Tangent said. "Where can I find Sam Leiberman?"

The bartender jerked a thumb. "Outside," he said. "Around in back. Flight of steps. Upstairs."

Tangent looked about. The melee had quieted. People were sitting and drinking. Just another bar, tavern, cabaret. A thin young man at an upright piano struck a chord. His eyelids were sequined. Conversation ceased.

"When they begin," the young man whispered, "the beguine . . ."

"Play it again, Sam," Tangent said.

"What?" the fat bartender asked.

Carrying the Johnnie Walker Red in a paper bag, Tangent trudged up the outside staircase and rapped at a frame door covered with cloth mosquito netting.

"Sweatpea is downstairs," a hoarse voice shouted.

"Sam?" Tangent shouted back. "Is that you? Sam Leiberman? It's Peter Tangent."

He heard sounds. A light flickered, went off, came on again. A gas lantern. The door opened.

A black girl, giggling, wearing a man's shirt that came almost to her knees.

"Good evening," he said, in Akan. "My name is Peter Tangent. I'd like—"

"Cut the crap and come on in," the harsh voice called. "She don't speak the language. You bring anything to drink?"

"Johnnie Walker," Tangent said, entering and peering about.

"Red or black?"

"Red."

"That's right," the voice said. Throaty laugh. "I saw your latest annual report. Profits are down."

Tangent stumbled into a smelly inner room, following the voice. Sam Leiberman was lying in a net-covered hammock.

"Give the hooch to the cunt," he said.

Tangent handed it over. Leiberman spoke to the girl in a language Tangent did not recognize.

"What's that?" he asked. "What are you speaking?"

"Boulé," Leiberman said. "She's from the Ivory Coast."

"Sam, how many languages do you speak?"

"Eighteen," Leiberman said. "But I dream in Yiddish. Throw the clothes off that chair."

Tangent removed the soiled shirts with his fingertips and sat down cautiously in a wicker armchair. He sat on the edge.

"Get your raw silk dirty?" Leiberman jeered. "You're something, you are. Little Lord Fauntleroy all grown up."

The girl came back with two small jelly jars. One for her, one for Tangent. Both filled with Scotch. The bottle went to Leiberman. A hairy, muscled arm came out from under the mosquito net. A strong hand grasped the neck of the bottle. It disappeared under the net. The girl curled onto the floor, alongside Leiberman's hammock.

"What's with the net?" Tangent asked.

"Habit," Leiberman said. "I can't afford Atabrine. Thanks for the booze. Looking at you."

There was a sound of a gross swallow, a deep belch.

"I can't even *see* you," Tangent said, trying to peer through the net.

"I'm here," Sam Leiberman said.

"Who is she?" Tangent asked.

"The cunt?" Leiberman said. "Don't worry; she doesn't coppish English. Would I call her a cunt if she could? Actually, she's a dear, sweet knish who has been a great comfort to me in my old age. King Lardass really broke it off in you at the palace this morning, didn't he?"

"My God," Tangent said, "does everyone in Asante know about that?"

"Not everyone," Leiberman said. "There are a few herders up in the hills who won't learn about it until tomorrow morning. Their goats will hear about it soon after. What do you want?"

"I wouldn't be here if I didn't know you can keep your mouth shut."

"Cut the shit," Leiberman said. "All right, you bought me a jug. What do you *want*?"

"Can you get papers for Togo?" Tangent asked.

"No," Leiberman said. "But I can get into Togo. No problem, if the price is right. What is it?"

"You'll have to go to Lomé. For a day or so."

"Okay. So now I'm in Lomé. Then what?"

"There's a reporter named St. Clair. René St. Clair. He works for the *Free Press*."

"St. Clair?" Leiberman said. "I know him. A crud."

"Right," Tangent said.

"Buy him a bottle of Algerian red," Leiberman said. "*Or* a carton of Luckies. *Or* a fat young boy with sphincter intact."

"That's the man."

"We all have our price," Leiberman said. "Mine is Johnnie Walker Red. When I was young, it was Johnnie Walker Black. But we all get old, Tangent. Did you know that?"

"The thought has crossed my mind on occasion. This is one of them. Now, listen carefully. I want—"

"Wait a minute."

The hairy arm came out of the mosquito net again. The meaty hand slid into the girl's shirt, clamped on her bony shoulder, dragged her up and under the net. She rolled into the hammock. Giggling.

"I'm listening, Tangent," Leiberman said.

Tangent had stock options with Starrett Petroleum Corp., an excellent pension plan, an annual bonus, and a salary of 65,000 American dollars. Sometimes he wondered if it was enough.

"St. Clair writes a column for the *Free Press*," he said. "Political gossip."

"Blackmail," Leiberman growled.

"Sure," Tangent agreed. "But it's popular. Widely read, all over West Africa. I've used it before."

"So?"

"Back in nineteen sixty-one, there was a big flap between Asante and Togo. Over who owned the island of Zabar. It almost came to war."

"War?" Leiberman scoffed. "In nineteen sixty-one they were still shooting arrows."

"Anyway, it went to UN arbitration. Asante got Zabar, and Togo got control of navigation on the Mono River. Follow?"

"Way ahead of you. You want me to get into Togo, go to Lomé, look up this crud St. Clair, and pay him enough to plant an item in his column saying there's been talk in high circles of the Togo government about reopening the whole Zabar question, and claiming rights to the island, adjacent territorial waters, and the oil underneath. You Jewish, Tangent?"

"No, I'm a goy."

"You dress British and think Yiddish. It might work. Worth a try."

"I just want an option, to give Starrett a chance to delay our answer. You sure she doesn't speak English?"

"I'm sure. She speaks mostly cock. You want to manufacture a flap."

"Right. A minor flap."

"Okay. How much?"

"A thousand francs. French. That's total. To you. For your expenses and the baksheesh to St. Clair. The lower you keep his dash, the more for you. But you've got to keep Starrett out of it. No connection."

"How about fifteen hundred?"

"No way. Well . . . maybe. For a little additional poop."

"Oh, you sly goyishe devil," Leiberman said. "You *will* work your evil way with me. What more do you want?"

"Captain Obiri Anokye," Tangent said. "Do you know him?"

"Sure."

"You've actually met him?"

"Sure. He looked me up. I had heard of him before that, of course."

"Why did he look you up?"

"Some of his men are equipped with reconditioned Garands. Okay, but old. He had read somewhere that during World War Two, the last *fun* war, some hotrods had modified the Garand to take a twenty-round magazine."

"Is that true?"

"Sure, it's true. Gun nuts will do *anything*. The twenty-round magazines worked fine—for maybe two fast firings. Then the barrel burned out or the bolt jammed or something. I liked him. A nice young wog. Small. They call him the Little Captain. Eager to learn. Strictly no-crap."

"What does he want?"

"Want? How the hell do I know what he wants? Just to be a good soldier boy, I guess."

"Is he into anything political?"

"Anokye? Not to my knowledge. Nothing I've heard about. He just does his job of work."

"The extra five hundred francs is to ask around about him," Tangent said. "His family, education, how much he spends, who he sleeps with, friends in high places . . . the whole shmear."

"No problem," Leiberman said.

"I'll be back down here in a couple of weeks," Tangent said. "By that time I'll expect you to have the St. Clair item in print or scheduled, and I'll want whatever you've dredged on Captain Obiri Anokye."

"It shall be done, O Great White Father," Leiberman said. "Now get lost. The bartender downstairs can put you next to Sweetpea."

Tangent rose, laughing. "That woman has the greatest advance billing since Jenny Lind."

"Worth it," Leiberman said. Then he simpered from under the net: "Oh, Peter . . ."

"Yes?"

"Leave the money on the mantel, dear boy."

7

Captain Anokye walked slowly through the soft darkness. This section of Mokodi was illuminated; corner street lamps with round globes leaked dim orange light, surrounded by frantic moths. Mid-block stretches were dark, but Anokye knew families lolled on screened porches, lay in outside, netted hammocks, perched on reed stools, sipped cold Benin beer, and watched his progress in the darkness. They knew; the Little Captain was on his way to visit Miss Yvonne at the Golden Calf. He could hear the gentle murmurs.

Beyond the business district, away from downtown, the Boulevard Voltaire became Asante Royal Highway No. 1, the nation's paved road running north 474 kilometers to Four Points. Intersecting roads were laterite, crushed stone, packed earth, or rutted one-track cart lanes leading away into the grasslands.

Less than a kilometer after street illumination ended was the Golden Calf, set in a handsome expanse of tended lawn and groomed acacia. It had formerly been the home of a wealthy *colon*. Now it was Mokodi's, and Asante's most renowned, and most expensive, house of pleasure.

Prostitution, in Asante, was not legal. But neither were prostitutes persecuted; they were simply ignored, providing tourists were not cheated, beaten, or robbed. All went smoothly. A uniformed member of Mokodi's gendarmerie was customarily stationed on the porch, near the front entrance of the Golden Calf. His presence lent a certain quiet dignity to the activities of the maison. It was understood that clients might misbehave only within the privacy of the individual chambers. Public impropriety was rare.

The Golden Calf was ostensibly owned and operated by Yvonne Mayer, daughter of a *colon* family from the Saar. Actually, as most Asantis knew, the Golden Calf was truly managed by Miss Yvonne, but she owned only a third. The remaining two-thirds were owned by the widow of the King's older brother. This lady lived most of the year in St. Tropez and visited Asante as infrequently as possible.

It was a wraith of a white building, gently illuminated, floating in the darkness. All pillars and gingerbread trim. It seemed to soar. There were gables and minarets. And soft laughter.

Captain Obiri Anokye walked up the chalk driveway and around to the kitchen entrance. He entered without knocking and mounted the back staircase. None of the busy cooks and waiters appeared to notice him, but he knew his arrival would be signaled to Miss Yvonne. So it was; she awaited him outside the door to her private chambers on the third floor.

She was wearing a peach-colored peignoir. Her spatulate feet were bare. In her fingers, twirling, were her unusual spectacles, half-glasses actually, American, the type called Benjamin Franklin.

"Obiri! How nice!" She leaned forward for his cheek kiss.

As usual, they spoke French.

"Please forgive me," he said. "I smell like a goat. I have been in the field all day. May I shower?"

"Of course," she said.

She drew him inside her apartment, closed and locked the door.

"I heard about your adventure," she said.

"What?"

"This morning. At Lake Volta."

"Oh, yes. That."

"You killed them all?"

"All," he said. "Those were my orders." Then he saw something in her face. "Only the men," he said. "The women and children lived."

"Good," she said. "A beer? Benin or Heinekens? Now or later?"

"Later," he said. "When I am clean. I sent a message to the Nyam to meet with me. Wherever he chooses. I will go alone, without weapons."

"Was that wise?" she asked.

"Wise, not wise." He shrugged. "I am becoming impatient. I must move. We will speak of this later. Go on with your work. No, wait . . ."

He moved her to him. Kissed her closed eyes. His fingers pressed her thin back.

"Goat!" she said.

"I know," he laughed. "I am."

He showered slowly and carefully. He lathered his short, squat body thoroughly, paying particular attention to his armpits and groin. As usual, the size of his penis bemused him: so small in repose, large and ardent when excited. The American, Sam Leiberman, the mercenary, had told him an amusing story about a man with a short penis. The final line had been: "It ain't the size that counts, it's the ferocity." That was true. And not only in fucking.

"May I wear your kimono?" he called from the bathroom.

"Of course," she called back. "Do you have to ask?"

He padded from the bathroom, took the Japanese robe from her closet. He left it unbelted. She was working at her desk, the funny glasses pushed down on her nose. He bent to rub his cheek against hers, to nibble her ear.

"Much better," she said approvingly, not looking up from her account book. "Now you smell clean and exciting."

"You are a blossom," he said, switching to Akan. "A white blossom blooming in the darkness, quivering to be plucked."

She spoke the language almost as well as he.

"Awaiting your fingers," she said. "To take me and press me in your heart."

He smiled, touched her lips. Then he went to the small office refrigerator. Benin was a light beer, tangy, Alsatian in flavor. He poured it slowly, admiring the froth. He brought the tall glass back to her desk. He sprawled in an armchair, the flowered kimono gaping open. He sipped, handed the glass to her. She took it absently, sipped, still peering at her ledger.

"A good month," she said. "Very good indeed."

"You work hard," he said. "You should own it all."

"Yes," she agreed. "But I cheat, you know."

"You'd be a fool not to."

"Still . . ." she said.

She took off the glasses, pushed the ledger away. She leaned forward to place her cupped palm lightly on his bared genitals.

"Love," she said.

They stared at each other. Nothing blocked them.

"What will you say to the Nyam?" she asked.

"At this time, I must tell every man what he wants to hear. I will tell him that I am his friend, that I desire what he desires—the end of the monarchy. Then I will tell him that he cannot succeed without me. That Okomfo was only one of many traitors in his camp. That I am aware of every move he makes, before he makes it. That I have been ordered to kill him. That he and many good men will die if he continues to provoke the King. That my way is best. For everyone."

"You think he will listen?"

"I believe so. He is not a fool. He will think to use me. Then, when I have helped him gain what he wishes—the liberation of Asante—he will kill me. That will be his thinking. What have you heard? Anything?"

"He met again with the man from Albania. Where are the arms? the Nyam wanted to know. Where are the weapons you promised? But the man from Albania was all soft apologies. Soon, he kept saying, soon . . ."

Captain Obiri Anokye laughed.

"They are having second thoughts," he said. "Perhaps they have invested in the wrong man. That is what they will think. Especially after what happened this morning at Lake Volta. The Nyam is a waste, they will think. The King's captain destroys him at his leisure. Why should we give such a victim valuable weapons? Another reason why the Nyam will speak with me."

"I love you," she said.

"Yes," he said. "Anything else?"

"A man has been asking questions about you."

"Oh? About me? Who?"

"A man named Peter Tangent. Do you know him?"

"I have never met him, but I know of him. The American from the oil company? Very tall, thin, elegant?"

"Yes. Too elegant."

Anokye looked at her, then showed his white teeth. "Just because he has never visited your girls and dresses well . . ."

"Bibi, I *know*."

"If you say so. What questions did he ask?"

"Who you are. Your family. What you want. Are you to be trusted. And so forth."

"Interesting. You believe Willi Abraham told him about me?"

"Yes. I think it may have something to do with the palace meeting this morning."

"About the oil lease."

"Yes. The King wanted seventy-five percent of future profits."

"But will settle for fifty-five with an additional ten to his Swiss account."

"That is what Willi guessed. Tangent wasn't happy."

"No, I do not believe he would be."

"He said he would have to talk to his people. Bibi, this American is very wise. He is in charge of all his company's African operations. But he never speaks of 'my company' or 'my corporation.' He always says 'My people.' That is smart in dealing with Africans. No, Bibi?"

"Yes," he agreed. "Very wise. You think this Tangent will come to me?"

"Yes," she said, "I think so. And I believe Willi thinks so. Tangent will come to you eventually. There is much money involved. The reports they showed the King are not true reports. There is oil there. Definitely. An ocean of oil."

He shook his head wonderingly. With great admiration.

"You know everything," he said.

"I listen," she said. "I listen and learn. My girls listen and tell me. Is anything a secret in Mokodi?"

"Not even in all Asante," he said. "The King sneezes in Mokodi, and in Four Points a border guard says, 'May your soul return.' "

She laughed and leaned back in her swivel chair. She pulled her peignoir up to her waist and spread her legs. Her pubic hair was flaxen.

"My home awaits you," she said, speaking in Akan. "I bid you enter and find peace."

"I would share your home with great honor and pleasure," he replied. "Please forgive the poor gifts I bring."

"Your presence is gift enough," she said.

They never wearied of entwining the black and the white: arms, torsos, legs, all of them. To form sweated, abstract patterns. His dark loins locked in her pale prison.

"Do you believe in me?" he asked her.

"Can you doubt it?" she said. "But your ambitions are not important. They are, of course. But I would love you if you were a sweeper."

He started to say, "That is not the truth," but caught himself, and said nothing.

He watched her slow tongue. Her long, slow tongue. Fire rose in him. Just as the sun had bloomed from the savanna that morning.

Just before he entered into her, he said, "I shall conquer."

"Oh yes," she said. "My king! Hurt me!"

8

Two days later Peter Tangent was back in England. A company limousine met
him at Heathrow, and he went directly to his suite at the Connaught. He had
lived most of his adult life in hotels, and if he had ever felt the need to put
down roots, he ascribed it to youthful romanticism. He might admire the
personally decorated apartments of friends, their suburban villas, country cottages, beach houses perched on stilts. But there was much to be said for hotel
living: its impersonality, instant service at the end of a phone, freedom from
owning many *things*, or more likely being owned by them.

He showered quickly, changed clothes, took up two attaché cases and went
back down again, to be driven to Starrett's London headquarters in an Edwardian town house in Mayfair.

"Good afternoon, Mr. Tangent," the uniformed commissionaire said, opening the limousine door. "Glad to have you back, sir."

"Glad to be back, John," Tangent said, and wondered if that was his first
lie of the day. No, he had complimented a maid at the Connaught on her
new hairdo. It had been dreadful. But that had been a white lie.

There it was again. White lie—small and innocent. Presumably a black lie
would be large and evil. He had trained himself never to make such gaffes
in his conversations with Africans. His thinking was something else again.
That it was essentially racist he had no doubt. A product of his education,
conditioning, growing up in Middle America. But at least he was aware of it.
Which was more than you could say of J. Tom Petty and the warm-smiled,
cold-eyed men from the Tulsa office.

There were no crises awaiting him. Most of Starrett's African fields had
long since shaken down into routine operations. It was only when leases had
to be negotiated, or when, following one of the frequent coups d'etat that
racked African nations, the new rulers had to be placated and assured of
Starrett's loyalty and support, that Tangent's personal intervention was required. In London oil circles, this latter process was sometimes casually referred to as "switching the dash."

"Where have you been, old boy?"

"South. Switching the dash."

"Ah."

On the afternoon of his return, Tangent found a confidential report awaiting him. It was his requested update on Asante's financial condition, prepared
for him by the foreign section of Starrett's London bank. Tangent flipped
through it quickly, automatically translating the cautious "bankese" and eval-
uating how it might affect Starrett's Asante investment.

The latest news was not encouraging. Asante's chronic balance of trade problem had worsened, exacerbated by the profligacies of King Prempeh IV and the ridiculous Asante tax structure which allowed the wealthy (mostly Prempeh's relatives) to escape income taxes almost completely if they established residence in a foreign land.

Most of Asante's bonds and short-term notes were held by French banks, investment funds, and institutions. The nation of Asante might have achieved political independence in 1958, but its economy did not. It was still heavily French-dominated. For instance, the Zabarian, Tangent's favorite restaurant, was French-owned. As were theaters, automobile agencies, insurance companies, the gold mine, office buildings, large cotton and corn plantations, the local Coca-Cola bottling plant, and many minor enterprises. The Asante National Bank—not the only Asante bank, but certainly the largest and most prestigious—was owned by a French-English-American banking consortium. The French had the largest share, by far.

So Tangent could understand why the French would be concerned by Asante's degenerating financial condition. He was certain that Anatole Garde, the King's personal secretary, was keeping the Quai d'Orsay informed as matters melted from bad to worse. Was it significant that Garde had directed him to Willi Abraham who had suggested the name of Captain Obiri Anokye? Did that mean France was giving tacit approval to the Little Captain? For what purpose?

Tangent put aside the financial report and flipped through phone messages that had accumulated during his absence. Most of the callers had left phone numbers, but not their names. Tangent recognized some of them, but not all. They would offer invitations to country weekends, request subscriptions to charities, announce gallery exhibitions. He tossed them all into his wastebasket. If they called again: "Sorry, my secretary must have slipped up; I didn't get your message." Then, standing at his desk, he dialed Tony Malcolm's private number on his outside line.

Malcolm's cover was unusual, a source of some amusement to members of Brindleys who knew the details.

In 1954, Virginia had invested in Schwarzkopf's Adventure Tours, a Liverpool-based travel agency, thinking to use it as a general cover for agents working Britain and Europe. The agency had been founded by Leon Schwarzkopf, an immigrant Pole, in 1950. His idea was to organize tours of European battlefields of World War II. He was certain British veterans would want to revisit the places where they had fought, suffered, and watched friends perish. They didn't. At least, not in the 1950s. Schwarzkopf's was kept alive by infusions of Virginia funds. Its premises were gradually enlarged, offices were added, certain structural changes were made, and specialized equipment installed.

Leon Schwarzkopf died in 1959, officially of cirrhosis of the liver, although Tony Malcolm always claimed it was from an overdose of kielbasy. Virginia then hired Mrs. Agatha Forbes-Smythe, the widow of a British brigadier, as manager. To their astonishment, Schwarzkopf's Adventure Tours began to succeed, to prosper, to boom. Part of this was due to Mrs. Forbes-Smythe's managerial prowess and part to Leon Schwarzkopf's basic concept. He had been correct, but ahead of his time. In the 1960s and thenceforth, British veterans *did* want to revisit scenes of their World War II adventures, and profitable tours were arranged to the battlefields of France, Belgium, Italy, Germany, North Africa, Greece, and Crete. Schwarzkopf grew into a very successful chain of travel agencies. Virginia, now the sole owner, was delighted; there was talk of going public.

Tony Malcolm's title was "Director of Client Relations" in the London Branch. He had a private entrance, his own small suite of offices, and a permanent staff of nine. The Schwarzkopf schedule of tours provided an excellent cover for moving mules, couriers, spooks, and sleepers all over Europe and Africa. Which had been the original idea, of course.

Tangent got through to Malcolm with no delay.

"Tony? Tangent here."

"Peter! Welcome back. And thank you."

"Oh, you got it. Like it?"

"Delightful. I'm building up quite a collection. Thanks to you."

"Dinner tonight?"

"Fine. The club?"

"Sure. I'll see if I can get our corner table for nine. Meet you at the bar around eight?"

"You're on."

Brindleys was an infant compared to other exclusive private clubs in London. It had been organized after World War II and was housed in a relatively new (1925) town house on Park Lane that had suffered only minor bomb damage during the war. It had been completely repaired and renovated before Brindleys took possession.

Brindleys was mainly a dining and drinking club, although the two upper floors offered small sleeping suites for members who lived outside London, or for overseas guests. It was a wealthy club and an expensive club, a matter of little consequence to most of the members since their companies, multinational corporations, banks, and embassies picked up the tick. The chef had been lured away from a three-star restaurant in Lyons, and the serving staff were mostly ex-British army batmen who knew a good thing when they saw one. Brindleys had a fashionable dull gloss, quiet and gently gleaming. The atmosphere, Tony Malcolm said, was one of "blatant restraint."

What distinguished Brindleys from other London clubs was the youth of its membership and their occupations: corporation executives, diplomats, international publishers, United Nations representatives, trade officials, high military officers, and a hard-to-define group of multilingual commission brokers who seemed to have no home base but circulated confidently across borders, selling, buying, cajoling, persuading, as interested in Russian gold as they were in Greek tankers, Spanish real estate, South African diamonds, and stolen Etruscan art. The business of the world was discussed and sometimes concluded in the bar, dining room, library, and salons of Brindleys. The members, in their carelessly elegant suits of banker's gray, subdued stripes, and gentle plaids, spun easily in the interlocking orbits of government, diplomacy, banking, international finance, oil . . . and espionage.

Listening to the shoptalk at the bar, Tony Malcolm said, "This place is the Establishment's establishment."

"More like the world's most expensive men's room," Tangent said.

They exchange only innocent gossip at the bar and, later, at their corner table. Talk of mutual acquaintances: who had been assigned where; who had succeeded and who had failed; marriages, divorces, and affairs; two unaccountable suicides, and one scarifying murder. They waited patiently, on their second brandy, until the surrounding tables were vacant before they got down to business.

"Did you see Bob Curtin?" Malcolm asked.

"Yes. For a short talk."

"What's your take?"

Tangent made a thumb-down gesture.

"Dump him, Tony," he advised. "He's lost his nerve. He'll fuck you up."

Malcolm sighed. "That's the word I get," he said. "Well . . . too bad. He was a good man."

"Good?"

"Good," Malcolm said, "not great. I'll get him on a stateside desk."

"An unimportant desk," Tangent said.

Malcolm looked at him, perplexed. He was a fleshy, pinkish man. He bounced rather than walked, and had the ebullient manner of a shoe salesman. He appeared to be a genial greeter and joiner, an intellectual lightweight, a grinning, slap-on-the-back chap, best company in the world. Believe all that, and you were doomed.

"Why so down on Curtin?" he asked.

"Something's going on there," Tangent said. "Curtin should be on top of it, and he's not."

He told Malcolm everything that had happened in Mokodi: the palace meeting, the mention of Captain Obiri Anokye, what he had been able to discover about the Little Captain. He told Malcolm he had hired Leiberman to dig further. He did not mention Leiberman's errand in Togo.

"Yes," Malcolm agreed, "something seems to be brewing. And Curtin should have been on to it. Peter, it'll take me a while to cancel him and break in a new bod. Will you keep me updated on what you get from Leiberman?"

"Of course. Can you get something for me from Virginia?"

"What is it?"

"What would their reaction be to destabilizing the Asante government?"

"All right," Malcolm said. "I should have word within a week."

"Think I should ask the French? I saw Ricard at the bar. I could go through him."

"Forget it," Malcolm said. "It'll take them a month of Sundays to come to any decision, and then your answer will be maybe yes, maybe no. If Garde sent you to see Abraham, then it stands to reason Paris won't object."

"Unless Abraham is playing his own game."

"Yes," Malcolm said, "there's that. Peter, you seem depressed."

"Oh . . . I don't know. Not so much depressed as subdued. A gray mood. One of those 'What does it all matter?' phases. You ever feel like that?"

"All the time," Malcolm said. "I know exactly what you need."

The two men stared at each other.

"You may be right," Tangent said.

"Let's go," Malcolm said.

Four days later, Tangent got a call at his Connaught suite.

"Peter? Tony Malcolm here."

"Yes, Tony."

"Feeling better?"

"Much."

"Good. That matter we discussed. The question you asked. At the club."

"I remember."

"I checked it out for you."

"And?"

"They couldn't care less."

9

On the following Saturday afternoon, Captain Obiri Anokye showered and dressed carefully at the Mokodi barracks. He donned his dress whites because he knew they would make his parents proud. Also, the whites would be easily identifiable later that night.

The dress uniform consisted of long trousers and a fitted tunic of white drill. A red ascot-type scarf was worn at the throat. A black, beaked officer's cap bore a brass Asante army insignia. Anokye wore two rows of ribbons and a gold aigulette signifying his staff status. The tunic's shoulder boards bore two small bars, captain's rank, and the trousers had an outside stripe of red. He was not armed.

Sgt. Yeboa waited in the Land Rover to drive him to the ferry slip.

"Yes *sah!*" the sergeant said, inspecting his captain. Both men laughed. It was their private joke.

They had been boyhood friends and had enlisted at the same time. In private, Sene Yeboa would never think of calling Anokye "sir." But they had seen many American films together, and the ones they liked best were war movies with Gary Cooper, David Niven, Douglas Fairbanks, Jr., Humphrey Bogart, etc. In these films, when the actors portrayed British officers in Africa and India, they gave commands, and their black soldiers, clad in khaki shorts and high stockings, stiffened to attention and snapped off a British salute, palm-faced, fingers together, the entire hand and upper arm quivering with tension. "Yes *sah!*" they always shouted. Anokye and Yeboa thought this hilarious. "Yes *sah!*" they kept shouting to each other as boys, and "Yes *sah!*" was still their private joke.

Yeboa was a thick man with the heavy neck and shoulder muscles of a born machine gunner. He lumbered, stooped, but his clumsiness was deceptive; he could move swiftly, lightly, silently, when needed. As the Little Captain knew. Yeboa had been "made in the bush," and was lighter in color than Anokye.

He drove slowly toward the port, hunched over the steering wheel. Anokye glanced at him, saw the puzzled frown, the furrowed brow.

"I must meet him alone, Sene," he said softly. "That was my word."

"I know. And without a weapon."

"Without a weapon," Anokye nodded.

"I could be there," Yeboa said. "In the shadows. They would not see me."

"Could you prevent my death?" the Little Captain asked. "Even if you were alongside me? They could use a long gun."

"Yes," Yeboa said miserably, "that is true. I fear for you, Bibi."

Captain Anokye touched the man's heavy shoulder.

"Do not fear, Sene," he said. "Auntie Tal cast the stones and saw a glorious future for me."

"Do you believe the stones of Auntie Tal?"

"No," the Little Captain said. "But still . . ."

At the ferry slip, Anokye got out, then leaned to speak through the open window.

"It will go well," he said to Yeboa. "Believe it."

"Will you then return to the barracks?"

"No. I have business elsewhere."

Yeboa nodded. "May the gods protect you," he said.

"And you," Anokye smiled. "My brother."

The trip to Zabar took almost half an hour, in a ferry that had once plied the waters of Chesapeake Bay. A refreshment stand that had formerly sold hot dogs, french fries, and Coca-Cola, now sold roasted yams, pepper chicken, and Coca-Cola. But there were few customers. Asantis had no money for ferryboat food.

At the slip in Zabar, Captain Anokye boarded a ramshackle bus to his village of Porto Chonin. He knew most of his fellow passengers, and there were warm greetings, embraces, jokes about his thinning hair, laughter. He took it as personal affection and was grateful; he knew their feelings toward the King, and he was the King's soldier.

At the village there were more friends to greet, a dozen invitations to decline regretfully. Little boys clustered about to stare wide-eyed at his splendid uniform. Old men and young pressed his clasped hands in theirs and muttered of prices, taxes, no work . . .

"Yes, yes," Anokye kept saying. "You speak the truth. I understand. These are evil times."

Finally he broke away, waving to all. He stopped at the butcher stand which offered a sad selection of three scrawny chickens, two miserably thin shoats, and a bony goat trembling as if with the ague. This butcher stand had once been the largest on Zabar. People came from other villages to buy its plump hens, cuts of bloody beef, and homemade pepper sausage greatly prized for stews. Now the poor stock, sagging tin roof, odor of spoiled meat gave evidence of its fate, of all Asante's fate.

Anokye picked out the largest of the chickens and watched while it was slaughtered, drained, gutted, plucked, wrapped in a week-old copy of the Mokodi *New Times*. He paid for it and started down toward the shore, holding the package away from him so it might not leak and stain his uniform.

"Uncle Bibi! Uncle Bibi!"

His older brother's children came running toward him, the four oldest racing like the wind, the baby stumbling after. They crowded around, hugging his legs, tugging at him, all speaking at once. He embraced them all, gave the oldest boy the chicken to carry, picked up the dusty toddler, and they all went down to their home, laughing and shouting.

First came the family. Then the sept, the tribe, the nation. But the family came first. The home was where a man was born and where he died. Between, if he was destined to journey to another place, he returned to the home and family to restore his strength and spirit. These were people *of* him. The same blood.

They were all there: grandmother, mother, father, older brother and his family, younger unmarried brother, younger unmarried sister. Also uncles, aunts, cousins, some old, some young. A huge crowd it seemed, impossible to feed. But somehow it was done. Obiri's chicken was cut up swiftly and added to the enormous cast-iron pot simmering on an ancient wood-burning stove that bore a little brass plaque (kept carefully shined by his mother as a kind of juju). It read: "J. B. Freebly, Kalamazoo, Mich." Kalamazoo. What a wonderful word! "Kalamazoo!" the children called to each other. What did it mean? "Kalamazooooo!"

Captain Anokye gave up trying to keep his dress whites clean. Impossible, with dripping crayfish, a fish stew (and Obiri's chicken) with onions, beans, okra, fufu, rice, greens. Fresh oranges and pineapple. He knew what this homecoming feast must have cost them; they would all live on rice for a week to make up for it. But he could not mention their sacrifice; it would diminish their pride and their enjoyment.

After, leaving the women to clean up, the men strolled down to the shore, and Obiri passed around a package of Gauloises blue he had brought. They all lighted up and puffed importantly, coughing.

They inspected the Anokye fishing boat, pulled up onto the beach on rollers. Obiri admired the repainting of the small figurehead: an Ashanti chief in war regalia. Then the men sat on the sand and talked politics.

Obiri listened carefully, trying to judge their temper. Times were bad, they agreed, and getting worse. Food was increasingly scarce in Zabar and in Mokodi, but in upland villages, it was said, people were starving, and the old were wandering off so as not to be a burden to their families. How could such things be? Taxes were increased once, twice, three times a year. Now a tax on salt and matches? It was unheard of! Where did the tax money go? They turned to Obiri for an answer: Where did all the tax money go?

He could have told them, but did not. What could he say: The King is a thief? So he urged them to be patient. He said that certain men in high places were aware of what was happening and were determined to make things better. If they would be patient and endure for six months, things would change for the better. He was certain of that. His confidence comforted them. They would repeat his words to their friends. Soon all of Zabar would know what Captain Obiri Anokye had said. Perhaps it would help keep men with hungry children from doing something foolish.

There was a brief silence after Obiri had spoken. They sat on the warm sands and gazed seaward. The night soothed them all. Far out they saw the lights of the *Starrett Explorer* rising and falling. The foreign ship searching for wealth beneath the sea. They dreamed of wells of francs, pounds, dollars—a constant flood of money pouring up from the center of the earth that would enrich them all.

Then it was time for Obiri to depart if he was to make the final ferry back to Mokodi. He embraced them all. There were tears, fond caresses. He finally tore himself away. His older brother, Zuni, accompanied him up the hill to the bus stop. They walked a few moments in silence. A half-moon paved the dirt path. Zuni was strong, slender with the sinewy muscles of a small-boat fisherman. He was darker than Obiri, burned black by the sun. He wore a small tuft of grayish beard. His forehead was already rippled with worry wrinkles; squint lines netted his eyes. An enormous blue marlin had left a pale scar along his right ribcage, from armpit to hip. Zuni had killed him. He rarely lost a big one.

"Our father grows old," Obiri said sadly.

"Yes," Zuni acknowledged, "but I cannot keep him from the boat. He demands to go. Every morning."

"I know," Obiri said. "Let him. What is he to do—sit and dream? You know he cannot do that."

"Nor can I," Zuni said. His voice was low. "When is it to be?"

"As I said, six months. Probably less."

"What may I do?"

"At this moment, do only what you have been doing. How many men can you count on?"

"Perhaps thirty men."

"Thirty *good* men?" Obiri asked.

"Yes. There are more, but some, I think, will not die."

"I understand."

"Weapons," Zuni said urgently. "We must have weapons."

"I know that, too. When the time comes, you shall have weapons. I promise you that."

"I believe you, Bibi. We all believe you."

"Kill me with your own hand if it is not so."

Zuni stopped, faced him on the dirt road, took him by the shoulders.

"Kill you?" he said. "You are my brother. How would I kill you?"

They embraced, and Captain Obiri Anokye left to return to Mokodi for his meeting with the Nyam.

During colonial times, the French had built a charming white boardwalk that ran along the shore from the foot of the Boulevard Voltaire to the site now occupied by the Mokodi Hilton. The boardwalk was wide, provided benches for the relaxation of sightseers, and afforded bathers access to the beach via several stairways decorated with ornate iron lighting fixtures.

Anokye's instructions, telephoned to him at his barracks office, had been precise: He was to be on the boardwalk, at the bench between the fourth and fifth lighted stairways, counting from the Boulevard Voltaire, at precisely 2400 hours.

He walked over from the ferry slip, sauntering slowly since he was early. It was a cleverly arranged rendezvous. Once on the boardwalk he would be in plain view of the Nyam's men on the beach or the landward dunes. If he was accompanied or followed, it would be noted. And the actual meeting of the two men at midnight would arouse no particular interest; a few bathers were still on the beach, a few tourists on the boardwalk and benches.

He paused to light a Gauloise before he crossed the wide Boulevard Voltaire. A movement to his left caught his eye. He turned slowly. Sgt. Sene Yeboa was standing in the shadows of the Asante National Bank building. Anokye looked at the night sky, strolled closer.

"Forgive me, Bibi," Yeboa whispered.

The Little Captain was silent.

"I can move *under* the boardwalk," Yeboa said eagerly. "On the sand. You know the hunter always looks ahead, behind, to right and left, but rarely up or down. They will not expect it."

Anokye did not speak.

"Do not feel anger toward me," Yeboa pleaded.

"I feel no anger," Anokye said. "Do what you must do. But do not interfere. Is that your word, Sene?"

"That is my word, Little Captain."

Anokye was quiet a moment.

"If I am killed," he said finally, "avenge me."

Yeboa nodded dumbly.

The Captain was moving past the second bench when two men rose and crowded him, one on either side. They were both wearing soiled tan raincoats and straw hats, the limp brims scraggly. They did not speak, but shouldered him roughly over to the seaside railing. Then, standing close to him, their bodies blocking him from the boardwalk, one held a knife point to the soft place beneath his chin while the other patted him down swiftly, expertly.

"I am without a weapon," Anokye said. "That was my word."

"Your word," the knifeman scoffed.

He was the taller and the angrier of the two. When the searcher reported Anokye was without weapons, the armed man pressed his point; Anokye felt it pierce his skin. Then the tall man removed his knife. Anokye touched his throat, wiped away a few drops of blood, licked his fingers.

"You have cut me," he said tonelessly.

"It won't show on your pretty red scarf," the rebel said. He revealed broken, blackened teeth. "The Nyam is waiting. March, soldier boy."

Below, crouched in shadow, looking up through the slatted planks of the boardwalk, Sgt. Yeboa saw what had happened and heard most of what was said. When Captain Anokye moved on along the boardwalk, Yeboa stayed motionless, watching the two rebel guards.

The Nyam was seated alone on the bench between the fourth and fifth lights. He was slumped far down, his legs thrust out before him. Like his men, he wore a soiled raincoat. A black beret was tilted rakishly over one ear.

Anokye sat down next to him. The two men turned to look at each other.

The Nyam showed a hard, coffin face, a thick, black mustache, fervid eyes. He had not the gift of repose; the long body hidden under the raincoat was in constant movement, twisting, turning, straightening, slumping. His hands, too: clenching, unclenching, stretching wide, then fingers flicking off his thumbs, one fingertip after another: a compulsive tic.

"It is true," he said. "You are a *Little* Captain."

Anokye said nothing.

"You wished to speak with me?" The Nyam said. "I am here. Speak."

"The killing must end," Anokye said softly. "We are all Asantis, all brothers. We should not spill each other's blood."

"You are the King's soldier," the Nyam said. But he used the Akan word for "animal" or "creature."

"The King," Captain Anokye said. "I cannot drink water with such a man. You must know that I have spies within your camp. Okomfo was only one of many. You cannot succeed. Your weapons are few and poor. Your people are hungry."

"So you say I should give my head to the King?"

"No," Anokye said. "I ask only that you end your foolish raids. They earn you nothing but the hatred of your victims. I want what you want—the end of the monarchy, the liberation of Asante. But your way is not the right way."

"We will fight on forever until the forces of democratic socialism defeat the imperialists and return the land to the popular will of the people," the Nyam recited.

"The words you speak are foreign words," Anokye said. "They are not the words of our people. But I did not come to debate political philosophy with you. I know your education and knowledge. You are wiser than I. I have no desire to change what you believe."

"Then?"

"I ask only for patience on your part, for an end to your raids and terrorism. When the time comes, you and I will join in creating a new Asante."

"And who will rule this new Asante?" the Nyam demanded.

"I am a soldier," the Little Captain said. "I told you, I have no experience in government. I know nothing of politics. My learning is not as deep as yours. But I can fight. That is all I propose, that we fight side by side to rid Asante of this evil that suffocates us all. Then, when the palace is ours, we may consider how best to rule our country so that the people do not starve and the rich do not steal our taxes for their personal gain."

There was silence then. The Nyam tilted back his head, stared at the night sky, his eyes moving back and forth as if to read an answer in the stars.

"You counsel patience," he said. "How long?"

"Six months," Anokye said.

"Too long," the Nyam said promptly.

"You have been fighting almost five years," Anokye said gently. "Are you any closer now to a free Asante?"

"More people come over to us every day," the Nyam said angrily.

"That may be true," Anokye acknowledged. "But where are your weapons? The men I killed at Lake Volta were armed with spears and one Lee Enfield rifle without ammunition. Is this how you intend to storm the palace and liberate Asante, with spears and guns without bullets?"

"What can you offer?" the Nyam demanded.

"I command Fourth Brigade," Anokye said. "You know that to be true. The Fourth will follow wherever I lead."

"And the King's cousin commands the Third," the Nyam said. "You mean to lead your men against Third Brigade?"

"That will not be necessary," Anokye said. "Many officers and men of the Third feel as we do. They would not die for the King. I propose that liberation be planned for a time when my brigade is stationed in the Mokodi barracks, and the Third is in the field, scattered and divided. The Fourth will then take Mokodi and occupy the palace. Your forces, and men who feel as we do, will attack Third Brigade in the field to prevent a march to retake Mokodi."

"Weapons," the Nyam said. "Where are we to find the weapons for such attacks?"

The Little Captain reached slowly into the side pocket of his tunic and drew out a ring of keys. He selected two heavy iron keys and held them close to the Nyam's face.

"Keys to the arsenals," he whispered. "Master keys to the arsenals of Mokodi, Kumasi, Gonja, Kasai, to every arsenal in Asante. Even the armory of the guards in the palace. Pistols, rifles, ammunition, grenades, mortars, machine guns . . ."

The Nyam's eyes glistened. He stared at the glittering keys, hypnotized.

"It could be done?" he asked hoarsely.

"It could be done," Captain Anokye said definitely. "It shall be done. With you or without you. But sooner with you, and with less shedding of Asante blood."

Again there was silence. Anokye did not replace the keys in his pocket but let them remain in his open hand. The Nyam could not take his eyes from those keys.

"I know you love Asante as I do," the Little Captain said, his voice low and urgent. "Together, with those who will follow us, we will liberate our poor, suffering country and create a great new nation where children do not starve, and men and women may live in dignity and peace with the respect of their elected leaders."

The Nyam drew a deep breath.

"I will think on it," he said.

"You will give me your answer soon?" Captain Anokye asked.

"Yes," the Nyam said. His eyes turned to the sky again. "By the time of the full moon."

"A good omen," Anokye said. "May the gods protect you, brother."

He stood abruptly, turned, strode quickly away, not looking back. When he came to the bench where the two bodyguards were seated, he passed without glancing at them. He marched down the boardwalk, dress whites gleaming in the moonlight.

Beneath the boardwalk, Sgt. Yeboa watched his captain depart safely. Then he returned his attention to the two rebel guards. They waited until the Nyam came up to them. The three men spoke a moment in low voices. They walked slowly toward the Boulevard Voltaire. At the main stairway, they spoke again, and separated. The Nyam departed with one guard, the other, the thin, gangling man who had held a knife to the Little Captain's throat, watched them go, then shambled toward the dock area. Sgt. Yeboa moved after him, slipping through shadows on the other side of the street.

The rebel entered the first cabaret he came to, a crowded place with a noisy jukebox that could be heard from the sidewalk. Yeboa waited patiently outside, across the street, in a dark doorway. It was almost an hour before the rebel came out. His shambling walk had become almost a stagger. He reeled down the street, touching a wall occasionally to keep his balance. He went deeper into the dock area, a dark place of shuttered warehouses, pier sheds, loading platforms, immobilized forklifts and cranes. He lurched into another café, this one small, dim, with dirty windows and a torn canvas awning hanging almost to the pavement.

Sgt. Yeboa waited a few moments, then crossed the street and peered through the grime-streaked window. Bartender. Three men scattered singly along the bar. And the rebel seated by himself at a table. There was a glass of beer before him. His head was nodding.

Yeboa stepped through the swinging door. The bartender and the men at the bar looked up. He stared at them. They saw his field uniform: dungarees, boots, forage cap, web belt, holster, pistol, and they quickly looked away.

He went to the bar, asked for a Benin, and paid for it immediately, leaving the bartender a small dash. Then he took his bottle and glass over to the rebel's table, to the man who had dared hold a knife to Captain Anokye's throat.

"Good evening, brother," Sgt. Sene Yeboa said politely. "Have I your permission to join you?"

He spoke loudly enough so that he would be overheard by the other men in the smoky room. The rebel looked up. Not drunk, but dazed. He made a gesture. Yeboa dragged over another stool, sitting so his body was clear of the table. He poured a half a glass of beer, raised it to the rebel.

"To your continued good health, brother," Yeboa said loudly.

The man muttered something, raised his glass, took a deep swallow, thumped the glass down again. Yeboa leaned toward him, his voice now low, confidential.

"Is it true that you fuck your mother?" he asked pleasantly. "So I have heard. And the other women of your family as well? That is strange since it is known you open your ass to any white man who pays."

The rebel's head came up slowly, features twisted with shock and sudden sobriety. He did not believe.

"Oh yes," Yeboa nodded sadly. "It is said you fuck your mother. And it is also said you—"

The rebel gave a great roar of fury and anguish. Men at the bar whirled around. The rebel staggered to his feet. His stool went over with a crash. An open knife was in his fist. He fell toward Sgt. Yeboa.

The sergeant remained seated to take the charge. His right knee came up almost to his chest. He planted his boot in the rebel's midsection at the same time his quick hands went under the knife and gripped wrist and elbow. Then Yeboa tipped back on his stool, using the attacker's momentum and weight, and cartwheeled him over his head onto an adjoining table, the straw hat flying. Wood splintered. The man was left stunned. Lying on his back in the wreckage. Eyes rolling dazedly.

Yeboa was on his feet then, standing over the fallen rebel. He brought one heavy boot high, slammed it down on the other's unprotected throat. Everyone in the room heard something break and crunch under Yeboa's grinding heel. The rebel's face empurpled. Blood welled from ears, eyes, nose, mouth. His chest made one rasping heave, caught, heaved again, stopped.

Sgt. Yeboa adjusted his forage cap, straightened web belt and holster, dusted camouflaged jacket and trousers. Then he looked at the frozen men at the bar.

"You all saw," he said coolly. "I spoke in friendship to this man. Yet he attacked a soldier of the King for no reason. Was he mad with drink? Who can say? But you all saw he drew his weapon and attacked me for no reason. Was that not how it happened?"

He looked slowly from man to man. Into their eyes. Each hastened to nod.

"It was so," one of them said. "I saw it. We all saw it. He attacked you for no reason."

They all agreed; it was so.

Captain Obiri Anokye was still charged when he arrived at the Golden Calf. He ran up the back staircase. Yvonne Mayer awaited him at the open doorway of her apartment.

"It went well?" she asked anxiously.

"I sold him his own tomatoes," Anokye said, paraphrasing an Akan proverb.

She laughed, drew him inside, closed and locked the door.

Within moments they were naked on her wide bed. His fears, tensions, turmoil, all were shoved within her. He thrust at life, hacking, splitting her wide with his fury. She wept with pleasure, urged him from crudity to cruelty, called him her "Little Captain," her "king," her "master." He continued to plunge, she to buck, until they were slippery with sweat and hot juices but could not stop their paroxysm until strength waned; they fell into a panting swoon, locked, insensate, teeth clamped to each other's fevered flesh.

Later, delirium faded, they showered, sat quietly a moment sharing a cold beer. Then they returned to the bed, which she spread with fresh sheets and pillowcases. He told her of his meeting with the Nyam.

"You have him in your basket," she said.

"I believe that is so," he laughed. "It was the keys that did it. He could not take his eyes from the keys. The keys to the arsenals. The keys to all his dreams."

"Could he steal the keys from you?" she asked.

"He could," Anokye said. "But to what purpose? The arsenals are empty."

"Empty?" she said. Astonished. "Bibi, all empty?"

"No weapons have been purchased for almost five years," he said. "And guns wear out, like shoes. Or are broken or lost. Ammunition is expended on the ranges, on maneuvers, in raids against the rebels. Money for new weapons goes instead to buy sports cars for the King's sons, diamonds for the King's wives and concubines, deposits to the King's account in Switzerland. The army's cupboard is bare."

"Then how will you get weapons?"

He quoted another Akan proverb: "Money is sharper than a sword."

"And where will you get the money?" she asked. "From Tangent, the oilman?"

"That is a possibility," he said. "Grade, at the palace, is another. There are others. Willi Abraham is a clever man. I do not despair. Do you?"

"Only when you are not with me."

She flung the covering sheet aside and began to lave him slowly with her tongue. He stared at the ceiling and listened to her tell what he might do to her.

10

Peter Tangent flew from London to Paris, and thence to Togo via Air Afrique. At the Lomé airport, the Starrett copter was awaiting him, per cabled instructions from his London office. An hour later he was asleep in one of the VIP suites at the Mokodi Hilton.

His phone rang a few minutes after 0800 the following morning.

"Tangent," he said.

"Sam here," Leiberman's hoarse voice answered. "You awake?"

"I am now. How did you know I was in town?"

"I smelled your cologne," Leiberman said. "When do we meet?"

Tangent considered a moment, staring at the morning sunlight filtering through fishnet drapes at the picture windows. The risk of meeting Leiberman in public seemed minimal.

"All right," he said. "In an hour on the Mokodi Hilton terrace."

Tangent showered slowly, shaved carefully, donned a suit of white linen, yellow cotton shirt, black tie of silk rep. His benchmade shoes (size 13-AA) were black suede-and-white. His wristwatch was a complicated gold Omega chronometer, showing the time in Asante, London, New York, and Tulsa. Also, phases of the moon.

The Mokodi Hilton dining terrace was a broad sweep of Italian ceramic tile, facing the ocean, the world beyond. It was furnished with umbrella tables of wrought iron, chairs padded with cushions covered in African cloth. The waiters, some of them over 70, were friendly, energetic, understanding. Tangent ordered iced tomato juice, a carafe of black coffee, two croissants, a wedge of chilled Persian melon served with slices of lime. He was starting the melon when Sam Leiberman arrived. He took the chair across from Tangent, in the shade of the fringed umbrella.

The mercenary was wearing a short-sleeved safari suit of starched and pressed chino. A clean white cotton T-shirt was underneath. Sprouting above that was a mat of chest hair like steel wool. He wore light tan bush boots and carried a brown paper bag.

"You look prosperous," Tangent said.

"I am," Leiberman said. "I'm being kept by a rich goy."

"Breakfast?"

"Espresso and cognac."

"Cognac? It's only nine o'clock."

"So?" Leiberman said. "Somewhere in the world it's noon."

Tangent turned his head. Before he could signal, the waiter was at his elbow. The two men sat silently until the copper pot of coffee and balloon of brandy appeared. They stared, squint-eyed, at the glitter: gently rolling ocean, the smooth strand before the hotel, twinkling palm fronds. They listened to the soft laughter of tourists, digging into their chilled mangoes at surrounding tables.

Leiberman drained his small cognac and took a sip of coffee. Tangent summoned the waiter again.

"I think the bottle would be best," he said.

Leiberman fished into his paper bag, brought out a copy of the Togo *Free Press*. It had been folded open, and the item in René St. Clair's column marked with a red grease pencil. Tangent took his glasses from a leather holder clipped inside his jacket pocket and read swiftly.

"Very nice," he said. "Just what I wanted. Is this copy for me?"

"Sure. I even have two extras."

"Good. How much did you have to pay him?"

"I didn't pay him anything."

They were silent while a bottle of Courvoisier was placed before Leiberman, resting in a silver wine coaster. Leiberman took up the bottle and filled his glass.

"Nothing?" Tangent said. He finished his melon, dabbed his lips with the stiff, pink linen napkin. "How did you get him to run it?"

"You wouldn't believe me if I told you."

"Don't tell me," Tangent said hastily. "But can I still use him?"

"Anything you want," Leiberman said. "He'll do anything for me."

Tangent stared at him. The mercenary was a heavy, brooding man. Gray

hair was brush-cut. Features were brutish: pig eyes, meaty nose, furrowed
brow and cheeks. Wet, turned-out lips. Massive jaw. Creased, sun-bronzed
neck. His bare arms were powerful, wrists particularly thick.

"You're not human," Peter Tangent said.

"Sure I am," Leiberman said. He took a swallow of his cognac. "That's my
problem: I'm *too* human. You got what you wanted, didn't you?"

"Yes."

"Then cut the shit about what I am or am not. Or I might have to take
you apart and see just how human *you* are. Would you enjoy that?"

"I doubt it," Tangent said.

"I do, too," Leiberman said.

They sipped their coffee. They looked out over the calm. Fishing boats,
rented catamarans, girls in bikinis dashing along the beach. Not only the sights
and sounds, but the scents of pleasure. Moneyed pleasure.

"How did you get on to him?" Leiberman asked.

"Who?"

"Anokye. Who tipped you off?"

"What the hell are you talking about?"

"Captain Obiri Anokye," Leiberman said. "Who told you what he's up to?"

"Will you start making sense?" Tangent said. "No one told me he's up to
anything. That's what I hired you to find out."

"What made him worth five hundred francs to you?"

"Someone mentioned his name. Said I might be interested in him."

"Who mentioned his name?"

Tangent hesitated a moment.

"Willi Abraham," he said finally. "The Minister of Finance."

"Oh-ho," Leiberman said. "That makes the cheese more binding. Now I
can put two and two together and come up with twenty-two. There's this
organization called Asante Brothers of Independence. The ABI. They're all
veterans of that shitty war against the French in fifty-eight. The Legion could
have kicked their asses into Lake Volta, but Asante wasn't worth the trouble.
Anyway, there's this Asante Brothers of Independence outfit. Branches in
every town and village. Every once in a while they have a rally or a parade.
But mostly they sit around their clubhouses and drink Benin and lie about
the good old days. Like veterans everywhere."

"Weapons?"

"No, but they'd know how to use them if they got them. Guess who's the
national leader."

"Captain Anokye?"

"Nah, he's too young. Willi Abraham."

Tangent signaled for another snifter and helped himself to brandy from
Leiberman's bottle. The mercenary pulled his chair closer, put his elbows on
the table.

"All right," he said. "Abraham has the ABI. A raggedy-assed bunch with no guns. But all the same, veterans and in every town. Anokye is CO of Fourth Brigade, a sharp outfit. His men love him. If he told them to cut off the King's balls, the fat bastard would be singing soprano before he knew what hit him. I went to see Anokye."

"You didn't!"

"Why not? Strictly a business proposition. I told him I know where I can get a thousand M3 burp guns, which I can, and asked him if the army and the palace might be interested. He said sure—which is a lot of shit. Asante hasn't got dime one for arms right now. But Anokye was interested in those guns—for himself."

"What does he want?"

"The Little Captain? He wants Asante. For starters."

"And then?"

"I'm not sure," Leiberman said. "The kid's got chutzpah. He's shacking up with Yvonne Mayer, who runs the fanciest cathouse in town. She wouldn't put out for a loser. Ever hear Anokye speak?"

"I've never met him," Tangent said. "Never even seen him."

"He'll mesmerize you. A great orator. Lots of drive, lots of power."

"Sam, he's just an army captain."

"And Hitler was just an army corporal. And Napoleon started out playing with toy soldiers. That's another thing."

"You're going too fast for me. What's another thing?"

"The toy soldiers. The chief teller of the Asante National Bank is a gimp named Alistair Greeley. A Limey. Got a clubfoot. His wife's a monster. Real hatchet face. Last year Greeley's younger sister came down to live with them. A looker. There's been talk."

"Talk? About what?"

"Greeley's pretty sister and Greeley's ugly wife. It's interesting—but not important. What is important is that Greeley is a war nut. A military expert. It's his hobby. Studies tactics, diagrams battles. All that crap. And he owns a valuable collection of antique lead soldiers. Anokye goes over there all the time, and he and Greeley move the toy soldiers around on maps. Isn't that cute? That would have been a big help to me in the Congo. My ass! Anyway, Greeley is palsy-walsy with Anokye. That any use to you?"

"Yesss," Tangent said slowly. "Could be. Starrett keeps a nice balance at Asante National. I think I'll wander over and renew the acquaintance of Mr. Alistair Greeley. Perhaps he'll be kind enough to invite me to his home so I can meet the Little Captain."

"Can I come?" Leiberman asked.

"No," Tangent said. "What for?" he asked.

"I want to meet the sister and wife and see if it's true."

"See if what's true?"

"What they say."

Tangent looked at him, then closed his eyes slowly. After the damp chill of London, the strong, deep sun of Asante was a glory. He could feel it seep into his body, melt his bones. He opened his eyes to see a flight of gulls wheel and soar against the blue. It was all hot, live, vibrant with light. Tulsa, New York, London were cold, dead, gray and gone.

"You're sore, aren't you?" Leiberman said.

"Sore?"

"About what I said. About taking you apart."

"Oh that," Tangent said. "Of course I'm not sore. If it pleases you to flex your muscles, it doesn't disturb me."

"You could make one phone call and have me put down," Leiberman said. "You know that, do you?"

"Sure," Leiberman said cheerfully.

"I think I better put you on the payroll," Tangent said.

"You're kidding?"

"Not the Starrett payroll, you idiot. My discretionary funds."

"I love it," Leiberman said. "How much?"

"Five hundred French francs a week."

"A thousand," Leiberman said.

"Seven-fifty."

"Done. Who gets the schlong?"

"Keep digging on Anokye and all his friends. And line up sources of weapons."

"Like what?"

"Small stuff. Infantry stuff. Pistols, rifles, machine guns, mortars, grenades, ammunition."

"How much of it?"

"Enough to take Asante," Tangent said dreamily.

"Oh-ho," Leiberman said.

"How will you get it in?" Tangent asked.

"No problem. Truck it over those open borders. Better yet, by lighter along the coast. Yes, that would be simpler. Money?"

"When needed. This is just exploratory. Make no commitments. Just make certain the stuff is available."

"Ah sahib, sahib, sahib," Leiberman sighed. "It is such a pleasure doing business with you, effendi."

"Go fuck yourself," Tangent said.

They finished the brandy. They watched two tall Swedish girls stride across the terrace, long blond hair whipping in the wind like flame. Out in the harbor were white yachts, brilliantly painted Asante fishing boats, the anchored *La Liberté*, showing a brave display of bright pennants. And above all, the endless Asante sky, the blazing Asante sun. Perfumed breeze: hot land, ripe land.

"It's not a bad country," Tangent said.

"Why don't you relax for once?" Leiberman said.

"Why don't you admit it's a beautiful country?"

"I don't want to get involved," Tangent said.

They both laughed.

11

Gonja sat astride Asante Royal Highway No. 1, almost halfway between Mo-kodi and Four Points. It was Asante's second largest city, the army's midland base. Nearby were the phosphate mines. But Gonja was primarily a market center, gathering produce from surrounding farms, plantations, orchards, and shipping it by truck down to Mokodi for sale or export.

It was a flat, sunbaked, graceless town. Scrawny dogs prowled the streets. Wooden buildings peeled and warped. The one movie theater was shuttered. In the few restaurants and cabarets still open, idle waiters flicked flies from barren tables, looking for customers who never came. There was nothing in Gonja for tourists. In days of despair, there was little for Gonjans.

As recently as two years ago, the monthly meeting of the Gonjan chapter of the Asante Brothers of Independence would have been a riotous evening of good food, palm wine, laughter. There would have been a whole stuffed lamb, roasted over open coals, with kenkey, curried rice, beans, greens, egg-plant, fufu, chicken, fish, crabs—as much as a man could eat. Later there would be speeches recalling the great victory over the French. Later still, some of the men, fired by food, wine, words, would leap to their feet and dance. Bare feet pounding on bare boards. To an intricate rhythm of clapped palms and a huffed chant.

But all that was two years gone. Now there was no feast, no wine, no dancing. Sullen, bewildered men hunched over plank tables and exchanged stories of hungry families, lost jobs, the cruelty of the King's tax collectors, who might seize a man's house—yes, even the clothes from his back and the food from his pot—if he could not deliver what the King commanded. Evil times. The veterans of Gonja agreed that Asante had fallen on evil times. Why had they fought and risked their lives? Had times been worse under French rule? No, they sadly concluded, times had been better.

Captain Obiri Anokye and Sgt. Sene Yeboa drove up from Mokodi in the Land Rover. The Little Captain was one of the scheduled speakers at the Gonjan ABI meeting. The other two were Professor Jean-Louis Duclos and Minister of Finance Willi Abraham. They had arrived earlier that afternoon in Abraham's limousine to consult with certain men.

The meeting was held in a deserted loading shed, the air thick with dust from bags of wheat, barley, rice. The hall was lighted by smoky kerosene lanterns. At one end, a platform of sorts had been constructed of planks set across small packing cases. Raw planks on trestles also served as tables and benches. There were not enough seats for all; many sat on the littered floor or hunkered on their hams, hugging their knees. Almost a hundred men waited patiently for spoken words that might lighten their misery.

The first speech, by Duclos, was a disaster. He spoke in French, in a fervent manner, with broad gestures. These men, most of whom were illiterate, had listened to griots from childhood. They respected the spoken word. It was sacred. It was their history, their meaning as a people.

But this downy black from across the seas could not move them. He spoke a lilting French they could scarcely comprehend. Worse, he seemed to be saying that all their troubles were the fault of the white man. They looked at each other in puzzlement. Was the King not black? And his ministers, his soldiers, his policemen? All black. And had they not agreed that their lives had been better under the rule of the white French?

But the whites were *still* in command, Duclos argued angrily. From behind the scenes, they manipulated their puppets. In Paris, white bankers owned Asante bonds. In Asante itself, whites owned the plantations, the factories, the shops. Asante was still a colony. All patriots must work for the day when blacks would truly control their own destinies. In Asante, in Africa, throughout the world.

His speech, too long and too loud, was greeted with silence. Too polite to boo or hiss, the assembled veterans merely let him finish and step down. The tax collectors were black; that was all they knew or needed to know. This man spoke the truth as he saw it. But it was *his* truth, not theirs.

The second speaker, Willi Abraham, was more to their liking. He was of their age, of their blood. He had fought with them, and spoke a French they could understand. There was little fervor in what he said, but it all made sense to them.

He said that Asante was a very small nation; it could never hope to rival Russia or the U.S.A. Still, the land was fertile, rainfall was plentiful, the people were prudent and hardworking. With proper management, there was no reason why Asante should not prosper. There would be sufficient food for all, and enough for export. Tourism was increasing. With the revenues from the newly discovered oil field off the coast of Zabar, Asante could become a modest paradise, a showcase for all of Africa, a stable and flourishing nation where every man might work as hard as he wished at the trade he desired, and live with his family in peace, happiness, and dignity.

They liked that, and leaped to their feet, shaking fists at him in delight, stamping, slapping their own bare shoulders. Willi Abraham was one of them, a wise man, and he spoke their truth.

Then Captain Obiri Anokye strode onto the platform and they quieted, grinning to welcome him. He stood erect, proud, in his dress whites with decorations. He was youth and power. He was as they had been when they fought the French.

"Bibi, Bibi, Bibi!" they chanted. "Little Captain! Brother!"

He smiled down on them, and gradually they stilled to hear his words. He spoke to them in Akan.

"You are great men," he said, starting slowly, in almost a whisper, so they had to lean toward him to hear. "You are the sons of great men, great warriors, the Ashanti. Noble blood flows in your veins. Your ancestors held land that could not be crossed by a swift-flying bird in the time of a moon's turning. These grasslands, mountains, lakes and rivers, coasts and rain forests, were once all Ashanti land." He paused to stare at his audience, meeting their eyes. "And who knows?" he said. "They may be yours once again."

He was not a trained orator, but instinctively had sought and developed an individual style, at once impressive to his audience, comfortable to him. He stood with feet firmly planted, slightly spread, rooted. Usually he spoke with hands on hips, torso bent slightly backward. His barrel chest was inflated, chin elevated. He nodded frequently. His few gestures were short and explosive: the right palm brought down, edge foremost, in a sharp chop, or the left fist clenched and brandished. Gestures of an impassioned warrior.

"These are troubled times," he told them. "Believe me, brothers, I know what you suffer, and what your women and children suffer, and I grieve with you. I say that our salvation, and that of Asante, lies in our dedication to our history, to our blood. We must return to the spirit of the old ones, to their wisdom, and their sacrifice. I tell you now, you are not alone. You are not lonely men to worry and despair. You are a people. Draw your strength from your knowledge of what your people have done in the past and will do in the future."

He spoke for another twenty minutes, recounting their history, retelling the deeds of the Ashantis, describing the great cities they had created, the laws, the arts. What these men and women had done, he told them, they could do. They were, most of them, knowledgeable and wise in the breeding of cattle and horses and goats. Even chickens! Were men any less? Blood would tell; they knew that to be true. And in their veins they bore the blood of mighty warriors, wise law-givers, statesmen, philosophers, artists, and a people who had worked a mighty civilization out of raw wilderness.

"Do not despair," he finished. "I pledge to you my honor as a soldier and my life as a man that you shall enjoy better times. And sooner than you think! Even sooner if you remember, always, that you spring from the seed of men who were not afraid to follow their destinies. Tomorrow belongs to us!"

They surged forward then, to engulf him on the platform, weeping and crying out, stamping their bare feet, stretching to touch him, to touch the magic. Bibi. The Little Captain. He, too, was of their blood. He was a brother. They were all a family. He would give his life for them, and they for him.

Later, Anokye drove back to Mokodi in Willi Abraham's limousine, leaving Sgt. Yeboa to return the Land Rover to the barracks. The Little Captain sat in back, with Abraham. Jean-Louis Duclos, slumped and disconsolate, sat in front with the chauffeur.

"Were there secret police in the audience?" Anokye asked.

"Undoubtedly," Abraham said. "But nothing was spoken of a seditious nature."

"Alistair Greeley called me this afternoon. He invites me to join his family at his home tomorrow evening for drink and talk. And to meet Peter Tangent. Shall I go?"

Willi Abraham offered Anokye a packet of short, fat Dutch cigars. When the Little Captain shook his head, Abraham lighted one for himself, slowly.

"Yes," he said finally. "I think that would be wise. Yesterday morning Tangent met with Sam Leiberman on the terrace of the Mokodi Hilton. They had a long talk. Do you know what that was about?"

"No," Anokye said. "I told you Leiberman came to me offering to sell M3s. I gave him the impression I was interested. Perhaps they spoke of that."

"Perhaps," Abraham said. "Go to Greeley's home tomorrow night. Speak with Tangent. I believe he merely wishes to meet you personally, to see for himself what kind of man you are. It is amusing that you should meet him through Greeley. That will infuriate Garde."

"Will Tangent make an offer?"

"Tomorrow night? I doubt it. He does not yet know who you are, what you plan. Men like Tangent move prudently. He will seek to learn as much as he can, then report all he has learned to his home office. The offer must come from there, through Tangent."

"Will he attempt to bribe me, Willi?"

"Perhaps. But in such a way that you could never say he had. Stop him. Immediately."

"Of course."

"Then he will be curious," Abraham laughed. "What kind of an African army officer is this who won't accept a bribe? It will intrigue him."

"Intrigue?"

"Interest him. Perplex him. And so we will keep him off balance."

They drove in silence then. Duclos was still slumped silently in the front seat next to the driver. Neither Anokye nor Abraham thought it wise to offer words of sympathy. They were approaching the outskirts of Mokodi before Willi Abraham spoke again.

"Bibi," he said. "I believe we will eventually receive an offer from Starrett, through Tangent, or from the French, through Garde. Or from both sources. When that time comes, it will be necessary to act. You agree?"

"Of course," Anokye said.

"You realize what it may mean to you and your family?"

"I realize. And you?"

"I realize. The Nyam desires the victory of the socialist proletariat. Duclos dreams of a racist war to remove every white from the sacred soil of Africa.

I wish only a liberated Asante which I may help to become self-sufficient, prosperous, and reasonably happy. And you, Bibi? What do you want?"

"I want what you want," the Little Captain said.

"Do you?" Willi Abraham said. "That speech of yours tonight . . . are you certain you don't yearn to withdraw into the Africa of the past, an Africa that can never again exist?"

Captain Anokye turned to look at the Finance Minister.

"No, Willi," he said gently. "I do not yearn for that. I told them what they wanted to hear."

12

In Peter Tangent's private file in his London office, Prime Minister Osei Ware of Asante had been thumbnailed:

"Venal and shrewd . . . a Muslim who prefers Dom Perignon . . . scorn of Christians . . . a private jihad? . . . compliment on rose garden . . . story from T.M. re torture of French prisoners at Gonja . . . Islamic dress . . . do not use sex jokes . . . rumor of Jewish mistress in Beirut (circa a long time ago) . . . two fingers missing left hand . . . bad French, better English . . . hashish?"

"Prime Minister," Tangent said, "if you will allow me . . ."

He reached into a canvas carryall and withdrew a bulbous object wrapped in plastic. He placed it carefully on the Prime Minister's desk.

"A cutting of a new American rose," he said. "It's called 'Independence Day.' If you will accept it, I hope it may bloom in that famous garden of yours and give you pleasure every day of your life."

"A small gift for me," Osei Ware said. "How nice." He smiled coldly, took up the package, peered through the plastic wrapping. "You remembered my poor flowers. I shall graft it immediately."

They were speaking English, seated in the Prime Minister's private office in the palace at Mokodi. The room was scented by two large, artful arrangements of roses in antique Asante jars. The ocher clay was decorated with black bands of stylized deer fleeing before spear-wielding hunters. As Tangent spoke, Prime Minister Osei Ware withdrew a pale yellow bloom from one of the vases and thrust his great hawk nose deep into the petals. He inhaled audibly, eyes lidding with pleasure.

"Prime Minister," Tangent said, "I have sought this audience because a matter of the gravest urgency has come to my attention, a matter I believe deserving of consideration at the highest levels of the Asante government."

He withdrew the copy of the Lomé *Free Press* from his carryall and placed it before the Prime Minister. He pointed at the item circled in red.

"Oh *that*," Ware said negligently. "A matter of little importance. It means nothing."

"With all due respect," Tangent said, "my people find it extremely upsetting. If that item accurately reflects the position of the Togo government, then our Zabarian investment is gravely threatened."

"The gossip of a journalist," Ware said. "It has no effect on our negotiations."

"But why should this man write such a story if there is no truth to it? What could his motive possibly be?"

"Who knows?" the Prime Minister shrugged. "Perhaps he is a writer of fiction. Perhaps he wishes to—what is the English expression—muddy the waters? And perhaps—" Here he raised his beak from the rose and looked directly at Tangent. Heavy lids; reptilian eyes. "—perhaps *you* persuaded him to write it."

"Excellency!" Tangent cried. Shocked. Horrified. "Do you know what you suggest? That I would deliberately endanger the friendly relations between two African nations for personal gain? Surely, Prime Minister, you know me better than that! My people, and I personally, desire nothing more than to develop a rich oil field in Zabarian waters, for the benefit of Asante—and for our benefit too, of course. But what are we to do now? If Togo brings this matter to the floor of the United Nations, the whole matter might be tied up in litigation for years. Dare we sign *any* lease agreement with Asante while this question remains unresolved? And I'm certain that other petroleum companies, of *whatever nation*, will feel the same. Quite frankly, Prime Minister, at this moment we don't know where we're at, or with whom we should deal."

"Togo signed a treaty in nineteen sixty-one relinquishing all claims to Zabar and its territorial waters."

"And the man who signed that treaty is now dead, as dead as the government he served. Why should the present rulers of Togo be fettered by the errors of the past? That, I fear, may be the way they feel. I know Your Excellency has had more than one experience with repudiated agreements. Governments change, and rulers, and circumstances. Perhaps rumors of a potentially profitable Zabarian oil field have reached Lomé, and that is the reason they talk of reopening the question of jurisdiction."

"Get to the point. What do you want?"

"Would it be possible for your government, through its ambassador, to make discreet inquiries in Lomé? To determine if that published item is, as you feel, the concoction of a scandalmonger, or if there is any truth to it?"

The Prime Minister slowly lowered his nose back into the rose petals. When he spoke, his voice was muffled, hardly understandable.

"Our man in Lomé is not famous for his discretion," he said. No hint of irony in his tone. "But perhaps you are right. Perhaps I should get to the bottom of this matter."

"Excellent, Prime Minister," Tangent said enthusiastically. "I assure you it would help expedite a decision by my people on the King's lease terms."

"Ah yes," the Prime Minister said. "The King's lease terms. In that case, it may be best for me to handle this matter personally. I have been working very hard lately. A short vacation in Lomé—a beautiful city—combining pleasure and business—not an official visit—could do no harm."

"A wise decision, Prime Minister," Tangent said. "Go in good health, and return in good health."

Again the heavy lids rose, the eyes were revealed.

"And who knows?" Osei Ware said. "I may be able to discover how this item in this newspaper came to be published."

So Peter A. Tangent had to make another trip to the smelly premises above Les Trois Chats. Once again Sam Leiberman was in his hammock, hidden under a mosquito net. The girl from the Ivory Coast was curled on the floor, working a cat's cradle.

"I'm afraid our friend in Lomé may prove an embarrassment," Tangent said.

"All right," Leiberman said. "I'll take care of it. How much?"

"Keep it cheap," Tangent said.

"I had no choice, did I?" Alistair Greeley said. "What? What? After all, he is one of our biggest depositors. Or his company is. What was I to say: 'Sorry, Mr. Tangent, you can't come to my home to meet Captain Anokye'? What? What?"

He spoke in a whining, aggrieved tone, the "What? What?" calling upon God and the world to witness that he was a cripple, helpless before the cruelty of others, unable to defend himself because of a wretched accident of birth that had robbed him of strength and dignity.

"No, I suppose not," Anatole Garde said.

He took a sip of his Pernod and water and regarded his companion with some distaste. Greeley was bent, crabbed, with a gray skin that ten years of Asante sun had failed to brighten. Grade felt guilty about his own erect carriage, bloomy youth, vitality.

They were seated in the small outdoor café of the Restaurant Cleopatra, a reasonably priced establishment recommended in the guidebooks for its "amusing Egyptian decor" and the spécialité de la maison: broiled grouper with pepper sauce.

"Actually," Garde said, "Abraham would have brought them together one way or another. Perhaps this is best."

Greeley blinked uneasily.

"You think Tangent knows of my connection with you? What? What?"

"Calm," Garde said soothingly. "Calm. How would he know? But perhaps we should not meet again in public. I can come to your place occasionally, late at night. Better yet, we will transact our business on the phone."

"There won't be any—any danger, will there? What?"

"Danger?" Garde said, astonished. "How could there be any danger?"

"All this violence," Greeley said muzzily. "I don't like it."

"What violence?"

"You know—the niggers. Always cutting each other."

"Yes," Garde said. "Almost as bad as Paris and New York."

"Well, Maud doesn't like it either."

Garde stared at him a moment. The other wouldn't meet his eyes.

"Just how much have you told your wife?" Garde asked finally.

"Nothing. I swear, I've told her nothing."

"And your sister?"

"Jane knows nothing either. All they know is that Anokye visits occasionally, just as a guest. I take him into the study, and we talk about military things. The women aren't interested."

"Good," Garde said. "Keep it that way."

"They couldn't care less," Greeley said bitterly. "They've got each other."

Garde looked away in embarrassment from the other man's pain. He watched the sauntering pedestrians, a fascinating parade of gorgeous colors, fanciful hairdos, brilliant costumes. Smiles, laughter, a dozen musical languages.

"Charming," Garde murmured.

"What? What?" Greeley demanded. Then, when Garde didn't reply, the chief teller asked, "I will get the bonus, won't I?"

"You'll get it," Garde said. "It will come through the bank: a Christmas bonus."

"Then I'll send Jane home on the first flight out."

"Isn't Asante your home?" Garde asked.

Greeley didn't hear, or paid no attention. He looked down at his glass of Scotch and Perrier.

"It's been hell," he muttered. "Hell. A man can stand so much. What? What?"

Garde watched him lift his glass and drain it suddenly in two heavy gulps. His throat worked convulsively. A little dribble ran from the corner of his mouth. Greeley wiped it away with the back of his hand.

"Has Anokye said anything to you about his plans?" Garde asked. "Any talk of a possible coup?"

"No. Nothing yet."

"He will," Garde said. "The Little Captain respects your expertise. Keep me informed."

"Then what? What happens then?"

Garde finished his Pernod. He rose, left money and a dash, adjusted his white Panama.

"I have to go back to the palace," he said. "Don't talk too much tonight. Just listen. Then call and tell me how it went."

Greeley watched him stride away. Moving lightly, blithely, almost bouncing. The chief teller looked down at his own right foot, encased in a great, ugly, misshapen black boot. It wasn't fair.

Alistair Greeley's home was more hacienda than house. In colonial days it had been the main building of a large cacao plantation. As the city of Mokodi grew, the land was sold off to developers and builders. Only Greeley's home, centered in a hectare plot, remained of the original farm. He rented; building and land were owned by one of the King's cousins.

It was a low, sprawling clapboard structure embellished with a screened veranda, gingerbread trim, a precisely organized flower garden in the rear. An additional embellishment—of some embarrassment to the British ambassador to Asante—was a steel flagpole, planted in concrete in the front lawn, from which Greeley insisted on flying the Union Jack on such occasions as the Queen's birthday and the anniversary of Nelson's victory at the Nile.

Peter Tangent left his rented black Opel in the gravel driveway and stepped around the flagstoned walk to the screened porch. There was an orange light burning; he smelled citronella. He glimpsed dim figures seated on the veranda. The door was pushed open suddenly.

"Come in quickly," Greeley said. "Can't let the bugs in! What? What?"

Tangent was introduced to the two women, neither of whom rose to greet him or offered a hand. He joined them, folding himself cautiously into a fragile rattan chair. He was provided with a glass of desperately weak and tepid lemonade.

"Anokye called," Greeley said. "He'll be a bit late. But better late than never. What? What?"

The younger woman, the sister, Jane, began to ask about London. How was dear old England? Had he been to the theater ("thee-ate-er") recently? Anything new and good? What were women wearing these days? Was it true that two ministers were involved in another call girl scandal? Had he ever been to Brighton? Were prices as bad as everyone said? And when would the Prince marry?

The questions came rapidly, in a brittle, almost accusatory tone. Tangent answered as best he could, trying to draw Greeley and his wife into the conversation. But Jane Greeley dominated.

In the orange light her face appeared drawn, cavernous. The odd light empurpled her sulky lips and blackened her painted fingernails and toenails. She was wearing a tie-dyed pagne, a kind of sarong that showed a wedge of smooth, tanned thigh. A lush body whispered within that loose garment. Nipples showed through thin cloth.

In contrast, Mrs. Greeley was a sour Victorian matron, wearing a high-necked, ankle-length garden gown of white linen. All pleats and ruffles, threaded through with girlish ribbons. Sam Leiberman had been right; hers was a hatchet face. And a thin, sharp body hidden behind that curtain of white. Sudden, jerky movements. Grimaces rather than expressions. Unable, for more than a moment, to take her puzzled stare away from her husband's sister.

"Are you in Asante permanently, Miss Greeley?" Tangent asked.

"No," Greeley said sharply. "Just a visit. She'll be going home shortly."

The silence that followed that pronouncement was so taut that Tangent had to break it before they flew at each other's throats, biting.

"I understand you collect toy soldiers, Mr. Greeley," Tangent said.

"*Model* soldiers," Greeley said angrily.

"Show Mr. Tangent your collection, Alistair," Maud Greeley said. "I'm sure he'll be interested in what's keeping us poor."

It was the first time she had spoken. Her voice was unexpectedly young, lilting, with an Aberdeen burr.

Muttering something, the chief teller hauled himself up with the aid of the chair arms. Dragging his foot behind him, he led the way inside his home. Tangent followed and looked about. A museum reproduction of a shabby, genteel English flat, complete with photos of the Royal Family. Even the dusty, tea-scented, stale smell was *right*. They had reproduced Birmingham in Mo-kodi.

In the study, lined with books in glass-fronted shelves, the host displayed his treasures. They were a revelation: Greeley's dream.

Most of the model soldiers were single figures in *ronde bosse*. But there was one stalwart squad of Prussian grenadiers and an entire mounted troop of French hussars. There were musketeers and dragoons, fusiliers and cuirassiers, drummers and pipers, lancers, pioneers, guardsmen, carabiniers, and many others. They stood frozen at parade rest, at attention, thrusting with pike or sword, rifle at shoulder, or charging at full gallop. Tangent had forgotten that men once dressed that brilliantly to die.

"Fascinating," he murmured. "Absolutely fascinating."

"What? What?"

Tangent donned his glasses and bent far over to inspect the models in bell jars and display cases. He clasped his hands firmly behind his back, the better to resist picking up one of the few bright figures standing uncovered in lonely splendor.

"Must have cost a mint," he said, not looking at Greeley.

"Oh yes," the chief teller said. He tried to laugh. "But when you're bitten, you're bitten. What? What?"

"Who is this chap?" Tangent asked, pointing. "With the curved plume."

"Bavarian cuirassier. About eighteen sixty-six."

"And this one, with the feathered hat?"

"Sardinian bersaglieri. About eighteen-sixty."

"Which are Captain Anokye's favorites?" Tangent asked casually.

"He seems most interested in the eighteen-sixty to eighteen-seventy period. About then."

"In Europe?"

"Yes. Now here are two you'll like. From your Civil War. Both are zouaves. The one on the right is Union, the Eleventh Indiana volunteers. On the left is the Confederate, from the Louisiana Tigers."

Tangent sighed, straightened up, removed his glasses.

"I can see how a hobby like this could take over a man," he said. "So you'd spend every franc you've got on it."

"Can you?" Greeley said eagerly. "Can you see that? Maud can't. Most fascinating hobby on eagerly. When you read about the wars and battles, you can see history come alive. What? What? How they dressed, their weapons, their equipment."

"I should think—" Tangent began, but there was a knock on the door, and he stopped.

"Come in," Greeley called.

The door opened slowly. Captain Obiri Anokye, wearing his dress whites, carrying his cap under his arm, stepped into the room, smiling faintly.

Tangent saw a short man, surely not more than five-four, heavy through the chest and shoulders, with a hint of corpulence to come in a thick torso that swelled his tunic. He carried himself with an erect, head-up posture, leaning backward slightly, chest inflated, chin elevated. He moved lightly and gracefully on small feet. He avoided pomposity, but there was an almost magisterial quality in his slow gestures, his manner of turning his head rather than moving his eyes.

He was a very dark brown, not a blue-black, with a ruddy burnish on his mahogany skin. He was without mustache or beard, his hair a tight toque of closely cropped curls. No appearance of gray. His hands were small but broad, palms and fingers squarish. He wore a ring on the index finger of his left hand. It was hammered silver set with a loin stone.

Brow was high; eyes large, liquid, deepest; nose slightly hooked. The full somewhat protuberant lips were delicately sculpted. Jaw was rounded, heavy, with a sharply defined chin line. His face was unlined except, occasionally, when two small vertical wrinkles appeared above the bridge of his nose. Small ears were set flat to his skull. Neck was thick and muscular.

He had an imperiousness that belied his size. It was not arrogance so much as assurance: resolution and confidence. If he had doubts, he hid them well. But then he was too young to have been tried by failure.

They seated themselves at one end of a refectory table. Greeley served small glasses of an indifferent port.

"I've been admiring this—this marvelous army," Tangent said, waving his hand at the model soldiers. He spoke French.

"Please, Mr. Tangent," Captain Anokye said, in English. "Could we speak English? I desire very much to improve my efficiency in that language."

"Of course," Tangent said, in English. "You're doing very well. Much better than my Akan!"

"Oh? You speak Akan?"

"Badly. It is a very delicate, very poetic language."

"That is true," Anokye nodded. "After speaking Akan, English seems— hard."

"The language of action?" Tangent suggested.

Anokye considered a moment.

"Perhaps," he nodded. "Yes, I believe that to be true."

"I hate French!" Greeley burst out. "All those swallowed sounds. Can't get my tongue around them. What? What?"

"Captain, Greeley tells me the eighteen-sixty to eighteen-seventy period in Europe is your favorite."

"Oh? Well, I do admire the uniforms of that time. So much more colorful than our plain whites and khakis."

"That was the period of unification, wasn't it? In Germany and Italy?"

"Yes, Mr. Tangent, I believe it was."

"Bismarck and Garibaldi, if I remember my history."

"You remember it very well."

"Great men," Tangent persisted. "I've often wondered if great men make history or if history, the times and circumstances, produce great men. How do you feel about that, Captain?"

Anokye was silent a moment, his head turning slowly to Tangent.

"I do not believe it is either/or, Mr. Tangent," he said softly. "The man must be ready to meet the challenges of his day, if he is to achieve."

"The right man in the right place at the right time?"

"Precisely," Anokye said. He was not smiling. "Of course, much depends on what you would call luck or good fortune."

"But what the Asantis might call destiny or fate?"

Then Anokye laughed. "Oh, the Akan concept of destiny and fate is very complex, very involved. There is a destiny of the people, a destiny of the family, and of the individual. One is impelled by one's own fate, the requirements of ancestors, the demands of the tribe. I am not certain I completely comprehend it myself."

"But a faith that can be completely comprehended is not a faith at all, is it, Captain?"

Anokye was puzzled. The two little lines appeared between his brows. Then his face smoothed.

"Yes," he said, "You speak the truth. You are a wise man, Mr. Tangent."

"Thanks, but not really," Tangent laughed. "Just a good memory. I read it somewhere. Do you read a great deal, Captain?"

"As much as I can."

"Reading can be a wonderful escape."

"I do not read to escape."

It was not spoken as a rebuke, and Tangent didn't take it so. He turned the conversation to another topic, a coup d'etat that had recently occurred in Chad.

The president of that nation, Ngarta Tombalbaye, after 15 years of increasingly mercurial rule, had made a radio speech accusing the Chadian armed forces of being a corrupt "state within a state" that abused citizens and acted like "a conquering force, an army of occupation."

Ten days later soldiers stormed the presidential palace in Ndjamena, killed Ngarta Tombalbaye, and set up a military-dominated commission to run the government.

Tangent asked Captain Anokye if he believed the French assisted in the coup. Chad had originally been a French colony and retained strong economic, military, and cultural ties with France.

Anokye said he doubted if French soldiers stationed in Chad (ostensibly to protect the nation from Muslim rebels of the north) actually took part in the coup. But he had no doubt that the Chadian armed forces moved only with the acquiescence of the French, only after they had been assured French troops would not defend the government and palace of President Tombalbaye.

"Taking the palace and killing the president is one thing," Tangent said. "Ruling the nation wisely is something else again."

"That is true," the Little Captain acknowledged. "Any coup or revolt or revolution contains within itself the seeds of its own destruction if it is not broadly based, attuned to the needs of the people, and willing and able to meet those needs. Otherwise, Chad is merely exchanging one group of despots for another, military for civilian."

"You believe the military are ever capable of ruling wisely, of understanding and answering the needs of the people?"

Anokye's eyes widened.

"Why not?" he asked. "Are military leaders of the higher ranks so different from high officials in government and business? Their training is quite similar."

"One big difference," Tangent said. "Officers are accustomed merely to giving commands and having their orders obeyed. Politics is another kettle of fish. In government, actions can only be taken and progress made by consensus. I'm speaking of governments other than dictatorships and absolute monarchies, of course. But in most governments, consultations, compromise, and agreement take the place of command."

"True," Anokye said. "But I see no vital discrepancy. History's great generals and admirals did not merely command, they led. Perhaps the processes of consultation, compromise, and agreement were not formalized, but they did exist. The military leaders realized, consciously or unconsciously, that their resolve was no stronger than the resolve of their men. Just as a ruler's resolve is no stronger than the resolve of the people he rules. Does what I speak make sense to you, Mr. Tangent?"

"A great deal. We call it feedback, a term used in computer technology. Now also used in sociology. If you will allow me, I would be happy to send you a book on the subject."

"I would like that very much, and I thank you."

After that, conversation became desultory. The port was finished, and since Greeley obviously had no intention of providing another bottle, of anything, and seemed uncomfortable in their presence, Captain Anokye and Peter Tangent rose almost simultaneously to thank their host and take their leave. Standing side by side, the two men made an odd picture. The slat-thin Tangent towered over the chunky Anokye. Neither man smiled at the disparity in their heights nor remarked on it. Tangent offered to drive the Little Captain back to the Mokodi barracks. Anokye accepted the invitation gratefully. The Greeley women were nowhere to be seen when they departed.

As they headed back to the Boulevard Voltaire, Tangent said: "Captain, must you return to the barracks immediately?"

"No," Anokye said. "Officially, I am not on duty until tomorrow morning."

"It's a lovely night. I thought perhaps we might take a short drive. Perhaps north toward Gonja."

"I would enjoy that," Anokye said. "This car is very comfortable. After our military vehicles."

"To get back to the coup in Chad for a moment," Tangent said. "I'd like your advice. As you may know, I am in charge of African operations for Starrett Petroleum. We now have operating installations in eight African nations, with several others in the talking stages. One of our problems, a big problem, is the impermanence of African governments. The Chad coup is an example. Did you know it is the thirty-sixth coup d'etat in Africa since World War Two?"

"I was not aware of that, no. But it does not surprise me."

"Naturally, my people would prefer to deal with stable governments. I, personally, would like to be certain that the men I negotiate with today will still occupy their offices tomorrow. Tell me, Captain, why are African governments so volatile?"

"Volatile?"

"So explosive. Liable to change suddenly, usually by violent overthrow."

"Volatile. I must remember that word. Mr. Tangent, your nation recently celebrated its two-hundredth birthday. I know you are accustomed to think of Africa as a very ancient continent. But the new Africa is actually quite young, no more than forty years old. We have, for the most part, thrown off the shackles of colonialism. Now you will find everything in Africa, from the most repressive dictatorship to a pure democracy. The revolts and coups are symptomatic of a people seeking, almost blindly, with few precedents to guide us, a form of government that is right for us, that uses what is best in Western Civilization but modified and reworked to fit our own unique traditions and culture and needs."

"In other words, Africa is suffering from growing pains?"

"You might say that. Perhaps, at this point in our development, a military dictatorship—as much as you might dislike such a form of government—is what is needed to bring an African nation into the mainstream of the modern world. Or perhaps a democracy or a constitutional monarchy or a socialist state would serve better to develop resources, build homes, end famines, improve health, educate the people. No one really knows. So there is much fumbling about, much experimenting. That is the reason for the political instability you find in Africa."

"But I gather you are confident of the future?"

"Oh yes, I am confident. We are young, and we are strong."

"And you shall overcome?"

"Yes," Anokye laughed. "We shall overcome."

They drove awhile in silence, passing the Mokodi barracks on Asante Royal Highway No. 1, and entering the unlighted stretch that led to Gonja.

"And Asante?" Tangent asked. "You have your problems here, too."

"Many problems," the Little Captain agreed. "Serious problems."

"But they will be solved?"

Anokye was quiet a moment, framing a careful answer.

"Our problems can be solved," he said finally. "I believe that. But perhaps, at the present time, we have not the resources to solve our problems by ourselves. It may be necessary to ask for outside assistance."

Now it was Tangent's turn to remain silent as he considered how far he might go.

"I presume," he said, "you mean such things as seeking financial assistance from other people?"

"Yes," Anokye said. "I believe that will prove necessary."

"I can understand why it might be," Tangent said cautiously. "But aren't you running a risk there? Surely no people would provide funds for Asante out of the goodness of their hearts. There would have to be a tradeoff, a quid pro quo."

Anokye smiled. " 'Quid pro quo.' Strange, I looked in the dictionary for that phrase less than a week ago. A something for a something. Is that correct, Mr. Tangent?"

"Yes, that's correct."

"Of course there would be a quid pro quo," Anokye said. "It could be arranged. When two parties want the same thing for different reasons, they form a partnership, so to speak, and make an arrangement. Is that not so?"

"Usually. And usually the arrangement is formalized in a signed agreement. It prevents misunderstandings later."

"I see no reason why that could not be done," Anokye said. "For the greater good of Asante."

"Of course," Tangent said. "You are very perceptive, Captain, very understanding. Would you care for a cigarette?"

"Thank you, no."

"Do you mind if I smoke?"

"Not at all."

"Would you hold the wheel a moment, please, while I light up?"

Tangent took longer than necessary to take a packet of Players from his inside jacket pocket, pick one out, light it slowly. As his foot pressed harder on the accelerator. But Anokye's hand was steady on the wheel; the car didn't waver, although they were driving swiftly on the dark, deserted road, tree trunks flashing by on both sides.

"These problems of Asante . . ." Tangent said, taking back the wheel. "It seems to me—this is just the opinion of an observer—that they are increasing in severity and should be resolved as soon as possible."

"Yes," Anokye said gravely, "that is so."

"Within a month or two?"

The Little Captain nodded.

"Perhaps my people could be of assistance," Tangent said tentatively. "There is little of substance I can tell them at the moment, but I might make an initial presentation to see if the desire exists to come to your aid."

"Asante's aid."

"Of course. If they decide to provide assistance, I will need more details on the extent of the aid and how best it can be administered."

Anokye nodded. "The information will be made available," he said.

"It surprises me that Asante would not seek help from the French," Tangent said.

"Asante will thankfully accept aid from whatever source," Anokye said.

"And you believe there are others in Asante who feel as you do?" Tangent asked.

Captain Anokye turned his head slowly to stare at him.

"Many others," he said. "Many, many. Enough. I speak the truth, Mr. Tangent."

"I'm sure you do, Captain," Tangent said. "And you believe, with outside aid, that Asante's problems may be solved?"

"Not *all* its problems, naturally. But its most serious problems."

Tangent slowed, stopped, backed onto the verge, turned around and headed the car back to Mokodi.

"Assuming Asante's problems are solved," he said. "Not only its most serious problem, but other problems as well . . . Assuming Asante becomes a thriving, prosperous nation. Then what?"

"Why then we might become a showcase," Captain Obiri Anokye said dreamily. "A model for all of Africa. Who knows, our most important export might become our system of government with other African nations—the poor and the rich—seeking to follow in our path. Is that impossible?"

"No," Tangent said. "Not impossible. Captain Anokye, what you say impresses me."

"Does it?"

"I wonder how a man of your obvious talents and learning and vision could be content as an army captain."

"I am content."

"But surely your salary cannot be great."

"No, it is not great."

"And your family is large?"

"I am not married, but my family is large."

"Do you never think of seeking a position that might offer more rewards? Or an arrangement that might augment your income?"

"I am content," Anokye repeated, and Tangent let it go at that, intrigued by this African army captain who would not accept a bribe.

Anokye asked Tangent to drop him a kilometer from the barracks gate. The American understood the Captain's motives and obediently pulled onto the shadowed verge and stopped. But the Little Captain made no immediate effort to get out of the car.

"Do you intend to stay in Asante long, Mr. Tangent?" he asked.

"This trip? Another day or two, at least."

Anokye sat in silence a few moments, considering.

"Mr. Tangent," he said finally, "there is an army general in Togo named Songo. Do you know him?"

"No. Never heard of him."

"A man of some influence in government. Very capable. His son, Jere Songo, was educated at St. Cyr. He has now returned to Togo and is a lieutenant in the Togolese army, assigned to his father's staff. He has been sent to Asante to observe our training techniques. A nice boy. He speaks French, Ewe, Twi, and Hausa. A little English. He is being escorted by Anatole Garde, the King's secretary. Tomorrow I will stage a military exercise for Lieutenant Songo. It is, I believe, the only one of its kind in the world. You may find it of interest. Would you care to join us as an observer? Lieutenant Songo will be present, of course, and Anatole Garde. It would be an honor to have you."

"Thank you," Tangent said. "You are very kind. I'd like to join you."

"I should warn you, you will have to cover a great distance on foot. Will that inconvenience you?"

This last was spoken politely, but the challenge was unmistakable.

"I think I can manage," Tangent said. "What shall I wear?"

"Dungarees, if you have them. Or old khakis. Certainly comfortable boots."

"I keep a change at the hotel," Tangent said. "Work clothes for my visits to the *Starrett Explorer*. They should do. A hat?"

"By all means. And sunglasses. I will provide a lunch. We start at exactly oh-eight-hundred."

"I'll be there."

"I will leave word with the gate guard at the Mokodi barracks to expect you. An escort will be provided to bring you to the staging area."

"I'm looking forward to it."

Captain Anokye got out of the car. He closed the door softly. He stood with hands on hips, torso bent slightly backward. His head was tilted up; he stared at the night sky a long moment. Then he leaned to speak through the open window.

"The moon is almost full," he said. "A good omen. A time to make important decisions. The sooner the better."

"I understand," Tangent said.

13

On the following morning, at 0745, Tangent drove his rented Opel up to the gate of the Mokodi barracks and stopped. A soldier immediately emerged from the guard hut and stalked toward him.

"How may I be of service, sir?" he called, in French.

"My name is Tangent. Captain Obiri Anokye said he'd leave word to expect me."

"Ah yes," the soldier grinned, not bothering to inspect the proffered passport. "Yes, yes. The Little Captain did say you are indeed to be admitted, Mr. Tangent, sir. You come to see the Hunt?"

"The Hunt?" Tangent asked. "Is that what it's called?"

"Ah yes!" the guard laughed. His mirth was so infectious that Tangent found himself smiling in return. "Much fun, the Hunt. Bim, bam, boom!"

His own words convulsed him, and Tangent had to wait until he calmed. Then he opened the gate and directed Tangent to the motor pool area where he would find parking space in the shade and where an escort would join him.

"Thank you very much," Tangent said.

"Bim, bam, boom!" the soldier repeated, and was still laughing as Tangent drove slowly inside the compound. He found the motor pool area, found a parking space in the shade of a large corrugated metal garage, and stepped out of the car, looking about curiously.

It was not his first visit to an African military installation. He was impressed with the neat cleanliness of this one: swept walks, trimmed foliage, no litter, garage windows washed. Good discipline and daily policing. There was a sign, in French, that read: "This is your home. Treat it so."

He was still looking about when an Asanti sergeant came around the corner of the garage, striding rapidly, right arm swinging, left arm crooked and holding a fly whisk clamped tightly between bicep and thick torso. He marched up to Tangent, froze to attention, saluted smartly.

"Mr. Peter Tangent, sir?"

"Yes, I'm Tangent."

"Sir, I am detailed as your escort for the day. My name is Sergeant First Class Sene Yeboa."

"Glad to meet you, Sergeant," Tangent said, proffering his hand—then, when Yeboa gripped it, trying not to sink to his knees in anguish.

"Is it all right to park here?" he asked, flexing his fingers behind his back.

"Perfectly A-OK," Yeboa grinned. "A guest of the Captain . . ." He left that sentence unfinished, then said, "A moment, sir." He looked into the rental car, reached through the opened window, removed the ignition key, and handed it to Tangent. "We would not like to leave temptation for a thoughtless child," he said, smiling. "This way, sir. I will take you first to the staging area. The other guests have already arrived."

The sergeant set a good pace, and Tangent lengthened his stride. They struck out across a wide parade ground, avoiding squads and platoons of soldiers going through close-order drill. They looked very professional to Tangent, and he told the sergeant so.

"They are indeed good soldiers, sir," Yeboa agreed. "But I would not care to tell them that."

Both men laughed.

"I understand this exercise is called the Hunt," Tangent said. "Is that correct?"

"Do you speak Ewe, sir?"

"No, I'm afraid not. Akan, and a little Kwa."

Yeboa immediately switched from French to Akan.

"In the Ewe language, the name for this exercise is a word that means hunt, search, or to fight on bravely—depending on how the word is used. We do indeed call it the Hunt, but it means other things as well."

The sergeant marched on steadily, slightly ahead and to the right of Tangent. They passed a row of wooden barracks where half-naked soldiers were washing clothes at iron troughs, airing bedding, playing with a couple of pye-dogs, reading the Asanti *New Times*, listening to a transistor radio, or just squatting on their hams in groups, gossiping and laughing.

"Free time for this company," Yeboa explained. "Soon they will be called to school."

"School? Weapons instruction?"

"Reading and writing," the sergeant said proudly. "Every Asanti soldier must know how to read and write."

"Oh?" Tangent said. "The whole army?"

"Oh no, sir," Yeboa said. "Only Fourth Brigade. It is Captain Anokye's order."

"Ah? Tell me, Sergeant, how do the enlisted men feel about Captain Anokye?"

Yeboa stopped suddenly and turned to stare at Tangent.

"We would die for him," he said, in such a tone that Tangent could not doubt it.

They passed through another guarded gate in the chain-link perimeter fence. Now they were in an area of scrub grass, dried gullies, rocky outcrops. Sgt. Yeboa proceeded rapidly along a barely defined path that led down into a ravine and up the other side. Tangent followed, thankful for broad-brimmed hat and sunglasses. He was beginning to feel the strength of the new sun.

They came up onto a large grassland plateau with wooded areas framing it on three sides, a horseshoe of trees with the open end on the dried riverbed they had just traversed. Almost precisely in the middle of this savanna, as if deliberately planted there, was a magnificent old iroko. In the shade of its thick trunk and branches, about 30 men stood or squatted or lay full-length on the ground. As Yeboa and Tangent came up to them, Captain Anokye walked forward smiling to shake Tangent's hand.

"Welcome," he said. "It promises to be a fair day."

"As always in Asante," Tangent replied.

He turned to greet Anatole Garde, and was then introduced to Lt. Jere Songo, the Togolese observer. Songo was a youth, open-faced, still flushing with pleasure at wearing a uniform and officer's bars, taking part in the world of men. He had a charming diffidence, a nervous laugh, an obvious anxiety not to behave badly.

The Captain glanced about, and without an order given, the lounging soldiers rose immediately to their feet, straightened, formed a loose circle around Anokye and his guests. The soldiers, Tangent noted, were not armed, but each carried a slung water bottle in a covering of woven straw and a stick about a meter in length, the thickness of a stick. Each stick was tied at one end with a bulbous wrapping of rags, tightly secured and dyed a bright red.

The Little Captain addressed his guests in French:

"The exercise you are about to witness is called the Hunt. I believe it is unique with us, although I have read of these coup sticks being used elsewhere in mock warfare. By your Red Indians, as a matter of fact, Mr. Tangent. As you all know, Asante is a small nation, and I try to design the military training of Fourth Brigade to fit our special and particular needs. It would be useless, for instance, to train for amphibious landings. To what purpose? We do not possess the needed equipment, and have no desire for it. Neither are we capable of staging maneuvers of large military units, of coordinating tank and artillery attacks, of practicing airborne invasions."

"What we are faced with in Asante is terrorism by Marxist guerrillas, the illegal traffic in smuggled goods and, of course, the basic need to protect our borders and national integrity from incursions and invasion."

"Because of the geography of our country and the small size of our armed forces, it is necessary that every man in uniform be skilled in the very fundamental arts of individual survival, of tracking and avoiding pursuit, of knowing the land as he knows the palm of his hand, and being able to use the land to carry out his assigned duty."

"So we have devised this exercise. A game of hide-and-seek. One soldier is assigned to act as the quarry. He is given a head start. His duty is to avoid capture. The remaining soldiers are the pursuers. Their duty is to track down and 'kill' the hunted man within eight hours. We do not kill the captured quarry, of course, since this is only practice. But the hunted man is considered 'killed' if one of his pursuers is able to get close enough to hit or touch him with a coup stick. That knob on the end of the stick has been dipped in a dye that will leave a mark, proving whether or not the hunted man has actually been tracked down and 'killed.'

"Before the Hunt begins, I shall point out the area in which the running man must stay. He can go anywhere in that area he wishes, hide wherever he likes—up a tree, in a cave, in a swamp. But he must remain free within that area for a period of eight hours. If he does remain undiscovered, he has won the Hunt and is rewarded with two days' extra liberty. If he is found and touched with a coup stick before the eight hours are up, he has lost—and must suffer the consequences."

The assembled soldiers burst out laughing, and several brandished their coup sticks, shaking them high in the air. Then the whole group clustered around a rough, hand-drawn map that Sgt. Yeboa spread on the ground. Captain Anokye pointed out the physical limits of the Hunt: the ravine behind them, Asante Royal Highway No. 1 to the west, a large wheat field on the north, a secondary dirt road to the east.

"Any questions?" Anokye asked.

There were none.

"Now it only remains to select the quarry," the Captain said. "Sergeant . . ."

Yeboa stepped forward and began to look slowly around the circle of grinning soldiers. It was obvious to Tangent that most of the men wished to be selected. They puffed their chests, pointed at themselves, even flexed their biceps, laughing. Finally Sgt. Yeboa pointed.

"Njonjo," he said. "You."

The chosen man gave a great roar of approval and leaped high into the air. He removed his boots and socks, handed his coup stick to a comrade, and immediately began a steady run toward the nearest shield of trees. Captain Anokye looked at his wristwatch.

"We allow the hunted man thirty minutes," he said.

The soldiers relaxed again, slumping onto the ground or squatting in groups. The Little Captain took Lt. Songo aside and spoke to him in a low voice. Tangent was left alone with Anatole Garde. The two men sat on the ground in the shade of the iroko, their backs against the massive trunk.

"Have you ever seen this before?" Tangent asked.

"No, never. I had heard of it, but I have never witnessed it."

"The Little Captain spoke of the consequences if the hunted man is found and touched with a coup stick before the eight hours are up. Then all of the soldiers laughed. What are the consequences—do you know?"

"Have no idea," Garde said. "Staying long?"

"This trip? No, not long. Another day or so."

"Any word from Tulsa?"

"Not yet. Is the King getting impatient?"

"What do you think?"

They were silent then. Tangent craned his head to look, but the quarry had disappeared into the forest.

"When do you think you'll hear?" Garde asked.

"This business in Togo . . ." Tangent said. He shook his head doubtfully. "It's fouled things up. It's made my people hesitant about making any deal."

"Nothing to it," Garde said. "You can sign."

"Well . . ." Tangent said hesitantly. "The Prime Minister is going to Lomé to check it out. I think we better wait until he returns."

"Time is running out on the lease," Garde said.

"I know," Tangent said pleasantly. "It's a problem, isn't it? What do you hear from Paris?"

"Hear from Paris? What do you mean?"

"That's where your family lives, isn't it?"

"Oh. Yes, that's right. All's well, as far as I know. As usual, they complain about high prices."

"They should visit London."

"So I understand. I was hoping to get back for a week's vacation."

"Oh?" Tangent said.

"But I think now I'll stick around until this lease thing is settled. One way or another."

"Ah," Tangent said.

They watched Anokye and Songo stroll slowly up and down, conversing quietly. The Captain was shorter than Songo, but his arm was up and about the young lieutenant's shoulders.

"Nice boy," Tangent said. "Any problems?"

"No," Garde said. "He's anxious to please."

"I understand his father's a hotshot general."

"Who told you that?"

"I heard."

"Anokye," Garde said definitely. "Must have been. How did you happen to meet him?"

"Through Alistair Greeley at the bank. He invited me over for a drink, and the Little Captain showed up. Interesting man."

"Isn't he. Don't underestimate him."

"I don't."

"For instance, he's invited Songo for dinner tonight, with his family, at his home in Zabar."

"So?" Tangent said. "That's neighborly."

"I told you not to underrate him," Garde said. He laughed. "The Little Captain has a young unmarried sister. Name of Sara."

"Oh-ho," Tangent said. "Wheels within wheels."

"That's the Little Captain," Garde agreed. "Sometimes I think he's way ahead of us all."

Finally, the soldiers becoming restive, Captain Anokye looked at his watch, then nodded to Yeboa. The sergeant strode forward, and the men rose to their feet and clustered about him eagerly.

"Corporal Kibasu will be in command of the Hunt," the sergeant said. "You will follow his orders as if they came from the Captain himself."

The corporal, a short, pudgy soldier with a delicately trimmed mustache, puffed his chest and held up a hand from which three rings flashed.

"Pay heed to what I shall tell you," he said pompously. "First, we know that Njonjo is cursed with left-handedness." The assembled men groaned at this evidence of perversity. "Usually, a right-handed man, when faced with a fork in the path or choosing a way to escape, will move to the right, and a left-handed man will move to the left. Is that not so?"

The listening men, now serious, nodded their agreement, and one called out, "It is so."

"*But!*" Corporal Kibasu said triumphantly. "Second, we know that Njonjo is a sly, devious fellow. Recall what the Little Captain has told us of the need to understand the feelings and desires of the enemy, of trying always to crawl within his skin. Njonjo knows we are aware of his left-handedness. Therefore, he will deliberately turn *right* whenever possible to throw us off his track. Remember this. We will now divide into three squads. I take the center, Jomo the left, Malloun the right. Select the leader of your choice."

After a few minutes of confusion, of milling about, the soldiers divided into three approximately equal squads.

"Go!" Corporal Kibasu shouted, and the three teams began trotting toward the point where their quarry had disappeared into the trees, gradually diverging as they advanced. Captain Anokye followed at a steady walk, along with Garde and Lt. Songo. Tangent and Sgt. Yeboa brought up the rear.

"Do you think Njonjo will escape?" Tangent asked.

"No," Sgt. Yeboa said. "Jomo's team will 'kill' him."

"Is Jomo the very thin soldier without a water bottle?"

"That is the man. He is one of our best trackers. He is said to have Masai blood. I do not believe that to be true, but Jomo is very skilled. He has been the quarry three times and has never been caught."

"Is he better than you?" Tangent said. He meant it humorously, but the sergeant answered seriously.

"No," he said. "I am the best."

It was not a boast, Tangent realized. Yeboa merely spoke his truth.

"That business about being left-handed," Tangent said. "I know how Africans feel about the left hand, but is Njonjo clever enough to do as Corporal Kibasu said he would?"

Sgt. Yeboa laughed. "Oh, that fool Kibasu!" he said. "Njonjo is more clever than that. He will know how Kibasu thinks—that he will turn right to confuse the hunters. Therefore, Njonjo will turn to the left. He will be one step ahead of Kibasu in his thinking. But Jomo will pay no attention to left or right. Jomo will follow only the signs. He will reject the false signs and follow only the true ones. You will see."

Then they were into the trees, not a true rain forest but thick enough. Sgt. Yeboa led the way, bringing Tangent up behind Jomo's squad, who were moving slowly and carefully, peering left, right, up, down, forward, back. There was an exclamation from one, and almost immediately Jomo was at his side, examining a twig that hung broken to the left. Tangent watched, fascinated, as Jomo waved the other men away and dropped to his knees. He sniffed the ground slowly, exactly as a bloodhound might. Then he rose to his feet, motioned directly ahead. The men moved off silently.

"How did Jomo know it was a false lead?" he asked Yeboa.

"When a green twig is broken deliberately in that manner, the stem is slightly pinched on both sides of the break by the man's fingers. Jomo saw that, and smelled no scent of human passing to the left. Now we will stay back a little. It is important the pursuers make as little noise as possible."

"Sorry," Tangent apologized, having just snapped a dried branch under his foot. "I'm afraid I'm not doing Jomo much good."

"No, no, it's all right," Yeboa assured him. "Njonjo is far ahead at this moment. But when they close in, we must move slowly and carefully and silently. If you become thirsty, please tell me."

"Thank you," Tangent said. "But not yet."

After hearing the Hunt described by Captain Anokye, Tangent had thought he would be bored. He was not. As the initial quartering settled down, and the trackers began moving stealthily through the forest about him, he found himself caught up in the chase.

There was a low whistle off to the left, and Sgt. Yeboa led him toward it. They came to a broad-trunked plane tree where Jomo was pointing out the direction he wanted his men to take.

Jomo saw Yeboa and Tangent come up and gestured briefly at the tree before disappearing again. Yeboa moved close to inspect the tree trunk.

"What do you see?" he whispered.

"A tree trunk," Tangent whispered back.

"Feel it."

Obediently Tangent ran his fingertips down the smooth-barked surface. "Dampish," he said.

"Now smell your fingers."

Tangent sniffed cautiously. "Sweat," he said. "Human sweat."

"Very good, sir," Yeboa chuckled. "We will make a tracker of you yet. Njonjo entered into the woods a distance and immediately set about laying false trails, doubling back to his starting place. He worked very hard, very fast. Now he is finished. He is sweating. He leans against this tree to catch his breath a moment, considering what his true path should be. This is his starting place, not where he entered the woods."

The morning went faster than Tangent could have believed. They moved slowly and deliberately, Yeboa following where Jomo's trackers led. After a while Tangent began to learn how to place his feet, how to avoid low-hanging limbs and refrain from scraping against rough surfaces. They waded quietly through several marshy areas, after Yeboa showed Tangent how to cinch his trouser cuffs inside his boot tops to keep leeches out.

The trail led generally northward, as far as Tangent could determine from infrequent glimpses of the sun overhead. Some of the wood was in dappled shadow; most was dimness with birdcalls, unexplained grunts, and occasionally the sudden crash of escaping animals.

"Warthogs?" Tangent asked. Somewhat nervously. "Deer, d'you suppose? Or what?"

Sgt. Yeboa didn't answer. He was too intent on following the path of the elusive Jomo, who was following the trail of the elusive Njonjo. Occasionally he pointed out the signs to Tangent: usually nothing more than a fallen leaf, or a forest orchid with one petal scraped loose and dangling. In one swampy area, apparently the hunted Njonjo had tripped over a submerged root and fallen. He had attempted to brush away the marks of his fall with a leafy branch, but time was running out; the branch itself had been concealed but the pale scar where it had been stripped from a sapling had not been smeared with earth; it gleamed whitely in the forest gloom. And the swept area of silky mud was apparent even to Tangent's untrained eye.

After moving northward, almost to the wheat field boundary, Njonjo had left several clever false trails, then returned to his junction to begin a wide circle westward toward the paved highway. The pace of the chase increased.

Sgt. Yeboa knelt suddenly to place his fingertips in a small depression in the leaf-rank earth.

"A heelmark," he whispered to Tangent. "Fresh and deep. Njonjo is getting careless. Now I think Jomo is no more than ten minutes behind him."

"Njonjo knows this?"

"Oh yes, Mr. Tangent. He hears things, feels things. Perhaps the birds are still as he passes, then chatter angrily, then are still again. Perhaps Njonjo hears the crash of animals behind him as Jomo advances. The hunter is close behind, so Njonjo runs and becomes careless. I think you will have your lunch sooner than you expected, Mr. Tangent."

Tangent found himself trembling, and not from fatigue.

"I would like to be in on the 'kill,' " he whispered.

Sgt. Yeboa looked at him a moment, then showed his teeth.

"Jomo moves very quickly, very silently," he said, "but I will try to move up on him. Please follow me closely."

"Where are the others?" Tangent asked. "Captain Anokye, Garde, Lt. Songo?"

"Behind us," Yeboa laughed. "Following Corporal Kibasu, who moves like a sleepy water buffalo. This way now, with care."

Tangent's khakis were sweated through, somewhere along the way he had lost his sunglasses, his face had been rasped with vines, and his bare forearms and hands oozed blood from a dozen small cuts and insect bites. He didn't care. He wanted Njonjo "killed."

They made a wide circle, moving faster now as the trees thinned, and there were grassy glades where Tangent could see the sun. Looking up, to judge their direction, he stumbled into a shallow ravine, fell, slid, went rolling to the bottom. He lay a moment, fighting for breath.

Sgt. Yeboa was at his side, hauling him to his feet.

"Are you all right, Mr. Tangent, sir?" he asked anxiously. "Shall we go back?"

"No, no," Tangent said. "I'm all right. I want to go on. How close are we now?"

"Jomo is directly ahead, and no more than five minutes behind Njonjo. I think Njonjo is heading to the grassland where we started. He means to enter the ravine and run along that. He hopes to gain time that way. But Jomo runs faster; you will see. There is no reason for quiet now, Mr. Tangent. Now he cannot escape Jomo."

The pace increased. Tangent found himself running with an agonizing stitch in his side. But that eased, he caught his second wind, and went crashing after the speeding Yeboa, marveling how lightly and effortlessly the heavy man moved.

Within a few moments they were in sight of Jomo, loping steadily ahead, scarcely pausing to glance at signs of the hunted man's passing. Jomo's head was up, he seemed to be sniffing the air. He turned suddenly to the left and began to run faster. Now he carried his coup stick shoulder-high, plunging back and forth like a barbed spear.

"He sees him," Yeboa shouted back over his shoulder. "He will 'kill' him before the ravine. Hurry, please, Mr. Tangent. Hurry! Hurry!"

Tangent dug in, disregarding the ache in his thighs, his straining lungs. Sweat stung his eyes, coursed in rivulets from scalp, neck, shoulders, back, groin. He smelled himself and didn't care. He ran dementedly. Everything was in the running.

Then they came bursting from the trees, out onto the wide savanna. Ahead was the iroko tree, shading three squatting soldiers who had brought bottles and boxes of drink and food for the Captain and his guests. They saw the running men, jerked to their feet, began to leap about excitedly and yell in a language Tangent could not understand.

Njonjo, the hunted, was in the lead. He saw he could not make the ravine and sprinted desperately across the grassed plateau, hoping to reach the forest on the other side. But Jomo, the pursuer, head still high, lengthened his stride; he seemed to be taking giant leaps, almost floating, both feet apparently off the ground. Now he carried his coup stick extended, the dyed knob forward. After him came Yeboa and Tangent, and then others burst from the forest behind them, calling and shouting, everyone running, screams rising in intensity, earth rumbling from the pounding feet, coup sticks brandished, torsos glistening with sweat, the hunted man frantically plunging, almost falling forward as the relentless Jomo gained on him, gained, gave a cry of triumph and made a final great lunge to slam the knob of his coup stick against Njonjo's back, the blow heavy enough to topple the fleeing man and send him somersaulting, rolling, twisting, until he came to rest on his back, spread-eagled, and then they were all on their backs, chests heaving, but yelling, screaming, cawing, barking, growling, Tangent as loud as the others.

Finally, slowly, they quieted, and men began to rinse their mouths with water, to pour water over their heads, to strip off sodden shirts and shorts, some to stand naked in socks and boots. Njonjo rose groggily to his feet, emptied a water bottle onto his upturned face. He clapped Jomo on the shoulder. The two men embraced, called each other "brother." Captain Anokye went to them and spoke quietly. Within a moment they were grinning, nodding, looking about proudly in hopes others had heard the Captain's praise. Tangent glanced at his watch. He was amazed to see it was 1500. The hunt had lasted almost six hours. He could hardly believe the time had run so swiftly.

Sgt. Yeboa stepped forward, gave a command in Ewe. The soldiers began to form two ranks, facing each other, a meter's space between. They reversed their coup sticks, gripping them with both hands just above the dyed knob. They held the staffs as men of other countries might hold bats or sledgehammers. The Little Captain came sauntering back to where Tangent, Lt. Songo, and Garde now stood in the shade of the iroko tree, nervously waiting.

"Running the gauntlet," Anokye said pleasantly, looking at Tangent. "An ancient custom, known in many lands. The price the loser must pay. He proves his manhood by how slowly he moves between the files. He may run swiftly or he may stroll. The choice is his to make."

Njonjo, head high, chose to stroll. The blows that fell upon his bare back were not light. They made a ripe, smacking sound, some of them powerful enough to knock him forward. But he never hurried his pace. Tangent saw that buttery black back suddenly riven with red. Then flowing. By the time Njonjo emerged from the gauntlet, now moving shakily, he was wearing a crimson cape, blood dripping onto his legs, onto the thirsty African soil. But he had not cried out. After the last blow had landed, the punished man turned to his tormentors, tried a grin, raised a wavering fist above his head.

Then a great roar of approval went up, coup sticks were tossed high into the air, his comrades rushed forward to hug his bloody torso. A sling of crossed fists was fashioned, Njonjo was seated, and the soldiers 'departed with the "killed" man carried aloft in triumph.

Tangent turned to Anatole Garde.

"What do you think of that?" he asked, his voice high.

"Appalling," Garde said. "You?"

"Thrilling," Tangent said.

14

In the past year or so, a strange thing had been happening to Josiah Anokye, the 82-year-old father of the Little Captain. His three sons—the oldest Zuni, Obiri, and the youngest Adebayo—had spoken of it amongst themselves. Their first thought was that their father, because of his age, was going soft in the head.

He would say odd, unexpected things that had nothing to do with what was being spoken at the moment. For instance, he might—very intent— suddenly say, "When the wind is from the west, as it is today, and it is difficult to breathe, and the clouds move fast and high, then pull the boat far up on the beach." Zuni, who captained the Anokye fishing boat, already knew this.

Or Josiah might say, "When a man you scarcely know becomes suddenly friendly and claps you on the shoulder, he plans mischief toward you." Or, "When gutting a fish, always move the blade away from you."

Or he might repeat ancient Akan proverbs: "Poverty has no friends," or, "When a rich man gets drunk, he is indisposed." (This latter very similar to the English-language saying: "The poor man is crazy; the rich man is eccentric.")

So his sons thought that Josiah, reciting these things at odd times, might be getting soft in the head. But then they realized it was not that. The old man sensed the onset of death, and since he had no wealth to leave to his sons, he was determined to leave them the accumulated experience and wisdom of his 82 years. He just wanted to help them; he was not soft in the head.

That night, for instance, the three sons and their father sat on the sandy beach of Zabar and watched as sister Sara and Lt. Jere Songo waded in the warm water up to their knees, laughing, chattering, whispering.

"He is a fine boy," Zuni said. "But shy."

"Yes," the Little Captain smiled. "But not with Sara."

"What do you know of his family?" Josiah asked.

"In his country," Obiri said, "his father is a man of importance, a general in the army and with power in the government."

"What would he pay for Sara?" the old man asked.

His face was a walnut, his head almost completely bald, covered always with a watch cap of blue knitted wool topped with a pompon that had once been red. The old man's body was all rope and twine, muscles and veins distinct through thin, wrinkled skin. He had once killed a shark with a knife, in the water with the big fish. That was the truth; men who had witnessed the fight still spoke of it with awe.

"Pay for Sara?" Obiri said. "It is too early to speak of such things."

"Not too early," Adebayo said in a low voice, hesitant to state his opinion in the presence of his elders. "See how he touches her hand? And she is drawn to him."

"How can you say?"

"She comes alive in his presence." Then, when they laughed, the young man said indignantly, "Well, is it not so? You see. She has a love for him."

"When I was their age," Josiah said, "we bought our wives. As I did your mother. That was the mark of a man's love: what he would pay for a woman. Now, today, this is said to be old-fashioned and bad. Now they must love each other, and that is enough. But I do not see that marriage is better for it. Love goes, but an investment lasts. A man who gives part of his wealth for his wife does not wish to be thought a fool for making a bad bargain. When he has given nothing of value for her, or she has brought no dowry, why should they remain together if their love goes? An investment insures the marriage will last until they are grown together, two edges of the same knife. Bibi, will you marry soon?"

"Yes, Father," Obiri said. "Soon. But I have work to do first."

"It goes well?" Zuni asked quietly.

"Yes."

"And the Nyam?"

"When a man wishes to take a wife," the old man intoned, "it is best to deal with an uncle, not the father. It may be necessary to say the woman desired is without beauty, she has a squint in one eye, she is a bad cook, and so forth. A father might respond to these things with anger. But an uncle, being once removed, will understand they are but bargaining, and he will praise the woman, pointing out her strength, her soft voice, how she always grinds the eggplant seeds."

"The Nyam sent word," Obiri said to Zuni. "He will end his terrorism, and will join us if we move within a period of one month."

"And if we do not act within a month?" Zuni asked.

"An uncle," Josiah nodded. "An older brother of the woman's father is best, since he has lived longer and has more experience. A gift is brought to him to prove good faith. He will then provide food and drink, a good meal to show the wealth of his family. Then the talk may begin. The man who wishes to marry should not speak for himself, but should be represented by his father, an older married brother, or by an uncle."

"Then the Nyam will resume his raids," Obiri said.

"You agreed to this, Bibi?" Adebayo asked hesitantly.

"Yes," the Little Captain nodded. "Since I had no choice. Also, things now move swiftly. I have been approached by a man named Tangent who represents the oil company. The money for the weapons may come from him. Or from the French, who are not happy with the reign of King Prempeh."

"The talk may take days, weeks, even months," Josiah said, remembering. "Your mother's sister, your Aunt Jemin, was not purchased until talk had continued for almost a year. It is not a matter to be taken lightly. But if the man and woman come from good families, an agreement may be reached that benefits both. Do not speak loudly or shake your fist or stamp the ground. Speak softly, gravely, and with respect. The other family will think more of you for this. Act with dignity. It is a matter of importance."

Zuni considered a moment, then addressed Obiri:

"You mean to play the oil company against the French?"

"Not I. But I believe that to be Abraham's plan. He has so acted that both Tangent and Anatole Garde, the King's secretary who represents the French, know of each other's interest. It is, I think, a good plan. Abraham is a wise man and knows more of these things than I do."

"You trust him?" Zuni asked.

"If the man truly wishes the woman, and cannot live his life without her, and would give all his wealth for her," Josiah went on steadily, "the man who speaks for him should not mention this. That is why it is best the man does not speak for himself. The man who speaks for him—the father, older brother, uncle—says only that man who wishes to marry is not certain in his own mind, that he wants only a woman to make his home, that he thinks frequently of other women. And so forth. The passion must be concealed. Or the price goes up."

"Abraham?" Obiri said. "Yes, I trust him. I must trust others; I cannot do it all myself. Abraham says he acts from his love of Asante, and I believe him. But he is not a simple man. He delights in riddles and puzzles. He plays chess very well. He wishes to solve problems. He finds pleasure in that."

"And he believes he can solve Asante's problems?"

"He believes so," the Little Captain nodded. "And I believe he can. Most of Asante's problems are money problems, and Abraham is skilled in moving money about. Like chess pieces."

"In the end," the father said, "it usually happens that the man gives more than he first intended. The time spent in talk has made him impatient. He wishes to make his home. The woman begins to seem more valuable to him as the bargaining continues. So, finally, defeated by desire, he offers more than he knows is wise, and his offer is accepted. Then he may become sorry, and wonder if he has acted the fool. But the agreement has been made, and he cannot withdraw. Usually it turns out well."

The four Anokye men were silent then, watching Sara and Lt. Jere Songo frolicking in the surf, splashing each other, laughing. Occasionally touching.

"You will marry soon, Bibi?" Josiah asked again.

"Soon, Father."

"Good," the old man said. "If not, who will make your fufu?"

15

Starrett Petroleum, Inc., leased a small suite at the Savoy for the convenience of transient VIPs. It was there the Man from Tulsa and the Man from New York stayed during their short visit to London. Tangent considered holding the conference dinner there or at a private dining room in Brindleys. But because of security problems, he finally decided to have them over to his Connaught suite. His premises were "swept" electronically twice a week. He was, he admitted to himself, paranoiac in his fear of shared secrets.

He had gone to a great deal of trouble and expense in planning the menu and selecting the wines.

"You're bribing us, Pete," the Man from Tulsa said, helping himself to more of the smoked salmon flown down from the north of Scotland.

"If I'm going to be bribed," the Man from New York said, holding his white beaujolais to the light, "this is the way to do it, Peter."

They were dressed like twins. Artfully tailored suits of some dark, sheeny material, pale blue shirts, silver satin ties. And tasseled black patent moccasins to prove their swinging informality. Their fingernail polish was colorless, but it was fingernail polish. They smiled frequently. Up to their eyes. They were not quite twins; one wore a toupee. But which, Tangent never could decide.

He had planned his presentation carefully. He waited until coffee and cognac had been brought, Cuban cigars offered, the door softly closed behind the departing serving staff. Then he listed their options.

"First," he said, "we can give Prempeh exactly what he wants—fifty-five to Asante and ten to him."

"Sheeyut," the Man from Tulsa said.

"On a two-year lease?" the Man from New York said. "And no guarantee that he won't raise the ante next time, or kick our ass out? No way."

"Second," Tangent said, "we can knock Prempeh. It could be bought. But to what purposes? He has five sons, a dozen bastards, countless brothers, uncles, cousins. Get rid of him, and we'd have another one just like him to deal with."

"Sheeyut," the Man from Tulsa said.

"Third," Tangent said, "withdraw from Asante completely."

They both stared at him, and he added hastily, "All right, all right, I just wanted to explore all our options, no matter how ridiculous."

The Man from New York ran a vividly red tongue around the rim of his brandy snifter.

"Peter," he said gently, "we know you didn't bring us three thousand miles to tell us to pick up our chips and go home. What are you finagling?"

"Spell it out, son," the Man from Tulsa said.

Tangent talked steadily for almost 20 minutes, telling them about Captain Obiri Anokye. He told them about the Little Captain's reputation in his own country, the loyalty he inspired, the bodies he owned. He spoke of the dreadful conditions in Asante, the poverty and starvation outside of Mokodi. He told them of the French investment, the role of Garde. He mentioned—casually, briefly—what he had already done to locate sources of weapons. He suggested Starrett finance a coup d'etat.

They were interested. The questions began.

"Did you check this out with State?"

"No. State is cold on Africa. No interest. I checked it out with Virginia. They couldn't care less."

"The French?"

"A problem. They hold the bonds. And they're jealous of their hegemony in Africa."

"Hegemony?" the Man from Tulsa asked.

"Power. I don't know how they'll jump."

"What guarantee would we have?"

"The very minimum would be a signed statement from Anokye before we started. X percentage for Y years. On paper and on tape. We get it first, or no guns. If he shits us, we release it to the world press. It would kill him in Asante."

"This Abraham—what's his gimmick?"

Tangent took a chance. "He wears dark suits, like yours. Blue shirts and silver ties, like yours. Tasseled patent moccasins, like yours. You can talk to him."

Both men laughed.

"Pete, you really are a red-ass," the Man from Tulsa said. "You know that?"

"All right," the Man from New York said. "Now let's get down to the nitty-gritty. How much?"

"Maybe a mil," Tangent said. "Maybe half a mil. Within those limits. I can't tell you exactly until I get a report from Leiberman. But in situations like this, I'd rather go for more than less. If we skimp, we're dead."

"Who gets the dineros?" the Man from Tulsa asked.

"Ah," Tangent said. "Good point. No one does. We buy the weapons and deliver to Anokye. That's my plan. I'll have to go through Leiberman, a thief. But his kickbacks will be mild compared to what we could lose delivering cash to a bunch of hungry niggers."

His language was brutal and deliberate. He knew his audience. But he had the uneasy feeling he might be trying slang in a foreign language. They'd know.

But—"Makes sense to me," the Man from Tulsa said.

"I'll buy that," the Man from New York said. "What about time?"

"Immediately," Tangent said. "I've stalled as long as I can with the Togo ploy. It's all smoke, but it served to scare off the competition. Now we've got to move. I don't want the French getting in before us."

The two men stared at each other a long time.

"Want me to leave the room?" Tangent asked.

"Don't be anal," the Man from New York said. "We're trying the permutations and combinations."

"There's a pisspot full of oil out there," the Man from Tulsa said. "You know that, don't you, Pete?"

"Sure."

There was silence again while Tangent poured a little more brandy into their balloons.

"How much can you get from Anokye?" the Man from New York finally asked.

"Forty-nine percent tops," Tangent said. "No one can get more. I'll stake my life on it. I'll ask for sixty, of course. And a twenty-year lease."

"And this lagniappe?" the Man from Tulsa asked.

Tangent stared at him, amazed that such a man should know such a word. Even if he pronounced it "lanny-yappy."

"Not a cent," he said. "I swear to that."

"Seems to me you're swearing to a lot tonight, Peter," the Man from New York said. Eyes cold. "And 'staking your life' on a lot. I'm just repeating what you've said."

"That's right," Tangent agreed. "I'm going all the way on this. My cock."

Again they were silent, but moving about, tasting cold coffee, warm brandy, crossing and recrossing their legs. Tangent said nothing.

"Your bottom line looks real good to us," the Man from Tulsa said finally.

"Glad to hear it," Tangent said.

Then the two men looked at each other. If a signal passed, Tangent didn't see it.

"Sheeyut," the Man from Tulsa said. "We got no choice, do we?"

"Keep the cost down," the Man from New York said. "We'll go a mil, but we'll scream. Over, and you're out. Half a mil will make us real happy."

"Got it," Tangent said, rising. "And now, gentlemen, I've lined up some entertainment for this evening that I don't think will disappoint you."

"Lead me to it," the Man from Tulsa said.

"I'll just call the ladies and see if they're ready," Tangent said. "Sorry I can't join you, but I want to get moving on this Asante thing. Cables, and so forth."

They didn't seen disappointed at his inability to spend the evening with them. Relieved, rather. Tangent felt it and turned back to address the Man from Tulsa.

"By the way," he said, "the lady you'll meet tonight really is a Lady."

"What?"

"She's a Lady. Peerage. Lady Sybil."

"Wow," the Man from Tulsa said.

"Six months ago she had a dose of the clap," Tangent said cruelly. "But I think she's okay now."

Two hours later Tangent was seated at a small banquette, with Tony Malcolm, in the grill at Brindleys. It was a Saturday night; the bar was crowded. The decibel count was satisfactorily high. They could lean toward each other and talk briskly.

"You're taking an awful risk, Peter," Malcolm said. "I mean *you*, personally."

"I know," Tangent agreed. "They as much as told me. If it goes sour, I'm out."

"Nice boys." Malcolm said.

"They do their job. I don't like them any more than they like me. But who says you have to like the people you work with?"

"Not me," Tony Malcolm said.

"They're such cold cruds," Tangent said, looking down at his glass, using the wet bottom to make interlocking circles on the wooden tabletop. "They make it all seem tawdry."

"What you're doing in Asante?"

"Yes," Tangent said. "No," Tangent said. "I'm not making much sense, am I?"

"No, you're not."

"How's this: When I'm in London, especially when I'm here at Brindleys, trading grins with all these slick movers and shakers, what I'm doing in Asante seems tawdry. Cut-and-dried. Cheap. But when I'm in Asante, I come alive. It's exciting, and worth the candle. It moves me."

"Moves you?" Malcolm said. "Oh boy."

"Yes, moves me," Tangent insisted. "You haven't met Captain Obiri Anokye."

"He moves you?"

"Yes, goddammit, he does. He believes in himself. Utterly. Do you or I? He's a complete man. No doubts. No doubts at all. Oh hell, I suppose that occasionally at three in the morning he wonders. But the impression he gives is of absolute purpose. That he can't miss."

"Can't miss what?"

"Taking Asante. And then on. And on. And on."

"Like what?"

"All of Africa."

"Peter, you're joking?"

"I swear I'm not. This is my take on the man. He sweats power. Tony, you know I'm very perceptive about people, and I tell you Anokye wants all of Africa, and if anyone can do it, he can. He's got balls. Did you get rid of Bob Curtin?"

"Goes home on Monday."

"Good. Replace him yet?"

"No."

"Don't until all this is over. Or Virginia will get blamed for it."

"We'll get blamed anyway," Malcolm said mournfully. "We always do."

"That's true," Tangent laughed. "Ready for another?"

When Malcolm nodded, Tangent looked around to signal the waiter. He pointed toward their empty glasses. A man at the bar caught his eye, smirked, winked lewdly.

"Julien Ricard's at the bar," Tangent said. "Drunk as a skunk."

"Oh?" Malcolm said. "This Little Captain of yours—how old is he?"

"Twenty-six."

"Twenty-six!"

"So?" Tangent said. "Napoleon was a general at twenty-four. Michelangelo finished the *David* at twenty-nine. Mozart—"

"All right, Peter, all *right*. You've made your point."

"And Keats—"

"Gotcha!" Malcolm said. He burst out laughing. "Keats was fucking *dead* at twenty-six."

"Well, you, know what I mean," Tangent said. "Anokye is alive and well and ambitious at twenty-six."

"A young Alexander," Malcolm murmured, and they were silent while their new drinks were served.

"How's he going to do it?" Malcolm asked.

"Anokye and Africa? I haven't the slightest at this stage. I doubt if he knows. But it's on his mind; I know it is. Tony, it makes sense. The whole continent is balkanized. Every time you pick up the *Times*, there's a new nation. And most of them smaller and poorer than Jersey City. They've got no political or economic clout. But the potential! Oil. Minerals. And a consumer market that hasn't even been tapped. Don't think the French don't know it. They want—"

"And speaking of the French," Malcolm said, rising. "Hello, Julien. Join us?"

"Thank-oo, no," Ricard said. "Siddown, siddown. Dropped by to see what mischief you two were plotting."

He stood before them, swaying slightly, his features trying for a sardonic smile. He settled for a vacuous grin.

"No mischief," Tangent said. "Just exchanging dirty jokes."

"I know a dirty joke," Ricard said, trying to drain a few drops from an empty glass.

"Tell us," Malcolm said.

"There's this Frenchman and this American and this Jew," Ricard mumbled.

"I like it already," Tangent said.

"How does it end?" Malcolm said.

Ricard stared at them. Slowly his face congealed into a scowl.

"Smartass," he said. "Isn't that what you'd say, Tangent?"

"No," Tangent said. "I really don't believe I'd say that."

"How does it end?" Ricard muttered. "You'll find out. And soon."

He turned abruptly, walked stiffly back to the bar, banged his glass down, shouted something. Men turned slowly to look at him with distaste.

"Nasty bastard when he's drunk," Tangent said.

"Isn't he?" Tony Malcolm said. "The French should stick to wine. By the way, Peter, there's another Frenchman I wanted to speak to you about. A man named St. Clair. In Togo. Do you know him?"

"St. Clair? René St. Clair? A newspaperman in Lomé? Writes a political column?"

"That's the man."

"Sure. I know him."

"He's dead. Died a few days ago."

"I'm sorry to hear that," Tangent said. "He did some favors for me. Years ago. Was it in the London papers?"

"Of course not. Our resident in Lomé sent me a bullet. St. Clair is supposed to have died in a car accident, but our resident doesn't think it was kosher."

"That's odd," Tangent said.

"Isn't it? St. Clair did some favors for us, too. I'm understandably concerned."

"Of course."

"Peter," Tony Malcolm said, "you *are* telling me everything you're doing down there, aren't you?"

"Tony, have I ever held out on you?"

"Not tonight—I hope."

16

Sam Leiberman, clean, sober, well-dressed, rented a Datsun in Mokodi and, with his Ivory Coast girl giggling beside him—her lap filled with presents for her relatives—drove at a sedate speed along the coastal road to Accra. At the border, he offered their passports, properly validated, each containing within its pages a "sincere dash," not too large, not too small. They were waved through with grave courtesy.

They spent the night at Sekondi-Takoradi, drank two bottles of Spanish white, ate four crayfish swimming in a sauce of cream, paprika, tiny shrimp, and little chunks of hot pork sausage. Then they made love on the floor of their hotel room. The Ivory Coast girl sat astride Sam Leiberman, squeezed his balls, and he had never been happier.

They were on the road again early the next morning (another bottle of chilled Spanish white on the seat between them), and were into Abidjan by 1400. Leiberman turned north and delivered his girl to her squealing family at Sikensi. Gifts were bestowed, the Spanish wine was finished along with a bottle of Algerian red, and by 1700 Leiberman, alone now, was eating a peppery fish stew at a hotel restaurant in Ndouci. He washed it down with two jugs of millet beer and couldn't stop belching.

He drove west from there, toward Agboville, and turned off the improved road onto a one-lane earth track. It led back into the rain forest and ended at wrought-iron gates suspended from two painted concrete pillars. One bore a brass plaque: "R. Firenza. Antiquities." Leiberman nudged the unlocked gate with the Datsun's front bumper, and the wings swung wide. He drove slowly onto a graveled driveway before a pillared mansion that resembled an antebellum Mississippi plantation home. Complete with verdant lawn and mossed trees.

"Frankly, my dear," Leiberman quoted aloud, "I don't give a damn."

He pulled the brass plunger, and the small black who answered the door let him in without question. Leiberman followed the ancient houseman into the shaded entrance hall, then moved closer and goosed him. The old man leaped, turned, grinned.

"Oh *you*!" he said in English.

"Me again," Leiberman said. "Stay loose, Saki."

Doctor Ramon Firenza was, as usual, in his paneled study, behind his splendid old American rolltop desk which had, somehow, found its way to this corner of Africa. And, as usual, the Doctor was examining a scarab with the aid of an enormous magnifying glass with a carved ivory handle.

"Ah," the Doctor said, looking up but not rising. "Peck's Bad Boy."

"Pecker's bad boy," Leiberman said. "Ask me to sit down and offer me a drink."

"Won't you sit down?" Firenza said. "And would you care for a glass of champagne?"

"Yes and yes," Leiberman said.

He flopped into a leather club chair and said nothing until the houseman brought a bottle of chilled Piper, two glasses, and served. Leiberman took a deep swallow, smacked his lips noisily, wiped his mouth on the back of his meaty hand, looked around at the museum. All small antiquities, displayed and mounted with loving care. Bone fragments, ivory chips, stone carvings, incised jewels, hammered gold, jade pendants, religious relics, raw diamonds.

"Worth a king's ransom," Leiberman said. "Except kings aren't worth much these days."

"True," Firenza chuckled. "They are not. And how may I serve you? Cleopatra's personal dildo? A shinbone from St. Peter? A Cro-Magnon horse? Perhaps Napoleon's penis, removed after his death on St. Helena. The provenance is impeccable. It's mummified now, of course."

"I've got one in the same condition," Leiberman said. "Actually, I'm looking for something a little more modern. How are you fixed for AR-15s? Or Kalashnikovs? Or Uzis?"

Doctor Firenza sighed. He was a tiny man, squirming in a shiny black alpaca suit. Leiberman didn't know what he was—Spanish, Portuguese, Berber, Egyptian, Lebanese; it was impossible to tell. He spoke dozens of languages, all with the accent of another. Once, as a joke, Leiberman had memorized a few phrases in Choctaw and tried them on the Doctor. He was answered immediately in that language, although later Firenza confessed he spoke Choctaw with a Cherokee accent.

"What is it, exactly, you desire?" he asked. Speaking French now, in a light, frilly voice.

Leiberman pulled his shirt from the front of his pants, unzipped a money belt, took out a folded square of onion-skin paper. He smoothed it out before he tossed it onto Firenza's desktop.

"My shopping list," the mercenary said.

The Doctor used his magnifying glass to read the numbers and types of weapons.

"You intend to invade Egypt?" he asked finally.

"Something like that," Leiberman said. "Well?"

"Most of it, but not all of it," Firenza said. "Where I cannot provide, suitable substitutions can be made."

"Let me be the judge of that," Leiberman said. "What about the mortars?"

"Most difficult."

"I didn't ask that. Can you get them?"

"I'll need time."

"How much time?"

"Three months."

"Forget. Give me my list. I'll try Darami."

"How soon then?"

"A month."

"Oi, vay," Doctor Ramon Firenza said. "A month? Well, of course, on special orders, the price goes up. Naturally."

"Naturally," Leiberman said. "I need an estimate to take to my people. How much? In American dollars?"

"In the neighborhood of a million," Firenza said.

"That's a rich neighborhood for a poor nebbish like me," Leiberman said. "Try again. Try a neighborhood of half a mil America. A real ghetto."

"Absurd," Firenza said. "But surely we can work something out. We each give a little, we each take a little. It's the story of civilization. Whatever we agree upon, I would prefer Swiss francs."

"It can be arranged," Leiberman said. "Delivery?"

"Oh no," Firenza said. "No no no. FOB Sassandra is the best I can do. After that, it's your problem."

"Keep the list," Leiberman said. "If it's go, I'll send a signal. See how I trust you, Doctor?"

Firenza spread his hands wide. He leaned toward Leiberman, sincere.

"Why should we not trust each other?" he asked. Earnestness in his voice. "Have we not worked together pleasantly and profitably in the past? Your five percent, of course. I accept that. I welcome it. You labor hard, you risk your life, you are entitled. But trust between us is everything. If we have no trust, then what have we? We deliver our lives to each other. Because we have faith in each other's integrity."

"You're fucking-ay right," Sam Leiberman said.

He drained his champagne and was about to rise when a French door leading to a patio opened suddenly. A youth stood posed. Soft, slender, tawny, wearing a tiny bright pink bikini brief.

"My ward," Doctor Ramon Firenza said hastily.

"Another one?" Leiberman said. "What a kind, generous man you are."

"Am I interrupting, Uncle?" the youth caroled. In Boulé.

"Not at all, Michael," Firenza said. "Come in, come in. Our business is concluded. This gentleman was just leaving."

The long-haired youth entered, came close to Firenza's side, pressed his nylon-sheathed load against the doctor's arm, slid a squid hand across the doctor's shoulder, caressed his neck.

Firenza blinked at Leiberman.

"It is not the fact that he is a boy," he said, in French. "It is the youth."

"I understand," Leiberman said gravely.

He drove away from the shaded mansion, down the dirt track, then stopped the Datsun about 100 meters before it joined the improved road. He got out of the car, raised the hood. Then he took three signet rings from the canvas musette bag on the rear seat. He put the rings on the index, middle, and third fingers of his right hand. One of the rings was steel, the other two a cheap pot metal. They were all heavy studs.

He waited patiently, sure, leaning against the warm front fender. It was almost 20 minutes before the trim Fiat sportscar came tearing down the earth track from the home of Doctor Ramon Firenza. Michael, the ward, was driving. He was wearing a yellow short-sleeved sports shirt with a little alligator embroidered on the breast, and white linen slacks. He slowed to a halt behind the parked Datsun. Leiberman walked toward him slowly, smiling.

"Something is not working," he said, bending at the window at the driver's side. "I have stalled and cannot get started. Do you know machinery?"

"No, I do not," Michael said crossly. "I must get on. I will push you off the road. Then I will send you a mechanic from Ndouci."

"Perhaps if you took a look . . . ?"

"I tell you I know nothing of machinery."

Leiberman sighed, jerked open the Fiat's door suddenly, grabbed a handful of the long hair, and dragged the shocked youth out onto the road. He spun him around, set him up, and crashed his armored fist twice, rapidly, into the boy's face. The nose broke on the first blow; blood sprayed. The second smash splintered the front teeth. The slender youth fell curling into the dust.

He wasn't carrying it, but Leiberman found it in the glove compartment of the Fiat: a sealed envelope addressed to M. Anatole Garde, Royal Palace, Mokodi, Asante. It was marked "Personal." Leiberman didn't even bother opening it; just tore it into small bits and tucked the pieces of paper into Michael's hip pocket.

Then he pulled the boy to his feet, propped him against the side of the car, slapped his face lightly. Michael didn't come around. Leiberman left him propped there, got a water bottle from his Datsun, poured some on the youth's head, some onto his face, some into his mouth. The blood thinned, running down the yellow sports shirt, the white linen slacks.

"Better?" Leiberman asked solicitously.

Michael nodded groggily.

"I think you better go back to Doctor Firenza," Leiberman said. "I think you better tell him what happened. Tell him his letter is in your hip pocket. Got that?"

The youth looked at him dazedly.

"Understand what I just said?" Leiberman asked.

Michael blinked his eyes.

"Good. Tell the Doctor I'll be in touch, and that trust between us is everything." Leiberman paused to inspect the boy's shattered face. "Mike," he said, "your career as a ward is ended. Sorry about that."

17

In France, in Paris, on the Avenue Montaigne, stands a restaurant that has had, during its distinguished history, one name, L'escargot d'Or, and a dozen façades—all of which have carefully preserved the scars of three musket balls fired into the original plaster during the French Revolution.

The two-star restaurant serves the public only on the ground floor. But there is a secluded dining room on the second floor available for private parties, conferences, discreet meetings of industrialists, labor leaders, church dignitaries, bankers, diplomats, etc. It is said that this dining room was once connected, via a secret sliding panel, to a bedchamber. But there is no evidence of that today.

On the third Wednesday of each month, the second floor of L'escargot d'Or was reserved for a banquet of Le Club des Gourmets. This prestigious association of food and wine fanciers never numbered more than 24. New members were elected only upon the death (frequent) or resignation (rare) of an existing member. Dues were nominal, but each member, in turn, was required to plan and pay for the monthly banquet at L'escargot d'Or for the entire Club.

A member's reputation as a gourmet depended upon the creativity of the dinner he provided, in consultation with the restaurant's master chef and executive staff. It was said that, on occasion, Club members had gone into debt to finance a memorable banquet. But it was also known that certain members had greatly advanced their careers by the originality and daring of the feasts they had furnished. Members of Le Club des Gourmets came mostly from the Bourse, Quai d'Orsay, Elysée Palace, and from multinational corporations and international cartels. There were also a few Parisian merchants, of newspaper publishing, auto making, asparagus canning.

The dining chamber itself was long and narrow, barely wide enough to accommodate table and chairs, and to allow room for serving. It was mostly dark mahogany and stained glass, both patinaed with the cigar smoke of generations. There were four rather scruffy chamois and mountain-goat heads mounted on the walls, and a series of faded chromolithographs showing the Eiffel Tower under construction. Otherwise, decoration was minimal. The business was eating.

On this particular Wednesday evening, the menu was the responsibility of Julien Ricard. It included pheasant pâté en croute, ris de veau à la financière en vol-au-vent, langoustes à la Parisienne, and riz à l'impératrice. But the only unusual dish was the soupe aux truffes Elysée. The original recipe was the creation of master chef Paul Bocuse for a luncheon at the Elysée Palace during which he was awarded the Legion of Honor by the President of France. The soup, baked with a pastry topping, had been craftily selected by Julien Ricard in homage to the Man from the Palace, one of Monsieur le President's closest advisers, and himself President of Le Club des Gourmets. Wines served included a '47 Château Margaux, Pouilly Fuissé, Krug '28. Coffee, Kirsch, Grand Marnier, and Remy Martin were offered from a sideboard after the cheese and sauterne. Cigars were available.

Members congratulated Ricard on his dinner, to his face. But amongst themselves, during private after-dinner conversations, most agreed that except for that truffle soup, it had been a pedestrian affair. Palatable, but undistinguished.

Unfortunately, Julien Ricard worked out of the same Quai d'Orsay office that employed Anatole Garde, in Asante. And the upper floor of L'escargot d'Or had been completely and cleverly equipped with listening devices and recording apparatus. So that on the following day, Ricard was able to hear tapes of the private comments of his fellow Club members. He was not amused.

The room had emptied out by midnight. The table had been cleared, lights dimmed. Julien Ricard remained. And two other men. Both were portly, wearing heavy, dark suits with high vests draped with golden chains. One, the Man from the Bourse, wore the ribbon of the Legion of Honor in his lapel. The other, the Man from the Palace, the President of the Club, had been a hero of the Resistance and bore the scars: a black patch over one eye, a steel hook for a hand. Thin white hair did not conceal a small metal plate set into his skull.

They dawdled over a final cognac while Ricard filled them in on what was happening in Asante. He spoke rapidly, vehemently, with the truculence they expected. He told them it was evident, from Garde's reports and other intelligence, that Asante was on the verge of a coup d'etat.

Ricard was a Cassius, dark, saturnine, with the body of a fencer. Nose and chin were long, skin olive, lips pale and compressed. No one doubted his intelligence or his patriotism; it was his judgment that was questioned in some quarters. He made his anti-Americanism superfluously evident, and it was known that on his frequent trips to England, he gambled heavily at a private London club. He seemed to win more often than he lost. But still . . . was it wise for a man in his position?

Ricard could not sit still, but paced about the darkened dining room, touching his birthmark as he related the most recent developments in Asante. The other two men, hands and steel claw folded comfortably over their bellies, listened in silence. They followed him with their eyes as he stalked about.

"As I see it," he said, "we have three alternatives. One: We can instruct Garde to do everything in his power to smash this coup and provide him the means for doing it. Two: We can take certain steps to remove Captain Anokye from the scene. It would be arranged. Three: We can offer assistance to this Anokye. In effect, take over the coup ourselves. Well?"

"Or four," the Man from Bourse rumbled, "we can do absolutely nothing."

"Nothing?" Ricard said angrily. "And let the Americans take over Asante?"

"Julien, Julien," the Man from the Palace said mildly. "You must not let your dislike of the Americans affect your good sense. Surely things are not as bad as you suggest. We agreed to let Starrett Petroleum develop Asante's oil resources. We had Prempeh's assurance they would eventually be expropriated. Let the Americans spend their dollars."

"And what if this Little Captain takes over with the aid of the Americans?" Ricard asked. "What guarantee do we have that he will honor Prempeh's assurance?"

"There is that, of course," the Man from the Bourse said. "Have representations been made to this man, this Anokye?"

"Nothing definite."

"Why not?"

"Because at this point we have no definite proof of his intentions. We have a hook into him: the chief teller of the bank, a man Anokye consults on military matters. So far, according to Garde, no mention has been made of a coup being planned. Still, the evidence is overwhelming: the economic condition of Asante, the starvation and unrest in outlying districts, the terrorism of Marxist guerrillas, Anokye's personal popularity, Abraham's leadership of the veterans' organization, Anokye's sudden friendship with Peter Tangent, who is Starrett's man in Asante. It all adds up to a military coup. We ignore all these danger signals at our peril."

"I think you exaggerate," the Man from the Bourse said. "As far as I can see, nothing has yet occurred to justify alarm."

"Still . . ." the Man from the Palace said.

"Prempeh is a dolt, a pig, a thief," the Man from the Bourse said.

"Agreed," the Man from the Palace said. "But rather the devil you know . . ."

"The loss might be considerable," the Man from the Bourse said. "But I have no wish to create a dangerous precedent. I need hardly tell you we have other interests in Africa, of more importance."

"And of more value," the Man from the Palace said.

"Gentlemen," Ricard said, the birthmark livid, "if your purpose is to confuse me, you are succeeding admirably."

Both men stared at him, without mirth.

"In situations like this," the Man from the Bourse said slowly, "my instinct is to preserve the status quo."

"I think I agree," the Man from the Palace said slowly.

"Therefore?" Ricard asked impatiently. "Shall we remove Anokye?"

"Oh, I wouldn't do that," the Man from the Bourse said. "Until it becomes absolutely necessary."

"Your first alternative," the Man from the Palace said. "Instruct Garde to do everything in his power to smash this coup. He's a clever chap; he'll know what to do. My wife's cousin, you know."

"I hadn't known that," the Man from the Bourse said. But he had. "I concur with your decision."

"Thank you, gentlemen," Ricard said gratefully. "Shall we finish the bottle?"

They begged off, and all departed and went their separate ways. Ricard drove first to his office at the Quai and dictated a long letter of instruction to Anatole Garde that would be included in the morning pouch. Then he nodded to his night staff and drove home alone to his apartment in the 16th Arrondissement, arriving at approximately 0200.

His Vietnamese wife roused sleepily.

"Julien?" she mumbled. "Is that you?"

"No," he said. "It is Mickey Mouse."

"That's nice," she giggled. "Come to bed, Mickey."

"Soon," he said. "In a moment, dear."

He waited for her soft snore before he went into his study and turned on the light. He composed a short, terse message revealing the decision regarding Asante that had been reached that evening in the private dining room of L'escargot d'Or. Then he transposed the message into code.

He used a book code, based on the number of page, paragraph, and word of a certain edition of "The Collected Works of Edgar Allan Poe." Ricard was charmed to find that he could select most of the words he required from "The Purloined Letter." He then tore up his original draft and flushed it down the toilet. The coded message he handled carefully, by the edges. He folded it, slid it into a plain white envelope, sealed it, stamped the envelope, addressed it to a box number in Liverpool, England.

Tony Malcolm should have it in a few days. He also admired Poe.

18

Minsiter of Finance Willi Abraham was not present at the palace conference. Tangent thought this curious, possibly significant. During a brief pause in King Prempeh's denunciation of Starrett's unwillingness to reach a decision, Tangent said:

"Your Majesty, with all due respect, my people are not unwilling to come to a decision, they are unable to. I am sure that if Finance Minister Willi Abraham was present, he would say—"

"I am not interested in anything Willi Abraham might say about this matter," Prempeh shouted. "You understand that? Do you?"

"Completely, Your Majesty," Tangent said humbly.

The others at the table—Prime Minister Osei Ware, General Opoku Tutu, Anatole Garde—all looked at Tangent coldly, trying to conceal the glee they felt at his humiliation. Their obvious enmity confirmed what Tony Malcolm had told him before he left London: Garde had been ordered to forestall the coup.

"Surely, Your Majesty," Tangent said, "under the circumstances, an extension of the current lease for three months would cause no hardship or loss of revenue to the Asante treasury."

"Not three months' extension," the Prime Minister thundered. "Not one month, not one week, not one day! Not even one hour's extension. The lease expires when our signed agreement says it expires."

"You take us for fools?" General Tutu screamed. "Poor little ignorant black boys? Your pickaninnies who know no better?"

"General, I assure you—"

"You assure me of nothing!" Here Tutu slammed a meaty hand down on the mahogany table. "I do not like you, Tangent. I hope I make that obvious. More important, I do not trust you."

"We don't need you," the Prime Minister continued the assault. "We do not need Starrett Petroleum, Incorporated. We have other friends, many friends. As wealthy as you."

"Wealthier," King Prempeh IV murmured. He was fondling his medals again. The gold Patek Philippe watch, Tangent's gift, was not on his wrist.

"But we are gentlemen," Osei Ware said. "We will observe every last detail of our signed agreement. No one will be able to say we are uncultured. But as for an extension—no, no, and no! If we have received no word from you by the expiration date, we will consider the lease null and void."

"And should that happen," King Prempeh said ominously, "should that happen, I suggest you make preparations to leave Asante within twenty-four hours. You personally, your staff, your ship, your helicopter, your equipment—everything. If you have no interest in Asante's welfare, then I have no interest in yours. If you remain on our soil more than twenty-four hours after the lease has expired, I cannot be responsible for you personal safety."

"Your Majesty! I wish—"

"No more. This audience is at an end."

Tangent was pleased to find he was not trembling. And during the taxi ride back to the Mokodi Hilton, he was able to chat quite casually with the driver about the mealy taste of frozen shrimp and the difficulty of finding properly ripened mangoes. Still, it was not easy to forget the hooded stare of Prime Minister Osei Ware, the lupine grin of General Opoku Tutu, the pity of triumph in the blue eyes of Anatole Garde.

Worst of all was the King's delight in his exhibit of naked power. Beheading was the punishment of those Asantis convicted of capital crimes. Tangent could imagine the vengeance Prempeh wreaked upon his political enemies. It would be as quick as decapitation.

He went at once to the office of Mai Fante, the Asanti legal counsel of Starrett Petroleum. Fante was on the phone, and waved Tangent to a deskside chair. It was obvious, from Fante's conversation, what the matter concerned. An Asanti fisherman claimed his boat had been scraped by the *Starrett Explorer* while it was changing position. His attorney had called Mai Fante, announcing that if damages of thirty-four dollars and fifty-two cents were not paid immediately, legal action would, of necessity, be initiated in Asante courts.

Mai Fante, urbane, confident, soft-spoken, replied by suggesting a personal meeting between himself and his caller to arrive at an equitable solution of this "tragic problem." It was not so much what the lawyer said that bemused Tangent as the language. Speaking Akan, Fante inquired after his caller's health and that of his family. Did he find the weather uncomfortably warm? And how was he enduring the grievous demands of the legal profession? Yes, surely, it was a difficult and yet a rewarding career. Justice was a fine ideal to which a man might devote a satisfactory life. The truth was worth fighting for, and who could deny that the law demanded much but offered more.

It went on and on, and Tangent listened with fascination as the Akan poetry spread its magic. It was truly a language designed for speaking: mellifluous, lilting, with delicate shades of meaning and emphasis indicated by change of voice pitch rather than breath force. The conversation ended by Mai Fante inviting the plaintiff's attorney to have lunch with him at the Zabarian.

"Beautiful," Tangent breathed, after Fante had hung up. "Do you know the man?"

"Never met him in my life," the lawyer grinned. "But before you came in, we discovered that his oldest uncle's cousin is married to my mother's aunt's youngest child. So you see, we are related! I think we shall come to a satisfactory agreement."

"Is everyone in Asante related to everyone else?" Tangent asked.

"Everyone in Africa," Fante said soberly.

He was a handsome, smooth-faced man, with features that seemed experienced in smiling. It was difficult to judge his age; he moved youthfully, step and gestures were full of bounce. But hair was gray, eyes old. He dressed with restraint, but the elegance was in the man himself, casual and sure.

"How may I be of service, Mr. Tangent?" he asked, in French.

"I wish to ask a favor of you," Tangent said, speaking Akan. "This is a personal matter and does not concern Starrett. If you cannot grant my request, I will understand completely, and it will in no way affect your employment or our friendship."

"Ah," Mai Fante said.

"I wish to meet with Captain Obiri Anokye," Tangent went on. "At a place and time of his choosing. As I say, this has nothing to do with Starrett. But for reasons I believe sufficient, I do not think it would be wise for me to call Captain Anokye at the Mokodi barracks."

"No," Fante said immediately. "That would not be wise."

He began to swing back and forth in his swivel chair, looking at the ceiling. Tangent waited patiently. Africa had a rhythm of its own. It was not Europe's rhythm, and even less America's. That did not make it better or worse; it was simply different.

"Yes," Mai Fante said suddenly. "I shall arrange it and let you know the details as soon as I learn them."

"My gratitude is poor reward," Tangent said.

"The pleasure is in serving," Fante replied gravely. Tangent rose to go.

"Mai," he said, "you're due for two weeks' vacation, are you not?" Now he spoke French.

"Yes," Fante nodded. "Beginning next month."

"Why don't you take four weeks?" Tangent said. "Take a nice, long trip. Perhaps to London. We can devise some reason for it. The company will pay. Take your wife and children. Get out of the country for a while. Give you a whole new perspective on things."

The two men stared at each other. Then Mai Fante resumed his gentle swinging back and forth in his swivel chair. But his eyes never left Tangent's.

"I thank you for your kind and generous offer, Mr. Tangent," he said. "You are a true friend."

Tangent made a gesture.

"But I believe I will remain in Asante," Fante said. "It is my home."

Tangent spent the next day drawing up a contingency plan, in case rapid evacuation of Starrett personnel became necessary. They would be flown by the Sikorsky copter to the *Starrett Explorer*, which would then haul ass for international waters. In case of attempted interception by Asante gunboats—well, that particular crisis would have to be handled when and if it arose. Tangent knew the *Explorer* carried only a small arsenal of handguns, rifles, and shotguns. But in its holds was an enormous store of dynamite, gelignite, nitroglycerine, and other explosives. In his imagination, Tangent saw the Starrett copter taking off from the ship's helipad to drop a huge bundle of short-fused explosives on an attacking launch crewed by Prempeh, Ware, Tutu, and Anatole Garde. It was a succulent fantasy.

Late in the afternoon he received his precise instructions, relayed through Mai Fante. He was to drive a dark-colored rental car to the Golden Calf, attempting to arrive at precisely midnight. Once inside, he would be accosted by a small black girl wearing a scarlet evening gown. Her name was Sbeth. Tangent was to accompany her upstairs, playing the part of a client. She would conduct him to a meeting with the Little Captain.

It went smoothly and without incident. Tangent entered the Golden Calf, barely had time to look about curiously, to note the surprisingly attractive interior, become conscious of the decorous, almost sedate atmosphere, when a small black girl wearing a scarlet evening gown was at his elbow. She smiled up at him, murmuring a crazy stream of copybook English as though she had memorized the phrases English as though she had memorized the phrases but had no idea of their meaning: "Hello, sir. How are you, sir? My name is Sbeth. I am well, thank you. Is it not a delightful evening? Shall we go upstairs, sir? Drink and food are also available at popular prices. Please to follow me, sir."

Tangent followed her up the wide, gracefully curved staircase. The second floor was active—clients arriving and departing, maids scurrying about with towels, waitresses hustling loaded trays—but Tangent's guide continued up to the third floor, and brought him to a closed door.

He offered her a dash, but she shook her head, smiled, slipped away.

The woman who answered his knock was pale-haired, pale-skinned. A curious face of cameo features with a tough, distrustful cast. Strong hands and long, bare feet. The body appeared slender, the naked arms were sinuous. She wore a bottlegreen cheongsam. The blond hair was plaited into two thick braids, small gold rings in her pierced ears. Tangent guessed her age at 32–35, in that range.

"Come in, Mr. Tangent," she said, not smiling. Her voice was unexpectedly resonant, deep. "I am Yvonne Mayer."

He stepped inside and while she closed and locked the door behind him, he looked about slowly. He knew who she was, and guessed this to be her personal apartment. He was about to compliment her on the comfortable charm of her sitting room when three men entered from an inner chamber. Captain Obiri Anokye led the file, followed by Willi Abraham, and a man introduced as Professor Jean Louis Duclos.

The four men drew up chairs about a small, round ormolu table. Yvonne Mayer sat at a desk, slightly with-drawn.

"Mr. Tangent," Captain Anokye said. "I have taken the liberty of asking these friends to be present during our discussion. They share my plans and my hopes. I vouch for all of them, completely."

Tangent nodded. He turned first to Willi Abraham. His challenge was almost brutal.

"Minister," he demanded, "are you in disfavor at the palace?"

"Yes," Abraham said promptly. "And I am fortunate it is no worse than 'disfavor.' I am protected by my association with the Asante Brothers of Independence; the King doesn't wish to antagonize the veterans. That is Anatole Garde's advice. Also, I am allowed to continue my work, to occupy my office. There are many things about the finances of Asante that only I know."

Then Tangent turned to Anokye.

"Captain, may I speak to you openly and honestly?"

"That is always best in the affairs of men," Anokye said.

Tangent looked at him sharply. Was the Little Captain putting him on? Anokye's expression seemed grave and intent. As did that of the others in the room.

"Are you planning a coup against the present regime in Asante?"

"I am."

"Do you intend to take over the government yourself?"

"I do. With the aid of those you see here, and others."

"What support do you have?"

"Fourth Brigade, without question. Certain officers and units of the Third. Amongst auxiliary companies—artillery, tanks, supply, and so forth—the most I can count on is neutrality, until they see how things are going. The same is true of navel and air personnel. But they are not numerous enough to be important. I also have the Asante Brothers of Independence. Trained men, but unarmed."

"What about the Marxist guerrillas?" Tangent asked.

"They will join us," Anokye said. "I have the Nyam's word. If we move within a month."

Tangent opened his mouth to speak, then closed it suddenly.

"Would you care for a glass of water?" Willi Abraham asked unexpectedly.

"Yes, thank you," Tangent said gratefully.

"Perhaps a glass of cold white wine?" Yvonne Mayer said, rising.

"Please don't go to any trouble."

"No trouble. I have it here."

She brought deep glasses and poured wine around to all. They lifted glasses in an unspoken toast, sipped, sipped again.

"You have a plan?" Tangent asked. "A military plan? Tactics, and so forth?"

"Only the basics," Anokye said. "That it must take place while the Fourth is in Mokodi, and the Third is in the field."

"You feel Mokodi is the key to Asante?" Tangent asked.

"Of course," Anokye said. "And the palace is the key to Mokodi."

"Difficult," Willi Abraham said.

"Why is that?"

"The palace guard," Abraham said. "A company of men, heavily armed. About two hundred, I think. Bibi?"

"Less than that," Anokye said. "Perhaps a hundred and fifty at full strength. But they are—as you would say, Mr. Tangent—very tough babies."

"I wouldn't say it," Tangent said, "but I know what you mean. Can they be bribed?"

"No," Anokye said. "They are all Muslims and will die happily for their faith. Particularly if they die while killing infidels. Then they will achieve paradise. Others in the army may be bribed, but not the palace guard."

"Then how do you intend to take the palace?" Tangent asked.

"I don't know," Anokye said frankly. "It would be foolish to plan until I know what weapons are available."

"Surely you could destroy the palace with mortars," Tangent suggested.

"Would you like your White House destroyed?" Professor Duclos said angrily.

"What Jean-Louis means," Willi Abraham said smoothly, "is that the palace is a symbol. The seat of government. Of law and authority. The heart of Asante. We would not care to see it reduced to a heap of rubble."

Tangent was silent, clinking his wineglass gently against his teeth. Finally he sighed, drew a deep breath.

"Let me tell you what my people want," he said. "Then you tell me what you want. Perhaps we can find a middle ground satisfactory to us both."

"No voice in our government," the Martinicain professor said determinedly. His fawny skin was flushed.

Anokye turned his head slowly. His gaze seemed to concentrate. Duclos lowered his head.

"We will listen to Mr. Tangent," the Little Captain said, mildly enough. "Then, as he has suggested, we will state our desires."

"We'll advance half a million American dollars," Tangent said, "for the purchase of arms, the exact number and types of weapons to be determined in consultation between Captain Anokye and our representative. The actual purchase will be done directly by us; no sums will be released to you. The weapons will be delivered where and when you want them. In return, my people want a twenty-year lease of the Zabarian oil fields with forty percent of the profits to Asante, and sixty percent to us. The moneys we advance to accomplish the coup will be subtracted from our first year's payment. And for Professor Duclos' benefit, we have absolutely no desire to interfere in any way in the government or interior affairs of the new Asante. All we want is oil. That does it, I think."

"Willi," Captain Anokye said.

"Let us take it point by point," the Minister of Finance said. "I see no objection in funds for the weapons being paid directly by your people. But we will require an additional two hundred thousand American dollars for other purposes. For propaganda, for instance; for bribery of staff members of the Asante *New Times* and the radio station. And gifts to certain army officers in return for either their loyalty or their neutrality. But most important, to provide food, medicine, and the basic necessities of life for our supporters in cities, towns, and outlying villages, to prove to them that we have the resources to answer their needs. When you are starving, Mr. Tangent, a tough chicken and an unripened melon mean more than all the political promises in the world. As for the Zabarian oil fields, we propose a five-year lease, with sixty percent of the profits to Asante, forty to you. I have finished."

"Now," Captain Anokye said, smiling faintly, "shall we get started?"

The bargaining continued for almost an hour. Voices rose gradually in volume, fists were clenched and brandished, palms were smacked together, feet were stamped, men rose and stalked about the room angrily. Yvonne Mayer quietly brought more cold wine and kept the glasses filled. The disputants drank thirstily, but were hardly aware of her presence.

Finally, they had narrowed the area of disagreement. Starrett was to purchase the weapons and provide a slush fund in cash, not to exceed one hundred thousand American dollars. The oil lease would run for twelve years. It was on the division of the profits that there was no meeting of minds. Abraham was willing to accept a minimum of 55 percent for Asante. Tangent was willing to accept the same minimum for Starrett. Neither would budge, and all were reduced to a morose silence, slumped in their chairs, staring moodily at nothing.

Finally, the Little Captain spoke:

"Mr. Tangent, to you this is a business proposition, and you seek the most favorable terms. As you said, all you want is oil. I do not condemn you for that. Indeed, you are to be congratulated; you have argued most persuasively. But you must understand that to us it is more than a business proposition. We are talking about the future of Asante, the future of our people. And we are talking about our own lives, which all of us are willing to sacrifice to make our dream of a new Asante come true. We have won many Asantis to our cause. We have done this by convincing them they are being robbed and cheated by rulers who care only for their personal wealth, who steal Asante taxes to fatten their Swiss bank accounts. Now, assuming the coup succeeds, and we become rulers of Asante, and we then announce that we have given more than half of the profits of Asante's oil to a foreign company—what would be the result of that? Would not the people feel that once again they have been robbed and cheated, that they have merely exchanged one gang of thieves for another? And would you blame them for feeling that way?"

There was silence again. Tangent sat hunched over, hands clasped between spread knees, head bowed. Finally he straightened up.

"All right," he said. "Fifty-one to Asante, forty-nine to us."

"Done," Willi Abraham said.

A sigh of relief ran around the room. The Asantis stretched wearily.

"Now," Tangent said, "I have another condition."

Duclos leaped angrily to his feet.

"We have come to an agreement," he shouted. "I, personally, feel we have given too much. But I will go along with the others. But no more conditions, no more demands! You take us for fools? Do you think we are poor little ignorant black boys?"

"Exactly what General Tutu screamed in the palace yesterday," Tangent said coldly. "I have not accused you of racism, Professor. Please have the courtesy not to accuse me."

"What is your new demand?" Willi Abraham asked.

"It is not *my* demand," Tangent said. "I have complete faith in what you have promised. But I am an employee—a servant, if you will—of a large, faceless corporation located thousands of miles away. I am empowered to make this agreement, yes, if I can provide proof that you—who are strangers to them—will honor this agreement if the coup is successful."

"*When* the coup is successful," Yvonne Mayer said, and they all looked at her in surprise, realizing it was the first time she had contributed to the discussion.

"What kind of proof?" Willi Abraham asked.

"A signed statement from Captain Anokye that he agrees to those terms affecting the oil lease. The twelve-year period. The fifty-one/forty-nine split. That he will honor those terms when he becomes ruler of Asante. Also, this statement must be repeated, in his voice, on tape."

The Little Captain burst out laughing. "Oh, Mr. Tangent," he said, "what kind of proof is this your people demand? What if I do not become ruler of Asante? What if the coup succeeds and Abraham becomes ruler? Or Duclos? Or any other man? Where is your proof then?"

Tangent stared at him. Gradually Anokye's mirth faded, the two small vertical wrinkles appeared above the bridge of his nose. His features took on that somber, magisterial quality Tangent remembered from their first meeting. Anokye may admire Garibaldi, the American reflected, but he resembles Mussolini.

"I'll take that gamble," Tangent said. "Will you sign and dictate such a statement?"

"I will," the Little Captain said.

The remainder of the meeting was spent in discussing ways and means. Willi Abraham named Mai Fante as the man he wanted to act as go-between, to deliver the Starrett slush fund and to obtain Captain Anokye's signed and recorded statements. Tangent named Sam Leiberman the man who would consult with Captain Anokye on the numbers and types of weapons available, and make arrangements for delivery.

All agreed on the necessity of secrecy and the need for fast action. The expiration date of Starrett's present lease was less than a month away.

"As is the Nyam's pledge," Captain Anokye remarked.

They were all, suddenly, sobered and shaken by the magnitude of the events they had set in motion. They could hardly meet each other's eyes as they shook hands and departed, one by one, at five-minute intervals. Duclos first, slipping down the back stairs. Then Tangent, stalking steadily down the main staircase, ignoring the music and dancing now going on in the main floor parlor. Then Abraham, out the front door, pausing on the porch to light a stubby Dutch cigar and gossip about the price of tobacco with the Mokodi gendarme on duty. Abraham gave him a cigar before he left, and the man never saw him.

Upstairs, Captain Obiri Anokye, his tunic unbuttoned, sat sprawled in the upholstered chair at the desk. Yvonne Mayer moved quietly about the room, straightening up, emptying ashtrays, collecting glasses, bottles, corks. She opened the windows wider. A vagrant breeze came in to dissolve the smoke, freshen the room with cool night air.

"More wine, Bibi?" she asked.

"Thank you, no. I am grateful for what you have done."

"I did nothing."

"Come here."

Obediently, she came over to him, sat on the floor at his feet. She grasped one calf, put her head against his knee. He stroked her smooth hair absently, then curled his fingers about one of her plaits, caressing it gently.

"What do you think of him?" he asked.

"Tangent? A very capable man. I would like to have him working for me. Think of what he has done for his people tonight. A twelve-year lease. Forty-nine percent of Asante's oil. And all moneys advanced to be repaid by Asante."

"Oh yes," Anokye agreed. "A hard bargain. But did we have a choice? We know from Garde's actions that we can expect no help from the French. They will continue to back Prempeh. Starrett was our only chance."

"Tangent knew this, of course."

"Of course. Yvonne, when you climb a steep ladder, it is foolish to take more than one step at a time. This agreement with Starrett is my first step. Tangent represents money and power. I need money and power if I am to succeed."

"You trust Tangent?" she asked.

"Why not? It is in his interest, the interest of his people, to see Prempeh overthrown."

"And after, when you become ruler of Asante? You mean to honor this agreement?"

"To the letter. There are other matters in which Tangent and his people may be of help. I must establish a relationship of trust with them. They must learn the kind of man I am."

"Why should they want to help you further?"

"If it is in their interest, if they can see profit or potential profit, they will help me. That is the nature of things." He was silent a moment, stroking her hair slowly. "This Tangent puzzles me. He said it was merely a business proposition, that he was interested only in the oil. But I have a feeling there is something else."

She rose to her knees, bowed her pliant back, rested her forearms on his thighs, looked up into his face.

"You saw that, did you, Bibi? I did too. He is excited by your plans."

"By the idea of a coup? Of overturning a government by force?"

"Nooo," she said thoughtfully. "Not entirely. I know men. Why should I not? Haven't I had enough experience? Yes, Tangent is excited by the violence of the coup. But he is also excited by you, Bibi. *You* excite him."

"I? Why should I excite him?"

"The same thing that excites me. Your sureness, your resolve, your ambition, your singlemindedness, your power. He senses all this, and he responds to it. It excites him because he knows he lacks it."

"I think you exaggerate."

"I did not. Bibi, would Tangent die for Starrett Petroleum, Incorporated?"

"Of course not."

"Because it is merely a job of work to him, nothing more. If not Starrett, then some other company or corporation. But you would die for Asante. He knows it. Since he cannot feel that, he wants to share the feeling of one who can and does. It makes him important. It is significant. There has been nothing of significance in his life until this."

He looked at her with wonder.

"You believe this to be true, Yvonne?"

"I do. I think you are right, that Starrett will continue to support you if they can see a profit in it. But Tangent's motive is more complex than that. You *must* succeed, and he will do everything in his power to help you. For if you are crushed, he is crushed. He loves you, Bibi. That is *his* profit."

"Now you speak nonsense," he murmured.

"No." She shook her head. "I speak the truth. I recognize it because that is the way I feel."

"Shall we go to bed now?" he asked.

"Of course."

"Let me shower first. Go to bed and wait for me."

"Don't be long. Please."

She lay naked in bed, staring at the ceiling, awaiting her lover. It was as she had said of Tangent; there had been nothing of significance in her life until Anokye. The pain she had known, the humiliation, fear, the dread—all had been endured. Repetition reduced them to a dull ache. But hope never died. Never. Not even in the starving or the condemned. The dying await the miracle. This man was hers.

He arranged her on hands and knees, her head down upon the pillow. He kneeled behind her, between her spread legs so that he might admire the sweet flare from narrow waist to smooth hips. He held her two braids as a rider might hold the reins of an eager, blooded horse.

When he entered into her, she cried out once and lurched back against him. He pulled on the plaits, and her head came up as though she held a bit. They rode with grunts and gasps, became sweated, their flesh raw and tumescent. They stopped a few moments and began again. They stopped a few moments and began again. They stopped a few moments and began again.

When, finally, they could pause no more, both victims of their lust, she called him, as she always did, her "master," her "king," her "ruler." He did not speak, but with intent ferocity rent the pale heart and continued to plunge even after she collapsed prone and boneless, a continent conquered by his hard blows.

19

The day's catch had been a good one—bluefish, bass, cod, a small tuna—and the Anokye family had a fine peppery stew from the best of the lot. The remainder were sold to a merchant in Porto Chonin. He would select the best of his purchase for his own table, and take the remainder across to Mokodi in his boat, for sale to hotels and restaurants. It was quite possible that Tangent, dining that night at the Zabarian, would eat a bass that had threshed futilely in the Anokye nets.

After the evening meal, Josiah, Zuni, and Adebayo went down to the beach to mend nets stretched over drying racks. Obiri stayed in the kitchen, listening to the talk of his sister Sara and their mother, who had been given the name Judith when her family converted to Christianity.

Sara was trying very hard to keep her conversation ladylike and dignified. But her youth defeated her. She was constantly breaking into an impish giggle, covering her blushing face with both hands, or betraying her delight with a smile of such radiance that it lighted the room. Judith and Obiri watched her and listened to her with loving indulgence; she was the youngest of the Anokye children, the beautiful "baby," and she could do no wrong.

The matter under discussion was this:

Lt. Jere Songo had returned to Lomé, to resume his duties with the Togolese army, on his father's staff. He had written a short letter to Josiah Anokye, as was proper, thanking him for the hospitality that had been shown him. The lieutenant had also written a personal letter to Sara. It was couched in most respectful terms. It mentioned his pleasure in meeting her and her family, and it concluded with an invitation to Sara to come to Lomé, to stay at his home and meet his family.

Sara, who had never been out of Asante, wanted very much to go. Her mother said it was completely, utterly, irrevocably out of the question; young girls did not travel alone to meet young men in another country, men they had met but once. Judith conceded that the lieutenant had made a good impression. He was open, cheerful, polite. Shy, too, of course. But that was to his credit; he did not push himself forward. Still . . .

It was more discussion than argument. There was never any possibility of Sara disobeying her mother's edict. But she wished to state her side, and in the process create a fantasy of the delightful new experiences that awaited her. Also, she was old enough to travel by herself. Also, how could she be expected to behave properly in the world outside Asante if she was not allowed to learn? And so forth . . .

She was sixteen, a tall, willowy girl-woman, tremulous with dreams but saved from sappiness by a ready sense of humor and a recognition of life's absurdities. She attended the lycée in Mokodi, and planned to become a teacher, nurse, secretary, airline stewardess, actress, fabric designer, or artist. All subject to change without notice. She was lively, the best swimmer of the Anokye children, and kept a picture of Alain Delon on the wall above her bed.

Then, the kitchen shining, pots and utensils set out for the morning meal, the two women sat down at the table and looked to Obiri expectantly, awaiting his judgment on the proper response to Lt. Songo's invitation. As usual he considered gravely and made no attempt to treat the matter lightly.

"Sara," he said finally, "join your father and brothers for a few minutes."

"I don't see why I—" she began indignantly, but the Little Captain rose and touched her twigged hair fondly.

"Please, Sara," he said. "We understand how you feel. Perhaps something can be worked out."

Satisfied with this vague promise, she flashed them both a bright grin and ran lightly from the room. They watched her go, smiling. It was impossible to resist her fresh charm.

Obiri sat down across the table from his mother. They stared at each other. She seemed suddenly smaller to him. Not older, but shrunken, the skin tighter on a body as corded as her husband's. She continued to work as hard as ever, her mind alert, but the rhythm of her life was slowing, slowing. Sometimes, late in the evening, she would sit silently, mending untouched in her lap, and stare about her home as if seeing it for the first time. Or the last.

"Sara cannot go to Togo," she told Obiri. He knew that tone well: the final judgment.

"Not alone," he agreed. "It would not be proper. But if you accompanied her . . ."

"I? No, I am too old."

"Nonsense. You would enjoy the trip. I would make all the arrangements."

For an instant her eyes brightened as she thought of the adventure. But her good sense conquered.

"No," she repeated. "I cannot leave Father. And now I am sometimes weary. Is it so important that Sara visit this boy?"

"And his family," Obiri said. "Yes, it is important. For her and me. For all of us. I would like you and Sara to be in Togo in about three weeks' time."

She knew his plans, of course; it was impossible to conceal anything from her, and he valued her counsel. Now she looked at him in much the same way Mai Fante had looked at Tangent when he suggested a vacation in London.

"So soon?" Judith breathed.

"Yes. I will feel better if you and Sara are not here."

The old woman thought a long moment.

"Sara may go," she said finally. "Zuni's wife will go with her. I will remain here."

"As you wish," Obiri said. "Also—"

He stopped speaking. But she knew his thoughts, as she always did.

"Also," she said, "it will be good for Sara to marry this boy. Then, if you succeed, you will have important relatives in Togo."

"Yes," he said, "that is my thinking."

"And Adebayo?" she asked ironically. "What do you plan for him?"

"Nothing, Mother," he said, smiling. "Not yet."

She shook her head, recognizing that this son had grown beyond her. He was engaged in enterprises, dangerous enterprises, foreign to her. She could not see the limits of his ambition, and what drove him she did not know. She knew only that he was her strongest, loneliest, and most loving child, and for that she could cherish him.

"Live a long life," she told him. "Be happy and do good in the sight of God."

He lifted her feather hand from the tabletop and kissed her worn fingers.

20

"Must you sit around like that?" Alistair Greeley said.

"What? What? You're half naked!"

"Oh, much more than that," Jane Greeley said languidly, and Maud laughed.

The chief teller glared at the two women, furious, feeling he should tell them a thing or two, but not knowing what—or how.

They sat on the hot, shadowed veranda; a pitcher of warm lemonade between them. Lately they had taken to spiking the insipid drink with sloe gin, ignoring Greeley's anguished reminders of what the gin cost. He dragged his clumsy boot up and down the porch, rehearsing in his mind all the clever, cutting things he might say.

"Oh, do sit down," his wife said. "You're making me nervous. You act like a Piccadilly tart waiting for her soldier boy."

This time his sister laughed. They were always laughing at him, one or the other or both. To his face or behind his back. He knew, he knew. They thought him a weak cripple, half a man. But they'd see, they'd see. When he got the bonus from Garde, they'd come sucking around, and then it would be his turn. What? What?

He waited impatiently for Captain Anokye, pacing, dragging his boot back and forth, pleased that he was annoying his wife. He avoided looking at his sister. She sat slumped far down in the cushioned wicker chair, her long bare legs thrust out. And spread! Between brief white shorts and a flowered scarf tied about her heavy breasts, a gap of soft, rippled flesh was insolently displayed. The whore! His own sister—a whore!

And his stick of a wife taking it all in with covetous eyes, leaning forward to murmur, touching the bare shoulder, playing up to the younger woman like a—like a—Greeley didn't know what. But it was poisonous to see. And even when he didn't look at them, even when he was away, at work in the bank, he knew they were together, alone in the big house, slopping down their gin and—and God knows what. Sickening!

"He's here," Greeley said loudly, watching Anokye's Land Rover pull into the driveway. "Jane, will you please straighten up and try to act like a lady for a change."

He thought she said, "Go flog yourself," but he wasn't sure, and didn't want to cause a scene with the Little Captain already mounting the steps.

"Good evening, Captain," he called out cheerily, flinging open the door. "Right on time. The only time you'll be late is for your own funeral. Then you'll be the late Captain Anokye. What? What?"

"That is true," the Little Captain smiled. "Good evening, ladies."

They nodded, and Greeley hustled his guest into the house.

"Strutting little peacock," Maud said.

"Oh, I don't know," Jane said lazily. "Some of those little men surprise you. Or maybe it just looks bigger because they're so small."

"Jane, I wish you wouldn't talk like that."

"Do you? I thought you liked pig-talk. Get me some more ice, there's a sweet."

Maud took longer than usual to return with a shallow bowl of stunted ice cubes.

"The fridge is acting up again," she reported. "I waited to hear if it clicked on, but it didn't. Do you suppose it's stopped completely?"

"Who cares?" Jane said. "Home, sweet home. Have another peg, sweetie. Good for what ails you."

"It makes me all perspiry," Maud said. "I'm all wet."

"The gin's not what makes you wet," Jane said. "I know what makes you wet."

"Oh you!" Maud said. "I could hear them plain as anything in the study. Always talking their wars and battles and soldiers. Like two little boys."

"Has the gimp said anything more to you about sending me back?"

"Not a word. But I know he's up to something. He gets that smirky look."

"Christ, I couldn't stand England again," Jane said. "Not after this sun. I'd like to spend the rest of my life in the sun. Lying naked in the sun. And you could keep me all oiled. Would you like that?"

"Oh yes," Maud whispered. "I would, I would."

Jane laughed throatily. "Not much chance of it if he sends me back," she said.

"He won't," Maud Greeley said fiercely. "I won't let him."

"I have a problem I hope you càn help me with, Mr. Greeley," Captain Anokye was saying.

"Of course, of course. Anything at all."

"Next month—say the first two weeks in August—I'd like to plan a brigade-strength tactical exercise, something designed to test the initiative of my junior officers and noncoms. Of course, being stationed in Mokodi, the area in which we can operate is necessarily limited. No farther north than Gonja, certainly. Any suggestions, sir?"

"Mmm, let me think," Greeley said. "I gather you're ruling out the reenactment of a set battle. What? What?"

"Oh yes, sir. It would have to be a situation in which small units—squad- and platoon-strength—would operate more or less independently, with only the most basic orders—assignment of objectives and time allowed."

"Tank and artillery units available?"

"No, sir. This will be mainly or wholly an infantry maneuver. You know approximately the number and type of vehicles assigned to Fourth Brigade."

"Yes, yes," Greeley nodded. He stumped about the study, turning his face away from the Little Captain. He was on fire, almost convinced Anokye was leading up to the planning of a coup, the action Anatole Garde had been waiting.

"Perhaps an invasion?" Greeley suggested. "An amphibious invasion with landings at the harbor?"

"No, I don't think so," Anokye said. "The area of hostilities would be too limited, and merchants would be certain to complain if we tied up traffic on the waterfront."

"True," Greeley said. "I hadn't thought of that. Ah, Captain, I have it! An insurrection! An attempted coup d'etat by the Nyam's rebels or any other bunch of crackpots. How does that strike you? What? What?"

"Yesss," Anokye said slowly. "That might do. We'll plan an imaginary coup, plant 'enemy' forces in certain key positions, and then see how effectively Fourth Brigade roots them out. Yes, Mr. Greeley, I think that will serve excellently. It can be staged in the area south of Gonja, and will necessitate several small units operating independently without specific tactical instructions."

"Good, good, good," Greeley chortled, rubbing his hands together. "Now let's get out the map and start planning how such a coup might take place. That's the first step. What? What?"

"Yes, Mr. Greeley," Captain Obiri Anokye said. "That's the first step."

. . .

After Captain Anokye departed, Alister Greeley announced he was going directly
to bed. After all, he said, he needed his sleep if he was to get to work the
next morning and earn enough money to keep them swilling sloe gin. He
waited for their rejoinder. When there was none, he slammed angrily back
into the house, leaving them sitting together on the dark veranda.

They assumed he had gone up to his bedroom, so when Maud Greeley
went into the kitchen to scrape more ice fragments from the stubborn refrigerator, she was surprised to hear her husband's voice coming from the study.
She pressed her ear against the wall.

"—doubt about it," Alistair Greeley was saying. "Certainly I'm sure, Mr.
Garde. He's pretending it will be a military exercise, a maneuver. What's
that? Next month. First two weeks in August, he said. Well, we'll plan the
coup as if it was actually taking place. The soldiers playing the 'enemy' will
take over the key positions selected. Then Anokye will designate teams to
retake the positions. But I'm sure he's not interested in that. All he wants is
my ideas on the coup itself—what positions to seize, vital crossroads, the
timing, and so forth. Well, of course, it's all a game. Maneuvers are supposed
to be a game. What? What? It's all play-acting. Practice for the real thing.
But in this case, it is the real thing, what? Of course, Mr. Garde. Yes, sir. No,
just preliminary work tonight, deciding exactly how we will approach the
problems of planning. Next time he will bring me the numbers of troops and
units involved in staging the coup, and the numbers assigned to the counter-
coup operation. Yes, Mr. Garde. Of course. I'll report every meeting. Yes, sir.
Thank you, sir."

Maud Greeley heard him hang up the phone. She went swiftly back to the
porch.

"Ice?" Jane asked.

"Sorry, no more," Maud said. She stood directly behind the other woman,
looking down at the naked shoulders. Gleaming. She stood there quite a long
time while her sister-in-law finished her warm drink. Then Jane rose, yawned,
stretched her full body like a satisfied cat. She looked curiously at the still
silent Maud.

"Penny for your thoughts," she said.

"Oh, they're worth more than that," Maud Greeley said. "Much more."

21

It began raining that night. It began suddenly; one moment the sky was clear,
the next it was clotted, and rain fell straight down, not driven by gusty winds
but simply dropping steadily, heavily, at the same rate for hour after hour. It
might, Asantis knew, continue for a day, three days, a week, two weeks. But

few complained. The rivers would gush full, trees would flower, the baked earth would bloom verdant overnight.

Tangent spent the afternoon in the office of J. Tom Petty at the Mokodi Hilton. He lounged on the leather couch, idly scanning the pages of the Asante *New Times*. Perhaps he was imagining it, but it seemed to him the tenor of local news articles had already changed perceptibly. The slush fund had been delivered only two days previously, yet there were such items as: "The Minister of Agriculture denies that near-starvation conditions exist in the northern provinces," and, "Authorities state supplies of beef, pork, veal, goat and chicken will be drastically reduced in the coming months due to a serious shortage of feed." Etc., etc. The items were cautiously worded to reflect the official position, but even mention of such matters was significant. Heretofore, the *New Times* had been a palace house organ.

Pleased with this early evidence of media manipulation, Tangent tossed the paper aside and turned to look out the window.

"It's never going to stop," J. Tom Petty said grumpily. "It's going to keep raining forever, and the whole goddamned country will float away."

The big man was in his shirtsleeves, seated in his swivel chair, hunched over the desk. He was smoking a fat cigar as he struggled with cost estimates and payrolls.

"The dry season starts in August," Tangent remarked.

"Bullshit," Petty said. "This place ain't got a dry season. Unless you call a week a season."

His phone rang, and he jerked it angrily off the hook.

"Yeah?" he said. "Yeah, he's here. Who? Okay. I'll tell him. Hold it a minute." He covered the transmitter with his palm. "Peter, you got a visitor. A lady. Says her name is Mrs. Greeley. Want to see her?"

Tangent unfolded slowly from the couch, straightened, tugged his jacket smooth.

"Why don't you run down to the bar and have a couple of slow ones, Tom?" he suggested. "Help you forget the paperwork and the rain."

"Best idea I've heard all day," Petty said. "Maybe there's some of that Swedish gash hanging around. Send the lady in?"

Tangent nodded, and Petty spoke over the phone. He grabbed his jacket and headed for the door. He was no sooner gone than an Asanti secretary ushered in Mrs. Greeley. She stood a moment, looking about in awe at the big, richly furnished room. She was wearing a clear plastic raincoat, a plastic hood. She carried a man's black umbrella.

Tangent came forward smiling.

"So nice to see you again, Mrs. Greeley," he said.

"What an unusual room," she said. "I've never seen anything like it."

"Marvelous view," Tangent said. "Except on days like this."

He took her wet hood, raincoat, umbrella, and hung them away. Then he conducted her on a short tour of the office, telling her something of the artwork displayed, pointing out rugs, drapes, and curtains of African fabrics and design.

She was wearing one of her calf-length Victorian gowns, white again, with the usual pleats and ruffles. She was, he decided, the kind of woman who didn't remove her undergarments until she had donned her nightdress. At the moment, she was visibly nervous, twisting her gold wedding band or reaching up to poke tendrils of hair into her spinsterish hairdo.

She did not seem the type of woman who would welcome informality. So rather than seat her on the couch, he drew up a club chair to the desk while he took Petty's swivel chair. Then he leaned forward, clasped his hands on the tabletop, smiled pleasantly.

"And how is your husband?" he asked. "And your sister-in-law?"

"All right," she said vaguely. "They're all right."

Then she was silent, looking down at her bony hands, twisting that ring again. Tangent stared at her, perplexed.

"Mrs. Greeley," he said, "how may I—"

She looked up suddenly.

"You're a good friend of Captain Anokye, aren't you?" she demanded.

Tangent leaned back slowly. He stopped smiling.

"I'd hardly call us good friends," he said. "I know him, certainly. I met him for the first time at your home."

"Well, I have some information that could be worth a lot of money to Captain Anokye," she said. Almost definately. He noted that she was blushing; deep pink blotches mottled face and neck.

"Oh?" Tangent said. "But why come to me? Why not go directly to Captain Anokye?"

She looked at him in astonishment.

"But he's a darky," she said.

"Ah, yes. I see."

"Besides," she said, "he's in the army. Men in the army don't have any money. Everyone knows that."

Tangent knew at least three millionaire colonels and one private first class worth a great deal more, but didn't feel the moment right to mention it.

"Do I understand you correctly, Mrs. Greeley?" he said gently. "You have some information you believe would be of value to Captain Anokye. You want to sell this information. But you don't wish to contact the Captain directly, and since you believe he could not afford to pay in any event, you have come to me, thinking I would pay you. Is that right?"

"Yes. That's right."

"Why on earth should I pay you for information about Captain Anokye?"

She became confused.

"I—I—I thought you were good friends. You left together. That night at our place. This is important information. I know it is. I need the money. I *need* it. I—"

Suddenly, to his discomfort, she began weeping. She bowed her head so he couldn't see the tears. But he heard her snuffling. She pulled a small square of white from her knitted handbag, held it to her face. She wasn't weeping because she needed the money desperately, he decided. It was the shame.

He waited patiently until she calmed. Finally she raised her head, lifted her chin, looked at him directly.

"I'm sorry," she said.

It was the wrong moment to offer sympathy. He looked at her sternly.

"I *may* be able to help you," he told her. "Right now, I don't know how, but perhaps it can be done. What is this information you have?"

"I get paid first," she said firmly.

"Oh no, Mrs. Greeley. No no no. That's not the way it's done. Why should Captain Anokye or I or anyone else buy a pig in a poke? What if, for instance, I pay you what you ask, and your information turns out to be worthless? I'd look a proper fool then, wouldn't I?"

"It's not worthless!" she cried. "I swear it's not."

"That's for the buyer to decide," he said grimly. "Either you reveal what you're selling, or I'm afraid this meeting must end."

"But that means I have to trust you!"

"Exactly," he nodded. "If you wish to profit from what you have, you must first reveal it. To me or someone else. Would you buy a home, a car, a dress, even a mango sight unseen?"

She was silent again, and he gave her all the time she wanted. He did not think her a stupid woman, but a troubled one. Under severe stress. Racked. He could guess her problem, but it was no concern of his. Everyone had problems. It was the name of the game.

"All right," she said finally. "Here it is: Captain Anokye came to our house last night. He went into the study with my husband. Then, later, he left. Mr. Greeley said he was going to bed, but he didn't. I went into the kitchen, and I heard him. He was in the study, talking on the telephone."

Then she recounted Greeley's conversation. To Tangent, it sounded like she was repeating it word for word, and he never doubted that such a conversation had taken place. He listened closely, his face expressionless. When she had finished, she looked at him expectantly. He leaned back in the swivel chair, arm outstretched, fingers toying with a steel letter opener. He sighed.

"Frankly, Mrs. Greeley," he said, "I fail to see why that conversation would be of value to Captain Anokye. I know it is certainly worth nothing to me. As far as I can tell, your husband was merely calling a Mr. Garde to tell of a military maneuver that is being planned. Nothing secret about that. Maneuvers are frequently held in the open, on public property, in the city or countryside, where anyone can witness them."

"But they talked about a coup!" she said desperately.

"I didn't get that impression at all," he said coldly. "It sounded to me, if you have repeated the conversation precisely, that the coup they discussed was merely to be—what was it your husband said?—'play-acting,' just an excuse for military practice. They do it all the time. Armies, I mean. They practice invading and repelling invasions, they run through old battles and devise new ones. Hardly valuable information."

She collapsed, defeated.

"However," he said, "I could be wrong, although I doubt it. Suppose we do this, Mrs. Greeley: Suppose I take your information to Captain Anokye. Perhaps his reaction will be different from mine, and he will be willing to pay you for your interest. How much were you thinking of asking?"

"Five thousand pounds," she said dully.

"Mmm," he said. "Quite a sum. Well . . . do you want me to try Captain Anokye?"

"Might as well," she said.

"All right. Suppose you call me at this number tomorrow afternoon. Here, I'll jot it down for you. Call about noon. I'll make it a point to be here, and I'll try to have some word for you."

"Thank you," she said, in a voice so low he could hardly hear. "You've been very kind."

"Not at all, not at all," he protested. "It's a pleasure to be of help."

He walked her to the elevator, talking enthusiastically of her husband's collection of model soldiers. When the doors closed her away, he hurried to the office of Mai Fante and burst in without knocking.

"Mai, I've got to see the man," he said. "The sooner the better."

"Tonight?"

"Has to be."

"I'll set it up," Fante said, "and get back to you. Trouble?"

"You might say that," Tangent said.

"That's the name of the game," Mai Fante said, and Tangent winced.

He drove slowly, hunched over the wheel, peering through the smear of the windshield wipers. Occasionally he reached to palm moisture from inside the glass. It didn't help much; it was almost midnight on Asante Royal Highway No. 1, on the unlighted stretch from Shabala north to Gonja. Tangent strained his eyes for the dirt track he had been instructed to seek. When he found it, it looked like a quagmire, and he feared bogging down if he made the turn. So he pulled onto the slightly raised shoulder of the road, keeping the left wheels on the paved highway.

He switched off the lights, kept the motor idling, opened the windows slightly to let in the cool, damp air, but not the rain. Then he waited . . .

Mai Fante had said "about midnight," but it was more than twenty minutes past the hour when he saw blurred headlights coming from the direction of Gonja. Gradually he made out the distinctive silhouette of a Land Rover, and when it was close, it slowed, crossed the road, and pulled up in front of him, bumper to bumper. Through the two windshields he could see a hand beckoning him. He dashed out into the rain, climbed hurriedly into the rear of the Land Rover, stretched his long legs sideways. Sgt. Sene Yeboa was driving. Captain Anokye sat beside him. The sergeant switched off motor and lights, and then they were all disembodied voices. It bothered Tangent that he could not see expressions, reactions, gestures.

Tangent was prepared to waste no time on preliminaries, to plunge right in. But the Little Captain inquired politely after his health, asked if the weather was inconveniencing him, assured him the rain was needed and welcome, and mentioned that he had had two satisfactory meetings with Sam Leiberman and they had reached an agreement on the numbers and types of weapons required. Tangent forced himself to reply in kind. Only after all courtesies had been exchanged did he begin to relate what had happened that afternoon. He did not question the presence of Sgt. Yeboa. If Anokye had brought him along to such a meeting, Tangent could speak freely.

The two soldiers listened to Tangent's rapid French without interrupting, though when Garde's name was mentioned, Tangent was conscious of Yeboa stirring restlessly in the driver's seat. When he had concluded, they all sat in silence at least a minute before Captain Anokye sighed.

"I have acted foolishly," he said.

"Not foolishly," Tangent said. "Carelessly, perhaps."

"I thank you for your kindness," Anokye said. "Greeley is a difficult man to like. Very difficult. But he is educated in military history and has an excellent tactical sense, though of course he has never seen active service. He has been of help to me several times in the past. I thought he enjoyed it—an opportunity to put his learning to the test. He never mentioned politics. I believed him to be nonpolitical."

"I think he probably is," Tangent said. "I don't think he is betraying you for ideological reasons."

"What then?"

"Money. I should have suspected him before this. The French control the Asante National Bank. Anatole Garde represents French interests in Asante. How better monitor your activities than through Greeley? I suppose he would do it for a promised promotion or raise in pay or something like that."

"For money," the Little Captain repeated in a low voice. "He did it for money."

"It's hardly catastrophic, Captain. There are several solutions."

"At the moment," Anokye said, "the only solution I desire is to eliminate Greeley."

"Yes *sah!*" Sgt. Yeboa said softly.

"But that is my blood talking," Anokye went on. "It would not be wise."

"No, it would not," Tangent agreed. "No matter how cleverly done. Garde would be suspicious, and angry. Can't you merely stop visiting Greeley? Give him some excuse—military secrecy, press of business, whatever. Simply end all personal contact with him. I'll tell Mrs. Greeley her information was of no value to you, and there's an end to it."

Again there was silence. Windows and curtains were closed; the interior of the car became oppressively hot. Tangent pulled his tie loose, opened his collar, struggled out of his jacket. And waited . . .

"May I light a cigarette?" he asked finally.

"Of course," the Little Captain said. "Strike your match near the floor, please, in your cupped hands. Probably an unnecessary precaution, but still . . ."

"You, Captain?"

"Thank you, no."

"Sergeant?"

"Thank you, sir."

Tangent bent far over, struck the match in cupped hands near the floor, lighted his Players. Then he handed a single cigarette to the sergeant and held the burning end of his own steady so Yeboa could light up. Now there was a slight illumination in the car. When Yeboa took a deep drag, Tangent could see his heavy, sensual features. Captain Anokye remained in shadow.

"My personal situation is delicate, Mr. Tangent," the Little Captain said slowly. "I have tried to move carefully, obey all orders, to make no speeches that could be considered seditious. But I am certain the secret police are aware of my association with Yvonne Mayer, with Minister Abraham and Professor Duclos. They cannot be unaware of the personal loyalty of my troops and my popularity with the Asante Brothers of Independence. I do not mean to boast; I merely state facts. We now know, from Garde's recent actions, that they fear an attempted coup. If I break off all contact with Greeley, the palace may feel their best course of action would be to arrest me. Or assassinate me."

A low growl came from Sgt. Yeboa.

"Yes," Tangent said. "I can see that. If they feel you are under adequate surveillance, that Greeley is reporting on your plans, they'll probably allow you to remain at liberty. For the time being, at least."

"Another factor also," Captain Anokye said, almost dreamily. "By maintaining my contact with Greeley, I will be able to pass along false information to Garde. On the plans for the coup, the numbers involved, the tactics to be employed, and most important, the timing."

Tangent smiled in the darkness.

"Congratulations, Captain," he said. "You have converted a difficulty into an opportunity."

"The mark of a professional soldier," Captain Anokye said. Then he added dryly, "Or so Alistair Greeley has told me."

22

They were in Abidjan, Ivory Coast, and their destination was on the road to Grand-Lahou, near the mouth of the Bandama River. Leiberman had described it to Tangent as a cluster of ramshackle safari cottages around a main restaurant-bar building.

"It was built for tourists," he explained, "but now it's a pirates' den. Every smuggler and nogoodnik along the coast drops by. We'll find our man there."

Leiberman had wanted to take a boat from the foot of the bridge in Treichville and make a lazy trip down the lagoon. Tangent had vetoed the plan as too time-consuming, and insisted on renting a Simca at the Hôtel Ivoire.

"You're running too close as it is," he told Leiberman.

"Deliberately," the mercenary said. "We're dealing with gonifs. The less time you give a gonif between making the deal and the delivery, the less time you give him to start brooding on how underpaid he is. Then you get the shaft."

"When are you scheduling the first delivery?"

"I told you—next Tuesday night."

"Did you coordinate that with Anokye?"

Leiberman was driving, and took his eyes off the road long enough to look sideways at Tangent.

" 'Coordinate,' " he repeated. "You guys kill me. I said we'd deliver at midnight on Tuesday, and Anokye said okay. If that's coordinating, then I coordinated."

"Where's the first drop?"

"Off Zabar. His brother is taking delivery. Just small arms and grenades."

"What do you think of him now?"

"The Little Captain? A pisscutter. He'll go far, if he stays alive."

"What do you mean by that?" Tangent asked.

"I've seen guys like him before. They think the bullet hasn't been made with their name on it. They die with the most surprised look on their faces. But the kid's got moxie, I'll give him that. I think he'll do all right."

"Your job is officially over after the last delivery is made," Tangent said. "But I'd feel better if you stay around until this thing comes off. I'll keep you on salary."

"Why not?" Leiberman said. "In for a penny, in for a fart. I want thirty percent combat pay plus a paid-up life insurance policy."

"All right," Tangent agreed. "I'll arrange it. Stick close to the Little Captain. We've got a lot riding on him."

"My cock, for starters," Leiberman said.

They drove in silence awhile, watching the north side of the road for a sign Leiberman said would indicate five kilometers to the Hôtel d'Azur.

"You know who puzzles me in this whole business?" he asked Tangent.

"Who?"

"You. I know you been involved in things like this before, but since when did you ever go along to make a deal? You leave that to expendables like me. Are you coming along on the delivery?"

"I think I may."

"What are you trying to prove?"

"I'm not trying to prove anything."

"Ho ho ho," Leiberman said. "And I suppose you'll be there in your raw silk suit and Countess Mara tie when the balloon goes up?"

"Yes," Tangent said determinedly. "I'll be there."

"What's the matter," Leiberman said, "backgammon lost its thrill? Listen, you're nuts, you know that? What can you do, except get in the way? Or get your ass shot off. Have you ever fired a gun?"

"Certainly I've fired a gun. I happen to be a rather good shot."

"With what?"

"A twenty-gauge Franchi over-and-under."

"Beautiful," Leiberman said. "I can tell you're a real killer."

They pulled into the small asphalt parking area. Leiberman rolled up the windows tightly and locked the doors.

"Take off your rings, sit on your wallet, and don't drink anything that doesn't come in sealed bottles," he advised Tangent. "And if you've got gold fillings, keep your teeth clenched. Let me do the talking."

Smells hit them first: human sweat of a dozen nationalities, frying oil, stale beer, spilled wine, spices, incense, pomade, hashish, and antique urine. Then the noise: shouted conversation, roared laughter, screamed delight, bellowed curses, a scratchy jukebox playing "The Last Time I Saw Paris," in English, competing with two live musicians, mandolin and drums, wailing an African lament, in Boulé. Then the sights: men and women, black, brown, tan, yellow, white, pink, wearing a thrift shop's inventory of costumes, mostly bright colors, jeweled with glass, hung with brass, flashing, twinkling, bare feet, naked torsos and bulging breasts, a zoo of ruffians and their women, a few dancing, kissing, rubbing, groping.

"It's the bishop's summer day-camp," Leiberman said. "Over here; we'll share."

They sat down in two empty chairs at a table for four. One of their partners was a tall, incredibly skinny black man wearing a red bandanna knotted about his head and a gold loop through the lobe of his left ear. The other man, wearing a seaman's cap, had his head down on his folded arms and was sleeping.

The black glanced up as they pulled out their chairs.

"Sam," he said.

"Yakubu," Leiberman said. "How they hanging?"

"Down," the black man said. "Who's your friend?"

"This is Pete," Leiberman said. "Pete, meet Yakubu, the best pimp in Abidjan."

"The best but not the richest," the black man said. "Buy me a beer?"

"Sure. How about your friend here?" he motioned toward the man flopped on the table, snoring gently.

"No friend of mine," Yakubu said. "He's out. I think someone rolled him."

"Oh? You checked, did you? Hey, waiter! Three Heinekens, the colder the better." He looked slowly around the crowded room. "Shagari been in?"

"He's here," Yakubu said. "Probably out in the kitchen trying to bang the cook."

"How's he doing these days?"

The black shrugged. "Eating thistles, I hear. You got something for him?"

"Could be."

"Need a hand?"

"Could be. What happened to your women?"

"They keep falling in love," Yakubu said. "Then they start giving it away. No business sense."

"Things are tough all over," Leiberman sympathized.

The beers were slammed down. Bottles, no glasses. Tangent paid.

"Take your beer and go find Shagari for me, will you?" Leiberman said to Yakubu. "And hang around; there may be something for you."

The black nodded, picked up his beer, slouched away.

"You know everyone here?" Tangent asked.

"Not everyone. Most of the bad boys."

"Is Shagari one of the bad boys?"

"Not so bad. Stupid, mostly. And a drunk. But his cousin is a fisherman, and he owns a trawler."

"How many men will you need?"

"Shagari and his cousin. Yakubu. And you and me. That should take care of it. They'll do the work; we'll ride shotgun."

"You don't anticipate any trouble, do you?"

"Always," Leiberman said. "I always anticipate trouble. Hello, Shagari, pull up a chair."

"You sonnenbitch Leiberman!" the man shouted. "You no good Jew bastard!"

"Not so loud," Leiberman said. "I'm trying to pass. Meet my friend, Pete."

"You sonnenbitch Pete!" the man shouted. He insisted on crushing their hands between his two filthy paws. Then he signaled wildly for the waiter, almost falling off his chair.

"You're in great shape," Leiberman said. "Too bad. I was going to offer you a job of work, but you couldn't navigate your way through a Tunnel of Love."

"You show me money, see how goddamned fast I sober up," Shagari said. "How's Dele?"

"Okay," Leiberman said. "She's out at your place. Dele's my girl," he explained to Tangent. "She's his daughter. He sold her to me."

"You beat her?" Shagari demanded.

"Only on national holidays," Leiberman said.

"Got more daughters," Shagari grinned at Tangent. "You want one?"

"Thank you, no."

"Sing, dance, cook, plenty push. Cheap."

Tangent shook his head, and Shagari shrugged. He was a short, dirty, walnut-colored man, wearing a sailor's blue dungarees and a soiled white singlet. He was barefoot, unshaven, gap-toothed, with dripping nose, rheumy eyes, ears stuffed with thick clumps of black hair. He smelled rankly of fish. Dead fish. Long-dead fish. Tangent had a sudden vision of the Man from Tulsa and the Man from New York stalking in unexpectedly and witnessing how Tangent was spending Starrett's money. He felt sick.

"Your cousin still got that trawler?" Leiberman asked.

"Sure."

"How's fishing?"

"Lousy."

"Maybe these waters are fished out," Leiberman said. "Maybe you can make money off Asante or Togo, around there."

True to his word, Shagari seemed to sober up instantaneously.

"What you got?" he asked in a hoarse whisper.

"Cargo."

"What cargo?"

"Farm implements."

"Where from?"

"Sassandra. Your cousin still got that electric winch aboard?"

"Sure."

"Good. These implements are heavy."

"What about crew?" Shagari asked.

"You, your cousin, Pete here, me, and Yakubu."

"Yakubu? Why him?"

"Because he's fast and don't give a damn."

"One trip?"

"One for starters. Maybe more if the price is right."

"When we go?"

"Figure on being off Lomé at midnight next Tuesday. Better give it two days. So we load next Sunday. You can make it in two days, can't you?"

"If weather holds."

"It'll hold," Leiberman assured him. "I slipped God a dash. For you, a thousand francs, French."

Suddenly Shagari was drunk again.

"Joke!" he shouted. "You make funny joke!" He pounded Leiberman on the back. "Plenty funny, Sam! Good laugh!"

They settled for 1,500 French francs, and Leiberman agreed to pay for fuel, food, and wine for the trip.

Later, Tangent said, "I hope it's a seaworthy boat."

"The *Queen Mary*," Leiberman assured him. "And you remember what a great swimmer *she* was."

They drank more beer, had some lunch, then rented one of the safari bungalows. They took a nap, fully clothed, on straw ticks covered with coarse unbleached muslin sheets. Leiberman got a man to come in and spray sheets, ticks and cots before he'd let Tangent take off his shoes.

"Can't send you back to London with crabs," he said cheerfully. "Give West Africa a bad name."

It was darkling when they awoke. They splashed water on their faces from a stained enamel basin, dried on a flour sack, combed their hair in a mirror tacked to the wall. It could be tacked because it was a disk of polished tin, looking like one end of a No. 10 can. Tangent told himself he was enjoying all this.

They went back into the restaurant-bar-tavern-cabaret. It was smellier, louder, dirtier, more crowded. Leiberman grabbed a table when two black men got up to dance together. When they came back, the mercenary told them to get lost.

"I cut you," one of them said menacingly. In English.

"Sure you will," Leiberman said.

"I slice you up."

"Of course," Leiberman said.

"I take you for a ride," the other one said.

"Naturally," Leiberman said.

"I rub you out."

Then they were all laughing, the blacks so hard they could hardly stand up. Tangent bought them drinks, thimbles of Pernod, and they went off, giggling and happy.

"Nice girls," Leiberman said. "Hold the fort, Pete. I'm going to explore the kitchen and see what I can promote. I'll send a bottle of wine from the bar. If I can find something that won't burn with a wick."

They had a meal of broiled chicken, one lobster they shared, yams, rice, fresh greens, cold papayas. Everything tasted good. The Algerian wine was harsh but palatable. Leiberman got some ice chips to put in their glasses, and that helped.

They were just finishing when Shagari returned, Dele trailing behind him. She was carrying a knotted scarf holding her personal belongings, ready for the trip back to Mokodi. She squealed with pleasure, jumped onto Leiberman, clamped her arms about his neck, kissed him frantically.

"Here, here," Leiberman said. "This ain't Paris, you know."

More chairs were pulled up. More food and wine were ordered. Friends and acquaintances of Leiberman came crowding around. The mandolin and drums struck up a mournful tune, and between swallows of chicken and rice, Dele sang the words for them, in Boulé, in a sad, sweet voice.

"It's about this woman who's going to marry a rich farmer," Leiberman translated for Tangent. "It's really his younger brother she loves, but her intended owns four pigs, three goats, and two cows. So she marries him. But his barn catches fire, and he and his pigs and his goats and his cows become overdone bacon. So she goes back to the younger brother and says it was him she loved all along, and he tells her to fuck off. It's a very romantic song."

"You're kidding me," Tangent said.

"I swear I'm not. It's called 'Four Pigs, Three Goats, Two Cows.' Right now, it's number one on the Hit Parade in Abidjan. Want a woman?"

"Not at the moment, thanks."

"Didn't think you would," Leiberman said.

"What the hell that supposed to mean?" Tangent demanded.

"Jesus Christ, don't be so goddamned touchy," Leiberman said. "Just that you look happy enough with your wine. My God, you're hostile."

"Sorry," Tangent said, and tried to grin.

They drank more. Tangent started out matching Leiberman glass for glass, and then decided that was a mistake, he better slow down. But it was too late; he was seeing everything through a pleasant haze of rosy smoke that swirled, billowed, bloomed.

"The cottage is second down on the right when you need it," Leiberman said.

"I know where the cottage is," Tangent said, speaking slowly and precisely.

"Sure you do," the mercenary said. "One more bottle and you won't be able to find your ass with a boxing glove."

People came and went. Once Tangent danced with Dele. He was so tall and she was so tiny that he tired of bending over her. So he picked her up and carried her gravely about the dance floor. People cheered and sent more drinks to their table. Only now it was three tables, pushed together, a great noisy banquet of sweating men and women, falling all over each other.

Tangent, beginning to slump, felt caution leak away. He was a long way from Brindleys, a long way, and he was delighted he could still feel joy. Fun. That's what had been lacking in his life.

"Fun!" he yelled at Sam Leiberman.

"You're fucking-ay right," Leiberman said, kissing Dele, who was sitting on his lap. "Who's your girlfriend?"

"Who?" Tangent said, confused.

"Next to you," Leiberman said, motioning.

Tangent turned slowly. A white woman was sitting close to him, rubbing the cloth of his jacket sleeve between her fingers.

"Nice material," she said, her voice low and husky. "You're in the business?" She spoke English.

"No," Tangent said. "I sell farm implements."

"That's good, too," she said. "How's business?"

"Fine," he said. "You in business?"

"Yes," she said.

"What do you sell?"

"I sell me," she said, not smiling.

"Oh," Tangent said. "Well, how's business?"

"Comme ci, comme ca," she said, flipping her hand. "Right now I'm having a seasonal slump, but it'll pick up in the fall."

"I hope you're watching your cash flow," he said, but it didn't faze her a bit.

"I'll get by," she said, "until the tourists return in the fall."

"Like the swallows to Capistrano?" he giggled.

"Exactly like the swallows," she nodded gravely.

He focused his eyes, with a conscious effort, and looked at her more closely. A fleshy woman, about 40, thickly made up. Black, oily hair. A shiny black dress cut low enough to reveal massive breasts pushed together. Sweat was trickling down her throat and chest, disappearing into the tight cleavage. Her body was heavy, but it did have shape. She stared at him with dark eyes.

"I know what you need," she said.

"What?"

She leaned forward and whispered in his ear. He listened intently. She pulled away and looked at him questioningly. He considered it carefully. It might be amusing. And pleasurable. As long as he didn't have to touch her. She might be diseased.

23

Professor Jean-Louis Duclos had been asked by Captain Obiri Anokye to submit ideas for the restructuring of the Asante government after the coup had destroyed the Prempeh monarchy. Duclos approached the task with none of the trepidation he had brought to all the other important challenges and decisions he had faced in his disappointing career. He had confidence in his own intelligence, ability, talent. But at the same time, a worm gnawed. The world's rejection of his merit mocked his self-assurance.

He ascribed this scurvy treatment to his color; it was that simple. Because of his skin pigmentation—only one of thousands of inherited physical and mental characteristics, and a minor one at that—he had been denied the prizes that should rightfully have been his. It was difficult not to despair—to hate!—when he saw white men of lesser quality reap money, honors, esteem, as if such rewards were their inalienable right.

But recognizing the accident of birth that seemingly doomed him was one thing; ignoring it or rebelling against it was quite another. Until he met Captain Obiri Anokye. Then hope flared that he might help change the unjust order of things. Blacks had once been great rulers, great leaders in Africa. As the Little Captain had said at Gonja (why couldn't *he* have spoken those inspiring words?), blacks had created African civilizations that had lasted for millennia and produced a culture equal to any that history recorded.

And now Captain Anokye had asked him to design the political foundation of a new nation that might one day produce a new civilization, a black civilization that would answer the needs of Africans and provide a vehicle by which Africa would become equal or superior to the other great world powers of the 20th century. Professor Jean-Louis Duclos opened a blank notebook, filled his fountain pen, and—a stack of reference books on the floor beside him, a bottle of wine on his desk—set to work with passion and delight.

Each day, because of his poverty, he was forced to teach summer classes at the lycée and to tutor the doltish sons of government officials. But even as he discharged these mechanical tasks, his brain was working feverishly, and he rushed home each evening to his growing pile of notebooks, fervid with new ideas, bold ideas. Never had he felt so creative, so masterful. A new world began to take form beneath his speeding pen, and the gnawing of self-doubt was vanquished.

During this period, he had little time for Mboa. He gulped down the food she put before him, answered her questions in monosyllables, discouraged her attempts at conversation, fled to his study as quickly as he could to refine and make elegant the political paradise he was designing.

There was one interruption when Captain Anokye summoned him to that meeting with the oilman, Tangent. Professor Duclos had done what he could to prevent a complete capitulation to the white interlopers, but all those military and financial details really did not concern him. He saw himself as a political scientist, and if *his* efforts did not succeed, the labyrinthine plans, hopes, and ambitions of the others would come to dust.

A second interruption in his vital work came that week in an engraved invitation (all the teachers of the lycée got one) to attend a reception at the palace given by King Prempeh IV to honor the new President of Dahomey. Such an invitation, of course, was tantamount to a command; there was no question but that he would attend. It infuriated him; an evening lost from his work.

Captain Anokye, who had also received an invitation (all officers of the armed forces had), promised to call for Professor Duclos in his Land Rover. All that remained was to dress as formally as his limited wardrobe allowed.

"Maria!" he wailed. "My white shirt! I can't find my white shirt. The one with the stiff collar."

Obediently, Mboa took the white shirt, wrapped in tissue paper, from the bottom dresser drawer. She also found his cuff links and black silk hose, polished his black shoes with a scrap of cloth and palm oil, whisked his shoulders, adjusted his maroon bow tie, and stepped back to admire him, smiling, her head cocked to one side.

"You are beautiful, Jean," she said softly.

"Handsome," he said. "Men are handsome, women are beautiful."

"To me, you are beautiful."

He inspected himself in the dresser mirror, squaring his shoulders. She came up close behind him, put her arms about him. He saw her face, over his shoulder, in the mirror. As always, her coal-blackness came as an unpleasant shock. Such a contrast to his tawniness. He was no darker than a sun-tanned white. A woman in Paris had told him that. In bed. Once.

"I wish I was going to the palace with you," she said sadly.

"Don't be silly," he said. "The invitation came to me, personally. It said nothing of bringing a guest."

"If we were married, it would be for both of us. Wouldn't it, Jean?"

"I suppose so. If we were married. Don't wait up for me; I may be late."

"I'll wait up. I want to hear all about it. I wish I was going. I could, if we were married."

He made a sound of impatience, broke the clutch of her arms, stepped away from her. He smoothed his jacket where her tight embrace had wrinkled it. He went to the front window to peer out, hoping Anokye would come soon.

"What are you going to do tonight?" he asked, his back still turned to her.

She didn't answer, and he turned to look at her. She was still standing in front of the mirror where he had left her. She was weeping, arms down at her sides, looking at her tearful image in the glass.

"Now what, for God's sake?" he shouted angrily.

"Nothing, Jean, nothing. I am sorry I am crying."

"What are you crying about?"

"Nothing. It is nothing."

He stared at her in baffled fury. She was wearing a sun-yellow lappa that made her skin even blacker. Her hair was still corn-rowed, a fashion he found detestable. "Jungle style," he called it. There was no denying the dignity in her slim body, but her features had a Negroid cast: wide-spread nose, protruding lips. Put bones through her ears, he thought, and brass rings about her neck, and she might paint her breasts and dance naked under the moon. He shook his head at the insanity of this vision, and without being aware of it, ran a finger down his own straight, patrician nose and lightly touched his delicate lips.

Then, thankfully, there was a short horn beep from outside.

"The Captain," he said loudly. "I'm on my way."

"Jean," she called, but he didn't turn back.

During the short ride to the palace in the Land Rover, chauffeured by Sgt. Sene Yeboa, Professor Jean-Louis Duclos lectured to Captain Anokye:

"History teaches us that most governments fail and fall because of inability or unwillingness to respond to the needs of the people. Governments—even new governments—by their very nature tend to become conservative, bureaucratized, slaves of the status quo. Political arteries harden. Government officials resist change, since change may threaten their power. Instead of serving the people, the government becomes a self-serving entity, its own continued existence its most important responsibility.

"What I have designed for the new Asante is not unusual in its organization, with one vital exception. Basically, Asante will be a republic, government by an elected chief executive, a unicameral legislature, and an independent judiciary. Universal suffrage, but with a literacy test for voters."

"Excellent," Captain Anokye said.

"The unique feature of my plan is this—and I have given it many hours of careful thought—the constitution submitted to the citizens for ratification would mandate change. For an initial period of, say, five years, the chief executive would have extraordinary powers. To overrule decisions of the judiciary, for instance. To veto laws passed by the legislature. The purpose of this is to provide a transitional period, from absolute monarchy to parliamentary democracy, to acquaint Asantis with participant government, to improve education in order to bring greater numbers into the electorate. During such a period of growth and confusion, a strong chief executive with almost unlimited powers would be a necessity.

"At the end of the initial five-year period, the chief executive's power would be greatly reduced. The powers of the legislature—representatives of the people—and the powers of an independent judiciary would be increased. The chief executive's veto could be overridden by a two-thirds vote of the legislature, for instance, and he could overrule decisions only of the courts of appeal and the highest court. During this middle period, greater freedom would be granted to the communications media and to opposition political parties.

"During the third five-year period and thereafter, the people would be granted unlimited freedom, of speech, worship, the press, political dissent, and so forth. The judiciary would be absolutely independent of the chief executive, and the legislature could override his veto by a simple majority.

"By this schedule, I hope to mandate change as the law of the land. I feel this design will not only be sensitive to the needs and desires of an increasingly sophisticated electorate, but it will reduce social unrest to a minimum. Why plan a revolt or revolution when the constitution clearly states the democratic goals you seek will become law within a few years?"

"Interesting," Captain Anokye said. "And I presume this constitution, after it has been ratified, could be amended, altered, or even totally rescinded?"

"Of course," Duclos said. "By plebiscite."

"Good," the Little Captain said. "That is what I wanted to hear."

The palace gleamed whitely in the glare of floodlights. Fountains splashed. From the flat roof hung garlands of flowers and huge national flags of Asante and Dahomey. Across the plaza, up to the palace door, a double file of guards stood at parade rest in their uniforms of black trousers with white spatter-dashes, red tunics, white kaffiyehs bound with agals of goat's hair. All were armed with MAT 49 submachine guns and Colt .45 automatics suspended from white leather holsters.

"Handsome turnout," Anokye said, returning the salute of the lieutenant in command.

"Thank you, sir," the guards officer said languidly, turning away, not at all interested in the opinion of a mere infantry captain.

A sergeant major at the door took their invitations, checked their names off on a master list, and motioned them to the grand ballroom on the ground floor. More prestigious guests were directed up the graceful mahogany stair-way to the second-floor landing where King Prempeh IV, the new President of Dahomey, and high-ranking officials of both nations formed a reception line.

"Was Willi Abraham invited?" Duclos whispered to Anokye.

"Oh yes. They were being most correct. He is probably upstairs."

The ballroom blazed with the light of three magnificent crystal chandeliers, inherited from the former governor. French doors to the terrace had been thrown wide, but the room was uncomfortably hot, crowded with at least two hundred perspiring guests. Palace servants circulated with trays of nonalco-holic drinks in paper cups, and a buffet offered sliced meats, side dishes, fresh fruits, and petit fours which, it was said, had been flown in from Paris that morning. A small military band, stationed on a platform at one end of the long room, played a medley of popular airs, one of which was, unaccountably, "Deep in the Heart of Texas."

The guests were predominantly male and predominantly black. There was an eye-blinking variety of costumes and uniforms, from embroidered girikes to European-style dinner jackets. The military attaché of the British Embassy wore trews and a white mess jacket, and a Yoruba chief wore a splendid cloak of fine furs and seemed the coolest man in the stifling room.

The few women present displayed as much variety in their dress and hair-dos. Curiously, most of the whites wore African fashions, and most of the black women wore Western-style evening gowns and tailored suits. Near the bandstand, a few couples danced sedately, but most of the guests merely stood or circulated slowly. Conversations were muted; even laughter was quiet.

Anokye and Professor Duclos were separated in the crush. The Captain moved casually about the room, nodding to acquaintances, stopping to exchange a few words with fellow officers. He was inspecting the platters of sliced meats on the buffet when he felt a light touch on his arm. He turned to face a white man clad in a dark suit of tropical worsted. The man had obviously suffered a bad sunburn; his entire face seemed to be scaling, and the shoulders of his jacket were covered with a thick scurf.

"Captain Obiri Anokye?"

"Yes."

The man held out a peeling hand.

"Jonathan Wilson. Cultural Attaché at the American Embassy." He spoke a lame French.

They shook hands.

"Too much Asante sun?" Anokye smiled.

"Like an idiot," Wilson nodded. "In bed three days. Didn't realize how close to equator we are. Stupid."

He seemed a pleasant enough young man, only a few inches taller than Anokye, but of a slender build, with narrow shoulders and a flat stomach.

"What happened to Curtin?" Anokye asked.

"Transferred," Wilson said. "Step outside a minute? Get a breath of air?"

The Little Captain nodded and followed Wilson through the crowd, out the French doors onto the tiled terrace. There were fewer people there; they were able to find a relatively secluded place at the balustrade, overlooking a beautifully groomed formal garden dominated by a fine beobab tree in full bloom.

"Tangent not invited," Wilson said. He was not facing Anokye, but spoke softly, his lips barely moving.

"No," Anokye said, "I did not think he would be."

"Asked me to look you up."

"Oh?"

"Said you might be interested."

"In what?"

"Know the French intervention force?"

"I have heard of it, yes. A division stationed near Toulouse?"

"Right. Just moved a regiment to Senegal. Paratroops."

There was a pause.

"I see," Anokye said slowly. "Thank you, Mr. Wilson."

"Pleased to meet you, Captain." Wilson waved, moving away. "Hope we meet again."

The Little Captain sauntered around the terrace. He looked up, but the floodlights obscured the stars. He followed the terrace to the rear of the palace and thence to the other side. There were few people there, some sitting in the shadows on iron settees. A servant came by with a tray, and Anokye took a paper cup of orange juice. It was warm.

He began to retrace his steps. In the rear of the palace, standing at the parapet, a young woman, short, rather plump, turned to face him. It would have been uncultured to ignore her.

"Good evening," he said.

"Good evening—" she said. She glanced at his shoulder insignia. "—captain. Is your drink as warm as mine?"

"Warmer." He smiled. "My name is Captain Obiri Anokye, Headquarters Staff, Fourth Asante Brigade."

"Happy to meet you, Captain," she said, holding out her hand. "I am Beatrice da Silva. From Dahomey."

"Da Silva?" he said. "Portuguese?"

"Yes," she laughed. "My family were Brazilians. Freed slaves."

"You were coming back when most of the others were going?"

She laughed again. "Just so," she said.

Her ring finger was bare.

"And your father?" he asked. "In the army?"

"No," she said. "Government. He's the new Premier."

"Ah," Anokye said, startled for a moment. "Then I presume he is upstairs with the President?"

"I suppose so. I was too, but it got so boring I came down."

"I fear it is not too exciting down here either. I have never been to Dahomey. Tell me about it."

"I don't know as much as I should. I've been away at school in France for the past ten years."

"And you are now home on vacation?"

"No, for good. I've graduated."

"Congratulations!"

"Thank you," she giggled. "There were times I didn't think I'd make it. Anyway, Mommy died last year, and Daddy needs a kind of hostess now, so I came back to stay."

"You miss France?"

"Of course, but I'll get over it. Dahomey is my home, and Daddy really needs me; he's so busy. We do a lot of entertaining. I like that."

They began to stroll slowly back to the ballroom.

"Brothers or sisters?" Anokye asked.

He learned a great deal about her, listening intently to everything she told him. Her ancestors originally came from Abomey, were sold to Portuguese slavers in Porto-Novo, and ended up in Brazil. In 1864 her great-grandparents were part of the exodus of liberated slaves returning to West Africa from South America. They were all called "Brazilians," and applied their new talents, skills, sophistication, and ambition to developing an elite managerial class that won wealth and privilege during the time Dahomey was under French control. After independence was granted, in 1960, the "Brazilians" continued to dominate, in government, business, education, and the arts.

She had two sisters and a brother, all younger than she. Her family was Catholic. Her father was very intelligent and worked very hard. She loved West African food, especially pepper chicken. French food was too bland. She liked to swim in the sea, but the undertow along the Dahomeyan coast could be treacherous. Green was her favorite color. She owned a bicycle. If he must know, she was eighteen and resigned to being an old maid. She had several male "friends," but wasn't serious about any. Had the Captain ever eaten crocodile meat?

All this came pouring from her in an open, ingenuous flow. As she chattered, he listened and, when they came to the lighted doorway to the ballroom, inspected her more closely.

She was almost as dark as he, but there was a rosy undertint to her skin while his had the deep glow of burnished cordovan. She *was* plump, but well-formed; she carried herself with a jaunty youthfulness. The short, beaded evening dress she wore (green, of course!) showed good legs; slender ankles, muscled calves.

Like his sister Sara's, her hair was twigged, braided into short plaits, a dozen at least, tied with small green ribbons. He thought perhaps she was wearing rouge, but no lipstick. Little jade chips hung from pierced ears on tiny golden chains. Her perfume was fruity and sweet.

Open brow. A smooth face, untouched by worry. Or even, he thought, reflection. Laughing mouth. A warm, bubbling, confiding manner. She touched his arm frequently. She was disappointed when he confessed he could not dance, and said, "I must teach you." Young. In years and in spirit.

They spent almost an hour together, a pleasant hour. He spoke little, but her conversation never flagged. He was amused by her often shrewd observations about passing guests:

"Look at that man over there by the buffet. First decent meal he's had in weeks. See how he chomps! There—that lieutenant! Is he holding his breath? No, he's wearing a corset! I swear it! See that woman? It's a wig; I can tell. And not even hair! Some kind of synthetic. Or perhaps wood shavings!"

A Dahomeyan major, wearing staff aigulettes, came up discreetly, bowed slightly, and informed Miss da Silva her father wished her to rejoin him.

"Bye!" she said to Captain Anokye, gripping his arm.

"Thanks for putting up with my nonsense. Will I see you again?"

"I hope so," he said.

She looked into his eyes, suddenly serious.

"Try," she said.

In a few minutes, there was silence from the military band, then a fanfare that seemed never to end. But it did, and at its conclusion, the closed doors to the entrance hall were thrown open, the band played the Asante national anthem, and King Prempeh IV waddled in, escorting the President of Dahomey. Following came dignitaries of both countries, generals and ministers, ambassadors and colonels, diplomats and majors. All ranked with stiff regard for precedence.

Captain Anokye, on tiptoe, trying to see over the crowd, caught a glimpse of Beatrice da Silva, walking solemnly beside a tall, distinguished man with gray hair and a silvered beard. She kept her eyes straight ahead, but seemed to be biting her lower lip. The Little Captain could guess how close she was to hilarity.

Then the speeches began. King Prempeh conferred upon his dearest friend, the President of Dahomey, the Asante Order of the Triumphant Lion with Laurel Crown. The President conferred upon King Prempeh a newly created Medal of Extreme Valor with Golden Cluster. They embraced. Applause was enthusiastic. Chairs magically appeared. The rulers and a few of their top ministers and aides sat down. Others in the ballroom pressed back to the walls to clear a space on the parquet floor.

Into this area came bounding members of the Asante Royal Dance Company, a troupe supported by the state, that had appeared to great critical acclaim in Moscow, Paris, London, New York, Tokyo, and many other cities. They presented an abbreviated version of their most famous dances: Harvest Celebration, Welcome Home to the Warriors, Full Moon, Young Love, To the Sea God, and River Magic. Accompaniment was provided by a band of flautists and drummers who played everything from tiny bongos to great hollowed logs. The audience responded to the ancient rhythms, clapping their hands, swaying, stamping their feet lightly, chanting softly.

When the entertainment ended, King Prempeh and his honored guests returned to the second floor where, it was said, a lavish state banquet for fifty was being served. The uninvited on the lower level began to straggle toward the exits. Captain Anokye looked about for Professor Duclos and finally found him, pacing impatiently outside the main doorway.

"What a waste of time," Duclos said angrily. "Ridiculous! Can you take me home?"

"Of course. Sene is waiting. This way."

Once again they passed between that double file of armed palace guardsmen. Captain Anokye looked at the Muslims closely and was impressed. Big men, with a professional air about them. Many mustached, with short tufts of beard. Hard eyes. He knew they would not die easily.

On the return trip the Little Captain said to Duclos, "Tell me more about the duties of the chief executive under this proposed constitution of yours. For instance, would he be commander of the armed forces?"

"Of course he would," the Professor said enthusiastically. "Commander-in-chief actually, ruling through a minister of defense."

"Could he conclude treaties with other nations on his own authority?"

"During the first five-year period, yes. During the second period and thereafter, he would require the consent of the legislature."

"Could he declare war?"

"The same conditions as pertain to treaties," Duclos said. "During the first period, the chief executive would be empowered to declare war on his own authority. After five years, he would require the consent of the legislature. An added factor: After ten years, the nation could not go to war without the approval of the electorate. A simple majority would suffice."

"But such things take time. What would the chief executive do in case of invasion or obvious threat of attack—wait for a vote?"

"Not at all. The chief executive would be empowered to use the full strength of the armed forces in time of invasion or national emergency without consulting the legislature or the electorate."

"I am glad to hear it," Captain Anokye said. No irony in his tone. "How many years does the chief executive serve?"

"Five," Duclos said. "He cannot serve two consecutive terms. But he may serve five years, remain out of office for five, then run again for another term. The same holds true for legislators. This is just another factor to insure change and growth, to make certain the government is constantly served by an infusion of new blood, fresh ideas, bold approaches to problems."

"You have thought of everything," the Little Captain said admiringly. "I presume the chief executive is served by a cabinet of ministers?"

"Naturally," Professor Duclos said. "During the first five-year period, the chief executive may appoint whom he pleases. During the second period, his choices must be confirmed by the legislature. During the third period, cabinet positions become elective posts. Everything has been designed to make the new Asante government a living, growing organism."

"You have all this written down?" Anokye asked.

"Yes. Roughly. In notebooks. I am almost finished. Then I will organize the material formally, type it up, and submit it for comment."

"I would not care to have it fall into the King's hands," Anokye said. "Guard it well."

"With my life!" Professor Jean-Louis Duclos said fervently.

As they turned into the road leading to Duclos' home, Sgt. Yeboa leaned forward suddenly, staring through the windshield.

"Captain," he said warningly.

Anokye and Duclos craned to look. At least twenty people milled about in the packed-earth yard in front of Duclos' house.

"What is it?" the Professor said. "What are they doing? What's happening?"

The crowd saw the Land Rover pull up, rushed to peer through the windows. When they saw Professor Duclos, a loud wail went up, and all began to jabber at once. Captain Anokye climbed from the car, faced the frenetic throng. All the men were speaking loudly at once, all the women were weeping, some rocking back and forth, aprons thrown over their heads in grief. The Captain held up a commanding hand.

"Silence!" he thundered. When they had quieted, he pointed at one man. "You, speak. Say what happened."

With frequent interruptions, the story came out. About an hour previously, neighbors had been startled and frightened to hear a loud scream from the

Duclos home. They had rushed to investigate and had found Mboa lying on the floor of the kitchen. Her slashed wrists were spouting blood. A fish-scaling knife lay nearby.

While some tried to tie rope and twine tightly about her arms, others had run to the corner fruit and vegetable market, which had the only telephone on the street. They had broken the locked door and had entered to call the gendarmerie.

"Nothing was stolen at the market," the speaker assured Captain Anokye.

A red squad car had soon arrived—"A matter of minutes, sir"—and the gendarmes had taken Mboa to the Mokodi Royal Hospital. Neighbors had called just a few minutes ago, and had been told that while she was still alive, her condition was critical and blood donors were needed. Immediately, several had set off to give blood for Mboa, but since they were walking, and the Hospital was at least two miles away, who knew if they would arrive on time?

As Jean-Louis Duclos listened to this report, his features grew ashen, and he slumped back against the car. Sgt. Yeboa moved to support him. Anokye went into the Duclos home. Stepping over a frighteningly large pool of blood on the kitchen floor, he took a bottle of wine from the cupboard, went back outside, and made Duclos take several small swallows. Then the Professor pushed the bottle away, put his hands to his face, began moaning.

"Sergeant," Anokye said, "take him to the Hospital. Stay with him as long as necessary. Then return to the barracks."

Yeboa assisted Duclos into the front seat of the Land Rover. The Professor seemed in shock.

"I love you, Maria," he kept repeating.

Anokye turned to the neighbors.

"You have done well," he told them. "I am proud of you."

They looked down, shuffled their feet, smiled shyly.

"Mboa is a fine girl," one of the women called loudly, and the others nodded.

"Always ready to help," another said.

"Yes," the Little Captain said. "Now please, return to your homes and pray for her recovery."

They dispersed slowly. He stood there until the street was empty, then went back into Duclos' home. He found the notebooks in full view on the desk in the study. He had to go back into that dreadful kitchen—flies and roaches already feasting on the spilled blood—to locate Mboa's string shopping bag. He put all the notebooks inside, then added several pages of rough notes and scribbled references. He turned off the lights and, carrying the bag, started walking to the Golden Calf.

He walked slowly; there was much to consider. And he knew, because of the many visitors in the city for the King's reception, Yvonne and her girls would be busy.

There were clouds moving slowly across the moon. The air smelled damply of rain. It intensified all the odors of Asante: the spicy aromas of cooking, perfume of sweet flowers, tangy scent of resinous wood, and beneath all, like a deep diapason, the stirring smell of the land itself, rich and fecund. It seemed to him a land that had lain fallow long enough and was now bursting to be sown.

As usual, he entered the Golden Calf through the kitchen. He went directly to Yvonne Mayer's apartment. She was not there, but the door was unlocked and he entered. He took off tunic, shoes, and socks, and sat down heavily at her desk. She came flying in breathlessly a few moments later, informed of his arrival. She kissed his cheek, told him the house was crowded, with clients waiting in the downstairs parlor, and that she must oversee everything for at least another hour or two.

"Of course," he said. "I understand."

"You promise to wait, Bibi?"

"I promise. Perhaps I shall take a short nap. Before you go back, would you put these notebooks in your safe? Duclos' work on the new government."

She locked them away in a heavy safe built into the wall behind a curtain. Then she kissed him again and was gone.

He locked the door behind her, went to her liquor cabinet and poured himself a small glass of Italian brandy. Then he undressed and, taking the brandy with him, went into the bathroom for a tepid shower. After he dried, he put on Yvonne's kimono, sat down again at her desk, and phoned the Mokodi Royal Hospital. He identified himself and was told that Mboa Aikpe—it was the first time he had heard her surname—was slightly improved, and the prognosis was now guardedly optimistic. Satisfied, he took a deep swallow of brandy. Then he sat stolidly, chin on chest, staring at the complex design of the Chinese rug.

He was still sitting thus, planning, rejecting, accepting, when Yvonne returned almost two hours later. Her face was slack with fatigue. She took the brandy glass from his hand, drained it, shuddered slightly, then smiled wanly.

"I feel tied in knots," she said. "I must have a hot bath. Come in and talk to me."

In the bathroom, he sat on the closed toilet seat and watched her loll in the sudsy water, steam rising. Her eyes closed in bliss. The oiled and scented water slicked her white arms and breasts. Beneath the glimmering surface, pale torso and legs wavered and moved feebly, like a limpid underwater plant bobbing on currents.

He made her laugh with her description of the reception, how the King had made his waddling entrance after a long fanfare of trumpets, how he had received a medal for "extreme valor" from a man he had met that day for the first time and to whom he referred as his "dearest friend."

He told her of what happened later, how they had returned to Duclos' home to discover what Mboa had done, or attempted to do. Yvonne's face showed shock, horror, pity. Her eyes brimmed with tears, but she wiped them away. She was encouraged by the report Anokye had received from the Hospital and vowed to visit Mboa the very next day.

Later, clad in nightgown and peignoir, she sat at the table with the Little Captain and shared a platter of "small things" she had sent up from the kitchen: radishes, cucumbers, pickled melon balls, squares of cold yam, goat cheese, chunks of smoked beef tongue. They cleaned it all up and traded belches. Then sat back, both quiescent, eyes lidded with weariness.

"What happened to Mboa," Anokye said, "is the result of Duclos not speaking what he felt. When he feared she might die, then he knew his love for her and would have spoken of it. But it was almost too late."

"You believe they will marry, Bibi?"

"If she lives, yes, I think so."

"It is a lesson to him," she said, almost angrily.

"A lesson for me, also," he said, looking at her. "I must tell you how I feel toward you."

Her eyes widened in alarm.

"You're leaving me?" she said. "You've come tonight to say goodbye?"

He smiled at her.

"No, Yvonne, not to say good-bye. But you must know I cannot marry you. If the coup succeeds or fails, no difference; we cannot marry."

"Oh *that*," she said, relieved. "I knew that from the start. I never expected it, never let myself think of it. I am content the way things are, Bibi. I want nothing more from you than what I already have."

"I speak to you this way because I love you," he said. "I do not believe it is your kind of love, but it is mine. I love you, my family, Sene Yeboa, Willi Abraham, Professor Duclos. Even Peter Tangent. Yes, I love you all."

"Surely you love me in a different way than you love the others?" she protested.

"No, Yvonne," he said gently. "I love you all for the faith you have in me."

"And in bed?" she asked. "Does that not count?"

"Surely, it counts," he said. "It is a great happiness for me, but it is not why I love you. Yvonne, I speak so truthfully because of what happened to Duclos tonight. Also, I know your intelligence, your knowledge of people and why they act as they do. I have told you more of my plans and hopes than I have told anyone else. Because I value your counsel and your friendship. You know this?"

"Yes."

"I want to continue that friendship. But I must tell you this: tonight at the reception I met a woman I wish to marry."

She stared at him, puzzled.

"You met her tonight? For the first time?"

"Yes. I do not know if she wishes to marry me, or will wish to if I am able to see her again. Or even if her father will allow her to marry me."

"Who is her father?"

"He is the new Premier of Dahomey."

"Ah!"

"Yes. At this time, there is no question of love between this woman and myself. I spoke to her for only an hour. But I feel she is interested in me. It would be an advantageous match. If I can convince her. And her father."

"If you wish to, you will," she said. "And me? If you marry?"

"I would want things to continue as they have been," he said. "That is my wish. But the decision is yours to make. That is why I tell you this now."

"But *could* we continue?" she asked. "It would be difficult."

"Difficult, yes," he agreed. "But I believe it could be done. If you desire it."

She tried to laugh.

"I knew you could not marry me and I was content," she said. "But now I am not so content, sharing you with another woman."

"I would not change to you."

"I know that, Bibi, but still . . ."

"I said it was your decision. If you wish not to see me again, I will accept that. It will sadden me, but I will understand."

"I don't know," she said. She rose, began to pace about the room. "I don't know what to do, what to say."

"It is not necessary to decide now, at this moment," he said. "Consider it for a time. I may never marry this woman."

"But if not her, then someone else?"

"Yes," he said, "that is true. Eventually. If not her, then someone else."

"Is she beautiful?"

"No, not as you. She is short, heavy, young."

"Oh!" she said bitterly. "Young!"

"It means nothing to me," he said. "You know that."

"But her father means something?"

"Yes. Will you consider it, Yvonne?"

"I suppose so."

"Do you wish me to leave now?"

"Yes. No. Yes. I don't know what I want. *Tell* me, Bibi!"

In bed, he lay beside her, a few inches away, their naked bodies not touching. But he stroked her with his strong fingers until her rigidity melted, the knot within her loosened, limbs relaxed, flesh became warm and yielding.

"I don't care," she said. "Don't care. I can't give you up. *Can't!* Please, Bibi, never go away from me. Swear it."

"I swear it."

She dug a hand, an arm, beneath him and pulled, tugged, until he rolled over on top of her. She spread her thighs wide, bent her knees, linked her ankles behind his back. She gripped his hair fiercely, pulled his face close to hers.

"If you desert me," she whispered, "if you deny what you have sworn to me, then I will do what Mboa did tonight. But I shall succeed. And after I am dead, I will come back and put a curse on you. All you have worked for and dreamed will come to nothing. You will fail. If you desert me."

He shivered and pressed closer.

"Do you believe what I have said?" she demanded.

"I believe."

Then she was all molten heat, seeking his brutality, clutching him and moaning and calling him "lord," and "King," and "master."

24

"No, no, Mr. Greeley," Captain Anokye said. "I don't think that would work at all."

"What? What?" the chief teller barked. Indignant.

They were standing at Greeley's study table, looking down at a map of Asante. Perched on the city of Mokodi, covering the suburbs and port area, was a French chasseur-à-cheval, a trooper of the 19th Century Imperial Guard. His little carbine and sword were finely detailed.

"In planning this military maneuver," Anokye patiently explained, "I have tired to put myself into the mind of a rebel leader planning a coup d'etat. I assume his resources are limited, perhaps no more than a few hundred trained and armed followers. Even granting the citizens were sympathetic to his cause, how could he hope to take Mokodi?"

"Strike for the jugular!" cried Alistair Greeley.

"No, sir," the Little Captain disagreed. "Not armed only with rifles and sidearms. Not when taking Mokodi means taking the palace. That would mean attacking the guard—superbly trained, well equipped, almost fanatical professionals. The rebellion would bleed to death on the plaza before they could get close enough to toss a single grenade through a palace window."

"Then what do you suggest? What? What?"

"Here," Anokye said. He lifted the model soldier gently and set it down so that it covered a circle marking the city of Gonja.

Greeley looked up in puzzlement. "Why there?"

"Gonja is almost in the exact center of Asante. It dominates the north-south Royal Highway. It is the hub of all these secondary roads—here, here, and here. Hardly a kilo of food reaches Mokodi that hasn't first passed through Gonja. In addition, the pipeline bringing fresh water from the north runs alongside the highway. The main pumping station is here, a few kilometers south of the city. If you control Gonja, you control the capital's food and water."

"Starve 'em out?" Greeley asked.

"Exactly. But there are other factors just as important. The Gonja armory is the largest in the country outside of the Mokodi barracks. If the rebels took Gonja, they'd have an excellent source of weapons and ammunition to supply their own needs and to arm their supporters. The Gonja garrison, including the arsenal, is lightly manned and guarded. A determined insurgent cadre could capture it easily. Then, with a greater force adequately armed, it could move down the highway to lay siege to Mokodi."

"Softening it up by cutting off the food supply and water?"

"Precisely. Under the circumstances, I think the public would force the capitulation of the government to the rebels' demands. The palace would be surrendered without a shot being fired."

"That is how you intend to do it?" Greeley asked. His eyes were wise.

"That is how I believe it *could* be done," Captain Anokey corrected him. "Do you agree with me, sir?"

"Absolutely!" Greeley cried. "Very ingenious, Captain. My congratulations."

"Your teaching," the Little Captain smiled. "You have repeated many times that 'War is geography.' "

"But what about Kumasi and Kasai?"

"Of minor importance. Once Gonja is taken, those towns would simply wither, to surrender after the capital falls. Besides, they are outside the physical area in which I will conduct this exercise."

"But you feel the rebels' main thrust would be at Gonja?"

"Correct," Captain Anokye nodded gravely. "The city itself, the garrison and arsenal, and the pumping station. This is the problem I mean to assign my junior officers the morning of the maneuver."

"And when will that be?" Greeley asked.

Captain Anokye, studying the map intently, looked up.

"Pardon me, sir? I didn't hear."

"When do you plan this maneuver to take place?"

"I've scheduled it for the twelfth of August. To start in the morning."

"The sooner the better," Greeley said excitedly. "What? What?"

"True, Mr. Greeley," Anokye said. "The sooner the better."

The agreement between Anokye and the Nyam specified that each could be accompanied by a single aide. The meeting was to be held in the back room of a waterfront bar. It happened to be the place where Sene Yeboa had stomped to death the rebel who had threatened the Little Captain. But the sergeant said nothing of this as he and Anokye drove directly to the rendezvous from the home of Alistair Greeley. The Captain and Yeboa wore civilian clothes. Both were armed. They parked several blocks away, locked the Land Rover, walked through the darkened streets to the bar.

The Nyam and his aide had already arrived, wearing soiled raincoats and black berets. They sat at one table in the empty, dimly lighted room. Anokye and the sergeant sat at a table facing them, about two meters away. No greetings were exchanged; no drinks were offered or ordered.

"The weapons?" the Nyam asked at once. "Where are the weapons?"

As before, he could not sit quietly, but thrust his feet out, drew them back, changed his position, straightening, slumping. His fingertips flicked off his thumbs constantly in a tic he could not control. But his burning eyes never left Anokye's face.

"You will receive them within a week," the Little Captain said. "A hundred Russian assault rifles with sufficient ammunition."

"Kalashnikovs?" the Nyam asked.

"Yes. Will you require instruction on their use?"

The Nyam's aide laughed suddenly, a brief, harsh sound in the shadowed room.

"No," the Nyam said. He showed large, yellowed teeth beneath the thick black mustache. "We know how to use them. What else?"

"That is all."

"All? No machine guns? No mortars?"

"Machine guns are primarily defensive weapons," Captain Anokye said. "You will have no need for them. The few mortars we have will not be available to you. But you will be able to obtain others?"

"Oh? And how may I do that?"

"By attacking and capturing the garrison and armory at Gonja. Whatever weapons you liberate are yours."

The Nyam straightened, leaned forward eagerly.

"And vehicles?"

"Vehicles also. Food. Equipment. Whatever the garrison contains."

"How many men are stationed there?"

"Sergeant?" Anokye said, turning his head slightly.

"Not more than fifty, sir," Yeboa said. "Probably less."

The Nyam, in turn, glanced at his aide. The rebel nodded briefly.

"A surprise assault," Anokye said. "You should have no problems. Discipline is lax in Third Brigade. There is one guard at the gate. No perimeter defense. The morning meal is at oh six hundred. I suggest you attack then."

"And where will you be?"

"In Mokodi."

"Ah? Taking the palace? Installing yourself as president—or king?"

"No, I will not be doing that," Anokye said sternly. "My men will be taking over the Mokodi barracks, neutralizing the navy and air force, the tank, engineer, and supply units, seizing the power station, newspaper and cable offices, and establishing control of all roads leading into the city. The assault on the palace will not commence until you and your men arrive from Gonja, after you have captured the garrison."

The Nyam stared at him a moment, his heavy lids drooping.

"You give your word on this?" he demanded.

"It is not a question of giving my word," Anokye said. "I will not have sufficient men to do everything that must be done and assault the palace by myself. I will need your help, and I will wait for it. I suggest that as soon as the Gonja garrison is taken, you bring your men to Mokodi as quickly as possible. In captured military vehicles or in commandeered civilian trucks and cars."

The Nyam thought awhile. Perhaps he had a mental image of a glorious armed convoy speeding south to Mokodi. Himself standing erect in the leading jeep, an automatic rifle cradled in his arms. Flags and pennants snapping. Citizens along the way cheering and throwing flowers . . .

Anokye and Yeboa waited patiently, expressionless.

"How do you intend to assault the palace?" the Nyam asked finally, and they knew they had won.

"With the mortars we have," Anokye said. "And those you bring."

"Good," the Nyam said, eyes glistening. "We will bury the running dogs of the colonial imperialists in a fitting tomb, the ruins of their own palace."

"Yes," the Little Captain said tonelessly. "Be prepared to move any day after the first of August. I will give you twenty-four hours' notice. Is that sufficient?"

"Yes, enough," the Nyam said. "Where will we receive the weapons?"

"Can you receive them on the coast? Or shall we truck them inland?"

Again the Nyam looked to his aide. The rebel bent forward, put his lips close to the Nyam's ear. The two men whispered a moment.

"The coast," the Nyam said finally. "We will make our own arrangements."

"As you wish. I will inform you when and where they will arrive. Is there anything else?"

"Yes," the Nyam said. "The King must die. Or he will remain a constant threat to the new Asante."

Captain Anokye shrugged. "What will be, will be. The battle itself will dictate who lives and who dies."

"Do you intend to take prisoners?" the Nyam demanded.

"The men of Third Brigade, yes. They are loyal Asantis, but badly led. I believe many will surrender and come to our side. The palace guard will not surrender. It will be necessary to kill them."

"Good," the Nyam said. "We will meet again before the attack?"

"Once again. To decide on timing, passwords, and so forth. Is there some way your people can be identified? By clothing or insignia? So my men will not fire upon them?"

The Nyam pondered a moment. The aide leaned forward again to whisper in his ear.

"Yes, good," the Nyam said. "Katsuva suggests a piece of red cloth tied around the right arm."

"Excellent," Anokye said. "I will have my people informed that those wearing red armbands are to be treated as brothers."

"Have you thought more on the organization of the new government?" the Nyam asked.

"No," the Little Captain said. "As I told you, I am a soldier, not a politico. I leave the formation of a new government to you. I would like to be commander of the armed forces."

"Of course," the Nyam said.

The Captain and Sgt. Yeboa departed first. The Nyam and his aide watched them go. They waited in silence a few moments. Katsuva went to the curtained doorway and peeked out, making certain the soldiers had departed. Then he came back to the Nyam.

"You trust him?" he asked.

"So far and no farther," the Nyam said, grinning. "We will capture the Gonja garrison, then go to Mokodi to assist in the destruction of the palace." He paused to stare at his aide. "As he said, the battle will dictate who lives and who dies. Can you take care of it?"

Katsuva nodded. "He will die a hero's death," he said. "All Asante will grieve."

"Mrs. Greeley!" Peter A. Tangent caroled. "What a pleasant surprise!"

As planned, they had met "accidentally" on the sidewalk near the Restaurant Cleopatra. It was their third meeting. At the second, they had agreed upon a final price of three thousand British pounds. Mrs. Greeley received half of this as a down payment. She was to receive an additional 500 each time she reported to Tangent on her husband's telephoned conversations with Anatole Garde, until the final payment had been made.

"In the event the number of your reports of the telephone calls exceeds the agreed-upon total payment of three thousand pounds," Tangent had explained precisely, "payment for the said additional reports will be made at a rate of fifty pounds per report. Is that satisfactory?"

"What?" Mrs. Greeley had said.

It was not that Tangent expected her betrayal of her husband to be of any further value. They already knew what they needed to know. It was just that he wanted to foreclose the possibility of her hawking her wares elsewhere. Like informing Anatole Garde of what she had told Tangent. He wanted her secure. Money would do it.

Now, chatting loudly for the benefit of any observer/listener, he steered her into the dim, cool interior of the Cleopatra. At that hour, the place was almost empty, as he knew it would be. They sat at a far corner table, and Tangent handed over his folded copy of the Asante *New Times*. Within its folds nestled her payment of 500 pounds. Without peeking, she put the paper into her tapestry knitting bag. When the waiter came up, she ordered a sloe gin fizz. Tangent had a vodka gimlet.

After the drinks had been served, he said, "Well?"

Like a schoolgirl reciting a memorized theme, she rattled off what her husband had said to Anatole Garde on the phone the previous evening. Tangent listened closely, not interrupting. When she had finished, they both took sips of their drinks. Then he leaned forward over the table. She leaned forward. Their heads almost touched.

"Two points," he said in a low voice. "You're certain he told Garde that the main attack would be at Gonja?"

"Absolutely."

"And he told him the maneuver would start on the morning of August twelfth?"

"Absolutely."

"Thank you." Tangent said back, smiling. "And how is your lovely sister-in-law?" he inquired.

"Very well, thank you," Maud Greeley said primly. She could not meet his eyes.

"A small problem, Mrs. Greeley," he said. "I'll be away for two or three days. So don't panic if you can't contact me. I expect to return by Wednesday morning. If you have anything to report, just save it till then."

"Taking a little vacation?" she said archly.

"Something like that," he said.

25

After that Walpurgisnacht at the Hôtel d'Azur, Peter Tangent was nagged by the fear that he had hired a bunch of drunken clowns. But when he boarded the trawler late that Sunday night at the Sassandra wharf, he was gratified to find an unexpectedly sober and professional crew of mercenaries.

They went about the task of loading with the ease of long experience. The boom swung in and out like a metronome, the electric winch whined efficiently, the wooden crates set down into the midships hold with a solid thump. The men rarely spoke. When they did, it was mostly in obscenities directed toward inanimate objects:

To a crate of rifles: "Get up there, you motherfucker."

To a coil of rope: "Get out of my way, you shit-brained cock sucker."

To a case of grenades that came apart: "I'll get you for that, you cunt-lapping whoreson."

And so forth . . .

Sam Leiberman was directing the loading with gestures and grunts. Yakubu, tall, skinny, still wearing his red bandanna and the gold ring in his left ear, manhandled the crates into the cargo net on the dock. Shagari, as dirty as before, a villain, unloaded the cargo net below. The winch was operated by Shagari's cousin, who seemed to be known to the others simply as "Cousin."

He was short, fat, wearing a dark green undershirt bulged by almost feminine breasts. He chomped a cold, wet cigar.

The whole operation seemed to be taking place with little effort at secrecy or concealment. Leiberman had assured Tangent that the dock watchman, the Ivory Coast gendarmes, and the harbor master had all been adequately dashed. But it still seemed incredible to Tangent that they were loading, quite openly, a shipment of arms to be used in overthrowing a legitimate African government. He felt, somehow, there should be bull's-eye lanterns, muttered passwords, armed lookouts.

When he mentioned this, the mercenary looked at him in astonishment.

"Guns go out of here every day in the week," he said. "For God's sake, it's *business*."

But Tangent's most serious doubts were reserved for the trawler itself. It was called *La Belle Dame*, and after one look, Tangent thought the *Sans Merci* could well be added.

It was certainly the strangest boat he had ever seen. He was ready for an old boat, even an ancient boat. And he guessed it would be filthy, cluttered, smelly, and uncomfortable. But he was not prepared for that design, if design it was and not just a crazy, haphazard joining of disparate sections.

A lofty pilothouse (with small cabin and engine room below) was shoved far aft. The foredeck, which appeared to be planked with sections of used crates still showing the original stenciling, extended only three meters back from the clumsy prow. Between this flimsy deck and the aft pilothouse was, almost literally, nothing. Only a large open hold from which a leaning mast and cargo boom protruded. On both sides of this enormous black hole, narrow catwalks ran fore and aft.

What worried Tangent was the freeboard, the distance between the surface of the water and the low gunnel of that midships hold. As *La Belle Dame* was loaded, it sank farther and farther until it seemed to Tangent that a wavelet in a park lake might be sufficient to lap over and swamp them, let alone the open sea.

He mentioned this to Leiberman.

"Nah. I been out in this tub before. She'll do."

"What if we run into rough weather?"

"Then she won't do. You want off?"

"No," Tangent said. "I can swim."

"Bully for you," Leiberman said. "I can't. But I'm not worried because my heart is pure. That's the last load. Now we add the fish."

And so they did. Not even bothering to use a tarp over the crates of weapons, but shoveling fish on top and spreading them around to make a reasonably effective cover. Within moments it appeared the trawler's hold was filled with a fine catch.

"Never stand any kind of inspection," Leiberman said, "but nothing else would either."

Final preparation included loading demijohns of wine and water, bread, cooked meats, some cold fufu, baked yams, fresh fruit, tins of sardines, cans of orange juice, paper cups and plates, etc. Coffee. Two bottles of Scotch and one of brandy. And two large cardboard cartons containing Leiberman's personal gear: an M3, two Uzis, three fragmentation grenades, an old Springfield with telescopic sight, a Colt .45, a Smith & Wesson .38, a delicate .22 with pearl grips, an old Very pistol with two flares, ammunition, a flashlight, a mayonnaise jar filled with a plastic explosive, caps, fuse, wire, a metal tea box filled with black gunpowder, binoculars, and a small tin mezuzah.

"Nearer, my God, to Thee," Leiberman said cheerfully.

They got underway about 0230, running lights rigged, and Tangent took as a good omen the fact that the engine farted into life almost immediately, and settled down to a comfortable pant. They headed out of the harbor, Cousin at the wheel, and within minutes were chugging slowly eastward, close enough to the coast to mark the lights of Sassandra, Grand-Lahou, Dabou, and Port Bouet.

"Ah, this is the life," Leiberman sighed. He was sitting on the midships catwalk, his legs dangling down into the hold. "Give me a stout ship, a merry crew, and a fair wind. Then Ho! for the Indies. How about a wee bit of the old nasty before we turn in?"

Tangent joined him, bringing a bottle of Scotch and paper cups. They filled their cups, then passed the bottle up to Shagari and Cousin in the pilothouse. Yakubu had taken a demijohn of wine to the foredeck and was sprawled out on his back, staring at the night sky and crooning softly.

"What's he singing?" Tangent asked.

"Some bush thing," Leiberman said. "About a warrior who turned into a snake. I know a guy who took a cunt for a drive and turned into a motel. Here's looking at you."

They sat silently awhile, sipping their Scotch.

"Nice night," Tangent said, looking about.

Leiberman grunted, leaning back against the gunnel. He held his paper cup atop his thick belly.

The offshore breeze brought the sultry smell of the land, sweet and stirring. The wake gurgled pleasantly. Above, the stars whirled their shining courses.

"So many," Tangent murmured. "So close. So much brighter than at home."

"Home?" Leiberman said. "Where you from, Tangent? Ohio?"

"Indiana."

"No shit? I never would have guessed it. You know how I tell guys from Indiana? They never untie their ties when they get undressed at night. They slip the knot down on the short end and pull the tie off over their heads. After a while the tie gets worn, and the stuffing starts to come out. You see a guy with the stuffing coming out of his tie, and the odds are ten to one he's from Indiana. Bet you can't guess where I'm from."

"Burbank, California," Tangent said.

Leiberman turned to look at him.

"You sonofabitch," he said softly. "You got a file on me, haven't you?"

"That's right," Tangent said equably. "I like to know who I'm hiring."

"How did you get in the oil business?"

"The money's good," Leiberman said. "If you live to collect. No pension, but you don't have to kiss too many asses. You're a queer duck."

"Queer? How?"

"I told you. I can't figure your angle on this Asante thing."

"Strictly business."

"Bullshit. You act like it's some kind of personal crusade."

"That's ridiculous," Tangent said. "Oil is what it's all about."

"If you say so," Leiberman sighed. "Get that bottle back; I need a refill. And get me another paper cup; this one is beginning to leak."

Tangent obeyed, rising cautiously and stepping carefully along the catwalk to the pilothouse deck. Shagari was asleep, wedged into a corner, snoring heavily. Cousin was still at the wheel, his eyes half-closed. The wet cigar, unlighted, was clamped in his teeth, chewed down to a butt. Tangent took the opened Scotch bottle and paper cups back to Leiberman.

"Married, Tangent?"

"No."

"Ever been?"

"No. How about you?"

"You mean it's not in that file of yours?" Leiberman jeered. "Shit, I got wives and kids all over the place. Of course, most of them were bush marriages, performed by some joker wearing a coconut mask and a feathered jock-strap. But I guess they made as much sense as saying 'I do' in a Stateside church and having a handful of rice tossed in your kisser."

"What's going to happen when you get old?" Tangent asked softly.

"In my business, no one gets old. But *no* one."

"How old are you?"

"On the sunny side of forty-five."

"Which side is that?"

"The other side," Leiberman said. "The down side. But I can still outfight and outfuck you any day of the week and twice on Sundays."

"I believe it," Tangent said. "Ever been scared? Not when you're fucking, when you're fighting."

"Scared?" Leiberman said. "Goddamned right. All the time. That's the kick. Feeling it and putting it away from you. Ever been in a firefight, Tangent?"

"No, I never have."

"If you go along with the Little Captain when he makes his move, you'll be in a firefight."

"I know."

"You're liable to shit your pants."

"I suppose so," Tangent sighed. "I'm not very brave."

"Who the hell is?" Leiberman asked. "The last party I went to—this was in the Congo—this big stud came at me with a sticker about ten feet long. I was carrying a machine pistol, some piece of Polish junk. So this guy came at me with this sticker, and I pulled the trigger, and the gun fell apart. I mean the whole goddamned gun literally fell apart. Lousy Polish joke."

"What did you do?" Tangent asked breathlessly.

"I started reciting the kaddish."

"No, no kidding, what happened?"

"He tripped," Leiberman said. "Can you believe it? This jungle-trained paskudnyak tripped over a vine and went flying ass over teakettle."

"Did you kill him?"

"Kill him, shit," Leiberman said. "I ran like a goosed golem. That's what I'm trying to tell you. There are times to be brave and times not to be stupid. Enough of this philosophy; let's get some sleep."

They slept in the tiny, bare cabin, taking off their shoes but not undressing. Tangent was certain he would be long awake in those strange surroundings. But he fell asleep almost instantly. He awoke once, toward dawn, and opened his eyes to see Leiberman up, yawning, trying to work the stiffness out of his shoulders and knees.

"Taking the wheel for a while," the mercenary whispered. "Go on back to sleep. I'll wake you if we sink."

Tangent closed his eyes and drowsed. After a while he awoke, looked at his watch, saw it was almost 0900. He heard Leiberman's footsteps overhead. It had to be Leiberman; the other three were barefoot. Tangent rose cautiously; he could not stand upright in the cramped cabin. Leaning against a bulkhead, he pulled on his shoes, then climbed the short ladder and stepped out onto the narrow deck that circled the pilothouse.

It was a blazing morning, hot and clear. To the westward, directly aft, the Atlantic Ocean stretched to a far horizon, heaving gently. Off the port beam was the green coast of Africa, a section of rain forest that came down almost to the sea. There were other boats in the area, small fishing craft, a rusty freighter directly ahead, and far out to starboard a white, rakeo-stack cruise ship. *La Belle Dame* chugged on, slowly and steadily. Tangent was pleased.

"Where are we?" he asked Yakubu.

"Off Ghana," the black said. "Past Cape Three Points. Coming up to Cape Coast."

"Right on the old kazoo," Sam Leiberman said. "We may have to kill some time before the meet. Have some breakfast."

Tangent had a can of warm orange juice, ate two slices of dry bread and a mango, drank three cups of black, chicory-laced coffee. Like the other men, he pissed over the side. There was a small head off the little cabin, the zinc toilet flushed by seawater, but the closet was so smelly that Sam Leiberman preferred to let down his pants and underdrawers and sit on the midships gunnel, his great white ass stuck out over the sea. Shagari said something to him in Boulé. Leiberman replied in kind, and the three blacks got hysterical.

"What was that about?" Tangent said.

"Shagari said a shark would come up out of the water and bite my ass off. I told him sharks won't eat kosher meat."

"Hilarious," Tangent said, and opted for self-imposed constipation before he would follow Leiberman's example or dare the stench of the below-decks head.

Cousin showed him the compass, pointed out the heading, and handed over the wheel without comment. He went below with Shagari. Yakubu went to his favorite spot on the foredeck. Leiberman began to disassemble and clean the tools of his trade on the pilothouse catwalk. Tangent was left alone, nervous at the wheel, making little adjustments to keep his course exact.

"Relax," Leiberman called from outside. "Take it easy. If you go off, you can always correct. We got plenty of bottom around here. You're not going to pile us up."

After that, it was fun. Standing erect at the wheel, feeling the throb of the engine through his soles. Most of the pilothouse windows were broken; a cool sea breeze came billowing through.

"Haul down your mains'l stays'l fores'l jib," Leiberman yelled. "Run out the port battery. You may fire when ready, Gridley."

Tangent grinned. He really did feel that way. He gripped the wheel firmly, surveyed the ocean grandly. In a few moments they ran into a brief rain squall, mild as mist. Then they were through, and he saw a rainbow. He didn't want to be anywhere else.

The day went pleasantly. By nightfall, they were coming up to Accra and nearing the coast of Asante. Cousin slowed the engine until they were barely making headway, sea mercifully calm, sky clear. Shagari put a line over the side and caught a nice bass which he gutted, skinned, and cut up. The three blacks and Leiberman ate it raw, but Tangent passed. He ate half a roast chicken, fufu, yams, and some canned fruit salad. He was ravenous.

At dusk, Leiberman took a loaded Uzi and extra magazines to the foredeck where he had a long, huddled conference with Yakubu. The weapon and ammunition were left there, concealed under a scrap of greasy canvas. Leiberman came back to the pilothouse. He pulled the Colt .45 from his box of tricks and handed it to Tangent.

"Ever fire one of these?"

"No," Tangent said. "My God, it's heavy."

"This little gizmo here is the safety. Off. On. There's another safety in the grip, so you've got to grab it hard or it won't fire. This dignus releases the magazine. See—full clip. You jack one into the chamber. When you want to fire, grab the gun with your right hand. Support your right hand with your left. Tight! Hold the gun out in front of you, two-handed. Try it."

Tangent did.

"Bend your elbows a little. Bring it in closer. That's it. Okay, let's say the safety is off. You're gripping it hard with both hands. Then you point it at what you want to hit, close your eyes, and blast away. Keep pulling that trigger until the gun is empty. And hang on, or the whole damned thing will go flying away over your right shoulder."

"You must think I'm some kind of an idiot," Tangent said.

"Behind a desk you're a genius," Leiberman said. "Out here you're an idiot."

"Why should I close my eyes before I fire?"

"Because you'll be too spooked to aim. Because you'll close them anyway after the first shot. This thing makes a noise like a one-oh-five howitzer. Just spray bullets. You may hit something. All right, give it back. I'll keep it for now."

They were nearing Asante waters, and Leiberman started giving orders. For the rest of the trip he wanted one man awake at the wheel and one man awake on the foredeck, as lookout. On the first four-hour trick, Shagari took the wheel, and Tangent went forward. At first, he liked it up there; the trawler was heading into the wind, and he couldn't smell the strong odor of rotting fish coming from the hold.

Like most African nights, this one came suddenly. One minute the swollen red sun was bobbing on the western horizon, the next minute it was gone. Darkness moved in; Tangent shivered. There was a waist-high rail about the prow. He hung on to that and strained his eyes for lights, shapes, anything. He kept turning, as Leiberman had instructed, making a 360-degree inspection of the sea about them. There were a few lights, far off, but these soon faded. Then *La Belle Dame* seemed alone in a black world, puffing quietly eastward, kicking up sprinkles of phosphorescence at bow and stern.

Tangent kept glancing at the luminous dial of his wrist-watch. He thought it had stopped, but it hadn't; time had. It was, he thought, the longest four hours of his life.

And the darkness was not only out there; it entered into him. Now he saw the Asante coup d'etat as an act of madness, doomed to failure. Captain Anokye was just another military opportunist. Sam Leiberman was an over-the-hill buffoon, not to be relied on. And Tangent himself was a foolish romantic, hoping to cure the sour desperation of his life with this wild fantasy, a comic opera of armed peasants coming down from the hills, singing; a gorgeously uniformed young officer flourishing a sword, singing; a fat bemedaled tyrant robbing Asante's treasury, singing. Sigmund Romberg could have plotted it. Or Victor Herbert. It lacked only a 40-piece orchestra and a blond heroine, singing, with Mary Pickford curls, six dirndl skirts, and a laced bodice.

Finally, the fantasia became so grotesque he began laughing, silently, and was still laughing when Yakubu relieved him, and he could go aft for a paper cup of whiskey and try to sleep.

There was a thick morning fog the next day, billowing right down to the surface. The sea moved oilily, not even a tiny whitecap to be seen. The fog burned off by noon, and they changed course to pass the island of Zabar to port. But they were close enough to see villages, fishing boats drawn up on the beach, donkey carts on the roads. Beyond, Mokodi was hidden in a shimmering haze, glowing. The Promised Land.

"We'll run down to Lomé to waste time," Leiberman decreed. "Turn around after sundown and run back. If anyone stops us before dark, we're on our way to Lagos."

"And if anyone stops us after dark?" Tangent asked.

Leiberman looked at him.

When they made their turn at dusk off Togo, Cousin took them farther out to sea so they might approach Zabar directly from the south, keeping the land mass of the island between them and Mokodi. Leiberman and Tangent went down into the stifling, fume-choked engine room. They smeared heavy black grease on their white faces, arms, backs of their hands. When they came back up on deck, Shagari was lowering the cargo boom to make it ready to swing over the port side. It would carry a green light, the signal for Zuni Anokye to bring out his fishing boats.

Leiberman handed the Colt .45 to Tangent. "Don't stick it in your belt," he advised. "You're liable to shoot your balls off. Stay inside the pilothouse. Sit on the deck. Make sure your head is below window level. Keep the gun close to you. Someplace where it won't slide around."

"Where will you be?"

"Don't worry about me. Just keep down out of sight. And stay there until I tell you otherwise."

Tangent obeyed, beginning to feel a tightness. Not fear, he told himself. It wasn't fear; it was just a tightness, a kind of tension.

"A tot of rum all around," Leiberman said, opening the second bottle of Scotch. "Cures the fantods and narrows the sphincter."

South of Zabar, out in the Gulf of Guinea, the sea was rougher. Waves began to lap over the midship gunnels, splashing down on the fish below. But then Cousin spun the wheel, changing course to head directly for Zabar. Then it was a following sea, and they shipped no more waves.

The engine was throttled down. Now it was almost purring. The trawler was barely moving.

Leiberman stood near Cousin in the pilothouse, staring directly ahead. He was holding a Uzi cradled in his arms. The S&W .38 was pushed halfway into his side pocket.

"Looking for three red lights," he explained to Tangent. "One on the beach, one farther inland, one on a hill. When we get them lined up, we're in position."

In a few moments, Cousin made a small sound and jerked his head to port. Leiberman went to a window.

"That's one all right," he said. "Bring her around a little, Cousin. There's another. Hold this course."

They finally found the third red light, almost hidden in the dim glow coming from a small village. Cousin worked the wheel carefully until they had the three red lights lined up. Then *La Belle Dame* retreated about two kilometers until the lights dimmed and could barely be seen. The engine was stopped, running lights extinguished. The boom was swung out over the port gunnel. At its end was fastened a battery-powered lantern showing a green light toward the shore of Zabar.

"Now we wait," Leiberman whispered. "Keep the noise down. No smoking. Tangent, what time you got?"

"Twenty-three forty-three."

"I make it forty-five. Close enough. If anything is copesetic, they should be here in ten-fifteen minutes."

"Anchor?" Tangent whispered.

"Nah. Probably too deep for what this tub carries. Besides, we might want to haul ass in a hurry."

They waited in the darkness. Sitting on the deck of the pilothouse, Tangent could see nothing but a dim night-glow through the broken windows. The tightness was swelling in him. His bladder felt full, and he realized he was gulping rapid, shallow breaths. He forced himself to breathe deeply, slowly.

Cousin hissed something, in Boulé.

"What?" Leiberman said.

Cousin repeated, louder.

"Son of a bitch," Leiberman said. "He says he hears a boat engine. Off to starboard. Not our boys. They got nothing but sails."

In a moment they all heard it: a faint rumble, growing louder. Yakubu shifted position on the foredeck, squatting on his hams near the scrap of canvas covering the Uzi. Shagari moved to lean against the pilothouse door.

The sound grew louder—a throaty cough. Cousin said something.

"He can see running lights," Leiberman reported to Tangent. "A launch, he thinks."

The sound increased—a burbling roar. Suddenly a searchlight snapped on. A yellow beam began to sweep the sea. It moved toward them slowly.

" 'Mother of God,' " Leiberman quoted, " 'is this the end of Rico?' "

He kneeled near Tangent, peering over a window ledge. But when the searchlight caught them, he ducked down, the Uzi held across his chest.

The light grew brighter, the engine louder, as the boat came up to them. Cousin muttered something.

"Asante navy," Leiberman whispered to Tangent. "One of their lousy motor launches. Looking for smugglers."

The launch came upon the starboard side. The engine diminished to a low growl. The searchlight probed back and forth slowly, finding Yakubu on the foredeck. Then it returned to glare on the pilothouse and remain there.

"Asante naval launch *Griselda*," someone shouted, in French. "Stop your engine."

"We are already stopped, excellency," Shagari yelled back. "We are not moving. Our engine has failed."

"Who are you?"

"Fishing trawler *La Bella Dame*, sir. Out of Accra."

"What are you doing in Asante waters?"

"We went to Lomé to sell our catch, excellency. But no one would buy. We were on our way back. But our engine died."

"Where are your lights?" the voice yelled.

"They went out when the engine failed, sir. All we have is that green battery lantern."

"Nice try but no cigar," Leiberman whispered to Tangent. "He'll know that's a lot of bullshit."

"How many men?" the voice called.

"Three, sir."

"Stand by. We are coming aboard."

"That does it," Leiberman muttered to Tangent. "Son of a *bitch!* Keep your head down."

The launch backed, then came forward slowly along the starboard rail. There were five men on deck. One sailor operated the searchlight; one stood behind a .30 caliber machine gun mounted on a swivel atop an eye-level pipe. A third was at the wheel in the open, lighted cockpit. An officer stood near him. The fifth sailor reached toward the trawler's gunnel with a boat hook.

"Whew! What a stink!" the officer yelled. "No wonder you could not sell your catch."

"We have been drifting out here all day in the hot sun, excellency."

"Why didn't you throw your fish overboard?"

"In Accra we can sell them for fertilizer," Shagari said. "Please not to come aboard, excellency. You will soil your uniforms."

For a moment, Leiberman thought it might work. But then the two boats crunched together.

"Go over and take a look," the officer commanded the sailor with the boat hook. "Make sure they have nothing but rotting fish."

Using his boat hook as a balancing pole, the sailor stepped up lightly onto the catwalk alongside the trawler's hold.

"Put the light down here," he called to the man on the launch.

The searchlight was lowered to illuminate the hold. The Asante sailor probed down with his boat hook, pushing it through the fish. Everyone heard the metal head strike the top of a crate.

"Lieutenant!" the sailor shouted excitedly. "Here is—"

Leiberman straightened suddenly.

"Yakubu!" he screamed.

He poked the muzzle of his Uzi through the pilothouse window and opened fire. Almost at the same instant Yakubu began firing from the foredeck. Tangent lurched to his feet, scrambled about wildly for the Colt.

Leiberman's first burst took out the man at the machine gun. Bullets stitched across his torso, slammed him backward, head thrown up, arms flying. Leiberman turned to the open cockpit, sweeping the muzzle back and forth. The helmsman's face and head exploded. His lifeless body fell forward over the wheel. The officer turned as if to dive overboard. Bullets ripped into his spine. His body arched, hands clawed around. He fell to his knees, crumpled forward.

Now Tangent was at the window next to Leiberman. He was vaguely conscious of Cousin and Shagari flat on the deck. He shoved the Colt .45 through the open window, held it in two hands, pointed it at the Asante motor launch, pulled the trigger again and again and again, not hearing his shots in the stuttering crack of Leiberman's machine pistol, next to his ear.

Yakubu's first burst killed the man at the searchlight. Now the light was swinging wildly, making swift patterns of light and dark across both boats. Yakubu's second target was the sailor who had come aboard with the boat hook. He was down, lying across the gunnel, legs over the side, his head, arms, shoulders dangling into the hold. The boats drifted slowly apart.

Suddenly, silence. Cousin and Shagari raised their heads cautiously. A final burst from Leiberman's gun shattered the searchlight. Then they were in darkness again, except for the green lantern at the end of the boom and the launch's running lights.

Tangent, numb, stood at the window. His arms and hands were outside, the automatic pistol still pointing at the launch. Leiberman put down his Uzi, pulled him gently back inside, helped him sit down on the deck. He tried to take the pistol from Tangent's grasp.

"Let go," he said.

"What?" Tangent said. "I can't hear you."

"Let go of the gun."

"I can't."

"Loosen your fingers."

"I just can't," Tangent said. "I can't move them. They're numb."

Leiberman worked the pistol back and forth, twisting. Finally it came free. Leiberman smelled the muzzle, then gave a hoarse bark.

"This little gizmo here," he said. "The safety. Off. On. Never mind. You tried. You did good."

He got his flashlight, switched it on. Cousin had tossed a small grappling hook onto the launch, caught its rail, pulled it close again. Leiberman jumped down onto the deck, his revolver held out in front of him. He inspected the two in the cockpit, then the sailors who had manned the machine gun and searchlight.

"Fini," he called back to the trawler. "Where's the other guy, the one with the boat hook?"

Yakubu, carrying his Uzi, began searching from the port catwalk. Leiberman looked down into the sea between the two boats.

"Where the hell is he?" he said angrily. "I don't like loose ends. Shagari, check the hold. Maybe he fell in on top of the fish."

Tangent had climbed shakily to his feet, stumbled out onto the pilothouse deck. Now he looked down, fighting sickness, and saw something in the water, something white.

"Here," he said weakly. But no one heard him. He tried again, louder: "Here he is. Back here."

Leiberman came running along the deck of the launch. Yakubu climbed the ladder to the pilothouse and stood alongside Tangent, peering down. The others joined them.

A white-clad arm came out of the water. Fingers scrabbled at the trawler's hull. The face of the sailor bobbed up, mouth gaping for air, eyes showing white completely around the iris.

"Grease him, Yakubu," Leiberman ordered.

The black fired a long burst. The sea churned a red froth. Jumping and dancing.

"Enough," Leiberman yelled. "He's finished."

The water calmed. The body was gone. Bits of white and gray stuff floated, bobbled, drifted away.

Leiberman came back aboard and gave orders to Cousin and Shagari, in Boulé. They went below, came back with an ax and a long crowbar. They jumped down into the launch and began opening the hull, jabbing, chopping, thrusting, letting in the sea.

"Did you have to do that?" Tangent demanded of Leiberman. "That last wounded sailor—did you have to kill him?"

"No," Leiberman said, "we could have fished him out, patched him, and you could have put him up at the executive suite of the Mokodi Hilton. Have your brains turned to shit? Witnesses we don't need. Are you going to be sick?"

"I don't think so."

"If you are, puke over the side. This tub stinks enough as it is."

The launch was already settling, water in the cockpit knee-deep, when Cousin and Shagari scrambled back aboard the trawler. They all lined the rail and watched as the launch went deeper and deeper, the sea rushing into the torn hull. It settled slowly, slowly, going down evenly. In the weak glow of Leiberman's flashlight they saw it sink below the surface, hesitate a moment, then it was gone. A few plank scraps swirled to the surface. An empty thermos bottle bobbed. A life preserver drifted. A sodden copy of the Asante *New Times* ...

"I could have used the grenades," Leiberman explained to Tangent, "but someone on Zabar or Mokodi might have heard or seen the explosions. This is as neat and clean as I could make it. The bodies may come up in a few days, but we'll be long gone by then."

Tangent said nothing.

Leiberman decided to remain where they were and wait.

They made a few efforts to destroy the evidence: tossed empty cartridge cases over the side, washed the sailor's blood from the starboard catwalk, chopped his boat hook into small pieces and flung them into the sea. Because the wood shaft had *Griselda* burned into it. Then they waited, Leiberman cleaning the Uzis and reloading. He made no effort to talk to Tangent.

They waited about an hour and were almost ready to give up when Cousin spotted a cluster of three white lights bobbing toward them slowly. Leiberman stood in the pilothouse, armed now with the M3. Yakubu returned to the foredeck with a cleaned and reloaded Uzi. Tangent held the Colt again, trying to remember—"Little gizmo. Off. On." Shagari and Cousin crouched on the pilothouse catwalk.

Cousin waited until the lights came close enough. Then he snapped on Leiberman's flashlight. Long enough to identify three brightly painted fishing boats. He turned off the light. The boats slipped up alongside, sails whispering down.

"Leiberman?" a voice called.

"My God," the mercenary said, "it's the man himself. Captain, is that you?" he called.

"Yes. We thought we heard firing. That is why we are late. Was it you? Trouble?"

"Nothing we couldn't handle. Can you come aboard? Need a ladder?"

"Thank you, we shall manage."

In a few moments, Obiri and Zuni Anokye were in the pilothouse, shaking hands with all, grinning.

"At the last minute, I decided to come along," the Little Captain said. "It was not that I felt Zuni could not do it"—here he put his hand on his brother's shoulder—"but it is the first delivery, and I wanted everything to go smoothly. Apparently it did not."

Leiberman shrugged. "Bad luck," he said. "The Asante navy picked this night to go cruising for smugglers."

"The navy?" Anokye said sharply. "Where are they now?"

"Sunk," Leiberman said. "No choice."

"Survivors?"

"No."

"Good. Any casualties here?"

"Only Tangent's pride."

The Little Captain turned. "How is that, Mr. Tangent?" he asked.

Tangent laughed shortly. "I forgot to take off the safety," he said. "I must have pulled the trigger a dozen times."

Anokye smiled. "I did exactly the same thing in my first action."

Tangent appreciated the lie.

"Next time you will remember," the Captain said. "My God, what is that stink?"

The flashlight was turned down into the hold.

"The guns are underneath," Leiberman said.

"Please," Captain Anokye said, "next time use bags of rice."

At Zuni's command, men came swarming over from the fishing boats. With Cousin at the electric winch, crates and cases began to fly up from the hold, to be deposited on a fishing boat's deck. As soon as one boat was loaded to capacity, it moved sluggishly away, and another took its place. In less than two hours, the trawler's hold was emptied of arms. Zuni Anokye insisted his men help clean up. Buckets of rotting fish were hoisted out and dumped overboard. Within minutes scavenging fish were in the area, darting, gobbling the unexpected banquet.

More handshakes as arrangements were confirmed for the next delivery. The last fishing boat slipped away into the darkness, the Little Captain waving. The trawler's boom was swung inboard and lashed, running lights were rigged, the engine was started. *La Belle Dame*, dancing high out of the water, headed back for the Ivory Coast. Full cups of brandy were poured. Tangent took his forward, sat on the foredeck, his back against a rail stanchion. He listened to the hiss of the cutwater, thinking back on what had happened that night, wondering what it meant, wondering if it meant anything.

But he found it difficult to think, impossible to concentrate. All he could feel was an immense weariness, physical, mental, nervous. So he sipped his brandy, conscious of his breathing, conscious of his heart pump, knew he was alive. At that moment it seemed enough.

Sam Leiberman came rolling carelessly along the catwalk, bringing the half-empty brandy bottle and fresh paper cups. He flopped down next to Tangent, poured him a new drink.

"Well," he said, "you didn't shit your pants after all."

"You seem to be anally oriented," Tangent said.

"Not me," Leiberman said. "I'm prickally oriented."

"Well, no one was firing at *me*," Tangent muttered.

"True," Leiberman said. "Still, it was hairy, and you tried to help. You didn't have to. No one asked you."

"Didn't do much good."

"Don't pick at it," Leiberman advised.

Tangent didn't answer, and they sat in silence a long time, finishing the brandy.

"What's eating you?" Leiberman asked finally.

"Nothing's eating me. A little shell-shocked, that's all. I've never seen— never been through anything like that before."

"Shocked to see what your money buys?" Leiberman asked.

"Yes," Tangent said.

"It's only the beginning," Leiberman said.

26

Sgt. Sene Yeboa was a great favorite with the Anokye family and relatives. Especially with the children, since he always brought gifts and delighted to teach them new games, new riddles, and such marvelous arts as building sand forts on the beach, making little boats from scraps of bark, and flying kites constructed of reeds and pages of old newspapers.

Since Yeboa had no family of his own, he had become an adopted son of the Anokyes and was encouraged to visit frequently. In return, he could not do enough for them. He insisted on helping all, even assisting Judith in the kitchen, cleaning fish, washing utensils, serving meals—women's work. The Anokye men were amused by this and called him "Auntie" Yeboa. But their jibes were without malice, and Sene took it all with elephantine good humor.

On Sunday morning, Sene Yeboa and the Anokyes walked to church, two kilometers west of Porto Chonin. Sara was missing since she was visiting Lt. Jere Songo in Togo, chaperoned by Zuni's wife.

The Baptists on Zabar had erected a one-room church, used as frequently for social gatherings as for religious services. It was a low, graceless structure, a weathered gray, but with adequate ventilation through wide doors at both ends and screened windows along both sides. A cloth-covered table on a low platform at one end served as a rude altar. The congregation sat on wooden benches. An ancient harmonium, foot-pumped, was placed at the right of the altar.

The usual Sunday service consisted of an opening hymn, a prayer, more hymns, the offertory, church announcements, and the award of colored picture cards to children who had distinguished themselves in Sunday School. Then it was the custom of this church to follow the minister's sermon with an address by a lay member.

It had been announced the previous week that Captain Obiri Anokye would speak on the following Sunday. As a result, by the time the Anokyes arrived the benches were almost full, with more people squeezing in every minute. When the wheezy organ sounded the chords of the first hymn, the church was jammed, all seats taken by children, women, and elders. Men stood at the back and along the walls. Many found no room inside, but clustered outside at the open windows and doors, waiting to hear the Little Captain speak.

He was introduced by the preacher with a quote from Isaiah: "A little one shall become a thousand, and a small one a strong nation." Captain Anokye's text came from Ecclesiastes: "Whatever thy hand findeth to do, do it with thy might."

He stood before them, wearing an undress uniform of khaki drill, an overseas cap tucked into his belt. His short-sleeved shirt was open at the throat. He assumed the familiar position: feet firmly planted, torso bent slightly backward, chest inflated, chin elevated. As he began speaking, in Akan, his hands rose to his hips and stayed there, except for the short, violent gestures he used to emphasize a point. He looked slowly about the church, locking eyes with his audience. They leaned forward eagerly, staring with fascination at those grave, magisterial features, impressed by his intensity.

"I am a soldier, as you know. Like soldiers everywhere, I am expected to do my duty, even though it might be difficult, it might be painful, even though it might result in my own suffering, or my own death.

"To whom do I owe this duty as a soldier? I owe it to our King. Is this duty absolute and supreme? It would be easy to say Yes. It would simplify a soldier's life, since then it would only be necessary to obey the orders of a superior officer to be a good soldier.

"But I say that my duty as a soldier of the King is not absolute and is not supreme. I believe that I have a higher duty, as you do, and you, and you. This duty, the *highest* duty, is to God.

"Our duty to God, as we know from the the Bible, is to walk in the paths of righteousness. That is no easy thing. But though we may fail occasionally—as fail we must since we are but human, with all the weaknesses of humans—that should not discourage us from seeking always to obey God's commandments and follow the teachings of Christ.

"Now I ask you this: What must a soldier do when the duty he owes his superior conflicts with the duty he owes to God? This is no simple matter to decide. For to disobey a superior officer, who speaks for the King, is a serious thing and, in some cases, may be punishable by death. And yet to disobey a commandment of God may condemn you to eternity in the fiery pit.

"When such a conflict arises, I say it is necessary for us all—soldiers and civilians alike—to listen to the voice of God and follow His orders. That is what I believe.

"How may one know what God commands? His order may not come from a voice from Heaven or a visitation of angels. But I believe each of us will feel it, will *know* it, in his soul. And since God is Our Father, that small whisper in our souls is His. There are so many of us and only one of Him, His voice and commands are divided amongst us all, and come to each of us only as a whisper. We deny God's whisper at great peril. He is telling us the way, and if we disregard His command, if we disobey, then we fail in our duty and will be punished for it.

"The time may come—sooner than you think—when it may be necessary for you to make this decision between duty to the King and duty to God. I urge you to listen to God's small whisper in your soul and then to think on how best you may obey His command. And whatsoever thy hand findeth to do, do it with thy might. To the greater glory of God."

With that he finished his address, and stepped down, taking his place along the wall with the other men. There was no applause. The congregation looked to each other in puzzlement, not certain what the Little Captain intended. In low voices they agreed it was an eloquent sermon, but he seemed to be hinting at more than he said. What did it all mean?

The Anokyes walked slowly home from church, the Little Captain alongside Sene Yeboa. Both had taken off boots and socks and luxuriated in the feel of the warm, powdery dirt beneath their bare toes.

"A good speech," Yeboa said.

"No, Sene, it was not," Captain Anokye said. "They did not understand. But the fault was mine. I could not make it clear to them. I am certain the secret police were there, listening. I went as far as I could. To say more would have endangered everything. But perhaps they will understand next week. Then they will remember what I said, and it will have meaning for them. Meanwhile, perhaps I have planted a seed."

"What seed is that?" Yeboa inquired innocently.

The Little Captain laughed. "That obedience to God's will sometimes demands disobedience to the King's. A revolutionary doctrine. I hope some day it does not return to haunt me. Now listen, Sene, here is what I want you to do . . ."

Briefly, concisely, he outlined Sgt. Yeboa's role in the coup d'etat. The big sergeant listened closely, interrupting frequently to ask questions, to make certain he understood precisely what would be expected of him.

"Bibi," he said finally, "Can't I be with you? In Mokodi?"

"You will be," Anokye patiently explained. "I will not start the assault until you and Leiberman join me. You have a very important part to play. You see that?"

"Yesss," Yeboa said. Dubiously.

"Another thing . . . If I am killed, or if I am wounded so badly that I cannot command—do not look at me so; such things may happen; you know that— the attack is to continue under the command of Willi Abraham. I expect you to give him the same loyalty you would give me. You agree? Sene? Well, do you?"

"I agree," Yeboa said in a low voice.

Anokye clapped him on the shoulder, the heavy, muscled machine gunner's shoulder. "But I do not intend to be killed or seriously wounded. That is *my* whisper from God. You and I shall live to enter the palace together."

"Yes *sah*!" Yeboa said, grinning.

The Sunday afternoon dinner was meager: a fish stew with mashed plantains. But the stew was mostly onions, tomatoes, beans, and okra. The fish scraps were just for seasoning; there was no meat on them.

After the pot had been scraped clean, Sene Yeboa passed around a packet of thin cigars he had brought as a treat. It would have been impolite to refuse, so even Judith lighted up one of the dark Spanish cigarillos.

The table was cleared, and Zuni spread a large, hand-drawn map of Zabar. It showed the island's roads, villages, and important installations, such as gendarme headquarters, ferry slip, a small army post, governor's office, etc. These had been marked with numerals indicating the order in which they would be captured by the Zabarian chapter of the Asante Brothers of Independence, commanded by Zuni Anokye.

Obiri and Sgt. Yeboa listened carefully as Zuni explained his plan of attack. He would first capture the telephone office to cut off all calls to the mainland. He would then take control of the ferry slip. From there, his men would move to gendarme headquarters, army post, and governor's office. They would move as rapidly as possible to surprise the King's forces on Zabar. Officers and officials would be jailed; soldiers and gendarmes would be given the option of joining the revolution or jail. Those offering resistance would be shot.

The Little Captain nodded agreement with this plan, knowing how easily Zuni's timetable could be bollixed by any number of things: an unexpected firefight, a truck that failed to start, excessive caution on the part of Zuni's men. He warned his brother of these things.

"You promised us weapons, and we received weapons," Zuni said. "I promise you Zabar."

Obiri reached up to touch his arm, smiling.

"I believe you, Zuni," he said, "and your plan is a good one. But do not be discouraged if things do not go as you have planned. You must be prepared to revise your tactics on the spot if circumstances dictate. You understand?"

"Of course."

"One final thing: If a ferry arrives while your attack is in progress, seize it and hold it here until you have taken control of Zabar. Then, if it is possible, send to me in Modoki as many armed men as you can spare. Not you. You will be needed here. But if you can send men, I can use them in Mokodi."

"I will go," Adebayo said excitedly. "I will lead the men to Mokodi."

Judith Anokye stretched out a hand seemed about to speak. Then her hand dropped, she said nothing.

Obiri looked at his younger brother.

"I can do it," Adebayo said defiantly. "I am not a boy. I have learned to shoot the rifle. I know how. I can help you in Mokodi."

"Zuni will decide who goes and who stays," Obiri said sternly. "You will take your orders from Zuni. You understand that?"

"I understand," Adebayo muttered, lowering his eyes.

"Then there is nothing more to be discussed." The Little Captain rose, pushed back his chair. "Sene and I must return to the barracks. Zuni, you will receive twenty-four hours' notice of the time to begin. That will be sufficient?"

"Yes, enough."

"Good. We shall not see you again before it starts. God bless you all and keep you well."

Then all rose. The family embraced Obiri and Sene with kisses and pattings, murmurings and hugs. Josiah began weeping, tears running down the deep walnut ravines of his face. The Little Captain took him aside and spoke softly to him a few moments, and the old man calmed.

Then Captain Anokye and Sgt. Yeboa departed, walking up the hill to the village. They turned once to look back. Judith, Josiah, Zuni, and Adebayo were standing outside the Anokye home, looking at them. No one waved.

27

The pastry crust of the Beef Wellington was soggy, but Peter Tangent was too excited to notice. Too excited, in fact, to do anything but stab at his dinner as he described the action off Zabar. Tony Malcolm listened, but didn't neglect his food. Finally, his dinner and Tangent's recital finished, he pointed at Tangent's plate and said, "Eat your food, Peter. If you insist on buckling swashes all over the place, you'll need your strength."

Then, when Tangent, blushing faintly, turned his attention to the rare beef, Malcolm said, "This Leiberman, he plays rough."

Tangent, talking around a mouthful, said, "That was my initial reaction. But then I started thinking about it. Tony, what else could he have done?"

"I suppose you're right," Malcolm murmured. "Still . . ."

"What amazed me," Tangent went on, chewing and still talking excitedly, "was how fast he reacted. Almost as if he had planned it."

"I imagine he had," Malcolm said. "Not consciously perhaps, but a man with his experience would have contingency plans. Do B in case of A. Do Y in case of X. So he was able to move almost instinctively."

The dining room at Brindleys was sparsely occupied; they were served at their favorite corner table with some degree of privacy. The other diners seemed as secretive as they; heads met over tables in whispered conversations.

"When is the coup scheduled?" Tony Malcolm asked.

"First week in August. I don't know the exact date. Garde has been told the twelfth. Have you heard anything more about what the French are up to?"

"They don't seem too concerned. Your Little Captain picked a good time. In August, everyone in Paris goes on vacation."

"The paratroops are still in Senegal?"

"As far as I know."

"Tony, I've got a wild idea I want to try on you. Would it be possible to put some of our ships in that area—just as a signal to the French?"

"No, it would not be possible."

"I'm not asking for the Sixth Fleet. I had in mind, say, a destroyer and a couple of escorts. Or perhaps a minelayer or two. Just showing the flag. A symbol of U.S. interest, that's all. It might make the French think twice before making a move."

Malcolm pondered a long moment, twirling the stem of his wineglass. For a plumpish man, he had unexpectedly long and elegant fingers.

"I could send a bullet to Virginia," he said finally. "But something like that would be bucked to State."

"Exactly," Tangent said eagerly, bending over the table. "And I could get Tulsa to have our man in D.C. lean on State. We've done them enough favors. My God, I'm not asking for the Marines—just a couple of small ships visiting, say, Accra, Lomé, or Lagos. Close enough to signal the French we have an interest in the Little Captain's coup and wouldn't take kindly to their dumping a regiment of paratroops on him."

Malcolm looked at him curiously.

"You're expanding this thing, Peter. It started out as just another army revolt in just another two-bit African country. Now you've got French troops on standby in Senegal, and you want some of our warships making an excursion into an area where the U.S. has no vested interest. Starrett Petroleum does, but not the U.S. Do you know what the hell you're doing?"

Tangent leaned back, took out his packet of Players, offered them to Malcolm. They both lighted up slowly, glancing about casually to see if anyone was interested in their conversation. No one was.

"I know exactly what I'm doing, Tony," Tangent said in a low voice. "Let me fill you in... There's a clique in the Secretariat for African Affairs in State that thinks the U.S. is missing the boat in Africa. Right now, most of the radicals are young and black and don't have much clout. They claim State and the White House are paying too much attention to West Europe, Russia, China, and the Middle East, and not enough attention to Africa. They argue it's an enormously rich continent, still largely uncommitted politically, and it's going to be a hell of a market in the future, besides being an incredible source of cereals, oil, minerals, and so forth. But all the White House does is give a free lunch to any African leader foolish enough to go to D.C. looking for help. Anyway, I happen to agree with the dissidents in African Affairs. I especially agree with their warning that we're letting African markets and raw materials go to France and Britain by default. I think Starrett's lobbyists in D.C. could work with this group and get State to okay a friendly cruise of a few piddling U.S. Navy ships off the Asante coast. If you could get Virginia's okay, it would be in the bag. It's not just Anokye's coup I'm interested in, Tony—although I admit it's important to me and important to Starrett. But it goes beyond Anokye. I want to see the U.S. make a dent in the French hegemony in Africa. If the Little Captain is successful—and I think he will be—we'll have Asante in our hip pocket. And with his ambition and drive, who knows where it might lead? Will you try Virginia?"

Malcolm considered a moment, staring into Tangent's eyes without seeing him.

"All right," he said finally. "I'll get off a request. No guarantee."

"Good enough," Tangent said happily. "And I'll get my people on it. I'll tell the Little Captain what we're attempting. Even if it doesn't come off, we'll make Brownie points for trying."

They were silent while the table was cleared, and coffee and brandy were served. Years later they were both to remember that dinner. It marked a turning point, though neither was aware of it at the time.

"What about tonight, Peter?" Malcolm asked lazily.

"Sorry, we'll have to let it go. I want to get a long cable off to Tulsa, and then I have to pack. I'm leaving for Asante again in the morning. Tell me, what does one wear to a coup d'etat?"

Malcolm shook his head. "You're demented, you know that? This Little Captain has scrambled your brains."

"Tony, if the coup comes off, I'd like you to come down to Asante."

"What for?"

"To meet Anokye. I think you should."

"Well . . . maybe. I'll have to get shots, won't I?"

"Shots? What for?"

"Tsetse flies. Rhinoceros bites. Things like that."

"Don't be an ass. Besides, there are no shots for what you're going to catch."

"And what's that?"

"Wait till you meet him. You'll see."

"Peter . . ."

"What?"

"I'm not going to try to talk you out of being there. During the action, I mean. I can see how excited you are. But listen, take care of yourself. Y'know?"

Tangent reached out to touch Tony Malcolm's arm.

"Thanks, Tony," he said softly. "Not to worry. I'm so skinny, they'll never hit me."

"Send me an update through Jon Wilson as soon as it's over. Win or lose."

"Will do."

"Hurry back," Malcolm said lightly.

28

They were all there in Yvonne Mayer's apartment at the Golden Calf: Anokye, Yeboa, Abraham, Duclos, Tangent, Fante, Leiberman—and Yvonne herself, withdrawn, saying little, listening. Her eyes followed Captain Anokye.

"The day after tomorrow," the Little Captain said. "The fifth of August. At oh six hundred. Is that clear to everyone? I will notify the Nyam myself, and my brother in Zabar. Minister, you, Duclos, Fante, and Sene will notify the others. Is that satisfactory?"

The men nodded.

"Now we will go through it once more," the Captain said. "The timing will make us or break us."

They clustered around the table, looking down at the map of Asante, studying the circles, the arrows, the routes of attack. Speaking in a cold, emotionless voice, Captain Obiri Anokye pointed out the sequence of actions that would culminate in the assault on the palace. It was his plan—no help from Alistair Greeley on this—but if he was apprehensive, nothing in his tone or manner revealed it. He spoke with steady authority, iron sureness.

There were questions: Leiberman wanted to know about transportation back to Mokodi from Gonja; Tangent asked about a weapon for himself; Duclos complained, briefly, of what he considered the trivial task assigned him—seizure of the Mokodi mosque. Even Willi Abraham had questions regarding his capture of the telephone exchange and cable office.

"Isolate the palace," Anokye ordered. "No calls can go out, but be sure they can receive calls. I suspect Anatole Garde may be in radio communication with Togo or Ghana from inside the palace, but there is nothing we can do about it. Any other questions?"

The men were silent.

"The important element is speed," the Little Captain said, studying the map. "With luck, all preliminaries should be concluded by noon, and the palace captured by nightfall. If we move quickly, if our complete control of Asante becomes obvious, I do not think the French will interfere. You know of the American warships off our coast. Mr. Tangent is to be thanked for that effort. But if the coup is not immediately successful, I believe the French may decide to come to the aid of Prempeh, regardless of the presence of those ships. So it is important to strike hard and strike swiftly. Avoid unnecessary killing, but do what must be done."

"Prisoners?" Leiberman asked.

"Preferably not," Anokye said shortly. "We do not have the men to guard them. But they should be given the opportunity to join us. Do not attempt to persuade them. Merely ask them—once. Do I make myself clear? Resistance must be met by annihilation. There is no other way. If you have no stomach for it, think of what *our* fate will be if we fail."

Little was said after that. There were handshakes, a few muttered words, and then the apartment gradually cleared as men slipped away. Finally, Anokye and Yvonne Mayer were alone, she in her corner chair, he still standing, hands on hips, staring down at the map of Asante.

"I have tried to anticipate every possibility and to prepare for it," he said aloud, almost speaking to himself. "But I know how important chance and accident can be. Do you pray, Yvonne?"

"No," she said. "Not for years."

"Nor I," he laughed.

"I thought you went to church?"

"I do. For the meaning it has to others. Well, if neither of us can pray, then I suppose we must put our faith in Russian rifles and American grenades."

He turned to her, grinning, and she rose and came to him, arms stretched wide. They embraced, but when he turned again to the map, she moved behind him, pressing tightly against him, her arms about his neck.

"I can do it," he said, voice low and urgent. "I know I can."

"You can," she whispered.

"It's in me," he said. "A fire to command. To rule. It drives me. You know that?"

"Yes," she said.

"I must obey," he went on, his eyes on the map but not seeing. "It is a kind of duty. To myself. Not to God, King, or country. But to me, my own destiny. I know, Yvonne, I *know* I will not be killed. I know I will succeed in this. I would be a traitor if I did not act, a traitor to myself. As far as I can. Wherever it leads. I can see no limits, no boundary I cannot cross. Energy. The need to act. The will to act! I cannot disobey that. That duty. I wish I could make you understand."

"I understand, Bibi,"

"Do you?" he said. He laughed shortly, excited. "I wonder if I do? It is something I cannot resist. A fever. An ache. How else can I describe it? That I was born for this. Auntie Tal cast the stones for me, and . . ."

"And what?"

"A great destiny. But that is all superstition. It means nothing. Still . . ."

They huddled quietly. He reached around behind her, gripped her buttocks so she came tighter to him, cleaving. She buried her face in his neck and shoulder. His stirring bull smell. She savored.

"How I wish I could see it," he mused. "All of it. My life outlined like this map. Circles and lines. Arrows and masses. The sequences and the climax. No, I would not want to see it. Where is the pleasure there? I must live it, make it unfold. Yvonne? You understand? Yes, you understand everything. I must believe in myself. Obey. My duty to myself. Follow it."

"I know," she murmured. "I know."

"I have no choice," he said. He turned slowly in her embrace until he was facing her. Widened eyes close. "No choice at all."

"Do you remember what I told you?" she whispered. "What I would do if you betrayed your promise to me?"

"I have not forgotten," he said.

"This future you see for yourself, this great destiny, it will all come to dust, Bibi, if you desert me. Do you believe that?"

"Yes," he said, shivering, "I believe it. But I shall not betray you, and I shall conquer. I swear it!"

In bed, he seemed charged with fury, a maniacal anguish he sought to exhaust inside her. He plunged, rutting, with a rage that drove her to a sweated convulsion, squirming slickly beneath him, trying to encompass and hold his frenzy.

He put a hand across her mouth to stifle her screams. Then he rent her brutally, oblivious to her pleasure or hurt, staring at her with burning eyes, gone from her and from himself, driven by a force he could not control, slave and master, crying out in pain in triumph.

29

Colonel Ramon de Blanca, cousin of King Prempeh, CO of 3rd Brigade, Asante Royal Army, spent the evening of August 4th in his Mokodi home. He enjoyed a delightful lamb curry, with all the side dishes, at a table shared with his father, grandfather, two uncles, three male cousins, and his two eldest sons. Later, stirred by the curry, he took pleasure with his second wife, who was five months pregnant.

At midnight, the Colonel headed back to Gonja, carrying a box of dates, raisins, figs, dried apricots, and a hand of green bananas. He nibbled these delicacies on the trip north. He was chauffeured by a Muslim corporal who was actually a member of the palace guard but had been temporarily detached to serve as Colonel de Blanca's bodyguard. And to report his activities personally to General Opoku Tutu, the Colonel had no doubt.

But he had nothing to fear. He had obeyed Tutu's orders, bringing in his brigade from the field and from village garrisons to concentrate more than 300 men in and around Gonja. There would be more in another week, and by August 12th, Colonel de Blanca did not believe any combination of rebels and dissidents would dare attack. He had already established a perimeter defense about the garrison and arsenal, including heavy machine guns. He had also detailed a reinforced platoon under the command of Lt. Rafael Mohammed to protect the pump station on the freshwater pipeline to Mokodi.

So the Colonel slept well that night, naked under the mosquito net in his private bedroom in officers' quarters above the Gonja arsenal. His last thoughts, before sleep took him, were a fantasy in which he crushed the expected rebellion, was awarded a higher rank, a raise in pay, medals, gifts from the King. Then he could afford a third wife.

The morning of August 5th was hot, vaporous, the blue sky scrimmed with white gauze. The air was a thin ocean; men awoke with bodies already sweated, eyes gummed, throats clogged. It was a day to move slowly, seek the shade, speak softly to avoid the angers that flared so easily in such cruel weather.

At 0600, rebels under the command of the Nyam approached the Bonja barracks in two troops, guiding on the paved highway. They had made a night march of more than ten miles over rough ground, but morale was high, the new Kalashnikov rifles were feathers in their hands, they looked forward eagerly to what they were to do.

The Nyam led almost 100 men, women, and a few children. Not all were Marxist rebels; there were perhaps 30 trained revolutionaries. The others had been won over with the rifles and glowing descriptions of the splendid victory that awaited them. There had been little military discipline on the march, but much laughter, calling back and forth, songs, even a few shots. It was of little importance, the Nyam assured Katsuva. The animals knew how to point the guns and pull the triggers. Their number, and their surprise attack, would overwhelm Gonja's defenders. Then the King's men would all be killed. Then the arsenal would be looted. Then the Nyam and his loyal 30 would push on to Mokodi. Then . . . A day of glory.

The Nyam himself approached the guard at the gate, his hands empty, stretched wide. He spoke in Twi, pleading for water, a scrap to eat, anything. As he begged, he moved slowly around, maneuvering the guard until the soldier's back was to the highway. Katsuva, running lightly on bare feet, came from the bushes, crossed the road, slid a knife into the soldier's back, to the left of the spine, upward, smoothly.

Then all the rebels came bursting across the road, shouting joyously, pointing their new rifles at the garrison buildings and firing at anything and everything. They screamed with delight at the noise of their guns. It was all as the Nyam had promised.

The wild rush carried them inside the fence. As planned, the Nyam and his trained men sprinted toward the corrugated iron building that housed the armory and officers' quarters. Katsuva led the recruits in a stampede to the main barracks, a long, low wooden building with wide screen doors and cloth netting nailed over open windows.

Alarmed by the shouting and firing, a few soldiers had come popping from the barracks. They saw the frenzied throng bearing down on them and turned to scramble back inside. A few made it; the bodies of the others fell on the porch, piling up in front of the doors.

The recruits rushed the doors, hurdling the dead and dying. Katsuva was first inside. He saw hundreds of men rising from plank benches and tables, from their morning meal. Most wore only shorts and singlets. Few had rifles. The NCOs carried sidearms. Almost all had razored glaives, swinging from belt scabbards.

The fire of the recruits slackened. They had been shown how to point their rifles and pull the trigger. They had not been taught to reload. It would not be necessary, the Nyam had insisted, not to surprise and destroy a garrison of 50 men. But here were hundreds of soldiers, staring wide-eyed at this civilian gang with red rags tied about their arms.

Then rifle fire dwindled and stopped. The recruits, laughing foolishly, began grabbing at the bread and rice and fufu and fruit on the tables. The soldiers roared, a single roar of fury, blood-lust. They surged forward with raised glaives, one animal, a steel porcupine.

They fell upon Katsuva and the recruits, glaives falling, cutting, piercing, slicing. Soldiers in the front ranks were pressed by those behind; the screaming mob was jammed out through the wide doors. Katsuva fell under a dozen blades, decapitated before his body ceased rolling.

The others, men, women, children, were pursued and cut down. New rifles were jerked from severed hands. Arms, ears, legs, heads sprang free and bounced. A woman was split upward to her waist, breasts sliced away. A child tottered fainting on bloodied legs until a mighty chop cut it in two. The lower half stood a moment, spouting, before crumpling.

Furious hacking continued even after the recruits, all, were dead. A red mist obscured the morning sun. Puddles soaked the dust. Pye-dogs nosed about ravenously. Flies gathered. Soldiers howled in their frenzy to find one enemy still alive. Glaives fell on lifeless limbs, on scraps of flesh. Heads were minced and flung, severed testicles kicked across the blood-soaked field. Soldiers' bare feet trampled hot meat. Then, at an officer's screamed command, maddened troops turned to the armory and with dripping glaives held high surged in a screaking charge.

Colonel Ramon de Blanca had been awakened by the crackling of rifle fire, by wild shouts. He lay a moment, sleep-fogged, struggling to understand what was happening. Then he rolled naked from under his mosquito net, rushed to the window. Men with red rags tied about their arms were running across the small parade ground. They were all carrying rifles and appeared to be led by a thin, mustached man waving them on.

The colonel was buckling his pistol belt about his bare waist when his bodyguard burst in to scream that the garrison was under attack.

"I know that, you fool," the colonel yelled at him. "Get the doors closed and barred. Put men at all the windows."

Then, realizing he was naked, Colonel de Blanca pulled on khaki pants, which meant he had to unbuckle his holster web, then put it on again over the trouser belt. Before he left his bedroom he ran to the window, cursing furiously, and fired two shots blindly at the advancing rebels. He hit nothing, he knew, but the action pleased him.

There was confusion downstairs. Men dashed about, pushing one another to find a firing position. The colonel got them sorted out, ordered a squad upstairs to fire from the windows there, unbarred the rear door long enough to send runners to bring in a machine gun crew from the perimeter defense and to recall Lt. Rafael Mohammed from the pump station.

The first grenade exploded outside the main door, but it held. The officers and men in the arsenal put up a steady fire from their window positions. Several rebels were seen to fall. The others sought what cover they could find behind trees and parked vehicles. A second grenade bounced off the arsenal wall and exploded. A splinter smashed the face of a soldier who had stood up to fire from a window.

The colonel estimated the attacking force at perhaps 40 or 50 men armed with automatic rifles. He hoped to hold out until the machine gun and Lt. Mohammed's platoon arrived. But suddenly the men at the windows were screaming wildly, jumping with excitement. Colonel de Blanca peered cautiously from below a ledge and saw a mob of his soldiers sprinting across the parade ground, shouting, attacking the rebels from the rear.

The enemy turned to face this threat. The colonel ordered the doors thrown open, and he personally led a determined charge toward the attackers. The rebels scattered, ran, were shot or cut down. Finally, a few threw their rifles away and stood with arms raised. Within moments the assault on the Gonja garrison was ended.

Seven rebels, including the mustached leader, still lived, standing, blank-faced, arms stretched high as 3rd Brigade soldiers danced about them laughing, poking rifle muzzles at them, sending glaives whistling by their heads. Then the captives were knocked down with rifle butts. Their elbows were wired tightly behind their backs, their ankles crossed and wired.

Order was slowly restored. Third Brigade had 11 dead and 23 wounded. Almost 100 rebels had been killed. And there were the seven live prisoners. A good morning's work. The colonel thought of his fantasy. It was all coming true. He hurried to the telephone in the Duty Office to call General Tutu at the palace and report how he, Colonel de Blanca, had crushed the rebellion.

Something was wrong with the phone. Twice he was disconnected, and when he finally got through to the palace, there was so much crackling on the line and so much background noise, he could hardly hear. It was a long time before General Tutu came on, and when he did, he refused to listen to the story of Colonel de Blanca's great victory. Instead, he shouted that a coup d'etat was in progress, the palace was under attack, and the colonel was to come to Mokodi at once, bringing every available man and weapon.

It took the colonel and his harried officers almost two hours to organize the convoy. There were not enough trucks and personnel carriers at the gar-

rison to transport all the 3rd Brigade troops, so men were sent into Gonja to
commandeer trucks, cars, taxis—any vehicle that could make it to Mokodi.

Finally, Colonel de Blanca had his men uniformed, fully equipped, and
loaded aboard transportation. He left twenty soldiers at the garrison, under
command of a master sergeant. Before he took his place in the lead jeep, the
colonel ordered the seven trussed rebels thrown in a heap. They were soaked
with two gallons of gasoline and set on fire. The 3rd Brigade convoy moved
off with soldiers laughing at the screams of the burning rebels and their frantic
efforts to roll out of the flames.

They drove through Gonja, Asantis standing silently alongside the road,
not responding to the soldiers' waves and whistles. Once outside the town,
the convoy picked up speed. Colonel Ramon de Blanca stood upright in the
lead jeep, an automatic rifle cradled in his arms. The hot wind tangled his
hair, rippled his shirt. He looked back proudly to see the line of packed
vehicles following him. Almost 300 armed men. A glorious moment.

But then, rounding a bend, the jeep slowed suddenly, and Colonel de
Blanca had to grab the windshield top to keep his balance. There was an
overturned produce truck, sideways across the road. It completely blocked the
highway.

The colonel's driver pulled up until his front bumper was only a few meters
from the underside of the tipped truck. The other vehicles in the convoy closed
in tightly and stopped, bumper to bumper.

"Get some men and drag that thing aside," the colonel ordered angrily.

Then the mortars opened up.

Captain Obiri Anokye had planned the ambush, and assigned Sam Leiberman and Sgt. Sene Yeboa to command. The three men had walked over
the ground and selected their positions.

"Emplace the mortars along this line," the Little Captain told Leiberman.
He held his arms out straight from his sides. "I will detail my best men, but
I want you to check elevations and corrections. You will be able to move along
this slight dip with reasonable concealment."

"Yeah," Leiberman said. "Reasonable."

"After the initial barrage, Third Brigade will retreat into the wheat field
on the other side of the road. They are poorly disciplined, and will run from
the mortars instead of attacking toward them. Sene, you will place the Gonjan
ABIs at the far edge of the wheat field, perhaps fifty meters beyond the grain,
in the clear. Plan overlapping fields of fire for your machine guns. Leiberman,
when you see them desert the trucks and run into the wheat field, increase
your range and herd them into Sene's guns. Does it sound good?"

"They all sound good," Leiberman said. "What if they come off the road
toward the mortars? What do I do then?"

"Run," the Captain said.

"Good," Leiberman said. "That's what I wanted to hear."

"But they will not do that," Anokye smiled. "I know my people. They will run into the wheat field, thinking to escape. Continue mortar fire even after you hear Sene's rifles and machine guns. I think then that many will surrender. Ask them if they wish to join us. But do not ask until all the officers have been killed. Is that clear, Sene?"

"Yes, Little Captain."

"All commissioned officers are to be killed immediately, regardless of rank. *Then* the men can be asked. With no officers alive to witness their defection, I believe many will come to us."

"And then we go to you in Mokodi?" Sgt. Yeboa asked eagerly.

"First, ask of your prisoners how many Third Brigade soldiers were left to guard the Gonja garrison. Then detail enough ABIs to capture it. You know the one they call the Leopard?"

"Yes, Bibi."

"Put him in command. The remainder of your forces should then come to Mokodi in whatever vehicles survive the mortar shelling. Come as quickly as you can. I shall be with the attack group at the palace."

"If we're late," Leiberman said, "start without us."

The first volley of 60 mm mortar shells that fell on the stalled 3rd Brigade convoy was an almost perfect straddle. Leiberman had carefully paced off the range, and the mortar crews Captain Anokye assigned to him were knowledgeable and eager. Watching the results through binoculars, Leiberman called out corrections, and before long all four mortar tubes were right on target, crews working swiftly, explosions following one another in a regular crump-crump-crump. The whole line of trucks and troops seemed to go up in dirty flame.

The first volley knocked Colonel Ramon de Blanca out of his jeep. When he climbed shakily to his feet, dazed but unwounded, he saw his command, those still alive, spilling from the transports and running into the wheat field. The colonel made one screaming effort to turn them around, to lead them in an attack toward the mortars. But it was hopeless. He joined the flight, plunging into the wheat.

Mortar shells pursued them; it was impossible to make a stand. Bodies and parts of bodies went flinging up against the morning sky, pinwheeling, falling back. The air filled with chopped grain, dust, the stink of burning trucks, of scorched flesh. Keens, too, of the wounded and the fearful living. They ran, ran, ran, tripping, falling, gasping, choking, weeping, pounding over the dead, over the crawling, lurching wounded. The mortar shells came after them, bloody blooms in golden wheat.

Until those who made it through the grain burst into the clear, still running wildly, rifles and helmets lost, thrown away. Then, from across the clearing, a line of rifle fire began to wink at them, machine guns sputtered, and men flopped on their faces, dug fingers into the hot earth, knew they were dead.

It seemed to Colonel de Blanca the noise would never end. But finally the mortars ceased, machine guns stuttered to a halt. He raised his head cautiously to see a line of riflemen advancing slowly. Lt. Rafael Mohammed, lying close to the colonel, jumped to his feet to fire his pistol at the approaching men. He got off two shots before he was cut down, bullets plucking at him, his face dissolving into a raw sponge.

Then what was left of 3rd Brigade was sitting with hands atop their heads, surrounded by at least a hundred silent men carrying good automatic rifles, machine pistols, burp guns. Grenades were slung from their belts and from ropes around their necks. Colonel de Blanca had time to note that none of these men wore red rags about their arms, but then a husky Asanti sergeant wearing the insignia of 4th Brigade came up to him, placed the muzzle of his Uzi close to the colonel's left side, and blew his heart away.

30

At 0800 the time lock on the vault of the Asante National Bank clicked off. M. Claude Bernard, the bank manager, spun the combination and twirled the big tumbler wheel. With the aid of Alistair Greeley, he swung the massive vault door open. Greeley entered to prepare the cash drawers. The assistant tellers began lining up at 0830, signed receipts for their trays, and went to their cages.

At precisely 0900, the manager nodded to the bank guard. The venetian blinds were pulled up, the front door unlocked, and the Asante National Bank was open for business.

First to enter was a 10-man squad of armed 4th Brigade troopers under command of a corporal. They knew exactly what to do: the bank guard was relieved of his revolver, two soldiers went immediately to the open vault and stood guard with rifles at port arms, and all employees of the bank were instructed to remain calm, leave the bank quietly, return to their homes, and listen to the radio for further news.

M. Claude Bernard, a plump, choleric man who wore white-piped waistcoats, demanded to know on what authority his bank was being seized.

"On this authority," the corporal said, showing the bank manager the muzzle of his rifle.

After the employees gathered their personal belongings and departed, they heard the front door being locked behind them and saw the venetian blinds rattle down.

"Madness!" the manager cried. "Madness! I must inform the palace at once."

Greeley watched him trot away. Then he looked about dazedly. The streets of Mokodi seemed calm, peaceful. Perhaps a few more people than usual, but nothing really extraordinary. Until two trucks loaded with soldiers rumbled by, heading toward the dock area. And softly on the morning breeze, Alistair Greeley heard a lazy popping of rifle fire from the direction of the palace.

Then a ramshackle flatbed truck came down the Boulevard Voltaire. There were at least a dozen shouting, singing civilians standing on the truck, throwing out handfuls of printed broadsides. One fluttered to the pavement at Greeley's feet. He didn't bother picking it up; he could read the headline easily: COUP D'ETAT!!! He felt sick.

He stood irresolutely outside the closed bank. The locked door and drawn blinds mocked him. He turned slowly away, eyes smarting with tears. The nigger had duped him. He, Alistair Greeley, an educated white man, duped and made a fool of by a smarmy nigger. It wasn't fair.

No hope of a bonus from Anatole Garde now. No hope of ridding his home of his whorish sister. No hope of anything. He'd be lucky to keep his position at the bank. Perhaps he would lose that, lose his home. Perhaps, even, lose his . . . Well, it was possible. If the Little Captain had deliberately fed him false information, then perhaps his relationship with Garde was known and he was on an "enemies of the state" list. Such things happened in these savage, uncivilized countries. Oh yes, it was possible.

He waited almost half an hour for his bus. He hardly saw the truckloads of soldiers trundling by. He was hardly conscious of the growing crowds of noisy, excited Asantis hurrying toward the palace. His own misery was a bile that sickened him. He retched dryly a few times, swallowing hard. His tongue felt swollen, teeth furry. He imagined he could smell his own tainted breath.

Then, when he realized the bus had not appeared, would not appear on this momentous day, he began the long walk home. He walked slowly, dragging that miserable boot that now seemed an intolerable weight holding him back, pulling him down. The sun rose slowly, sought him out, seared his eyes. He sweated through his black alpaca suit. Dust puffed from the unpaved road with every scuffling step, and the world wavered.

Three times he stopped to rest, twice in the shade of scrawny trees and once merely sitting on the open road, head bowed, tears making crazy rivulets in his mask of dust. He was staggering when his home came into view. The last hundred meters were a lurching nightmare. The glaring sun was inside his head, a molten core that threatened to grow, pulsing, until it consumed him.

He made it up the steps, but tripped on the worn rag rug on the porch and fell heavily to his knees.

"Maud," he called weakly. "Maud. Help me."

He made it inside on hands and knees, then clawed himself upright, pulling on the door frame. He stumbled into the kitchen, struggled out of his filthy jacket, pulled off his sodden tie, unbuttoned his shirt. He opened the tap, splashed water onto his face. Then he bent far over, letting the tepid water pour into his thin hair, onto his neck, soak his shirt and the cotton singlet he wore beneath.

He held a glass under the tap with a trembling hand, but could hardly swallow, it was so warm. He found a small bottle of Perrier water in the fridge. He struggled with the cap, almost weeping again with his weakness and frustration. Finally, he got it open, drank from the bottle, gulping greedily, water spilling from his mouth. He set the empty bottle aside, trying to catch his breath.

"Maud," he gasped. "Maud, where are you?"

He sat down on a kitchen chair to unlace and remove his boots. The molten core inside him was beginning to shrink, but he still felt fluttery. His hands still trembled as he filled a pitcher at the tap, then added a few broken slivers of ice from the laboring fridge.

"Maud," he called, louder now. "Are you home, Maud?"

The water was barely cooled, but he drank off half the pitcher and put the remainder inside the fridge. He shuffled into the living room, flopped into a morris chair with soiled cushions. He closed his eyes.

"Maud," he called once. Then stopped. She wasn't home. Jane wasn't home. Both probably in town to see the excitement. To see Captain Obiri Anokye make a fool of Alistair Greeley, an educated white man. Oh God. What would Garde say? What would Garde do? He had little doubt now that not only had Anokye lied about the date of the coup, he had lied about everything else: the numbers involved, the weapons available, the tactics to be used. Everything.

Telephone Garde. That was the thing to do. Call and explain that he was as much an innocent victim as Garde. Anokye had lied to him. Anokye had led him by the nose. The dirty wog had cheated him. It wasn't Greeley's fault. It was the treachery of the Little Captain. Yes. Garde could see that, couldn't he?

He dragged himself into his study. But when he picked up the phone, he heard nothing but the sound of his own heavy breathing. The line was dead. Groaning, Greeley let the phone slip from his grasp and dangle on its cord. But then, for some reason, it reminded him of a hanged man, and he hastily hauled it up and replaced it in its cradle.

"Maud!" he yelled furiously. "Maud!"

He turned away and saw the white envelope. It was on a small end table, propped against a display case of two model soldiers.

"What?" Alistair Greeley said aloud. "What?"

The envelope was inscribed: Alistair—Personal. In Maud's spidery script. It was sealed. He tore it open and read it swiftly. He didn't understand.

"What?" he said again. "What?"

He read it twice more, the second time slowly because, somehow, it was gratifying to feel such complete anguish, to be so utterly abased, to be thoroughly and finally destroyed and have nothing left. There was a curious kind of peace in that. In annihilation. A blank quiet with foolish hope dead once and for all.

She and Jane had gone away together, and it was no use searching for them because he would never find them, and even if he did, they had no intention of returning to his house, and the best thing he could do would be to try to forget them and make a new life, as they intended to do, and she was sorry for any unhappiness this might cause, but things couldn't continue as they had been, could they, and this was the best way, and surely he could see that, and both of them wished him good luck and all the best and hoped he might find happiness in the future, and there was a beef pie on the bottom shelf of the fridge he might warm up for dinner. Sincerely yours. Maude.

He started to read it again, but his hands were shaking so, his eyes so smeary with tears, that he could make out none of it; the letter fell from limp fingers onto the floor.

He seemed to know instinctively what he must do, the one effective act of an ineffectual life, and stumbled to the desk. In the lower drawer, far back, was a Webley .38 revolver, an enormous, long-barreled weapon he had owned for years and never fired. There was a small box of cartridges, but when he opened it he saw the bullets were green, furry with tarnish, and he had trouble sticking one into the cylinder. But he fumbled it into place, turned the loaded chamber into firing position and, using both hands, succeeded in pulling the rusty hammer back to full cock.

Moving quickly now, while his spasm of resolve lasted, he sat in the swivel chair behind the desk. He raised the heavy revolver. He pointed the wavering barrel at his right temple. He took a deep breath. He closed his eyes. He yanked the trigger.

There was an enormous explosion. He felt a blast of hot gas scorch his cheek. The lid of his right eye stung and quivered. His right ear rang shrilly. He smelled heat, gunpowder, burning hair. Dazed, he turned slowly and saw that he had shot the head off the antique model of an 1812 British captain of the King's Own Regiment of Dragoons.

31

The junior officers and NCOs crowded into Captain Anokye's office leaned forward eagerly to hear his words. Never before had they seen him so tense, never had he spoken so fiercely.

"Do not think it will be easy," he warned them. "The palace, the city, the nation will not be won without a bitter struggle. Many of the King's men will die rather than surrender. I may die. You may die. Be prepared for this and be willing to accept it, knowing our cause is just, and our people look to us for a better life."

There was a murmur of approval from the assembled soldiers. They were uniformed, armed, ready to go.

"No quarter asked, none given," the Little Captain said harshly. "If we fail, we and our families perish. Our blood will soak the earth, vultures will feed on our guts. But if we win, the rewards of the victors will be ours. I promise you this: I shall never forget those who stood beside me on this day. Trust me! It is important that we move swiftly. Do not hesitate to kill those who offer resistance, even those who merely delay you. Carry out the orders you have been given. Strike hard and strike fast. Have no doubt of the—"

There was an interruption; Captain Anokye stopped speaking. The office door opened, Major Etienne Corbeil entered slowly, leaning heavily on a silver-headed cane. Behind him, hovering solicitously, came his aide, Lt. Lebrun.

The Major, a holdover from the days of French rule, was nominal CO of 4th Brigade during the extended absences of Colonel Onya Nketia, the King's youngest son, who preferred Paris to Mokodi. Major Corbeil was pushing 70, a small, frail, pale-haired, pale-skinned soldier, only somewhat senile. He looked about vaguely, eyes dimmed, frame wasted but still erect. He appeared startled when all the men in the room snapped noisily to attention.

"Would you care to join us, Major?" Captain Anokye asked softly.

"No, no," Corbeil said, making a short waving gesture. "Carry on, carry on. Forgive the intrusion. Just looking about . . ."

He was seen so rarely away from his air-conditioned office that Anokye's junior officers and noncoms stared at him curiously. He wore the old French colonial uniform: high choker collar, fitted tunic, braided kepi. Decorations from a dozen wars covered his left breast.

"We are planning an action, Major," Anokye said, "and I would deem—"

"Ah," the old soldier said, eyes suddenly gleaming. "An action!" He drew himself up, looked about sternly. "Soldiers of France," he said in a whispery voice, "on your brave shoulders rests the reputation of the French army. Do not forget the heroes who have gone before, and those to come. Napoleon, Foch, Pétain. Orléans, Austerlitz, Verdun. The roll call of great battles and great victories is a constant reminder of our heritage. And now, the eyes of all France are on you today as you once again prove the valor of French arms. Remember, you . . ."

They stared with astonishment at this antique as he spoke eloquently of la gloire! la patrie! urging them to attack with vigor, to fight with determination, and to have their gas masks with them at all times. They were to remember always that they were citizens of France, with the tradition of French courage and élan.

Captain Anokye was silent, letting the old man finish. The others, too, listened politely.

"Soldiers of France!" Major Etienne Corbeil cried out in conclusion, "I salute you:"

He raised a trembling hand to the brim of his kepi. Then he turned slowly and shuffled away, his aide close to his elbow.

They waited silently until the door was again closed. Then Captain Anokye took a deep breath, glanced at his watch.

"It is time," he said.

There were almost twenty men in the room, but he insisted on embracing and speaking a few quiet words to each. Lieutenants, sergeants, corporals. The room gradually emptied as officers and NCOs departed to join their commands. Finally the Little Captain was alone. He sat a moment at his desk. He heard the shouted orders outside, the grind of trucks starting up, the solid stamp of armed men advancing on packed ground. Then he stood, buckled on his pistol belt, donned his helmet. Concealed in the helmet, between liner and steel, was a small bundle of white feathers from the hackle of a cock, bound with a crimson thread.

The Asante Royal Tank Corps was quartered within a fenced compound large enough to contain a corrugated iron garage, a repair shop, a combination barracks and mess hall, and several small outbuildings. The Corps consisted of thirty men commanded by Capt. Jim Nkomo, with Lt. Seko second in command. The garage housed the two new French AMX-30 tanks that constituted the Royal Tank Corps. There was also an ancient British half-track personnel carrier, inoperative, and two jeeps of World War II vintage, both in working order but rarely used because of the Corps' limited fuel allotment.

The same shortage of fuel kept the tanks immobilized most of the time, though they were featured in parades and during the annual King's Day when all the armed forces paraded in review. The AMX-30 tanks were less than a year old and had been customized in France to operate in Asante's climate and on Asante's soft roads.

Captain Obiri Anokye pulled up outside the fenced compound, riding in the cab of a truck that held twenty-five 4th Brigade soldiers. The Captain alighted slowly and moved casually around to the back. He ordered Sgt. Sebako to get the men disembarked and lined up in two files outside the gate. While this was going on, several tankers inside moved up to the fence and stared curiously at the troopers wearing battle dress. Many of the tankers had been engaged in early morning housekeeping assignments, washing clothes, policing the Corps area. Most of them wore only shorts. All wore the dark green Tank Corps beret, a mark of distinction.

When his men were formed, the Little Captain approached the uniformed guard inside the fence. The armed tanker came to attention and saluted.

Anokye returned the salute. "Open the gate," he said.

The guard hesitated a moment, eyes rolling in indecision. Then he lifted the heavy steel bar on his side and pulled half the gate inward. Captain Anokye motioned to his men. He marched inside the compound. They followed him. No one was grinning.

The tankers watched in bewilderment as Sgt. Sebako stationed the men at three-meter intervals along the inside of the fence. The soldiers stood at port arms. More halfclad tankers came out of the barracks building to stare at this unusual proceeding. At first there was a confused chatter. Then the tankers fell silent, moving uneasily, not taking their eyes from the armed men.

Captain Anokye waited patiently until Sgt. Sebako had placed the soldiers in a wide semicircle, all facing inward. They covered the fronts and sides of the compound buildings.

An unarmed tanker officer came hurrying from the garage toward Captain Anokye. It was Lt. Seko, a thin, pinched-face, light-skinned man, a Muslim, old for a lieutenant, wearing steel-rimmed spectacles. He looked in astonishment at the armed troopers inside the fence, his eyes flicking from Captain Anokye to the soldiers, then back again. Finally he saluted slowly, hand trembling slightly. Anokye returned the salute gravely.

"Captain," Seko faltered, "is there—"

"Is Nkomo on duty?" the Little Captain interrupted.

"Well, not exactly on," Seko mumbled. He licked his lips nervously. "In his quarters. I'm not sure. He may still be."

"Take me to him," Anokye said. "Now."

He motioned Sgt. Sebako to remain in position, then followed Lt. Seko to the barracks. They went to the far end where plywood partitions halfway to the ceiling formed small bedrooms for the two officers and an even smaller duty office.

They paused before one of the openings. Capt. Jim Nkomo was sitting naked on the edge of his bed. He was holding a shard of mirror, and with a small pair of manicure scissors, he was delicately trimming his heavy black beard. It was an enormous beard, covering his neck, almost reaching his chest. But it was difficult to tell where the beard ended; Nkomo's body was covered with a thick mat of black hair: chest, shoulders, back, legs. His penis and testicles were almost hidden.

He glanced up as the two men paused at the doorway. He looked at Anokye, looked at his helmet, looked at the pistol holster hanging from the web belt.

"Captain Anokye," he said. Voice loud, booming, echoing in the small bedroom. "Good morning."

"Good morning."

"To what fortunate concatenation of events do I owe the honor of this unexpected visitation?"

"His men are all around," Lt. Seko reported angrily. "Inside the fence. Battle gear."

"We have a de facto invasion of the premises, do we?" Nkomo said. He didn't seem perturbed. He held the mirror before his face again and continued clipping gently at his beard. "Captain Anokye, can you provide a reason for this unusual and somewhat incomprehensible course of action?"

"I want your tanks," Anokye said coldly. "Both of them. Fueled and manned. Under my orders."

Nkomo lowered the mirror to stare at the Little Captain. Then he tossed mirror and scissors aside. He stood slowly, unfolding to his full height. A heavy man, blue-black, straight up and down, no waist. Large teeth gleamed whitely in the tangle of mustache and beard. Anokye supposed it was meant to be a smile, but Capt. Nkomo's eyes weren't smiling.

"You want my tanks, do you?" he asked. "I presume you have a legitimate order from a superior officer to that effect?"

"No," Captain Anokye said. He withdrew his pistol, let it hang from his hand alongside his right leg. "I have no order. I have twenty-five armed men."

Nkomo's eyes flickered to the pistol, then rose again to Anokye's face.

"Precisely what the fuck is this?" he asked gently. "Surely you can't seriously believe I will turn over command of my tanks to you without a legitimate order from a superior officer?"

"Yes," Anokye said. "I seriously believe you would be wise to do exactly that."

There was silence, inside the little room and outside. The two tankmen looked at each other, then back to Anokye.

"The palace is presently under attack," Captain Anokye said. "I need the tanks for the final assault. I intend to take the palace, Mokodi, all of Asante. I have the men to do it."

There was a moment of silence again, the two tankers considering this. Then Nkomo sighed noisily.

"Oh-ho," he said. "Oh-ho. May I have permission to call the palace, Captain? The phone is right next door, in the duty office."

Anokye raised the pistol, trained it on Nkomo's hairy middle.

"Make your call," he said. "No sudden movements. From either of you."

"We are both unarmed," Nkomo shrugged. "As you can easily perceive."

The three men moved next door to the duty office. Capt. Jim Nkomo, still naked, stood at the desk, absently scratching his ribs, and called the palace. It took almost five minutes to get through to General Opoku Tutu. The conversation was brief. Nkomo listened, murmured a few words, replaced the phone slowly.

"Yes," he nodded. "It is as you stated. The palace is indeed under attack. Heavy rifle fire. I am ordered to bring up my tanks and drive off the attackers. Now that presents me with a rather difficult if not insuperable problem, wouldn't you say?"

"Don't do it," Lt. Seko cried furiously. "He can't use the tanks without us."

Anokye shifted the pistol muzzle slightly toward Seko.

"A dead hero?" he asked. "Is that your wish? I could kill you both now. Your men would then do as I command. They would follow me."

"Ah, yes," Capt. Nkomo agreed thoughtfully. "I rather imagine they would." He pondered a moment, head lowered, beard mingling with chest hair. "What about Third Brigade?" he asked finally.

"Being engaged right now at Gonja. By the Nyam's rebels and the Asante Brothers of Independence. All armed with automatic weapons. And mortars."

"Oh-ho," Nkomo said again, teeth flashing. "Long planning, Captain?"

"Yes. Long and careful. The bank is being taken now. And the cable office, telephone exchange, radio station, dock area, newspaper. And Zabar."

Lt. Seko cursed, a long stream of bitter futility.

"Ah, the coup I have heard rumored," Nkomo said. "But early. That, too, was part of your plan?"

"Yes."

"And if you succeed, you become the new king?"

"No one will be king," Anokye said. "Asante will become a republic. A new constitution. Everyone will vote. An elected legislature. Well? Please decide quickly."

"If I should choose to link my destiny with yours, Captain," Nkomo said, "to become your humble and obedient servant, how may I profit?"

"I suggest we discuss that at another time, in private. Make up your mind, man. What is it to be?"

Capt. Nkomo turned to Seko.

"Fuel the tanks, Lieutenant," he said briskly. "I'll take the lead with A Team. You follow with B."

Seko stared at him, shocked.

"Captain—" he started.

Nkomo sighed. "Lieutenant, as I have reiterated to you on several occasions, you must discipline yourself to reason coolly and logically, as the white man reasons. If we refuse Captain Anokye's request, we are dead. And to no purpose, as he gets the tanks without us. If we join him and he is defeated, then we are also dead. Ergo, our only logical choice is to join him and exert our energies to the utmost to insure his success. Only then may we hope to remain alive."

Lt. Seko made a strangled sound, turned, ran down the barracks toward the garage.

"Now it is another time and we are alone," Nkomo said. "I repeat, how may I profit personally from joining this crusade of yours?"

"What do you want?" the Little Captain asked. "Money?"

"Always welcome, of course. But what I really desire is an expanded Tank Corps. Perhaps an armored brigade. More equipment, sufficient fuel, more men, a higher rank. *Colonel* Nkomo would be a great honor."

"Agreed," Captain Anokye said promptly. "You have my word."

"I know it is to be trusted," Nkomo nodded. "You may replace your pistol now. I assure you that—"

They felt the heavy explosion through the floor of the barracks. Then heard a reverberating boom that fluttered the walls. Somewhere glass shattered. They heard yells from outside, a few shots.

Capt. Jim Nkomo gave a great roar of fury and dashed naked down the barracks. Anokye ran after him.

Flames and heavy black smoke poured from the open doors of the garage. The roof had been blown twenty meters away. The tankmen were running about frantically, throwing canvas buckets of water onto the garage walls, trying to operate two small fire extinguishers. The heat drove them back. Finally they stopped trying; tankers and soldiers watched with awe as small explosions continued to belch. One wall fell inward, then another . . .

Sgt. Sebako and three soldiers were holding Lt. Seko tightly by the arms. His steel-rimmed spectacles had been knocked awry. They hung crazily from one ear.

"He did it, Captain," Sgt. Sebako said excitedly. "Went into the garage. Then came running out. He started for the back fence. I fired at him. But it was too late. The garage blew up. It knocked him down."

Capt. Jim Nkomo shielded his eyes, trying to peer into the smoke and flames. He turned slowly away.

"My beauties," he said to the Little Captain. "Oh, the lovelies. Not a scratch on them. Worthless junk now. He filled them with fuel all right. Down the hatch."

"Long live King Prempeh!" Lt. Seko shouted loudly. "Long live Asante!"

"But not long live you," Nkomo said grimly. "May I borrow your pistol, Captain?"

Anokye handed it to him, butt foremost.

"Stand aside," Nkomo ordered.

Sgt. Sebako and the other soldiers dropped Lt. Seko's arms and scrambled hastily out of the way. Capt. Jim Nkomo stepped close, aimed carefully, fired three times into Seko's genitals. The lieutenant crumpled onto the ground, still alive, still conscious. He looked up meekly.

"No one offer him succor," Nkomo commanded. "Let the foul traitor decay slowly." He returned the Walther to Anokye. "Will you be able to assault the palace without the aid of the tanks, Captain?"

"Somehow," the Little Captain said. "But it will be difficult."

"Trucks," Capt. Nkomo said, grinning. "The biggest trucks we can find, and the bulldozer belonging to the Department of Transportation. Infantry can follow them up to the palace doors."

"Suicide for the drivers," Anokye said.

"Perhaps not. We may be able to rig wood shielding. Heavy planks."

"Excellent," the Little Captain nodded. "Will you see what can be done? My command post will be the telephone exchange across the Boulevard from the palace. Report to me there."

"As soon as possible. I'll get on it at once."

"I suggest you cover your nakedness first," Anokye smiled.

"Before I do that . . ." said Capt. Jim Nkomo, and began to urinate on the dying Lt. Seko.

Prior to his efforts at the Royal Tank Corps, Captain Obiri Anokye had led the bulk of 4th Brigade, more than 200 men, to the neighborhood of the palace. He had directed the placement of his troops, armed with rifles, machine pistols, machine guns, and rifle grenades, in previously selected positions. They were on the ground and higher floors of office buildings, stores, hotels, restaurants, cabarets, and residences surrounding the palace plaza.

These premises were commandeered, the occupants of the buildings told to leave immediately. Many of the positions selected were a floor or two higher than the palace. All windows overlooking the palace grounds were manned by armed troopers of 4th Brigade. Streets were cleared of pedestrians, and guards posted to prevent civilians from entering the siege area.

At 0800, the order was given to open fire, and the attack against the Asante Royal Palace began. All its windows were shattered almost immediately; doors were hastily slammed shut as the heavy barrage continued steadily. After making an inspection tour of the firing positions, the Little Captain temporarily turned command over to Lt. Solomon, a stolid, unimaginative officer who knew only how to obey orders. Captain Anokye then departed on his unsuccessful attempt to obtain the tanks.

Others active in the coup, including Minister of Finance Willi Abraham and Professor Jean-Louis Duclos, had been given subsidiary assignments and sufficient personnel to carry them out. Abraham, for instance, captured the cable office and telephone exchange. Duclos seized the Mokodi mosque. Certain employees of the Asante *New Times* and the national radio station took over control of their offices without military assistance. They had been beneficiaries of the Starrett Petroleum slush fund. Continuous radio broadcasts began at once, predicting the imminent downfall of King Prempeh in joyous tones. The presses of the *New Times* turned out broadsides informing the populace of the coup and hailing the birth of a free Asante.

Small additional detachments of troops had been sent to the homes of a selected list of high government and secret police officials. These included most of King Prempeh's relatives and ministers of his regime. The individuals were placed under house arrest with armed guards posted inside and out. Prime Minister Osei Ware was taken while tending roses in his garden. Anatole Garde was arrested while sleeping with Sbeth in an upper bedroom of the Golden Calf. Soldiers sent to the home of Commander of the Armed Forces Opoku Tutu reported the general was absent. It was later determined that he was inside the palace when the attack started. It was determined by the simple expedient of calling him on the telephone.

During the previous evening, fragmentary and confusing reports had begun filtering into headquarters of the secret police, located in the palace cellar. The reports dealt with the observed movement of the Nyam's rebels toward Gonja, unexpected gatherings of several chapters of the Asante Brothers of Independence, unusual nighttime activities at the Mokodi barracks, etc. The chief of the secret police, an organization that also provided intelligence to the armed forces, thought it best to alert General Tutu at 0200.

The general, grumbling, left a pleasant party with several old friends and new boys being held aboard *La Liberté* and went to the palace to hear in person an assessment of the situation by the "Nutcracker," the chief of the secret police. Tutu then made the decision to alert the palace guard. The entire guard, with battle gear, was brought into the palace. When King Prempeh awoke, he was informed of this action. He and General Tutu were discussing at breakfast what further measures should be taken when, at 0800, the palace came under heavy rifle fire.

From the volume of shots, it was almost immediately apparent to both men that this was not the sniping of a few dissidents but the start of the coup that Anatole Garde had warned them was coming. They cursed the inaccuracy of the time schedule he had predicted as (with some difficulty on the King's part) they flopped onto the floor and crawled under the dining table. In a few moments they cautiously raised their heads far enough to watch palace guards rush into the room and begin firing at targets of opportunity from the palace windows.

Stooping low, making a wild dash, and then sliding under the table to join them, the colonel of the guard told King Prempeh that his wives and children had been escorted to the cellar. He recommended the King and General Tutu join them there as soon as possible. No windowed room in the palace was safe, he said, and some of the bullets apparently were being fired from positions higher than the palace; plunging fire made even the floors unsafe.

It took the King and General Tutu almost an hour to make the perilous trip downstairs. It was particularly difficult for the obese Prempeh because he could not run; he could, at best, hurry. And bending double was impossible. The sight of several dead and unattended wounded lying on the palace floor did not increase his confidence; he was gray with fright, gasping for breath, and sweating profusely when he finally burst into cellar headquarters of the secret police. Slithering along corridors and down stairs had dislodged most of his medals. He was immediately surrounded by wives and children, all of them weeping, screaming, clutching at him for comfort.

He slapped his way through the frantic mob to grab up a phone and call the French embassy. But after several clicks and much static, the dial tone returned. The same thing happened when General Tutu attempted to call the Royal Tank Corps and the Gonja garrison. It was only when a call came through from the gendarmerie on Zabar, reporting they were under attack, that it became evident the telephone exchange had been captured; the palace could receive calls but not make them.

In the small inner office of the chief of the secret police, the colonel of the palace guard delivered his assessment of the situation. It was not reassuring. He said the palace was surrounded by a large force of concealed riflemen, and it appeared impossible to summon rescuers.

"So far they are using only rifles, Your Majesty," the colonel said. "If they have mortars and artillery, I cannot guarantee we'll be able to hold out."

"Can you send runners?" Tutu asked. "Slip them out back doors or terrace windows? To call Colonel de Blanca at Gonja?"

The colonel shook his head. "We tried it, General. Three men at different times. All shot down before they had taken ten steps."

"What about our ammunition?"

"Plenty of that, sir. And machine guns, grenades, and two bazookas. But at the moment we have no satisfactory targets."

"How many men have you?"

"Counting the secret police, about a hundred and sixty. Fourteen casualties at last count."

King Prempeh rose, and the other two men automatically jerked to their feet. The King slammed a pudgy fist down on the rickety table.

"I will not hide here and be threatened," he thundered. "Go out there and kill them!"

The two soldiers looked at him in astonishment. Even in this cellar room they could hear the constant crackle of gunfire.

"A sortie, Your Majesty?" the colonel asked. "Where? In what direction? Against what? They are all around us."

"I command you to go out there and kill them!" the King screamed. "I *command* you!"

"Yes, Your Majesty. At once, Your Majesty."

At the door, General Tutu whispered, "No more than ten men." The colonel nodded grimly and departed.

King Prempeh sat down heavily on a wooden chair that creaked and groaned beneath his weight. General Opoku Tutu stood at his right.

"The French embassy will learn of our situation, Your Majesty. They will come to our aid."

The King looked up hopefully. "Do you really think so?"

"Oh yes, Your Majesty. If we can just hold out, paratroops can be here in a few hours."

"How many hours?" the King demanded.

"I don't know the exact disposition of French forces," General Tutu acknowledged. "But surely by tonight."

"Tonight? We may all be dead by tonight. Who is it, Tutu? Who's leading them? That captain Garde told us about?"

"Probably, Your Majesty. Captain Anokye."

"We should have taken him," the King groaned. "We should have killed him. I was too kind."

"Yes, Your Majesty."

"Get me some food," Prempeh said nervously. "I am hungry."

General Tutu went to the door and motioned to the King's chamberlain. "The King is hungry," he told him. "Bring some food."

The man was shocked. "But I'll have to go upstairs for it, General."

"Then go, you fool! Or send a servant. But get it!"

There was a heavier burst of firing from upstairs. General Tutu heard a few distant shouts. And dimly, he thought, he heard the chatter of machine guns. In a few moments the colonel of the guard came down the cellar steps, dark face coated with plaster dust. He was carrying a Colt .45.

"We tried, General," he reported. "Ten men. They didn't even get halfway across the plaza. Machine guns."

Tutu nodded glumly. "I heard," he said.

"Where's my food?" King Prempeh roared.

But 30 minutes later their plight didn't seem so serious. Colonel de Blanca had called from the Gonja garrison and Capt. Nkomo had called from the Royal Tank Corps compound. Both had promised to come at once to the relief of the palace.

"More chicken!" screamed King Prempeh IV.

The insurgents' command post was established on the second floor of the telephone exchange, captured by Willi Abraham's task force. Here, during the long morning of August 5th, the first results of the Asante coup d'etat were reported.

Other than failure at the Royal Tank Corps, events were proceeding as Captain Obiri Anokye had planned. By 1300, it was learned that the Nyam had been killed and his force of Marxist rebels destroyed. Third Brigade had been decimated south of Gonja; Sam Leiberman and Sgt. Sene Yeboa had already arrived in Mokodi, bringing 50 men on trucks with another 70 following on foot. The Gonja garrison had been secured, as had those at Kasai, Kumasi, and all the smaller towns and villages where chapters of the Asante Brothers of Independence existed.

The Royal Highway from Mokodi to Four Points was under control of insurgent forces, as were the freshwater pumping stations in the north. Property of the King's relatives had been seized, including the phosphate mines where many political prisoners were released. La Liberté and the Royal Navy's motor launches had been surrendered by their crews without serious resistance. The three planes and the small airfield used by the Royal Air Force were taken without a shot fired.

Finally, most gratifying to Captain Anokye, a telephoned message from his brother Zuni reported the island of Zabar captured and secured. Zuni's forces had suffered only two men killed and five wounded. He promised to send immediately 20 armed men to assist in the attack on the palace.

By 1400, the reinforcements brought by Leiberman and Sgt. Yeboa had been posted in additional firing positions; the palace was surrounded by a tight ring of riflemen reinforced by several machine-gun crews. Leiberman had brought along the mortars, but the Little Captain again refused to use them against the palace.

Meanwhile, the crowds of excited civilians had grown and were being restrained with difficulty behind army barricades. It was Leiberman who suggested using the civilians in an assault on the palace.

"There must be five thousand out there," he told Anokye. "Why don't you turn them loose? A human wave. The palace guard can't kill 'em all."

The Captain shook his head. "It would probably work," he said, "but politically it would be unsatisfactory. I want only the army to carry out this coup—carry it out to a successful conclusion. I want the nation to remember the courage and sacrifice of the army."

Leiberman stared at him a moment, then nodded. "I guess you know what you're doing."

Later, Leiberman murmured to Peter Tangent: "The black bwana is way ahead of us all. Nice to be on the winning side for a change."

Tangent, following instructions of Captain Anokye, had remained close to Willi Abraham during the early hours of the coup. He had peeked nervously from a telephone exchange window while the armed cordon was thrown around the palace. And he had watched, fascinated, when a squad of guards, sallying bravely from the palace, were shot down in minutes. Some of the men, struck by the fusillade, had gone into balletic poses and steps, pirouetting, rising on their toes, whirling, arms lifted high, legs flung in their death leaps.

Tangent had made a determined effort to keep out of the soldiers' way and to refrain from asking too many questions. Sam Leiberman had told him of the action south of Gonja, and Willi Abraham had kept him informed as messages came in from outlying localities, reporting the insurgents' success.

Tangent did ask Willi Abraham: "Does Anokye intend to kill the King?"

"Oh yes," Abraham nodded. "It is necessary. A living Prempeh, in Asante or abroad, would represent a constant danger, a threat. He would never cease plotting his return to power. And, of course, by killing the King personally, the Little Captain inherits his strength, spirit, and wisdom."

"Do you believe that?" Tangent asked.

"Many in Asante do," Abraham said. "Captain Anokye is aware of it. So Prempeh must die."

Then, perhaps sensing Tangent's reaction, Abraham glanced down at the 9 mm Parabellum automatic Tangent was wearing in a brand-new leather holster.

"Surely, Mr. Tangent," the Minister of Finance said gently, "you did not expect this to be a bloodless coup? In South America perhaps. Not in Africa."

At approximately 1430, Capt. Jim Nkomo reported to the command post in high good humor. The bearded tank officer had been unable to obtain the Department of Transportation bulldozer—as usual, it was down for repairs—

but he had rounded up six heavy trucks, military and civilian, and equipped the cabs with shielding: thick planks across the windshields with just a crack between them where the driver could peer out.

It took 30 minutes to plan the first truck assault on the palace. It would be driven across the plaza alongside the flagstoned walk leading up to the front steps and doorway. Driver and a man armed with a machine pistol in the cab. Twenty men standing on the truck bed, concealed but not protected by the canvas covering. Thirty men to follow on foot directly behind the truck. All the assault troops to be armed with automatic weapons.

Captain Anokye said he would command the assault personally. Attempts were made to dissuade him, by Abraham, Tangent, Capt. Nkomo. Sgt. Sene Yeboa begged permission to lead the truck assault. The Little Captain listened to them all patiently, then shook his head.

"This is my decision," he said firmly. "I will go. Willi, you will be in command here. The moment the truck starts, lay down fire against every doorway and window of the palace."

The truck assault was a disaster. As it rumbled across the plaza, going slowly to provide cover for the foot soldiers who followed, a heavy rifle barrage was brought to bear against the palace windows. But it did not prevent a well-directed return fire from the guards against the lumbering truck. The tires were shot out first and, as the truck wobbled forward, enfilade fire from the wings of the palace killed most of the men aboard the truck.

Then a lucky shot into the gas tank brought the truck to a flaming halt halfway across the parade ground. The few troopers on the truck still alive leaped off screaming, burning bundles. The soldiers following, led by Captain Anokye, retreated to the protection of the telephone exchange. It was not an orderly retreat. Seventeen men returned safely, several with wounds and burns. The Little Captain was unharmed.

He first saw to the care of the wounded, then gathered his aides about the desk in the office of the director of the telephone exchange. Spread on the desk was a hand-drawn map of the palace, the plaza, the surrounding buildings.

"We will try again," the Little Captain said grimly. "This time we will use two trucks, one to the front door, one to the rear. To divide their fire. No men on foot following the trucks. So they will be able to speed across the plaza, as fast as possible, carrying as many men as we can squeeze aboard. Captain Nkomo, drain the tanks of surplus gas. Leave just enough to get across the grounds to the palace itself. Everyone understand?"

The dual assault was organized by 1600. At 20 minutes past the hour, precisely, a truckload of soldiers raced across the plaza toward the front door of the palace as another truckload sped toward the rear entrance. The front truck was manned by 4th Brigade troopers, the rear by veterans of the ABI. A heavy covering fire was laid down by riflemen and machine gunners in the surrounding buildings.

The guard proved equal to the challenge. In the front of the palace and in the rear, bazookamen poked the snouts of their tubes over ledges of windows on the ground floor and fired their rockets at short range at the approaching trucks. The one speeding to the rear of the palace was destroyed by two direct hits. All aboard were casualties.

The truck lurching toward the front door evaded the first rocket, was stopped by the second, survived two close misses and another direct hit, and then was tipped over on its side by a sixth rocket. The soldiers came spilling out. Being closer to the palace than to the protection of the buildings beyond the plaza, about ten 4th Brigade troopers ran forward frantically and sought cover by throwing themselves onto the ground at the base of the palace terrace. Here they could not be hit by rifle fire from the palace windows.

But the guard solved this problem; they pulled pins from fragmentation grenades and rolled them across the tiled terrace to drop amongst the cowering soldiers on the far side.

Captain Obiri Anokye and the others watched this massacre from windows in the telephone exchange. After several grenades had exploded and no movement was seen amongst the attackers huddled at the base of the palace terrace, the Little Captain said tonelessly to Lt. Solomon, "Resume intermittent fire."

Then he stood somberly with folded arms as the fire against the palace from soldiers in protected positions dwindled to a light popping. Willi Abraham stepped to Anokye's side, murmured a few words, led him away from the open window back to the safety of the interior office. The others clustered about the desk again, looking down at the map, not wanting to see Anokye's face.

Finally: "The mortars, Captain?" Leiberman asked softly.

"We have three more trucks," Capt. Nkomo offered.

Captain Anokye took his familiar stance: hands on hips, torso bent slightly backward, chin elevated. The small vertical wrinkles appeared between his brows. He looked slowly around the circle of aides.

"We have several alternatives," he said quietly. "We could cut off their freshwater supply and simply sit here and starve them out. But time is the determining factor. I am certain the French are now aware of Prempeh's predicament. I want to present Paris with a fait accompli before they decide to come to the King's aid. Also, the guard will undoubtedly take advantage of darkness to make potentially dangerous sallies from the palace against our positions. So the palace must be taken as soon as possible. Certainly before nightfall. We will use every man available in a coordinated charge. The three remaining trucks will attack at the same time."

"Casualties will be high, Bibi," Willi Abraham said.

"Yes," Anokye agreed, "but it must be done. It is the only way. I will personally lead the attack."

There was silence again as all stared down at the map on the table, envisioning the raw, frontal attack. The palace grounds were already littered with the smoking debris of battle: burned-out trucks and burned-out men. They could hear the diminishing screams of the wounded. If they dared look, they could see, here and there, arms raised in supplication from the twisted and blackened heaps. They could imagine what reeking garbage the new attack would create.

Peter Tangent cleared his throat. "Captain," he said hesitantly, "may I make a suggestion?"

"Of course, Mr. Tangent."

"Starrett has a helicopter. A Sikorsky. Seats twelve plus two-man crew. We use it to transport personnel and matériel from the roof of the Mokodi Hilton to the helipad on the *Starrett Explorer*."

When they all looked at him, waiting, Tangent added: "The palace has a flat roof."

Then they all turned to look at Captain Anokye. He was staring at Tangent, large eyes partly lidded as he regarded the American thoughtfully.

"And Starrett would make the helicopter available to us?" he asked softly.

"I don't believe it would be wise for me to *volunteer* the copter, Captain. But if you commandeered it at gunpoint, I would have no choice, would I?"

Captain Anokye drew his Walther P38 and pointed it at Tangent. "I demand you make the Starrett helicopter available," he said.

"That's good enough for me," Tangent said hurriedly. "All of you are witnesses that I am complying under duress. Now let me call and see if it's at the hotel or out on the ship."

He put a call through to J. Tom Petty at the Mokodi Hilton.

"What the hell's happening?" Petty demanded excitedly. "We can hear the gunfire. There's soldier boys in the lobby. Where are you? Is Prempeh out on his fat ass?"

"Almost," Tangent said. "The palace is surrounded. Just a question of time. Where's the chopper?"

"What?"

"Where's the helicopter?"

"Right here. Upstairs. On the roof."

"The army wants it to land troops on the palace roof."

"Beautiful. You going to give it to them?"

"I have no choice."

"Oh-ho, it's like that, is it? Well, let them borrow it if it means getting rid of those royal shitheads."

"Where's the crew?"

"Down in the bar, hustling gash."

"You think they'll fly soldiers onto the palace?"

"Sure they will."

"Pay them as much as they want."

"Pete, they're *Australians*, for God's sake. They'll do it for a case of beer."

Sam Leiberman called the plan "organized chaos," but seemed to think none the less of it for that. As improvised by Captain Anokye, the attack on the palace would consist of three elements:

Leiberman and Sgt. Yeboa would select 10 men of 4th Brigade, soldiers known for their vigor and resourcefulness. All twelve men, armed with submachine guns and fragmentation grenades, would be taken by truck to the Mokodi Hilton. There they would board Starrett's helicopter for the trip back to the palace roof.

When the copter came in over the palace and was letting down, the three remaining trucks under the command of Capt. Jim Nkomo would begin their assault. All would aim for the front entrance to the palace, hoping that one or two might escape bazooka rockets by offering more than one target.

After the trucks began their wild dash, Captain Obiri Anokye and Lt. Solomon would lead the charge of foot soldiers. This attack would come from all sides, ringing the palace. It would be preceded by a barrage of rifle grenades aimed to land on the terrace and drive the defenders back from the windows.

By 1700, the three forces were organized, the helicopter squad on its way to board the Sikorsky at the Mokodi Hilton.

"See you in the throne room," Leiberman said to Peter Tangent.

"We'll be waiting for you," Tangent said, with more confidence than he felt.

Then Tangent and the other aides, officers, and noncoms joined the Little Captain at the desk while Minister of Finance Willi Abraham drew quick floor plans of the palace, pointing out stairways, chambers, the entrance to the cellar, the door to the armory, offices, and apartments.

"After we are inside," Anokye said to Capt. Nkomo, "I will take my men down to the cellar. You and Solomon clear out the upstairs. Remember, Leiberman and Yeboa will be coming down from the roof. Be certain of your targets. Willi, please stay here with the reserve. If we need you, a messenger will be sent. Mr. Tangent, I suggest you stay with the Minister. There is no need to endanger yourself. Anything else? I think not. It will all be over in an hour. One way or another."

Then they waited in silence. The few soldiers remaining at the windows kept up a desultory fire against the palace. But most of the attacking troops were gathered out of sight on the ground floors of the protecting buildings. Captain Obiri Anokye let himself be seen as much as possible by the waiting soldiers, moving about, smiling, joking, slapping a few men atop their helmets, saying things to make them laugh. Several reached out to touch him briefly.

"Juju," Willi Abraham murmured to Tangent. "They think he has magic, that he is invincible. By touching him, they may share it."

Then, sooner than Tangent had expected, they heard the whump-whump-whump of the copter. It approached the palace from the rear, coming in low. It made a tight circle, tilting steeply downward, then straightened over the palace roof, slowed, hovered a moment, began to let down.

"Now!" the Little Captain shouted to Nkomo. "Go!"

The bearded tanker waved, swung into the cab of the lead truck. Its horn began blaring steadily. The three trucks ground into gear, accelerated across the Boulevard Voltaire, bounced over the curb, started speeding across the grassed plaza toward the palace.

"Rifle grenades!" Anokye shouted. "Fire!"

A few seconds later a ragged circle of explosions burst around the palace. Only a few grenades hit the building itself or landed on the terrace. But their blooms of earth and flame served as a signal. With a feral roar, almost 200 armed men burst from cover, began a wild charge toward the palace, legs driving, knees lifted high, guns firing. In the forefront ran Captain Anokye, carrying a Thompson submachine gun. And close behind him, to his own amazement, pounded the tall, lanky figure of Peter Tangent, wondering just what the hell he thought he was doing.

At almost the moment the copter touched down, the door was flung open. Leiberman jumped onto the palace roof. After him came Sgt. Yeboa. Then the remainder of the squad, leaping, staggering, falling.

They heard the ragged crump of rifle grenades. Then the whine of truck engines. Explosions. The roar of the attack. The rotor began its dazzling spin again, the helicopter took off and tilted swiftly away. No escape now.

Leiberman glanced around the roof, led the way to a hutlike structure, opened the door cautiously. A narrow staircase led down to a dusty, dimly lighted attic. He started down, step by step, holding a Uzi chest-high. The others followed in file.

The attic was stacked with cartons and crates. At the far end, a three-sided railing marked the stairway. Leiberman ran forward. Almost there when head and shoulders poked above floor level. A startled face stared. A rifle barrel began swinging to level.

Leiberman triggered a short burst. The guard's head exploded like a hammered melon. Then, grenades into the stairway opening, down on the floor, explosions, up, rush, thunder of boots, down to the next floor, a corridor door, Yeboa and Leiberman working as a team, opened door, tossed grenade, slammed door, explosion, open again, debouchment into the corridor, guards popping from doorways, spray of bullets, all the squad in action now, spreading, kicking doors open, rolling grenades, automatic weapons chattering from hip, chest, shoulder, leaning into the kick, piercing smell of cordite, men rushing, falling, skidding on the polished floor, a guard clapping his eyes, screaming, out again, in, down a staircase, a soldier shot and looping over a banister to fall spread-eagled, curses, shout of triumph, shriek of terror, steel whispers in the air, glass shattering, solid thunk of bullets, defecation of the dying, invisible fingers plucking, two men straining against each other, embracing, bodies tight until one slides away, eyes glazing, down, guards rushing, doors smashed open, grenades floating upward, whine of splinters, and more doors, corridors, rooms, splinters from the walls and moldings, plaster dropping, a shrill whistle cut off suddenly, faces of fear, faces of fury, men clutching chests, throats, bellies, another staircase, wide, and Yeboa and Leiberman, sobbing, shivering, bloodied, sodden, halted their remaining men, reloaded again, knelt, peered downward, the noise of the battle below growing in intensity.

Two of Capt. Nkomo's trucks were taken out by bazooka rockets. The third, with Nkomo in the cab, hit the steps, front tires blew, rear wheels churned, the truck bounced up the steps, across the terrace, slammed into the front doors, smashed them open, stopped, steam rising from the cracked radiator.

Then Nkomo and his men were through the doors, into the palace. Down on the polished floor as an arc of fire from inside doorways poured into them. Grenades skidded back and forth, dead men were lifted and flung by the blasts, ropes of red festooned the walls. Nkomo sprayed his gun ahead of him, deafened by the noise, despairing of gaining the wide stairway that led upward. But then Anokye's foot soldiers were pouring through the shattered doors behind him, through windows, and running, screaming from the rear of the palace. The guards retreated, some backing up the stairway, as more and more soldiers pressed them, closer, glaives flashing now, fingers, hands, arms, legs springing free and rolling. The screams were of victory, as more soldiers rushed the stairway, the remaining guards were trapped between death above and death below and stood in their last fury to club with rifle butts and went down to bloody puddles, kicked, stamped, riddled again and again, killed a dozen times, as a screamed chant of triumph burst from a hundred throats, and the head of a guard, kaffiyeh still in place, was booted the length of a corridor, glaived through an eye, hoisted aloft with a scream of exultation even as explosions from the cellar rumbled and walls quivered.

Running men following Captain Anokye took heavy casualties as they crossed the plaza. But they saw Nkomo's truck crash the doors, heard the sounds of battle from the helicopter squad. As they neared the palace, fire from the windows slackened. They knew the day was theirs.

Anokye came to the terrace wall, leaped for a handhold, slipped, fell back, and Tangent was beside him, bending over, hands on knees, offering his back. The Little Captain understood, stepped on Tangent's back, hauled himself up by the balustrade, leaned down to grab Tangent's hand, pull him scrabbling up. And the other soldiers leaped, formed human ladders, swarmed up and over to the palace windows and French doors, tossing grenades, firing at anything and everything, Anokye into the main ballroom, Tangent and others crowding him, skidding, sliding, falling, rolling, killing the guards who crouched and died along the walls, keening a battle cry. Out into the corridor, remembering the floor plan, around a corner, a dozen guns chopping down a guards officer who loomed, then blasting the lock from the cellar door, crushing it off the hinges, a stumbling rush downward, women and children cowering in a corner, a guards colonel coolly leveling his pistol as chunks of his shoulder shred away, his eyes and ears spouting blood, and melting down he goes, to another doorway, inner room, General Tutu smashed away with a rifle butt, fat Prempeh caught in the arms of his chair, struggling to rise, as Captain Obiri Anokye steps close and stitches the bulging belly and chest, bullets making neat holes like fingers poking deep in dough, slamming the King backward as one plump, beringed hand floats up in lazy protest and a final burst from the Little Captain's gun ends the reign of King Prempeh IV.

32

During the evening of August 5th, following the capture of the royal palace of Mokodi by insurgent forces under command of Captain Obiri Anokye, Mai Fante escorted an unharmed Anatole Garde to the French embassy and delivered him to the Ambassador.

Fante spent an hour with embassy officials and, using his considerable forensic skills and even more considerable charm, assured them the new Asante government would desire nothing but the closest friendship with France. French investments in Asante were secure, the Asante National Bank could reopen in the morning with not a franc missing, no French assets would be seized, no French citizen would be harmed or threatened. And, Mai Fante reminded the Ambassador, Captain Anokye had been educated at the lycée and owed his military expertise to Major Etienne Corbeil. The Little Captain would not forget his friends.

Much mollified, the Ambassador immediately sent off a long cable to Paris. There, at a meeting on the second floor of L'escargot d'Or of those most closely concerned with the Asante problem, it was decided to make no decision for the time being. This, as Tony Malcolm later remarked to Peter Tangent, was a classically Gallic action: a decision not to make a decision. In any event, no intervention or opposition by French forces was anticipated, and none developed.

Also in the hours following the coup d'etat, a number of men and a few women were brought to the Mokodi barracks by armed guards. The prisoners included former Prime Minister Osei Ware, General Opoku Tutu, several high officials of the Prempeh regime, several of the late King's close relatives, the few members of the palace guard still alive, the chief of the secret police and all his subordinates who could be rounded up, and a mixed bag of police spies, informers, executives of the phosphate mines, etc.

Around midnight, the prisoners were marched to a distant field and executed by gunfire, but not before their captors had a little fun with them.

In the days and weeks following the coup, Captain Obiri Anokye moved swiftly to consolidate his power. He appointed an interim cabinet, including Willi Abraham as Premier, Mai Fante as Attorney General, and Professor Jean-Louis Duclos as Minister of State. Other official positions were fairly parceled out to animists, Christians, and Muslims. All were black. In addition to serving as president pro tem, Captain Anokye assumed the powers and duties of Commander-in-Chief of the Armed Forces.

A month after the coup d'etat, the new constitution was submitted to the electorate along with a ballot of candidates for election to the executive and legislative branches of the new government. Anyone who wished might run for national office, and several slates of candidates were submitted to the voters. The Little Captain and those he supported won easily.

During this period, Starrett Petroleum brought over two offshore drilling rigs and began sinking delineation wells to determine the size of the Zabarian oil field. When President-elect Anokye announced his intention to celebrate his inauguration with a national festival, Starrett (at Peter Tangent's suggestion) offered to pay the cost of the entire celebration that would include free food and drink, fireworks, and dancing in the streets. Starrett also presented President-elect Anokye with a fine piece of Steuben glass depicting a lion, rampant, on a ground of dead serpents.

The inaugural ceremony and the celebration that followed were planned and carried out under the direction of a public relations expert Peter Tangent persuaded Anokye to employ. The expert, from PR Afrique in Monrovia, Liberia, suggested to the Little Captain that during the inaugural ceremony and afterward he continue to wear the uniform of an officer of the Asante army, but without any indication of rank or decorations. Anokye readily agreed.

It seemed to Tangent that the entire population of Asante gathered in Mokodi to witness the inauguration of Obiri Anokye as President of the Asante Republic. The crowds waited patiently while oaths of office were taken by the legislature and newly appointed judiciary. Finally, when the Little Captain swore to "uphold, maintain, and further" the principles of the constitution, the Asantis greeted their new President and new nation with such noisy joy that foreign correspondents, in their dispatches, could only use such phrases as "mad delight," "hysterical pleasure," "thunderous approval," and so forth.

That night the main boulevards of Mokodi were lighted by the blaze of the palace and the brilliant flare of fireworks overhead. There was, indeed, dancing in the streets, and a sense of unreserved delight as a whole people threw off the tyranny of the past and celebrated their limitless future. Food for all. Jobs for all. Fun for all.

During the early hours of the evening, President Anokye moved through the crowds of civilians thronging the open ground floor of the palace and enjoying the free food and drinks, dancing to the music of three bands, singing the new National Anthem ("Asante, land of our fathers/our hearts belong to thee . . ."). The President was escorted closely at all times by several aides and an armed and alert Sgt. Sene Yeboa. He had refused promotion to officers rank but had accepted a large increase in salary and assignment as commander of President Anokye's personal guard.

Later in the evening, the President left the public chambers to join a smaller throng on the second floor of the palace. The damage caused during the battle of August 5th had been sufficiently repaired so that President Anokye was able to entertain friends and honored guests in elegant chambers and to join them at a generous buffet.

The President's family was present, of course, conducting themselves with quiet dignity. Squiring Sara Anokye was Lt. Jere Songo of the Togolese army, who had received a personal invitation to the inaugural from the President himself. Another recipient of a gracefully written request from the President was the Premier of Dahomey, Benedicto da Silva. He was accompanied by his daughter Beatrice.

The young girl's greeting to Anokye was a mixture of hesitant formality and youthful delight. "I left you a captain and find you a president," she laughed, holding out a soft hand. "Anyway, congratulations, Mr. President."

"Things have moved quickly," he smiled in return. "I am very happy to see you again. What a lovely gown!"

"Do you really like it? I had it made specially for your inaugural."

"I like it very much. As you said, green is your color."

"You remember!"

She glowed with pleasure. They stood a moment without speaking, looking into each other's eyes. But then Peter Tangent and Jonathan Wilson, the American cultural attaché, came up to offer their congratulations. They introduced a third man, Anthony Malcolm, described merely as "a resident of London." In turn, the President introduced Beatrice da Silva, and the five chatted easily a few minutes until the Little Captain excused himself and moved away to greet Jean-Louis Duclos and Mboa, who had announced their intention to wed.

It was almost an hour before the President was able to maneuver through the crush to the side of Benedicto da Silva.

"Premier," he murmured, "may I have a few moments of your time?"

"With pleasure, Mr. President," da Silva said, and followed Anokye out into the corridor and to a room at the rear of the palace.

"Please excuse the confusion here, Premier," Anokye said, switching on the overhead light and closing the door behind them. "This room is being redecorated as a study. I have an office downstairs, but I felt the need for more private quarters. For quiet talks, or just to be alone for a few moments."

"I understand, Mr. President. For a man in your position, public appearances can become onerous. One sometimes needs solitude to think."

"Yes, that is so."

"A cigar, Mr. President?"

"Thank you, I will."

They sat on a leather couch, lighted the long, thin cigars.

"Excellent tobacco," Anokye said. "Cuban?"

"Sumatran. I expect a shipment soon. Please accept the poor gift of a box."

"Thank you. With pleasure."

They sat in silence, puffing slowly, watching the white smoke bloom up to the high ceiling.

"I hope our nations may continue to enjoy cordial relations," Anokye said. "I see no reason why this cannot be."

"Nor I, Mr. President," the Dahomeyan Premier said. "I look forward to a closer relationship in the future."

"Yes. You have heard of the oil field found in our waters?"

"All Africa knows of it, Mr. President. And envies your good fortune!"

"Premier, I am aware of the economic situation in your country. We have not yet started to receive revenues from our oil. When we do, perhaps we may find a way to be of assistance to you."

"We would welcome such assistance with sincere thanks, Mr. President."

"But that is all in the future. I asked you to join me here to discuss a more immediate matter." President Anokye turned slowly to look at the Premier. "A more personal matter."

Benedicto da Silva said nothing, waiting. He was a tall, slender man, with gray hair naturally curled, lying in waves along his elegantly shaped head. The silvered Vandyke was beautifully trimmed, the mustache waxed. Like his daughter, his skin was dark with a rosy undertint. He smelled faintly of a woodsy cologne.

His black silk suit was artfully tailored, shoes gleaming, linen impeccable. His manner was assured. But behind the smooth urbanity, graceful gestures, fluent speech, were craggy jaw, firm lips, flinty eyes.

"Premier, I had the pleasure of meeting your daughter several weeks ago during a reception in this palace."

"So she informed me, Mr. President."

"I found her a lovely and charming young lady."

"Thank you, Mr. President. Since the death of my wife, Beatrice has taken over duties not usually the responsibility of one so young. I find her assistance invaluable."

"I am certain you do. Premier, I would like to see her more frequently. On a personal basis. I would not do that without your permission."

The Premier's eyes narrowed slightly. But he showed no obvious surprise. He did not smile.

"You do my daughter great honor, Mr. President," he said softly. "And show me great respect, for which I am grateful."

"I would do nothing to endanger our friendship, Premier. Or the friendship between our countries. In matters of this kind, I believe it is best to speak openly and honestly."

"I agree. I hope you will understand if I speak as openly and honestly."

"Of course."

"Your history and background, to my knowledge, are altogether admirable. With few advantages to start with, you have worked hard, developed your talents, and earned an enviable reputation in Asante. Knowing your past record. I am confident you will prove to be a wise and effective leader of your people. However, there *is* something that makes me hesitate to grant immediately the approval you seek."

"Oh? And that is?"

"Mr. President, please forgive my candor, but it has come to my attention that you are involved with a woman who is a subject of public comment. A public woman, in fact. A white woman. May I ask if this is true?"

"It is true."

"I appreciate your honesty. Ordinarily, your relationship with this woman, or any woman, would be no business of mine. After all, it hardly concerns me. But in view of what you are asking, it suddenly becomes my business and does concern me. Me and mine. Do I make myself clear, Mr. President?"

"Perfectly."

Anokye stood and began to pace about the littered room, head lowered, hands clasped behind him. The Premier sat quietly, knees crossed, the crease of his trousers precisely adjusted. Finally the Little Captain sighed, raised his head, looked directly at the other man.

"Premier," he said, "if I promised you to end the relationship to which you refer, if I gave you my word that never again will I meet with this woman, would you then grant me permission to see your daughter?"

"I would, Mr. President, and gladly."

"I now give you that promise and pledge my honor that I will immediately end my—my relationship with this woman."

"Then I welcome your relationship for my daughter. But I must warn you: My approval may not guarantee hers! She has a mind of her own, and in matters of this nature I would not attempt to influence her—unless she asks for my advice, of course."

"I understand that."

"So, in effect, Mr. President, you are on your own. But I cannot believe my daughter's love will prove more difficult for the Little Captain to capture than the royal palace of Asante!"

The two men laughed, shook hands, finished their cigars, and returned arm in arm to the inaugural reception.

By midnight, most of the guests had departed or were queuing up to leave. President Anokye stood at the doorway, shaking hands, embracing his family, exchanging salaams with Muslim guests, placing palms against palms with certain old friends who retained the ancient ways. To some men he murmured a few words, so that when the last visitor had departed and servants moved in to clean the room, President Anokye returned to his private study to find waiting for him Sgt. Yeboa, Peter Tangent, Sam Leiberman, Colonel Jim Nkomo, Willi Abraham, Jean-Louis Duclos, and Mai Fante.

As instructed, Sgt. Yeboa was serving brandy and black coffee. The men were gathered around a small table on which was displayed Peter Tangent's personal gift to President Obiri Anokye to commemorate his inauguration.

It was a set of handsomely designed and crafted model soldiers wearing the dress uniforms of a captain and nine enlisted men of the Asante army. Made by Bulwer & Knightley of London, the beautifully detailed models gleamed with bright colors and sparkling accoutrements. The gift had pleased the Little Captain enormously.

He joined the circle of men admiring the models and picked up the figure of the captain to hold it high in the air, turning it this way and that to catch the light, grinning unaffectedly with delight. He held on to the soldier even as he motioned the men into a circle about the desk and unfolded a large colored map of Africa.

They stared down, fascinated, at the mosaic of the giant continent.

"So many nations," said Willi Abraham.

"So many poor nations," said Jean-Louis Duclos.

"So many weak nations," said Sam Leiberman.

"Many small, poor, and weak nations," President Anokye repeated slowly. "Yes, they are that. With governments as evil as Prempeh's—and worse. With ignorant and greedy rulers torturing the land and the people. Africa, my Africa! How many nations now? I have lost count? Sixty? More? And singly they are nothing. Spits of impoverished land. Even those with natural riches see their children die and their spirit dwindle." He paused to look around the circle of silent, spellbound men. "You know I speak the truth. Some so poor they have nothing to offer but their thin blood. But Africans all! Our brothers. I have thought much on this. So when I stare at this map I no longer see the blotches of individual countries and the lines of boundaries. I see one Africa, one land, one great continent unified and strong. Wait! Do not say to me that this is an impossible dream. Was our resolve to free Asante impossible? Was our capture of this palace a dream? What we may conceive, we may do—if we believe in our destiny. I say to you we can create *one* Africa. We can weld all these fragile links into one mighty chain that no enemy can break. A chain of blood, of common heritage and tradition, a chain of history and culture that once joined might last a thousand years or for all eternity. I would give my life with joy to help create such a human monument. I ask you to think on what I have said, and you will know in your hearts it is so. Africa *can* be united. Africa *shall* be united. If not by us, then by others. As for me, I want only to end my days not as an Asante but as an *African*, a citizen of a great new nation. Tangent, there are profits awaiting you and the men you represent. Leiberman, there is adventure without end. Nkomo, there is fame. Abraham, Fante, Duclos, there is opportunity to put your theories into practice, to create a world power of wise laws, prosperous people, and fertile lands. Sene, I know, shares my destiny and my dreams. The future is ours if we but have the strength and confidence and courage that won the Fifth of August. Together, we can create from this poor, shattered land one nation from the Indian Ocean to the South Atlantic, from the Mediterranean to the Cape. I *know* it can be done. I *know* I am the man to do it. I ask now for your help and your dedication. I need not spell out what such a resolve will demand of you. But if you make the greatest sacrifice a man can make, is there not content in that, for a man to give his life to such a cause? Compared to that purpose, all else seems feeble and without value. I can think of no better life— short or long—than one spent freely, gladly for the future of Africa. Think of it! One land, one government, one people. The world's second-largest continent become the world's first nation! How do you answer me?"

Transfixed by his words, they stood shaken and silent. If they thought they had guessed his ambition, their guesses were water compared to the blood of his true desire. Now they stared at him with wonder, seeing the fire, hearing the glory. They could not resist him.

"Whatever you ask," Peter Tangent said.

"I'm in," Sam Leiberman said.

"I pledge to you," said Nkomo.

And Abraham, Duclos, Mai Fante nodded their agreement.

President Obiri Anokye exhaled in a slow sigh, but gave no sign that he had ever doubted their assent. He turned the map of Africa until he was facing the west coast.

"When viewed from where I now stand," he said.

"Africa looks exactly like a gun, a cocked gun, and Asante is the trigger."

Suddenly he slammed the model of an Asante army captain onto the map of Africa.

"We turn south," he said.

"Yes *sah!*" said Sgt. Yeboa.

The Tangent Factor

1

The nightclub had originally been a barn. Stalls had been converted to booths. The loft had been ripped away to expose splintery beams, now festooned with ropes of onions and red peppers. Feeding troughs were planted with plastic orchids in bark chips. An unpainted plywood bar ran the length of the back wall, facing the dance floor and tables. The acrid odor of manure lingered, mixing with the edgy scents of hashish, the sweat of dancers, fruity perfume.

Yakubu was the only customer at the bar. He wore a red bandanna knotted about his head. A small gold loop hung from the lobe of his left ear. His blue workshirt was open to the navel. A necklace of yellowed shark teeth gleamed on smooth black skin.

He lifted his eyes to glance at the other customers in the club: two black men sitting at a far table. They wore white shirts, flowered ties, sedate suits of European cut. They sat quietly, finishing a carafe of Algerian red.

Yakubu motioned to the bartender. The man came over slowly, polishing a glass with a towel made from an opened flour sack. He had a walleye that stared at the rafters. Yakubu found it difficult not to look up there, to see what was happening.

"Would you care for an additional beer, sir?" the bartender asked.

He spoke Twi. Yakubu replied in that language.

"Thank you, no," he said. "That man at the table . . . The large one with his back against the wall. . . . I have seen him before. Is it possible you know the name?"

"Ah, that one," the bartender said. "You are not of Togo, sir?"

"I do not have that good fortune. But the man seems familiar."

"Perhaps you have seen his image in the Lomé newspaper," the bartender said. "He is Nwabala. A politico."

"Oh yes," Yakubu nodded. "The very man. I have read of him. He wishes to join the land of Benin to Togo. He leads a band of followers."

"So it is said. The man with him is his bodyguard. Very ill-tempered, that one."

Yakubu smiled. He finished his beer, left the bartender a small dash, sauntered out of the cabaret. The two men at the back table watched him go, but he didn't glance in their direction.

Ten minutes later, a white woman walked into the club. She paused, looked about curiously, then moved to the bar. Her long blonde hair was braided into a single plait, coiled, pinned atop her head. She wore a tie-dyed brown Apollo, the loose shift ending just above her knees. Her legs were bare, hairless, pale.

"Scotch whisky and Perrier, if you please," she said to the bartender, speaking French.

"At once, madam. Does the lady desire ice? It is available."

"Thank you, no. No ice."

At the far table, the two men straightened slowly in their chairs. Nwabala lifted the glass of wine to his lips, staring over the rim at the blonde.

"A sympathetic woman," he said to his companion. "She is a tourist?" He spoke Hausa.

The bodyguard shrugged. He was younger, thinner, harder.

"Undoubtedly a tourist," he said. "She wonders, Is it true what they say about black men? So she comes to West Africa to find out."

The big man laughed. "Perhaps I can help her. Go to the bar. Ask her if she wishes to join us for a drink. Speak to her politely in French."

The younger man glared angrily, then pushed back his chair with a clatter. He strode to the bar, spoke to the woman a moment, then returned to the table.

"She does not wish to join us," he said.

Nwabala stared at him a moment.

"Fool," he said. "You do not know how to speak to a white woman. You spoke to her in an uncultured manner."

Nwabala rose to his feet. He was tall, heavy, with long, dangling arms, big hands.

"Could she have a weapon?" he asked.

The bodyguard looked at him, then turned away without speaking.

Nwabala went to the bar, bowed to the woman. In a moment, they were smiling, shaking hands. They chatted easily, laughing occasionally. The wall-eyed bartender had retreated to the end of the bar, leaving them alone.

After a few minutes, Nwabala smiled, lifted the woman's hand, kissed the knuckles. Then he returned to the table. He sat down, picked up his wine.

"She is French," he said in a low voice. "Parisienne. Her name is Yvonne. Staying for two weeks in a bungalow she has rented. I will join her there in thirty minutes. See how easy it is if you speak in a cultured manner?"

They sipped their wine slowly. They watched as the white woman paid for her drink, left a dash, and departed. Soon after, they finished their wine and moved to the bar to settle their bill.

Nwabala paused at the doorway. "Take a look," he said. "A good look."

The younger man went outside alone. He looked up and down the deserted street. It was almost 0200. Thin clouds slid oilily across a watery moon. The bodyguard strolled to the corner, staring about. He checked the alley alongside the cabaret. He peered into shadows. Then he returned to the club.

"All clear," he reported.

They drove in a black Peugeot, doors locked and windows up, although the night was muffled with heat. Beads of moisture gathered on the hood.

The bungalow sat alone, deserted, on a small plot of land halfway to Porto-Seguro. The earth around it was packed hard, treeless. Bare dirt gleamed whitely.

The bodyguard drove the Peugeot off the road, stopped next to the little porch. Lights were on in the bungalow, coming through narrow chinks in the closed venetian blinds.

"Take a look around," Nwabala ordered.

The bodyguard got out of the car. He slid a hand into the right pocket of his suit jacket. He made a complete circuit of the house, then returned to the car.

"All clear," he said.

"Inside too, you fool," Nwabala said.

The younger man went up the porch steps, knocked on the screened door. In a moment, the inner door was opened. The white woman stood there. She was wearing a blue peignoir over a lighter blue nightgown. Her feet were bare.

"I must search your house," the bodyguard said stolidly. He spoke a harsh French.

She looked beyond him to the parked Peugeot. Behind the closed glass, Nwabala waved to her and smiled. She waved back and unlatched the screened door, letting the bodyguard inside. Then she went to sit on a couch. She crossed her legs, adjusted the peignoir carefully to cover her knees.

The bodyguard didn't look at her. He marched slowly through the living room, kitchen, bathroom. He pulled drapes aside and opened closet doors. Then he went into the bedroom. There was a chest of drawers, chair, small dressing table and bench, and the bed. There was one closet door, louvered, with a loop of soiled string hanging from the hole where the knob should have been.

The bodyguard pulled the loop of string slowly. The door opened. Yakubu stood inside, arms folded. The two men stared at each other a moment. Then Yakubu handed over an unsealed envelope. The bodyguard took it, opened the flap, counted the CFA francs slowly with blunt fingers. He nodded, tucked the envelope into an inside pocket, swung the closet door shut on Yakubu. Then he went back outside.

"All clear," he said.

Nwabala climbed out of the car.

"Wait here for me," he said. "An hour. Perhaps two or three. It depends . . ."

He went into the bungalow. The woman locked the door behind him. She had a bottle of Italian brandy uncorked, two little paper cups beside it.

"Yvonne!" Nwabala said. "But how nice!"

Twenty minutes later they were naked in bed. She had unpinned her hair. It hung about her shoulders. He was enchanted to see that her pubic hair was also flaxen.

He lay atop her.

"Am I too heavy?" he inquired solicitously.

"No, no," she breathed. "Oh no."

He spread her smooth thighs, pulled up her knees.

"Oh, you're so big," she recited. "Oh, what a man you are. Oh, I've never had a lover like you before."

And so on. He grinned with pleasure.

She put her arms about his broad, buttery back. She hooked ankles and feet behind his knees.

"Hold me," she whispered fiercely. "Hold me tight!"

Obediently he slid his arms beneath her. Her weight locked them there. Her arms and knees held him imprisoned.

"Oh!" she cried. "Now!"

The closet door opened silently. Yakubu crossed to the bed in one smooth step, flowing, the knife held knuckles down. It was not a heavy blow, but a graceful thrust, the blade going in alongside the spine, angled upward. In, in, until forefinger and thumb pressed soft flesh. Yvonne watched Nwabala's eyes as he realized he was dead.

Yakubu helped her roll the body away. It thumped to the floor. Then Yakubu went outside and got into the front seat of the Peugeot, next to the driver.

"It went well?" the bodyguard asked.

Yakubu nodded and offered a Gitane. Both men lighted up and smoked slowly, not speaking. The car windows were open now. The night air seemed to be clearing, a fresh wind blowing from the west.

Twenty minutes later Yvonne came out of the house. She was wearing the brown Apollo and carrying a small overnight case. She turned off the final light, locked the door, left the key on a ledge over the porch window. Then she came down to the car. She sat alone in the back seat. No one spoke. They drove directly to the airport. The bodyguard let them out and drove away.

An hour later the Piper Aztec landed at the new Mokodi International Airport in Asante. They taxied to a remote section of the field used by the Asante National Air Force. Yvonne was met by Sgt. Sene Yeboa, who took her bag and led her to a waiting Land-Rover. Yakubu alighted and looked around. A bright red Volkswagen was parked in the dim light coming from the corrugated iron hangar. A bare arm extended through the opened sunroof and beckoned. He walked over and got in alongside Sam Leiberman.

The mercenary had a pint bottle of American whisky. He handed it to Yakubu, waited patiently while the black took three slow swallows. Then Leiberman took one deep gulp and belched.

"How'd it go?" he asked.

"As you planned," Yakubu said.

"He died happy," Leiberman said. "Now what? You going back to pimping in Abidjan?"

"Ah . . . well, no," Yakubu said. "Not Abidjan. I have a little trouble there."

"*Little* trouble?" Leiberman scoffed. "And death is an inconvenience. What in Christ's name made you take on a Muslim girl?"

"I didn't go to her. She came to me."

"Her brothers catch you, they'll pound a tent peg up your ass."

"I know," Yakubu said mournfully.

"Want to stay in Mokodi?" Leiberman asked.

"Can I?"

"I can arrange it," Leiberman nodded. "But we'll have to get you a respectable job. How would you like to manage a whorehouse?"

2

The Asante National Army was passing in review on the parade ground of the Mokodi barracks. Newly armed with American-made M16A1 automatic rifles, three brigades of black soldiers stepped smartly past the reviewing stand, weapons carried at port arms. Flags and guidons snapped on the fiery morning wind. Toward the rear, growl of engines increasing to a roar as they approached the stand, came the Asante National Tank Corps. Ten new AMX-30 tanks, hatches open, tankers at the salute.

On the reviewing stand was the guest of honor, Gen. Kumayo Songo of the Togolese army. Standing at his left was his son and aide, Capt. Jere Songo. On his right was the President of Asante, Obiri Anokye, wearing an army uniform without decorations or indication of rank.

As the tanks clanked past, Anokye told General Songo that the commander, the tall, bearded man in the lead tank, was Col. Jim Nkomo. "Very capable," Anokye said.

The President spoke French as did his guests.

"A formidable man," the general smiled. "A veteran of your coup?"

"Yes. He was with me."

A company of machine gunners came last, trundling their heavy .50 Browning M2 guns on two-wheeled carts, and then the parade was at an end.

"Very impressive, Mr. President," General Songo said. "You have accomplished wonders in a short time. I congratulate you."

"Thank you. But there is still much to be done. Particularly in weapons training."

"Morale?"

"Excellent," President Anokye said. "To be an Asante soldier is a thing of pride. Our people are grateful to the army for ending the tyranny of King Prempeh."

"Of course," Songo nodded. "And no doubt the new rifles also help morale?"

"That is true," Anokye said. "You still have the MAS?"

"Still," Songo said disgustedly. "And old Garands and Mannlichers, even a few Lebels. My country has money for everything but new guns."

"I know," the President said sympathetically. "It is a problem. Shall we seek the shade?"

He led the two officers down the wooden stairway. The stand was surrounded by a cordon of the President's personal guard, commanded by Sgt. Sene Yeboa. The guardsmen wore khaki with white spatterdashes and white silk ascots. They carried Thompson submachine guns and Colt .45 sidearms in white leather holsters.

"Captain," Anokye said, "would you please ask the sergeant to call the cars?"

"Of course, sir. At once, sir."

The young Songo moved away briskly. The President led the general into the shade beneath the reviewing stand. Anokye, still called "the Little Captain" by Asantis, was only five feet four. He easily stood erect beneath the planked platform. Songo, a brooding, slumpish man with his brown leather belt cinched under a heavy paunch, had to duck his head. He appeared to be in obeisance to the Little Captain.

"General, I deeply regret you must cut short your visit."

"I also, sir. This Nwabala business.... My government is much concerned."

"I understand," Anokye said gravely. "But surely it was a personal matter? It is said the man was a womanizer."

"He may have been," Songo said angrily. "But it was no jealous husband or lover who killed him. This was a political assassination."

"Political?" the President said. "Can you be certain?"

"The bodyguard has fled to Benin," Songo said grimly. "We have demanded his return, but they refuse. The border has been closed. On both sides."

Anokye shook his head sorrowfully. "I do not like to see neighbors in angry confrontation. We are all brothers, all Africans."

"Sir, it is not the first time they have tried our patience," Songo said. "They have much to answer for. There is only one way to answer a bully, and that is to stand up to him. We must bring an end to these insults and provocations against the people and government of Togo."

"And you believe the killing of Nwabala was a Benin plot?"

"I know it was," the general said furiously. "He spoke for peace between Togo and Benin, a closer relationship, perhaps even a merger of the two countries. His death was their answer. Very well. If they don't desire peace, they must suffer the consequences."

"Please be assured of my understanding," President Anokye said gently. "I am ready to help in any way I can. Will you convey my sympathy to your government?"

"I shall be happy to, Mr. President," General Songo said. "Ah, here are the cars . . ."

"One moment more, if you please, general. I was happy to hear of your son's promotion. A fine boy."

"Thank you, sir."

"You are aware of his interest in my younger sister Sara?"

"Aware of it and welcome it, sir," Songo said. "A charming girl."

"Thank you. I hope our families may become better acquainted. Who knows . . ."

They moved out from under the platform into bright sunlight and crossed to the waiting cars. Guardsmen stood at attention by opened doors.

"With God's smile, go in good health and return in good health," President Anokye said, speaking Akan.

"May Allah bless your days and your family," General Songo replied, in Twi. Then he switched again to French. "Thank you, Mr. President, for your generous hospitality. I was much impressed by the discipline and training of your fine army."

"We progress," Anokye said gravely. "I hope to have four fully armed brigades within six months. One difficulty . . ."

"Oh?" Songo said. "What is that?"

"A critical shortage of dependable field and general officers. I myself, of course, am Commander in Chief of the Armed Forces. I have personally planned and directed the reorganization of the army following the end of the Prempeh regime. But I find my time increasingly spent on affairs of state. Domestic politics, foreign relations, matters of finance, and so forth. Yet I have no generals of education, training, and experience to whom I can safely entrust this new army. You are a graduate of St.-Cyr, are you not, general?"

"Yes," Songo said, straightening his shoulders, pulling in his paunch, "that is true, Mr. President."

"Ah," Obiri Anokye said softly, "if only Asante had a commander like you."

The Songos' limousine left for the airport a few moments later, but not before a blushing, stammering Captain Songo had asked the President of Asante to give a folded note to his sister Sara.

"But I am too old to be playing Cupid," Anokye said solemnly. "But perhaps plump enough." Then, when the young captain blushed even more, Anokye laughed and said, "I shall deliver it with pleasure, captain. I know I speak for Sara—and all my family, of course—when I express the hope you may return soon for a longer visit."

After the Togolese departed, President Anokye entered his black Mercedes-Benz limousine. He was driven across the parade ground to the barracks gate, chauffeured by Sgt. Sene Yeboa. Preceding them was a military Land-Rover with four guardsmen. Both vehicles flew small Asante flags from their front fenders.

The cars moved slowly south on Asante National Highway No. 1, the country's only paved road, then swung west on a laterite road, avoiding the built-up section of Mokodi. They made a wide circle, and approached the city again, through a section of large estates bordered with bougainvillea hedges. At a deserted place on the road, the cars stopped and were exchanged. The four guardsmen drove the limousine back to the Asante National Palace, flags whipping. President Anokye and Sergeant Yeboa got into the Land-Rover, after removing the fender flags.

They went on for a few kilometers, then pulled into the pebbled driveway of a handsome private home. It was stucco painted a light pink, on a single level, gracefully rambling, with several small wings. Yeboa drove the Land-Rover around to the back, through the open door of a galvanized iron garage. Both men got out and walked the few steps to the back door of the house. They entered without knocking. The sergeant remained in the kitchen. President Anokye went down a hallway to the living room. Yvonne Mayer was waiting for him, wearing a blue peignoir over a lighter blue nightgown. Her feet were bare. Her hair was down.

"Bibi!" she said, holding wide her arms.

Later, sated and sweated, they lay in bed on their backs and watched the mad motes dance. Once, lying thus, Anokye had stared down at their naked bodies and said, "We are night and day." It was true; the abstract patterns formed when black and white entwined never failed to bemuse them.

His skin was dark, as cordovan, with a ruddy burnish. He was stoutly made, already inclining to corpulence, thick waist, a layer of softness over the muscles of chest, shoulders, thighs. The young power was still there, but with the yield of padded suede. Black hair at armpits, chest, groin, was hard, with the spring of wire.

The woman, taller than he, was whalebone, as resilient. Blonde hair, pale skin. Arms and legs slender and sinuous. Strong hands and long, prehensile feet. A curious face: cameo features with a tough, distrustful cast. Her breasts were small shields with stiff pink bosses. All of her as sinewy as a vine.

"Bibi," she said lazily, "how did it go—the Nwabala business?"

"As I hoped," he said. "General Songo is furious. Togo has demanded the return of the bodyguard. Benin refuses. The borders have been closed."

"The bodyguard may speak."

"And reveal his own complicity? I do not believe so. Yvonne, there is a long history of enmity between these two countries. Borders have been closed a dozen times. I remember when it was necessary to go to Lagos in Nigeria in order to get into Benin. No visas were issued for travel from Togo. No, the bodyguard will remain in Benin. They will reject Togo's demands."

"I am glad—that what I did helps you."

"Yes, it helps. Did it bother you?"

"Nwabala? No. I have done worse things."

He turned his head slowly on the pillow to stare at her.

"Did you enjoy it?" he asked softly.

"Enjoy?" She shrugged. "A job of work. Yakubu was very good; fast and without useless talk afterward."

"He has moved into the Golden Calf?"

"Yes, into my old apartment. I think he will work out well. The girls like him. He is hard with them but does not demand special favors. You understand? He brings me the books every week. I believe he is stealing about five percent. I don't think that's too much, do you, Bibi?"

"No, let him have it. But no more than five."

"He wishes to raise rates. With all the Texas oilmen in town, he says we can charge more."

"How do you feel about it? The Golden Calf belongs to you."

"Yes, I think we can increase prices. Business has been very good."

"Do as you think best. Men came from London to speak with Willi Abraham. They wish to build a gambling casino on the beach, west of the Mokodi Hilton, near the Zabarian Restaurant. Sam Leiberman says these men are connected with a crime syndicate. But he says they are honest in money matters. What do you think?"

She considered a few moments. "Asante will share?" she asked.

"Yes. A percentage of the net to be negotiated."

"No," she said, "don't do that. They will hide all kinds of expenses and big salaries and skimming in figuring their net. Ask for a percentage of the gross."

"Then you think we should grant a license?"

"Yes, if Asante gets a percentage of the gross. And the tables must be completely straight. The house percentage is enough with honest games and wheels. And all employees including croupiers, are to be Asantis. Insist on that."

"Yes," he nodded. "Good. I can always depend on you for excellent advice. Yvonne, I have to leave soon; I have a staff meeting at the palace. But first I wish to speak about us, about you."

Now she turned her head to look at him. Their eyes locked.

"What do you wish to say, Bibi?"

"You are happy with this house?"

"Oh yes, it is very fine. I have hired a housekeeper and cook, a maid, and a man to see to the grounds."

"Good. And as I promised, the Golden Calf is completely yours. Just be certain to pay your taxes!"

"I shall," she smiled.

"Now . . . oil from the Zabarian wells will begin to flow a week from next Friday. Actually, it has already begun to flow, but on that day we will have an official ceremony and celebration. The public relations man from Monrovia is arranging it. I will push a button, and everyone will see oil flow through a clear plastic pipe. Starrett executives are coming from America. Peter Tangent has arranged that. It will give me the chance to meet them and speak with them about my plans. Also, I am inviting Premier Da Silva of Benin."

"Ah," she said, still staring into his eyes. "And his daughter Beatrice?"

"Yes. His daughter Beatrice. I will ask to marry her while they are here. Ask him and ask her."

She shivered. Her eyes slid away. She stared at nothing over his shoulder.

"So soon, Bibi?" she murmured.

"It must be done," he said. "You know my plans. You agreed."

"To the marriage," she said reluctantly. "But I told you what I would do if you left me—I will destroy myself and put a curse on you and your plans."

It was his turn to shiver.

"I do not like to hear you speak of such things," he said. "I will not leave you; that I have sworn. But Da Silva knows of you, of us, and the only way I may win his friendship, and his daughter, is to make it appear to him that I have given you up. That is why I have taken you from the Golden Calf and given you this home. But it is not enough. You know there is little I do in Mokodi, in Asante, that can be hidden for long. Da Silva will learn that I am visiting you here. I cannot let that happen. So . . ."

"So?" she asked.

"I wish to make a suggestion. Just a suggestion. I want you to consider it carefully. I wish you to marry Sene Yeboa. Then this will become his home. And I will be able to visit without gossip. He is the commander of my guard and my oldest personal friend. He is my brother. It would be perfectly natural if I was seen—"

Her eyes flicked back to his, and widened.

"No," she said. "No, no, and no. Find another way. I don't want to marry Sene Yeboa, or any other man. I want only you. I want to love only you."

"Please listen to what I speak," he said patiently. "Sene is a good man. I have not suggested it to him until I spoke to you, but I am certain he will do as I wish. He follows me in everything. Since we were boys together. He will agree to marry you. He will—"

"No," she said fiercely. "No, no no."

"He will not wish to make love to you," Anokye said quietly. "He has many other women. He is a bull. He will understand it is a marriage of—of convenience."

"Your convenience!"

"Yes," he agreed. "But what is good for me is also good for you, for all of you. You have sworn allegiance to me, to my destiny."

"I will not do it," she cried. "Not not *not!*"

"Then the love you speak of means nothing," he said, beginning to anger. "Bibi, whatever you ask. Bibi, I will do anything for you. Bibi, I will die for you.' And so forth. But now I ask, and you say, 'No no no.' That is what your love means."

She struck his chest with her fist.

"And you?" she shouted. "What does your love mean? That I should marry another man?"

It went on and on, rising in intensity. Her blows against his chest and shoulders became harder, more frantic. He attempted to pin her arms. She squirmed to escape. He rolled his weight atop her. She wept with anger, head whipping from side to side, hair flinging. He caught her flailing legs between his. He crushed her torso within his arms.

And slowly, slowly, their disordered fury turned to a different frenzy. He smacked her jaw with the heel of his hand, ravaged her flesh with his teeth, fell violently upon her and forced penetration as her blows turned to a nailed grasp and her whippy body lurched up to meet his rage, and once more she called him, "My captain!" "My King!" "My master!" and what began as rape ended as . . . if not love, then need.

When, finally, they were finished and lay slackly, bruised and swollen, they stared at each other with dulled eyes. Both, not wishing to part in anger, moved about fretfully on the bed, each hoping the other might speak first. Or make a signal. She did, taking his fingers in hers, shifting to be close to him, head on his shoulder, her fine flaxen hair entangled in his black wire. He took a deep breath, held her body tightly, their slicked skin damply pressed.

"Bibi . . ." she murmured, stopped what she was about to say and instead said, "Bibi, this General Songo—you trust him?"

"He is a simple man," the Little Captain said. "A good soldier but a simple man. He can be valuable."

"And Sene Yeboa—is he a simple man?"

He looked at her a long moment.

"Many believe so. That is the impression he gives. But Sene Yeboa is not a simple man. Sene is deep, and he yearns."

"Yearns? For what?"

"Ask him after you are married."

"I will think about it," she said, and they left it at that.

The Land-Rover, flags replaced in fender sockets, headed back toward the Asante National Palace. President Obiri Anokye sat sprawled in the front seat, alongside Sgt. Sene Yeboa. The Little Captain's left arm was extended across the back of the driver's seat, touching the sergeant's thick shoulders.

"Sene," he asked, "it goes well with the mercenary? There are no problems?" As usual when they were alone, they spoke Akan.

"No problems, Bibi," the sergeant replied. "Leiberman makes many jokes. I must laugh at him. But he is a wise man. And brave. He plans well."

"He plans very well," Anokye agreed. "But he is white. Sene, as my plans grow, we must select special men."

"Special?"

"Prempeh had his secret police. We killed them all, but now I see why such men are necessary."

"You desire to have secret police, Bibi?"

"We would not call them that, of course. But I need men I can trust. These men would provide me with information of what happens in Asante, things I might not otherwise know. You understand? Who says what. Who plots against me. Who assembles guns. And so forth. But also, I need men in other countries, my men who could learn and tell me what I need to know. These men must be black. White men could not talk and listen and make friends and go to certain places in Africa. Leiberman could not."

"You speak the truth, Little Captain."

"Sene, I want you to find men who can do these things and who will be willing to serve me. We will pay them generously, for their tasks will not be easy. Perhaps dangerous."

"Yakubu is such a man."

"That is true. He kills well and has no fear. Can you find other such men?"

"I will find them. Little Captain. There are a few who serve in the guard. Quick men who do not fear death."

"Good. And then you must go to Lomé, to Cotonou, and find such men there. And perhaps other places."

Yeboa considered carefully a long moment. Finally he said, "I believe it would be better to select Asantis for the task and send them to other places rather than to select men of those countries. Then the men who serve can be trusted. They will be of our blood."

"Brother," Anokye said, and squeezed the sergeant's heavy shoulder. "You speak wisely."

They drove a few moments in silence. Then Yeboa spoke again.

"You asked the woman, Bibi?"

"I did," Anokye said. "I told her I had not yet spoken to you about it."

"What was her answer?"

"She will think on it. Sene, you are certain you are willing to do this thing for me?"

"I will do it, Little Captain."

They turned into the Boulevard Voltaire, passed the American embassy, circled the palace plaza, and pulled into the rear driveway. President Anokye glanced sideways at the sergeant. The husky soldier, with a machine gunner's massive neck and shoulder muscles, was hunched over the wheel, his thick, sensuous features intent and solemn.

"You are troubled, Sene?" Anokye asked gently.

"Little Captain," Yeboa said earnestly, "she is your woman. If I should marry with her, I would not go to her. You know that?"

"I know."

"But if she comes to me?"

"She will," Anokye said. "In time."

"Then what am I to do?"

President Obiri Anokye slapped a hand down on the man's broad knee.

"Are we not brothers?" he said.

"Yes *sah!*" said Sergeant Yeboa.

The palace and the ground had been repaired and restored following the violent coup d'etat of August 5th. Armed guardsmen still stood at the entrances and patrolled the plaza, but the ground floor of the palace and certain chambers in the upper floors were open from 1000 to 1500 to all Asantis and tourists. An exhibition of Asanti art was currently on display in the main ballroom, and once a week the Asante National Dance Company presented a free performance of their most famous dances.

President Obiri Anokye had moved his aged mother and father, and his younger brother Adebayo and sister Sara, into chambers on the third floor. His older brother Zuni and his wife had elected to remain, with their children, in the original Anokye home on the island of Zabar, off the Asante shore, connected to Mokodi by a thrice-a-day ferry.

On this morning, the palace was already open to the public, the main floor corridors were crowded with Asantis and tourists. President Anokye was recognized and greeted with a spattering of applause. He smiled and stopped frequently to speak a few words with visitors, to exchange handshakes, salaams, bows. Anokye spoke French and Akan fluently, English carefully, some German and Italian, several African languages.

He welcomed a tour group of tall Swedes, speaking to them in English. He stood in his familiar stance; feet apart and firmly rooted, short torso bent slightly backward, erect, chest inflated, chin elevated and thrust forward, hands on hips.

He told them of his pleasure in seeing them in Asante. He said he hoped they would visit all of his nation, including the cooler hill country, and urged them particularly to seek the opportunity to meet with and come to know the friendly Asanti people. He said that with the revenue from the new oil wells beneath the sea off Zabar, plans were being made to provide more attractions for tourists. He said he hoped to make Asante a showcase for all of Africa, where citizens would enjoy the blessings of liberty and prosperity, and be free to work out their own destinies, whatever they might desire. The tourists were impressed.

"Mr. President," one of the Swedes asked, "do you believe there will be war between Togo and Benin?"

Anokye turned grave. "I pray to God it may not be so," he said. "We are all Africans, all brothers, and we must learn to live in peace with each other. Thank you again for visiting us, and I hope you may return home with many fond memories of our beautiful country."

Then he left them and marched up the wide mahogany staircase to his second floor conference room. He was closely followed by Sgt. Sene Yeboa, who never ceased glancing about, a hand hovering near his holstered pistol.

They were all waiting for him: his inner circle, the men who had been with him through the bloody events of August 5th and had proved their loyalty. The blacks were Premier Willi Abraham, Minister of State Professor Jean-Louis Duclos, Attorney General Mai Fante, and Col. Jim Nkomo. These men were Asantis except for Duclos, a fawn-skinned Martinicain. The two whites in the room were Sam Leiberman and Peter A. Tangent. Leiberman was a mercenary, currently under contract to Asante as a "military advisor." Tangent was still on salary with the Starrett Petroleum Corp., headquartered in Tulsa, Oklahoma, and New York. He was their Chief of African Operations, working out of Starrett's London office.

The Little Captain greeted his friends and insisted on shaking hands all around. He apologized for having kept them waiting, then settled into the high-backed chair behind his wide desk. The legs of the chair had been lengthened so that he would be on eye level with visitors. All drew up chairs except for Sergeant Yeboa, who stood with his back against the single door.

Heavy drapes had been drawn across the tall windows, blocking out the fierce Asante sun. The air conditioning was going full-blast, a chilled breeze circulated by a four bladed fan suspended from the ceiling. The fans had been installed by the French governor who built the palace. After Asante achieved independence in 1958, King Prempeh IV had the palace air-conditioned, but in one of his many extravagances, had kept the old-fashioned fans. Obiri Anokye had retained them.

He picked up a desk ornament, a lead model of a black officer in the dress uniform of an Asanti captain. This, with nine models of Asanti enlisted men, had been Peter Tangent's personal gift to President Obiri Anokye to commemorate his inauguration. The gift had pleased the former army captain enormously. He fondled the little soldiers as he spoke.

"About the casino project," he began abruptly, speaking French. "Willi, we will take our percentage from the gross rather than the net. Do you approve?"

Premier Abraham, a small, fine-boned, grey-haired man wearing a suit of dark tropical worsted beautifully tailored in a European cut, nodded at once.

"Good, Bibi. They will object, but they will finally agree."

"More profits for the whites," the Minister of State said angrily.

The Little Captain had a habit of turning his entire head in a magisterial way instead of shifting his eyes. Now he turned to stare at Duclos.

"We know how you feel, Jean," he said softly. "But there is an English saying about learning to walk before you can run. Is that not so, Peter?"

"Something like that," Tangent said.

"Besides," Anokye went on, "we will insist that all employees of the casino, including croupiers, be Asantis. It will aid employment here and give us knowledge of their gross revenues."

"I'm not certain they'll agree to that, Bibi," Willi Abraham said dubiously. "They are hard men."

"Leiberman?" Anokye asked.

"They'll probably agree to Asantis for waiters, porters, bartenders, bouncers, cooks, and so on," Sam Leiberman said. "And I'd guess they'll be willing to train Asantis as croupiers. But they'll want their own guys at the top; pit bosses, the spooks behind the walls with glasses, cashiers, accountants, managers, and so on."

"All right," Anokye said. "We will settle for that. I am anxious this casino should be built. I believe it will help tourism and our balance of payments. Anything else before we hear Peter's report?"

"The personnel carriers?" Col. Jim Nkomo offered.

"I will discuss that with you personally," the President said. "It is a military matter. Anything else?"

"This Togo-Benin matter," said Mai Fante slowly.

"Yes?"

"There is talk of their submitting their differences to the Organization of African Unity for arbitration."

"Talk?" Anokye said sharply. "From where? Who talks?"

"I received a call from Benin," Mai Fante said. "A friend. He says it is under discussion. He asks our reaction. The call was to sound us out."

"We welcome any move that will insure peace," President Anokye said. "Any move that will help remove causes of dispute between Togo and Benin. That is our official reaction. Our public position. Is that clear to everyone? Good. Anything else? No? All right, Peter; take the floor. Tell us the bad news."

"Not entirely bad," Peter Tangent said. He rose to his skinny six feet five, seeming to unkink as he straightened up. He lounged about the paneled study as he spoke. Once he paused to pull a packet of Players from his inside pocket, lighted up, then passed the cigarettes about, Fante, Nkomo, Leiberman, and Sergeant Yeboa accepted. President Anokye shook his head, but took a package of Gauloise Blue from his top desk drawer and sat listening with an unlighted cigarette between his lips.

Tangent was wearing a suit of navy blue silk, a white cotton shirt with button-down collar, a maroon Countess Mara tie. He had a gold Omega chronometer loosely chained about his left wrist. His tasseled black loafers gleamed with a dull gloss. Tangent's skin was pale, cheekbones lightly freckled. Across his high forehead was a discernible red mark; the panama he habitually wore pressed too tightly.

"The meeting was held in Tulsa," he began, speaking rapidly. "Present were five men besides myself. The vice president and the general manager of the Tulsa office. They handle domestic operations. And the vice president and general manager of the New York office, responsible for overseas operations. The fifth man was old Ross Starrett himself, chairman of the board. He's the son of the original owner of the company, Sherm Starrett, who died about twenty years ago. Ross himself is no spring chicken. Pushing eighty, I'd guess. I hadn't seen him for several years, and he looked like death warmed over. Suffers terribly from rheumatoid arthritis. But the brain is still keen. Surprisingly, I found him the most sympathetic. Just a feeling I had. He let the others carry the ball and went along with their judgment. But I got a definite feeling of interest from him. I'm very perceptive to vibrations in the executive suite, and I got the impression that Ross Starrett was curious and interested. Perhaps even intrigued.

"In any event, I made my presentation, using a big map of Africa. I had the research department of our London office look up some numbers for me, and I threw them fast: population of Africa, land area, present and projected GNP, existing and estimated mineral deposits, petroleum fields discovered and suspected, cereal grains, everything. Then we got down to the nitty-gritty: what, exactly, you wanted.

"Here I was hampered by your instructions, Mr. President. I was to mention Togo and Benin, and nothing else. They are not stupid men, and the general manager of the New York office had done his homework and had all the answers. The tribal volatility of the two countries, their frequent changes of government, their lack of a solid economic base; no oil, no gold, no diamonds, no phosphates to speak of. Just palm oil and cassava. As he pointed out, both countries would have been down the drain years ago if it wasn't for the subsidies from France. No argument there.

"To make this as brief as possible, they have no interest in Togo or Benin. As the veep of Tulsa pointed out, Shell had great hopes for offshore Benin wells but has nothing to show for it but a string of dry holes and a gusher of red ink. So it's no-go for any investment on Starrett's part. But as expected, they're perfectly willing to advance limited sums against anticipated revenue from Asante's Zabarian wells."

"The same bargain they made on the coup," Professor Jean-Louis Duclos cried bitterly. "They are kind enough to lend us our own money!"

"We are not that badly off," Willi Abraham said. "We don't need Starrett for loans. With oil production about to begin, many sources of ready cash are open to us."

"I know all that," Tangent said patiently, "and I explained it to them. I said what you sought was a kind of partnership: an outright grant against future licenses to explore for oil and prospect for minerals in lands that came under Asante's hegemony. But since all I could offer was Togo and Benin, they said no way. Too poor. Not enough evidence of a potential return to justify the gamble. Then old Ross Starrett said something that made me realize he was interested, and way ahead of the others. He said their answer might be different if you had other countries in mind."

President Anokye looked up quickly.

"Did he mention any specific countries, Peter?"

"Yes, he did. Nigeria and Zaire."

The men in the room looked at each other, smiling. The Little Captain leaned back in his chair. He finally lighted his cigarette and smoked slowly, blowing plumes at the ceiling.

"Sene," he said dreamily, "how do you feel about all this?" He straightened, leaned forward over the desk, spoke to the others. "I trust Sene's judgment. He is bushwise. Perhaps he does not know economics, but he knows men and why they act as they do. Sene, what do you say?"

"Do not borrow their money," Yeboa said immediately. "If it is needed, get it elsewhere. If we crawl, pan in hand, they will think themselves our masters. If they are not willing to take the risk, they should not share the profit."

"Very good, Sene," Anokye said approvingly. "Exactly how I feel. The rest of you?"

They all nodded in agreement.

"And how did you leave it?" the President asked Tangent.

"I told them their decision would anger you, and might cause complications. That is the word I used: 'complications.' I implied that after hearing their decision, you might have second thoughts about the lease arrangements on the Zabarian wells."

"Good," Willi Abraham said. "And their reaction?"

"Concern," Tangent said. "They were definitely concerned. That was when I suggested a man from Tulsa and a man from New York come over for the ceremony when the oil flow officially starts. I suggested they speak to you in person. They readily agreed. Ross Starrett was most anxious for them to come. He said, 'Maybe something can be worked out.' I quote his exact words."

"Sounds like my kind of guy," Leiberman said.

"He's almost twice as old as the others," Tangent said, "and has twice their nerve. He's an old man now, but still a wildcatter at heart."

"What do you suggest we do now?" the Little Captain asked. "What would be our wisest course of action?"

"I see several options," Tangent said, lighting another cigarette. "One: we can go elsewhere for the funds needed for the Togo-Benin campaign. Willi says they would be easily available."

"They would be," Abraham nodded. "Not for the purpose intended, of course, but we could say the money was needed for schools or hospitals or whatever."

"Two:" Tangent went on, "when the Starrett men come over for the oil ceremony, you could tell them in confidence, Mr. President, that our objective is actually Nigeria. If you decide to do that, I can state confidently that funds will be made available on a no-strings basis."

"Why shouldn't they?" Duclos burst out. "Nigeria—the richest nation in Africa!"

"No," Anokye said, "I do not believe it would be wise to reveal our plans to others at this time. It is enough that we alone know of it."

"There is one other option available," Tangent said. "I cannot say how viable it is, since I will not be consulted in the decision, but here it is. . . . While I was in the Tulsa office, I stopped by to say hello to old friends in production and development. We talked shop, of course, and I learned that Starrett's overseas operations are becoming increasingly strained by a shortage of refining capacity. To put it in a simplified way, the oil taken from Asante's waters will be shipped by tanker to Starrett's Ireland refinery. There the petroleum is broken down into gasoline, naphtha, kerosene, petrochemicals, whatever, and then must be shipped again by tanker to the end markets. In other words, if Africa wishes to buy Starrett gasoline or diesel oil, then Asante crude must be shipped thousands of miles and then shipped back again as finished products. Very uneconomical. So Starrett is investigating several areas where a refinery might be built to service all of Africa, a profitable market and a growing one. Asante is one of the areas under consideration as a possible refinery site. There is no way I can influence the decision. All the pertinent data is fed into a computer to find the location that maximizes profits. But since Starrett's leases with Asante and other oil producing African nations deal only with the drilling and pumping of petroleum, not refining, it occurs to me that the offer of generous terms to Starrett in granting a refinery license might result in a no-strings grant to Asante for the Togo-Benin campaign."

"Who do you work for?" Minister of State Duclos cried out. "Asante or Starrett?"

Tangent turned to look at him coldly. The young professor had jerked to his feet. His slight figure was quivering with fury. He shook a finger at the oilman.

"How do we know—" He tried to speak, choked on his rage, started again. "How do we know this is not a plot by your employer? Something they suggested you offer? In order to get favorable terms for their refinery? That will pollute our air and water? How do we know that? Eh? Eh?"

"My loyalty is with Asante and Obiri Anokye," Tangent said tightly. He turned to the desk. "Mr. President, if you do not believe that, then my value to you is at the end. I swear that no one at Starrett Petroleum brought up the subject of the refinery in connection with your request for funds. It was entirely my own idea. If you feel I am playing a double game, then I will withdraw at once."

"Peter, Peter," Obiri Anokye said soothingly, "I do not believe that for an instant. I have no doubts of your loyalty. To me and to my dream of a united

Africa. Jean!" he spoke sharply to his Minister of State. "Sit down and do not speak. You shame me and my home by these false accusations. Peter has said the decision as to where the refinery will be located has not been made, and he cannot influence that decision. Perhaps it will be built in Guinea or Liberia or Ghana or Gabon. Is that not true, Peter?"

"That is correct, Mr. President. The matter has not yet been determined by the computer. But I felt you should be made aware of the possibility that Asante may be selected so that if it is, you may take full advantage of it."

"A refinery in Asante," Willi Abraham said, eyes gleaming. "It would help employment immeasurably."

"Only during construction," Tangent warned. "After it's in operation, it's almost fully automated, requiring only a minimal staff."

"Still," Mai Fante said enthusiastically, "it would be a boon to our balance of trade. Perhaps the harbor will be dredged and enlarged."

"Undoubtedly," Tangent said. "But it is too early to speak of such things. At the moment, our only two viable options are to take a loan from Starrett or seek it elsewhere, or to reveal the plan to conquer Nigeria and request a cash grant."

"Thank you, Peter," President Anokye said. "You have done well, performed a valuable service to Asante and to me personally. I will give the matter much thought. I will probably not reach a decision until after the visit of the Starrett people during the oil ceremony. If they bring up the matter of the refinery, then we will meet again and discuss it further. I thank you all. This meeting is at an end. Peter, will you remain a moment, please."

They filed from the room, excited and voluble. Duclos was still flushed with anger. When the room had emptied, Anokye made a motion of his head, and Sgt. Sene Yeboa also withdrew, to take up his station outside. He closed the door behind him.

"Peter, sit down and relax," the Little Captain said. "Here, next to the desk. Give me one of your cigarettes, please. How is it an American smokes English cigarettes?"

"Acquired taste," Tangent shrugged, still tense. He leaned forward to hold a flame for Anokye. "This lighter is French. My shoes are made in Spain. The suit is Italian."

"But your heart belongs to Africa?" Anokye said wryly.

"Yes," Tangent laughed, relaxing, "my heart belongs to Africa. As a matter of fact, that is the truth. I first saw Africa more than ten years ago, and I fell in love with it then. I have not changed."

"What do you love?"

"First it was the physical things. Incredible space. Unbelievable sky. The land itself. Then the people. Their humanness. More recently it's been the African way of life that attracts me. The soul of Africa. The spoken, visual, instinctive, *feeling* culture. A welcome alternative to my dull, unfeeling, mechanical world. Warm emotion as against chilly reason. Do I make sense?"

"Oh yes," Anokye nodded. "A great deal. Peter, I wish to apologize for Jean-Louis' outburst. It was not you, personally, he assaulted. In his eyes, no white man is capable of loyalty, sacrifice or, in fact, any unselfish motive."

"I understand the way he feels."

"Do you? I doubt it. Understand in your mind perhaps, but not in your heart. I assure you that I do not understand Jean's feelings. I have never hated the whites. Never. Perhaps because I never met a white I could not outwit."

"I'll remember that," Tangent laughed.

"Yes," Anokye said, showing his teeth, "do that." He sat back a moment, pondering. "Poor Jean. He does not realize how his hatred of the whites limits him. But he can be of value to me. In certain places. There are nations in Africa where the black leaders feel as he does, with better reason. In Rhodesia, for example. In South Africa. Zaire perhaps. Kenya. He will be a good representative for me in those places. Tell me, Peter—something that puzzles me—when you pleaded my cause before your employers in Tulsa, did they not suspect that your loyalty was now with me, and no longer with them?"

"It would never occur to them."

"Oh? Why not?"

"Because they could never believe that a white man would link his future to that of a black, would work for a black man."

"Ahh," Anokye said. He shook his head more in incredulity than disgust. "The reason I ask is that I wish to be certain that you know that should your employment with Starrett be terminated, I would want you to serve Asante full time. You will be an 'advisor' of one kind or another. At a very generous salary, I assure you. Admittedly, at this moment you are more valuable to me as the representative of Starrett Petroleum in Asante. But your value will not cease when your Starrett connection ends, if it should. You understand that?"

"I do, Mr. President, and I thank you."

"You think there is a chance of the refinery coming to Asante?"

"I think there is a very good chance. Asante is approximately halfway down the west coast of Africa. Starrett sells petroleum products from Morocco to Botswana. If that computer has any sense at all, it will select Asante for the refinery site."

"Yes, geography is everything, it is not? Look at this . . ."

He stood and led Tangent to the facing wall where, on a section of smooth hardwood paneling, a map had been taped. It was the *Michelin* No. 153, *Afrique Nord et Quest*. The borders of Togo and Benin had been heavied with a red grease pencil. Anokye pointed at them.

"Why do you think I selected these two countries as the first targets of my drive southward?"

Tangent shrugged. "Because they are the closest to Asante? Because they are small and relatively weak?"

"Only partly that. If I had the military strength, I would strike directly at Nigeria or Zaire. Where wealth exists. Those are prizes worth the gamble.

But to conquer those countries would require massive invasions. I may soon have sufficient soldiers, well armed and trained, but I do not have the means of invasion. It would require troop-carrying ships and amphibious craft to invade Nigeria from Asante, and probably a large air force to take Zaire. As conquests, Togo and Benin mean nothing economically. They are poor nations. Your men in Tulsa were quite right. But if I take Togo and Benin, then what do I have? Here . . . see? A border with Nigeria. There are roads across that border. I can go overland, on foot or in trucks. I can use tanks. No need for ships or aircraft. Togo leads to Benin, which leads to Nigeria. Once that is ours, all the southern half of Africa opens up. Perhaps, with Nigeria's wealth, I can leap-frog to Zaire or Angola."

"But Mr. President," Tangent protested, "Angola is in a state of rebellion."

"Peter," Obiri Anokye said gently, "all of Africa is in a state of rebellion."

3

The Mokodi Hilton, located on the beach west of the port area, was the highest building in Asante. Starrett Petroleum had leased the entire penthouse floor. It had been converted to offices and living quarters for J. Tom Petty, general manager of Starrett's Zabarian operation, and his staff. In addition, several suites were available for visiting VIPs. It was here Peter Tangent stayed during his frequent visits to Mokodi.

He had returned to the Starrett office following the palace conference, and had plunged immediately into a series of meetings with Petty and the chief engineers of the two offshore drilling rigs that straddled the ocean southwest of Zabar like steel spiders. Sitting in on the confabs were the technicians responsible for the temporary pipeline leading to a jerry-built floating dock in Mokodi harbor. For the time being, it would serve as a delivery site for the Starrett tankers that already floated high in the water a few miles offshore, waiting for the official ceremony before loading began.

Tangent listened to the progress reports, most of them delivered in the harsh twang of West Texas or the softer drawl of Oklahoma. Then he listened to the indignant complaints: the unreliability of Asante contractors, laziness of the niggers, high cost of American bourbon, shortage of matériel, thievery of cab drivers, African heat, the impossibility of getting a good bowl of chili. . . .

"WAWA," Tangent said finally, and when they looked at him in puzzlement, he explained, "West Africa Wins Again. Don't fight it; go along with it. These are good people. Their way of life is not ours, but we'll get further faster if we respect their method of doing things. You're a long way from Tulsa and Houston. Relax. You'll get better results if you treat them as equals. They've got a great sense of humor. A good joke will get you more than blowing your stack. Remember, it's their country. We're here on sufferance. You're all making big money. Starrett expects you to do your job, grin and bear it, then go home. Everyone get the message?"

After they left, grumbling, Tangent spent the remainder of the afternoon on paperwork. He had a plate of chicken sandwiches sent up from room service, and munched on those as he worked, washing them down with two bottles of Evian mineral water. Finally, about 2030, he stuffed documents into an attaché case to take back to London, and went into his suite to pack.

He was suddenly faced with empty hours, a realization so abrupt and so painful he felt like weeping. He did not know the cause. He was deeply involved with the plans of Obiri Anokye, and this had meaning for him. But his strength came from the passion of others. His hours alone seemed to have no more significance than ticking, the slow passage of time.

At the big picture window, drapes pulled back, he looked out and down onto the lighted terrace. There tourists dined, and he could imagine warm talk, cunning lies, loud laughter. Life. And beyond was the black sea, shirred with whitecaps. And farther beyond were the twinkling lights of the oil rigs and the island of Zabar. All, all, cheerful enough. Then why depression?

When the phone rang he moved slowly, still pondering his gloom. Almost savoring it. A bittersweet hurt he could not define.

"Tangent," he said.

"Leiberman here. Come have a drink with us. Dele and me. We're going to the Zabarian. They've got a new singer. A cunt from Accra."

"Thanks, but I can't," Tangent said. "I'm taking a morning flight out, and I've got a lot of work to do."

"Cut the shit," Leiberman said. "There's more to life than a barrel of oil and Sulka pajamas. Meet you at the Zabarian in an hour."

"All right," Tangent said.

Dele was Leiberman's Ivory Coast girl, a little bundle of giggling wickedness. She sat between Tangent and the mercenary at the bar at the Zabarian and rubbed knees with both of them. She and Leiberman and Felah, the bartender, carried on an uproarious conversation in Boulé, laughing continually. Tangent couldn't understand a word of it, but he felt better.

After a while the lights dimmed, the crowd quieted, a spotlight came on, and the singer walked out. She was carrying a mandolin. There was some polite applause.

She seemed enormously tall—Tangent guessed almost six feet—and was stalk-thin. No breasts. No ass. She was wearing a silver-grey silk gown, hung from her bony shoulders with rhinestone straps. The shimmering stuff was loose, but touched hard nipples, narrow hips. Her naked arms were eels.

Her color was brown-black, deep, with no undertint. Just matte. Black curls fitted her long skull like a tight toque. A big, splayed nose, thick lips turned outward. Heavy cheekbones, a chin like an elbow. Wide eyes somewhat slanted. The entire face an African mask. Tangent looked for tribal tattoos, but there were none. Big gold hoops hung from pierced ears.

Leiberman leaned across to Tangent. "The queen of spades," he whispered, in English.

She strummed a few chords, then began to sing. Tangent listened a moment, then leaned across to Leiberman. "What is it?"

"Yoruba. About her guy who went to war and got greased. Very sad. Jesus, what a lousy voice. Great bod, lousy voice."

He was right, Tangent decided; the voice was bad: reedy, as mechanical as an old Victrola. But she could move. The sinuous body swayed. Arms lifted. The long throat was muscled ebony. Taut. There was something there, something. . . . But not the voice.

After a while, people began talking again and ordering drinks. She kept singing, and Tangent felt sorry for her.

"What is her name?" he asked Felah, in French.

"Amina Dunama, Mr. Tangent, sir."

"Where from?"

Felah rolled his eyes in his Rastus act.

"Here, there, everywhere. Mr. Tangent, sir. She up in Ghana before she come here. I think she Lagos-born."

"Let's have her over for a drink," Leiberman said.

"No," Tangent said.

Leiberman said, "Felah, though I've belted you and flayed you . . ."

"By the living God that made you . . ." Felah said.

"Get her skinny ass over here," Leiberman said.

"A duty and a pleasure, bwana," Felah said solemnly.

"Up yours," Leiberman said, "and have one on me."

"Oh, I had that a long time ago, Mr. Leiberman, sir," Felah said, and when the singer finished, to polite applause, he went to fetch her.

Leiberman and Tangent stood when she joined them. Felah made the introductions. Dele moved over so the singer could sit next to Tangent. But for a moment, he and Amina Dunama stood side by side.

"Look at you," Sam Leiberman said, "I could thread both of you through one needle. What're you drinking, toots—hot goat's blood?"

She laughed and ordered a dry Beefeater Gibson, up. Her speaking voice was better than her singing voice: smooth, casual, mellifluous. Her French was fluent. A lot of Parisian argot.

"I enjoyed your songs, Miss Dunama," Tangent said politely.

"Thank you," she said.

"You got a terrible voice," Leiberman said. "You were lousy."

Tangent was embarrassed, but Amina Dunama looked at Leiberman with interest. "You're right," she said. "If it wasn't for the tourists, I'd starve."

"It's the carcass that gets them, honey," the mercenary nodded.

She looked down at her bodice.

"You think I should get silicone?" she asked.

"Nah," Leiberman said. "That stuff shifts. You're liable to end up a Babinga."

She threw back her head and laughed, long and hard. Her throat was thick, much bigger than her upper arm. A thigh of a throat.

Tangent looked from her to Leiberman and back, not understanding the exchange that made her laugh.

"Babinga?" he asked.

"Pygmies," Leiberman explained. "Some of them have steatopygia. Enormous great asses. You wouldn't believe."

"Oh," Tangent said.

Dele discovered that Amina spoke Boulé. The two women began to chatter. Leiberman got off his bar stool and came over to stand behind Tangent. He put a meaty arm across Tangent's shoulders.

"You drunk?" Tangent said, shrugging off the arm.

"Sure I am," Leiberman said cheerfully. "And loving every minute of it. I happen to be a very sweet drunk." Then he switched to English. "You fancy the beautiful cunt?" he asked.

Amina Dunama turned slowly and looked at the mercenary. "I also speak English," she said in that language.

"So?" Leiberman said. "I just asked him an innocent question."

The singer shifted her stare to Tangent.

"Why don't you give him an innocent answer?" she said.

"Yes," Tangent said, "I fancy the beautiful lady."

Amina leaned forward and thrust a wet tongue into his left ear.

"Mazel tov!" Leiberman shouted. "May all your troubles be little ones. Felah!"

"Sir?" the bartender cried.

"But when it comes to slaughter . . ." Leiberman recited.

"You will do your work on water . . ." Felah answered.

"And you'll lick the bloomin' boots of 'im that's got it," they finished in unison, and Leiberman said, "The hell you will. Another round, chappie, and let joy be unrefined."

"I'm afraid he's drunk, Miss Dunama." Tangent said.

She looked into his eyes.

"Why are you afraid?" she asked softly.

They left Leiberman and his Ivory Coast girl at the bar. The loud, red-faced mercenary had attracted a circle of admiring tourists who were buying him drinks. Sam was regaling them with old *colon* jokes. ("When you first come to Africa, you pick a fly out of your beer. After six months in Africa, you swill the beer down, fly and all. After a year in Africa, you put a fly *in* your beer, for the protein!")

Amina was staying at the Mokodi Hilton. They strolled slowly back along the boardwalk. A three-quarter moon had come over. It laid a silver swath across the gently rolling sea. She had a fishnet scarf across her bare shoulders, but the mild night wind was warm and scented.

He wanted to ask her about her life, singing, home, childhood, likes, dislikes, everything. . . . But he was too content to speak, and she was silent.

They came into the lighted lobby, stopped, faced each other. He did not have to stoop to look into her eyes.

"I would ask you for lunch or dinner, Miss Dunama," he said, "but I must return to London tomorrow morning."

"Oh," she said.

"But I'll be back in a week," he said hastily. "Perhaps less than that. Will you be here?"

"For two weeks," she said. "Then on to Lomé."

"We'll have dinner when I return?"

"Of course."

"Can I bring you anything from London? I have no problems with customs."

"Just yourself," she said. They had been speaking French. Now she switched to Akan: "Go in good health and return in good health."

"The memory of your beauty shall keep me young and happy," he replied, and they both smiled. Then he said in French, "May I escort you to your door?"

"Please," she said. "Fourth floor."

At her door, he held out his hand.

"Thank you for a very pleasant evening, Miss Dunama."

She looked at the proffered hand in surprise, then looked up into his eyes.

"You're not coming in?" she said.

"Well . . . ah," he said. Then: "I haven't been invited," he giggled.

"Would you care to come in, Mr. Tangent?"

"Well . . . yes. For a moment."

Her hotel room was a shambles. Clothing tossed everywhere. Cosmetics. Perfumes. Cigarette butts. Used tissues. Half-empty glasses. A sandwich with one bite taken out, red lip rouge around the crescent. The bed mussed. She made no apologies.

"Let me see . . ." she said. "I think I have some banana liqueur. Or we can call room service."

"No, no," he said hurriedly. "Nothing, thank you."

"I have some cigars."

"Cigars?"

"Yes. I smoke cigars. Are you shocked?"

"Of course not," he said.

"Would you like a cigar?"

"All right," he said bravely. "I'll have a cigar."

They were really Spanish cigarillos, long, thin, black. They lighted up solemnly. Not bad. She threw clothes off chairs, and they sat close, puffing importantly. After a moment she reached up and switched off the lamp. But her balcony was over the lighted terrace; they could see each other dimly, in outline. Highlights: her bare shoulders, his tilted head.

"What Leiberman said..." he began. "You're really a good singer, Miss Dunama."

"I am not," she said without rancor. "He spoke the truth. I like him. He's alive."

"Then why..."

"Why do I continue? Because it allows me independence."

"But what is..."

"What is to become of me? What is to happen? I never fear of that. Do you know any African who plans the future, Mr. Tangent?"

"Yes," he said.

"Well, I do not."

"I would like to call you Amina, if I may."

"Of course."

"And my name is Peter."

"I know. But may I call you Mr. Tangent?"

"You may, of course. But why so formal?"

"I prefer Mr. Tangent."

"All right," he said equably. "If you prefer."

"In English, 'tangent' means going away from a straight line, does it not?"

"That's one meaning," he said shortly.

She got up, cigar clamped between her teeth, hiked up her silver-grey skirt, sat down in his lap. He squirmed about to accommodate her weight.

"Do you have a woman, Mr. Tangent?" she asked. "In London?"

"No."

"In Africa?"

"No."

"Anywhere?"

"No. No woman anywhere."

"That is sad."

"Yes," he said. "Sad."

"Would you like me to be your woman?"

His reply surprised him. Not what he said so much as how quickly he said it.

"Yes," he said. "I would like you to be my woman."

"All right, Mr. Tangent," she said.

She stunned him.

"Look here..." he said.

"Look where?" she asked innocently.

"I don't understand," he said.

"Don't understand what?"

"You. What you said. I don't understand why you would wish to be my woman."

"Will you pay?" she asked.

He drew a deep breath, pondered a long moment.

"Yes," he said.

She laughed.

"I don't wish payment," she said.

"You're mischievous," he said.

"Yes," she said, "I am. But I can save you."

"Save me?" he said indignantly. He shook his head. "Are you playing with me? Save me how? From what? What makes you think I need saving?"

"Don't you?"

"Of course not. From anything."

"Good," she said.

She stood and turned her back to him.

"The zipper," she said.

Obediently he pulled it down. It whispered derisively.

"Should we put out our cigars?" he asked nervously.

"What for?" she said.

He undressed shyly. He would not look at the naked wave on the rumpled sheet. He hung his jacket and shirt over chair backs. He shook out his trousers and draped them over a table edge.

"The socks," she said. "Rolled and tucked into the shoes."

He turned to her angrily.

"You think me a fool," he cried.

"Yes," she said. "A sweet fool. Now come to me."

He did, gingerly, rolling close to her.

"Oh my," she said. "So pale."

"Yes," he said.

"Freckled."

"Some," he said. "I can't go out in the sun. My skin can't take it. I used to go out in the sun all the time, but I reacted. Doctors told me that if I insisted on going out in—"

"Shut up," she said.

"All right," he said meekly.

After a while, he said, "I'm not going to make it."

"Is it so important?" she said.

"No," he said. "It's not," he said. With wonderment.

4

Tangent flew Air Afrique to Paris, planning to switch to Air France for the hop to London. There was food and drink all the way on the Mokodi-Paris flight, but he wasn't interested. Strapped into his seat in a half-empty cabin, he took a blank pad from his attaché case and stared at it.

He reviewed what he had said and done in Mokodi. The palace conference. He had made a mistake in admitting he was powerless to influence Starrett's decision on the refinery site. One did not publicly confess weakness. At worst, he should have said, "I'll see what I can do." He had not thought it through. Now, pondering, he saw that perhaps he might shape events. He grunted with pleasure, made a few cryptic notes.

Then, his writing hand reminding him of a white squid, something dead and apart from him, he put the ballpoint pen aside. He closed his eyes. He thought of Amina Dunama. Black wave on rumpled sheet. There again he had confessed weakness. Displayed it. But that was something entirely different. No power play there. Or if it was, of a different kind. And Amina had not cared. Said she did not care. Appeared not to care. It was difficult. He sighed, and dozed off.

The company limousine met him at Heathrow. He went immediately to Starrett's headquarters in an Edwardian townhouse in Mayfair. Only a minimal night shift was on duty, mostly in the communications center. But there was coffee steaming in a big perc and a tin of stale biscuits. Tangent helped himself to both, then placed a person-to-person call to Ed Gianelli in Tulsa. The time was right: about 2100 in London, 1500 in Oklahoma. The call went through without delay.

"Ed? Peter Tangent in London."

"Hey, Peter! And happy fish-and-chips to you."

"How're you, Ed? And the wife and bambinos?"

"Couldn't be better. You?"

"Fine, thanks. Ed, small problem. . . . You remember that thing we talked about when I was over—the refinery?"

"Yes?"

"It's out of the bag. A reporter from the London *Times* has been on my neck. He says he hears, quote, from an unimpeachable source, unquote, that it's going to Liberia. Anything to it?"

"No way. The choice right now is either Gabon or Asante. But not decided yet. At least that's what I hear."

"Good. I'll deny the report. Better yet, I'll just say, 'No comment.'"

"Right you are. When in doubt, keep your mouth shut."

"Thanks, Ed. Love to all."

Tangent rang off, grinning. Gabon or Asante. Interesting. He called Schwarzkopf's Adventure Tours, the travel agency that served as Tony Malcolm's cover. The phone was answered on the first ring; a canned voice began: "Hello. This is a recorded message. There is no one in the office at present. But if you—"

Tangent hung up and called Malcolm's unlisted home phone. No answer. Then he tried Brindleys. Mr. Malcolm had signed in; "Just a moment, sir, and we will try to locate him." Finally, he was switched to the bar, and Malcolm came on.

"Who?" he said.

"Tangent. Hi, Tony."

"Peter! You're back. Or are you calling from darkest Africa?"

"I'm back. What're you drinking?"

"A bottle of Chateau Tannic Acid, vintage of yesterday."

"If I stand you a bottle of Latour fifty-three, will you meet me in the library in an hour?"

"Latour fifty-three? I'll meet you on the roof!"

Brindleys was a private club for gentlemen, in a refurbished townhouse on Park Lane. It was small, and expensive, although most members' bills were picked up by their corporations, embassies, trade organizations, etc., as a legitimate business expense. It was true that the world's business was frequently discussed and sometimes concluded at Brindleys. But it also offered an excellent kitchen and what was said to be the third largest wine cellar in London. Prices were not reasonable.

There were four men at the coppered bar when Peter Tangent strode in: Tony Malcolm down at the far end; the Stavros brothers in the middle, nursing little glasses of ouzo; and near the entrance, Julien Ricard hunched and glowering over a small balloon of brandy. Tangent hoped to slip by the Frenchman unobserved, but Ricard's hand shot out, he clutched Tangent's arm.

"Buy you drink," he said thickly.

"Raincheck," Tangent said, trying to smile pleasantly. "Got some business with Tony Malcolm."

Ordinarily at Brindleys, mention of "business" was sufficient excuse. For anything. But Ricard would not be put off; he did not release Tangent's arm. The American thought, not for the first time, what an unattractive fellow his captor was: dark, peevish, with a great livid birthmark that ran down his right cheek on to his neck.

"You're in plastics, aren't you, Tangent?" Ricard said, though he knew better.

"In a manner of speaking," Tangent said. "Oil, actually. You're in snails, aren't you, Ricard?"

"Import-export," Ricard said angrily.

"Ah yes," Tangent said. "Snails *and* ticklers."

He jerked his arm away, and stalked down to Tony Malcolm. He nodded to the Stavros brothers as he passed. God only knew what *they* were in. Everything, probably.

"Tony," he said. "Let's go into the library. Can't stand that man!"

"He's a bit much," Malcolm said sympathetically. "I expect it's the birth-mark that makes him so nasty."

"No excuse," Tangent said, regaining his good humor. "I've got the world's shortest cock, but I'm as nice a fellow as you'd want to meet."

Malcolm laughed, and led the way.

There was only one other member in Brindleys library: a gaffer deep in a leather club chair pulled up before the fireplace. He was staring into the flames and giggling. Tangent and Tony Malcolm sat far back in a secluded corner. They watched Harold reverently uncork the Latour.

"Should let it catch its breath, gentlemen," the old waiter said. He poured a bit into a glass, paused expectantly as Tangent sniffed and sipped.

"Loverly," Tangent said.

"It has a nice nose," Harold said, filling their glasses halfway. "Please give it some time, gentlemen. We're on the last case of this lot."

Malcolm savored.

"Velvet," he said. "Moonlight. Rembrandt. Mozart."

"How about Donald Duck?" Tangent asked.

"Philistine. When did you get back?"

"A few hours ago."

"See the papers?"

"Not yet."

"Starrett is up another three," Malcolm said. "Think I should hang on?"

"Definitely," Tangent said. "I am. It'll bounce even higher in a week or so. We're planning a refinery in Africa."

"Oh? Where?"

"Ah," Tangent said. "That's the reason for the wine."

"Didn't think it was my damp, white body," Malcolm said. "What's up?"

There was little point in trying to deceive; Virginia had good men in Togo and Benin, and Malcolm would guess what was going on. He looked like a plump, affable shoe salesman. But his brain, as Tangent once remarked, was "pure Borgia."

He told Malcolm of President Obiri Anokye's planned takeover of Togo and Benin. He mentioned nothing of Nigeria. He described Starrett's pro-jected African refinery, and how it might affect Anokye's shortage of funds.

"I think they'll come through with the money he wants," Tangent said, "if he agrees to good terms on the refinery license."

"How do you know they'll build in Asante?"

"I checked with a friend in Tulsa. Just an hour ago. The choice has nar-rowed down to Asante or Gabon. That's where you come in."

"Is it?" Malcolm said lazily. He held his glass up to the dim light, peered through it, twirled it slowly. "You're really gung-ho for the Little Captain, aren't you?"

"Oh yes," Tangent admitted. "Burned my bridges. Metaphorically speaking. Look, Tony, this man has a great dream. A vision. He wants to unite all of Africa. All those sixty or so poor, suffering, undeveloped countries into one great nation, from the Mediterranean to the Cape, from the Atlantic to the Indian Ocean. That's something, isn't it?"

"You think he can do it?"

"I think he can do it," Tangent nodded. "You were impressed, weren't you, when you met him at the inaugural?"

"Yes," Malcolm admitted, "but I'm easily impressed."

"And shrimp can fly," Tangent scoffed. "You're the most realistic man I know. And you think he has a chance—don't you?"

"A lot of ifs, Peter," Malcolm sighed. "If he gets the money. If he gets backing from a powerful friend. If he keeps winning. If he isn't blown away himself. It's far from a sure thing."

"Didn't say it was. But the possibility is there, and the game is worth the candle. I'm not going to rend your heart with a recital of all the good things the Little Captain can do for the African people. Decent food, housing, health, education. All that. Just look at it from a balance sheet point of view. Minerals and oil discovered or not yet found. Millions of acres of underdeveloped or misused land. Great forests. Rivers and falls for hydroelectric plants. What a source of raw materials and cheap labor! What a potential market! Right now Africa is about where the U.S. was in eighteen-fifty. Just opening up . . ."

"I'm not certain Virginia should get involved," Malcolm said slowly.

"You'll be involved sooner or later, whether you want to be or not. I see the U.S. as that powerful friend you mentioned who's going to lead Africa into the Twenty-first Century. When the time is right, I'm going to start beating the drums in D.C. You know Starrett has some valuable contacts there. I think that if the Little Captain keeps winning, we can get State to pay more attention to Africa, to back Anokye politically and economically. We can become a world power!"

" 'We'?"

"I mean Africa and President Anokye and the men backing him. Including me. The immediate problem is money. For arms, bribes, and so forth. That's why this Starrett refinery is important."

"And what do you want Virginia to do?"

"The choice is between Asante and Gabon—right? Well, Gabon is as French as the Champs-Elysées. I mean, they *own* the country. Oh, I know Gabon is supposed to be an independent republic, but the French run everything. Their advisors are everywhere, and I assure you that nothing big gets built in Gabon, no large investment is made, without a nod of approval from the Quai d'Orsay."

"Oh-ho," Malcolm said. "I begin to see your fine Italianate hand."

"Tony, you know how to do it. Just have Virginia leak to the—"

"All right, Peter, all right. You don't have to spell it out."

"It's worth a try, isn't it?"

"I'll think about it."

"Do that," Tangent said. "And always remember, the wine was a fifty-three."

"You conniving bastard!" Malcolm laughed.

Tangent pleaded weariness—"Only four hours' sleep in the last thirty-six"—and left Malcolm in the library. There was still a third of the precious bottle remaining. When the gaffer dragged himself out, still giggling, Malcolm took his place in the warmed club chair before the open fire. He sipped the wine slowly, staring into the flames.

Anthony Malcolm was a fleshy, pinkish chap who cultivated a manner of great good-humor. Candid, open, a genial fellow who was always delighted to stand a drink, tell a joke, offer a loan. Few of his pals at Brindleys would believe he had once killed a man with an umbrella. A very special umbrella.

Finally, sighing, he rose and took his final glass into the bar. The Stavros brothers had departed, but Julien Ricard still sat at one end, slumped over his brandy. He looked up as Malcolm entered from the library corridor. Malcolm looked at him and, no one else being present, the bartender busy with his accounts, jerked his head slightly. He drained his wine, left the glass on the bar, walked through the swinging door into the men's lavatory.

While he waited, Malcolm looked under the doors of the three toilet compartments. Then, just to make certain, he opened the three doors and glanced within. It was an old-fashioned loo with walls of white ceramic tiles and fixtures of cracked enamel: urinals as big as altars, sinks like baptismal fonts. Malcolm stood at one of the urinals, fly unzipped, and lighted a cigarette.

After a few moments, Julien Ricard came sauntering in. He glanced about, went to one of the huge sinks, began to soap his hands slowly.

"Poor Tangent," he said. "I give him a hard time."

"Keep it up," Malcolm said. "You're doing fine. You have anything for me?"

"Nothing since my last letter," Ricard said. "You received it? The new actuator?"

"Yes, I received it. We already had the actuator, but it's always comforting to get confirmation. Nothing else?"

"No. Nothing."

"Devaluation?"

"No, nothing on that as yet. Pending."

"Everything in France is pending," Malcolm said equably.

"True, my friend, true," Ricard chuckled. "We make haste slowly." He dried his hands on the roller towel. He looked into the mirror and began to comb his long, black hair, carefully, palm following the comb. Malcolm zipped up his fly, came over to a sink, began to rinse his hands.

"I have something for *you*," he said.

"Oh?" Ricard said.

"Starrett Petroleum is planning to build a refinery. In Gabon."

"Ah?" Ricard said. Then, "Tangent told you this?"

"In confidence. Apparently preliminary approaches have already been made in Libreville. In secret."

"Interesting," Ricard said.

"I thought you'd find it so," Malcolm said. "Your people should find it interesting, too. Help you score Brownie points."

"Brownie points?"

"American expression. Means getting credit for achievement."

"Brownie points," Ricard repeated. "Incredible."

5

In Paris, on the avenue Montaigne, stands l'Escargot d'Or, a restaurant mentioned both in history books ("Bears on its facade the scars of musket balls fired during the French Revolution") and in the *Guide Michelin* (two stars).

L'Escargot d'Or serves the public on the ground floor. The smaller dining room on the second floor is available only for private parties, conferences, discreet meetings of publicly antagonistic politicos, industrialists, labor leaders, bankers, church dignitaries, etc. The second floor dining room is also the scene of the monthly banquet of Le Club des Gourmets, a prestigious association of food and wine connoisseurs.

Two nights following the meeting of Tony Malcolm and Julien Ricard amidst the urinals of Brindleys, a not very successful dinner of Le Club des Gourmets was held at l'Escargot d'Or. The Beluga caviar was not properly chilled, the soufflé de homard à l'américaine was definitely chewy, and bits of shell were found in the Mont Blanc aux marrons. As for the wines— whispers of *"Merde!"* were heard. The hapless bishop who had provided the dinner (the twenty-four members of Le Club des Gourmets each planned and paid for the monthly banquet, in turn) was all apologies as Club members departed. They tried to be polite to the monseigneur, but there was little doubt that they would not soon forget this affront to their palates.

Left behind in the dimmed dining salon were Julien Ricard, the Man from the Palace, and the Man from the Bourse. The last two were portly men, wearing heavy, dark suits with high vests draped with golden chains. The Man from the Bourse wore the ribbon of the Legion of Honor. The Man from the Palace had been a hero of the Resistance. He had a black patch over one eye, a steel machine for a hand. Thin white hair did not conceal a metal plate set into his skull.

The three dawdled over minuscule glasses of kirschwasser and cups of espresso. They sat placidly until the table had been cleared and the waiters gone. Then Ricard rose and began to speak. He paced about the dim hall, occasionally pausing to look up at one of the scruffy chamois heads decorating the walls, or to touch his birthmark as a man might stroke a growing mustache.

"The original intelligence came from a friend in London," he told the others. "He has a valuable contact within Starrett itself. I am inclined to credit the report on those grounds. But to confirm, I sent Anatole Garde to Gabon. He speaks Fang and a few Bantu dialects. So far, he is unable either to confirm or deny. Those in government he has spoken to swear they have not been approached, in secret or openly, by Starrett representatives. Which means, of course, absolutely nothing."

"What do you recommend, Julien?" the Man from the Palace rumbled, hand and hook clasped comfortably across his paunch.

"I believe we should treat it as a matter of some consequence," Ricard said. "After what happened in Asante, we can no longer tolerate intrusions by the Americans into our sphere."

"What happened in Asante?" the Man from the Bourse asked blandly. "Merely a change of government. Hardly a world-shaking event. It was a change, incidentally, which has resulted in no loss to us."

Ricard was indignant.

"You think President Anokye will honor Prempeh's pledge to expropriate the oil wells?"

"He may or he may not," the Man from the Palace shrugged. "Meanwhile, Asante is becoming prosperous, which benefits us, of course. Subsidies will no longer be needed."

"But we're losing clout," Ricard cried angrily.

"'Clout,'" the Man from the Bourse smiled. "For a man who dislikes the Americans as much as you profess, dear Julien, you adopt Americanisms quickly. But no matter . . . let us get back to Gabon. Assuming the worst, that Starrett is attempting to maneuver secretly, what do you propose?"

"First, that we make the strongest representations possible to Libreville that we would view very dimly indeed any unilateral action on their part in negotiating this Starrett refinery. Second, that we make the strongest representations possible to the Americans that we would view very dimly indeed any attempts by one of their grotesque corporations to interfere without consultation in what is universally recognized as our sphere."

The Man from the Bourse sighed. "Julien, that is a formidable amount of 'strongest representations possible.'"

"Also," the Man from the Palace added, "a formidable amount of 'viewing very dimly indeed.' Still . . ."

The two looked at each other.

"I see no harm . . ." the Man from the Bourse began cautiously.

"Even if the report is without substance..." the Man from the Palace offered.

"True. The Americans want very much that nothing should delay the Geneva conference."

"At the moment, they desire to be pleasant and cooperative on all matters."

"What better time to express our wish, delicately of course, that Starrett Petroleum should not take precipitous action within our legitimate sphere?"

"...That might, possibly, affect our interests and compromise the current spirit of cooperation and friendship that exists between France and the United States."

Ricard stroked his birthmark frantically.

"Well?" he asked. "Well?"

"Yes," the Man from the Palace said judiciously. "I think certain discreet representations may be made."

"Yes," the Man from the Bourse said thoughtfully. "We must treat the whole matter in an offhand manner, casually. But leaving no doubt of our concern and of our intentions."

Ricard sighed. "Thank you, gentlemen," he said, and wondered if he had scored Brownie points.

6

Peter Tangent checked in at the Mokodi Hilton at about 1600 and went immediately to the Starrett offices on the penthouse floor. There he was handed a note that Jonathon Wilson had called, at 1330 that day, and requested that Tangent call back. Wilson was Cultural Attaché of the U.S. Embassy, having replaced the ineffectual Bob Curtin. He was Virginia's man in Asante.

Tangent called immediately.

"Wilson? Peter Tangent here."

"Hi. Good flight?"

"Good enough. An hour's delay in Conakry, for no apparent reason."

"Buy you a drink?"

Tangent paused a second. Then: "Sure. Where and when?"

"Cleopatra. Outside. In an hour?"

"Fine. See you then."

The Cleopatra, across from the palace on the Boulevard Voltaire, was a reasonably priced restaurant. "You will be amused," said the guidebooks, "by its Egyptian decor." Plaster sphinxes or not, its sidewalk café offered a most pleasant panorama of Mokodi. Handsome men and beautiful women of a dozen tribes, in costumes ranging from funereal European, to jeans and T-shirts, to brilliant native dress: bright gbariyes, flowing saparas, encrusted gur-iles. Head coverings from berets to fezzes, turbans to labarikas. Skin colors from fish-belly white to tunnel black. Flashing teeth. Cutting eyes. People moving to an inner rhythm. Scents that assaulted the nose, beguiled, sickened, wooed. Warm voices, warm laughter.

"Wilson," Tangent smiled, proffering a hand, taking a chair at the attaché's outdoor table. "Watching the passing parade?"

"Can't get enough of it," Wilson said, awed.

"I know exactly how you feel," Tangent said. "What're you drinking?"

"Gin sling."

"Very good," Tangent approved. "Won't cure the screaming trots, but makes 'em endurable. So it's said." He signaled the hovering waiter, pointed at Wilson's glass, held up two fingers. Then he stared at the Cultural Attaché. "The last time I saw you, you were peeling."

"Yes," Wilson laughed. "A mess. Tanning now. Finally."

"You are indeed. Are you enjoying Asante?"

"Very much," Wilson said, cutting short the "sir."

Tangent sympathized. This slight, eager young man wasn't sure of Tangent's status. Was he just another Yankee businessman? Or an undercover Virginia agent? Or an American executive offering close cooperation? A sleeper? A mule? A courier? A spook? What, exactly, was he? And not knowing, Wilson couldn't be certain what he might say—or even ask.

"Had a bullet," he said finally. "From Malcolm. For you."

"Oh?" Tangent said. "When?"

"Noon. Today."

They were silent while their drinks were served. They raised glasses in an unspoken toast, sipped gently.

"I'm glad you suggested this," Tangent said genially. "It tastes fine."

"Malcolm says to tell you the wine is working," Wilson said. "Mean anything?"

"The wine is working?" Tangent repeated. "Yes. Thank you."

"Good news? I hope."

Tangent flipped a hand back and forth, but didn't answer.

"That's all he sent," Wilson said. "For you." He looked out onto the street where as many strolled along the Boulevard, in traffic, as crowded the paved sidewalk. "What a country!" he said. "Marvelous!"

"Isn't it?" Tangent said. "I'm glad you like it. Getting on, are you?"

"Think so," Wilson said. "But slowly."

"Ah, yes," Tangent said. "A different rhythm here. Where were you before?"

"Copenhagen."

"My God!" Tangent laughed. "*Totally* different. Is there any way I can help?"

"Oh ..." Wilson said, troubled. Not knowing how far to go. "President Anokye. Know him, don't you?"

"Oh yes. I have an appointment in the morning."

"Met him once or twice," Wilson said. "Official things. Embassy receptions. So forth." He leaned across the table, earnest, ingenuous. "What can you tell me about him?"

"Very ambitious," Tangent said promptly. "Very talented. An incredible orator. Sweep you off your feet. He's brave, as he proved during the coup. The people love him. The Little Captain. Very broad-based support. He's learning government as he goes along."

"He's also learning Portuguese."

"Is he?"

"I don't know where that fits in," Wilson said lamely. "Do you?"

"No, I don't."

"Marxist?"

"Anokye? No way. Starrett wouldn't be here if he was. No, we can work with him. A pragmatic man."

"Knowing anything about his personal life?"

"Very little. He smokes occasionally. He has a drink now and then. Never to excess, to my knowledge."

"Women?"

"I wouldn't know about that," Tangent said.

"Hear he was sleeping with a white woman," Wilson said, blushing faintly beneath his tan. "Ran a local cathouse. The Golden Calf. But now she's out. A black man is running the place."

"Ever been there?"

"What? Where?"

"The Golden Calf."

"Oh," Wilson said, blushing even deeper. "Ah . . . no. Not yet."

"What happened to her?" Tangent asked. "The woman?"

"Living in a big, expensive house out in the Evogu district. Talk is she's going to marry a soldier. Sergeant. Commander of the President's personal guard."

"You do get around," Tangent said slowly. "Ready for another?"

"All right. One more. You know anything of this?"

"No," Tangent said. "Nothing."

"Story is that Anokye dumped the white woman—Yvonne Mayer, her name is—so he can marry the daughter of the premier of Benin."

"Interesting," Tangent said.

"Fascinating!" Wilson said enthusiastically. "Larger than life. Italian opera."

Tangent laughed and paid for the drinks.

"What else have you heard?" he asked the keen young man.

"Well . . ." Jonathan Wilson said, leaning forward again, carried away by his own prescience. "Some evidence that Anokye is organizing a kind of secret police."

"Oh?"

"Not secret police exactly. Domestic spies. To keep a tab on things. No one's been arrested or tortured. Nothing like that. Yet. Just a few men. No uniforms. They go around and, you know, ask questions. At the moment, it's all very vague."

Tangent nodded. "You're filing all this with Virginia, aren't you?" he asked casually.

"Of course."

"Good," Tangent said, reflecting ruefully that Tony Malcolm knew more of what was going on in Asante than he did.

He spent the early evening with J. Tom Petty, reviewing plans for the oil ceremony. There would be a luncheon at noon—Starrett had reserved the entire Zabarian—with President Anokye and other honored guests attending. Then, after the ceremony and speeches in the afternoon, guests would be welcomed to an open house at the palace, culminating in an evening gala with music, dancing, fireworks.

"It's shaping up to be a real brawl," Petty said enthusiastically. "My boys can hardly wait."

"Try to keep them under control," Tangent said, somewhat nervously.

"Oh hell, Pete, you know what oilmen are like. If they get too rough, we'll kick their asses back to the rigs. I'll have the small boats standing by. That sergeant—what's his name? The light-colored nig in the palace?"

"Yeboa?"

"Yeah, Yeboa. He promised his guards would take it easy. No one gets locked up unless they start tearing the place apart."

"Good," Tangent said. "It's important that everything goes well. What about the booze?"

"It won't run out," Petty assured him. "And if it does, the hotel manager said we can draw on him. Jesus, this is going to be a blast!"

He was a hulking man with a bourbon complexion.

Muscles running to flab. Clothing perpetually rumpled and sweat-stained. On the rigs, or on the *Starrett Explorer* anchored offshore, he was a tiger, and needed. In an executive suite, he was too big, too raucous, too everything, including chewed cigars.

"Listen, Peter," he said, frowning importantly, "these hotshots coming in from Tulsa and New York . . ."

"Yes?"

"You reckon they'll want tail?"

Tangent paused. "I hadn't thought of it. I suppose they will."

"They go for caramel ass, y'suppose?"

Tangent reflected a long moment.

"I'd guess so," he said finally, with some distaste. "Exotic Africa. Something to tell the boys about back home. Can you line it up?"

"Sure I can."

"Not too black," Tangent said hastily. "High yaller. Clean, for God's sake. The last thing in the world we want . . ." He left the sentence unfinished.

"Gotcha," Petty said. "I'll have something sweet up here waiting for them when they come back from the palace. That way they won't have to be seen in public with the cunts."

"That's good," Tangent said faintly. "You take care of it."

But was it, he thought mournfully, any worse than what he had done when the Man from Tulsa and the Man from New York had visited London? He remembered his mother saying, "Everyone has to eat a peck of dirt before they die." Sometimes his peck seemed bottomless.

He finally got back to his own suite, took off jacket, loosened tie, kicked off tasseled moccasins. He mixed a gin sling at the little bar, and carried it over to the bed. He called her room number.

"Amina? Peter Tangent."

"Mr. Tangent! You're back! How nice."

"Are you working tonight?"

"Yes, I am."

"Time for some food? Before or after?"

"After would be just right," she said. "But I have a late show. I'll be through about one o'clock. Too late for you?"

"Oh no. Suppose I meet you at the Zabarian?"

"We'll eat there?"

"If you like," he said. "Or we could come back here. The terrace serves until four. Or any place you prefer."

"Why, Mr. Tangent," she said, mocking, "you mean you don't mind being seen with me in public?"

"No," he said happily, "I don't mind."

He took a nap, awoke, showered, dressed carefully and, about midnight, strolled along the boardwalk toward the Zabarian. He could have gone earlier and caught her act. He felt guilty about that—but not very; she really had no singing voice at all.

Amina was just finishing her last set when he entered. He sat at the bar, exchanged greetings with Felah, ordered another gin sling. He took a handful of salted ground nuts, swiveled to look at her.

Tonight she was wearing an off-the-shoulder gown of bottle green. A lot of flounces. It was too much for her stick body. Still, those marvelous arms were bare. And when she turned slowly, in time to strummed chords, her bare back was revealed. To below the waist. A hard, sinuous back. Polished. Rippled with muscle.

"Much woman," Felah whispered.

"Yes," Peter Tangent said.

She finished to apathetic applause. She saw Tangent at the bar, came over, handed her mandolin to Felah.

"I wowed them tonight," she said, picking up Tangent's drink and taking a deep swallow. "How are you, Mr. Tangent, sir?"

"Very well, thank you. And you, Amina?"

"Jack-dandy," she said.

"Jim-dandy," he said.

"What's jack-dandy?"

"There isn't any. There's Jack Daniels. That's an American whisky."

"Gee, Mr. Tangent," she said, "you know everything. Going to feed me?"

"I am," he said. "Where?"

"You say," she said. "I'm too tired to care. Can I have a drink here?"

"Of course."

"What you're having. I liked that."

Tangent ordered, and asked Felah if Sam Leiberman had been around. Felah said no, Mr. Leiberman had been scarce lately. Probably busy moving. Moving where? Tangent wanted to know. Felah said Mr. Leiberman felt his quarters over Les Trois Chats were not suitable for an advisor to the Asante national government, so he had rented a larger apartment over Le Café du Place, a slightly more reputable cabaret located behind the French embassy, near the palace.

"He's living over *another* nightclub?" Tangent marveled.

"That's what he say," Felah chuckled. "He say, 'If I have my life to live over again, I want to live it over a bar.'"

"That's Leiberman," Tangent smiled.

"Can we have a party?" Amina Dunama asked. Her hand was on Tangent's arm. "With him and Dele? I liked them."

"Sure," he said. "I'll look him up tomorrow. Will you be here for the oil ceremony?"

"No," she said. "I'm moving on to Lomé."

"Sadness," he said. "But you'll come back?"

"Maybe," she said. She looked into his eyes. "Or maybe you come to Lomé, Mr. Tangent?"

"Maybe," he said, feeling a shiver.

He felt very happy with her, very relaxed. A few tourists were staring at them, whispering. But there was no hassle. They talked about . . . later, he couldn't remember. He did remember that she wanted him to put two cigarettes in his mouth, light both from one match, then give her one. Just like an American movie star she had seen. He couldn't do it, he told her, he just couldn't; it was too silly. But he mollified her by lighting one cigarette between his lips and placing it between hers.

They sauntered slowly back to the Mokodi Hilton, and he learned a little about her. She was a Nigerian Hausa, but from a rural animist family, not Muslim. She spoke Hausa, of course, and Yoruba, some Akan and Ewe, and less of Fond, Dende, Mina, Edo, and others. Also, French and English.

"Also love, Mr. Tangent, sir," she said. "I also speak the language of love."

"Do you now?" he said.

They dined on the tiled terrace of the Mokodi Hilton and watched a gecko lizard dart between the empty tables. An old morose waiter, whose bare feet obviously pained him, listened to their order in silence, then brought them what was available at that late hour: a pot of pepper chicken, a salad of oiled greens, a bottle of Asti Spumante. A few others were dining, but the terrace was uncrowded, so hushed they could hear the gush of sea on the strand beneath the terrace wall.

"Why isn't there a moon?" he said crossly.

Still, the breeze was warm and scented, the ocean heaved gently, palm fronds rattled a bit. It was, he judged, oh, about 80°F., a smell of rain in the air. The lights of the oil rigs and the island of Zabar twinkled offshore. A fishing boat went bobbing past. What more do I want? he asked himself. What *more*?

She tucked in to the food. As she nibbled, he watched her, fascinated. Her strong white teeth stripped the meat away and, once, cracked the bones. Then she sucked the juice.

"I'm glad you're not hungry," he said. She giggled, but didn't pause. He could not understand where it all went; she was as skinny as he, and harder. She finished everything, sopping up the remainder of the chicken sauce with cold fufu. Then she sighed, patted her napkin to her lips, took a swallow of wine, and belched.

"Take me," she said. "I'm yours."

"Not if you eat that way all the time," he said. "I couldn't afford you."

"Being with you makes me ravenous," she said.

He was about to ask her what she meant, but thought better of it.

He learned a few other things. She came from a large family: three sisters and four brothers. Many, many aunts, uncles, cousins. All living in Nigeria. In the west. She had the Nigerian equivalent of a grade school education, then had gone to work in the kitchen of a village bar-cabaret-restaurant.

"And then it was onward and upward?" he asked.

"Mostly outward," she laughed. "I wanted to see the world. The whole wide world."

"And have you?"

"I've seen West Africa. Have you been to Paris, Mr. Tangent?"

"Yes. Many times."

"Tell me about it."

He did, telling the things he thought she wanted to hear. Her eyes glistened as he spoke; her thick lips parted.

"Oh," she said. "Oh. Some day . . ."

"Yes," he said.

They had a liqueur, some peppermint atrocity, then rose to leave. She chatted a moment with the old waiter.

"What were you speaking?" Tangent asked, as they strolled into the hotel.

"Twi," she said. "His feet hurt. He's tired."

"I guessed that," he said.

"I'm tired, too," she said. "My feet hurt."

"Then I'll say good-night, Amina," he said holding out his hand.

She looked at him.

"Mr. Tangent, sir," she said, "I just mentioned I was weary. I did not mean you should depart from me."

"Oh," he said, feeling foolish, "I thought . . ."

"Leave the thinking to me," she said. "And the singing to you."

He thought that the funniest thing he had heard in a long time, was still laughing when they entered her room and she locked the door behind them. She kicked off her shoes, went padding through the mess.

"I'm going to turn off the air conditioner and open the balcony door," she said. "Okey-dokey?"

"Okey-dokey," he said.

"What's wrong?" she said.

"Nothing's wrong."

"Your voice sounded strange."

"You're very quick, Amina," he said. "It's just that—uh—well, 'okey-dokey'—it's—it's dated."

"I like it," she said.

"Oh, I do, too," he said hastily. "Nothing wrong with it."

"Okey-dokey," she said. "Say it."

"Okey-dokey," he said obediently.

She undressed in the dimness, pulling a zipper somewhere in those ridiculous flounces.

"Lousy dress," she said. "Is 'lousy' okey-dokey?"

"Applied to that dress, 'lousy' is definitely okey-dokey."

She was naked then, and unconcerned. A glinting shadow moving gracefully. She went out onto the little balcony, and he followed. Nervous. Hesitant. She slumped into a chair with plastic webbing.

"You'll get a waffle pattern on your ass," he giggled.

She didn't answer, but closed her eyes. He stood a moment, then knelt before her, fully clothed, and began gently to massage her long, bony feet.

"I like that, Mr. Tangent," she murmured.

"Must you call me 'Mr. Tangent'?"

"Yes."

The balcony hung over the terrace, blocked from view from above and the sides. They were floating in space. Alone in the night. After a while, he put her feet softly aside and sat down next to her. He rested his cheek against the warm velvet of her knee and thigh. Her fingers absently tangled in his hair.

"I thought of you," he said. "Amina."

"Did you?"

"Are you falling asleep?"

"No."

"I thought of you."

"Did you?"

"Raise your knees."

"All right."

She raised her knees, spread them slowly, hooked heels onto the edge of the chair. She let her long, slender arms rest along the chair back. Her forearms drooped limply. She looked like some great black bat, hovering. She looked down at him gravely.

"Oh, Mr. Tangent," she said.

"Shut up," he said.

"Yes, sir."

She had a smoky flavor, dark and savory. Like nothing he had ever tasted before. Neither wine nor food nor anything. Almost metallic, he thought. Almost cocky. Almost the taste of loam. Almost a lot of things. But not quite. Different.

Her spine stiffened with delight, head bent back, heavy throat hard. She stared dreamily at wavery reflections of the sea on the balcony above. Her body began to move, to twist, to squirm. His tongue pursued, and he knew her flow, the pour within her, an easy rhythm ending in a deep, deep paroxysm, then onward, upward, outward to the whole wide world. He looked up and she looked down to see hard nipples and flat breasts tight and sheened.

"Mr. Tangent," she breathed. "Sir."

"Yes," he said. "Oh yes."

The reception desk was in the entrance lobby, flanked by two stolid palace guardsmen. The receptionist was a plump, middle-aged Asanti lady wearing a neat black dress with white collar and cuffs. Her hair was precisely cornrowed.

"Good morning, Mr. Tangent," she said. Her smile revealed three gold teeth and a gap, waiting.

"Good morning, Mrs. Odunsi," he said. In Akan, he asked, "Do you have health?"

"I have health," she replied, and asked, "Do you have sadness?"

"I have no sadness," he said, completing the ritual, then switching back to French: "And how is your father feeling?"

"He recovers, thanks to Allah."

"I am happy to hear it. Is there anything I may do to help? Perhaps medicine from London?"

"I thank you, Mr. Tangent, but he has what is needed. Now it is just a matter of waiting."

"The hardest part," he said. "And speaking of waiting, may I see the President? I have an appointment."

"Just a moment, please, sir." She called on her desk phone and spoke softly, then replaced the receiver. "You may go right up, Mr. Tangent. Second floor conference room."

Sgt. Sene Yeboa opened the door at his knock, grinning, and shook hands formally. He motioned Tangent to a chair near the door. President Anokye and Sam Leiberman were standing behind the big mahogany desk. They raised their hands in greeting.

"In a moment," Anokye called.

"No hurry," Tangent said.

Yeboa went back to the desk. The three men bent intently over what appeared to Tangent to be a pile of maps. They conversed in low voices. At one point, they appeared to be arguing. Finally, the Little Captain began to speak in a somewhat louder tone, his forefinger tracing a route on the top map. The other two listened carefully. When the President stopped speaking and looked at them in turn, Yeboa to Leiberman, they nodded. More than consent, Tangent thought; they nodded approval.

Anokye straightened up, and now he spoke in normal tones; Tangent could hear. "The timing is most important," Anokye said. Then he folded the maps, slipped them into his top desk drawer. He shook hands with Sam Leiberman. The mercenary picked up a floppy linen hat, started for the door, paused at Tangent's chair.

"Balles de golf!" he said. "You look like the cat that ate the canary."

"Something like that," Tangent said. "Going to be around for a while, Sam?"

"Why?"

"Thought we might get together for a party."

"Not before the ceremony," Leiberman said. "Maybe after."

"Too late," Tangent said. Then, in a lower voice, "She'll be gone by then."

Leiberman stared at him.

"The singer?" he said finally.

Tangent nodded, feeling ridiculously proud.

Leiberman laughed and slapped a meaty hand on his shoulder.

"You sly goyische devil," he said. "Now you know what they mean by 'the white man's burden.' "

He went out laughing, shaking his head. Tangent rose and, when Anokye motioned, took the lounge chair in front of the desk. The President murmured something to Yeboa, and the sergeant departed—to take up his station, Tangent was certain, outside the door. Anokye sat down in his long-legged chair and took a deep breath.

"Perhaps I was happier as an army captain," he said.

"I cannot believe that, Mr. President," Tangent smiled.

"No, of course it is not true," Anokye said. "It is simply that I do not have enough hours in the day to do what must be done."

"Perhaps you need more people," Tangent suggested. "A larger staff."

"That, certainly. But people I can trust."

"I understand the difficulty," Tangent said. "But surely it can be done. In addition, perhaps your administration should be reorganized. I am not speaking of the government now; I mean only your own activities. Perhaps they require restructuring, better organization."

Anokye was interested.

"I had not thought of that. How would I go about it?"

"Call in professionals," Tangent said promptly. "There are good management consultants in London and New York. They have experience in such work. They will come in, study your setup, make recommendations for changes they feel will result in increased efficiency."

"I like that," President Anokye nodded. "Yes, very much. They charge a fee, of course?"

"Of course. But I don't believe your operation here is so extensive, as yet, to require a lot of time and a big fee. Perhaps this is the right moment to have it done. So you may expand your activities in an orderly manner. Shall I put someone in touch with you?"

"Please do. What is the word I want? Modernize? Yes, I will modernize my administration."

"According to proved managerial concepts," Tangent said.

"Yes. Excellent idea. I thank you. Now . . . what did you wish to discuss?"

"I hope this may prove to be good news, Mr. President," Tangent said. "It concerns the refinery Starrett plans to build in Africa."

He told the Little Captain of how he had learned that Starrett's choices had narrowed to Asante and Gabon. He said he had spoken to a friend about the matter, a friend in a position to alert the French to fictitious secret negotiations between Starrett and the Gabonese.

"You can imagine the reaction of the French to such a report," Tangent said. "I felt they would take steps immediately to make their displeasure known both to Libreville and to Starrett, through diplomatic channels. I received a message yesterday from London saying that is indeed what the French are doing. I cannot guarantee it, Mr. President, but I think it likely that when the Starrett executives come here for the oil ceremony, they will wish to sound you out on the possibility of building the refinery in Asante. Should that happen, you will be in a stronger position knowing they have already been warned away from Gabon. Under those circumstances, your chances of getting a no-strings grant for the Togo-Benin operation are considerably enhanced."

Obiri Anokye listened to this recital without change of expression. But when Tangent had finished, he rose to his feet, grinning. Tangent also stood up. The two men shook hands warmly, then sat down again.

"I recognize and declare my debt to you," Anokye said. "But who assisted?"

"A certain friend," Tangent said.

The Little Captain thought a moment.

"The gentleman from London who attended my inauguration?" he asked.

"I didn't think you'd remember," Tangent said.

"I remember," Anokye said. "I thought then he was not what he appeared to be, but more. I would like to reward him."

"He won't take money," Tangent said.

"What, then?"

"Well . . . he collects African art."

"Ah," President Anokye said. "I will select something fine. You will deliver it?"

"Of course."

"Tell him it is only a small token of friendship. I still consider myself in his debt. He may call on me."

"He will understand."

"And my congratulations to you on a very elegant plan."

"Thank you, Mr. President. And speaking of congratulations—are mine in order?"

Anokye stared at him.

"On what?" he asked.

"Perhaps I am being premature, Mr. President. But I have heard rumors of your impending marriage to the daughter of the Benin premier."

A different look came into Obiri Anokye's eyes. A deepening. Darkening. Then his glance cleared, he smiled coldly. He rose slowly, sauntered to the long window overlooking the palace plaza. He put his hands on his hips, stared down. His back was to Tangent.

"Congratulations?" he said. "Well . . . possibly. Premier Da Silva comes for the oil ceremony. Then we shall see."

"May your every wish be granted," Tangent said, in Akan.

"And may your smallest dream come true," Anokye replied solemnly in the same language. Then he returned to English: "It is very difficult to keep a personal secret in Asante."

"That is true, Mr. President," Tangent said.

"For instance," Anokye said, almost lazily. "This singer . . . Amina Dunama? You enjoy her company, Peter?"

Tangent gulped. "Yes, sir," he said.

"Nigerian?"

"Yes, sir. Hausa. But not a Muslim."

Anokye nodded, still staring down from the window.

"I am looking now at the exact spot where we came running across the plaza," he said dreamily. "Screaming and firing our weapons. I remember how surprised I was when I glanced around and you were right behind me. I had ordered you to remain in the telephone exchange."

"I apologize for disobeying your orders, Mr. President."

"I am thankful you did," Anokye said. He laughed softly. "I would never have gained the terrace if you had not offered your back. Why did you charge with us? It was not your war."

"I've asked myself that question several times," Tangent said. "I just don't know."

"To prove something?"

"Partly that perhaps. Partly the noise and excitement and madness of the moment."

"Maybe you wished to determine what kind of a man you are?" Anokye said thoughtfully.

"There may have been that also, Mr. President."

Anokye turned slowly, came back to the desk, sat down again. He leaned forward, elbow on the desk, heavy chin cupped in his palm. He looked at Tangent, into his eyes, through and beyond.

He sat in silence, and the American marveled that this young man (Anokye was now twenty-seven; Tangent, ten years older) should possess such gravity, such deep weightiness. His seriousness, somehow, invested life with significance. It was not to be flung to wine and roses, but measured out gravely with an acknowledgment of the consequences of one's acts.

"Physical courage is a curious thing," Obiri Anokye mused. "Those whose physical courage has never been tried believe it is not so important. I have read the words of men—wise, honored men—who have said that moral courage is the equal or superior of physical courage. That is not the truth, Peter. Physical courage is the root of all else. It is certainly the root of my success. Everything I have done, and shall do, grows from physical courage. That is why I must lead my men. Always. In person. On the field. I cannot rule from behind a desk. Then my power would surely fall away, and they would turn to a braver leader. And all my political and economic dreams for Africa would come to nothing. Men respect physical courage, and I must exhibit it."

He paused, but Tangent was silent.

"I believe you are a brave man, Peter," Anokye said suddenly.

"Thank you, Mr. President. Coming from you, that is praise indeed."

"But courage and foolhardiness are different," the Little Captain said gently. His thousand-yard stare shortened until his eyes were locked with Tangent's. "You must not be foolhardy."

"I don't intend to be," Tangent said stoutly.

"Good," the President of Asante said, still in that quiet, silky voice. "I am happy to hear that."

The meeting was concluded, and Tangent departed with an indefinable impression that he had been warned. But of what, he could not have said.

7

The Border between Togo and Benin remained closed. Though he now had a diplomatic passport identifying him as an official advisor to the Republic of Asante, Sam Leiberman thought it best to enter Benin from Nigeria. So he flew from Mokodi to Lagos on the twin-engined Piper Aztec, pride of the Asante National Air Force. Their other two planes were aged Broussards. Airworthy, but just.

In Lagos, he rented a Citroën 2-CV. Not very elegant transportation, but sturdy. He figured the dusty car would blend perfectly with Cotonou's taxi fleet. He drove up through the Nigerian rain forest on an improved road and crossed the Benin border without incident. He was carrying no weapon, nor anything else that might endanger his assignment. He came down to the coast road at Porto-Novo. He drove through the sleepy capital without stopping and arrived in Cotonou before noon. The siesta had just started; Benin's largest city appeared as somnolent as the capital.

Leiberman had a vague plan in mind, not detailed but sufficient to get him started. He drove directly to Akpapa, across the Nokoue lagoon. He registered at a crummy hotel he had stayed at once before when he had no choice. He rented a single room and wasn't surprised to find he was sharing it with flies, mosquitos, roaches, bedbugs, lizards, spiders, and a goodly selection of other African fauna. The stained toilet was down the hall, and you provided your own paper. Leiberman had come prepared. The hotel had one advantage: the other residents were thieves, pimps, whores, and drunks. Questions would not be asked.

He changed to a short-sleeved shirt in a wild batik pattern. It hung loosely outside maroon slacks. He suspended a cheap Japanese camera from a leather thong about his neck. He put on a pair of big green sunglasses with white plastic frames. He replaced his shoes with strap sandals over white cotton socks.

He took all his valuables and identification with him. He left only a cheap cardboard suitcase, a few items of clothing, and toilet articles in the room. The door had a lock, but he knew a determined push would spring it.

He drove back to Cotonou, down to the waterfront. After a few false turns, he found what he was looking for. He parked a few squares away and walked back. The siesta was ending; yawning dogs were getting up from the middle of the street.

It had once been a ships' chandler. The original sign, faded, chipped, still swung over the doorway on rusted iron chains. It read ARMAND DUBOIS ET CIE. But up and down the coast of West Africa, from Dakar to Douala, the place was now known as Harry Chime's.

The owner's name was nowhere displayed, but the dust-encrusted, bug-spattered windows bore many hand-lettered cardboard signs: U NAME IT, OUI HAVE IT; WE BUY JUNK AND SELL ANTIQUES; IF YOU DON'T FIND IT HERE, YOU WON'T FIND IT ANYWHERE.

The last was not an empty boast; Harry Chine's was a cluttered warehouse of clothing and hardware, kitchen utensils and camping gear, boat fittings and plumbing supplies, cordage and wire, tools and cutlery ... and everything else. All piled higgledy-piggledy in a confusion that only the proprietor could solve. Nothing was new; everything had passed through one, three, a dozen owners, and was now torn, rotted, broken, dented, rusted, or bent. No matter. Some of the things could be found nowhere else in West Africa. Harry bought from anyone and sold to anyone. He did very well indeed.

When Sam Leiberman entered, the door struck a bell that jangled loudly in the cluttered shed. But the owner, sitting behind a scarred counter, didn't look up. He was busy prizing blue stones from a tarnished copper bracelet with the point of an awl.

"Hello, you stinking Limey shit," Leiberman called.

Startled, the man looked up, the awl clattered to the counter, he stared at the mercenary.

"Hello, you lousy Jew bastard," he said finally. "Where's my hundred francs?"

"Right here," Leiberman said. He walked to the counter. He took a roll of bills from his trouser pocket and counted off 100 CFAs. Harry Chime grabbed the notes, but couldn't take his tiny, tiny eyes off the roll. He was saddened when it disappeared back into Leiberman's pocket.

"Prosperous?" he asked.

"Sure. I'm being kept by a wealthy Montenegrin countess."

"And I shall be Queen of the May," Harry Chime said. "What's with the clown suit?"

"You mean *Tailor & Cutter* wouldn't approve? I'm Terre Haute, for God's sake. Can't you tell? Close up shop and let's go in the back room and talk business."

"Sure," Chime said. He locked the street door and put up a sign: CLOSED BECAUSE OF DEATH IN THE FAMILY. Then he led the way toward the rear, threading a path through the piles of jumbled merchandise.

He was as tall as Leiberman, but about a hundred pounds heavier. He wore soiled khaki jeans, the fly straining at its buttons. The seat had been let out and patched with a wedge-shaped section of stained blue denim. On his bare feet were ripped U.S. Army combat boots of World War II. The top straps were unbuckled and flapped about as Chime walked, showing punky ankles. He also wore a sweated dark blue undershirt, revealing a billowing belly and bulbous breasts.

He led Leiberman into a small back room used for sleeping and cooking. It smelled like it. Leiberman sat down at a rickety wooden table and waited while Harry Chime dug out two jelly glasses and a demijohn of wine in a wicker basket. The outside bore the label of a good Italian volpolicella, but inside was Benin palm wine. Leiberman wasn't surprised. Chime sat down heavily, filled the two jars, and they drank.

"Losing a little weight, aren't you?" Leiberman said.

"Maybe a few pounds," Chime said.

Leiberman leaned across the table and dug a cruel thumb into Chime's belly.

"When was the last time you saw your cock, Harry?" he said.

"June 21, 1958," Chime said. "You come in here to feel me up or to talk business?"

They spoke a crude argot all their own, a mixture of several languages. "Donne-moi the fuckin' botella of vino, mein imbecile." They gossiped about old mercs. Who had died, and how. Who was down with bilharzia. Who had disappeared. Who was fighting where for how much. Most of their comrades from the disastrous Biafran campaign were now shooting at each other in Angola.

"You got anything besides this piss?" Leiberman asked, draining his jelly jar.

"Maybe some rum," Chime said reluctantly.

"Ho-ho-ho," Leiberman said. "Bring it out, Harry, or I'll take my business to Monoprix."

"Take it to Harrod's for all I care," Chime said, but he dug a half-full quart of Meyer's dark from under his littered sink and put it on the table. Leiberman filled his jelly jar. Chime poured some into what was left of his palm wine.

"What's going on around here?" Leiberman wanted to know.

"Aagh, they got this thing with Togo," Chime said disgustedly. "Ever since that wog got knifed in Lomé. The border's closed. How the hell did you get in?"

"I waltzed," Leiberman said. "What else?"

"Aagh, the fuckin' Reds are all over the place."

"No kidding?" Leiberman said. "I thought the French had the first mortgage."

"Still do," Chime said, "but the place is crawling with Russians and Chinks."

"Interesting, but not very," Leiberman said. "Enough of this bullshit. Harry, I need some stuff. A few little items."

"Like what?"

"Odds and ends."

"Pick out anything you want," Chime said, the rum getting to him. "No cost. Absolutely no cost to you, Sam."

"Thanks, Harry."

Leiberman sucked in his gut, opened the top of his trousers, unzipped a silk money belt. He carefully extracted a small square of onion-skin paper. He slid it across the table to Chime.

"Here's my list."

Chime rooted around in the table drawer and found a pair of glasses with bent wire frames. He put them on and scanned Leiberman's list. Then he looked up, blinking through thick magnifying glass.

"*This* will cost you," he said, and when Leiberman laughed, Chime said, "What the hell." He read the list again. "What's the thermite for?"

"I'm blowing the bank," Leiberman said.

"The hell you are," Chime said. "The government's taken it over. The place is full of barefoot soldiers."

"Goodbye bank," Leiberman said. "They'll suck it dry in a month. You got this stuff?"

"Most of it."

"The thermite, too?"

"Well . . . it's not new."

"How old?"

"Thirty, maybe forty years."

"Jesus Christ, Harry!"

"Best I can do."

"What is it?" Leiberman asked.

"Incendiary grenades. Wehrmacht potato mashers. Some of the stuff abandoned when Montgomery and Rommel were chasing each other across the desert."

"It's not leaking, is it?" Leiberman asked.

"Maybe a little corroded. Just a little. I'll throw in a pair of gloves."

"That's sweet," Leiberman said. "Thanks, but no thanks."

They sat staring at each other. Chime looked down at the list again, looked up and said, "Fuse?"

"Just what I was thinking," Leiberman said. "You got it?"

"Miles of it," Chime assured him.

"Fast or slow?"

Chime shrugged. "Who the hell knows? Cut off a piece and time it."

"Okay," Leiberman said. "Now something that's not on the list—I need a piece."

"Aagh, that's hard," Harry Chime said. "This ain't New York, you know. You want to rent it or buy it?"

Leiberman considered a moment.

"Buy, I guess," he said finally. "What can you get?"

"A 'thirty-four Baretta."

"Lousy vintage. How about a 'fifty-one?"

"Haven't got."

"This 'thirty-four Beretta—it works?"

"Sam, would I sell you defective merchandise?"

"Sure you would," Leiberman said cheerfully.

"Well . . . maybe it jams a bit."

"Beautiful."

"But all you do is smack the butt on the heel of your hand, and it unjams."

"And blows my balls off," Leiberman said. "All right. And two loaded magazines."

"When?"

Leiberman told him he'd pick up everything that evening at 2100. At that time he would inspect what he was buying, and they'd arrive at a price.

"Cash," Harry Chime said. "No tickee, no shirtee."

Sam Leiberman drove north on the improved road that ran up the length of Benin like a spine. It was tarred as far as Bohicon, about 150 kilometers north of Cotonou. But before Bohicon, and the turnoff for Abomey, was the village of Ighobo. And the Musée Ethnographique. Perhaps not as large as the one in Porto-Novo. But Ighobo's museum had an older and more valuable collection. And, as the Little Captain had pointed out, it was in a small village and probably lightly guarded.

The museum was housed in a whitewashed mud-brick, one-story building said to have been a collection center for slaves, before they were marched south to be sold to European traders at Porto-Novo. Rusted chains and manacles still hung from the rough-hewn posts supporting the thatched roof. A wooden floor had been added in modern times.

A tour bus had arrived just before Leiberman pulled into the dirt parking area. There were at least thirty tourists, mostly Canadians, and the mercenary was happy to note that many of the men were dressed in costumes not unlike his own: demented shirts, maroon slacks, strap sandals, necklaces of cameras. He casually fell in at the rear of the group as they followed their French-speaking Benin guide into the museum.

The L-shaped building had been divided by plywood partitions into a dozen small galleries, each devoted to the ancient arts and crafts of one of Benin's many tribes: Fulani, Bariba, Fon, Yoruba, Adj, etc. Objects were hung from walls and partitions, stood upright on the wooden floor, or were displayed in open cases.

Following the gawking tour group, listening to the enthusiastic spiel of the Benin guide, Sam Leiberman understood why Obiri Anokye had sent him on this mission, and not a black man. The Musée Ethnographique was an awesome treasurehouse of African culture. Marvelously carved Gelede masks. Wood and bronze sculpture. Ceremonial robes of shell and feathers. Intricate ironwork. Brilliant Glélé tapestries. Arms for court rituals and arms for battle. Thrones carved from a single block of mahogany. Kings' stools. Bracelets and necklaces of ivory, copper, gold. Grave ornaments. Phallic staves. Monoliths and deities.

But it was the juju charms and the grisgris that would keep this sacred place safe from despoilment by most black Africans. The spirits of ancestors dwelt here. Their clothing was here, their jewelry, arms, grave markers, images of the gods they worshiped. To defy the amulets, to scorn the fetishes, was to court doom in this world, the next, and all worlds to come. So Sam Leiberman, white mercenary, unbeliever, had been sent. He appreciated the Little Captain's reasoning.

But he was not totally immune to the shivery appeal of this art. It stirred the same fear and devotion he had felt as a boy watching the solemn ceremony in his father's temple, seeing the sacred objects and hearing the chants of exaltation. But that had been in another time, in another world, and now his faith was dead and gone. Not even a corpse left behind.

He came out into the bright sunlight and wandered around to the rear of the museum. He held his camera near his chin, as if seeking a suitable scene to photograph. There was an outdoor toilet, remarkably like a Chic Sale. And there was a kind of open shed, no more than a tilted thatched roof supported by four rough-hewn posts. In the shade squatted a single Benin soldier, barefoot, tending a charcoal fire within a clay pot. He hunkered comfortably on his hams, blowing into the embers of his fire pot. On the bare ground alongside him were three small yams and a chicken leg, most of the feathers still attached. Leaning against one of the posts was the soldier's rifle. It appeared to Leiberman to be a MAS 49. He strolled closer, and the soldier looked up.

Leiberman smiled, lifted his camera, pointed at the soldier and nodded hopefully. The soldier scowled and shook his head no. He did not want his soul captured on film and taken from him. He was a young man, no more than twenty. His khaki shorts and short-sleeved shirt were clean. He wore a shoulder patch Leiberman could not identify. He carried no sidearms. Just the rifle.

Leiberman made a circle of the museum. As far as he could see, there was no alarm system. Several of the glass windows were broken. There was a side door, but it had been padlocked from the outside. Hasp and lock were rusty. Leiberman completed his circuit and returned to the parking area. The tourists were piling back into their bus. He waited a few moments, then drove slowly back to Cotonou behind the bus. He thought the young soldier, or another, would probably be on guard all night. He tried to figure a way to avoid killing him, but could not.

He followed the bus into Cotonou. When he saw where the tourists were staying, he parked the Citroën and walked back to the hotel dining room. He was greeted in English by a maître d' who knew Terre Haute when he saw it. Leiberman stayed in character by ordering *bifteck aux pomme frites*, with a bottle of Löwenbräu dark. He dawdled over a second beer, but it was only 1800 when he finished; he had three hours to fill.

He strolled along the dirt sidewalks, watching the laughing Cotonais hurry home to their town *quartiers*. He stopped at the poolside bar of the Hôtel du

Port and had a double arak. It didn't help. He kept thinking about the African art now standing in lonely splendor in the locked museum. Brilliant enough to light up the night. He thought of that, and of the young soldier on guard.

He went back to the Citroën and drove to his sleazy hotel in Akpapa to change and pack. There was a small restaurant and smaller bar attached. The place was almost empty: a few villains drinking millet beer, a handsome black fegela eating a cold rice salad, a white woman sitting at the bar. She must have been pushing fifty, Leiberman guessed. A French tart from the looks of her. He sat at the other end of the counter and avoided glancing in her direction. He didn't need her. It would make him like men he knew who couldn't go into action unless they were half smashed.

A half-hour later he and the French tart were naked under the mosquito net in his cruel room. She had shaved her pubic hair, and across her bristly groin was tattooed, in French, ALL HOPE ABANDON YE WHO ENTER HERE. He laughed to think that Harry Chime was putting his crazy signs everywhere.

He was at Chime's at 2100, changed back into his khakis. He had given the tart ten dollars Yank, and she had been grateful. He never had learned her name, thought no more of her, and would not—unless in a few days he found himself wearing his pickle in a brown paper bag.

Bamboo shades were down across the windows. Leiberman knocked and waited. Eventually, the fat man unlocked, let him in, relocked the door, and led the way to the back room. He had everything ready in there. Leiberman sat down at the table to inspect what he was buying.

He stripped the Beretta. "Just to make sure there are no old cigarette butts in here." The parts of the gun appeared worn but serviceable. The barrel was clear. Leiberman had lived with guns most of his adult life and had respect for them, figuring that anything enabling an ounce of lead to waste 200 pounds of flesh deserved respect.

He reassembled the pistol. He unloaded the two magazines and tested the springs. They weren't as strong as he would have liked, but he thought they'd do. He reloaded the magazines, slammed one into the butt of the gun, jacked a round into the chamber, put loaded gun and extra magazine into the pockets of his bush jacket.

"Piece of shit," he growled.

"Beggars can't be choosers," Chime said smugly.

"And a fuck in a bed is worth two in the bush," Leiberman said.

He took up the coil of fuse and measured a length from his wrist to his elbow, and cut it off. He put the piece on the floor, lighted one end, glanced at his watch. He and Chime watched the fuse sputter to the end. It took fifty seconds to burn. It also left a scar across the kitchen-bedroom floor. Chime made no objection.

"Fifty seconds," Leiberman said. "That's slow."

"Is it?" Chime said.

"Slow enough," Leiberman said. "I'll need, oh, say twenty-five feet."

Then he inspected the three battered gasoline cans. A gallon in each. He sloshed the contents, unscrewed the caps, sniffed cautiously.

"Not that you'd sell me sea water," Leiberman said.

"Aagh," Chime said.

Leiberman examined the metal Togolese army badge. It seemed to be authentic; he'd have to gamble on that. The sap was a good one: a canvas tube about a foot long, filled with sand and stitched with heavy, waxed twine. The canvas was sweat-stained. One end looked like it had been dipped in brown paint. But it wasn't paint.

Leiberman swung it experimentally a few times.

"Very nice," he said. "Reminds me of my days as a Boy Scout. Okay, Harry, now much for the lot?"

"Well now—" Chime started.

"Forget it," Leiberman said. "I'll give you half that."

After ten minutes of peppery argument, they agreed on 875 French francs, and Leiberman paid. Chime helped him carry the stuff out to the car, after carefully scouting the street.

"Thanks, Harry," Leiberman said. "You've been a great help."

"Tell your friends," Chime said.

"Not likely," Leiberman said. "That's another thing: you haven't seen me for years, have you?"

Chime looked at him.

"I don't see you now," he said.

"Very good," Leiberman approved. "Keep it that way."

To get into the car, he had to brush close to Chime.

"Tell me something, Harry," he said. "You ever take a bath?"

"What the hell for?" Chime said. "I sleep alone."

He drove north slowly toward Ighobo. Dark, dark. A quarter moon dimmed by thick overcast. Moisture on the tarred road. Rains coming; maybe soon. Not too soon, he hoped. Turned off for the Musée Ethnographique. Headlights out. A dim glow behind the building: the guard's fire.

Turned, drove back again. Nothing to be seen. All quiet. Parked a hundred meters down the road to Cotonou. Backed off the verge, partly into the bush. Got out. Locked the car. Everything inside. Took only the Beretta, extra magazine.

Walked on the road. Then cut into the bush. Moved slowly. Circled wide. Came up from the rear. Crouched. Saw the outhouse silhouetted in the small fire they had going. *They*. Two of them. Two guards, two rifles. Should have known: African soldiers don't like the night. Fight badly at night. So two guards, for company when the shadows close in.

Retreated. Went back to the car. Got the canvas sap. Went back to the museum again. Sap in hip pocket, gun in hand. Again, silent approach, circling, crawling the last few meters. Stopped short of the cleared area of packed dirt.

What were the children doing? Kneeled, lifted his head to see. Cavorting in firelight. Striking poses. Shouting things. What? Then rushing to flip pages of a tattered magazine near the firepot. Looked at pictures. Then took a stance. "EEEYAH!" Answered by "HEEYUH!" Then hands chopping at each other. Feet kicking. Laughing and giggling. The one he had seen during the day and another just like him. Two young boys.

"EEEYAH!"

"HEEYUH!"

Then a spatter of howled Fon.

Got it. Practicing karate or judo. Martial arts magazine. Screaming with laughter as they assumed the rigid poses, made the formal moves. Fun.

Studied the scene. Two rifles leaning against posts of the shed. Fire in clay pot. Bottle of water or palm wine. No handguns or machetes. He moved cautiously. Coming closer to thatched-roof shed. But too far to use the Beretta. Get them apart. Take them one at a time. How?

Hunkered down on his heels. Watched. Waited, waited. No more karate now. No dancing about. Quiet. Both near the cook pot. Lying on packed earth. Talking softly. Grinning. Good palaver. Thirty minutes. Hour. No action. No inspection tour of museum. Sleep? Go to sleep, for Christ's sake. For your sake.

Then, finally, one gets up. Stretches. Says something. Other laughs. Standing soldier ambles toward privy. Built for tourists. Luxury for soldiers. Leiberman is on his feet, crouching, hot. Moves to edge of cleared area. Soldier goes into outhouse. Door closes.

Chance now. Good chance. Moves fast. Lightly. Runs across clearing. Gun out. Kicks rifles away. Spins to face astonished soldier rising to his feet.

Soldier rushes him. Eyes swollen. Teeth wet. Hand held high like a cleaver. "EEEYAH!"

"Sonny, sonny," Leiberman groans sadly. He shoots. Three in the face. Fast. Slams boy backward. Crashing onto cook pot. Leiberman runs to privy. Waits at side. Crouching. Sweat dripping. Door smashes open. Soldier stumbles out. Pulling up shorts. Eyes glaring. Mouth open. Doesn't see Leiberman. Swish of sap. Down hard across back of skull. Soldier crumples. Doesn't move. Alive, but out.

Then Leiberman worked fast, whistling a merry tune. Left the soldiers where they lay. Ran along the road to car. Backed up to museum area. Parked on road in front. Quickly now. Found the front door locked. Good lock. New. Back to the car for a tire iron. Ripped away old padlock and hasp on side door. When he yanked, the entire door came off rusted hinges.

Inside with first can of gasoline. Dribbled a path in and out of galleries.

Gas soaking into dried flooring. Never raised his eyes to icons on the walls. Second can completed the soaked trail around interior walls. Third can pouring a dark trace out the side door.

Heeled depression in packed earth. Filled with last of gas. Propped end of fuse between two stones. Suspended in fumes over gas pool. Carefully uncoiled fuse toward road. Three gasoline cans inside museum. Placed Togolese army insignia near outflung hand of dead soldier. Live one still out. Not stirring.

Check his pockets. Gun, extra magazine, sap. Final look around. Lighted end of fuse with wooden kitchen match flicked on thumbnail. Fuse caught. Started to sputter. Flame began to crawl. Glanced at watch.

He drove slowly toward Cotonou for five minutes. Stopped on the verge. Got out of the car. Lighted a cigarette. Gauloise. Looked back. Waiting. Very patient. No panic. Waiting. Then, heard a distant "*whump*!" Saw a crimson ball of flame float up into the night sky.

He got back into the Citroën and drove steadily, at a legal speed, through Cotonou and Porto-Novo. Just before he came to the Nigerian border, he stopped on a deserted section of road in the rain forest and threw Beretta, extra magazine, and sap far out into the bush. Then he drove on and crossed the Nigerian border without incident. As he came into Lagos, it began to rain, heavily. But it was too late.

8

The late King Prempeh IV had been a Muslim, with four wives, a plenitude of children, a superfluity of poor relations. To accommodate this mob in the living quarters on the third and fourth floors of the palace at Mokodi, jerry-built interior walls and partitions had been erected. They destroyed the fine proportions of the original sleeping chambers and family rooms designed by a French architect for the first governor of Asante.

When Obiri Anokye deposed the King and became President of the Republic, one of his first acts was to order the removal of Prempeh's alternations; the spacious old rooms were restored, as closely as possible, to their original splendor. Only one of King Prempeh's additions was retained: an enormous electric refrigerator installed in a corner of the family dining room. Its shiny white bulk contrasted oddly with oak parquet floors and damascened walls. But the palace kitchen was on the floor below, next to the state dining room, and meals were brought up to the living quarters by a dumbwaiter operated by a rope pull. It was an awkward arrangement; the convenience of the General Electric refrigerator was undeniable.

Whenever possible, President Obiri Anokye dined with his family. He was almost certain to be present for the morning meal, shared with his parents, Judith and Josiah, his younger sister Sara and younger brother Adebayo. An older brother, Zuni, his wife, Magira, and their children chose to remain in the Anokye home near Porto-Chonin on the island of Zabar.

On the Friday morning of the oil ceremony, breakfast in the palace was a light meal: melon, fresh croissants from the new pâtisserie on the Place de la Concorde, and chicory-laced coffee lightened with condensed milk. The Anokye family, in robes and pajamas, was served by a lean, grave, ebony-skinned butler. He was a Fulani, a Muslim, and wore a starched white dickey with a rather rusty black swallowtail. The Anokyes saw nothing strange in the fact that his long feet were bare. And, being a Fulani, he wore several rings and a handsome necklace of cat's-eye shells. His name was Ajaka.

The Little Captain waited until second cups of coffee had been poured and Ajaka had bowed himself gracefully from the room, closing the door gently.

"The luncheon at the Zabarian begins at noon," the President told the others. "Please be downstairs thirty minutes sooner. A car will be waiting."

"How shall I dress, Obiri?" Sara asked timidly. "Is it to be a dress-up?"

"Dress as you wish," he said. "Lightly, I suggest. The Zabarian is air-conditioned, but then we must go to the port area for the turning-on of the oil. There will be speeches. And no shade."

"You will speak, Obiri?" his mother asked.

"Oh yes," he said. "As briefly as possible," he added, smiling. "Then we will return here. The gala begins in the evening, so you will have the opportunity to rest and change. If you wish."

"Zuni?" the old man said vaguely. "Where is Zuni?"

"Zuni will join us at the Zabarian, father," Anokye explained patiently. "And after the ceremony, he will return with us to the palace. He and Magira."

"Is the boat all right?" Josiah asked anxiously. "What did Zuni say of the boat?"

"The boat is fine," the President of Asante assured him. "Zuni goes out every morning at dawn."

Then, seeing the old man's crumpled sadness, Anokye said, "Is it not better to sleep late?" And immediately cursed his stupidity for having compounded the original error.

Something had changed in his relationship with his family. He had not changed, of that he was certain. But, since his becoming President of Asante, their manner toward him had altered. He was no longer "Bibi," but was "Obiri." And frequently they avoided direct address, as if they felt "Obiri" too familiar and yet "Mr. President" too coldly formal for members of the family.

They looked at him differently, too; he was aware of it. There was love, of course, but now there was also respect and awe. Sometimes he wondered if there was not fear in their eyes as well. And if someone had suggested it was closer to dread than fear, he would have been saddened but not surprised.

They spoke awhile of Zuni's activities. The older brother continued to work as a fisherman, as Josiah had, and his father before him. Zuni was leader of the Zabarian chapter of the Asante Brothers of Independence, a veterans' organization that had aided in the Little Captain's coup. And Zuni was also head of the League of Liberty on Zabar. The League was Asante's largest political party, founded by Obiri Anokye, subservient to his wishes, dependent on his personal popularity for its success at the polls.

"Obiri," Judith said slowly, eyes lowered, "perhaps we—your father and I—should return to Zuni's home. To Zabar."

"For a visit?"

She raised her eyes then.

"I think we should return there to live," she said.

He set his coffee cup down carefully, looked at his mother and father tenderly. Age, a lifetime of hard work, a marriage of more than fifty years, had made them sister and brother, almost twins. Both with crinkled shell faces. Both with seamed skin over corded tendon and stretched muscle. Both seemingly shrunken as if they were dwindling away to the size of children, and regaining the irrational desires and petulances of children.

"You are not happy here?" he asked softly.

"The palace is very fine," his mother sighed. "But still . . ."

"Has anyone shown you disrespect?"

"No no," she said hastily. "But your father misses the boat. I miss my kitchen and Zuni's children. All the family. Our old friends. The church. We are not needed here, Obiri."

The room was still. A few flies buzzing. Far-off hum of traffic on the Boulevard Voltaire. Distant drone of an airliner coming in for a landing at the airport. Something fading . . .

"I need you," he said gently.

She made a gesture, a small wave that said he spoke as a dutiful son. But she knew he did not need them. Or anyone.

"If you are not happy," he said finally, "do as you wish. Return to Zabar. Perhaps, after a time, you will wish to return here again. That would give me happiness."

Josiah beamed. "I will send you the best fish," he said.

The Little Captain smiled, turned to his sister. "You, Sara? Do you also wish to return to Zabar?"

"Oh no," she said quickly, "I like it here."

"And you, Adebayo?"

"I would stay with you, Obiri."

"I want you to," the President said. "You must both continue your studies. But there are ways you can be of help to me. Perhaps we should all go now to dress for the luncheon."

His mother and father rose so eagerly, moved so spryly to the doorway, that he wondered if they might not be relieved to be out of his presence. But things could never again be as they had been, and he was incapable of regret.

He called Sara and Adebayo back to the table. He waited until their parents had left the room.

"I want both of you to go to Togo," he told them. "Stay in Lomé a few days. I will have arrangements made. Sara," he smiled, "call Captain Songo and tell him you and your brother will visit."

She giggled, glanced down at her twisting fingers. She was a tall, willowy girl, hair twigged, each braid bound with a bright yellow ribbon. Her smile was of such radiant charm that it kindled the room.

"Call him now," he suggested. "You will be there Monday morning."

She paused to press her cheek against his, then flew to call her swain.

"Adebayo," the Little Captain said, "I have a task for you. An important thing you must do."

He looked steadily at the youth. Adebayo was already as tall as Obiri, almost as broad through the shoulders. His skin was darker, his features crisper. Because he wished to emulate his older brother, he was preternaturally grave, almost solemn. He tried to think deeply and speak profoundly. Only occasionally did youthful high spirits shatter that sober mien. Laughter seemed to shame him, and he bit it back.

"What is it I am to do, Obiri?"

"Escort your sister to Togo. See to her safety and comfort. It is time you learned how you must act away from home. Also, I shall give you a sealed envelope, a letter, to deliver to General Kumayo Songo, Jere's father. You are to hand it to him personally. I would prefer you give it to him in private. If that is not possible, then it will be sufficient if you hand it to him personally. Do you understand that?"

"Yes, Obiri."

"If you lose the letter, if it falls into other hands, the results will be damaging. To me and to Asante. I trust you, Adebayo."

"I will deliver the letter only to General Songo. I will not lose it, I swear it. Will he send a reply?"

"Perhaps, perhaps not. Follow his instructions."

"I will do as you say, Obiri."

The President rose, put his arms about Adebayo, pulled him to a close embrace.

"Brother," he said.

Outside, in the second floor corridor, two guardsmen stood at parade rest alongside the closed door to the conference room. Inside, President Obiri Anokye sat behind his broad desk, bending forward intently, hands clasped on the blotter. Facing him, in a semicircle of leather club chairs, were Minister of State Jean-Louis Duclos, Benin Premier Benedicto da Silva, and the Premier's aide and executive secretary, Christophe Michaux.

Duclos and Michaux were seated next to each other, having discovered during the introductions that both were Martinicains, Duclos from St.-Pierre and Michaux from Trinité. Neither had returned to his homeland after his first trip to Paris.

President Anokye sighed, unclasped his hands, leaned back into his armchair.

"There can be no doubt it was the work of Togo?" he asked. The question was directed to Da Silva, but when the Premier answered, Anokye's glance slid away to Michaux.

"No doubt whatsoever, Mr. President," Da Silva said stonily. "A Togolese army insignia was found at the scene. The murder and fire were obviously in retaliation for the killing of Nwabala. In which affair, I assure you, Mr. President, we were totally innocent."

"I find it difficult to believe that black Africans could be guilty of such sacrilege," Anokye said. "The museum was a holy place to all Africans. Centuries of our history and culture..."

"Exactly, Mr. President," Michaux burst out excitedly. "In my mind I, too, cannot believe this was an act of vandalism committed by blacks against blacks."

Anokye stared at him.

"But why..." he began, then was silent.

"Why?" Da Silva said bitterly. "Exactly—why? Who stood to profit from his insult? Who but the Togolese would have any reason to despoil the Benin national heritage? Who else could possibly benefit from such desecration? No, no, gentlemen. Togo intended it as a deliberate provocation. There is no other explanation."

Professor Duclos shook his head sorrowfully. "That blacks should commit such aggression against blacks... We should be forging stronger ties against the common enemy."

"With all due respect, Premier," Christophe Michaux said, "I must agree with Minister Duclos. I feel we should move cautiously in this matter, with great deliberation. We have no proof of the complicity of Togo in the attack. Surely we should wait to learn their reaction. Perhaps the fire was the work of a psychopath. Or of one who wishes to create ill-feeling between Benin and Togo."

"For what reason?" Anokye asked.

"I cannot answer that, Mr. President. But I am far from certain in my own mind that this was Togo's work. The finding of the army badge on the scene is too pat. It smells of contrivance. I am almost certain in my own mind that Togo is innocent in this affair."

Michaux was almost as light as Duclos. He was taller than the Minister of

State, slender, with long, limp hands he used frequently when speaking. His hair, bleached or sun-streaked, lay flat in oiled billows, sculpted and scented. He was a young man but affected a goatee. Arched eyebrows and the spiked beard gave his triangular face a Mephistophelian cast. One looked for cloven hooves and found Gucci loafers.

"In my own mind—" he began.

"Please, Christophe," Premier Da Silva said, holding up a palm. "I don't wish to appear unkind, but what is in your own mind is of less interest to me at the moment than the political realities. Benin and Togo were already on a collision course before the burning of the museum. Whether or not Togo is actually guilty is of less importance than the fact that most Benin are firmly convinced they are. Already there is talk of reprisals. Even a war."

"Surely not that," Duclos protested. "There are other options available. The Organization of African Unity. The United Nations. Arbitration by a third party who enjoys the confidence of both Benin and Togo. Surely all these should be explored before we speak of the possibility of war."

"There are those in my country who would gladly march tonight if the command was given," Da Silva said grimly. "How many provocative insults are we obliged to accept? Gentlemen, there is only one way to handle a bully: stand up to him. That is the advice I intend to give my government in the strongest possible terms."

"Is there any way I may be of service in this unfortunate situation?" President Anokye asked gravely.

"Mr. President," the Premier said, "I assure you every effort will be made to resolve this conflict between my country and Togo without recourse to combat. But if all peaceable means fail and open warfare becomes inevitable, where does Asante stand? What will be your reaction?"

The Little Captain drew a deep breath.

"A difficult question," he said slowly. "And one to which I cannot give you an answer now, this minute. I must give the problem careful consideration. Gentlemen, it is drawing on to noon. I suggest we adjourn and leave for the Zabarian as soon as possible. Perhaps we will have a chance to discuss the matter further this afternoon. Premier, could I have a few words with you in private? It should not take long. Jean, will you and Mr. Michaux wait for us at the cars?"

When the two Martinicains had departed, the door closed behind them, Obiri Anokye rose and stood behind his desk.

"Premier," he said abruptly, almost curtly, "several months ago, in this room, on the evening of my inaugural, I spoke to you regarding my affection for your daughter Beatrice and my desire to see her more often, to learn more about her and give her the opportunity to learn more about me."

Premier Benedicto da Silva stirred restlessly, crossed and recrossed his knees. He was a dark man, sheened skin with a ruddy underglow. Silvered hair and beard were elegantly trimmed, linen a dazzling white, all of him polished and gleaming, precisely pressed and creased. Flinty eyes saved him from soft foppishness.

"I recall that conversation, Mr. President," he said tonelessly.

"Yes. Since then, as you know, I have seen more of Beatrice, in Cotonou and Mokodi. Each time I have met with her, I have come to cherish her more. She is lovely, charming, and—and intelligent. With your permission, Premier, I wish to ask Beatrice to be my wife. To ask her tonight."

Da Silva sighed gently.

"She is so young," he said.

"Yes," Anokye agreed. "Younger than I, certainly. But old enough to marry."

"I suppose so," Da Silva said. "Although it is a difficult thing for a father to realize and admit. Since the death of my wife, Beatrice has managed my home. I know I am being selfish to hope that it might continue awhile longer, but still . . ."

Anokye was silent.

"And then there is a matter of religion," the Premier said, almost desperately.

"I would be willing for our children to be raised in the Catholic faith," Anokye said. "If you insist," he added, "I will become a Catholic."

Da Silva drew a deep breath.

"Ah, Mr. President," he said hesitantly, "during our conversation at your inaugural, I brought up the matter of your relationship with a certain public woman. A white woman."

"That is true. I made a promise to you at that time, a promise that I can now state has been fulfilled. The problem could not be resolved immediately. Such matters rarely can. I am certain you appreciate that. But the woman in question is no longer employed in a—a public house. I have ended my relationship with her. In fact, she is about to marry the commander of my personal guard."

"Oh?"

"So you see, your conditions have been met. Have I permission now to marry your daughter?"

"You believe Beatrice will accept you?"

"Yes, I believe it. But you have not answered my question, Premier. Will *you* accept me?"

Da Silva rose, smoothed the wrinkles from his jacket, began to pace slowly back and forth before Anokye's desk. His head was bowed, his eyes seemed to study the design of the blood-red Sarouk. He stopped suddenly, shoulders stooped, hands thrust into his pockets.

"Mr. President," he said in a low voice, "may I suggest an engagement of, perhaps, a year? To enable the families to meet and become better acquainted, to allow—"

"No," Obiri Anokye said. "A short engagement. No more than three months. I desire to marry Beatrice as soon as possible."

"Three months?" Da Silva said. His head came up. He looked directly at Anokye. "Surely such haste is unnecessary, Mr. President. I am so involved with this Togo business that I would prefer it if—"

"This Togo business," Anokye said. "Ah, yes. Premier, Benin is on Togo's eastern border. Asante is on Togo's western border. If indeed, as you fear, it comes to open warfare, why we might stand together. We might be brothers. Possibly . . ."

There was silence. The two men stared at each other.

"Three months?" the Premier said hoarsely. "Agreed."

Obiri Anokye accompanied Da Silva into the corridor. He ordered one of the guards to escort the Premier to his car. Then the President of Asante returned to his private office alone.

From the back of his top desk drawer he carefully withdrew a small tissue-wrapped package. He unfolded it slowly. A coin, a gold coin, that had been drilled and threaded onto a loop of string. It had been given to him by Auntie Tal. She told him its history. As she had been told. And her teller before her.

Centuries ago, perhaps two millennia, on this stretch of West African coast, a fleet of six ships with triangular sails had appeared, coming through the Gulf of Guinea from the north. The men who sailed these ships were white, burned by the sun, thinned by hunger. They came ashore. They spoke an unknown language. By gesture, they asked for food and drink. It was brought, and as was the custom in that place, the ancient system of dumb barter was begun.

Grain and palm wine were set out by Ashantis, who then retreated a distance. The foreigners advanced to inspect the victuals. They put down gold coins, bars of copper, knives of bronze, strings of glittering red beads. All this was placed alongside the provisions. Then the white men retreated. The Ashantis advanced to inspect what had been left. It was not enough. They retreated in silence. The strange men came forward and added more gold coins, more bronze knife blades, and retreated once more.

This happened yet again. Then the Ashantis, satisfied with the bargain, picked up the trade good and departed. The white men loaded their grain and palm wine and sailed away. They were never seen again. They were small men, wiry and strong, with protruding lips and long, bent noses.

One of the gold coins left by these voyagers of centuries ago was the amulet given to Obiri Anokye by Auntie Tal. It had been rubbed smooth by many fingers, centuries of fingers, but the pressed images were still discernible. On one side was a leaping ibex. On the other was the head of a man. His nose was heavy and curved like a scimitar. His hair was in ringlets, rows of curls bound with a crown of laurel. His beard was also curled, but cut off squarely at the bottom. A tapering spade of a beard. Auntie Tal said this man was a great king, ruler of all the world.

Obiri Anokye unbuttoned his shirt, slipped the loop of string over his head, hung the grisgris upon his bare chest, buttoned his shirt over it. He did not believe in these things: amulets, grisgris, fetishes, juju. But he did not *not* believe.

"Honored guests," Peter A. Tangent said, in French. "Ladies and gentlemen. It is a great privilege for me, and an even greater pleasure, to present the President of Asante, Obiri Anokye."

The luncheon guests at the Zabarian Restaurant leaped to their feet, applauding enthusiastically. The Little Captain rose slowly, shook Tangent's hand, then turned to the acclamation, smiling faintly. He stood silently, looking about the crowded room, waiting patiently until the hand-clapping ended; the guests sat down, turning their chairs so they all faced him. Black faces, white faces. All shades, all hues. Waiting . . .

"Friends," Obiri Anokye said. "Brothers and sisters. I thank you all for your respect and affection. I give you my love and my gratitude. Gladly and without limit." He then repeated this greeting in English and in Akan.

They bent forward, already won by his solemn words, by his grave manner. He had the gift of making the moment, and those who shared it, seem intense and significant. Even the Man from Tulsa and the Man from New York were impressed. They leaned to him as eagerly as the others, not wanting to miss a word, gesture, expression; mesmerized by this short, stocky man wearing the khakis of an Asante soldier, without decoration or indication of rank.

"Within the hour we shall witness the start of commercial production of oil from Asante waters. It is the end of a long, difficult period of exploration, discovery, and development. Success would not have been possible without the resolution and labor of Mr. Peter Tangent and his associates of the Starrett Petroleum Corporation. All Asantis are grateful for what they have done."

There was a splatter of applause. The oilmen in the audience looked at each other and grinned happily.

"But if today's ceremony marks the end of one period, it signals the start of another. A beginning. A birth. Of a new day for our beloved country. We have been blessed with a great national resource. It will enable us to provide a better life for all Asantis. Our people fed, clothed, and housed. Our children educated to the limits of their ability and talents. The land itself respected, nurtured, and made more beautiful. If we plan wisely and work diligently with love and understanding, we may create an Asante that will serve as a model for all of Africa, and that will prove to the world that Africa has the faith and determination to create a civilization of the future to rival the greatest of the past."

Then, slowly, the Little Captain assumed his familiar speaking posture: feet spread and planted, hands on hips, torso bent slightly backward, chest inflated, chin elevated so he seemed to stare at his listeners broodingly from under heavy brows. His low voice gained power:

"Africa . . . My Africa . . . *Our* Africa! So beset by trials and problems. Poor and ill. The people and the land impoverished. Drained of our wealth for so many years by others. And now struggling to create a new continent, free of the fears of the past. And yet chained to the past. It is the chain of separatism, a cruel shackle that prevents us from realizing our true destiny.

"Family against family. Tribe against tribe. Creed against creed. Race against race. Nation against nation, I tell you this infamy must end! We shall never succeed until we recognize we are Africans. Before all, *Africans!* Races means nothing. Creed nothing. Tribe nothing. Borders nothing. But our sacred land is all, demanding our total loyalty, our hearts, minds and, if need be, blood.

"I stand before you today not as an Asanti, a Christian, or a black. I am an African! And I plead with you all to renounce the evil of separatism that enfeebles our holy soil. I call upon you to give your talents, your love, your soul, every minute of the life that is in you, to the future of Pan-Africa: one beautiful continent, one strong nation, one magnificent people, one glorious future!"

With the approval of President Anokye, employees of PR Afrique, the Liberian public relations firm on retainer to the Republic of Asante, planned the evening gala to be an informal, festive affair. The palace at Mokodi, gleaming in floodlights, was festooned with garlands of fresh flowers and bunting in the national colors. Illuminated fountains on the plaza tossed sparkles into the night sky. Bands played jazz and le rock-and-roll in the streets. Vendors were allowed to set up stands on the Boulevard Voltaire, selling palm wine, millet beer, pepper chicken, and fufu. The strolling gendarmerie even smiled indulgently at games of chance flourishing on side streets.

The ardent night air was alive with the scent of sun-baked skin, exploding firecrackers, perfumed water squirted from syringes onto unsuspecting passersby. It was a noisy, good-natured crowd celebrating Asante's new wealth. There was indeed dancing in the streets, and singing, laughter, the close mingling of black natives and white tourists, all intent on enjoying the carnival mood of this memorable night. Many, in fact, wore masquerade, their outlandish costumes dimmed by the brilliance of tribal dress.

The same mood of informal gaiety prevailed inside the palace. Rather than a sit-down state dinner, a bountiful buffet had been provided in the main ballroom on the ground floor. Three bands played in as many rooms, waiters hustled to provide whatever drink might be desired and, best of all, no formal program or speeches had been planned.

Yet it was a speech that dominated the excited gathering—the short speech of President Obiri Anokye at the Zabarian. The luncheon had been covered by representatives of Reuters and Agence France-Presse. Both had taken down the Little Captain's words in shorthand. Better than that, the man from PR Afrique had tape-recorded the speech. With Anokye's permission, a transcript was made, copies were run off and distributed in answer to many requests. The only change the President made was to label his words "extempore remarks" rather than "formal speech."

Whatever he wished to call it, Anokye's ideas and phrases aroused the most intense interest in Asante's diplomatic community. Copies of the speech were sent off immediately to home offices with analyses by ambassadors and consuls stationed in Mokodi.

It was the significance of the President's remarks that caused so much spirited discussion at the palace gala. Anokye seemed to have included whites—"all races, all colors, all creeds"—in his plea for Pan-Africa. Yet he had made an obvious reference to the evils of white colonialism. And was he serious in his suggestion for "one continent, one nation, one people, one future"? In his condemnation of separatism, he went far beyond the plans of others who asked for an African unity based on a loose federation of sovereign states. Did he really mean to eliminate national boundaries in Africa? What exactly did he mean—and how did he propose it be achieved?

These questions, and others, were debated heatedly, not only by the representatives of other African countries but by diplomats of the Americas, Western Europe, the Soviet Bloc, the Far East. In fact, by everyone. And when the author of the perplexing speech was asked directly for explanation or amplification, he would only smile slightly and murmur, "Surely the meaning is evident in the words." The only consensus arrived at was that Obiri Anokye had voiced new ideas important to Africa, and to the world, and by this one short speech had marked himself a young statesman to be reckoned with. The PR representative was kept busy providing copies of the President's official biography to the world's capitals and communication media.

The ballroom was thronged, pulsing with a life of its own, the crowd growing and diminishing as guests moved to other palace rooms or out onto the terrace. Eventually they returned, drawn by the magnetic presence of President Anokye himself. He stood poised in one corner of the enormous room, Sgt. Sene Yeboa and two other guardsmen in mufti standing at his back. He greeted guests affably, thanked them graciously for their good wishes and congratulations on his speech. He sipped, occasionally, from a glass of champagne. Though he remained standing in this one spot for almost two hours, he showed no fatigue. And in spite of the demands made upon his time and attention, he seemed completely aware of what was going on in the crowded room. Once, he quietly instructed a guardsman to ask the ballroom band to moderate their volume. And once he beckoned Beatrice da Silva to his side to whisper a few words into her ear that made her blush with pleasure.

Nearby, Minister of State Jean-Louis Duclos, his wife, Mboa, and the Benin Christophe Michaux watched the President's performance with admiration.

"Poor Bibi," Mboa said. "He must be so weary."

"Bibi?" Michaux asked, greatly amused. "You call him that?"

Mboa clapped a palm over her mouth for a second.

"I should not have said that," she confessed. "But Jean and I knew him well before the coup. I still think of him as a good friend, as Bibi."

"You must address him as 'Mr. President,'" Duclos said severely.

"Yes, Jean," she said, lowering her eyes.

She was a petite woman, coal-black, wearing an Apollo shift in a blue tie-dyed design. Despite her husband's objections, she wore her hair corn-rowed. Her experiments with makeup (at his urging) had ended so disastrously that now she wore none. She had graduated from the Mokodi lycée, where Duclos had taught in precoup days, but she shared none of his political interests, and seemed content.

He had married her after her attempted suicide. As, he thought, she lay dying, he had realized his love, and declared it when she recovered. But now, sometimes, in moments when her placid Negro-ness infuriated him, he wondered if that attempted suicide was not a trick, as another woman might feign pregnancy to insure marriage. Mboa—or Maria, as he called her—might not be intellectual but she had, he admitted, bush shrewdness, jungle wisdom. If only she were not so black!

He was black too, of course. But so light in color that several women in Paris had told him he could easily pass. That, he would never do. He was, he told himself, proud of his blood. Still, meeting the smartly dressed white wives of foreign diplomats, imposing women who could discuss social, political, and economic theory with verve and knowledgeableness, he sometimes wondered if he had made a horrible mistake, fettering himself to this small, coal-black woman with enormous eyes and gleaming teeth, who needed only a plate in her lower lip or rings of brass about an elongated neck to qualify for a full-page portrait in *National Geographic*. Topless, of course.

"And what did you think of the President's speech, Mrs. Duclos?" Christophe Michaux asked.

She was confused for a moment.

"He wants only what is best for all of us," she said in a low voice. "I trust him."

"Do you?" he smiled loftily, a smile directed at the Minister of State, a smile of sympathy and complicity. Duclos found himself responding to that smile. Here was a man who understood.

"What was your reaction to the speech?" he asked Michaux.

The Benin Premier's aide sobered immediately, features freezing into an expressionless diplomatic mask.

"There were several things that troubled me," he said thoughtfully. "In my own mind, I cannot resolve certain contradictions. Apparently, he was saying 'Africa for the Africans.' Yet he said race was of no importance. Does he think white settlers, white colonials, are Africans?"

"It troubled me also," Duclos confessed.

"He has never discussed this idea of Pan-Africa with you, Minister?"

"Well, ah . . . no. At least not in the terms he expressed today."

"Do you agree with it?"

"Well . . . I sympathize with his vision, Mr. Michaux, but—"

"Christophe, please."

"Christophe. Thank you. As I say, I sympathize with his vision, his dream, but I believe he errs in including race as a sin of separatism. I cannot conceive of a new Africa based on anything but the highest ideals of negritude."

Michaux looked at him with interest.

"Perhaps," he said softly, "you and I hold the same beliefs. Not identical, certainly, but similar. I, for instance, in my own mind believe that the tyranny of class rather than separatism is the main obstacle to African progress."

"Class?" Duclos said. "Are you a Marxist, Christophe?"

"Oh no," Michaux laughed merrily. "No no no. I merely feel that white hegemony in Africa, economic hegemony, must be ended before we Africans may call our souls our own."

"But you are both Martinicains," Mboa said bravely. "How can you be Africans?"

They looked at her in astonishment.

"Don't be stupid, Maria," Duclos said angrily.

"All blacks are Africans," Michaux said. The lofty smile. "Originally. Whatever their birthplace."

"Jean," Mboa said earnestly, "are there not blacks in Australia? The islands of the Pacific? So you taught us at the lycée. Did they come originally from Africa?"

"Don't confuse the issue," he said furiously. "You don't have the intelligence to discuss such matters."

They stood without speaking a few moments, embarrassed. The celebration swirled about them. Music. Dancing. Laughter as brittle as shattered glass.

"Tell me, Minister," Michaux said, "how do you suppose President Anokye intends to implement his scheme?"

"Scheme?"

"His suggestion for Pan-Africa. How is it to be achieved?"

"I believe the President intended it as an ideal, a hope for the future. I do not believe it is a concrete program."

"Oh? I thought perhaps he had a plan . . ."

"A plan, Christophe? Oh no. Nothing like that, I'm sure."

"You should know," Michaux said dryly. "Who better than the Asanti Minister of State? You don't find some of his ideas—well . . . dangerous?"

"How dangerous? To whom?"

Michaux shook his head. "I cannot say. But in my own mind, I have a vague fear that the President's obvious love of Africa, his sympathy, and compassion for the masses, may lead him astray. He is such a persuasive man.

What presence! It would be a sad thing if he should employ his enormous gifts only to prolong Africa's servitude to the international white power infrastructure."

"He would never do that."

"Not deliberately, Minister. Of course not. Such an implication was farthest from my thoughts. But his great personal popularity and Asante's new wealth may blind him to the realities of the racial situation in Africa today. I would not care to see him become a puppet of the whites."

"Nor I."

Michaux put a limp hand on Duclos' arm. "How happy I am to find a man of your talents in Asante who sees things so clearly. We must speak of this again. I would deem it a great honor and pleasure, Minister, if you could visit me in Cotonou. Is such a thing possible in your busy schedule?"

"Thank you, Christophe," Duclos said, blushing with pride. "I believe it could be arranged."

"Excellent, excellent! There are some men I would like you to meet. Intelligent men with many fresh and provocative ideas. I'm sure you'll enjoy speaking with them. Mrs. Duclos, I hope you will be able to accompany your husband to Benin."

"No," Duclos said shortly. "I'm afraid that's impossible. Maria doesn't wish to fly in a plane."

"We could drive, Jean," she said timidly.

"No," he said again. "Ah . . . the President is looking at us."

The others turned to see. President Obiri Anokye was indeed staring at them. But then they realized he was not actually looking at them. He was deep in conversation with the French ambassador and was merely staring in their direction without seeing them. Or so it seemed.

Thirty minutes before midnight, the Little Captain beckoned Beatrice da Silva to his side. Making his apologies to the diplomats and oilmen surrounding him, he stepped clear of the crowd, guiding Beatrice with a light touch on her elbow. Sgt. Sene Yeboa stalked a few steps after them.

President Anokye led her from the ballroom, down a corridor toward the rear of the palace, through a suite of staff offices, and out French doors onto the terrace. Yeboa stood posted at the open door as Obiri and Beatrice strolled to the balustrade overlooking the plaza.

Because of the warmth of his manner and the ardor of his glances, the woman was certain, in her heart, that the man would ask her to marry him this evening. And when she saw he had selected the exact spot where they had first met—on the terrace, during a reception held by the late King Prempeh IV—she was filled with love. For his thoughtfulness, for his perception, for *him*.

Actually, he had selected this place for other reasons. It was a position that could be easily observed by Sergeant Yeboa and guards posted on the palace grounds below. And he was not certain how modern young women reacted to proposals of marriage; the semi-public nature of this place, with other guests occasionally sauntering by, precluded any uncultured romantic violence on her part.

"I hope you are enjoying the gala, Beatrice," he said politely. "Is there anything you wish? A glass of champagne, perhaps? A piece of chicken?"

"Oh no," she said, giggling nervously. "I've had so much. It's good to be away from the crowd. For a few minutes."

"Your accommodations are satisfactory?"

"Marvy," she said. "A whole suite for daddy and me. Did I thank you for the flowers? They're beautiful."

He suspected they had been provided by the manager of the Mokodi Hilton, but made a casual gesture: it was nothing.

"I loved your speech at the Zabarian," she said. "Just loved, loved, loved it."

He made the gesture again, with the sudden realization of what his married life with this silly, good-natured woman might be like. But he concealed his dread and took her fingers into his. Her soft, warm, boneless fingers.

She had, he thought, gained a few pounds since he last saw her; it was not a welcome presage of what the years would bring. But now, this moment, plump flesh was springy and young, dark skin glowed. Her unlined, untouched face was alive with excitement, half-fearful, half-yielding sensuality. He was conscious of her fruity scent. Her entire body seemed bursting with expectation and hope, leaning to him. He loved her more because he knew the pain he would cause her. If not pain, then disappointment. But there would be compensations. For her and for him. They would work it out. And besides, her legs were good.

"What a wonderful night," she said. "The most wonderful night of my life!"

As always, in her superlatives, youth burbled. He thought it might be good for him, this unthinking joy. It might leaven his life, dilute his gravity, complete him. He had a sudden succulent fantasy of the smell of baked bread, a broad-bosomed wife and mother, sticky-fingered children screaming with laughter and grabbing at his legs. Home.

"Beatrice, there is something I must say to you. Ask you."

"Yes?"

"I have spoken to your father and have his permission."

"What is it, Bibi?"

"I want you to—"

He stopped. Suddenly, as she stared into his eyes, she saw the depth change. He was gone from the moment, from her.

"I must leave you a moment," he said. "Please stay here. I will return in only a minute or two."

He turned and strode away from her. She stared after him, shocked and puzzled. Had he lost his nerve? Did he need to relieve himself? What had happened to him? Why had he deserted her at such a moment?

He drew Sergeant Yeboa into the staff offices.

"Bring Sam Leiberman to me," he said. "At once. Here."

Yeboa looked at him doubtfully.

"Little Captain, you will be alone."

"Go, Sene," Anokye smiled tightly. "For a few minutes I will defend myself. You know I can."

He waited patiently, almost five minutes. Neither pacing nor smoking. Finally Yeboa returned, Leiberman following. Anokye motioned, and the mercenary came close.

"Sir?" he said.

"The aide to the Premier of Benin," President Anokye said. "Christophe Michaux. Did you meet him?"

"Yeah," Leiberman said. "I met him."

"What do you think?"

"A weasel," Leiberman said. "Or a butterfly. Or maybe a weasel *and* a butterfly."

"I want to know about him," Anokye said. "I have no one in our embassy there I can trust. Can you do it?"

Leiberman thought a moment, then nodded.

"Not me personally," he said, "but I can get it."

"Good," Anokye said. "I want everything."

"Of course," Leiberman said.

The Little Captain rejoined Beatrice da Silva at the terrace balustrade. She was almost weeping with vexation. He took her hands in his.

"Please forgive me," he said gently. "As I was saying, I have spoken to your father and have his permission to ask you."

"To ask me what?"

"If you will marry me. If you will be my wife. Will you?"

"Oh yes, Bibi! Yes yes yes!"

She flung her arms around him, drew him to her, all soft heart. And, as if arranged by the PR man from Monrovia, at that precise instant there was a loud explosion high in the sky, a crown of multi-colored torches curved out in a graceful spray. The fireworks display had started, and their lips peeled away, sideways, as their startled eyes followed the brilliant succession of red rockets, green streamers, white dripping fire, yellow falling stars, blue whirling discs, cracking, booming, thudding, snapping, roaring in the night sky over Mokodi.

Outside, from the streets of Mokodi, came the occasional crack of an exploding firecracker, a bit of song, a high drunken yell of delight. But the city was going to bed, to love or to sleep. Confetti scattering down gutters before a warm night wind. Wisps of clouds sliding across a lemon moon. From somewhere, the baritone cough of a boat whistle, siren cut off in mid-wail. And dimly, dimly, endless splash of the sea.

By 0200 the crowd in the palace ballroom had dwindled to a dozen dreamy-eyed couples. Revolving slowly to Edith Piaf tunes. Played by a somnolent band. Waiters shuffled wearily about, cleaning up the littered buffet, overflowing ashtrays, spilled drinks and broken glass. Ancient sweepers, moving in time to the draggy music, pushed their rag brooms over the parquet floors.

In the first floor audience chamber, the barefoot Ajaka placed a silver tray of coffee and brandy on the long mahogany table, then went bowing, yawning, off to bed. They crowded around to help themselves.

"Mighty fine celebration, Mr. President," the Man from Tulsa said.

"Can't remember a better one," the Man from New York said.

"I am happy you gentlemen enjoyed it," Anokye said. "I hope you will return frequently and see more of our beautiful country."

He did not take his chair at the head of the table but selected one midway on the side. Premier Willi Abraham sat on his right, Attorney General Mai Fante on his left. The oilmen sat across from them, Peter Tangent between the Man from Tulsa and the Man from New York. For a few moments no one spoke; they sipped cautiously at hot, black coffee or touched brandy to their lips.

"I hope we're not inconveniencing you, Mr. President," the Man from New York said.

"But we're grabbing a morning flight," the Man from Tulsa said. "And this seemed like the only time to have our confab."

"No inconvenience at all," the Little Captain assured them. "I frequently work through the night. I find it more productive while everyone else sleeps."

They looked at him sharply, but there was nothing in his manner to suggest he was implying more than he had stated.

Tangent had briefed Oribi Anokye on these two Starrett Petroleum executives.

"I think of them as twins," he had told the President. "One speaks with the accent of Oklahoma, and one of New York. But they are almost identical in appearance and style. They'll wear black silk suits, light blue shirts, with either silver or striped ties. If striped, they'll be ties of British army regiments. But if I ever suggested to them that it was infra dig to wear the colors of a military regiment to which one did not belong, they'd look at me as if I were some kind of a nut. The ties come from England, don't they? The British are helping their balance of payments by selling their regimental stripes and clan tartans around the world, aren't they? So? I only mention this, Mr. President, because it is indicative of their mentality. The Bottom Line Mentality. Profit is good, loss is bad. Profit is smart, loss is dumb. So I suggest you deal with them on those terms. Like most international businessmen, they are apolitical.

But do not take them lightly; they are very hard, very practical men. Shrewd as Lebanese rug merchants or Amsterdam diamond dealers. They mean to use you."

The Little Captain had looked at Tangent curiously.

"Is that so unnatural?" he asked.

Now, sitting across from them, Anokye could understand why Tangent thought of them as twins. Both American executives had a polished gloss, faces in which age and experience had apparently left no interpretable marks. In spite of a long day's festivities, they were sober, spotlessly clean, unrumpled, alert and keen. The Little Captain found himself wishing he had such men working for him. They were second-rank men, but good ones.

"Mr. President," Tangent started, "we have asked for this audience to learn your reaction to a project Starrett is exploring."

"I'm glad Peter said 'exploring,' " the Man from New York said. "It's still in the talking stage."

"All smoke so far," the Man from Tulsa said. "But it's a possibility. For the future."

"What Starrett is considering," Tangent went on, "is building an oil refinery somewhere on the west coast of Africa so that crude taken from Asante wells can be broken down into marketable products in this area instead of shipping it to our Ireland refinery."

"It makes buck sense," the Man from Tulsa said. "Saves transportation costs."

"And brings us closer to our end markets in Africa," the Man from New York said. "Good for everyone. For us, of course, and because of the savings, for the consumer. Eventually."

"But refineries don't come cheap," the Man from Tulsa said.

"Far from it," the Man from New York said.

"I see," President Anokye said slowly. "And where is this refinery to be built?"

"That's the purpose of this meeting," Tangent said quickly. "As I understand it, several excellent sites are under consideration. Is that correct?"

He looked left and right, and both Starrett executives nodded.

"Several excellent sites," Tangent repeated. "We are now in the process of talking to the governments involved. Naturally, we want the most advantageous lease terms we can obtain. You understand that, Mr. President, I'm sure."

"Of course."

"One of the sites under consideration is Asante, I'm happy to say. So this is in the nature of an exploratory discussion. If we can arrive at an equitable arrangement, it's possible the refinery will be built here, and Asante will benefit from having one of the most modern, productive and profitable installations of its type anywhere in Africa."

"No doubt about that," the Man from New York said. "With a lot of local labor needed during construction, of course. That should help your employment numbers."

"With the outside technicians spending their dinero right here in Asante," the Man from Tulsa said. "To say nothing of new roads, port facilities, and other goodies."

"I see," Anokye said thoughtfully. "And you say several sites are under consideration?"

"That's right, Mr. President," the Man from Tulsa said cheerfully. "No guarantee Asante gets the prize."

"Wherever we get the best terms, like Peter said," the Man from New York nodded. "It's business."

"Well . . ." the Little Captain said doubtfully, "while I appreciate Starrett considering Asante, I'm not sure. . . . Willi, what is your reaction?"

"I'm afraid I can't express too much enthusiasm, Mr. President," the well-coached Abraham said. "While the industrializing of Asante would have some obvious benefits, I fear it would adversely affect tourism, which accounts for a very substantial part of our annual income. Tourists come to Asante because they seek a simpler, unspoiled way of life. They want to see the green hills of Africa, our villages, a lifestyle that once existed, perhaps, in their home countries, but is now gone forever. I fear we could not lure visitors if our main attraction was an oil refinery. It's exactly the sort of thing they hope to get away from, to leave behind them when they come to Asante."

"You speak the truth," Anokye nodded, very grave. "Mai, how do you feel?"

"Much as Premier Abraham, Mr. President. I must also add that the building of a refinery on Asante soil would have serious social and political repercussions. We have a growing and very vocal organization of environmentalists in Asante who would be certain to react to a proposed oil refinery with outrage. They would point out the polluting effects on their clean air and pure water. Joined in their opposition, no doubt, by fishermen and owners of coastal hotels. I'm very dubious about this project for Asante, Mr. President."

Anokye sighed. "What you say substantiates my own judgment." He looked at the three oilmen, back and forth. "I thank you for your kind offer, gentlemen, but I must request that Asante be eliminated as a possible site of your new oil refinery."

After recovering from their initial shock, the two Starrett executives moved swiftly to the attack. Tangent said little, content to—content?—*delighted* to watch and listen to this snappish dialogue.

They wheedle. Anokye scorns. They bark. He thunders. They threaten. He shrugs. They implore. He rejects. Tangent sees it as a verbal ballet—approaches and retreats, spins and leaps. To be concluded by a graceful bow from all, roses tossed from the darkness.

Aware of the professional expertise of the Man from New York and the Man from Tulsa, Tangent was exhilarated by the implacableness of the Little

Captain. He was caught up in the ebb, the flow, the clash, the withdrawal, and was hardly aware of when, or by what means, Obiri Anokye introduced his demand for a no-strings grant for "national expansion."

The battle surged again, the overseas visitors rising and stalking angrily about the room. Until Anokye's steadfastness simply wore them down, physically and emotionally, and they flopped back into their chairs and asked him how much he wanted, and Tangent realized, with awe, that the Little Captain had won: he had his no-strings grant, and Asante's environmentalists disappeared as quickly as they had been invented.

The winner sat back, solemn, not gloating, and let Willi Abraham and Mai Fante hammer out the terms: Starrett got their Asante refinery site for three and a half million American dollars, to be paid in six installments over a period of eighteen months, the cash payments to be disguised in a variety of ways: advances on anticipated oil revenues, investments in worthless Asante real estate, contributions to schools and hospitals, the establishment of a Friends of West Africa foundation in the U.S. Abraham and Fante had done their homework.

When the final agreement was reached, close to 0400, the two beaten Starrett executives ceremoniously shook hands with President Obiri Anokye.

"Mr. President," the Man from New York said, "if you ever get tired of running Asante, there's a place for you at Starrett Petroleum."

"Any time," the Man from Tulsa said. "Anywhere in the world. Just tell us how much you want. Don't ask—*tell!*"

Smiling gently, the Little Captain bid them good-night and wished them a safe and speedy trip home.

Tangent drove them back to their VIP suites at the Mokodi Hilton, wondering, with savage satisfaction, if they had enough energy remaining to enjoy the pleasures J. Tom Petty had arranged for them.

Yvonne Mayer sat on the middle cushion of a wicker couch. It was covered with a rough twill in a batik pattern of harsh yellow, orange, brown, clashing with the peach-colored peignoir she wore. Her legs were crossed; she peered down through Benjamin Franklin glasses as she filed her nails with an emery board. Beside her was the evening edition of the Mokodi *New Times*, the only newspaper in Asante. It carried the President's Zabarian speech on the front page.

"It was on the radio every hour until the station went off the air," she said. "Bibi, was it wise?"

"Wise, not wise," he shrugged. "I think many Africans will react favorably. It is time to make myself known in other countries, to make friends. I cannot do it alone, from Asante. I must have men in other countries who know me, know my ideas, believe in me."

He and Sgt. Sene Yeboa had taken off their shoes and socks. They sat sprawled wearily in cushioned wicker armchairs, drinking Star beer. A single lamp burned dimly. But already, through the east windows, the black sky was thinning.

"Sene, do you have any men ready?"

"Three, Little Captain. And two more in a week's time."

"Good. We will send two to Lomé, two to Cotonou, one to Lagos. I will give them their instructions and provide funds."

"Did you ask her?" Yvonne said, not looking up from her nails.

"Yes," Anokye said. "I asked her."

"She said yes, of course?"

"She said yes."

"I had her pointed out to me at the oil ceremony," Yvonne said, finally raising her eyes to stare at him over her spectacles. "She is a dumpling."

Anokye said nothing.

"In a few years she will be a pig."

He looked at her coldly. The peignoir had fallen open. He saw her smooth knees, waxen legs. He remembered her body. Like a shaved snake. Sene Yeboa kept his eyes on his beer.

"The marriage will be within three months," he said. "My marriage. Yours will be sooner."

She made a moue and started on the other hand.

"We have the money," he told her. "From Starrett."

"How much?"

"Enough. Nkomo and I will begin examining weapons immediately. When it is learned we wish to buy and have the funds, there will be no problems."

He spoke to himself as much as to her.

"Perhaps you could go to Cotonou," he said. "No, not yet. There is a certain man, the aide to the Premier. But I will wait for Leiberman's report; then I will decide. I am tired. It has been a long day."

"You will sleep here?"

"Yes. No. Well, perhaps for an hour or two. A nap. Then I will return to the palace. There is much to be done. Much . . ."

There was silence, and when she looked up from her nails, she saw he had fallen asleep in the armchair, his chin on his chest.

"Poor Bibi," she breathed softly. "Sene, help me get him into the bedroom."

Between them, they supported the drowsing, stumbling, mumbling President of Asante into the bedroom and lowered him gently onto the bed, on his back.

"Thank you, Sene," Yvonne whispered. "I will let him sleep a few hours. Will you wait for him?"

"Oh yes. I must drive him back to the palace."

"If you wish to sleep, go to the guest room. I will wake you when he awakes."

"I am not sleepy."

"There is some beer in the kitchen, and food if you are hungry. Take anything."

"Thank you, Yvonne."

She rose up on her bare toes to kiss his cheek swiftly. He stood a moment, frozen, then smiled at her, shy and puzzled. He turned, marched from the room. She closed the door behind him.

The room was not lighted, but the bamboo shades were up, drapes open. Enough illumination to enable her to unbutton Anokye's shirt, his trousers, pull them off. He made groaning, protesting sounds as she pushed and hauled at him, trying to roll him free. Finally he was naked, lying on his back, legs spread, arms flung wide. His great, hairy chest pumped slowly. She could almost see tense force flow from his limbs as the flesh slackened, sank into sleep. He twitched a few times, moaned a few times. Then he was still. Almost, she thought, with the stillness of death.

She sat alongside him, on the edge of the bed, staring down at his dark majesty. She put her palm lightly, fingers spread, on his thigh. His skin was hot. Her white hand looked like a fulgent sun, beams radiating.

Her hand drifted; she touched the black staff cautiously. He did not stir. She held it delicately upright, as one might hold the stem of a wine glass. At the same time her other hand pried beneath her peignoir, between her legs. She touched herself. Almost immediately she felt a flow, slick wetness.

Lost, she bent over him slowly, touched her lips to him. Her eyes were turned upward; she watched his face anxiously. It was important that he not awake. All her movements, on him and in herself, were small, sly, and without passion. The moment seemed to her of a bittersweetness she could not comprehend. As piercing as a farewell.

When his penis began to harden, she stopped immediately. She withdrew her fingers, from him and from herself. She rose cautiously, slipped quietly to the door, closed it gently behind her. In the living room she lighted one of his Gauloises, and stepped out onto the front porch. The eastern sky was greying now, changing as she watched. New sun, new day. The air smelled of it, all fresh and dewy. Flowered air, perfumed world. Hugging her elbows, cigarette dangling from her lips, she strolled around to the rear of the house, feeling the damp grass beneath her bare feet, kicking her way through a tangle of low wet groundcover whose name she did not know and a stand of tall flowers whose name she could not recall.

When she reentered the house, through the back door into the kitchen, Sene Yeboa was crouched, a snubby Smith & Wesson .38 swallowed in his huge fist, pointing toward the door. When he saw her, he slid the revolver smoothly back into a black belt holster, sat down, took up his beer and sandwich again.

"I'm sorry," she said humbly.

He chewed, grinned, waved her to the chair across from him. She took a bottle of Star from the refrigerator and joined him.

He swallowed heavily, took a gulp of beer.

"The Little Captain sleeps?"

She nodded.

"Good. A long day. He had to smile at many people. I could not have done it."

She looked at him closely. A blunt, heavy man, not as dark as Anokye. He had, Obiri said, been "made in the bush": white father, black mother. Though who they were, he did not know. Raised in a Christian mission. A silent, brooding boy. But when he was sent to the Mokodi lycée, he met Obiri Anokye, and his life began. Boyhood friends, and into the army together. He had killed for the Little Captain, and would willingly die for him.

He was Bibi's age, but without the Little Captain's magisterial quality. There was sensuousness in his dense, almost brutish features. Wide nostrils flared. Thick lips turned out, showing wet red inner skin. The smooth jaw seemed never to need a shave. Small, narrowed eyes. Wide neck. Rounded, bunchy shoulders. A blunt body. "A bull," Anokye had called him. It was there in the truculent forward tilt of head and torso. Ready to charge.

"And you, Sene?" she asked. "Are you not weary?" They spoke Akan now. Before, in the living room with Anokye, they had spoken English. The President insisted on it, wanting to improve his proficiency.

Yeboa shrugged those massive shoulders.

"I will sleep tomorrow," he said. "When I can. Yvonne, the Little Captain's marriage troubles you?"

It was her turn to shrug.

"I accept it," she said.

"Good," he said heartily, as if that settled the matter. "He will work it out for your happiness; you will see."

"My happiness?"

"Of course," he said. He waved his hand about. "You have this fine house. Servants. Now you own the Golden Calf. Is not all this better?"

She said nothing, but something in her eyes made him stare.

"You miss the life?" he asked.

She saved sympathy and kindness as another person might put money in the bank. For a rainy day.

"How did you know?" she asked. "My family came to Africa from the Saar. Not came. Were driven. My father was a thief, my mother an alcoholic. All I can remember were the hunger and beatings. So I ran away."

None of this was true, and she wondered why she said it.

"Yes, I miss the life," she said. "Not the men. The girls. The friends. It was like a family, a home. I never had any."

She had said the right thing. His eyes glistened with tears. His hand crept across the table to cover hers.

"I also," he said. Voice low and choked. "No home, no family. Until I met Bibi. Then I could go to his family, his home. But not my own."

She nodded dumbly.

"What men are you sending to Lomé and Cotonou?" she asked.

"The Little Captain wants men he can trust in other countries. To find out things. And also here in Asante, I have men to listen and learn what is going on. Like Prempeh's secret police."

"Bibi has put you in command of all this?" she asked.

"Oh yes," he said proudly. "He wishes me to recruit and train these men. They will all report to me. It is a very important task. And difficult. I do not know if I can do it."

"Do it," she said, turning her hand over so she clasped his. "I will help you."

9

In Mokodi, the Rue Dumas runs parallel to the Boulevard Voltaire, one square west. It is, for the length of four squares, a popular shopping center, especially for tourists. It is dominated by Monoprix, the French equivalent of Woolworth, and by the offices of American Express and several foreign consulates.

At the corner of a narrow east-west street called Shinbone Alley is the curio shop of Lum Fong. In its small windows are displayed splendid examples of Hong Kong Renaissance: lacquered salad bowls, transistor radios, silken flowers, wire banzai trees, painted shells, bamboo backscratchers, tobacco jars shaped like human skulls, brass jewelry, "African" amulets, bead curtains, and ashtrays in the form of Negro hands, stamped SOUVENIR OF ASANTE.

When Sam Leiberman stepped into the incense-scented interior, a lissome Chinese girl came eagerly forward. She was wearing a cheongsam of electric blue silk.

"Good morning, sir," she said brightly. "Is there something I can show you?"

"Yeah," Leiberman said. "Is it true?"

She averted her eyes. "May I be of service, sir?"

"I want to see Lum Fong."

"I shall tell the master you are here," she said.

"Master of what?" he called after her. "Plastic chopsticks?"

Lum Fong followed her from an inner office. He was a wizened Chinese with wispy chin whiskers. He wore a gorgeous brocaded gown with a high collar and braided frog closures. His tiny feet were in heelless velvet slippers. He touched his long fingernails and bowed deeply.

"Ahh, Reiberman," he said. "My insignificant shop is honored by your august presence."

"Cut the Mandarin shit and talk straight," Leiberman said. "Let's go in back."

Fong led the way through a bead curtain into a large office. Larger than the shop.

Leiberman said, "You can start by offering me a thimbleful of that plum brandy you keep in the red lacquer cabinet."

The Chinese made a sound deep in his throat, a cat's purr. Leiberman supposed it was meant to be an amused chuckle.

"You forget nothing," Fong said.

"Nothing important, I don't," Leiberman agreed.

He sat in an ornately carved armchair before the desk and watched the Chinese carefully dole out minuscule teacups of the brandy. Leiberman took his, sniffed, sipped appreciatively.

"That'll put lead in your pencil," he said. He lolled back, hooked one knee over the chair arm.

The mercenary was a heavy, meatish man. Arms were thick, hairy, wrists powerful. His short-sleeved safari jacket revealed a whitened scar running from right bicep to forearm, across the elbow. He was burned a deep brick-red. Stiff iron-grey hair cut en brosse. Squinty eyes. Small, flat ears. Nose was broad, lips protuberant. A rude face. Gravelly voice. Clotted laugh.

"How's business?" he asked.

Lum Fong shrugged. "I survive."

"Don't we all," Leiberman said. "The nose candy coming in okay?"

The other's expression didn't change.

"I do not understand what you mean, Reiberman," he said softly.

"Sure you do," Leiberman said genially. "I'm working out of the palace now; you know that. I couldn't care less about your little sideline, but I don't think El Presidente would approve. He might even have that tough sergeant of his reach up your asshole and pull you inside out. I don't think you'd enjoy that, Lummy baby."

The Chinese sat back and sighed.

"What do you want, Reiberman?"

"A small favor. Muy poco. You got cousins in Benin?"

Lum Fong nodded.

"Cotonou or Porto-Novo?" Leiberman asked.

"Both."

"Good," Leiberman said. "There's a politico named Christophe Michaux. Tall, skinny, color of sand. Greasy, marcelled hair. Looks bleached to me. Little goatee. He's the secretary or aide to the Premier. I want a rundown on him. Things *Who's Who* wouldn't be interested in printing. You coppish?"

Again Lum Fong nodded. "That is all?" he asked.

"That's all," Leiberman said. "As soon as you can. Now that wasn't so bad, was it?"

He drained his brandy, unhooked his knee, stood up. Lum Fong rose behind the desk. He touched his long fingernails, bowed so deeply the wispy chin whiskers touched the brocaded gown.

"My humble abode has been honored by your sublime presence," he said.

"Ahh, Jesus," Leiberman sighed. "Fu Manchu strikes again."

10

"It's Beautiful," Tony Malcolm said. "Did you see it?"

"No," Peter Tangent said, "it was crated when I picked it up."

"A Benin bronze," Malcolm said. "Brilliant work. Ten thousand. At least. Maybe twenty."

"A small token of the President's esteem," Tangent smiled. "For your help on the refinery thing. He said to tell you he still feels obligated."

"I'm beginning to see the Little Captain in a new light," Malcolm said.

Tangent laughed. "Thought you might," he said. "Ready to order?"

They were at their favorite corner table at Brindleys. They were wearing dinner jackets, part of the pre-theatre crowd. They were going to see *She Would If She Could*, an American musical based on *Antony and Cleopatra*, which one London critic had described as "A bird for the Bard—turkey."

"What're you having?" Tangent asked, scanning the deckle-edged menu.

"Dover sole."

"I'll buy that. How about a Muscadet?"

"Why not? It'll dull the pain of the play. It's supposed to be a clinker."

"Then why are we going?"

"We don't seem to have much else to do together these nights, do we?"

"No, we don't," Tangent said. Somewhat sadly. "Ah well . . ."

He gave the order to Harold, their superannuated waiter, then glanced casually about the crowded room. Men and women in formal dress. Most of them young, handsome, glittering. The rattle of smart talk.

"I'm in Africa," he said to Malcolm, "the land of sweat-stained khaki. Then a few hours later I'm in the middle of this. A crazy kind of jet-lag. Call it culture-lag. Difficult to adjust so quickly."

"You're complaining?"

"Oh God, no. Tony, I didn't ask if you want an appetizer. They have smoked salmon tonight."

"Thanks, no; I'll skip. Up two pounds this morning."

"So is our stock."

They smiled at each other, comfortable again, and watched Harold lovingly uncork their wine.

"Bit of all right this is, gentlemen," he said. "Dust on the tongue, flint on the teeth."

"And acid on the liver," Malcolm said, taking a sip. "Mmm, good. So he got his refinery? And his money?"

"He surely did," Tangent said. "He's looking at guns now. The Galil system from Israel. You know it?"

"Oh yes. Very fine. As good as the Uzi. Converts to submachine gun, sniper's rifle, grenade launcher, and so forth. I think it'll go."

"He's buying more tanks and personnel carriers from France. Wants to keep them happy."

"Very wise. He thinks of everything, doesn't he?"

"Everything. He also wants some stuff from us."

"Us?"

"The U.S. Exotic stuff."

"Like what?"

"Sound-activated mines, electronic monitors, recoilless rifles, rocket launchers. Especially the eighty-seven. And a few TOW missiles."

"The TOW? That's an antitank missile. What does he want that for?"

"Who the hell knows?" Tangent said. "Maybe he just likes to play with toys. Ah, here we are. Looks good, Harold."

"Caught today, gentlemen."

"Us or the fish?" Malcolm asked, and Harold put a finger alongside his nose.

"Good," Tangent said, after trying a bite. "How's yours?"

"Okay," Malcolm said. "Caught yesterday, if not frozen."

"Eh, oui," Tangent sighed. "You can help—if you want to."

Malcolm didn't stop eating.

"He doesn't need my help to buy weapons."

"Well . . . you know. There may be some questions asked about why a two-bit African nation needs antitank missiles and helicopter gunships."

Malcolm stopped eating.

"Gunships?" he said. "You didn't mention those."

"Didn't I?" Tangent said innocently. "Slipped my mind. How about it? If Virginia gets behind it, the export licenses will go through with no problems."

"Oh, I don't know," Malcolm said. He patted his lips with his napkin and sat back. "I'd like to know a little more about it."

"About what?"

"Why he needs the heavy artillery. His plans."

"I've already told you what I know."

"I doubt that."

"Well, your man down there probably knows more than I do."

"Some. Wilson's eager."

"Then you can guess the rest." Tangent put down his knife and fork, leaned forward, stared earnestly at Malcolm. "Tony, please don't ask me. I have an obligation to you, but I have a bigger one to him. I know you can put it together by yourself. From what I tell you and what Jonathon Wilson sends you. Isn't that enough?"

"Apparently it'll have to be," Malcolm said. "They have tortoni tonight. Ever have a big cup of espresso with a spoonful of tortoni in it?"

"Never have."

"Magnificent."

"What about your diet?"

"Screw my diet. Let's have it."

They waited in silence while the table was cleared. Harold brought the tortoni, cups, the copper espresso pot.

"Please give it a few minutes to filter, gentlemen," he said.

"What's in it for me?" Malcolm asked.

"If Virginia makes sure the permits go through?" Tangent said. "Let's see what I've got to trade . . ." He thought a minute. "Is Wilson doing a good job down there?"

"Good enough. His embassy cover is blown, of course."

"How would you like someone inside? Inside the palace?"

Malcolm straightened up.

"How?" he asked.

"The Little Captain was complaining how busy he was. I suggested he bring in a management consultant to take a look at his operation and sort it out for him. You know—make recommendations for staff reorganization, office design, work flow, paper forms, and so forth. He liked the idea. Wants to modernize his administration. His word: 'modernize.' Virginia could send someone down under cover of a legit London firm, couldn't you?"

Malcolm tested the espresso pot, found it was pouring, filled Tangent's cup and his own.

"Just a spoonful of the tortoni," he said. "Float it on top. Like this . . ."

Tangent tried it.

"You were right," he said. "Magnificent."

"Life's little pleasures," Malcolm said. "Get enough of them, they add up, and you can endure. Interesting idea. About a management consultant in the palace. I could arrange that. Will you tell Anokye he's a Virginia spook?"

Tangent thought a long moment.

"Difficult to know where one's loyalties lie," he said.

"Always has been," Malcolm said.

"No, I won't tell him," Tangent decided. "For two reasons: one, I think he's smart enough not to reveal anything important. To *anyone*. Two, I want Virginia on his side. Not only now, but in the future."

"Clever bastard," Malcolm grumbled. "All right, I'll send a recommendation to Virginia. No guarantee. At least they'll know who he is. That speech of his kicked up a lot of dust."

They sipped their tortoni-creamed coffee. Again, Tangent looked casually about. At a nearby table there was a young, chestnut-haired woman wearing a black silk evening gown with plunging dècolletage. Around her neck was a double strand of large pearls. They hung down into the cleavage between her heavy breasts.

Tangent had a sudden, shattering fantasy of a naked Amina Dunama wearing only a rope of white pearls. Glistening against her black skin. The vision was so sharp, so painful, that he caught his breath.

"What?" he said.

"Where have you been?" Tony Malcolm asked. "I said we better think about leaving. Curtain going up."

"Yes," Peter Tangent said. "Curtain going up. Tony, tell me something . . . I know you're Virginia, and half the members of Brindleys know it. Doesn't it bother you that your cover's so thin?"

"No, it doesn't bother me," Malcolm said. He smiled faintly. "It's designed that way."

"Designed?"

"Sure. I take the heat. What makes you think my group is the only one in England?"

"You mean there are other—other cells in deep cover?"

"Of course."

"Do you have any communication with them?"

"No."

"Who coordinates?"

"Virginia."

"You mean," Tangent repeated incredulously, "there are other Virginia groups here and maybe in Africa?"

"That's what I mean."

"My God. It never occurred to me. There may be another Tony Malcolm operating in Asante right now."

"There may be," Malcolm acknowledge.

"Any idea who he could be?" Tangent asked.

Malcolm looked at him queerly.

"Maybe you," he said.

11

Togo, like its neighbors, Asante and Benin, is a northsouth slat of land. The three of them stand side by side, pickets on the west coast of Africa. And like its neighbors, Togo has a single main highway, running from Lomé on the coast to Dapango at the north. Many crossroads and trails connect the three improved highways of Asante, Togo, and Benin.

Where these east-west roads passed across frontiers, border guards were stationed. Otherwise, national boundaries were unfenced and unguarded—the "green borders" strolled across by smugglers who had their own network of unimproved crossroads, tracks, and trails.

President Obiri Anokye's letter to Gen. Kumayo Songo, of Togo, delivered by Adebayo Anokye, had requested a clandestine meeting with the general, at a place and time of his choosing. The general had sent a reply by Adebayo: Tuesday noon at a deserted village called Alampa, south of Pagala in Togo. It was not too far inside the Togolese border. Anokye could drive over the hills from Asante on a single-lane unimproved road in about thirty minutes. Or, if he elected to walk along smugglers' trails, he could be there in about two hours.

"We shall go on foot," the Little Captain told Sgt. Sene Yeboa. "I am stifled by this office. I need to get into the field again. We will take the Land-Rover to Gonja, and hike from there. Just the two of us. It will be like old times."

"Yes *sah!*" Sergeant Yeboa grinned. "Water bottles? Food?"

"No. Nothing. We will prove the good life has not softened us."

Yeboa grinned again. "Weapons, Little Captain?"

"Oh yes," Anokye nodded. "Bring the Uzi."

He would have been as elated as Yeboa at the prospect of this "outing" if it had not been for the selection of deserted Alampa for the meeting. He knew the place, and feared it. A roughly circular collection of thatched huts surrounding a packed earth compound. No one knew when this village had been inhabited, or when or why it had been abandoned. It was located near the bank of a small, sweet stream that fed into the Mono River. It was sited on a slight elevation: green land, cool breeze.

Yet the people who once lived there had walked away from it, driving their cows and goats, trundling their personal belongings, carrying squawking chickens in flopping sacks. They had left ancient fire stones, empty huts, a few rags fluttering in the wind, silence. Grass and trees had moved back in. Once-tilled fields were overgrown. Domed huts, beaten by storm, baked by the sun, had fallen in upon themselves, like shrinking old people.

Perhaps a pestilence had come. Perhaps a prolonged drought had dried the stream and withered the crops. Or perhaps, as some in nearby Pagala said, a curse had been put on the place. By a shaman, an unfriendly god, or maybe by the sins of the inhabitants. Whatever, Alampa was deserted. And despite the attractiveness of the site, no one, ever, showed the slightest desire to dwell in those crumbling huts again. The place was accursed.

But Anokye had to recognize its value as the scene of a secret meeting. No casual visitors. No wandering herdsmen. It was, in Africa, a no-man's-land.

The smugglers' trail led into and over the hills. The climb strained thigh and calf muscles. But cramps thawed on this hot, sweat-popping day, and after a while it became an excursion. They settled down to a good pace, Yeboa leading. But they played games in the bush: running madly down smooth, clear slopes, moving silently up to feeding warthogs, trying to snap the legs of feeding birds. It was their element; it was like coming home.

It was close to noon when they came up to Alampa, their camouflaged dungarees soaked. They had tracked on Pagala and then turned south. All this without map or compass. They separated then and circled the deserted village from opposite directions. No sign of visitors. No ambush indicated. They hunkered on their hams in the shade of a ruined hut, smoked crumpled Gauloises, waited without speaking. They heard no bird calls, no sounds of small animals snuffling in the bush. Only the hushed and vacant air. Finally the sound of a car moving along the Pagala-Akaba road. They listened. The motor stopped.

"Watch," Anokye said.

Yeboa nodded, unslung his Uzi, disappeared. One moment he was there, the next instant he was gone. Vanished into the green. The Little Captain heeled a depression for their cigarette butts in the dry, powdery earth, covered them over. He stepped deeper into the shadows of the dilapidated hut. He loosened the Walther P-38 in its hip holster.

Gen. Kumayo Songo came alone, puffing up the slight rise from road to village. He wore khaki uniform, peaked cap, Sam Browne belt. President Anokye watched him approach, expressionless, noting the rounded shoulders, protruding paunch, stumbling gait. The man was a clump; the bush was not his home. He came up wheezing, stopped, looked around warily. He was, Anokye realized, frightened.

He stepped slowly from the concealment of the ruined hut.

"Good morning, general," he said softly.

Songo whirled, stared, took off his cap, wiped his hand across his sweated forehead, replaced his cap, tugged down his uniform jacket, tried to smile, and bowed slightly—all this in one rapid, nervous movement.

"Good morning, Mr. President," he said.

"The shade?" Anokye gestured. "I fear we must stand. But what I have to say should not take much time."

Obediently, Songo followed him into the dimness. He was still breathing heavily. There were semicircles of stain beneath his armpits, and more sweat stains along the edges of his tightly cinched belt.

"I turst you are in good health?" Anokye inquired politely. He spoke Twi.

"I am well, praise to Allah," Songo replied. "Do you know happiness?"

"Thanks to God," Anokye returned, then switched to French. "Your family, is well, I hope?"

"They are well, thank you. And yours?"

"In good health. Your son—please extend my best wishes."

"I shall."

"My sister Sara speaks of him fondly. Frequently."

"And he of her." Songo's breathing had steadied. Now he tried a small laugh. "I think perhaps we may become related."

Anokye echoed the general's small laugh.

"I think so too. How would you feel about that, general?"

"I would welcome it," Songo said promptly. He peered at Anokye in the dimness.

"I also," the Little Captain said. "There is the problem of religion. But such things can be worked out when the only desire is for the happiness of all."

"My feelings exactly," Songo said.

"If your son should come to me," Anokye said, "although he should rightfully apply to my father, I can assure you he will not be disappointed."

"Thank you, Mr. President," Songo said gratefully. "He is my oldest son; I want only the best for him."

"Of course," the Little Captain said. "And I for Sara. But that is not the reason I asked for this meeting."

"Oh?" Songo said.

The gloom bothered President Anokye. He could not see the other man's reactions, changes of expression, shift of eyes. He led the way back outside, pausing where a frayed overhang of thatch provided a latticed shade. Spindles of light illuminated Kumayo Songo's lumpish features, hairline mustache, sweaty jowls.

"What I wish to say to you," Anokye said rapidly, "must be held in the strictest confidence."

"Of course. If you say so, Mr. President."

"I must tell you that you are the only man in Togo I trust. All the others—the politicos, the diplomats, the *civilians*"—Anokye poured contempt into this last—"these men I do not trust."

As expected, General Songo swelled with pride. The paunch below his brown leather belt disappeared to inflate his chest above. His head lifted, chin elevated.

"Civilians," he repeated. "Exactly!"

"General, in all honesty I must say to you that I feel the leaders of your government are not aware of the true situation. I speak now, as you must know, of the relations between Togo and Benin."

Songo groaned softly. "Mr. President, I have tried to tell them. Many times . . ."

"I am sure you have, general. You are a military man. You assess the situation clearly. Without emotion and without sentiment. But I must also tell you, general, that it is more serious than even you believe. As you know, I am privy to secret reports from my embassies. Also, I have had in the last two weeks certain private conversations with persons at the highest level of the Benin government. One of the purposes of this meeting, general, is to warn you."

"Warn?" Songo almost shouted. "Of what? What?"

"I only relay this information because of our close personal friendship, the high regard I have for your patriotism, and the hope I know we both share for an even closer relationship in the future through your son Jere and my sister Sara."

"Warn me of what?" Songo agonized.

"Within the past two weeks," Anokye said solemnly, "a high representative of the Benin government asked me what Asante's reaction would be in the event of open warfare between Benin and Togo."

Songo hissed slowly.

"I gave him no direct reply," Anokye went on. "I told him Asante wanted only peace between the two nations. Between *all* African nations. But I felt I would be derelict in my obligation to our friendship if I did not tell you of this. Knowing you are the only man in Togo to whom I can speak so freely. The only man I can be certain of understanding the gravity of the situation. The civilians who control your government would . . ." He shrugged and left the sentence unfinished.

Gen. Kumayo Songo took a deep breath. He was sweating again, his forehead beading, stains in his uniform deepening.

"They mean to attack?" he asked hoarsely.

"That I cannot say. But their question to me indicates the possibility."

"Oh yes," Songo said bitterly. "They plan it, they plan it!"

"I do not know what you can do," Anokye said sadly. "You are a general, true. You command the armed forces. But you . . ."

"Not the entire army," Songo said angrily. "There are units not under my command."

"Of course," Anokye said. "But you have the northern zone. Your forces, in numbers, are the largest in Togo, are they not?"

"That is true."

"Unfortunately, you have no direct voice in foreign policy. Nevertheless, I thought it my duty to warn you."

General Songo stepped forward and placed one large, damp hand on the Little Captain's shoulder.

"For which I extend my thanks and the thanks of my people," he said portentously.

Anokye nodded gravely. "It was my duty," he repeated. "A soldier's duty. I only wish there was some way you could alert your government to the seriousness of the situation."

General Songo gave a short, mean bark of laughter. "They won't become alert to the situation until Benin rockets land in Lomé."

"Ahh," President Obiri Anokye said slowly, as if a solution had just occurred to him. "That presents a possibility. Let us discuss it . . ."

He led the general out farther into the cruel sunlight, knowing how the blaze would weaken the man, deafen him to reason, scramble his wit, and make him eager to conclude any foolish agreement so that he might seek shade and comfort.

"It was the burning of the museum at Ighobo that aroused Benin," Anokye said. "Personally, I do not feel that Togo was guilty of that desecration. But what I believe is of no importance. The Benin believe you did it, and prepare for war. Would not a similar attack by Benin within your borders convince those ostrich civilians who head your government that your nation is in peril?"

Songo looked at him, wet features twisted, not comprehending.

"Well...certainly, Mr. President. A direct attack on Togo would surely make our politicos realize the dangers we face."

"You believe, in the event of war, that Togo could defeat Benin?"

"Of course."

"So do I." Here Anokye paused a moment, poked his head forward, stared at Songo keenly. "Especially with the troops and weapons of Asante."

The general caught his breath. "What are you suggesting, Mr. President?"

"That we, you and I, create an incident that will make war between Togo and Benin inevitable. That when that war begins, troops, tanks, and weapons of Asante are made immediately available—under your command, of course—to aid Togo in that war. That upon the successful completion of hostilities, you yourself—again with Asante's aid—take control of the Togolese government, nation, and people. I did it in Asante; there is no reason why you cannot do it in Togo."

This bright prospect did not stagger Gen. Kumayo Songo. Anokye was certain the man had dreamed it himself. Many times.

Songo began pacing, chin in hand, the other hand supporting the elbow. He did not look at Anokye.

"Possible," he murmured. "Possible. Not for myself, of course. But to rescue my beloved country."

"To be sure," the Little Captain said.

"The poor," Songo said. "The hungry."

"The impoverished masses," President Obiri Anokye added. "With Asante's oil money behind you, so much could be done to forge a great, strong nation. And after the military had stabilized the country, it could be returned to civilian rule. Limited civilian rule. The military would remain strong, a vital policy-making force in government."

"But Mr. President," Songo said, somewhat bewildered, "it all hinges on convincing our present politicians that war with Benin is inevitable. You mentioned creating an incident...?"

President Anokye said he had some ideas on that.

12

Peter Tangent, in England, cabled President Obiri Anokye, in Asante, that he had contacted the management counseling firm of Fisk, Twiggs & Sidebottom, Ltd., of London, and suggested they send a personal representative to Mokodi to learn first-hand from the President what services he required.

Bemused by the names, Anokye rather hoped Mr. Sidebottom would appear. But it was Mr. Samuel Fisk who presented his credentials at the palace and requested an audience with the President. He was a portly, imposing man, clad in a white linen suit, white shirt, white tie, white socks, white shoes. He resembled movie actor Sidney Greenstreet. Just to see him conjured up visions of peacock chairs, beaded curtains, fezzed waiters, and Turkish cigarettes smoked in long ivory holders.

He addressed Anokye as "Dear sir," and was voluble and confident as he outlined what Fisk, Twiggs & Sidebottom, Ltd., could do for the Republic of Asante and for President Anokye personally. A complete on-the-scene examination of all government operations, chain of command, areas of responsibility, work flow, paper handling, production norms, future needs, and so forth. The study would be made by a senior investigator and his assistant, would require a minimum of four weeks and, preferably, would include a time study of the President's daily activities.

"Indispensably necessary, dear sir," Mr. Fisk said. That was the way he talked. Economic factors were "importantly significant." The senior investigator was "knowledgeably experienced." Even Asante was "fruitfully verdant."

At the completion of the survey, the investigators would return to London with the raw data. There, senior analysts would construct a computer model of the present Asante government, including President Anokye's role. By feeding various suggestions to the computer, they could then evolve an improved model that optimized efficiency, minimized intramural conflicts, and futurized consumer needs and production requirements. Recommendations would then be sent to the President outlining a specific program of changes in methodology to achieve the ideal, computer-created Asante.

Somewhat bedazzled by all this, Anokye signed contracts, shook the firm hand of Mr. Samuel Fisk, and showed him to the door, reflecting hopefully that the projected analysis could do no harm, even if it proved useless.

A week later, the senior investigator of Fisk, Twiggs & Sidebottom, Ltd., appeared at the palace in Mokodi, trailed by his assistant. If Mr. Fisk had been Sidney Greenstreet, Ian Quigley was Ronald Colman, and assistant Joan Livesay was Claudette Colbert. And if the Little Captain saw all these personae as movie stars, it was, he decided, because the entire project had a fictional, dream-like quality about it, theatrical and faintly ridiculous.

Quigley was English, though much given to Americanisms—"nuts and bolts," "the nitty-gritty," "separate the men from the boys," "meaningful dialogue," "viable scenario," and so forth. He was a slender, quick man of medium height. Brown hair receding into a widow's peak. Innocent brown eyes. A warm smile and affable manner. His shoes were rubber-soled. And he wore paisley waistcoats and seemed unaffected by the Asante sun.

The assistant, Joan Livesay, was also English, though her accent was subtly different from Quigley's. (Tangent later told Anokye that Quigley's accent was upper, but that of Joan Livesay was "more upper.") She was, perhaps, five centimeters taller than the Little Captain. After her first meeting with him, she was careful to wear flat-heeled shoes or sandals. She also wore white gloves. Constantly. She was a young, quiet, pleasant woman, subdued in appearance, but with a wry wit. She sometimes made him laugh, for which he was grateful. He liked her hair: brown mixed with grey, cut like a boy's, parted on the left and brushed flat to her skull.

During their initial meeting with the President, they explained how they hoped to operate. Ian Quigley would roam all over the place, inspecting staff offices inside the palace and government installations outside. He would ask questions of everyone, armed with a letter of authorization from the President. Joan Livesay would dog the footsteps of Obiri Anokye, keeping a careful account of his daily activities: where he went, what he did, the officials he saw, etc.

"Please understand, Mr. President," Ian Quigley said briskly, "I have no desire to intrude in those areas that are off-limits for reasons of national security. Or for any reasons you deem sufficient. And Miss Livesay has no need to eavesdrop on any conversations or conferences of a confidential nature. Goodness, that's three 'cons' in one sentence. You'll think me a con man. Ha! But in those cases where you desire secrecy, it would help if we could be told the general nature of the work being done. That is, if it concerns foreign relations or military, economic, social, political, or personal matters. Even that much would help us to finalize our report."

"I believe that could be done," Anokye agreed. "Miss Livesay, I fear you will find following me about something of a trial. Not very exciting."

"I'm sure it will prove very interesting, Mr. President," she said politely. Her voice was low and agreeable, and she usually kept her eyes cast down. He thought her possibly shy. Or perhaps it was a professional trick: by self-effacement to fade, as it were, into the walls, so he might come to forget or ignore her presence, and act more naturally, speak more freely.

So the project began. Ian Quigley was here, there, everywhere. He carried a pocket tape recorder into which he dictated low-voiced comments as he roamed. Occasionally he whipped out a miniature Japanese camera and took photographs of office layouts, filing facilities, the exterior of the Mokodi barracks, the fleet of cars used by palace personnel, and so forth.

Each morning, when he came down from his third-floor bedroom to his second-floor office, Obiri Anokye found Joan Livesay awaiting him, steno notebook ready, pen poised. She looked as eager as a sparrow, and after a few days he found himself welcoming her bright, "Good morning, Mr. President!" He had requested that both investigators speak English in his presence. But occasionally Miss Livesay essayed a word or phrase in Akan. She told him she was fascinated by the language and determined to learn it.

By the time Peter Tangent returned to Mokodi, the representatives of Fisk, Twiggs & Sidebottom, Ltd., had become familiar sights about Mokodi, and their presence at palace receptions caused no comment, other than frequently expressed curiosity if they slept together. And if so, did she remove her white gloves and he his paisley waistcoat? There wasn't much else to talk about in Mokodi.

Tangent introduced himself to Ian Quigley at the Mokodi Hilton bar. His first reaction was favorable; he thought Tony Malcolm had selected a good man. Quigley was easy in manner, bright, open. Nothing obviously devious or quirky about him.

Tangent asked, idly, if he had yet made the acquaintance of Jonathon Wilson, the American Cultural Attaché. Quigley said he had not. Tangent proposed bringing them together at an informal dinner.

"You'll like him," he told Quigley. "Your kind of man." There was no reaction to this, but Tangent expected none. He went on: "He knows a lot about Asante, and the government in particular. Might be able to help you out."

"Good," Quigley said. "I need all the help I can get. Very kind of you. Speaking of help, what're my chances of taking a look at those oil rigs of yours?"

"Just say when," Tangent said. "I'll make the arrangements."

"Thank you. Right now I'm trying to get the overview. The oil seems important to Asante's economy."

"Essential," Tangent said. "But I'm prejudiced," he laughed. "Anything else I can do for you?"

"Nooo, not at the moment, thanks. Joan may have some questions."

"Joan?"

"Joan Livesay. My Girl Friday. She's doing the time study on the President's activities. Poor girl—he works late. Was at it till midnight last night. And then, I understand, he took work up to his bedroom."

"Well, she can't follow him there!" Tangent said.

"Not likely," Quigley said. An amused smile. "Not her cup of tea at all, at all. Bit of a mouse, our Joan."

They chatted pleasantly for two drinks. Then Quigley excused himself to go upstairs to his room and transcribe his recorded notes.

"I hope you're getting some useful stuff," Tangent said, looking into the investigator's eyes.

"No doubt about it," Quigley said, staring back at him. "I think the home office will be satisfied."

At the same time Tangent and Ian Quigley were meeting in the Mokodi Hilton bar, Joan Livesay was seated in a straight chair in the palace corridor outside the President's second-floor office and conference room. The chair had been placed there for her convenience during meetings at which her presence, however silent and unobtrusive, was not desired. She accepted this banishment as part of her job; it did not offend her. The chair was placed slightly away from the two armed soldiers guarding the room. It was not a particularly comfortable chair, but she had patience and the gift of repose. She spent her time studying a dictionary of Akan, trying the liquid syllables in a low voice.

About an hour previously, Col. Jim Nkomo, Sam Leiberman, and Sgt. Sene Yeboa had arrived within a few minutes of each other and were immediately admitted to the President's office. The visitors had already met Joan Livesay and greeted her in a friendly fashion, the two blacks calling her "Miss Livesay," and Leiberman calling her "Toots." After the three were present, Anokye had asked her to step outside.

When the three finally emerged, nothing in their expression or manner indicating if they were happy or unhappy with the conference, they nodded good-night to her and stalked away, conversing in low voices. When she reentered the office, President Anokye was replacing in his top desk drawer a sheaf of what appeared to her to be multi-colored maps. He motioned her, not to her usual station on a leather couch in a far corner of the room, but to an armchair at the side of his desk.

"Please forgive the length of the meeting," he said. "But we had much to discuss. It concerned matters of national security."

"May I list the hour as being devoted to military matters, Mr. President?" she asked.

He thought a moment. "Yes," he said. "Military. That should cover it. I think my official day is at an end, Miss Livesay. But first I intend having a cup of coffee. Will you join me."

"Thank you," she said, pleased. "That would be nice."

He lifted his phone and spoke to someone, ordering coffee—and brioche, if they were available.

"That is certainly one improvement needed," he smiled at her after he hung up. "Please make a note in your journal that when the President of Asante desires a cup of coffee in his office, he must call the main-floor receptionist, who then relays the order to the kitchen. I have no direct contact."

"I have already noted it, Mr. President," she said softly. "The palace needs a good intercom system."

"You are very efficient," he said admiringly. "Perhaps some good will come of this after all."

"I'm sure it will," she murmured.

She sat silently while he flipped through the evening edition of the Mokodi New Times. He was, she thought, an attractive man. Not handsome in a conventional way, but—well . . . exciting. There was no mistaking his blunt force. Much of that was physical; his energy seemed limitless. But there was something else. Psychical. His sureness, his absolute certainty. He had the same oneness Ajaka had. But in the butler it was dandyism. In Obiri Anokye it was solemnity of purpose, and absolute belief in his own destiny. She could understand his popularity, why he held so many in thrall. He was complete.

He tossed the paper aside when Ajaka knocked and came padding in with a tray of coffee and pastries.

"Good evening, my president," the butler said, in French. "Good evening, missy."

"Good evening, Ajaka," Miss Livesay said. Of all the people she had met since her arrival in Asante, Ajaka was one of her favorites. She admired the elegance with which he moved, admired his natural, flamboyant display of jewelry, admired his presence, his completeness as a human being. He obviously saw nothing menial in his job, but was proud of his smooth deftness with creamer and sugar tongs.

When the butler had bowed himself out, Anokye and Miss Livesay settled back with coffee cups. No brioche had been available, but Ajaka had brought fresh petit fours.

"You like him?" Anokye said, looking at her shrewdly.

"Ajaka? Oh yes."

"The man is an actor," he laughed. "All Fulani are actors. Fulani is Ajaka's tribe."

"I can't keep the tribes straight," she confessed. "So many of them."

"Tribes are no longer important," he said.

"So you said in your Zabarian speech, Mr. President."

"Oh?" he said. "You read my speech? I am honored. Was the speech noted in London?" He knew very well.

"It surely was," she said. "Printed in full in the *Times*."

"A speech by an African in the *Times*," he marveled.

"Only because it was so short," she said, her smile taking the sting from her words, and they both laughed.

"I am a great believer in short speeches," he said. "If one speaks at length, there is danger of saying too much."

"Or putting your audience to sleep," she said.

"Yes," he agreed. "That, too. Are you familiar with Abraham Lincoln's Gettysburg Address?"

"I've heard of it," she said dryly.

"Very short," he said. "Very powerful."

She leaned forward to select a pastry from the tray on the desk. Sitting slightly to one side of her, he saw the bulge of her breast. It shocked him. He had never noticed her body, never considered her as a woman. She wore prim, cover-up dresses, loosely fashioned, concealing bosom, thighs, buttocks. And those white gloves signaled memsahib to all of Africa, the Middle and Far East. Now he was suddenly conscious of what might exist beneath. Not only beneath the tent-dresses, but beneath the shy, quiet, withdrawn manner. Was there something there?

"You have never been married?" he asked her bluntly.

"No, Mr. President, I never have."

"But you are young. You will be."

"Shall I? I am not certain I wish to be. Some people, I think, should not marry."

He brooded on that for a moment.

"Yes," he said, "that is true. But sometimes it is necessary."

"I haven't yet congratulated you on your approaching marriage, Mr. President."

"Thank you. I hope you will have the opportunity to meet my fiancée. A charming girl."

"I'm sure she is. Will you be working upstairs tonight, Mr. President?"

"Working? Well, if reading is working, then I will be working. And perhaps some correspondence. Personal letters."

"What are you reading? This is not for my notebook. Just personal curiosity."

"What am I reading? Let me see. . . . It is my habit to keep two or three books going at once. Tonight I think I shall read more of a history of the ancient Persian empire. Do you enjoy history?"

"Oh yes. Very much."

"What is your favorite era?"

"Eighteenth-century Europe."

"Oh? My interests, at the moment, go farther back than that. Almost prehistory. Miss Livesay, may I trouble you to draw the drapes for me?"

It was such an odd request, so out of character for him, that she was startled. But obediently she set empty coffee cup and saucer on the desk, rose, walked to the windows, reached up, twitched the drapes closed.

He watched her move. The haunch showing briefly beneath the stuff of her skirt. When she reached high, he saw the strength of her back, indentation of waist. Fine hair clung to her skull like a helmet.

"Thank you," he said, rising. "Your coffee is finished? Then perhaps we will end the day and I will say good-night. I will see you again in the morning."

She had memorized a blessing in Akan. "May you awake stronger and younger," she said.

He looked at her in pleased surprise.

"*Very* good, Miss Livesay," he said, in English. Then he spoke a sentence in Akan.

She shook her head.

"I'm sorry. I didn't catch a word of it."

"I said, 'May your dreams of tonight become the happiness of tomorrow.' "

"Oh," she said faintly. Blushing. "Thank you."

13

"Ahh, this is the life," Sam Leiberman sighed. "I wonder what the poor folks are doing?"

He lolled back in the passenger seat of the white air-conditioned Mercedes-Benz limousine belonging to Starrett Petroleum Corp. Tangent was driving.

With some trepidation, he had invited Leiberman and Dele to join him on a jaunt to Lomé to have dinner with Amina Dunama. They would stay for her performance, perhaps have a few drinks later.

Now the Ivory Coast girl sat happily, cross-legged and alone on the brocaded back seat, working a cat's cradle, while Leiberman slouched comfortably next to Tangent. He smoked a bent Italian cigar, watched the world whiz by as they sped along the coast road to the Togolese border.

"I thought we'd play it by ear," Tangent said casually. "If we're having a good time, we can stay over. No need to drive back tonight."

Leiberman turned his head to look at him, then laughed. "You're as hard to read as a billboard at five paces. Does the cunt know you're coming?"

"Don't call her that," Tangent said sharply.

"Pardon me all to hell, bwana. Does Miss Amina Dunama know you are arriving?"

"No," Tangent said. "I wanted to surprise her."

"Oh, you'll surprise her," Leiberman said. "Probably in the sack with some big black stud. Is that why you brought me along—in case there's trouble?"

"Don't be silly," Tangent said. Wondering if Leiberman was right. "What trouble? If she doesn't want to see me, she doesn't have to. My God, Sam, we're just friends. Acquaintances, really."

"Oh sure," Leiberman said. "And Dele is my mother. Hey, look at that—that's new."

He jerked a thumb at a roadside stand offering le hot dog and les hamburgeurs.

"Haven't seen a McDonald's yet," Leiberman said, "but it's just a question of time. Jesus, how Africa is changing. And so fast. Right in front of my eyes."

"How long have you been out, Sam?"

"Since World War the Second." He was silent a moment, then continued dreamily: "You should have seen it then. All open. Miles and miles of miles and miles. Nothing. I mean nothing. It was glorious. Now witchdoctors get around on Honda motorcycles. Well, what the hell; it had to happen. There was a lot of shit in the old days. Still is, but getting less. Now they got air pollution, hard drugs, and television commercials, just like every other civilized country. Know what did it?"

"What?" Tangent asked.

"Dry martinis," Leiberman said. "Once every gook bartender learned to mix a martini, I knew the end was near."

Tangent laughed. "Wait'll they hear about Harvey Wallbangers."

"Don't tell me," Leiberman said. "I don't want to know."

Armed with their Asante passports (handed over folded on a dash) and official documents, they had no trouble at the border.

"You dig this c—this Amina lady?" Leiberman asked.

"I enjoy her company," Tangent said carefully.

"Tell me, do you really know what the hell you're doing?"

"No," Tangent said.

"Good on you," Leiberman said. "Maybe there's more in your veins than bunker oil number six. Let me tell you something about African women..."

"Tell me, daddy."

"Screw it," Leiberman said. "Learn the hard way—like I did."

Traffic slowed them as they came into Lomé.

"Early for dinner," Leiberman said. "But we can have a few drinks somewhere while you call your ebony Cleopatra."

"Uh," Tangent said. "As a matter of fact, I took a suite at the Europa. I thought it would be handier."

"Oh, you sly goyische devil!"

"Well, they can take care of the car, and we can freshen up."

"Freshen up. Beautiful."

"Shut up," Tangent said. "It has two bedrooms and a sitting room."

"Two bedrooms," Leiberman said. "That *is* handy. One for Dele and Amina, and one for you and me."

"I'm sorry I invited you," Tangent said.

"Well, I do hope you ordered flowers for my room," Leiberman said.

But an hour later, all were in their glory. Leiberman had taken one look at the hotel suite, intoned, "Eminently habitable," had taken off jacket, tie, and shoes, and immediately called room service. Soon he was confortable with a quart of malt Scotch, a siphon of soda, a tub of cubes. Dele, curled on the floor, was spooning madly into a liter of pistachio ice cream. And, after several increasingly desperate phone calls, Peter Tangent had located Amina Dunama, who laughed delightedly when she heard his voice and promised to join them within the hour.

Which she did. Wearing strap sandals on those long, elegant feet Tangent remembered so well. She was also wearing something called "elephant pants"—big, green, floppy slacks that she made at once amusing, chic, and sexy. And a tightly fitted tanktop of bright purple cotton. Gold hoops in her ears. A fake jewel pasted onto the flare of a nostril. Ebony Cleopatra indeed! With a kiss for Dele, a kiss for Sam. A kiss for Peter Tangent.

Laughter. Disco music from a local radio station. And—Tangent pushing his luck—four bottles of champagne brought up and iced by a grinning waiter who became their slave when he discovered that Leiberman spoke Hausa. It was, Tangent decided, going to be all right.

He got her over to a corner, supplied her with a glass of champagne, one of his Players, and placed a hand lightly on her bare shoulder.

"I thought of you," he said in a low voice. "Did you think of me?"

"What was your name again?" she asked.

"Mr. Tangent, sir," he said.

"No." She shook her head. "Sorry. Never heard of such a name."

He had kept a perfect memory of her: the tall, bony, spindliness. Brown skin's midnight sheen at fold of elbow, crease of neck. High cheekbones, high brow. Black curls fitting as snugly as a knitted cap. Slanted, luminous eyes, and a smile so wide, so deep, that the pink gum showed above perfect teeth. And eely arms. He did not think it was her exoticness that moved him. But he was not sure.

"You have been well?" he asked.

"Oh yes. I am never ill. And you?"

"Fine. We came to hear you sing."

"Such a long trip just to hear me sing!"

"Not so long. Can you have dinner with us first?"

"Of course. As usual, I am hungry."

They turned back to Dele and Sam, who were dancing, together but separately, to rhumba rhythm.

"The hippo and the gazelle," Tangent said.

"Whites dance the step, blacks dance the beat," she said.

"And never the twain shall meet," he said.

"Do you believe that?"

"Would I be here if I did? All right, everybody, dinner-time! Where to?"

But their party seemed to be kindling its own joyous momentum, and the business of moving on would halt it. Or so they felt. Dinner in the suite would be the solution. Their very own dining room. Private service. The grinning Hausa waiter was summoned.

They plied him with malt Scotch chased with champagne, and he planned a marvelous dinner for them: prawns in a pepper sauce, whole roast kid with white truffles, baked yams and mashed plantains, a cold salad of imported asparagus and endive. This banquet would be theirs, he assured them, within minutes. And weaved his way out the door.

After thirty minutes had passed, and not even the peppered prawns had put in an appearance, Tangent got on the phone. Not only was their dinner not being prepared, but it had not even been ordered from the kitchen. In any event, a whole roast kid was not available at the Hotel Europa.

Tangent was elected, by acclamation, to investigate. Putting on his dignity with his raw silk jacket, he descended to the hotel kitchen to discover their Hausa waiter had disappeared. He was found, eventually, sleeping peacefully in the laundry room, a smile twitching his lips. After consultation with the chef, Tangent ordered four large broiled veal chops, backed yams, and a salad of mixed greens.

He returned to the suite to find that hunger pains had not diminished the hilarity. His description of the unconscious waiter produced another paroxysm, and they were still laughing, and drinking, when their dinner was wheeled in.

It was escorted by the assistant manager of the Hotel Europa, a fat, fluttery Swiss wearing a morning coat and striped trousers. Because the suite had been reserved in the name of Starrett Petroleum Corp., he had arrived to offer his personal apologies. He couldn't have been sweeter, and Sam Leiberman insisted on kissing him to prove they harbored no ill-will toward him or the Hotel Europa for the loss of their whole roast kid.

The dinner was uproarious, a polyglot contest of English, French, Akan, Yoruba, and Boulé. Leiberman declaimed a limerick in Swahili he said was so obscene that it defied translation. Amina sang a ditty in Fon. Dele chanted a short school verse in Pidgin English. And not to be outdone, Tangent recited, in Latin, the opening paragraph of Caesar's *Gallic Wars*.

Finally, it was time for Amina's performance. She was doing one show a night at a scruffy nightclub out toward Porto-Séguro. It was, in fact, though not even Leiberman was aware of it, the same nightclub where Yakubu had located the politico Nwabala and where Yvonne Mayer had lured him to his doom.

It was crowded that night, plywood bar jammed, most of the tables occupied. The floor creaked and groaned under the stamping feet of frenzied dancers. The air was milky with smoke and smelled of hashish.

"Throats cut while you wait," Leiberman commented.

Tangent paid a healthy dash, and they were escorted to what had originally been a stall, set with a scarred table and two rickety benches. Leiberman insisted they order something sealed. Surprisingly, the harried waiter brought them a half-gallon jug of California zinfandel.

"Now how did this get here?" Tangent wondered.

"Probably a disaster-aid shipment from the U.S.," Leiberman said. "When I was in Biafra, a shipment came in that was ten thousand tubes of shaving cream and sixteen crates of sanitary napkins."

After a while the three-piece band stopped playing and picked up their bottles of millet beer. Some of the dancers returned to the bar or tables. Many just wandered about, carrying their drinks, greeting friends. The crowd was mostly black, but with a dusting of tourists talking loudly and looking as if they expected to be staked out on an anthill any minute.

A waiter made a half-hearted effort to clear the dance floor. He didn't succeed, but there was a small, empty circle for Amina Dunama when she came strolling out slowly, carrying her mandolin. She was wearing the same gown she wore when Tangent first saw her—the silver-grey silk number, hung from her bony shoulders with rhinestone straps. The audience quieted. She strummed a few chords and began to sing.

Something had happened to her voice since Tangent last heard her. Perhaps it was just this one night. Perhaps it was due to the cigarettes she had smoked in the hotel suite, the loud talk and shouted laughter. Whatever the cause, her voice had lost that annoyingly thin, reedy sound, the mechanical phrasing. Now it was low, husky, befitting such a large woman. Maybe he imagined it, since he could not understand the language, but it seemed to him there was genuine feeling, something deepfelt in her that stirred the audience. She ended her song to enthusiastic applause.

"Son of a bitch," Leiberman said. "She's better. Did you hear it?"

"Of course I heard it," Tangent said. "What was it?"

"A love song in Ewe. Hey, she's all right. If she can keep it up."

She did. The wildly applauding audience kept her on for more than an hour. She did several types of things: ballads, fast rhythm numbers, laments. She concluded with a repetitive, guttural, half-screamed song that had the crowd yelling and stamping their feet.

"Dendi war chant," Leiberman said. "Let's go and chop their nuts off—or words to that effect. She's something, isn't she?"

She came over to their table, breathing hard and sweating. She pushed in next to Tangent, waving at the audience who were still yelling and holding their glasses up to her.

Dele, bouncing up and down in excitement, said something to her in Boulé. Amina replied in that language, and both women laughed.

"I told her my voice is changing because of the cigars I smoke," she explained to Tangent. "What did you think?"

"Wonderful," he said warmly. "I think you should stick to the blues numbers. The slow, sad things. Edith Piaf."

"Yes," she nodded. "I think so, too. I am so dry. Some wine, please?"

He filled her glass. Before she drank, she spilled a few drops onto the dusty floor.

"I haven't seen that since I got kicked out of Zambia," Leiberman said. "It's for her ancestors."

"And for good fortune," Amina said. She held up her glass. "For all of us, good fortune."

"I'll drink to that," Leiberman said. "And to anything else anyone would care to mention."

They finished the half-gallon of wine and left the nightclub, Amina still wearing her costume, Tangent carrying her mandolin. There were cabs waiting, and they selected a Peugeot they could all fit in. The driver, speaking a rapid, hissed French, offered marijuana, hashish, heroin, cocaine, opium, penicillin, quinacrine, absinthe with wormwood, milk of magnesia, or love potions. Leiberman told him to fuck off.

Tangent had devised several clever ploys to get Amina back to the hotel. He was about to essay the least fantastic when she said, "Let's go back to the hotel and have something to eat."

"My God, where do you put it?" Leiberman marveled. "You're so skinny that if you swallowed an olive you'd look pregnant. Well, I'll go for coffee and a brandy. Pete?"

"Fine with me," Tangent said carelessly.

The kitchen of the Hotel Europa was closed but a bellhop, made sympathetic with a generous dash, went hunting for an open café, and returned with a cardboard box of pepper chicken, fried shrimp, and something Leiberman called "African matzoh balls."

They sipped coffee and nibbled, more from politeness than hunger. But

Amina worked her way steadily through the contents of the grease-stained box.

"Yum," she said finally, wiping her lips on the edge of the tablecloth. She dumped the naked bones into the box and clapped on the lid. "Now I feel human. What's to drink?"

"Coffee, champagne, brandy," Tangent said. "Which?"

"Everything," she said, and they stared in fascination as she first drained a cup of black coffee, then had a glass of champagne and brandy, mixed half-and-half.

"I can't watch any more of this," Leiberman said. "I hate to see a woman cry."

"I never cry," Amina said.

"Tomorrow you'll cry," he assured her. "Unless you remember that the only sure preventative for a hangover is not to stop drinking." He held the brandy bottle up to the light, then poured a large water tumbler full. "You take the glass," he told Tangent, "and I'll take the bottle. You can have what's left of the champagne."

"Where are you going?"

"Dele and I are going into the bedroom to discuss the International Monetary Fund. Care to join us?"

"No, thanks."

"Ta-ta, all," Leiberman said. "Sleep tight; don't let the bedbugs bite."

He and Dele kissed Amina. They walked slowly, hand in hand, into one of the bedrooms. Their door closed.

"Suddenly everyone's sober," Tangent said, wondering if they had ever been drunk. Not really, he decided. Just high on joy and laughter.

Amina kicked off her sandals, fished the long, thin cigars from her batik bag. She offered him one, but he shook his head. She lighted up, sprawled in a cushioned armchair. She slumped far down, sitting on the edge of her spine, long legs spread beneath the silk gown.

"Tired?" he asked.

She nodded. "Only an hour each night, but it wearies me. That is strange."

"Where do you go next?"

"They're keeping me here for another two weeks. Then on to Cotonou. A nicer place. A hotel lounge. Will you come to see me?"

"Yes," he said immediately.

"Good. I want you to. You are good luck for me."

"Am I?" he said, pleased.

She held out her glass. He divided the remaining champagne between them.

"Brandy?" he asked.

"Later," she said. "Mr. Tangent, sir."

"Oh, you do remember the name?"

She grinned, the wide open, toothy grin that ignited her entire face.

"I have a present for you," he said. "I brought it from London."

"Good," she said. "I like presents. When do I get it?"

"Now if you like."

"No," she said. "Later. After."

"After what?"

"Ho-ho," she said.

She lazily lifted a hand, pointed a long forefinger at him, thumb up, like a cocked gun. Her nails were painted green. How had he not seen her hands before? Slender hands and articulated. Nails curved like talons. Boned, supple hands. Tight knuckles shining. The pink palms were maps.

"Where in the United States were you born, Mr. Tangent?"

"Indiana."

"Is that near California?"

"Not very. It's more in the middle of the country."

"What is it like?"

"Where I was born? Flat farmland. Like most of Asante and Togo."

"Did you like it?"

"No."

"So you left to see the whole, wide world," she said, laughing and clapping her hands delightedly. "Just like me."

"Oh yes," he nodded. "Then I went east to school. Two years in the army. Back to school for two more years of business administration. Then onward and upward. Just like you."

It was the first time he had told a woman the story, the dull story, of his life. He tried to keep it short and make it amusing. But she didn't smile. Just listened intently.

"The army?" she said. "Did you fight in the army? Did you kill?"

"Oh God, no. I made out payrolls."

"But you fought in the Asante coup."

"How do you know that?"

"All of West Africa knows."

"Would you like your present now?"

"No."

"Why not?"

"Because if you give it to me now, you will think what I give to you after is a debt to be paid."

"That's nonsense," he said angrily. "I won't think anything of the sort. You owe me no obligation."

"You are a generous white man being kind to a poor, benighted heathen?"

He groaned, leaped to his feet, raced to her chair, stooped, kissed her upturned lips.

"Oh Mr. Tangent, sir," she breathed, and her tongue flickered like wet flame.

In the bedroom, naked together, she ministered to him, saying, "Hush,

hush," to his moans, like a mother soothing a fretful child. His body was lean, smooth, sprinkled with freckles and tiny black moles. Ribs and vertebrae pressed the skin, and she scraped the bones with her talons, moved her teeth lightly across fluttering abdomen, trembling chest.

"So thin," she murmured. "So white."

Her gaping mouth scrubbed him like a small sponge. When he knew he could not endure, he tried to move her head away, but she imprisoned his hands, hissing faintly, and her tongue stabbed his breast. He looked down upon her and saw a negative of himself, embraced himself, loved himself. He could not comprehend.

He gave her the pearls then, and thought reality equaled expectation for the first time in his life. She was delighted, and doubled the long rope so that chill white spheres dripped about her neck, down between her muscled breasts, coiled about empurpled nipples, rolled into a warm navel as large as a second mouth.

He put his tongue to cool pearls and fevered flesh, his eyes glistening. He lifted one loop of beads from around her neck. Then it hung in a single rope, long enough so that pale moons gleamed between night legs. He took it all into him, night and moon, dry land and moving sea. The taste was tart, spiced, tingling on the tongue, and he didn't care.

In the morning she was gone. Nothing left of her but a dark scent on the pillow, which he kissed like a poet.

He found Dele and Leiberman in the hotel restaurant, having breakfast. He joined them wordlessly and ordered what they were having: melon, croissants, coffee, cognac.

"You can stay a few days if you like," Tangent said. "It's on Starrett."

"Nah," Leiberman said. "Thanks anyway. Let's check out. I have to get back."

"Oh?" Tangent said, not looking at him. "What's happening?"

"Fun and games," Leiberman said.

14

Obiri Anokye would have been astonished if anyone aware of his actions had accused him of corrupting Gen. Kumayo Songo of Togo. Patiently, the Little Captain would have pointed out there was no corruption involved; he had merely made clear to Songo how his interests and those of Anokye coincided, and how the plan he proposed would further those interests. It was simply a matter of mutual benefit. The President had not spoken falsehoods for the sake of his own ambitions; Songo was to become preeminent in Togo, though perhaps not in the role he imagined.

In any event, having been won over, General Songo's cooperation was enthusiastic. He supplied the Little Captain with excellent maps, and revealed information concerning the strength, disposition, weapons, and combat readiness of the Togolese armed forces. Anokye did not think it wise or necessary to inform Songo of the tactics and timing of the "created incident." That way, he assured the general, he could with truth deny detailed knowledge of the raid. And though the Little Captain did not mention it, the lack of detailed knowledge would also prevent a last-minute change of heart and betrayal by the general.

Working with Colonel Nkomo, Sergeant Yeboa, and Sam Leiberman, President Anokye then planned the operation. His first inclination had been to send Leiberman in command of a group of civilian cutthroats, such as Yakubu. Then, if any should fall into Togolese hands, or be killed or wounded on Togolese soil, no proved connection with Asante could be established. (It was true that Leiberman was presently an official advisor to the Asante Government, and if captured might talk. But he was widely known in Africa as a mercenary, available to the highest bidder. Furthermore he was white and, naturally, not to be trusted.)

But as the plan evolved, it became apparent that a military operation was called for. So Anokye decided to send Nkomo, Yeboa, and Leiberman, each commanding a two-man team drawn from a special assault company Anokye had organized in 4th Brigade. It was modeled after the Commando-Ranger concept. The Little Captain hoped eventually to increase it to battalion size with amphibious and airborne landing capabilities.

The personnel having been decided upon, it remained only to plan the approach, attack, and return. The nine men would wear civilian khaki or work clothes with no labels of national origin. They would carry no incriminating identification. Obiri Anokye specified the weapons. This was the kind of thing he did well and enjoyed most.

At midnight, the three three-man teams slipped across the unguarded "green border" into Togo at a point where that country was scarcely 100 km. Wide. The time of the raid had been planned to take advantage of the light of a full moon, and they spent the hours till dawn moving eastward, climbing and descending the north-south chain of the Togo Hills. They used smugglers' trails, Sergeant Yeboa's team leading the way, Leiberman's in the middle, Colonel Nkomo's in the rear. They moved strung out on the trail, the moonlight strong enough to maintain visual contact. By dawn, they had come down onto the flat savanna, and took time out to rest, drink water, eat some food, and relieve themselves in the tall grass.

Within an hour, the three teams had separated and were on their way again, carrying their weapons in flour sacks, burlap bags, or cheap cardboard suitcases strapped to their backs. They hoped to pass as farmers coming from market or itinerants looking for work. If stopped and questioned, Leiberman was prepared to impersonate a drunken white man who had "gone native," a role in which he needed no coaching.

The Little Captain's orders allowed them considerable latitude in their method of traveling, the only requirement being that they arrive at their destination on time. So all three teams, at some point during the day, took advantage of "mammy wagons," a popular mode of transportation in West Africa, particularly favored by the market women who, in some areas, ruled the local economy.

Mammy wagons were ramshackle flatbed trucks with makeshift stake sides and wooden benches. Usually operating on no fixed schedule, stopping whenever and wherever a passenger wished to climb on or off, the rattling trucks offered perfect anonymous transport for the Asante attack teams who blended in with the motley crowds aboard. Their weapons bags attracted no attention; practically everyone else was carrying similar burdens.

As planned, all three teams passed their destination late in the evening and went on close to the border of Benin. Here, at a predetermined map position, they rendezvoused in a wooded area, drank water, ate, slept, and waited for nightfall.

The most important factor of the assault against the selected Togolese army post was that it be made from the east, as if from Benin. Tricky business, since it required that some of the Togolese defenders be allowed to live in order to report the direction from which the attack had come.

The assault was scheduled for 0200, just before the guard was changed. Anokye reasoned that at that hour, despite the alert of Togolese army units ordered since the trouble with Benin began, many of the sentries would be bored with their uneventful tour of duty, nodding on post, or actually asleep.

The Asante force checked their weapons and gear at midnight and, with Yeboa again leading the way, began the final approach. They moved slowly in three columns of three men each, in a rough arrowhead formation, the point (Yeboa) guiding on an unimproved road leading from the Benin border inland to the Togolese army post south of the village of Kamina.

According to information supplied by Gen. Kumayo Songo, the normal strength of the garrison was thirty to thirty-five men commanded by a captain. Weapons were mostly aged bolt-action rifles, a few sidearms, and one antiquated Hotchkiss Modele 1916 machine gun. Perimeter defense was expected to be no more than five sentries. The post was not equipped with floodlights or searchlights, and the transportation was as old as the weapons: a single Ford truck, circa 1950, and the captain's personal Citroën 2-CV.

The six Asante soldiers were armed with Kalashnikov assault rifles. Of the team leaders, Yeboa and Leiberman carried Uzi submachine guns, and Nkomo a Thompson. All the attacking force wore Colt .45 pistols in holsters suspended from web belts, and each team carried a specific type of grenade: fragmentation, incendiary, and smoke. The three team leaders had combat knives. Their men were armed with glaives, the short, razor-sharp machete-swords issued to all Asante soldiers. These were carried in canvas scabbards (with one metal edge), usually worn slung across the back with the glaive hilt protruding above the man's left shoulder for an easy draw.

The Little Captain had ordered that the 4th Brigade assault company be given special training in night operations—not usual for African troops—and this attack group moved through the darkness with confidence and almost complete silence. Visual contact was maintained, and since every man's part in the action had been worked out by Anokye on a sand table at 4th Brigade headquarters, there was little need for verbal communication during the final advance.

In a tactical situation of this nature, convention required surrounding the sleeping army post, or at least making a simultaneous attack from three sides. But as the Little Captain remarked, "Strategy dictates tactics." (He was fond of quoting military aphorisms.) So the attack was made only from the east, from the direction of the Benin border.

Col. Jim Nkomo was an enormous man, tall and broad, with a solid belief in his own invincibility. This, during battle, he translated into laughing courage. He grew a heavy black beard and a mustache that almost obscured his lips. His body, too, was covered with a pelt of thick, wiry hair. Leiberman called him "King Kong," a title he cherished. His tank corps were proud of him, although their respect was tinged with fear that he would, one day, get their ass shot off.

The Little Captain had selected Nkomo to lead the assault, Yeboa and Leiberman on the flanks.

The moon had set. As they came silently up to the compound, only the light of a small fire illuminated the dim outlines of the post itself: a low building of mud brick with a thatched roof. Two smaller outbuildings. The parked vehicles. The Asantis halted while Nkomo studied the terrain. Two uniformed men slept near the fire. After a few moments, a third soldier came from one of the smaller buildings and joined them, sitting on the ground, hugging his knees.

Nkomo sent his men to left and right to scout for additional sentries. The other Asantis lay full-length in undergrowth just short of the cleared compound. Nkomo's men returned within five minutes. They shook their heads. Nkomo then rose to a crouch and looked to both sides. Yeboa and Leiberman signaled their readiness.

The colonel straightened up. He threw a fragmentation grenade at the sentries' fire. He hurled it in a curious manner, not the recommended put-toss. He pitched it half-underhand, half-sidearm: a cross between an American softball pitcher and a British cricket bowler. The grenade sailed through the air. It exploded almost directly in the sentries' fire.

The two sleeping men were hit by splinters and died without waking, their relaxed bodies absorbing the steel like bundles of rags taking axe blows. The sitting man was flung backward, his heart exposed by a small section of the serrated grenade that cut him open as neatly as a glaive.

All the Asantis were on their feet then, crouching. Leiberman's team hurled incendiary grenades onto the roofs of the main barrack, the outbuildings, the vehicles. Anokye's orders. When half-dressed and naked men came stumbling out into the night, Yeboa's team killed them with short bursts from automatic weapons.

The first Togolese soldiers were without guns. But those who came dashing out a few moments later fired rifles into the darkness, aiming at their attackers' gun flashes. A few weapons began to wink from the post's windows and doorways.

Nkomo pitched another grenade and, waving his men on, rushed after it, firing his Thompson, grinning. The roof of the post was aflame now; both sides could see their targets clearly.

Leiberman led his men in a rush, firing his Uzi in staccato bursts. He was not surprised to find he was screaming as wildly as the Asantis. He dropped to one knee, spraying the windows and doorways from which most of the return fire was coming. More fragmentation grenades exploded inside the main building. The roof seemed to rise a few inches, then collapsed inside the walls.

A grossly fat Togolese soldier came tiptoeing in a dainty way from the flaming ruins, firing his rifle as quickly as he could work the bolt. His face was squinched with fear and shock. He was naked. His obese body glistened; the pores seemed to exude grease. Several Asanti guns were brought to bear on this huge target, as if the attackers feared a single bullet could never bring down that great hulk. But down he went, falling face-forward into the dust, billows of suet pocked with a score of holes that oozed blood slowly.

The Asantis closed on a tight line. Anokye's orders. But not without casualties. One of Nkomo's men went spinning backward, jaw shot away. One of Leiberman's men sat down suddenly, hands pressing his belly in bewilderment. Still they crushed forward, driving the Togolese back. They were reddened by flames, blood, fury.

Into the burning building itself. Men pressed thigh to thigh, hot and screaming, eyes glaring. A few defenders battered and scrambled their way out over the crumbling rear wall. Those who chose to stand held up empty rifles in an attempt to ward off the flashing glaives. An entire head went sailing, the trunk standing a moment, spouting blood from the severed neck before crumpling to earth. An arm lying by itself in the dust, fingers slowly flexing. An ear. Things.

Then all Togolese within the post were down. The Asantis heard the sound of survivors crashing through the bush westward, heard a long, keening wail that seemed never to end.

They killed all the wounded, they mutilated all the dead. Anokye's orders. Then they regrouped. Nkomo's man, the one with the jaw shot away, was dead. Leiberman's soldier, the one with the belly wound, was still alive and conscious. He looked up at them meekly. Sergeant Yeboa stooped over him, patted his cheek, put his Colt .45 close to the man's temple, pulled the trigger once. They threw their two casualties into the burning building. There were other wounds, but minor. Everyone alive could move under his own power.

They tossed a ring of smoke grenades in case brave survivors attempted pursuit. They retreated eastward to pick up their gear, to conceal weapons in sacks, bags, suitcases. Then the teams separated, moved south as planned, struck out westward, heading home in mammy wagons.

15

Beatrice Da Silva, mistress of her father's home, sat at the foot of the long glass table and peremptorily rang a small crystal bell. Immediately, three servants— one Ewe, two Cabrai—entered and began deftly to clear the table of the dinner dishes. Obiri Anokye looked admiringly at Beatrice. She sat haughty, upright, watching the servants' movements with keen eyes. He began to get a new insight into what she might be: a slave in the bedroom, a tyrant in the kitchen. He was not displeased.

She was plumpish and jolly, more girl than woman. A ruddy glow beneath the dark brown of her skin. Deep-bosomed, wide-hipped, with smooth, exciting legs. A face unmarked by experience or reflection. A tittering laugh, a swollen-eyed engrossment in anything a man might say to her. To which she would reply, "Really? Fantastic! How marvelous!" and so on. Anokye believed her a virgin, burning.

Premier Benedicto da Silva sat regally at the head of the table. President Anokye on his right. On Anokye's right, Asante Minister of State Jean-Louis Duclos. Across from them, in casual loneliness, Christophe Michaux, the Premier's aide. He touched his little goatee occasionally, once or twice patted his marcelled and oiled hair. The significant glances he aimed at Duclos did not go unnoticed by Anokye. But he was watching for them, alerted by Sam Leiberman's report.

"This Michaux cat, Mr. President," Leiberman had said. "The way I get it, he's playing footsie with the Reds. The Russians, not the Chinese. There's both varieties in Benin right now, lots of them, and more coming in. The way I hear it, Michaux is King Shit with Moscow. Maybe they're grooming him to take over."

"Da Silva is aware of this?"

"My source says no. Da Silva knows his secretary leans to the left, but he thinks Michaux is just a brainy kid kicking up his heels. I mean, Michaux isn't an out-and-out Marxist. Not in public, he ain't. He covers it with an 'Africa for the Africans' line. Solidarity forever and let's kill all the whites. That kind of crap."

"His private life?"

"That's where it gets sticky. Back in the States they call 'em chickenhawks. Meaning he likes little boys. We all like little boys, Mr. President, but not the way Michaux does. I mean he *likes* them."

"I see," Anokye said. "Thank you."

Premier Da Silva looked at his daughter, and she immediately rose.

"Please don't get up, gentlemen," she said, smiling sweetly. She spoke a very Parisian French. "Continue your conversation. I'll see to coffee."

"Perhaps the Portuguese brandy," her father said.

"Of course, daddy," she nodded, and was gone.

"An excellent meal, Premier," President Anokye said. "I thank you."

The others also murmured their appreciation. They spoke in generalities of the problems in Angola while coffee was served, brandy poured into proper snifters. When the servants had departed, door closed, Premier Da Silva addressed Anokye directly, his face drawn and solemn.

"I pledge you my word of honor, Mr. President," he said in a somewhat hollow, shaky voice. "We had nothing to do with it."

He spoke, of course, of the cruel raid on the Togolese army post. Men mutilated. A massacre that had brought Togo and Benin close to war.

Anokye made a gesture, as if to say he accepted Da Silva's word without question.

"But I must ask you this, Premier," he said, "is it possible the attack could have been planned and executed by your military without your knowledge? By hotheads who would like nothing better than a declared war?"

Da Silva was troubled.

"I will not say we do not have such men in our military," he said slowly. "What country does not? But I cannot believe they would go to such lengths. Christophe?"

"I agree with you, Premier," Michaux said promptly. "In my own mind I cannot conceive of any Benin engaging in such an insane act."

"Nationalists?" Doclos suggested. "Fanatics? Terrorists?"

Michaux waved the suggestion away.

"A few minor groups," he said. "Ineffectual. Ridiculous, really. And constantly under watch. They are not capable of such an attack."

Obiri Anokye looked at him directly.

"Then what is your explanation?"

"I simply do not know, Mr. President. But in my own mind, I have a—a foreboding that we are being manipulated. By an outside force. The CIA, perhaps."

"Nonsense," Da Silva said curtly. "Next you will be blaming them for our lack of rainfall."

"It is possible they staged the raid, Premier," Michaux said stubbornly. "They move in hidden ways. And, of course, they have the money to buy these things—the murder of Nwabala, the burning of our museum, the massacre at Kamina."

"For what purpose?" Anokye asked softly.

"Who can tell, Mr. President? Perhaps they merely wish to make mischief, to provoke a war that ruins both countries. Then they step in and take over."

"Take over the ruins?" Anokye said. "Why would the U.S. or any other power desire to control Togo and Benin? With all due respect, Premier, your country and Togo are not economically sound. Your national resources are not sufficient to attract any of the great powers. But you are aware of this . . ."

"Unfortunately," nodded Da Silva mournfully. "Christophe, I cannot swallow your theory. As president Anokye said, we and Togo, together, do not represent one fish large enough to tempt anyone to cast bait. No, I do not believe the CIA is involved."

Michaux would not give up.

"Their motives do not become clear until later," he said, his words sounding foolish even to his own ears.

Then they sat in silence. Anokye was content, letting it grow. Knowing the gloom of the Benin. Finally he looked at Duclos, at Michaux.

"Please," he said gently, "I would like a few moments alone with the Premier. Jean, I will see you on the plane in the morning."

The two aides rose, murmured something polite, withdrew. Anokye waited until the door closed behind them. Then he hitched his chair closer to Da Silva.

"Courage, brother," he said. "Things are not as desperate as they may seem."

"Not desperate," Da Silva said, waving his hand. "But bleak. Depressing."

"May we speak frankly? As brothers?"

"Of course."

"I have heard, from various sources, that Russian agents are active in your country. Very active. Is that true?"

"Yes."

"I have heard further that it may be a serious attempt to subvert the government of Benin. Do you have any information on that?"

"It—it may well be," Da Silva admitted. "They have won many friends in high places. They have made loans, taken over farms, factories, banks. They are now a force to be reckoned with."

"How do you feel about this?"

"Need you ask, Mr. President? I am a Benin, wanting only the continued independence of my country. And now there is this business with Togo. On top of our economic problems. It is all complex. Messy."

"All life is complex and messy, Premier. We find simplicity in the grave. Meanwhile, we must look for solutions."

Da Silva looked up hopefully.

"You have a solution, Mr. President?"

"Only a suggestion. A suggestion I wish you to consider carefully. You and I are close and will soon be closer, after my marriage to your daughter. You know of Asante's wealth from the oil. That wealth could help solve your economic problems. I have also modernized the Asante armed forces. They grow stronger every day. More men. New Weapons. Powerful. The best in the world. Those men and those weapons could insure the victory of Benin in the event of open war with Togo."

Da Silva began to brighten, almost growing before Anokye's eyes. He straightened in his chair, sat erect. His eyes glistened. Even the silvered beard seemed to bristle.

"So now we have solved two of the problems that beset you," Anokye went on relentlessly. "Asante wealth will help you make your economy viable. Asante weapons will guarantee you victory in case of a war with Togo. Now, how may we assure the sovereignty of Benin against the aggression of the Marxists?"

The Premier listened to this lecture with fascination. The Little Captain was saying everything he wanted to hear. It seemed to him that this evening, this talk, might prove to be a turning point. In his country's destiny, and in his own career.

"I tell you frankly," Anokye said, "and I speak the truth, you are the only man I trust."

He spoke this last in Portuguese. Da Silva was touched.

"Excellent, Mr. President," he said, in French. "Your accent is improving."

"Thank you. I study hard. But in any language, my meaning is the same: you, I trust. The others, the politicos, I do not trust. They are not aware of the true situation."

"They are not," Da Silva said hoarsely. "I agree."

"I will not pledge Asante wealth and Asante weapons to a country in whose government I do not have the most complete confidence," Anokye said sternly. "Do you condemn me for this?"

"Of course not, Mr. President," the Premier said hastily. "It is only common sense."

"Exactly. Common sense. Now I shall tell you what my price is for Asante francs to shore up your economy and for Asante men and weapons to insure your victory over the Togolese."

"The price?" Da Silva said. He feared the worst. This man might demand—God only knew what this resolute man might demand! "What is your price, Mr. President?"

"That you become the leader of Benin. You are a man I can trust. We shall soon be related. I know that with you in control, I can be confident that the very considerable investment I am willing to make in Benin will not be wasted on fools or those who follow foreign ideologies."

Benedicto da Silva groaned with relief and gratification. He could hardly believe his good fortune. He knew, he *knew*, all the good things he could do if he was head of state. And for agreeing to take on this task—awesome and onerous though it might be—he would guarantee his nation the beneficence of a wealthy and powerful friend.

"Mr. President," he said, rising, "I want only what is best for my country."

"I knew I could count on you," the Little Captain said, also rising. The two men shook hands, staring gravely into each other's eyes. "And now the hour is becoming late, and I must leave. I thank you for your hospitality. But I would also like to thank Beatrice. A few words before I return to Mokodi. I think I would enjoy a final cigarette on your lovely patio. If you would—?"

"I'll send her out to you, Mr. President," Premier Benedicto da Silva said quickly, "At once, sir."

Anokye strolled up and down, smoking his Gauloise and looking at the stars. They belonged to him. One told men what they wanted to hear; it was as simple as that. But still, one never spoke a falsehood, which was a sin. Da Silva would become preeminent in Benin, just as General Songo would in Togo. And both bound to him by ties stronger than political expediency. Blood. Family. It was history, in all the books. Not dates and events. History was people.

"Bibi!" she said, coming to him with outspread arms. "You are leaving? So soon!"

"So late," he grinned, tossing his cigarette away. He pressed her to him. "First, the dinner. . . . It was a thing to remember. But I beseech you, when we are married, we cannot eat like that every night. Look at this . . ."

He patted his growing paunch. Then smiled when she patted it, too.

"I promise," she said. "Only mixed greens and perhaps some cold rice."

"Well . . ." he said. "Occasionally, the broiled grouper as you served it tonight."

"Oh!" she said, delighted. "I knew you would like it. And the chicken?"

"Magnificent," he said. "With white wine?"

"Yes," she nodded. "And bits of this and that. I learned in Paris. At school."

They strolled up and down together, his arm about her waist. She was wearing a flowing chiffon gown. Tent-like. In green. Her favorite color. Her scent was so young, so fruity. He thought of the juices.

"You set the date," he said. "As soon as possible. Within two months."

"So much to do," she said, and shivered slightly. Not so much troubled by the planning as by the sudden vision of lying naked in bed with this man. This stranger. "I don't know where it should be."

"In Asante," he said. "The palace." He laughed. "I will declare a national holiday. We shall receive many fine gifts. From all over the world."

"Oh Bibi," she sighed. "I love you so much. We're going to have such a fantastic life."

He didn't answer, but embraced her again. Kissed her warm lips. Her mouth opened to his in surrender. As his fingers pressed her back, her soft back, her soft, yielding back. All of her yielding, and soft, and warm. Conquered.

To his surprise, Jean-Louis Duclos discovered that Christophe Michaux was driving a Renault 30TS. On the way back to Cotonou from Premier Da Silva's home near Ouidah, Duclos expressed his pleasure at riding in such a luxurious car.

"So expensive," he murmured, believing it to be a government vehicle that Michaux had borrowed for the evening.

"I was going to get a light blue," Michaux said casually. "Then decided on the black. So much more tasteful, don't you think?"

"Oh yes."

"Black is beautiful," Michaux laughed.

He drove with careless ease, relaxed, fingertips barely touching the wheel. Duclos was conscious of his scent. Sandalwood perhaps.

"I was surprised President Anokye did not desire your presence during his conference with the Premier," Michaux said. He kept his eyes on the road.

Duclos stirred restlessly.

"Sometimes more is accomplished between two men, with no third party present," he said.

"Of course," Michaux said. He laughed suddenly. "Best to have no witnesses, eh?" When Duclos said nothing, Michaux continued: "The Premier, on occasion, has not desired my presence during a conversation. But I can usually guess what is going on. I imagine their conversation tonight concerns the Togo matter. No?"

"Perhaps," Duclos said, uneasy with this conversation. "Or the marriage of President Anokye to the Premier's daughter."

"Or that," Michaux admitted. "Or both. Together. President Anokye is a very—I was about to use the word 'devious,' but I don't mean that at all. A very *complex* man. Yes, that is better. Don't you agree he is complex?"

"No, I do not," Duclos said shortly. "It seems to me his aims are quite clear. As stated in his Zabarian speech."

"Ah yes," Michaux said. "But I was not speaking of his stated aims. I had in mind his motives; his desires. But of course you would know more of that than I. You said you have been friends for many years? Even before the coup?"

"That is true. He has been to my home frequently."

"A friend of the family, so to speak. Please forgive me for not having asked sooner, but how is Mrs. Duclos? Well, I hope?"

"Thank you, yes. In good health."

"I am delighted to hear it. I gathered from our short conversation that she has no particular interest in the business of government. Am I wrong?"

"No, you are quite right. Maria is interested only in domestic things. Our home . . ."

"A charming lady. You are to be congratulated, minister, for selecting an African woman to be your wife. It offends me to see so many African leaders sniffing after white bitches. Forgive the coarseness of my language, but I must speak what is in my mind. To me, negritude is of primary importance."

"To me also," Duclos said.

"Good," Michaux said. "The men we are about to meet feel as we do. I think you will like them. Not much farther now."

Jean-Louis Duclos had the right to call himself "Professor." He had been, and now he was Minister of State of the Republic of Asante. By law, he was third in rank in the Asante government, following only President Obiri Anokye and Premier Willi Abraham. His was an office of some consequence, remarkable for one as light-skinned as he. In addition, he was a Martinicain, not an African, by birth.

So, in view of these honors, why, he asked himself, should he feel such inferiority to this Christophe Michaux? The man was almost as light-skinned as he, also a Martinicain, and no more than a premier's aide. Practically a secretary. He was, he decided finally, daunted by Michaux's almost insolent self-assurance. When speaking of Obiri Anokye, his tone verged almost on contempt. As if he knew something Duclos did not know.

In addition, Duclos was as disturbed by certain portions of the Little Captain's Zabarian speech as Michaux. The Minister of State was aware that Anokye was an expedient man. The coup would not have been successful if he were not. But now, in a position of great power, president of a wealthy African state, Anokye had no need to compromise with his enemies. Whites. Yet in his speech Anokye had publicly favored a united Africa, shared by all races, colors, creeds. It was troublesome. More so because Michaux made no effort to hide his disapproval. And Duclos, in good conscience, could not defend the Little Captain.

He had supposed the premier's aide had invited him to an informal party, a get-together. He recognized almost immediately that he was attending a meeting of sorts.

It was held in a secluded private home, near the sea, off the Porto-Novo road. There were several cars already parked in the driveway when they arrived. A few government cars and two obviously military vehicles. It was also apparent to Jean-Louis Duclos that he and Michaux were the last arrivals expected; the proceedings began as soon as Duclos was introduced to the host, a glass of warm orange juice passed to him, and the lights dimmed.

The speaker, a thin, ascetic black, introduced himself to the twenty men in the room as Sumaila Jakpa, a citizen of Benin. He had, he said, recently returned from two years in the Soviet Union, during which he had been enrolled as a student of political science in Moscow University. In answer to many requests, he was presenting this short lecture—more of a personal account, really—on his experiences in Russia.

The first part of the presentation consisted of a series of color slides (of professional quality) showing various views of the Soviet Union: the Kremlin, Moscow streets, restaurants, and hotels, a tractor factory, a resort on the Black Sea, closeup portraits of several of the many ethnic types who composed the Union of Soviet Socialist Republics.

Then the lights were turned up again. The speaker delivered a fluent précis of his experiences in the Soviet Union: the food (unusual but palatable), the weather (extremely cold but invigorating), the hospitality of the Russian people (superlative), racism (non-existent), and sympathy for the African cause (overwhelming). The meeting was then thrown open to questions.

Q: How was his two years' stay in Moscow financed?

A: By personal funds and a scholarship from the Soviet Union, available to students from all over the world.

Q: During his studies in political science, were efforts made to convert him to socialism?

A: Absolutely not. The lectures were historical in nature, and it was frequently emphasized that students were expected to return to their native countries and make their newfound knowledge and skills available to their governments, whatever their position in the political spectrum.

Q: Had attempts ever been made to recruit him into a Soviet intelligence apparat?

A: Never. Nor was he ever, to his knowledge, spied upon, followed, his mail intercepted, or his rights of free movement and expression interfered with.

He concluded by saying:

"I do not wish to leave you with the impression that the USSR is a paradise. Of course it is not. They have many problems, serious problems, not the least of which is the constant military threat posed by the USA and China. This requires Russia to devote an inordinately large share of its gross income to national defense. This is money they would much prefer to spend for such things as schools, hospitals, housing, consumer goods, and so forth. Just as we Africans would like to do.

"One final word: At no time during my two years' stay, *no* time, was I ever insulted or made to feel inferior because of my color or national origin. At a final party, when all the black students met with our professor, he reiterated in the strongest terms the Soviet Union's interest in and sympathy for black hegemony, wherever in the world blacks were still being exploited and suffering under the grinding heel of white colonialism. And he said—I remember this well—he said, 'All we ask is that you judge us by our deeds, not our words. A helping hand will always be extended from the USSR to people of any race or color groaning under oppressive tyranny. These people, in Africa and elsewhere, will find in us a good friend who desires only to free them from the tyrants' yoke and enable them to determine their own destiny as free and independent nations.' Stirring words. I shall never forget them."

The formal program then ended, and the meeting broke up into several small groups. All were talking excitedly, most of the guests trying to press close to the speaker to ask additional questions. Duclos found himself led aside by Michaux, to be introduced to two men in the Benin government. One was a statistician attached to the Ministry of Agriculture, the other an assistant to the Minister of Transportation and Communication. Like Duclos and Michaux, both government employees wore black suits, white shirts, sedate ties. They chatted a few moments, exchanging their reactions to the presentation of the Benin student.

"What did *you* think, minister?" Michaux asked.

"Very impressive," Duclos nodded. "If we can believe what they say."

"Of course," one of the others said. "But as his professor said: 'Judge us by our deeds, not our words.' And it is worthy of note that the USSR owns not a foot of African soil, and has shown no desire for any. It may be true that they have a few minor installations here and there—refueling stations for their navy, that kind of thing—but only on sufferance of the host nation."

"I was particularly interested in his comments on their views of African hegemony," Michaux said. "Africa for the Africans. Did you find that struck a sympathetic chord, minister?"

"Oh yes," Duclos agreed. "If we can trust them. After all, they too are white."

Following the student's presentation, iced highballs, cocktails, and wine had been offered in place of the warm orange juice. And after two heavy gin and bitters, Duclos found himself with senses heightened, well able to cope with whatever subjects were introduced or questions asked by these elegant men who were so obviously respectful of his station and anxious to learn his views.

The conversation bubbled. It was years since Jean-Louis Duclos had engaged in such lively discussion and debate. He was intoxicated by it, made drunk with words, the clash of ideas, the blaze of intellects, the display of philosophical depths. He was proud of these black brothers, proud of their wit, their obvious concern for the welfare and future of black Africa. And he was proud of himself, taking another gin and bitters from Michaux's outstretched hand, proud of the things he said, the way he fielded their questions, refuted their illogic, scored intellectual points. He was, he felt, their superior in political history and political science. Somehow, the conversation came around to Obiri Anokye's Zabarian speech.

"An excellent speech," one of the Benin officials declared. "Still, I wish President Anokye had stated more clearly how he intends to achieve his dream of Pan-Africa."

"He will make it plain," Duclos said wisely. "All in good time."

"But surely, minister, you can appreciate that his comments have caused concern in some quarters. Now I specifically refer to his embracement of the whites. No one can argue against the ideal of solidarity for the African continent. But why need it include whites?"

"True," Michaux said. "And what whites does he wish to include? Rhodesian whites? South African whites? The whites who own the oil wells in his own country—the American whites?"

"A point there," the other government official said. "We cannot condemn all 'white devils' and refuse to accept aid from any."

"Still," Michaux said, "the slaves went to America, not to Russia. But I have no objection to white aid, providing it does not diminish our independence. Do you agree, minister?"

"Absolutely," Duclos said. Vaguely conscious it came out. "Abslutey." "We have all suffered enough from white barbarism. Economic barbarism. Military savagery. Insults. Dedegration. Degradation. There must be an end to it."

"I am glad to hear you say that," Christophe Michaux said warmly. He placed his hands on Duclos' shoulders and stared solemnly into his eyes. "You have a marvelous gift of expression. You put into exact words what we all feel. We are brothers."

"Brothers!" said Duclos. So loudly that several others in the room stopped speaking and turned to glance at him.

Michaux handed him another gin and bitters, then raised his own glass.

"Death to our enemies," he said.

16

The residents of Mokodi might view the activities of Ian Quigley with amusement (calling him "Supersnoop"), but there was little doubt that the chief investigator for Fisk, Twiggs & Sidebottom, Ltd., approached his assignment with energy and zeal. He was everywhere with his tape recorder and little camera, clocking the traffic flow on the Boulevard Voltaire, inspecting the phosphate mines, charting the course of a passport application, timing the unloading, storage, and sale of perishables from the Gonjan markets.

Armed with the letter of authorization from Obiri Anokye, he was even able to inspect military installations and armories, board the several small craft of the Asante National Navy, and review operations of the air force.

"He will end up knowing more about Asante than I do," President Anokye said to Joan Livesay. "Mr. Leiberman tells me Quigley went far to the north, almost to Four Points, to do something called a time-motion study on goat herdsmen."

Livesay laughed. Anokye liked her laugh. Sturdy and resonant.

"I think Mr. Leiberman exaggerates," she said. "Ian did go north, but only to get a first-hand look at the economy of the region. I suppose goat-herding is a part of that economy."

It was Anokye's turn to laugh.

"In some areas, it *is* the economy," he said. "From the goat comes milk, cheese, meat, hair, skins. A very valuable national asset. How much longer will you and Mr. Quigley continue?"

"We hope to finish up in two weeks."

"I imagine you will be happy to see the last of Asante."

"Not at all, Mr. President. I can't speak for Ian, but this has been one of the happiest months of my life. I've enjoyed every minute of it."

"I am glad to hear that, Joan. You like Asante, do you?"

"Very, very much. The sun. The sea. But mostly the friendliness of the people."

"Yes. They are good people."

She looked down at the notebook in her lap, fingers twisting.

"Your friendliness, Mr. President," she said in a low voice. "It has been a great help. I know it hasn't been pleasant for you having me hang about all the time. You have been very kind."

He waved her thanks away.

"It is for my own benefit," he said. "If it aids you to—what is it Mr. Quigley says?—to optimize my performance."

He said it so wryly that she looked up at him smiling. It was early evening, the office lights not yet on. He would, he had told her, soon have a private conference with Willi Abraham, Jean-Louis Duclos and Mai Fante, concerning foreign relations. Followed by a meeting with the Minister of Tourism regarding publicity on the new gambling casino being built—a meeting she was welcome to attend. This would be followed by his weekly lesson in Portuguese, tutored by a junior clerk from the Portuguese Embassy. This would be followed by a private conversation with Peter Tangent. She could mark in her notebook that it would concern economic matters. Oil revenues. And finally, he would motor to the Mokodi barracks to observe a night operation by the special attack company of 4th Brigade.

"Where do you find the energy?" she marveled.

"I was born strong," he said. "That is to God's credit, not mine. But also, I have the—the determination."

"That is to your credit," she said softly.

They sat quietly in the dimness, comfortable in each other's presence. He stared at the sleek helmet of her hair. She had the perfect complexion of so many Englishwomen, rosied now by the Asante sun. He saw the crisp features in silhouette. Her chin and throat seemed to him so tender that if he touched them, ever so gently, they might retain the impress of his fingers. He wondered, idly, how old she was. Older than he, he guessed. By a few years.

"And what will you do when you return to England, Joan?"

"Finish up my part of the report. Make my recommendations. I'll probably have a holiday, a few days, before my next job."

"You have family?"

"Only a father living. And some distant cousins."

"You live with your father?"

"No," she said. Something in her eyes. "He is in a nursing home. A kind of hospital."

"I am sorry to hear that. It must be lonely for you."

"I try to keep busy."

"That is best," he nodded. "But you have friends, of course?"

"Of course."

"And what do you do in London? Parties? The theatre?"

"Oh yes. And museums. Concerts. Things of that sort."

"So it is not so lonely?"

"Sometimes," she said.

"For all of us, Joan," he said. "Sometimes."

Then they sat together in silence a few close moments. Their reverie was ended by the arrival of Abraham, Duclos, and Fante. The Attorney General was carrying a small black gripsack, something like a doctor's bag. As Joan Livesay was moving to her chair outside in the corridor, Sgt. Sene Yeboa arrived, and smiled at her. He went into the President's office for a moment and then emerged carrying the black bag that had been brought by Fante. Then the door of the study closed and was locked from the inside. Joan Livesay opened her dictionary and began to whisper Akan verbs.

President Anokye made his guests comfortable in armchairs facing his desk. He put out cigarettes, a box of Sumatran cigars, a decanter of Italian brandy. He lounged back in his swivel chair, picked up the painted model of the Asante army captain, turned it slowly in his fingers.

"The Togo-Benin operation goes well," he reported to them. "Please forgive me for not informing you of what has been done, but so far all activities have been of a military nature, and I did not desire that you be involved. Your time is too valuable to be spent on details better left to military professionals."

How like the Little Captain, Willi Abraham thought. To tell them they had no need to know, and to soften this implied denigration of their status by telling them they were too important to be involved.

"If all goes well," Anokye continued, "we can count on de facto control of both countries within a month or so."

There was a hissing intake of breath. Anokye looked up to see who had reacted. His gaze settled on Fante.

"Mai," he said, "you are surprised?"

"Only at the timing, Mr. President. So soon?"

"Oh yes," Anokye nodded gravely. "It must be done quickly. These things have a rhythm of their own. If we dawdle, we are lost."

"Assuming all goes as you plan, Bibi," Abraham said, "then what?"

"Precisely, Willi: Then what? The reason I have asked you here tonight. Jean, you remember that when the coup was still in the planning stage, I asked you to begin designing the government of the new Asante. So when we succeeded in overthrowing Prempeh, we were able almost immediately to present to the Asante people a complete constitution for the republic, tailored to their needs and desires. Some mistakes were made, true, but generally I feel the constitution is working well."

"Remarkably well, Mr. President," Mai Fante said. "Hardly a week goes by without my receiving a request from an African nation for a copy of our constitution, codes of civil and criminal law, and so forth."

"Very encouraging. You have worked hard, Mai. You all have. I think the stability of the country proves you have worked well."

"Thank you, Mr. President," the Attorney General said proudly. "We still have far to go, but the way forward is shorter than the road already traveled."

He was a clear-eyed older man, silver-haired, who moved lithely, youthfully. He wore suits of polished grey silk, always casual, always elegant. It was said he was related, closely or distantly, by blood or by marriage, to half the citizens of Asante. There was no doubt he had the natural politician's gift for remembering names, faces, familial ties. Which was one reason Obiri Anokye had appointed him national chairman of the League of Liberty, the Little Captain's political party.

"To continue," President Anokye said. "I believe the time has come to consider how we may administer the governments of Togo and Benin. And other countries that come under our hegemony in the future. Not only in the best interests of those countries, but to further our aim of a Pan-Africa. You three men are my best trusted advisors. You know I speak the truth. I ask you now for your ideas on the nature of the union we must form with other African nations. Jean?"

"A—a sort of United States of Africa?" Duclos said slowly. "Based on the American model of several states joined in a partnership by and to a federal government?"

"Not another USA," Willi Abraham smiled. "We would have to call it United African States, UAS, to avoid confusion. But I am not certain the American model is suitable for Africa."

"Nor I," Anokye said.

"Perhaps a looser federation," Mai Fante suggested. "Similar to the British Commonwealth."

"Too loose," Duclos said. "That is just a sentimental club of sovereign states."

"I think," Anokye said, "rather than attempt to adopt or adapt an existing system, it would be best if we first decide what characteristics we desire our system to possess, and then design it with those requirements in mind."

"Very sound, Bibi," Abraham nodded approvingly. "As usual, you go to the basics. I will start off. Our federation, first of all, must have a single monetary system."

"Good," Anokye said. "I agree. Now you, Mai."

"A single code of law," Fante said promptly.

The others were silent.

"Desirable," Abraham said finally, "but unrealistic, considering tribal customs. Perhaps a very brief, basic code of criminal and civil law, but loose enough to allow local interpretation. Elastic enough to cover the traditions and habits of different areas and different peoples."

He was a small, neat man, somber in dress, educated at the Wharton School of Finance, very hard, incorruptible. His calm bravery and cool assurance during the coup had contributed greatly to the outcome. And his had been the chess player's brain behind the financing of Anokye's coup.

"I will accept that, Willi," the Little Captain said. "Jean, you wish to add something?"

Duclos rubbed a palm across his forehead.

"Some form of democratic participation in the government. Perhaps elected legislatures in each country, but with the chief executive appointed by you, Mr. President. It is a very difficult problem that requires much thought and careful planning."

"Which is why I want to get started on it at once," President Anokye said. "I hereby appoint you gentlemen a committee of three to draw up a blueprint for the new—well, for the time being, let us call it the United African States. The UAS. It is not a bad name. I would like from you a design, as detailed as possible, of exactly how this union will be constituted."

"And when do you want this, Bibi?" Abraham asked.

"Two weeks," Anokye said. "No later."

He smiled at their groans, and rose to his feet. They stood up promptly and moved toward the door. But they stopped when he spoke.

"None of you has asked what my requirement is for the new union," he asked.

"What do you suggest, Mr. President?" Mai Fante asked.

"One army," Obiri Anokye said. "One uniform. One flag. The army of the United African States to be headquartered in Asante. Under my command."

Yvonne Mayer and Sgt. Sene Yeboa had been married in a quiet civil ceremony, presided over by a magistrate of the Asante National Judiciary. The only witnesses were President Obiri Anokye, best man, and Mboa Duclos, matron of honor. Following the brief wedding, the Yeboas returned to the home of the bride for a short, sedate reception attended by a dozen of their friends. The guests included a few of the girls from the Golden Calf and some of the sergeant's army buddies. Everyone behaved well.

Yvonne and Sene then settled down to a quiet, contented married life. To all appearances. They both seemed intent upon acting in what Asante's social arbiters called "a cultured manner." The wife, with the aid of servants, kept a clean, cheerful home for her husband. There was hot food awaiting him whatever time he arrived, and cold beer in the refrigerator. In turn, he allowed her to handle all their finances, spoke to her in a respectful tone, never beat her or struck her in anger or drunkenness. It was known in Mokodi, via testimony of the servants, that the Yeboas slept in separate bedrooms.

But no one, ever, doubted the manhood of Sene Yeboa. Bush wisdom decreed that it was only a question of time before the door between their adjoining chambers was unlocked, thrown open. It was said that in the Mokodi barracks, wagers had been made on when this event might occur.

On the evening that President Anokye met with his advisors to begin planning the United African States, Sergeant Yeboa returned home about 2130. He had not left the palace until, as usual, he had satisfied himself that the guards assigned to the Little Captain for the remainder of the night were adequate, armed, sober, and mindful of their responsibility. "Mother Yeboa," he was called. Not, of course, to his face.

When he entered his home, through the rear entrance that led directly into the kitchen, Yvonne was waiting for him with a warm smile and a cold bottle of Star. It was difficult for him to choose which gave him more pleasure, the friendly greeting or the frosty beer. But as Yvonne took from him the gripsack he carried, he leaned forward to kiss her scented, flaxen hair. She laughed and patted his cheek. He felt very good.

Only one servant, Chantal, the maid, lived in. But this was Chantal's weekly night off. She spent it moonlighting at the Golden Calf. She liked the opportunity of earning extra money, of having fun. And she also served as an unwitting spy for Yvonne, enabling her mistress better to estimate revenue and calculate the malfeasance of the sly Yakubu.

So this evening, Yvonne, having already dined, served her husband's dinner with her own hands. The main dish was pepper chicken, prepared in a way she knew pleased Sene: enough hot spices to bring sweat to his scalp. But there was beer to cool his palate and, if he wished, brandy afterward in the living room, and a good cigar.

He did so wish, and they relaxed together, both barefoot. Sene puffed importantly on his cigar, touching the brandy balloon to his lips occasionally. Yvonne had taught him that it was uncultured to toss the drink down in one wild gulp.

She, with her own gin sling, sat coiled at the opposite end of the couch. Watching him with amused affection. She did feel affection for him. As one might feel affection for a splendid stallion. Or even a massive bear, shambling on its hind legs.

"What is in the black bag, Sene?" she asked casually.

"Money," he said, grinning at her. "Much money. French francs."

She was very quick.

"It goes to Togo and Benin?"

"Yes," he admitted. "To men who favor war. You understand?"

"Of course. The Little Captain plans well."

"He does," Sene agreed. "I must assemble the packages tonight. Tomorrow I will cross the borders and deliver them."

"You alone?"

"Bibi wishes his brother Adebayo to accompany me. He says the boy must learn."

"Adebayo?" she said. "A child."

"Not so much a child. Already taller than the Little Captain. When he puts meat on his bones, he will be a good man. Strong."

"You can trust him?"

"Adebayo? Of course. Bibi has told him to follow my orders in all things. Adebayo learns quickly. He speaks little, but he listens carefully. And he never complains."

"Adebayo," she repeated. "I still think of him as a child. Does he have a woman?"

"Ho!" he laughed. "Give the lad time."

In truth, he was not enamored of brandy; it was too small, gone too soon, and did nothing to calm the fire of the pepper chicken. So when the snifter was empty, he fetched another cold beer from the kitchen and brought Yvonne a fresh gin sling.

"The Little Captain has left it to me to decide how much money the men in Togo and Benin are to receive," he told her. "It is a great responsibility. Will you help me?"

"Of course," she said. "Need you ask? But what of your men here in Asante? Do you also pay them?"

"I pay them, personally, but Bibi has set the amount each man gets."

"You pay them, and they report to you?"

"That is true."

"How many men do you have, Sene? Here in Asante and in other countries? In your entire private army?"

"Now? Today? I cannot say exactly. Perhaps fifty men. And Bibi says we must have more."

"Interesting," she said thoughtfully. "Let me get my glasses, and we will decide how the money is to be divided."

She had been wearing a man's sapara of unbleached muslin, the voluminous folds cinched at the waist with a narrow scarf of vermilion silk. She had learned the off-hand, taunting chic of African women, their high-rumped flair. And she made the plain sapara a ballgown. But when she came from the bedroom, wearing her glasses, she had changed into a blue pegnoir over a lighter blue nightgown. The same costume she had worn to invite Nwabala to his death.

They sat close together at the teak table in the dining area, and she began to organize his affairs. He had pockets of paper scraps, jotted notes, some hastily scrawled hieroglyphics that even he could not decipher. But gradually, as they worked, she was able to draw up lists, of names and assignments.

They opened a jug of palm wine, poured it over ice cubes, and sipped occasionally as they worked. He supplied her with details, furrowing his heavy brow as he sought to recall the personalities, virtues and vices, of the men who worked for him. They did not include members of the President's personal guard, who were uniformed Asanti soldiers. They dealt only with Yeboa's secret army, the domestic spies and the agents who had been sent abroad, to Togo and Benin, Nigeria, one to Zaire, one to Gabon, one to Cameron.

When they had finished, they stared in astonishment at their lists. Many more than fifty. Sene personally commanded almost a hundred men in undercover work in Asante and beyond the borders. Gathering information. Funneling it only to Sergeant Yeboa.

"I didn't know," he admitted, ashamed of his inefficiency. "But it has all happened so quickly. The Little Captain tells me more men, more men, more places. I want to know everything, everywhere."

"I am glad you spoke to me of this," she said, putting a comforting hand on his arm. "From now on, you must tell me everything. Whenever a man is added, or when a man is sent from here to there, you must tell me, and I will keep a record of it. I will set up a file for each man."

"Good," he said gratefully. "Who each man is, how much has been paid, if he is to be trusted, and so forth. Yvonne, you will do this for me?"

"Of course," she said. She laughed lightly. "It is exactly what I need to keep busy."

He looked at her, understanding. The first few weeks of their marriage had been difficult for her. He knew that. When she realized, slowly realized, that Obiri Anokye was not coming to their home, not coming to her bed, ever again. But she was no stranger to pain, physical or emotional, and had the stripped sinews of a survivor.

"Now you must do something for me," she said. "Tell Bibi you need more men. Men to gather information. To go everywhere in Africa. If he wishes to create one nation, he must have friends in Angola and Kenya and South Africa and Mali and Chad. Everywhere. Tell him this, and he will agree. Never fear. He will find the money for all these men."

He looked at her a long, long moment. Then his hand crept across the tabletop, a dark beast walking on strong fingers. It clamped about her wrist.

"I will tell him that," he said. Throaty voice. "I will do as you say, Yvonne."

"Good," she said. "Also, I wish you to hold a higher title than sergeant. I know Bibi has offered you officer's rank. I want you to accept it."

His eyes went opaque; she felt something close to fear. Perhaps because she could not read what he was thinking.

"No, Yvonne," he said softly, still holding her wrist. "It is something to be a sergeant in the Asante army. The President is called the Little Captain and is proud of it. I will not ask him for officer's rank."

She had not been a successful whore for nothing. She knew when to be hard, when to be soft.

"All right," she said. "Do not ask him. But if Bibi suggests it again, grumble but accept. You agree?"

"I agree," he said grudgingly. "But only if he suggests it."

"He will," she said. "I know the Little Captain," she added bitterly. She twisted her wrist in his grasp, bent her fingers down, stroked his pink palm with her fingertips. Then scraped with her nails. "And now we shall go to bed," she said staring into his eyes.

"Yes," he said.

She had never seen him naked before, and caught her breath. His blunt body was a geography of scars: thin rivers of white, puckered valleys, torn ravines and crooked crevices. Bullet wounds, knife cuts, purpled blows. She could hardly believe that his flesh had borne this punishment. Like her, he was a survivor.

He made love like the splendid stallion engorged, the massive bear maddened and no longer exhibiting his tame tricks. He showed his teeth, and she surrendered willingly beneath that ferocious assault. She could not counter his brute strength, his grunting fury. But opened her pale and hairless thighs to him, wondering if she would die from that throbbing bludgeon that rent her, split her, and drove her steaming.

"My master!" she gasped. "My ruler! My king!"

"I do not wish to be paranoid about the French," President Obiri Anokye told Peter Tangent. "Still, I know they are aware of the situation between Togo and Benin, and it must puzzle them."

"I'm sure it does, Mr. President. You anticipate interference? By the French?"

"No," Anokye said. "Not really. But it—what is the English word?—it frets me. Yes. Frets. I thought perhaps there is something I can do. We can do. I leave as little to chance as possible. I would not care to see a thousand French paratroops dropping on Mokodi."

He stood suddenly and began stalking about his office. He glanced, several times, at the gold Patek Philippe he had taken from the wrist of the dead King Prempeh IV. The band had been shortened, and the Little Captain wore the watch—originally a gift to Prempeh from Peter Tangent—with comfort and pride.

"I'm already late for a night operation at the barracks," he said, almost angrily. "They are waiting for me. We must conclude this quickly. I have only one thought on the matter. The Russian Marxists are active in Benin. Also, somewhat, in Togo. But in recent months, very heavily in Benin. I know this to be true. Do you think the French are aware of it?"

"Undoubtedly, Mr. President."

"This is my idea: Is there any way we can convince the French that the Togo-Benin dispute is the result of a Communist plot? To divide the two countries. Inflame hatreds that will lead to open warfare. So that, in the resulting confusion, the Marxists may come to power, or perhaps act as arbitrator, enforcing their own policies, elevating their own men. Could the French be made to believe this?"

Peter Tangent smiled slowly. "A red herring," he said softly.

"Red herring? I do not know the meaning, Peter."

"In my country, the phrase has two meanings, Mr. President. Primarily, it means a false trail. But in government circles, it also means using the Red Menace as a means of promoting policies—appropriations, and so forth—that might otherwise have no viability. You understand, Mr. President?"

"Of course. Very ingenious. We will give the French a red herring. Could your friend in London be of assistance to us in this matter?"

Tangent considered a few moments.

"I think he could," he said finally. "But I do not believe he would be willing to act only on my word, on my assurance of the Russians' complicity in the Togo-Benin dispute. If we could present him with evidence . . ."

"Evidence? You mean, perhaps, a statement by a third party? A confession? Perhaps a document that has come into our possession?"

"Something like that."

"I will provide it," President Anokye said.

"And perhaps another gift of African art," Tangent said.

"That, too," the Little Captain said.

17

The Popular "Haut Monde" column in the Mokodi *New Times* carried the following account:

Mokodi society, and even the au courant of the hinterlands of Gonja and Kumasi, are all atwitter over the visit to Asante of General and Mrs. Kumayo Songo and their oldest son, Capt. Jere. Songo père commands the northern zone of the Togolese army, and Songo fils serves as his father's Chief of Staff. The beautiful and gracious Mrs. Songo, the former Bakwa Bawo of Bassari, is active in Lomé society and renowned for her many charitable activities. Last season, the Songos hosted the annual Society Club Ball at their lovely home near Ountivou. It was a glittering event that brought together the very brightest ornaments of West African society, with glamorous party-goers galore arriving from such distant locales as Senegal and Gabon.

Haut Monde has learned from a usually reliable source that the visit of the Songos to Mokodi has nothing to do with military matters or foreign relations. No, indeed! It is rumored that the oh-so-handsome Capt. Jere and Sara, the lovely younger sister of President Obiri Anokye, are an item, and an announcement of their engagement is expected to be made shortly, perhaps during a formal dinner being given in the visitors' honor tonight at the palace.

Best wishes to all!

The "usually reliable source" mentioned by the author of "Haute Monde" was the public relations man retained by the Asante government, and the newspaper account was reasonably accurate. The dinner was a family affair, attended by the three Songos and the complete Anokye clan, including Judith and Josiah, and Zuni and his wife, Magira, who had come over from Zabar on the afternoon ferry. And, of course, Sara and Adebayo.

Sara and Captain Jere were seated side by side at the long table in the state dining room. They were the center of attraction, blushing targets of mild joking, embarrassed recipients of dire warnings of the pitfalls of marriage.

Sara had never looked lovelier. She wore a long gown of russet silk, with ribbons of the same material threaded through her twigged hair. The excitement of the evening gave her eyes a brilliance, her smile a flash. She attempted to appear composed and mature, but youthful high spirits broke out in giggles and snorts of laughter. Once, when Zuni warned Captain Jere that his bride-to-be could not boil water without burning it, Sara covered her face with her palms in uncontrollable mirth.

The captain blushed as frequently. He was shy, almost to the point of inarticulateness. But "Haute Monde" had not exaggerated; he was "oh-so-handsome" and, in his dress uniform, was a prince charming perfectly capable of making Sara forget the photograph of Alain Delon that hung above her bed.

After dessert and coffee were finished, President Anokye nodded to Ajaka, and champagne was served. The Songos were Muslims, but happily ignored the prohibition on alcohol in honor of this festive occasion. The Little Captain rose to his feet at the head of the table, and the others quieted.

Speaking French, he said: "I ask you all to join me in celebrating the engagement of my beloved sister, Sara Anokye, to Captain Jere Songo." He raised his glass. "To this charming young couple. May they know happiness for the remainder of their days, and may their union be blessed by Allah, God, and all the gods of our ancestors. Sara and Jere, you have all our love and all our hopes for a long life of good fortune."

All drank to that, willingly, and then clustered around to embrace and kiss Sara, who was now weeping with joy, and to shake the grinning captain's hand, slap his back, congratulate him and wish him well. Even the servants in the room came forward to kiss Sara's hand and the captain's, and to bestow blessings in several tribal dialects. Ajaka made a cabalistic sign over the young couple and whirled thrice, rapidly, on his bare feet.

"A moment of your time, general?" President Anokye murmured, touching Songo's elbow.

"Of course, Mr. President."

The Little Captain led him from the dining room down the corridor to his office. Joan Livesay was sitting outside with her Akan dictionary. She looked up briefly as the two men approached, then went back to her book. Anokye made no attempt to explain her presence, and Songo didn't ask.

Inside, the door locked, the President took maps from the top drawer of his desk, rolled them open, motioned the general close.

"You can depend upon the loyalty of the Army of the North Zone?" he asked abruptly.

"Absolutely, Mr. President," Songo said, somewhat shocked by the question.

"And the South Zone?"

The general hesitated. "That I cannot say with certainty. I would guess they will remain neutral."

"Or wait until they see how you progress in the north. Then, if you appear to be succeeding, they will join the attack."

"That is possible, Mr. President."

"Yes. Possible. But I count only on their neutrality for a short period of time. I ask only that they do nothing. You understand?"

"Of course, Mr. President."

"Now," the Little Captain went on, pointing to wide red arrows marked on the map with grease pencil. "I wish you to advance in this area south of the hills. A three-pronged attack from Sokodé, Kpessi, and Atakpamé. All three columns are to strike directly eastward into Benin, guiding on these roads here, here, and here. Any objections so far?"

"It is wise to divide my forces, Mr. President?"

"It would not be if a single large force of the enemy was in position to oppose you. But intelligence reports indicate there are only a few scattered outposts in this area of Benin. The only place that might give you trouble is here, at Savalou. If you meet determined resistance, I advise you to flank the village and continue your advance. Try, in all events, to avoid a confrontation. Move as swiftly as you can. Your objective is to slice directly across to the Nigerian border. Cut the north-south highway and divide Benin in two, so that troops cannot be brought south to the coast from Kandi and Parakou. Is that clear?"

"Yes, Mr. President."

"I will coordinate my attack with yours. By moving in vehicles on the improved coastal road, I should be in Ouidah, Cotonou, and Porto-Novo before you are well inside Benin. You see my plan now, general?"

"A classic pincer," Songo said admiringly. "You striking northward from the coast, and I striking coastward from the north!"

"Exactly," the Little Captain said. "But do not begin your move southward until your advance troops have reached the Nigerian border. I will send you word when to turn southward. I can count on you to await that word?"

"You can."

"Good. I anticipate hard fighting in the Ouidah-Cotonou-Porto-Novo area. It is where the bulk of the Benin army is presently positioned. But I have the men and weapons to move them, to shove them northward. Then, after you have cut the country in half, you will make your ninety-degree turn southward. We will have the enemy trapped between us. And we will smash him."

"Excellent, Mr. President! A brilliant plan! There is but one thing..."

"And that is?"

"To reach Benin, your army must come through Togo on the coastal road. You said you ask only the neutrality of the officers and men of the Army of the South Zone. But what if they should offer resistance to this invasion by the Asante army?"

"Hardly an invasion, general. We will merely be passing through to Benin."

"I understand that, Mr. President, but will they? All they will see are armed men pouring into Togo from Asante. They may fight. It is something to be considered."

Obiri Anokye straightened. He tossed down the pencil he had been using as a pointer. He stood at the map, feet firmly planted, hands on hips, chest inflated. His head was lowered; he stared at the map broodingly from under his brows.

"I have already considered it," he told General Songo. "I have made contact with certain officers of the Army of the South Zone. Money has changed hands. Pledges have been made. They will remain neutral. There will be no resistance offered to Asante forces passing through to Benin."

Gen. Kumayo Songo looked at the Little Captain with wonder.

"You think of everything, Mr. President."

Anokye didn't answer, and after a moment of silence, Songo became uneasy.

"You intend to lead your troops in person, Mr. President?" he asked nervously.

"I do. I will be with Colonel Nkomo's tank corps. I will try to keep you informed of my progress. During the next two weeks, you will receive several private messages from me. These will concern timing, passwords, radio wavelengths, flare signals, and so forth. The messages will be delivered to you personally by my brother Adebayo. If you wish to reply, he will carry your letters back to me. After your return to Togo tomorrow, I suggest we have no more direct communication by telephone or mail."

"I agree, Mr. President."

"Begin organizing your striking forces at once. Please keep me informed of your progress and exact dispositions. I expect you to be ready to move within two weeks."

"Two weeks!"

"It can be done."

"I am not certain I can . . ."

Songo's voice faltered. President Anokye raised his head. He stared coldly at the general, starting at his feet, and letting expressionless eyes move slowly upward: bandy legs, bulging paunch, uniform straining at breast and arms, tight collar, fat neck, flushed face glistening with sweat, damp hair. Then lowered to stare at Songo's rapidly blinking eyes.

"But I am certain you can," he said softly. "I have great faith in you, general. I would not care to find that faith has been misplaced. Two weeks. After that, be prepared to move on twenty-four hours' notice. You will be informed of the code word that will signal the attack. And twenty-four hours after *that*, Benin will be crushed, and you will be the leader of Togo."

"Nothing can stop us!" General Songo said excitedly, regaining his nerve.

"Nothing," Obiri Anokye said gravely. He replaced the maps in his desk and started toward the door. Then he paused. "One other small thing," he said casually. "I need a certain document from you. . . ."

18

They sat like landed gentry in the library of Brindleys in London. Slumped in deep leather armchairs. Nursing their brandies. Feet up on a brass fender before the fireplace. Genial flames flickering, lighting ruddy faces in the darkened room. Peter A. Tangent from Crawfordsville, Indiana. Anthony J. Malcolm from Altoona, Pennsylvania. And there they were . . .

"A beautiful mask from the Congo," Tony Malcolm said lazily. "Shells and ivory, human hair and odd things. Must be centuries old. I'm embarrassed by his generosity. And to think he wants nothing in return."

Peter Tangent laughed. Lightly.

"Cynical bastard," he said. "As a matter of fact, he wants to do something for you."

"Does he, now?"

"Well . . . something for the French, actually. But he thought it might benefit you if you brought it to their attention."

"Very kind of the Little Captain."

"He can't go directly to the French with it, you see, because he fears their embassy in Mokodi is riddled with Marxists. Makes sense, doesn't it?"

"Peter," Malcolm said dreamily, staring squint-eyed into the dancing flames, "just what the fuck are you talking about?"

"This . . ." Tangent said. He took an envelope from his inside jacket pocket, withdrew a folded sheet of paper. He shook it open, held it out to Malcolm. "Read this," he said.

"Must I?" Tony murmured.

"You must. I assure you, you'll find it interesting."

Malcolm sighed, straightened up in his chair. He took a pair of rimless spectacles from his breast pocket and put them on as slowly as a fussy book-keeper. Then he took the paper from Tangent's hand. He turned sideways in his chair to illuminate it by firelight.

"You read French?" Tangent asked.

"My mother tongue," Malcolm said, and Tangent chuckled.

Malcolm read it through, then read it again. He raised his eyes to stare at Tangent over his glasses.

"Let's see if I've got this straight," he said. "This document is submitted to me as being a photostatic copy of the third page of a three-page Top Secret report sent to the Togolese Minister of Defense in Lomé by a certain General Kumayo Songo, and signed by him. The report concerns an investigation carried out under the general's orders into the circumstances of a raid by persons unknown on a Togolese army base near the village of Kamina. In their investigation of the unprovoked attack, the general's men discovered the body of one of the attacking force. He was identified, by papers found on the corpse, as being one Indris Obodum, a Benin student who was also, apparently, a card-carrying member of the Benin Communist Party. Have I understood all this correctly?"

"You have," Tangent said solemnly. "The document came into the posses-sion of President Anokye by means that need not concern us. You are aware of the Marxist activity in Benin?"

"I am aware," Malcolm said.

"So is President Anokye. And very concerned about it. I need hardly tell you. He believes this document is added evidence that the Reds are fo-menting the trouble between Togo and Benin. He thought he should bring this document to the attention of the French, who still consider Togo and Benin in their sphere of influence. For the reasons I've already stated. Anokye prefers to do it this way—to ask you to inform the French of the Communist plot."

Tony Malcolm took off his glasses, folded them slowly, tucked them back into his jacket pocket.

"You fucking amateurs," he said softly.

"What?" Tangent said, jerking upright. "What do you mean?"

Malcolm rose to a crouch, leaned forward, scaled the paper into the flames.

"What are you doing?" Tangent cried.

The paper burst into flames, curled, crisped. In a few moments it was ashes. The two men settled back in their club chairs, heads turned so they could stare at each other.

"A piece of bumf," Tony Malcolm said calmly. "The French could make one phone call and discover it was as phony as a three-dollar bill. I'm surprised at you, Peter. Is that what you think my business is like? Falsified documents?

Micro-miniaturized bugs and cameras in cigarette lighters? Unspeakable torture and fiendishly clever assassination?"

"Well, I—well, isn't it?" Tangent said confusedly.

"About five percent," Malcolm said.

"And the other ninety-five?"

"People. Just people. Getting them to tell you what you want to know. To do what you want done."

"Manipulating them, in other words?"

"Nonsense. Most of them are quite aware of what they're doing. Do it voluntarily, happily."

"But . . . *why*?"

"Why do they do it?" Malcolm asked rhetorically. "Idealism. The dream of a better world. They feel they can strike a blow against the forces of evil and darkness, make some small contribution to a future of freedom and liberty, a world in which political fear and tyranny no longer exist."

His speech began to take on the singsong accents of an evangelist. Tangent listened with astonishment, wondering if (1) it was an elaborate put-on; (2) Malcolm really believed this shit; or (3) the man was crazed with drink.

"There *are* good people in this world," Malcolm continued what sounded like a soliloquy. "People determined to leave this life just a little better than they found it. If I am able, in some small way, to harness that high resolve, to further it, then I feel it is my moral duty to do exactly that. But I will not aid in any way whatsoever the advancement of those dark forces of political absolutism that threaten everything I and the people who work for me hold dear."

Tangent, seeing a side of Malcolm he never knew existed, was thoroughly flummoxed.

"Then I gather," he said, "that you know what the Little Captain is trying to do."

"Of course," Malcolm said. "He doesn't want the French to make any good guesses about what he's up to. So he's trying to sell them the Russians as the *agents provocateurs* behind the Togo-Benin dispute."

"Something like that," Tangent said grimly. "Another drink?" he asked, determined to be polite.

"Why not?"

The bottle of Remy-Martin was on the floor alongside Tangent's chair. He poured a finger or two into their glasses. Malcolm was in charge of the soda siphon. He gave them each a splash. They settled back again, slumping down onto their spines.

"Oh well," Tangent sighed. "You win one, you lose one."

"What makes you think you've lost this one?" Malcolm said.

Tangent's head jerked around. He stared at Malcolm again.

"If you make confusion a deliberate policy," he said, "you're succeeding admirably. Whee! You mean, after that lecture, you're willing to—"

"The document was stupid. It would never have convinced the French. Except that Anokye has this General Songo in his hip pocket."

"But now you say you'll—"

"That I'll do it? Yes, I'll help the Little Captain. Tell him that. I'll get the French all excited about the Red threat in Togo and Benin."

"And how will you do that?"

"Trade secret," Malcolm said smugly.

"Come on, Tony, you can tell me. How will you do it?"

Malcolm considered a moment, then smiled sweetly.

"I'll tell them," he said. "That's all. Just tell them to beware the Russians."

Tangent looked at him in wonderment.

"And they'll believe you?" he asked. "Just like that?"

"Just like that," Malcolm nodded. "They know I'm a very honest fellow."

"Ho-ho," Tangent said. "Tell me, honest fellow, why are you willing to do this for the Little Captain?"

"I like the gifts he sends me," Tony Malcolm said. "I'm building up one of the finest private collections of African art in the world."

"Bullshit!" Peter Tangent said promptly. "There's something more . . ."

The two men sat in silence for almost five minutes. Once, a uniformed attendant came into the library, and they took their feet off the fender to allow him to lift another small log onto the fire. Then, without speaking, went back to their former positions, their brandies and soda.

"Got it!" Tangent said finally.

"Oh?"

"You've heard from Ian Quigley. He's filed with Virginia. You think the Little Captain is going to pull this off, and you want to be on the winning side. That's why you're willing to help."

"Is that what you think?" Tony Malcolm said sleepily.

Shortly afterward, drink finished, Tangent rose, stretched, yawned. He mumbled something about a busy tomorrow, told Malcolm he was welcome to whatever remained of the Remy-Martin, and made his exit. Tony Malcolm flapped a languid hand in farewell.

Tangent left the club through the bar. There were several men there, including the Frenchmen Julien Ricard. Tangent kept his head down and hurried past. For once Ricard didn't grab his arm and start another of his unpleasant conversations. The club's commissionaire whistled up a cab, and Tangent headed back for his suite at the Connaught, phrasing in his mind the tender, clever letter he would write that night to Amina Dunama.

"He's gone?" Tony Malcolm said, as Julien Ricard slid into the armchair vacated by Tangent.

"Took off in a cab," Ricard said. He laughed shortly. "Rushed past me like a thief. Learn anything?"

"Yes," Tony Malcolm said, staring again into the flames. "Tell your people in Paris that the Russians are stirring up the trouble between Togo and Benin."

"I don't believe that," Ricard said, touching the purple birthmark that glowed in firelight.

Malcolm turned slowly to look at him.

"You don't have to believe it," he said coldly. "You played at Canby's last night, didn't you?"

"You know I did," Julien Ricard said surlily.

"And you won, didn't you?"

"I did," Ricard said. "But not enough."

"Don't get greedy," Tony Malcolm said.

19

The limousine came directly from the airport. When it arrived, President Obiri Anokye was waiting on the steps of the palace. He was flanked by Premier Willi Abraham, Minister of State Jean-Louis Duclos, and Col. Jim Nkomo.

The long, black Mercedes-Benz rolled slowly to a stop. Guards hurried forward to open the doors. Out stepped Premier Benedicto da Silva of Benin, his daughter Beatrice, his aide Christophe Michaux, and a Benin army officer, Col. Kwasi Sitobo, whose aiguillettes denoted his staff rank.

President Anokye moved down the steps smiling, holding his arms wide in welcome. He embraced Beatrice first; a chaste kiss on her cheek.

"Welcome to your new home!" he said, and then laughed when she did.

He shook hands formally with Da Silva and Michaux, and then was introduced to Colonel Sitobo, a dark, thin man with fiery eyes. In turn, Anokye presented his aides to all the others. After introductions, the party was sorted out:

Col. Jim Nkomo commandeered the limousine and took Colonel Sitobo off to a review of the Asante tank corps, planned in the visitor's honor.

Premier Abraham and Minister of State Duclos took charge of Da Silva and Michaux, and led them to the main floor audience chamber for preliminary discussions on a cash loan President Anokye had promised to make to Benin.

The Little Captain escorted Beatrice up the wide mahogany staircase to the second floor where his sister Sara was waiting, Joan Livesay hovering in the background. The two fiancées, who had met several times before, embraced and kissed with expressions of girlish delight. Joan Livesay was introduced to Beatrice, and the three women were shooed off to the upper regions of the palace that, everyone agreed, needed redecoration—new rugs, new drapes, new furniture—before they would be suitable for a married president.

"Go spend the taxpayers' money," Anokye called, in high good humor, and the three women went upstairs giggling, already chattering about color schemes and the pros and cons of calling in a professional decorator.

Obiri Anokye had an hour to himself in his office. He spent it reviewing, once again, the maps and battle orders he had prepared for the Togo-Benin campaign.

There had been a time, not too long ago, when he would not have planned a military operation of any magnitude without the counsel of the Englishman Alistair Greeley, chief teller of the Asante National Bank. Greeley, a strange man, a cripple, had one passion in life: military history and his collection of antique model soldiers. And it was with the aid of those brilliantly painted miniatures, moved about on maps and diagrams, that Captain Anokye and Greeley had plotted the attacks against the Marxist rebels in Asante.

But the rebels were destroyed now, or at least reduced to insignificant numbers. And Greeley was gone, faded away, after his wife and sister deserted him, together. Some said he was in South Africa. There were rumors he had been seen in the slums of Durban, filthy and besotted. But no matter. No one cared.

His advice was no longer needed. Obiri Anokye, alone, had planned and commanded the successful coup d'etat that deposed King Prempeh IV. The Little Captain himself had devised the tactics, sent these men here, those men there. And then, in person, had led the final assault on the palace.

That victory made him his own man. He knew now what he must do, and how he must do it. If he patterned his fighting style after any military leader's it was that of the American general Ulysses S. Grant: move in the greatest force you could muster, bulldoze, crush, take your losses without faltering and come on, implacable, unstoppable, a juggernaut.

This did not mean that you should not be adroit in your planning. But cleverness took you only to the instant the first gun was fired. Then planlessness took over, and winning then depended on resolve, instinct, and a kind of fury. All growing from a belief in your own invincibility. "I fight: therefore I am." The philosophy of every successful general.

So Obiri Anokye, the Little Captain, pondered his maps, diagrams, orders. Knowing this was only the start, the beginning. Intelligent enough to question what drove him, what lashed him on. It was an odd thing, he acknowledged, for a man to be in awe of himself. And yet he was.

Africa was filled with captains, and colonels, and generals. Some commanding numbers of men ridiculous in the blue eyes of white military leaders. An African captain might command ten, a colonel fifty, a general a few hundred. Sometimes African soldiers wore the castoffs of the world's armies. Weapons were frequently ancient, and malfunctioned. An army might need a dozen calibers of rifle ammunition. Close-order drill was a laugh. Discipline lasted until the first mortar round landed. And yet ... And yet ...

Obiri Anokye knew all this, worked within these limits. He knew the men who served under him, their shortcomings and their capabilities. Knew all these things better than his foes. But he could see no reason why a well-trained, well-fed, well-uniformed, well-armed, proud African soldier could not be the equal of any soldier on earth. Superior, perhaps, if the man with the rifle could be won to the Little Captain's dream: one nation, one people, one Africa.

So he was awed by his own ambition, his hunger. Knowing he could not hesitate nor doubt. He was familiar with Shakespeare's "There is a tide ..." and was determined his life would not be leaked out in shallows and miseries. Auntie Tal had cast the stones for him and had seen a glorious future. He could not deny his destiny.

Col. Jim Nkomo's personal tank was called "Ami," the name painted on the side in crimson script. And it was from the opened turret of *Ami* that the bearded Nkomo and visiting Benin colonel Kwasi Sitobo reviewed the maneuvers of the Asante tank corps. After a corps parade, they watched through field glasses as a V-formation of the new AMX-30 tanks plunged down into a ravine, raced up the other slope, and blasted away with their 105mm cannon at paper targets, scoring impressive hits.

Colonel Sitobo growled softly.

"Now here is something that may interest you," Jim Nkomo said casually. "Our first TOW missile from America. You are familiar with this weapon?"

Sitobo nodded uncertainly.

"Wire-guided," Nkomo said. "Designed for antitank work, but useful on anything within a thirty-five-hundred-meter range. Especially moving targets. Crew of four. All the gunner has to do is keep his crosshairs on the target. A computer makes in-flight corrections. The missile can't miss. About fifteen centimeters in diameter. Speed is about a thousand kilometers per hour. The warhead is shaped. Armor-piercing. We have this one on a portable tripod mount. The ones on order will be mounted on Jeeps. I understand the Americans have also had good results with the TOW on helicopter gunships. Watch this."

They stood in the turret of *Ami* and stared through their field glasses as a squad of soldiers, somewhat apprehensively, dragged the burned-out hulk of a Volkswagen on a long rope across an open field. A thousand meters away, the TOW crew worked swiftly.

"Three launches in ninety seconds," Nkomo murmured. "If needed ..."

The TOW gunner brought his crosshairs to bear. Pressed the trigger. There was a surprisingly small whoosh as the missile streaked toward the moving target. The gunner worked his sights; the missile, uncoiling its wire from two spools, curved toward the hauled Volkswagen body. It hit squarely; the rusted hulk dissolved in an explosion of steel and earth. The squad pulling the target fell to the ground, then rose shakily to their feet.

Col. Kwasi Sitobo made a sound.

"Nice," Nkomo said. "Well, that concludes our little show. I'm afraid the limousine has returned to the palace, but I can run you back in one of our Berliet armored personnel carriers. A fine piece of machinery. I think you'll like it."

Colonel Sitobo sighed.

The guests arrived promptly, wooed by an invitation to "a Portuguese evening" in honor of visiting Premier Benedicto da Silva of Benin. They gathered for a pre-dinner drink at one end of the grand ballroom. A rum-and-lemon punch was served, and appetizers included hot peppers, marinated hearts of palm, black olives, pickled mushrooms, and tiny prawns in a garlic sauce. At the other end of the long room, a five-piece African band played rhumbas, sambas, and mambos in execrable rhythm.

As usual, the guests soon divided into two gossiping groups: men and women. Only Joan Livesay and Ian Quigley stood together, a bit apart from the others.

"No punch, Ian?" she asked. "It's quite good."

"I'll pass," he said. "I'm hoping to work tonight, and a buzz I don't need. Where's his nibs?"

"Upstairs. Locked in his office with the visiting premier and that funny little colonel who never speaks."

"Ah?" Quigley said. "That's interesting. Wonder what they're up to?"

"Foreign relations," Livesay said. "At least, that's what President Anokye told me. Said he'd join us at dinner."

"Decent of him to invite us," he said. "Makes me feel less of a nuisance. Ready to go home?"

"Whenever you say."

"A week perhaps. Maybe less."

"Then you've got everything you want?"

"Just about. A few more details. What do you think of the Little Captain's fiancée?"

"A child," Joan Livesay said. "Still has her baby fat."

"Maybe that's what he fancies," Quigley laughed.

"Don't be crude, Ian."

"Sorry, old girl. One of these days you must draw me a blueprint of that high moral sense of yours. So I'll know—"

"Oh, shut up," she said.

"Where's Bibi?" Beatrice da Silva asked, looking about anxiously. "I hope he won't be late."

"He's upstairs with your father," Sara Anokye told her. "I'm sure they won't be long. Mboa, you look so pretty. I love your Apollo. Did you make it?"

Mrs. Duclos flushed with pleasure.

"Thank you, Sara. Yes, I printed the cloth myself. You do not think it is too—too crazy?"

"Of course not. It's fun!"

"Jean says it is crazy," Mboa said sorrowfully. "His friend, that man Michaux, agrees."

"They're both full of beans," Sara said. Then she giggled. "Or they will be after dinner. That's what we're having—beans. Feijoada."

"Feijoada!" Beatrice da Silva exclaimed, clapping her hands. "How wonderful! How thoughtful of Bibi to have this for us."

"Where is the President?" Christophe Michaux asked, looking about, frowning. "He appears to be missing. And Premier Da Silva."

"I believe they are upstairs," Jean-Louis Duclos said. "In conference."

"Ah? And where is Colonel Sitobo? He is also in conference?"

"I believe so."

"Interesting," Michaux said. "I must say that in my own mind I am somewhat annoyed that we weren't asked to join them. Are you not annoyed?"

"Perhaps it is a private matter, Christophe. The marriage . . ."

"A private matter with Sitobo present? I doubt it. It must concern military matters. They are planning something?"

"I don't know."

"Don't know or won't say?" Michaux laughed lightly. "I'm afraid you do not—" But then he stopped what he was about to say.

"What is your impression of Premier Da Silva's aide?" Mai Fante asked Willi Abraham in a low voice.

"Michaux?" Abraham said. "A capable man." He turned slowly to glance at Duclos and Michaux deep in conversation. "Very knowledgeable. He was shrewd in the negotiations this morning. But there is something about him . . ."

"Exactly," Mai Fante said. "Something. . . . My reaction exactly. You think he may make trouble?"

"Let him," Abraham shrugged. He quoted an Akan proverb: "Let the child pick up a live coal; you won't have to tell him to drop it."

"Well, I hope Jean is keeping his mouth tight," Fante said.

"He'd better," Willie Abraham said grimly. "I have seen the Little Captain in anger. Mai, do me the honor to exchange favors?"

"What may that be?"

"If I talk to your wife, will you talk to mine?"

"Done," Fante laughed.

. . .

In his private office, the door locked, President Obiri Anokye stood behind his desk and traced map positions with a blunt forefinger. It was not the same map he had shown to Gen. Kumayo Songo. Now the red arrows ran from east to west, from Benin into Togo.

"A broad attack in the north," he was saying. "Aimed toward Sokodé, Kpessi, Atakpamé. Your objective is to cut the north-south highway, divide the country in two so that reinforcements cannot be brought south to the coast from Sansanne-Mango and Lama-Kara. Is this plan clear to you so far?"

Premier Da Silva stroked his silvery Vandyke and looked to Col. Kwasi Sitobo. The colonel, his eyes on the map, bobbed his head and grunted. Anokye took the sound for acquiescence.

"I will coordinate my attack with yours," the Little Captain went on. "I will come down the coast road to Lomé. I, personally, with Colonel Nkomo's tank corps in the lead. I believe you saw with your own eyes what that force is capable of, Colonel. Infantry will follow the tanks. I intend to take Lomé and push the enemy northward along the improved road. When you have achieved your objective, colonel, and Togo is cut in two, turn south and we will have what is left of the Togolese army between us, and we will smash them."

Colonel Sitobo looked up briefly, eyes flashing. Obiri Anokye had a profile on him, supplied by the Asante embassy in Porto-Novo and by Sergeant Yeboa's agents in Cotonou. On the strength of this information, he had instructed Premier Da Silva to select Sitobo as his military chief.

This Sitobo was a young hawk, fierce. Apparently, he was apolitical, but combined excessive patriotism with excessive zeal for military ideals: discipline, discipline, and discipline. It was said he had once shot and killed one of his own men when his orders were disobeyed. Surprisingly, in one whose whole existence was devoted to command, he had a ridiculously high-pitched voice and spoke as infrequently as possible.

"During the next two weeks," President Anokye continued, "you will receive a number of messages, delivered by my brother Adebayo. These will concern timing, code signals, radio wavelengths, and so forth. I want you ready to move in two weeks. You can do this?"

Again Da Silva looked to Sitobo. The colonel nodded.

"Good," Anokye said. "At the end of two weeks, be prepared to begin your attack on twenty-four hours' notice. I believe it will only take us another twenty-four hours to crush Togo completely and end this threat to your national security."

Col. Kwasi Sitobo spoke for the first time.

"I agree," he squeaked.

The crystal chandeliers in the state dining room gleamed wickedly. The table was trigly dressed with stiff napery and polished silver. A staff of grinning servants, commanded by the lordly Ajaka, skipped merrily about to keep glasses filled with Portuguese wine, to rush in more and more platters, bowls, and kettles of the fabulous feijoada.

A dish as much African as Brazilian, feijoada is an orchestration of tangy flavors: garlic and pigs' tails, onion and smoked fatback, collard greens and ham hocks, spareribs and manioc, pigs' ears and rice, fufu and Tabasco, black beans and sausage. It is a kitchen sink of a dish. Prepared for a company as large as this one, it took the palace cooks almost two days to prepare; the Piper Aztec of the Asante National Air Force was dispatched to Cotonou for the paio sausage, to Accra for the smoked beef tongue.

Feijoada is a festive dish, and suited the mood of the guests, appetites already whetted by the rum punch and spicy things. Platters were passed, bowls spooned, kettles ladled, and great mounds of feijoada grew on the plates of the diners, to be hacked away, whittled down, demolished, as the beaming waiters scurried in with more steaming rice, more greens, more hot sauce, more peppers and jerked beef.

President Anokye looked on benignly from the head of the table, making certain no guest was in want. Premier Da Silva was to his right, Beatrice to his left. The others sat along the sides, men and women alternating, with Sara at the foot of the table, learning to act as hostess.

The room was noisy with the loud appreciation of the diners, clash of cutlery, clink of bottle against glass, clack of spoon on bowl, ladle on kettle.

"The best, Mr. President," Premier Da Silva said, closing his eyes in rapture. A smear of garlic sauce clung to his silvery beard. He raised his glass to Anokye. "I swear to you, the best I have ever tasted. It is an evening to remember." He leaned across the table to Sitobo. "Well, colonel, what do you think of this? Eh? Eh?"

Sitobo grunted, not pausing to look up, shoveling into his waiting mouth yet another spoonful of black turtle beans.

Even the ladies, who had started picking daintily at their food in a cultured manner, could not resist the contrast of succulent flavors. Soon they ate as energetically as the men, calling for more salt pork, more cold orange salad, more hot malagueta peppers. Then women and men alike were sweating from the spices and from their labors. Chilled Mateus and beer were brought, and bowls of ice chunks which some of the guests rubbed across their fevered foreheads.

Obiri Anokye selected carefully, avoiding the beans and rice, filling up on beef, tongue, spareribs.

"You are not eating, Bibi," Beatrice chided.

"Enough," he protested. "Well, perhaps a few ribs more and some sausage. I must store up strength. After we are married, it will be only cold rice and green salad. We agreed!"

"Of course," she giggled. "Oh, it's so good!"

"Your suite at the Mokodi Hilton is satisfactory?" he asked, leaning toward her to be heard above the hubbub.

She nodded, wide-eyed, her white teeth too busy gnawing a pig's foot to reply.

"And Colonel Sitobo and Christophe Michaux—they are comfortable?"

She paused a moment to dab her greasy lips with a starched napkin.

"I'm sure the colonel is," she said. "But he never says anything about anything!"

Anokye smiled, nodded understandingly.

"And Michaux?" he said.

"Oh, he didn't want to stay at the Hilton. Said it was too American. He's staying in a safari bungalow at the Hôtel Africain. Do you know it?"

"Oh yes," the Little Captain nodded slowly. "I know it."

Then, when they could eat no more, when every guest swore another mouthful, a bite, a nibble, would cause him to burst asunder, the plates, platters, bowls and kettles were whisked away, the table cleared, and mounds of sherbet were served, in three flavors, with chilled Madeira to reduce the possibility of their palates' igniting. Champagne, beer, and brandy were also available, and chicory-coffee, tea, and Perrier water.

As usual, Obiri Anokye drank sparingly, touching a glass of cold Star beer to his lips. He sat back comfortably, hearing the happy, chattering company. Soft smile on his lips. Eyes away somewhere.

But not so far away that he was not the first in the room to see Sgt. Sene Yeboa standing framed in the suddenly opened door to the dining room. The Little Captain rose immediately to his feet, murmured quiet apologies to right and left, and was gone from the table before most of the guests realized their host was leaving. He drew Yeboa out into the corridor, closed the door against the noise.

"What is it, Sene?" he demanded.

But the sergeant's eyes were brimming with tears. Massive shoulders slumped. Muscled arms dangled.

The Little Captain gripped him, shook him gently.

"What is it, man?"

"Your father," Yeboa whispered, his eyes turning slowly downward. "Forgive me, Bibi."

Anokye looked at him.

"Dead?" he asked.

Yeboa nodded dumbly.

"When?" Anokye asked.

"Not so long ago, Little Captain. Zuni called the duty officer here. I was out at the barracks. They called me. Then I spoke to Zuni. He said Josiah was helping to pull the boat up onto the sand. And then he fell over and was dead. Bibi, I . . ."

Anokye nodded. The two men embraced, holding each other tightly.

"He was my father, too," Yeboa said, his voice muffled and shaky.

"I know, Sene, I know. You have done well. Now there is more you must do. Call the naval base. Have a launch prepared. Sara and I will go at once."

"May I go also, Bibi?"

"Of course. You are family. Go now and have the launch ready. I will tell Sara. Thank you, brother."

They embraced again. Then Yeboa turned away and began to run. Anokye stopped a servant about to enter the dining room and asked him to send his sister Sara out to him. She was with him in a moment. He told her. She fell into his arms, her wails of anguish smothered in his shoulder. He comforted her as best he could, saying their father was an old man, it was to be expected, he had lived a good life and harmed no one, now he was with God, and so forth.

When she had calmed, he told her to go to her room and pack a suitcase to take to Zabar; her mother would need her, for how long no one could say. When she ran upstairs, he took a deep breath and reentered the dining room. The guests, surprised by the sudden, unexpected departure of the two Anokyes, looked at him, silent and troubled.

"Dear friends," he said in a steady voice, "I regret that a family matter has arisen that requires the presence of my sister Sara and myself. I apologize for our absence. Please do not concern yourselves, but finish your dinner and enjoy the evening. Premier Abraham, may I ask you to serve as host in my absence?"

"Of course, Mr. President."

"I thank you all for your company," Obiri Anokye said, smiling bleakly. "Please do not let this unfortunate interruption spoil your pleasure."

"What a tragedy," Jean-Louis Duclos mourned. "The Little Captain will be devastated."

"He was an old man, wasn't he?" Christophe Michaux said.

"Very old."

"Well then?"

Sitting alone in the back seat of the Duclos' Simca, Mboa listened to the conversation and decided she did not like this man Michaux. She hoped he would stay for only one drink at their home, and then depart. Black he may have been, but he was not African; there was no feeling in him for Bibi's loss.

"Is there a grog shop on the way?" Michaux asked.

"Yes," Duclos said, "but there's no need to stop. I have wine, beer..."

"Let me get you something good," Michaux said.

When they stopped in front of the lighted store, Michaux hopped out and went inside.

"Jean—" Mboa began.

"Maria, do not tell me I have already had enough to drink," he said angrily. "I am in no mood for lectures tonight."

"When have I ever lectured you?" she asked.

"Your manner," he said furiously. "Your silent, reproachful manner. It is lecture enough."

"I do not understand," she said faintly.

Michaux came bouncing out, carrying a string bag containing bottles wrapped in old newspaper.

"Two Beefeater gin," he said, "and one Glenlivet Scotch whisky. That should be sufficient."

"Raw-ther," Duclos drawled in a burlesque English accent, and both men laughed hysterically.

They pulled up before the Duclos' home, on an ordinary street off the Boulevard Voltaire. In this section, the sidewalks were unpaved, the roads laterite or packed earth.

"We're looking for a new place," Duclos said casually, "but haven't been able to find anything suitable. With all the oilmen in town, good housing is scarce."

"The Americans spoil everything," Michaux said.

Inside, the premier's aide looked about amusedly. "Roughing it?" he laughed. He patted his marcelled waves. "You do have ice, I trust?"

"Of course," Duclos said angrily. "Maria, two glasses with ice."

"As I recall from Cotonou," Michaux said languidly, "you fancy gin and bitters. Do you have bitters?"

"No," Duclos said shortly. Then he brightened. "But two fine fresh limes. We shall have gin gimlets."

"Enchanting," Michaux drawled.

Mboa went into the bedroom, closed the door. She sat on the edge of the bed, stared down at her clenched fists.

"Maria!" Duclos bawled from the living room. "Where are you? Glasses! Ice!"

She rose, changed into a nondescript housedress, a loose shift of unbleached muslin laundered so many times it was as thin as silk. It clung to hips, haunch, nipples. She went padding out in bare feet, deliberately the African slattern.

She fetched the men their glasses. Fetched their ice. Sliced a lime and fetched that. Fetched a small pillow to put behind the back of Christophe Michaux so he might be more comfortable in the raddled armchair. Then she retired to the kitchen and sat quietly in the darkness, listening.

She was a small woman. Flat-breasted, lean-shanked, tunnel-black. But there was a slim sinuousness to her body. A grace. Her features were classically African: convoluted lips and nostrils boldly splayed. Eyes liquid and almost Oriental. Nose strong and almost Semitic. She was a Hausa. Proud women. And, when need be, stone. In the darkness of her kitchen she sat as stone, motionless and listening.

"How will the death of his father affect President Anokye?" asked Christophe Michaux.

"Affect him?"

"His public activities," Michaux said impatiently. "Will there be a period of public mourning? Will the loan talks be postponed?"

"Oh no, no," Duclos said hurriedly. "It is a private matter. I imagine the President will want the day-to-day activities of the government to continue without interruption."

Michaux laughed shortly. "You imagine," he said ironically. "Duclos, exactly how much do you know of what Anokye intends?"

"I know his intentions," Duclos said hotly. "I am as close to him as any man in the Asante government."

"Of course, of course," Michaux soothed. "I did not mean to imply you were not. But surely you will admit he may have plans which he has not revealed to you. Military plans, for instance."

Duclos grumbled something unintelligible, swilling his gin, sulking.

"How I wish I could have a private audience with the Little Captain," Michaux mused. "A short audience. There is so much I would like to ask."

Duclos looked up with interest.

"Ask him what?"

"Oh . . . about his political philosophy. How he intends to achieve the Pan-Africa of his Zabarian speech. Whether his inclusion of all races is something he really believes, or is just expediency. Public relations."

"The President is an expedient man," Duclos acknowledged. "But is that to be condemned? All the world's great political leaders have been pragmatists."

"I couldn't agree with you more," Michaux said warmly. "With your deep knowledge of history and political science, who would dare disagree?"

He laughed lightly, and Duclos laughed in return, feeling better. He poured himself another drink after noting that the premier's aide still had half a glass.

"Expediency," Michaux nodded. "Now, that is wise. I believe almost any compromise might be justifiable if the goal can be achieved. The end justifies the means—what?"

"Oh yes," Duclos agreed. "But not always. No obsalutes. Absolutes."

"Correct, minister!" Michaux cried. "Not always, and no absolutes. For instance, if I knew in my own mind that the unification of Africa could be achieved by the inclusion of whites in high political and economic posts. I would be tempted. I admit it, I-would-be-tempted."

"Wouldn't we all?" Duclos muttered.

"But knowing the past history of whites in Africa, their cruelty and racism, could we dare include them? Could we in all conscience include them? I say no."

"No," Duclos said.

"A dilemma, is it not? We agree the end justifies the means, but here is one means we reject out of hand. What to do? You know, Duclos, with all my heart I hope Obiri Anokye has solved this problem. That he has devised a way to achieve African solidarity with the aid of whites without the danger of giving them a stranglehold on our future."

"He has!" Duclos shouted, beaming. "He has!"

"Has he, now?" Michaux said smoothly. "That's encouraging. I think I'll have a refill."

Duclos poured gin with a wavering hand. Michaux added ice and a squeezed lime wedge. He stirred the drink slowly with a long forefinger and polished nail. Then he settled back, stroking his little goatee lovingly.

"I can't tell you what a pleasure this is," he said. "To have such a stimulating conversation with a man of your learning. Just to listen to your words, minister, gives me renewed faith in Africa's destiny."

"Thank you," Duclos said, preening. " 'Preciate that."

"Africa, Africa," Michaux sighed. "What are we to do with her? But I am glad to hear that at least one man knows the answer. Obiri Anokye can unite the continent if any man can."

"Correct!" the Minister of State said excitedly. "He has not told me this, mind you . . . This is strictly my own idea. . . ."

"Of course, minister."

"But I believe Bibi—the President, that is—unconsciously senses an evolution of political form. That is to say, no man of intelligence believes democracy is the ideal form of government for every country, regardless of its stage of political and economic sophit—sophistication. That is to say, in India, for example, authoritarian rule may be necessary, temporarily. And then, evolving, we arrive at a limited monarchy, constitutional monarchy, something of the sort. And then, when the electorate has been educated and is capable of understanding the issues involved and choosing representatives wisely to deal with those issues, why then we—you understand what I'm getting at?"

"Of course, of course," Michaux said enthusiastically. "Government not as stasis, but a growing organism, evolving as the people evolve."

"Exactly!" Duclos said. "Christophe, you've grasped it immediately. The state growing as the people grow. Say, from a military dictatorship to a fully participant democracy. Over a period of years, naturally."

"Naturally," Michaux said. He hunched forward on his chair, hands on knees, staring at Duclos intently. "And you feel this is what President Anokye believes? Unconsciously, of course."

"Induti—indubitably," Duclos said. "The Little Captain has faith in the inherent good sense of the comman man."

"The common man," Michaux repeated. "His inherent good sense. How right you are! But first, a start must be made. Even if it's a military dictatorship. Correct?"

"Correct," Duclos said, staring at his guest somewhat glassily. "It's only a start. A first step."

"Granted. Toward something much better. Much finer. I agree. But how is this first step to be made? Africa is an enormous continent. More than sixty nations. How would one take the first step? To bring all these diverse nations and peoples under one rule?"

"Ah!" Jean-Louis Duclos exclaimed. He held up a finger, shaking it. "Impossible for any other man. But Obiri Anokye can do it. He has a plan!"

"Oh-ho," Christophe Michaux nodded, as if with satisfaction. "A plan. And what might that be?"

The Asante Minister of State began to talk.

Mboa, huddled in the kitchen, listened with dismay. She knew little of history, nothing of Realpolitik. But she knew her husband was drinking too much, and talking too much to a man from another country. A man she did not trust. One did not have to be a professor to know this. Or a politico. One had only to be a smart bush nigger—which was, she acknowledged, exactly what she was—to know that her husband, whom she loved, was acting the fool. And fools in Africa were no different from fools in America, France, or Esquimau-land. Fools anywhere could bring to nothing all the agonized thinking and careful planning of wise men. A smart bush nigger knew that from the age of three.

So she let her husband talk, and drink, and did not interrupt. She merely sat tensely, noting grimly how Michaux flattered her foolish husband, massaged his ego, agreed with him in all things, and drew from him, eventually, the story of how Obiri Anokye intended to become the ruler of both Togo and Benin in two weeks' time.

Finally, after another drink—Mboa had lost count—her husband fell asleep in his chair, snoring softly. Christophe Michaux took the empty glass gently from the limp fingers. "Maria!" he said imperiously.

When she entered the room, he stretched lazily and tried to yawn.

"Good talk," he said. "What is it you say—good palaver? I have enjoyed it. As you can see, your husband is asleep." He laughed. "The cares of state," he said. "I must get back to my hotel. Call a taxi for me."

"They do not run at this hour," she said stonily. "I shall drive you."

He looked at her bare feet.

"Well, well, well," he said. "Will wonders never cease?"

She put on sandals to drive the Simca. Michaux sat close beside her. It seemed to her he sat too close.

"It is a delight to see an African woman capable of handling modern machinery," he said. "You drive very well."

When she said nothing, he poked around in his jacket and came up with a packet of cigarettes.

"Would you care for a smoke?" he asked. She shook her head, and he laughed and said, "Not strong enough for you?"

The cigarette had a sickening, perfumish odor. She leaned her head toward the open window to escape the smoke.

"You are a funny little woman, Maria," he said. "Or would you prefer that I call you Mboa?"

"Whatever pleases you," she said.

"What pleases me?" he said. "Are you good at pleasing men, Mboa? Are you an expert?"

Suddenly she realized this evil man was as big a fool as her husband. Bigger. She had a vagrant thought that perhaps these light-skinned Martinicains, these pale-skinned men, had been bled of their sense as well as their color.

"I like to please men," she said boldly, determined to test the depth of his stupidity.

"Do you?" he chuckled. His hand fell onto her thigh. "Would you like to please me, Mboa?"

"Perhaps," she said archly, and he laughed.

She knew the way. South on the Boulevard Voltaire, and then west on the coastal road past the Mokodi Hilton. It was quite late; there was little traffic.

When they came to the turnoff to the Hôtel Africain, he directed her along the laterite road to the row of safari bungalows. His was last in line, the one farthest west. She had heard talk about this hotel, but could not recall it. Idle gossip was of no interest to her.

His soft hand had remained on her thigh. When she switched off the motor and killed the lights, the hot hand moved upward.

"I find you African women very understanding," he said. "Very sympathetic. I am so alone, Mboa. So lonely."

"No man should be alone," she said, knowing she ran no risk.

Then he did laugh, his hands fondling her small breasts roughly through the thin cloth.

"Nigger whore," he said, still laughing. "No, Mboa. I already have company. And I would not soil myself with you. Now drive carefully going back, sweetie. Tuck hubby into bed and play with yourself awhile."

Still laughing, he got out of the car, unlocked the door of his cottage, entered. She heard the door lock behind him. She leaned from the car window, spat on his track, muttered a curse in Hausa.

Then she started the car and drove directly to the home of Yvonne and Sene Yeboa.

His wife, Judith, and Zuni's wife, Magira, had washed and patted dry the corpse. Scented it with cloves and spices artfully placed. Dressed it in clean linen and a shiny black suit. Now the small, dead body lay on the kitchen table, arms crossed on the chest. The eyelids had been lowered. A small bundle of white cock feathers, bound with Judith's hair, had been concealed beneath the shirt, over the heart. The Baptist burial had been scheduled for early morning. In that climate, it was wise.

Obiri Anokye, Sara, and Sene Yeboa had arrived. They had waded ashore from a launch of the Asante National Navy. Under orders, it rode at anchor, bobbing, a hundred meters off the Zabarian beach. They embraced Judith, Magira, Zuni. Then kissed the wrinkled cheek of the dead man. The family sat about the corpse in the kitchen, drinking coffee and discussing funeral arrangements.

"Bibi, you will speak over the grave?" Judith asked.

Obiri looked to Zuni. He was the oldest son; it was his right.

"You, Bibi," Zuni said. "It will be more honor if the President of Asante speaks."

"I will speak," Obiri nodded. "You have arranged for the carriage? The grave?"

"Pastor Moeller has promised to take care of all," Zuni said. "We asked for a private burial, but he said friends will wish to be there and we cannot say no."

"Let them come," the Little Captain said. "He had many friends. Let them show their grief."

"Bibi," Sene Yeboa said in a low voice, "an honor guard? Rifles fired over the grave?"

"No, Sene," Obiri said gently. "Nothing like that. Let us keep it simple and quiet. Mother, you are tired?"

She shrugged. "I will sit up," she said.

"No, no," he said quickly. "You are all tired. You have had much to do. Go to bed. I will keep vigil."

"And I," Yeboa said.

"And Sene," the President said. "Sene and I will sit together. The rest of you go to your beds."

"I will not sleep," Judith warned.

"Then rest," Obiri smiled. "Just rest. Tomorrow, you will need your strength."

She was as old, as worn and wrinkled, as her dead husband. Veins, sinews, tendons pressing out the parchment skin. But her eyes were unclouded. As lively as Sara's. And her children knew her determination. She might, they hoped, live on another ten years or more, struggling against death as she had struggled all her life, never questioning the need.

"Adebayo?" she asked suddenly.

"I have sent him to Togo," Obiri Anokye said. "He cannot be recalled in time."

She looked at him but said nothing. She rose slowly. The others followed her from the room. Obiri and Sene were left alone with the corpse. They took off their shoes, jackets, loosened their collars. The Little Captain poured them more coffee.

"Sene, call the palace duty officer and tell him where we are."

When he had become President, he had insisted that a telephone be installed in Zuni's home. It was the second phone in the village of Porto-Chonin. The other belonged to the fish merchant.

Yeboa spoke briefly, then returned to take a chair to the right of the Little Captain and slightly behind him.

"The dinner has ended," he reported. "The guests have all departed. Premier Da Silva wishes to convey his condolences. And the others, also."

Anokye nodded. The two men settled down, in comfortable silence. They both had the ability to wait, in quiet and tranquillity. On the trail, ambush, or whatever the circumstances. Waiting, patiently, was a gift as important as fury in battle. Acceptance was the other side of resolve.

Obiri Anokye stared at the body of his dead father. He saw the old man's face in profile. Features already softening. Waxen sheen of blood stopped. Ironic expression of repose.

Death did not come new to him. Neither natural death: among kin or friends, field or road, face whirled suddenly to the sun, soil warm beneath the back. Nor violent death: the body torn and shocked, ripped from life. The Little Captain knew it all.

"Sene," he said slowly, "do you fear death?"

"Fear it?" Yeboa said, just as slowly. "No, I do not, Bibi. We go to a better world. The sun shines. The rain is sufficient, and so there is food. Old friends and laughter. How should I fear it? Millet beer and palm wine. All a man can drink. And the hunt of splendid animals. The hunt might take the turning of the sun, but in the end the beast is slain. And a good-hearted woman who cooks well and never complains. The sea is there, also. Fish. The hills. Great savannas of grass and forests of green trees. Everything a man could want. In the next world. Do I speak the truth, Little Captain?"

"You speak the truth," Anokye said.

"It is true I have not always been a good man," Yeboa went on in his stubborn way. "I have killed. But always for sufficient reason, Bibi."

"I believe it."

"Other things I have done I did from bad feelings or drunkenness or from weakness. But Little Captain, if we are all God's creatures, as our church says, then God has given us the bad feelings and the weakness. The drunkenness, I admit, might be mine. But if we are truly God's creatures, then we must do what we must do, and the fault is not in us. Is that not true?"

"It is true, Sene."

"So we do what we must do," Yeboa nodded, satisfied. "I am a sergeant, and you are a captain. But God is the general who commands us all. And we obey His orders because we are good soldiers. That is how I see it."

"You are a wise man, Sene."

"No, Bibi, not so wise. I am just a soldier."

Their palaver ceased then. Neither slept, but both sat upright with the corpse of Josiah Anokye since it would not be seemly for the dead man to be left alone before his interment. It was long past midnight when the new phone shrilled. Neither man was startled, but both turned slowly to stare at the black instrument. Yeboa rose to answer it, and Anokye watched his expression.

"Yes? Yes, Yvonne, he is here and awake. Yes. Tell me; I listen."

He listened a long time, turning his head to stare at President Anokye.

"All right, Yvonne," he said finally. "Now you must repeat what you told me to Bibi. Yes, it is necessary. I want him to hear it in your words."

His eyes had become blank, his face frozen. He held the phone out to the Little Captain.

"It is Yvonne," he said, his voice cold. "From our home."

Anokye rose and took the phone.

"Yes, Yvonne?" he said.

First she expressed condolences on the death of his father, for which he thanked her. Then she told him what she had just told her husband: that Mboa Duclos had come to the Yeboa home and awakened her. That Mboa had told her that Minister of State Jean-Louis Duclos had become befuddled with drink and had spoken foolishly to Christopher Michaux. That Duclos had revealed details of the Togo-Benin campaign to the premier's aide. That Mboa believed Michaux was an evil man who was Obiri Anokye's enemy, and Mboa wished Yvonne to tell all this to the President.

"Thank you, Yvonne," Anokye said evenly. "You and Mboa have done well. I shall not forget it. She is there now?"

"Yes. Weeping."

"Keep her there. Sene and I will be with you in an hour. You understand?"

"Yes, Bibi."

He hung up and turned to Yeboa.

The sergeant stared at him and imagined he saw, far in the back of Obiri Anokye's dark eyes, a red light begin to flame. No larger than a candle in a tunnel, but burning, burning . . .

"Call Sam Leiberman," Anokye said. Voice hard and without tone. "Tell him to meet us at the naval base. A black car. Not a government car. A full tank of fuel."

The sergeant nodded.

"I will wake Zuni to keep vigil with our father. Then I will go down to the beach and signal the launch to come in for us. Meet me there. We must move as quietly as we can. I do not wish to awaken the women."

He started from the room, then turned back.

"Sene, are you armed?"

"I have a revolver, Little Captain."

"Good. But I have nothing. Tell Leiberman to bring me a weapon. A Uzi."

"Yes *sah!*" said Sgt. Yeboa.

Sam Leiberman was waiting for them at the head of the ramp. The car he had brought was an old, bulge-bodied Buick. It had been repainted a dozen times.

The top coat was a dulled, grainy black, covering ancient dents and scars. Even the pitted chrome had been painted over. President Anokye and Sergeant Yeboa climbed into the wide back seat.

Leiberman turned, arm resting on the back of the front seat.

"Listen," he said roughly to the Little Captain, "about your old man—I'm sorry."

Anokye patted the meaty arm.

"Thank you, Sam," he said. "Your father is still living?"

"Who the hell knows?" Leiberman said. "He took off when I was a kid." He bent over, picked up the Uzi from the floor at his feet, handed it across to Anokye. "The safety's on," he said. "I cleaned it. Full magazine. It throws a little high and to the right."

"I'll remember," Anokye nodded.

"Where to now?"

"First to Sene's home. Here is what has happened . . ."

Mboa was still there, no longer weeping. President Anokye took her aside and spoke gently to her a long time. Holding her hands, looking into her eyes as he questioned her. Leiberman, Sene, and Yvonne sat in the kitchen, smoking Gauloises and drinking Star beer. Leiberman told them a funny story of how, while serving with the U.S. Army in Sicily, he had fallen out of a truck, dead drunk, broken his arm, and had been awarded the Purple Heart. Then Mboa and the Little Captain came into the kitchen.

"We will need two cars," the President said. "Sam, you and Sene and I will go in yours. The women will follow in Mboa's Simca. When we get to the turnoff for the Hôtel Africain, switch off your lights. Michaux is in the last safari cottage, the one farthest west."

Leiberman finished his beer in two heavy gulps and belched. He rose to his feet, hitched up his pants.

"We go there first?" he asked, knowing.

"No," Obiri Anokye said. He turned slowly, looked at the trembling figure of Mboa. "First we go to the Duclos' home and take Jean."

She took a quick step forward, put a hand hesitantly on his arm.

"Bibi?" she said. "Please?"

They stared at each other. The others did not speak. Did not move.

Then Obiri Anokye touched the woman's cheek and nodded once.

"For you," he said.

The door of the Duclos' home was unlocked. They went in fast, grabbed Minister of State Jean-Louis Duclos from where he sat, still snoring gently in the armchair. They hustled him out of there, stumbling, grumbling, legs flopping under him. They threw him into the back seat of the Buick. Leiberman drove sedately toward the Hôtel Africain.

The windows were down. A cool night breeze came billowing in. Duclos gulped, came awake, shook his head, looked about. Puzzled. Not yet fearing.

"Sene?" he said. "Bibi—Mr. President?"

"Yes," Anokye said.

"What—where are we going?"

"To visit your good friend Christopher Michaux," the Little Captain said. The fire in his dark eyes blazed brighter. He leaned close to Duclos. Face to face. "You understand?"

Duclos looked into those eyes. Then he feared.

"Thank your wife that you live," Anokye said. "I do it for her. She is correct; you are a fool."

"A fool," Duclos agreed, beginning to weep. "I am a fool."

Anokye thrust the man from him, turned his face away. They drove the rest of the way without speaking; the only sounds were Duclos' sobs and snuffles. The Simca followed closely.

They came to the turnoff. Switched off their lights. They toured slowly down the line of separated bungalows. Coasted silently to a stop near the last.

"Wait here," Anokye whispered.

He slipped out of the Buick, faded into shadows. They sat patiently. Duclos had stopped crying. Now he sat bent far over, face hidden in his hands. In a few moments, Anokye returned.

"Lights," he reported in a low voice. "Two of them inside. Michaux and another. In the rear of the cottage. The door is locked, but not strong. Here is how we shall do it: I go in first. If I cannot kick the door open, I will shoot the lock."

"Bibi—" Sene Yeboa started.

"No, Sene," Anokye said sternly. "I go first. You two bring Duclos between you. Close behind me. We go in very fast. Is all understood?"

They got out of the car. Reached in, hauled out Duclos. He was blubbering again. Hardly able to stand. Leiberman and Yeboa got a good grip under his arms. Hustled him after Anokye, feet barely touching the ground. They moved quickly around to the front door.

Anokye glanced back. In the darkness the whites of his eyes seemed enormous. Flaming centers. Entire face old and stretched.

"Ready?" he asked. Voice gritty.

They nodded. He drew up his right leg. Knee almost touching chin. Uzi held in firing position across his chest. Heavy boot drove forward. Wood splintered. Lock wrenched off. Door went slamming backward, Anokye rushed, crouching. Muzzle of gun searching. He ran short, quick steps toward the lighted bathroom. The moaning Duclos was pulled after him.

Bathroom door slammed back. Into the scented room. A naked black boy, ten perhaps, or twelve, in the water. Lolling. Head over the tub rim. Michaux atop him. Glistening. Looking back over his shoulder. Face coming apart. The full tub soaped and steamy. Bubbles of bath oil. Perfume.

Anokye stepped to one side. Duclos was dragged to the doorway. Yeboa grabbed his hair. Yanked his head back so he must look. Obiri Anokye opened fire.

The Uzi thundered in the small room. He held the trigger depressed and ran through the entire twenty-five-round magazine. Back and forth. Bodies of the two stitched again and again. Leaping first. Then twisting. Turning. Driven back. Down. Under. Soapy water churned to bloody froth. Mouths open but no screams. No sound but thunder. The 9mm slugs hit, pierced, broke, hammered, killed.

Sudden silence. Christopher Michaux, one arm draped over the tub edge. Head out. Silky goatee dripping crimson soap. Eyes staring at the floor. The boy completely under. Swirling. Floating in ink.

Obiri Anokye turned away, motioned to the others. They supported the gagging, retching Jean-Louis Duclos outside, threw him into the back seat of the Simca. Mboa got in alongside him, cradled him in her arms.

"Thank you," she said softly to Anokye. "The other?"

He stared at her a moment, slowly calming. Then he nodded.

"Good," she said.

President Anokye turned to Leiberman and Yeboa.

"Handle it," he said. "For those who have heard the gunfire, it is a police matter, not to be questioned. Forget the damage. The manager will wish to keep his license for this shit pot. But give him money also."

"It shall be done, Bibi," Sergeant Yeboa said. "As for the bodies, there are deserted phosphate pits up near Gonja."

"I know them," the Little Captain nodded. "Excellent. Better than the sea. Questions will be asked about the disappearance of the premier's aide and the boy. An exhaustive investigation will be made by the gendarmerie. Take care of it, Sene. Sam, here is your Uzi. Thank you. You are correct; it throws high and to the right."

He got into the front seat of the Simca, next to Yvonne. She drove back to the Yeboa home. She and Anokye got out. Then Mboa drove her husband back to their home. Yvonne and the Little Captain got into the sergeant's military Land-Rover. Yvonne drove him back to the naval base.

"I am in your debt," he said shortly. He drummed fingers on his knee. "Yours and Sene's. Is there anything you wish?"

"Yes," she said promptly, and he turned in surprise. "Sene wishes to become an officer."

"I offered him rank after the coup," he told her. "Sene said he wished to remain a sergeant."

"I think he now knows he made a mistake," she said. "But Sene is a proud man. You must ask him again."

"Yes," Anokye agreed, "Sene is proud. I shall ask him again. How does Captain Yeboa sound?"

"Colonel Yeboa sounds better," she said.

He laughed at her impudence and touched her arm lightly.

"Very well," he said. "Colonel Yeboa. Now you shall be the colonel's lady."

"So I shall," she said.

They drove the rest of the way in silence. She pulled up at the ramp at the naval base. Anokye reached over, turned off the engine, the lights.

"Yvonne," he said. "You and Sene. . . . All goes well?"

"Very well," she nodded. "Better than I expected."

"Good. Yvonne, you are still in my heart. I have not deserted you. You know that?"

"I know it, Bibi. You will marry soon?"

"Yes. Very soon."

"I hope you and your wife will be as happy as Sene and I."

"Thank you," he said. They had been speaking French. He switched to Akan: "May you have happiness all the days of a long life."

"May good health be yours," she replied in the same language. She paused. "And may the gods grant all you deserve," she added.

When he was in the launch, heading out to Zabar, he looked back. The Land-Rover was still parked at the head of the ramp. He thought he could see her pale face. Staring at him from the opened window.

Once again he waded ashore. When he came into the kitchen of the Anokye home, his older brother was seated next to the corpse. But Zuni's head was down on folded arms on the table. Judith Anokye sat nearby, awake and erect. She looked up as Obiri came in.

"There has been trouble?" she asked anxiously.

"A matter of no importance," he said. "Please return to bed."

She rose wearily to her feet. She seemed to him so old, so worn by life, that he took her into his arms, held her tightly. Refusing to weep.

"You are not happy, Bibi?" she asked.

"Yes, yes. I know happiness. All goes well, mother."

"You are not happy," she decided, and sighed.

He would not argue, but stroked her cheek and pushed her gently off to bed. Then he awoke Zuni and told him he would resume the vigil. His older brother nodded, embraced him sleepily, started out. He turned, the two of them standing on opposite sides of their father's corpse.

"A good catch today, Bibi," Zuni said muzzily.

Obiri Anokye, fisherman's son, was immediately interested.

"I have heard the runs have been good," he said. "What did you get?"

"Bass, grouper, and three fine, fat tuna. Tomorrow, I will send the fattest tuna to the palace for you."

"Thank you, brother."

Zuni departed, and Obiri took his chair next to their dead father. Who, the Little Captain knew, would have been pleased by this short conversation between his two oldest sons. He took off his wet shoes and socks again, removed his jacket. He stared at the blurred, dissolving features of Josiah Anokye. He began, in his mind, to compose the eulogy he would deliver at the burial of this good man.

20

There was a hard knock on the office door. Anokye frowned, slid the maps he was working on into his top desk drawer, called out, "Come in." The guard on corridor duty stepped inside, snapped off a sharp salute. "My president," he said, "the English lady wished to speak with you."

"Livesay?" the Little Captain said. "Yes, it is all right. Show her in."

He rose and moved from behind his desk. She came into the room flustered and, he thought, blushing. She was wearing the white gloves again.

"Joan," he said, smiling, "I thought you had gone back to the hotel to pack?"

"I had, Mr. President," she said, trying to smile. "But now Ian tells me we're flying out quite early in the morning. I was afraid I wouldn't have a chance to see you again, and I did want to say goodbye and thank you for your kindness. I'm sure it was a very trying time for you."

He made a gesture.

"Come sit down. for a moment, Joan," he said. "You do have a moment?"

"Oh yes."

"Good. Sit here on the couch."

He crossed the room to close the door firmly, then went to the cabinet behind his desk.

"Now here is an excellent Italian brandy," he said. "Shall we have a drink together and toast our friendship and also, perhaps, our meeting again soon?"

"Thank you," she said faintly. "I'd like that."

He poured them each a small bit, then sat on the couch with her. Each turned sideways to look at the other. Raised glasses.

"Go in good health and return in good health," he said in Akan.

"May you know happiness," she said in the same language. They touched glasses and sipped.

"Your Akan is very good," he said, in English. "I hope you will continue your studies."

"Oh yes," she said. "I intend to."

"Good," he said. "I think you will find that after you have mastered Akan, then all the others—Twi, Ewe, Hausa, and so forth—all will come much easier. But of course, you must return to Asante to practice!"

She smiled, looking down at her glass.

"I hope I'm not keeping you from your work, Mr. President."

"Not at all. I was about to finish up. It is late, is it not?"

"Yes. Almost midnight. But I don't suppose you consider that very late."

"No, I do not," he laughed. "There is still some reading I must do. Upstairs. In my chamber."

"Oh," she said. "Then I'll just stay a moment."

"As long as you wish," he said gallantly. "Tell me, Joan, have you decided what recommendations to make? How things may be improved in Asante?"

"I have some ideas, Mr. President," she nodded. "I really shouldn't mention them to you because the analysts in London may turn them down. They'll run them through the computer, you see, to determine if they're sound. Economically sound, you know, or justified in view of Asante's priorities. The 'overview.' They're always talking of judging suggestions in relation to the 'overview.' "

"I understand that," he said. "But what suggestions will you make?"

"Mostly small things," she confessed. "Like efficient intercom systems for the palace and other staff offices and ministries. A centralized government motor pool. Better organization of the school system. More bus routes. And have you considered a railroad from Mokodi to the north?"

"It has been discussed off and on for many years," he said. "But it hardly seems necessary with the paved highway going all the way to Four Points. Trucking takes care of all our needs."

"It does today," she agreed. "But phosphate production increases every year, and so does the shipment of hardwoods from the hills. Perhaps in five or ten years, a railroad would prove valuable. It would certainly help open the north country. New villages. New factories."

He was bemused by her insistence. "Perhaps you are right," he said doubtfully. "But I would have to see the results of a study by transportation specialists. Projection of future needs."

"And a television station," she said. "I think Asante should have TV."

"A television station! But would that not be very costly?"

"Very," she acknowledged. "But I was wondering if you might get a big British or American or French or German company to build it for you. In return for an exclusive franchise to sell their sets in Asante."

He looked at her admiringly.

"Clever," he said. "Very clever, Joan."

"You have so little time for domestic politics, Mr. President. It is an area that, frankly, I think you neglect. Not because you fail to recognize its importance, but simply because you don't have the time to travel all over the country giving speeches and meeting voters. Television might be the answer."

"Yes," he said thoughtfully, "that is true. And would I also be able to appear on television sets in neighboring countries? Say, Ghana and Togo?"

She shook her head, the short, fine hair bouncing about her ears.

"I don't know the answer to that, Mr. President. You would need technicians to tell you. But your speeches could always be taped for showing in other African countries. And overseas, too, of course."

"Yes," he said. "An interesting idea. You will suggest this to your company in London?"

"I intend to."

"Good. Do you have any more recommendations?"

"Just in the organization of your personal office, Mr. President." She took a deep breath, a sip of brandy, another deep breath, and plunged ahead. "I think you need a private aide. An executive secretary. Someone like that. To oversee a personal staff. To relieve you of all the day-to-day details of your office. About a week ago you spent most of one morning straightening out a squabble between your cook and the man who delivers fresh vegetables to the palace. There were other times when you had to call repeatedly to get a car or make certain the plane would go to Cotonou to pick up Premier Da Silva and your fiancée. Your time is too valuable to spend on such matters. A good executive staff could take care of those annoying details."

"Oh, what a blessing that would be!" he exclaimed. "Joan, you are a very intelligent, honest, and understanding young woman. I believe your suggestions are going to be a great help, and for that I thank you. Would you care for more brandy?"

"Well . . . all right," she said shyly. "A wee bit, thank you. I really just came to say goodbye."

He poured them each a little more. Then sat back in the corner of the couch, crossed his legs. He sniffed his brandy, regarded her with some puzzlement. She sat on the edge of the leather couch, back straight, knees together, elbows close to her body. Her head was bent. He could see the curved nape of her neck, a halo of fine hair outlined in the lamplight. There was about her, in that child's pose, a tenderness, a soft vulnerability.

As usual, her loose dress revealed nothing. It fell in generous pleats and folds, billows of cloth. She could be a stick beneath. Or a child. Or a naked woman. And beneath the blushing manner, the hesitant wit, might be . . . what?

He stood suddenly and put his brandy glass aside. He came over to stand directly in front of her. She looked up. He took her glass from her and set that aside also. Then he cupped her head in his hands, lightly, feeling the sheen of her hair. Pressing. Still she looked up at him, rigid, but showing no fear. Slowly her hands rose and clamped about his wrists. Not pulling him away. Pulling him closer.

He leaned from the hips, lowering his head until their faces almost touched. So he could stare directly into her deep, swimming eyes. She raised her chin slightly and brushed his lips with hers. A swift brush. A pause. Then her lips returned. A pause. And brushed again. And again. Until they lingered. Her hands gripping his wrists harder, pulling. Then leaping suddenly to the back of his head, his neck. Straining. Lips . . . tongue . . .

Still leaning, still kissing, he unbuttoned her high-collared dress, slipped a hand inside. Heard her sound. Felt her move. Touched a naked breast. As slick as silk. Large, coolly limpid, with a peak that hardened instantly between his blunt, twisting fingers.

"Is the door locked?" she said.

21

Asante, a former French Colony, achieved independence in 1958. King Prempeh IV was crowned first ruler of the new monarchy, and as a gesture of goodwill, the French gave Asante a small corvette. Of Le Fouqueux class, the craft was 52 meters long and displaced 325 tons. It was powered by four Pielstick diesels, and had a range of 3,000 miles at 12 knots. Main armament included two 40mm Bofors and two 20mm antiaircraft guns, as well as deck mortars and depth charge racks.

The gift turned out to be a shrewd investment for the French. The profligate Prempeh spent almost five million francs in Toulon shipyards converting the fighting craft to a pleasure yacht with luxurious sleeping accommodations, a grand piano, marble bathtubs, and bidets in the Asante national colors. The pride of the Asante Royal Navy, it was renamed *La Liberté*, and was reserved for the King's exclusive use. Prempeh made several short cruises, close to shore, but by the time the conversion was completed, Asante's balance sheet was in a deplorable state; little money was available for fuel. So *La Liberté* was moored at the Mokodi naval base, and used as a setting for diplomatic receptions or as a kind of private club for the King's relatives and cronies, who, all being Muslims, welcomed the opportunity to escape occasionally from the suffocating presence of their many wives and the strictures of their faith against the use of alcohol.

When Obiri Anokye deposed, and killed, King Prempeh IV, and became the first president of the Republic of Asante, *La Liberté* was one of the prizes that fell undamaged into the hands of the dissidents. President Anokye was more interested in guns than colorful bidets, and during the early months of his regime, *La Liberté*'s armament was restored to working order. The baroque furnishings, gilt-framed paintings, grand piano, tapestried bulkhead panels, and Oriental rugs were taken to the presidential palace. Because of the cost of removal, it was decided that the marble bathtubs (and the famous bidets) would remain in situ. But generally *La Liberté* was returned to fighting trim. Instructors were brought from Toulon to teach Asante sailors how to operate the antiaircraft batteries, deck mortars, and depth charge racks. With Asante's treasury beginning to show signs of wealth, money was available for practice ammunition. And money was available for fuel.

It was a hazy, sun-spangled morning when the crew of *La Liberté* cast off lines from the Mokodi pier and headed slowly southward out to sea, under the proud command of young Capt. Niblo Ojigi, highest ranking officer of the Asante navy. (There were only five other officers, all lieutenants, three of whom commanded motor launches.)

Aboard, in addition to officers and crew, were President Obiri Anokye,

Col. Sene Yeboa, Col. Jim Nkomo, Peter Tangent, and Sam Leiberman. Despite the shimmering glory of the day, and the special provisions brought aboard, this was not intended as a pleasure cruise. It was, in fact, to be the final planning session for the Togo-Benin campaign.

In the main wardroom, where the late King Prempeh had once shown Laurel and Hardy films and Chaplin comedies, the men gathered about a long steel table bolted to the deck. President Obiri Anokye spread his maps and outlined his plan to pit Togolese and Benin armies against each other in the central areas of both countries while Asante forces invaded and occupied the centers of government on the coast.

They listened with growing amazement as Anokye's scheme became clear to them. Sam Leiberman, in particular, was almost hysterical with amusement.

"I love it," he said, coughing and holding his ribs. "It's going to be a fucked-up as a Chinese fire drill. How long do you think it'll take them to coppish what's happening?"

"By the time they understand," Anokye said, "It will be too late. We will have taken Lomé, Cotonou, and Porto-Novo."

"And then?" Colonel Nkomo asked. "Surely they will turn south? Come at us?"

"Let them try," Sene Yeboa growled. He was wearing his new gold leaf with pride.

"Possibly they will turn south," Anokye nodded. "Probably. But I believe they will be bloodied. Demoralized from having found a hard fight when they expected to be unopposed. If they come south, then we must fight on two fronts. In Togo *and* Benin. It will be necessary to divide our forces. But with the new tanks, trucks, and personnel carriers, we have mobility. They do not. I will shift men and weapons as events develop. Now here is our first order of battle. Listen closely and learn your assignments. Ask questions if everything is not clear. It is the timing that concerns me most. We must move swiftly, hit hard, move on again . . ."

They spent three hours in preliminary discussions as *La Liberté* continued cruising, cutting smoothly through a calm sea. South of the island of Zabar, Captain Ojigi set a new course, on the second leg of a triangle that would bring his ship, eventually, back to the Mokodi base.

Shortly after noon, the wardroom was locked. President Anokye and his guests went topside for an alfresco luncheon on the afterdeck. The cold chicken, sandwiches, salad and fruit had been prepared in the palace kitchen and packed into individual boxes. Chilled beer was available from *La Liberté*'s capacious refrigerator.

They sat on the teak deck between depth charge racks and mortars, and looked about at the curious day. The sky was pearlescent, sea a thin milk. They merged at the horizon with no juncture. So all the world seemed a steamy, lustrous globe, slightly bluish, faintly gleaming, and *La Liberté* was its center. All else revolved slowly, dazzling and dreamy. They fell silent, drank their beer, and felt dizzy, transported.

Finally, they returned to the wardroom, and in the cool dimness regained their purpose and resolve. They bent over the maps once again.

"I will lead the attack personally with Nkomo's tank corps," the Little Captain told them. "Following us will be Fourth and Sixth brigades in trucks and personnel carriers. We will pause in Togo only long enough to neutralize Lomé. Then we advance across the Benin border to take Cotonou and Porto-Novo. Hopefully, during the siesta. Sam, you and Sene, with the Third and Fifth brigades, will remain in Togo. When the coastal section is secure, begin moving northward in case Songo discovers what has happened and turns south in an attempt to retake Lomé. Jim and I shall do the same in Benin to counter Colonel Sitobo. I do not underestimate that man. I am assigning you field artillery and the TOW missiles that are operable. We shall be in constant communication on radio. Broadcast in clear. I do not care. If you face a situation you cannot handle, tell me and I will send tanks. In addition, *La Liberté* will cruise off Lomé. The Bofors may prove of value in the event buildings near the coast must be shelled."

"What are you leaving in Asante?" Leiberman asked curiously.

"Very little," Anokye admitted. "The Corps of Engineers, the palace guard, the gendarmerie. Border guards. The country will be practically stripped bare, undefended for at least twenty-four hours. A calculated risk. With the aid of Peter and his friends, we have done all that can be done to turn the attention of the French elsewhere. But if they decide to drop paratroops or bring in a landing party, they will stroll into the palace, probably without firing a shot. But we cannot allow that possibility to affect our plans. Sene, I want you and Sam to work out your attack and movement toward the north tonight. I will go over your maps tomorrow morning at the palace."

"When does the balloon go up?" Leiberman asked. Then, when Anokye looked at him, puzzled, the mercenary said, "When does the party begin?"

"I have determined, after studying all the factors involved, that we shall move at dawn on August the seventh. Almost exactly a year to the day after the coup. An auspicious date."

He wondered what their reaction (particularly that of the whites) might be if they knew "all the factors involved" included secret consultations with certain astrologers, necromancers, and Auntie Tal, who had cast her magical stones to determine the most favorable time to launch an undertaking of great magnitude, importance, and danger.

"I want every Asante soldier to wear clean camouflaged dungarees," the Little Captain went on. "Polished boots. Regulation headgear. All weapons to be inspected. Extra magazines. We have spelled it out in a general order to be distributed to all officers and noncoms."

He continued to speak in flat, emotionless tones, all the more dramatic for that, but Peter Tangent was no longer listening. It was Anokye's unexpected use of the royal "we" that had caught his attention and started him wondering. He moved quietly away from the map table. Left the others discussing the logistics of the attack and wandered to one of the windows. Prempeh had them installed in the main wardroom in place of portholes. Tangent stood looking out, bending slightly from the waist. He watched Asante come up on the starboard bow.

At this distance, the land rose from the sea like a green dream. Cloud puffs hung almost motionless in a pellucid sky. Palms along the shore were as sharply etched as Japanese prints; and beyond, the white ribbon of the coastal road and the haze of the city. It was a floating fantasy, a vision of what all the world might be, perfumed and verdant.

"A beautiful land," Obiri Anokye said quietly at his elbow. "You agree, Peter?"

"Oh yes. Beautiful."

"But not your land. I do not expect you to die for it. That is why I have not planned your participation."

"I noticed that."

"I am sure you did. You have already done much to make our plan possible. I am in your debt; you know that, I do not think it wise if an American citizen, a representative of the oil company, joins Asante in this invasion of other African nations."

"You're probably right," Tangent sighed. "Still . . ."

"Still?"

"I would like to be there. To take part."

He turned to face Anokye. The two men stared gravely at each other.

"If that is your wish," the Little Captain said softly, "I cannot say no." He thought a moment. "Where is your lady? The singer? Amina Dunama?"

"She is presently in Cotonou, Mr. President. I believe she is performing in a hotel lounge."

Anokye nodded. "Perhaps you might join her there. A day or two before the attack. When we arrive at Cotonou, you might then join us. As an observer. Would that please you?"

"Very much, Mr. President."

Anokye grinned suddenly, clapped Tangent on the shoulder. "Good. I told you once you bring me luck. I will be happy to have you with me. But be cautious. You need not die to prove your manhood. There are other ways."

"Ah?" Peter Tangent said. "Ah," he agreed sadly.

22

She was still sleeping when he awoke. He lay motionless, staring at the ceiling. He thought, this is the day I may die. He waited to feel something significant, but felt nothing. He slid cautiously from the bed. The sheet had wadded on his side. She slept naked, back bowed, knees drawn up. She made an elegant Z shape. The pearls were still around her neck and hidden beneath her body.

He padded quietly to the hotel window, parted the curtains cautiously, peeked down. A dusty Cotonou street. A few people shuffling slowly on the shady side. A car now and then. Dogs. A woman with a frayed market basket balanced on her head. Two soldiers laughing and pushing each other. Tangent listened intently, but heard nothing. No gunfire. He looked at his watch. Coming up to noon.

He went into the bathroom. He recalled reading somewhere that men going into battle should, if possible, wash thoroughly and wear clean clothing. To help prevent the infection of wounds. Like having your head blown off, he thought sourly. Still, he soaped and scrubbed more thoroughly than usual, brushed his teeth, shaved carefully. The dandy preparing for an assignation.

When he came out, a towel modestly knotted about his thin hips, Amina Dunama was awake. Lying on her back, legs spread wide. She was smoking one of her long cigarillos. He bent to kiss her cheek.

"Good morning, darling," he said.

She grunted, but when he started to straighten up, she grabbed his head, pulled him down again, kissed his lips.

"I'm hungry," she said.

"Oh boy," he sighed. "Last night, after that half a cow you ate, you said you'd never be hungry again."

"That was last night," she said. "Mr. Tangent, sir."

"I thought you agreed to drop that 'Mr. Tangent, sir' crap," he said.

"When did I agree to that?"

"About two o'clock this morning."

"I didn't know what I was saying," she said lazily. "I was crazed with lust."

"Yes," he said, laughing. "So you were. Do you remember standing on your head?"

"Did I?" she said. "I thought it was you who was upside down."

He went to the window again, looked at his watch again.

"Got a date?" she asked.

"No, no. Just seeing what kind of a day it is."

"What kind is it?"

"Usual. Hot. Sunshiny."

"What is it?" she asked.

"What is what?"

"You. You're acting funny."

"Funny?"

"Well . . . strange. All wound-up."

"Nonsense. I'm the same sweet, understanding, calm, dependable, lovable slob I've always been."

"Come to bed," she said. "Mr. Tangent, slob."

"Well, ah, no," he said. "I don't think so. Not at the moment. I have to dress."

"Why?"

"People usually do. Sooner or later."

"What's wrong with later?"

"Come on," he said. "You're hungry; you said so. Let's dress and get a big a big breakfast. Maybe bifteck aux pommes frites. How does that sound?"

"Look at me," she said.

He turned to look at her. She was doing his favorite stunt: sitting up in bed, bending forward, her ankles hooked behind her neck. Her bearded vulva protruded like a pouting mouth. She looked up at him meekly. He couldn't help laughing, went over to sit on the edge of the bed, kissed the insides of her thighs.

"One of these days you're going to get stuck in that position," he said. "Spend the rest of your life like that. A little boy will have to pull you around on a cart."

She unhooked her ankles, curled around, put her head in his lap.

"There was a leper in my village like that," she said. "He had no legs. Or hands either, for that matter. Or ears. A child pulled him around on a little cart."

"I don't want to hear about it," he said stiffly.

She slowly raised her head. Slowly straightened up. Stared at him.

"Don't want to *hear* about it?" she said. "Lepers. People with their bodies eaten away. Also elephantiasis. Ever see a man who had to carry his balls in a wheelbarrow?"

"Why are you talking like this?" he said angrily.

"You think you know Africa," she said.

"Did I ever say I knew Africa?" he demanded. "You're determined to quarrel, aren't you?"

"You don't know Africa," she said sullenly. "Never will."

He stood, stalked away, ripped his towel off. He began to dress, tried to step into his undershorts, got his toes caught, had to hop about.

"Now we get it," he said furiously. "White men can never understand the secret heart of Africa. Englishmen can never understand Italians. Protestants can never understand Catholics. But everyone in the whole wide world understands the crass, money-grubbing, vulgar Americans. Right?"

"Go fuck yourself," she said coldly.

"Except, the first chance they get, they see American movies, read American novels, eat American food, drive American whisky. They have nothing but contempt for American culture, and they'll tell me all about it while eating a hotdog and drinking a Coke."

"I didn't say a word about Americans," she said. "All I said was you'll never know Africa. Not if mention of leprosy makes you sick. Just the *mention* of it. Let alone getting outside the Mokodi Hilton and trying to see what this country is really like."

"Eyeball to eyeball with a tsetse fly?" he said. "You think I don't know the sickness and the hunger and the poverty? You want me to wallow in it, is that it? Go into the villages and cry over the lepers, weep because children have swollen bellies from starvation, despair because some tribes eat the livers of the enemies they kill? Would that satisfy you?"

"You *don't* understand," she cried.

"*You* don't understand," he said hotly. "I'm helping bring dollars to Africa. And the only reason there's not more being done with those dollars is because you've got the most rotten, most venal, most corrupt political leaders in the world, and you damn well know it!"

They glared at each other, quivering with their fury. Eyes bulging. Fists clenched. She sitting naked on the bed, trembling. He in his long white cotton drawers, knobby knees shaking. But the moment was too taut to hold. It twanged tight and broke.

"What are we arguing about?" she asked.

He shook his head bewilderedly.

"Beats me," he said.

She leaped out of bed, raced across to him, pearls streaming behind her. She jumped up onto him, arms about his neck, long black legs curling about his hips. He staggered back and just did manage to keep his balance. She plastered her lips to his, and at the precise instant their darting tongues touched, there was a rumble of thunder in the distance, a high-pitched warble overhead and, in the street below, someone began to scream and seemed never to stop.

She slid down him, like coming off a greased pole, and ended up sitting on the floor at his feet. They stared at each other, mouths still open, tongues still protruding.

"Now what the hell?" she said.

He strode quickly to the window, looked down, saw a deserted street. He came back, pulled her roughly to her feet. He held her close, staring into her eyes.

"Listen carefully," he said. "Stay right here. Stay inside. Lock the door after I leave, and keep it locked. Don't go out. You understand that?"

She looked at him.

"It's an invasion," he said. "Asante soldiers are coming. Are here. There may be fighting in Cotonou. I don't know. I want you right here."

"Where are you going?" she said quietly.

"I'm going," he said. "I'll be back. But don't you go anyplace. Stay right here. Wait for me."

He began to dress, pulling on clothes she had not seen before, clothes she didn't know he had in his suitcase: khaki jeans, bush jacket, denim cap, heavy woolen socks, boots. And a 9mm Parabellum automatic in a shiny new holster. He tucked pistol and holster into his belt, under his jacket.

He went to the window again, pulled the curtain aside, searched the empty street. The scream had ended. There was no more warbling overhead. But the thunder of guns was louder now, coming from the west. As he stood at the window, realizing he had planned no way to join Anokye's forces, wondering how he might get to them, Amina Dunama came up behind him.

"Going off to war, are you?" she said.

"Ah yes," he said, still peering down. "Into the breach, lads, for Harry and for England. Shot and shell. And all that."

"Well, well, well," she said. Alongside him now. Staring out the window with him. "My conquering hero. Braving death. Then dying with my name on his lips."

"Something like that," he said lamely. "You know—machismo. Or whatever."

She pushed his shoulder suddenly, spun him around, struck him across the face with her clenched knuckles. His head flung back, and he blinked.

"You," she said. "*You!* But what about *me?*"

Then she was in his arms, and they were both weeping. He was saying, "I must I must I must," and she was saying, "I know I know I know."

In this area of West Africa, distances between national capitals are short: little more than 180 kilometers between Mokodi, in Asante, and Porto-Novo, in Benin. The invasion could have been made on foot. But the Little Captain insisted on tanks, personnel carriers, and trucks. Not for the comfort of his troops, but to achieve speed and surprise. And to overwhelm the enemy with the abundance of new Asante vehicles and weapons.

It was almost 0700 before the long column began to move. But Anokye had allowed for slippage in his schedule; the delay was not important. If all was going well, Gen. Kumayo Songo of Togo and Col. Kwasi Sitobo of Benin were beginning their attacks at approximately the same time.

President Obiri Anokye led the Asante invasion, riding in the front seat of a Jeep preceding Col. Jim Nkomo's tank corps. Following orders, Asante border guards had closed the coastal road to traffic from Ghana on the west and Togo on the east at midnight of August 6th. The only vehicles encountered were the cars of Asante citizens or tourists in Asante. These were ordered off the road by Mokodi gendarmerie on motorcycles, acting as outriders for the military column.

At the border, Togolese guards took one look at the rumbling file of AMX-30 tanks and hastily raised their barricades. The tanks clanked through. A squad of infantrymen, detailed for the duty, dropped off to take possession of Togolese border installations. No shots had yet been fired.

At the juncture of a secondary north-south road before the approach of Lomé, a company of 3rd Brigade moved out of the column and took up positions to guard against a flank attack. This force was commanded by Lieutenant Solomon, who was also assigned three 105mm M-50 howitzers and three 60mm mortars.

The main invasion force continued rolling eastward and, at 0749, on the outskirts of Lomé, came under intermittent rifle fire, badly aimed. Col. Sene Yeboa then led an assault company of 5th Brigade troopers who advanced on a skirmish line, firing their Kalashnikovs briskly over open ground. Opposition melted away and, as far as could be determined, no casualties resulted, on either side.

Lomé itself proved to be undefended. The airfield, railroad terminal, and presidential palace were seized without serious resistance, although there was a great deal of shouting, shoving, and brandishing of weapons by the Togolese gendarmerie and troops assigned to the capital.

But the sight of Nkomo's enormous tanks had the desired effect. As did the truckloads of smartly uniformed, well-armed Asante infantrymen. Within an hour, all important government offices were occupied. The railroad station and airfield were temporarily closed to traffic. Asante troops held the power station, telephone exchange, and cable office. The newspaper and radio stations were closed down. The port area was patrolled by armed guards.

Under strict orders, Asante soldiers treated the curious (but not fearful) populace with grave courtesy. The sophisticated Togolese were no strangers to coups and assassinations. They did not find this invasion of soldiers of another land particularly alarming, especially since the "foreigners" spoke French, Ewe, Twi, and Hausa, just as they did, and most of them were animists, as they were. So the business of Lomé continued uninterrupted, for the most part; restaurants, cafés, and shops remained open, the tourist hotels were not affected, and vendors on the Rue du Commerce did a brisk business with the invading army. Raising prices, naturally.

A command post was established on the Rue Pelletier in a building housing the Asante Embassy, where communications equipment had gradually been accumulated in the week preceding the invasion. After making a quick tour of the key targets, to make certain they were firmly in Asante hands, President Obiri Anokye wished Col. Sene Yeboa and Sam Leiberman good luck, and set out for Benin, once more leading the tank corps, followed by 4th and 6th brigades.

Yeboa and Leiberman set up a loose perimeter defense of Lomé and established roadblocks on the two main highways leading into the city from the north. They then formed company-strength probes to provide advance warning of any attack in force from General Songo's troops to the north. Yeboa led the 3rd Brigade foray in person, and Leiberman headed the 5th Brigade reconnaissance. The white mercenary, commanding forty men in two trucks, proceeded up the improved highway. He came under heavy rifle and machine gun fire near the village of Tsévié. The time was approximately 1045.

They were far from being the Wehrmacht, Leiberman knew. And maybe they weren't as good as a company of Ibo scouts he had led in Biafra. But those men knew they were dead, and didn't give a damn. Still, these Asantis were okay soldiers and would be even better after a few firefights. Preferably wins. Leiberman had helped train them; he knew what they could do, and what would be foolish to expect.

When the guns opened up, they didn't panic. But they didn't waste any time getting off the trucks, down into a foul-smelling ditch alongside the paved road. Then they scuttled back to a scraggly growth of oleander, elephant grass, and thorn bush, Leiberman right along with them. They had a tendency to bunch up, like all new soldiers, so he got them spread out in a line paralleling the highway. The fire from the other side hadn't slackened. It was directed mostly against the two deserted trucks. One of them blew with a crimson whoosh of exploding gas and black smoke. Grenades and extra ammunition left behind kept cracking off after the flames dwindled.

Leiberman was happy to see his radioman nearby. His backslung equipment appeared intact. The mercenary slithered along the ground and told the radioman to stay put. He then pointed out two two-man teams, and told them what he wanted them to do: one team drift to the right flank, the other to the left. They were to determine the size and position of the enemy force. The only way to do this was to fire their weapons directly ahead and see if that drew return fire. If not, they had to stand, or at least crouch, to draw enemy fire. They weren't happy about this assignment. Leiberman didn't blame them.

He waited patiently, repeatedly cautioning his men not to fire since, from their position, they could see no targets. The raised roadbed hid their enemy. It also, of course, provided effective cover. As far as Leiberman could determine, his casualties so far were two men killed jumping from the trucks. Their bodies lay on the road. A brindled pyedog came nosing around.

His flanking teams eventually returned and reported. Allowing for their exaggeration, and adding what he could judge from the volume of rifle fire, Leiberman estimated he was pinned down by a force of fifty to seventy-five men armed with bolt-action rifles and two light machine guns. They seemed to be spread along a 100-meter line, slightly bowed, the two ends closer to the road than the middle. The mercenary did not believe they had mortars, or they would already have used them.

He knew Sene Yeboa was moving along an improved road that ran northwestward. The farther Yeboa went, the farther he moved from Leiberman's position. Consulting the Michelin map he carried, Leiberman saw there was an earth track connecting Yeboa's road and his.

Assuming the colonel had not been bushwacked, and his trucks were still rolling, he could turn eastward at Assahoun, go through Gape to Agbélouve. There he would join the highway that Leiberman was on. By turning south, Yeboa could come in behind the Togolese force that had ambushed the mercenary. Yeboa had about fifty men with him, and two 87mm rocket launchers. If they could join forces, Leiberman figured he and Yeboa could take the Togolese, who were still wasting ammunition on the other side of the road. According to the map, Sene could be there in an hour.

He motioned the radioman over and tried to raise the colonel, calling in clear. Nothing. Either the radios were kaput—hardly unusual in Africa's climate—or Yeboa's radioman was fucking off. Or dead. Lots of possibilities. Leiberman then tried the command post in Lomé. This time he got through. Much interference, but he was able to explain his predicament and ask them to contact the colonel. They said they would. The operator in Lomé signed off by crying, "Long live Asante!" and Leiberman grinned sourly.

He told his men help was on the way. He felt a lot better about the situation, and settled back behind the thickest tree trunk he could find. He was about to light a black, twisted Italian cigar when a grenade came sailing across the road, exploded, killed one of his men, wounded three, and he bit his cigar in two.

Grenades were an added factor; he pulled his men farther back into the bush and had them cover the crest of the road. If a rush came, it had to come from there, and for a very brief time, the attackers would be silhouetted against the sky. If Leiberman's force couldn't stop them there, the only alternative was to run. As fast and as far as they could.

The mercenary did what he could for the wounded. One of his corporals had been designated as a medic. In addition to his AR-15, he carried sterile pads, sulfa powder, quinine pills, and morphine syrettes. Leiberman gave each of the wounded men a shot. After a while they stopped screaming.

Another grenade came lobbing across the road, but fell short and did no damage. But Leiberman had two men send up shrieks of terrible anguish. It did no harm and just possibly might make the attackers overconfident and careless. They were using their grenades so sparingly, tossing one at a time, that Leiberman figured their supply was limited.

He also figured the Togolese on the other side of the road, still firing at nothing, were not part of Songo's disciplined forces, coming down from the north, but were just a ragtag outfit, perhaps from a garrison at Tsévié, who had heard about the invasion and wanted to get in on the fun. He hoped he was correct. In Africa, it was hard to judge. Maybe right now they were getting a snootful of hemp or something stronger, and listening to a shaman tell them they were impervious to bullets. If all that happened, they'd come floating across the road, silly grins on their faces, and if there were enough of them, they'd waltz right through Leiberman's troops, kill them all, and gnaw on their roasted knuckles. It was possible.

The firing from the other side of the road suddenly ceased. Leiberman heard a shrilling, exultant screams, battle cries, wails that went up and down the scale. He didn't have to tell his men what that meant. They aimed their weapons at the road, pressed their bodies harder against the warm African earth, waited. No one bugged out. He loved them then.

Togolese came over the road in a long, leaping line, capering and shouting. Even as he raised his Uzi, he thought it was bad leadership; they should have hit in a single, hard-driving wedge. They'd have gone right through him. As it was, his men had a field day. They cut down the attackers with short bursts, as they had been taught. A few Asantis even rose to their feet to pursue the fleeing Togolese. Leiberman had to scream them back.

He looked again at his watch. Yeboa had to be nearing the paved highway, soon to turn south. *Had* to be. Then Leiberman checked what was left. Four more dead, seven more wounded. But three of the wounded were still able to function. He redistributed weapons and ammunition. He called Lomé again. They swore they had passed his first message on to Yeboa, and the colonel had acknowledged. There must have been something in Leiberman's voice; this time the operator didn't cry, "Long live Asante!"

They waited, shifting uneasily. Showing their teeth to each other. Leiberman watched them carefully. It wouldn't do to let one man break. The others would stampede after him. With the mercenary bringing up the rear, bellowing, but running just as hard as his men. No one broke. No one ran. But he saw the amulets and grisgris were out. His men were preparing to die.

The second attack came in silence. A sudden wave of high-stepping men coming over the road, down into the ditch, up and into the grass, through the thorn, firing wildly. The Asantis shot them down again. But not all, not all. Men leaped to their feet, glaives flashing. Leiberman, back against a tree, half a cold Italian cigar clamped in his teeth, potted targets as they came, turning left and right, but never sure if he was doing any good. It was all hot and close, grunts and cries of fury, smells of blood and sweat, burning things. And shit. And fear.

A few fled back across the road. This time no one attempted to pursue. Half his men were gone, dead or staring wide-eyed at the empty sky, holding arms, legs, chests, bellies, faces, while blood bubbled out between their fingers. The flies were there.

Once more, he thought. That's all it will take. If they have the will to come across that road one more time, they have our livers.

He lighted his cigar stub. He moved up and down his punished line.

The Little Captain is with you, he told them. He told them they should stay and fight to the death for the Little Captain. He will know of your bravery, he assured them. He will honor you as great Asanti soldiers. As great as the Ashanti warriors of the past. Do not run now, he said to them. Your brothers will be with you soon. The Little Captain has great magic, great juju. Fight and die bravely for the Little Captain, he urged them.

He spoke to them in Akan. They listened and nodded their agreement, pledging their blood. Not to him, he knew, but to the Little Captain. And to Asante. Son of a bitch, he thought suddenly. With faithful, trusting children like these, a man could go anywhere, do anything. Win the world.

He never questioned why he was staying. If you got paid for a job, you did the job. He admitted the stupidity of that. But all men were stupid—in different ways. Staying was his brand of stupidity. He reloaded and wished he had been kinder to Dele, his Ivory Coast girl.

When the third attack came over the road, he and all his remaining men stood. Even the wounded dragged themselves to their feet, those who could, and there was a tight action so confused he was conscious of nothing but explosions, screams, cries of terror, cries of triumph.

And then, unmistakably, he heard the rush of a rocket on the other side of the road, a fresh screeching of fury. He was aware of more men, many men, in clean Asante uniforms. There was a great silvery flashing of glaives, stuttering of automatic weapons, a Hausa chant of victory he recognized, and he wondered—theirs or ours?

He straightened, turned toward the road, and something hit his back, low, whirled him, slammed him down. The Uzi bounced from his limp fingers. He tasted dirt and bile in his mouth, rolled, said aloud, "Goodbye, goodbye."

He lay there on his back, fully conscious, listening to the slowly quieting sounds of battle. His pants felt full of blood. He raised his head slowly, saw the dark stain spreading across his groin. His first thought was that his genitals had been shot away. He opened his belt and fly with fumbling, nerveless fingers. His penis and testicles were still there.

"Hi, fellers," he said.

He felt around to the back with cautious fingers, probing through the greasy blood. The pain was starting, but nothing he couldn't handle.

He discovered what had happened: he had been shot through both buttocks, from right to left, the slug apparently exiting. Mortifying, but comforting. He would play the violin again—if the wounds were treated before his ass turned green.

He was lying on his stomach, pants and drawers down, trying to stop the blood with strips torn from his shirt, when he saw a pair of dusty combat boots planted next to him. He looked up. Col. Sene Yeboa.

"You grinning ape," Leiberman said to him. "Get me some sulfa powder and a morphine shot."

Yeboa nodded, trying not to laugh, and not succeeding.

"Sam," he said, "I think you eat standing up for a while."

"Ah, what the hell," Leiberman said. "I'm young again. I got dimples in my ass."

.   .   .

From Lomé, the Asante invasion force rolled eastward along the coastal road, President Obiri Anokye leading. Baguida and Anécho fell without resistance. The border of Benin came into view. Anokye signaled a halt. Men slapped dust from their uniforms, sought the shade, drank some water, beer, or palm wine.

Offshore, *La Liberté* moved slowly along the coast. Since the corvette had not been needed in Lomé, Anokye had signaled Captain Ojigi to proceed eastward and stand off Cotonou. Escorted by three motor launches, *La Liberté* moved on ahead of the halted column, an oversize Asante flag whipping back from the mainmast.

The Little Captain remained in his Jeep, listening to his field radio. Since leaving Baguida, he had been aware of the ambush of Sam Leiberman's force below Tsévié. He had heard the mercenary's first laconic call for aid. The relay to Sene Yeboa, Leiberman's second, more desperate plea, and Yeboa's assurance he was on the way.

Then there was silence. Anokye sat stolidly, not revealing his tension to his driver or radioman. He could easily visualize what had happened, what was happening. He believed in the skill and loyalty of Leiberman and Yeboa, but it was difficult to resist the temptation to turn around, lead his force in a dash to the rescue, flags snapping, plunge into the battle, fight, *win*.

But during the brief halt before the Benin border, the radio crackled into life. Anokye learned that Yeboa had arrived in time. Leiberman was wounded, but not seriously. Opposition had been annihilated.

The Little Captain sat back, but could not relax. He mused on how his destiny was coming to depend more upon the faithfulness and bravery of others. Before the coup, he had been a junior army officer relying on his own determination and the belief of a few. Today he led an invasion of thousands, tomorrow a political crusade of millions. He could not do everything himself; he needed the minds, strength and blood of others.

The problem was trust. His own family he could trust without limit. Sene Yeboa perhaps. The Asantis, his brothers. But now there were others: Yvonne Mayer, Sam Leiberman, Peter Tangent. And soon there would be his wife, Beatrice, Benedicto da Silva, Kumayo Songo. And then many, many more not of his family, blood, or people.

They would cleave to him because they wished to share his destiny. But he was realist enough to know that he must give to each what no one else could offer. Always there was the peril of a higher bidder. Obiri Anokye stared at the shaved neck of the Jeep driver in front of him, and thought this man might very well turn suddenly and empty his pistol into his president's face. Because another had bought his loyalty with a bigger reward or a greater promise.

He sighed with sorrow, knowing he would never be sure, of anyone. But he could never let doubt hobble his will. He must be alert, constantly, and secretly command one to watch the other. And so, by turning his aides and confederates against each other, he might escape the consequences of their greed, venom, ambition, or jealousy. It was not a way that was sweet on the tongue, but he saw no other choice.

He signaled the advance. In a few moments, the men returned to their vehicles, the column rolled forward. Obviously, news of the Asante invasion had spread; Benin border guards fired upon them with rifles. Anokye waved one of Nkomo's tanks forward. Machine guns spat. The border guards were killed, and Obiri Anokye crossed into Benin.

Now speed was increased and Anokye's Jeep pulled out of line to let the giant AMX-30 tanks take the lead. They raced through Comé and Guézin, and although there was no resistance, Anokye ordered his men to spray automatic rifle fire at guard huts and gendarmerie offices. Heavily armed squads were dropped off at each village captured, and a reinforced platoon, a tank, and an armored personnel carrier were left in Ouidah. The airfield outside of Cotonou was taken after a brisk skirmish with soldiers and guards. Anokye took his first casualties here—two men of 4th Brigade killed, four wounded—but he seized the airport and plunged on.

The Little Captain commanded that a roadblock be set up at the juncture of the coastal road and the tarred north-south highway. Then 6th Brigade, reinforced with two tanks, a TOW missile, and a mortar company, was sent on a wide sweep north of Cotonou to attack Porto-Novo, the capital. In addition to the government buildings, their mission was to occupy the customs post at the Nigerian border.

Anokye and 4th Brigade moved against Cotonou, ponderously and in force. When the invaders were fired upon from gendarmerie headquarters, the gaudy presidential palace, ministries, and from buildings in the Akpakpa area, the Little Captain radioed *La Liberté* to fire 40mm rounds into the city.

When resistance continued, Col. Jim Nkomo's tanks brought their 105mm cannon to bear. The tanks clanked slowly ahead through deserted streets, turrets questing, turning this way and that, blasting. Several buildings crumbled; others shuddered from point-blank hits, but stood shakily, showing blue sky through holes in walls and roofs. Casualties included civilians.

Within an hour, all resistance ceased; a Benin official approached under a white flag and surrendered the city. Asantis took control of the radio stations, and repeated broadcasts were made—in French, Yoruba, Dendi, Fon, and Mina—asking the populace to remain calm. The telephone exchange and power station were occupied. Asanti soldiers patrolled the streets. Gradually, slowly, the Cotonois peeked out, ventured out, picked up the tempo of their daily lives.

Peter Tangent joined President Obiri Anokye by strolling along dusty streets past the Hôtel de la Plage. He approached the tanks drawn up in the parking lot before the Hall des Congrès. He waved jauntily. A grinning Little Captain. Came out to meet him. They shook hands.

A few moments later, Tangent was seated alongside Anokye in the back of the President's Jeep. They led a convoy of tanks and trucks back to the north-south highway. The Piper Aztec of the Asante National Air Force, scouting the Abomey-Bohicon area, had reported a large force of troops, in trucks and on foot, moving south toward the coast.

"That will be Colonel Sitobo," Anokye said grimly. "He has guessed what is happening. He has reacted very quickly. A good man."

Col. Kwasi Sitobo's attack had kicked off on schedule, at 0600 that day, and had almost immediately run into trouble. The advance westward, which President Anokye had assured him would be against undefended or lightly defended areas of Togo, slammed head-on into strong columns of Togolese apparently on the march eastward.

If Sitobo was surprised, the only thing that saved him was that the Togolese forces seemed just as shocked. Both sides, after sharp skirmishes, drew back cautiously. The Benin colonel ordered a series of small reconnaissance probes. By 1100, he had learned that three columns of Togolese had crossed the border under orders to seize the north-south highway in Benin and press on to the Nigerian frontier. Most of this intelligence was obtained from a captured Togolese lieutenant whose initial obduracy disappeared before the first strip of skin was wholly peeled from his chest. He began chattering. Within minutes, Sitobo had the details of Gen. Kumayo Songo's plans.

Shortly after that, a radio broadcast from Cotonou reported the Asante invasion of Togo and the capture of Lomé. Subsequent bulletins said the border of Benin had been breached, Ouidah had fallen, the airport seized, and Asante tanks were approaching Cotonou. The radio station then went off the air.

Col. Kwasi Sitobo was a man of such fervent nationalism that the thought of foreign troops on the sacred soil of Benin was as great an abomination to him as another man's hands on his body. He wasted no time in considering whether or not Benedicto da Silva might be a party to this plot; his only desire was to defend his country, drive out the invaders and, if possible, drink the blood of Obiri Anokye.

He moved swiftly. He left a dangerously light screening force in the Savalou area to counter Togolese attacks, and then marshaled the bulk of his troops and vehicles on the highway for a dash southward to defend Cotonou. There was a small plane overhead, identified as a Piper Aztec belonging to the Asante National Air Force. Sitobo had no doubt that the Little Captain would be kept informed of his position and strength. He didn't care. The sooner the battle was joined, the sooner Benin would once again be free.

His column rolled south on the highway, through Bohicon. He picked up additional troops from Abomey, a few kilometers away, and continued the advance through the great palm groves of Zogbodomé. At Ouagbo he learned that Cotonou was under attack. At Allada he learned that Cotonou had fallen. He halted the column and called his officers to a conference at his Jeep.

At the junction of the coastal road and the north-south highway, Obiri Anokye halted his Jeep and called his officers to him again. He spread his maps on the hot, pinging hood, and they clustered around to learn his orders.

The majority of Col. Jim Nkomo's tanks were needed in Togo, and at Ouidah, Cotonou, and Porto-Novo. But two AMX-30s could be spared, with a single armored personnel carrier, and enough trucks to carry sixty men. This mobile force was assigned rocket launchers and recoilless rifles, and designated Task Group Able, under command of Colonel Nkomo. He was ordered to proceed westward to Ouidah, then to turn northward on a secondary improved road to Allada. With luck, Task Group Able might take the tarred north-south highway behind Sitobo's force. Exactly the same tactics that had worked for Leiberman and Yeboa in Togo. Anokye was willing to try it once again, but doubted if Nkomo could arrive on time to influence a pitched infantry battle he now saw as inevitable.

As for him, he would command what remained of 4th Brigade in a march northward to stop Sitobo. He sent a captain of the special assault company and three troopers on ahead in the presidential Jeep, to serve as advance point. Then he led his troops on foot, setting a steady pace, guiding on the tarred highway. Peter Tangent walked alongside him, looking about curiously as the heavily armed men trudged steadily, dust rising as they cut along the borders of fields of cotton, corn, coffee, and a precisely planned, beautifully groomed orange grove.

"Probably Chinese," Anokye commented, pointing at the gently curving rows of trees. "Africans could never be that neat!"

"Is this the type of terrain where you expect to meet up with Sitobo, Mr. President?"

"It will probably be similar, Peter. I do not know this land as well as I would like. I know the palm groves are farther north, and the rice fields to the east. This section is mostly plantations. Some orchards. All flatland."

"Not much cover," Tangent said.

"No," Anokye agreed, "not much cover. But it is not always possible to select an advantageous site. We must manage with what exists."

They tramped on, Anokye leading his men farther west, off the road. He explained to Tangent that by the time he turned to meet Sitobo, the sun would be setting, and he wanted it at his back, so that Benin riflemen would be dazzled and blinded by the fulgent rays.

The late afternoon was hot, caught in the stillness of a wind-shift. Dust raised by the marching men hung almost motionless in the air, chalked their faces, clogged their throats. The sky was cloudless, a salt-rimmed blue, and, if one looked upward, seemed sprinkled with a million twinkling points of white light, diamonds or dancing motes.

"Mr. President," Tangent said hesitatingly, "if Sitobo is coming south, then he must be aware of your presence in Benin."

"That is true. Probably from the radio before we captured Cotonou."

"If it had been broadcast that Premier Da Silva was the new ruler of Benin, do you think Sitobo would still have reacted?"

"Probably not," Anokye said blithely. "He is a fanatical patriot. It is the thought of foreign troops in his country that maddens him. If I had broadcast Da Silva's elevation to power, I believe Sitobo would have accepted a fait accompli. I considered such a course, but rejected it."

Tangent said nothing; they hiked on in silence. At this time of day, the sun cooling, it seemed the greater heat came from the baked earth itself, radiating upward in glassy waves. They swam through this sea, uniforms soaked, bare skin raw and swollen.

Perhaps Anokye took Tangent's silence for rebuke. He said: "I told you that personal bravery, in combat, is the root of political power in Africa. It is so for men and so for nations. It is necessary that Asante fight a battle and win it, if we are to be respected and feared. What is the Oriental expression—a paper tiger? We cannot allow ourselves to be thought a paper tiger. A decisive military victory now will save lives in the future. It will dismay our enemies, hearten our friends. It will encourage the Asante army."

"And help spread the legend of your magic," Tangent said, without irony.

"Yes," Anokye said tonelessly. "That too."

Tangent looked about. He estimated about 150 men were in the line of march. It seemed incredible to him that a commander would lead these soldiers into a needless battle for such intangibles. He stared at the short, stocky figure of Obiri Anokye, striding ahead so purposefully, and wondered if he would ever get to the end of this man.

The presidential Jeep came bouncing off the highway, across a field of reaped wheat. Anokye held up an arm; the marching column halted, men hunkered on their hams or leaned on their rifles. Several stood casually on one foot, the other knee bent with the sole of the foot pressed against the inside of the straight knee. Like cranes. They could stand so for hours without strain.

The Captain commanding the advance point leaped from the Jeep, came trotting, saluting Anokye as he came. He was a short, muscular man, wearing a black beret, chewing on a kola nut. He carried an M-16 under his arm as easily as a swagger stick.

"Made contact, my president," he said laconically. "Drew fire. Here is the situation . . ."

He squatted, and Anokye squatted next to him. Other officers came up, and they squatted, sitting comfortably on their heels. Only Tangent remained standing. The captain drew a combat knife from a scabbard inside his boot and used the point to sketch a diagram in the earth.

"The coastal road is here," he said. "The tarred highway runs slightly northeast, then turns northwestward to Allada. Here. This is your position. Soon you will come to the village of Abomey-Calavi. The news of your coming has spread; the village is deserted."

"And the enemy?"

"South of Allada, just before the bend in the road. About here. On a front extending across the road and into the fields on both sides. Through the glasses I saw no tanks or artillery. But at least five machine guns. Perhaps more. Far behind are parked trucks. Perhaps there are men in the trucks. A reserve. I do not know. The men I saw appear well-armed. Grenades. Automatic weapons."

"Mortars?"

"I saw none."

"They are advancing?"

"No, my president. They are sitting or lying down. Resting. There is a picket line out in front of the main force. The pickets are standing, patrolling."

"How many men in all?"

"I would guess two hundred, my president. There may be more in the trucks."

"You have done well."

Anokye studied the rough sketch drawn in the dust. No one spoke. Then Anokye took the combat knife from the captain's hand and pointed with the tip.

"Here, where the road turns northwest—is it a sharp turn?"

"Perhaps forty-five degrees, my president."

"Good. We will take them at that turn. Half the men on this side below the turn; half on the other side above the turn."

"But they are not moving southward, my president."

"So you said. I will take the assault company up the road, make a frontal attack. Their flanks will wheel and close in. I will then retreat down the road to the turn. They will follow, smelling victory. Then we will spring the trap."

"Let me take the assault company, my president."

"No. I will command. How far to their position?"

"Perhaps fifteen kilometers if you go by road. But if you go northward across country from this position, then only half that."

"Then we will go across country. Quickly now, before it grows dim. Here are your orders, and this will be our timing."

He gave commands rapidly, showing officers on the earth sketch where troops were to be placed at the turn so their fire would enfilade the road.

"Give me two hours, precisely," Anokye said. "If I have not returned within that time, then I am dead. If that should happen, wait for the arrival of Task Group Able, and smash them between you."

The officers nodded, went to their commands. The specially trained assault company, thirty men, stood, slung their weapons.

"May I come?" Peter Tangent asked.

"If you wish," Anokye shrugged. "We will move fast. If you cannot keep up, we must leave you."

"I understand."

"Do you have a weapon?"

"I have a pistol," Tangent said.

"Unfortunately we have no extra rifles," Anokye said. Then he added, "Later, there will be many extra rifles."

The Little Captain took one quick glance at the setting sun, turned, set off at a fast pace. Not quite a jog or trot, but stretching his legs in a ground-covering stride across plowed fields, through orchards, down rows of corn, over paths, into and out of shallow ravines, drainage ditches, irrigation canals. Tangent tried to keep up, stumbling, breathing heavily through his nose. The heat was beginning to melt his knees, drain his reserve. After them came the Asante soldiers, stolidly pounding in a steady rhythm all their own, rifles and equipment clanking, picking up a cadence of boots thudding on packed earth.

Anokye did not look at the men behind him, and did not stop. A Kalashnikov assault rifle was slung across his back. He swung his arms as he hiked, the momentum pulling him forward. To Tangent, the Little Captain seemed to be leaning, always in danger of falling, his feet coming up at the last second to smack the earth, peel back, tilt him on, push him ahead.

They marched steadily for almost an hour, dust swirling about their churning legs, and never exchanged a word. They stopped when they came to the highway. Anokye signaled everyone down. They fell limply to the ground, chests heaving, mouths open, throats taut in the hunger to suck in air. But the Little Captain took his rest standing, his weapon now in his hands. His eyes searched the road ahead, a stretch of bougainvillea, a stand of dusty eucalyptus trees.

Slowly, one by one, the soldiers climbed to their feet, checked their weapons. Anokye looked at them, then at Tangent.

"All right?" he asked.

Tangent nodded.

They moved up the road cautiously in two files, along the verges, five meters between them. Anokye led, crouched, head swirling. Then he held up a hand, signaled down. They crawled then, bellies and knees scraping loose gravel. The Little Captain signaled a halt. Tangent raised his head slowly, fearfully.

On the road ahead, two Benin soldiers stood close together, rifles slung. They were lighting cigarettes. Anokye came up to one knee, looked back. With hand signals, he moved his men out into the fields on either side of the road, then waved them forward until they formed a ragged line.

The Benin sentinels had separated, were strolling into the fields. Anokye stood up. Fired a short burst to left. Then to right. He jerked the barrel of his gun forward. His men began screaming, firing, plunging ahead.

They raced on, cutting down the pickets. A hundred meters away, the main body of troops scrambled to their feet, shouting, grabbing up weapons. Tangent, followed closely, saw the Little Captain go down, fire a burst, roll swiftly to the right, fire another burst. He tried to do the same, popping away with his pistol, the sound lost in the crackle of fire all around him.

Then they were all down, reloading, setting up to take the first charge of Sitobo's troops. They came howling across the fields, firing their automatic weapons in long, unaimed blasts, leaping as if demented, and shrieking in warbling wails.

The disciplined fire of the Asantis slowed them, halted them, killed them. Some ran. Some threw away their weapons. But behind them came more, and more, and more. Tangent heard the sound of motors starting; the trucks in the far background began to move. Anokye stood bent, turned, waved his men to withdraw. Tangent saw his face: lips tightened in death's head grin. Wet teeth. Eyes blazing. They pulled back, turned, fired, retreated, turned, fired.

Then they began to run—those still alive. Not in the fields now, but pounding down the highway, sobbing, reloading as they ran, turning to fire wildly, blindly, and running again. Men dropped and crawled. Men dropped and lay still. But no one paused to give aid or comfort. The Benin trucks were in sight now, gears grinding, and the pursuing enemy foot soldiers were close enough so Tangent could glimpse faces, glaring eyes, straining chests, mouths open and screaming.

Pistol empty, Tangent flung it insanely at men who wanted him dead, and without breaking stride swooped and snatched up an AR-15 from a fallen Asanti. He saw Anokye was still on his feet, still functioning, the last to pull back, the man closest to the enemy. He thought that if the Little Captain lived, then he would live, and he kept pulling the trigger of the unfamiliar weapon, not aiming it, but just pointing it and firing and cursing and filling with a wildness he had never known before because now he was on the edge, and felt it, and perhaps he was sobbing, but whether from hot joy or cold fear or both, he did not care.

Then they were coming to the sharp bend in the highway, and pounding around, the trucks closing now, the running enemy scenting the kill and pressing harder. Then they were through the turn, the road soft beneath their jolting feet, and as Tangent started a scream of exaltation, the guns of 4th Brigade opened up, a hurricane, and Tangent was slammed down by the thunder, fell, rolled, ended up on his face, hands crossed atop his head, and couldn't stop whimpering.

The storm would not end, but grew, and now there were louder explosions, and gradually a feral roar as 4th Brigade rose up and came on, glaives catching the last crimson light, and there was Peter A. Tangent, white man, oil executive, native of Crawfordsville, Indiana, on his feet again, right along with them, bony knees pumping, thin arms waving crazily, a glaive in his fist now, and not seeing or hearing or knowing, but wading like the others into the madness, his own shriek lost in the world, a face looming up, a slash, and the face opening like a sliced casaba, eyes springing apart, and then 4th Brigade was through, turned, came back, winnowed the ground again and again, until the enemy was not only dead but minced, shredded, hacked, kicked, stomped and made to vanish utterly from the earth, including the patriot, Col. Kwasi Sitobo, and when it was over, the Little Captain had to twist the glaive hilt from Tangent's frozen fingers, and patted his cheek with a bloody hand.

It was almost 2100 before Peter Tangent returned to Cotonou. He had watched, a fascinated observer, as Obiri Anokye met with his officers and diplomatic staffs, and issued orders to consolidate his power in Togo and Benin. Army units were dispatched to the northernmost sections of both countries, beyond the Atacora Mountains, to insure the loyalty of small, isolated villages and outposts. Meetings were scheduled with Gen. Kumayo Songo and Benedicto da Silva. Statements were released to Reuters and Agence France-Presse claiming that the "Twelve-Hour War" had ended; Asante, Togo, and Benin were at peace, and Obiri Anokye wanted nothing but close friendship with all nations, "in the true spirit of equality and brotherhood."

Tangent hitched a ride back to Cotonou in a black Citroën belonging to the Asante Embassy. His fellow passengers were embassy officials who could not stop exclaiming in wonder at the day's events and extolling the wisdom and bravery of the Little Captain. When one referred to the new Asante as a "world power," the others took up the phrase with delight. Tangent listened to these young, elegant Asantis chatter of hegemonic spheres, axes of influence, and dichotomous interactions. It saddened him, but he supposed it was inevitable. Something gained; something lost.

The hotel seemed untouched by the change of government. The air-conditioned lobby was bustling, the bar jammed, a line waiting for tables in the crowded dining room. Tangent couldn't see the merry, jostling, brightly dressed throng. His mind was clogged with denser images: hot, earth-colored, without laughter.

He was about to open the door of his suite, then stopped, hearing an odd sound. He put an ear close to the panel. A dull chant, almost a singsong mumble, in a language he could not understand. Yoruba, he guessed, or perhaps Adj. He opened the door slowly. The short hallway was in darkness. But a dim, flickering glow came from the sitting room. He closed the door softly, moved quietly.

Amina Dunama, naked, her basalt body gleaming with oil, sat crouching on her thighs before a small clay lamp in which scented fuel burned bluely. The rope of pearls was doubled about her thin waist. On her high brow, cheeks, and breasts were strokes of what appeared to be grey ash. On the rug in front of her were several things: a small bundle of feathers, a stone, a bone, a brass amulet ...

Her head was back, face lifted. Her body swayed slightly as she droned the endless dirge. Tangent could guess what it was: ritual for the dead in battle. His eyes stung. Then he moved silently back to the outside door. He opened it, slammed it loudly shut. When he entered the sitting room again, she was standing, staring at him with enormous eyes.

He looked at her, then down at the objects on the floor. She bent swiftly and snuffed the little lamp. Now the room was in darkness, faint illumination coming from the street through drawn curtains.

"You thought I was dead?" he asked.

"You didn't return," she said. "So ..."

He was fretted by the sudden notion that they were speaking as strangers, meeting as strangers. Whatever they had been to each other in the past was eliminated, gone. They were starting anew, having to fumble their way to a fresh relationship. Better than the old or worse than the old. But different.

He stumbled his way to an armchair, sat heavily. He saw her crouching on hands and knees in front of him. Light gathered on her oiled back, curved spine stretching the skin.

She opened his pants, took the tip of his penis between her lips. More gesture than caress. Then she moved close to him, clasped his legs.

"They say the Little Captain has great magic," she said. "Is that true?"

"It's true," he nodded. "Even in my country it would be recognized. In one day he has conquered two nations."

"And sent you back to me."

"Yes."

"He knows of us?"

"Oh yes."

"He approves?"

"I think so. I think he believes it is another link that ..."

He didn't finish the sentence.

"That chains you to Africa?" she said.

"That is what I was about to say, but that is not what I feel. May I turn on the light?"

"If you wish."

He reached up to turn on a table lamp. In the bright light he saw something else on the floor. With the bone, feathers, amulet, was a long, dry, black thing, wrinkled and mummified. She saw him staring at it.

"It is very old," she said. "Very holy. A relic."

"What is it?"

"Very old," she said evasively. "Why do you smile so strangely?"

"An odd thought. This ceremony in a hotel that takes American Express credit cards. You were right this morning. I shall never understand Africa."

She unbuckled his boots, took them off. Peeled away his wool socks.

"Your feet are all red and swollen," she said.

"We marched," he said.

"And fought?"

"Yes."

"But you are alive," she said, with satisfaction.

"Sort of," he said.

"Do you wish to talk about it? Palaver?"

"No palaver now. Maybe later. Now I wish to shower and be clean."

She took off the pearls and came with him into the shower. She soaped him and herself, scrubbed both their bodies with a sponge. She handled him gently, patted him dry, powdered him. When they came out of the bathroom, she led him by the hand to the bed.

He wanted to beg off, to plead weariness, or to say honestly that love was of no interest to him at the moment. But she knew better, and her instinct was true. Kaleidoscopic visions of that bloody day stretched his mind, and almost against his will he became turgid and hard. He was astonished, but she was not.

She put him into her with delicate thumb and forefinger. She was hot, hot and tight, and he pressed himself down upon her swallowing body as he had sought the protection of the earth when death came howling across the field.

She clamped him with strong muscles inside her. She grasped his buttocks to pull him deeper. Her hips began to move, to pump slowly. Her long, sleek legs hooked about his waist. She raised her head from the pillow, and with closed eyes, swollen lips, whispered obscenities into his ear. Which was exactly what he wanted.

23

Fog hung low over the Thames. It swirled across parks, rolled down narrow streets in billows of grey lambs' wool, greasy and clinging. The sun was gone forever; air stuffed the throat. The sky itself pressed down, an enormous weight that bowed heads, curved backs.

In spite of the day's gloom, the two men sauntered through Green Park, careless boulevardiers. They were identically clad: putty-colored Burberry topcoats, black bowlers. They both carried tightly furled umbrellas. They might have been twins—or refugees from a chorus line of flashers.

"Were you surprised?" Peter Tangent asked.

"Not really," Tony Malcolm said.

"Ah," Tangent nodded wisely. "Ian Quigley tipped you off what to expect, eh?"

Malcolm didn't answer. They strolled on in silence.

Finally, Malcolm said: "I suppose Anokye will go after Nigeria next."

"What makes you say that?"

"It's obvious, isn't it? Togo and Benin weren't worth the tick, except to get a border contiguous with Nigeria. *That's* worth the tick."

"Don't know," Tangent said shortly. "I really don't, Tony. I know nothing of his military plans. Hasn't Ian Quigley given you a clue?"

"No," Malcolm said. "By the way, did you see the report Fisk, Twiggs and Sidebottom submitted to the Little Captain?"

"Yes, I saw it."

"What was your reaction?"

"Some excellent recommendations. Some silly stuff. But all in all, worth the cost."

"That's what I thought. Well, Quigley is a professional."

"You should know," Tangent said.

Tony Malcolm stopped abruptly at an empty bench. "Let's sit a minute."

"Tony, look at it; it's all wet."

"Nonsense," Malcolm said. "Just a bit dampish." He took a clean white handkerchief from his jacket cuff, wiped off the seat rapidly. "There you are. All dry."

"Nut," Tangent said, but he sat down cautiously. "We look a couple of proper cuckoos, we do, sitting on a park bench in this weather."

He offered Malcolm a Players. The two men sat quietly, smoking.

"How is he going to organize it?" Malcolm asked. "Do you know?"

"Well . . ." Tangent said hesitantly, "I really shouldn't talk about it, but it won't be a secret for long. The United African States, a federation of semi-sovereign nations. Each with its own chief executive appointed by Anokye, but with national legislatures elected by popular vote. One law code for the entire UAS, but elastic enough to allow for local traditions and tribal customs. A single monetary system. One flag. One army."

"Commanded by Anokye, of course?"

"Of course."

"He remains president of Asante?"

"No, he becomes president of the United African States. The chief executive of each member nation is actually a governor. Zuni Anokye—he's Obiri's older brother—takes over in Asante."

"Interesting," Malcolm said. "What about taxes?"

"Each nation collects its own, with a percentage going to the UAS. Willi Abraham is setting it up, putting in his own men."

"Naturally. I think the Little Captain has been reading Persian history."

"Why do you say that?"

"The whole shmear is right out of Cyrus. Satrapies."

"Could be. He reads a lot of history."

"Perhaps he'll be able to avoid the Persians' mistakes," Malcolm said.

"Do I detect a note of hope?" Tangent asked sardonically. "Are you really on his side?"

"All the world loves a winner," Malcolm said.

"My, we are sententious today. As a matter of fact, you're right. He's already received confidential inquiries from Sierra Leone and Niger asking on what terms they might join the United African States."

"Why not?" Malcolm said. "With all that oil money he's got. More, if he takes Nigeria."

Tangent leaned over to stub out his cigarette on the park path. He spoke while still bent over, his voice muffled.

"Going to back him then?" he asked casually. He straightened up, looked at Malcolm.

"Thinking about it," Malcolm said.

"Don't think too long," Tangent advised. "I'd like you to get in first. Before the French or British. Or anyone else. He'd be a valuable friend in Africa for the U.S. That's the line I'm going to sell in Washington. You can help."

"I'll think about it," Malcolm repeated.

They sat in silence a moment, hunched over, poking at the ground with their umbrellas. Then Tangent glanced at his watch, rose to his feet.

"I've got to get back," he said. "Give you a lift?"

"Thanks, no," Malcolm said. "Think I'll sit here awhile and enjoy the damp."

"All right," Tangent laughed. "Dinner Saturday? At nine? The club?"

"Sounds good."

"See you then," Tangent nodded, and stalked off.

Tony Malcolm sat quietly, hardly moving. He didn't even stir when a woman wearing a plaid mackintosh took the seat vacated by Tangent. Her head was uncovered; droplets of moisture glistened in her sleek hair.

"I thought he'd never leave," Joan Livesay said.

"My sentiments exactly," Malcolm said. "Well, you're looking fit. Nice tan."

"I never get much darker than this. That sun was glorious."

"I can imagine. The deposit was made to your account."

"I know. Thank you. Was everything all right?"

"Everything was fine."

"I had some trouble with that bloody camera. Thought I'd botched it."

"No, no," he assured her. "Everything was quite clear."

"The maps?"

"Especially the maps."

"Good. What are you going to do with that lot?"

"Oh . . ." Malcolm said vaguely. "File it all away somewhere. You never know . . ."

"Anokye's quite a man, isn't he, Tony?"

"Oh yes. Quite a man."

"I got a letter from him this morning. At the office."

He turned slowly to stare at her.

"Did you, now? About what?"

"Guess."

"I like guessing games," he smiled. "How many do I get?"

"One," she said.

"The Little Captain wants you to return to Asante as his executive secretary."

It was her turn to stare at him.

"You son of a bitch," she said.

He laughed. "A little respect for your elders, dear."

"What do you think I should do?" she asked him.

"It's your choice," he told her. "Go or don't go. You're a freelancer; you can do anything you effing well please."

"Watch your effing language," she said. "I just don't know what to do. The salary he offers is splendid. That, plus what you'd pay me. . . . You would pay, wouldn't you? For more of the same?"

"Oh yes, I'd pay for more of the same. You need money badly?"

She nodded violently, teeth gnawing her upper lip.

"Your father?" he asked gently.

"They put on a new attendant at the home. My father gave him five pounds to smuggle in a bottle. Doctor Gaither said it almost killed him. He's back where he was a year ago."

"I'm truly sorry," he said softly.

She turned suddenly to glare at him, eyes widening.

"You didn't plant that new attendant in there, did you?"

"I? Joan!"

"To bring dad the bottle? So I'd have to . . ."

He groaned. "Do you really think I'd do such a thing?"

She wasn't entirely convinced. "Well . . . you are a bastard at times, you know."

"My, my," he said. "A son of a bitch *and* a bastard within ten minutes. This *is* my lucky day."

She sat forlornly, and he said nothing. He looked at her twisting hands, bowed head, the fog-slicked hair.

"Well?" he said finally. "What have you decided?"

Her head rose slowly. Face turned upward. Eyes searched for the Asante sun. But the sky was falling.

"I'll go back," she said.

"That's best," said Tony Malcolm.